the Collector's Bookshelf

Books by Joseph Raymond LeFontaine

Investors Guide to Rare Books

You Can Write Yourself a Fortune

The International Book Collector's Directory

Turning Paper to Gold

A Handbook for Booklovers

Official Identification and Price Guide to Collectible Books

the Collector's Bookshelf

Joseph Raymond Le Fontaine

Prometheus Books • Buffalo, New York

THE COLLECTOR'S BOOKSHELF. Copyright © 1990 by Joseph Raymond LeFontaine. All rights reserved. No part of this book may be reproduced in any manner whatsoever without written permission, except in the case of brief quotations embodied in critical articles and reviews. Inquiries should be addressed to Prometheus Books, 700 E. Amherst Street, Buffalo, New York 14215, 716-837-2475.

The publisher and the author assume no liability, implied or otherwise, in the use of the information presented in this book.

94 93 92 91 90   5 4 3 2 1

Library of Congress Cataloging-in-Publication Data

LeFontaine, Joseph Raymond, 1927-
    The collector's bookshelf / by Joseph Raymond LeFontaine.
       p.   cm.
    ISBN 0-87975-605-5
    1. Book collecting—Handbooks, manuals, etc. 2. American literature—Bibliography. 3. English literature—Bibliography. 4. Popular literature—Bibliography. 5. Fiction—Bibliography. I. Title
Z987.L37   1990
002'.074—dc20   90—45897
                                                                                                 CIP

Printed in the United States of America on acid-free paper.

For
Rosalie

Contents

Preface   9

Acknowledgments   11

Introduction   13

Section I.   How to Use This Book   17
Section II.   The Master Author Index   21
Section III. The Authors and Their Books   35

Appendix A.   A Reading Guide   331

Appendix B.   About the Collector's Bookshelf Value Guide   335

Preface

People love or collect books for various reasons. You may simply love to read, and having read a book have no further interest in that book as a material object. You want to go on to the next one—perhaps another book by the same author or another of the same genre by a different author.

Or perhaps you are a book collector! You may or may not have an organized plan for collecting. Perhaps you're interested in any book from a particular genre, be it romantic novels or the scariest horror stories. Maybe you only want to collect books by certain authors you admire.

You may also be involved in the academic or business aspects of the world of books and authors.

Whichever category you fit into, this book is for you. Nowhere else will you find gathered together in a single volume the information that is now at your fingertips. A book like this has never been published before. Here is a directory that will lead you to the pleasures of over 33,000 books, mostly fiction, written by hundreds of authors since the mid-19th century. The information provided is for the first edition or printing of each book. However, the vast majority of these books were also published in later editions, both in the United States and in Great Britain.

You don't need a first edition to enjoy reading a book—usually any edition will do. But because first editions are usually of greater value than later editions, you should be able to identify them if you have any. Often they are of considerable value. Knowing this value can benefit you in several ways as I'll explain in the Introduction.

There are 33,614 individual book titles in this directory, written by 931 authors who used a total of 1,764 different names, including pseudonyms, or pen names. Of these 931 authors, 596 (or 64 percent) are male and 335 are female. Sixty percent of these authors (556) are American; 375 are of other nationalities, primarily British.

At an average value of $25 for one copy of each book listed, the value today of all the books listed is over $800,000. If the collective value of all these books were to double in, say, ten years they would then be worth 1.6 million dollars.

If you could accumulate one copy of each title listed, you would need over 2,800 feet of shelving, and the books would weigh nearly seventeen tons. If you were able to read one book each day the year 'round, it would take you 92 years to read them all. That's a lot of books and a lot of reading.

Yet this represents only a small portion of all the books that have been published during the past 500-odd years. For the past several years between 40 and 50 thousand new books have been published each year. If an average of 3,000 hardbound copies of each title are printed and sold, this means between

120 and 150 million books have been printed each year. How many trees are cut down to accomplish that, do you suppose?

Why do I ask that question in a book devoted to exalting books, both past and present? Because I think we have to do a much better job of managing this particular resource in the future. Our supply of trees is finite. Our need for knowledge and entertainment is not. And every year the gap between the two will grow larger.

As the population of the world inexorably increases, the market for books as entertainment or for scholarly use will also increase. So our need for forest products will also increase. At some point in the future we will reach that finite point I mentioned earlier. What then? What are the alternatives?

One is electronic publishing of the spoken word. Recorded books are now available on tape and compact disk. Although the effort in this direction is still small, it will become increasingly important in the future. Another alternative is books published as computer programs on compact disks, which can then be read on a computer display monitor (screen) or even an ordinary television screen. An encyclopedia and several other types of reference works are already available in this form.

Such changes in the not too distant future will have an effect on printed books currently in existence. Used copies of printed books will become increasingly valuable. We may reach a point when we simply won't be able to print additional copies of popular and classic books, some of which have been continuously in print for hundreds of years. This will increase the value of used copies of hundreds of thousands of titles by thousands of authors—many of which are already of considerable value due to scarcity and demand.

That's why this book—and more like it—is needed now and in the future.

Acknowledgments

Many thanks are due Charles Opper and Gail Pieronski, whose dedication and perseverance helped to turn a substantial portion of an enormous database into a viable reference book. Any errors of omission or commission remain mine, however, and I will be most appreciative if they are called to my attention so they can be corrected in future editions.

I must also acknowledge that I could not have attempted this project without a personal computer and suitable software. The manuscript was prepared using Ashton-Tate's word-processing software program MultiMate, version 4.0.

The computer system used was CompuAdd AT/286s running at 12 Mhz under MS-DOS Version 3.3, and 71 megabyte hard disks. Hardcopy printout was from a Hewlett Packard LaserJet IIP.

Introduction

One of the most difficult problems that faces readers, collectors, librarians, and booksellers is locating additional information about authors and their books. When we discover an author we admire and enjoy reading, most of us want to read more. But where do we go to find the titles of other books a given author has published? Where and when were they published? If we do need this information, is it possible for us to find out which of the authors' titles are still in print and which are out-of-print?

There is another important piece of information that book owners should have access to. That is: How much are their books worth in the marketplace? This is particularly true for out-of-print books by authors who have become collectible and whose first editions are wanted by collectors and libraries.

In this book I have more or less arbitrarily selected authors, who have written over 33,000 books, using 833 pseudonyms as well as their 931 true names. A companion book to this one, *The Collector's Bookshelf Value Guide,* provides the current (October, 1990) estimated market value for all these titles. If you could purchase a single copy of every one of these books, as described, it would require an investment of nearly one million dollars.

Even though you can begin to put this book to use immediately just by browsing through it in search of your favorite authors, you will find a great deal of useful information in the first section, "How to Use This Book." Take the time to read it—it will enhance your searches and the overall usefulness of the book.

If you find this book useful in helping you toward greater enjoyment and wider scope in your reading or collecting, I would appreciate hearing from you. Any comment you care to make will be welcome.

The Availability of Books

Books are first available in new condition from the various bookstores throughout the country and, in many cases, directly from the publisher. This has been true since pre-Revolutionary days. Very few, if any, stores are able to stock all of the 40 to 50 thousand new titles published each year.

Many of these new titles are also marketed throughout the country through mass-marketing methods. These are primarily the paperbacks, which are seen in racks in food markets, airport shops, etc.

New books are also available in libraries throughout the country, but again, no library other than the Library of Congress is able to stock a copy of every new title published each year in the United States.

A further source of books are those companies that purchase publisher's overstocks of books and market them at discounts, usually through mail-order catalogs but also in many of the chain bookstores. An example of a mail-order marketer is Publisher's Clearinghouse. Millions of people receive its catalogs each year. Chains such as B. Dalton and Waldenbooks also market these books under the category of "remainders." When a publisher "remainders" a book title by selling all remaining copies to one of these companies, the book then becomes out-of-print, meaning it is no longer available from the original publisher. So we then have a class of books which are "new but out-of-print." It occasionally happens that books of this type will rise in value above the original published price.

A third source of books is the used-book market, including stores that sell used books. Here, there is a wide variety of sources and vast range of values; we need to distinguish between two categories of books.

The first is used copies of books that are still in print. This means that new copies of the book are still available from the publisher in bookstores. As a rule the fair market value for these books is half of the new book price if the book is in like-new condition. This is an important rule for you to remember. It applies to hardcover as well as paperback books. It will help if you actually know or can determine whether the book is still in print.

Most chain bookstores and libraries have available a multivolume set of books called *Books in Print,* which is published annually. This set lists all of the books that are in print by hundreds of publishers in the United States that year. The set is indexed by author, title, and subject. You can determine from *Books in Print* if any particular title you are interested in is currently in print. There is a comparable set for paperbacks.

What you must keep in mind, however, is that many books are kept in print for many, many years by repeatedly printing them. These are known as reprints; many books have been reprinted hundreds of times and not always by the original publisher. Reprints generally have little added monetary value and follow the rule of half the cost of a new copy. They do, however, have an intrinsic value for anyone who simply wants to read the book for pleasure or knowledge. Examples of this type of book are the many titles by Mark Twain, such as *Tom Sawyer,* and classic children's books such as *Black Beauty* or the Oz books by L. Frank Baum.

The second category is the one we're concerned about in this book: used copies of books in which the original edition is out of print. The original edition is commonly referred to as the first edition. All the book titles listed in this book provide the place of publication and date for the original, or first, edition. These are the books whose value has risen above the cost of later reprints and are thus collectible, or valued, because reprint editions are not available for replacing them in libraries.

Who Sells Used Books?

There are many sources for used books that are collectible or valued for other reasons. The first source is the stores that style themselves "antiquarian booksellers." Most of these are found in the larger cities and are operated as "open-to-the-public" stores, though many of them also sell by mail via catalogs. There are also hundreds of booksellers, some located in small communities, who sell only by mail via catalogs or lists. Generally, the people who operate these types of stores are knowledgeable about books and authors as well as proper values.

Another type of store is the used-merchandise store, which may sell only used books and other printed paper goods or may sell all sorts of used merchandise. Examples are the stores operated by the Salvation Army and Goodwill Industries. The pricing in most stores of this type can range from ridiculously low to atrociously high. As the rule, little or no knowledge of books, authors, or values is available from store personnel.

Other sources are antique stores (very little knowledge normally present), flea markets, garage, attic and yard sales, and country auctions.

If you buy for any reason other than reading or research, do not buy books that are in less than very good condition, including the dust jacket. Don't buy books that have any kind of library markings on them, unless you want to be a nice person and return them to the library they came from.

There are many opportunities for making money by buying used books, if you use *The Collector's Bookshelf* to buy wisely. But you must bear in mind some basic facts. First, the values shown in *The Collector's Bookshelf Value Guide* are for books in very good to fine condition, including dust jackets. They are retail values that are based on prices realized in large cities such as New York, Los Angeles, and Chicago. Values will be much lower in most other parts of the country.

Second, unless you can sell directly to a collector who wants the book, you will have to sell to a dealer, who will not normally pay more than half of these values and will probably offer much less. It depends on whether the dealer has an immediate customer for the book or is buying it for stock.

So, you must buy the book at a low enough price to make it worth your while even at that level. As a rule, you should not pay more than half the price you can reasonably hope to sell a book for, or about one-fourth the value shown in the *Value Guide*. If you are a collector, however, these are the prices you might expect to pay to a knowledgeable dealer or that you might ask for if you are selling to another collector. These are also the prices you might have to pay to replace these books if you become involved in an insurance claim.

Please be sure to read the "How to Use This Book" section. Good hunting!

Section I

How to Use This Book

The Master Author Index

In order to make it easier for you to locate the information you need, I have provided a Master Author Index. This is where you should begin any name search because it lists *all* names—true or pseudonymous. If the name is a pseudonym, you will be referred to the true name in the main directory, "The Authors and Their Books," which also provides place and date of publication.

Pseudonyms are always followed by a reference to the true name of the author or the name under which all books by that author are listed. Here's an example:

Adams, Chuck. See E.C. Tubb.

This indicates that Chuck Adams is a pseudonym used by the writer E.C. Tubb and that you will find Tubb, E.C. listed in Section III, "The Authors and Their Books." When you turn to Tubb, E.C. in Section III, you will find the other pseudonyms used by him, as well as the books written under his various pseudonyms and under his true name.

The Master Author Index also lists all the true-name-author entries that will be found in Section III. These names are printed in boldface to make it easier for you to locate them. The number enclosed in parentheses is the total number of book titles for each author. Thus **Adams, Andy** (8) means Andy Adams will be found in Section III and that there are eight book titles listed there.

If an author name is not listed in The Master Author Index, you need look no further. You will have to go to other reference sources for whatever information you require.

The Authors and Their Books

This is the heart of the book. This section contains the names of 931 authors and the titles of most, and in some cases, all, of the books published by that author.

Each author entry lists books written by the author, using his or her true name as well as those written under pseudonyms. To sum up, I have included the following information for each author:

1. the author's name as it is customarily used on books;
2. the remainder of the name or the author's full true name if different in any way from the customary name;
3. the author's national origin if known
4. the author's birth date if known and the death date if known and applicable
5. a list of the pseudonyms, if any, used for any of the books listed (this is not necessarily all of the pseudonyms an author may have used for nonbook publications such as magazine articles or stories);
6. a code number which cross indexes each title to a current market value listed in *The Collector's Bookshelf Value Guide;*
7. the titles of the author's books and any pseudonyms used (books are listed in chronological order of publication);
8. the place or places and date of publication for the first printing (or edition) of each title.

Here is an example of a typical listing. Each element is coded with a letter in parentheses following it; these are explained in the key below.

Hunter, Elizabeth (a) [Elizabeth Mary Theresa Hunter] (b)
American (c), born in 1934 (d)
Pseudonym: Isobel Chace (e)
1. (f) *African Mountain* (g), as Isobel Chace (h). London (i), 1962 (j)

   (a) The author's name as it customarily appears on the title page of books not written under a pseudonym;
   (b) The author's full true name (the brackets indicate that the full true name was not used for any of the books listed);
   (c) the national origin of the author;
   (d) the birth date of the author (the death date is included when applicable or when known);
   (e) the pseudonym used, if applicable to any book listed (some authors used a great many pseudonyms, as you will see);
   (f) the number used with *The Collector's Bookshelf Value Guide;*
   (g) the title of the book as it appears on the title page. It is not unusual for the title on the cover to differ from the one on the title page. The correct title is the one on the title page;
   (h) the pseudonym used, if applicable;
   (i) the place of first publication;
   (j) the date of first publication.

In most cases, I have listed all of an author's fiction works if the author is deceased, as well as many nonfiction works. Obviously, these lists are not complete if the author is still living, since more books may be forthcoming. In all cases I have listed the author's first book since this is normally the key book in any collection and is usually the most difficult to obtain.

You may have already noticed, if you've browsed through Section III, that a great many of the authors are British and that their books were first published in England. These authors are included because they are also popular in the United States, and their books were also published in the United States after English publication. This means that for most of these books there is also an

American first edition, but it will not be the true first edition.

If you have a book whose publication information differs from the information I have provided, you do not have a true first edition. You may, however, have a first American edition or a first English edition.

When a book is published in both England and the United States in the same year I have noted this. Thus, "London and New York, 1939," would indicate that initial publication occurred in both countries in 1939, perhaps simultaneously or perhaps one before the other during that year. It is beyond the scope of this book to provide that information, but it may be available from a bibliography that includes that author's works. In the example above, listing London before New York indicates that the primary, or lead, publisher was British.

Hardcover and Paperback Books

A common misperception is that paperback books are always reprints and thus of little value. This is not true. In fact, the most valuable American book, *The Murders in the Rue Morgue* by Edgar Allan Poe, is a paperback. During the 19th century, thousands of books were published with paper covers, but in those days they were referred to as *wrappers*.

After World War II the modern version of the paperback emerged with its slick and often gaudy stiff paper cover, and many millions have been published since then. A very significant percentage of them were, of course, reprints of hardcover books. This is still true. It has become customary to reprint most hardcover bestsellers as paperbacks, usually about a year after the first hardcover publication.

However, there has always been a significant portion of new books originally published as paperbacks. That is, the first edition is a paperback edition. This is particularly true for genre novels. In fact, in recent years, some publishing houses have been publishing a paperback edition first, followed by a hardcover edition.

The point I'm making is that thousands of the books listed in Section III are paperback first editions. So in your search for titles, do not ignore paperbacks. You can usually tell if a paperback is a reprint by inspecting the title page and the copyright page. If there is a reference to the first publication by another publisher then you have a reprint. If not, you may well have a first edition. Sometimes this will be stated on the title or copyright page.

The Condition of Books

The value of any used book is based on many factors. Scarcity, desirability, and condition are among the most important. Unless a book is extremely scarce, condition is the primary factor. Unless you want a book only for reading purposes, do not spend your money on books that are not in very good to fine condition. This means clean, unscuffed, not written in other than a neat owner's name or a bookplate, and with the dust jacket, if it is a hardcover book, in the same condition as the book itself.

Paperbacks are more fragile than hardcover books, and it's often quite difficult to find them in top condition. Nevertheless, the preceding statement is still applicable.

Section II

Master Author Index

A., Dr. See Isaac Asimov
Aarons, Edward S. (76)
Abbey, Edward (16)
Abbot, Sara. See Charlotte Zolotow
Adams, Andy (8)
Adams, Annette. See Donald S. Rowland
Adams, Bart. See David Bingley
Adams, Chuck. See E.C. Tubb
Adams, Cleve F. (15)
Adams, Clifton (50)
Adams, Justin. See Lou Cameron
Adams, Richard (6)
Adlard, Mark (4)
Agee, James (13)
Ahlswede, Ann (3)
Aiken, Joan (65)
Ainsbury, Ray. See A. Hyatt Verrill
Ainsworth, Harriett. See Elizabetth Cadell
Ainsworth, Patricia (8)
Ainsworth, Ruth (57)
Aird, Catherine (9)
Airlie, Catherine. See Jean S. MacLeod
Albanesi, Madame (259)
Albert, Marvin H. (48)
Alding, Peter. See Roderic Jeffries
Aldiss, Brian Wilson (53)
Alexander, Lloyd Chudley (25)
Algren, Nelson (12)
Allan, Mabel Esther (133)
Allardyce, Paula. See Ursula Torday
Allan, Luke. See Lacey Amy
Allbeury, Ted (14)
Allen, Grant (88)
Allen, Henry Wilson (53)
Allen, Hugh. See St. George Rathborne
Allen, Hervey (19)
Allingham, Margery (48)
Allyson, Kym. See Katheryn Kimbrough
Almedingen, E.M. (78)
Ambler, Eric (29)
Ames, Jennifer. See Maysie Greig
Amis, Kingsley (34)
Amy, Lacey (45)
Andersen, Doris (3)
Anderson, Chester (6)
Anderson, Colin (2)

Anderson, Frederick Irving (5)
Anderson, James (6)
Anderson, Poul (85)
Andrew, Prudence (22)
Andrews, Lucilla (25)
Angelo, Valenti (17)
Anglund, Joan Walsh (22)
Anthony, Evelyn (34)
Anthony, Piers (13)
April, Steve. See Ed Lacy
Arbor, Jane (56)
Archer, A.A. See Archie Joscelyn
Archer, Frank. See Richard O'Connor
Archer, Ron. See Ted White
Ard, William (41)
Ardies, Tom (7)
Ardizzone, Edward (23)
Arlen, Leslie. See Andrew York
Arlen, Michael (20)
Armour, Richard (55)
Armstrong, Charlotte (37)
Armstrong, Richard (35)
Armstrong, William H. (16)
Arnett, Caroline. See Anne Eliot
Arnold, Edwin L. (12)
Arnold, Elliott (28)
Arnold, Joseph H. See Joseph Hayes
Arre, Helen. See Zola Ross
Arthur, Frank (12)
Arthur, Ruth (27)
Arthur, T.S. (3)
Arundel, Honor (12)
Ash, Fenton (10)
Ashe, Mary Ann. See Christianna Brand
Ashford, Jeffrey. See Roderic Jeffries
Ashley, Bernard (9)
Ashley, Ellen. See Elizabeth Seifert
Ashley, Fred. See Fenton Ash
Ashton, Ann. See Katheryn Kimbrough
Ashton, Elizabeth (44)
Ashton, Sharon. See Helen Van Slyke
Asimov. Isaac (53)
Asprin, Robert (6)
Asquith, Nan (23)
Astley, Juliet. See Norah Lofts
Aston, James. See T.H. White

Athanas, Verne (3)
Atherton, Gertrude (51)
Atkins, John (17)
Atkinson, M.E. (31)
Atkinson, Mary. See Mollie Hardwick
Atwater, Richard (3)
Aubrey, Frank. See Fenton Ash
Audemars, Pierre (34)
August, John. See Bernard De Voto
Austin, Frank. See Frederick Faust
Austin, Mary (39)
Avallone, Michael (142)
Averill, Esther (23)
Averill, H.C. See Charles H. Snow
Avery, Gillian (21)
Avery, Lynn. See Anne Eliot
Aydy, Catherine. See Emma Tennant
Ayer, Jacqueline (5)
Ayres, Paul. See Edward S. Aarons
Ayres, Ruby M. (151)

Bachelor of Arts, A. See Phyliss Bentley
Babson, Marian (13)
Bagby, George. See Aaron Marc Stein
Bagley, Desmond (13)
Bailey, H.C. (80)
Baker, Asa. See Davis Dresser
Baldwin, Faith (104)
Baldwin, Gordo. See Gordon C. Baldwin
Baldwin, Gordon C. (30)
Ball, John (23)
Ballard, P.D. See Willis Todhunter Ballard
Ballard, Willis Todhunter (79)
Ballew, Charles. See Charles H. Snow
Ballinger, Bill S. (34)
Balmer, Edwin (26)
Bannon, Peter. See Paul Durst
Barbette, Jay. See Bart Spicer
Barclay, Ann. See Jennifer Greig-Smith
Barclay, Florence L. (15)
Barclay, Marguerite. See Countess Barcynska
Bardwell, Denver. See James Denson Sayers
Barcynska, Countess (148)
Barker, S. Omar (17)
Barrie, Susan (61)
Barrington, E. See L. Adams Beck
Barry, Jane (6)
Barton, Jon. See John B. Harvey
Bassett, Jack. See Donald S. Rowland
Bawden, Nina (32)
Baxt, George (7)
Baxter, George Owen. See Frederick Faust
Baxter, Hazel. See Donald S. Rowland
Baxter, Valerie. See Laurence Meynell
BB. See D.J. Watkins-Pitchford
Beach, Rex (40)
Beagle, Peter S. (2)
Bean, Amelia (4)
Beaty, Betty (24)
Beauclerk, Helen (7)
Bechdolt, Frederick R. (15)
Bechko, P.A. (8)
Beck, L. Adams (40)
Bedford, John. See Phyliss Hastings
Beeding, Francis. See John Leslie Palmer
Beeding, Francis. See Hilary Adam St. George Saunders
Behn, Noel (3)
Bell, Catherine. See Rosemary Weir

Bell, Eric Temple (29)
Bell, Josephine (70)
Bellah, James Warner (26)
Bellairs, George (59)
Bellem, Robert Leslie (5)
Benet, Stephen Vincent (5)
Bennett, Dwight. See D.B. Newton
Bennett, Margot (11)
Bennetts, Pamela (44)
Benson, Ben (19)
Benson, E.F. (116)
Benteen, John. See Ben Haas
Bentley, E.C. (13)
Bentley, Nicolas (23)
Bentley, Phyliss (49)
Benton, Karla. See Donald S. Rowland
Benton, Kenneth (10)
Berckman, Evelyn (37)
Beresford, Elisabeth (79)
Berger, Thomas (12)
Bergman, Andrew (3)
Berkeley, Anthony. See A.B. Cox
Berry, Don (5)
Berry, Helen. See Donald S. Rowland
Bertin, Jack. See Barry Cord
Betteridge, Anne. See Margaret Potter
Bevan, Gloria (18)
Bexar, Phil. See Jack Borg
Beynon, John. See John Wyndham
Bickham, Jack M. (55)
Biggers, Earl Derr (13)
Bindloss, Harold (131)
Bingham, John (21)
Bingley, David (127)
Birney, Hoffman (26)
Black, Gavin. See Oswald Morris Wynd
Black, Laura (5)
Black, Mansell. See Elleston Trevor
Blackburn, John (30)
Blackmore, Jane (57)
Blackstock, Charity. See Ursula Torday
Blackstock, Lee. See Ursula Torday
Blackwood, Algernon (49)
Blaisdell, Anne. See Elizabeth Linington
Blake, Forrester (5)
Blake, Nicholas. See C. Day Lewis
Blake, Stephanie (8)
Blanc, Suzzane (4)
Bleeck, Oliver. See Ross Thomas
Bloch, Robert (49)
Blochman, Lawrence G. (25)
Block, Lawrence (32)
Blood, Matthew. See Davis Dresser
Bloom, Ursula (402)
Blunt, Don. See Edwin Booth
Bodkin, M. M'Donnell (36)
Boland, John (34)
Bonett, John and Emery. See John H.A. Coulson
Bonett, Emery. See John H.A. Coulson
Bonham, Frank (48)
Bonner, Michael. See Anne Glasscock
Bonner, Parker. See Willis Todhunter Ballard
Bookman, Charlotte. See Charlotte Zolotow
Booth, Edwin (46)
Borg, Jack (63)
Borgenicht, Miriam (10)
Borland, Hal (36)
Bosworth, Allan R. (22)

Boucher, Anthony (15)
Bouma, J.L. (14)
Bourne, Lesley. See Jean Marsh
Bowden, Jim. See Bill Spence
Bowen, Marjorie (131)
Bower, B.M. (74)
Bower, Barbara. See Barbara Euphan Todd
Bowie, Sam. See Willis Todhunter Ballard
Box, Edgar. See Gore Vidal
Boyd, Alamo. See Allan R. Bosworth
Boyd, Frank. See Frank Kane
Boyle, Jack (1)
Bradbury, Ray (34)
Bradford, Richard (2)
Brady, William S. See John B. Harvey
Bragg, W.F. (21)
Brahms, Caryl (32)
Bramah, Ernest (18)
Bramwell, Charlotte. See Katheryn Kimbrough
Brand, Christianna (26)
Brand, Max. See Frederick Faust
Brandon, John G. (120)
Branson, H.C. (9)
Brant, Lewis. See Donald S. Rowland
Braun, Lillian Jackson (3)
Braun, Matt (21)
Bray, Alison. See Donald S. Rowland
Brayce, William. See Donald S. Rowland
Brean, Herbert (15)
Brent, Madeleine (7)
Brett, John Michael. See Miles Tripp
Brett, Michael. See Miles Tripp
Brett, Simon (7)
Brewer, Gil (33)
Bridge, Ann (28)
Bridger, Adam. See David Bingley
Bridges, Victor (44)
Brittain, William (2)
Brock, Lynn (24)
Brock, Stuart. See Louis Trimble
Brockley, Fenton. See Donald S. Rowland
Bromfield, Louis (24)
Bronson, Oliver. See Donald S. Rowland
Brown, Carter. See A.G. Yates
Brown, Peter Carter. See A.G. Yates
Brown, Dee (27)
Brown, Fredric (1)
Brown, J.P.S. (4)
Buchanan, Chuck. See Donald S. Rowland
Bude, John. See Ernest Elmore
Burchardt, Bill (10)
Burford, Eleanor. See Victoria Holt
Burford, Lolah (6)
Burgess, Anthony (4)
Burgess, Gelett (4)
Burgess, Trevor. See Elleston Trevor
Burke, John (91)
Burke, John. See Richard O'Connor
Burke, Jonathan. See John Burke
Burke, Owen. See John Burke
Burnett, Frances Hodgson (5)
Burnett, W.R. (37)
Burns, Sheila. See Ursula Bloom
Burns, Tex. See Louis L'Amour
Burns, Walter Noble (6)
Burroughs, Edgar Rice (79)
Burt, Katharine (30)
Busch, Niven (13)

Bush, Christopher (95)
Butler, Gwendoline (39)
Butler, Nathan. See Jerry Sohl
Butler, Octavia (5)
Butler, Richard. See Ted Allbeury
Butler, Walter C. See Frederick Faust

Cade, Robin. See Christopher Nicole
Cadell, Elizabeth (59)
Caine, Hall (33)
Caird, Janet (10)
Caldwell, Taylor (44)
Caley, Rod. See Donald S. Rowland
Cameron, Julie. See Lou Cameron
Cameron, Lou (49)
Campbell, Karen. See Betty Beaty
Campbell, Margaret. See Marjorie Bowen
Cannon, Curt. See Evan Hunter
Canuck, Abe. See David Bingley
Capps, Benjamin (11)
Carder, Leigh. See Eugene Cunningham
Carlton, Roger. See Donald S. Rowland
Carpenter, John Jo. See John Reese
Carr, Philippa. See Victoria Holt
Carstairs, Cathleen. See Jacques Pendower
Carter, Ashley. See Harry Whittington
Carter, Felicity (16)
Carter, Forrest (7)
Carter, Nick. Michael Avallone
Carter, Nick. See Willis Todhunter Ballard
Carter-Brown, Peter. See A.G. Yates
Carver, Henry. See David Bingley
Cary, Jud. See E.C. Tubb
Case, David (12)
Case, Robert Ormond (21)
Castell, Megan. See Jeanne Williams
Cassidy, George. See William E. Vance
Cather, Willa (29)
Caudwell, Christopher. See Christopher St. John Sprigg
Cavendish, Peter. See Sydney Horler
Chace, Isobel. See Elizabeth Hunter
Challis, George. See Frederick Faust
Chance, Stephen. See Philip Turner
Chandos, Fay. See Theresa Charles
Chapman, Walter. See Robert Silverberg
Charbonneau, Louis (36)
Charles, Anita. See Susan Barrie
Charles, Franklin. See Robert Leslie Bellem
Charles, Franklin. See Cleve F. Adams
Charles, Theresa (252)
Chase, Borden (7)
Chatham, Larry. See David Bingley
Chelton, John. See Paul Durst
Chesham, Henry. See David Bingley
Chisholm, A.G. (13)
Chisholm, Matt. See Peter Watts
Cholmondeley, Alice. See Elizabeth
Christie, Agatha (158)
Christian, Frederick H. See Frederick Nolan
Clare, Ellen. See Olga Sinclair
Clark, Curt. See Donald E. Westlake
Clark, Walter Van Tilburg (7)
Clarkson, Helen. See Helen McCloy
Clarkson, J.F. See E.C. Tubb
Clerihew, E. See E.C. Bentley
Cleve, Brian (31)
Cleve, Janita. See Donald S. Rowland
Clifton, Oliver Lee. See St. George Rathborne

Clinton, Jeff. See Jack M. Bickham
Coates, Sheila. See Sheila Holland
Coburn, Walt (39)
Cochran, Jeff. See Paul Durst
Cockrell, Marian (9)
Cody, John. See Ed Earl Repp
Cody, Stetson (24)
Coe, Tucker. See Donald E. Westlake
Coffin, Peter. See Jonathan Latimer
Coffman, Virginia (75)
Coldsmith, Don (4)
Cole, Robert. See Charles H. Snow
Collins, Hunt. See Evan Hunter
Colt, Clem. See Nelson Nye
Colt, Zandra. See Florence Stevenson
Coltman, Will. See David Bingley
Comfort, Will (29)
Coniston, Ed. See David Bingley
Conner, Ralph (39)
Constiner, Merle (17)
Conway, Troy. See Michael Avallone
Cook, Will (58)
Cook, William Wallace (41)
Cookson, Catherine (66)
Coolidge, Dane (47)
Cooper, Courtney Ryley (35)
Cord, Barry (49)
Corelli, Marie (50)
Corle, Edwin (17)
Cort, Van (4)
Costain, Thomas B. (22)
Coulson, Juanita (14)
Coulson, John H.A. (15)
Courtney, Caroline (12)
Court, Sharon. See Donald S. Rowland
Courtney, Robert. See C. Daly King
Cowen, Frances (61)
Cox, A.B. (33)
Cox, William R. (66)
Craig, Alisa. See Charlotte McLeod
Craig, Vera. See Donald S. Rowland
Craig, M.S. See Mary Francis Craig
Craig, Mary Francis (30)
Craille, Wesley. See Donald S. Rowland
Crane, Robert. See Frank C. Robertson
Crecy, Jeanne. See Dorothy Jeanne Williams
Crom a Boo. See M. M'Donnell Bodkin
Cromwell, Elsie. See Elsie Lee
Cross, Stewart. See Harry Sinclair Drago
Cross, Victor. See Virginia Coffman
Crowe, Cecily (6)
Cullum, Ridgewell (40)
Culp, Jr., John Hewett (8)
Culver, Kathryn. See Davis Dresser
Culver, Timothy J. See Donald E. Westlake
Cunningham, Cathy. See Chet Cunningham
Cunningham, Chet (28)
Cunningham, Eugene (26)
Curry, Peggy Simson (5)
Curtin, Philip. See Marie Lowndes
Curtis, Peter. See Norah Lofts
Curtis, Tom. See Jacques Pendower
Curwood, James Oliver (44)
Curzon, Lucia. See Florence Stevenson
Cushman, Dan (33)

Daemer, Will. See Robert Wade
Dailey, Janet (70)

D'Allard, Hunter. See Willis Todhunter Ballard
Dalton, Priscilla. See Michael Avallone
Dane, Mark. See Michael Avallone
Dane, Mary. See Nigel Morland
Daniels, Dorothy (157)
Daniels, John S. See Wayne D. Overholser
Daniels, Max. See Roberta Gellis
Daniels, Norman. See Elsie Lee
Darcy, Clare (14)
Davenport, Marcia (9)
Davis, Don. See Davis Dresser
Daviot, Gordon. See Josephine Tey
Davis, Dorothy Salisbury (18)
Davis, H.L. (8)
Dawson, Peter (29)
Dawson, Peter. See Frederick Faust
Day, Robert S. (1)
Dean, Dudley (29)
Dean, Shelley. See Lucy Walker
Debrett, Hal. See Davis Dresser
Decker, William (2)
de Pre, Jean-Anne. See Michael Avallone
Deeping, Warwick (88)
Deer, M.J. See George Henry Smith
Delafield, E.M. (45)
Delaney, John. See Donald S. Rowland
Dell, Ethel M. (44)
Delmar, Vina (26)
Delving, Michael. See Jay Williams
Deming, Kirk. See Harry Sinclair
Deminjohn, Thom. See John Sladeck
Denver, Rod. See J.T. Edson
Denver, Drake C. See Nelson Nye
Denver, Lee (19)
De Rosso, H.A. (6)
De Voto, Bernard (23)
DeWeese Wehen, Joy (7)
Dewlen, Al (8)
Dexter, Martin. See Frederick Faust
Dillard, James. See Charles H. Snow
Doctorow, E.L. (7)
Dominic, R.B. See Emma Lathen
Domino, John. See Esther Averill
Donovan, John. See Nigel Morland
Dorman, Luke. See David Bingley
Dorsett, Danielle. See Dorothy Daniels
Dorset, Richard. See Richard Sharpe Shaver
Douglas, Thorne. See Ben Haas
Dower, Penn. See Jacques Pendower
Dowler, James R. (4)
Downes, Quentin. See Michael Harrison
Drago, Harry Sinclair (130)
Draper, Hastings. See Roderick Jefferies
Dresser, Davis (112)
Drew, Nicholas. See Robert Harling
Drinkrow, John. See Mollie Hardwick
Dryden, John. See Donald S. Rowland
Dryden, Lennox. See Marguerite Steen
Dudley, Nancy. See Anne Eliot
Dudley-Smith. See Elleston Trevor
Duncan, Duke. See St. George Rathborne
Durham, David. See Roy C. Vickers
Durham, Marilyn (3)
Durrant, Theo. See Anthony Boucher
Durst, Paul (28)
Dunnett, Dorothy (16)
Duval, Jeanne. See Virginia Coffman
DuVaul, Virginia C. See Virginia Coffman

Dwight, Allen. See Anne Eliot
Dymoke, Juliet (21)

Eastlake, William (8)
Easton, Robert (9)
Eberhart, Mignon G. (69)
Eden, Dorothy (52)
Edgar, Josephine. See Mary Howard
Edson, J.T. (114)
Edwards, Norman. See Ted White
Egan, Lesley. See Elizabeth Linington
Ehrlich, Jack (13)
Elder, Evelyn. See Milward Roden Kennedy Burge
Eliot, Anne (28)
Elizabeth (24)
Ellerbeck, Rosemary (14)
Elmore, Ernest (37)
Elston, Allen Vaughan (40)
Erdman, Loula Grace (20)
Ermine, Will. See Harry Sinclair Drago
Ertz, Susan (27)
Esteven, John. See Samuel Shellabarger
Esmond, Harriet. See John Burke
Essex, Mary. See Ursula Bloom
Estleman, Loren D. (12)
Estoril, Jean. See Mabel Esther Allan
Estridge, Robin (25)
Eton, Robert. See Laurence Meynell
Euphan. See Barbara Euphan Todd
Evan, Paul. See Paul Evan Lehman
Evans, Evan. See Frederick Faust
Evans, Max (10)
Evans, Tabor. See Harry Whittington
Evarts, Sr., Hal G. (19)
Evarts, Jr., Hal (28)
Ewing, Frederick R. See Theodore Sturgeon
Eyre, Annette. See Anne Worboys

Faire, Zabrina. See Florence Stevenson
Fallon, George. See David Bingley
Fallon, Martin. See Hugh Marlowe
Farnol, John Jeffery (55)
Farr, John. See Jack Webb
Farrow, James S. See E.C. Tubb
Faust, Frederick (215)
Fecher, Constance. See Constance Heaven
Felton, Ronald (20)
Fenner, James R. See E.C. Tubb
Fenton, Freda. See Donald S. Rowland
Field, Charles. See Donald S. Rowland
Field, Frank Chester. See Frank C. Robertson
Field, Gans T. See Manly Wade Wellman
Field, Rachel (41)
Finley, Glenna (34)
Fisher, Clay. See Henry Wilson Allen
Fiske, Sharon. See Pamela Hill
Fitzalan, Roger. See Elleston Trevor
Fleming, Caroline. See Anne Mather
Fleming, Oliver. See Philip MacDonald
Forbes, Aleck. See St. George Rathborne
Forbes, Daniel. See Michael Kenyon
Ford, Elbur. See Victoria Holt
Ford, Elizabeth. See Mary Ann Gibbs
Ford, Kirk. See Bill Spence
Ford, Lewis. See Lewis Bedford Patten
Forrest, Allen. See Charles H. Snow
Forrest, Felix C. See P.M.A. Linebarger
Forrest, Norman. See Nigel Morland

Foster, Jeanne. See Dorothy Jeanne Williams
Fowler, Sydney. See Sydney Fowler Wright
Franken, Rose (29)
Frazer, Andrew. See Milton Lesser
Frederick, John. See Frederick Faust
Freeman, Cynthia (6)
French, Paul. See Isaac Asimov
Friend, Ed. See Richard Edward Wormser
Freyer, Frederic. See Bill S. Ballinger
Frost, Frederick. See Frederick Faust

Gage, Wilson. See Mary Steele
Gallagher, Patricia (11)
Galway, Robert Conington. See Philip McCutchan
Gant, Jonathan. See Clifton Adams
Garner, Graham. See Donald S. Rowland
Garnett, Roger. See Nigel Morland
Garrison, Fredrick. See Upton Sinclair
Garvice, Charles (187)
Gaskin, Catherine (19)
Gavin, Catherine (19)
Gellis, Roberta (16)
Gentlewoman, A. See Doris Langley Moore
George, Jonathan. See John Burke
Gibbons, Margaret. See Mrs. Patrick MacGill
Gibbs, Henry (76)
Gibbs, Mary Ann (65)
Gibson, Charles. See Charles Garvice
Gilbert, Anna (7)
Gilbert, Manu. See Joyce Tarlton West
Giles, Janice Holt (24)
Glasscock, Anne (4)
Gluyas, Constance (14)
Glyn, Elinor (40)
Godden, Rumer (51)
Gordon, Diana. See Lucilla Andrews
Gordon, Ethel Edison (8)
Gordon, Jane. Elsie Lee
Gordon, Lew. See Gordon C. Baldwin
Gordon, Rex. See S.B. Hough
Goudge, Elizabeth (45)
Grady, Tex. See Jack Webb
Graeme, Roderic. See Roderic Jeffries
Graham, Charles S. See E.C. Tubb
Graham, James. See Hugh Marlowe
Grandower, Elissa. See Hilary Baldwin Waugh
Grange, Peter. See Christopher Nicole
Grant, Margaret. Rose Franken
Gray, Angela. See Dorothy Daniels
Gray, Elizabeth Janet. See Elizabeth Gray Vining
Gray, Ellington. See Naomi Jacobs
Greaves, Richard. See George Barr McCutcheon
Greig, Maysie (228)
Grey, Brenda. See Leila Mackinlay
Grey, Charles. See E.C. Tubb
Gridban, Volsted. See E.C. Tubb
Griff, Alan. See Donald Suddaby
Griffin, David. See Robin Maugham
Grimstead, Hettie (76)
Grinnel, David. See Donald Allen Wollheim
Grundy, Mabel Barnes (24)

Haas, Ben (26)
Haddon, Christopher. See John Leslie Palmer
Haggard, H. Rider (75)
Haggard, William (26)
Hagon, Priscilla. See Mabel Esther Allan
Haines, Pamela (4)

Hall, Adam. See Elleston Trevor
Hall, Oakley Maxwell (19)
Hall, Evan. See E.E. Halleran
Haller, Bill. See P.A. Bechko
Halleran, E.E. (38)
Halliday, Brett. See Davis Dresser
Halliday, Dorothy. See Dorothy Dunnet
Halls, Geraldine. See G.M. Jay
Hamill, Ethel. See Jean Francis Webb
Hamilton, Donald (32)
Hamilton, Priscilla. See Roberta Gellis
Hammett, Dashiell (25)
Hampson, Anne (94)
Hannon, Ezra. See Evan Hunter
Hanshew, Thomas W. (20)
Harbage, Alfred B. (15)
Hardin, Clement. See Dwight Bennet Newton
Hardwick, Mollie (42)
Hardy, Laura. See Sheila Holland
Hardy, Russ. See Charles Horace Snow
Hardy, W.G. (13)
Harling, Robert (14)
Harlow, John. See Charles Horace Snow
Harrington, Joseph (5)
Harris, J.B. See John Wyndham
Harris, Johnson. See John Wyndham
Harris, Herbert (4)
Harris, Marilyn (12)
Harris, Rosemary (23)
Harrison, Chip. See Lawrence Block
Harrison, Elizabeth (13)
Harrison, Michael (56)
Harrison, Whit. See Harry Whittington
Hart, Caroline. See Charles Garvice
Hart, Jon. See John B. Harvey
Harte, Marjorie. See Marjorie McEvoy
Harvester, Simon. Henry Glbbs
Harvey, Caroline. See Joanna Trollope
Harvey, John B. (61)
Harvey, Rachel. See Ursula Bloom
Hastings, Graham. See Roderic Jeffries
Hastings, Phyllis (45)
Haycox, Ernest (63)
Hawk, Alex. See Elmer Kelton
Hayes, Joseph (37)
Haygood, G. Arnold. See Frank G. Slaughter
Hazard, Jack. See Edwin Booth
Heald, Tim (9)
Heaven, Constance (23)
Heckelmann, Charles Newman (27)
Held, Peter. See Jack Vance
Hendryx, James B. (63)
Henry, O. (28)
Henry, Will. See Henry Wilson Allen
Herbert, Henry K. See Henry Herbert Knibbs
Heritage, Martin. See Sydney Horler
Herron, Shaun (9)
Heuman, William (73)
Hewes, Cady. See Bernard De Voto
Heyer, Georgette (58)
Hichens, Robert (68)
Higgins, George V. (9)
Higgins, Jack. See Hugh Marlowe
Highland, Dora. See Michael Avallone
Hildick, E.W. See Wallace Hildick
Hildick, Wallace (72)
Hill, Alexis. See Mary Francis Craig
Hill, Grace Livingston (109)

Hill, Pamela (22)
Hill-Lutz, Grace Livingston. See Grace Livingston Hill
Hillerman, Tony (8)
Hilton, James (28)
Himes, Chester (21)
Hintze, Naomi A. (8)
Hobart, Donald Bayne (25)
Hoch, Edward D. (11)
Hockaby, Stephen. See Gladys Mitchell
Hocking, Anne (60)
Hodemart, Peter. See Pierre Audemars
Hodge, Jane Aiken (19)
Hodgson, William Hope (17)
Hodson, Arthur. See Arthur Nickson
Hoffman, Lee (22)
Hogan, Ray (133)
Holding, Elisabeth Sanxay (29)
Holding, James (14)
Holland, Isabelle (23)
Holland, Kel. See Harry Whittington
Holland, Sheila (76)
Holman, C. Hugh (15)
Holmes, H.H. See Anthony Boucher
Holt, Tex. See Archie Jocelyn
Holt, Victoria (157)
Holton, Leonard. See Leonard Wibberley
Home, Michael. See Christopher Bush
Homes, Geoffrey. See Daniel Mainwaring
Hope, Anthony (47)
Hope, Margaret. See Alanna Knight
Hopkins, Hiram. See Charles Alden Seltzer
Hopley, George. See Cornell Woolrich
Hopson, William (53)
Horgan, Paul (45)
Horler, Sydney (176)
Horner, Lance (14)
Hornung, E.W. (36)
Horsley, David. See David Bingley
Hosken, Clifford (23)
Hough, Emerson (35)
Hough, S.B. (30)
Household, Geoffrey (33)
Houston, Tex (3)
Howard, Captain. See Luis Senarens
Howard, Linden. See Audrie Manley-Tucker
Howard, Mark. See Howard Rigsby
Howard, Mary (62)
Howard, Robert E. (49)
Howard, Vechel. See Howard Rigsby
Howatch, Susan (10)
Hoy, Elizabeth (71)
Huffaker, Clair (16)
Hufford, Susan (9)
Hughes, Dorothy B. (20)
Hughes, Matilda. See Charlotte MacLeod
Hull, E.M. (8)
Hull, Richard (15)
Hume, Fergus (141)
Humphrey, William (10)
Hunt, Clarence. See C. Hugh Holman
Hunt, Francesca. See Isabelle Holland
Hunt, Gill. See E.C. Tubb
Hunt, Harrison. See Willis Todhunter Ballard
Hunter, Elizabeth (61)
Hunter, Evan (86)
Hunter, Hall. See Edison Marshall
Hunter, John. See Willis Todhunter Ballard
Hurst, Fannie (31)

Hutten, Baroness von (41)
Huxley, Elspeth (32)
Hyde, Eleanor. See Frances Cowan

Iles, Francis. See A.B. Cox
Inglis, Susan (23)
Innes, Michael. See J.I.M. Stewart
Irish, William. See Cornell Woolrich
Irwin, G.H. See Richard Sharpe Shaver
Irwin, Margaret (27)

Jackson, E.F. See E.C. Tubb
Jackson, Shirley (17)
Jacob, Naomi (78)
Jacobs, Leah. See Roberta Gellis
Jacobs, T.C.H. See Jacques Pendower
Jakes, John (69)
James, Cy. See Peter Watts
James, Dan. See James Denson Sayers
James, Margaret. See Pamela Bennetts
James, P.D. (8)
James, Will (24)
James, William M. See John B. Harvey
Jarrett, Cora (8)
Jason, Jerry. See George Henry Smith
Jason, Veronica. See Velda Johnston
Jay, Charlotte. See G.M. Jay
Jay, G.M. (16)
Jefford, Bat. See David Bingley
Jeffries, Roderic (91)
Jenkins, W.F. (73)
Jenks, George C. (6)
Jepson, Selwyn (37)
Jessup, Richard (23)
Johnson, Barbara Ferry (5)
Johnson, Dorothy M. (20)
Johnson, E. Richard (9)
Johnston, Mary (28)
Johnston, Norma (24)
Johnston, Velda (24)
Jones, Annabel. See Christianna Brand
Jones, Douglas C. (9)
Jones, Luke. See Peter Watts
Jones, Joanna. See John Burke
Jones, Nard (17)
Jorgensen, Ivar. See Robert Silverberg
Joscelyn, Archie (220)

Kane, Frank (44)
Kane, Henry (82)
Kane, Jim. See Barry Cord
Kantor, MacKinlay (51)
Kavanaugh, Cynthia. See Dorothy Daniels
Kavanagh, Paul. See Lawrence Block
Keating, H.R.F. (25)
Keene, Day (49)
Keene, Faraday. See Cora Jarrett
Keene, James. See William Everett Cook
Keene, Lieutenent. See St. George Rathborne
Kelland, Clarence Budington (70)
Kellow, Kathleen. See Victoria Holt
Kelton, Elmer (26)
Kennedy, Jr., Cody. See John Reese
Kennedy, Margaret (25)
Kennedy, Milward (23)
Kennedy, Robert Milward. See Milward Kennedy
Kenrick, Tony (10)
Kent, Pamela. See Susan Barrie

Kenyon, Michael (15)
Keppel, Charlotte. See Ursula Torday
Kern, Gregory. See E.C. Tubb
Kerr, Ben. See William Ard
Kersh, Gerald (41)
Kesey, Ken (4)
Ketchum, Philip L. (52)
Kevern, Barbara (4)
Keverne, Richard. See Clifford Hosken
Keyes, Frances Parkinson (51)
Kidd, Flora (42)
Kimbro, Jean. See Katheryn Kimbrough
Kimbrough, Katheryn (52)
King, C. Daly (8)
King, General Charles (57)
King, Rufus (36)
Kingston, Syd. See David Bingley
Kinkaid, Matt. See Clifton Adams
Kirk, Michael. See Bill Knox
Kirk, Russell (9)
Knibbs, H.H. (20)
Knight, Alanna (17)
Knox, Bill (59)
Knox, Calvin. See Robert Silverberg
Knox, Ronald A. (39)
Knye, Casandra. See John Sladek
Kramer, George. See William Heuman
Krause, Herbert (5)
Kroll, Burt. See Donald S. Rowland
Kyd, Thomas. See Alfred Bennett Harbage
Kyle, Sefton. See Roy C. Vickers
Kyne, Peter B. (38)

Lacy, Ed. See Len Zinberg
La Farge, Oliver (23)
Laker, Rosalind. See Barbara Ovstedal
Lamb, Charlotte. See Sheila Holland
L'Amour, Louis (84)
Lancaster, Sheila. See Sheila Holland
Lance, Leslie. See Theresa Charles
Lane, Roumelia (20)
Lang, King. See E.C. Tubb
Langley, Helen. See Donald S. Rowland
Langley, John (17)
Lansing, Henry. See Donald S. Rowland
Lant, Harvey. See Donald S. Rowland
Lantry, Mike. See E.C. Tubb
Lathen, Emma (23)
Latimer, Jonathan (13)
La Tourrette, Jacqueline (7)
Lattin, Anne. See Anne Eliot
Lawless, Anthony. See Philip MacDonald
Lawrence, Hilda (6)
Lawrence, P. See E.C. Tubb
Lawson, Chet. See E.C. Tubb
Lea, Tom (18)
Lear, Peter. See Peter Lovesey
Leasor, James (37)
Leaver, Ruth. See Ruth Tomalin
le Carre, John (10)
Lee, Elsie (41)
Lee, Ranger. See Charles H. Snow
Lee, Wayne (50)
Lehman, Paul Evan (73)
Leigh, Roberta. See Rachel Lindsay
Leighton, Lee. See Wayne D. Overholser
Leighton, Lee. See Lewis Bedford Patten
Leinster, Murray. See W.F. Jenkins

Lemarchand, Elizabeth (11)
LeMay, Alan (19)
Leonard, Elmore (23)
Le Queux, William (214)
LeSeig, Theo. See Dr. Seuss
Leslie, Doris (36)
Leslie, Miriam. See Philip L. Ketchum
Lesser, Milton (49)
L'Estrange, Anna. See Rosemary Ellerbeck
Levin, Ira (11)
Lewin, Michael Z. (8)
Lewis, Alfred Henry (22)
Lewis, C. Day (86)
Lewis, J.R. See Roy Lewis
Lewis, Maynah (22)
Lewis, Roy (36)
Lewty, Marjorie (21)
Ley, Alice Chetwynd (14)
Leyton, Sophie. See Sheila Walsh
Lin, Frank. See Gertrude Atherton
Linebarger, P.M.A. (18)
Linden, Oliver. See Caryl Brahms
Lindsay, Rachel (74)
Linington, Elizabeth (66)
Little, Constance and Gwyneth (23)
Livingston, Grace. See Grace Livingston Hill
Lofts, Norah (65)
Logan, Ford. See D.B. Newton
Logan, Mark. See Christopher Nicole
Lomax, Bliss. See Harry Sinclair Drago
London, Jack (83)
London, Laura (5)
Lord, Nancy. See Eve Titus
Loring, Emilie (54)
Loring, Peter. See Samuel Shellabarger
Lorrimer, Clair (55)
Lovell, Marc. See Mark McShane
Lovesey, Peter (14)
Low, Dorothy Mackie (11)
Lowndes, Marie (66)
Ludlow, Geoffrey. See Laurence Meynell
Ludlum, Robert (10)
Lurgan, Lester. See May Wynne
Luther, Martin. See Arthur Sellings
Lyall, Gavin (8)
Lynch, Eric. See David Bingley
Lynn, Irene. See Donald S. Rowland
Lynn, Margaret (6)

Macardle, Dorothy (11)
MacDonald, John D. (75)
Macdonald, Marcia. See Grace Livingston Hill
MacDonald, Philip (44)
MacGill, Mrs. Patrick (21)
MacInnes, Helen (20)
Mackinlay, Leila (89)
Mackinlock, Duncan. See Peter Watts
MacLean, Alistair (33)
Maclean, Arthur. See E.C. Tubb
MacLeod, Charlotte (20)
MacLeod, Jean S. (119)
MacLeod, Robert. See Bill Knox
MacNeil, Duncan. See Philip McCutchan
MacNeil, Neil. See Willis Todhunter Ballard
Maddocks, Margaret (18)
Maddox, Carl. See E.C. Tubb
Madison, Hank. See Donald S. Rowland
Mainwaring, Daniel (18)

Maling, Arthur (11)
Manley-Tucker, Audrie (27)
Manly, Marline. See St. George Rathborne
Mann, Deborah. See Ursula Bloom
Mann, James. See John B. Harvey
Manning, David. See Frederick Faust
Manning, Marsha. See Hettie Grimstead
Manning, Roy. See Tom West
Manor, Jason. See Oakley Hall
Marchant, Catherine. See Catherine Cookson
Marcus, Joanna. See Lucilla Andrews
Markham, Robert. See Kingsley Amis
Marlowe, Dan J. (27)
Marlowe, Derek (10)
Marlowe, Hugh (57)
Marlowe, Stephen. See Milton Lesser
Marquand, John. (37)
Marsh, Jean (23)
Marsh, Ngaio (41)
Marshall, Edison (54)
Marshall, Gary. See Charles H. Snow
Marshall, Rosamond (16)
Marsten, Richard. See Evan Hunter
Martell, James. See David Bingley
Martin, Rhona (2)
Martin, Stella. See Georgette Heyer
Mason, A.E.W. (39)
Mason, Chuck. See Donald S. Rowland
Masterson, Whit. See Robert Wade
Masur, Harold Q. (14)
Mather, Anne (85)
Mather, Berkely (16)
Maugham, Robin (36)
Maugham, W. Somerset (102)
Maxwell, Vicky. See Anne Worboys
May, Wynne (15)
Maybury, Anne (77)
Mayfield, Julia. See Phyliss Hastings
Mayo, Jim. See Louis L'Amour
McBain, Ed. See Evan Hunter
McBain, Laurie (5)
McCall, Anthony. See Henry Kane
McCall, Vincent. See Nigel Morland
McCloy, Helen (34)
McClure, James (9)
McCoy, Horace (7)
McCutchan, Philip (71)
McCutcheon, George Barr (47)
McDonald, Gregory (7)
McElroy, Lee. See Elmer Kelton
McEvoy, Marjorie (34)
McGivern, William P. (30)
McHugh, Stuart. See Donald S. Rowland
McLaglen, John J. See John B. Harvey
McKenna, Evelyn. See Archie Joscelyn
McNeile, H.C. (36)
McShane, Mark (32)
Meade, L.T. (243)
Meade, Richard. See Ben Haas
Meggs, Brown (3)
Melville, Anne. See Margaret Potter
Melville, Jennie. See Gwendoline Butler
Merlin, Christina. See Constance Heaven
Messer, Mona. See Anne Hocking
Meyer, Nicholas (4)
Meynell, Laurence (157)
Michaels, Kristin. See Jeanne Williams
Michaels, Steve. See Michael Avallone

Miles, John. See Jack M. Bickham
Miles, Lady (11)
Millar, Margaret (26)
Miller, Wade. See Robert Wade
Miller, Warne, M.D. See St. George Rathborne
Millhiser, Marlys (5)
Milne, A.A. (68)
Mitchell, Gladys (79)
Mitchell, Margaret (2)
Mitchum, Hank. See D.B. Newton
Monahan, John. See W.R. Burnett
Moore, Doris Langley (20)
Moran, Mike. See William Ard
Moresby, Louis. See L. Adams Beck
Morgan, G.J. See Donald S. Rowland
Morgan, Glebe. See Donald S. Rowland
Morgan, Mark. See Wayne D. Overholser
Morice, Anne. See Felicity Shaw
Morland, Nigel (101)
Morland, Peter Henry. See Frederick Faust
Morris, Sara. See John Burke
Morrison, Roberta. See Jean Francis Webb
Morrissey, J.L. (5)
Mossop, Irene. See Theresa Charles
Murray, Edna. See Donald S. Rowland
Murray, Frances (8)
Myers, Harriet Kathryn. See Harry Whittington

Newman, Margaret. See Margaret Potter
Neihardt, John G. (26)
Newton, D.B. (67)
Nickson, Arthur (54)
Nichols, John (8)
Nicholson, Christina. See Christopher Nicole
Nicholson, Jane. See Marguerite Steen
Nicole, Christopher (50)
Nile, Dorothea. See Michael Avallone
Niven, Frederick (40)
Nolan, Chuck. See J.T. Edson
Nolan, Frederick (37)
Noone, Edwina. See Michael Avallone
North, Colin. See David Bingley
North, Howard. See Elleston Trevor
Norris, Frank (21)
Nye, Nelson (143)

Obets, Bob (2)
O'Conner, Jack (19)
O'Conner, Kevin. See Frank O'Rourke
O'Conner, Patrick. See Leonard Wibberley
O'Connor, Richard (52)
Olsen, T.V. (41)
O'Malley, Frank. See Frank O'Rourke
O'Malley, Patrick. See Frank O'Rourke
O'Neill, Egan. See Elizabeth Linington
Onstott, Kyle (17)
O'Rourke, Frank (69)
Osborne, David. See Robert Silverberg
Ostenso, Martha (18)
Overholser, Wayne D. (101)
Ovstedal, Barbara (21)
Owen, Caroline Dale. See Caroline Dale Snedeker
Owen, Dean. See Dudley Dean
Owen, Hugh. See Frederick Faust
Owen, Tom. See Peter Watts

Page, Lorna. See Donald S. Rowland
Palmer, John Leslie (64)

Paradise, Mary. See Dorothy Eden
Parkes, Lucas. See John Wyndham
Patten, Lewis B. (101)
Patterson, Harry. See Hugh Marlowe
Patterson, Olive. See Donald S. Rowland
Pattullo, George (13)
Paul, Barbara. See Barbara Ovstedal
Paye, Robert. See Marjorie Bowen
Payne, Alan. See John Jakes
Pender, Marilyn. See Jacques Pendower
Peace, Frank. See Will Cook
Pendower, Jacques (107)
Penn, Anne. See Jacques Pendower
Perry, George Sessions (12)
Peters, Bill. See William P. McGivern
Peters, Roy. See Arthur Nickson
Pickard, John Q. See Jack Borg
Pilgrim, Anne. Mabel Esther Allan
Pilgrim, David. See John Leslie Palmer
Pilgrim, David. See Hilary Adam St. George Saunders
Plaidy, Jean. See Victoria Holt
Plummer, Ben. See David Bingley
Pocock, Roger (19)
Porlock, Martin. See Philip MacDonald
Porter, Alvin. See Donald S. Rowland
Portis, Charles McColl (3)
Potter, Margaret (37)
Powell, James (6)
Powers, M.L. See E.C. Tubb
Prebble, John (21)
Preedy, George. See Marjorie Bowen
Prescott, Caleb. See David Bingley
Prescott, John (11)
Pritchard, John Wallace (13)
Prole, Lozania. See Ursula Bloom
Pryor, Vanessa. See Chelsea Quinn Yarbro
Putnam, J. Wesley. See Harry Sinclair Drago
Purdum, Herbert R. (2)

Quarry, Nick. See Marvin H. Albert
Queen, Jr., Ellery. See James Holding
Queen, Ellery. See Jack Vance
Queen, Ellery. See Theodore Sturgeon
Queen, Ellery (60)
Quin. See Alfred Henry Lewis

Raine, William MacLeod (113)
Randall, Clay. See Clifton Adams
Random, Alex. See Donald S. Rowland
Rathborne, St. George (188)
Rattray, Simon. See Elleston Trevor
Rayner, Olive Pratt. See Grant Allen
Rebel, Adam. See Tom Roan
Reed, Eliot. See Eric Ambler
Reese, John (41)
Reeve, Joel. See William R. Cox
Reiner, Max. See Taylor Caldwell
Remington, Mark. See David Bingley
Reno, Clint. See Willis Todhunter Ballard
Renton, Cam. See Richard Armstrong
Repp, Ed Earl (14)
Rhodes, Eugene Manlove (20)
Richards, Henry. See J.L. Morrissey
Richmond, Hugh. See Gordon Young
Richmond, Roe (29)
Richter, Conrad (22)
Ridgway, Jason. See Milton Lesser
Rigsby, Howard (20)

Rimmer, W.J. See Donald S. Rowland
Ringold, Clay. See Ray Hogan
Ripley, Jack. See John Wainwright
Rix, Donna. See Donald S. Rowland
Roan, Tom (20)
Roberts, John. See David Bingley
Roberts, Wayne. See Wayne D. Overholser
Robertson, Frank C. (147)
Robins, Patricia. See Clair Lorrimer
Rockwell, Matt. See Donald S. Rowland
Roderus, Frank (12)
Rogers, Floyd. See Bill Spence
Roland, Mary. See Christianna Brand
Rome, Anthony. See Marvin H. Albert
Romney, Steve. See David Bingley
Ronns, Edward. See Edward S. Aarons
Roscoe, Charles. See Donald S. Rowland
Rosetti, Minerva. See Donald S. Rowland
Ross, Barnaby. See Ellery Queen
Ross, Catherine. See Betty Beaty
Ross, Helaine. See Dorothy Daniels
Ross, Sinclair (6)
Ross, Z.H. See Zola Ross
Ross, Zola (29)
Rowen, Deirdre. See Jeanne Williams
Rowland, Donald S. (348)
Rowlands, Effie. See Madame Albanesi
Rushing, Jane Gilmore (6)
Russell, Charles M. (8)
Ryan, Marah Ellis (19)
Ryder, Jonathan. See Robert Ludlum
Ryder, Thom. See John B. Harvey

Sabastian, Lee. See Robert Silverberg
Sabatini, Rafael (55)
Saberhagen, Fred (22)
Sachs, Marilyn (12)
St. George, Harry. See St. George Rathborne
St. John, Nicole. See Norma Johnston
Sale, Richard (15)
Salkey, Felix (17)
Sallis, James (2)
Sanborn, B.X. See Bill S. Ballinger
Sanders, Dorothy (43)
Sanders, Lawrence (11)
Sandon, J.D. See John B. Harvey
Sandoz, Mari (23)
Sands, Martin. See John Burke
Santee, Ross (13)
Sandys, Oliver. See Countess Barcynska
Sapper. See H.C. McNeile
Sarban (4)
Sargent, Pamela (5)
Saunders, John. See Arthur Thomas Nickson
Saunders, Mack. See Philip L. Ketchum
Saville, Malcolm (66)
Sawyer, Ruth (35)
Saunders, Hilary Adam St. George (45)
Saxon, John A. See Robert Leslie Bellem
Saxon, Richard. See J.L. Morrissey
Saxton, Josephine (5)
Sayers, Dorothy L. (37)
Sayers, James Denson (23)
Scarborough, Dorothy (9)
Scarry, Richard (68)
Schachner, Nat (6)
Schaefer, Jack (19)
Scherf, Margaret (32)

Schlee, Ann (5)
Schlein, Miriam (55)
Schmidt, Stanley (3)
Schmitz, James H. (11)
Schofield, Paul. See E.C. Tubb
Scortia, Thomas N. (8)
Scotland, Jay. See John Jakes
Scott, Anthony. See Davis Dresser
Scott, Dan. See S. Omar Barker
Scott, Janey. See Rachel Lindsay
Scott, Norford. See Donald S. Rowland
Scott, R.T.M. (9)
Scott, Valerie. See Donald S. Rowland
Scott, Warwick. See Elleston Trevor
Seale, Sara (50)
Seare, Nicholas. See Rod Whitaker
Searls, Hank (11)
Seed, Jenny (22)
Seeley, Mabel (10)
Seelye, John (4)
Segundo, Bart. See Donald S. Rowland
Seifert, Elizabeth (97)
Selden, George (11)
Sellings, Arthur (9)
Seltzer, Charles Alden (55)
Selwyn, Francis (5)
Senarens, Luis (218)
Sendak, Maurice (12)
Seredy, Kate (12)
Serling, Rod (11)
Serviss, Garrett P. (8)
Seton, Anya (13)
Seton, Ernest Thompson (41)
Seuss, Dr. (54)
Severn, David (28)
Sewell, Helen (9)
Seymour, Alan. See S. Fowler Wright
Shane, Bart. See Donald S. Rowland
Shane, John. See Paul Durst
Shannon, Monica (6)
Shannon, Dell. See Elizabeth Linington
Shannon, Steve. See J.L. Bouma
Sharkey, Jack (5)
Sharmat, Marjorie Weinman (25)
Sharp, Margery (38)
Shaul, Frank. See Donald S. Rowland
Shaver, Richard S. (1)
Shaw, Bob (16)
Shaw, Brian. See E.C. Tubb
Shaw, Felicity (15)
Shearing, Joseph. See Marjorie Bowen
Sheckley, Robert (30)
Sheldon, Lee. See Wayne Lee
Sheldon, Roy. See E.C. Tubb
Shellabarger, Samuel (22)
Shelley, John L. (11)
Shepherd, John. See Willis Todhunter Ballard
Shepherd, Michael. See Robert Ludlum
Shepherd, Neal. See Nigel Morland
Sheridan, Lee. See Elsie Lee
Sherriff, R.C. (2)
Shiras, Wilmar H. (2)
Short, Luke (68)
Shrake, Edwin (6)
Shura, Mary Francis. See Mary Francis Craig
Shute, Nevil (28)
Siller, Van (28)
Silver, Nicholas. See Frederick Faust

Silverberg, Robert (135)
Silvester, Frank. See David Bingley
Simak, Clifford D. (40)
Simon, Roger L. (5)
Simpson, Helen (22)
Sims, George (12)
Sims, John. See William Hopson
Sinclair, Grant. See Harry Sinclair Drago
Sinclair, Olga (18)
Sinclair, Upton (135)
Singer, Isaac Bashevis (32)
Sladek, John (13)
Slaughter, Frank G. (72)
Slesar, Henry (7)
Sloane, Sara. See Ursula Bloom
Sloane, William M. (13)
Slobodkin, Louis (42)
Slobodkina, Esphyr (14)
Smith, Caesar. See Elleston Trevor
Smith, Carmichael. See P.M.A. Linebarger
Smith, Clark Ashton (22)
Smith, Cordwainer. See P.M.A. Linebarger
Smith, E.E. (19)
Smith, George H. (25)
Smith, George O. (16)
Smith, Joan (16)
Smith, Shelley (19)
Smith, Wade. See Charles H. Snow
Snedeker, Caroline Dale (15)
Snow, Charles H. (419)
Snyder, Zilpha Keatley (14)
Sobol, Donald J. (15)
Sohl, Jerry (23)
Somers, Susanne. See Dorothy Daniels
Sorensen, Virginia (16)
Spain, John. See Cleve F. Adams
Speare, Elizabeth George (6)
Spearman, Frank H. (20)
Spellman, Roger G. See William R. Cox
Spence, Bill (32)
Spence, Duncan. See Bill Spence
Spencer, John. See Roy C. Vickers
Sperry, Armstrong (21)
Spicer, Bart (23)
Spillane, Mickey (25)
Spinrad, Norman (14)
Sprigg, Christopher St. John (13)
Springfield, David. See Roy Lewis
Spurr, Clinton. See Donald S. Rowland
Spykman, E.C. (5)
Stableford, Brian M. (36)
Stafford, Jean (13)
Stairs, Gordon. See Mary Austin
Stanfield, Anne. See Virginia Coffman
Stanley, Bennet. See S.B. Hough
Stanton, Vance. See Michael Avallone
Stark, Joshua. See T.V. Olsen
Stark, Richard. See Donald E. Westlake
Starr, Henry. See David Bingley
Starr, Roland. See Donald S. Rowland
Starrett, Vincent (39)
Stasheff, Christopher (3)
Steel, Danielle (15)
Steele, Mary Q. (15)
Steele, William O. (35)
Steelman, Robert J. (18)
Steen, Marguerite (45)
Stegner, Wallace (22)

Stein, Aaron Marc (110)
Steinbeck, John (37)
Steptoe, John (6)
Stevens, Blaine. See Harry Whittington
Stevens, Dan J. See Wayne D. Overholser
Stevens J.D. See Donald S. Rowland
Stevens, James (8)
Stevens, John. See E.C. Tubb
Stevenson. Anne (8)
Stevenson, Florence (38)
Stewart, J.I.M. (88)
Stewart, Mary (17)
Stewart, Will. See Jack Williamson
Stine, Hank (3)
Stockton, Frank R. (49)
Stoker, Bram (23)
Stolz, Mary (43)
Stone, Hampton. See Aaron Marc Stein
Stong, Phil (42)
Storm, Christopher. See T.V. Olsen
Storm, Virginia. See Theresa Charles
Stout, Rex (69)
Strange, John Stephen (34)
Strete, Craig (3)
Stribling, T.S. (16)
Stuart, Clay. See Harry Whittington
Stuart, Ian. See Alistair MacLean
Stuart, Sidney. See Michael Avallone
Sturgeon, Theodore (32)
Sublette, C.M. (5)
Suddaby, Donald (15)
Suffling, Mark. See Donald S. Rowland
Sullivan, Sean Mei. See Jerry Sohl
Summers, Diana. See George Henry Smith
Swarthout, Glendon (18)
Symons, Julian (47)

Taine, John. See Eric Temple Bell
Talbot, Kay. See Donald S. Rowland
Tall, Stephen (3)
Tate, Ellalice. See Victoria Holt
Tate, Joan (69)
Tate, Peter (6)
Tattersall, Jill (14)
Taylor, H. Baldwin. See Hillary Waugh
Taylor, Phoebe Atwood (33)
Taylor, Robert Lewis (11)
Taylor, Sydney (8)
Taylor, Theodore (9)
Telfair, Richard (11)
Tempest, Jan. See Theresa Charles
Temple, Dan. See D.B. Newton
Tenn, William (8)
Tennant, Emma (9)
Terry, C.V. See Frank G. Slaughter
Tevis, Walter (4)
Tey, Josephine (13)
Thames, C.H. See Milton Lesser
Thane, Elswyth (29)
Thayer, Geraldine. See Dorothy Daniels
Thayer, Lee (79)
Thomas, Ross (20)
Thomason, John Jr. (10)
Thompson, China. See Christianna Brand
Thompson, Thomas (17)
Thomson, Basil (31)
Thomson, Edward. See E.C. Tubb
Thomson, June (7)

Thorne, Nicola. See Rosemary Ellerbeck
Thorpe, Kay (32)
Thorpe, Sylvia (29)
Thurber, James (28)
Tidyman, Ernest (15)
Tilton, Alice. See Phoebe Atwood Taylor
Tippette, Giles (15)
Titus, Eve (18)
Todd, Barbara Euphan (36)
Tolbert, Frank X. (7)
Tolkien, J.R.R. (17)
Tomalin, Ruth (15)
Tompkins, Walter A. (48)
Torday, Ursula (81)
Torrie, Malcolm. See Gladys Mitchell
Townsend, John Rowe (19)
Traherne, Michael. See D.J. Watkins-Pitchford
Train, Arthur (49)
Tranter, Nigel (95)
Travers, Col. J.M. See St. George Rathborne
Travers, P.L. (14)
Travers, Will. See Donald S. Rowland
Travis, Gerry. See Louis Trimble
Treadgold, Mary (16)
Trease, Geoffrey (76)
Treat, Lawrence (20)
Tredgold, Nye. See Nigel Tranter
Treece, Henry (68)
Trench, John (6)
Tresselt, Alvin (51)
Trevanian. See Rod Whitaker
Trevor, Elleston (88)
Trevor, Glen. See James Hilton
Trevor, Meriol (31)
Trimble, Louis (65)
Tripp, Miles (23)
Tring, A. Stephen. See Laurence Meynell
Trollope, Joanna (6)
Troy, Katherine. See Anne Maybury
Troy, Simon. See Thurman Warriner
Tubb, E.C. (123)
Tucker, Link. See David Bingley
Tucker, Wilson (25)
Tudor, Tasha (19)
Tunis, John R. (32)
Turkle, Brinton (9)
Turner, Philip (17)
Turner, Clay. See Willis Todhunter Ballard
Tuttle, W.C. (90)
Twain, Mark (149)
Tyre, Nedra (9)

Uchida, Yoshiko (22)
Ude, Wayne (2)
Udry, Janice (23)
Uhnak, Dorothy (6)
Underwood, Michael (31)
Ungerer, Tomi (21)
Unwin, Nora S. (10)
Upfield, Arthur W. (43)
Upton, Bertha (15)
Updyke, James. See W.R. Burnett

Vaizey, Mrs. George de Horne (33)
Valentine, Douglas. See Valentine Williams
Valentine, Jo. See Charlotte Armstrong
Van Slyke, Helen (12)
Van Stockum, Hilda (22)

Vance, Jack (54)
Vance, Louis Joseph (41)
Vance, William E. (20)
Van Dine, S.S. (23)
van Vogt, A.E. (70)
Varley, John (6)
Vedette. See Valentine Williams
Verney, John (12)
Vernon, Roger Lee (2)
Verrill, A. Hyatt (76)
Veryan, Patricia (7)
Vickers, Roy C. (76)
Vidal, Gore (31)
Vine, Sarah. See Donald S. Rowland
Vinge, Joan D. (4)
Vining, Elizabeth Gray (29)
Vinson, Elaine. See Donald S. Rowland
Viorst, Judith (18)
Vonnegut, Kurt, Jr. (14)

Waber, Bernard (20)
Wade, Alan. See Jack Vance
Wade, Bob. See Robert Wade
Wade, Henry (24)
Wade, Jennifer. See Joy DeWeese-Wehen
Wade, Robert (53)
Wagoner, David (26)
Wahl, Jan (56)
Wainwright, John (51)
Waldo, Dave (11)
Walker, David (19)
Walker, Harry. See Hillary Waugh
Walker, Lucy. See Dorothy Lucy Sanders
Walker, Max. See Michael Avallone
Wallace, Edgar (200)
Wallace, Ian. See John Wallace Pritchard
Walling, R.A.J. (55)
Walsh, J.M. (89)
Walsh, Sheila (7)
Walsh, Thomas (11)
Walters, Hugh (27)
Walters, Rick. See Donald S. Rowland
Wambaugh, Joseph (5)
Wandrei, Donald (6)
Warborough, Martin Leach. See Grant Allen
Ward, Jonas. See William R. Cox
Ward, Jonas. see William Ard
Wardle, Dan. See Charles H. Snow
Warre, Mary Douglas. See Jennifer Greig-Smith
Warren, Charles Marquis (3)
Warren, Mary Douglas. See Jennifer Greig-Smith
Warriner, Thurman (20)
Waterloo, Stanley (12)
Waters, Frank (20)
Watkins, William Jon (10)
Watkins-Pitchford, D.J. (46)
Watson, Clyde (5)
Watson, Colin (16)
Watson, Ian (11)
Watts, Peter (125)
Waugh, Hillary (43)
Way, Margaret (43)
Wayland, Patrick. See Richard O'Connor
Wayne, Anderson. See Davis Dresser
Wayne, Jenifer (20)
Wayne, Joseph. See Wayne D. Overholser
Wayne, Joseph. See Lewis Bedford Patten
Webb, Christopher. See Leonard Wibberly

Webb, Jack (19)
Webb, Jean Francis (38)
Webb, Neil. See Donald S. Rowland
Webster, Jean (10)
Webster, Noah. See Bill Knox
Weinbaum, Stanley G. (7)
Weir, Rosemary (43)
Welch, James (3)
Welch, Ronald. See Ronald Felton
Welcome, John (20)
Wellman, Manly Wade (71)
Wellman, Paul I. (34)
Wells, Carolyn (163)
Wells, H.G. (155)
Wells, Hondo. See Harry Whittington
Wentworth, Patricia (87)
Wersba, Barbara (11)
West, Joyce (12)
West, Kingsley (9)
West, Tom (58)
West, Ward. See Hal Borland
West, Wallace George (19)
Westerman, Percy (176)
Westlake, Donald E. (63)
Westland, Lynn. See Archie Joscelyn
Westmacott, Mary. See Agatha Christie
Weston, Carolyn (7)
Weston, Helen Gray. See Dorothy Daniels
Westwood, Gwen (19)
Wharton, Anthony. See Lynn Brock
Wheatley, Dennis (77)
Whitaker, Rod (6)
White, Eliza Orne (38)
White, E.B. (19)
White, Ethel Lina (23)
White, Harry. See Harry Whittington
White, James (18)
White, Jon Manchip (25)
White, Jonathan. See John B. Harvey
White, Lionel (35)
White, Stewart Edward (58)
White, Ted (14)
White, T.H. (25)
Whitechurch, Victor L. (26)
Whitfield, Raoul (8)
Whitney, Hallam. See Harry Whittington
Whitney, Phyllis A. (62)
Whitson, John H. (29)
Whittington, Harry (120)
Wibberley, Leonard (101)
Wick, Carter. See Collin Wilcox
Wigan, Christopher. See David Bingley
Wiggin, Kate Douglas (34)
Wigg, T.I.G. See Philip McCutchan
Wilcox, Collin (17)
Wilder, Laura Ingalls (9)
Wilhelm, Kate (19)
Will, Thomas. See William Ard
Willard, Barbara (26)
Williams, J.R. See Jeanne Williams
Williams, Claudette (14)
Williams, Gordon (16)
Williams, Jay (67)
Williams, Jeanne (45)
Williams, John (6)
Williams, John A. (16)
Williams, Robert Moore (28)
Williams, Ursula Moray (59)

Williams, Valentine (37)
Williamson, Jack (37)
Willis, Ted (25)
Willoughby, Cass. See T.V. Olsen
Willoughby, Lee Davis. See Jean Francis Webb
Wills, Cecil M. (27)
Wills, Chester. See Charles H. Snow
Wilmer, Dale. See Robert Wade
Wilson, Barbara Ker (19)
Wilson, Colin (51)
Wilson, Harry Leon (21)
Wilson, Richard (5)
Wilson, Robert Anton (5)
Winch, John. See Marjorie Bowen
Winsor, Kathleen (6)
Winspear, Violet (61)
Winstan, Matt. See Arthur Nickson
Winston, Daoma (49)
Winther, Sophus K. (6)
Wister, Owen (22)
Witting, Clifford (19)
Wolfe, Gene (8)
Wollheim, Donald A. (9)
Wood, Lorna (21)
Woodiwiss, Kathleen E. (4)
Woods, Sara (30)
Woolf, Douglas (9)
Woolrich, Cornell (50)
Worboys, Anne (30)
Worboys, Anne Eyre. See Anne Worboys
Wormser, Richard (40)
Wren, P.C. (47)
Wright, Austin Tappan (1)
Wright, Harold Bell (19)
Wright, Rowland. See Carolyn Wells
Wright, S. Fowler (62)
Wrightson, Patricia (10)
Wylie, Philip (45)
Wynd, Oswald (32)
Wyndham, John (29)
Wyndham, Lee (41)
Wynne, Brian. See Dudley Dean
Wynne, May (207)

Yarbro, Chelsea Quinn (15)
Yates, A.G. (38)
Yates, Dornford (39)
Yates, Elizabeth (48)
Yerby, Frank (32)
Yolen, Jane (38)
Yorke, Andrew. See Christopher Nicole
Yorke, Katherine. See Rosemary Ellerbeck
Yorke, Margaret (22)
Yorke, Roger. See David Bingley
Young, Delbert Alton (5)
Young, Carter Travis. See Louis Charbonneau
Young, Collier. See Robert Bloch
Young, Gordon (42)
Young, Wilson. See Giles Tippette
Yuill, P.B. See Gordon Williams

Zagat, Arthur Leo (1)
Zangwill, Israel (61)
Zebrowski, George (5)
Zelazny, Roger (27)
Zinberg, Len (39)
Zindel, Paul (6)
Zion, Gene (14)
Zolotow, Charlotte (57)

Section III

The Authors and Their Books

Aarons, Edward S. (Sidney)
American, born 1916 in Philadelphia, died June 16, 1975
Pseudonyms: Paul Ayres, Edward Ronns
1. *Death In a Lighthouse,* as Edward Ronns. New York, 1938
2. *Murder Money,* as Edward Ronns. New York, 1938
3. *The Corpse Hangs High,* as Edward Ronns. New York, 1939
4. *No Place to Live,* as Edward Ronns. Philadelphia, 1947
5. *Terror in the Town,* as Edward Ronns. Philadelphia, 1947
6. *Gift of Death,* as Edward Ronns. Philadelphia, 1948
7. *Nightmare.* Philadelphia, 1948
8. *Dead Heat,* as Paul Ayres. Drexel Hill (PA), 1950
9. *The Art Studio Murders,* as Edward Ronns. Kingston (NY), 1950
10. *Catspaw Ordeal,* as Edward Ronns. New York, 1950
11. *Dark Memory,* as Edward Ronns. Kingston, 1950
12. *Million Dollar Murder,* as Edward Ronns. New York, 1950
13. *State Department Murders,* as Edward Ronns. New York, 1950
14. *The Decoy,* as Edward Ronns. New York, 1950
15. *I Can't Stop Running,* as Edward Ronns. New York, 1951
16. *Escape to Love.* New York, 1952
17. *Don't Cry, Beloved,* as Edward Ronns. New York, 1952
18. *Passage to Terror,* as Edward Ronns. New York, 1952
19. *Come Back, My Love.* New York, 1953
20. *The Sinners.* New York, 1953
21. *Dark Destiny,* as Edward Ronns. Hasbrouck Heights (NJ), 1953
22. *The Net,* as Edward Ronns. Hasbrouck Heights, 1953
23. *Say It with Murder,* as Edward Ronns. Hasbrouck Heights, 1954
24. *Girl on the Run.* New York, 1954
25. *Assignment to Disaster.* New York, 1955
26. *They All Ran Away,* as Edward Ronns. Hasbrouck Heights, 1955
27. *Assignment—Suicide.* New York, 1956
28. *Assignment—Treason.* New York, 1956
29. *Point of Peril,* as Edward Ronns. New York, 1956
30. *Assignment—Budapest.* New York, 1957
31. *Assignment—Stella Marni.* New York, 1957
32. *Death Is My Shadow,* as Edward Ronns. New York, 1957
33. *Pickup Alley,* as Edward Ronns. New York, 1957
34. *Assignment—Angelina.* New York, 1958
35. *Assignment—Madeleine.* New York, 1958
36. *Gang Rumble,* as Edward Ronns. New York, 1958
37. *The Lady Takes a Flyer,* as Edward Ronns. New York, 1958
38. *Assignment—Carlotta Cortez.* New York, 1959
39. *Assignment—Helene.* New York, 1959
40. *Assignment—Lili Lamaris.* New York, 1959
41. *The Big Bedroom,* as Edward Ronns. New York, 1959
42. *The Black Orchid,* as Edward Ronns. New York, 1959
43. *But Not for Me,* as Edward Ronns. New York, 1959
44. *Assignment—Mara Tirana.* New York, 1960
45. *Hell to Eternity.* New York, 1960
46. *Assignment—Zoraya.* New York, 1960
47. *Assignment—Ankara.* New York, 1961
48. *Assignment—Lowlands.* New York, 1961
49. *The Defenders.* New York, 1961
50. *Assignment—Burma Girl.* New York, 1962
51. *Assignment—Karachi.* New York, 1962
52. *The Glass Cage,* as Edward Ronns. New York, 1962
53. *Assignment—Sorrento Siren.* New and London, 1963
54. *Assignment—Manchurian Doll.* New York, 1963
55. *Assignment—Sulu Sea.* New York, 1964
56. *Assignment—The Girl in the Gondola.* New York, 1964
57. *Assignment—The Cairo Dancers.* New York, 1965
58. *Assignment—Palermo.* New York, 1966
59. *Assignment—Cong Hai Kill.* New York, 1966
60. *Assignment—School for Spies.* New York, 1966
61. *Assignment—Black Viking.* New York, 1967
62. *Assignment—Moon Girl.* New York, 1967
63. *Assignment—Nuclear Nude.* New York, 1968
64. *Assignment—Peking.* New York, 1969
65. *Assignment—Star Stealers.* New York and London, 1970
66. *Assignment—White Rajah.* New York and London, 1970
67. *Assignment—Tokyo.* New York and London, 1971
68. *Assignment—Bangkok.* New York and London, 1972
69. *Assignment—Golden Girl.* New York and London, 1972
70. *Assignment—Maltese Maiden.* New York, 1972
71. *Assignment—Ceylon.* New York, 1973
72. *Assignment—Silver Scorpion.* New York, 1973
73. *Assignment—Amazon Queen.* New York, 1974
74. *Assignment—Sumatra.* New York, 1974
75. *Assignment—Black Gold.* New York, 1975
76. *Assignment—Quayle Question.* New York, 1975.

Abbey, Edward
American, born in 1927
1. *Jonathan Troy.* New York, 1954
2. *The Brave Cowboy.* New York, 1956
3. *Fire on the Mountain.* New York, 1962
4. *Desert Solitaire: A Season in the Wilderness.* New York, 1968

5. *Appalachian Wilderness: The Great Smoky Mountains.* New York, 1970
6. *Slickrock: The Canyon Country of Southeast Utah,* with Philip Hyde. New York, 1971
7. *Black Sun.* New York, 1971
8. *Cactus Country.* New York, 1973
9. *The Monkey Wrench Gang.* Philadelphia, 1975
10. *The Hidden Canyon: A River Journey.* New York, 1977
11. *The Journey Home: Some Words in Defense of the American West.* New York, 1977
12. *Desert Images: An American Landscape.* New York, 1978
13. *Back Roads of Arizona.* Flagstaff (AZ), 1978
14. *Abbey's Road: Take the Other.* New York, 1979
15. *Good News.* New York, 1980
16. *Down the River.* New York, 1982.

Adams, Andy
American, born in 1859, died September 26, 1935
1. *The Log of a Cowboy.* Boston and London, 1903
2. *A Texas Matchmaker.* Boston and London, 1904
3. *The Outlet.* Boston and London, 1906
4. *Cattle Brands: A Collection of Western Camp-Fire Stories.* Boston and London, 1906
5. *Reed Anthony, Cowman: An Autobiography.* Boston, 1907
6. *Wells Brothers, The Young Cattle Kings.* Boston and London, 1911
7. *The Ranch of the Beaver.* Boston, 1927
8. *Why the Chisholm Trail Fords and Other Tales of the Cattle Country.* Austin (TX), 1956.

Adams, Cleve F. (Franklin)
American, born in 1895, died December 28, 1949
Pseudonyms: Franklin Charles, John Spain
1. *And Sudden Death.* New York, 1940
2. *Sabotage.* New York, 1940
3. *The Black Door.* New York, 1941
4. *Decoy.* New York, 1941
5. *The Vice Czar Murders,* as Franklin Charles, with Robert Leslie Bellem. New York, 1941
6. *Dig Me a Grave,* as John Spain. New York, 1942
7. *The Private Eye.* New York, 1942
8. *What Price Murder.* New York, 1942
9. *Up Jumped the Devil.* New York, 1943
10. *Death Is Like That,* as John Spain. New York, 1943
11. *The Crooking Finger.* New York, 1944
12. *The Evil Star,* as John Spain. New York, 1944
13. *Contraband.* New York, 1950
14. *No Wings on a Cop.* Kingston (NY), 1950
15. *Shady Lady.* New York, 1955

Adams, Clifton
American, born in 1919
Pseudonyms: Jonathan Gant, Matt Kinkaid, Clay Randall
1. *The Desperado.* New York, 1950
2. *A Noose for the Desperado.* New York, 1951
3. *The Colonel's Lady.* New York, 1952
4. *Six-Gun Boss,* as Clay Randall. New York, 1952
5. *When Oil Ran Red,* as Clay Randall. New York, 1953
6. *Whom Gods Destroy.* New York, 1953
7. *Hardcase,* as Matt Kinkaid. New York, 1953
8. *Two-Gun Law.* New York, 1954
9. *Gambling Man.* New York, 1955
10. *Death's Sweet Song.* New York, 1955
11. *The Race of Giants,* as Matt Kinkaid. New York, 1956
12. *Never Say No to a Killer,* as Jonathan Gant. New York, 1956
13. *Law of the Trigger.* New York, 1956
14. *Outlaw's Son.* New York, 1957
15. *Boomer,* as Clay Randall. New York, 1957
16. *Killer in Town.* New York, 1959
17. *Stranger in Town.* New York, 1960
18. *The Legend of Lonnie Hall.* New York, 1960
19. *The Very Wicked.* New York, 1960
20. *Day of the Gun.* New York, 1962
21. *Reckless Men.* New York, 1962
22. *The Moonlight War.* New York and London, 1963
23. *Hogan's Way.* New York, 1963
24. *The Dangerous Days of Kiowa Jones.* New York, 1963
25. *The Oceola Kid,* as Clay Randall. New York, 1963
26. *Hardcase for Hire,* as Clay Randall. New York, 1963
27. *The Long Vendetta,* as Jonathan Gant. New York, 1963
28. *Amos Flagg—Lawman,* as Clay Randall. New York, 1964
29. *Doomsday Creek.* New York, 1964
30. *The Hottest Fourth of July in the History of Hangtree County.* New York, 1964
31. *Amos Flagg—High Gun,* as Clay Randall. New York, 1965
32. *The Grabhorn Bounty.* New York, 1965
33. *Shorty.* New York and London, 1966
34. *The Most Dangerous Profession.* New York, 1967
35. *Amos Flagg—Bushwhacked,* as Clay Randall. New York and London, 1967
36. *Amos Flagg Rides Out,* as Clay Randall. New York and London, 1967
37. *Amos Flagg Has His Day,* as Clay Randall. New York, 1968
38. *A Partnership with Death.* New York and London, 1968
39. *Amos Flagg—Showdown,* as Clay Randall. New York, 1969
40. *Dude Sheriff.* New York, 1969
41. *Tragg's Choice.* New York, 1969
42. *The Last Days of Wolf Garnett.* New York, 1970
43. *Biscuit-Shooter.* New York, 1971
44. *Rogue Cowboy.* New York, 1971
45. *The Badge and Harry Cole.* New York, 1972
46. *Concannon.* New York, 1972
47. *Hard Times and Arnie Smith.* New York, 1972
48. *Once an Outlaw.* New York, 1973
49. *The Hard Time Bunch.* New York, 1973
50. *Hassle and the Medicine Man.* New York, 1973

Adams, Richard
British, born in 1920
1. *Watership Down.* London, 1972
2. *Shardik.* London, 1974
3. *Nature Through the Seasons,* with Max Hooper. London, 1975
4. *The Tyger Voyage.* London and New York, 1976
5. *The Ship's Cat.* London and New York, 1977
6. *The Plague Dogs.* London, 1977

Adlard, Mark
British, born in 1932
1. *Interface.* London, 1971
2. *Volteface.* London, 1972
3. *Multiface.* London, 1975
4. *The Greenlander.* London, 1978

Agee, James
American, born in 1905, died in 1955
1. *Permit Me Voyage.* New Haven (CT), 1934
2. *Let Us Now Praise Famous Men.* Boston, 1941
3. *Knoxville: Summer of 1915. . . .* New York, 1949
4. *The Morning Watch.* Boston, 1951
5. *A Death In the Family.* New York, 1957
6. *Agee On Film.* New York, 1958
7. *Agee on Film—Volume Two.* New York, 1960
8. *Letters of James Agee to Father Flye.* New York, 1962

9. *A Way of Seeing.* New York, 1965
10. *Many Are Called.* Boston, 1966
11. *The Collected Poems of James Agee.* Boston, 1968
12. *The Collected Short Prose of James Agee.* Boston, 1968
13. *The Last Letter of James Agee to Father Flye.* Boston, 1969

Ahlswede, Ann
American, born in 1928
1. *Day of the Hunter.* New York, 1960
2. *Hunting Wolf.* New York, 1960
3. *The Savage Land.* New York, 1962

Aiken, Joan (Delano)
British, born in 1924
1. *All You've Ever Wanted and Other Stories.* London, 1953
2. *More Than You Bargained For and Other Stories.* London, 1955
3. *The Kingdom and the Cave.* London and New York, 1960
4. *The Wolves of Willoughby Chase.* London, 1962
5. *Black Hearts in Battersea.* New York, 1964
6. *The Silence of Herondale.* New York, 1964
7. *The Fortune Hunters.* New York, 1965
8. *Nightbirds of Nantucket.* London and New York, 1966
9. *Beware of the Banquet.* New York, 1966
10. *Trouble with Product X.* London, 1966
11. *Dark Interval.* New York, 1967
12. *Hate Begins at Home.* London, 1967
13. *The Ribs of Death.* London, 1967
14. *The Crystal Crow.* New York, 1968
15. *A Necklace of Raindrops and Other Stories.* London and New York, 1968
16. *The Whispering Mountain.* London, 1968
17. *Armitage, Armitage, Fly Away Home.* New York, 1968
18. *A Small Pinch of Weather and Other Stories.* London, 1969
19. *Night Fall.* London, 1969
20. *The Windscreen Weepers and Other Tales of Horror and Suspense.* London, 1969
21. *The Embroidered Sunset.* London and New York, 1970
22. *Smoke From Cromwell's Time and Other Stories.* New York, 1970
23. *The Green Flash and Other Tales of Horror, Suspense, and Fantasy.* New York, 1971
24. *The Cuckoo Tree.* London and New York, 1971
25. *The Kingdom under the Sea and Other Stories.* London, 1971
26. *All and More.* London, 1971
27. *Died On a Rainy Sunday.* London and New York, 1972
28. *A Harp of Fishbones and Other Stories.* London, 1972
29. *Arabel's Raven.* London, 1972
30. *The Butterfly Picnic.* London, 1972
31. *A Cluster of Separate Sparks.* New York, 1972
32. *Winterthing.* New York, 1972
33. *The Escaped Black Mamba.* London, 1973
34. *The Mooncusser's Daughter.* New York, 1973
35. *All But a Few.* London, 1974
36. *The Bread Bin.* London, 1974
37. *Midnight Is a Place.* London and New York, 1974
38. *Not What You Expected: A Collection of Short Stories.* New York, 1974
39. *Voices In An Empty House.* London and New York, 1975
40. *Mortimer's Tie.* London, 1976
41. *A Bundle of Nerves.* London, 1976
42. *The Skin Spinners.* New York, 1976
43. *Castle Barebane.* London and New York, 1976
44. *The Far Forests.* New York, 1977
45. *Go Saddle the Sea.* London and New York, 1977
46. *Last Movement.* London, 1977
47. *The Five-Minute Marriage.* London, 1977
48. *The Faithless Lollybird.* London, 1977
49. *Tale of a One-Way Street.* London, 1977
50. *The Smile of the Stranger.* London and New York, 1978
51. *Mice and Mendelson.* London, 1978
52. *Mortimer and the Sword Excalibur.* London, 1979
53. *The Spiral Stair.* London, 1979
54. *A Touch of Chill.* London, 1979
55. *Arabel and Mortimer.* London, 1979
56. *The Lightning Tree.* London, 1980
57. *The Shadow Guests.* New York, 1980
58. *The Weeping Ash.* New York, 1980
59. *Mortimer's Portrait on Glass.* London, 1980
60. *Mr. Jones' Disappearing Taxi.* London, 1980
61. *The Stolen Lake.* London and New York, 1981
62. *The Young Lady from Paris.* London, 1982
63. *The Girl From Paris.* New York, 1982
64. *A Whisper in the Night.* London, 1982
65. *The Way to Write for Children.* London, 1982

Ainsworth, Patricia [Patricia Nina Bigg]
1. *The Flickering Candle.* London, 1968
2. *The Candle Rekindled.* London, 1969
3. *Steady Burns the Candle.* London, 1970
4. *The Devil's Hole.* London, 1971
5. *Portrait in Gold.* London, 1971
6. *A String of Silver Beads.* London, 1972
7. *The Bridal Lamp.* London, 1975
8. *The Enchanted Cup.* London, 1980

Ainsworth, Ruth
British, born in 1908.
1. *Tales about Tony.* London, 1936
2. *Mr. Popcorn's Friends.* London, 1938
3. *The Gingerbread House.* London, 1938
4. *The Ragamuffins.* London, 1939
5. *Richard's First Term.* London, 1940
6. *All Different.* London, 1947
7. *Five and a Dog.* London, 1949
8. *"Listen with Mother" Tales.* London, 1951
9. *Rufty Tufty the Golliwog.* London, 1952
10. *The Evening Listens.* London, 1953
11. *Rufty Tufty at the Seaside.* London, 1954
12. *Charles Stories and Others, from "Listen with Mother."* London, 1954
13. *More about Charles and Other Stories, from "Listen with Mother."* London, 1954
14. *Three Little Mushrooms: Four Puppet Plays.* London, 1955
15. *More Little Mushrooms: Four Puppet Plays.* London, 1955
16. *The Snow Bear.* London, 1956
17. *Rufty Tufty Goes Camping.* London, 1956
18. *Rufty Tufty Runs Away.* London, 1957
19. *Five "Listen with Mother" Tales about Charles.* London, 1957
20. *Nine Drummers Drumming.* London, 1958
21. *Rufty Tufty Flies High.* London, 1959
22. *Cherry Stones: A Book of Fairy Stories.* London, 1960
23. *Rufty Tufty's Island.* London, 1960
24. *Lucky Dip: A Selection of Stories and Verses.* London, 1961
25. *Rufty Tufty and Hattie.* London, 1962
26. *Far-Away Children.* London, 1963
27. *The Ten Tales of Shellover.* London, 1963
28. *The Wolf Who Was Sorry.* London, 1964
29. *Rufty Tufty Makes a House.* London, 1965
30. *Daisy the Cow.* London, 1966
31. *Horse on Wheels.* London, 1966
32. *Jack Frost.* London, 1966
33. *Roly the Railway Mouse.* London, 1967
34. *The Aeroplane Who Wanted to See the Sea.* London, 1968

35. *Boris the Teddy Bear.* London, 1968
36. *Dougal the Donkey.* London, 1968
37. *More Tales of Shellover.* London and New York, 1968
38. *Mungo the Monkey.* London, 1968
39. *The Old Fashioned Car.* London, 1968
40. *The Rabbit and His Shadow.* London, 1968
41. *The Noah's Ark.* London, 1969
42. *Roly the Railroad Mouse.* New York, 1969
43. *The Bicycle Wheel.* London, 1969
44. *Look, Do and Listen.* London and New York, 1969
45. *The Ruth Ainsworth Book.* London and New York, 1970
46. *The Phantom Cyclist and Other Stories.* London and Chicago, 1971
47. *Dandy the Donkey.* London, 1971
48. *The Wild Wood.* London, 1971
49. *Fairy Gold: Favourite Tales Retold for the Very Young.* London, 1972
50. *Another Lucky Dip.* London, 1973
51. *The Phantom Fisherboy: Tales of Mystery and Magic.* London, 1974
52. *Bedtime Book.* Maidenhead (Eng), 1974
53. *Three's Company.* London, 1974
54. *Three Bags Full.* London, 1975
55. *The Bear Who Liked Hugging People and Other Stories.* London, 1976
56. *The Phantom Roundabout and Other Stories.* London, 1977
57. *Up the Airy Mountain.* London, 1977

Aird, Catherine [Kinn Hamilton McIntosh]
British, born June 20, 1930
1. *The Religious Body.* New York, 1966
2. *A Most Contagious Game.* New York, 1967
3. *Henrietta Who?* New York, 1968
4. *The Complete Steel.* London, 1969
5. *The Stately Home Murder.* New York, 1970
6. *A Late Phoenix.* New York, 1971
7. *His Burial Too.* New York, 1973
8. *Slight Mourning.* New York, 1976
9. *Parting Breath.* New York, 1978

Albanesi, Madame [Effie Adelaide Maria Albanesi]
British, born in 1859, died October 16, 1936
Pseudonym: Effie Rowlands
1. *Margery Daw,* anonymously. London and New York, 1886
2. *The Spell of Ursula,* as Effie Rowlands. Philadelphia, 1894
3. *The Woman Who Came Between,* as Effie Rowlands. London, 1895
4. *At Great Cost,* as Effie Rowlands. New York, 1895
5. *Little Kit,* as Effie Rowlands. New York, 1895
6. *A Faithful Traitor,* as Effie Rowlands. London and Philadelphia, 1896
7. *The Fault of One,* as Effie Rowlands. London and Philadelphia, 1897
8. *The Blunder of an Innocent.* London, 1899
9. *The Kingdom of a Heart,* as Effie Rowlands. London and New York, 1899
10. *They Laugh That Win,* as Effie Rowlands. London and New York, 1899
11. *A Woman Scorned,* as Effie Rowlands. New York, 1899
12. *A King and a Coward,* as Effie Rowlands. New York, 1899
13. *Little Lady Charles,* as Effie Rowlands. New York, 1899
14. *The Heart of Hetta,* as Effie Rowlands. Chicago, 1900
15. *Husband and Foe,* as Effie Rowlands. New York, 1900
16. *Beneath a Spell,* as Effie Rowlands. New York, 1900
17. *A Charity Girl,* as Effie Rowlands. New York, 1900
18. *The Man She Loved,* as Effie Rowlands. New York, 1900
19. *One Man's Evil,* as Effie Rowlands. New York, 1900
20. *Brave Barbara.* New York, 1901
21. *Peter, A Parasite.* London, 1901
22. *Love and Louisa.* London and Philadelphia, 1902
23. *Susannah and One Elder.* London, 1903
24. *Susannah and One Other.* New York, 1904
25. *For Ever True,* as Effie Rowlands. New York, 1904
26. *Capricious Caroline.* London, 1904
27. *A Love Almost Lost,* as Effie Rowlands. London, 1905
28. *Angel of Evil,* as Effie Rowlands. New York, 1905
29. *Her Husband and Her Love,* as Effie Rowlands. New York, 1905
30. *So Like a Man,* as Effie Rowlands. New York, 1905
31. *The Splendid Man,* as Effie Rowlands. New York, 1905
32. *Marian Sax.* London, 1905
33. *The Brown Eyes of Mary.* London, 1905
34. *The Wiles of a Siren,* as Effie Rowlands. New York, 1906
35. *The End Crowns All,* as Effie Rowlands. New York, 1906
36. *A Shadowed Happiness,* as Effie Rowlands. New York, 1906
37. *For Love of Sigrid,* as Effie Rowlands. New York, 1906
38. *Love's Greatest Gift,* as Effie Rowlands. New York, 1906
39. *My Lady of Dreadwood,* as Effie Rowlands. New York, 1906
40. *A Wife's Triumph,* as Effie Rowlands. New York, 1906
41. *Sweet William.* London, 1906
42. *I Know a Maiden.* London, 1906
43. *A Little Brown Mouse.* London, 1906
44. *A Young Man from the Country.* London, 1906
45. *Love-in-a-Mist.* London, 1907
46. *The Strongest of All Things.* London, 1907
47. *Simple Simon.* London, 1907
48. *Pretty Penelope,* as Effie Rowlands. London, 1907
49. *The Forbidden Road.* New York, 1908
50. *The Laughter of Life.* New York, 1908
51. *Sister Anne.* London, 1908
52. *The Rose of Yesterday.* London, 1908
53. *Drusilla's Point of View.* London, 1908
54. *Pretty Polly Pennington.* London, 1908
55. *The Invincible Amelia, or, The Polite Adventuress.* London, 1909
56. *A Question of Quality.* London, 1909
57. *Envious Eliza.* London, 1909
58. *The Marriage of Margaret.* London, 1909
59. *The Glad Heart.* London, 1910
60. *For Love of Anne Lambert.* London, 1910
61. *Maisie's Romance.* London, 1910
62. *Her Punishment,* as Effie Rowlands. London, 1910
63. *The Man She Married,* as Effie Rowlands. London, 1910
64. *After Many Days,* as Effie Rowlands. London, 1910
65. *Contrary Mary,* as Effie Rowlands. London, 1910
66. *A Dangerous Woman,* as Effie Rowlands. London, 1910
67. *For Love of Speranza,* as Effie Rowlands. London, 1910
68. *The Game of Life,* as Effie Rowlands. London, 1910
69. *Her Heart's Longing,* as Effie Rowlands. London, 1910
70. *Her Kingdom,* as Effie Rowlands. London, 1910
71. *John Galbraith's Wife,* as Effie Rowlands. London, 1910
72. *Love for Love,* as Effie Rowlands. London, 1910
73. *A Loyal Man's Love,* as Effie Rowlands. London, 1910
74. *The Master of Lynch Towers,* as Effie Rowlands. London, 1910
75. *The Mistress of the Farm,* as Effie Rowlands. London, 1910
76. *Bitter Sweet,* as Effie Rowlands. London, 1910
77. *A Splendid Destiny,* as Effie Rowlands. London, 1910
78. *Barbara's Love Story,* as Effie Rowlands. London, 1911
79. *Brave Heart,* as Effie Rowlands. London, 1911
80. *Carlton's Wife,* as Effie Rowlands. London, 1911
81. *Dare and Do,* as Effie Rowlands. London, 1911
82. *False Faith,* as Effie Rowlands. London, 1911
83. *For Ever and a Day,* as Effie Rowlands. London, 1911
84. *A Girl with a Heart,* as Effie Rowlands London, 1911

85. *Her Mistake*, as Effie Rowlands. London, 1911
86. *Leila Vane's Burden*, as Effie Rowlands. London, 1911
87. *A Life's Love*, as Effie Rowlands. London, 1911
88. *Love's Harvest*, as Effie Rowlands. London, 1911
89. *The Madness of Love*, as Effie Rowlands. London, 1911
90. *The Man at the Gate*, as Effie Rowlands. London, 1911
91. *The One Woman*, as Effie Rowlands. London, 1911
92. *The Power of Love*, as Effie Rowlands. London, 1911
93. *Splendid Love*, as Effie Rowlands. London, 1911
94. *White Abbey*, as Effie Rowlands. London, 1911
95. *A Wild Rose*, as Effie Rowlands. London, 1911
96. *A Woman Worth Winning*, as Effie Rowlands. London, 1911
97. *A Woman's Heart*, as Effie Rowlands. London, 1911
98. *The Young Wife*, as Effie Rowlands. London, 1911
99. *Love's Fire*, as Effie Rowlands. London, 1911
100. *The Triumph of Love*, as Effie Rowlands. London, 1911
101. *A Wonder of Love*. London, 1911
102. *Poppies in the Corn*. London, 1911
103. *Heart of His Heart*. London, 1911
104. *On the Wings of Fate*, as Effie Rowlands. New York, no date
105. *Andrew Leicester's Love*, as Effie Rowlands. New York, no date
106. *Carla*, as Effie Rowlands. New York, no date
107. *Change of Heart*, as Effie Rowlands. New York, no date
108. *False and True*, as Effie Rowlands. New York, no date
109. *For Love and Honor*, as Effie Rowlands. New York, no date
110. *The Girl's Kingdom*, as Effie Rowlands. New York, no date
111. *Interloper*, as Effie Rowlands. Chicago, no date
112. *Kinsman's Sin*, as Effie Rowlands. New York, no date
113. *Love's Cruel Whim*, as Effie Rowlands. New York, no date
114. *Selina's Love Story*, as Effie Rowlands. New York, no date
115. *Siren's Heart*, as Effie Rowlands. New York, no date
116. *Spurned Proposal*, as Effie Rowlands. New York, no date
117. *Temptation of Mary Barr*, as Effie Rowlands. New York, no date
118. *Tempted by Love*, as Effie Rowlands. New York, no date
119. *With Heart So True*, as Effie Rowlands. New York, no date
120. *Woman Against Her*, as Effie Rowlands. New York, no date
121. *Woman Against Woman*, as Effie Rowlands. New York, no date
122. *Woman Scorned*, as Effie Rowlands. New York, no date
123. *A Golden Dawn*, as Effie Rowlands. London, 1912
124. *A Heart's Triumph*, as Effie Rowlands. London, 1912
125. *Hester Trefusis*, as Effie Rowlands. London, 1912
126. *The House of Sunshine*, as Effie Rowlands. London, 1912
127. *In Love's Land*, as Effie Rowlands. London, 1912
128. *A Love Match*, as Effie Rowlands. London, 1912
129. *The Love of His Life*, as Effie Rowlands. London, 1912
130. *The Rose of Life*, as Effie Rowlands. London, 1912
131. *Temptation*, as Effie Rowlands. London, 1912
132. *To Love and to Cherish*, as Effie Rowlands. London, 1912
133. *The Wooing of Rose*, as Effie Rowlands. London, 1912
134. *His One Love*, as Effie Rowlands. London, 1912
135. *Lavender's Love Story*, as Effie Rowlands. London, 1912
136. *Love Wins*, as Effie Rowlands. London, 1912
137. *A Modern Witch*, as Effie Rowlands. London, 1912
138. *Olivia Mary*. London, 1912
139. *The Beloved Enemy*. London, 1913
140. *One of the Crowd*. London, 1913
141. *Cissy*. London, 1913
142. *Beth Mason*, as Effie Rowlands. London, 1913
143. *Elsie Brant's Romance*, as Effie Rowlands. London, 1913
144. *Hearts at War*, as Effie Rowlands. London, 1913
145. *The Joy of Life*, as Effie Rowlands. London, 1913
146. *Lady Patricia's Faith*, as Effie Rowlands. London, 1913
147. *Love's Mask*, as Effie Rowlands. London, 1913
148. *Margaret Dent*, as Effie Rowlands. London, 1913
149. *Ruth's Romance*, as Effie Rowlands. London, 1913
150. *Stranger Than Truth*, as Effie Rowlands. London, 1913
151. *The Surest Bond*, as Effie Rowlands. London, 1913
152. *Through Weal and Through Woe*, as Effie Rowlands. London, 1913
153. *In Daffodil Time*, as Effie Rowlands. London, 1913
154. *The Heart of a Woman*, as Effie Rowlands. London, 1913
155. *Judged by Faith*, as Effie Rowlands. London, 1913
156. *The Cap of Youth*. London, 1914
157. *The Sunlit Hills*. London, 1914
158. *The Hand of Fate*, as Effie Rowlands. London, 1914
159. *Her Husband*, as Effie Rowlands. London, 1914
160. *An Irish Lover*, as Effie Rowlands. London, 1914
161. *Money or Wife?*, as Effie Rowlands. London, 1914
162. *On the High Road*, as Effie Rowlands. London, 1914
163. *Two Waifs*, as Effie Rowlands. London, 1914
164. *At Her Mercy*, as Effie Rowlands. London, 1914
165. *The Price Paid*, as Effie Rowlands. London, 1914
166. *Prudence Langford's Ordeal*, as Effie Rowlands. London, 1914
167. *Love's Young Dream*, as Effie Rowlands. London, 1914
168. *Above All Things*, as Effie Rowlands. London, 1915
169. *Sunset and Dawn*, as Effie Rowlands. London, 1915
170. *The Woman's Fault*, as Effie Rowlands. London, 1915
171. *Hearts and Sweethearts*. London, 1916
172. *The Girl Who Was Brave*, as Effie Rowlands. London, 1916
173. *When Michael Came to Town*. London, 1917
174. *The Splendid Friend*, as Effie Rowlands. London, 1917
175. *The Heart of Angela Brent*, as Effie Rowlands. London, 1917
176. *Truant Happiness*. London, 1918
177. *Diana Falls in Love*. London, 1919
178. *Tony's Wife*. London, 1919
179. *Punch and Judy*. London, 1919
180. *A Strange Love Story*, as Effie Rowlands. London, 1919
181. *Patricia and Life*. London, 1920
182. *John Helsby's Wife*, as Effie Rowlands. London, 1920
183. *The House That Jane Built*. London, 1921
184. *Mary Dunbar's Love*, as Effie Rowlands. London, 1921
185. *Roseanne*. London, 1922
186. *Truth in a Circle*. London, 1922
187. *Against the World*, as Effie Rowlands. London, 1923
188. *The Flame of Love*, as Effie Rowlands. London, 1923
189. *The Garland of Youth*, as Effie Rowlands. London, 1923
190. *A Bird in a Storm*. London, 1924
191. *Young Hearts*, as Effie Rowlands. London, 1924
192. *The Life Line*, as Effie Rowlands. London, 1924
193. *Real Gold*, as Effie Rowlands. London, 1924
194. *Sally in Her Alley*. London, 1925
195. *The Shadow Wife*. London, 1925
196. *Out of a Clear Sky*, as Effie Rowlands. London, 1925
197. *The Way of Youth*, as Effie Rowlands. London, 1925
198. *The White in the Black*. London, 1926
199. *Brave Love*, as Effie Rowlands. London, 1926
200. *A Bunch of Blue Ribbons*, as Effie Rowlands. London, 1926
201. *Lady Feo's Daughter*, as Effie Rowlands. London, 1926
202. *Sally Gets Married*. London, 1927
203. *The Green Country*. London, 1927.
204. *The Gates of Happiness*, as Effie Rowlands. London, 1927
205. *A Man from the West*, as Effie Rowlands. London, 1927
206. *Fateful Promise*, as Effie Rowlands. London, no date
207. *Her Golden Secret*, as Effie Rowlands. New York, no date
208. *Hero for Love's Sake*, as Effie Rowlands. New York, no date
209. *Unhappy Bargain*, as Effie Rowlands. New York, no date

210. *The Moon Through Glass.* London, 1928
211. *Claire and Circumstances.* London, 1928
212. *Fine Feathers,* as Effie Rowlands. London, 1928
213. *Lights and Shadows,* as Effie Rowlands. London, 1928
214. *Meggie Albanesi.* London, 1928
215. *Gold in the Dust.* London, 1929
216. *A Heart for Sale.* London, 1929
217. *Spring in the Heart,* as Effie Rowlands. London, 1929
218. *While Faith Endures,* as Effie Rowlands. London, 1929
219. *The Clear Stream.* London, 1930
220. *Loyalty.* London, 1930
221. *The Courage of Love.* London, 1930
222. *White Flame.* London, 1930
223. *Coulton's Wife,* as Effie Rowlands. London, 1930
224. *Dorinda's Lovers,* as Effie Rowlands. London, 1930
225. *The Fighting Spirit,* as Effie Rowlands. London, 1930
226. *Sunlight Beyond,* as Effie Rowlands. London, 1930
227. *Coloured Lights.* London, 1931
228. *Wings of Chance,* as Effie Rowlands. London, 1931
229. *Princess Charming,* as Effie Rowlands. London, 1931
230. *All's Well with the World.* London, 1932
231. *In Love with Claire.* London, 1932.
232. *The Laughter of Life.* New York, ca.1932.
233. *The Moon of Romance.* London, 1932
234. *Snow in Summer.* London, 1932
235. *Green Valleys,* as Effie Rowlands. London, 1932
236. *A Loyal Defence,* as Effie Rowlands. London, 1932
237. *A Star in the Dark.* London, 1933
238. *Sweet and Lovely.* London, 1933
239. *White Branches.* London, 1933
240. *A Ministering Angel,* as Effie Rowlands. London, 1933
241. *Through the Mist.* London, 1934
242. *The Half Open Door.* London, 1934
243. *Frances Fights for Herself,* as Effie Rowlands. London, 1934
244. *A School for Hearts,* as Effie Rowlands. London, 1934
245. *An Unframed Portrait.* London, 1935
246. *A World of Dreams,* as Effie Rowlands. London, 1935
247. *The One Who Paid,* as Effie Rowlands. London, 1935
248. *As a Man Loves.* London, 1936
249. *The Hidden Gift.* London, 1936
250. *A Leaf Turned Down.* London, 1936
251. *The Heart Line,* as Effie Rowlands. London, 1936
252. *The Lamp of Friendship,* as Effie Rowlands. London, 1936
253. *The Little Lady.* London, 1937
254. *The Love That Lives.* London, 1937
255. *The One Who Counted.* London, 1937
256. *Her Father's Wish,* as Effie Rowlands. London, 1937
257. *The Top of the Tree,* as Effie Rowlands. London, 1937

Albert, Marvin H.
American, born probably early 1920s
Pseudonyms: Nick Quarry, Anthony Rome
1. *Lie Down with Lions.* New York, 1955
2. *The Law and Jake Wade.* New York, 1956
3. *Becoming a Mother,* with Theodore R. Seidman. New York, 1956
4. *Apache Rising.* New York, 1957
5. *Broadsides and Boarders.* New York, 1957
6. *The Long White Road: Ernest Shackleton's Antarctic Adventures.* New York, 1957
7. *Party Girl.* New York, 1958
8. *The Bounty Killer.* New York, 1958
9. *Renegade Posse.* New York, 1958
10. *The Hoods Come Calling,* as Nick Quarry. New York, 1958
11. *Trail of a Tramp,* as Nick Quarry. New York, 1958
12. *That Girl from Maine.* New York, 1959
13. *Pillow Talk.* New York, 1959
14. *Rider from Wind River.* New York, 1959
15. *The Reformed Gun.* New York, 1959
16. *The Girl with No Place to Hide,* as Nick Quarry. New York, 1959
17. *All the Young Men.* New York, 1960
18. *No Chance in Hell,* as Nick Quarry. New York, 1960
19. *Till It Hurts,* as Nick Quarry. New York, 1960
20. *Some Die Hard,* as Nick Quarry. New York, 1961
21. *Miami Mayhem,* as Anthony Rome. London, 1961
22. *The Lady in Cement,* as Anthony Rome. London, 1962
23. *My Kind of Game,* as Anthony Rome. New York, 1962
24. *Lover Come Back.* New York, 1962
25. *The VIP's.* New York, 1963
26. *Move Over, Darling.* New York, 1963
27. *Palm Springs Week-end.* New York, 1963
28. *Under the Yum-Yum Tree.* New York, 1963
29. *The Outrage.* New York, 1964
30. *Goodbye Charlie.* New York, 1964
31. *The Pink Panther.* New York, 1964
32. *Honeymoon Hotel.* New York, 1964
33. *Posse at High Pass.* New York, 1964
34. *What's New, Pussycat?* New York, 1965
35. *Strange Bedfellows.* New York, 1965
36. *Do Not Disturb.* New York, 1965
37. *The Great Race.* New York, 1965
38. *A Very Special Flavor.* New York, 1965
39. *The Divorce.* New York, 1965
40. *Duel at Diablo.* London, 1966
41. *Tony Rome,* as Anthony Rome. New York, 1967
42. *Come September.* New York, 1971
43. *The Don Is Dead,* as Nick Quarry. New York and London, 1972
44. *The Vendetta,* as Nick Quarry. New York, 1973
45. *The Gargoyle Conspiracy.* New York, 1975
46. *The Dark Goddess.* New York, 1978
47. *Clayburn.* New York, 1979
48. *The Medusa Complex.* New York, 1982

Aldiss, Brian Wilson
British, born in 1925
1. *The Brightfount Diaries.* London, 1955
2. *Space, Time, and Nathaniel: Presciences.* London, 1957
3. *Non-Stop.* London, 1958
4. *No Time Like Tomorrow.* New York, 1959
5. *Starship.* New York, 1959
6. *Vanguard from Alpha.* New York, 1959
7. *The Canopy of Time.* London, 1959
8. *Galaxies Like Grains of Sand.* New York, 1960
9. *Bow Down to Nul.* New York, 1960
10. *The Male Response.* New York, 1961
11. *The Primal Urge.* New York, 1961
12. *Equator.* London, 1961
13. *The Interpreter.* London, 1961
14. *Hothouse.* London, 1962
15. *The Long Afternoon of Earth.* New York, 1962
16. *The Airs of Earth.* London, 1963
17. *The Dark Light-Years.* London and New York, 1964
18. *Greybeard.* London and New York, 1964
19. *Starswarm.* New York, 1964
20. *Best Science Fiction Stories of Brian Aldiss.* London, 1965
21. *Earthworks.* London, 1965
22. *Who Can Replace a Man?* New York, 1966
23. *The Saliva Tree and Other Strange Growths.* London, 1966
24. *Cities and Stones: A Traveller's Jugoslavia.* London, 1966
25. *An Age.* London, 1967
26. *Report on Probability A.* London, 1968
27. *Cryptozoic!* New York, 1968
28. *Barefoot in the Head.* London, 1969
29. *Intangibles Inc. and Other Stories.* London, 1969

30. *Neanderthal Planet.* New York, 1970
31. *The Moment of Eclipse.* London, 1970
32. *The Hand-Reared Boy.* London and New York, 1970
33. *The Shape of Further Things: Speculation On Change.* London, 1970
34. *A Soldier Erect; or, Further Adventures of the Hand-Reared Boy.* London and New York, 1971
35. *The Book of Brian Aldiss.* New York, 1972
36. *Frankenstein Unbound.* London, 1973
37. *Billion Year Spree: A History of Science Fiction.* London, and New York, 1973
38. *The Eighty-Minute Hour.* London and New York, 1974
39. *Excommunication.* London, 1975
40. *Science Fiction Art.* New York, 1975
41. *The Malacia Tapestry.* London, 1976
42. *Last Orders and Other Stories.* London, 1977
43. *Brothers of the Head.* London, 1977
44. *Enemies of the System.* London and New York, 1978
45. *A Rude Awakening.* London, 1978
46. *Science Fiction As Science Fiction.* Frome (Eng), 1978
47. *New Arrivals, Old Encounters.* London, 1979
48. *Brothers of the Head, and Where the Lines Converge.* London, 1979
49. *Pile: Petals From St. Klaed's Computer.* London and New York, 1979
50. *This World and Nearer Ones: Essays Exploring the Familiar.* London, 1979
51. *Life In the West.* London, 1980
52. *Moreau's Other Island.* London, 1980
53. *An Island Called Moreau.* New York, 1981

Alexander, Lloyd Chudley
Born Philadelphia, Pennsylvania, in 1924
1. *And Let the Credit Go.* New York, 1955
2. *My Five Tigers.* New York and London, 1956
3. *Border Hawk: August Bondi.* New York, 1958
4. *Janine is French.* New York, 1958
5. *The Flagship Hope: Aaron Lopez.* Philadelphia, 1960
6. *My Love Affair With Music.* New York, 1960
7. *Park Avenue Vet,* with Louis J. Camuti. New York and London, 1962
8. *Time Cat: The Remarkable Journeys of Jason and Garath.* New York, 1963
9. *Nine Lives.* London, 1963
10. *The Book of Three.* New York, 1964
11. *Fifty Years in the Doghouse.* New York, 1964
12. *Send for Ryan!* London, 1965
13. *The Black Cauldron.* New York, 1965
14. *Coll and His White Pig.* New York, 1965
15. *The Castle of Llyr.* New York, 1966
16. *Taran Wanderer.* New York, 1967
17. *The High King.* New York, 1968
18. *The Marvelous Misadventures of Sebastian: Grand Extravaganza, Including a Performance By the Entire Cast of the Gallimaufry-Theatricus.* New York, 1970
19. *The King's Fountain.* New York, 1971
20. *The Four Donkeys.* New York, 1972
21. *The Cat Who Wished to Be a Man.* New York, 1973
22. *The Foundling and Other Tales of Prydain.* New York, 1973
23. *The Wizard in the Tree.* New York, 1975
24. *The Town Cats and Other Tales.* New York, 1977

Algren, Nelson
American, born in 1909, died in 1983
1. *Somebody In Boots.* New York, 1935
2. *Never Come Morning.* New York, 1942
3. *The Neon Wilderness.* New York, 1947
4. *The Man with the Golden Arm.* New York, 1949
5. *Chicago: City on the Make.* New York, 1951
6. *A Walk on the Wild Side.* New York, 1956
7. *The Jungle.* New York, 1957
8. *Nelson Algren's Own Book of Lonesome Monsters.* New York, 1962
9. *Who Lost An American?* London, 1963
10. *Notes from a Sea Diary.* New York, 1965
11. *The Last Carousel.* New York, 1973
12. *The Devil's Stocking.* New York, 1983

Allan, Mabel Esther
British, born in 1915
Pseudonyms: Jean Estoril, Priscilla Hagon, Anne Pilgrim
1. *The Glen Castle Mystery.* London, 1948
2. *The Adventurous Summer.* London, 1948
3. *The Wyndhams Went to Wales.* London, 1948
4. *Mullion.* London, 1949
5. *Cilia of Chiltern's Edge.* London, 1949
6. *Trouble at Melville Manor.* London, 1949
7. *Holiday at Arnriggs.* London, 1949
8. *Chiltern Adventure.* London, 1950
9. *Jimmy John's Journey.* London, 1950
10. *Over the Sea to School.* London, 1950
11. *School Under Snowdon.* London, 1950
12. *Everyday Island.* London, 1950
13. *Seven in Switzerland.* London, 1950
14. *The Exciting River.* London, 1951
15. *Clues to Connemara.* London, 1952
16. *The MacIains of Glen Gillean.* London, 1952
17. *Return to Derrykereen.* London, 1952
18. *A School in Danger.* London, 1952
19. *The School On Cloud Ridge.* London, 1952
20. *The School On North Barrule.* London, 1952
21. *The Secret Valley.* Leeds (Eng), 1953
22. *Room For the Cuckoo: The Story of a Farming Year.* London, 1953
23. *Three Go to Switzerland.* London, 1953
24. *Lucia Comes to School.* London, 1953
25. *Strangers at Brongwerne.* London, 1953
26. *Meric's Secret Cottage.* London, 1954
27. *Adventure Royal.* London, 1954
28. *Here We Go Round: A Career Story For Girls.* London, 1954
29. *Margaret Finds a Future.* London, 1954
30. *New Schools For Old.* London, 1954
31. *The Summer at Town's End.* London, 1954
32. *Adventures in Switzerland.* London, 1955
33. *The Mystery of Derrydane.* Huddersfield (Eng), 1955
34. *Changes for the Challoners.* London, 1955
35. *Glenvara.* London, 1955
36. *Judith Teaches.* London, 1955
37. *Swiss School.* London, 1955
38. *Adventure in Mayo.* London, 1956
39. *Balconies and Blue Nets: The Story of a Holiday in Brittany.* London, 1956
40. *Lost Lorrenden.* London, 1956
41. *Strangers in Skye.* London, 1956
42. *Two in the Western Isles.* London, 1956
43. *The Vine-Clad Hill.* London, 1956
44. *Flora at Kilroinn.* London, 1956
45. *The Amber House.* London, 1956
46. *Ann's Alpine Adventure.* London, 1956
47. *At School in Skye.* London, 1957
48. *Black Forest Summer.* London, 1957
49. *Sara Goes To Germany.* London, 1957
50. *Ballet for Drina,* as Jean Estoril. London, 1957
51. *Murder at the Flood.* London, 1957
52. *Drina's Dancing Year,* as Jean Estoril. London, 1958

Allan, Mabel Esther

53. *Blue Dragon Days.* London, 1958
54. *The Conch Shell.* London, 1958
55. *The House by the Marsh.* London, 1958
56. *Rachel Tandy.* London, 1958
57. *Drina Dances in Exile,* as Jean Estoril. London, 1959
58. *Drina Dances in Italy,* as Jean Estoril. London, 1959
59. *Amanda Goes to Italy.* London, 1959
60. *Catrin in Wales.* London, 1959
61. *A Play to the Festival.* London, 1959
62. *Shadow Over the Alps.* London, 1960
63. *A Summer in Brittany.* London, 1960
64. *Tansy of Tring Street.* London, 1960
65. *Drina Dances Again,* as Jean Estoril. London, 1960
66. *Drina Dances in New York,* as Jean Estoril. London, 1961
67. *Holiday of Endurance.* London, 1961
68. *Bluegate Girl.* London, 1961
69. *The First Time I Saw Paris,* as Anne Pilgrim. London and New York, 1961
70. *Pendron Under the Water.* London, 1961
71. *Clare Goes to Holland,* as Anne Pilgrim. London, 1962
72. *Drina Dances in Paris,* as Jean Estoril. London, 1962
73. *Home to the Island.* London, 1962
74. *Signpost to Switzerland.* London, 1962
75. *Drina Dances in Madeira,* as Jean Estoril. London, 1963
76. *A Summer in Provence,* as Anne Pilgrim. London, and New York, 1963
77. *The Ballet Family.* London, 1963
78. *Kate Comes to England.* London, 1963
79. *New York for Nicola.* New York, 1963
80. *The Sign of the Unicorn: A Thriller for Young People.* London and New York, 1963
81. *Drina Dances in Switzerland,* as Jean Estoril. London, 1964
82. *Strangers in New York.* London, and New York, 1964
83. *It Happened in Arles.* London, 1964
84. *The Ballet Family Again.* London, 1964
85. *Fiona on the Fourteenth Floor.* London, 1964
86. *Mystery in Arles.* New York, 1964
87. *Drina Goes On Tour,* as Jean Estoril. Leicester (Eng), 1965
88. *A Summer at Sea.* London and New York, 1965
89. *Cruising to Danger,* as Priscilla Hagon, Cleveland (OH), 1966
90. *Dancing to Danger,* as Priscilla Hagon. Cleveland, 1966
91. *The Way Over Windle.* London, 1966
92. *Skiing to Danger.* London, 1966
93. *Mystery of the Ski Slopes.* New York, 1966
94. *In Pursuit of Clarinda.* London, 1966
95. *It Started in Madeira.* London, 1967
96. *The Mystery Began in Madeira.* New York, 1967
97. *Missing in Manhattan.* London, 1967
98. *Selina's New Family,* as Anne Pilgrim. London and New York, 1967
99. *We Danced in Bloomsbury Square,* as Jean Estoril. London, 1967
100. *Mystery at Saint-Hilaire,* as Priscilla Hagon. Cleveland, 1968
101. *The Wood Street Secret.* London, 1968
102. *The Kraymer Mystery.* New York, 1969
103. *Mystery at Villa Bianca,* as Priscilla Hagon. New York, 1969
104. *Climbing to Danger.* London, 1969
105. *The Mystery of the Secret Square,* as Priscilla Hagon. New York, 1970
106. *Dangerous Inheritance.* London, 1970
107. *The Wood Street Group.* London, 1970
108. *Christmas at Spindle Bottom.* London, 1970
109. *The Secret Dancer.* London, 1971
110. *The May Day Mystery.* New York, 1971
111. *The Wood Street Rivals.* London, 1971
112. *Mystery in Wales.* New York, 1971
113. *An Island in a Green Sea.* New York, 1972
114. *Behind the Blue Gates.* London, 1972
115. *Time to Go Back.* London and New York, 1972
116. *Mystery in Rome.* New York, 1973
117. *The Wood Street Helpers.* London, 1973
118. *A Formidable Enemy.* London, 1973
119. *Crow's Nest.* London, 1974
120. *A Chill in the Lane.* Nashville, 1974
121. *The Night Wind.* New York, 1974
122. *Ship of Danger.* London and New York, 1974
123. *The Secret Players.* Leicester (Eng), 1974
124. *Bridge of Friendship.* London, 1975
125. *Romansgrove.* New York, 1975
126. *The Flash Children.* London and New York, 1975
127. *The Bells of Rome.* London, 1975
128. *Away From Wood Street.* London, 1976
129. *Trouble in the Glen.* London, 1976
130. *The Rising Tide.* London, 1976
131. *The Sound of Cowbells.* London, 1977
132. *My Family's Not Forever.* London, 1977
133. *The View Beyond My Father.* London, 1977

Allbeury, Ted [Theodore Edward le Bouthillier Allbeury]
British, born in 1917
Pseudonym: Richard Butler

1. *A Choice of Enemies.* New York, 1972
2. *Snowball.* London and Philadelphia, 1974
3. *Palomino Blonde.* London, 1975
4. *The Special Collection.* London, 1975
5. *Where All the Girls Are Sweeter,* as Richard Butler. London, 1975
6. *Omega Minus.* New York, 1975
7. *Italian Assets,* as Richard Butler. London, 1976
8. *Moscow Quadrille.* London, 1976
9. *The Only Good German.* London, 1976
10. *The Man with the President's Mind.* London, 1977
11. *The Lantern Network.* London, 1978
12. *The Alpha List.* London, 1979
13. *Consequence of Fear.* London, 1979

Allen, Grant [Charles Grant Blairfindie Allen]
British, born in 1848, died October 28, 1899
Pseudonyms: Cecil Power, Olive Pratt Rayner, Martin Leach Warborough

1. *Physiological Aesthetics.* London, 1877
2. *The Colour-Sense: Its Origin and Development: An Essay in Comparative Psychology.* London and Boston, 1879
3. *Anglo-Saxon Britain.* London and New York, 1881
4. *The Evolutionists at Large.* London, 1881
5. *Vignettes From Nature.* London, 1881
6. *The Colours of Flowers, as Illustrated in the British Flora.* London and New York, 1882
7. *Colin Clout's Calendar: The Record of a Summer, April-October.* London, 1882
8. *Flowers and Their Pedigrees.* London, 1883
9. *Nature Studies,* with others. London and New York, 1883
10. *Philistia,* as Cecil Power. London, 3 vols, and New York, 1 vol., 1884
11. *Strange Stories.* London, 1884
12. *Biographies of Working Men.* London, 1884
13. *Babylon,* as Cecil Power. London, 3 vols., and New York, 1 vol., 1885
14. *Charles Darwin.* London and New York, 1885
15. *Kalee's Shrine,* with May Cotes. Bristol (Eng), 1886
16. *The Sole Trustee.* London, 1886
17. *For Maimie's Sake.* London and New York, 1886
18. *The Beckoning Hand and Other Stories.* London, 1887
19. *A Terrible Inheritance.* London, 1887
20. *Common Sense Science.* Boston, 1887

21. *In All Shades.* London, 3 vols., and Chicago, 1 vol., 1888
22. *This Mortal Coil.* London, 3 vols., and New York, 1 vol., 1888
23. *The White's Man's Foot.* London, 1888
24. *The Devil's Die.* London, 3 vols., and New York, 1 vol., 1888
25. *A Half-Century of Science,* with T.H. Huxley. New York, 1888
26. *Force and Energy: A Theory of Dynamics.* London, 1888
27. *The Jaws of Death.* London, 1889
28. *The Tents of Shem.* London, 3 vols., and New York, 1 vol., 1889
29. *Dr. Palliser's Patient.* London, 1889
30. *A Living Apparition.* London, 1889
31. *Falling in Love, with Other Essays on More Exact Branches of Science.* London, 1889
32. *Individualism and Socialism.* Glasgow, 1890(?)
33. *The Great Taboo.* London, 1890
34. *Wednesday the Tenth.* Boston, 1890
35. *Recalled to Life.* Bristol and New York, 1891
36. *What's Bred in the Bone?* London and Boston, 1891
37. *Dumaresq's Daughter.* London, 3 vols., and New York, 1 vol., 1891
38. *The Duchess of Powysland.* London, 3 vols., and Boston, 1 vol., 1892
39. *The General's Will and Other Stories.* London, 1892
40. *Science in Arcady.* London, 1892
41. *The Tidal Thames.* London, 1892
42. *Ivan Greet's Masterpiece.* London, 1893
43. *The Scallywag.* London, 3 vols., and New York, 1 vol., 1893
44. *Michael's Crag.* London and Chicago, 1893
45. *Blood Royal.* London and New York, 1893
46. *An Army Doctor's Romance.* London and New York, 1893
47. *At Market Value.* London, 2 vols., and Chicago, 1 vol., 1894
48. *The Lower Slopes: Reminiscences of Excursions round the Base of the Hellicon.* London and Chicago, 1894
49. *Post-Prandial Philosophy.* London, 1894
50. *The British Barbarians: A Hill-Top Novel.* London and New York, 1895
51. *The Desire of the Eyes and Other Stories.* London, 1895
52. *The Woman Who Did.* London and Boston, 1895
53. *Under Sealed Orders.* London, 3 vols., 1895
54. *In Memoriam: George Paul MacDonell.* London, 1895
55. *The Story of the Plants.* London, 1895
56. *A Bride From the Desert.* New York, 1896
57. *A Splendid Sin.* London, 1896
58. *Moorland Idylls.* London, 1896
59. *An African Millionaire.* London and New York, 1897
60. *The Type-Writer Girl,* as Olive Pratt Rayner. London, 1897
61. *The Evolution of the Idea of God: An Inquiry Into the Origins of Religions.* London and New York, 1897
62. *Tom, Unlimited: A Story for Children,* as Martin Leach Warborough. London, 1897
63. *Paris.* London, 1897
64. *Florence.* London, 1897
65. *Cities of Belgium.* London, 1897
66. *The Curse of the Albatross; or, When Was Wednesday the Tenth?* Boston, 1898
67. *Linnet.* London, 1898
68. *The Incidental Bishop.* London and New York, 1898
69. *Venice.* London, 1898
70. *Flashlights on Nature.* New York, 1898
71. *Twelve Tales, With a Headpiece, A Tailpiece, and an Intermezzo, Being Select Stories.* London, 1899
72. *Rosalba: The Story of Her Development,* as Olive Pratt Rayner. London and New York, 1899
73. *Miss Cayley's Adventures.* London and New York, 1899
74. *The European Tour: A Handbook For Americans and Colonists.* London and New York, 1899
75. *Hilda Wade.* London and New York, 1900
76. *The New Hedonism.* New York, 1900
77. *Plain Words on the Woman Question.* Chicago, 1900
78. *The Type-Writer Girl.* New York, 1900
79. *In Nature's Workshop.* London and New York, 1901
80. *County and Town in England, Together With Some Annals of Churnside.* London and New York, 1901
81. *Sir Theodore's Guest and Other Stories.* Bristol (Eng), 1902
82. *The Indian Mystery.* New York, 1902
83. *Belgium: Its Cities.* Boston, 2 vols., 1903
84. *Evolution in Italian Art.* London and New York, 1908
85. *The Plants.* New York, 1909
86. *The Hand of God and Other Posthumous Poems.* London, 1909
87. *The Reluctant Hangman and Other Stories.* Boulder (CO), 1973

Allen, Henry Wilson
American, born in 1912
Pseudonyms: Clay Fisher, Will Henry

1. *No Survivors,* as Will Henry. New York, 1950
2. *Red Blizzard,* as Clay Fisher. New York, 1951
3. *Wolf-Eye, the Bad One,* as Will Henry. New York, 1951
4. *Santa Fe Passage,* as Clay Fisher. Boston, 1952
5. *War Bonnet,* as Clay Fisher. Boston, 1953
6. *Yellow Hair,* as Clay Fisher. Boston, 1953
7. *To Follow a Flag,* as Will Henry. New York, 1953
8. *Death of a Legend,* as Will Henry. New York, 1954
9. *The Fourth Horseman,* as Will Henry. New York, 1954
10. *The Tall Men,* as Clay Fisher. Boston, 1954
11. *Who Rides with Wyatt,* as Will Henry. New York, 1955
12. *The Brass Command,* as Clay Fisher. Boston, 1955
13. *The Big Pasture,* as Clay Fisher. Boston, 1955
14. *The North Star,* as Will Henry. New York, 1956
15. *Pillars of the Sky,* as Will Henry. New York, 1956
16. *The Blue Mustang,* as Clay Fisher. Boston, 1956
17. *Yellowstone Kelly,* as Clay Fisher. Boston, 1957
18. *The Texas Rangers,* as Will Henry. New York, 1957
19. *The Crossing,* as Clay Fisher. Boston, 1958
20. *Reckoning at Yankee Flat,* as Will Henry. New York, 1958
21. *The Seven Men at Membres Springs,* as Will Henry. New York, 1958
22. *Orphan of the North,* as Will Henry. New York, 1958
23. *Where the Sun Now Stands,* as Will Henry. New York, 1960
24. *Journey to Shiloh,* as Will Henry. New York, 1960
25. *Nino: The Legend of Apache Kid,* as Clay Fisher. New York, 1961
26. *The Return of the Tall Man,* as Clay Fisher. New York, 1961
27. *The Feleen Brand,* as Will Henry. New York and London, 1962
28. *The Pitchfork Patrol,* as Clay Fisher. New York, 1962
29. *The Oldest Maiden Lady in New Mexico and Other Stories,* as Clay Fisher. New York, 1962
30. *San Juan Hill,* as Will Henry. New York, 1962
31. *The Gates of the Mountains,* as Will Henry. New York, 1963
32. *Mackenna's Gold,* as Will Henry. New York, 1963
33. *Valley of the Bear,* as Clay Fisher. Boston, 1964
34. *In the Land of the Mandans,* as Will Henry. Philadelphia, 1965
35. *The Last Warpath,* as Will Henry. New York, 1966
36. *Custer's Last Stand,* as Will Henry. Philadelphia, 1966
37. *Songs of the Western Frontier,* as Will Henry. Philadelphia, 1966

38. *One More River to Cross,* as Will Henry. New York, 1967
39. *Alias Butch Cassidy,* as Will Henry. New York, 1968
40. *Maheo's Children,* as Will Henry. Philadelphia, 1968
41. *The Day Fort Larking Fell,* as Will Henry. Philadelphia, 1968
42. *Genesis Five.* New York, 1968
43. *Tayopa!* New York, 1970
44. *See How They Run.* New York, 1970
45. *Outcasts of Canyon Creek,* as Clay Fisher. New York, 1972
46. *Chiricahua,* as Will Henry. Philadelphia, 1972
47. *The Bear Paw Horses,* as Will Henry. Philadelphia, 1973
48. *Apache Ransom,* as Clay Fisher. New York and London, 1974
49. *I, Tom Horn,* as Will Henry. Philadelphia, 1975
50. *Black Apache,* as Clay Fisher. New York and London, 1976
51. *Summer of the Gun,* as Will Henry. Philadelphia, 1978
52. *Nine Lives West,* as Clay Fisher. New York, 1978
53. *Seven Card Stud,* as Clay Fisher. New York, 1981

Allen, Hervey [William Hervey Allen, Jr.]
American, born in 1889, died December 28, 1949
1. *Ballads of the Border.* Privately printed, 1916
2. *Wampum and Old Gold.* New Haven (CT), 1921
3. *Carolina Chansons: Legends of the Low Country,* with Du Bose Hayward. New York, 1922
4. *The Bride of Huitzil: An Aztec Legend.* New York, 1922
5. *Christmas Epithalamium.* Privately printed, 1923
6. *Earth Moods and Other Poems.* New York, 1925
7. *Israfel: The Life and Times of Edgar Allan Poe.* New York, 2 vols., 1926
8. *Toward the Flame: A War Diary.* New York, 1926
9. *Du Bose Hayward: A Critical and Biographical Sketch.* New York, 1927
10. *New Legends.* New York, 1929
11. *Sarah Simon, Character Atlantean.* New York, 1929
12. *Songs for Annette.* New York, 1929
13. *Anthony Adverse.* New York and London, 1933
14. *Action at Aquila.* New York and London, 1938
15. *It Was Like This: Two Stories of the Great War.* New York, 1940
16. *The Forest and the Fort.* New York and London, 1943
17. *Bedford Village.* New York and London, 1944
18. *Toward the Morning.* New York, 1948
19. *The City in the Dawn.* New York, 1950

Allingham, Margery (Louise)
British, born in 1904, died June 30, 1966
1. *Blackerchief Dick: A Tale of Mersea Island.* London and New York, 1923
2. *The White Cottage Mystery.* London, 1928
3. *The Crime at Black Dudley.* London, 1929
4. *The Black Dudley Murder.* New York, 1930
5. *Mystery Mile.* London and New York, 1930
6. *Look to the Lady.* London, 1931
7. *The Gyrth Chalice Mystery.* New York, 1931
8. *Police at the Funeral.* London, 1931
9. *Sweet Danger.* London, 1933
10. *Kingdom of Death.* New York, 1933
11. *The Fear Sign.* New York, 1933
12. *Death of a Ghost.* London and New York, 1934
13. *Flowers for the Judge.* London and New York, 1936
14. *Six Against the Yard,* with others. London, 1936
15. *Six Against Scotland Yard.* New York, 1936
16. *Dancers in Mourning.* London and New York, 1937
17. *The Case of the Late Pig.* London, 1937
18. *Mr. Campion, Criminologist.* New York, 1937
19. *The Fashion in Shrouds.* London and New York, 1938
20. *Mr. Campion and Others.* London, 1939
21. *Black Plumes.* London and New York, 1940
22. *Traitor's Purse.* London and New York, 1941
23. *The Oaken Heart.* London and New York, 1941
24. *Dance of the Years.* London, 1943
25. *The Gallantrys.* Boston, 1943
26. *Who Killed Chloe?* New York, 1943
27. *The Sabotage Murder Mystery.* New York, 1943
28. *Coroner's Pidgin.* London, 1945
29. *Pearls Before Swine.* New York, 1945
30. *Wanted: Someone Innocent.* No place, 1946
31. *The Case Book of Mr. Campion.* New York, 1947
32. *More Work for the Undertaker.* London, 1948
33. *Legacy in Blood.* New York, 1949
34. *Deadly Duo.* New York, 1949
35. *Take Two at Bedtime.* Kingswood (Eng), 1950
36. *The Tiger in the Smoke.* London and New York, 1952
37. *No Love Lost.* Kingswood and New York, 1954
38. *The Beckoning Lady.* London, 1955
39. *The Estate of the Beckoning Lady.* New York, 1955
40. *Hide My Eyes.* London, 1958
41. *Tether's End.* New York, 1958
42. *Ten Were Missing.* New York, 1959
43. *The China Governess.* New York, 1962
44. *The Mysterious Mr. Campion.* London, 1963
45. *The Mind Readers.* London and New York, 1965
46. *Mr. Campion's Lady.* London, 1965
47. *Cargo of Eagles.* London and New York, 1968
48. *The Allingham Case-Book.* London and New York, 1969

Almedingen, E.M. [Martha Edith von Almedingen]
British, born in 1898, died March 5, 1971
1. *The Catholic Church in Russia Today.* London and New York, 1923
2. *The English Pope, Adrian IV.* London, 1925
3. *Women under Fire: Six Months in the Red Army.* London, 1930
4. *St. Gregory the Great.* Dublin, 1930
5. *The Wanderer.* Dublin, 1930
6. *Clear Skies at Last.* Dublin, 1931
7. *Destiny.* Dublin, 1931
8. *God in the Soviet.* Dublin, 1931
9. *From Rome to Canterbury.* London and Milwaukee, 1933
10. *The Pilgrimage of a Soul.* London and Milwaukee, 1934
11. *Through Many Windows Opened by the Book of Common Prayer.* London and Milwaukee, 1935
12. *Young Catherine.* London, 1937
13. *The Lion of the North.* London, 1938
14. *She Married Pushkin.* London, 1939
15. *Rus.* London and New York, 1939
16. *Tomorrow Will Come.* London and Boston, 1941
17. *Poloniae Testamentum.* London, 1942
18. *Out of Seir.* London, 1943
19. *Frossia.* London, 1943
20. *Dasha.* London, 1944
21. *Dom Bernard Clements: A Portrait.* London, 1945
22. *The Almond.* London, 1947
23. *The Inmost Heart.* London, 1949
24. *The Golden Sequence.* Philadelphia, 1949
25. *Within the Harbour.* London, 1950
26. *Flame on the Water.* London, 1952
27. *Storm at Westminster.* London and New York, 1952
28. *Late Arrival.* Philadelphia, 1952
29. *The Rock.* London, 1953
30. *Stand Fast, Beloved City.* London, 1954
31. *Ground Corn.* London, 1955
32. *Fair Haven.* London, 1956
33. *Stephen's Light.* London, 1956
34. *The Scarlet Goose.* London, 1957

35. *Russian Fairy Tales.* London, 1957
36. *Life of Many Colours: The Story of Grandmother Ellen.* London, 1958
37. *A Very Far Country.* New York, 1958
38. *So Dark a Stream: A Study of the Emperor Paul I of Russia, 1754-1801.* London, 1959
39. *The Little Stairway.* London, 1960
40. *The Winter in the Heart.* New York, 1960
41. *The Young Pavlova.* London, 1960
42. *Dark Splendour.* London, 1961
43. *The Batsford Colour Book of Kittens.* London, 1961
44. *Kittens in Color.* New York, 1961
45. *Catherine, Empress of Russia.* New York, 1961
46. *Catherine the Great: A Portrait.* London, 1963
47. *The Empress Alexandra, 1872-1918: A Study.* London, 1961
48. *The Emperor Alexander II: A Study.* London, 1962
49. *Russian Folk and Fairy Tales.* New York, 1963
50. *One Little Tree: A Christmas Card of a Finnish Landscape.* London, 1963
51. *The Knights of the Golden Table.* London, 1963
52. *The Young Leonardo da Vinci.* London, 1963
53. *A Picture History of Russia.* London and New York, 1964
54. *The Treasure of Siegfried.* London, 1964
55. *The Emperor Alexander I.* London, 1964
56. *An Unbroken Unity: A Memoir of Grand Duchess Serge of Russia, 1864-1918.* London, 1964
57. *The Young Catherine the Great.* London, 1965
58. *The Ladies of St. Hedwigs.* London, 1965
59. *The Unnamed Stream and Other Poems.* London, 1965
60. *Little Katia.* London, 1966
61. *The Retreat from Moscow.* London, 1966
62. *The Romanovs: Three Centuries of an Ill-Fated Dynasty.* London and New York, 1966
63. *Katia.* New York, 1967
64. *The Story of Gudrun, Based on the Third Part of the Epic of Gudrun.* New York, 1967
65. *Young Mark.* London, 1967
66. *Francis of Assisi: A Portrait.* London, 1967
67. *St. Francis of Assisi: A Great Life in Brief.* New York, 1967
68. *Charlemagne: A Study.* London, 1968
69. *A Candle at Dusk.* London and New York, 1969
70. *I Remember St. Petersburg.* London, 1969
71. *Leonardo da Vinci: A Portrait.* London, 1969
72. *My St. Petersburg: A Reminiscence of Childhood.* New York, 1970
73. *Fanny.* London and New York, 1970
74. *Ellen.* New York, 1970
75. *Too Early Lilac.* London, 1970
76. *Rus into Muscovy: The History of Early Russia.* London, 1971
77. *Land of Muscovy.* New York, 1972
78. *Anna.* London and New York, 1972

Ambler, Eric
British
Pseudonym: Eliot Reed, with Charles Rodda
1. *The Dark Frontier.* London, 1936
2. *Uncommon Danger.* London, 1937
3. *Background to Danger.* New York, 1937
4. *Epitaph for a Spy.* London, 1938
5. *Cause for Alarm.* London, 1938
6. *The Mask of Dimitrios.* London, 1939
7. *A Coffin for Dimitrios.* New York, 1939
8. *Journey into Fear.* London and New York, 1940
9. *Skytip,* as Eliot Reed. New York, 1950
10. *Tender to Danger,* as Eliot Reed. New York, 1951
11. *Judgment on Deltchev.* London and New York, 1951
12. *Tender to Moonlight,* as Eliot Reed. London, 1952
13. *The Maras Affair,* as Eliot Reed. London and New York, 1953
14. *The Schirmer Inheritance.* London and New York, 1953
15. *Charter to Danger,* as Eliot Reed. London, 1954
16. *The Night-Comers.* London, 1956
17. *State of Siege.* New York, 1956
18. *Passport to Panic,* as Eliot Reed. London, 1958
19. *Passage of Arms.* London, 1959
20. *The Light of Day.* London, 1962
21. *The Ability to Kill and Other Pieces.* London, 1963
22. *Topkapi.* New York, 1964
23. *A Kind of Anger.* London and New York, 1964
24. *Dirty Story.* London and New York, 1967
25. *The Intercom Conspiracy.* New York, 1969
26. *The Levanter.* London and New York, 1972
27. *Doctor Frigo.* London and New York, 1974
28. *Send No More Roses.* London, 1977
29. *The Siege of the Villa Lipp.* New York, 1977.

Amis, Kingsley (William)
British, born in 1922
Pseudonym: Robert Markham
1. *Bright November.* London, 1947
2. *A Frame of Mind.* Reading (Eng), 1953
3. *Poems.* Oxford (Eng), 1954
4. *Lucky Jim.* London and New York, 1954
5. *That Uncertain Feeling.* London, 1955
6. *A Case of Samples: Poems 1946-1956.* London, 1956
7. *Socialism and the Intellectuals.* London, 1957
8. *I Like It Here.* London and New York, 1958
9. *New Maps of Hell: A Survey of Science Fiction.* New York, 1960
10. *Take a Girl Like You.* London, 1960
11. *The Evans Country.* Oxford, 1962
12. *Penguin Modern Poets 2,* with Don Moraes and Peter Porter. London, 1962
13. *One Fat Englishman.* London, 1963
14. *My Enemy's Enemy.* London, 1962
15. *The Egyptologists,* with Robert Conquest. London, 1965
16. *The James Bond Dossier.* London and New York, 1965
17. *The Anti-Death League.* London and New York, 1966
18. *A Look round the Estate: Poems 1957-1967.* London, 1967
19. *Colonel Sun: A James Bond Adventure,* as Robert Markham. New York, 1968
20. *I Want It Now.* London, 1968
21. *Lucky Jim's Politics.* London, 1968
22. *The Green Man.* London, 1969
23. *What Became of Jane Austen?, and Other Questions.* London, 1970
24. *Girl, 20.* London, 1971
25. *On Drink.* London, 1972
26. *Penguin Modern Stories II,* with others. London, 1972
27. *Dear Illusion.* London, 1972
28. *The Riverside Villas Murder.* London and New York, 1973
29. *Ending Up.* London and New York, 1974
30. *Kipling and His World.* New York, 1975
31. *The Alteration.* London, 1976
32. *The Darkwater Hall Mystery.* Edinburgh (Scotland), 1978
33. *Jake's Thing.* London, 1978
34. *Collected Poems, 1944-1979.* London, 1979.

Amy, Lacey [William Lacey Amy]
Canadian, died in 1962
Pseudonym: Luke Allan
1. *The Blue Wolf: A Tale of the Cypress Hills,* as Luke Allan. London, 1913
2. *Blue Pete, Half Breed: A Story of the Cowboy West.* London, 1920

3. *The Lone Trail.* London. 1921
4. *The Return of Blue Pete.* London, 1922
5. *The Westerner.* London, 1923
6. *The Beast.* London, 1924
7. *The Pace.* London, 1926
8. *The White Camel.* London, 1926
9. *The Sire.* London, 1927
10. *Blue Pete, Detective.* London, 1928
11. *The Masked Stranger.* Bristol, 1930
12. *Murder at Midnight.* Bristol, 1930
13. *Jungle Crime.* Bristol, 1931
14. *The End of the Trail.* Bristol, 1931
15. *The Many-Coloured Thread.* London, 1932
16. *The Dark Spot.* Bristol, 1932
17. *The Fourth Dagger.* Bristol, 1932
18. *The Traitor.* Bristol, 1933
19. *Murder at the Club.* Bristol, 1933
20. *Five for One.* Bristol, 1934
21. *Behind the Wire Fence.* Bristol, 1935
22. *The Black Opal.* Bristol, 1935
23. *The Case of the Open Drawer.* Bristol, 1936
24. *Scotland Yard Takes a Holiday.* Bristol, 1937
25. *The Man on the Twenty-Fourth Floor.* London, 1937
26. *The Ghost Murder.* London, 1937
27. *Beyond the Locked Door.* London, 1938
28. *Blue Pete, Horsethief.* London, 1938
29. *The Tenderfoot.* London, 1939
30. *The Vengeance of Blue Pete.* London, 1939
31. *Blue Pete, Rebel.* London, 1940
32. *Blue Pete Pays a Debt.* London, 1942
33. *Blue Pete Breaks the Rules.* London, 1943
34. *Blue Pete, Outlaw.* London, 1944
35. *Blue Pete's Dilemma.* London, 1945
36. *Blue Pete to the Rescue.* London, 1947
37. *Blue Pete's Vendetta.* London, 1947
38. *Blue Pete and the Pinto.* London, 1948
39. *Blue Pete Works Alone.* London, 1948
40. *Blue Pete, Unofficially.* London, 1949
41. *Blue Pete, Indian Scout.* London, 1950
42. *Blue Pete at Bay.* London, 1952
43. *Blue Pete and the Kid.* London, 1953
44. *Blue Pete Rides the Foothills.* London, 1953
45. *Blue Pete in the Badlands.* London, 1954

Andersen, Doris
Canadian, born in 1909
1. *Blood Brothers.* Toronto, New York, and London, 1967
2. *Ways Harsh and Wild.* Vancouver (Canada), 1973
3. *Slave of the Haida.* Toronto, 1974

Anderson, Chester
American, born in 1932
1. *Colloquy.* San Francisco, 1960
2. *A Liturgy for Dragons.* New York, 1961
3. *The Pink Palace.* New York, 1963
4. *Ten Years to Doomsday,* with Michael Kurland. New York, 1964
5. *The Butterfly Kid.* New York, 1967
6. *Fox and Hare.* Glen Ellen (CA), 1980

Anderson, Colin
British
1. *Boon.* London, 1964
2. *Magellan.* New York and London, 1970

Anderson, Frederick Irving
American, born in 1877
1. *The Farmer of Tomorrow.* New York, 1913
2. *The Adventures of the Infallible Godahl.* New York, 1914
3. *Electricity for the Farm.* New York, 1915
4. *The Notorious Sophie Lang.* London, 1925
5. *The Book of Murder.* New York, 1930

Anderson, James
1. *Assassin.* London, 1969
2. *The Alpha List.* London, 1972
3. *The Abolition of Death.* London, 1974
4. *The Affair of the Blood-Stained Egg Cosy.* London, 1975
5. *Appearance of Evil.* London, 1977
6. *Angel of Death.* London, 1978

Anderson, Poul (William)
American, born in 1926
1. *Vault of the Ages.* Philadelphia, 1952
2. *The Broken Sword.* New York, 1954
3. *Brain Wave.* New York, 1954
4. *No World of Their Own.* New York, 1955
5. *Planet of No Return.* New York, 1956
6. *Star Ways.* New York, 1956
7. *Earthman's Burden,* with Gordon R. Dickson. New York, 1957
8. *The Snows of Ganymede.* New York, 1958
9. *War of the Wing-Men.* New York, 1958
10. *Virgin Planet.* New York, 1959
11. *The War of Two Worlds.* New York, 1959
12. *We Claim These Stars!* New York, 1959
13. *The Enemy Stars.* Philadelphia, 1959
14. *Perish By the Sword.* New York, 1959
15. *Murder in Black Letter.* New York, 1960
16. *The Golden Slave.* New York, 1960
17. *Rogue Sword.* New York, 1960
18. *The High Crusade.* New York, 1960
19. *Earthman, Go Home.* New York, 1960
20. *Guardians of Time.* New York, 1960
21. *Strangers From Earth.* New York, 1961
22. *Twilight World.* New York, 1961
23. *Mayday Orbit.* New York, 1961
24. *Orbit Unlimited.* New York, 1961
25. *Three Hearts and Three Lions.* New York, 1961
26. *After Doomsday.* New York, 1962
27. *The Makeshift Rocket.* New York, 1962
28. *Un-Man and Other Novellas.* New York, 1962
29. *Murder Bound.* New York, 1962
30. *Let the Spacemen Beware!* New York, 1963
31. *Shield.* New York, 1963
32. *Is There Life on Other Worlds?* New York and London, 1963
33. *Thermonuclear Warfare.* Derby (CT), 1963
34. *Three Worlds to Conquer.* New York, 1964
35. *Time and Stars.* New York and London, 1964
36. *Trader to the Stars.* New York, 1964
37. *Agent of the Terran Empire.* Philadelphia, 1965
38. *The Corridors of Time.* New York, 1965
39. *Flandry of Terra.* Philadelphia, 1965
40. *The Star Fox.* New York, 1965
41. *The Trouble Twisters.* New York, 1966
42. *Ensign Flandry.* Philadelphia, 1966
43. *World Without Stars.* New York, 1966
44. *The Fox, the Dog, and the Griffin: A Folk Tale Adapted from the Danish of Christian Molbech.* New York, 1966
45. *The Horn of Time.* New York, 1968
46. *The Rebel Worlds.* New York, 1969
47. *Beyond the Beyond.* New York, 1969
48. *Seven Conquests.* New York and London, 1969
49. *Satan's World.* New York, 1969
50. *The Infinite Voyage: Man's Future in Space.* New York and London, 1969

51. *A Circus of Hells.* New York, 1970
52. *Tau Zero.* New York, 1970
53. *Tales of the Flying Mountains.* New York, 1970
54. *The Byworlder.* New York, 1971
55. *The Dancer From Atlantis.* New York, 1971
56. *Operation Chaos.* New York, 1971
57. *There Will Be Time.* New York, 1972
58. *The Day of Their Return.* New York, 1973
59. *Hrolf Kraki's Saga.* New York, 1973
60. *The People of the Wind.* New York, 1973
61. *The Queen of Air and Darkness.* New York, 1973
62. *Inheritors of Earth,* with Gordon Eklund. Radnor (PA), 1974
63. *Fire Time.* New York, 1974
64. *A Midsummer's Tempest.* New York, 1974
65. *A Knight of Ghosts and Shadows.* New York, 1974
66. *Star Prince Charlie,* with Gordon R. Dickson. New York, 1975
67. *The Winter of the World.* New York, 1975
68. *Homeward and Beyond.* New York, 1975
69. *Homebrew.* Cambridge (MA), 1976
70. *The Best of Poul Anderson.* New York, 1976
71. *Mirkheim.* New York, 1977
72. *The Avatar.* New York, 1978
73. *Two Worlds.* New York, 1978
74. *The Book of Poul Anderson.* New York, 1978
75. *The Long Way Home.* New York, 1978
76. *The Night Face and Other Stories.* Boston, 1978
77. *Question and Answer.* New York, 1978
78. *The Peregrine.* New York, 1978
79. *The Man Who Counts.* New York, 1978
80. *The Night Face.* New York, 1978
81. *Commander Flandry.* London, 1978
82. *The Merman's Children.* New York, 1979
83. *The Devil's Game.* New York, 1980
84. *Knight Flandry.* London, 1980
85. *The Last Viking Book 2: The Road of the Sea Horse.* New York, 1980

Andrew, Prudence (Hastings)
British, born in 1924
1. *The Hooded Falcon.* London, 1960
2. *Ordeal by Silence: A Story of Medieval Times.* London and New York, 1961
3. *Ginger over the Wall.* London, 1962
4. *A Question of Choice.* London and New York, 1962
5. *Ginger and Batty Bill.* London, 1963
6. *The Earthworms.* London, 1963
7. *The Constant Star.* New York, 1964
8. *Ginger and Number 10.* London, 1964
9. *A Sparkle from the Coal.* London, 1964
10. *The Christmas Card.* London, 1966
11. *Ginger among the Pigeons.* London, 1966
12. *Mr. Morgan's Marrow.* London, 1967
13. *A New Creature.* London and New York, 1968
14. *Dog!* London, 1968
15. *A Man with Your Advantages.* London, 1970
16. *Mr. O'Brien.* London, 1972
17. *Una and Grubstreet.* London, 1972
18. *Rodge, Silvie, and Munch.* London, 1973
19. *Goodbye to the Rat.* London, 1974
20. *The Heroic Deeds of Jason Jones.* London, 1975
21. *Una and the Heaven Baby.* Nashville, 1975
22. *Where Are You Going To, My Pretty Maid?* London, 1977

Andrews, Lucilla (Mathew)
British
Pseudonyms: Diana Gordon, Joanna Marcus
1. *The Print Petticoat.* London, 1954
2. *The Secret Armour.* London, 1955
3. *The Quiet Wards.* London, 1956
4. *The First Year.* London, 1957
5. *A Hospital Summer.* London, 1958
6. *My Friend the Professor.* London, 1960
7. *Nurse Errant.* London, 1961
8. *The Young Doctors Downstairs.* London, 1963
9. *Flowers for the Doctor.* London, 1963
10. *The New Sister Theatre.* London, 1964
11. *The Light in the Ward.* London, 1965
12. *A House for Sister Mary.* London, 1966
13. *Hospital Circles.* London, 1967
14. *A Few Days in Endel,* as Diana Gordon. London, 1968
15. *Highland Interlude.* London, 1968
16. *The Healing Time.* London, 1969
17. *Edinburgh Excursion.* London, 1970
18. *Ring o'Roses.* London, 1972
19. *Silent Song.* London, 1973
20. *In Storm and in Calm.* London, 1975
21. *No Time for Romance: An Autobiographical Account of a Few Moments in British and Personal History.* London, 1977
22. *The Crystal Gull.* London, 1978
23. *One Night in London.* London, 1979
24. *Marsh Blood,* as Joanna Marcus. London, 1980
25. *A Weekend in the Garden.* London, 1981

Angelo, Valenti
American, born in 1897
1. *Nino.* New York, 1938
2. *Golden Gate.* New York, 1939
3. *Paradise Valley.* New York, 1940
4. *The Splendid Gift.* New York, 1940
5. *A Battle in Washington Square.* New York, 1942
6. *Hill of Little Miracles.* New York, 1942
7. *Look out Yonder.* New York, 1943
8. *The Rooster Club.* New York, 1944
9. *The Bells of Bleecker Street.* New York, 1949
10. *The Marble Fountain.* New York, 1951
11. *Big Little Island.* New York, 1955
12. *The Acorn Tree.* New York, 1958
13. *The Honey Boat.* New York, 1959
14. *The Candy Basket.* New York, 1960
15. *Angelino and the Barefoot Saint.* New York, 1961
16. *The Merry Marcos.* New York, 1963
17. *The Tale of a Donkey.* New York, 1966

Anglund, Joan Walsh
American, born in 1926
1. *A Friend Is Someone Who Likes You.* New York, 1958
2. *Look Out the Window.* New York, 1959
3. *The Brave Cowboy.* New York and London, 1959
4. *Love Is a Special Way of Feeling.* New York and London, 1960
5. *In a Pumpkin Shell: A Mother Goose ABC.* New York, 1960
6. *Christmas Is a Time of Giving.* New York, 1961
7. *Cowboy and His Friend.* New York and London, 1961
8. *Nibble Nibble Mousekin: A Tale of Hansel and Gretel.* New York, 1962
9. *Cowboy's Secret Life.* New York, 1963
10. *Spring Is a New Beginning.* New York, 1963
11. *Childhood Is a Time of Innocence.* New York, 1964
12. *A Pocketful of Proverbs.* New York, 1964
13. *Morning Is a Little Child.* New York, 1969
14. *What Color Is Love?* New York, 1966
15. *A Year Is Round.* New York, 1966
16. *A Cup of Sun: A Book of Poems.* New York, 1967
17. *A Is for Always: An ABC Book.* New York, 1968

18. *A Slice of Snow: A Book of Poems.* New York, 1970
19. *Do You Love Someone?* New York, 1971
20. *The Cowboy's Christmas.* New York, 1972
21. *A Child's Book of Old Nursery Rhymes.* New York, 1973
22. *Goodbye, Yesterday: A Book of Poems.* New York, 1974

Anthony, Evelyn [Evelyn Bridget Patricia Ward-Thomas]
British, born in 1928
1. *Imperial Highness.* London, 1953
2. *Rebel Princess.* New York, 1953
3. *Curse Not the King.* London, 1954
4. *Royal Intrigue.* New York, 1954
5. *Far Flies the Eagle.* New York, 1955
6. *Anne Boleyn.* London and New York, 1957
7. *Victoria and Albert.* London, 1958
8. *Victoria.* London, 1959
9. *Elizabeth.* London, 1960
10. *All the Queen's Men.* New York, 1960
11. *Charles the King.* London and New York, 1963
12. *Clandara.* London and New York, 1963
13. *The Heiress.* London and New York, 1964
14. *The French Bride.* New York, 1964
15. *Valentina.* London and New York, 1966
16. *The Rendezvous.* London, 1967
17. *Anne of Austria.* London, 1968
18. *The Cardinal and the Queen.* New York, 1968
19. *The Legend.* London and New York, 1969
20. *The Assassin.* London and New York, 1970
21. *The Tamarind Seed.* London and New York, 1971
22. *The Poellenberg Inheritance.* London and New York, 1972
23. *The Occupying Power.* London, 1973
24. *Stranger at the Gates.* New York, 1973
25. *The Malaspiga Exit.* London, 1974
26. *Mission to Malaspiga.* New York, 1974
27. *The Persian Ransom.* London, 1975
28. *The Persian Price.* New York, 1975
29. *The Silver Falcon.* London and New York, 1977
30. *The Return.* London and New York, 1978
31. *The Grave of Truth.* London, 1979
32. *The Janus Imperative.* New York, 1980
33. *The Defector.* London, 1980
34. *The Avenue of the Dead.* London, 1981

Anthony, Piers [Piers Anthony Dillingham Jacob]
British, born in 1934
1. *Chthon.* New York, 1967
2. *Omnivore.* New York, 1968
3. *The Ring,* with Robert E. Margroff. New York, 1968
4. *So's the Rope.* New York, 1968
5. *Macroscope.* New York, 1969
6. *The E.S.P. Worm,* with Robert E. Margroff. New York, 1970
7. *Orn.* New York, 1970
8. *Prostho Plus.* London, 1971
9. *Var the Stick.* London, 1972
10. *Race Against Time.* New York, 1973
11. *Rings of Ice.* New York, 1974
12. *Neq the Sword.* London, 1975
13. *All.* New York, 1978

Arbor, Jane
British
1. *This Second Spring.* London, 1948
2. *Each Song Twice Over.* London, 1948
3. *Ladder of Understanding.* London, 1949
4. *Strange Loyalties.* London, 1949
5. *By Yet Another Door.* London, 1950
6. *No Lease for Love.* London, 1950
7. *The Heart Expects Adventure.* London, 1951
8. *Eternal Circle.* London, 1952
9. *Memory Serves My Love.* London, 1952
10. *Flower of the Nettle.* London, 1953
11. *Such Frail Armour.* London, 1953
12. *Jess Mawney, Queen's Nurse.* London, 1954
13. *Dear Intruder.* London, 1955
14. *Folly of the Heart.* London, 1955
15. *Towards the Dawn.* London, 1956
16. *City Nurse.* London, 1956
17. *Yesterday's Magic.* London, 1957
18. *Far Sanctuary.* London, 1958
19. *Nurse Harlowe.* Toronto, 1959
20. *Sandflower.* London, 1959
21. *Consulting Surgeon.* Toronto, 1959
22. *No Silver Spoon.* London, 1959
23. *Queen's Nurse.* Toronto, 1960
24. *A Girl Named Smith.* London, 1960
25. *Nurse of All Work.* London and Toronto, 1962
26. *Nurse in Waiting.* London and Toronto, 1962
27. *Desert Nurse.* London, 1963
28. *Jasmine Harvest.* London and Toronto, 1963
29. *Lake of Shadows.* London, 1964
30. *Kingfisher Tide.* London and Toronto, 1965
31. *High Master of Clere.* London and Toronto, 1966
32. *Summer Every Day.* London, 1966
33. *Golden Apple Island.* London, 1967
34. *Stranger's Trespass.* London, 1968
35. *The Cypress Garden.* London and Toronto, 1969
36. *The Feathered Shaft.* London and Toronto, 1970
37. *Walk into the Wind.* London and Toronto, 1970
38. *The Other Miss Donne.* London and Toronto, 1971
39. *The Linden Leaf.* London and Toronto, 1971
40. *The Flower on the Rock.* London, 1972
41. *Wildfire Quest.* London and Toronto, 1972
42. *Roman Summer.* London and Toronto, 1973
43. *The Velvet Spur.* London and Toronto, 1974
44. *Meet the Sun Halfway.* London and Toronto, 1974
45. *The Wide Fields of Home.* London and Toronto, 1975
46. *Tree of Paradise.* London, 1976
47. *Smoke into Flame.* Toronto, 1976
48. *Flash of Emerald.* London, 1977
49. *Two Pins in a Fountain.* London and Toronto, 1977
50. *A Growing Moon.* London, 1977
51. *Late Rapture.* London, 1978
52. *Return to Silbersee.* London, 1978
53. *Pact Without Desire.* London, 1979
54. *The Devil Drives.* London, 1979
55. *One Brief Sweet Hour.* London, 1980
56. *Where the Wolf Leads.* London, 1980

Ard, William (Thomas)
American, born on July 7, 1922, died March 12, 1960
Pseudonyms: Ben Kerr, Mike Moran, Thomas Wills, Jonas Ward
1. *The Perfect Frame.* New York, 1951
2. *.38.* New York, 1952
3. *And So to Bed.* Derby (CT), 1952
4. *The Diary.* New York, 1952
5. *You'll Get Yours,* as Thomas Wills. New York, 1952
6. *Shakedown,* as Ben Kerr. New York, 1952
7. *A Girl for Danny.* New York, 1953
8. *A Private Party.* New York, 1953
9. *You Can't Stop Me.* New York, 1953
10. *Double Cross,* as Mike Moran. New York, 1953
11. *This Is Murder.* London, 1954
12. *Don't Come Crying to Me.* New York, 1954
13. *No Angels for Me.* New York, 1954

14. *Rogue's Murder.* London, 1955
15. *Hell Is a City.* New York, 1955
16. *Mr. Trouble.* New York, 1955
17. *Mine to Avenge,* as Thomas Wills. New York, 1955
18. *Down I Go,* as Ben Kerr. New York, 1955
19. *The Name's Buchanan,* as Jonas Ward. New York, 1956
20. *Cry Scandal.* New York, 1956
21. *Damned If He Does,* as Ben Kerr. New York, 1956
22. *I Fear You Not,* as Ben Kerr. New York, 1956
23. *Buchanan Says No,* as Jonas Ward. New York, 1957
24. *The Root of His Evil.* New York, 1957
25. *Club 17,* as Ben Kerr. New York, 1957
26. *The Blonde and Johnny Malloy,* as Ben Kerr. New York, 1958
27. *Deadly Beloved.* New York, 1958
28. *One-Man Massacre,* as Jonas Ward. New York, 1958
29. *Buchanan Gets Mad,* as Jonas Ward. New York, 1958
30. *All I Can Get.* Derby, 1959
31. *As Bad as I Am.* New York, 1959
32. *Wanted: Danny Fontaine.* New York, 1960
33. *Like Ice She Was.* Derby, 1960
34. *When She Was Bad.* New York, 1960
35. *The Sins of Billy Serene.* Derby, 1960
36. *The Naked and the Innocent.* London, 1960
37. *Buchanan's Revenge,* as Jonas Ward. New York and London, 1960
38. *Buchanan on the Prod,* as Jonas Ward. New York, 1960
39. *Babe in the Woods.* Derby, 1961
40. *Make Mine Mavis.* Derby, 1961
41. *Give Me This Woman.* Derby, 1962

Ardies, Tom
American, born August 5, 1931
1. *Their Man in the White House.* New York, 1971
2. *This Suitcase Is Going to Explode.* New York, 1972
3. *Pandemic.* New York, 1973
4. *Kosygin Is Coming.* New York, 1974
5. *Russian Roulette.* London, 1975
6. *In a Lady's Service.* New York, 1976
7. *Palm Springs.* New York, 1978

Ardizzone, Edward
British, born in 1900
1. *Little Tim and the Brave Sea Captain.* London and New York, 1936
2. *Lucy Brown and Mr. Grimes.* London and New York, 1937
3. *Lucy and Tim Go to Sea.* London and New York, 1938
4. *Baggage to the Enemy.* London, 1941
5. *Nicholas and the Fast-Moving Diesel.* London, 1947
6. *Paul, The Hero of the Fire.* London, 1948
7. *Tim to the Rescue.* London and New York, 1949
8. *Tim and Charlotte.* London and New York, 1951
9. *Tim in Danger.* London and New York, 1953
10. *Tim All Alone.* London and New York, 1956
11. *Johnny the Clockmaker.* London and New York, 1960
12. *Tim's Friend Towser.* London and New York, 1962
13. *Peter the Wanderer.* London, 1963
14. *Diana and Her Rhinoceros.* London and New York, 1964
15. *Sarah and Simon and No Red Paint.* London, 1965
16. *Tim and Ginger.* London and New York, 1965
17. *Tim to the Lighthouse.* London and New York, 1968
18. *The Wrong Side of the Bed.* New York, 1969
19. *Johnny's Bad Day.* London, 1970
20. *The Young Ardizzone: An Autobigraphical Fragment.* London and New York, 1970
21. *Tim's Last Voyage.* London, 1972
22. *Diary of a War Artist.* London, 1974
23. *Ship's Cook Ginger.* London, 1977

Arlen, Michael
British, born in 1895 in Bulgaria, died June 23, 1956
1. *The London Venture.* London and New York, 1920
2. *The Romantic Lady.* London and New York, 1921
3. *Piracy: A Romantic Chronicle of These Days.* London, 1922
4. *The Green Hat: A Romance for a Few People.* London and New York, 1924
5. *These Charming People.* London, 1923
6. *May Fair, in Which Are Told the Last Adventures of These Charming People.* London and New York, 1925
7. *Young Men in Love.* London and New York, 1927
8. *The Man with the Broken Nose and Other Stories.* London, 1927
9. *The Ace of Cads and other Stories.* London, 1927
10. *Ghost Stories.* London, 1927
11. *Lily Christine.* New York, 1928
12. *Babes in the Wood.* London and New York, 1929
13. *The Ancient Sin and Other Stories.* London, 1930
14. *Men Dislike Women: A Romance.* London and New York, 1931
15. *A Young Man Comes to London.* Privately printed, 1931
16. *Man's Mortality.* London and New York, 1933
17. *The Short Stories.* London, 1933
18. *Hell! Said the Duchess: A Bed-Time Story.* London and New York, 1934
19. *The Crooked Coronet and Other Misrepresentations of the Real Facts of Life.* London and New York, 1937
20. *Flying Dutchman.* London and New York, 1939

Armour, Richard (Willard)
American, born in 1906
1. *Barry Cornwall: A Biography of Bryan Waller Procter.* Boston, 1935
2. *The Literary Recollections of Barry Cornwall.* Boston, 1936
3. *Yours for the Asking: A Book of Light Verse.* Boston, 1942
4. *To These Dark Steps,* with Brown Adams. New York, 1943
5. *Privates' Lives: Verses.* Boston, 1944
6. *Leading with My Left.* New York, 1946
7. *Golf Bawls.* New York, 1946
8. *Writing Light Verse.* Boston, 1947
9. *For Partly Proud Parents: Light Verse about Children.* New York, 1950
10. *It All Started with Columbus.* New York, 1953
11. *Light Armour: Playful Poems.* New York, 1954
12. *It All Started with Europa.* New York, 1955
13. *It All Started with Eve.* New York, 1956
14. *Twisted Tales from Shakespeare.* New York, 1957
15. *It All Started with Marx.* New York, 1958
16. *Nights with Armour: Lighthearted Light Verse.* New York, 1958
17. *Drug Store Days: My Youth among the Pills and Potions.* New York, 1959
18. *Pills, Potions and Granny.* London, 1960
19. *The Classics Reclassified.* New York, 1960
20. *A Safari into Satire.* Los Angeles, 1961
21. *Golf is a Four-Letter Word.* New York and London, 1962
22. *Armour's Almanac.* New York, 1962
23. *Through Darkest Adolescence.* New York, 1963
24. *American Lit Relit.* New York, 1964
25. *An Armoury of Light Verse.* Boston, 1964
26. *The Year Santa Went Modern.* New York, 1964
27. *Our Presidents.* New York, 1964
28. *The Adventures of Egbert the Easter Egg.* New York, 1965
29. *Going Around in Academic Circles.* New York, 1965
30. *Punctured Poems: Famous First and Infamous Second Lines.* Englewood Cliffs (NJ), 1966
31. *Animals on the Ceiling.* New York, 1966
32. *It All Started with Hippocrates.* New York, 1966

33. *A Dozen Dinosaurs.* New York, 1967
34. *A Satirist Looks at the World.* Ann Arbor (MI), 1967
35. *It All Started with Stones and Clubs.* New York, 1967
36. *Odd Old Mammals: Animals After the Dinosaurs.* New York, 1968
37. *My Life with Women.* New York, 1968
38. *English Lit Relit.* New York, 1969
39. *A Diabolical Dictionary of Education.* New York, 1969
40. *On Your Marks: A Package of Punctuation.* New York, 1969
41. *All Sizes and Shapes of Monkeys and Apes.* New York, 1970
42. *A Short History of Sex.* New York, 1970
43. *Who's in Holes?* New York, 1971
44. *Writing Light Verse and Prose.* Boston, 1971
45. *Out of My Mind.* New York, 1972
46. *All in Sport.* New York, 1972
47. *The Strange Dreams of Rover Jones.* New York, 1973
48. *It All Started with Freshman English.* New York, 1973
49. *Sea Full of Whales.* New York, 1974
50. *Going Like Sixty: A Lighthearted Look at the Later Years.* New York, 1974
51. *The Academic Bestiary.* New York, 1974
52. *The Spouse in the House.* New York, 1975
53. *The Happy Bookers: A History of Librarians and the World.* New York, 1976
54. *It All Would Have Startled Columbus.* New York, 1976
55. *It All Started with Nudes.* New York, 1977

Armstrong, Charlotte
American, born in 1905, died July 18, 1969
Pseudonym: Jo Valentine
1. *Lay On, MacDuff!* New York, 1942
2. *Ring Around Elizabeth.* New York, 1942
3. *The Case of the Weird Sisters.* New York and London, 1943
4. *Death Filled the Glass.* London, 1945
5. *The Innocent Flower.* New York, 1945
6. *The Unsuspected.* New York, 1946
7. *The Chocolate Cobweb.* New York, 1948
8. *Mischief.* New York, 1950
9. *The Black-Eyed Stranger.* New York, 1951
10. *Catch-as-Catch-Can.* New York, 1952
11. *The Trouble in Thor,* as Jo Valentine. New York and London, 1953
12. *Walk Out on Death.* New York, 1954
13. *And Sometimes Death,* as Jo Valentine. New York, 1954
14. *The Better to Eat You.* New York and London, 1954
15. *Murder's Nest.* New York, 1954
16. *The Dream Walker.* New York and London, 1955
17. *Alibi for Murder.* New York, 1956
18. *A Dram of Poison.* New York and London, 1956
19. *The Albatross.* New York, 1957
20. *Mask of Evil.* New York, 1958
21. *The Seventeen Windows of Sans Souci.* New York and London, 1959
22. *Duo: The Girl with a Secret, Incident at a Corner.* New York, 1959
23. *Something Blue.* New York, 1962
24. *Who's Been Sitting in My Chair.* New York, 1962
25. *Then Came Two Women.* New York, 1962
26. *A Little Less Than Kind.* New York, 1963
27. *The Mark of the Hand.* New York, 1963
28. *The One-Faced Girl.* New York, 1963
29. *The Witch's House.* New York, 1963
30. *The Turret Room.* New York and London, 1965
31. *Dream of Fair Woman.* New York and London, 1966
32. *I See You.* New York, 1966
33. *The Gift Shop.* New York and London, 1967
34. *Lemon in the Basket.* New York, 1967
35. *The Balloon Man.* New York and London, 1968
36. *Seven Seats to the Moon.* New York and London, 1969
37. *The Protege.* New York and London, 1970

Armstrong, Richard
British, born in 1903
Pseudonym: Cam Renton
1. *The Mystery of Obadiah.* London, 1943
2. *Sabotage at the Forge.* London, 1946
3. *The Northern Maid.* London, 1947
4. *Sea Change.* London, 1948
5. *The Whinstone Drift.* London, 1951
6. *Passage Home.* London, 1952
7. *Wanderlust: Voyage of a Little White Monkey.* London, 1952
8. *Danger Rock.* London, 1955
9. *Cold Hazard.* Boston, 1956
10. *The Lost Ship: A Caribbean Adventure.* London, 1956
11. *No Time for Tankers.* London, 1958
12. *Sailor's Luck.* London, 1959
13. *Another Six.* Oxford (Eng), 1959
14. *The Lame Duck.* London, 1959
15. *Before the Wind.* Oxford, 1959
16. *Horseshoe Reef.* London, 1960
17. *Ship Afire!* New York, 1961
18. *Out of the Shallows.* London, 1961
19. *Trial Trip.* London, 1962
20. *The Ship Stealers,* as Cam Renton. Penhurst (Eng), 1963
21. *Island Odyssey.* London, 1963
22. *Storm Path.* London, 1964
23. *Big-Head,* as Cam Renton. Penhurst, 1964
24. *The Big Sea.* London, 1964
25. *Grace Darling, Maid and Myth.* London, 1965
26. *The Greenhorn.* London, 1965
27. *The Secret Sea.* London and New York, 1966
28. *Fight for Freedom: An Adventure of World War II.* New York, 1966
29. *A History of Seafaring: The Early Mariners.* London, 1967
30. *A History of Seafaring: The Discoverers.* London, 1968
31. *The Mutineers.* London and New York, 1968
32. *A History of Seafaring: The Merchantmen.* London and New York, 1969
33. *The Albatross.* London and New York, 1970
34. *Themselves Alone: The Story of Men in Empty Places.* London and Boston, 1972
35. *Powered Ships: The Beginnings.* London, 1975

Armstrong, William H. (Howard)
American, born in 1914
1. *Study Is Hard Work.* New York, 1956
2. *Through Troubled Waters.* New York, 1957
3. *People of the Ancient World,* with Joseph Ward Swain. New York, 1959
4. *87 Ways to Help Your Child in School.* New York, 1961
5. *Tools of Thinking.* New York, 1961
6. *Word Power in Five Easy Lessons.* New York, 1969
7. *Sounder.* New York, 1969
8. *Barefoot in the Grass: The Story of Grandma Moses.* New York, 1970
9. *Animal Tales.* New York, 1970
10. *Sour Land.* New York, 1971
11. *The MacLeod Place.* New York, 1972
12. *Hadassah: Esther, the Orphan Queen.* New York, 1972
13. *The Mills of God.* New York, 1973
14. *My Animals.* New York, 1974
15. *The Education of Abraham Lincoln.* New York, 1974
16. *Study Tapes.* New York, 1975

Arnold, Edwin L. [Edwin Lester Linden Arnold]
British, born in 1857, died March 1, 1935
1. *A Summer Holiday in Scandinavia.* London, 1877
2. *On the Indian Hills; or, Coffee-Planting in Southern India.* London, 2 vols., 1881
3. *Coffee: Its Cultivation and Profit.* London, 1886
4. *Bird Life in England.* London, 1887
5. *England as She Seems, Being Selections from the Notes of an Arab Hadji.* London, 1888
6. *The Wonderful Adventures of Phra the Phoenician.* London, 3 vols.; New York, 1 vol., 1890
7. *The Constable of St. Nicholas.* London, 1894
8. *The Story of Ulla and Other Tales.* London and New York, 1895
9. *Lepidus the Centurian: A Roman of To-Day.* London, 1901
10. *Lieut. Gulliver Jones: His Vacation.* London, 1905
11. *The Soul of the Beast.* London, 1960
12. *Gulliver of Mars.* New York, 1964

Arnold, Elliott
American, born September 13, 1912, died May 13, 1980
1. *Two Loves.* New York, 1934
2. *Personal Combat.* New York, 1936
3. *Only the Young.* New York, 1939
4. *Nose for News: The Way of Life of a Reporter.* Evanston (IL), 1941
5. *Finlandia: The Story of Sibelius.* New York, 1941
6. *The Commandos.* New York, 1942
7. *First Comes Courage.* New York, 1943
8. *Mediterranean Sweep: Air Stories from El Alamein to Rome,* with Richard Thruelsen. New York, 1944
9. *Tomorrow Will Sing.* New York, 1945
10. *Big Distance,* with Donald Hough. New York, 1945
11. *Blood Brother.* New York, 1947
12. *Everybody Slept Here.* New York, 1948
13. *Deep in My Heart: A Story Based on the Life of Sigmund Romberg.* New York, 1949
14. *Walk with the Devil.* New York, 1950
15. *Time of the Gringo.* New York, 1953
16. *Broken Arrow.* New York, 1954
17. *White Falcon.* New York, 1955
18. *Rescue!* New York, 1956
19. *Flight from Ashiya.* New York and London, 1959
20. *Brave Jimmy Stone.* New York, 1962
21. *A Night of Watching.* New York and London, 1967
22. *A Kind of Secret Weapon.* New York, 1969
23. *Code of Conduct.* New York and London, 1970
24. *Forests of the Night.* New York, 1971
25. *The Spirit of Cochise.* New York, 1972
26. *Proving Ground.* New York, 1973
27. *The Camp Grant Massacre.* New York, 1976
28. *Quicksand.* New York, 1977

Arthur, Frank [Arthur Frank Ebert]
British, born in 1902
1. *Who Killed Netta Maul?* London, 1940
2. *The Suva Harbour Mystery.* London, 1948
3. *Time's a Thief.* London, 1952
4. *Twenty Minutes with Mrs. Oakentubb.* London, 1955
5. *She Would Not Dance.* London, 1956
6. *Another Mystery in Suva.* London, 1956
7. *Murder in the Tropic Night.* London, 1961
8. *The Throbbing Dark.* London, 1963
9. *The Abandoned Woman: The Story of Lucy Walter (1630-1658).* London, 1964
10. *The Profit from Murder.* London, 1974
11. *Confession to Murder.* London, 1974
12. *Captain Rocco Rides to Sheffield.* London, 1975

Arthur, Ruth (Mabel)
British, born in 1905
1. *Friendly Stories.* London, 1932
2. *The Crooked Brownie.* London, 1936
3. *Pumpkin Pie.* London, 1938
4. *Mother Goose Stories.* London, 1938
5. *The Crooked Brownie in Town.* London, 1942
6. *The Crooked Brownie at the Seaside.* London, 1942
7. *Cowslip Mollie.* London, 1949
8. *Carolina's Holiday and Other Stories.* London, 1957
9. *The Daisy Cow and Other Stories of the Channel Islands.* London, 1958
10. *Carolina's Golden Bird and Other Stories.* London, 1958
11. *A Cottage for Rosemary.* London, 1960
12. *Carolina and Roberto.* London, 1961
13. *Dragon Summer.* London, 1962
14. *Carolina and the Sea Horse, and Other Stories.* London, 1964
15. *My Daughter Nicola.* New York, 1965
16. *A Candle in Her Room.* London and New York, 1966
17. *Requiem for a Princess.* London and New York, 1967
18. *Portrait of Margarita.* London and New York, 1968
19. *The Whistling Boy.* London and New York, 1969
20. *The Saracen Lamp.* London and New York, 1970
21. *The Little Dark Thorn.* London and New York, 1971
22. *The Autumn People.* London and New York, 1973
23. *After Candlemas.* London and New York, 1974
24. *On the Wasteland.* London and New York, 1975
25. *The Autumn Ghosts.* London, 1976
26. *Candlemas Mystery.* London, 1976
27. *An Old Magic.* London and New York, 1977

Arthur, T.S.
1. *Words for the Wise.* Philadelphia, 1851
2. *True Riches.* Boston, 1852
3. *Ten Nights in a Bar-Room, and What I Saw There.* Philadelphia, 1854

Arundel, Honor (Morfydd)
British, born in 1919
1. *The Freedom of Art.* London, 1965
2. *Green Street.* London, 1966
3. *The High House.* London, 1966
4. *Emma's Island.* London, 1968
5. *The Two Sisters.* London, 19689
6. *The Amazing Mr. Prothero.* London, 1968
7. *The Longest Weekend.* London, 1969
8. *The Girl in the Opposite Bed.* London, 1970
9. *Emma in Love.* London, 1970
10. *The Terrible Temptation.* London and New York, 1971
11. *A Family Failing.* London and Nashville (TN), 1972
12. *The Blanket Word.* London, 1973

Ash, Fenton [Frank Atkins]
British
Other pseudonyms: Fred Ashley, Frank Aubrey
1. *The Devil Tree of El Dorado,* as Frank Aubrey. London, 1896
2. *A Studio Mystery,* as Frank Aubrey. London, 1897
3. *Strange Stories of Hospitals,* as Frank Aubrey. London, 1898
4. *A Queen of Atlantis,* as Frank Aubrey. London and Philadelphia, 1899
5. *King of the Dead,* as Frank Aubrey. London, 1903
6. *The Radium Seekers; or, The Wonderful Black Nugget.* London, 1905
7. *The Temple of Fire; or, The Mysterious Islands,* as Fred Ashley. London, 1905

8. *A Trip to Mars.* London, 1909
9. *By Airship to Ophir.* London, 1911
10. *The Black Opal.* London, 1915

Ashley, Bernard
British, born in 1935
1. *Don't Run Away.* London, 1965
2. *Wall of Death.* London, 1966
3. *Space Shot.* London, 1967
4. *The Big Escape.* London, 1967
5. *The Men and the Boats: Britain's Life-Boat Service.* London, 1968
6. *Weather Men.* London, 1970
7. *The Trouble with Donovan Croft.* London, 1974
8. *Terry on the Fence.* London, 1975
9. *All My Men.* London, 1977

Ashton, Elizabeth
British
1. *The Pied Tulip.* London, 1969
2. *The Benevolent Despot.* London and Toronto, 1970
3. *Parisian Adventure.* London and Toronto, 1970
4. *Cousin Mark.* London and Toronto, 1971
5. *The Enchanted Wood.* London, 1971
6. *Sweet Simplicity.* London, 1971
7. *Flutter of White Wings.* London and Toronto, 1972
8. *A Parade of Peacocks.* London, 1972
9. *Scorched Wings.* London, 1972
10. *The Rocks of Arachenza.* London, 1973
11. *Sigh No More.* London, 1973
12. *The Bells of Bruges.* London, 1973
13. *Alpine Rhapsody.* Toronto, 1973
14. *Errant Bride.* London, 1973
15. *Moorland Magic.* London and Toronto, 1973
16. *Dark Angel.* London and Toronto, 1974
17. *The House of the Eagles.* London, 1974
18. *Dangerous to Know.* London, 1974
19. *The Road to the Border.* London, 1974
20. *The Scent of Sandalwood.* London, 1974
21. *Miss Nobody from Nowhere.* London and Toronto, 1975
22. *The Willing Hostage.* London, 1975
23. *Crown of Willow.* London, 1975
24. *The Player King.* London and Toronto, 1975
25. *Sanctuary in the Desert.* London, 1976
26. *My Lady Disdain.* London and Toronto, 1976
27. *Mountain Heritage.* London, 1976
28. *Lady in the Limelight.* Toronto, 1976
29. *Aegean Quest.* Toronto, 1977
30. *Voyage of Enchantment.* Toronto, 1977
31. *Green Harvest.* Toronto, 1977
32. *Breeze from the Bosphorus.* Toronto, 1978
33. *The Garden of the Gods.* London, 1978
34. *The Golden Girl.* London and Toronto, 1978
35. *The Questing Heart.* London and Toronto, 1978
36. *Rendezvous in Venice.* London and Toronto, 1978
37. *The Joyous Adventure.* London, 1979
38. *Moonlight on the Nile.* London and Toronto, 1979
39. *Reluctant Partnership.* London, 1979
40. *Borrowed Plumes.* London, 1980
41. *The Rekindled Flame.* London and Toronto, 1980
42. *Sicilian Summer.* London, 1980
43. *Silver Arrow.* London, 1980
44. *Rebel Against Love.* London and Toronto, 1981

Asimov, Isaac
American, born in 1920
Pseudonyms: Dr. A, Paul French
1. *Pebble in the Sky.* New York, 1950
2. *I, Robot.* New York, 1950
3. *The Stars, Like Dust.* New York, 1951
4. *Foundation.* New York, 1951
5. *Foundation and Empire.* New York, 1952
6. *The Currents of Space.* New York, 1952
7. *David Starr: Spaceranger,* as Paul French. New York, 1952
8. *Second Foundation.* New York, 1953
9. *Lucky Starr and the Pirates of the Asteroids,* as Paul French. New York, 1953
10. *The Caves of Steel.* New York and London, 1954
11. *The Rebellious Stars.* New York, 1954
12. *Lucky Starr and the Oceans of Venus,* as Paul French. New York, 1954
13. *The Martian Way and Other Stories.* New York, 1955
14. *The End of Eternity.* New York, 1955
15. *The 1,000-Year Plan.* New York, 1955
16. *The Man Who Upset the Universe.* New York, 1955
17. *Lucky Starr and the Big Sun of Mercury,* as Paul French. New York, 1956
18. *Earth Is Room Enough.* New York, 1957
19. *The Naked Sun.* New York, 1957
20. *Lucky Starr and the Moons of Jupiter,* as Paul French. New York, 1957
21. *The Death Dealers.* New York, 1958
22. *Lucky Starr and the Rings of Saturn,* as Paul French. New York, 1958
23. *Nine Tomorrows: Tales of the Near Future.* New York, 1959
24. *The Rest of the Robots.* New York, 1964
25. *Of Time and Space and Other Things.* New York, 1965
26. *Fantastic Voyage.* Boston and London, 1966
27. *Through a Glass Clearly.* London, 1967
28. *A Whiff of Death.* New York and London, 1968
29. *Asimov's Mysteries.* New York and London, 1968
30. *Nightfall and Other Stories.* New York, 1969
31. *The Isaac Asimov Treasury of Humor.* Boston, 1971
32. *The Sensuous Dirty Old Man,* as Dr. A. New York, 1971
33. *The Early Asimov; or, Eleven Years of Trying.* New York, 1972
34. *The Gods Themselves.* New York and London, 1972
35. *The Best of Isaac Asimov (1939-1972).* London, 1973
36. *Tales of the Black Widowers.* New York, 1974
37. *Have You Seen These?* Cambridge (MA), 1974
38. *Lecherous Limericks.* New York, 1975
39. *Buy Jupiter and Other Stories.* New York, 1975
40. *The Heavenly Host.* New York, 1975
41. *More Lecherous Limericks.* New York, 1976
42. *The Bicentennial Man and Other Stories.* New York, 1976
43. *More Tales of the Black Widowers.* New York, 1976
44. *Murder at the ABA.* New York, 1976
45. *Authorized Murder.* London, 1976
46. *The Dream, Benjamin's Dream, Benjamin's Blast.* Privately printed, 1976
47. *Good Taste.* Topeka (KS), 1976
48. *Still More Lecherous Limericks.* New York, 1977
49. *Asimov's Sherlockian Limericks.* Yonkers (NY), 1978
50. *Limericks: Too Gross,* with John Ciardi. New York, 1978
51. *The Collected Fiction: The Far Ends of Time and Earth, Prisoners of the Stars.* New York, 2 vols., 1979
52. *The Road to Infinity.* New York, 1979
53. *Casebook of the Black Widowers.* New York, 1980

Asprin, Robert (Lynn)
American, born in 1946
1. *The Cold Cash War.* New York and London, 1977
2. *Another Fine Myth.* Virginia Beach (VA), 1978
3. *The Bug Wars.* New York, 1979
4. *Tambu.* New York, 1979

5. *Mirror Friend, Mirror Foe,* with George Takei. Chicago, 1979
6. *Myth Conceptions.* Virginia Beach, 1979

Asquith, Nan [Nancy Evelyn Pattinson]
British
1. *My Dream Is Yours.* London, 1954
2. *With All My Heart.* London, 1954
3. *Believe In To-morrow.* London, 1955
4. *Only My Heart to Give.* London, 1955
5. *The Certain Spring.* London, 1956
6. *Honey Island.* London, 1957
7. *The House on Brinden Water.* London, 1958
8. *The Time for Happiness.* London, 1959
9. *Time May Change.* London, 1961
10. *The Doctor Is Engaged.* Toronto, 1962
11. *The Way the Wind Blows.* London, 1963
12. *The Quest.* London, 1964
13. *The Summer at San Milo.* London, 1965
14. *Doctor Robert Comes Around.* Toronto, 1965
15. *Dangerous Yesterday.* London, 1967
16. *The Garden of Persephone.* London, 1967
17. *The Admiral's House.* London, 1969
18. *Turn the Page.* London and Toronto, 1970
19. *Beyond the Mountain.* London, 1970
20. *Carnival at San Cristobal.* London, 1971
21. *Out of the Dark.* London, 1972
22. *The Girl From Rome.* London and Toronto, 1973
23. *The Sun in the Morning.* London, 1974

Athanas, Verne [William Verne Athanas]
American, born August 13, 1917, died June 21, 1962
1. *The Proud Ones.* New York, 1952
2. *Rogue Valley.* New York, 1953
3. *Maverick.* New York, 1956

Atherton, Gertrude
American, born October 30, 1857, died June 14, 1948
Pseudonym: Frank Lin
1. *What Dreams May Come,* as Frank Lin. Chicago, 1888
2. *Hermia Suydam.* New York, 1889
3. *Los Cerritos: A Romance of the Modern Times.* New York, 1890
4. *A Question of Time.* New York, 1891
5. *The Doomswoman.* New York, 1893
6. *Before the Gringo Came.* New York, 1894
7. *A Whirl Asunder.* New York, 1895
8. *Patience Sparhawk and Her Times.* New York, 1897
9. *His Fortunate Grace.* New York, 1897
10. *American Wives and English Husbands.* New York, 1898
11. *The Californians.* New York, 1898
12. *The Valiant Runaways.* New York, 1898
13. *A Daughter of the Vine.* New York, 1899
14. *Senator North.* New York, 1900
15. *The Aristocrats, Being the Impressions of Lady Helen Pole During Her Sojourn in the Great North Woods.* New York, 1901
16. *The Conqueror, Being the True and Romantic Story of Alexander Hamilton.* New York, 1902
17. *Heart of Hyacinth.* New York, 1903
18. *Rulers of Kings.* New York, 1904
19. *The Bell in the Fog and Other Stories.* New York, 1905
20. *The Travelling Thirds.* New York, 1905
21. *Rezanov.* New York, 1906
22. *Ancestors.* New York, 1907
23. *The Gorgeous Isle: A Romance: Scene, Nevis, B.W.I., 1842.* New York, 1908
24. *Tower of Ivory.* New York, 1910
25. *Julia France and Her Times.* New York, 1912
26. *Perch of the Devil.* New York, 1914
27. *California: An Intimate History.* New York, 1914
28. *Mrs. Balfame.* New York, 1916
29. *Live in the War Zone.* New York, 1916
30. *The Living Present.* New York, 1917
31. *The White Morning: A Novel of the Power of the German Women in Wartime.* New York, 1918
32. *The Avalanche: A Mystery Story.* New York, 1919
33. *Transplanted.* New York, 1919
34. *The Sisters-in-Law: A Novel of Our Time.* New York, 1921
35. *Sleeping Fires.* New York, 1922
36. *Dormant Fires.* London, 1922
37. *Black Oxen.* New York and London, 1923
38. *The Crystal Cup.* New York, 1925
39. *The Immortal Marriage.* New York, 1927
40. *The Jealous Gods: A Processional Novel of the Fifth Century B.C. (Concerning One Alcibiades).* New York, 1928
41. *Dido, Queen of Hearts.* London, 1929
42. *The Sophisticates.* New York, 1931
43. *Adventures of a Novelist.* New York, 1932
44. *The Foghorn: Stories.* Boston, 1934
45. *Golden Peacock.* Boston, 1936
46. *Rezanov and Dona Concha.* New York, 1937
47. *Can Women Be Gentlemen?* Boston, 1938
48. *The House of Lee.* New York, 1940
49. *The Horn of Life.* New York, 1942
50. *Golden Gate Country.* New York, 1945
51. *My San Francisco: A Wayward Biography.* Indianapolis, 1946

Atkins, John (Alfred)
British, born in 1916
1. *The Distribution of Fish.* London, 1941
2. *The Diary of William Carpenter.* London, 1943
3. *Experience of England.* London, 1943
4. *Walter de la Mare: An Exploration.* London, 1947
5. *Cat on Hot Bricks.* London, 1950
6. *The Art of Ernest Hemingway: His Work and His Personality.* London, 1952
7. *Rain and the River.* London, 1954
8. *George Orwell: A Literary Study.* London, 1954
9. *Tomorrow Revealed.* London, 1955
10. *Arthur Koestler.* London and New York, 1956
11. *Aldous Huxley: A Literary Study.* London and New York, 1956
12. *Graham Greene.* London and New York, 1957
13. *A Land Fit for Eros,* with J.B. Pick. London, 1957
14. *The Erotic Impulse in Literature.* London, 1970
15. *The Classical Experience of the Sexual Impulse.* London, 1973
16. *Six Novelists Look at Society . . .* London and Dallas (TX), 1977
17. *The Medieval Experience.* London, 1978

Atkinson, M.E. (Mary Evelyn)
British, born in 1899
1. *Here Lies Matilda.* London, 1931
2. *Beginner's Luck.* London and Boston, 1932
3. *Patchwork.* London and Boston, 1933
4. *The Chimney Corner.* London and Boston, 1934
5. *The Day's Good Cause.* London and Boston, 1935
6. *Crab-Apple Harvest.* London and Boston, 1936
7. *Going Rustic.* London and Boston, 1936
8. *August Adventure.* London, 1936
9. *Mystery Manor.* London, 1937
10. *Little White Jumbo.* London, 1937
11. *The Compass Points North.* London, 1938

12. *Smugglers' Gap.* London, 1939
13. *Can the Leopard?* London and Boston, 1939
14. *Going Gangster.* London, 1940
15. *Crusoe Island.* London, 1941
16. *Challenge to Adventure.* London, 1942
17. *The Monster of Widgeon Weir.* London, 1943
18. *The Nest of the Scarecrow.* London, 1944
19. *The Lights Go Up.* London, 1945
20. *Problem Party.* London, 1945
21. *Chimney Cottage.* London, 1947
22. *The House on the Moor.* London, 1948
23. *The Thirteenth Adventure.* London, 1949
24. *Steeple Folly.* London, 1950
25. *Castaway Camp.* London, 1951
26. *Hunter's Moon.* London, 1952
27. *The Barnstormers.* London, 1953
28. *Riders and Raids.* London, 1955
29. *Unexpected Adventure.* London, 1955
30. *Horseshoes and Handle Bars.* London, 1958
31. *Where There's a Will.* London, 1961

Atwater, Richard (Tupper)
American, born in 1892, died in 1938
1. *Rickety Rimes of Riq.* Chicago, 1925
2. *Doris and the Trolls.* Chicago, 1931
3. *Mr. Popper's Penguins.* Boston, 1938

Audemars, Pierre
British, born in 1909
Pseudonym: Peter Hodemart
1. *Night Without Darkness.* London, 1936
2. *Hercule and the Gods.* London, 1944
3. *The Temptation of Hercule.* London, 1945
4. *Fate and Fernand.* London, 1945
5. *When the Gods Laughed.* Hounslow (Eng), 1946
6. *The Obligation of Hercule.* London, 1947
7. *The Confessions of Hercule.* London, 1947
8. *Wrath of the Valley,* as Peter Hodemart. London, 1947
9. *The Thieves of Enchantment.* London, 1956
10. *The Two Imposters.* London, 1958
11. *The Fire and the Clay.* London, 1959
12. *The Turns of Time.* London, 1961
13. *The Crown of Night.* London and New York, 1962
14. *The Dream and the Dead.* London, 1963
15. *The Wings of Darkness.* London, 1963
16. *The Street of Grass.* New York, 1963
17. *Fair Maids Missing.* London, 1964
18. *Dead with Sorrow.* London, 1964
19. *A Woven Web.* New York, 1965
20. *Time of Temptation.* London and New York, 1966
21. *A Thorn in the Dust.* London, 1967
22. *The Veins of Compassion.* London, 1967
23. *The White Leaves of Death.* London, 1968
24. *The Flame in the Mist.* London, 1969
25. *A Host for Dying.* London, 1970
26. *Stolen Like Magic Away.* London, 1971
27. *The Delicate Dust of Death.* London, 1973
28. *No Tears for the Dead.* London, 1974
29. *Nightmare in Rust.* London, 1975
30. *And One for the Dead.* London, 1975
31. *The Healing Hands of Death.* London, 1977
32. *Now Dead Is Any Man.* London, 1978
33. *A Sad and Savage Dying.* London, 1978
34. *Slay Me a Sinner.* London, 1979

Austin, Mary
American, born September 9, 1868, died August 13, 1934
Pseudonym: Gordon Stairs
1. *The Land of Little Rain.* Boston, 1903
2. *The Basket Woman: A Book of Fanciful Tales for Children.* Boston, 1904
3. *Isidro.* Boston, 1905
4. *The Flock.* Boston, 1906
5. *Santa Lucia: A Common Story.* New York, 1908
6. *Lost Borders.* New York, 1909
7. *Outland,* as Gordon Stairs. London, 1910
8. *The Arrow-Maker.* New York, 1911
9. *A Woman of Genius.* New York, 1912
10. *Masterpieces.* New York, 1912
11. *Christ in Italy, Being the Adventures of a Maverick among Masterpieces.* New York, 1912
12. *The Lovely Lady.* New York, 1913
13. *The Green Bough: A Tale of Resurrection.* New York, 1913
14. *California, The Land of the Sun.* New York and London, 1914
15. *Love and the Soul Maker.* New York, 1914
16. *Suffrage and Government . . . with Special Reference to Nevada and Other Western States.* New York, 1914
17. *What the Mexican Conference Really Means.* New York, 1915
18. *The Man Jesus, Being a Brief Account of the Life and Teaching of the Prophet of Nazareth.* New York, 1915
19. *The Ford.* Boston, 1917
20. *The Trail Book.* Boston, 1918
21. *The Young Woman Citizen.* New York, 1918
22. *Outland.* New York, 1919
23. *No. 26 Jayne Street.* Boston, 1920
24. *The American Rhythm.* New York, 1923
25. *The Land of Journey's Ending.* New York, 1924
26. *Everyman's Genius.* Indianapolis, 1925
27. *The Children Sing in the Far West.* Boston, 1928
28. *Taos Pueblo,* with Ansel Adams. San Francisco, 1930
29. *Starry Adventure.* Boston, 1931
30. *Experiences Facing Death.* Indianapolis and London, 1931
31. *Earth Horizon.* Boston, 1932
32. *One-Smoke Stories.* Boston, 1934
33. *Indian Pottery of the Rio Grande.* Pasadena (CA), 1934
34. *Can Prayer Be Answered?* New York, 1934
35. *When I Am Dead.* Privately printed, 1935
36. *Mother of Felipe and Other Early Stories.* San Francisco, 1950
37. *Mary Austin on the Art of Writing: A Letter to Henry James Foreman.* Los Angeles, 1961
38. *One Hundred Miles on Horseback.* Los Angeles, 1963
39. *Literary America 1903-1934: Mary Austin Letters.* Westport (CT), 1979

Avallone, Michael [Michael Angelo Avallone, Jr.]
American, born in 1924
Pseudonyms: Nick Carter, Troy Conway, Priscilla Dalton, Mark Dane, Jean-Anne de Pre, Dora Highland, Steve Michaels, Dorothea Nile, Edwina Noone, Vance Stanton, Sidney Stuart, Max Walker
1. *The Spitting Image.* New York, 1953
2. *The Tall Dolores.* New York, 1953
3. *Dead Game.* New York, 1954
4. *Violence in Velvet.* New York, 1956
5. *The Case of the Bouncing Betty.* New York, 1957
6. *The Case of the Violent Virgin.* New York, 1957
7. *The Crazy Mixed-Up Corpse.* New York, 1957
8. *The Voodoo Murders.* New York, 1957
9. *Meanwhile Back at the Morgue.* New York, 1960
10. *All the Way Home.* New York, 1960
11. *The Little Black Book.* New York, 1961
12. *Stag Stripper.* New York, 1961
13. *Women in Prison.* New York, 1961
14. *The Alarming Clock.* London, 1961

15. *Flight Hostess Rogers.* New York, 1962
16. *Never Love a Call Girl.* New York, 1962
17. *The Platinum Trap.* New York, 1962
18. *Sex Kitten.* New York, 1962
19. *Sinners in White.* New York, 1962
20. *Lust at Leisure.* Beacon (NY), 1963
21. *The Bedroom Bolero.* New York, 1963
22. *There Is Something About a Dame.* New York, 1963
23. *Shock Corridor.* New York, 1963
24. *The Doctor's Wife.* Beacon, 1963
25. *Tales of the Frightened.* New York, 1963
26. *And Sex Walked In.* Beacon, 1963
27. *The Main Attraction,* as Steve Michaels. New York, 1963
28. *The Living Bomb.* London, 1963
29. *Lust is No Lady.* New York, 1964
30. *Station Six—Sahara.* New York, 1964
31. *The China Doll,* as Nick Carter. New York, 1964
32. *Run Spy Run,* as Nick Carter. New York, 1964
33. *Saigon,* as Nick Carter. New York, 1964
34. *The Night Walker,* as Sidney Stuart. New York, 1964
35. *Felicia,* as Mark Dane. New York, 1964
36. *Young Dillinger,* as Sidney Stuart. New York, 1965
37. *The Thousand Coffins Affair.* New York and London, 1965
38. *Corridor of Whispers,* as Edwina Noone. New York, 1965
39. *Dark Cypress,* as Edwina Noone. New York, 1965
40. *Heirloom of Tragedy,* as Edwina Noone. New York, 1965
41. *The Brutal Kook.* London, 1965
42. *The Darkening Willows,* as Priscilla Dalton. New York, 1965
43. *90 Gramercy Park,* as Priscilla Dalton. New York, 1965
44. *The Silent, Silken Shadows,* as Priscilla Dallton. New York, 1965
45. *Daughter of Darkness,* as Edwina Noone. New York, 1966
46. *The Second Secret,* as Edwina Noone. New York, 1966
47. *The Victorian Crown,* as Edwina Noone. New York, 1966
48. *Edwina Noone's Gothic Sampler.* New York, 1966
49. *The Birds of a Feather Affair.* New York, 1966
50. *The Blazing Affair.* New York, 1966
51. *Kaleidoscope.* New York, 1966
52. *The Evil Men Do,* as Dorothea Nile. New York, 1966
53. *Mistress of Farrondale,* as Dorothea Nile. New York, 1966
54. *Terror at Deepcliff,* as Dorothea Nile. New York, 1966
55. *The Fat Death.* London, 1966
56. *The February Doll Murders.* London, 1966
57. *Madame X.* New York, 1966
58. *The Felony Squad.* New York, 1967
59. *The Man from A.V.O.N.* New York, 1967
60. *Assassins Don't Lie in Bed.* New York, 1968
61. *The Coffin Things.* New York, 1968
62. *Hawaii Five-O.* New York, 1968
63. *The Incident.* New York, 1968
64. *Come One, Come All,* as Troy Conway. New York, 1968
65. *The Man-Eater,* as Troy Conway. New York, 1968
66. *Seacliffe,* as Edwina Noone. New York, 1968
67. *The Vampire Cameo,* as Dorothea Nile. New York, 1968
68. *The Horrible Man.* London, 1968
69. *The Big Broad Jump,* as Troy Conway. New York, 1969
70. *Mannix.* New York, 1968
71. *Hawaii Five-O: Terror in the Sun.* New York, 1969
72. *The Killing Star.* London, 1969
73. *A Good Peace,* as Troy Conway. New York, 1969
74. *The Flower-Covered Corpse.* London, 1969
75. *Had Any Lately?* as Troy Conway. New York, 1969
76. *The Doomsday Bag.* New York, 1969
77. *Missing.* New York, 1969
78. *I'd Rather Fight than Swish,* as Troy Conway. New York, 1969
79. *Krakatoa, East of Java.* New York, 1969
80. *Killer's Highway.* London, 1970
81. *The Last Escape,* as Max Walker. New York, 1970
82. *The Blow-Your-Mind Job,* as Troy Conway. New York, 1970
83. *The Cunning Linguist,* as Troy Conway. New York, 1970
84. *The Cloisonne Vase,* as Edwina Noone. New York, 1970
85. *A Bullet for Pretty Boy.* New York, 1970
86. *One More Time.* New York, 1970
87. *Beneath the Planet of the Apes.* New York, 1970
88. *The Doctors.* New York, 1970
89. *Hornets' Nest.* New York, 1970
90. *The Haunted Hall.* New York, 1970
91. *Keith, the Hero.* New York, 1970
92. *The Partridge Family.* New York, 1970
93. *The Ultimate Client.* London, 1971
94. *When Were You Born?* Paris, 1971
95. *The Night Before Chaos.* Paris, 1971
96. *The Craghold Legacy,* as Edwina Noone. New York, 1971
97. *All Screwed Up,* as Troy Conway. New York, 1971
98. *The Penetrator,* as Troy Conway. New York, 1971
99. *A Stiff Proposition,* as Troy Conway. New York, 1971
100. *Keith Partridge, Master Spy,* as Vance Stanton. New York, 1971
101. *Death Dives Deep.* New York and London, 1971
102. *Little Miss Murder.* New York, 1971
103. *A Sound of Dying Roses,* as Jean-Anne de Pre. New York, 1971
104. *The Third Woman,* as Jean-Anne de Pre. New York, 1971
105. *The Fat and Skinny Murder Mystery,* as Vance Stanton. New York, 1972
106. *The Walking Fingers,* as Vance Stanton. New York, 1972
107. *Who's That Laughing in the Grave?,* as Vance Stanton. New York, 1972
108. *Aquarius, My Evil,* as Jean-Anne de Pre. New York, 1972
109. *Die, Jessica, Die,* as Jean-Anne de Pre. New York, 1972
110. *Shoot It Again, Sam.* New York, 1972
111. *The Girl in the Cockpit.* New York, 1972
112. *London Bloody London.* New York, 1972
113. *The Living Bomb.* New York, 1972
114. *The Craghold Creatures,* as Edwina Noone. New York, 1972
115. *The Craghold Curse,* as Edwina Noone. New York, 1972
116. *The Bolero Murders.* London, 1972
117. *The Craghold Crypt,* as Edwina Noone. New York, 1973
118. *The Beast with Red Hands,* as Sidney Stuart. New York, 1973
119. *Kill Her—You'll Like It.* New York, 1973
120. *The Hot Body.* New York, 1973
121. *Killer on the Keys.* New York, 1973
122. *The X-Rated Corpse.* New York, 1973
123. *Love Comes to Keith Partridge.* New York, 1973
124. *The Third Shadow,* as Dorothea Nile. New York, 1973
125. *Warlock's Woman,* as Jean-Anne de Pre. New York, 1973
126. *The Moving Graveyard.* London, 1973
127. *153 Oakland Street,* as Dora Highland. New York, 1973
128. *Fallen Angel.* New York, 1974
129. *The Werewolf Walks Tonight.* New York, 1974
130. *The Girls in Television.* New York, 1974
131. *Ed Noon in London.* London, 1974
132. *Death Is a Dark Man,* as Dora Highland. New York, 1974
133. *Devil, Devil.* New York, 1975
134. *Only One More Miracle.* New York, 1975
135. *CB Logbook of the White Knight.* New York, 1977
136. *The Big Stiffs.* London, 1977
137. *Carquake.* London, 1977
138. *Where Monsters Walk.* New York, 1978
139. *Five Minute Mysteries.* New York, 1978
140. *Dark on Monday.* London, 1978
141. *Name That Movie.* New York, 1978
142. *Son of Name That Movie.* New York, 1978

Averill, Esther (Holden)
American, born in 1902
Pseudonym: John Domino
1. *Powder: The Story of a Colt, The Duchess, and a Circus.* Paris, New York, and London, 1933
2. *Flash: The Story of a Horse, a Coach-Dog, and the Gypsies.* Paris, New York, and London, 1934
3. *Fable of a Proud Pony,* as John Domino. Paris, 1934
4. *Political Propaganda in Children's Books of the French Revolution.* New York, 1935
5. *The Voyages of Jacques Cartier.* New York, 1937
6. *The Cat Club: or, The Life and Times of Jenny Linsky.* New York and London, 1944
7. *The Adventures of Jack Ninepins.* New York and London, 1944
8. *The School for Cats.* New York and London, 1947
9. *Jenny's First Party.* New York and London, 1948
10. *Jenny's Moonlight Adventure.* New York, 1949
11. *King Philip: The Indian Chief.* New York, 1950
12. *When Jenny Lost Her Scarf.* New York, 1951
13. *Jenny's Adopted Brothers.* New York, 1952
14. *How the Brothers Joined the Cat Club.* New York, 1953
15. *Jenny's Birthday Book.* New York, 1954
16. *Cartier Sails the St. Lawrence.* New York, 1956
17. *Jenny Goes to Sea.* New York, 1957
18. *Jenny's Bedside Book.* New York, 1959
19. *The Fire Cat.* New York, 1960
20. *The Hotel Cat.* New York, 1969
21. *Eyes of the World: The Story and Work of Jacques Collot.* New York, 1969
22. *Captains of the City Streets.* New York, 1972
23. *Jenny and the Cat Club.* New York, 1973

Avery, Gillian (Elise)
British, born in 1926
1. *The Warden's Niece.* London, 1957
2. *Trespassers at Charlcote.* London, 1958
3. *James Without Thomas.* London, 1959
4. *The Elephant War.* London, 1960
5. *To Tame a Sister.* London, 1961
6. *Mrs. Ewing.* London, 1961
7. *The Greatest Gresham.* London, 1962
8. *The Peacock House.* London, 1963
9. *The Italian Spring.* London, 1964
10. *Nineteenth Century Children: Heroes and Heroines in English Children's Stories, 1780-1900,* with Angela Bull. London, 1965
11. *Call of the Valley.* London, 1966
12. *Victorian People in Life and Literature.* London and New York, 1970
13. *A Likely Lad.* London and New York, 1971
14. *Ellen's Birthday.* London, 1971
15. *Ellen and the Queen.* London, 1972
16. *Jemima and the Welsh Rabbit.* London, 1972
17. *The Echoing Green: Memories of Victorian and Regency Youth.* London and New York, 1974
18. *Book of Strange and Odd.* London, 1975
19. *Childhood's Pattern: A Study of the Heroes and Heroines of Children's Fiction, 1770-1950.* London, 1975
20. *Freddie's Feet.* London, 1976
21. *Huck and Her Time Machine.* London, 1977

Ayer, Jacqueline (Brandford)
American, born in 1932
1. *Nu Dang and His Kite.* New York, 1959
2. *A Wish for Little Sister.* New York, 1960
3. *The Paper-Flower Tree.* New York, 1962
4. *Little Silk.* New York, 1970
5. *Oriental Costume.* London, 1974

Ayres, Ruby M. (Mildred)
British, born in 1883, died November 14, 1955
1. *Castles in Spain: The Chronicles of an April Month.* London, 1912
2. *Richard Chatterton, V.C.* London, 1915
3. *The Long Lane to Happiness.* London, 1915
4. *The Making of a Man.* London, 1915
5. *The Road That Bends.* London, 1916
6. *Paper Roses.* London, 1916
7. *A Man of His Word.* London, 1916
8. *The Year After.* London, 1916
9. *The Littl'st Lover.* London, 1917
10. *The Black Sheep.* London, 1917
11. *The Winds of the World.* London, 1918
12. *The Remembered Kiss.* London, 1918
13. *For Love.* London, 1918
14. *Invalided Out.* London, 1918
15. *The Second Honeymoon.* New York, 1918
16. *The Phantom Lover.* New York, 1919
17. *The One Who Forgot.* London, 1919
18. *A Bachelor Husband.* London and New York, 1920
19. *The Master Man.* London, 1920
20. *The Woman Hater.* London, 1920
21. *The Beggar Man.* London, 1920
22. *The Dancing Master.* London, 1920
23. *The Scar.* London, 1920
24. *The Marriage of Barry Wicklow.* London, 1920
25. *The Uphill Road.* New York, 1921
26. *The Waif's Wedding.* London, 1921
27. *The Fortune Hunter.* London, 1921
28. *Her Way and His.* London, 1921
29. *The Highest Bidder.* London, 1921
30. *His Word of Honour.* London, 1921
31. *The Love of Robert Dennison.* London, 1921
32. *Brown Sugar.* London, 1921
33. *A Loveless Marriage.* London, 1921
34. *The Making of a Lover.* London, 1921
35. *The Man's Way.* London, 1921
36. *Nobody's Lovers.* London, 1921
37. *The One Unwanted.* London, 1921
38. *The Street Below.* London, 1922
39. *Our Avenue and Other Stories.* London, 1922
40. *A Gamble with Love.* London, 1922
41. *The Little Lady in Lodgings.* London, 1922
42. *The Lover Who Died.* London, 1922
43. *The Matherson Marriage.* London, 1922
44. *The Romance of a Rogue.* London and New York, 1923
45. *Love and a Lie.* London, 1923
46. *The Man Without a Heart.* London, 1923
47. *The One Who Stood By.* London, 1923
48. *The Eager Search.* London, 1923
49. *Candle Light.* London and New York, 1924
50. *Ribbons and Laces.* London, 1924
51. *Paul in Possession.* London, 1924
52. *The Man the Women Loved.* London, 1925
53. *The Marriage Handicap.* London, 1925
54. *Overheard.* London, 1925
55. *Charity's Chosen.* London and New York, 1926
56. *Spoilt Music.* London and New York, 1926
57. *The Faint Heart.* London, 1926
58. *The Planter and the Tree.* London, 1926
59. *Wynne of Windwhistle.* London, 1926
60. *By the Gate of Pity.* New York, 1927
61. *The Luckiest Lady.* London and New York, 1927
62. *Life Steps In.* London, 1928
63. *Broken.* London and New York, 1928
64. *The Family.* London, 1928
65. *Lovers.* London and New York, 1929

66. *The Heartbreak Marriage.* London, 1929
67. *One Month at Sea, Together with George Who Believed in Allah.* London, 1929
68. *In the Day's March.* London and New York, 1930
69. *One Summer.* London and New York, 1930
70. *Giving Him Up.* London, 1930
71. *My Old Love Came.* London, 1930
72. *The Big Fellah.* London and New York, 1931
73. *Men Made the Town.* London and New York, 1931
74. *The Little Man.* London, 1931
75. *The Princess Passes.* London, 1931
76. *Love Comes to Mary.* New York, 1932
77. *By the World Forgot.* London, 1932
78. *Changing Pilots.* London and New York, 1932
79. *So Many Miles.* New York, 1932
80. *Look to the Spring.* London, 1932
81. *Always Tomorrow.* London, 1933
82. *Come to My Wedding.* London and New York, 1933
83. *Love Is So Blind.* London, 1933
84. *All Over Again.* New York, 1934
85. *From This Day Forward.* London and New York, 1934
86. *Much-Loved.* London and New York, 1934
87. *Than This World Dreams Of.* London, 1934
88. *Happy Endings.* London, 1935
89. *Between You and Me.* London, 1935
90. *Feather.* New York, 1935
91. *The Man in Her Life.* London and New York, 935
92. *Some Day.* London and New York, 1935
93. *The Sun and the Sea.* London and New York, 1935
94. *Our Avenue and Other Stories.* New York, 1936
95. *Compromise.* London and New York, 1936
96. *After-Glow.* London and New York, 1936
97. *Follow the Shadow.* London, 1936
98. *High Noon.* London, 1936
99. *Somebody Else.* New York, 1936
100. *Too Much Together.* London and New York, 1936
101. *Living Apart.* New York, 1937
102. *Owner Gone Abroad.* London and New York, 1937
103. *Silver Wedding.* London, 1937
104. *Unofficial Wife.* New York, 1937
105. *Winner Takes All.* New York, 1937
106. *The Tree Drops a Leaf.* London and New York, 1938
107. *Return Journey.* New York, 1938
108. *And Still They Dream.* New York, 1938
109. *One to Live With.* London and New York, 1938
110. *There Was Another.* London and New York, 1938
111. *Big Ben.* New York, 1939
112. *The Moon in the Water.* New York, 1939
113. *The Thousandth Man.* London and New York, 1939
114. *Week-End Woman.* London and New York, 1939
115. *Little and Good.* London and New York, 1940
116. *The Little Sinner.* London and New York, 1940
117. *Wallflower.* London and New York, 1940
118. *Sometimes Spring is Late.* London, 1941
119. *Sunrise for Georgie.* London, 1941
120. *Still Waters.* London and New York, 1941
121. *The Constant Heart.* New York, 1941
122. *Rosemary—For Forgetting.* London, 1941
123. *Young Is My Love.* New York, 1941
124. *The Young at Heart.* London, 1942
125. *Nothing Lovelier.* London, 1942
126. *Starless Night.* London, 1943
127. *Lost Property.* New York, 1943
128. *Man Friday.* London, 1943
129. *Love Comes Unseen.* New York, 1943
130. *The Lady from London.* London, 1944
131. *The Dreamer Wakes.* London, 1945
132. *April's Day.* London, 1945
133. *Where Are You Going?* London, 1946
134. *Salt of the Earth.* London, 1946
135. *Young Shoulders.* London, 1947
136. *Missing the Tide.* London, 1948
137. *The Story of John Willie.* London, 1948
138. *Steering by a Star.* London, 1949
139. *The Day Comes Round.* London, 1949
140. *The Man from Ceylon.* London, 1950
141. *The Man Who Lived Alone.* London, 1950
142. *Autumn Fires: Two Love Stories.* London, 1951
143. *The Story of Fish and Chips.* London, 1951
144. *Twice a Boy.* London, 1951
145. *The Youngest Aunt.* London, 1952
146. *One Sees Stars.* London, 1952
147. *One Woman Too Many.* London, 1952
148. *Bright Destiny.* New York, 1952
149. *Love Without Wings.* London, 1953
150. *Old-Fashioned Heart.* New York, 1953
151. *Dark Gentleman.* London, 1953

Babson, Marian
American, born in Massachusetts
1. *Cover-Up Story.* London, 1971
2. *Murder on Show.* London, 1972
3. *Pretty Lady.* London, 1973
4. *The Stalking Lamb.* London, 1974
5. *Unfair Exchange.* London, 1974
6. *Murder Sails at Midnight.* London, 1975
7. *There Must Be Some Mistake.* London, 1975
8. *Untimely Guest.* London, 1976
9. *The Lord Mayor of Death.* London, 1977
10. *Murder, Murder, Little Star.* London, 1977
11. *Tightrope for Three.* London, 1978
12. *So Soon Done For.* London, 1979
13. *The Twelve Deaths of Christmas.* London, 1979

Bagley, Desmond
British, born October 29, 1923
1. *The Golden Keel.* London, 1963
2. *High Citadel.* London and New York, 1965
3. *Wyatt's Hurricane.* London and New York, 1966
4. *Landslide.* London and New York, 1967
5. *The Vivero Letter.* London and New York, 1968
6. *The Spoilers.* London, 1969
7. *Running Blind.* London, 1970
8. *The Freedom Trap.* London, 1971
9. *The Mackintosh Man.* New York, 1973
10. *The Tightrope Men.* London and New York, 1973
11. *The Snow Tiger.* London, 1974
12. *The Enemy.* London, 1977
13. *Flyaway.* London, 1978

Bailey, H.C. (Henry Christopher)
British, born February 1, 1878, died March 24, 1961
1. *My Lady of Orange.* London and New York, 1901
2. *Karl of Erbach.* New York, 1902
3. *The Master of Gray.* London and New York, 1903
4. *Rimingtons.* London, 1904
5. *Beaujeu.* London, 1905
6. *Under Castle Walls.* New York, 1906
7. *Springtime.* London, 1907
8. *Raoul, Gentleman of Fortune.* London, 1907
9. *A Gentleman of Fortune.* New York, 1907
10. *The God of Clay.* London and New York, 1908
11. *Colonel Stow.* London, 1908
12. *Colonel Greatheart.* Indianapolis, 1908
13. *Storm and Treasure.* London and New York, 1910
14. *The Lonely Queen.* London and New York, 1911

15. *The Suburban.* London, 1912
16. *The Sea Captain.* New York, 1913
17. *The Gentleman Adventurer.* London, 1914
18. *Forty Years After: The Story of the Franco-German War, 1870.* London, 1914
19. *The Highwayman.* London, 1915
20. *The Gamesters.* London, 1916
21. *All the Young Lovers.* London, 1917
22. *The Pillar of Fire.* London, 1918
23. *Barry Leroy.* London, 1919
24. *His Serene Highness.* London, 1920
25. *Call Mr. Fortune.* London, 1920
26. *The Fool.* London, 1921
27. *The Plot.* London, 1922
28. *Mr. Fortune's Practice.* London, 1923
29. *The Rebel.* London, 1923
30. *Knight at Arms.* London, 1924
31. *Mr. Fortune's Trials.* London, 1925
32. *The Golden Fleece.* London, 1925
33. *Mr. Fortune, Please.* London, 1927
34. *The Merchant Prince.* London, 1926
35. *Bonaventure.* London, 1927
36. *Judy Bovenden.* London, 1928
37. *Mr. Fortune Speaking.* London, 1929
38. *The Roman Eagles.* London, 1929
39. *Mr. Fortune Explains.* London, 1930
40. *Garstons.* London, 1930
41. *The Garston Murder Case.* New York, 1930
42. *Mr. Cardonnel.* London, 1931
43. *The Red Castle.* London, 1932
44. *The Red Castle Mystery.* New York, 1932
45. *Case for Mr. Fortune.* London and New York, 1932
46. *Mr. Fortune Wonders.* London and New York, 1933
47. *The Man in the Cape.* London, 1933
48. *Shadow on the Wall.* London and New York, 1934
49. *The Sullen Sky Mystery.* London and New York, 1935
50. *Mr. Fortune Objects.* London and New York, 1935
51. *A Clue for Mr. Fortune.* London and New York, 1936
52. *Mr. Fortune's Case Book.* London, 1936
53. *Black Land, White Land.* London and New York, 1937
54. *Clunk's Claimant.* London, 1937
55. *The Twittering Bird Mystery.* New York, 1937
56. *The Great Game.* London and New York, 1939
57. *The Veron Mystery.* London, 1939
58. *Mr. Clunk's Text.* New York, 1939
59. *The Bottle Party.* New York, 1940
60. *The Bishop's Crime.* London, 1940
61. *Mr. Fortune Here.* London and New York, 1940
62. *The Little Captain.* London, 1941
63. *Orphan Ann.* New York, 1941
64. *Dead Man's Shoes.* London, 1942
65. *Nobody's Vineyard.* New York, 1942
66. *No Murder.* London, 1942
67. *The Apprehensive Dog.* New York, 1942
68. *Meet Mr. Fortune.* New York, 1942
69. *Mr. Fortune Finds a Pig.* London and New York, 1943
70. *The Best of Mr. Fortune.* New York, 1943
71. *Slippery Ann.* London, 1944
72. *The Queen of Spades.* New York, 1944
73. *The Cat's Whisker.* New York, 1944
74. *Dead Man's Effects.* London, 1945
75. *The Wrong Man.* New York, 1945
76. *The Life Sentence.* London and New York, 1946
77. *Honour among Thieves.* London and New York, 1947
78. *Saving a Rope.* London, 1948
79. *Save a Rope.* New York, 1948
80. *Shrouded Death.* London, 1950

Baldwin, Faith
American, born October 1, 1893, died March 18, 1978
1. *Mavis of Green Hill.* Boston and London, 1921
2. *Laurel of Stonystream.* Boston, 1923
3. *The Maid of Stonystream.* London, 1924
4. *Magic and Mary Rose.* Boston, 1924
5. *Sign Posts.* Boston, 1924
6. *Thresholds.* Boston, 1925
7. *Those Difficult Years.* Boston, 1925
8. *Three Women.* New York, 1926
9. *Departing Wings.* New York, 1926
10. *Rosalie's Career.* New York, 1928
11. *Betty.* New York and London, 1928
12. *Alimony.* New York, 1928
13. *The Incredible Year.* New York, 1929
14. *Garden Oats.* New York, 1929
15. *Broadway Interlude,* with Achmed Abdullah. New York, 1929
16. *Judy: A Story of Divine Corners.* New York, 1930
17. *Make-Believe.* New York, 1930
18. *The Office Wife.* New York and London, 1930
19. *Skyscraper.* New York, 1931
20. *Today's Virtue.* New York, 1931
21. *Babs: A Story of Divine Corners.* New York, 1931
22. *Mary Lou: A Story of Divine Corners.* New York, 1931
23. *Skyscraper Souls.* New York, 1932
24. *Myra: A Story of Divine Corners.* New York, 1932
25. *Self-Made Woman.* New York, 1932
26. *Week-End Marriage.* New York and London, 1932
27. *Girl on the Make,* with Achmed Abdullah. New York and London, 1932
28. *District Nurse.* New York, 1932
29. *White-Collar Girl.* New York, 1933
30. *Beauty.* New York and London, 1933
31. *Love's a Puzzle.* New York, 1933
32. *Innocent Bystander.* New York, 1934
33. *Within a Year.* New York and London, 1934
34. *Honor Bound.* New York, 1934
35. *Wife vs. Secretary.* New York, 1934
36. *American Family.* New York, 1935
37. *Conflict.* London, 1935
38. *The Puritan Strain.* New York and London, 1935
39. *The Moon's Our Home.* New York, 1936
40. *Men Are Such Fools!* New York, 1936
41. *Private Duty.* New York, 1936
42. *That Man Is Mine.* London, 1936
43. *The Heart Has Wings.* New York, 1937
44. *Twenty-Four Hours a Day.* New York, 1937
45. *Manhattan Nights.* New York, 1937
46. *Hotel Hostess.* New York, 1938
47. *Enchanted Oasis.* New York, 1938
48. *Rich Girl, Poor Girl.* New York, 1938
49. *White Magic.* New York, 1939
50. *Station Wagon Set.* New York, 1939
51. *The High Road.* New York, 1939
52. *Career by Proxy.* New York, 1939
53. *Letty and the Law.* New York, 1940
54. *Medical Center.* New York, 1940
55. *Rehearsal for Love.* New York, 1940
56. *Something Special.* New York, 1940
57. *Temporary Address: Reno.* New York, 1941
58. *And New Stars Born.* New York, 1941
59. *The Heart Remembers.* New York, 1941
60. *Blue Horizons.* New York, 1942
61. *Breath of Life.* New York, 1942
62. *The Rest of My Life with You.* New York, 1942
63. *Five Women.* New York, 1942
64. *You Can't Escape.* New York, 1943
65. *Washington, U.S.A.* New York, 1943

66. *Change of Heart*. New York, 1944
67. *He Married a Doctor*. New York, 1944
68. *A Job for Jenny*. New York, 1945
69. *Arizona Star*. New York, 1945
70. *No Private Heaven*. New York, 1946
71. *Woman on Her Own*. New York, 1946
72. *Give Love the Air*. New York, 1947
73. *Sleeping Beauty*. New York, 1947
74. *Marry for Money*. New York, 1948
75. *They Who Love*. New York, 1948
76. *The Golden Shoestring*. New York, 1949
77. *Look Out for Liza*. New York, 1950
78. *Tell Me My Heart*. New York, 1950
79. *The Whole Armor*. New York, 1951
80. *The Juniper Tree*. New York, 1952
81. *Widow's Walk: Variations on a Theme*. New York, 1954
82. *Face Toward the Spring*. New York, 1956
83. *Three Faces of Love*. New York, 1957
84. *Many Windows: Seasons of the Heart*. New York, 1958
85. *Blaze of Sunlight*. New York, 1959
86. *Testament of Trust*. New York, 1960
87. *Harvest of Hope*. New York, 1962
88. *The West Wind*. New York, 1962
89. *The Lonely Man*. New York, 1964
90. *The Lonely Doctor*. London, 1964
91. *Living by Faith*. New York, 1964
92. *Echoes of Another Spring*. New York, 1965
93. *There Is a Season*. New York, 1966
95. *Evening Star*. New York, 1966
95. *The Velvet Hammer*. New York and London, 1969
96. *Take What You Want*. New York, 1970
97. *Any Village*. New York, 1971
98. *One More Time*. New York, 1972
99. *No Bed of Roses*. New York, 1973
100. *Time and the Hour*. New York, 1974
101. *New Girl in Town*. New York, 1975
102. *Thursday's Child*. New York, 1976
103. *Hold On to Your Heart*. London, 1976
104. *Adam's Eden*. New York, 1977

Baldwin, Gordon C. (Cortis)
American, born June 5, 1908
Pseudonyms: Gordo Baldwin, Lew Gordon
1. *Trouble Range*. London, 1956
2. *Trail North*. London, 1956
3. *Range War at Sundown*. London, 1957
4. *Trail North*. New York, 1957
5. *Powdersmoke Justice*. London, 1957
6. *Sundown Country*. New York, 1959
7. *Trouble Range*. New York, 1959
8. *Roundup at Wagonmound*. New York and London, 1960
9. *Brand of Yuma*. New York, 1960
10. *Ambush Basin*, as Gordo Baldwin. New York, 1960
11. *Ambush Basin*, as Lew Gordon. London, 1965
12. *Wyoming Rawhide*, as Gordo Baldwin. New York, 1961
13. *Powdersmoke Justice*, as Lew Gordon. New York, 1961
14. *America's Buried Past: The Story of North American Archaeology*. New York, 1962
15. *The Ancient Ones: Basketmakers and Cliff Dwellers of the Southwest*. New York, 1963
16. *The World of Prehistory: The Story of Man's Beginnings*. New York, 1963
17. *The Riddle of the Past: How Archaeological Detectives Solve Prehistoric Riddles*. New York, 1965
18. *The Warrior Apaches: A Story of the Chiricahua and Western Apache*. Tucson (AZ), 1965
19. *Race Against Time: The Story of Salvage Archaeology*. New York, 1966
20. *Strange People and Stranger Customs*. New York, 1967
21. *Calendars to the Past: How Science Dates Archaeological Ruins*. New York, 1967
22. *How Indians Really Lived*. New York, 1967
23. *Games of the American Indian*. New York, 1969
24. *Indians of the Southwest*. New York, 1970
25. *Talking Drums to Written Word: How Early Man Learned to Communicate*. New York, 1970
26. *Schemers, Dreamers, and Medicine Men: Witchcraft and Magic amomg Primitive People*. New York, 1971
27. *Pyramids of the New World*. New York, 1971
28. *Inventors and Inventions of the Ancient Worlds*. New York, 1973
29. *The Apache Indians: Raiders of the Southwest*. New York, 1978
30. *Wyoming Rawhide*. London, 1965

Ball, John [John Dudley Ball, Jr.]
American, born July 8, 1911
1. *Operation Springboard*. New York, 1958
2. *Operation Space*. London, 1960
3. *Spacemaster*. New York, 1960
4. *Edwards: Flight Test Center of the U.S.A.F*. New York, 1962
5. *Judo Boy*. New York, 1964
6. *In the Heat of the Night*. New York, 1965
7. *Arctic Showdown*. New York, 1966
8. *The Cool Cottontail*. New York, 1966
9. *Rescue Mission*. New York, 1966
10. *Miss 1000 Spring Blossoms*. Boston, 1968
11. *Johnny Get Your Gun*. Boston, 1969
12. *Dragon Hotel*. New York, 1969
13. *Last Plane Out*. Boston, 1970
14. *The First Team*. Boston, 1971
15. *Five Pieces of Jade*. Boston and London, 1972
16. *The Eyes of the Buddha*. Boston, 1976
17. *Death for a Playmate*. New York, 1972
18. *The Fourteenth Point*. Boston, 1973
19. *Mark One—The Dummy*. Boston, 1974
20. *The Winds of Mitamura*. Boston, 1975
21. *Phase Three Alert*. Boston, 1977
22. *Police Chief*. New York, 1977
23. *The Killing in the Market*, with Bevan Smith. New York, 1978

Ballard, Willis Todhunter
American, born December 13, 1903, died in 1980
Pseudonyms: P.D. Ballard, Parker Bonner, Sam Bowie, Nick Carter, Hunter D'Allard, Harrison Hunt, John Hunter, Neil MacNeil, Clint Reno, John Shepherd, Clay Turner
1. *Say Yes to Murder*. New York, 1942
2. *Murder Can't Stop*. Philadelphia, 1946
3. *Murder Picks the Jury*, as Harrison Hunt. New York, 1947
4. *Dealing Out Death*. Philadelphia, 1948
5. *Two-Edged Vengeance*. New York, 1951
6. *Incident at Sun Mountain*. Boston, 1952
7. *Walk in Fear*. New York, 1952
8. *The Circle C Feud*. London, 1952
9. *West of Quarantine*. Boston, 1953
10. *High Iron*. Boston, 1953
11. *Showdown*, with James C. Lynch. New York, 1953
12. *Rawhide Gunman*. New York, 1954
13. *West of Justice*, as John Hunter. Boston, 1954
14. *Trigger Trail*. New York, 1955
15. *Blizzard Range*. New York, 1955
16. *The Package Deal*. New York, 1956
17. *Gunman from Texas*. New York, 1956
18. *Guns of the Lawless*. New York, 1956

19. *Roundup.* New York, 1957
20. *Trail Town Marshall.* New York, 1957
21. *Ride the Wind South,* as John Hunter. New York, 1957
22. *Saddle Tramp.* New York, 1958
23. *Chance Elson.* New York, 1958
24. *The Marshall from Deadwood,* as John Hunter. New York, 1958
25. *Death Takes an Option,* as Neil MacNeil. New York, 1958
26. *Fury in the Heart.* Derby (CT), 1959
27. *Trouble on the Massacre.* New York, 1959
28. *Badlands Buccaneer,* as John Hunter. New York, 1959
29. *Third on a Seesaw,* as Neil MacNeil. New York, 1959
30. *Two Guns for Hire,* as Neil MacNeil. New York, 1959
31. *Thunderland Range,* as Sam Bowie. Derby, 1959
32. *The Long Trail Back.* New York, 1960
33. *Hot Damn,* as Neil MacNeil. New York and London, 1960
34. *The Death Ride,* as Neil MacNeil. New York, 1960
35. *Lights, Camera, Murder,* as John Shepherd. New York, 1960
36. *Gunman from Texas.* New York, 1960
37. *The Night Riders.* New York, 1961
38. *Pretty Miss Murder.* New York, 1961
39. *Badlands Buccaneer,* as John Hunter. London, 1961
40. *Gopher Gold.* New York, 1962
41. *Mexican Slayride,* as Neil MacNeil. New York, 1962
42. *The Long Sword,* as Hunter D'Allard. New York, 1962
43. *Gold Fever in Gopher.* London, 1962
44. *The Demise of a Louse,* as John Shepherd. New York, 1962
45. *The Seven Sisters.* New York, 1962
46. *Westward the Monitors Roar.* New York and London, 1963
47. *Three for the Money.* New York, 1963
48. *Guns of the Lawless.* New York, 1963
49. *Desperation Valley.* New York, 1964
50. *End of a Millionaire,* as P.D. Ballard. New York, 1964
51. *Tough in the Saddle,* as Parker Bonner. Derby, 1964
52. *Gold in California!* New York, 1965
53. *Duke,* as John Hunter. New York, 1965
54. *The Man from Yuma,* as John Hunter. New York, 1965
55. *The Spy Catchers,* as Neil MacNeil. New York, 1966
56. *Murder Las Vegas Style.* New York, 1967
57. *The Man Who Stole a University,* with Phoebe Ballard. New York, 1967
58. *How to Defend Yourself, Your Family, and Your Home.* New York, 1967
59. *Gunlock,* as Sam Bowie. New York and London, 1968
60. *Look to Your Guns,* as Parker Bonner. New York, 1969
61. *The Californian.* New York, 1971
62. *Nowhere Left to Run.* New York, 1972
63. *Brothers in Blood,* as P.D. Ballard. New York, 1972
64. *Outlaw Brand,* as Parker Bonner. New York, 1972
65. *Applegate's Gold.* New York, 1973
66. *Loco and the Wolf.* New York, 1973
67. *Angel of Death,* as P.D. Ballard. New York, 1973
68. *The Death Brokers,* as P.D. Ballard. New York, 1973
69. *The Kremlin File,* as Nick Carter. New York, 1973
70. *The Burning Land,* as John Hunter. New York, 1973
71. *Gambler's Gun,* as John Hunter. New York, 1973
72. *Home to Texas.* New York, 1974
73. *Go West Ben Gold!* as Clay Turner. New York, 1974
74. *Gold Goes to the Mountain,* as Clay Turner. New York, 1974
75. *Sun Mountain Slaughter,* as Clint Reno. New York, 1974
76. *Trouble on the Massacre.* New York, 1974
77. *Trails of Rage.* New York, 1975
78. *Sheriff of Tombstone.* New York, 1977
79. *Fight or Die.* New York, 1977

Ballinger, Bill S. [William Sanborn Ballinger]
American, born March 13, 1912
Pseudonyms: Frederic Freyer, B.X. Sanborn

1. *The Body in the Bed.* New York, 1948
2. *The Body Beautiful.* New York, 1949
3. *Portrait in Smoke.* New York, 1950
4. *The Darkening Door.* New York, 1952
5. *Rafferty.* New York and London, 1953
6. *The Beautiful Trap.* New York, 1955
7. *The Black, Black Hearse,* as Frederic Freyer. New York, 1955
8. *The Case of the Black, Black Hearse.* New York, 1955
9. *The Tooth and the Nail.* New York and London, 1955
10. *The Longest Second.* New York, 1957
11. *The Wife of the Red-Haired Man.* New York and London, 1957
12. *The Deadlier Sex.* London, 1958
13. *Beacon in the Night.* New York, 1958
14. *Formula for Murder.* New York, 1958
15. *The Doom-Maker,* as B.X. Sanborn. New York and London, 1959
16. *The Blonde on Borrowed Time.* Rockville Centre (NY), 1960
17. *The Fourth of Forever.* New York and London, 1963
18. *The Chinese Mask.* New York, 1965
19. *Not I, Said the Vixen.* New York, 1965
20. *The Spy in Bangkok.* New York, 1965
21. *The Spy in the Jungle.* New York, 1965
22. *The Heir Hunters.* New York, 1966
23. *The Spy at Angkor.* New York, 1966
24. *The Spy in the Java Sea.* New York, 1966
25. *The Source of Fear.* New York, 1968
26. *The 49 Days of Death.* Los Angeles, 1969
27. *Heist Me Higher.* New York, 1969
28. *The Lopsided Man.* New York, 1969
29. *Triptych.* Los Angeles, 1971
30. *The Corsican.* New York, 1974
31. *The Law.* New York, 1975
32. *The Ultimate Warrior.* New York, 1975
33. *Lost City of Stone.* New York, 1978
34. *The California Story.* Dubuque (IA), 1979

Balmer, Edwin
American, born July 26, 1883, died March 21, 1959
1. *Waylaid by Wireless.* Boston, 1909
2. *The Science of Advertising.* Chicago, 1909
3. *The Achievements of Luther Trant,* with William McHarg. Boston, 1910
4. *The Surakarta,* with William McHarg. Boston, 1913
5. *A Wild-Goose Chase.* New York, 1915
6. *The Blind Man's Eyes,* with William McHarg. Boston and London, 1916
7. *The Indian Drum,* with William McHarg. Boston, 1917
8. *Ruth of the U.S.A.* Chicago, 1919
9. *Resurrection Rock.* Boston and London, 1920
10. *Her Great Moment.* London, 1921
11. *The Breath of Scandal.* Boston, 1922
12. *Keeban.* Boston and London, 1923
13. *Fidelia.* New York, 1924
14. *That Royle Girl.* New York, 1925
15. *Dangerous Business.* New York, 1927
16. *Flying Death.* New York, 1927
17. *Five Fatal Words,* with Philip Wylie. New York, 1932
18. *When Worlds Collide,* with Philip Wylie. New York and London, 1933
19. *After Worlds Collide,* with Philip Wylie. New York and London, 1934
20. *The Golden Hoard,* with Philip Wylie. New York, 1934
21. *Dragons Drive You.* New York, 1934
22. *The Shield of Silence,* with Philip Wylie. New York, 1936
23. *The Torn Letter.* New York, 1941
24. *In His Hands.* New York, 1954

25. *The Candle of the Wicked.* New York, 1956
26. *With All the World Away.* New York, 1958

Barclay, Florence L. (Louisa)
British. Born December 2, 1862, died March 10, 1921
Pseudonym: Brandon Roy
1. *Guy Mervyn,* as Brandon Roy. 3 volumes. London, 1891
2. *A Notable Prisoner.* London, 1905
3. *The Wheels of Time.* New York, 1908
4. *The Rosary.* New York and London, 1909
5. *The Mistress of Shenstone.* New York and London, 1910
6. *The Following of the Star.* New York and London, 1911
7. *Through the Postern Gate.* New York and London, 1912
8. *The Upas Tree.* London and New York, 1912
9. *The Broken Halo.* London and New York, 1913
10. *The Wall of Partition.* London and New York, 1914
11. *My Heart's Right There.* London and New York, 1914
12. *The Golden Censer.* London and New York, 1914
13. *In Hoc Vince: The Story of a Red Cross Flag.* London and New York, 1915
14. *The White Ladies of Worcester.* London and New York, 1917
15. *Returned Empty.* London and New York, 1920

Barcynska, Countess [Marguerite Florence Jervis]
British, born in 1894, died March 10, 1964
Other pseudonyms: Marguerite Barclay, Oliver Sandys
1. *The Woman in the Firelight,* as Oliver Sandys. London, 1911
2. *The Activities of Lavie,* as Marguerite Barclay, with Armiger Barclay. London, 1911
3. *Chicane,* as Oliver Sandys. London, 1912
4. *Letters from Fleet Street,* as Marguerite Barclay, with Armiger Barclay. London, 1912
5. *Where There Are Women,* as Marguerite Barclay, with Armiger Barclay. London, 1915
6. *The Honey Pot: A Story of the Stage.* London and New York, 1916
7. *Peter Day-by-Day,* as Marguerite Barclay, with Armiger Barclay. London, 1916
8. *If Wishes Were Horses.* London and New York, 1917
9. *Love Maggy.* London, 1918
10. *Sanity Jane.* London, 1919
11. *Love's Last Reward.* London, 1920
12. *Pretty Dear: A Romance.* London, 1920
13. *Rose o' the Sea.* Boston, 1920
14. *Jackie.* London and Boston, 1921
15. *The Garment of Gold,* as Oliver Sandys. London, 1921
16. *Chappy—That's All,* as Oliver Sandys. London, 1922
17. *Ships Come Home.* London, 1922
18. *Webs.* London, 1922
19. *The Green Caravan,* as Oliver Sandys. London, 1922
20. *Tesha, A Plaything of Destiny.* London, 1923
21. *We Women!* London, 1923
22. *Old Roses,* as Oliver Sandys. London, 1923
23. *The Pleasure Garden,* as Oliver Sandys. London, 1923
24. *The Russett Jacket: A Story of the Turf.* London, 1924
25. *Sally Serene,* as Oliver Sandys. London, 1924
26. *Tilly-Make-Haste,* as Oliver Sandys. London, 1924
27. *Twenty-One.* London, 1924
28. *Back to the Honey-Pot: A Story of the Stage.* London, 1925
29. *Hand Painted.* London, 1925
30. *Blinkeyes,* as Oliver Sandys. London, 111 1925
31. *Mr. Anthony,* as Oliver Sandys. London, 1925
32. *Decameron Cocktails.* London, 1926
33. *The Curled Hands,* as Oliver Sandys. London, 1926
34. *The Ginger Jar,* as Oliver Sandys. London, 1926
35. *Mint Walk.* London, 1927
36. *The Crimson Ramblers,* as Oliver Sandys. London, 1927
37. *The Sorcerers,* as Oliver Sandys. London, 1927
38. *The Golden Snail and Other Stories.* London, 1927
39. *A Certified Bride.* London, 1928
40. *Milly Comes to Town.* London, 1928
41. *Mops,* as Oliver Sandys. London, 1928
42. *Vista, The Dancer,* as Oliver Sandys. London, 1928
43. *S.O.S. Queenie and Other Stories,* as Oliver Sandys. London, 1928
44. *He Married His Parlourmaid.* London, 1929
45. *Cherry,* as Oliver Sandys. London, 1929
46. *The Champagne Kiss,* as Oliver Sandys. London, 1929
47. *Running Free and Other Stories.* London, 1929
48. *Fantoccini.* London, 1930
49. *Bad Lad,* as Oliver Sandys. London, 1930
50. *Mr. Scribbles,* as Oliver Sandys. London, 1930
51. *Sally of Sloper's,* as Oliver Sandys. London, 1930
52. *The Joy Shop.* London, 1931
53. *A Woman of Experience.* London, 1931
54. *Jinks,* as Oliver Sandys. London, 1931
55. *Misty Angel,* as Oliver Sandys. London, 1931
56. *Butterflies,* as Oliver Sandys. London, 1932
57. *Squire,* as Oliver Sandys. London, 1932
58. *The Five-Hooded Cobra,* as Oliver Sandys. London, 1932
59. *I Loved a Fairy.* London, 1933
60. *Under the Big Top.* London, 1933
61. *Just Lil,* as Oliver Sandys. London, 1933
62. *Sir Boxer,* as Oliver Sandys. London, 1933
63. *Exit Renee.* London, 1934
64. *Happy Day,* as Oliver Sandys. London, 1934
65. *Spangles,* as Oliver Sandys. London, 1934
66. *Publicity Baby.* London, 1935
67. *Tiptoes,* as Oliver Sandys. London, 1935
68. *Pick Up and Smile.* London, 1936
69. *The Curtain Will Go Up,* as Oliver Sandys. London, 1936
70. *The Show Must Go On,* as Oliver Sandys. London, 1936
71. *God and Mr. Aaronson.* London, 1937
72. *Keep Cheery.* London, 1937
73. *Angel's Kiss,* as Oliver Sandys. London, 1937
74. *The Happy Mummers,* as Oliver Sandys. London, 1937
75. *Prince Charming,* as Oliver Sandys. London, 1937
76. *Hearts for Gold.* London, 1938
77. *Sweetbriar Lane.* London, 1938
78. *Crinklenose,* as Oliver Sandys. London, 1938
79. *Love Is a Flower,* as Oliver Sandys. London, 1938
80. *Mud on My Stockings,* as Oliver Sandys. London, 1938
81. *Writing Man.* London, 1939
82. *That Troubled Piece!* London, 1939
83. *Hollywood Honeyman,* as Oliver Sandys. London, 1939
84. *Old Hat,* as Oliver Sandys. London, 1939
85. *Whatagirl,* as Oliver Sandys. London, 1939
86. *Calm Waters,* as Oliver Sandys. London, 1940
87. *Singing Uphill,* as Oliver Sandys. London, 1940
88. *Let the Storm Burst.* London, 1941
89. *Jack Be Nimble,* as Oliver Sandys. London, 1941
90. *Wellington Wendy,* as Oliver Sandys. London, 1941
91. *Full and Frank: The Private Life of a Woman Novelist,* as Oliver Sandys. London, 1946
92. *Black-Out Symphony.* London, 1942
93. *The Wood Is My Pulpit.* London, 1942
94. *Lame Daddy,* as Oliver Sandys. London, 1942
95. *Meadowsweet,* as Oliver Sandys. London, 1942
96. *Swell Fellows,* as Oliver Sandys. London, 1942
97. *Joy Comes After.* London, 1943
98. *Love Never Dies.* London, 1943
99. *Merrily All the Way,* as Oliver Sandys. London, 1943
100. *No Faint Heart,* as Oliver Sandys. London, 1943

101. *Astrologer*. London, 1944
102. *The Tears of Piece*. London, 1944
103. *Miss Paraffin*, as Oliver Sandys. London, 1944
104. *Poppet & Co.*, as Oliver Sandys. London, 1944
105. *Love Is a Lady*. London, 1945
106. *Deputy Pet*, as Oliver Sandys. London. 1945
107. *Caradoc Evans*. London, 1946
108. *Learn to Laugh Again*, as Oliver Sandys. London, 1947
109. *We Lost Our Way*. London, 1948
110. *Unbroken Thread: An Intimate Journal*. London, 1948
111. *Gorgeous Brute*. London, 1949
112. *The Constant Rabbit*, as Oliver Sandys. London, 1949
113. *Dot on the Spot*, as Oliver Sandys. London, 1949
114. *Conjuror*. London, 1950
115. *Shining Failure*, as Oliver Sandys. London, 1950
116. *Yesterday Is Tomorrow*, as Marguerite Barclay. London, 1950
117. *Bubble Over Thorn*. London, 1951
118. *Those Dominant Hills*. London, 1951
119. *Bachelor's Tonic*, as Oliver Sandys. London, 1951
120. *Kiss the Moon*, as Oliver Sandys. London, 1951
121. *Let's All Be Happy*, as Oliver Sandys. London, 1952
122. *Quaint Place*, as Oliver Sandys. London, 1952
123. *Sunset Is Dawn*, as Marguerite Barclay. London, 1953
124. *Shine My Wings*, as Oliver Sandys. London, 1954
125. *Beloved Burden*. London, 1954
126. *Suffer to Sing*, as Oliver Sandys. London, 1955
127. *The Happiness Stone*, as Oliver Sandys. London, 1956
128. *Miss Venus of Aberdovey*. London, 1956
129. *The Miracle Stone of Wales*, as Marguerite Barclay. London, 1957
130. *Angel's Eyes*. London, 1957
131. *The Jackpot*. London, 1957
132. *A New Day*, as Oliver Sandys. London, 1957
133. *Dear Mr. Dean*, as Oliver Sandys. London, 1957
134. *Butterflies In the Ruin*, as Oliver Sandys. London, 1958
135. *Two Faces of Love*. London, 1958
136. *Prince's Story*. London, 1959
137. *Cherry Stones*, as Oliver Sandys. London, 1959
138. *The Tinsel and the Gold*, as Oliver Sandys. London, 1959
139. *Black Harvest*. London, 1960
140. *These Changing Years*. London, 1961
141. *The Wise and the Steadfast*, as Oliver Sandys. London, 1961
142. *The Golden Flame*, as Oliver Sandys. London, 1961
143. *The Poppy and the Rose*, as Oliver Sandys. London, 1962
144. *The Happy Hearts*, as Oliver Sandys. London, 1962
145. *Laughter and Love Remain*, as Oliver Sandys. London, 1962
146. *I Was Shown Heaven*. London, 1962
147. *Smile in the Mirror*. London, 1963
148. *Madame Adastra*, as Oliver Sandys. London, 1964

Barker, S. Omar [Squire Omar Barker]
American, born June 16, 1894
Pseudonym: Dan Scott
1. *Vientos de las Sierras, Winds of the Mountains*. No place, 1922
2. *Buckaroo Ballads*. Privately printed, 1928
3. *Born to Battle*. Albuquerque (NM), 1951
4. *Songs of the Saddlemen*. Denver, 1954
5. *Sunlight Through the Trees*. Las Vegas (NM), 1954
6. *The Mystery of Ghost Canyon*, as Dan Scott. New York, 1960
7. *The Secret of Hermit's Peak*, as Dan Scott. New York, 1960
8. *The Range Rodeo Mystery*, as Dan Scott. New York, 1960
9. *The Mystery of Rawhide Gap*, as Dan Scott. New York, 1960
10. *The Secret of Fort Pioneer*, as Dan Scott. New York, 1961
11. *The Mystery of Blizzard Mesa*, as Dan Scott. New York, 1961
12. *The Mystery of the Comanche Caves*, as Dan Scott. New York, 1962
13. *The Phantom of Wolf Creek*, as Dan Scott. New York, 1963
14. *The Mystery of Bandit Gulch*, as Dan Scott. New York, 1964
15. *Little World Apart*. New York, 1966
16. *The Cattleman's Steak Book: Best Beef Recipes*. New York, 1967
17. *Rawhide Rhymes: Singing Poems of the Old West*. New York, 1968

Barrie, Susan
British
Pseudonyms: Anita Charles, Pamela Kent
1. *Mistress of Brown Furrows*. London, 1952
2. *The Gates of Dawn*. London, 1954
3. *Marry a Stranger*. London, 1954
4. *Carpet of Dreams*. London, 1955
5. *Hotel Stardust*. London, 1955
6. *Moon Over Africa*, as Pamela Kent. London, 1955
7. *Dear Tiberius*. London, 1956
8. *The House of the Laird*. London, 1956
9. *So Dear to My Heart*. London, 1956
10. *Desert Doorway*, as Pamela Kent. London, 1956
11. *The Black Benedicts*, as Anita Charles. London, 1956
12. *Air Ticket*. London, 1957
13. *Four Roads to Windrush*. London, 1957
14. *City of Palms*, as Pamela Kent. London, 1957
15. *Sweet Barbary*, as Pamela Kent. London, 1957
16. *My Heart at Your Feet*, as Anita Charles. London, 1957
17. *One Coin in the Fountain*, as Anita Charles. London, 1957
18. *Heart Specialist*. London, 1958
19. *The Stars of San Cecilio*. London, 1958
20. *Meet Me in Istanbul*, as Pamela Kent. London, 1958
21. *Interlude for Love*, as Anita Charles. London, 1958
22. *The Moon and Bride's Hill*, as Anita Charles. London, 1958
23. *Flight to the Stars*, as Pamela Kent. London, 1959
24. *The Wings of the Morning*. London, 1960
25. *Nurse Nolan*. Toronto, 1961
26. *Bride in Waiting*. London, 1961
27. *Moon at the Full*. London, 1961
28. *The Chateau of Fire*, as Pamela Kent. London, 1961
29. *Dawn on the High Mountain*, as Pamela Kent. London, 1961
30. *Royal Purple*. London, 1962
31. *Journey in the Dark*, as Pamela Kent. London, 1962
32. *A Case of Heart Trouble*. London and Toronto, 1963
33. *Bladon's Rock*, as Pamela Kent. London, 1963
34. *The Dawning Splendour*, as Pamela Kent. London, 1963
35. *Autumn Wedding*, as Anita Charles. London, 1963
36. *The King of the Castle*, as Anita Charles. London, 1963
37. *White Rose of Love*, as Anita Charles. London, 1963
38. *Mountain Magic*. London, 1964
39. *Hotel at Treloan*. Toronto, 1964
40. *Enemy Lover*, as Pamela Kent. London, 1964
41. *Castle Thunderbird*. London, 1965
42. *No Just Cause*. London, 1965
43. *The Gardenia Tree*, as Pamela Kent. London, 1965
44. *Gideon Faber's Choice*, as Pamela Kent. London, 1965
45. *Star Creek*, as Pamela Kent. London, 1965
46. *Master of Melincourt*. London, 1966
47. *The Quiet Heart*. London, 1966
48. *Rose in the Bud*. London, 1966
49. *Cuckoo in the Night*, as Pamela Kent. London, 1966
50. *White Heat*, as Pamela Kent. London, 1966
51. *Accidental Bride*. London, 1967
52. *Victoria and the Nightingale*. London, 1967
53. *Beloved Enemies*, as Pamela Kent. London, 1967

54. *The Man Who Came Back,* as Pamela Kent. London and Toronto, 1967
55. *The Marriage Wheel.* London, 1968
56. *Wild Sonata.* London and Toronto, 1968
57. *Desert Gold,* as Pamela Kent. London and Toronto, 1968
58. *Return to Tremarth.* Toronto, 1969
59. *Man from the Sea,* as Pamela Kent. London, 1968
60. *Night of the Singing Birds.* London and Toronto, 1970
61. *Nile Dusk,* as Pamela Kent. London, 1972

Barry, Jane
American, born August 25, 1925
1. *The Long March.* New York, 1955
2. *The Carolinians.* New York, 1959
3. *A Time in the Sun.* New York, 1962
4. *A Shadow of Eagles.* New York, 1964
5. *Maximilian's Gold.* New York, 1966
6. *Grass Roots.* New York, 1968

Bawden, Nina [Nina Mary Mabey Bawden]
British, born January 19, 1925
1. *Who Calls the Tune.* London, 1953
2. *Eyes of Green.* New York, 1953
3. *The Odd Flamingo.* London, 1954
4. *Change Here for Babylon.* London, 1955
5. *The Solitary Child.* London, 1956
6. *Devil by the Sea.* London, 1957
7. *Just Like a Lady.* London, 1960
8. *Glass Slippers Always Pinch.* Philadelphia, 1960
9. *In Honour Bound.* London, 1961
10. *Tortoise by Candlelight.* London and New York, 1963
11. *The Secret Passage.* London, 1963
12. *Under the Skin.* London and New York, 1964
13. *The House of Secrets.* Philadelphia, 1964
14. *On the Run.* London, 1964
15. *Three on the Run.* Philadelphia, 1965
16. *A Little Love, A Little Learning.* London and New York, 1966
17. *The White Horse Gang.* London and Philadelphia, 1966
18. *The Witch's Daughter.* London and Philadelphia, 1966
19. *A Woman of My Age.* London and New York, 1967
20. *A Handful of Thieves.* London and Philadelphia, 1967
21. *The Grain of Truth.* London and New York, 1968
22. *The Runaway Summer.* London and Philadelphia, 1969
23. *The Birds on the Trees.* London, 1970
24. *Squib.* London and Philadelphia, 1971
25. *Anna Apparent.* London and New York, 1972
26. *Carrie's War.* London and Philadelphia, 1973
27. *George Beneath a Paper Moon.* London and New York, 1974
28. *The Peppermint Pig.* London and Philadelphia, 1975
29. *Afternoon of a Good Woman.* London and New York, 1976
30. *Rebel on a Rock.* London and Philadelphia, 1978
31. *The Robbers.* London and New York, 1979
32. *Familiar Passions.* London and New York, 1979

Baxt, George
American, born June 11, 1923
1. *A Queer Kind of Death.* New York, 1966
2. *Swing Low, Sweet Harriet.* New York, 1967
3. *A Parade of Cockeyed Creatures; or, Did Someone Murder Our Wandering Boy?* New York, 1967
4. *Topsy and Evil.* New York, 1968
5. *"I" Said the Demon.* New York and London, 1969
6. *The Affair at Royalties.* London, 1971
7. *Burning Sappho.* New York and London, 1972

Beach, Rex (Ellingwood)
American, born September 1, 1877, died December 7, 1949
1. *Pardners.* New York, 1905
2. *The Spoilers.* New York, 1906
3. *The Barrier.* New York, 1908
4. *The Silver Horde.* New York, 1909
5. *Going Some: A Romance of Strenuous Affection.* New York, 1910
6. *The Ne'er-Do-Well.* New York and London, 1911
7. *The Net.* New York and London, 1912
8. *The Iron Trail: An Alaskan Romance.* New York and London, 1913
9. *The Auction Block: A Novel of New York Life.* New York and London, 1914
10. *Heart of the Sunset.* New York and London, 1915
11. *The Crimson Gardenia and Other Tales of Adventure.* New York and London, 1916
12. *Rainbow's End.* New York and London, 1916
13. *Laughing Bill and Other Stories.* New York, 1917
14. *The Winds of Chance.* New York and London, 1918
15. *Too Fat to Fight.* New York, 1919
16. *Oh, Shoot! Confessions of an Agitated Sportsman.* New York, 1921
17. *Flowing Gold.* New York and London, 1922
18. *Big Brother and Other Stories.* New York, 1923
19. *Going Some.* New York, 1923
20. *North of Fifty-Three.* New York, 1924
21. *The Goose Woman and Other Stories.* New York and London, 1925
22. *Padlocked.* New York, 1926
23. *The Miracle of Coral Gables.* No place, 1926
24. *The Mating Call.* New York, 1927
25. *Confessions of a Sportsman.* New York, 1927
26. *Don Careless, and Birds of Prey.* New York, 1928
27. *Son of the Gods.* New York, 1929
28. *Money Mad.* New York and London, 1931
29. *Men of the Outer Islands.* New York and London, 1932
30. *Beyond Control.* New York, 1932
31. *Masked Women.* New York, 1934
32. *The Hands of Dr. Locke.* New York, 1934
33. *Jungle Gold.* New York, 1935
34. *Alaskan Adventures.* New York, 1935
35. *Wild Pastures.* New York and London, 1935
36. *Valley of Thunder.* New York, 1939
37. *The Tower of Flame: An Oil Fields Story; Jaragu of the Lost Islands: A High Seas Story.* Los Angeles, 1940
38. *Personal Exposures.* New York, 1941
39. *The World in His Arms.* New York, 1946
40. *Woman in Ambush.* New York, 1951

Beagle, Peter S.
1. *A Fine and Private Place.* New York, 1960
2. *The Last Unicorn.* New York, 1968

Bean, Amelia [Myrtle Amelia Bean]
American
1. *The Fancher Train.* New York, 1958
2. *The Vengeance Trail.* London, 1958
3. *The Feud.* New York, 1960
4. *Time for Outrage.* New York, 1967

Beaty, Betty
British
Pseudonyms: Karen Campbell, Catherine Ross
1. *South to the Sun.* London, 1956
2. *Maiden Flight.* London, 1956
3. *Amber Five.* London, 1958
4. *The Butternut Tree.* London, 1958
5. *From This Day Forward,* as Catherine Ross. London, 1959
6. *The Top of the Climb.* London, 1962
7. *The Colours of the Night,* as Catherine Ross. London, 1962

8. *The Path of the Moonfish*. London, 1964
9. *The Trysting Tower*, as Catherine Ross. London, 1966
10. *The Atlantic Sky*. London, 1967
11. *Suddenly, In the Air*, as Karen Campbell. London, 1969
12. *Miss Miranda's Walk*. London and Toronto, 1967
13. *The Swallows of San Fedora*. London, 1970
14. *Love and the Kentish Maid*. London, 1971
15. *Head of Chancery*. London, 1972
16. *Thunder on Sunday*, as Karen Campbell. London, 1972
17. *Master at Arms*. London, 1973
18. *Wheel Fortune*, as Karen Campbell. London, 1973
19. *Fly Away, Love*. London, 1975
20. *Death Descending*, as Karen Campbell. London, 1976
21. *Battle Dress*, as Catherine Ross. London, 1979
22. *The Bells of St. Martin*, as Karen Campbell. London, 1979
23. *Exchange of Hearts*. London, 1980
24. *Wings of the Morning*, with David Beaty. New York and London, 1982

Beauclerk, Helen [Helen Mary Dorothea Bellingham]
British, born September 20, 1892, died in 1969
1. *The Green Lacquer Pavilion*. London and New York, 1926
2. *The Love of the Foolish Angel*. London and New York, 1929
3. *The Mountain and the Tree*. London, 1935
4. *So Frail a Thing: Love Scenes of the Twentieth Century*. London, 1940
5. *Shadows on a Wall*. London, 1941
6. *Where the Treasure Is*. London, 1944
7. *There Were Three Men*. London, 1949

Bechdolt, Frederick R. (Ritchie)
American, born July 27, 1874, died April 12, 1950
1. *9009*, with James Hopper. New York, 1908
2. *The Hard Rock Man*. New York, 1910
3. *When the West Was Young*. New York, 1922
4. *Tales of the Old-Timers*. New York, 1924
5. *Mutiny: An Adventure Story*. New York, 1927
6. *Giants of the Old West*. New York, 1930
7. *Riders of the San Pedro*. New York, 1931
8. *Horse Thief Trail*. New York, 1932
9. *The Tree of Death*. New York, 1937
10. *Bold Raiders of the West*. New York, 1940
11. *Danger on the Border*. New York, 1940
12. *Riot at Red Water*. New York, 1941
13. *Hot Gold*. New York, 1941
14. *The Hills of Fear*. New York, 1943
15. *Drygulch Canyon*. New York, 1946

Bechko, P.A. (Peggy Anne)
American, born August 26, 1950
Pseudonym: Bill Haller
1. *Night of the Flaming Guns*. New York, 1974
2. *Gunman's Justice*. New York, 1974
3. *Blown to Hell*. New York, 1976
4. *Dead Man's Feud*. New York, 1976
5. *Sidewinder's Trail*, as Bill Haller. New York, 1976
6. *The Winged Warrior*. New York, 1977
7. *Omaha Jones*. London, 1979
8. *Hawke's Indians*. New York, 1979

Beck, L. Adams [Lily Adams Beck]
British, died January 3, 1931
Pseudonyms: E. Barrington, Louis Moresby
1. *The Key of Dreams*. New York, 1922
2. *The Ninth Vibration and Other Stories*. New York, 1922
3. *The Ladies: A Shining Constellation of Wit and Beauty*, as E. Barrington. Boston, 1922
4. *The Perfume of the Rainbow and Other Stories*. New York, 1923
5. *The Chaste Diana*, as E. Barrington. New York and London, 1923
6. *The Treasure of Ho*. New York, 1924
7. *The Gallants*, as E. Barrington. Boston, 1924
8. *The Divine Lady*, as E. Barrington. New York, 1924
9. *Glorious Apollo*, as E. Barrington. New York, 1925
10. *The Way of Stars: A Romance of Reincarnation*. New York, 1925
11. *Dreams and Delights*. New York, 1926
12. *The Exquisite Perdita*, as E. Barrington. New York and London, 1926
13. *The Glory of Egypt*, as Louis Moresby. New York and London, 1926
14. *The Splendour of Asia: The Story and Teaching of the Buddha*. New York, 1926
15. *The House of Fulfillment*. New York and London, 1927
16. *The Thunderer*, as E. Barrington. New York and London, 1927
17. *Rubies*, as Louis Moresby. New York, 1927
18. *Rubies*. London, 1927
19. *The Empress of Hearts*, as E. Barrington. New York and London, 1928
20. *Captain Java*, as Louis Moresby. New York and London, 1928
21. *The Story of Oriental Philosophy*. New York, 1928
22. *The Way of Power: Studies in the Occult*. New York, 1928
23. *The Garden of Vision*. New York, 1929
24. *The Laughing Queen: A Romance of Cleopatra*, as E. Barrington. New York and London, 1929
25. *The Openers of the Gate: Stories of the Occult*. New York, 1930
26. *The Duel of Queens*, as E. Barrington. New York and London, 1930
27. *The Openers of the Gate: Stories of the Occult*. New York, 1930
28. *The Joyous Story of Astrid*. New York, 1931
29. *The Irish Beauties*, as E. Barrington. New York and London, 1931
30. *Anne Boleyn*, as E. Barrington. New York and London, 1932
31. *The Great Romantic*, as E. Barrington. New York and London, 1933
32. *The Ghost Plays of Japan*. New York, 1933
33. *Cleopatra*, as E. Barrington. New York, 1934
34. *The Wooing of the Queens*, as E. Barrington. London, 1934
35. *The Graces*, as E. Barrington. London, 1934
36. *Dream Tea*. London, 1934
37. *The Crowned Lovers*, as E. Barrington. London, 1935
38. *The Life of the Buddha*. London, 1939

Behn, Noel
American, born January 6, 1928
1. *The Kremlin Letter*. New York and London, 1966
2. *The Shadowboxer*. New York, 1969
3. *Big Stick-Up at Brink's!* New York, 1977

Bell, Eric Temple
American, born February 7, 1886, died December 21, 1960
Pseudonym: J.T., John Taine, J.T. Boston
1. *The Cyclotomic Quinary Quintic*. New York, 1912
2. *Recreations*, as J.T. Boston, 1915
3. *An Arithmetic Theory of Certain Numerical Functions*. Seattle (WA), 1915
4. *The Singer*, as J.T. Boston, 1916
5. *The Purple Sapphire*, as John Taine. New York, 1924
6. *Quayle's Invention*, as John Taine. New York, 1927

7. *The Gold Tooth,* as John Taine. New York, 1927
8. *Algebraic Arithmetic.* New York, 1927
9. *Green Fire,* as John Taine. New York, 1928
10. *The Greatest Adventure,* as John Taine. New York, 1929
11. *The Iron Star,* as John Taine. New York, 1930
12. *Debunking Science.* Seattle, 1930
13. *The Queen of the Sciences.* Baltimore (MD), 1931
14. *Numerology.* Baltimore, 1933
15. *Before the Dawn,* as John Taine. Baltimore, 1934
16. *The Handmaiden of the Sciences.* Baltimore and London, 1937
17. *Men of Mathematics.* New York and London, 1937
18. *Man and His Lifebelts.* Baltimore, 1938
19. *The Development of Mathematics.* New York, 1940
20. *The Time Stream,* as John Taine. Providence (RI), 1946
21. *The Magic of Numbers.* New York, 1946
22. *The Forbidden Garden,* as John Taine. Reading (PA), 1947
23. *The Cosmic Geoids, and One Other,* as John Taine. Los Angeles, 1949
24. *Seeds of Life,* as John Taine. Reading, 1951
25. *Mathematics, Queen and Servant of Science.* New York, 1951
26. *The Crystal Horde,* as John Taine. Reading, 1952
27. *G.O.G. 666,* as John Taine. Reading, 1954
28. *The Last Problem.* New York, 1961
29. *White Lily,* as John Taine. New York, 1966

Bell, Josephine [Doris Bell Ball]
British, born December 8, 1897
1. *Murder in Hospital.* London, 1937
2. *Death on the Borough Council.* London, 1937
3. *Fall over Cliff.* London, 1938
4. *The Port of London Murders.* London, 1938
5. *Death at Half-Term.* London, 1939
6. *From Natural Causes.* London, 1939
7. *All Is Vanity.* London, 1940
8. *The Bottom of the Well.* London, 1940
9. *Martin Croft.* London, 1941
10. *Trouble at Wrekin Farm.* London, 1942
11. *Alvina Foster.* London, 1943
12. *Death at the Medical Board.* London, 1944
13. *Compassionate Adventure.* London, 1946
14. *Total War at Haverington.* London, 1947
15. *Wonderful Mrs. Marriott.* London, 1948
16. *The Whirlpool.* London, 1949
17. *Death in Clairvoyance.* London, 1949
18. *The Summer School.* London, 1950
19. *Backing Winds.* London, 1951
20. *To Let, Furnished.* London, 1952
21. *Bombs in the Barrow.* London, 1953
22. *Cage-Birds.* London, 1953
23. *Two Ways to Love.* London, 1954
24. *Fires at Fairlawn.* London, 1954
25. *Hell's Pavement.* London, 1955
26. *Death in Retirement.* London and New York, 1956
27. *The China Roundabout.* London, 1956
28. *Double Doom.* London, 1957
29. *The Seeing Eye.* London, 1958
30. *The House above the River.* London, 1959
31. *Easy Prey.* London and New York, 1959
32. *A Well-Known Face.* London and New York, 1960
33. *The Convalescent.* London, 1960
34. *New People at the Hollies.* London and New York, 1961
35. *Crime in Our Time.* London, 1961
36. *Adventure with Crime.* London, 1962
37. *Safety First.* London, 1962
38. *A Flat Tyre in Fulham.* London, 1963
39. *Fiasco in Fulham.* New York, 1963
40. *The Hunter and the Trapped.* London, 1963
41. *The Upfold Witch.* London and New York, 1964
42. *Room for a Body.* New York, 1964
43. *Stranger on a Cliff.* New York, 1964
44. *The Alien.* London, 1964
45. *Curtain Call for a Corpse.* New York, 1965
46. *Murder on the Merry-Go-Round.* New York, 1965
47. *No Escape.* London, 1965
48. *Death on the Reserve.* London and New York, 1966
49. *The Catalyst.* London, 1966
50. *Tudor Pilgrimage.* London, 1967
51. *Death of a Con Man.* London and Philadelphia, 1968
52. *The Fennister Affair.* London, 1969
53. *The Wilberforce Legacy.* London and New York, 1969
54. *Jacobean Adventure.* London, 1969
55. *Over the Seas.* London, 1970
56. *A Hydra with Six Heads.* London, 1970
57. *A Hole in the Ground.* London, 1971
58. *The Dark and the Light.* London, 1971
59. *To Serve a Queen.* London, 1972
60. *Death of a Poison-Tongue.* London, 1972
61. *In the King's Absence.* London, 1973
62. *A Question of Loyalties.* London, 1974
63. *A Pigeon among the Cats.* London, 1974
64. *Victim.* London, 1975
65. *The Trouble in the Hunter Ward.* London, 1976
66. *Such a Nice Client.* London, 1977
67. *Stroke of Death.* New York, 1977
68. *A Swan Song Betrayed.* London, 1978
69. *Treachery in Type.* New York, 1979
70. *Wolf! Wolf!* London, 1979

Bellah, James Warner
American, born September 14, 1899, died in 1976
1. *Sketch Book of a Cadet from Gascony.* New York, 1923
2. *These Frantic Years.* New York, 1927
3. *The Sons of Cain.* New York, 1928
4. *Gods of Yesterday.* New York, 1928
5. *Dancing Lady.* New York, 1932
6. *White Piracy.* New York, 1933
7. *The Brass Gong Tree.* New York, 1936
8. *South by East a Half East.* Privately printed, 1936
9. *This Is the Town.* New York, 1937
10. *7 Must Die.* New York, 1938
11. *The Bones of Napoleon.* New York, 1940
12. *Ward Twenty.* New York, 1946
13. *Irregular Gentleman.* New York, 1948
14. *Massacre.* New York, 1950
15. *Rear Guard.* New York, 1951
16. *The Apache.* New York, 1951
17. *Divorce.* New York, 1952
18. *The Valiant Virginians.* New York, 1953
19. *Ordeal at Blood River.* New York, 1959
20. *Sergeant Rutledge.* New York and London, 1960
21. *A Thunder of Drums.* New York, 1961
22. *Soldier's Battle—Gettysburg.* New York, 1962
23. *The Man Who Shot Liberty Valance.* New York, 1962
24. *Reveille.* New York, 1962
25. *Fighting Men U.S.A.* Evanston (IL), 1963
26. *The Journal of Colonel De Lancey.* Philadelphia, 1967

Bellairs, George [Harold Blundell]
British, born April 19, 1902
1. *Littlejohn on Leave.* London, 1941
2. *The Four Faithful Servants.* London, 1942
3. *Death of a Busybody.* London, 1942
4. *The Dead Shall Be Raised.* London, 1942
5. *Murder Will Speak.* New York, 1943

6. *Turmoil in Zion.* London, 1943
7. *The Murder of a Quack.* London, 1943
8. *Death Stops the Frolic.* New York, 1944
9. *Calamity at Harwood.* New York, 1945
10. *He'd Rather Be Dead.* London, 1945
11. *Death in the Night Watches.* London, 1945
12. *The Crime at Halfpenny Bridge.* London, 1946
13. *The Case of the Scared Rabbits.* London, 1947
14. *The Case of the Seven Whistlers.* London and New York, 1948
15. *Death on the Last Train.* London, 1948
16. *The Case of the Famished Parson.* London and New York, 1949
17. *Outrage on Gallows Hill.* London, 1949
18. *The Case of the Demented Spiv.* London, 1949
19. *The Case of the Headless Jesuit.* London, 1950
20. *Death Brings In the New Year.* New York, 1951
21. *Death March for Penelope Blow.* London and New York, 1951
22. *Death in Dark Glasses.* London and New York, 1952
23. *Crime in Lepers' Hollow.* London, 1952
24. *A Knife for Harry Dodd.* London, 1953
25. *Half-Mast for the Deemster.* London, 1953
26. *Corpses in Enderby.* London, 1954
27. *The Cursing Stone Murders.* London, 1954
28. *Death in Room Five.* London, 1955
29. *Death Treads Softly.* London, 1956
30. *Death Drops the Pilot.* London, 1956
31. *Death on High Provence.* London, 1957
32. *Death Sends for the Doctor.* London, 1957
33. *Corpse at the Carnival.* London, 1958
34. *Murder Makes Mistakes.* London, 1958
35. *Bones in the Wilderness.* London, 1959
36. *Toll the Bell for Murder.* London, 1959
37. *Death in the Fearful Night.* London, 1960
38. *Death in Despair.* London, 1960
39. *Death of a Tin God.* London, 1961
40. *The Body in the Dumb River.* London, 1961
41. *Death Before Breakfast.* London and New York, 1962
42. *The Tormentors.* London, 1962
43. *Death in the Wasteland.* London, 1963
44. *Surfeit of Suspects.* London, 1964
45. *Death of a Shadow.* London, 1964
46. *Death Spins the Wheel.* London, 1965
47. *Intruder in the Dark.* London, 1966
48. *Strangers among the Dead.* London, 1966
49. *Death in Desolation.* London, 1967
50. *Single Ticket to Death.* London, 1967
51. *Fatal Alibi.* London, 1968
52. *Murder Gone Mad.* London, 1968
53. *Tycoon's Death-Bed.* London, 1970
54. *The Night They Killed Joss Varran.* London, 1970
55. *Pomeroy, Deceased.* London, 1971
56. *Murder Adrift.* London, 1972
57. *Devious Murder.* London, 1973
58. *Fear round About.* London, 1975
59. *Close All Roads to Sospel.* London, 1976

Bellem, Robert Leslie
American, born in 1902, died in 1968
Pseudonyms: Franklin Charles, with Cleve F. Adams; John A. Saxon
1. *Blue Murder.* New York, 1938
2. *The Window with the Sleeping Nude.* Kingston (NY), 1940
3. *The Vice Czar Murders,* as Franklin Charles. New York, 1941
4. *Half-Past Mortem,* as John A. Saxon. New York, 1947
5. *No Wings on a Cop.* Kingston, 1950

Benet, Stephen Vincent
American, born July 22, 1898, died March 13, 1943
1. *Merchants from Cathay and Other Poems.* New York, 1913
2. *Five Men and Pompey.* Boston, 1915
3. *John Brown's Body.* New York, 1928
4. *The Devil and Daniel Webster.* New York, 1937
5. *Nightmare at Noon.* New York, 1940

Bennett, Margot
British, born in 1912
1. *Time to Change Hats.* London, 1945
2. *Away Went the Little Fish.* London and New York, 1946
3. *The Golden Pebble.* London, 1948
4. *The Widow of Bath.* London and New York, 1952
5. *Farewell Crown and Good-Bye King.* London, 1953
6. *The Long Way Back.* London, 1954
7. *The Man Who Didn't Fly.* London, 1955
8. *Someone from the Past.* London and New York, 1958
9. *That Summer's Earthquake.* London, 1964
10. *The Intelligent Woman's Guide to Radiation.* London, 1964
11. *The Furious Masters.* London, 1968

Bennetts, Pamela
British
Pseudonym: Margaret James
1. *The Borgia Prince.* London, 1968
2. *The Borgia Bull.* London, 1968
3. *The Venetian.* London, 1968
4. *The Suzerain.* London, 1968
5. *The Adversaries.* London, 1969
6. *The Black Plantagenet.* London, 1969
7. *Envoy from Elizabeth.* London, 1970
8. *Richard and the Knights of God.* London, 1970
9. *The Tudor Ghosts.* London, 1971
10. *Royal Sword at Agincourt.* London and New York, 1971
11. *A Crown for Normandy.* London, 1971
12. *Bright Son of York.* London, 1971
13. *The Third Richard.* London, 1972
14. *The Angevin King.* London, 1972
15. *The de Montfort Legacy.* London and New York, 1973
16. *The Lords of Lancaster.* London and New York, 1973
17. *The Barons of Runnymede.* London and New York, 1974
18. *A Dragon for Edward.* London and New York, 1975
19. *My Dear Lover England.* London and New York, 1975
20. *The She-Wolf.* London, 1975
21. *Death of the Red King.* London and New York, 1976
22. *Stephen and the Sleeping Saints.* London and New York, 1977
23. *The House in Candle Square.* London, 1977
24. *The Haunting of Sara Lessingham,* as Margaret James. New York, 1978
25. *Don Pedro's Captain.* London and New York, 1978
26. *Ring the Bell Softly.* London, 1978
27. *Ring the Bell Softly,* as Margaret James. New York, 1978
28. *One Dark Night.* London, 1978
29. *Footsteps in the Fog.* London, 1979
30. *Footsteps in the Fog,* as Margaret James. New York, 1979
31. *Marionette.* London, 1979
32. *Marionette,* as Margaret James. New York, 1979
33. *A Voice in the Darkness.* London, 1979
34. *A Voice in the Darkness,* as Margaret James. New York, 1979
35. *Amberstone.* London, 1980
36. *Amberstone,* as Margaret James. New York, 1980
37. *The Quick and the Dead.* London, 1980
38. *The Quick and the Dead,* as Margaret James. New York, 1980
39. *Lucy's Cottage.* London, 1981

40. *Lucy's Cottage,* as Margaret James. New York, 1981
41. *Beau Barron's Lady.* London, 1981
42. *The Marquis and Miss Jones.* London, 1981
43. *Regency Rogue.* London, 1981
44. *The Michaelmas Tree.* London, 1982

Benson, Ben [Benjamin Benson]
American, born in 1915, died April 29, 1959
1. *Hoboes of America: Sensational Life Story and Epic Life on the Road,* by Hobo Benson. New York, 1942
2. *Beware the Pale Horse.* New York, 1951
3. *Alibi at Dusk.* New York, 1951
4. *Lily in Her Coffin.* New York, 1952
5. *Stamped for Murder.* New York, 1952
6. *Target in Taffeta.* New York, 1953
7. *The Venus Death.* New York, 1953
8. *The Girl in the Cage.* New York, 1954
9. *The Burning Fuse.* New York, 1954
10. *Broken Shield.* New York, 1955
11. *The Silver Cobweb.* New York, 1955
12. *The Ninth Hour.* New York, 1956
13. *The Black Mirror.* New York, 1957
14. *The Running Man.* New York, 1957
15. *The Affair of the Exotic Dancer.* New York, 1958
16. *The Blonde in Black.* New York, 1958
17. *The End of Violence.* New York and London, 1959
18. *Seven Steps East.* New York, 1959
19. *The Frightened Ladies.* New York, 1960
20. *The Huntress Is Dead.* New York, 1960

Benson, E.F. (Edward Frederic)
British, born July 24, 1867, died February 29, 1940
1. *Dodo: A Detail of the Day.* London, 2 vols., and New York, 1893
2. *The Rubicon.* London, 2 vols., and New York, 1893
3. *Six Common Things.* London, 1893
4. *A Double Overture.* Chicago, 1894
5. *The Judgement Books.* London and New York, 1895
6. *Limitations.* London and New York, 1896
7. *The Babe, B.A.* London, 1896
8. *The Vintage.* London and New York, 1898
9. *The Money Market.* Bristol (Eng) and Philadelphia, 1898
10. *The Capsina.* London and New York, 1899
11. *Mammon and Co.* London and New York, 1899
12. *The Princess Sophia.* London and New York, 1900
13. *The Luck of the Vails.* London and New York, 1901
14. *Scarlet and Hyssop.* London and New York, 1902
15. *Daily Training,* with E.H. Miles. London, 1902
16. *The Book of Months.* London and New York, 1903
17. *The Valkyries.* London, 1903
18. *The Relentless City.* London and New York, 1903
19. *An Act in a Backwater.* London and New York, 1903
20. *The Challoners.* London and Philadelphia, 1904
21. *Two Generations.* London, 1904
22. *Diversions Day by Day.* London, 1905
23. *The Angel of Pain.* Philadelphia, 1905
24. *The Image in the Sands.* London and Philadelphia, 1905
25. *Paul.* London and Philadelphia, 1906
26. *The House of Defence.* New York, 1906
27. *Sheaves.* New York, 1907
28. *The Blotting Book.* London and New York, 1908
29. *The Climber.* London, 1908
30. *English Figure Skating.* London, 1908
31. *A Reaping.* London and New York, 1909
32. *Daisy's Aunt.* London, 1910
33. *The Fascinating Mrs. Halton.* New York, 1910
34. *Margery.* New York, 1910
35. *The Osbornes.* London and New York, 1910
36. *Juggernaut.* London, 1911
37. *Account Rendered.* London and New York, 1911
38. *Mrs. Ames.* London and New York, 1912
39. *The Room in the Tower and Other Stories.* London, 1912
40. *Bensoniana.* London, 1912
41. *Winter Sports in Switzerland.* London and New York, 1913
42. *Thoughts from E.F. Benson.* London, 1913
43. *The Weaker Vessel.* London and New York, 1913
44. *Dodo's Daughter.* New York, 1913
45. *Thorley Weir.* London and Philadelphia, 1913
46. *Dodo the Second.* London, 1914
47. *Arundel.* London, 1914
48. *The Oakleyites.* London and New York, 1915
49. *David Blaize.* London and New York, 1916
50. *Mike.* London, 1916
51. *Michael.* New York, 1916
52. *The Freaks of Mayfair.* London, 1916
53. *An Autumn Sowing.* London, 1917
54. *Mr. Teddy.* London, 1917
55. *The Tortoise.* New York, 1917
56. *Thoughts from E.F. Benson.* London, 1917
57. *Deutschland uber Allah.* London, 1917
58. *Poland and Mittel-Europa.* London and New York, 1918
59. *The White Eagle of Poland.* London, 1918
60. *Crescent and Iron Cross.* London and New York, 1918
61. *Up and Down.* London and New York, 1918
62. *David Blaize and the Blue Door.* London, 1918
63. *Robin Linnet.* London and New York, 1919
64. *Across the Stream.* London and New York, 1919
65. *Queen Lucia.* London and New York, 1920
66. *The Countess of Lowndes Square and Other Stories.* London and New York, 1920
67. *Our Family Affairs 1867-1896.* London, 1920
68. *Lovers and Friends.* London and New York, 1921
69. *Dodo Wonders.* London and New York, 1921
70. *Miss Mapp.* London, 1922
71. *Peter.* London and New York, 1922
72. *Colin.* London and New York, 1923
73. *Visible and Invisible.* London, 1923
74. *And the Dead Spake —, and The Horror-Horn.* New York, 1923
75. *Expiation, and Naboth's Vineyard.* New York, 1924
76. *The Face.* New York, 1924
77. *Spinach and Reconciliation.* New York, 1924
78. *David of King's.* London, 1924
79. *David Blaize of King's.* New York, 1924
80. *Alan.* London, 1924
81. *Rex.* London and New York, 1925
82. *Colin II.* London and New York, 1925
83. *A Tale of an Empty House, and Bagnell Terrace.* New York, 1925
84. *The Temple.* New York, 1925
85. *Mother.* London, 1925
86. *Mezzanine.* London and New York, 1926
87. *Pharisees and Publicans.* London, 1926
88. *Lucia in London.* London, 1927
89. *Sir Francis Drake.* London and New York, 1927
90. *Spook Stories.* London, 1928
91. *The Life of Alcibiades.* London, 1928
92. *Paying Guests.* London and New York, 1929
93. *Ferdinand Magellan.* London, 1929
94. *The Male Impersonator.* London, 1929
95. *As We Were: A Victorian Peep-Show.* London and New York, 1930
96. *The Inheritor.* London and New York, 1930
97. *The Step.* London, 1930
98. *Mapp and Lucia.* London and New York, 1931
99. *Secret Lives.* London and New York, 1932

100. *As We Are: A Modern Revue.* London and New York, 1932
101. *Charlotte Bronte.* London and New York, 1932
102. *King Edward VII: An Appreciation.* London and New York, 1933
103. *Travail of Gold.* London and New York, 1933
104. *The Outbreak of War, 1914.* London, 1933
105. *Raven's Brood.* London and New York, 1934
106. *More Spook Stories.* London, 1934
107. *Lucia's Progress.* London, 1935
108. *The Worshipful Lucia.* New York, 1935
109. *Queen Victoria.* London and New York, 1935
110. *The Kaiser and English Relations.* London and New York, 1936
111. *Old London.* 4 vols. New York, 1937
112. *Queen Victoria's Daughters.* New York, 1938
113. *Daughters of Queen Victoria.* London, 1939
114. *Trouble for Lucia.* London and New York, 1939
115. *Final Edition: Informal Autobiography.* London and New York, 1940
116. *The Horror Horn and Other Stories.* London, 1974

Bentley, E.C. [Edmund Clerihew]
British, born in 1875, died March 30, 1956
Pseudonym: E. Clerihew
1. *Biography for Beginners,* as E. Clerihew. London, 1905
2. *Trent's Last Case.* London, 1913
3. *The Woman in Black.* New York, 1913
4. *Peace Year in the City, 1918-1919: An Account of the Outstanding Events in the City of London During Peace Year.* Privately printed, 1920
5. *More Biography.* London, 1929
6. *Trent's Own Case,* with H. Warner Allen. London and New York, 1936
7. *Trent Intervenes.* London and New York, 1938
8. *Baseless Biography.* London, 1939
9. *Those Days: An Autobiography.* London, 1940
10. *Elephant's Work: An Enigma.* London and New York, 1950
11. *Clerihews Complete.* London, 1951
12. *Far Horizon: A Biography of Hester Dowden, Medium and Psychic Investigator.* London and New York, 1951
13. *The Chill.* New York, 1953

Bentley, Nicolas [Nicolas Clerihew]
British, born in 1907, died August 14, 1978
1. *Die? I Thought I'd Laugh: A Book of Pictures.* London, 1936
2. *The Time of My Life.* London, 1937
3. *Ballett-Hoo.* London, 1937
4. *Gammon and Espionage.* London, 1938
5. *Second Thoughts on First Lines and Other Poems.* London, 1939
6. *Le Sport.* London, 1939
7. *Animal, Vegetable, and South Kensington: A Book of Bentley's Pictures.* London, 1940
8. *The Tongue-Tied Canary.* London, 1948
9. *The Floating Dutchman.* London, 1950
10. *Third Party Risk.* London, 1953
11. *How Can You Bear to Be Human?* London, 1957
12. *A Choice of Ornaments.* London, 1959
13. *A Version of the Truth.* London, 1960
14. *Book of Birds: An Avian Alphabet.* London, 1965
15. *The Victorian Scene: A Picture Book of the Period 1837-1901.* London, 1968
16. *Don't Do-It-Yourself: A Fantasy of Exporters.* London, 1970
17. *Golden Sovereigns, and Some of Lesser Value, from Boadicea to Elizabeth II.* London, 1970
18. *Tales from Shakespeare.* London, 1972
19. *The Events of That Week.* London and New York, 1972
20. *Inside Information.* London, 1974
21. *Edwardian Album: A Photographic Excursion into a Lost Age of Innocence.* London and New York, 1974
22. *Pay Bed.* London, 1976
23. *The History of the Circus.* London, 1977

Bentley, Phyliss (Eleanor)
British, born in 1894, died June 27, 1977
Pseudonym: A Bachelor of Arts
1. *The World's Bane and Other Stories.* London, 1918
2. *Pedagomania; or, The Gentle Art of Teaching,* as A Bachelor of Arts. London, 1918
3. *Environment.* London, 1922
4. *Cat-in-the-Manger.* London, 1923
5. *The Spinner of the Years.* London, 1928
6. *The Partnership.* London, 1928
7. *Carr.* London, 1929
8. *Trio.* London, 1930
9. *Sounding Brass.* Halifax (Eng), 1930
10. *Inheritance.* London and New York, 1932
11. *A Modern Tragedy.* London and New York, 1934
12. *The Whole of the Story.* London, 1935
13. *Freedom, Farewell!* London and New York, 1936
14. *Sleep in Peace.* London and New York, 1938
15. *Take Courage.* London, 1940
16. *The Power and the Glory.* New York, 1940
17. *Manhold.* London and New York, 1941
18. *Here Is America.* London, 1941
19. *The English Regional Novel.* London, 1941
20. *The Rise of Henry Morcar.* London and New York, 1946
21. *Some Observations on the Art of Narrative.* London, 1946
22. *Colne Valley Cloth from the Earliest Times to the Present Day.* Huddersfield (Eng), 1947
23. *The Brontes.* London, 1947
24. *Life Story.* London and New York, 1948
25. *Quorum.* London, 1950
26. *The Bronte Sisters.* London, 1950
27. *Panorama: Tales of the West Riding.* London and New York, 1952
28. *The House of Moreys.* London and New York, 1953
29. *Noble in Reason.* London and New York, 1955
30. *Love and Money: Seven Tales of the West Riding.* London and New York, 1957
31. *Crescendo.* London and New York, 1958
32. *Kith and Kin: Nine Tales of Family Life.* London and New York, 1960
33. *The Young Brontes.* London and New York, 1961
34. *"O Dreams, O Destinations": An Autobiography.* London and New York, 1962
35. *Committees.* London, 1962
36. *Enjoy Books: Reading and Collecting.* London, 1964
37. *Public Speaking.* London, 1964
38. *The Adventures of Tom Leigh Macdonald.* London, 1964
39. *Tales of the West Riding.* London, 1965
40. *A Man of His Time.* London and New York, 1966
41. *Ned Carver in Danger.* London, 1967
42. *Oath of Silence.* New York, 1967
43. *Gold Pieces.* London, 1968
44. *Forgery!* New York, 1968
45. *Ring in the New.* London, 1969
46. *The Brontes and Their World.* London and New York, 1969
47. *Sheep May Safely Graze.* London, 1972
48. *The New Venturers.* London, 1973
49. *More Tales of the West Riding.* London, 1974

Benton, Kenneth (Carter)
British, born in 1909
1. *Twenty-Fourth Level.* London, 1969

2. *Sole Agent.* London, 1970
3. *Peru's Revolution from Above.* London, 1970
4. *Spy in Chancery.* London, 1972
5. *Craig and the Jaguar.* London, 1973
6. *Craig and the Tunisian Tangle.* London, 1974
7. *Death on the Appian Way.* London, 1974
8. *Craig and the Midas Touch.* London, 1975
9. *A Single Monstrous Act.* London, 1976
10. *The Red Hen Conspiracy.* London, 1977

Berckman, Evelyn (Domenica)
American, born October 18, 1900, died September 18, 1978
1. *The Evil of Time.* New York, 1954
2. *The Beckoning Dream.* New York, 1955
3. *The Strange Bedfellow.* New York, 1956
4. *The Blind Villain.* New York, 1957
5. *The Hovering Darkness.* New York, 1957
6. *Worse Than Murder.* New York, 1957
7. *No Known Grave.* New York, 1958
8. *Lament for Four Brides.* New York, 1959
9. *Do You Know This Voice?* New York, 1960
10. *House of Terror.* New York, 1960
11. *Blind-Girl's-Buff.* New York and London, 1962
12. *Nelson's Dear Lord: A Portrait of St. Vincent.* London, 1962
13. *A Thing That Happens to You.* New York, 1964
14. *A Simple Case of Ill-Will.* London, 1964
15. *Keys from a Window.* London, 1965
16. *Stalemate.* London and New York, 1966
17. *The Heir of Starvelings.* New York, 1967
18. *A Case of Nullity.* London, 1967
19. *Jewel of Death.* New York, 1968
20. *The Long Arm of the Prince.* London, 1968
21. *She Asked for It.* New York, 1969
22. *The Voice of Air.* New York, 1970
23. *A Finger to Her Lips.* London and New York, 1971
24. *The Stake in the Game.* London, 1971
25. *The Fourth Man on the Rope.* London and New York, 1972
26. *The Victorian Album.* London and New York, 1973
27. *Wait.* London, 1973
28. *Wait, Just You Wait.* New York, 1973
29. *The Hidden Navy.* London, 1973
30. *Creators and Destroyers of the English Navy.* London, 1974
31. *Indecent Exposure.* London, 1975
32. *The Nightmare Chase.* New York, 1975
33. *The Crown Estate.* New York, 1976
34. *The Blessed Plot.* London, 1976
35. *Be All and End All.* London, 1976
36. *Journey's End.* New York, 1977
37. *Victims of Piracy: The Admiralty Court 1575-1678.* London, 1979

Beresford, Elisabeth
British
1. *The Television Mystery.* London, 1957
2. *The Flying Doctor Mystery.* London, 1958
3. *Trouble at Tullington Castle.* London, 1958
4. *Cocky and the Missing Castle.* London, 1959
5. *Gappy Goes West.* London, 1959
6. *The Tullington Film-Makers.* London, 1960
7. *Two Gold Dolphins.* London, 1961
8. *Danger on the Old Pull 'n Push.* London, 1962
9. *Strange Hiding Place.* London, 1962
10. *Paradise Island.* London, 1963
11. *Diana in Television.* London, 1963
12. *The Missing Formula Mystery.* London, 1963
13. *The Mulberry Street Team.* Penhurst (Eng), 1963
14. *Escape to Happiness.* London, 1964
15. *Awkward Magic.* London, 1964
16. *The Flying Doctor to the Rescue.* London, 1964
17. *Holiday for Slippy.* Penhurst, 1964
18. *Roses round the Door.* London and New York, 1965
19. *The Magic World.* Indianapolis, 1965
20. *Game, Set, and Match.* London, 1965
21. *Knights of the Cardboard Castle.* London, 1965
22. *Travelling Magic.* London, 1965
23. *The Hidden Mill.* London, 1965
24. *Island of Shadows.* London, 1966
25. *Peter Climbs a Tree.* London, 1966
26. *Veronica.* London, 1967
27. *A Tropical Affair.* London, 1967
28. *The Vanishing Garden.* New York, 1967
29. *Fashion Girl.* London, 1967
30. *The Black Mountain Mystery.* London, 1967
31. *Looking for a Friend.* London, 1967
32. *Saturday's Child.* London, 1968
33. *The Island Bus.* London, 1968
34. *Sea-Green Magic.* London, 1968
35. *The Wombles.* London, 1968
36. *David Goes Fishing.* London, 1969
37. *Gordon's Go-Kart.* London, 1970
38. *Stephen and the Shaggy Dog.* London, 1970
39. *Vanishing Magic.* London, 1970
40. *The Wandering Wombles.* London, 1970
41. *Love Remembered.* London, 1970
42. *Love and the S.S. Beatrice.* London, 1972
43. *Dangerous Magic.* London, 1972
44. *The Invisible Womble and Other Stories.* London, 1973
45. *The Secret Railway.* London, 1973
46. *The Wombles in Danger.* London, 1973
47. *The Wombles at Work.* London, 1973
48. *Invisible Magic.* London, 1974
49. *The Wombles Go to the Seaside.* London, 1974
50. *Pandora.* London, 1974
51. *The Wombles Annual 1975-1978.* London, 4 vols., 1974-77
52. *The Wombles Gift Book.* London, 1975
53. *The Snow Womble.* London, 1975
54. *Snuffle to the Rescue.* London, 1975
55. *Tomsk and the Tired Tree.* London, 1975
56. *Wellington and the Blue Balloon.* London, 1975
57. *Orinoco Runs Away.* London, 1975
58. *The Wombles Make a Clean Sweep.* London, 1975
59. *The Wombles to the Rescue.* London, 1975
60. *The MacWomble's Pipe Band.* London, 1976
61. *Bungo Knows Best.* London, 1976
62. *Tobermory's Big Surprise.* London, 1976
63. *The Wombles Go round the World.* London, 1976
64. *Madame Cholet's Picnic Party.* London, 1976
65. *The World of the Wombles.* London, 1976
66. *Wombling Free.* London, 1978
67. *Toby's Luck.* London, 1978
68. *Secret Magic.* London, 1978
69. *Tropical Affairs.* New York, 1978
70. *Thunder of Her Heart.* New York, 1978
71. *Echoes of Love.* New York, 1979
72. *The Happy Ghost.* London, 1979
73. *The Treasure Hunters.* London and New York, 1980
74. *The Steadfast Lover.* London, 1980
75. *The Silver Chain.* London, 1980
76. *Curious Magic.* London and New York, 1980
77. *The Four of Us.* London, 1981
78. *The Animals Nobody Wanted.* London, 1982
79. *The Restless Heart.* New York, 1982

Berger, Thomas (Louis)
American, born July 20, 1924
1. *Crazy in Berlin.* New York, 1958
2. *Reinhart in Love.* New York, 1962
3. *Little Big Man.* New York, 1964
4. *Killing Time.* New York, 1967
5. *Vital Parts.* New York, 1970
6. *Regiment of Women.* New York, 1973
7. *Sneaky People.* New York, 1975
8. *Who Is Teddy Villanova?* New York and London, 1977
9. *Arthur Rex: A Legendary Novel.* New York, 1978
10. *Neighbors.* New York, 1980
11. *Reinhart's Women.* New York, 1981
12. *The Feud.* New York, 1983

Bergman, Andrew
American
1. *The Big Kiss-Off of 1944.* New York, 1974
2. *Hollywood and Le Vine.* New York, 1975
3. *James Cagney.* New York, 1975

Berry, Don
American, born January 23, 1932
1. *Trask.* New York and London, 1960
2. *A Majority of Scoundrels: An Informal History of the Rocky Mountain Fur Company.* New York, 1961
3. *Moontrap.* New York, 1962
4. *To Build a Ship.* New York, 1963
5. *Mountain Men: The Trappers of the Great Fur-Trading Era 1822-1843.* New York, 1966

Bevan, Gloria
Australian
1. *The Distant Trap.* London, 1969
2. *The Hills of Maketu.* London and Toronto, 1969
3. *Beyond the Ranges.* London, 1970
4. *Make Way for Tomorrow.* London and Toronto, 1971
5. *It Began in Te Rangi.* London, 1971
6. *Vineyard in a Valley.* London and Toronto, 1972
7. *Flame in Fiji.* London and Toronto, 1973
8. *The Frost and the Fire.* London and Toronto, 1973
9. *Connelly's Castle.* London and Toronto, 1974
10. *High-Country Wife.* London, 1974
11. *Always a Rainbow.* London and Toronto, 1975
12. *Dolphin Bay.* London and Toronto, 1976
13. *Bachelor Territory.* London and Toronto, 1977
14. *Plantation Moon.* London, 1977
15. *Fringe of Heaven.* London and Toronto, 1978
16. *Kowhai Country.* London, 1979
17. *Half a World Away.* London, 1980
18. *Master of Mahia.* London and Toronto, 1981

Bickham, Jack M. (Miles)
American, born September 2, 1930
Pseudonyms: Jeff Clinton, John Miles
1. *Gunman's Gamble.* New York, 1958
2. *Feud Fury.* New York, 1959
3. *Killer's Paradise.* New York, 1959
4. *The Useless Gun.* New York, 1960
5. *Dally with a Deadly Doll.* New York, 1960
6. *Hangman's Territory.* New York, 1961
7. *Gunmen Can't Hide.* New York, 1961
8. *The Fighting Buckaroo,* as Jeff Clinton. New York, 1961
9. *Range Killer,* as Jeff Clinton. New York, 1962
10. *Wildcat's Rampage,* as Jeff Clinton. New York, 1962
11. *Wildcat Against the House,* as Jeff Clinton. New York, 1963
12. *Troubled Trails,* as John Miles. New York, 1963
13. *Wildcat's Revenge,* as Jeff Clinton. New York, 1964
14. *Trip Home to Hell.* New York, 1965
15. *Killer's Choice,* as Jeff Clinton. New York, 1965
16. *Wildcat Takes His Medicine,* as Jeff Clinton. New York, 1966
17. *Wanted: Wildcat O'Shea,* as Jeff Clinton. New York, 1967
18. *Wildcat on the Loose,* as Jeff Clinton. New York, 1967
19. *Wildcat's Witch Hunt,* as Jeff Clinton. New York, 1967
20. *The Padre Must Die.* New York, 1967
21. *The War on Charity Ross.* New York, 1967
22. *The Shadowed Faith.* New York, 1968
23. *Target: Charity Ross.* New York, 1968
24. *Watch Out for Wildcat,* as Jeff Clinton. New York, 1968
25. *Wildcat Meets Miss Melody,* as Jeff Clinton. New York, 1968
26. *Build a Box for Wildcat,* as Jeff Clinton. New York, 1969
27. *A Stranger Named O'Shea,* as Jeff Clinton. New York, 1970
28. *Decker's Campaign.* New York, 1970
29. *Fletcher.* New York, 1971
30. *Jilly's Canal.* New York, 1971
31. *The Apple Dumpling Gang.* New York, 1971
32. *The Sheriff's Campaign.* London, 1971
33. *Ambush Vengeance.* London, 1971
34. *Wildcat's Claim to Fame,* as Jeff Clinton. New York, 1971
35. *Bounty on Wildcat,* as Jeff Clinton. New York, 1971
36. *Dopey Dan.* New York, 1972
37. *Hang High, O'Shea,* as Jeff Clinton. New York, 1972
38. *Katie, Kelly, and Heck.* New York, 1973
39. *The Night Hunters,* as John Miles. Indianapolis, 1973
40. *Baker's Hawk.* New York, 1974
41. *Texas Challenge.* London, 1974
42. *Emerald Canyon,* as Jeff Clinton. New York, 1974
43. *The Silver Bullet Gang,* as John Miles. Indianapolis, 1974
44. *The Blackmailer,* as John Miles. Indianapolis, 1974
45. *The Invisible Plague.* New York, 1975
46. *Hurry Home, Davey Clock.* New York, 1975
47. *A Boat Named Death.* New York, 1975
48. *Showdown at Emerald Canyon,* as Jeff Clinton. New York, 1975
49. *Operation Nightfall,* as John Miles, with Tom Morris. Indianapolis, 1975
50. *Twister.* New York, 1976
51. *The Winemakers.* New York, 1977
52. *The Excalibur Disaster.* New York, 1978
53. *Dinah, Blow Your Horn.* New York, 1979
54. *The Regensburg Legacy.* New York, 1980
55. *All the Days Were Summer.* London, 1982

Biggers, Earl Derr
American, born in 1884, died April 5, 1933
1. *Seven Keys to Baldpate.* Indianapolis, 1913
2. *Love Insurance.* Indianapolis, 1914
3. *Inside the Lines,* with Robert Welles Ritchie. Indianapolis, 1915
4. *The Agony Column.* Indianapolis, 1916
5. *The House Without a Key.* Indianapolis, 1925
6. *The Chinese Parrot.* Indianapolis, 1926
7. *Fifty Candles.* Indianapolis, 1926
8. *Behind That Curtain.* Indianapolis and London, 1928
9. *The Black Camel.* Indianapolis, 1929
10. *Charlie Chan Carries On.* Indianapolis, 1930
11. *Second Floor Mystery.* New York, 1930
12. *Keeper of the Keys.* Indianapolis and London, 1932
13. *Earl Derr Biggers Tells Ten Stories.* Indianapolis, 1933

Bindloss, Harold (Edward)
British, born in 1866
1. *In the Niger Country.* Edinburgh, 1898
2. *A Wide Dominion.* London, 1900

3. *Ainslee's Ju-Ju: A Romance of the Hinterland.* London, 1900
4. *A Sower of Wheat.* London, 1901
5. *Sunshine and Snow.* London, 1902
6. *The Concession-Hunters.* London, 1902
7. *The Mistress of Bonaventure.* London, 1903
8. *His Master Purpose.* London, 1903
9. *Daventry's Daughter.* London, 1904
10. *The League of the Leopard.* London, 1904
11. *True Grit: The Adventure of Two Lads in Western Africa.* London, 1904
12. *Alton of Somasco.* London, 1905
13. *The Imposter.* London, 1905
14. *In the Misty Seas: A Story of the Sealers of Behring Strait* London, 1905
15. *Beneath Her Station.* London, 1906
16. *A Damaged Reputation.* London, 1906
17. *The Cattle-Baron's Daughter.* London and New York 1906
18. *Delilah of the Snows.* London, 1907
19. *The Young Traders.* New York, 1907
20. *The Dust of Conflict.* London and New York, 1907
21. *His Lady's Pleasure.* London, 1907
22. *By Right of Purchase.* London and New York, 1908
23. *Long Odds.* Boston, 1908
24. *For Jacinta.* New York, 1908
25. *Thrice Armed.* London and New York, 1908
26. *The Liberationist.* London, 1908
27. *Lorimer of the Northwest.* New York 1909
28. *The Greater Power.* London and New York, 1909
29. *The Gold Trail.* London and New York 1910
30. *The Boy Ranchers of Puget Sound.* New York 1910
31. *Rancher Carteret.* London, 1910
32. *The Opium Smuggler.* London, 1910
33. *Thurston of Orchard Valley.* New York, 1910
34. *Sydney Carteret, Rancher.* New York 1911
35. *Hawtrey's Deputy.* London, 1911
36. *Masters of the Wheat-Lands.* New York 1911
37. *The Protector.* London, 1911
38. *Vane of the Timberlands.* New York, 1911
39. *The Pioneer.* London, 1912
40. *The Long Portage.* New York 1912
41. *The Trustee.* London, 1912
42. *The Wastrel.* London, 1913
43. *Prescott of Saskatchewan.* New York 1913
44. *Ranching for Sylvia.* New York, 1913
45. *The Allinson Honour.* London, 1913
46. *For the Allinson Honor.* New York, 1913
47. *Blake's Burden.* London, 1914
48. *The Secret of the Reef.* London and New York, 1914
49. *The Intriguers.* New York, 1914
50. *A Risky Game.* London, 1915
51. *The Coast of Adventure.* New York, 1915
52. *Harding of Allenwood.* New York, 1915
53. *The Intruder.* London, 1915
54. *The Borderer.* London, 1916
55. *Johnstone of the Border.* New York, 1916
56. *Alison's Adventure.* London, 1917
57. *A Prairie Courtship.* New York 1917
58. *Sadie's Conquest.* London, 1917
59. *The Girl from Keller's.* New York, 1917
60. *Crossthwaite of Banisdale.* London, 1917
61. *Carmen's Messenger.* London and New York, 1917
62. *Agatha's Fortune.* London, 1918
63. *The Lure of the North.* New York, 1918
64. *Askew's Victory.* London, 1918
65. *The Buccaneer Farmer.* New York, 1918
66. *Wyndham's Partner.* London, 1919
67. *Wyndham's Pal.* New York, 1919
68. *Deerham's Inheritance.* London, 1919
69. *Partners of the Out-Trail.* New York 1919
70. *Stayward's Vindication.* London, 1920
71. *The Head of the House.* London, 1920
72. *The Wilderness Mine.* New York 1920
73. *Lister's Great Adventure.* New York, 1921
74. *The Man from the Wilds.* London, 1921
75. *Musgrave's Luck.* London, 1921
76. *Kit Musgrave's Luck.* New York, 1921
77. *The Mountaineers.* London, 1922
78. *Northwest!* New York 1922
79. *The Wilderness Patrol.* London and New York 1923
80. *The Keystone Block.* London, 1923
81. *The Bush-Rancher.* New York, 1923
82. *The Boys of Wildcat Ranch.* London and New York, 1924
83. *The Lute Player.* London, 1924
84. *Carson of Red River.* New York 1924
85. *Andrew's Folly.* London, 1924
86. *Green Timber.* New York, 1924
87. *The Broken Net.* London, 1925
88. *Prairie Gold.* New York 1925
89. *A Debt of Honour.* London, 1925
90. *Cross Trails.* New York, 1925
91. *Helen the Conqueror.* London, 1926
92. *Pine Creek Ranch.* New York 1926
93. *Sour Grapes.* London, 1926
94. *The Broken Trail.* New York, 1926
95. *Footsteps.* London, 1927
96. *The Ghost of Hemlock Canyon.* New York 1927
97. *The Dark Road.* London and New York, 1927
98. *Halford's Adventure.* London, 1928
99. *Mystery Reef.* New York, 1928
100. *The Firm Hand.* London, 1928
101. *The Lone Hand.* New York, 1928
102. *Frontiersman.* London, 1929
103. *The Frontiersman.* New York 1929
104. *The Harder Way.* London, 1929
105. *Larry of Lonesome Lake.* New York, 1929
106. *Harden's Escapade.* London, 1930
107. *The Man at Willow Ranch.* New York 1930
108. *A Moorside Feud.* London, 1930
109. *Rancher Jim.* New York, 1930
110. *The Lean Years.* London, 1931
111. *The Prairie Patrol.* New York 1931
112. *Carter's Triumph.* London, 1931
113. *The Border Trail.* New York 1931
114. *Jungle Gold.* New York, 1932
115. *Right of Way.* London and New York, 1932
116. *The Loser Pays.* London, 1933
117. *The Stain of the Forge.* London, 1933
118. *Fenwick's Trail.* London, 1933
119. *Sonalta Gold.* London, 1934
120. *Valley Gold.* New York 1934
121. *The Lady of the Plain.* London, 1935
122. *Sweetwater Ranch.* New York 1935
123. *Fellside Folk.* London, 1937
124. *Posted Missing.* London, 1938
125. *Valeria Goes West.* London, 1939
126. *What's Mine I Hold!* London, 1940
127. *The Call of the Soil.* London, 1941
128. *The Secret of the Scree.* London, 1942
129. *Caverhills.* London, 1943
130. *The Laird of o'Borrans.* London, 1945
131. *Richardsons of the Forge.* London, 1946

Bingham, John [John Michael Ward Bingham, Lord Clanmoris]
British, born in 1908
1. *My Name Is Michael Sibley.* London and New York, 1952
2. *Five Roundabouts to Heaven.* London, 1953

3. *The Tender Poisoner.* New York, 1953
4. *The Third Skin.* London and New York, 1954
5. *The Paton Street Case.* London, 1955
6. *Inspector Morgan's Dilemma.* New York, 1956
7. *Murder off the Record.* New York, 1957
8. *Murder Is a Witch.* New York, 1957
9. *Marion.* London, 1958
10. *Murder Plan Six.* London, 1958
11. *Night's Black Agent.* London and New York, 1961
12. *A Case of Libel.* London, 1963
13. *A Fragment of Fear.* London, 1965
14. *The Double Agent.* London, 1966
15. *I Love, I Kill.* London, 1968
16. *Good Old Charlie.* New York, 1969
17. *Vulture in the Sun.* London, 1971
18. *The Hunting Down of Peter Manuel, Glasgow Multiple Murderer,* with William Muncie. London, 1973
19. *God's Defector.* London, 1976
20. *Ministry of Death.* New York, 1977
21. *The Marriage Bureau Murders.* London, 1977

Bingley, David (Ernest)
British, born April 16, 1920
Pseudonyms: Bart Adams, Adam Bridger, Abe Canuck, Henry Carver, Larry Chatham, Henry Chesham, Will Coltman, Ed Coniston, Luke Dorman, George Fallon, David Horsley, Bat Jefford, Syd Kingston, Eric Lynch, James Martell, Colin North, Ben Plummer, Caleb Prescott, Mark Remington, John Roberts, Steve Romney, Frank Silvester, Henry Starr, Link Tucker, Christopher Wigan, Roger Yorke

1. *Mossyhorn Trail,* as Christopher Wigan. London, 1957
2. *Operation Pedestal,* as David Horsley. London, 1957
3. *Tinfish Running!,* as David Horsley. London, 1958
4. *Showdown at Cedar Springs,* as Christopher Wigan. London, 1958
5. *The Ocean, Their Grave,* as David Horsley. London, 1958
6. *Torpedoes in the Wake,* as David Horsley. London, 1958
7. *Vinegar Johnny,* as David Horsley. London, 1958
8. *The Decoys,* as David Horsley. London, 1959
9. *Living Death,* as David Horsley. London, 1959
10. *The Thirty Eight Days,* as David Horsley. London, 1959
11. *Don't Compel Me!* as David Horsley. London, 1960
12. *The Time of the Locust,* as David Horsley. London, 1960
13. *Dive, Dive—Dive,* as David Horsley. London, 1960
14. *Malayan Adventure.* London, 1962
15. *The Restless Breed,* as Larry Chatham. London, 1963
16. *Trails of Destiny,* as Larry Chatham. London, 1963
17. *Timber Wolves Trail,* as Larry Chatham. London, 1964
18. *Railtown Round-Up,* as Syd Kingston. London, 1964
19. *Showdown at the Lazy T,* as John Roberts. London, 1964
20. *The Bar T Brand,* as Dave Carver. London, 1964
21. *Johnny Pronto,* as David Horsley. London, 1964
22. *The Man from Casagrande,* as Christopher Wigan. London, 1964
23. *The Trail-Blazer,* as Christopher Wigan. London, 1964
24. *Gunsmoke at Nester Creek.* London, 1964
25. *Sons of the Diamond V.* London, 1964
26. *Famous Storybook Heroes.* London, 1964
27. *Gunsmoke County,* as Ben Plummer. London, 1964
28. *Short Trigger Valley,* as Henry Starr. London, 1964
29. *The Border Brigands,* as Henry Starr. London, 1965
30. *The Railroad Renegades,* as Ben Plummer. London, 1965
31. *The Necktie Trail,* as Syd Kingston. London, 1965
32. *Trail of Reckoning,* as Larry Chatham. London, 1965
33. *The Reluctant Renegade,* as David Horsley. London, 1965
34. *Counterfeit Trail,* as Adam Bridger. London, 1965
35. *Bullhead's Canyon,* as Frank Silvester. London, 1965
36. *Hellion's Roost,* as Mark Remington. London, 1965
37. *The Reluctant Gunman,* as Colin North. London, 1965
38. *Little Pecos Trail,* as James Martell. London, 1965
39. *The Iron Trail,* as Roger Yorke. London, 1965
40. *Renegade's Blade,* as Luke Dorman. London, 1965
41. *Gunsmoke Lawyer,* as Steve Romney. London, 1965
42. *Bar X Bandit,* as Ed Coniston. London, 1965
43. *Renegade Valley,* as Link Tucker. London, 1965
44. *Naples, or Die!,* as Henry Chesham. London, 1965
45. *Elusive Witness,* as D.E. Bingley. London, 1966
46. *Caribbean Crisis,* as D.E. Bingley. London, 1966
47. *Buzzard's Breed,* as Luke Dorman. London, 1966
48. *Guadalupe Bandit,* Roger Yorke. London, 1966
49. *Renegade Trail,* as James Martell. London, 1966
50. *Trail of Tragedy,* as Colin North. London, 1966
51. *Silver City Showdown,* as Mark Remington. London, 1966
52. *Gunsmoke Gorge,* as Adam Bridger. London, 1966
53. *Flying Horseshoe Trail,* as David Horsley. London, 1966
54. *Buckboard Bandit,* as David Horsley. London, 1966
55. *Gunsmoke Gambler,* as Henry Carver. London, 1966
56. *Colorado Gun Law,* as John Roberts. London, 1966
57. *Settlers' Stampede,* as Frank Silvester. London, 1966
58. *Owlhoot Raiders,* as Bart Adams. London, 1966
59. *The Torrington Trail,* as Will Coltman. London, 1966
60. *The Ruthless Renegades,* as Caleb Prescott. London, 1966
61. *Creek Town Killer,* as Bat Jefford. London, 1966
62. *The Rioting Renegades,* as Abe Canuck. London, 1966
63. *Skyborne Sapper,* as Henry Chesham. London, 1966
64. *Pecos River Posse,* as Caleb Prescott. London, 1967
65. *Sawbones' City,* as Steve Romney. London, 1967
66. *The Elusive Renegade,* as Ed Coniston. London, 1967
67. *Circle M Showdown,* as Link Tucker. London, 1967
68. *Renegades' Stampede,* as Bart Adams. London, 1967
69. *South Fork Showdown,* as Eric Lynch. London, 1967
70. *Rendezvous in Rio,* as George Fallon. London, 1967
71. *Murder Mesa,* as Eric Lynch. London, 1968
72. *Badman's Bounty,* as Bat Jefford. London, 1968
73. *Study Book of Bridges.* London, 1969
74. *Silvertown Trail,* as Abe Canuck. London, 1969
75. *Killer's Creek,* as Will Coltman. London, 1969
76. *Owlhoot Bandits,* as Roger Yorke. London, 1969
77. *Trailtown Trickster,* as Colin North. London, 1969
78. *The Palomino Kid,* as Frank Silvester. London, 1969
79. *Renegade Range,* as Adam Bridger. London, 1969
80. *El Yanqui's Gold,* as Mark Remington. London, 1969
81. *Boulder Creek Trail,* as Ed Coniston. London, 1969
82. *Hellions at Large,* as Link Tucker. London, 1969
83. *Silver Creek Trail,* as Bat Jefford. London, 1970
84. *Six Shooter Junction,* as Caleb Prescott. London, 1970
85. *Ghost Town Killer,* as Will Coltman. London, 1970
86. *The Coyote Kids,* as Bart Adams. London, 1970
87. *Showdown City,* as Steve Romney. London, 1970
88. *Salt Creek Showdown,* as James Martell. London, 1970
89. *Red Rock Renegades,* as Luke Dorman. London, 1970
90. *Renegades' Retreat,* as Eric Lynch. London, 1971
91. *Hellions' Hostage,* as Abe Canuck. London, 1971
92. *Cowtown Kidnap,* as James Martell. London, 1971
93. *Two Horse Trail,* as Larry Chatham. London, 1971
94. *Remuda's Renegades,* as Christopher Wigan. London, 1971
95. *Rustlers' Moon.* London, 1972
96. *The Kid from Cougar,* as Syd Kingston. London, 1972
97. *Trailmen's Truce,* as John Roberts. London, 1972
98. *The Diamond Kid,* as David Horsley. London, 1972
99. *Cowtown Killers,* as Ben Plummer. London, 1972
100. *Lawman's Lament,* as Henry Starr. London, 1972
101. *Killer's Canyon,* as Christopher Wigan. London, 1973
102. *Hangtown Heiress,* as Larry Chatham. London, 1973
103. *The Judge's Territory,* as Larry Chatham. London, 1973
104. *Renegade River,* as Henry Carver. London, 1973

105. *Red Bluff Renegades*, as Frank Silvester. London, 1973
106. *Alias Jack Dollar*, as Syd Kingston. London, 1974
107. *Hellions' Hideaway*. London, 1974
108. *Redman Range*, as David Horsley. London, 1975
109. *The Man from Abilene*. London, 1975
110. *Lopez's Loot*, as Christopher Wigan. London, 1975
111. *Hideaway Heist*, as Syd Kingston. London, 1975
112. *The Place of the Chins*, as Henry Chesham. London, 1975
113. *Rogue's Remittance*, as Frank Silvester. London, 1976
114. *Sunset Showdown*, as David Horsley. London, 1977
115. *A Surfeit of Soldiers*, as Henry Chesham. London, 1978
116. *Brigand's Blade*, as David Horsley. London, 1978
117. *Adam of Pendle Grange*. London, 1979
118. *The Beauclerc Brand*, as David Horsley. London, 1979
119. *Trouble Shooter on Trial*, as David Horsley. London, 1980
120. *Salt Creek Killing*, as David Horsley. London, 1981
121. *Smith's Canyon*, as Larry Chatham. London, 1981
122. *Buckboard Barber*, as Christopher Wigan. London, 1981
123. *Greenhorn Gorge*, as Frank Silvester. London, 1981
124. *The Angry Atoll*, as Henry Chesham. London, 1981
125. *Badlands Bonanza*, as David Horsley. London, 1982
126. *Boot Hill Bandit*, as Syd Kingston. London, 1982
127. *The Long Siesta*, as David Horsley. London, 1983

Birney, Hoffman [Herman Hoffman Birney]
American, born in 1891
Pseudonym: David Kent
1. *King of the Mesa*. Philadelphia, 1927
2. *The Masked Rider*. Philadelphia, 1928
3. *Steeldust: The Story of a Horse*. Philadelphia, 1928
4. *Vigilantes*. Philadelphia, 1929
5. *The Pinto Pony: A Real Horse Story*. Philadelphia, 1930
6. *Roads to Roam*. Philadelphia, 1930
7. *The Canon of Lost Waters*. Philadelphia, 1930
8. *The Canyon of Lost Waters*. London, 1930
9. *Two Little Navajos: A Tale of the Children of the Painted Desert*. Philadelphia, 1931
10. *Zealots of Zion*. Philadelphia, 1931
11. *Kudlu, The Eskimo Boy*. Philadelphia, 1932
12. *Tu'kwi of the Peaceful People*. Philadelphia, 1933
13. *Barrier Ranch*. Philadelphia, 1933
14. *Grim Journey: The Story of the Adventures of the . . . Donner Party. . . .* New York, 1934
15. *Forgotten Canon*. Philadelphia, 1934
16. *Holy Murder: The Story of Porter Rockwell*, with Charles Kelly. New York, 1934
17. *Eagle in the Sun*. New York, 1935
18. *Ay-chee, Son of the Desert*. Philadelphia, 1935
19. *A Stranger in Black Butte*. Philadelphia and London, 1936
20. *Dead Man's Trail*. Philadelphia, 1937
21. *Mountain Chief: An Indian Legend for Children*. Philadelphia, 1938
22. *Ann Carmeny*. New York, 1941
23. *Jason Burr's First Case*, as David Kent. New York, 1941
24. *Brothers of Doom: The Story of the Pizarros of Peru*. New York, 1942
25. *A Knife Is Silent*, as David Kent. New York, 1947
26. *The Dice of God*. New York, 1956

Black, Laura
1. *Glendraco*. New York and London, 1977
2. *Ravenburn*. New York, 1978
3. *Castle Raven*. London, 1978
4. *Wild Cat*. New York and London, 1979
5. *Strathgallant*. New York and London, 1981

Blackburn, John (Fenwick)
British, born in 1923
1. *A Scent of New-Mown Hay*. London and New York, 1958
2. *Sour Apple Tree*. London, 1958
3. *Broken Boy*. London, 1959
4. *Dead Man Running*. London, 1960
5. *The Gaunt Woman*. London and New York, 1962
6. *Blue Octavo*. London, 1963
7. *Bound to Kill*. New York, 1963
8. *Colonel Bogus*. London, 1964
9. *Packed for Murder*. New York, 1964
10. *The Winds of Midnight*. London, 1964
11. *Murder at Midnight*. New York, 1964
12. *A Ring of Roses*. London, 1965
13. *A Wreath of Roses*. New York, 1965
14. *Children of the Night*. London, 1966
15. *The Reluctant Spy*. London, 1966
16. *The Flame and the Wind*. London, 1967
17. *Nothing But the Night*. London, 1968
18. *The Young Man from Lima*. London, 1968
19. *Bury Him Darkly*. London, 1969
20. *Blow the House Down*. London, 1970
21. *The Houseold Traitors*. London, 1971
22. *Devil Daddy*. London, 1972
23. *For Fear of Little Men*. London, 1972
24. *Deep Among the Dead Men*. London, 1973
25. *Our Lady of Pain*. London, 1974
26. *Mister Brown's Bodies*. London, 1975
27. *The Face of the Lion*. London, 1976
28. *The Cyclops Goblet*. London, 1977
29. *Dead Man's Handle*. London, 1978
30. *The Sins of the Father*. London, 1978

Blackmore, Jane
British
1. *Towards Tomorrow*. London, 1941
2. *They Carry a Torch*. London, 1943
3. *It Happened to Susan*. London, 1944
4. *Snow in June*. London, 1947
5. *The Square of Many Colours*. London, 1948
6. *So Dark the Mirror*. London, 1949
7. *The Nine Commandments*. London, 1950
8. *The Bridge of Strange Music*. London, 1952
9. *Beloved Stranger*. London, 1953
10. *Perilous Waters*. London, 1954
11. *Three Letters to Pan*. London, 1955
12. *The Closing Door*. London, 1956
13. *Storm in the Family*. London, 1956
14. *A Woman on Her Own*. London, 1957
15. *The Lonely House*. London, 1957
16. *Beware the Night*. London, 1958
17. *Dangerous Love*. London, 1958
18. *Tears in Paradise*. London, 1959
19. *The Missing Hour*. London, 1959
20. *Bitter Honey*. London, 1960
21. *A Trap for Lovers*. London, 1960
22. *The Night of the Stranger*. London, 1961
23. *The Dark Between the Stars*. London, 1961
24. *Two in Shadow*. London, 1962
25. *It Couldn't Happen to Me*. London, 1962
26. *Joanna*. London, 1963
27. *That Night*. London, 1963
28. *Flight into Love*. London, 1964
29. *Return to Love*. London, 19674
30. *Girl Alone*. London, 1965
31. *Man of Power*. London, 1966
32. *Miranda*. London, 1966
33. *Gold for My Girl*. London, 1967
34. *Raw Summer*. London, 1967
35. *The Other Room*. London, 1968

36. *Deed of Innocence.* New York, 1969
37. *The Velvet Trap.* New York, 1969
38. *The Lilac Is for Sharing.* London, 1969
39. *Lonely Night.* London, 1969
40. *Broomstick in the Hall.* New York, 1970
41. *Dance on a Hornet's Nest.* London, 1970
42. *Hunter's Mate.* London, 1971
43. *Stephanie.* New York, 1972
44. *The Room in the Tower.* London, 1972
45. *The Deep Pool.* London and New York, 1972
46. *My Sister Erica.* London, 1973
47. *The Cresselly Inheritance.* London, 1973
48. *A Love Forbidden.* London, 1974
49. *Angel's Tear.* New York, 1974
50. *Night of the Bonfire.* London and New York, 1974
51. *And Then There Was Georgia.* London and New York, 1975
52. *Lord of the Manor.* London, 1975
53. *Ravenden.* London, 1976
54. *Hawkridge.* New York, 1976
55. *Silver Unicorn.* London, 1977
56. *Of Wind and Fire.* Loughton (Eng), 1980
57. *Wildfire Love.* Loughton, 1980

Blackwood, Algernon (Henry)
British, born in 1869, died December 10, 1951
1. *John Silence, Physician Extraordinary.* London, 1908
2. *Jimbo: A Fantasy.* London and New York, 1909
3. *The Education of Uncle Paul.* London, 1909
4. *The Human Chord.* London and New York, 1910
5. *The Lost Valley and Other Stories.* London, 1910
6. *The Centaur.* London and New York, 1911
7. *Pan's Garden.* London and New York, 1912
8. *A Prisoner in Fairyland: The Book That "Uncle Paul" Wrote.* London and New York, 1913
9. *Incredible Adventures.* London and New York, 1914
10. *Ten Minute Stories.* London and New York, 1914
11. *The Extra Day.* London and New York, 1915
12. *Julius Le Vallon.* London and New York, 1916
13. *The Wave: An Egyptian Aftermath.* London and New York, 1916
14. *Day and Night Stories.* London and New York, 1917
15. *The Garden of Survival.* London and New York, 1918
16. *The Promise of Air.* London and New York, 1918
17. *Karma: A Re-incarnation Play,* with Violet Pearn. London and New York, 1918
18. *Through the Crack,* with Violet Pearn. London and New York, 1920
19. *The Bright Messenger.* London, 1921
20. *The Wolves of Gods and Other Fey Stories,* with Wilfred Wilson. London and New York, 1921
21. *Episodes Before Thirty.* London, 1923
22. *Tongues of Fire and Other Sketches.* London, 1924
23. *The Dance of Death and Other Tales.* London, 1927
24. *Ancient Sorceries and Other Tales.* London, 1927
25. *Sambo and Snitch.* Oxford (Eng) and New York, 1927
26. *Mr. Cupboard.* Oxford, 1928
27. *Dudley and Gilderoy: A Nonsense.* London and New York, 1929
28. *Full Circle.* London, 1929
29. *Strange Stories.* London, 1929
30. *Stories.* London, 1930
31. *By Underground.* Oxford, 1930
32. *The Willows and Other Queer Tales.* London, 1932
33. *The Italian Conjuror.* Oxford, 1932
34. *Maria—of England—in the Rain.* Oxford, 1933
35. *Adventures Before Thirty.* London, 1934
36. *The Fruit Stoners.* London, 1934
37. *Sergeant Poppett and Policeman James.* Oxford, 1934
38. *Shocks.* London, 1935
39. *How the Circus Came to Tea.* Oxford, 1936
40. *The Tales of Algernon Blackwood.* London, 1938
41. *Selected Tales: Stories of the Supernatural and the Uncanny.* London, 1942
42. *The Doll and One Other.* Sauk City (WI), 1946
43. *Tales of the Uncanny and Supernatural.* London, 1949
44. *In the Realm of Terror: 8 Haunting Tales.* New York, 1957
45. *Selected Tales.* London, 1964
46. *Tales of Terror and the Unknown.* New York, 1965
47. *The Insanity of Jones and Other Stories.* London, 1966
48. *Ancient Sorceries and Other Stories.* London, 1968
49. *Tales of the Mysterious and Macabre.* London, 1968

Blake, Forrester (Avery)
American, born in 1912
1. *Riding the Mustang Trail.* New York, 1935
2. *Denver, Rocky Mountain Capital.* Denver, 1945
3. *Johnny Christmas.* New York, 1948
4. *Wilderness Passage.* New York, 1953
5. *The Franciscan.* New York, 1963

Blake, Stephanie
1. *Flowers of Fire.* Chicago, 1977
2. *Daughter of Destiny.* Chicago, 1977
3. *Blazon of Passion.* Chicago, 1978
4. *So Wicked My Desire.* Chicago and Feltham (Eng), 1979
5. *Secret Sins.* Chicago, 1980
6. *Wicked Is My Flesh.* Chicago, 1980
7. *Scarlet Kisses.* Chicago, 1981
8. *Unholy Desires.* Chicago, 1981

Blanc, Suzzane
American
1. *The Green Stone.* New York, 1961
2. *The Yellow Villa.* New York, 1964
3. *The Rose Window.* New York, 1967
4. *The Sea Troll.* New York, 1969

Bloch, Robert
American, born in 1917
Pseudonym: Collier Young
1. *The Opener of the Way.* Sauk City (WI), 1945
2. *Sea-Kissed.* London, 1945
3. *The Scarf.* New York, 1947
4. *The Scarf of Passion.* New York, 1948
5. *The Kidnapper.* New York, 1954
6. *Spiderweb.* New York, 1954
7. *The Will to Kill.* New York, 1954
8. *Shooting Star.* New York, 1958
9. *Terror in the Night and Other Stories.* New York, 1958
10. *Psycho.* New York, 1959
11. *Pleasant Dreams—Nightmares.* Sauk City, 1959
12. *The Dead Beat.* New York, 1960
13. *Firebug.* Evanston (IL), 1961
14. *Blood Runs Cold.* New York, 1961
15. *Nightmares.* New York, 1961
16. *More Nightmares.* New York, 1961
17. *The Couch.* New York, 1962
18. *Terror.* New York, 1962
19. *Yours Truly, Jack the Ripper: Tales of Horror.* New York, 1962
20. *The Eighth Stage of Fandom: Selections from 25 Years of Fan Writing.* Chicago, 1962
21. *Atoms and Evil.* New York, 1962
22. *Horror-7.* New York, 1963
23. *Bogey Men.* New York, 1963

24. *Tales in a Jugular Vein.* New York, 1965
25. *The House of the Hatchet and Other Tales of Horror.* London, 1965
26. *Torture Garden.* London, 1965
27. *The Skull of the Marquis de Sade and Other Stories.* New York, 1965
28. *Chamber of Horrors.* New York, 1966
29. *The Living Demons.* New York, 1967
30. *Ladies Day/This Crowded Earth.* New York, 1968
31. *The Star Stalker.* New York, 1968
32. *The Todd Dossier,* as Collier Young. New York and London, 1969
33. *Dragons and Nightmares.* Baltimore (MD), 1969
34. *Bloch and Bradbury.* New York, 1969
35. *Fever Dream and Other Fantasies.* London, 1970
36. *It's All in Your Mind.* New York, 1971
37. *Sneak Preview.* New York, 1971
38. *Fear Today—Gone Tomorrow.* New York, 1971
39. *Night-World.* New York, 1972
40. *American Gothic.* New York, 1974
41. *Cold Chills.* New York, 1977
42. *The King of Terrors.* Yonkers (NY), 1977
43. *The Best of Robert Bloch.* New York, 1977
44. *The Laughter of the Ghoul.* West Warwick (RI), 1977
45. *Out of the Mouths of Graves.* Yonkers, 1978
46. *The Serpent Was Cunning.* New York, 1979
47. *Strange Eons.* Browns Mills (NJ), 1979
48. *Such Stuff as Screams Are Made Of.* New York, 1979
49. *Mysteries of the Worm.* New York, 1979

Blochman, Lawrence G. (Goldtree)
American, born in 1900, died January 22, 1975
1. *Bombay Mail.* Boston and London, 1934
2. *Bengal Fire.* London, 1937
3. *Red Snow at Darjeeling.* London, 1938
4. *Midnight Sailing.* New York, 1938
5. *Blow-Down.* New York, 1939
6. *Wives to Burn.* New York and London, 1934
7. *See You at the Morgue.* New York, 1941
8. *Diagnosis Homocide.* Philadelphia, 1950
9. *Death Walks in Marble Halls.* New York, 1951
10. *Pursuit.* New York, 1951
11. *Menace.* London, 1951
12. *Rather Cool for Mayhem.* Philadelphia, 1951
13. *Recipe for Homicide.* Philadelphia, 1952
14. *Here's How! A Round-the-World Bar Book.* New York, 1957
15. *Doctor Squibb: The Life and Times of a Rugged Idealist.* New York, 1958
16. *My Daughter, Maria Callas,* with Evangelina Callas. New York, 1960
17. *Alone No Longer,* with Stanley Stein. New York, 1963
18. *Clues for Dr. Coffee.* Philadelphia, 1964
19. *Are You Misunderstood?* with Harlan Logan. New York, 1965
20. *The Power of Life or Death,* with Michael V. DiSalle. New York, 1965
21. *Second Choice,* with Michael V. DiSalle. New York, 1966
22. *Understanding Your Body.* New York, 1968
23. *Wake Up Your Body.* New York, 1969
24. *Help Without Psychoanalysis,* with Herbert Fensterheim. New York, 1971
25. *Mister Mayor,* with A.J. Cervantes. Los Angeles, 1974

Block, Lawrence
American, born in 1938
Pseudonyms: Chip Harrison, Paul Kavanagh
1. *Death Pulls a Double Cross.* New York, 1961
2. *Mona.* New York, 1961
3. *The Case of the Pornographic Photos.* New York, 1961
4. *Markham: The Case of the Pornographic Photos.* New York, 1965
5. *The Girl with the Long Green Heart.* New York, 1965
6. *A Guide Book to Australian Coins.* Racine (WI), 1965
7. *Swiss Shooting Talers and Medals,* with Delbert Ray Krause. Racine, 1965
8. *The Cancelled Czech.* New York, 1966
9. *The Thief Who Couldn't Sleep.* New York, 1966
10. *Deadly Honeymoon.* New York, 1967
11. *Tanner's Twelve Swingers.* New York, 1967
12. *Two for Tanner.* New York, 1967
13. *Here Comes a Hero.* New York, 1968
14. *Tanner's Tiger.* New York, 1968
15. *After the First Death.* New York, 1969
16. *The Specialists.* New York, 1969
17. *Such Men Are Dangerous,* as Paul Kavanagh. New York, 1969
18. *Me Tanner, You Jane.* New York, 1970
19. *No Score,* as Chip Harrison. New York, 1970
20. *The Triumph of Evil,* as Paul Kavanagh. Cleveland (OH), 1971
21. *Ronald Rabbit Is a Dirty Old Man,* as Chip Harrison. New York, 1971
22. *Chip Harrison Scores Again,* as Chip Harrison. New York, 1971
23. *Make Out with Murder,* as Chip Harrison. New York, 1974
24. *Not Comin' Home to You.* New York, 1974
25. *The Topless Tulip Caper,* as Chip Harrison. New York, 1975
26. *In the Midst of Death.* New York, 1976
27. *Sins of the Fathers.* New York, 1977
28. *Time to Murder and Create.* New York, 1977
29. *Burglars Can't Be Choosers.* New York, 1977
30. *The Burglar in the Closet.* New York, 1978
31. *The Burglar Who Liked to Quote Kipling.* New York, 1979
32. *Writing the Novel: From Plot to Print.* Cincinnati, 1979

Bloom, Ursula
British, died October 29, 1984
Pseudonyms: Sheila Burns, Mary Essex, Rachel Harvey, Deborah Mann, Lozania Prole, Sara Sloane
1. *Tiger.* Privately printed, ca.1903
2. *Winifred.* Privately printed, 1903
3. *Girlie.* Privately printed, 1904
4. *The Cherry Hat.* Privately printed, 1904
5. *The Great Beginning.* London, 1924
6. *Vagabond Harvest.* London, 1925
7. *The Driving of Destiny.* London, 1925
8. *Our Lady of Marble.* London, 1926
9. *The Judge of Jerusalem.* London, 1926
10. *Spilled Salt: The Story of a Spy.* London, 1927
11. *Candleshades: The Story of a Soul.* London, 1927
12. *Base Metal: The Story of a Man.* London, 1928
13. *An April After.* London, 1928
14. *Tomorrow for Apricots.* London, 1929
15. *The Eternal Tomorrow.* New York, 1929
16. *Veneer.* New York, 1929
17. *Tarnish.* London, 1929
18. *The Secret Lover.* London, 1930
19. *The Passionate Heart.* London, 1930
20. *A Lamp in the Darkness: A Series of Essays on Religion.* London, 1930
21. *The Gossamer Dream.* London, 1931
22. *Pack Mule.* London, 1931
23. *Trackless Way.* London, 1931
24. *Fruit on the Bough: The Story of a Brother and Sister.* London, 1931

25. *Flood of Passion.* New York, 1932
26. *The Pilgrim Soul.* London, 1932
27. *Breadwinners.* London, 1932
28. *The Cypresses Grow Dark.* London, 1932
29. *Love's Playthings.* London, 1932
30. *The Log of a Naval Officer's Wife.* London, 1932
31. *Rose Sweetman.* London, 1933
32. *Spread Wings.* London, 1933
33. *Better to Marry.* New York, 1933
34. *Wonder Cruise.* London, 1933
35. *Enchanted Journey.* London, 1933
36. *Love Is Everything.* London, 1933
37. *Love, Old and New.* New York, 1933
38. *Crazy Quilt: A Volume of Stories.* London, 1933
39. *Mistress of None.* London, 1933
40. *Mediterranean Madness.* London, 1934
41. *The Questing Trout.* London, 1934
42. *Pastoral.* London, 1934
43. *Young Parent.* London, 1934
44. *Holiday Mood.* London, 1934
45. *This Is Marriage.* London, 1935
46. *Harvest of a House.* London, 1935
47. *The Gipsy Vans Come Through.* London, 1936
48. *The Laughing Lady.* London, 1936
49. *Laughter in Cheyne Walk.* London, 1936
50. *Marriage of Pierrot.* London, 1936
51. *The Passionate Adventure,* as Sheila Burns. London, 1936
52. *Three Cedars.* London, 1937
53. *Leaves Before the Storm.* London, 1937
54. *Dream Awhile,* as Sheila Burns. London, 1937
55. *Take a Chance,* as Sheila Burns. London, 1937
56. *The Golden Venture.* London, 1938
57. *Lily-of-the-Valley.* London, 1938
58. *Honeymoon Island,* as Sheila Burns. London, 1938
59. *Lady! This Is Love,* as Sheila Burns. London, 1938
60. *The Brittle Shadow.* London, 1938
61. *Without Make-Up.* London, 1938
62. *The ABC of Authorship.* London, 1938
63. *A Cad's Guide to Cruising.* London, 1938
64. *Beloved Creditor.* London, 1939
65. *These Roots Go Deep.* London, 1939
66. *Week-end Bride,* as Sheila Burns. London, 1939
67. *Wonder Trip,* as Sheila Burns. London, 1939
68. *Letters to My Son.* London, 1939
69. *Trailing Glory.* London, 1940
70. *The Woman Who Was To-morrow.* London, 1940
71. *The Flying Swans.* London, 1940
72. *Adventurous Heart,* as Sheila Burns. London, 1940
73. *Meet Love on Holiday,* as Sheila Burns. London, 1940
74. *Haircut for Samson,* as Mary Essex. London, 1940
75. *The Log of No Lady, Being the Story of a London Woman Evacuated Before the Outbreak of War.* London, 1940
76. *Spring in September.* London, 1941
77. *Silver Orchids.* London, 1941
78. *The Virgin Thorn.* London, 1941
79. *Dinah's Husband.* London, 1941
80. *The Golden Flame.* London, 1941
81. *Romance Is Mine,* as Sheila Burns. London, 1941
82. *The Stronger Passion,* as Sheila Burns. London, 1941
83. *Nesting Cats,* as Mary Essex. London, 1941
84. *Eve Didn't Care,* as Mary Essex. London, 1941
85. *The Housewife's Beauty Book.* London, 1941
86. *Marry To Taste,* as Mary Essex. London, 1942
87. *Age Cannot Wither.* London, 1942
88. *Lovely Shadow.* London, 1942
89. *Bridal Sweet,* as Sheila Burns. London, 1942
90. *Thy Bride Am I,* as Sheila Burns. London, 1942
91. *Time, Tide and I.* London, 1942
92. *Romantic Fugitive,* as Sheila Burns. London, 1943
93. *No Lady Buys a Cot.* London, 1943
94. *Marriage in Heaven.* London, 1943
95. *A Robin in a Cage.* London, 1943
96. *Bride Alone,* as Sheila Burns. New York, 1943
97. *Freddy for Fun,* as Mary Essex. London, 1943
98. *Wartime Beauty.* London, 1943
99. *A Paymaster in Every Family.* London, 1943
100. *One Wedding, Two Brides.* London, 1943
101. *Nightshade at Morning.* London, 1944
102. *No Lady in Bed.* London, 1944
103. *The Fourth Cedar.* London, 1944
104. *Romance of Jenny W.R.E.N.,* as Sheila Burns. London, 1944
105. *The Amorous Bicycle,* as Mary Essex. London, 1944
106. *Me—After the War: A Book for Girls Considering the Future.* London, 1944
107. *Divorce? Of Course,* as Mary Essex. London, 1945
108. *The Painted Lady.* London, 1945
109. *The Faithless Dove.* London, 1945
110. *Jenny W.R.E.N.,* as Sheila Burns. New York, 1945
111. *Vagrant Lover,* as Sheila Burns. London, 1945
112. *The Changed Village.* London, 1945
113. *The Little Fir Tree.* London, 1945
114. *Rude Forefathers.* London, 1945
115. *Questions Answered about Knitting; about Beauty.* London, 2 vols., 1945-46
116. *Hold Hard, My Heart,* as Sheila Burns. London, 1946
117. *Bride—Maybe,* as Sheila Burns. London, 1946
118. *Three Sons.* London, 1946
119. *A Garden for My Child.* London, 1946
120. *Ursula's Cook Book for the Woman Who Has No Time to Spare.* London, 1946
121. *No Lady with a Pen.* London, 1947
122. *Adam's Daughters.* London, 1947
123. *Alien Corn.* London, 1947
124. *Desire Is Not Dead,* as Sheila Burns. London, 1947
125. *What's in a Name? A Nativity Play.* London, 1947
126. *No Lady Meets No Gentleman.* London, 1947
127. *Pumpkin the Pup.* London, 1947
128. *Smugglers Cave.* London, 1947
129. *Caravan for Three.* London, 1947
130. *Displaced Person.* London, 1948
131. *Young Kangaroos Prefer Riding,* as Mary Essex. London, 1948
132. *Six Fools and a Fairy,* as Mary Essex. London, 1948
133. *The Chance Romance,* as Sheila Burns. London, 1948
134. *Air Liner,* as Sheila Burns. London, 1948
135. *Tomorrow Is Eternal,* as Sheila Burns. London, 1948
136. *Facade.* London, 1948
137. *Next Tuesday.* London, 1949
138. *No Lady in the Cart.* London, 1949
139. *Gipsy Flower.* London, 1949
140. *Faint with Pursuit,* as Sheila Burns. London, 1949
141. *No Trespassers in Love,* as Sheila Burns. London, 1949
142. *Full Fruit Flavour,* as Mary Essex. London, 1949
143. *The Herring's Nest,* as Mary Essex. London, 1949
144. *Our Dearest Emma,* as Lozania Prole. London, 1949
145. *Cookery.* London, 1949
146. *The Cuckoo Never Weds,* as Sheila Burns. London, 1950
147. *Primula and Hyacinth.* New York, 1950
148. *Not Free to Love,* as Sheila Burns. London, 1950
149. *The King's Wife.* London, 1950
150. *Eleanor Jowitt, Antiques.* London, 1950
151. *The Song of Philomel.* London, 1950
152. *An Apple for the Doctor,* as Mary Essex. London, 1950
153. *Tea Is So Intoxicating,* as Mary Essex. London, 1950
154. *The Magnificent Courtesan,* as Lozania Prole. New York, 1950

155. *Three Girls Come to Town.* London, 1950
156. *Dark Gentleman, Fair Lady,* as Mary Essex. London, 1951
157. *A Gentleman Called James,* as Mary Essex. London, 1951
158. *How Dark, My Lady! A Novel Concerning the Life of William Shakespeare.* London, 1951
159. *Pavilion.* London, 1951
160. *Nine Lives.* London, 1951
161. *Orange Blossom for Sandra.* London, 1951
162. *The Sentimental Family.* London, 1951
163. *Heaven Lies Ahead,* as Sheila Burns. New York, 1951
164. *Hold Back the Heart,* as Sheila Burns. New York, 1951
165. *Rosebud and Stardust,* as Sheila Burns. London, 1951
166. *Emma Hart,* as Lozania Prole. Toronto, 1951
167. *Mum's Girl Was No Lady.* London, 1951
168. *NY World round the Corner.* London, 1951
169. *Live Happily—Love Song,* as Sheila Burns. London, 1952
170. *Love Me To-morrow,* as Sheila Burns. London, 1952
171. *As Bends the Bough.* London, 1952
172. *Twilight of a Tudor.* London, 1952
173. *Romantic Intruder,* as Sheila Burns. London, 1952
174. *She Had What It Takes,* as Mary Essex. London, 1952
175. *Forty Is Beginning,* as Mary Essex. London, 1952
176. *For the Bride.* London, 1952
177. *Tomorrow We Marry,* as Mary Essex. London, 1953
178. *Beloved and Unforgettable,* as Sheila Burns. London, 1953
179. *Moon Song.* London, 1953
180. *Sea Fret.* London, 1953
181. *Marriage of Leonora.* London, 1953
182. *The First Elizabeth.* London, 1953
183. *Pretty, Witty Nell!* as Lozania Prole. London and New York, 1953
184. *Matthew, Mark, Luke, and John.* London, 1954
185. *Please Burn After Reading,* as Sheila Burns. London, 1954
186. *Danielle, My Darling,* as Mary Essex. London, 1954
187. *The Fabulous Nell Gwynne,* as Lozania Prole. Toronto, 1954
188. *To-night, Josephine!* as Lozania Prole. London and New York, 1954
189. *The King's Pleasure,* as Lozania Prole. London and New York, 1954
190. *Trilogy.* London, 1954
191. *Curtain Call for the Guv'nor: A Biography of George Edwardes.* London, 1954
192. *The Girls' Book of Popular Hobbies.* London, 1954
193. *Hitler's Eva.* London, 1954
194. *How Dear Is My Delight,* as Sheila Burns. London, 1955
195. *Adventure in Romance,* as Sheila Burns. London, 1955
196. *Daughters of the Rectory.* London, 1955
197. *The Gracious Lady.* London, 1955
198. *The Girl Who Loved Crippen.* London, 1955
199. *The Silver Ring.* London, 1955
200. *The Enchanting Courtesan,* as Lozania Prole. London, 1955
201. *The Tides of Spring Flow Fast.* London, 1956
202. *Romantic Summer Sea,* as Sheila Burns. London, 1956
203. *The Sweet Impulse,* as Sheila Burns. London, 1956
204. *The Passionate Springtime,* as Mary Essex. London, 1956
205. *My Wanton Tudor Rose: The Love Story of Lady Katheryn Howard,* as Lozania Prole. London, 1956
206. *Victorian Vinaigrette.* London, 1956
207. *How Rich Is Love?,* as Sheila Burns. London, 1957
208. *The Beloved Man,* as Sheila Burns. London, 1957
209. *Brief Springtime.* London, 1957
210. *Forbidden Fiance,* as Mary Essex. London, 1957
211. *The Dark Lover,* as Mary Essex. London, 1957
212. *The Little Victoria,* as Lozania Prole. London, 1957
213. *A Queen for England,* as Lozania Prole. London, 1957
214. *The Elegant Edwardians.* London, 1957
215. *The Abiding City.* London, 1958
216. *Monkey Tree in a Flower Pot.* London, 1958
217. *This Dragon of Desire,* as Sheila Burns. London, 1958
218. *A Nightingale Once Sang,* as Mary Essex. London, 1958
219. *It's Spring, My Heart!,* as Mary Essex. London, 1958
220. *Harry's Last Love,* as Lozania Prole. London, 1958
221. *The Stuart Sisters,* as Lozania Prole. London, 1958
222. *Down to the Sea in Ships.* London, 1958
223. *He Lit the Lamp: A Biography of Professor A.M. Low.* London, 1958
224. *Wanting to Write: A Complete Guide for Would-Be Writers.* London, 1958
225. *The Storm Bird,* as Sheila Burns. London, 1959
226. *Undarkening Green.* London, 1959
227. *Romance of Summer,* as Mary Essex. London, 1959
228. *This Man Is Not for Marrying,* as Mary Essex. London, 1959
229. *Consort to the Queen,* as Lozania Prole. London, 1959
230. *The Little Wig-Maker of Bread Street,* as Lozania Prole. London, 1959
231. *The Inspired Needle.* London, 1959
232. *Youth at the Gate.* London, 1959
233. *The Romance of Charles Dickens.* London, 1960
234. *The Thieving Magpie.* London, 1960
235. *The Lasting Lover,* as Sheila Burns. London, 1960
236. *Doctor Gregory's Partner,* as Sheila Burns. London, 1960
237. *The Fugitive Romantic,* as Mary Essex. London, 1960
238. *The Love Story of Dr. Duke,* as Mary Essex. London, 1960
239. *For Love of the King,* as Lozania Prole. London, 1960
240. *The Tudor Boy,* as Lozania Prole. London, 1960
241. *The Woman Called Mary,* as Deborah Mann. London, 1960
242. *Sixty Years at Home.* London, 1960
243. *The Cactus Has Courage.* London, 1961
244. *Prelude to Yesterday.* London, 1961
245. *Doctor to the Rescue,* as Sheila Burns. London, 1961
246. *The Dishearted Doctor,* as Sheila Burns. London, 1961
247. *A Sailor's Love,* as Mary Essex. London, 1961
248. *Doctor on Call,* as Mary Essex. London, 1961
249. *The Queen's Midwife,* as Lozania Prole. London, 1961
250. *My! My Little Queen!,* as Lozania Prole. London, 1961
251. *War Isn't Wonderful.* London, 1961
252. *Harvest-Home Come Sunday.* London, 1962
253. *Ship in a Bottle.* London, 1962
254. *Dr. Irresistible, M.D.,* as Sheila Burns. London, 1962
255. *The Eyes of Doctor Karl.* London, 1962
256. *Date with a Doctor,* as Mary Essex. London, 1962
257. *Dr. Guardian of the Gate,* as Mary Essex. London, 1962
258. *A King's Plaything,* as Lozania Prole. London, 1962
259. *Queen Guillotine,* as Lozania Prole. London, 1962
260. *Nurse from Killarney,* as Mary Essex. London, 1963
261. *Heartbreak Surgeon,* as Sheila Burns. London, 1963
262. *Theatre Sister in Love,* as Sheila Burns. London, 1963
263. *The Gated Road.* London, 1963
264. *A Strange Patient for Sister Smith,* as Mary Essex. London, 1963
265. *The Sangor Hospital Story,* as Mary Essex. London, 1963
266. *The Ghost That Haunted a King,* as Lozania Prole. London, 1963
267. *The Wild Daughter,* as Lozania Prole. London, 1963
268. *Daughter of the Devil,* as Lozania Prole. London, 1963
269. *Mrs. Bunthorpe's Respects: A Chronicle of Cooks.* London, 1963
270. *Parson Extraordinary.* London, 1963
271. *The Hard-Hearted Doctor,* as Mary Essex. London, 1964
272. *Doctor and Lover,* as Mary Essex. London, 1964
273. *The Ring Tree.* London, 1964
274. *The House That Died Alone.* London, 1964
275. *When Doctors Love,* as Sheila Burns. London, 1964
276. *Doctor's Distress,* as Sheila Burns. London 1964

277. *Doctor Delightful,* as Sheila Burns. London, 1964
278. *Henry's Golden Queen,* as Lozania Prole. London, 1964
279. *The Three Passionate Queens,* as Lozania Prole. London, 1964
280. *The Rose of Norfolk.* London, 1964
281. *The Quiet Village.* London, 1965
282. *The Ugly Head.* London, 1965
283. *Dare-Devil Doctor,* as Mary Essex. London, 1965
284. *Romantic Theatre Sister,* as Mary Essex. London, 1965
285. *Sweet Nell,* as Lozania Prole. London, 1965
286. *Marlborough's Unfair Lady,* as Lozania Prole. London, 1965
287. *The Haunted Headsman,* as Lozania Prole. London, 1965
288. *Price above Rubies.* London, 1965
289. *The Dandelion Clock.* London, 1966
290. *Doctor Called David,* as Sheila Burns. London, 1966
291. *Doctor Devine,* as Sheila Burns. London, 1966
292. *A Surgeon's Sweetheart,* as Sheila Burns. London, 1966
293. *Hospital of the Heart,* as Mary Essex. London, 1966
294. *The Dangerous Husband,* as Lozania Prole. London, 1966
295. *Nelson's Love,* as Lozania Prole. London, 1966
296. *A Woman Called Mary,* as Deborah Mann. London, 1966
297. *Rosemary for Stratford-on-Avon.* London, 1966
298. *The Mightier Sword.* London, 1966
299. *The Little Nurse,* as Mary Essex. London, 1967
300. *The Romance of Dr. Dinah,* as Mary Essex. London, 1967
301. *Assistant Matron,* as Mary Essex. London, 1967
302. *The Beauty Surgeon,* as Sheila Burns. London, 1967
303. *The Flying Nurse,* as Sheila Burns. London, 1967
304. *The Old Adam.* London, 1967
305. *Two Pools in a Field.* London, 1967
306. *Romantic Cottage Hospital,* as Sheila Burns. London, 1967
307. *The Dark-Eyed Queen,* as Lozania Prole. London, 1967
308. *King Henry's Sweetheart,* as Lozania Prole. London, 1967
309. *The Queen Who Was a Nun,* as Lozania Prole. London, 1967
310. *The Village Nurse,* as Rachel Harvey. London, 1967
311. *A Roof and Four Walls.* London, 1967
312. *The Dark-eyed Sister,* as Sheila Burns. London, 1968
313. *Casualty Ward,* as Sheila Burns. London, 1968
314. *Acting Sister,* as Sheila Burns. London, 1968
315. *Yesterday's Tomorrow.* London, 1968
316. *The Dragonfly.* London, 1968
317. *The Adorable Doctor,* as Mary Essex. London, 1968
318. *The Ghost of Fiddler's Hill,* as Mary Essex. London, 1968
319. *The Sympathetic Surgeon,* as Mary Essex. London, 1968
320. *The Greatest Nurse of Them All,* as Lozania Prole. London, 1968
321. *Prince Philanderer,* as Lozania Prole. London, 1968
322. *The Loves of a Virgin Princess,* as Lozania Prole. London, 1968
323. *Now Barrabas Was a Robber,* as Deborah Mann. London, 1968
324. *Dearest Doctor,* as Rachel Harvey. London, 1968
325. *Weep Not for Dreams,* as Rachel Harvey. London, 1968
326. *The Flight of the Falcon.* London, 1969
327. *The Hunter's Moon.* London, 1969
328. *Surgeon at Sea,* as Sheila Burns. London, 1969
329. *Doctor on Duty Bound,* as Mary Essex. London, 1969
330. *When a Woman Doctor Loves,* as Mary Essex. London, 1969
331. *Sister Marie-Antoinette,* as Lozania Prole. London, 1969
332. *The Boutique of the Singing Clocks,* as Lozania Prole. London, 1969
333. *The Song of Salome,* as Deborah Mann. London, 1969
334. *The Little Matron of the Cottage Hospital,* as Rachel Harvey. London, 1969
335. *The House of Kent.* London, 1969
336. *The Nurse Who Shocked the Matron,* as Sheila Burns. London, 1970
337. *The Tune of Time.* London, 1970
338. *The Dangerous Doctor,* as Mary Essex. London, 1970
339. *The Enchanting Princess,* as Lozania Prole. London, 1970
340. *The Last Tsarina,* as Lozania Prole. London, 1970
341. *Darling District Nurse,* as Rachel Harvey. London, 1970
342. *Nurse on Bodwin Moor,* as Rachel Harvey. London, 1970
343. *Rosemary for Frinton.* London, 1970
344. *Perchance to Dream.* London, 1971
345. *The Caravan of Chance.* London, 1971
346. *Sister Loving Heart,* as Sheila Burns. London, 1971
347. *Heart Surgeon,* as Mary Essex. London, 1971
348. *Judas Iscariot—Traitor!,* as Lozania Prole. London, 1971
349. *A Queen for the Regent,* as Lozania Prole. London, 1971
350. *The Two Queen Annes,* as Lozania Prole. London, 1971
351. *Doctor Called Harry,* as Rachel Harvey. London, 1971
352. *Sister to a Stranger,* as Rachel Harvey. London, 1971
353. *The Great Tomorrow.* London, 1971
354. *Rosemary for Chelsea.* London, 1971
355. *The Fascinating Doctor,* as Mary Essex. London, 1972
356. *The Nurse Who Fell in Love,* as Mary Essex. London, 1972
357. *Edwardian Day-Dream.* London, 1972
358. *Cornish Rhapsody,* as Sheila Burns. London, 1972
359. *Romance and Nurse Margaret,* as Sheila Burns. London, 1972
360. *The Ten-Day Queen,* as Lozania Prole. London, 1972
361. *Taj Mahal, Shrine of Desire,* as Lozania Prole. London, 1972
362. *Love Has No Secrets,* as Rachel Harvey. London, 1972
363. *The Duke of Windsor.* London, 1972
364. *The Cheval Glass.* London, 1973
365. *The Old Rectory.* London, 1973
366. *A Nurse Called Lisa,* as Mary Essex. London, 1973
367. *The Queen's Daughters,* as Lozania Prole. London, 1973
368. *The Gipsy Lover,* as Rachel Harvey. London, 1973
369. *Requesting the Pleasure.* London, 1973
370. *Princesses in Love.* London, 1973
371. *Mirage on the Horizon.* London, 1974
372. *The Old Elm Tree.* London, 1974
373. *The Dark Farm,* as Mary Essex. London, 1974
374. *A Doctor's Love,* as Mary Essex. London, 1974
375. *Albert the Beloved,* as Lozania Prole. London, 1974
376. *The Last Love of a King,* as Lozania Prole. London, 1974
377. *The Doctor Who Fell in Love,* as Rachel Harvey. London, 1974
378. *The Twisted Road.* London, 1975
379. *The Lass a King Loved,* as Lozania Prole. London, 1975
380. *The King's Daughter,* as Lozania Prole. London, 1975
381. *The Love Story of Nurse Julie,* as Rachel Harvey. London, 1975
382. *The Royal Baby.* London, 1975
383. *The Turn of Life's Tide.* London, 1976
384. *The Bells Still Ring,* as Sheila Burns. London, 1976
385. *When Paris Fell,* as Lozania Prole. London, 1976
386. *Pilate's Wife,* as Deborah Mann. London, 1976
387. *Life Is No Fairy Tale.* London, 1976
388. *The Great Queen Consort.* London, 1976
389. *The House on the Hill.* London, 1977
390. *The Fire and the Rose.* Canoga Park (CA), 1977
391. *Edward and Victoria.* London, 1977
392. *The Woman Doctor.* London, 1978
393. *Bittersweet.* Canoga Park, 1978
394. *Born for Love.* Canoga Park, 1978
395. *Mirage of Love.* Canoga Park, 1978
396. *Sunday Love.* Canoga Park, 1978
397. *A Change of Heart.* Canoga Park, 1979
398. *Forever Autumn.* Canoga Park, 1979
399. *Gypsy Flame.* Canoga Park, 1979
400. *Honor's Price.* Canoga Park, 1979

401. *The Queen's Affair.* Canoga Park, 1979
402. *Sweet Spring of April.* Canoga Park, 1979

Bodkin, M. M'Donnell [Matthias M'Donnell Bodkin]
Irish, born 1850, died June 7, 1933
Pseudonym: Crom a Boo
1. *Poteen Punch, Strong, Hot, and Sweet, Being a Succession of Irish After-Dinner Stories,* as Crom a Boo. Dublin, 1890
2. *Pat o' Nine Tales and One Over.* Dublin and New York, 1894
3. *Lord Edward Fitzgerald.* London, 1896
4. *White Magic.* London, 1897
5. *A Stolen Life.* London, 1898
6. *Paul Beck, The Rule of Thumb Detective.* London, 1898
7. *The Rebels.* London, 1899
8. *Dora Myrl, The Lady Detective.* London, 1900
9. *A Bear Squeeze; or, Her Second Self.* London, 1901
10. *A Modern Miracle.* London, 1902
11. *Shillelagh and Shamrock.* London, 1902
12. *A Modern Robin Hood.* London, 1903
13. *In the Days of Goldsmith.* London, 1903
14. *Patsey the Omadawn.* London, 1904
15. *A Madcap Marriage.* London, 1905
16. *A Trip Through the States and a Talk with the President.* Dublin, 1907
17. *The Quests of Paul Beck.* London, 1908
18. *The Capture of Paul Beck.* London, 1909
19. *True Man and Traitor; or, The Rising of Emmet.* London, 1910
20. *Young Beck: A Chip of the Old Block.* London, 1911
21. *Grattan's Parliament, Before and After.* London, 1912
22. *His Brother's Keeper.* London, 1913
23. *The Test.* London, 1914
24. *Behind the Picture.* London, 1914
25. *Recollections of an Irish Judge: Press, Bar, and Parliament.* London and New York, 1914
26. *Pigeon Blood Rubies.* London, 1915
27. *Old Rowley.* London, 1916
28. *Famous Irish Trials.* Dublin, 1918
29. *When Youth Meets Youth.* Dublin and New York, 1920
30. *Another Considered Judgement: Second Report of Judge Bodkin.* Dublin, 1921
31. *Hunt the Hare.* Dublin, 1926
32. *Kitty the Madcap.* Dublin, 1927
33. *The Lottery,* as Crom a Boo. Dublin, 1927
34. *Guilty ot Not Guilty?* Dublin, 1929
35. *Paul Beck, Detective.* Dublin, 1929

Boland, John [Bertram John Boland]
British, born in 1913, died November 9, 1976
1. *White August.* London and New York, 1955
2. *No Refuge.* London, 1956
3. *Queer Fish.* London, 1958
4. *The League of Gentlemen.* London, 1958
5. *Mysterious Way.* London, 1959
6. *Bitter Fortune.* London, 1959
7. *Operation Red Carpet.* London, 1959
8. *The Midas Touch.* London, 1960
9. *Negative Value.* London, 1960
10. *Free-Lance Journalism.* London, 1960
11. *Short-Story Writing.* London, 1960
12. *The Gentlemen Reform.* London, 1961
13. *Inside Job.* London, 1961
14. *Vendetta.* London, 1961
15. *The Golden Fleece.* London, 1961
16. *The Gentlemen at Large.* London, 1962
17. *Fatal Error.* London, 1962
18. *Counterpol.* London, 1963
19. *The Catch.* London, 1964
20. *Counterpol in Paris.* London, 1964
21. *The Good Citizens.* London, 1965
22. *The Disposal Unit.* London, 1966
23. *The Gusher.* London, 1967
24. *Painted Lady.* London, 1967
25. *Breakdown.* London, 1968
26. *The Fourth Grave.* London, 1969
27. *The Shakespeare Curse.* London, 1969
28. *Kidnap.* London, 1970
29. *The Big Job.* London, 1970
30. *The Trade of Kings.* Crowborough (Eng), 1972
31. *Murder in Company,* with Philip King. London, 1973
32. *Short Story Technique.* Crowborough, 1973
33. *Elementary, My Dear,* with Philip King. London, 1975
34. *Who Says Murder?* with Philip King. London, 1975

Bonham, Frank
American, born February 25, 1914
1. *Lost Stage Valley.* New York, 1948
2. *Bold Passage.* New York, 1950
3. *Blood on the Land.* New York, 1952
4. *Snaketrack.* New York, 1952
5. *The Outcast of Crooked River.* London, 1953
6. *Night Raid.* New York, 1954
7. *The Feud at Spanish Ford.* New York, 1954
8. *The Wild Breed.* New York, 1955
9. *Rawhide Guns.* New York, 1955
10. *Border Guns.* London, 1956
11. *Defiance Mountain.* New York, 1956
12. *Hardrock.* New York, 1958
13. *Tough Country.* New York and London, 1958
14. *Last Stage West.* New York and London, 1959
15. *Sound of Gunfire.* New York, 1959
16. *One for Sleep.* New York, 1960
17. *Burma Rifles: A Story of Merrill's Marauders.* New York, 1960
18. *The Skin Game.* New York, 1961
19. *War Beneath the Sea.* New York, 1962
20. *Trago.* New York, 1962
21. *By Her Own Hand.* New York, 1963
22. *Deepwater Challenge.* New York, 1963
23. *Honor Bound.* New York, 1963
24. *The Loud, Resounding Sea.* New York, 1963
25. *Cast a Long Shadow.* New York, 1964
26. *Logan's Choice.* New York, 1964
27. *Speedway Contender.* New York, 1964
28. *Durango Street.* New York, 1965
29. *Mystery in Little Tokyo.* New York, 1966
30. *Mystery of the Red Tide.* New York, 1966
31. *The Ghost Front.* New York, 1968
32. *Mystery of the Fat Cat.* New York, 1968
33. *The Nitty Gritty.* New York, 1968
34. *The Vagabundos.* New York, 1969
35. *Viva Chicano.* New York, 1970
36. *Chief.* New York, 1971
37. *Cool Cat.* New York, 1971
38. *The Friends of the Loony Lake Monster.* New York, 1972
39. *Hey Big Spender!* New York, 1972
40. *A Dream of Ghosts.* New York, 1973
41. *The Golden Bees of Tulami.* New York, 1974
42. *The Missing Persons League.* New York, 1976
43. *The Rascals at Haskell's Gym.* New York, 1977
44. *Devilhorn.* New York, 1978
45. *The Forever Formula.* New York, 1979
46. *Gimme an H, Gimme an E, Gimme an L, Gimme a P.* New York, 1980

47. *Break for the Border.* New York, 1980
48. *Fort Hogan.* New York, 1980

Booth, Edwin
American, born in Nebraska
Pseudonyms: Don Blunt, Jack Hazard
1. *Showdown at Warbird.* New York, 1957
2. *Jinx Rider.* New York, 1957
3. *Boot Heel Range.* New York, 1958
4. *The Man Who Killed Tex.* New York, 1958
5. *The Trail to Tomahawk.* New York, 1958
6. *Wyoming Welcome.* New York, 1959
7. *Danger Trail.* New York, 1959
8. *Danger on the Trail.* London, 1960
9. *Lost Valley.* New York, 1960
10. *The Broken Window.* New York, 1960
11. *The Desperate Dude.* New York, 1960
12. *Return to Apache Springs.* New York, 1960
13. *Crooked Spur,* as Jack Hazard. New York, 1960
14. *Reluctant Lawman.* New York, 1961
15. *Outlaw Town.* New York, 1961
16. *The Troublemaker.* New York, 1961
17. *Short Cut,* as Don Blunt. New York, 1962
18. *Sidewinder.* New York, 1962
19. *Valley of Violence.* New York, 1962
20. *Hardcase Hotel.* New York, 1963
21. *Dead Giveaway,* as Don Blunt. New York, 1963
22. *John Sutter, Californian.* Indianapolis, 1963
23. *Devil's Canyon.* New York, 1964
24. *The Dry Gulchers.* New York, 1964
25. *The Stolen Saddle.* New York, 1964
26. *Renegade Guns.* New York, 1965
27. *Trouble at Tragedy Springs.* New York, 1966
28. *Triple Cross Trail.* New York, 1967
29. *Shoot-Out at Twin Buttes.* New York, 1967
30. *No Spurs for Johnny Loop.* New York, 1967
31. *One Man Posse.* New York, 1967
32. *The Man from Dakota.* New York, 1968
33. *Stranger in Buffalo Springs.* New York, 1969
34. *The Backshooters.* New York, 1969
35. *The Prodigal Gun.* New York, 1971
36. *Grudge Killer.* New York, 1971
37. *Hardesty.* New York, 1971
38. *Stage to San Felipe.* New York, 1972
39. *Bushwhack.* New York, 1974
40. *Small Spread.* New York, 1974
41. *The Colt-Packin' Parson.* New York, 1975
42. *Ambush at Adams Crossing.* New York, 1976
43. *Crossfire.* New York, 1977
44. *The Colorado Gun.* New York, 1980
45. *Leadville.* New York, 1980
46. *Rebel's Return.* New York, 1980

Borg, Jack [Phillip Anthony John Borg]
British
Pseudonyms: Phil Bexar, John Q. Pickard
1. *Sheriff of Clinton.* London, 1954
2. *Hellbent Trail.* London, 1954
3. *Big Cherokee.* London, 1955
4. *The Cannon Kid.* London, 1955
5. *Bushwhack Canyon.* London, 1956
6. *Sheriff's Deputy.* London, 1956
7. *Law of the Six-Gun,* as Phil Bexar. London, 1957
8. *Storm in the Saddle,* as Phil Bexar. London, 1957
9. *Bronco Justice.* London, 1957
10. *Gunsmoke Feud.* London, 1957
11. *The Cherokee Trail.* London, 1958
12. *Guns over Texas,* as Phil Bexar. London, 1958
13. *Showdown in Gunsmoke,* as Phil Bexar. London, 1958
14. *Kansas Trail.* London, 1958
15. *Rawhide Tenderfoot.* London, 1958
16. *Outlaw Marshall,* as Phil Bexar. London, 1959
17. *Six-Gun Fury,* as Phil Bexar. London, 1959
18. *Badlands Fury.* London, 1959
19. *Rustler's Range.* London, 1959
20. *The Lone Prairie,* as Phil Bexar. London, 1960
21. *Range Wolves.* London, 1960
22. *Saddle Tramp.* London, 1960
23. *Trail to Slaughter Creek,* as Phil Bexar. London, 1961
24. *Cowtown Fury,* as Phil Bexar. London, 1961
25. *Horsethieves Hang High.* London, 1961
26. *Kid with a Colt.* London, 1961
27. *Cowtown Marshall,* as Phil Bexar. London, 1962
28. *Texas Terror,* as Phil Bexar. London, 1962
29. *Guns of the Lawless.* London, 1962
30. *Trail of Fury,* as John Q. Pickard. London, 1962
31. *Medicine Pony,* as John Q. Pickard. London, 1962
32. *The Trail Drivers.* London, 1963
33. *Sixgun for Sale,* as John Q. Pickard. London, 1963
34. *Gone to Texas,* as John Q. Pickard. London, 1963
35. *Maverick Gunfighter,* as Phil Bexar. London, 1963
36. *Cast a Wide Loop.* London, 1963
37. *Texas Wolves.* London, 1963
38. *Rustler Guns,* as Phil Bexar. London, 1964
39. *Gun Feud at Sun Creek.* London, 1964
40. *Cactus Maverick,* as John Q. Pickard. London, 1964
41. *Black Hawk,* as John Q. Pickard. London, 1964
42. *Whistling Bone Creek,* as John Q. Pickard. London, 1965
43. *The Gringo,* as John Q. Pickard. London, 1965
44. *Rope for a Rustler.* London, 1965
45. *Stagecoach to Concho.* London, 1966
46. *Pistol Wages,* as John Q. Pickard. London, 1966
47. *Richer Than Tombstone,* as John Q. Pickard. London, 1966
48. *Blood Creek,* as John Q. Pickard. London, 1967
49. *The Horsethieves,* as John Q. Pickard. London, 1967
50. *Buzzard Bait,* as John Q. Pickard. London, 1968
51. *Comanche Crossing,* as John Q. Pickard. London, 1968
52. *The Banks of the Sacramento,* as Phil Bexar. London, 1968
53. *Dry Valley War.* London, 1968
54. *The Owlhooter.* London, 1968
55. *Hardcase Prodigal,* as Phil Bexar. London, 1969
56. *The Long-Ropers.* London, 1969
57. *Tumbleweed Man.* London, 1972
58. *The Man from San Antonio.* London, 1972
59. *Badman's Shadow.* London, 1972
60. *Badman Headed North.* London, 1974
61. *The Calico Kid.* London, 1974
62. *Showdown at Sweet Springs.* London, 1975
63. *Trail of Dead Men.* London, 1975

Borgenicht, Miriam
American, born in 1915
1. *A Corpse in Diplomacy.* New York, 1949
2. *Ring and Walk In.* New York and London, 1952
3. *Don't Look Back.* New York, 1956
4. *To Borrow Trouble.* New York, 1965
5. *Extreme Remedies.* New York, 1967
6. *Margin for Doubt.* New York, 1968
7. *The Tomorrow Trap.* New York, 1969
8. *A Very Thin Line.* New York, 1970
9. *Roadblock.* Indianapolis, 1973
10. *No Bail for Dalton.* Indianapolis, 1974

Borland, Hal [Harold Glen Borland]
American, born May 14, 1900
Pseudonym: Ward West

1. *Heaps of Gold.* Privately printed, 1922
2. *Rocky Mountain Tipi Tales.* New York and London, 1924
3. *Valor.* New York, 1934
4. *Trouble Valley,* as Ward West. New York, 1934
5. *Halfway to Timberline,* as Ward West. New York, 1935
6. *Wapiti Pete.* New York, 1938
7. *What Is America?,* with Philip Dunning. New York, 1942
8. *America Is Americans.* London, 1942
9. *An American Year: Country Life and Landscapes Through the Seasons.* New York, 1946
10. *Rustler's Trail,* as Ward West. London, 1948
11. *How to Write and Sell Non-Fiction.* New York, 1956
12. *High, Wide, and Lonesome.* Philadelphia, 1956
13. *The Amulet.* Philadelphia, 1957
14. *This Hill, This Valley.* New York, 1957
15. *The Enduring Pattern.* New York, 1959
16. *The Seventh Winter.* Philadelphia, 1960
17. *The Dog Who Came to Stay.* Philadelphia, 1961
18. *Beyond Your Doorstep: A Handbook to the Country.* New York, 1962
19. *The Youngest Shepherd: A Tale of the Nativity.* Philadelphia, 1962
20. *When the Legends Die.* Philadelphia, 1963
21. *Sundial of the Seasons: A Selection of Outdoor Editorials from the New York Times.* Philadelphia, 1964
22. *King of Squaw Mountain.* Philadelphia, 1964
23. *Countryman: A Summary of Belief.* Philadelphia, 1965
24. *Hill Country Harvest.* Philadelphia, 1967
25. *Homeland: A Report from the Country.* Philadelphia, 1969
26. *Plants of Christmas.* New York, 1969
27. *Country Editor's Boy.* Philadelphia, 1970
28. *Borland Country.* Philadelphia, 1971
29. *Penny: The Story of a Free-Soul Basset Hound.* Philadelphia, 1972
30. *Seasons.* Philadelphia, 1973
31. *This World of Wonder.* Philadelphia, 1973
32. *The History of Wildlife in America.* Washington (DC), 1975
33. *Hal Borland's Book of Days.* New York, 1976
34. *A Place to Begin: The New England Experience.* San Francisco, 1976
35. *The Golden Circle: A Book of Months.* New York, 1977
36. *Hal Borland's Twelve Moons of the Year.* New York, 1979

Bosworth, Allan R. (Rucker)
American, born October 29, 1901
Pseudonym: Alamo Boyd
1. *Wherever the Grass Grows.* New York, 1941
2. *Steel to the Sunset,* as Alamo Boyd. New York, 1941
3. *Full Crash Dive.* New York, 1942
4. *Hang and Rattle.* New York, 1947
5. *Border Roundup.* New York, 1947
6. *Double Deal.* New York, 1947
7. *A Cabin in the Hills.* New York, 1947
8. *Sancho of the Long, Long Horns.* New York, 1947
9. *Murder Goes to Sea.* London, 1948
10. *Bury Me Not.* New York, 1948
11. *Ladd of the Lone Star.* New York, 1952
12. *Ginza-Go, Papa-san.* Rutland (VT), 1955
13. *Only the Brave.* New York, 1955
14. *The Drifters.* New York, 1956
15. *The Lovely World of Richi-san.* New York and London, 1960
16. *The Crows of Edwina Hill.* New York, 1961
17. *New Country.* New York, 1962
18. *Ozona Country.* New York, 1964
19. *Storm Tide.* New York, 1965
20. *America's Concentration Camps.* New York, 1967
21. *My Love Affair with the Navy.* New York, 1969
22. *The Submarine Signalled—Murder!* New York, no date

Boucher, Anthony [William Anthony Parker White]
American, born in 1911, died October 31, 1968
Other Pseudonyms: Theo Durrant, with others; H.H. Holmes
1. *The Case of the Seven of Calvary.* New York and London, 1937
2. *The Case of the Crumpled Knave.* New York and London, 1939
3. *The Case of the Baker Street Irregulars.* New York, 1940
4. *Nine Times Nine,* as H.H. Holmes. New York, 1940
5. *The Case of the Solid Key.* New York, 1941
6. *The Case of the Seven Sneezes.* New York, 1942
7. *Rocket to the Morgue,* as H.H. Holmes. New York, 1942
8. *The Marble Forest,* as Theo Durrant. New York and London, 1951
9. *Ellery Queen: A Double Profile.* Boston, 1951
10. *The Big Fear,* as Theo Durrant. New York, 1953
11. *Blood on Baker Street.* New York, 1953
12. *Far and Away: Eleven Fantasy and Science-Fiction Stories.* New York, 1955
13. *The Compleat Werewolf and Other Stories of Fantasy and Science Fiction.* New York, 1969
14. *Multiplying Villainies: Selected Mystery Criticism, 1942-1968.* Boston, 1973
15. *Sincerely, Tony/Faithfully, Vincent: The Correspondence of Anthony Boucher and Vincent Starrett.* Chicago, 1975

Bouma, J.L. (Johanas L.)
American
Pseudonym: Steve Shannon
1. *Danger Trail.* New York, 1954
2. *Texas Spurs.* New York, 1955
3. *Border Vengeance.* New York, 1956
4. *The Hell-Fire Kid,* as Steve Shannon. New York, 1957
5. *Burning Valley.* New York, 1957
6. *The Avenging Gun.* New York, 1958
7. *Outlaw Frenzy.* New York, 1967
8. *Bitter Guns.* New York, 1972
9. *Slaughter at Crucifix Canyon.* Canoga Park (CA), 1975
10. *Vengeance.* New York, 1976
11. *Six-Gun Mule-Skinner.* Canoga Park, 1976
12. *Ride to Violence.* New York, 1978
13. *Longrider.* New York, 1978
14. *Beyond Vengeance.* New York, 1979

Bowen, Marjorie [Gabrielle Margaret Vere Campbell]
British. Born October 29, 1886, died December 23, 1952
Other pseudonyms: Margaret Campbell, Robert Paye, George Preedy, Joseph Shearing, John Winch
1. *The Viper of Milan.* London and New York, 1906
2. *The Glen o'Weeping.* London, 1907
3. *The Master of Stair.* New York, 1907
4. *The Sword Decides!* London and New York, 1908
5. *Black Magic: A Tale of the Rise and Fall of Antichrist.* London, 1909
6. *The Leopard and the Lily.* New York, 1909
7. *I Will Maintain.* London, 1910
8. *Defender of the Faith.* London and New York, 1911
9. *God and the King.* London, 1911
10. *Lovers' Knots.* London, 1912
11. *The Quest of Glory.* London and New York, 1912
12. *The Rake's Progress.* London, 1912
13. *The Soldier from Virginia.* New York, 1912
14. *God's Playthings.* London, 1912
15. *The Governor of England.* London, 1913
16. *A Knight of Spain.* London, 1913
17. *The Two Carnations.* London and New York, 1913
18. *Price and Heretic.* London, 1914

19. *Because of These Things* London, 1915
20. *Mister Washington.* London, 1915
21. *The Carnival of Florence.* London and New York, 1915
22. *William, By the Grace of God—.* London, 1916
23. *Shadows of Yesterday: Stories from an Old Catalogue.* London and New York, 1916
24. *The Third Estate.* London, 1917
25. *Curious Happenings.* London, 1917
26. *The Burning Glass.* London, 1918
27. *Kings-at-Arms.* London, 1918
28. *Mr. Misfortunate.* London, 1919
29. *Crimes of Old London.* London, 1919
30. *The Cheats.* London, 1920
31. *The Haunted Vintage.* London, 1921
32. *Rococo.* London, 1921
33. *The Pleasant Husband and Other Stories.* London, 1921
34. *The Jest.* London, 1922
35. *Affairs of Men.* London, 1922
36. *Stinging Nettles.* London and Boston, 1923
37. *Seeing Life! and Other Stories.* London, 1923
38. *The Presence and the Power.* London, 1924
39. *Five People.* London, 1925
40. *Boundless Water.* London, 1926
41. *Nell Gwyn: A Decoration.* London, 1926
42. *Mistress Nell Gwyn.* New York, 1926
43. *The Seven Deadly Sins.* London, 1926
44. *Five Winds.* London, 1927
45. *The Pagoda: Le Pagode de Chanteloup.* London, 1927
46. *Dark Ann and Other Stories.* London, 1927
47. *The Countess Fanny.* London, 1928
48. *The Golden Roof.* London, 1928
49. *General Crack,* as George Preedy. London and New York, 1928
50. *Dickon.* London, 1929
51. *The Gorgeous Lover and Other Tales.* London, 1929
52. *Sheep's-Head and Babylon, and Other Stories of Yesterday and Today.* London, 1929
53. *The English Paragon.* London, 1930
54. *The Devil's Jig,* as Robert Paye. London, 1930
55. *Old Patch's Medley; or, A London Miscellany.* London, 1930
56. *Bagatelle and Some Other Diversions,* as George Preedy. London, 1930
57. *A Family Comedy.* London, 1930
58. *The Prince's Darling,* as George Preedy. New York, 1930
59. *The Rocklitz,* as George Preedy. London, 1930
60. *Brave Employments.* London, 1931
61. *Withering Fires.* London, 1931
62. *Grace Latouche and the Warringtons: Some Nineteenth-Century Pieces, Mostly Victorian.* London, 1931
63. *Tumult in the North,* as George Preedy. London and New York, 1931
64. *The Pavilion of Honour,* as George Preedy. London, 1932
65. *Violante: Circe and Ermine,* as George Preedy. London, 1932
66. *The Devil Snar'd,* as George Preedy. London, 1932
67. *The Shadow on Mockways.* London, 1932
68. *Dark Rosaleen.* London, 1932
69. *Passion Flower.* London, 1932
70. *Beneath the Passion Flower,* as George Preedy. New York, 1932
71. *Idler's Gate,* as John Winch. London and New York, 1932
72. *Fond Fancy and Other Stories.* London, 1932
73. *The Last Bouquet: Some Twilight Tales.* London, 1932
74. *Forget-Me-Not,* as Joseph Shearing. London, 1932
75. *Lucile Clery,* as Joseph Shearing. New York, 1932
76. *Julia Roseingrave,* as Robert Paye. London, 1933
77. *I Dwelt in High Places.* London, 1933
78. *Set with Green Herbs.* London, 1933
79. *The Stolen Bride.* London, 1933
80. *The Veil'd Delight.* London, 1933
81. *The Knot Garden: Some Old Fancies Re-Set,* as George Preedy. London, 1933
82. *Dr. Chaos, and The Devil Snar'd,* as George Preedy. London, 1933
83. *Double Dallilay,* as George Preedy. London, 1933
84. *Album Leaf,* as Joseph Shearing. London, 1933
85. *The Triumphant Beast.* London, 1934
86. *Queen's Caprice,* as George Preedy. New York, 1934
87. *The Autobiography of Cornelius Blake, 1773-1810, of Ditton See, Cambridgeshire,* as George Preedy. London, 1934
88. *The Spider in the Cup,* as Joseph Shearing. New York, 1934
89. *Moss Rose,* as Joseph Shearing. London, 1934
90. *Laurell'd Captains,* as George Preedy. London, 1935
91. *Trumpets at Rome.* London, 1936
92. *The Poisoners,* as George Preedy. London, 1936
93. *The Golden Violet: The Story of a Lady Novelist,* as Joseph Shearing. London, 1936
94. *My Tattered Loving,* as George Preedy. London, 1937
95. *A Giant in Chains: Prelude to Revolution—France 1775-1791.* London, 1938
96. *God and the Wedding Dress.* London, 1938
97. *Orange Blossoms,* as Joseph Shearing. London, 1938
98. *Painted Angel,* as George Preedy. London, 1938
99. *Mr. Tyler's Saints.* London, 1939
100. *The Circle in the Water.* London, 1939
101. *The Fair Young Widow,* as George Preedy. London, 1939
102. *Dove in the Mulberry Tree,* as George Preedy. London, 1939
103. *Blanche Fury; or, Fury's Ape,* as Joseph Shearing. London and New York, 1939
104. *Exchange Royal.* London, 1940
105. *Primula,* as George Preedy. London, 1940
106. *Aunt Beardie,* as Joseph Shearing. London and New York, 1940
107. *Laura Sarelle,* as Joseph Shearing. London, 1940
108. *Today Is Mine.* London, 1941
109. *Black Man—White Maiden,* as George Preedy. London, 1941
110. *Findernes' Flowers,* as George Preedy. London, 1941
111. *The Strange Case of Lucile Clery,* as Joseph Shearing. New York, 1941
112. *The Crime of Laura Sarelle,* as Joseph Shearing. New York, 1941
113. *Lyndley Waters,* as George Preedy. London, 1942
114. *The Fetch,* as Joseph Shearing. London, 1942
115. *The Spectral Bride,* as Joseph Shearing. New York, 1942
116. *Lady in a Veil,* as George Preedy. London, 1943
117. *Airing in a Closed Carriage,* as Joseph Shearing. London and New York, 1943
118. *The Fourth Chamber,* as George Preedy. London, 1944
119. *Nightcap and Plume,* as George Preedy. London, 1945
120. *The Abode of Love,* as Joseph Shearing. London, 1945
121. *No Way Home,* as George Preedy. London, 1947
122. *For Her to See,* as Joseph Shearing. London, 1947
123. *So Evil My Love,* as Joseph Shearing. New York, 1947
124. *Mignonette,* as Joseph Shearing. New York, 1948
125. *The Bishop of Hell and Other Stories.* London, 1949
126. *The Sacked City,* as George Preedy. London, 1949
127. *Within the Bubble,* as Joseph Shearing. London, 1950
128. *To Bed at Noon,* as Joseph Shearing. London, 1951
129. *Julia Ballantyne,* as George Preedy. London, 1952
130. *The Man with the Scales.* London, 1954
131. *The Heiress of Frascati,* as Joseph Shearing. New York, 1966

132. *Eugenie.* London, 1971
133. *The King's Favourite* London, 1971
134. *Night's Dark Secret,* as Margaret Campbell. New York, 1975

Bower, B.M. (Bertha Muzzy)
American, born November 15, 1871, died July 23, 1940
1. *Chip, of the Flying U.* New York, 1906
2. *Her Prairie Knight, and Rowdy of the "Cross L."* New York, 1907
3. *The Lure of the Dim Trails.* New York, 1907
4. *The Range Dwellers.* New York and London, 1907
5. *The Lonesome Trail.* New York, 1909
6. *The Long Shadow.* New York, 1909
7. *The Happy Family.* New York, 1910
8. *Good Indian.* Boston, 1912
9. *Lonesome Land.* Boston, 1912
10. *The Uphill Climb.* Boston, 1913
11. *The Gringo.* Boston, 1913
12. *Flying U Ranch.* New York, 1914
13. *The Ranch at the Wolverine.* Boston, 1914
14. *The Flying U's Last Stand.* Boston, 1915
15. *Jean of the Lazy A.* Boston, 1915
16. *The Heritage of the Sioux.* Boston, 1916
17. *The Phantom Herd.* Boston, 1916
18. *The Lookout Man.* Boston, 1917
19. *Starr, Of the Desert.* Boston, 1917
20. *Skyrider.* Boston, 1918
21. *Cabin Fever.* Boston, 1918
22. *Rim o'the World.* Boston, 1919
23. *The Thunder Bird.* Boston, 1919
24. *The Quirt.* Boston, 1920
25. *Cow-Country.* Boston and London, 1921
26. *Casey Ryan.* Boston, 1921
27. *Sawtooth Ranch.* London, 1921
28. *The Trail of the White Mule.* Boston, 1922
29. *The Parowan Bonanza.* Boston, 1923
30. *The Voice at Johnnywater.* Boston and London, 1923
31. *The Bellehelen Mine.* Boston, 1924
32. *The Eagle's Wing.* Boston and London, 1924
33. *Meadowlark Basin.* Boston, 1925
34. *Desert Brew.* Boston and London, 1925
35. *Black Thunder.* Boston and London, 1926
36. *The Adam Chasers.* Boston and London, 1927
37. *Outlaw Paradise.* London, 1927
38. *White Wolves.* Boston and London, 1927
39. *Points West.* Boston and London, 1928
40. *Hay-Wire.* Boston and London, 1928
41. *Rodeo.* Boston and London, 1929
42. *The Swallowfork Bulls.* Boston and London, 1929
43. *Fool's Goal.* Boston and London, 1930
44. *Tiger Eye.* Boston and London, 1930
45. *Dark Horse: A Story of the Flying U.* Boston, 1931
46. *The Long Loop.* Boston and London, 1931
47. *Laughing Water.* Boston and London, 1932
48. *Rocking Arrow.* Boston and London, 1932
49. *The Whoop-Up Trail.* Boston, 1933
50. *Trails Meet.* Boston and London, 1933
51. *Open Land.* Boston and London, 1933
52. *The Flying U Strikes.* Boston and London, 1934
53. *The Haunted Hills.* Boston, 1934
54. *The Dry Ridge Gang.* Boston and London, 1935
55. *Trouble Rides the Wind.* Boston, 1935
56. *Five Furies of Leaning Ladder.* Boston, 1936
57. *The Five Furies.* London, 1936
58. *Shadow Mountain.* Boston and London, 1936
59. *Van Patten.* Boston, 1936
60. *The North Wind Do Blow.* Boston, 1937
61. *North Wind.* London, 1937
62. *Pirates of the Range.* Boston, 1937
63. *The Wind Blows West.* Boston, 1938
64. *A Starry Night.* Boston and London, 1939
65. *The Singing Hill.* Boston and London, 1939
66. *Man on Horseback.* Boston and London, 1940
67. *Spirit of the Range.* Boston and London, 1940
68. *Sweet Grass.* Boston and London, 1940
69. *Kings of the Prairie.* London, 1941
70. *The Family Failing.* Boston, 1941
71. *Border Vengeance.* New York, 1951
72. *Gun Fight at Horsethief Range.* New York, 1951
73. *Outlaw Moon.* New York, 1952
74. *Trigger Vengeance.* New York, 1953

Boyle, Jack
American
1. *Boston Blackie.* New York, 1919

Bradbury, Ray (Douglas)
American, born in 1920
1. *Dark Carnival.* Sauk City (WI), 1947
2. *The Martian Chronicles.* New York, 1950
3. *The Illustrated Man.* New York, 1951
4. *The Silver Locusts.* London, 1951
5. *The Golden Apples of the Sun.* New York and London, 1953
6. *Fahrenheit 451.* New York, 1953
7. *The October Country.* New York, 1955
8. *Switch on the Night.* New York and London, 1955
9. *Dandelion Wine.* New York and London, 1957
10. *A Medicine for Melancholy.* New York, 1959
11. *The Day It Rained Forever.* London, 1959
12. *Something Wicked This Way Comes.* New York, 1962
13. *The Small Assassin.* London, 1962
14. *R Is for Rocket.* New York, 1962
15. *The Anthem Sprinters.* New York, 1963
16. *The Anthem Sprinters and Other Antics.* New York, 1963
17. *The Machineries of Joy: Short Stories.* New York and London, 1964
18. *The Vintage Bradbury.* New York, 1965
19. *The Autumn People.* New York, 1965
20. *Tomorrow Midnight.* New York, 1966
21. *The Day It Rained Forever.* New York, 1966
22. *The Pedestrian.* New York, 1966
23. *S Is for Space.* New York, 1966
24. *I Sing the Body Electric!* New York, 1969
25. *Old Ahab's Friend, and Friend to Noah, Speaks His Piece: A Celebration.* Privately printed, 1971
26. *The Halloween Tree.* New York, 1972
27. *The Wonderful Ice-Cream Suit and Other Plays.* New York, 1972
28. *When Elephants Last in the Dooryard Bloomed: Celebrations for Almost Any Day of the Year.* New York, 1972
29. *Mars and the Mind of Man.* New York, 1973
30. *Zen and the Art of Writing.* Santa Barbara (CA), 1973
31. *That Son of Richard III.* Glendale (CA), 1974
32. *Long after Midnight.* New York, 1976
33. *Pillar of Fire and Other Plays.* London, 1976
34. *Where Robot Mice and Robot Men Run Round in Robot Towns: New York Poems Both Light and Dark.* New York, 1977

Bradford, Richard (Roark)
American, born May 1, 1932
1. *Red Sky at Morning.* Philadelphia, 1968
2. *So Far from Heaven.* Philadelphia, 1973

Bragg, W.F. (William Frederick)
American, born in 1892

1. *Starr of Wyoming*. London, 1936
2. *Smoke Joe*. New York, 1949
3. *Mountain Maverick*. New York, 1950
4. *Gun Trouble*. New York, 1950
5. *Range Camp*. New York, 1950
6. *Sagebrush Lawman*. New York, 1951
7. *Texas Fever*. New York, 1953
8. *Bullet Song*. New York, 1953
9. *Stampede Jones*. New York, 1954
10. *Maverick Showdown*. New York, 1954
11. *Guns of Roaring Fork*. New York, 1954
12. *Wildcat Brand*. New York, 1955
13. *Bullet Proof*. New York, 1955
14. *Ghost Mountain Guns*. New York, 1955
15. *Badlands Basin*. New York, 1956
16. *Buckskin Rider*. New York, 1956
17. *Buzzard's Roost*. New York, 1956
18. *Ride On, Cowboy!* New York, 1956
19. *Poison Creek Posse*. New York, 1957
20. *Rawhide Roundup*. New York, 1957
21. *Outlaw Moon*. New York, 1958

Brahms, Caryl [Doris Caroline Abrahams]
British, born in 1901
Other pseudonym: Oliver Linden
1. *The Moon on My Left*. London, 1930
2. *Sung Before Six*, as Oliver Linden. London, 1931
3. *Curiouser and Curiouser*. London, 1932
4. *A Bullet in the Ballet*, with S.J. Simon. London, 1937
5. *Casino for Sale*, with S.J. Simon. London, 1938
6. *Murder a la Stroganoff*, with S.J. Simon. New York, 1938
7. *The Elephant Is White*, with S.J. Simon. London, 1939
8. *Don't, Mr. Disraeli!* with S.J. Simon. London, 1940
9. *Envoy on Excursion*, with S.J. Simon. London, 1940
10. *No Bed for Bacon*, with S.J. Simon. London, 1941
11. *Robert Helpmann, Choreographer*. London, 1943
12. *No Nightingales*, with S.J. Simon. London, 1944
13. *Titania Has a Mother*, with S.J. Simon. London, 1944
14. *Six Curtains for Stroganova*, with S.J. Simon. London, 1945
15. *Six Curtains for Natasha*, with S.J. Simon. Philadelphia, 1946
16. *Trottie True*, with S.J. Simon. London, 1946
17. *Coppelia: The Story of the Ballet Told for the Young*, as Caryl Brahms. London, 1946
18. *To Hell with Hedda! and Other Stories*, with S.J.Simon. London, 1947
19. *You Were There*, with S.J. Simon. London, 1950
20. *A Seat at the Ballet*. London, 1951
21. *Away Went Polly*. London, 1952
22. *Cindy-Ella*, with Ned Sherrin. London, 1962
23. *No Castanets*. London and New York, 1963
24. *The Rest of the Evening's My Own*. London, 1964
25. *Rappel 1910*, with Ned Sherrin. London, 1964
26. *Benbow Was His Name*, with Ned Sherrin. London, 1967
27. *Ooh! La-la!* with Ned Sherrin. London, 1973
28. *Gilbert and Sullivan: Lost Chords and Discords*. London and Boston, 1975
29. *After You, Mr. Feydeau!* with Ned Sherrin. London, 1975
30. *Reflections in a Lake: A Study of Chekhov's Greatest Plays*, as Caryl Brahms. London, 1976
31. *A Mutual Pair*, with S.J. Simon. London, 1976
32. *Enter a Dragon, Stage Centre*. London, 1979

Bramah, Ernest [Ernest Bramah Smith]
British, born in 1868, died June 27, 1942
1. *English Farming and Why I Turned It Up*. London, 1894
2. *The Wallet of Kai Lung*. London and Boston, 1900
3. *The Mirror of Kong Ho*. London, 1905

4. *What Might Have Been: The Story of a Social War*. London, 1907
5. *The Secret of the League*. London, 1909
6. *Max Carrados*. New York, 1914
7. *Kai Lung's Golden Hours*. London, 1922
8. *The Eyes of Max Carrados*. London, 1923
9. *The Specimen Case*. London, 1924
10. *Max Carrados Mysteries*. London, 1927
11. *The Story of Wan and the Remarkable Shrub and The Story of Ching-Kwei and the Destinies*. New York, 1927
12. *Kai Lung Unrolls His Mat*. London and New York, 1928
13. *A Little Flutter*. London, 1930
14. *The Moon of Much Gladness*. London, 1932
15. *The Bravo of London*. London, 1934
16. *The Return of Kai Lung*. New York, 1938
17. *Kai Lung Beneath the Mulberry Tree*. London, 1940
18. *Best Max Carrados Detective Stories*. New York, 1972

Brand, Christianna [Mary Christianna Milne Brand]
British, born in 1909
Pseudonyms: Mary Ann Ashe, Annabel Jones, Mary Roland, China Thompson
1. *Death in High Heels*. London, 1941
2. *Heads You Lose*. London, 1941
3. *Green for Danger*. New York, 1944
4. *The Crooked Wreath*. New York, 1946
5. *The Single Pilgrim*, as Mary Roland. London and New York, 1946
6. *Suddenly at His Residence*. London, 1947
7. *Death of a Jezebel*. New York, 1948
8. *Danger Unlimited*. New York, 1948
9. *Welcome to Danger*. London, 1950
10. *Cat and Mouse*. London and New York, 1950
11. *London Particular*. London, 1952
12. *Fog of Doubt*. New York, 1953
13. *Tour de Force*. London and New York, 1955
14. *The Three-Cornered Halo*. London and New York, 1957
15. *Starrbelow*, as China Thompson. London and New York, 1958
16. *Heaven Knows Who*. London and New York, 1960
17. *Nurse Matilda*. Leichester (Eng) and New York, 1964
18. *Nurse Matilda Goes to Town*. Leicester, 1967
19. *What Dread Hand?* London, 1968
20. *Court of Foxes*. London, 1969
21. *Brand X*. London, 1974
22. *The Radiant Dove*, as Annabel Jones. London, 1974
23. *Nurse Matilda Goes to Hospital*. London and New York, 1974
24. *A Ring of Roses*, as Mary Ann Ashe. London, 1976
25. *Alas for Her That Met Me!* as Mary Ann Ashe. London, 1976
26. *The Honey Harlot*. London, 1978

Brandon, John G. (Gordon)
Australian, born in 1879, died in 1941
1. *The Big Heart*. London and New York, 1923
2. *Young Love*. London, 1925
3. *The Joy Ride*. London and New York, 1927
4. *Red Altars*. London, 1928
5. *The Secret Brotherhood*. New York, 1928
6. *The Silent House*. London and New York, 1928
7. *Nighthawks!* London, 1929
8. *Th' Big City*. London and New York, 1930
9. *The Black Joss*. London, 1931
10. *West End!* London, 1933
11. *The Taxi-Cab Murder*. London, 1933
12. *The Survivor's Secret*. London, 1933
13. *The Tragedy of the West End Actress*. London, 1933

14. *The Championship Crime.* London, 1934
15. *The Chink's Victim.* London, 1934
16. *The Case of the Gangster's Moll.* London, 1934
17. *The Glass Dagger.* London, 1934
18. *Murder in Mayfair.* London, 1934
19. *Murder on the Stage.* London, 1934
20. *Under Police Protection.* London, 1934
21. *The Mystery of the Three City's.* London, 1934
22. *On the Midnight Beat.* London, 1934
23. *The One-Minute Murder.* London, 1934
24. *The Yellow Mask.* London, 1935
25. *By Order of the Tong.* London, 1935
26. *The Case of the Murdered Commissionnaire.* London, 1935
27. *The Riverside Mystery.* London, 1935
28. *The Red Boomerang.* London, 1935
29. *The Downing Street Discovery.* London, 1935
30. *Murder in Y Division.* London, 1935
31. *The Victim of the Thieves' Den.* London, 1936
32. *The Pawnshop Murder.* London, 1936
33. *The Mystery of the Murdered Blonde.* London, 1936
34. *The Mystery of the Three Acrobats.* London, 1936
35. *The Case of the Night Club Queen.* London, 1936
36. *Dead Man's Evidence.* London, 1936
37. *Murder on the Fourth Floor.* London, 1936
38. *The "Snatch" Game.* London, 1936
39. *The Case of the Withered Hand.* London, 1936
40. *Death Tolls the Gong.* London, 1936
41. *The Dragnet.* London, 1936
42. *McCarthy, C.I.D.* London, 1936
43. *Murder at the "Yard.".* London, 1936
44. *The Girl Who Knew Too Much.* London, 1936
45. *The Bond Street Murder.* London, 1937
46. *The Bond Street Raiders.* London, 1937
47. *The Crime in the Kiosk.* London, 1937
48. *Death in Downing Street.* London, 1937
49. *The Diamond of Ti Lingo.* London, 1937
50. *The Mystery of the Murdered Sentry.* London, 1937
51. *The Mystery of X20.* London, 1937
52. *The Spy from Spain.* London, 1937
53. *The Tattooed Triangle.* London, 1937
54. *The Victim of the Secret Service.* London, 1937
55. *The Hand of Seeta.* London, 1937
56. *The Mail-Van Mystery.* London, 1937
57. *The Man from Italy.* London, 1937
58. *The Melbourne Mystery.* London, 1937
59. *Murder in Soho.* London, 1937
60. *Murder on the High Seas.* London, 1938
61. *The Mystery of the Dead Man's Wallet.* London, 1938
62. *The Mystery of the Murdered Ice Cream Man.* London, 1938
63. *The Mystery of the Street Musician.* London, 1938
64. *The Night Club Murder.* London, 1938
65. *The Pigeon Loft Crime.* London, 1938
66. *The Regent Street Raid.* London, 1938
67. *The Roadhouse Mystery.* London, 1938
68. *Bonus for Murder.* London, 1938
69. *The Clue of the Tattooed Man.* London, 1938
70. *The Cork Street Crime.* London, 1938
71. *The False Alibi.* London, 1938
72. *The 50 Marriage Case.* London, 1938
73. *The 250 Marriage Case.* London, 1954
74. *The Frame-Up.* London, 1938
75. *The Mark of the Tong.* London, 1938
76. *The Crooked Five.* London, 1939
77. *Death on Delivery.* London, 1939
78. *Fatal Forgery.* London, 1939
79. *Finger-Prints Never Lie!* London, 1939
80. *The Great Taxi-Cab Ramp.* London, 1939
81. *In the Hands of Spies.* London, 1939
82. *The Gunboat Mystery.* London, 1939
83. *The Man from Singapore.* London, 1939
84. *The Man with Jitters.* London, 1939
85. *Mr. Pennington Comes Through.* London, 1939
86. *Murder on the Ice Rink.* London, 1939
87. *The Mystery of the Green Bottle.* London, 1939
88. *The Riddle of the Greek Financier.* London, 1940
89. *The Riddle of the Dead Man's Bay.* London, 1940
90. *On Ticket of Leave.* London, 1940
91. *A Scream in Soho.* London, 1940
92. *The Terror of the Pacific.* London, 1940
93. *Yellow Gods.* London, 1940
94. *The Black Swastika.* London, 1940
95. *Crook's Cargo.* London, 1940
96. *Death in the Ditch!* London, 1940
97. *Gang War!* London, 1940
98. *Mr. Pennington Goes Nap.* London, 1940
99. *The Death in the Quarry.* London, 1941
100. *Mr. Pennington Barges In.* London, 1941
101. *Under Secret Orders.* London, 1941
102. *The Transport Murders.* London, 1942
103. *The Blue-Print Murders.* London, 1942
104. *Murder for a Million.* London, 1942
105. *Mr. Pennington Sees Red.* London, 1942
106. *Death in Jermyn Street.* London, 1942
107. *Death in "D" Division.* London, 1943
108. *Death in Duplicate.* London, 1945
109. *Candidate for a Coffin!* London, 1946
110. *"M" for Murder.* London, 1949
111. *The Case of the Would-Be Widow!* London, 1950
112. *The Corpse Rode On.* London, 1952
113. *Murderer's Stand-In.* London, 1953
114. *The Call Girl Murders.* London, 1954
115. *Death of a Greek.* London, 1955
116. *Murder on the Beam.* London, 1956
117. *Death of a Socialite.* London, 1957
118. *Murder in Pimlico.* London, 1958
119. *The Corpse from "the City"!* London, 1958
120. *Death Stalks in Soho!* London, 1959

Branson, H.C. (Henry Clay)
American
1. *I'll Eat You Last.* New York, 1941
2. *I'll Kill You Last.* New York, 1942
3. *The Pricking Thumb.* New York, 1942
4. *Case of the Giant Killer.* New York, 1944
5. *The Fearful Passage.* New York, 1945
6. *Last Year's Blood.* New York, 1947
7. *The Leaden Bubble.* New York, 1949
8. *Beggar's Choice.* New York, 1953
9. *Salisbury Plain.* New York, 1965

Braun, Lillian Jackson
American
1. *The Cat Who Could Read Backwards.* New York, 1966
2. *The Cat Who Ate Danish Modern.* New York, 1967
3. *The Cat Who Turned On and Off.* New York, 1968

Braun, Matt (Matthew)
American, born November 15, 1932
1. *Mattie Silks.* New York, 1972
2. *Black Fox.* New York, 1972
3. *The Savage Land.* New York, 1973
4. *El Paso.* New York, 1973
5. *Noble Outlaw.* New York, 1975
6. *Bloody Hand.* New York, 1975
7. *Cimarron Jordan.* New York, 1975

8. *Kinch.* New York, 1975
9. *Buck Colter.* New York, 1975
10. *The Kincaids.* New York, 1976
11. *The Second Coming of Lucas Brokaw.* New York, 1977
12. *The Save-Your-Life Defense Handbook.* Old Greenwich (CT), 1977
13. *Hangman's Creek.* New York, 1979
14. *Lords of the Land.* New York, 1979
15. *The Stuart Women.* New York, 1980
16. *Jury of Six.* New York, 1980
17. *Tombstone.* New York, 1981
18. *The Spoilers.* New York, 1981
19. *The Manhunter.* New York, 1981
20. *Deadwood.* New York, 1981
21. *The Judas Tree.* New York, 1982

Brean, Herbert
American, born in 1907, died May 7, 1973
1. *Wilders Walk Away.* New York, 1948
2. *The Darker the Night.* New York, 1949
3. *Hardly a Man Is Now Alive.* New York, 1950
4. *How to Stop Smoking.* New York, 1951
5. *The Clock Strikes Thirteen.* New York, 1952
6. *A Matter of Fact.* New York, 1956
7. *Collar for the Killer.* London, 1957
8. *Dead Sure.* New York, 1958
9. *How to Stop Drinking.* New York, 1958
10. *The Traces of Brillhart.* New York, 1960
11. *The Life Treasury of American Folklore.* New York, 1961
12. *The Music of Life,* with others. New York, 1962
13. *A Handbook for Drinkers—and for Those Who Want to Stop.* New York, 1963
14. *The Only Diet that Works.* New York, 1965
15. *The Traces of Merrilee.* New York, 1966

Brent, Madeleine
British
1. *Tregaron's Daughter.* London and New York, 1971
2. *Moonraker's Bride.* London and New York, 1973
3. *Kirby's Changeling.* London, 1975
4. *Stranger at Wildings.* New York, 1976
5. *Merlin's Keep.* London, 1977
6. *The Capricorn Stone.* London, 1979
7. *The Long Masquerade.* London, 1981

Brett, Simon (Anthony Lee)
British, born in 1945
1. *Cast, In Order of Disappearance.* London, 1975
2. *So Much Blood.* London, 1976
3. *Star Trap.* London, 1977
4. *An Amateur Corpse.* London and New York, 1978
5. *Frank Muir.* London, 1978
6. *A Comedian Dies.* London and New York, 1979
7. *A Second Frank Muir Goes into* London, 1979

Brewer, Gil
American
1. *13 French Street.* New York, 1951
2. *Satan Is a Woman.* New York, 1951
3. *So Rich, So Dead.* New York, 1951
4. *Flight to Darkness.* New York, 1952
5. *Hell's Our Destination.* New York, 1953
6. *A Killer Is Loose.* New York, 1954
7. *Some Must Die.* New York, 1954
8. *The Squeeze.* New York, 1955
9. *77 Rue Paradise.* New York, 1955
10. *And the Girl Screamed.* New York, 1956
11. *The Angry Dream.* New York, 1957
12. *The Brat.* New York, 1957
13. *Little Tramp.* New York, 1957
14. *The Girl from Hateville.* Rockville Center (NY), 1958
15. *The Bitch.* New York, 1958
16. *The Red Scarf.* New York, 1958
17. *The Vengeful Virgin.* New York, 1958
18. *Wild.* New York, 1958
19. *Sugar.* New York, 1959
20. *Angel.* New York, 1960
21. *The Three-Way Split.* New York, 1960
22. *Backwoods Teaser.* New York, 1960
23. *Nude on Thin Ice.* New York, 1960
24. *Appointment in Hell.* Derby (CT), 1961
25. *A Taste of Sin.* New York, 1961
26. *Memory of Passion.* New York, 1963
27. *Play It Hard.* Derby, 1964
28. *The Hungry One.* New York, 1966
29. *Sin for Me.* New York, 1967
30. *The Tease.* New York, 1967
31. *The Devil in Davos.* New York, 1969
32. *Mediterranean Caper.* New York, 1969
33. *Appointment in Cairo.* New York, 1970

Bridge, Ann [Mary Dolling O'Malley]
British, born in 1889, died March 9, 1974
1. *Peking Picnic.* London and Boston, 1932
2. *The Ginger Griffin.* London and Boston, 1934
3. *Illyrian Spring.* London and Boston, 1935
4. *The Song in the House.* London, 1936
5. *Enchanter's Nightshade.* London and Boston, 1937
6. *Four-Part Setting.* London and Boston, 1939
7. *Frontier Passage.* London and Boston, 1942
8. *Singing Waters.* London, 1945
9. *And Then You Came.* London, 1948
10. *The Selective Traveller in Portugal,* with Susan Lowndes. London, 1949
11. *The Dark Moment.* London, 1951
12. *The House in Kilmartin.* London, 1951
13. *A Place to Stand.* London and New York, 1953
14. *Portrait of My Mother.* London, 1955
15. *A Family of Two Worlds.* New York, 1955
16. *The Lighthearted Quest.* London and New York, 1956
17. *The Portuguese Escape.* London and New York, 1958
18. *The Numbered Account,* with Susan Lowndes. London and New York, 1960
19. *Julia Involved.* New York, 1962
20. *The Tightened String.* London and New York, 1962
21. *The Dangerous Islands.* New York, 1963
22. *Emergency in the Pyrenees.* London and New York, 1965
23. *The Episode at Toledo.* New York, 1966
24. *Facts and Fictions: Some Literary Recollections.* London and New York, 1968
25. *The Malady in Madeira.* New York, 1969
26. *Moments of Knowing: Some Personal Experiences Beyond Normal Knowledge.* London and New York, 1970
27. *Permission to Resign: Goings-On in the Corridors of Power* London, 1971
28. *Julia in Ireland.* New York, 1973

Bridges, Victor [George de Freyne]
British, born in 1878, died November 29, 1972
1. *Camping Out, for Boy Scouts and Others.* London, 1910
2. *Another Man's Shoes.* London and New York, 1913
3. *The Man from Nowhere.* London, 1913
4. *Jetsam.* London, 1914
5. *A Rogue by Compulsion.* London and New York, 1915
6. *Mr. Lyndon at Liberty.* London, 1915
7. *The Lady from Long Acre.* London, 1918

8. *The Cruise of the "Scandal" and other Stories.* New York, 1920
9. *Greensea Island.* London and New York, 1922
10. *Another Pair of Spectacles.* London, 1923
11. *A Handful of Verses.* London, 1924
12. *The Red Lodge.* London and New York, 1926
13. *The Girl in Black.* London, 1926
14. *Deadman's Pool,* with T.C. Bridges. London, 1929
15. *The Green Monkey.* London, 1929
16. *The King Comes Back.* London, 1930
17. *The Secret of the Creek.* London and Boston, 1930
18. *Edward FitzGerald and Other Verses.* London, 1932
19. *Three Blind Mice.* London, 1933
20. *The Happy Murderers.* London, 1933
21. *I Did Not Kill Osborne.* Philadelphia, 1934
22. *Peter in Peril.* London and Philadelphia, 1935
23. *Blue Silver.* London, 1936
24. *It Happened in Essex.* London, 1938
25. *The Seven Stars.* London, 1939
26. *Dusky Night.* London, 1940
27. *The House on the Saltings.* London, 1941
28. *The Man Who Butted In.* London, 1942
29. *The Gulls Fly Low.* London, 1943
30. *It Never Rains.* London, 1944
31. *Trouble on the Thames.* London, 1945
32. *The Man Who Limped.* London, 1947
33. *Accidents Will Happen.* London, 1948
34. *Quite Like Old Days.* London, 1949
35. *The Tenth Commandment.* London, 1951
36. *We Don't Want to Lose You.* London, 1952
37. *All Very Irregular.* London, 1953
38. *The Man Who Vanished.* London, 1954
39. *The Secret of the Saltings.* London, 1955
40. *What the Doctor Ordered.* London, 1956
41. *Exit Mr. Marlowe.* London, 1957
42. *The Creaking Gate.* London, 1958
43. *Secrecy Essential.* London, 1959
44. *The Girl from Belfast.* London, 1961

Brittain, William
American, born in 1930
1. *Survival Outdoors.* Derby (CT), 1977
2. *All the Money in the World.* New York, 1979

Brock, Lynn [Alister McAllister]
Irish, born in 1877
Other Pseudonym: Anthony Wharton
1. *At the Barn,* as Anthony Wharton. London and New York, 1912
2. *13, Simon Street,* as Anthony Wharton. London and New York, 1913
3. *Nocturne,* as Anthony Wharton. London and New York, 1913
4. *Joan of Overbarrow,* as Anthony Wharton. New York, 1921
5. *The Man on the Hill,* as Anthony Wharton. London, 1923
6. *The Deductions of Colonel Gore.* London, 1924
7. *Be Good, Sweet Maid,* as Anthony Wharton. London and New York, 1924
8. *Colonel Gore's Second Case.* London, 1925
9. *Colonel Gore's Third Case: The Kink.* London, 1925
10. *The Two of Diamonds.* London, 1926
11. *Evil Communications,* as Anthony Wharton. London, 1926
12. *The Slip-Carriage Mystery.* London and New York, 1928
13. *The Dagwort Combe Mystery.* London, 1929
14. *The Stoke Silver Case.* New York, 1929
15. *The Mendip Mystery.* London, 1929
16. *Murder at the Inn.* New York, 1929
17. *Q.E.D.* London, 1930
18. *Murder on the Bridge.* New York, 1930
19. *Nightmare.* London, 1932
20. *The Barrington Mystery.* London, 1932
21. *The Silver Sickle Case.* London, 1938
22. *Fourfingers.* London, 1939
23. *The Riddle of the Roost.* London, 1939
24. *The Stoat.* London, 1940

Bromfield, Louis
American, born December 27, 1896, died March 18, 1956
1. *The Green Bay Tree.* New York, 1924
2. *Possession.* New York, 1925
3. *Early Autumn.* New York, 1926
4. *A Good Woman.* New York, 1927
5. *The Strange Case of Miss Annie Spragg.* New York, 1928
6. *Awake and Rehearse.* New York, 1929
7. *Tabloid.* New York, 1930
8. *Twenty-Four Hours.* New York, 1930
9. *A Modern Hero.* New York, 1932
10. *The Farm.* New York, 1933
11. *Here Today and Gone Tomorrow: Four Short Novels.* New York, 1934
12. *The Man Who Had Everything.* New York, 1935
13. *The Rains Came: A Novel of Modern India.* New York, 1937
14. *It Takes All Kinds.* New York, 1939
15. *Night in Bombay.* New York, 1940
16. *Wild Is the River.* New York, 1941
17. *Until the Day Break.* New York, 1942
18. *Mrs. Parkington.* New York, 1943
19. *The World We Live In: Stories.* New York, 1944
20. *What Became of Anna Bolton.* New York, 1944
21. *Kenny.* New York, 1947
22. *Colorado.* New York, 1947
23. *The Wild Country.* New York, 1948
24. *Mr. Smith.* New York, 1951

Brown, Dee (Alexander)
American, born February 28, 1908
1. *Wave High the Banner.* Philadelphia, 1942
2. *Fighting Indians of the West,* with Martin F. Schmitt. New York, 1948
3. *Trail Driving Days.* New York, 1952
4. *Grierson's Raid.* Urbana (IL), 1954
5. *The Settler's West,* with Martin F. Schmitt. New York, 1955
6. *Yellowhorse.* Boston, 1956
7. *Cavalry Scout.* New York, 1958
8. *The Gentle Tamers: Women of the Old Wild West.* New York, 1958
9. *The Bold Cavaliers: Morgan's 2nd Kentucky Cavalry Raiders.* Philadelphia, 1959
10. *They Went Thataway.* New York, 1960
11. *Fort Phil Kearny: An American Saga.* New York, 1962
12. *The Galvanized Yankees.* Urbana, 1963
13. *The Girl from Fort Wicked.* New York, 1964
14. *Showdown at Little Big Horn.* New York, 1964
15. *The Year of the Century: 1876.* New York, 1966
16. *Action at Beecher Island.* New York, 1967
17. *Bury My Heart at Wounded Knee.* New York and London, 1971
18. *The Fetterman Massacre.* London, 1972
19. *Andrew Jackson and the Battle of New Orleans.* New York, 1972
20. *Tales of the Warrior Ants.* New York, 1973
21. *The Westerners.* New York and London, 1974
22. *Women of the Wild West.* London, 1975
23. *Hear That Lonesome Whistle Blow: Railroads in the West.* New York and London, 1977

24. *Teepee Tales of the American Indian.* New York, 1979
25. *Campfire Tales of the American Indians.* London, 1979
26. *Creek Mary's Blood.* New York and London, 1980
27. *Lonesome Whistle.* New York, 1980

Brown, Fredric
American, born in 1906, died March 11, 1972
1. *The Fabulous Clipjoint.* New York, 1947.

Brown, J.P.S. (Joseph Paul Summers)
American, born August 25, 1930
1. *Jim Kane.* New York, 1970
2. *The Outfit: A Cowboy's Primer.* New York, 1971
3. *Pocket Money.* London, 1972
4. *The Forests of the Night.* New York, 1974

Burchardt, Bill (William Robert)
American, born August 16, 1917
1. *The Wildcatters.* New York, 1963
2. *Yankee Longstraw.* New York, 1965
3. *Shotgun Bottom.* New York, 1966
4. *The Birth of Logan Station.* New York, 1974
5. *The Mexican.* New York, 1977
6. *Buck.* New York, 1978
7. *Oklahoma.* Portland (OR), 1979
8. *Medicine Man.* New York and London, 1980
9. *The Lighthorseman.* New York, 1981
10. *Black Marshall.* New York, 1981

Burford, Lolah
American, born in 1931
1. *Vice Avenged: A Moral Tale.* New York, 1971
2. *The Vision of Stephen: An Elegy.* New York, 1972
3. *Edward, Edward.* New York, 1973
4. *MacLyon.* New York, 1974
5. *Alyx.* New York, 1977
6. *Seacage.* New York, 1979

Burgess, Anthony
British, born February 25, 1917
1. *The Doctor Is Sick.* London, 1960
2. *A Clockwork Orange.* London, 1962
3. *Honey for the Bears.* London, 1963
4. *Nothing Like the Sun: A Story of Shakespeare's Love-Life.* London and New York, 1964

Burgess, Gelett [Frank Gelett Burgess]
American, born in 1866, died September 18, 1951
1. *Vivette, or the Memoirs of the Romance Association.* Boston, 1897
2. *The Nonsense Almanack for 1900.* New York, 1899
3. *Goops and How To Be Them.* New York, 1900
4. *Are You a Bromide?* New York, 1906.

Burke, John (Frederick)
British, born in 1922
Pseudonyms: Jonathan Burke; Owen Burke; Harriet Esmond, with his wife Jean; Jonathan George, Joanna Jones, Sara Morris, Martin Sands
1. *Swift Summer,* as John and Jonathan Burke. London, 1949
2. *Another Chorus,* as John and Jonathan Burke. London, 1949
3. *These Haunted Streets,* as John and Jonathan Burke. London, 1950
4. *The Outward Walls,* as John and Jonathan Burke. London, 1952
5. *Chastity House,* as John and Jonathan Burke. London, 1952
6. *Dark Gateway,* as John and Jonathan Burke. London, 1953
7. *The Echoing World,* as John and Jonathan Burke. London, 1954
8. *Twilight of Reason,* as John and Jonathan Burke. London, 1954
9. *Pattern of Shadows,* as John and Jonathan Burke. London, 1954
10. *Hotel Cosmos,* as John and Jonathan Burke. London, 1954
11. *Deep Freeze,* as John and Jonathan Burke. London, 1955
12. *Revolt of the Humans,* as John and Jonathan Burke. London, 1955
13. *Alien Landscape: Science Fiction Stories,* as John and Jonathan Burke. London, 1955
14. *Pursuit Through Time,* as John and Jonathan Burke. London, 1956
15. *The Poison Cupboard,* as John and Jonathan Burke. London, 1956
16. *The Happy Invaders: A Picture of Denmark in Springtime,* with William Luscombe. London, 1956
17. *Corpse to Copenhagen,* as John and Jonathan Burke. London, 1957
18. *Nurse Is a Neighbour,* as Joanna Jones. London, 1958
19. *Nurse on the District,* as Joanna Jones. London, 1959
20. *Echo of Barbara,* as John and Jonathan Burke. London, 1959
21. *Fear by Installments,* as John and Jonathan Burke. London, 1960
22. *The Entertainer,* as John and Jonathan Burke. London, 1960
23. *Look Back in Anger,* as John and Jonathan Burke. London, 1960
24. *The Angry Silence,* as John and Jonathan Burke. London, 1961
25. *A Widow for the Winter,* as Sara Morris. London, 1961
26. *The Lion of Sparta,* as John and Jonathan Burke. London, 1961
27. *The 300 Spartans,* as John and Jonathan Burke. London, 1961
28. *Flame in the Streets,* as John and Jonathan Burke. London, 1961
29. *Teach Yourself Treachery,* as John and Jonathan Burke. London, 1962
30. *Deadly Downbeat,* as John and Jonathan Burke. London, 1962
31. *The Boys,* as John and Jonathan Burke. London, 1962
32. *Private Potter,* as John and Jonathan Burke. London, 1962
33. *The World Ten Times Over,* as John and Jonathan Burke. London, 1962
34. *The Man Who Finally Died,* as John and Jonathan Burke. London, 1963
35. *The Artless Flat-Hammer,* as Joanna Jones. London, 1963
36. *Guilty Party,* as John and Jonathan Burke. London, 1963
37. *The Twisted Tongues,* as John and Jonathan Burke. London, 1964
38. *The System,* as John and Jonathan Burke. London, 1964
39. *A Hard Day's Night,* as John and Jonathan Burke. New York, 1964
40. *The Artless Commuter,* as Joanna Jones. London, 1965
41. *That Magnificent Air Race,* as John and Jonathan Burke. London, 1965
42. *Those Magnificent Men and Their Flying Machines,* as John and Jonathan Burke. New York, 1965
43. *Only the Ruthless Can Play,* as John and Jonathan Burke. London, 1965
44. *Dr. Terror's House of Horrors,* as John and Jonathan Burke. London, 1965
45. *The Weekend Girls,* as John and Jonathan Burke. London, 1966
46. *Goodbye Gillian,* as John and Jonathan Burke. New York, no date

47. *Echo of Treason*, as John and Jonathan Burke. New York, 1966
48. *The Trap*, as John and Jonathan Burke. London, 1966
49. *The Hammer Horror Omnibus*, as John and Jonathan Burke. London, 1966
50. *The Power Game*, as John and Jonathan Burke. London, 1966
51. *The Second Hammer Horror Film Omnibus*, as John and Jonathan Burke. London, 1967
52. *Gossip to the Grave*, as John and Jonathan Burke. London, 1967
53. *The Jokers*, as Martin Sands. London, 1967
54. *Maroc 7*, as Martin Sands. London, 1967
55. *Privilege*, as John and Jonathan Burke. London and New York, 1967
56. *The Suburbs of Pleasure*, as John and Jonathan Burke. London and New York, 1967
57. *Till Death Us Do Part*, as John and Jonathan Burke. London, 1967
58. *Chitty Chitty Bang Bang: The Story of the Film*, as John and Jonathan Burke. London, 1968
59. *Smashing Time*, as John and Jonathan Burke. London, 1968
60. *Someone Lying, Someone Dying*, as John and Jonathan Burke. London, 1968
61. *Rob the Lady*, as John and Jonathan Burke. London, 1969
62. *Moon Zero Two: The Story of the Film*, as John and Jonathan Burke. London, 1969
63. *The Smashing Bird I Used to Know*, as John and Jonathan Burke. London, 1969
64. *All the Right Noises*, as John and Jonathan Burke. London, 1970
65. *Four Stars for Danger*, as John and Jonathan Burke. London, 1970
66. *Strange Report*, as John and Jonathan Burke. London and New York, 1970
67. *The Killdog*, as Jonathan George, with George Theiner. London and New York, 1970
68. *Suffolk*. London, 1971
69. *England in Colour*. London and New York, 1972
70. *Expo 80*, as John and Jonathan Burke. London, 1972
71. *Dead Letters*, as Jonathan George. London, 1972
72. *Darsham's Tower*, as Harriet Esmond. New York, 1973
73. *Darsham's Folly*, as Harriet Esmond. London, 1974
74. *Sussex*. London, 1974
75. *An Illusrated History of England*. London, 1974
76. *South East England*. London, 1975
77. *The Eye Stones*, as Harriet Esmond. London and New York, 1975
78. *English Villages*. London, 1975
79. *Suffolk in Photographs*. London, 1976
80. *Beautiful Britain*. London, 1976
81. *Czechoslovakia*. London, 1976
82. *The Devil's Footsteps*, as John and Jonathan Burke. London and New York, 1976
83. *Luke's Kingdom*, as John and Jonathan Burke. London, 1976
84. *The Florian Signet*, as Harriet Esmond. London, 1977
85. *The Black Charade*, as John and Jonathan Burke. London and New York, 1977
86. *Historic Britain*. London, 1977
87. *Life in the Castle in Mediaeval England*. London and Totowa (NJ), 1978
88. *Life in the Villa in Roman Britain*. London, 1978
89. *Ladygrove*, as John and Jonathan Burke. London and New York, 1978
90. *The Prince Regent*, as John and Jonathan Burke. London, 1979
91. *The Figurehead*, as Owen Burke. London, 1979

Burnett, Frances Hodgson
American, born November 24, 1849, died October 29, 1924
1. *That Lass O'Lowrie's*. New York, 1877
2. *Little Lord Fauntleroy*. New York, 1886
3. *Editha's Burglar*. Boston, 1888
4. *The Drury Lane Boys' Club*. Washington, 1892
5. *The Secret Garden*. New York, 1911

Burnett, W.R. (William Riley)
American, born November 25, 1899, died April 25, 1982
Pseudonyms: John Monahan, James Updyke
1. *Little Caesar*. New York and London, 1929
2. *Saint Johnson*. New York, 1930
3. *Iron Man*. New York and London, 1930
4. *The Silver Eagle*. New York, 1931
5. *The Giant Swing*. New York, 1932
6. *Dark Hazard*. New York, 1933
7. *Goodbye to the Past: Scenes from the Life of William Meadows*. New York, 1934
8. *The Goodhues of Sinking Creek*. New York, 1934
9. *King Cole*. New York, 1936
10. *Six Days' Grace*. London, 1937
11. *The Dark Command: A Kansan Iliad*. New York and London, 1938
12. *High Sierra*. New York and London, 1940
13. *The Quick Brown Fox*. New York, 1942
14. *Nobody Lives Forever*. New York, 1943
15. *Tomorrow's Another Day*. New York, 1945
16. *Romelle*. New York, 1946
17. *The Asphalt Jungle*. New York, 1949
18. *Stretch Dawson*. New York, 1950
19. *Little Men, Big World*. New York, 1951
20. *Vanity Row*. New York, 1952
21. *Adobe Walls*. New York, 1953
22. *Big Stan*, as John Monahan. New York, 1954
23. *Captain Lightfoot*. New York, 1954
24. *It's Always Four O'Clock*, as James Updyke. New York, 1956
25. *Pale Moon*. New York, 1956
26. *Underdog*. New York and London, 1957
27. *Bitter Ground*. New York and London, 1958
28. *Mi Amigo*. New York, 1959
29. *Conant*. New York, 1961
30. *Round the Clock at Volari's*. New York, 1961
31. *The Widow Barony*. London, 1962
32. *The Goldseekers*. New York, 1962
33. *Sergeants Three*. New York, 1962
34. *The Abilene Samson*. New York, 1963
35. *The Winning of Mickey Free*. New York, 1965
36. *The Roar of the Crowd*. New York, 1965
37. *The Cool Man*. New York, 1968

Burns, Walter Noble
American, born October 24, 1872, died April 15, 1932
1. *A Year with a Whaler*. New York, 1913
2. *The Saga of Billy the Kid*. New York, 1926
3. *Billy the Kid*. London, 1926
4. *Tombstone: An Iliad of the Southwest*. New York, 1927
5. *The One-Way Ride: The Red Trail of Chicago Gangland from Prohibition to Jake Lingle*. New York and London, 1931
6. *The Robin Hood of El Dorado: The Saga of Joaquin Murrieta, Famous Outlaw of California's Age of Gold*. New York, 1932

Burroughs, Edgar Rice
American, born September 1, 1875, died March 19, 1950
1. *Tarzan of the Apes*. Chicago, 1914

2. *The Return of Tarzan.* Chicago, 1915
3. *The Beasts of Tarzan.* Chicago, 1916
4. *The Son of Tarzan.* Chicago, 1917
5. *A Princess of Mars.* Chicago, 1917
6. *The Gods of Mars.* Chicago, 1918
7. *Tarzan and the Jewels of Opar.* Chicago, 1918
8. *The Warlord of Mars.* Chicago, 1919
9. *Jungle Tales of Tarzan.* Chicago and London, 1919
10. *Thuvia, Maid of Mars.* Chicago, 1920
11. *Tarzan the Untamed.* Chicago and London, 1920
12. *Tarzan the Terrible.* Chicago and London, 1921
13. *The Mucker.* Chicago, 1921
14. *The Mucker and The Man Without a Soul.* 2 vols. London, 1921-22
15. *The Chessmen of Mars.* Chicago, 1922
16. *At the Earth's Core.* Chicago, 1922
17. *Pellucidar.* Chicago, 1923
18. *Tarzan and the Golden Lion.* Chicago, 1923
19. *The Girl from Hollywood.* New York, 1923
20. *Tarzan and the Ant Men.* Chicago, 1924
21. *The Land That Time forgot.* Chicago, 1924
22. *The Bandit of Hell's Bend.* Chicago, 1925
23. *The Eternal Lover.* Chicago, 1925
24. *The Cave Girl.* Chicago, 1925
25. *The Moon Maid.* Chicago, 1926
26. *The Mad King.* Chicago, 1926
27. *The War Chief.* Chicago, 1927
28. *The Outlaw of Torn.* Chicago and London, 1927
29. *The Tarzan Twins.* Joliet (IL), 1927
30. *Tarzan, Lord of the Jungle.* Chicago and London, 1928
31. *The Master Mind of Mars.* Chicago, 1928
32. *The Monster Men.* Chicago, 1929
33. *Tarzan and the Lost Empire.* New York, 1929
34. *Tarzan at the Earth's Core.* New York, 1930
35. *Tanar of Pellucidar.* New York, 1930
36. *A Fighting Man of Mars.* New York, 1931
37. *Tarzan the Invincible.* Tarzana (CA), 1931
38. *Tarzan Triumphant.* Tarzana, 1931
39. *Jungle Girl.* Tarzana, 1932
40. *Tarzan and the City of Gold.* Tarzana, 1933
41. *Apache Devil.* Tarzana, 1933
42. *Tarzan and the Golden Lion.* Chicago, 1933
43. *Tarzan and the Lion-Man.* Tarzana, 1934
44. *Pirates of Venus.* Tarzana, 1934
45. *Lost on Venus.* Tarzana, 1935
46. *Tarzan and the Leopard Men.* Tarzana, 1935
47. *Tarzan's Quest.* Tarzana, 1936
48. *Swords of Mars.* Tarzana, 1936
49. *Tarzan and the Tarzan Twins, with Jad-Bal-Ja, the Golden Lion.* Racine (WI), 1936
50. *Back to the Stone Age.* Tarzana, 1937
51. *The Oakdale Affair; The Rider.* Tarzana, 1937
52. *Tarzan and the Forbidden City.* Tarzana, 1938
53. *The Lad and the Lion.* Tarzana, 1938
54. *Carson of Venus.* Tarzana, 1939
55. *Tarzan the Magnificent.* Tarzana, 1939
56. *Official Guide of the Tarzan Clans of America.* Privately printed, 1939
57. *Synthetic Men of Mars.* Tarzana, 1940
58. *The Deputy Sheriff of Comanche County.* Tarzana, 1940
59. *Land of Terror.* Tarzana, 1944
60. *Escape on Venus.* Tarzana, 1946
61. *Tarzan and the Foreign Legion.* Tarzana, 1947
62. *Llana of Gathol.* Tarzana, 1948
63. *Beyond Thirty.* Privately printed, 1955
64. *The Man-Eater.* Privately printed, 1955
65. *The Moon Men.* New York, 1962
66. *Savage Pellucidar.* New York, 1963
67. *John Carter of Mars.* New York, 1964
68. *Tarzan and the Castaways.* New York, 1964
69. *Tarzan and the Madman.* New York, 1964
70. *Beyond the Farthest Star.* New York, 1964
71. *The Girl from Farris's.* Kansas City (MO), 1965
72. *The Efficiency Expert.* Kansas City, 1966
73. *I Am a Barbarian.* Tarzana, 1967
74. *Pirate Blood,* as John Tyler McCulloch. New York, 1970
75. *The Wizard of Venus.* New York, 1970

Burt, Katharine
American, born in 1882, died in 1977
1. *The Branding Iron.* Boston and London, 1919
2. *The Red Lady.* Boston and London, 1920
3. *Hidden Creek.* Boston, 1920
4. *Snow-Blind.* Boston, 1921
5. *"Q".* Boston, 1922
6. *Quest.* Boston, 1925
7. *The Grey Parrot.* London, 1926
8. *Body and Soul.* New York, 1927
9. *Cock's Feather.* Boston, 1928
10. *The Men of Moon Mountain.* London, 1930
11. *A Man's Own Country.* Boston, 1931
12. *The Tall Ladder.* Boston, 1932
13. *Beggar's All.* Boston, 1933
14. *This Woman and This Man.* New York, 1934
15. *Rapture Beyond.* New York, 1935
16. *When Beggars Choose.* Philadelphia, 1937
17. *Safe Road.* Philadelphia, 1938
18. *If Love I Must.* Philadelphia, 1939
19. *No Surrender.* Philadelphia, 1940
20. *Fatal Gift.* Philadelphia, 1941
21. *Captain Millett's Island.* Philadelphia, 1944
22. *Lady in the Tower.* Philadelphia, 1946
23. *Close Pursuit.* New York, 1947
24. *Still Water.* Philadelphia, 1948
25. *Strong Citadel.* New York, 1949
26. *Escape from Paradise.* New York, 1952
27. *Smarty.* New York, 1965
28. *Girl on a Broomstick.* New York, 1967
29. *One Silver Spur.* New York, 1968
30. *A Very Tender Love.* New York, 1975

Busch, Niven
American, born April 26, 1903
1. *Twenty-One Americans, Being Profiles of Some Famous People in Our Time, Together with Silly Pictures of Them Drawn by De Miskey.* New York, 1930
2. *The Carrington Incident.* New York, 1941
3. *They Dream of Home.* New York, 1944
4. *Duel in the Sun.* New York, 1944
5. *Day of the Conquerors.* New York, 1946
6. *The Furies.* New York, 1948
7. *The Hate Merchant.* New York and London, 1953
8. *The Actor.* New York and London, 1955
9. *California Street.* New York and London, 1959
10. *The San Franciscans.* New York, 1962
11. *The Gentleman from California.* New York, 1965
12. *The Takeover.* New York, 1973
13. *Continent's Edge.* New York, 1980

Bush, Christopher [Charlie Christmas Bush]
British, born ca.1888, died September 21, 1973
Other pseudonym: Michael Home
1. *The Plumley Inheritence.* London, 1926
2. *The Perfect Murder Case.* London and New York, 1929
3. *Murder at Fenwold.* London, 1930
4. *Dead Man Twice.* London and New York, 1930

5. *The Death of Cosmo Revere*. New York, 1930
6. *Dancing Death*. London and New York, 1931
7. *Dead Man's Music*. London, 1931
8. *Cut Throat*. London and New York, 1932
9. *The Case of the Unfortunate Village*. London, 1932
10. *The Case of the Three Strange Faces*. London, 1933
11. *The Case of the April Fools*. London and New York, 1933
12. *Return*, as Michael Home. London, 1933
13. *God and the Rabbit*, as Michael Home. London, 1934
14. *The Case of the Dead Shepherd*. London, 1934
15. *The Tea Tray Murders*. New York, 1934
16. *The Case of the 100% Alibis*. London, 1934
17. *The Kitchen Cake Murder*. New York, 1934
18. *The Case of the Chinese Gang*. London and New York, 1935
19. *This String First*, as Michael Home. London, 1935
20. *The Case of the Bonfire Body*. London, 1936
21. *The Body in the Bonfire*. New York, 1936
22. *The Case of the Monday Murders*. London, 1936
23. *Murder on Mondays*. New York, 1936
24. *The Questing Man*, as Michael Home. London, 1936
25. *The Harvest Is Past*, as Michael Home. London, 1937
26. *The Case of the Hanging Rope*. London, 1937
27. *The Wedding Night Murder*. New York, 1937
28. *The Case of the Missing Minutes*. London, 1937
29. *Eight O'Clock Alibi*. New York, 1937
30. *David*. London, 1937
31. *July at Fritham*, as Michael Home. London, 1938
32. *The Case of the Tudor Queen*. London and New York, 1938
33. *The Case of the Leaning Man*. London, 1938
34. *The Leaning Man*. New York, 1938
35. *The Case of the Green Felt Hat*. London and New York, 1939
36. *The Case of the Flying Ass*. London, 1939
37. *The Case of the Climbing Rat*. London, 1940
38. *The Place of Little Birds*, as Michael Home. London, 1941
39. *The Case of the Murdered Major*. London, 1941
40. *The Case of the Fighting Soldier*. London, 1942
41. *Attack in the Desert*, as Michael Home. London, 1942
42. *The House of Shade*, as Michael Home. London and New York, 1942
43. *The Case of the Kidnapped Colonel*. London, 1942
44. *The Case of the Magic Mirror*. London, 1943
45. *City of the Soul*, as Michael Home. London, 1943
46. *The Case of the Running Mouse*. London, 1944
47. *The Case of the Platinum Blonde*. London, 1944
48. *Autumn Fields*. London, 1944
49. *The Case of the Corporal's Leave*. London, 1945
50. *The Cypress Road*, as Michael Home. London, 1945
51. *Spring Sowing*. London, 1946
52. *The Case of the Second Chance*. London, 1946
53. *The Case of the Missing Men*. London, 1946
54. *The Case of the Curious Client*. London, 1947
55. *The Strange Prisoner*, as Michael Home. London, 1947
56. *The Case of the Haven Hotel*. London, 1948
57. *The Case of the Housekeeper's Hair*. London, 1948
58. *The Case of the Seven Belts*. London, 1949
59. *The Case of the Purloined Picture*. London, 1949
60. *No Snow Is Latching*, as Michael Home. London, 1949
61. *The Case of the Happy Warrior*. London, 1950
62. *Grain of the Wood*, as Michael Home. London, 1950
63. *The Soundless Years*, as Michael Home. London, 1951
64. *The Case of the Frightened Mannequin*. New York, 1951
65. *The Case of the Fourth Detective*. London, 1951
66. *The Case of the Corner Cottage*. London, 1951
67. *The Case of the Happy Medium*. London and New York, 1952
68. *The Brackenford Story*, as Michael Home. London and New York, 1952
69. *The Case of the Counterfeit Colonel*. London, 1952
70. *The Case of the Burnt Bohemian*. London, 1953
71. *The Case of the Silken Petticoat*. London, 1953
72. *The Auber File*, as Michael Home. London, 1953
73. *The Case of the Three Lost Letters*. London, 1954
74. *The Case of the Red Brunette*. London, 1954
75. *The Case of the Amateur Actor*. London, 1955
76. *The Case of the Benevolent Bookie*. London, 1955
77. *That Was Yesterday*, as Michael Home. London, 1955
78. *The Case of the Extra Man*. London, 1956
79. *The Case of the Flowery Corpse*. London, 1956
80. *The Case of the Russian Cross*. London, 1956
81. *The Case of the Treble Twist*. London, 1958
82. *The Case of the Triple Twist*. New York, 1958
83. *The Case of the Running Man*. London, 1958
84. *The Case of the Careless Thief*. London, 1959
85. *The Case of the Sapphire Brooch*. London, 1960
86. *The Case of the Extra Grave*. London, 1961
87. *The Case of the Dead Man Gone*. London and New York, 1962
88. *The Case of the Three-Ring Puzzle*. London, 1962
89. *The Case of the Heavenly Twin*. London, 1963
90. *The Case of the Grand Alliance*. London, 1964
91. *The Case of the Jumbo Sandwich*. London, 1965
92. *The Case of the Good Employer*. London, 1966
93. *Winter Harvest: A Norfolk Boyhood*. London, 1967
94. *The Case of the Deadly Diamonds*. London, 1967
95. *The Case of the Prodigal Daughter*. London, 1968

Butler, Gwendoline
British
Pseudonym: Jennie Melville
1. *Receipt for Murder*. London, 1956
2. *Dead in a Row*. London, 1957
3. *The Dull Deed*. London, 1958
4. *The Murdering Kind*. London, 1958
5. *The Interloper*. London, 1959
6. *Dine and Be Dead*. New York, 1960
7. *Death Lives Next Door*. London, 1960
8. *Make Me a Murderer*. London, 1961
9. *Coffin in Oxford*. London, 1962
10. *Come Home and Be Killed*, as Jennie Melville. London, 1962
11. *Burning Is a Substitute for Loving*, as Jennie Melville. London, 1963
12. *Coffin for Baby*. London and New York, 1963
13. *Coffin Waiting*. London, 1963
14. *Coffin in Malta*. London, 1964
15. *Murderer's Houses*, as Jennie Melville. London, 1964
16. *There Lies Your Love*, as Jennie Melville. London, 1965
17. *Nell Alone*, as Jennie Melville. London, 1966
18. *A Nameless Coffin*. London, 1966
19. *A Different Kind of Summer*, as Jennie Melville. London, 1967
20. *Coffin Following*. London, 1968
21. *Coffin's Dark Number*. London, 1969
22. *The Hunter in the Shadows*, as Jennie Melville. London, 1969
23. *A New Kind of Killer, An Old Kind of Death*, as Jennie Melville. London, 1970
24. *A Coffin from the Past*. London, 1970
25. *Ironwood*, as Jennie Melville. London and New York, 1972
26. *Nun's Castle*, as Jennie Melville. New York, 1973
27. *A Coffin for Pandora*. London, 1973
28. *A Coffin for the Canary*. London, 1974
29. *Olivia*. New York, 1974

30. *Sarsen Place.* New York, 1974
31. *The Vesey Inheritance.* New York, 1975
32. *Raven's Forge,* as Jennie Melville. London and New York, 1975
33. *Dragon's Eye,* as Jennie Melville. New York, 1976
34. *Meadowsweet.* New York, 1977
35. *The Brides of Friedberg.* London, 1977
36. *Tarot's Tower,* as Jennie Melville. New York, 1978
37. *Axwater,* as Jennie Melville. London, 1978
38. *The Red Staircase.* New York, 1979
39. *Murder Has a Pretty Face,* as Jennie Melville. London, 1981

Butler, Octavia E. (Estelle)
American, born June 22, 1947
1. *Patternmaster.* New York, 1976
2. *Mind of My Mind.* New York, 1977
3. *Survivor.* New York and London, 1978
4. *Kindred.* New York, 1979
5. *Wild Seed.* New York and London, 1980

Cadell, Elizabeth [Violet Elizabeth Cadell]
British, born November 10, 1903
Pseudonym: Harriet Ainsworth
1. *My Dear Aunt Flora.* London, 1946
2. *Last Straw for Harriet.* New York, 1947
3. *Fishy, Said the Admiral.* London, 1948
4. *River Lodge.* London, 1948
5. *Gay Pursuit.* New York, 1948
6. *Iris in Winter.* New York, 1949
7. *Sun in the Morning.* New York, 1950
8. *Brimstone in the Garden.* New York, 1950
9. *The Greenwood Shady.* London, 1951
10. *Enter Mrs. Belchamber.* New York, 1951
11. *The Frenchman and the Lady.* London, 1952
12. *Men and Angels.* London, 1952
13. *Crystal Clear.* New York, 1952
14. *Spring Green.* London, 1953
15. *Journey's Eve.* London, 1953
16. *The Cuckoo in Spring.* New York and London, 1954
17. *Around the Rugged Rock.* New York, 1954
18. *The Gentlemen Go By.* London, 1954
19. *The Lark Shall Sing.* New York and London, 1955
20. *The Blue Sky of Spring.* London, 1956
21. *I Love a Lass.* New York, 1956
22. *Consider the Lillies,* as Harriet Ainsworth. London, 1956
23. *Bridal Array.* London, 1957
24. *The Green Empress.* London, 1958
25. *Shadows on the Water,* as Harriet Ainsworth. London, 1958
26. *Shadows on the Water.* New York, 1958
27. *Sugar Candy Cottage.* London, 1958
28. *Alice, Where Art Thou?* London, 1959
29. *The Yellow Brick Road.* London and New York, 1960
30. *Honey for Tea.* London, 1961
31. *Six Impossible Things.* London and New York, 1961
32. *Language of the Heart.* London, 1962
33. *The Toy Sword.* New York, 1962
34. *Letter to My Love.* London, 1963
35. *Mixed Marriage: The Diary of a Portugese Bride.* London, 1963
36. *Be My Guest.* London, 1964
37. *Death Among Friends,* as Harriet Ainsworth. London, 1964
38. *Come Be My Guest.* New York, 1964
39. *Canary Yellow.* London and New York, 1965
40. *The Fox from His Lair.* London, 1965
41. *The Corner Shop.* London, 1966
42. *The Stratton Story.* London, 1967
43. *Mrs. Westerby Changes Course.* New York, 1968
44. *The Golden Collar.* London and New York, 1969
45. *The Friendly Air.* London, 1970
46. *The Past Tense of Love.* London and New York, 1970
47. *Home for the Wedding.* London, 1971
48. *The Haymaker.* London, 1972
49. *Royal Summons.* New York, 1973
50. *Deck with Flowers.* London, 1973
51. *The Fledgling.* London and New York, 1975
52. *Game in Diamonds.* London and New York, 1976
53. *Parson's House.* London and New York, 1977
54. *Round Dozen.* London and New York, 1978
55. *Family Gathering.* London, 1979
56. *Return Match.* London and New York, 1979
57. *The Marrying Kind.* London and New York, 1980
58. *Any Two Can Play.* New York, 1981
59. *A Lion in the Way.* London and New York, 1982

Caine, Hall [Thomas Henry Hall Caine]
British, born May 14, 1858, died August 31, 1931
1. *Richard III and Macbeth Dramatic Study.* London, 1877
2. *Recollections of Dante Gabriel Rossetti.* London, 1882
3. *Cobwebs of Criticism.* London, 1883
4. *The Shadow of a Crime.* London and New York, 3 vols., 1885
5. *She's All the World to Me.* New York, 1885
6. *The Deemster.* London, 3 vols., 1887
7. *Life of Samuel Taylor Coleridge.* London, 1887
8. *A Son of Hagar.* London, 1887
9. *The Bondman: A New Saga.* New York, 1889
10. *The Prophet: A Parable.* London, 1890
11. *The Scapegoat.* London, 2 vols., 1891
12. *The Little Manx Nation.* London and New York, 1891
13. *Mary Magdalene: The New Apocrypha.* Privately printed, 1891
14. *Cap'n Davy's Honeymoon, The Last Confession, The Blind Mother.* London, 1892
15. *Cap'n Davey's Honeymoon.* New York, 1892
16. *The Last Confession, The Blind Mother.* New York, 1892
17. *The Manxman.* London and New York, 1894
18. *The Mahdi; or, Love and Race.* New York and London, 1894
19. *The Little Man Island: Scenes and Specimen Days in the Isle-of-Man.* Douglas (Eng), 1894
20. *The Christian.* London and New York, 1897
21. *The Eternal City.* London and New York, 1901
22. *The Prodigal Son.* London and New York, 1904
23. *Drink: A Love Story on a Great Question.* London, 1906
24. *My Story.* London, 1908
25. *The White Prophet.* London, 2 vols., 1909
26. *Why I Wrote "The White Prophet."* Privately printed, 1909
27. *King Edward: A Prince and A Great Man.* London, 1910
28. *The Woman Thou Gavest Me.* London and Philadelphia, 1913
29. *The Drama of Three Hundred Sixty Five Days: Scenes in the Great War.* London and Philadelphia, 1915
30. *Our Girls: Their Work for the War.* London, 1916
31. *The Master of Man.* London and Philadelphia, 1921
32. *The Woman of Knockaloe: A Parable.* London and New York, 1923
33. *Life of Christ.* London and New York, 1938

Caird, Janet (Hinshaw)
British, born April 24, 1913
1. *Angus the Tartan Partan.* London, 1961
2. *Murder Reflected.* London, 1965
3. *In a Glass Darkly.* New York, 1966
4. *Perturbing Spirit.* London and New York, 1966
5. *Murder Scholastic.* London, 1967

6. *The Loch.* London, 1968
7. *Murder Remote.* New York, 1973
8. *The Shrouded Way.* New York, 1973
9. *Some Walk a Narrow Path.* Edinburgh, 1977
10. *The Umbrella-Maker's Daughter.* Scotland and New York, 1980

Caldwell, Taylor [Janet Miriam Taylor Holland Caldwell]
American, born September 7, 1900
Pseudonym: Max Reiner
1. *Dynasty of Death.* New York, 1938
2. *The Eagles Gather.* New York and London, 1940
3. *Time No Longer,* as Max Reiner. New York, 1941
4. *The Earth Is the Lord's.* New York and London, 1941
5. *The Strong City.* New York and London, 1942
6. *The Arm and the Darkness.* New York and London, 1943
7. *The Turnbulls.* New York, 1943
8. *The Final Hour.* New York, 1944
9. *The Wide House.* New York, 1945
10. *This Side of Innocence.* New York, 1946
11. *There Was a Time.* New York, 1947
12. *Melissa.* New York, 1948
13. *Let Love Come Last.* New York, 1948
14. *The Balance Wheel.* New York, 1951
15. *The Beautiful Is Vanished.* London, 1951
16. *The Devil's Advocate.* New York, 1952
17. *Maggie, Her Marriage.* New York, 1953
18. *Your Sins and Mine.* New York, 1955
19. *Tender Victory.* New York and London, 1956
20. *Never Victorious, Never Defeated.* New York and London, 1956
21. *The Sound of Thunder.* New York, 1957
22. *Dear and Glorious Physician.* New York and London, 1959
23. *The Listener.* New York, 1960
24. *The Man Who Listens.* London, 1961
25. *A Prologue to Love.* New York, 1961
26. *Grandmother and the Priests.* New York, 1963
27. *To See the Glory.* London, 1963
28. *The Late Clare Beame.* New York, 1963
29. *A Pillar of Iron.* New York, 1965
30. *Wicked Angel.* New York, 1965
31. *No One Hears But Him.* New York and London, 1966
32. *Dialogues with the Devil.* New York, 1967
33. *Testimony of Two Men.* New York, 1968
34. *Great Lion of God.* New York and London, 1970
35. *On Growing Up Tough.* Old Greenwich (CT), 1971
36. *Growing Up Tough.* London, 1971
37. *Captains and the Kings.* New York, 1972
38. *Glory and the Lightning.* New York, 1974
39. *To Look and Pass.* London, 1974
40. *The Romance of Atlantis,* with Jess Stearn. New York, 1975
41. *Ceremony of the Innocent.* New York, 1976
42. *I, Judas,* with Jess Stearn. New York, 1977
43. *Bright Flows the River.* New York, 1978
44. *Answer as a Man.* New York and London, 1981

Cameron, Lou
American, born June 20, 1924
Pseudonyms: Justin Adams, Julie Cameron
1. *Angel's Flight.* New York, 1960
2. *The Big Red Ball.* New York, 1961
3. *The Sky Divers.* New York, 1962
4. *The Empty Quarter.* New York, 1962
5. *The Bastard's Name Is War.* New York, 1963
6. *The Black Camp.* New York and London, 1963
7. *Not Even You, Mother.* New York, 1963
8. *The Green Fields of Hell.* New York, 1964
9. *The Block Busters.* New York, 1964
10. *None But the Brave.* New York, 1965
11. *The Dirty War of Sargeant Slade.* New York, 1966
12. *Iron Men with Wooden Wings.* New York, 1967
13. *The Dragon's Spine.* New York, 1968
14. *File on a Missing Redhead.* New York, 1968
15. *The Good Guy.* New York, 1968
16. *The Outsider.* New York, 1969
17. *Before It's Too Late.* New York, 1970
18. *The Amphorae Pirates.* New York, 1970
19. *Behind the Scarlet Door.* New York, 1971
20. *Spurhead.* New York, 1971
21. *Cybernia.* New York, 1972
22. *The Girl with the Dynamite Bangs.* New York, 1973
23. *The First Blood.* New York, No date
24. *Hannibal Brooks.* New York, No date
25. *Mistress Bayou Labelle.* New York, No date
26. *Mud War.* New York, No date
27. *Tipping Point.* New York, No date
28. *Tunnel War.* New York, No date
29. *Califonia Split.* New York, 1974
30. *Barca.* New York and Henley on Thames (Eng), 1974
31. *The Closing Circle.* New York, 1974
32. *Devil in the Pines,* as Julie Cameron. New York, 1975
33. *The Darklings.* New York, 1975
34. *Tancredi.* New York, 1975
35. *Doc Travis.* New York, 1975
36. *North to Cheyenne.* New York, 1975
37. *The Guns of Durango.* New York, 1976
38. *The Spirit Horses.* New York, 1976
39. *Dekker.* New York, 1976
40. *Drop into Hell.* New York, 1976
41. *Chains,* as Justin Adams. New York, 1977
42. *How the West Was Won.* New York, 1977
43. *Code Seven.* New York, 1977
44. *The Big Lonely.* New York, 1978
45. *The Cascade Ghost.* New York, 1978
46. *The Subway Stalker.* New York, 1980
47. *This Fever in My Blood.* New York, 1980
48. *The Wilderness Seekers.* New York, 1980
49. *The Track Stalker.* New York, 1980

Capps, Benjamin (Franklin)
American, born June 11, 1922
1. *Hanging on Comanche Wells.* New York, 1962
2. *The Trail to Ogallala.* New York, 1964
3. *Sam Chance.* New York, 1965
4. *A Woman of the People.* New York, 1966
5. *The Brothers of Uterica.* New York, 1967
6. *The White Man's Road.* New York, 1969
7. *The True Memoirs of Charley Blankenship.* Philadelphia, 1972
8. *The Indians.* New York, 1973
9. *The Warren Wagontrain Raid.* New York, 1974
10. *The Great Chiefs.* New York, 1975
11. *Woman Chief.* New York, 1979

Carter, Felicity (Winifred)
British, born in 1906
Pseudonyms: John and Emery Bonett, with John H.A. Coulson; Emery Bonett, with John H.A. Coulson
1. *A Girl Must Live,* as Emery Bonett. London, 1936
2. *Never Go Dark.* London, 1940
3. *Make Do with Spring,* as Emery Bonett. London, 1941
4. *High Pavement,* as Emery Bonett. London, 1944
5. *Old Mrs. Camelot,* as Emery Bonett. Philadelphia, 1944
6. *Dead Lion,* as John and Emery Bonett. London and New York, 1949
7. *A Banner for Pegasus,* as John and Emery Bonett. London, 1951

8. *Not in the Script,* as John and Emery Bonett. New York, 1951
9. *No Grave for a Lady,* as John and Emery Bonett. New York, 1959
10. *Better Dead,* as John and Emery Bonett. London, 1964
11. *Better Off Dead,* as John and Emery Bonett. New York, 1964
12. *The Private Face of Murder,* as John and Emery Bonett. London and New York, 1966
13. *This Side Murder?,* as John and Emery Bonett. London, 1967
14. *Murder on the Costa Brava,* as John and Emery Bonett. New York, 1968
15. *The Sound of Murder,* as John and Emery Bonett. London, 1970
16. *No Time to Kill,* as John and Emery Bonett. London and New York, 1972

Carter, Forrest
American, born in 1925
1. *The Rebel Outlaw, Josey Wales.* Gantt (AL), 1973
2. *Gone to Texas.* New York and London, 1975
3. *The Outlaw Josey Wales.* New York, 1976
4. *The Vengence Trail of Josey Wales.* New York, 1976
5. *The Education of Little Tree.* New York, 1976
6. *Watch for Me on the Mountain.* New York, 1978
7. *Cry Geronimo.* New York, 1980

Case, David
American
1. *The Cell: Three Tales of Horror.* New York, 1969
2. *The Cell and Other Tales of Horror.* London, 1969
3. *Fengriffen: A Chilling Tale.* New York, 1970
4. *Fengriffen and Other Stories.* London, 1971
5. *And Now the Screaming Starts.* London, 1973
6. *Plumb Drillin'.* New York, 1975
7. *The Fighting Breed.* New York, 1980
8. *Wolf Tracks.* New York, 1980
9. *The Third Grave.* Sauk City (WI), 1981
10. *Guns of Valentine.* New York, 1982
11. *Gold Fever.* New York, 1982
12. *Among the Wolves and Other Tales.* Sauk City, 1982

Case, Robert Ormond
American, born October 8, 1895
1. *Just Buckaroos.* New York, 1927
2. *Riders of the Grande Ronde.* New York, 1928
3. *Dynamite Smith—Cowboy.* New York, 1930
4. *The Yukon Drive.* New York, 1930
5. *Whispering Valley.* New York, 1932
6. *Buckaroo Partners.* London, 1934
7. *A Pair o' Mavericks.* London, 1934
8. *Big Timber.* Philadelphia, 1937
9. *Timber Joe.* London, 1938
10. *Wings North.* New York and London, 1938
11. *The Golden Hills.* London, 1939
12. *River of the West: A Story of Opportunity in the Columbia Empire.* Portland (OR), 1940
13. *Golden Portage.* New York, 1940
14. *West of Barter River.* New York, 1941
15. *White Victory.* New York, 1943
16. *Last Mountains: The Story of the Cascades.* New York, 1945
17. *The Empire Builders.* New York, 1947
18. *We Called it Culture: The Story of Chautauqua,* with Victoria Chase. New York, 1948
19. *Buccaneer of the Barrens.* London, 1953
20. *Cold Gold.* London, 1956
21. *Bootleg Gold.* London, 1957

Cather, Willa (Sibert)
American, born December 7, 1873, died April 24, 1947
1. *April Twilights.* Boston, 1903
2. *The Troll Garden.* New York, 1905
3. *Alexander's Bridge.* Boston and London, 1912
4. *O Pioneers!* Boston and London, 1913
5. *My Autobiography,* by S.S. McClure (ghostwritten by Cather). New York, 1914
6. *The Song of the Lark.* Boston, 1915
7. *My Antonia.* Boston, 1918
8. *Youth and the Bright Medusa.* New York, 1920
9. *One of Ours.* New York, 1922
10. *April Twilights and Other Poems.* New York, 1923
11. *A Lost Lady.* New York, 1923
12. *The Professor's House.* New York and London, 1925
13. *My Mortal Enemy.* New York, 1926
14. *Death Comes for the Archbishop.* New York and London, 1927
15. *Shadows on the Rock.* New York, 1931
16. *The Fear That Walks by Noonday.* New York, 1931
17. *Obscure Destinies.* New York and London, 1932
18. *Lucy Gayheart.* New York and London, 1935
19. *Not Under Forty.* New York and London, 1936
20. *Sapphira and the Slave Girl.* New York, 1940
21. *The Old Beauty and Others.* New York, 1948
22. *On Writing: Critical Studies as an Art.* New York, 1949
23. *Writings from Willa Cather's Campus Years.* Lincoln (NB), 1950
24. *Willa Cather in Europe, Her Own Story of the First Journey.* New York, 1956
25. *Early Stories of Willa Cather.* New York, 1957
26. *Collected Short Fiction 1892-1912.* Lincoln, 1965
27. *The Kingdom of Art: Willa Cather's First Principles and Critical Statements 1893-1896.* Lincoln, 1967
28. *The World and the Parish: Willa Cather's Articles and Reviews 1893-1902.* Lincoln, 2 vols., 1970
29. *Uncle Valentine and Other Stories: Willa Cather's Uncollected Short Fiction 1915-1959.* Lincoln, 1973

Charbonneau, Louis (Henry)
American, born January 20, 1924
Pseudonym: Carter Travis Young
1. *No Place on Earth.* New York, 1958
2. *Night of Violence.* New York and London, 1959
3. *Nor All Your Tears.* New York, 1959
4. *The Time of Desire.* London, 1960
5. *The Trapped Ones.* London, 1960
6. *The Wild Breed,* as Carter Travis Young. New York, 1960
7. *The Sudden Gun,* as Carter Travis Young. London, 1960
8. *The Savage Plain,* as Carter Travis Young. New York, 1961
9. *Shadow of a Gun,* as Carter Travis Young. New York, 1961
10. *Corpus Earthling.* New York, 1960
11. *The Bitter Iron,* as Carter Travis Young. New York, 1964
12. *The Sentinel Stars.* New York and London, 1964
13. *Psychedelic-40.* New York, 1965
14. *Long Boots, Hard Boots,* as Carter Travis Young. New York, 1965
15. *Way Out.* London, 1966
16. *Down to Earth.* New York, 1967
17. *Antic Earth.* London, 1967
18. *Why Did they Kill Charley?* as Carter Travis Young. New York and London, 1967
19. *The Specials.* London, 1967
20. *The Sensitives,* as Carter Travis Young. New York, 1968
21. *Down from the Mountain.* New York, 1969
22. *Winchester Quarantine,* as Carter Travis Young. New York, 1970
23. *And Hope to Die.* New York, 1970

24. *Barrier World.* New York, 1970
25. *The Pocket Hunters,* as Carter Travis Young. New York, 1972
26. *Winter of the Coup,* as Carter Travis Young. New York, 1972
27. *The Captive,* as Carter Travis Young. New York, 1973
28. *Guns of Darkness,* as Carter Travis Young. New York, 1974
29. *Blaine's Law,* as Carter Travis Young. New York, 1974
30. *From a Dark Place.* New York, 1974
31. *Embryo.* New York, 1976
32. *Red Grass.* New York, 1976
33. *Intruder.* New York, 1979
34. *The Liar.* New York, 1979
35. *Winter Drift,* as Carter Travis Young. New York, 1980
36. *The Brea.* New York, 1983

Charles, Theresa [Irene Maude Swatridge]
British
Other pseudonyms: Fay Chandos, Leslie Lance, Irene Mossop, Virginia Storm, Jan Tempest
1. *Well Played, Juliana!* as Irene Mossop. London, 1928
2. *Prunella Plays the Game,* as Irene Mossop. London, 1929
3. *Freesia's Feud,* as Irene Mossop. London, 1930
4. *The Luck of the Oakleighs,* as Irene Mossop. London, 1930
5. *Chris in Command,* as Irene Mossop. London, 1930
6. *Sylvia Sways the School,* as Irene Mossop. London, 1930
7. *Theresa's First Term,* as Irene Mossop. London, 1930
8. *Vivien of St. Val's,* as Irene Mossop. London, 1931
9. *Charm's Last Chance,* as Irene Mossop. London, 1931
10. *Nicky—New Girl,* as Irene Mossop. London, 1931
11. *Rona's Rival,* as Irene Mossop. London, 1931
12. *A Rebel at "Rowan's",* as Irene Mossop. London, 1932
13. *Barbara Black-Sheep,* as Irene Mossop. London, 1932
14. *Una Wins Through,* as Irene Mossop. London, 1932
15. *Feud in the Fifth,* as Irene Mossop. London, 1933
16. *Hilary Leads the Way,* as Irene Mossop. London, 1933
17. *The Taming of Pickles,* as Irene Mossop. London, 1933
18. *The Fifth at Cliff House,* as Irene Mossop. London, 1934
19. *The Four V's,* as Irene Mossop. London, 1934
20. *The Fourth at St. Faith's,* as Irene Mossop. London, 1934
21. *Play Up, Pine House!* as Irene Mossop. London, 1934
22. *Theresa on Trial,* as Irene Mossop. London, 1935
23. *Theda Marsh,* as Irene Mossop. London, 1935
24. *Stepmother of Five,* as Jan Tempest. London, 1936
25. *Someone New to Love,* as Jan Tempest. London, 1936
26. *Be Still My Heart!,* as Jan Tempest. London, 1936
27. *Kiss—and Forget,* as Jan Tempest. London, 1936
28. *Believe Me, Beloved—,* as Jan Tempest. London, 1936
29. *All This I Gave,* as Jan Tempest. London, 1937
30. *The Gay Adventure.* London, 1937
31. *No Other Man—,* as Jan Tempest. London, 1937
32. *Grow Up Little Lady!* as Jan Tempest. London, 1937
33. *Carey Come Back!* as Jan Tempest. London, 1937
34. *If I Love Again,* as Jan Tempest. London, 1937
35. *No Limit to Love,* as Fay Chandos. London, 1937
36. *No Escape from Love,* as Fay Chandos. London, 1937
37. *Man of My Dreams,* as Fay Chandos. London, 1937
38. *Before I Make You Mine,* as Fay Chandos. London, 1938
39. *Wife for a Wager,* as Fay Chandos. London, 1938
40. *Gay Knight I Love,* as Fay Chandos. London, 1938
41. *Face the Music—for Love,* as Jan Tempest. London, 1938
42. *Man—and Waif,* as Jan Tempest. London, 1938
43. *Because My Love Is Come,* as Jan Tempest. London, 1938
44. *When First I Loved,* as Jan Tempest. London, 1938
45. *Hilary in His Heart,* as Jan Tempest. London, 1938
46. *Say You're Sorry,* as Jan Tempest. London, 1939
47. *My Only Love,* as Jan Tempest. London, 1939
48. *Uninvited Guest,* as Jan Tempest. London, 1939
49. *I'll Try Anything Once,* as Jan Tempest. London, 1939
50. *All I Ask,* as Fay Chandos. London, 1939
51. *Another Woman's Shoes,* as Fay Chandos. London, 1939
52. *When Three Walk Together,* as Fay Chandos. London, 1939
53. *The Man Who Wasn't Mac,* as Fay Chandos. London, 1939
54. *Husband for Hire,* as Fay Chandos. London, 1940
55. *You Should Have Warned Me,* as Fay Chandos. London, 1940
56. *When We Two Parted,* as Fay Chandos. London, 1940
57. *Substitute for Sherry,* as Fay Chandos. London, 1940
58. *Top of the Beanstalk,* as Jan Tempest. London, 1940
59. *The Broken Gate,* as Jan Tempest. London, 1940
60. *Why Wouldn't He Wait?* as Jan Tempest. London, 1940
61. *Little Brown Girl,* as Jan Tempest. London, 1940
62. *The Distant Drum,* with Charles Swatridge. London, 1940
63. *Alice, Where Are You?* as Leslie Lance. London, 1940
64. *Take a Chance,* as Leslie Lance. London, 1940
65. *My Enemy and I,* with Charles Swatridge. London, 1941
66. *Always Another Man,* as Jan Tempest. London, 1941
67. *The Moment I Saw You,* as Jan Tempest. London, 1941
68. *The Unknown Joy,* as Jan Tempest. London, 1941
69. *Ghost of June,* as Jan Tempest. London, 1941
70. *Women Are So Simple,* as Fay Chandos. London, 1941
71. *Only a Touch,* as Fay Chandos. London, 1941
72. *Awake, My Love!* as Fay Chandos. London, 1942
73. *A Letter to My Love,* as Fay Chandos. London, 1942
74. *No Time for a Man,* as Jan Tempest. London, 1942
75. *Romance on Ice,* as Jan Tempest. London, 1942
76. *If You'll Marry me,* as Jan Tempest. London, 1942
77. *A Prince for Portia,* as Jan Tempest. London, 1943
78. *Wife after Work,* as Jan Tempest. London, 1943
79. *The Long Way Home,* as Jan Tempest. London, 1943
80. *Eve and I,* as Fay Chandos. London, 1943
81. *A Man to Follow,* as Fay Chandos. London, 1943
82. *Away from Each Other,* as Fay Chandos. London, 1944
83. *Made to Marry,* as Fay Chandos. London, 1944
84. *Just a Little Longer,* as Fay Chandos. London, 1944
85. *"Never Again!" Said Nicola,* as Jan Tempest. London, 1944
86. *The One Thing I Wanted,* as Jan Tempest. London, 1944
87. *Utility Husband,* as Jan Tempest. London, 1944
88. *Westward to My Love,* as Jan Tempest. London, 1944
89. *Love While You Wait,* as Jan Tempest. London, 1944
90. *Not for This Alone,* as Jan Tempest. London, 1945
91. *Last Year's Roses,* as Fay Chandos. London, 1945
92. *To Be a Bride,* as Fay Chandos. London, 1945
93. *A Man for Margaret,* as Fay Chandos. London, 1945
94. *Three Roads to Romance,* as Fay Chandos. London, 1945
95. *When Time Stands Still,* as Fay Chandos. London, 1946
96. *Home Is the Hero,* as Fay Chandos. London, 1946
97. *The Orange Blossom Shop,* as Jan Tempest. London, 1946
98. *Happy with Either,* as Jan Tempest. London, 1946
99. *House of the Pines,* as Jan Tempest. London, 1946
100. *Bachelor's Bride,* as Jan Tempest. London, 1946
101. *Lovely, Though Late,* as Jan Tempest. London, 1946
102. *To Save My Life,* with Charles Swatridge. London, 1946
103. *The Dark Stranger,* as Leslie Lance. London, 1946
104. *Happy Now I Go,* with Charles Swatridge. London, 1947
105. *Close Your Eyes,* as Jan Tempest. London, 1947
106. *Teach Me to Love,* as Jan Tempest. London, 1947
107. *Because I Wear Your Ring,* as Fay Chandos. London, 1947
108. *Cousins May Kiss,* as Fay Chandos. London, 1947
109. *Lost Summer,* as Fay Chandos. London, 1948
110. *Since First We Met,* as Fay Chandos. London, 1948
111. *How Can I Forget?* as Jan Tempest. London, 1948
112. *Cinderella Had Two Sisters,* as Jan Tempest. London, 1948
113. *Short-Cut to the Stars,* as Jan Tempest. London, 1949
114. *Never Another Love,* as Jan Tempest. London, 1949

115. *Promise of Paradise*, as Jan Tempest. London, 1949
116. *Man-Made Miracle*, with Charles Swatridge. London, 1949
117. *June in Her Eyes*, as Fay Chandos. London, 1949
118. *For a Dream's Sake*, as Fay Chandos. London, 1949
119. *Fugitive from Love*, as Fay Chandos. London, 1950
120. *There Is a Tide*, as Fay Chandos. London, 1950
121. *The Ugly Prince*, with Charles Swatridge, as Virginia Storm. London, 1950
122. *Nobody Else—Ever*, as Jan Tempest. London, 1950
123. *A Match Is Made*, as Jan Tempest. London, 1950
124. *Now and Always*, as Jan Tempest. London, 1950
125. *Until I Find Her*, as Jan Tempest. London, 1950
126. *First I Must Forget*, as Virginia Storm. London, 1951
127. *Two Loves for Tamara*, as Jan Tempest. London, 1951
128. *This Time It's Love*, as Fay Chandos. London, 1951
129. *First and Favourite Wife*, as Fay Chandos. London, 1952
130. *Families Are Such Fun*, as Fay Chandos. London, 1952
131. *Open the Door to Love*, as Jan Tempest. London, 1952
132. *Without a Honeymoon*, as Jan Tempest. London, 1952
133. *Happy Is the Wooing*, as Jan Tempest. London, 1952
134. *At a Touch I Yield*, with Charles Swatridge. London, 1952
135. *Man of the Family*, as Leslie Lance. London, 1952
136. *Fairer Than She*. London, 1953
137. *Meet Me By Moonlight*, as Jan Tempest. London, 1953
138. *Give Her Gardenias*, as Jan Tempest. London, 1953
139. *Leave It to Nancy*, as Fay Chandos. London, 1953
140. *The Other One*, as Fay Chandos. London, 1953
141. *Leave It to Nancy*, as Fay Chandos. London, 1953
142. *Find Another Eden*, as Fay Chandos. London, 1953
143. *Just Before the Wedding*, as Fay Chandos. London, 1954
144. *Doctors Are Different*, as Fay Chandos. London, 1954
145. *Enchanted Valley*, as Jan Tempest. London, 1954
146. *First-Time of Asking*, as Jan Tempest. London, 1954
147. *My Only Love*, with Charles Swatridge. London, 1954
148. *The Kinder Love*, with Charles Swatridge. London, 1955
149. *Where the Heart Is*, as Jan Tempest. London, 1955
150. *Husbands at Home*, as Fay Chandos. London, 1955
151. *Ask Me Again*, as Jan Tempest. London, 1955
152. *Hibiscus House*, as Fay Chandos. London, 1955
153. *So Nearly Married*, as Fay Chandos. London, 1956
154. *For Those in Love*, as Jan Tempest. London, 1956
155. *Wedding Bells for Willow*, as Jan Tempest. London, 1956
156. *The Burning Beacon*, with Charles Swatridge. London, 1956
157. *Craddock's Kingdom*, as Jan Tempest. London, 1957
158. *Will Not Now Take Place*, as Jan Tempest. London, 1957
159. *The Romantic Touch*, as Fay Chandos. London, 1957
160. *Partners Are a Problem*, as Fay Chandos. London, 1957
161. *Model Girl's Farm*, as Fay Chandos. London, 1958
162. *The Youngest Sister*, as Jan Tempest. London, 1958
163. *Because There Is Hope*, as Jan Tempest. London, 1958
164. *Because My Love Is Coming*, as Jan Tempest. London, 1958
165. *The Ultimate Surrender*, with Charles Swatridge. London, 1958
166. *A Girl Called Evelyn*, with Charles Swatridge. London, 1959
167. *Romance for Rose*, as Jan Tempest. London, 1959
168. *Wild Violets*, as Fay Chandos. London, 1959
169. *Stranger to Love*, as Jan Tempest. London, 1960
170. *No Through Road*, with Charles Swatridge. London, 1960
171. *Spun by the Moon*, as Leslie Lance. London, 1960
172. *Sisters in Love*, as Leslie Lance. London, 1960
173. *A Summer's Grace*, as Leslie Lance. London, 1961
174. *Mistress of Castle Mount*, as Jan Tempest. London, 1961
175. *The Turning Point*, as Jan Tempest. London, 1961
176. *When Four Ways Meet*, as Fay Chandos. London, 1961
177. *Sister Sylvan*, as Fay Chandos. London, 1962
178. *House on the Rocks*, with Charles Swatridge. London, 1962
179. *Ring for Nurse Raine*, with Charles Swatridge. London, 1962
180. *Springtime for Sally*, as Leslie Lance. London, 1962
181. *Spreading Sails*, as Leslie Lance. London, 1963
182. *Widower's Wife*, with Charles Swatridge. London, 1963
183. *Patient in Love*, with Charles Swatridge. London, 1963
184. *That Nice Nurse Nevin*, as Jan Tempest. London and Toronto, 1963
185. *The Madderleys Married*, as Jan Tempest. London, 1963
186. *Two Other People*, as Fay Chandos. London, 1964
187. *The Flower and the Fruit*, as Jan Tempest. London, 1964
188. *Nurse Incognito*, as Fay Chandos. Toronto, 1964
189. *Nurse Alice in Love*, with Charles Swatridge. London, 1964
190. *The Young Curmudgeon*, as Leslie Lance. London, 1964
191. *I'll Ride Beside You*, as Leslie Lance. London, 1965
192. *Bright Winter*, as Leslie Lance. London, 1965
193. *The Man for Me*, with Charles Swatridge. London, 1965
194. *Nurse Willow's Ward*, as Jan Tempest. London, 1965
195. *The Way We Used to Be*, as Jan Tempest. London, 1965
196. *Jubilee Hospital*, as Jan Tempest. London, 1966
197. *The Lonesome Road*, as Jan Tempest. London, 1966
198. *How Much You Mean to Me*, with Charles Swatridge. London, 1966
199. *The Shrouded Tower*, with Charles Swatridge. New York, 1966
200. *Lady in the Mist*, with Charles Swatridge. New York, 1966
201. *Return to Terror*, with Charles Swatridge. New York, 1966
202. *Don't Give Your Heart Away*, as Fay Chandos. London, 1966
203. *Stranger in Love*, as Fay Chandos. London, 1966
204. *No Summer Beauty*, as Leslie Lance. London, 1967
205. *Return to King's Mere*, as Leslie Lance. London, 1967
206. *Bride of Emersham*, as Leslie Lance. New York, 1967
207. *Farm by the Sea*, as Fay Chandos. London, 1967
208. *Proud Citadel*, with Charles Swatridge. London and New York, 1967
209. *The Way Men Love*, with Charles Swatridge. London, 1967
210. *Meant to Meet*, as Jan Tempest. London, 1967
211. *Dark Legacy*, with Charles Swatridge. London, 1968
212. *The Shadowy Third*, with Charles Swatridge. London, 1968
213. *Lyra, My Love*, as Jan Tempest. London, 1969
214. *From Fairest Flowers*, with Charles Swatridge. London, 1969
215. *Nurse in the Woods*, as Leslie Lance. London, 1969
216. *The Summer People*, as Leslie Lance. London, 1969
217. *Nurse Verenain Weirwater*, as Leslie Lance. London, 1970
218. *Wayward as the Swallow*, with Charles Swatridge. London, 1970
219. *Second Honeymoon*, with Charles Swatridge. London, 1970
220. *The Three of Us*, as Fay Chandos. London, 1970
221. *My True Love*, with Charles Swatridge. London, 1971
222. *No Laggard in Love*, as Leslie Lance. London, 1971
223. *Therefore Must Be Loved*, with Charles Swatridge. London, 1972
224. *Sweet Rosemary*, as Fay Chandos. London, 1972
225. *Castle Kelpiesloch*, with Charles Swatridge. London, 1973
226. *The New Lord Whinbridge*, as Leslie Lance. London, 1973
227. *Now I Can Forget*, as Leslie Lance. London, 1973
228. *The Love That Lasts*, as Leslie Lance. London, 1974
229. *Nurse By Accident*, with Charles Swatridge. London, 1974
230. *House of Pines*, as Jan Tempest. London, 1975
231. *The Flower and the Nettle*, with Charles Swatridge. London, 1975
232. *Trust Me, My Love*, with Charles Swatridge. London, 1975
233. *The Maverton Heiress*, as Leslie Lance. London, 1975
234. *The Return of the Cuckoo*, as Leslie Lance. London, 1976
235. *Romance at Wrecker's End*, as Leslie Lance. London, 1976
236. *Island House*, as Leslie Lance. London, 1976
237. *One Who Remembers*, with Charles Swatridge. London, 1976
238. *Rainbow after Rain*, with Charles Swatridge. London, 1977

239. *Crisis at St. Chad's,* with Charles Swatridge. London, 1977
240. *Cousins by Courtesy,* as Leslie Lance. London, 1977
241. *The Family at the Farm,* as Leslie Lance. London, 1978
242. *Orchid Girl,* as Leslie Lance. London, 1978
243. *Just for One Weekend,* with Charles Swatridge. London, 1978
244. *Surgeon's Reputation,* with Charles Swatridge. London, 1979
245. *The Girl in the Mauve Mini,* as Leslie Lance. London, 1979
246. *The Rose Princess,* as Leslie Lance. London, 1979
247. *Doctor in the Snow,* as Leslie Lance. London, 1980
248. *The House in the Woods,* as Leslie Lance. London, 1980
249. *Hawk's Head,* as Leslie Lance. London, 1981
250. *With Somebody Else,* with Charles Swatridge. London, 1981
251. *Surgeon's Sweetheart,* with Charles Swatridge. London, 1981
252. *Someone Who Cares,* as Leslie Lance. London, 1982

Chase, Borden
American
1. *East River.* New York, 1935
2. *Sandhog.* Philadelphia, 1938
3. *Diamonds of Death.* New York and London, 1947
4. *Blazing Guns on the Chisholm Trail.* New York, 1948
5. *Red River.* New York, 1948
6. *Lone Star.* New York, 1952
7. *Viva Gringo!* New York, 1961

Chisholm, A.M. (Arthur Murray)
Canadian, born in 1872, died January 24, 1960
1. *The Boss of Wind River.* New York, 1911
2. *Precious Waters.* New York, 1913
3. *Desert Conquest.* New York, no date
4. *The Land of Strong Men.* New York, 1919
5. *When Stuart Came to Sitkum.* New York, 1924
6. *The Land of Big Rivers: A Novel of the Northwest.* New York and London, 1924
7. *Black Powder Dan.* London, 1925
8. *The Red Headed Kids: An Adventure Story.* New York, 1925
9. *The Red Heads.* London, 1926
10. *Yellow Horse.* London, 1926
11. *Prospectin' Fools.* London, 1927
12. *Red.* London, 1927
13. *Red Bill.* New York, 1930

Christie, Agatha (Mary Clarissa)
British, born September 15, 1890, died January 12, 1976
Pseudonym: Mary Westmacott
1. *The Mysterious Affair at Styles.* London, 1920
2. *The Secret Adversary.* London and New York, 1922
3. *The Murder on the Links.* London and New York, 1923
4. *The Man in the Brown Suit.* London and New York, 1924
5. *Poirot Investigates.* London, 1924
6. *The Secret of Chimneys.* London and New York, 1925
7. *The Road of Dreams.* London, 1925
8. *The Murder of Roger Ackroyd.* London and New York, 1926
9. *The Big Four.* London and New York, 1927
10. *The Mystery of the Blue Train.* London and New York, 1928
11. *The Seven Dials Mystery.* London and New York, 1929
12. *Partners in Crime.* London and New York, 1929
13. *The Under Dog.* London, 1929
14. *The Murder at the Vicarage.* London and New York, 1930
15. *The Mysterious Mr. Quin.* London and New York, 1930
16. *Giants Bread,* as Mary Westmacott. London and New York, 1930
17. *The Floating Admiral.* London, 1931
18. *The Sittaford Mystery.* London, 1931
19. *The Murder at Hazelmoor.* New York, 1931
20. *Peril at End House.* London and New York, 1932
21. *The Thirteen Problems.* London, 1932
22. *Lord Edgeware Dies.* London, 1933
23. *Thirteen at Dinner.* New York, 1933
24. *The Sunningdale Mystery.* London, 1933
25. *The Tuesday Club Murders.* New York, 1933
26. *The Hound of Death and Other Stories.* London, 1933
27. *Why Didn't They Ask Evans?* London, 1934
28. *Murder on the Orient Express.* London, 1934
29. *Murder in the Calais Coach.* New York, 1934
30. *Murder in Three Acts.* New York, 1934
31. *Parker Pyne Investigates.* London, 1934
32. *Mr. Parker Pyne, Detective.* New York, 1934
33. *The Listerdale Mystery and Other Stories.* London, 1934
34. *Black Coffee.* London and Boston, 1934
35. *Unfinished Portrait,* as Mary Westmacott. London and New York, 1934
36. *Three Act Tragedy.* London, 1935
37. *Death in the Clouds.* London, 1935
38. *Death in the Air.* New York, 1935
39. *The A.B.C. Murders.* London and New York, 1936
40. *Cards on the Table.* London, 1936
41. *Murder in Mesopotamia.* London and New York, 1936
42. *Death on the Nile.* London, 1937
43. *Dumb Witness.* London, 1937
44. *Poirot Loses a Client.* New York, 1937
45. *Murder in the Mews and Three Other Poirot Cases.* London, 1937
46. *Dead Man's Mirror and Other Stories.* New York, 1937
47. *Appointment with Death.* London and New York, 1938
48. *Hercule Poirot's Christmas.* London, 1938
49. *Murder for Christmas.* New York, 1939
50. *Murder Is Easy.* London, 1939
51. *Easy to Kill.* New York, 1939
52. *Ten Little Niggers.* London, 1939
53. *The Regatta Mystery and Other Stories.* New York, 1939
54. *And Then There Were None.* New York, 1940
55. *One, Two, Buckle My Shoe.* London, 1940
56. *Sad Cypress.* London and New York, 1940
57. *The Mystery of the Blue Geranium and Other Tuesday Club Murders.* New York, 1940
58. *Evil under the Sun.* London and New York, 1941
59. *The Patriotic Murders.* New York, 1941
60. *N or M?* London and New York, 1941
61. *The Body in the Library.* London and New York, 1942
62. *The Moving Finger.* New York, 1942
63. *Five Little Pigs.* London, 1942
64. *Murder in Retrospect.* New York, 1942
65. *The Mystery of the Baghdad Chest.* Los Angeles, 1943
66. *The Mystery of the Crime in Cabin 66.* Los Angeles, 1943
67. *Poirot and the Regatta Mystery.* Los Angeles, 1943
68. *Poirot on Holiday.* London, 1943
69. *Problem at Pollensa Bay, and Christmas Adventure.* London, 1943
70. *Death Comes as the End.* New York, 1944
71. *Towards Zero.* London, 1944
72. *The Veiled Lady, and The Mystery of the Baghdad Chest.* London, 1944
73. *Ten Little Niggers.* London, 1944
74. *Absent in the Spring,* as Mary Westmacott. London and New York, 1944
75. *Sparkling Cyanide.* London, 1945
76. *Remembered Death.* New York, 1945
77. *The Hollow.* London and New York, 1946
78. *Poirot Knows the Murderer.* London, 1946
79. *Poirot Lends a Hand.* London, 1946
80. *Ten Little Indians.* New York, 1946

Christie, Agatha

81. *Come, Tell Me How You Live.* London and New York, 1976
82. *A Holiday for Murder.* New York, 1947
83. *The Labours of Hercules.* London and New York, 1947
84. *Taken at the Flood.* London, 1948
85. *There Is a Tide.* New York, 1948
86. *The Witness for the Prosecution and Other Stories.* New York, 1948
87. *Murder on the Nile.* London and New York, 1948
88. *The Rose and the Yew Tree,* as Mary Westmacott. London and New York, 1948
89. *Crooked House.* London and New York, 1949
90. *The Mousetrap and Other Stories.* New York, 1949
91. *A Murder Is Announced.* London and New York, 1950
92. *Three Blind Mice and Other Stories.* New York, 1950
93. *They Came to Baghdad.* London and New York, 1951
94. *The Under Dog and Other Stories.* New York, 1951
95. *A Daughter's a Daughter,* as Mary Westmacott. London, 1952
96. *They Do It with Mirrors.* London, 1952
97. *Murder with Mirrors.* New York, 1952
98. *Mrs. McGinty's Dead.* London and New York, 1952
99. *Blood Will Tell.* New York, 1952
100. *The Hollow.* London and New York, 1952
101. *After The Funeral.* London, 1953
102. *Funerals Are Fatal.* New York, 1953
103. *A Pocket Full of Rye.* London, 1953
104. *An Overdose of Death.* New York, 1953
105. *Destination Unknown.* London, 1954
106. *Murder after Hours.* New York, 1954
107. *The Mousetrap.* London and New York, 1954
108. *Witness for the Prosecution.* London and New York, 1954
109. *So Many Steps to Death.* New York, 1955
110. *Hickory, Dickory, Dock.* London, 1955
111. *Hickory, Dickory, Death.* New York, 1955
112. *The Burden,* as Mary Westmacott. London, 1956
113. *Dead Man's Folly.* London and New York, 1956
114. *Appointment with Death.* London, 1956
115. *4:50 from Paddington.* London, 1957
116. *What Mrs. McGillicuddy Saw!* New York, 1957
117. *Spider's Web.* London and New York, 1957
118. *Towards Zero.* New York, 1957
119. *Ordeal by Innocence.* London, 1958
120. *Verdict.* London, 1958
121. *The Unexpected Guest.* London, 1958
122. *Cat among the Pigeons.* London, 1959
123. *The Adventure of the Christmas Pudding, and Selection of Entrees.* London, 1960
124. *Go Back for Murder.* London, 1960
125. *The Pale Horse.* London, 1961
126. *Murder She Said.* New York, 1961
127. *Double Sin and Other Stories.* New York, 1961
128. *13 for Luck! A Selection of Mystery Stories for Young Readers.* New York, 1961
129. *The Mirror Crack'd from Side to Side.* London, 1962
130. *The Mirror Crack'd.* New York, 1963
131. *The Clocks.* London, 1963
132. *Murder at the Gallop.* London, 1963
133. *Rule of Three: Afternoon at the Seaside, The Patient, The Rats.* London, 3 vols., 1963
134. *A Caribbean Mystery.* London, 1964
135. *At Bertram's Hotel.* London, 1965
136. *Ten Little Indians.* New York, 1965
137. *Surprise! Surprise! A Collection of Mystery Stories with Unexpected Endings.* New York, 1965
138. *Star over Bethlehem and Other Stories,* as Agatha Christie Mallowan. London and New York, 1965
139. *Third Girl.* London, 1966
140. *The Alphabet Murders.* New York, 1966
141. *13 Clues for Miss Marple.* New York, 1966
142. *Endless Night.* London, 1967
143. *By the Pricking of My Thumbs.* London and New York, 1968
144. *Hallowe'en Party.* London and New York, 1969
145. *Passenger to Frankfurt.* London and New York, 1970
146. *Nemesis.* London and New York, 1971
147. *The Golden Ball and Other Stories.* New York, 1971
148. *Elephants Can Remember.* London and New York, 1972
149. *Postern of Fate.* London and New York, 1973
150. *Akhnaton.* London and New York, 1973
151. *Poems.* London and New York, 1973
152. *Poirot's Early Cases.* London, 1974
153. *Hercule Poirot's Early Cases.* New York, 1974
154. *Curtain: Hercule Poirot's Last Case.* London and New York, 1975
155. *Sleeping Murder.* London and New York, 1976
156. *An Autobiography.* London and New York, 1977
157. *The Mousetrap and Other Plays.* New York, 1978
158. *Miss Marple's Final Cases and Two Other Stories.* London, 1979

Clark, Walter Van Tilburg
American, born August 3, 1909, died November 10, 1971
1. *Christmas Comes to Hjalsen,* Reno (NV), 1930
2. *Ten Women in Gale's House and Shorter Poems.* Boston, 1932
3. *The Ox-Bow Incident.* New York, 1940
4. *The City of Trembling Leaves.* New York, 1945
5. *The Track of the Cat.* New York, 1949
6. *The Watchful Gods.* New York, 1950
7. *Tim Hazard.* London, 1951

Cleve, Brian (Talbot)
Irish, born November 22, 1921
1. *The Far Hills.* London, 1952
2. *Portrait of My City.* London, 1952
3. *Birth of a Dark Soul.* London, 1953
4. *Colonial Policies in Africa.* Johannesburg (South Africa), 1954
5. *The Night Winds.* Boston, 1954
6. *Assignment to Vengeance.* London, 1961
7. *Death of a Painted Lady.* London, 1962
8. *Death of a Wicked Servant.* London, 1963
9. *Vote X for Treason.* London, 1964
10. *Dark Blood, Dark Terror.* New York, 1965
11. *The Judas Goat.* London, 1966
12. *Counter Spy.* New York, 1966
13. *The Horse Thieves of Ballysaggert and Other Stories.* Cork (Ireland), 1966
14. *Vice Isn't Private.* London, 1966
15. *Violent Death of a Bitter Englishman.* New York, 1967
16. *Dictionary of Irish Writers.* Cork, 3 vols., 1967-71
17. *You Must Never Go Back.* New York, 1968
18. *Exit from Prague.* London, 1970
19. *Cry of Morning.* London, 1971
20. *The Triumph of O'Rourke.* New York, 1972
21. *Tread Softly in This Place.* London and New York, 1972
22. *Escape from Prague.* New York, 1973
23. *The Dark Side of the Sun.* London, 1973
24. *A Question of Inheritance.* London, 1974
25. *For Love of Crannagh Castle.* New York, 1975
26. *Sara.* London and New York, 1976
27. *Kate.* London and New York, 1977
28. *Judith.* London and New York, 1978
29. *Hester.* London, 1980
30. *The House on the Rock.* London, 1980
31. *The Seven Mansions.* London, 1980

Coburn, Walt [Walter J. Coburn]
    American, born October 23, 1889, died May 24, 1971
1. *The Ringtailed Rannyhans.* New York, 1927
2. *Mavericks.* New York, 1929
3. *Barb Wire.* New York, 1931
4. *The Four Aces.* New York, 1931
5. *Cartridges Free.* New York, 1931
6. *Paths to Glory.* New York, 1931
7. *The Maverick Legion.* New York, 1931
8. *Law Rides the Range.* New York, 1935
9. *Sky-Pilot Cowboy.* New York, 1937
10. *Pardners of the Dim Trails.* Philadelphia, 1951
11. *The Way of a Texan.* New York, 1953
12. *Drift Fence.* New York, 1953
13. *The Burnt Ranch.* London, 1954
14. *Gun Grudge.* London, 1954
15. *Wet Cattle.* London, 1955
16. *The Square Shooter.* London, 1955
17. *The Renegade.* Toronto, 1956
18. *Cayuse.* London, 1956
19. *Border Jumper.* London, 1956
20. *Beyond the Wild Missouri.* New York, 1956
21. *One Step Ahead of the Posse.* New York, 1956
22. *The Night Branders.* New York, 1957
23. *Stirrup High.* New York, 1957
24. *Fear Branded.* London, 1957
25. *Buffalo Run.* London, 1958
26. *Guns Blaze on Spiderweb Range.* New York, 1958
27. *Free Rangers.* London, 1959
28. *Branded.* New York, 1959
29. *Fast Gun.* New York, 1959
30. *Fued Valley, and Sleeper Marked: Two New Westerns.* London, 1960
31. *The Ramrod, and Sons of Gunfighters: Two New Westerns.* London, 1960
32. *La Jornado.* London, 1961
33. *Invitation to a Hanging.* New York, 1963
34. *Man from Montana.* New York, 1966
35. *The Kansas Killers.* New York, 1966
36. *Tough Texan.* New York, 1966
37. *El Hombre.* New York, 1967
38. *Reckless.* New York, 1968
39. *Pioneer Cattleman in Montana: The Story of the Circle C Ranch.* Norman (OK), 1968

Cockrell, Marian
    American, born March 15, 1909
1. *Yesterday's Madness.* New York, 1943
2. *Lillian Harley.* New York, 1943
3. *Dark Waters,* with Frank Cockrell. Cleveland, 1944
4. *Shadow Castle.* New York, 1945
5. *Something Between.* New York, 1946
6. *The Revolt of Sara Perkins.* New York, 1965
7. *Mixed Blessings.* New York, 1978
8. *The Misadventures of Bethany Price.* New York, 1979
9. *Mixed Company.* New York, 1979

Cody, Stetson
1. *Cactus Clancey Rides.* London, 1949
2. *The Range Hawk.* London, 1950
3. *Texas Triggers.* London, 1951
4. *Wolf Trail.* London, 1952
5. *Cactus Justice.* London, 1952
6. *Overland Guns.* London, 1953
7. *Vengeance Rider.* London, 1954
8. *Rawhide Range.* London, 1955
9. *Branding Bullets.* London, 1956
10. *Gunsmoke at Necktie.* London, 1957
11. *Moon River Outlaw.* London, 1957
12. *Double X Ranch.* London, 1958
13. *Renegade Triggers.* London, 1959
14. *Sagebrush Bandit.* London, 1959
15. *Colt Fever.* London, 1960
16. *Hair-Trigger Justice.* London, 1961
17. *The Violent Breed.* London, 1962
18. *The Fast Gun.* London, 1963
19. *Trouble Shooter.* London, 1964
20. *The Wide Loop.* London, 1964
21. *Lawdog's Bite.* London, 1965
22. *The Gunslick Code.* London, 1965
23. *Sinister Valley.* London, 1967
24. *Guns Along the Ruthless.* London, 1973

Coffman, Virginia (Edith)
    American, born July 30, 1914
    Pseudonyms: Victor Cross, Jeanne Duval, Virginia C. DuVaul, Anne Stanfield
1. *Moura.* New York, 1959
2. *The Affair of Alkali.* New York, 1960
3. *Neveda Gunslinger.* London, 1962
4. *The Beckoning.* New York, 1965
5. *Curse of the Island Pool.* New York, 1965
6. *Castle Barra.* New York, 1966
7. *Black Heather.* New York, 1966
8. *The High Terrace.* New York, 1966
9. *Castle at Witches' Coven.* New York, 1966
10. *A Haunted Place.* New York, 1966
11. *The Demon Tower.* New York, 1966
12. *The Devil Vicar.* New York, 1966
13. *The Shadow Box.* New York, 1966
14. *Blood Sport,* as Victor Cross. New York, 1966
15. *The Secret of Shower Tree.* New York, 1966
16. *Richest Girl in the World.* New York, 1967
17. *The Small Tawny Cat.* New York, 1967
18. *The Chinese Door.* New York, 1967
19. *The Rest Is Silence.* New York, 1967
20. *A Few Fiends to Tea.* New York, 1967
21. *The Hounds of Hell.* New York, 1967
22. *One Man Too Many.* New York, 1968
23. *The Villa Fountains.* New York, 1968
24. *The Mist at Darkness.* New York, 1968
25. *Call of the Flesh.* New York, 1968
26. *The Candidate's Wife.* New York, 1968
27. *The Dark Gondola.* New York, 1968
28. *To Love a Dark Stranger.* London, 1969
29. *Of Love and Intrigue.* New York, 1969
30. *The Devil's Mistress.* New York, 1969
31. *Isle of the Undead.* New York, 1969
32. *Voodoo Widow.* London, 1970
33. *Priestess of the Damned.* New York, 1970
34. *The Devil's Virgin.* New York, 1970
35. *The Beach House.* New York, 1970
36. *Masque by Gaslight.* New York, 1970
37. *The Vampyre of Moura.* New York, 1970
38. *Masque of Satan.* New York, 1971
39. *Chalet Diabolique.* New York, 1971
40. *The Master of Blue Mire.* New York, 1971
41. *Masque by Gaslight,* as Virginia C. DuVaul. London, 1971
42. *Vicar of Moura.* New York, 1972
43. *From Satan, With Love.* New York, 1972
44. *Night at Sea Abbey.* New York, 1972
45. *The House on the Moat.* New York, 1972
46. *Mistress Devon.* New York, 1972
47. *The Cliffs of Dread.* New York, 1972
48. *The Dark Palazzo.* New York, 1973
49. *Garden of Shadows.* New York, 1973

50. *A Fear of Heights.* New York, 1973
51. *The Evil at Queens Priory.* New York, 1973
52. *Survivor of Darkness.* New York, 1973
53. *The House of Sandalwood.* New York, 1974
54. *Hyde Place.* New York, 1974
55. *The Ice Forest.* New York, 1975
56. *Veronique.* New York, 1975
57. *Marsanne.* New York, 1976
58. *Strange Secrets.* New York, 1976
59. *The Alpine Coach.* New York, 1976
60. *Careen.* New York, 1977
61. *Enemy of Love.* New York, 1977
62. *The Beckoning from Moura.* New York, 1977
63. *The Stalking Terror.* New York, 1977
64. *The Dark Beyond Moura.* New York, 1977
65. *Fire Dawn.* New York, 1977
66. *The Gaynor Women.* New York, 1978
67. *Looking-Glass.* New York, 1979
68. *Legacy of Fear.* New York, 1979
69. *The Lady Serena,* as Jeanne Duval. New York, 1979
70. *Looking-Glass.* New York, 1979
71. *Dinah Faire.* New York, 1979
72. *Pacific Cavalcade.* New York, 1980
73. *The Ravishers,* as Jeanne Duval. New York, 1980
74. *The Golden Marguerite,* as Anne Stanfield. New York, 1981
75. *The Lombard Cavalcade.* New York, 1982

Coldsmith, Don [Donald C. Coldsmith]
American, born February 28, 1926
1. *Horsin' Around.* Texas, 1975
2. *Trail of the Spanish Bit.* New York, 1980
3. *Buffalo Medicine.* New York, 1981
4. *The Elk-Dog Heritage.* New York, 1982

Comfort, Will (Levington)
American, born January 17, 1878, died November 2, 1932
1. *Trooper Tales: A Series of Sketches of the Real American Private Soldier.* New York, 1899
2. *The Lady of Fallen Star Island.* New York and London, 1902
3. *Routledge Rides Alone.* Philadelphia, 1910
4. *Sue Buildeth Her House.* Philadelphia, 1911
5. *Fate Knocks at the Door.* Philadelphia, 1912
6. *Down among Men.* New York, 1913
7. *The Road of Living Men.* Philadelphia, 1913
8. *Sport of Kings.* Philadelphia, 1913
9. *Fatherland.* New York, 1914
10. *Midstream: A Chronicle at Halfway.* New York, 1914
11. *Lost and Company.* New York, 1915
12. *Red Fleece.* New York, 1915
13. *The Last Ditch.* New York, 1916
14. *Child and Country: A Book of the Younger Generation.* New York and London, 1916
15. *The Hive.* New York, 1918
16. *The Shielding Wing.* Boston, 1918
17. *The Yellow Lord.* Boston, 1919
18. *Magic Hours: A Romance of the East and the Desert.* London, 1920
19. *Son of Power,* with Zamin Ki Dost. New York, 1920
20. *Nine Great Little Books.* Privately printed, 1920
21. *The Will Levington Comfort Letters.* Privately printed, 2 vols., 1920-21
22. *This Man's World.* New York, 1921
23. *The Public Square.* New York, 1923
24. *Somewhere South of Sonora.* Boston, 1925
25. *Samadhi.* Boston, 1927
26. *Apache.* New York, 1931
27. *Mangus Colorado.* London, 1931
28. *The Pilot Comes Aboard.* New York, 1932
29. *A Man Is at His Best.* Privately printed, 1953

Conner, Ralph [Charles William Gordon]
Canadian, born September 13, 1860, died October 31, 1937
1. *Gwen's Canyon.* Toronto, 1898
2. *Beyond the Marshes.* Toronto, 1898
3. *Black Rock: A Tale of the Selkirks.* Toronto, New York, and London, 1898
4. *The Sky Pilot: A Tale of the Foothills.* Toronto, Chicago, and London, 1899
5. *Michael McGrath, Postmaster.* London, 1900
6. *The Prospector: A Tale of Crow's Nest Pass.* Toronto, 1901
7. *The Man from Glengarry.* Toronto and Chicago, 1901
8. *Glengarry School Days: A Story of Early Days in Glengarry.* Toronto and Chicago, 1902
9. *The Swan Creek Blizzard.* Chicago, 1904
10. *Gwen: An Idyll of the Canyon.* Chicago and London, 1904
11. *Breaking the Record.* New York, 1904
12. *The Pilot at Swan Creek.* London, 1905
13. *The Doctor: A Tale of the Rockies.* Toronto and Chicago, 1906
14. *The Doctor of Crow's Nest.* London, 1906
15. *The Settler: A Tale of Saskatchewan.* New York and London, 1906
16. *The Life of James Robertson, Missionary Superintendent in the Northwest Territories,* as Charles William Gordon. Toronto, Chicago, and London, 1908
17. *The Angel and the Star.* Toronto, New York, and London, 1908
18. *The Dawn by Galilee: A Story of the Christ.* Toronto, New York, and London, 1909
19. *The Foreigner: A Tale of Saskatchewan.* Toronto, New York, and London, 1909
20. *The Recall of Love: A Message of Hope.* Toronto, New York, and London, 1910
21. *Christian Hope.* London, 1912
22. *Corporal Cammeron: A Tale of the North-West Mounted Police.* Toronto and New York, 1912
23. *The Patrol of the Sundance Trail.* New York and London, 1914
24. *A Fight for Freedom.* Toronto, 1917
25. *The Major.* Toronto, New York, and London, 1917
26. *To Him That Hath.* New York, 1921
27. *The Gaspards of Pine Croft: A Romance of the Windermere.* Toronto, New York, and London, 1923
28. *Treading the Winepress.* Toronto, New York, and London, 1925
29. *The Friendly Four and Other Stories.* New York, 1926
30. *The Runner: A Romance of the Niagaras.* Toronto and New York, 1929
31. *The Rock and the River: A Romance of Quebec.* Toronto and New York, 1931
32. *The Arm of Gold—le Bras d'or.* Toronto and New York, 1932
33. *The Girl from Glengarry.* Toronto and New York, 1933
34. *The Glengarry Girl.* London, 1934
35. *Torches Through the Bush: A Tale of Glengarry.* Toronto and New York, 1934
36. *The Rebel Loyalist.* Toronto and New York, 1935
37. *He Dwelt Among Us.* Toronto, New York, and London, 1936
38. *The Gay Crusader: A Romance of Quebec.* Toronto and New York, 1936
39. *Postscript to Adventure: Autobiography of Ralph Conner—Charles W. Gordon.* New York and London, 1938

Constiner, Merle
1. *Hearse of a Different Color.* New York, 1952

2. *Last Stand at Anvil Creek.* New York, 1957
3. *The Fourth Gunman.* New York, 1958
4. *Short-Trigger Man.* New York, 1964
5. *Wolf on Horseback.* New York, 1965
6. *Guns at Q Cross.* New York, 1965
7. *Outrage at Bearskin Forks.* New York, 1966
8. *Meeting at the Merry Fifer.* New York, 1966
9. *Rain of Fire.* New York, 1966
10. *Top Gun from the Dakotas.* New York, 1966
11. *The Action at Redstone Creek.* New York, 1967
12. *Two Pistols South of Deadwood.* New York, 1967
13. *Killer's Corral.* New York, 1968
14. *The Rebel Courier and the Redcoats.* New York, 1968
15. *Sumatra Alley.* Camden (NJ), 1971
16. *Steel-Jacket.* New York, 1972
17. *The Four from Gila Bend.* New York, 1974

Cook, Will [William Everett Cook]
Born in 1921, died July 1964
Pseudonyms: Wade Everett, James Keene, Frank Peace
1. *Frontier Feud.* New York, 1954
2. *Prairie Guns.* New York, 1954
3. *Fury at Painted Rock.* New York, 1955
4. *Apache Ambush.* New York, 1955
5. *Bullet Range.* New York, 1955
6. *The Texas Pistol,* as James Keene. New York, 1955
7. *The Brass and the Blue,* as James Keene. New York, 1956
8. *Sabrina Kane: A Novel of Frontier Illinois.* New York, 1956
9. *Easy Money,* as Frank Peace. New York, 1956
10. *The Brass Brigade,* as Frank Peace. New York, 1956
11. *The Fighting Texan.* New York, 1956
12. *Trumpets of the West.* New York, 1956
13. *Lone Hand from Texas.* New York, 1957
14. *Justice, My Brother!* as James Keene. New York, 1957
15. *Gunman's Harvest,* as James Keene. New York, 1957
16. *Seven for Vengeance,* as James Keene. New York, 1958
17. *Badman's Holiday.* New York, 1958
18. *Guns of North Texas.* New York, 1958
19. *The Wind River Kid.* New York, 1958
20. *Elizabeth, By Name.* New York, 1958
21. *Outcast of Cripple Creek.* New York, 1959
22. *We Burn Like Fire.* New York, 1959
23. *McCracken in Command,* as James Keene. New York, 1959
24. *Posse for Gunlock,* as James Keene. New York, 1959
25. *First Command,* as Wade Everett. New York, 1959
26. *Fort Starke,* as Wade Everett. New York, 1959
27. *Last Scout,* as Wade Everett. New York, 1960
28. *Sixgun Wild,* as James Keene. New York, 1960
29. *Iron Man, Iron Horse,* as James Keene. New York, 1960
30. *Killer Behind a Badge.* New York, 1960
31. *The Wranglers.* New York, 1960
32. *Comanche Captives.* New York, 1960
33. *The Peacemakers.* New York, 1961
34. *Two Rode Together.* New York, 1961
35. *Big Man, Big Mountain,* as Wade Everett. New York, 1961
36. *The Big Drive,* as Wade Everett. New York, 1962
37. *Killer,* as Wade Everett. New York, 1962
38. *Ambush at Antler's Spring.* New York, 1962
39. *The Tough Texan.* New York, 1963
40. *Gunnison's Empire,* as James Keene. New York, 1963
41. *The Breakthrough.* New York, 1963
42. *The Speed Merchants.* New York, 1964
43. *Last Command.* New York, 1964
44. *Shotgun Marshal,* as Wade Everett. New York and London, 1964
45. *Temporary Duty,* as Wade Everett. New York and London, 1964
46. *Texas Ranger,* as Wade Everett. New York and London, 1964
47. *Top Hand,* as Wade Everett. New York, 1964
48. *Cavalry Recruit,* as Wade Everett. New York, 1965
49. *Bullets for the Doctor,* as Wade Everett. New York, 1965
50. *The Outcasts.* New York, 1965
51. *Texas Yankee,* as Wade Everett. New York, 1966
52. *Vengeance,* as Wade Everett. New York, 1966
53. *The Warrior,* as Wade Everett. New York, 1967
54. *The Apache Fighter.* New York, 1967
55. *The Horse Trader,* as Wade Everett. New York, 1968
56. *The Drifter.* New York, 1969
57. *Broken Gun,* as Wade Everett. New York, 1970
58. *Bandit's Trail.* New York, 1974

Cook, William Wallace
American, born April 11, 1867, died July 20, 1933
1. *His Friend the Enemy.* New York, 1903
2. *Castaway at the Pole.* New York, 1904
3. *Adrift in the Unknown.* New York, 1905
4. *A Quarter to Four.* New York, 1909
5. *The Desert Argonaut.* New York, no date
6. *The Goal of a Million.* New York, no date
7. *The Gold Gleaners.* New York, no date
8. *Innocent Outlaw.* New York, no date
9. *Jim Dexter, Cattleman.* New York, no date
10. *Montana.* New York, no date
11. *Frisbie of San Antone.* New York, no date
12. *Trailing of Josephine.* New York, no date
13. *At Daggers Drawn.* New York, no date
14. *Back from Bedlam.* New York, no date
15. *Billionaire pro Tem and the Trail of the Billy Doo.* New York, no date
16. *Catspaw.* New York, no date
17. *Cotton Bag.* New York, no date
18. *A Deep Sea Game.* New York, no date
19. *Eighth Wonder.* New York, no date
20. *Fateful Seventh.* New York, no date
21. *His Audacious Highness.* New York, no date
22. *In the Wake of the Scimitar.* New York, no date
23. *In the Web.* New York, no date
24. *Juggling with Liberty.* New York, no date
25. *Little Miss Vasar.* New York, no date
26. *Marooned in 1492.* New York, no date
27. *The Mysterious Mission.* New York, no date
28. *Paymaster's Special.* New York, no date
29. *River Tangle.* New York, no date
30. *Rogers of Butte.* New York, no date
31. *A Round Trip to the Year 2000.* New York, no date
32. *Running the Signal.* New York, no date
33. *The Spur of Necessity.* New York, no date
34. *Testing of Noyes.* New York, no date
35. *Thorndyke of the Bonita.* New York, no date
36. *Dare of Darling & Co.* New York, no date
37. *The Deserter.* New York, no date
38. *Fools for Luck.* New York, no date
39. *Wanted: A Highwayman.* New York, no date
40. *Plotto: A New Method of Plot Suggestion for Writers of Creative Fiction.* Battle Creek (MI), 1928
41. *The Sheriff of Broken Bow.* London, 1939

Cookson, Catherine
British, born June 20, 1906
Pseudonym: Catherine Marchant
1. *Kate Hannigan.* London, 1950
2. *The Fifteen Streets.* London, 1952
3. *Colour Blind.* London, 1953
4. *A Grand Man.* London, 1954
5. *Maggie Rowan.* London, 1954
6. *The Lord and Mary Ann.* London, 1956

7. *Rooney.* London, 1957
8. *The Devil and Mary Ann.* London, 1958
9. *The Menagerie.* London, 1958
10. *Slinky Jane.* London, 1959
11. *Fanny McBride.* London, 1959
12. *Fenwick Houses.* London, 1960
13. *Love and Mary Ann.* London, 1961
14. *The Garment.* London, 1962
15. *Life and Mary Ann.* London, 1962
16. *Heritage of Folly,* as Catherine Marchant. London, 1962
17. *The Fen Tiger,* as Catherine Marchant. London, 1963
18. *House of Men,* as Catherine Marchant. London, 1963
19. *The Blind Miller.* London, 1963
20. *Marriage and Mary Ann.* London, 1964
21. *Hannah Massey.* London, 1964
22. *Mary Ann's Angels.* London, 1965
23. *Matty Doolin.* London, 1965
24. *The Long Corridor.* London, 1965
25. *The House on the Fens,* as Catherine Marchant. New York, 1965
26. *The Mists of Memory,* as Catherine Marchant. New York, 1965
27. *Evil at Roger's Cross,* as Catherine Marchant. New York, 1966
28. *The Unbaited Trap.* London, 1966
29. *Mary Ann and Bill.* London, 1967
30. *Katie Mulholland.* London and Indianapolis, 1967
31. *The Round Tower.* London, 1968
32. *Joe and the Gladiator.* London, 1968
33. *Our Kate: An Autobiography.* London, 1969
34. *The Glass Virgin.* Indianapolis, 1969
35. *The Nice Bloke.* London, 1969
36. *The Nipper.* London and New York, 1970
37. *The Invitation.* London, 1970
38. *The Dwelling Place.* London and Indianapolis, 1971
39. *Feathers in the Fire.* London, 1971
40. *Pure as the Lily.* London, 1972
41. *Blue Baccy.* London, 1972
42. *The Mallen Girl.* New York, 1973
43. *The Mallen Streak.* London and New York, 1973
44. *Our John Willy.* London and New York, 1974
45. *The Mallen Lot.* New York, 1974
46. *The Mallen Litter.* London, 1974
47. *The Invisible Cord.* London and New York, 1975
48. *The Gambling Man.* London and New York, 1975
49. *Miss Martha Mary Crawford,* as Catherine Marchant. London, 1975
50. *The Slow Awakening,* as Catherine Marchant. London, 1976
51. *The Iron Facade,* as Catherine Marchant. London, 1976
52. *The Husband.* New York, 1976
53. *The Tide of Life.* London and New York, 1976
54. *Mrs. Flannagan's Trumpet.* London, 1976
55. *Go Tell It to Mrs. Golightly.* London, 1977
56. *The Girl.* London and New York, 1977
57. *The Cinder Path.* London and New York, 1978
58. *The Man Who Cried.* London and New York, 1979
59. *The Mallen Novels.* London, 1979
60. *Tilly Trotter.* London, 1980
61. *Tilly.* New York, 1980
62. *Tilly Trotter Wed.* London, 1981
63. *Tilly Wed.* New York, 1981
64. *Lanky Jones.* London and New York, 1981
65. *Tilly Trotter Widowed.* London, 1982
66. *Tilly Alone.* New York, 1982

Coolidge, Dane
American, born March 24, 1873, died August 8, 1940
1. *Hidden Water.* Chicago, 1910
2. *The Texican.* Chicago, 1911
3. *Bat Wing Bowles.* New York, 1914
4. *The Desert Trail.* New York, 1915
5. *Rimrock Jones.* New York, 1917
6. *The Fighting Fool.* New York, 1918
7. *Silver and Gold.* New York, 1919
8. *Shadow Mountain.* New York, 1919
9. *Wunpost.* New York, 1920
10. *The Man-Killers.* New York, 1921
11. *Lost Wagons.* New York, 1923
12. *The Scalp-Lock.* New York and London, 1924
13. *Lorenzo the Magnificent (The Riders from Texas).* New York, 1925
14. *Not-Afraid.* New York, 1926
15. *Under the Sun.* New York, 1926
16. *Gun-Smoke.* New York, 1928
17. *War-Paint.* New York and London, 1929
18. *The Navajo Indian,* with Mary Roberts Coolidge. Boston, 1930
19. *Horse-Ketchum.* New York and London, 1930
20. *Other Men's Cattle.* New York, 1931
21. *Maverick Makers.* New York, 1931
22. *Sheriff Killer.* New York and London, 1932
23. *Fighting Men of the West.* New York, 1932
24. *Navajo Rugs,* with Mary Roberts Coolidge. Pasadena (CA), 1933
25. *Jess Roundtree, Texas Ranger.* New York, 1933
26. *The Texas Ranger.* London, 1933
27. *The Fighting Danites.* New York and London, 1934
28. *Silver Hat.* New York, 1934
29. *Long Rope.* New York and London, 1935
30. *Wolf's Candle.* New York, 1935
31. *Rawhide Johnny.* New York and London, 1936
32. *Snake Bit Jones.* New York, 1936
33. *Ranger Two-Rifles.* New York, 1937
34. *The Trail of Gold.* New York and London, 1937
35. *Texas Cowboys.* New York, 1937
36. *Death Valley Prospectors.* New York, 1937
37. *Arizona Cowboys.* New York, 1938
38. *Hell's Hip Pocket.* New York, 1938
39. *Comanche Chaser.* New York, 1938
40. *Redskin Trail.* London, 1938
41. *Old California Cowboys.* New York, 1939
42. *The Last of the Seris,* with Mary Roberts Coolidge. New York, 1939
43. *Wally Laughs-Easy.* New York, 1939
44. *Gringo Gold.* New York, 1939
45. *Bloody Head.* New York, 1940
46. *Yaqui Drums.* New York, 1940
47. *Bear Paw.* New York, 1941

Cooper, Courtney Ryley
American, born October 31, 1886, died September 29, 1940
1. *Us Kids: Verses.* Kansas City (MO), 1910
2. *The Eagle's Eye: A True Story of the Imperial German Government's Spies and Intrigues in America.* New York, 1918
3. *The Quick Lunch Cabaret: A Versical Omelette in One Scramble for Male Quartette.* Chicago, 1918
4. *Memories of Buffalo Bill,* with Mrs. Louisa Frederici Cody. New York, 1919
5. *The Cross-Cut.* Boston, 1921
6. *The White Desert.* Boston, 1922
7. *The Jungle Behind Bars.* London, 1923
8. *The Last Frontier.* Boston, 1923
9. *The Far Frontier.* Boston, 1923
10. *Under the Big Top.* Boston, 1923
11. *Lions 'n' Tigers 'n' Everthing.* Boston, 1924

12. *The Avalanche*. London, 1925
13. *Oklahoma*. Boston, 1926
14. *High Country: The Rockies Yesterday and To-day*. Boston, 1926
15. *With the Circus*. Boston, 1927
16. *Annie Oakley, Woman at Arms*. New York, 1927
17. *The Drowned Bonanza*. London, 1927
18. *Builders of Cities*. London, 1927
19. *The Golden Bubble*. Boston, 1928
20. *The Challenge of the Bush*. Boston, 1929
21. *The Mystery of the Four Abreast*. London, 1929
22. *Ghost Country*. London, 1929
23. *Go North, Young Man!* Boston, 1929
24. *Trigger Finger*. London, 1930
25. *Caged*. Boston, 1930
26. *End of Steel*. New York and London, 1931
27. *Circus Day*. New York, 1931
28. *Pike's Peak*. London, 1931
29. *Boss Elephant*. Boston, 1934
30. *Ten Thousand Public Enemies*. Boston and London, 1935
31. *Poor Man's Gold*. Boston and London, 1936
32. *Here's to Crime*. Boston, 1937
33. *The Pioneers*. Boston and London, 1938
34. *Designs in Scarlet*. Boston, 1939
35. *Action in Diamonds*. Philadelphia, 1942

Cord, Barry [Peter B. Germano]
American, born May 17, 1913
Other pseudonyms: Jack Bertin, Jim Kane
1. *Trail Boss from Texas*. New York and London, 1948
2. *The Gunsmoke Trail*. New York, 1951
3. *Shadow Valley*. New York, 1951
4. *Mesquite Johnny*. New York, 1952
5. *Trail to Sundown*. New York, 1953
6. *Cain Basin*. New York, 1954
7. *The Sagebrush Kid*. New York, 1954
8. *Boss of Barbed Wire*. New York, 1955
9. *Dry Range*. New York, 1955
10. *The Rustlers of Dry Range*. London, 1956
11. *The Guns of Hammer*. New York, 1956
12. *The Gunshy Kid*. New York, 1957
13. *Sheriff of Big Hat*. New York, 1957
14. *Savage Valley*. New York, 1957
15. *The Prodigal Gun*. New York, 1957
16. *Concho Valley*. New York, 1958
17. *Gun-Proddy Hombre*. New York, 1958
18. *The Iron Trail Killers*. New York, 1959
19. *Starlight Range*. New York, 1959
20. *The Third Rider*. New York, 1959
21. *Six Bullets Left*. New York, 1959
22. *War in Peaceful Valley*. New York, 1959
23. *Maverick Gun*. New York, 1959
24. *Last Chance at Devil's Canyon*. New York, 1959
25. *Gunman's Choice*, as Jim Kane. New York, 1960
26. *Renegade Rancher*, as Jim Kane. New York, 1961
27. *Two Guns to Avalone*. New York, 1962
28. *The Masked Gun*. New York, 1963
29. *Spanish Gold*, as Jim Kane. New York, 1963
30. *Tangled Trails*, as Jim Kane. 1963
31. *Lost Canyon*, as Jim Kane. New York, 1964
32. *Red River Sheriff*, as Jim Kane. New York, 1965
33. *Rendezvous at Bitter*, as Jim Kane. New York, 1966
34. *Last Stage to Gomorrah*. New York, 1966
35. *A Ranger Called Solitary*. New York, 1966
36. *Canyon Showdown*. New York, 1967
37. *Gallows Ghost*. New York, 1967
38. *The Long Wire*. New York, 1968
39. *Trouble in Peaceful Valley*. New York, 1968
40. *The Interplanetary Adventures*, as Jack Bertin. New York, 1970
41. *The Doublecross Gun*, as Jim Kane. New York, 1970
42. *Texas Warrior*, as Jim Kane. New York, 1971
43. *The Coffin Fillers*. New York, 1972
44. *Brassado Hill*. New York, 1972
45. *Desert Knights*. New York, 1973
46. *The Running Iron Samaritans*. New York, 1973
47. *Hell in Paradise Valley*. New York, 1978
48. *Gun Junction*. New York, 1979
49. *Deadly Amigos: Two Graves for a Gunman*. New York, 1979

Corelli, Marie [Mary Mackay]
British, born May 1, 1855, died April 21, 1924
1. *A Romance of Two Worlds*. London, 2 vols., 1886
2. *Vendetta; or, The Story of One Forgotten*. London, 3 vols., 1886
3. *Thelma: A Society Novel*. London, 3 vols., 1887
4. *Ardath: The Story of a Dead Self*. London, 3 vols., 1889
5. *My Wonderful Wife: A Study in Smoke*. London, 1889
6. *Wormwood: A Drama of Paris*. London, 3 vols., 1890
7. *The Hired Baby and Other Stories and Social Sketches*. Leipzig (Germany), 1891
8. *The Soul of Lilith*. London, 3 vols., 1892
9. *The Silver Domino; or, Side-Whispers, Social and Literary*. London, 1892
10. *Barabbas: A Dream of the World's Tragedy*. London, 3 vols., 1893
11. *The Sorrows of Satan; or, The Strange Experiences of One Geoffrey Tempest, Millionaire: A Romance*. London, 3 vols., 1895
12. *The Murder of Delicia*. London and Philadelphia, 1896
13. *Three Wise Men of Gotham*. Philadelphia, 1896
14. *Cameos*. London and Philadelphia, 1896
15. *The Mighty Atom*. London and Philadelphia, 1896
16. *Ziska*. Bristol (Eng) and Chicago, 1897
17. *Jane: A Social Incident*. London and Philadelphia, 1897
18. *The Song of Miriam and Other Stories*. New York, 1898
19. *Boy*. London and Philadelphia, 1900
20. *The Master-Christian*. London and New York, 1900
21. *Patriotism or Self-Advertisement? A Social Note on the War*. London and Philadelphia, 1900
22. *The Greatest Queen in the World: A Tribute to the Majesty of England 1837-1900*. London, 1900
23. *An Open Letter to His Eminence Cardinal Vaughan*. London, 1900
24. *A Christmas Greeting of Various Thoughts, Verses, and Fancies*. London, 1901
25. *The Passing of the Great Queen*. London and New York, 1901
26. *The Vanishing Gift: An Address on the Decay of the Imagination*. Edinburgh (Scotland), 1902
27. *Temporal Power: A Study in Supremacy*. London and New York, 1902
28. *The Plain Truth of the Stratford-upon-Avon Controversy*. London, 1903
29. *God's Good Man: A Simple Love Story*. London and New York, 1904
30. *The Strange Visitation of Josiah McNason: A Christmas Ghost Story*. London, 1904
31. *Free Opinions Freely Expressed on Certain Phases of Modern Social Life and Conduct*. London and New York, 1905
32. *The Treasure of Heaven: A Romance of Riches*. London and New York, 1906
33. *Woman or Suffragette? A Question of National Choice*. London, 1907

Corelli, Marie

34. *Holy Orders.* London and New York, 1908
35. *The Devil's Motor.* London and New York, 1910
36. *The Life Everlasting: A Reality of Romance.* London and New York, 1911
37. *The Strange Visitation.* London, 1912
38. *Innocent: Her Fancy and His Fact.* London and New York, 1914
39. *Is All Well with England?* London, 1917
40. *Eyes of the Sea.* London, 1917
41. *Delicia.* London and Philadelphia, 1917
42. *The Young Diana: An Experience of the Future.* London and New York, 1918
43. *My "Little Bit."* London and New York, 1919
44. *The Love of Long Ago and Other Stories.* London, 1920
45. *The Secret Power.* London and New York, 1921
46. *Praise and Prayer: A Simple Home Service.* London, 1923
47. *Love—and the Philosopher: A Study in Sentiment.* London and New York, 1923
48. *Open Confession to a Man from a Woman.* London, 1924
49. *Poems.* London, 1925
50. *Harvard House Guide Book,* with Percy S. Brentnall and Bertha Vyver. Privately printed, 1931

Corle, Edwin
American, born May 7, 1906, died June 11, 1956
1. *Fig Tree John.* New York, 1935
2. *People on Earth.* New York, 1937
3. *Burro Valley.* New York, 1938
4. *Solitaire.* New York, 1940
5. *Virginia's Double Life—Solitaire.* London, 1940
6. *Desert Country.* New York, 1941
7. *Coarse Gold.* New York, 1942
8. *Listen, Bright Angel.* New York, 1946
9. *Three Ways to Mecca.* New York, 1947
10. *The Story of the Grand Canyon.* London, 1948
11. *John Studebaker: An American Dream.* New York, 1948
12. *In Winter Light.* New York, 1949
13. *The Royal Highway (El Camino Real).* Indianapolis, 1949
14. *The Gila, River of the Southwest.* New York, 1951
15. *Billy the Kid.* New York, 1953
16. *Mojave: A Book of Stories.* New York, 1934
17. *Death Valley and the Creek Called Furnace.* Los Angeles, 1962

Cort, Van
1. *The Rangers of Bloody Silver.* New York, 1941
2. *Blood on the Moon.* London, 1941
3. *Mail Order Bride.* New York, 1964
4. *Journey of the Gun.* New York, 1966

Costain, Thomas B. (Bertram)
American, May 8, 1885, died October 8, 1965
1. *For My Great Folly.* New York, 1942
2. *Joshua, Leader of a United People,* with Rogers MacVeagh. New York, 1943
3. *Ride with Me.* New York, 1944
4. *The Black Rose.* New York, 1945
5. *The Moneyman.* New York, 1947
6. *High Towers.* New York and London, 1949
7. *The Conquerors.* New York, 1949
8. *Son of a Hundred Kings.* New York, 1950
9. *The Magnificent Century.* New York, 1951
10. *The Silver Chalice.* New York, 1952
11. *The White and the Gold: The French Regime in Canada.* New York, 1954
12. *The Mississippi.* New York, 1955
13. *The Tontine.* New York, 2 vols., 1955
14. *Below the Salt.* New York, 1957
15. *The Three Edwards.* New York, 1958
16. *The Darkness and the Dawn.* New York, 1959
17. *William the Conquerer.* New York, 1959
18. *The Chord of Steel: The Story of the Invention of the Telephone.* New York, 1960
19. *All About William the Conquerer.* London, 1961
20. *The Last Plantagenets.* New York, 1962
21. *The Conquering Family.* New York, 1962
22. *The Last Love.* New York, 1963

Coulson, Juanita
American, born Feruary 12, 1933
1. *Crisis on Cheiron.* New York, 1967
2. *The Singing Stones.* New York, 1968
3. *The Secret of Seven Oaks.* New York, 1972
4. *Door into Terror.* New York, 1972
5. *Stone of Blood.* New York, 1975
6. *Unto the Last Generation.* Toronto, 1975
7. *Space Trap.* Toronto, 1976
8. *Fear Stalks the Bayou.* New York and Skirden (Eng), 1976
9. *Dark Priestess.* New York, 1977
10. *The Web of Wizardry.* New York, 1978
11. *Fire of the Andes.* New York, 1979
12. *The Death God's Citadel.* New York, 1980
13. *Tomorrow's Heritage.* New York, 1981
14. *Outward Bound.* New York, 1982

Coulson, John H.A.
British, born in 1906
Pseudonyms: John and Emery Bonett, with Felicity Winifred Carter; Emery Bonett, with Felicity Winifred Carter
1. *A Girl Must Live,* as Emery Bonett. London, 1936
2. *Make Do with Spring,* as Emery Bonett. London, 1941
3. *High Pavement,* as Emery Bonett. London, 1944
4. *Old Mrs. Camelot,* as Emery Bonett. Philadelphia, 1944
5. *Dead Lion,* as John and Emery Bonett. London and New York, 1949
6. *A Banner for Pegasus,* as John and Emery Bonett. London, 1951
7. *Not in the Script,* as John and Emery Bonett. New York, 1951
8. *No Grave for a Lady,* as John and Emery Bonett. New York, 1959
9. *Better Dead,* as John and Emery Bonett. London, 1964
10. *Better Off Dead,* as John and Emery Bonett. New York, 1964
11. *The Private Face of Murder,* as John and Emery Bonett. London and New York, 1966
12. *This Side Murder?,* as John and Emery Bonett. London, 1967
13. *Murder on the Costa Brava,* as John and Emery Bonett. New York, 1968
14. *The Sound of Murder,* as John and Emery Bonett. London, 1970
15. *No Time to Kill,* as John and Emery Bonett. London and New York, 1972

Courtney, Caroline
1. *Duchess in Disguise.* New York and London, 1979
2. *A Wager for Love.* New York and London, 1979
3. *Love Unmasked.* New York and London, 1979
4. *Guardian of the Heart.* New York and London, 1979
5. *Dangerous Engagement.* New York and London, 1979
6. *The Fortunes of Love.* New York and London, 1980
7. *Forbidden Love.* New York, 1980
8. *Love Triumphant.* New York, 1980
9. *The Romantic Rivals.* New York, 1980
10. *Love's Masquerade.* London, 1981

11. *Heart of Honour*. London, 1982
12. *Libertine in Love*. London, 1982

Cowen, Frances
British, born December 27, 1915
Pseudonym: Eleanor Hyde
1. *In the Clutch of the Green Hand*. London, 1929
2. *The Wings That Failed*. London, 1931
3. *The Plot That Failed*. London, 1933
4. *The Milhurst Mystery*. London, 1933
5. *The Conspiracy of Silence*. London, 1935
6. *The Perilous Adventure*. London, 1936
7. *Children's Book of Pantomimes*. London, 1936
8. *Laddies Way: The Adventures of a Fox Terrier*. London, 1939
9. *The Girl Who Knew Too Much*. London, 1940
10. *Mystery Tower*. London, 1945
11. *Honor Bound*. London, 1946
12. *Castle in Wales*. London, 1947
13. *The Secret of Arrivol*. Huddersfield (Eng), 1947
14. *Mystery of the Walled House*. London, 1951
15. *The Little Countess*. London, 1954
16. *The Riddle of the Rocks*. London, 1956
17. *Clover Cottage*. London, 1958
18. *The Secret of Grange Farm*. London, 1961
19. *The Little Heiress*. London, 1961
20. *The Balcony*. London, 1962
21. *A Step in the Dark*. London, 1962
22. *The Desperate Holiday*. London, 1962
23. *The Secret of the Loch*. London, 1963
24. *The Elusive Quest*. London, 1965
25. *The Bitter Reason*. London, 1966
26. *Scented Danger*. London, 1966
27. *The One Between*. London, 1967
28. *The Gentle Obsession*. London, 1968
29. *The Fractured Silence*. London, 1969
30. *The Daylight Fear*. London, 1969
31. *The Shadow of Polperro*. London, 1969
32. *Edge of Terror*. London, 1970
33. *The Hounds of Carvello*. London, 1970
34. *The Nightmare Ends*. London, 1970
35. *The Lake of Darkness*. London, 1971
36. *The Unforgiving Moment*. London, 1971
37. *Tudor Maid*, as Eleanor Hyde. London, 1972
38. *Tudor Masquerade*, as Eleanor Hyde. London, 1972
39. *Tudor Mayhem*, as Eleanor Hyde. London, 1973
40. *The Curse of the Clodaghs*. London, 1973
41. *Shadow of Theale*. London and New York, 1974
42. *The Village of Fear*. London, 1974
43. *Tudor Mystery*, as Eleanor Hyde. London, 1974
44. *The Secret of Weir House*. London, 1975
45. *The Dangerous Child*. London, 1975
46. *The Haunting of Helen Farley*. London, 1976
47. *The Medusa Connection*. London, 1976
48. *Sinister Melody*. London, 1976
49. *Tudor Myth*, as Eleanor Hyde. London, 1976
50. *Tudor Mausoleum*, as Eleanor Hyde. London, 1977
51. *Tudor Murder*, as Eleanor Hyde. London, 1977
52. *The Silent Pool*. London, 1977
53. *The Lost One*. London, 1977
54. *Gateway to Nowhere*. London, 1978
55. *The House Without a Heart*. London, 1978
56. *Tudor Mansion*, as Eleanor Hyde. London, 1978
57. *Tudor Malice*, as Eleanor Hyde. London, 1979
58. *The Princess Passes*, as Eleanor Hyde. London, 1979
59. *House of Larne*. London, 1980
60. *Wait for Night*. London, 1980
61. *The Elusive Lover*. London, 1981

Cox, A.B. (Anthony Berkeley)
British, born in 1893, died March 9, 1971
Pseudonyms: Anthony Berkeley, Francis Iles
1. *The Layton Court Mystery*, as Anthony Berkeley. London, 1925
2. *The Family Witch: An Essay in Absurdity*. London, 1925
3. *Brenda Entertains*. London, 1925
4. *Jugged Journalism*. London, 1925
5. *The Wychford Poisoning Case*, as Anthony Berkeley. London, 1926
6. *The Professor on Paws*. London, 1926
7. *Roger Sheringham and the Vane Mystery*, as Anthony Berkeley. London, 1927
8. *The Mystery at Lovers' Cave*, as Anthony Berkeley. New York, 1927
9. *Mr. Priestley's Problem*. London, 1927
10. *The Amateur Crime*, as Anthony Berkeley. New York, 1928
11. *The Silk Stocking Murders*, as Anthony Berkeley. London and New York, 1928
12. *The Piccadilly Murder*, as Anthony Berkeley. London, 1929
13. *The Poisoned Chocolates Case*, as Anthony Berkeley. London and New York, 1929
14. *The Second Shot*, as Anthony Berkeley. London, 1930
15. *Top Storey Murder*, as Anthony Berkeley. London and New York, 1931
16. *The Floating Admiral*, as Anthony Berkeley, et al. London, 1931
17. *Malice Aforethought*, as Francis Iles. London and New York, 1931
18. *Murder in the Basement*, as Anthony Berkeley. London and New York, 1932
19. *Before the Fact*, as Francis Iles. London and New York, 1932
20. *Ask a Policeman*, as Anthony Berkeley, et al. London and New York, 1933
21. *Jumping Jenny*, as Anthony Berkeley. London, 1933
22. *Dead Mrs. Stratton*, as Anthony Berkeley. New York, 1933
23. *Panic Party*, as Anthony Berkeley. London, 1934
24. *Mr. Pidgeon's Island*, as Anthony Berkeley. New York, 1934
25. *O England!* London, 1934
26. *Six Against the Yard*, as Anthony Berkeley, et al. London, 1936
27. *Six Against Scotland Yard*, as Anthony Berkeley, et al. New York, 1936
28. *Trial and Error*, as Anthony Berkeley. London and New York, 1937
29. *Not to Be Taken*, as Anthony Berkeley. London, 1938
30. *A Puzzle in Poison*, as Anthony Berkeley. New York, 1938
31. *Death in the House*, as Anthony Berkeley. London and New York, 1939
32. *As for the Woman*, as Francis Iles. London and New York, 1939
33. *A Pocketful of One Hundred New Limericks*. Privately printed, 1960

Cox, William R. (Robert)
American, born April 14, 1901
Pseudonyms: Joel Reeve, Roger G. Spellman, Jonas Ward
1. *Make My Coffin Strong*. New York, 1954
2. *The Lusty Men*. New York, 1957
3. *The Tycoon and the Tigress*. New York, 1958
4. *Hell to Pay*. New York, 1954
5. *Five Were Chosen: A Basketball Story*. New York, 1956
6. *Gridiron Duel*. New York, 1959
7. *Comanche Moon: A Novel of the West*. New York, 1959
8. *Murder in Vegas*. New York, 1960
9. *Death Comes Early*. New York, 1961
10. *Luke Short and His Era*. New York, 1961

Cox, William R.

11. *Luke Short, Famous Gambler of the Old West.* London, 1962
12. *Death on Location.* New York, 1962
13. *The Duke.* New York, 1962
14. *The Outlawed.* New York, 1963
15. *Bigger than Texas.* New York and London, 1963
16. *The Wild Pitch.* New York, 1963
17. *The Mets Will Win the Pennant.* New York, 1964
18. *Tall on the Court.* New York, 1964
19. *Third and Eight to Go.* New York, 1964
20. *Big League Rookie.* New York, 1965
21. *Tall for a Texan,* as Roger G. Spellman. New York, 1965
22. *The Gunsharp.* New York, 1965
23. *Frank Merriwell, Freshman Quarterback.* New York, 1965
24. *Frank Merriwell, Freshman Pitcher.* New York, 1965
25. *Frank Merriwell, Sports Car Racer.* New York, 1965
26. *Way to Go, Doll Baby!* New York, 1966
27. *Trouble at Second Base.* New York, 1966
28. *The Valley Eleven.* New York, 1966
29. *Goal Ahead,* as Joel Reeve. New York, 1967
30. *Black Silver.* No place, 1967
31. *Day of the Gun.* New York, 1967
32. *Firecreek.* New York, 1968
33. *Jump Shot Goal.* New York, 1968
34. *Moon of Cobre.* New York, 1969
35. *Law Comes to Razor Edge.* New York, 1970
36. *Buchanan's War,* as Jonas Ward. New York, 1970
37. *Rookie in the Back Court.* New York, 1970
38. *Big League Sandlotters.* New York, 1971
39. *Third and Goal.* New York, 1971
40. *Trap for Buchanan,* as Jonas Ward. New York, 1971
41. *The Sixth Horseman.* New York, 1972
42. *Buchanan's Gamble.* New York, 1972
43. *Jack o' Diamonds.* New York, 1972
44. *Buchanan's Siege.* New York, 1972
45. *Playoff.* New York, 1972
46. *Gunner of the Court.* New York, 1972
47. *The Running Back.* New York, 1972
48. *Chicano Cruz.* New York, 1972
49. *The Backyard Five.* New York, 1973
50. *Game, Set and Match.* New York, 1973
51. *Navajo Blood.* New York, 1973
52. *Hot Times.* New York, 1973
53. *Buchanan on the Run.* New York, 1973
54. *Get Buchanan.* New York, 1973
55. *The Ginshop.* New York, 1973
56. *Buchanan Takes Over.* New York, 1974
57. *The Unbeatable Five.* New York, 1974
58. *Buchanan Calls the Shots.* New York, 1975
59. *Buchanan's Big Showdown.* New York, 1975
60. *Buchanan's Texas Treasure.* New York, 1976
61. *Buchanan's Stolen Railway.* New York, 1977
62. *Battery Mates.* New York, 1978
63. *Buchanan's Manhunt.* New York, 1978
64. *Buchanan's Range War.* New York, 1979
65. *Home Court Is Where You Find It.* New York, 1980
66. *Buchanan's Big Fight.* New York, 1980

Craig, Mary Francis
American, born February 27, 1923
Pseudonyms: M.S. Craig, Alexis Hill, Mary Francis Shura

1. *Simple Spigott,* as Mary Francis Shura. New York, 1960
2. *The Garret of Greta McGraw,* as Mary Francis Shura. New York, 1961
3. *Mary's Marvelous Mouse,* as Mary Francis Shura. New York, 1962
4. *The Nearsighted Knight,* as Mary Francis Shura. New York, 1964
5. *The Riddle of Raven's Gulch,* as Mary Francis Shura. New York, 1964
6. *Run Away Home,* as Mary Francis Shura. New York, 1965
7. *Shoe Full of Shamrock,* as Mary Francis Shura. New York, 1965
8. *A Tale of Middle Length,* as Mary Francis Shura. New York, 1966
9. *Backwards for Luck.* New York, 1967
10. *Pornada,* as Mary Francis Shura. New York, 1968
11. *The Valley of the Frost Giants,* as Mary Francis Shura. New York, 1971
12. *The Seven Stone,* as Mary Francis Shura. New York, 1972
13. *Topcat of Tam,* as Mary Francis Shura. New York, 1972
14. *The Shop on Threnody Street,* as Mary Francis Shura. New York, 1972
15. *A Candle for the Dragon.* New York, 1973
16. *Ten Thousand Several Doors.* New York, 1973
17. *The Cranes of Ibycus.* New York, 1974
18. *Mistress of Lost River.* New York, 1976
19. *Shadows of the Past.* New York, 1976
20. *The Riddle of Raven's Hollow,* as Mary Francis Shura. New York, 1976
21. *The Season of Silence,* as Mary Francis Shura. New York, 1976
22. *The Gray Ghosts of Taylor Ridge,* as Mary Francis Shura. New York, 1978
23. *Were He a Stranger.* New York, 1978
24. *Passion's Slave,* as Alexis Hill. New York, 1979
25. *Mister Wolf and Me,* as Mary Francis Shura. New York, 1979
26. *The Barkley Street Six-Pack,* as Mary Francis Shura. New York, 1979
27. *Chester,* as Mary Francis Shura. New York, 1980
28. *The Untamed Heart,* as Alexis Hill. New York, 1980
29. *Happles and Cinnamunger,* as Mary Francis Shura. New York, 1981
30. *The Chicagoans: Dust to Diamonds,* as M.S. Craig. New York, 1981

Crowe, Cecily
American

1. *Miss Spring.* New York, 1953
2. *The Tower of Kilraven.* New York, 1965
3. *Northwater.* New York, 1968
4. *The Twice-Born.* New York, 1972
5. *Abbeygate.* New York, 1977
6. *The Talisman.* New York, 1979

Cullum, Ridgewell
British, born August 13, 1867, died November 3, 1943

1. *The Devil's Keg.* London, 1903
2. *The Story of the Foss River Ranch.* Boston, 1903
3. *The Hound from the North.* London and Boston, 1904
4. *The Brooding Wild.* London, 1905
5. *In the Brooding Wild.* Boston, 1905
6. *The Night-Riders: A Romance of Western Canada.* London, 1906
7. *The Watchers of the Plains.* London, 1908
8. *The Compact.* London and New York, 1909
9. *The Sheriff of Dyke Hole.* London and Philadelphia, 1909
10. *The Trail of the Axe.* London and Philadelphia, 1910
11. *The One-Way Trail.* London and Philadelphia, 1911
12. *The Twins of Suffering Creek.* London and Philadelphia, 1912
13. *The Night-Riders: A Romance of Early Montana.* Philadelphia, 1913
14. *The Golden Woman.* London and Philadelphia, 1913
15. *The Law-Breakers.* London and Philadelphia, 1914

16. *The Way of the Strong.* London and Philadelphia, 1914
17. *The Son and His Father.* London and Philadelphia, 1915
18. *The Men Who Wrought.* London and Philadelphia, 1916
19. *The Triumph of John Kars.* London and Philadelphia, 1917
20. *The Purchase Price.* London and Philadelphia, 1917
21. *The Forfeit.* Philadelphia, 1917
22. *The Law of the Gun.* London and Philadelphia, 1918
23. *The Heart of Unaga.* London and New York, 1920
24. *The Man in the Twilight.* London and New York, 1922
25. *The Luck of the Kid.* London and New York, 1923
26. *The Saint of the Speedway.* London and New York, 1924
27. *The Riddle of Three-Way Creek.* London and New York, 1925
28. *The Candy Man.* London, 1926
29. *Child of the North.* New York, 1926
30. *Foss River Ranch.* London, 1927
31. *The Wolf Pack.* London and Philadelphia, 1927
32. *The Mystery of the Barren Lands.* London and Philadelphia, 1928
33. *The Tiger of Cloud River.* London and Philadelphia, 1929
34. *The Treasure of Big Waters.* London and Philadelphia, 1930
35. *The Bull Moose.* London and Philadelphia, 1931
36. *Sheets in the Wind.* London and Philadelphia, 1932
37. *The Flaming Wildness.* London and Philadelphia, 1934
38. *The Vampire of N'Gobi.* London, 1935
39. *One Who Kills.* London and Philadelphia, 1938
40. *The Man from Lias River.* London, 1950

Culp, John H. [John Hewett Culp, Jr.]
American, born August 31, 1907
1. *Born of the Sun.* New York, 1959
2. *The Men of Gonzales.* New York, 1960
3. *The Restless Land.* New York, 1962
4. *The Bright Feathers.* New York, 1965
5. *A Whistle in the Wind.* New York, 1968
6. *Timothy Baines.* New York, 1969
7. *The Treasure of the Chisos.* New York, 1971
8. *Oh, Valley Green!* New York, 1972

Cunningham, Chet
American, born December 9, 1928
Pseudonym: Cathy Cunningham
1. *Bushwackers at Circle K.* New York, 1969
2. *Killer's Range.* New York, 1970
3. *The Gold Wagon.* New York, 1972
4. *Blood on the Strip.* New York, 1973
5. *Fatal Friday.* No place, 1973
6. *The Demons of Highpoint House,* as Cathy Cunningham. New York, 1973
7. *Dead Start Scramble.* New York, 1973
8. *Your Wheels: How to Keep Your Car Running.* New York, 1973
9. *Baja Bike.* New York, 1974
10. *Hijacking Manhattan.* New York, 1974
11. *Terror in Tokyo.* New York, 1974
12. *Bloody Gold.* New York, 1975
13. *Your Bike: How to Keep Your Motorcycle Running.* New York, 1975
14. *The Patriots.* New York, 1976
15. *The Gold and the Glory.* New York, 1977
16. *The Power and the Price.* New York, 1977
17. *Seeds of Rebellion.* New York, 1977
18. *The Poker Club.* Westport (CT), 1978
19. *Beloved Rebel.* New York, 1978
20. *Rainbow Saga.* New York, 1979
21. *This Splendid Land.* New York, 1979
22. *Devil's Gold.* New York, 1980
23. *Die of Gold.* New York, 1980
24. *222 Ways to Save Gas and Get the Best Possible Mileage.* Englewood Cliffs (NJ), 1981
25. *Cheyenne Payoff.* New York, 1981
26. *Gold Train.* New York, 1981
27. *The Silver Mistress.* New York, 1981
28. *Tuscon Temptress.* New York, 1981

Cunningham, Eugene
American, born November 29, 1896, died October 18, 1957
Pseudonym: Leigh Carder
1. *The Regulation Guy.* New York, 1922
2. *Gypsying Through Central America.* New York and London, 1922
3. *The Trail to Apacaz.* New York and London, 1924
4. *Famous in the West.* El Paso (TX), 1926
5. *Riders of the Night.* Boston, 1932
6. *Buckaroo.* Boston, 1933
7. *Diamond River Man.* Boston and London, 1934
8. *Texas Sheriff.* Boston, 1934
9. *Triggernometry: A Gallery of Gunfighters.* New York, 1934
10. *Redshirts of Destiny.* New York, 1935
11. *Quick Triggers.* Boston, 1935
12. *Trail of the Macaw.* Boston and London, 1935
13. *Border Guns,* as Leigh Carder. New York, 1935
14. *Bravo Trail,* as Leigh Carder. New York, 1935
15. *Outlaw Justice,* as Leigh Carder. New York, 1935
16. *Pistol Passport.* Boston, 1936
17. *Whistling Lead.* Boston, 1936
18. *The Ranger Way.* Boston, 1937
19. *Texas Triggers.* Boston, 1938
20. *The Trail from the River.* London, 1939
21. *Gun Bulldogger.* Boston, 1939
22. *Red Range.* Boston, 1939
23. *Spiderweb Trail.* Boston, 1940
24. *Diamond River Range.* New York, 1949
25. *Mesquite Maverick.* New York, 1955
26. *Riding Gun.* Boston, 1956

Curry, Peggy Simson
British, born December 30, 1911
1. *Fire in the Water.* New York, 1951
2. *So Far from Spring.* New York, 1956
3. *The Oil Patch.* New York, 1959
4. *Creative Fiction from Experience.* Boston, 1964
5. *A Shield of Clover.* New York, 1970

Curwood, James Oliver
American, born June 12 1878, died August 13, 1927
1. *The Courage of Captain Plum.* Indianapolis, 1908
2. *The Wolf Hunters: A Tale of Adventure in the Wilderness.* Indianapolis, 1908
3. *The Gold Hunters: A Story of Life and Adventure in the Hudson Bay Wilds.* Indianapolis, 1909
4. *The Great Lakes, The Vessels That Plough Them, Their Owners, Their Sailors, and Their Cargoes, Together with a Brief History of Our Inland Seas.* New York, 1909
5. *The Danger Trail.* Indianapolis, 1910
6. *Phillip Steele of the Royal Northwest Mounted Police.* Indianapolis, 1911
7. *The Honor of the Big Snows.* Indianapolis, 1911
8. *Flower of the North: A Modern Romance.* New York, 1912
9. *Isobel: A Romance of the Northern Trail.* New York, 1913
10. *Kazan.* Indianapolis, 1914
11. *Kazan the Wolf-Dog.* London, 1914
12. *The Beloved Murderer.* New York, 1914
13. *Ice-Bound Hearts.* London, 1915
14. *God's Country—and the Woman.* New York and London, 1915

15. *The Valley of Gold.* London, 1916
16. *The Grizzly King: A Romance of the Wild.* New York, 1916
17. *The Grizzly.* London, 1916
18. *The Hunted Woman.* New York, 1916
19. *Baree, Son of Kazan.* New York, 1917
20. *Son of Kazan.* New York, 1917
21. *The Treasure Hunters.* London, 1917
22. *The Girl Beyond the Trail.* London, 1917
23. *The Courage of Marge O'Doone.* New York, 1918
24. *The Golden Snare.* London, 1918
25. *Nomads of the North: A Story of Romance and Adventure under the Open Stars.* New York and London, 1919
26. *The River's End: A New Story of God's Country.* New York, 1919
27. *The Valley of Silent Men: A Story of the Three River Country.* New York, 1920
28. *Back to God's Country and Other Stories.* New York, 1920
29. *Swift Lightning: A Story of Wild-Life Adventure in the Frozen North.* London, 1920
30. *The Flaming Forest: A Novel of the Canadian Northwest.* New York, 1921
31. *The Country Beyond: A Romance of the Wilderness.* New York and London, 1922
32. *The Last Frontier.* London, 1923
33. *The Alaskan: A Novel of the North.* New York, 1923
34. *A Gentleman of Courage: A Novel of the Wilderness.* New York and London, 1924
35. *The Ancient Highway: A Novel of High Hearts and Open Roads.* New York and London, 1925
36. *The Black Hunter: A Novel of Old Quebec.* New York and London, 1926
37. *The Crippled Lady of Peribonkz.* London, 1927
38. *The Plains of Abraham.* New York and London, 1928
39. *The Glory of Living: The Autobiography of an Adventurous Boy Who Grew into a Writer and a Lover of Life.* London, 1928
40. *Green Timber.* New York, 1930
41. *Faulkner of the Inland Sea.* Indianapolis, 1931
42. *Son of a Hero.* London, 1931
43. *Son of the Forests: An Autobiography.* New York, 1939
44. *Steele of the Royal Mounted.* New York, 1946

Cushman, Dan
American, born June 9, 1909
1. *Montana, Here I Be!* New York, 1950
2. *Badlands Justice.* New York, 1951
3. *Naked Ebony.* New York, 1951
4. *Jewel of the Java Sea.* New York, 1951
5. *Savage Interlude.* New York, 1952
6. *The Ripper from Rawhide.* New York, 1952
7. *Stay Away Joe.* New York, 1953
8. *Timberjack.* New York, 1953
9. *Jungle She.* New York, 1953
10. *The Fabulous Finn.* New York, 1954
11. *Tongking!* New York, 1954
12. *Port Orient.* New York, 1955
13. *The Fastest Gun.* New York, 1955
14. *The Old Copper Collar.* New York, 1957
15. *The Silver Mountain.* New York, 1957
16. *Tall Wyoming.* New York, 1957
17. *The Forbidden Land.* New York, 1958
18. *Goodbye, Old Dry.* New York and London, 1959
19. *The Con Man.* New York, 1960
20. *The Half-Caste.* London, 1960
21. *Brothers in Kickapoo.* New York, 1962
22. *Boomtown.* London, 1962
23. *On the Make.* New York, 1963
24. *Opium Flower.* New York, 1963
25. *4 for Texas.* New York, 1963
26. *The Grand and the Glorious.* New York, 1963
27. *North Fork to Hell.* New York, 1964
28. *The Great North Trail: America's Route of the Ages.* New York, 1966
29. *Cow Country Cook Book.* Great Falls (MT), 1967
30. *The Long Riders.* New York, 1967
31. *Montana: The Gold Frontier.* Great Falls, 1973
32. *Plenty of Room and Air.* Great Falls, 1975
33. *The Muskrat Farm.* Great Falls, 1977

Daley, Janet
American, born May 21, 1944
1. *No Quarter Asked.* London, 1974
2. *Savage Land.* London, 1974
3. *Something Extra.* London, 1975
4. *Fire and Ice.* London, 1975
5. *Boss Man from Ogallala.* London, 1975
6. *After the Storm.* London, 1975
7. *Land of Enchantment.* London, 1975
8. *Sweet Promise.* London, 1976
9. *The Homeplace.* London and Toronto, 1976
10. *Dangerous Masquerade.* London, 1976
11. *Show Me.* London, 1976
12. *Valley of the Vapours.* London, 1976
13. *The Night of the Cotillion.* London, 1976
14. *Fiesta San Antonio.* London and Toronto, 1977
15. *Bluegrass King.* London and Toronto, 1977
16. *A Lyon's Share.* London and Toronto, 1977
17. *The Widow and the Wastrel.* London and Toronto, 1977
18. *The Ivory Cane.* London, 1977
19. *Six White Horses.* London, 1977
20. *To Tell the Truth.* London, 1977
21. *The Master Fiddler.* London, 1977
22. *Giant of Mcdabi.* London and Toronto, 1978
23. *Beware of the Stranger.* London and Toronto, 1978
24. *Darling Jenny.* London and Toronto, 1978
25. *The Indy Man.* London and Toronto, 1978
26. *Reilly's Woman.* London and Toronto, 1978
27. *For Bitter or Worse.* London, 1978
28. *Tidewater Lover.* London, 1978
29. *The Bride of the Delta Queen.* London, 1978
30. *Green Mountain Man.* London, 1978
31. *Sonora Sundown.* London and Toronto, 1978
32. *Summer Mahogany.* London, 1978
33. *The Matchmakers.* London and Toronto, 1978
34. *Big Sky Country.* London and Toronto, 1978
35. *Low Country Liar.* London and Toronto, 1979
36. *Strange Bedfellow.* London and Toronto, 1979
37. *For Mike's Sake.* London and Toronto, 1979
38. *Sentimental Journey.* London and Toronto, 1979
39. *Bed of Grass.* London, 1979
40. *That Boston Man.* London, 1979
41. *Kona Winds.* London, 1979
42. *A Land Called Deseret.* London and Toronto, 1979
43. *Touch the Wind.* London, 1979
44. *Sweet Promise.* London and Toronto, 1979
45. *Difficult Decision.* London and Toronto, 1980
46. *Enemy in Camp.* London and Toronto, 1980
47. *Heart of Stone.* London and Toronto, 1980
48. *The Mating Season.* London and Toronto, 1980
49. *Southern Nights.* London and Toronto, 1980
50. *The Thawing of Mara.* London and Toronto, 1980
51. *One of the Boys.* London and Toronto, 1980
52. *Wild and Wonderful.* London, 1980
53. *Lord of the High Lonesome.* London and Toronto, 1980
54. *The Rogue.* London and Toronto, 1980

55. *Ride the Thunder.* London and Toronto, 1981
56. *A Tradition of Pride.* London and Toronto, 1981
57. *The Travelling Kind.* London and Toronto, 1981
58. *Dakota Dreamin'.* London and Toronto, 1981
59. *The Hostage Bride.* New York, 1981
60. *Night Way.* New York, 1981
61. *Lancaster Men.* New York, 1981
62. *For the Love of God.* New York, 1981
63. *This Calder Sky.* New York, 1981
64. *This Calder Range.* New York, 1982
65. *Stands a Calder Man.* New York, 1982
66. *Northern Magic.* London and Toronto, 1982
67. *With a Little Luck.* London and Toronto, 1982
68. *That Carolina Summer.* London and Toronto, 1982
69. *Terms of Surrender.* New York, 1982
70. *Wildcatter's Woman.* New York, 1982

Daniels, Dorothy
American, born July 1, 1915
Pseudonyms: Danielle Dorsett, Angela Gray, Cynthia Kavanaugh, Helaine Ross, Suzanne Somers, Geraldine Thayer, Helen Gray Weston

1. *The Caduceus Tree,* as Suzanne Somers. New York, 1961
2. *A Nurse for Doctor Keith.* New York, 1962
3. *House of Eve,* as Suzanne Somers. New York, 1962
4. *The Dark Rider,* as Geraldine Thayer. New York, 1962
5. *Jennifer James, R.N.* New York, 1962
6. *No Tears Tomorrow,* as Helaine Ross. New York, 1962
7. *Eve Originals.* New York, 1962
8. *Cruise Ship Nurse.* New York, 1963
9. *Country Nurse.* New York, 1963
10. *Image of Truth,* as Suzanne Somers. New York, 1963
11. *World's Fair Nurse.* New York, 1964
12. *Island Nurse.* New York, 1964
13. *The Tower Room.* New York, 1965
14. *The Leland Legacy.* New York, 1965
15. *Shadow Glen.* New York, 1965
16. *Marriott Hall.* New York, 1965
17. *Darkhaven.* New York, 1965
18. *The Unguarded.* New York, 1965
19. *The Mistress of Falcon Hill.* New York, 1965
20. *Dance in Darkness.* New York, 1965
21. *Cliffside Castle.* New York, 1965
22. *The Lily Pond.* New York, 1965
23. *Marble Leaf.* New York, 1966
24. *Midday Moon.* New York, 1966
25. *Knight in Red Armor.* New York, 1966
26. *Nurse at Danger Mansion.* New York, 1966
27. *Danger Mansion.* New York, No date
28. *Dark Villa.* New York, 1966
29. *Bride of Lenore,* as Cynthia Kavanaugh. New York, 1966
30. *The Deception,* as Cynthia Kavanaugh. New York, 1966
31. *Mystic Manor,* as Helen Gray Weston. New York, 1966
32. *The Templeton Memoirs.* New York, 1966
33. *This Ancient Evil.* New York, 1966
34. *The Last of the Mansions.* New York, 1966
35. *The Mists of Morning,* as Suzanne Somers. New York, 1966
36. *House of False Faces,* as Helen Gray Weston. New York, 1967
37. *House of Stolen Memories.* New York, 1967
38. *The Sevier Secrets.* New York, 1967
39. *Screen Test for Laurel.* New York, 1967
40. *Traitor's Road.* New York, 1967
41. *House of Seven Courts.* New York, 1967
42. *The Eagle's Nest.* New York, 1967
43. *Mostly by Moonlight.* New York, 1968
44. *Blue Devil Suite.* New York, 1968
45. *Affair at Marrakesh.* New York, 1968
46. *Candle in the Sun.* New York, 1968
47. *Lady of the Shadows.* New York, 1968
48. *Duet.* New York, 1968
49. *Survivors of Darkness.* New York, 1969
50. *Mansion of Lost Memories.* New York, 1969
51. *Strange Paradise.* New York, 1969
52. *Affair in Hong Kong.* New York, 1969
53. *Voice on the Wind.* New York, 1969
54. *The Carson Inheritance.* New York, 1969
55. *The Tormented.* New York, 1969
56. *The Marble Angel.* New York, 1970
57. *The Curse of Mallory Hall.* New York, 1970
58. *The Man from Yesterday.* New York, 1970
59. *The Dark Stage.* New York, 1970
60. *Emerald Hill.* New York, 1970
61. *Willow Weep.* New York, 1970
62. *Island of Evil.* New York, 1970
63. *Raxl, Voodoo Princess.* New York, 1970
64. *The Raging Waters.* New York, 1970
65. *The Attic Rope.* New York, 1970
66. *The Unearthly.* New York, 1970
67. *Journey into Terror.* New York, 1971
68. *Key Diablo.* New York, 1971
69. *The House of Many Doors.* New York, 1971
70. *The Bell.* New York, 1971
71. *Diablo Manor.* New York, 1971
72. *Witch's Castle.* New York, 1971
73. *The Beaumont Tradition.* New York, 1971
74. *The Lattimer Legend.* New York, 1971
75. *Shadows of Tomorrow.* New York, 1971
76. *The Romany Curse,* as Suzanne Somers. New York, 1971
77. *The Ghost Dancers,* as Angela Gray. New York, 1971
78. *The Golden Packet,* as Angela Gray. New York, 1971
79. *The Lattimore Arch,* as Angela Gray. New York, 1971
80. *Blackwell's Ghost,* as Angela Gray. New York, 1972
81. *Duelling Oaks,* as Danielle Dorsett. New York, 1972
82. *The Spanish Chapel.* New York, 1972
83. *Conover's Folly.* New York, 1972
84. *The House of Broken Dolls.* New York, 1972
85. *The Lanier Riddle.* New York, 1972
86. *Castle Morvant.* New York, 1972
87. *Maya Temple.* New York, 1972
88. *The Larrabee Heiress.* New York, 1972
89. *Shadows from the Past.* New York, 1972
90. *The House on Circus Hill.* New York, 1972
91. *Dark Island.* New York, 1972
92. *Witch's Island.* New York, 1972
93. *The Stone House.* New York, 1973
94. *The Duncan Dynasty.* New York, 1973
95. *The Silent Halls of Ashenden.* New York, 1973
96. *The Possession of Tracy Corbin.* New York, 1973
97. *Hills of Fire.* New York, 1973
98. *The Prisoner of Malville Hall.* New York, 1973
99. *Jade Green.* New York, 1973
100. *The Caldwell Shadow.* New York, 1973
101. *Image of a Ghost.* New York, 1973
102. *The House on Thunder Hill,* as Suzanne Somers. New York, 1973
103. *Touch Me,* as Suzanne Somers. Los Angeles, 1973
104. *Ashes of Falconwyck,* as Angela Gray. New York, 1973
105. *The Watcher in the Dark,* as Angela Gray. New York, 1973
106. *Nightmare at Riverview,* as Angela Gray. New York, 1973
107. *Ravenswood Hall,* as Angela Gray. New York, 1973
108. *The Warlock's Daughter,* as Angela Gray. New York, 1973
109. *Until Death,* as Suzanne Somers. New York, 1973
110. *The Apollo Fountain.* New York, 1974
111. *Island of Bitter Memories.* New York, 1974
112. *Child of Darkness.* New York, 1974

113. *Ghost Song.* New York, 1974
114. *The Two Worlds of Peggy Scott.* New York, 1974
115. *The Exorcism of Jenny Slade.* New York, 1974
116. *A Web of Peril.* New York, 1974
117. *Illusion at Haven's Edge.* New York, 1975
118. *The Possessed.* New York, 1975
119. *The Guardian of Willow House.* New York, 1975
120. *The Unlamented.* New York, 1975
121. *The Tide Mill.* New York, 1975
122. *Shadow of a Man.* New York, 1975
123. *Marble Hills.* New York, 1975
124. *Blackthorn.* New York, 1975
125. *Whistle in the Wind.* New York, 1976
126. *Night Shade.* New York, 1976
127. *The Vineyard Chapel.* New York, 1976
128. *Circle of Guilt.* New York, 1976
129. *Juniper Hill.* New York, 1976
130. *Portrait of a Witch.* New York, 1976
131. *The Summer House.* New York, 1976
132. *Terror of the Twin.* New York, 1976
133. *Dark Heritage.* New York, 1976
134. *Twilight at the Elms.* New York, 1976
135. *Poison Flower.* New York, 1977
136. *Nightfall.* New York, 1977
137. *Wines of Cyprien.* New York, 1977
138. *A Woman in Silk and Shadows.* New York, 1977
139. *In the Shadows.* New York, 1978
140. *The Lonely Place.* New York, 1978
141. *Hermitage Hill.* New York, 1978
142. *Perrine.* New York, 1978
143. *The Magic Ring.* New York, 1978
144. *Meg.* New York, 1979
145. *The Cormac Legend.* New York, 1979
146. *Yesterday's Evil.* New York, 1979
147. *Veil of Treachery.* New York, 1979
148. *The Purple and the Gold.* New York, 1980
149. *Legend of Death.* New York, 1980
150. *Valley of the Shadows.* New York, 1980
151. *The Love of the Lion,* as Angela Gray. New York, 1980
152. *Bridal Black.* New York, 1980
153. *House of Silence.* New York, 1980
154. *Nicola.* New York, 1980
155. *Sisters of Valcour.* New York, 1981
156. *Saratoga.* New York, 1981
157. *Monte Carlo.* New York, 1981

Darcy, Clare
American
1. *Georgina.* New York, 1971
2. *Cecily; or, A Young Lady of Quality.* New York, 1972
3. *Lydia; or, Love in Town.* New York, 1973
4. *Victoire.* New York, 1974
5. *Allegra.* New York, 1975
6. *Lady Pamela.* New York, 1975
7. *Regina.* New York, 1976
8. *Elyza.* New York, 1976
9. *Cressida.* New York, 1977
10. *Eugenia.* New York, 1977
11. *Gwendolen.* New York, 1978
12. *Rolande.* New York, 1978
13. *Letty.* London and Toronto, 1980
14. *Caroline and Julia.* New York, 1982

Davenport, Marcia
American, born June 9, 1903
1. *Mozart.* New York, 1932
2. *Of Lena Geyer.* London and Toronto, 1936
3. *The Valley of Decision.* New York, 1942
4. *East Side, West Side.* New York, 1947
5. *Lena Geyer.* London, 1949
6. *My Brother's Keeper.* London and Toronto, 1954
7. *Garibaldi, Father of Modern Italy.* New York, 1957
8. *The Constant Image.* London and Toronto, 1960
9. *Too Strong for Fantasy.* New York, 1967

Davis, Dorothy Salisbury
American, born April 26, 1916
1. *The Judas Cat.* New York, 1949
2. *The Clay Hand.* New York, 1950
3. *A Gentle Murderer.* New York, 1951
4. *A Town of Masks.* New York, 1952
5. *Men of No Property.* New York, 1956
6. *Death of an Old Sinner.* New York, 1957
7. *A Gentleman Called.* London and Toronto, 1958
8. *Old Sinners Never Die.* New York, 1959
9. *The Evening of the Good Samaritan.* New York, 1961
10. *Black Sheep, White Lamb.* New York, 1963
11. *The Pale Betrayer.* New York, 1965
12. *Enemy and Brother.* New York, 1966
13. *God Speed the Night,* with Jerome Ross. New York, 1968
14. *Where the Dark Streets Go.* New York, 1969
15. *Shock Wave.* New York, 1972
16. *The Little Brothers.* New York, 1973
17. *A Death in the Life.* New York, 1976
18. *Scarlet Night.* New York, 1980

Davis, H.L. (Harold Lenoir)
American, born October 18, 1894, died October 31, 1960
1. *Honey in the Horn.* London and Toronto, 1935
2. *Proud Rider and Other Poems.* New York, 1942
3. *Harp of a Thousand Strings.* New York, 1947
4. *Beulah Land.* New York, 1949
5. *Winds of Morning.* London and Toronto, 1952
6. *Team Bells Woke Me and Other Stories.* New York, 1953
7. *The Distant Music.* New York, 1957
8. *Kettle of Fire.* New York, 1959

Dawson, Peter [Jonathan H. Glidden]
American, born in 1907
1. *The Crimson Horseshoe.* London and Toronto, 1941
2. *The Stageline Feud.* New York, 1941
3. *Gunsmoke Graze.* New York, 1942
4. *Long Ride.* New York, 1942
5. *Time to Ride.* London, 1943
6. *Trail Boss.* New York, 1943
7. *High Country.* London and Toronto, 1947
8. *Royal Gorge.* New York, 1948
9. *Renegade Canyon.* New York, 1949
10. *The Stirrup Boss.* New York, 1949
11. *Battle Royal.* London, 1949
12. *Canyon Hell.* New York, 1949
13. *Guns on the Santa Fe.* New York, 1950
14. *The Outlaw Longbow.* New York, 1950
15. *Ruler of the Range.* New York, 1951
16. *High Lonesome.* New York, 1951
17. *The Wild Bunch.* New York, 1953
18. *Dead Man Pass.* New York, 1954
19. *Leashed Guns.* New York, 1955
20. *Big Outfit.* New York, 1955
21. *Man on the Buckskin.* New York, 1957
22. *Treachery at Rock Point.* New York, 1957
23. *The Savages.* New York, 1959
24. *Yancey.* New York, 1960
25. *The Texas Slicks.* New York, 1961
26. *The Half-Breed.* New York, 1962
27. *Bloody Gold.* New York, 1963

28. *The Showdown.* New York, 1964
29. *A Pride of Men.* New York, 1966

Day, Robert S.
American, born in 1941
1. *The Last Cattle Drive.* London and Toronto, 1977

Dean, Dudley [Dudley Dean McGaughy]
American
Other pseudonyms: Dean Owen, Brian Wynne
1. *Guns to the Sunset,* as Dean Owen. New York, 1948
2. *Point of a Gun,* as Dean Owen. New York, 1953
3. *The Man from Boot Hill,* as Dean Owen. New York, 1953
4. *Ambush at Rincon.* New York, 1953
5. *The Man from Riondo.* New York, 1954
6. *Rifle Pass,* as Dean Owen. New York, 1954
7. *Brush Rider,* as Dean Owen. New York, 1955
8. *The Broken Spur.* New York, 1955
9. *Tough Hombre.* New York, 1956
10. *Son of the Gun.* London, 1956
11. *Six-Gun Vengeance.* New York, 1956
12. *The Diehards.* New York, 1956
13. *The Gunpointer,* as Dean Owen. New York, 1956
14. *Last-Chance Range,* as Dean Owen. New York, 1957
15. *Border Renegade.* New York, 1957
16. *Gun in the Valley.* New York, 1957
17. *Rawhider from Texas,* as Dean Owen. Derby (CT), 1958
18. *This Range Is Mine,* as Dean Owen. New York, 1959
19. *Lawless Guns.* New York, 1959
20. *Gun Shy,* with Les Savage. New York, 1959
21. *Lila My Lovely.* New York, 1960
22. *Rebel Ramrod,* as Dean Owen. New York, 1960
23. *Killer's Bargain,* as Dean Owen. London, 1961
24. *The Sam Houston Story,* as Dean Owen. Derby, 1961
25. *Cross of Rope.* New York, 1963
26. *Trail of the Hunter.* New York, 1963
27. *Gun the Man Down.* New York, 1971
28. *Lone Star Roundup.* New York, 1972
29. *Gunslick Territory,* as Brian Wynne. New York, 1973

Decker, William
American, born in 1926
1. *To Be a Man.* Boston, 1967
2. *The Holdouts.* Boston, 1979

Deeping, Warwick [George Warwick Deeping]
British, born May 28, 1877, died April 20, 1950
1. *Uther and Igraine.* London and New York, 1903
2. *Love Among the Ruins.* London and New York, 1904
3. *The Seven Streams.* London, 1905
4. *The Slanderers.* New York, 1905
5. *Bess of the Woods.* London and New York, 1906
6. *A Woman's War.* London and New York, 1907
7. *Bertrand of Brittany.* London and New York, 1908
8. *Mad Barbara.* London, 1908
9. *The Red Saint.* London, 1909
10. *The Return of the Petticoat.* London and New York, 1909
11. *The Lame Englishman.* London, 1910
12. *The Rust of Rome.* London, 1910
13. *Fox Farm.* London, 1911
14. *Joan of the Tower.* London, 1911
15. *Sincerity.* London, 1912
16. *The Strong Hand.* London, 1912
17. *The House of Spies.* London and New York, 1913
18. *The White Gate.* London and New York, 1913
19. *The King Behind the King.* London and New York, 1914
20. *The Pride of Eve.* London, 1914
21. *Marriage by Conquest.* London and New York, 1915
22. *Unrest.* London, 1916
23. *Bridge of Desire.* New York, 1916
24. *Martin Valliant.* London and New York, 1917
25. *Valour.* London, 1918
26. *Second Youth.* London, 1919
27. *Countess Glika and Other Stories.* London, 1919
28. *The Prophetic Marriage.* London, 1920
29. *Lantern Lane.* London, 1921
30. *Orchards.* London, 1922
31. *Apples of Gold.* London, 1923
32. *The Secret Sanctuary; or, The Saving of John Stretton.* London, 1923
33. *Suvla John.* London, 1924
34. *Three Rooms.* London, 1924
35. *Sorrell and Son.* London, 1925
36. *Doomsday.* London and New York, 1927
37. *Kitty.* London and New York, 1927
38. *Old Pybus.* London and New York, 1928
39. *Roper's Row.* London, 1929
40. *Martyrdom, with The House Behind the Judas Tree.* London, 1929
41. *The Short Stories of Warwick Deeping.* London, 1930
42. *Stories of Love, Courage, and Compassion.* New York, 1930
43. *Exiles.* London, 1930
44. *Exile.* New York, 1930
45. *The Ten Commandments.* New York, 1931
46. *The Road.* London, 1931
47. *The Challenge of Love.* New York, 1932
48. *Old Wine and New.* London and New York, 1932
49. *Smith.* London and New York, 1932
50. *The Eyes of Love.* New York, 1933
51. *Two Black Sheep.* London and New York, 1933
52. *The Captive Wife.* New York, 1933
53. *The Man on the White Horse.* London and New York, 1934
54. *Seven Men Came Back.* London and New York, 1934
55. *Sackcloth into Silk.* London, 1935
56. *The Golden Chord.* New York, 1935
57. *Two in a Train and Other Stories.* London, 1935
58. *Three Stories of Romance.* London, 1936
59. *No Hero—This.* London and New York, 1936
60. *Blind Man's Year.* London and New York, 1937
61. *These White Hands.* New York, 1937
62. *The Woman at the Door.* London and New York, 1937
63. *The Malice of Men.* London and New York, 1938
64. *Fantasia.* London, 1939
65. *Bluewater.* New York, 1939
66. *Shabby Summer.* London, 1939
67. *Folly Island.* New York, 1939
68. *The Man Who Went Back.* London and New York, 1940
69. *The Shield of Love.* London and New York, 1940
70. *Corn in Egypt.* London, 1941
71. *The Dark House.* London and New York, 1941
72. *I Live Again.* London and New York, 1942
73. *Slade.* London and New York, 1943
74. *Mr. Gurney and Mr. Slade.* London, 1944
75. *The Cleric's Secret.* New York, 1944
76. *Reprieve.* London and New York, 1945
77. *The Impudence of Youth.* London and New York, 1946
78. *Laughing House.* London, 1946
79. *Portrait of a Playboy.* London, 1947
80. *The Playboy.* New York, 1948
81. *Paradise Place.* London, 1949
82. *Old Mischief.* London, 1950
83. *Time to Heal.* London, 1952
84. *Man in Chains.* London, 1953
85. *The Old World Dies.* London, 1954
86. *Caroline Terrace.* London, 1955

87. *The Serpent's Tooth*. London, 1956
88. *The Sword and the Cross*. London, 1957

Delafield, E.M. [Edmee Elizabeth Monica De la Pasture]
British, born June 9, 1890, died December 2, 1943
1. *Zella Sees Herself*. London and New York, 1917
2. *The War Workers*. London and New York, 1918
3. *The Pelicans*. London, 1919
4. *Consequences*. London and New York, 1919
5. *Tension*. London and New York, 1920
6. *The Heel of Achilles*. London and New York, 1921
7. *Humbug*. London, 1921
8. *The Optimist*. London and New York, 1922
9. *A Reversion to Type*. London and New York, 1923
10. *Mrs. Harter*. London, 1924
11. *Messalina of the Suburbs*. London, 1924
12. *The Chip and the Block*. London, 1925
13. *Jill*. London, 1926
14. *The Way Things Are*. London, 1926
15. *The Entertainment*. London and New York, 1927
16. *The Suburban Young Man*. London, 1928
17. *What Is Love?* London, 1928
18. *Woman Are Like That: Short Stories*. London, 1929
19. *First Love*. London, 1929
20. *Turn Back the Leaves*. London and New York, 1930
21. *Diary of a Provincial Lady*. London, 1930
22. *Challenge to Clarissa*. London, 1931
23. *House Party*. New York, 1931
24. *Thank Heaven Fasting*. London, 1932
25. *A Good Man's Love*. New York, 1932
26. *The Provincial Lady Goes Further*. London, 1932
27. *The Provincial Lady in London*. New York, 1933
28. *Gay Life*. London and New York, 1933
29. *General Impressions*. London, 1933
30. *The Provincial Lady in America*. London and New York, 1934
31. *The Bazalgettes: A Tale* (published anonymously). London, 1935
32. *Faster! Faster!* London and New York, 1936
33. *Nothing Is Safe*. London and New York, 1937
34. *Ladies and Gentlemen in Victorian Fiction*. London and New York, 1937
35. *As Others Hear Us: A Miscellany*. London, 1937
36. *Straw Without Bricks: I Visit Soviet Russia*. London, 1937
37. *I Visit the Soviets: The Provincial Lady Looks at Russia*. New York, 1937
38. *When Women Love*. New York, 1938
39. *Love Has No Resurrection and Other Stories*. London, 1939
40. *Three Marriages*. London, 1939
41. *The Provincial Lady in War-Time*. London and New York, 1940
42. *People You Love*. London, 1940
43. *This War We Wage*. New York, 1941
44. *No One Now Will Know*. London and New York, 1941
45. *Late and Soon*. London and New York, 1943

Dell, Ethel M. (Mary)
British, born August 2, 1881, died September 19, 1939
1. *The Way of an Eagle*. New York, 1911
2. *The Knave of Diamonds*. London and New York, 1913
3. *The Rocks of Valpré*. New York, 1913
4. *The Swindler and Other Stories*. London and New York, 1914
5. *The Desire of His Life*. London, 1914
6. *The Keeper of the Door*. London and New York, 1915
7. *The Bars of Iron*. London and New York, 1916
8. *The Hundredth Chance*. London and New York, 1917
9. *The Rose of Dawn*. New York, 1917
10. *The Safety-Curtain and Other Stories*. London and New York, 1917
11. *Greatheart*. London and New York, 1918
12. *The Lamp in the Desert*. London and New York, 1919
13. *The Tidal Wave and Other Stories*. London, 1919
14. *The Top of the World*. London and New York, 1920
15. *The Princess's Game*. London, 1920
16. *The Lucky Number*. New York, 1920
17. *The Obstacle Race*. London and New York, 1921
18. *Rosa Mundi and Other Stories*. London and New York, 1921
19. *The Odds and Other Stories*. London and New York, 1922
20. *Charles Rex*. London and New York, 1922
21. *Tetherstones*. London and New York, 1923
22. *Verses*. London and New York, 1923
23. *The Unknown Quantity*. London and New York, 1924
24. *A Man Under Authority*. London, 1925
25. *The Passerby and Other Stories*. London and New York, 1925
26. *The Black Knight*. London and New York, 1926
27. *The House of Happiness and Other Stories*. London and New York, 1927
28. *By Request*. London, 1927
29. *Peggy by Request*. New York, 1928
30. *The Gate Marked "Private."* London and New York, 1928
31. *The Altar of Honour*. London, 1929
32. *Storm Drift*. London, 1930
33. *Pullma*. London, 1930
34. *The Live Bait and Other Stories*. London and New York, 1932
35. *The Silver Wedding*. London, 1932
36. *The Silver Bride*. New York, 1932
37. *The Prison Wall*. London, 1932
38. *Dona Celestis*. London and New York, 1933
39. *The Electric Torch*. London and New York, 1934
40. *Where Three Roads Meet*. London, 1935
41. *Honeyball Farm*. London and New York, 1937
42. *The Juice of the Pomegranate*. London and New York, 1938
43. *The Serpent in the Garden*. London and New York, 1938
44. *Sown Among Thorns*. London and New York, 1939

Delmar, Vina
American, born January 29, 1905
1. *Bad Girl*. New York, 1928
2. *Loose Ladies*. New York, 1929
3. *Women Who Pass By*. London, 1929
4. *Kept Woman*. New York, 1929
5. *The Other Woman*. London, 1930
6. *Women Live Too Long*. New York and London, 1932
7. *The Restless Passion*. New York, 1947
8. *The Marriage Racket*. New York and London, 1933
9. *Mystery at Little Heaven*. Los Angeles, 1933
10. *The End of the World*. New York, 1934
11. *The Love Trap*. New York, 1949
12. *New Orleans Lady*. New York, 1949
13. *About Mrs. Leslie*. New York, 1950
14. *Strangers in Love*. New York, 1951
15. *The Marcaboth Women*. New York, 1951
16. *The Laughing Stranger*. New York, 1953
17. *Ruby*. New York, 1953
18. *Beloved*. New York, 1956
19. *The Breeze from Camelot*. New York, 1959
20. *The Big Family*. New York, 1961
21. *The Enchanted*. New York, 1965
22. *Grandmere*. New York, 1967
23. *The Becker Scandal: A Time Remembered*. New York, 1968
24. *The Freeways*. New York, 1971
25. *A Time for Titans*. New York, 1974
26. *McKeever*. New York, 1976

Denver, Lee
1. *Gun Feud at Sunrock.* London, 1951
2. *Outlaw Range.* London, 1952
3. *Owl Hoot Trail.* London, 1953
4. *Six-Gun Deadline.* London, 1954
5. *Red Sky at Warpaint.* London, 1960
6. *Saddlerock Canyon.* London, 1960
7. *Trail to Maverick.* London, 1965
8. *Pay Off for Wells Fargo.* London, 1967
9. *Posse Thunder.* London, 1967
10. *Showdown at Sandy Gulch.* London, 1968
11. *The Hungry Gun.* London, 1970
12. *Cheyenne Swings a Wide Loop.* London, 1971
13. *The Gun Code of Cheyenne Jones.* London, 1971
14. *Three Slugs for Cheyenne.* London, 1971
15. *Cheyenne Pays in Lead.* London, 1972
16. *Lone Trail for Cheyenne.* London, 1973
17. *Cheyenne Bucks the Law.* London, 1975
18. *Cheyenne Jones, Maverick Marshal.* London, 1977
19. *Cheyenne's Sixgun Justice.* London, 1980

De Rosso, H.A. (Henry Andrew)
American, born in 1917
1. *.44.* New York, 1953
2. *The Gun Trail.* New York, 1953
3. *End of the Gun.* New York, 1955
4. *The Man from Texas.* New York, 1957
5. *The Dark Brand.* New York, 1963
6. *Killer's Brand.* New York, 1968

De Voto, Bernard (Augustine)
American, born January 11, 1897, died November 13, 1955
Pseudonyms: John August, Cady Hewes
1. *The Crooked Mile.* New York, 1924
2. *The Chariot of Fire.* New York, 1926
3. *The House of Sun-Goes-Down.* London and Toronto, 1928
4. *The Writer's Handbook: A Manual of English Composition,* with others. New York, 1928
5. *Mark Twain's America.* Boston, 1932
6. *We Accept with Pleasure.* Boston, 1934
7. *Forays and Rebuttals.* Boston, 1936
8. *Troubled Star,* as John August. Boston, 1939
9. *Rain Before Seven,* as John August. Boston, 1940
10. *Minority Report.* Boston, 1940
11. *Mark Twain at Work.* Cambridge (MA), 1942
12. *Advance Agent,* as John August. Boston, 1942
13. *The Year of Decision 1846.* Boston, 1943
14. *The Literary Fallacy.* Boston, 1944
15. *The Woman in the Picture,* as John August. Boston, 1944
16. *Mountain Time.* Boston, 1947
17. *Across the Wide Missouri.* Boston, 1947
18. *The World of Fiction.* Boston, 1950
19. *The Course of Empire.* Boston, 1952
20. *Westward the Course of Empire.* London, 1953
21. *The Easy Chair.* Boston, 1955
22. *Women and Children First,* as Cady Hewes. Boston, 1956
23. *The Letters of Bernard De Voto.* New York, 1975

DeWeese-Wehen, Joy
Anglo-American, born October 31, 1936
Pseudonym: Jennifer Wade
1. *Stairway to a Secret.* New York, 1953
2. *The Tower in the Sky.* New York, 1955
3. *Stranger at Golden Hill.* New York, 1961
4. *The Golden Hill Mystery.* New York, 1964
5. *The Silver Cricket.* New York, 1966
6. *So Far from Malabar.* New York, 1970
7. *The Singing Wind,* as Jennifer Wade. New York, 1977

Dewlen, Al
American, born November 30, 1921
1. *The Night of the Tiger.* New York, 1956
2. *The Bone Pickers.* New York, 1958
3. *The Golden Touch.* New York, 1959
4. *Twilight of Honor.* New York, 1961
5. *Ride Beyond Vengeance.* New York, 1966
6. *Servants of Corruption.* New York, 1971
7. *Next of Kin.* New York, 1977
8. *The Session.* New York, 1981

Doctorow, E.L. (Edgar Laurence)
American, born January 6, 1931
1. *Welcome to Hard Times.* New York, 1960
2. *Bad Man from Bodie.* London, 1961
3. *Big as Life.* New York, 1966
4. *The Book of Daniel.* New York, 1971
5. *Ragtime.* London and Toronto, 1975
6. *Drinks Before Dinner.* New York, 1979
7. *Loon Lake.* London and Toronto, 1980

Dowler, James R. (Ross)
American, born April 19, 1925
1. *Partner's Choice.* New York, 1958
2. *Fiddlefoot Fugitive.* New York, 1970
3. *Laredo Lawman.* New York, 1970
4. *The Copperhead Colonel.* New York, 1972

Drago, Harry Sinclair
American, born March 20, 1888, died October 25, 1979
Pseudonyms: Stewart Cross, Kirk Deming, Will Ermine, Bliss Lomax, J. Wesley Putnam, Grant Sinclair
1. *Whoso Findeth a Wife,* as J. Wesley Putnam. New York, 1914
2. *The Hidden Things,* as J. Wesley Putnam. New York, 1915
3. *Suzanna: A Romance of Early California.* New York, 1922
4. *Whispering Sage,* with Joseph Noel. New York, 1922
5. *Smoke of the .45.* New York, 1923
6. *Out of the Silent North.* New York, 1923
7. *Following the Grass.* New York, 1924
8. *Playthings of Desire,* as J. Wesley Putnam. New York, 1924
9. *The Snow Patrol.* New York, 1925
10. *The Woman Thou Art,* as Grant Sinclair. New York, 1925
11. *Wild Fruit,* as Grant Sinclair. New York, 1926
12. *The Desert Hawk.* New York, 1927
13. *Borrowed Reputations,* as J. Wesley Putnam. New York, 1928
14. *Where the Loon Calls.* London and Toronto, 1928
15. *Where East Is East,* with Tod Browning. New York, 1929
16. *Rio Rita.* New York, 1929
17. *The Trespasser.* New York, 1929
18. *The Singer of Seville.* New York, 1930
19. *Madam Satan.* New York, 1930
20. *Divorce Trap.* New York, 1930
21. *Women to Love.* New York, 1931
22. *The Champ.* London and Toronto, 1932
23. *Guardian of the Sage.* New York, 1932
24. *Desert Water.* New York, 1933
25. *This Way to Hell,* as Stewart Cross. New York, 1933
26. *Longhorn Empire,* as Will Ermine. New York, 1933
27. *Laramie Rides Alone,* as Will Ermine. London and Toronto, 1934
28. *The Wild Bunch.* New York, 1934
29. *Montana Road.* New York, 1935
30. *Trigger Gospel.* London and Toronto, 1935
31. *Rustlers Ranch,* as Will Ermine. London, 1935
32. *Lobo Law,* as Will Ermine. New York, 1935
33. *Plundered Range,* as Will Ermine. London and Toronto, 1936

34. *Prairie Smoke*, as Will Ermine. New York, 1936
35. *Wind River Outlaw*, as Will Ermine. New York, 1936
36. *Closed Range*, as Bliss Lomax. New York, 1936
37. *Canyon of Golden Skulls*, as Bliss Lomax. New York, 1937
38. *The Law Bringers*, as Bliss Lomax. New York, 1937
39. *Barbed Wire Empire*, as Will Ermine. New York, 1937
40. *Colt Lightning*, as Kirk Deming. New York, 1938—London, 1935
41. *Grass Means Fight*, as Kirk Deming. New York, 1938
42. *Lawless Legion*, as Will Ermine. London and Toronto, 1938
43. *Mavericks of the Plains*, as Bliss Lomax. New York, 1938
44. *Trail Trouble*, as Will Ermine. New York, 1938
45. *Singing Lariat*, as Will Ermine. New York, 1939
46. *Rustlers' Moon*, as Will Ermine. London and Toronto, 1939
47. *Colt Comrades*, as Bliss Lomax. New York, 1939
48. *Cowboy, Say Your Prayers*, as Will Ermine. New York, 1939
49. *Boss of the Plains*, as Will Ermine. New York, 1940
50. *Rider of the Midnight Range*, as Will Ermine. London and Toronto, 1940
51. *The Leather Burners*, as Bliss Lomax. New York, 1940
52. *Gringo Gunfire*, as Bliss Lomax. New York, 1940
53. *Secret of the Wastelands*, as Bliss Lomax. New York, 1940
54. *Watchdog of Thunder River*, as Will Ermine. New York, 1941
55. *Pardners of the Badlands*, as Bliss Lomax. New York, 1942
56. *My Gun Is My Law*, as Will Ermine. New York, 1942
57. *Buckskin Empire*. New York, 1942
58. *Stagecoach Kingdom*. New York, 1943
59. *Brave in the Saddle*, as Will Ermine. New York, 1943
60. *Busted Range*, as Will Ermine. London and Toronto, 1944
61. *The Iron Bronc*, as Will Ermine. New York, 1944
62. *Boss of the Badlands*, as Will Ermine. London, 1944
63. *Horsethief Creek*, as Bliss Lomax. New York, 1944
64. *Rusty Guns*, as Bliss Lomax. New York, 1944
65. *Saddle Hawks*, as Bliss Lomax. New York, 1944
66. *Outlaw River*, as Bliss Lomax. New York, 1945
67. *Buckskin Marshal*, as Will Ermine. New York, 1945
68. *War on the Saddle Rock*, as Will Ermine. New York, 1945
69. *River of Gold*. New York, 1945
70. *Outlaw on Horseback*, as Will Ermine. New York, 1946
71. *The Phantom Corral*, as Bliss Lomax. New York, 1946
72. *Trail Dust*, as Bliss Lomax. New York, 1947
73. *My Gun Is Law*, as Will Ermine. London, 1947
74. *The Drifting Kid*, as Will Ermine. New York, 1947
75. *Last of the Longhorns*, as Will Ermine. New York, 1948
76. *Laramie Rides Again*, as Will Ermine. New York, 1948
77. *Shadow Mountain*, as Bliss Lomax. New York, 1948
78. *The Lost Buckaroo*, as Bliss Lomax. New York, 1949
79. *Sage Brush Bandit*, as Bliss Lomax. New York, 1949
80. *Gunsmoke and Trail Dust*, as Bliss Lomax. New York, 1949
81. *Rustler's Bend*, as Will Ermine. New York, 1949
82. *Love Toy*. New York, 1949
83. *The Fight for the Sweetwater*, as Bliss Lomax. New York, 1950
84. *The Law Busters*, as Bliss Lomax. New York, 1950
85. *Apache Crossing*, as Will Ermine. New York, 1950
86. *The Silver Star*, as Will Ermine. New York, 1951
87. *Arizona Gunsmoke*, as Will Ermine. London, 1951
88. *Guns Along the Yellowstone*, as Bliss Lomax. London, 1952
89. *Riders of the Buffalo Grass*, as Bliss Lomax. New York, 1952
90. *Honky-Tonk Woman*, as Bliss Lomax. New York, 1955
91. *Ambush at Coffin Canyon*, as Bliss Lomax. New York, 1954
92. *Their Guns Were Fast*. New York, 1955
93. *Top Hand with a Gun*. New York, 1955
94. *Frenchman's River*, as Will Ermine. New York, 1955
95. *Pay-off at Black Hawk*. New York, 1956
96. *The Loner*, as Bliss Lomax. New York, 1956
97. *Lone Stranger*, as Bliss Lomax. London, 1956
98. *Stranger with a Gun*, as Bliss Lomax. New York, 1957
99. *Decision at Broken Butte*. New York, 1957
100. *Wild Grass*. New York, 1957
101. *Guns in the Night*, as Will Ermine. London, 1957
102. *Buckskin Affair*. New York, 1958
103. *Showdown at Sunset*. New York, 1958
104. *Last Call for a Gunfighter*, as Bliss Lomax. New York, 1958
105. *Call for a Gunfight*, as Bliss Lomax. London, 1959
106. *Appointment on the Yellowstone*, as Bliss Lomax. New York, 1959
107. *Fenced Off*. New York, 1959
108. *Rebel Basin*. New York, 1959
109. *It Happened at Thunder River*, as Bliss Lomax. New York, 1959
110. *The Lawless Guns*, as Bliss Lomax. New York, 1960
111. *Wild, Woolly, and Wicked: The History of the Kansas Cow Towns and the Texas Cattle Trade*. New York, 1960
112. *A Gun for Cantrell*. New York, 1961
113. *The Long Trail North*. New York, 1961
114. *The Trail of Johnny Dice*. New York, 1961
115. *Sun in Their Eyes*. New York, 1962
116. *Wild, Woolley, and Wicked*. New York, 1962
117. *Buckskin Meadows*. New York, 1962
118. *Red River Valley: The Mainstream of Frontier History from the Louisiana Bayous to the Texas Panhandle*. New York, 1962
119. *Avenger from Texas*, as Will Ermine. New York, 1964
120. *Outlaws on Horseback*. New York, 1964
121. *Great American Cattle Trails: The Story of the Old Cow Paths of the East and Longhorn Highways of the Plains*. New York, 1965
122. *Lost Bonanzas: Tales of the Legendary Lost Mines of the American West*. New York, 1966
123. *Many Beavers*. New York, 1967
124. *The Steamboaters: From the Early-Wheelers to the Big Packets*. New York, 1967
125. *Roads to Empire: The Dramatic Conquest of the American West*. New York, 1968
126. *Notorious Ladies of the Frontier*. New York, 1969
127. *The Great Range Wars: Violence on the Grasslands*. New York, 1970
128. *Canal Days in America*. New York, 1972
129. *Road Agents and Train Robbers: Half a Century of Western Banditry*. New York, 1973
130. *The Legend Makers: Tales of the Old Time Peace Officers and Desperadoes of the Frontier*. New York, 1975

Dresser, Davis
American, born July 31, 1904, died February 4, 1977
Pseudonyms: Asa Baker, Matthew Blood, Kathryn Culver, Don Davis, Hal Debrett, Brett Halliday, Anthony Scott, Anderson Wayne

1. *Mardi Gras Madness*, as Anthony Scott. New York, 1934
2. *Test of Virtue*, as Anthony Scott. New York, 1934
3. *Love Is a Masquerade*, as Kathryn Culver. New York, 1935
4. *Ten Toes Up*, as Anthony Scott. New York, 1935
5. *Virgin's Holliday*, as Anthony Scott. New York, 1935
6. *Stolen Sins*, as Anthony Scott. New York, 1936
7. *Ladies of Chance*, as Anthony Scott. New York, 1936
8. *Too Smart for Love*, as Kathryn Culver. New York, 1937
9. *Million Dollar Madness*, as Kathryn Culver. New York, 1937
10. *Let's Laugh at Love*. New York, 1937
11. *Romance for Julie*. New York, 1938
12. *Mum's the Word for Murder*, as Asa Baker. New York, 1938

13. *Satan Rules the Night,* as Anthony Scott. New York, 1938
14. *Temptation,* as Anthony Scott. New York, 1938
15. *Green Path to the Moon,* as Kathryn Culver. New York, 1938
16. *Once to Every Woman,* as Kathryn Culver. New York, 1938
17. *Girl Alone,* as Kathryn Culver. New York, 1939
18. *The Kissed Corpse,* as Asa Baker. New York, 1939
19. *Dividend on Death,* as Brett Halliday. New York, 1939
20. *The Private Practice of Michael Shane,* as Brett Halliday. New York, 1940
21. *The Uncomplaining Corpses,* as Brett Halliday. New York, 1940
22. *Return of the Rio Kid,* as Don Davis. New York, 1940
23. *Death on Treasure Trail,* as Don Davis. London, 1940
24. *Death Rides the Pecos.* London and Toronto, 1940
25. *The Hangmen of Sleepy Valley.* New York, 1940
26. *The Masked Riders.* London, 1941
27. *Gunsmoke on the Mesa.* London and Toronto, 1941
28. *Lynch-Rope Law.* New York, 1941
29. *Rio Kid Justice,* as Don Davis. New York, 1941
30. *Two-Gun Rio Kid,* as Don Davis. New York, 1941
31. *Tickets for Death,* as Brett Halliday. New York, 1941
32. *Bodies Are Where You Find Them,* as Brett Halliday. New York, 1941
33. *Michael Shayne Takes Over,* as Brett Halliday. New York, 1941
34. *The Corpse Came Calling,* as Brett Halliday. New York, 1942
35. *The Case of the Walking Corpse,* as Brett Halliday. New York, 1943
36. *Murder Wears a Mummer's Mask,* as Brett Halliday. New York, 1943
37. *Blood on the Black Market,* as Brett Halliday. New York, 1943
38. *Michael Shayne Investigates,* as Brett Halliday. London, 1943
39. *Michael Shayne Takes a Hand,* as Brett Halliday. London, 1944
40. *Michael Shayne's Lost Chance,* as Brett Halliday. New York, 1944
41. *Murder and the Married Virgin,* as Brett Halliday. New York, 1944
42. *Murder Is My Business,* as Brett Halliday. London and Toronto, 1945
43. *Marked for Murder,* as Brett Halliday. New York, 1945
44. *Dead Man's Diary, and Dinner at Dupre's,* as Brett Halliday. New York, 1945
45. *Blood on Biscayne Bay,* as Brett Halliday. Chicago, 1946
46. *Counterfeit Wife,* as Brett Halliday. Chicago, 1947
47. *Blood on the Stars,* as Brett Halliday. New York, 1948
48. *A Taste for Violence,* as Brett Halliday. New York, 1949
49. *Call for Michael Shayne,* as Brett Halliday. New York, 1949
50. *Before I Wake,* as Hal Debrett, with Kathleen Rollins. New York, 1949
51. *A Lonely Way to Die,* as Hal Debrett, with Kathleen Culver. New York, 1950
52. *This Is It, Michael Shayne,* as Brett Halliday. New York, 1950
53. *Framed in Blood,* as Brett Halliday. New York, 1951
54. *Murder Is a Habit,* as Brett Halliday. New York, 1951
55. *When Dorinda Dances,* as Brett Halliday. New York, 1951
56. *Charlie Dell,* as Anderson Wayne. New York, 1952
57. *The Avenger,* as Matthew Blood, with Ryerson Johnson. New York, 1952
58. *What Really Happened,* as Brett Halliday. New York, 1952
59. *One Night with Nora,* as Brett Halliday. New York, 1953
60. *Murder on the Mesa.* London, 1953
61. *The Lady Came by Night,* as Brett Halliday. London, 1954
62. *Death Is a Lovely Dame,* as Matthew Blood, with Ryerson Johnson. New York, 1954
63. *She Woke to Darkness,* as Brett Halliday. New York, 1954
64. *Death Has Three Lives,* as Brett Halliday. London and Toronto, 1955
65. *Stranger in Town,* as Brett Halliday. New York, 1955
66. *The Blonde Cried Murder,* as Brett Halliday. New York, 1956
67. *In a Deadly Vein,* as Brett Halliday. New York, 1956
68. *Weep for a Blonde,* as Brett Halliday. New York, 1957
69. *Shoot the Works,* as Brett Halliday. New York, 1957
70. *Heads You Lose,* as Brett Halliday. New York, 1958
71. *Murder and the Wanton Bride,* as Brett Halliday. New York, 1958
72. *Fit to Kill,* as Brett Halliday. New York, 1958
73. *Date with a Dead Man,* as Brett Halliday. New York, 1959
74. *Target: Mike Shayne,* as Brett Halliday. New York, 1959
75. *A Time to Remember.* New York, 1959
76. *Die Like a Dog,* as Brett Halliday. New York, 1959
77. *Murder Takes No Holiday,* as Brett Halliday. New York, 1960
78. *Dolls are Deadly,* as Brett Halliday. New York, 1960
79. *The Homicidal Virgin,* as Brett Halliday. New York, 1960
80. *Killer from the Keys,* as Brett Halliday. New York, 1961
81. *Murder in Haste,* as Brett Halliday. New York, 1961
82. *The Careless Corpse,* as Brett Halliday. New York, 1961
83. *Michael Shayne's Torrid Twelve,* as Brett Halliday. New York, 1961
84. *Pay-Off in Blood,* as Brett Halliday. New York, 1962
85. *Murder by Proxy,* as Brett Halliday. New York, 1962
86. *Never Kill a Client,* as Brett Halliday. New York, 1962
87. *Too Friendly, Too Dead,* as Brett Halliday. New York, 1963
88. *The Corpse That Never Was,* as Brett Halliday. New York, 1963
89. *The Body Came Back,* as Brett Halliday. New York, 1963
90. *A Redhead for Mike Shane,* as Brett Halliday. New York, 1964
91. *Shoot to Kill,* as Brett Halliday. New York, 1964
92. *Michael Shayne's 50th Case,* as Brett Halliday. New York, 1964
93. *Dangerous Dames,* as Brett Halliday. New York, 1965
94. *The Violent World of Michael Shayne,* as Brett Halliday. New York, 1965
95. *Nice Fillies Finish Last,* as Brett Halliday. New York, 1965
96. *Murder Spins the Wheel,* as Brett Halliday. New York, 1966
97. *Armed . . . Dangerous. . . . ,* as Brett Halliday. New York, 1966
98. *Mermaid on the Rocks,* as Brett Halliday. New York, 1967
99. *Guilty as Hell,* as Brett Halliday. New York, 1967
100. *So Lush, So Deadly,* as Brett Halliday. New York, 1968
101. *Violence Is Golden,* as Brett Halliday. New York, 1968
102. *Lady Be Bad,* as Brett Halliday. New York, 1969
103. *Six Seconds to Kill,* as Brett Halliday. New York, 1970
104. *Count Backwards to Zero,* as Brett Halliday. New York, 1971
105. *I Come to Kill You,* as Brett Halliday. New York, 1971
106. *Caught Dead,* as Brett Halliday. New York, 1972
107. *Kill All the Young Girls,* as Brett Halliday. New York, 1973
108. *Blue Murder,* as Brett Halliday. New York, 1973
109. *Last Seen Hitchhiking,* as Brett Halliday. New York, 1974
110. *At the Point of a .38,* as Brett Halliday. New York, 1974
111. *Million Dollar Handle,* as Brett Halliday. New York, 1976
112. *Win Some, Lose Some,* as Brett Halliday. New York, 1976

Durham, Marilyn
American, born September 8, 1930
1. *The Man Who Loved Cat Dancing.* London and Toronto, 1972

2. *Dutch Uncle.* London and Toronto, 1973
3. *Flambard's Confession.* New York, 1982

Durst, Paul
American, born April 23, 1921
Pseudonyms: Peter Bannon, John Chelton, Jeff Cochran, John Shane
1. *Die, Damn You!* New York, 1952
2. *Bloody River.* New York, 1953
3. *Trail Herd North.* New York, 1953
4. *Guns of Circle 8,* as Jeff Cochran. New York, 1954
5. *Along the Yermo Rim,* as John Shane. London, 1954
6. *My Deadly Angel,* as John Chelton. New York, 1955
7. *Showdown.* London, 1955
8. *Justice.* New York, 1956
9. *Kid from Canadian.* Kingswood (Eng), 1956
10. *Prairie Reckoning.* New York, 1956
11. *Sundown in Sundance,* as John Shane. London, 1956
12. *Six-Gun Thursday,* as John Shane. London, 1956
13. *Gunsmoke Dawn,* as John Shane. London, 1957
14. *John Law, Keep Out.* New York, 1957
15. *Ambush at North Platte.* London, 1957
16. *The River Flows West.* London, 1957
17. *They Want Me Dead,* as Peter Bannon. London, 1958
18. *If I Should Die,* as Peter Bannon. London, 1958
19. *Kansas Guns.* New York, 1958
20. *Dead Man's Range.* London, 1958
21. *The Gun Doctor.* New York, 1959
22. *Johnny Nation.* London, 1960
23. *Whisper Murder Softly,* as Peter Bannon. London, 1963
24. *Backlash.* London, 1967
25. *Badge of Infamy.* London, 1968
26. *Intended Treason: What Really Happened in the Gunpowder Plot.* London, 1970
27. *A Roomful of Shadows.* London, 1975
28. *The Florentine Table.* New York, 1980

Dunnett, Dorothy
British, born September 7, 1913
Pseudonym: Dorothy Halliday
1. *The Game of Kings.* New York, 1961
2. *Queens Play.* London and New York, 1964
3. *The Disorderly Knights.* London and New York, 1966
4. *Dolly and the Singing Bird,* as Dorothy Halliday. London, 1968
5. *The Photogenic Soprano.* Boston, 1968
6. *Pawn in Frankincense.* London and New York, 1969
7. *Dolly and the Cookie Bird,* as Dorothy Halliday. London, 1970
8. *Murder in the Round.* Boston, 1970
9. *The Ringed Castle.* London, 1971
10. *Dolly and the Doctor Bird,* as Dorothy Halliday. London, 1971
11. *Match for a Murderer.* Boston, 1973
12. *Dolly and the Starry Bird,* as Dorothy Halliday. London, 1973
13. *Murder in Focus.* Boston, 1973
14. *Checkmate.* London and New York, 1975
15. *Dolly and the Nanny Bird,* as Dorothy Halliday. London, 1976
16. *King Hereafter.* London, 1982

Dymoke, Juliet [Juliet Dymoke de Schanschieff]
British, born June 28, 1919
1. *The Sons of the Tribune: An Adventure on the Roman Wall.* London, 1956
2. *London in the 18th Century.* London, 1958
3. *The Orange Sash.* London, 1958
4. *Born in Victory.* London, 1960
5. *Treason in November.* London, 1961
6. *Bend Sinister.* London, 1962
7. *The Cloisterman.* London, 1969
8. *Of the Ring of Earls.* London, 1970
9. *Henry of the High Rock.* London, 1971
10. *Serpent in Eden.* London, 1973
11. *The Lion's Legacy.* London, 1974
12. *Prisoner of Rome.* London, 1975
13. *Shadows on a Throne.* London, 1976
14. *A Pride of Kings.* London, 1978
15. *The Royal Griffon.* London, 1978
16. *The White Cockade.* London, 1979
17. *Lady of the Garter.* London, 1979
18. *The Lion of Mortimer.* London, 1979
19. *The Lord of Greenwich.* London, 1980
20. *The Sun in Splendour.* London, 1980
21. *A Kind of Warfare.* London, 1981

Eastlake, William (Derry)
American, born July 14, 1917
1. *Go in Beauty.* New York, 1956
2. *The Bronc People.* New York, 1958
3. *Portrait of an Artist with Twenty-Six Horses.* New York, 1963
4. *Castle Keep.* New York, 1965
5. *The Bamboo Bed.* New York, 1969
6. *A Child's Garden of Verses for the Revolution.* New York, 1971
7. *Dancers in the Scalp House.* New York, 1975
8. *The Long, Naked Descent into Boston: A Tricentennial Novel.* New York, 1977

Easton, Robert (Olney)
American, born July 4, 1915
1. *The Happy Man.* New York, 1943
2. *Lord of Beasts: The Sage of Buffalo Jones,* with McKenzie Brown. Tucson (AZ), 1961
3. *The Book of the American West,* with others. New York, 1963
4. *California Condor: Vanishing American,* with Dick Smith. Charlotte (NC), 1964
5. *Max Brand, The Big Westerner.* Norman (OK), 1970
6. *Black Tide: The Santa Barbara Oil Spill and Its Consequences.* New York, 1972
7. *Guns, Gold, and Caravans: The Extraordinary Life of Fred Meyer Schroder.* Santa Barbara (CA), 1978
8. *China Caravans.* Santa Barbara (CA), 1982
9. *This Promised Land.* Santa Barbara (CA), 1982

Eberhart, Mignon G. (Good)
American, born July 6, 1899
1. *The Patient in Room 18.* New York and London, 1929
2. *The Mystery of Hunting's End.* New York, 1930
3. *While the Patient Slept.* New York and London, 1930
4. *From This Dark Stairway.* New York, 1931
5. *Murder by an Aristocrat.* New York, 1932
6. *The Dark Garden.* New York, 1933
7. *The White Cockatoo.* New York and London, 1933
8. *The Cases of Susan Dare.* New York, 1934
9. *Murder of My Patient.* London, 1934
10. *Death in the Fog.* London, 1934
11. *The House on the Roof.* New York and London, 1935
12. *Fair Warning.* New York and London, 1936
13. *Danger in the Dark.* New York, 1937
14. *Hand in Glove.* London, 1937
15. *The Pattern.* New York and London, 1937
16. *The Glass Slipper.* New York and London, 1938

17. *Hasty Wedding.* New York, 1938
18. *320 College Avenue,* with Fred Ballard. New York, 1938
19. *Brief Return.* London, 1939
20. *The Chiffon Scarf.* New York, 1939
21. *The Hangman's Whip.* New York, 1940
22. *Strangers in Flight.* Los Angeles, 1941
23. *Speak No Evil.* New York and London, 1941
24. *With This Ring.* New York, 1941
25. *Eight O'Clock Tuesday,* with Robert Wallsten. New York, 1941
26. *Deadly Is the Diamond.* New York, 1942
27. *Wolf in Man's Clothing.* New York, 1942
28. *The Man Next Door.* New York, 1943
29. *Unidentified Woman.* New York, 1943
30. *Escape the Night.* New York, 1944
31. *Wings of Fear.* New York, 1945
32. *Five Passengers from Lisbon.* New York and London, 1946
33. *The White Dress.* New York, 1946
34. *Another Woman's House.* New York, 1947
35. *Pattern of Murder.* New York, 1948
36. *Five of My Best: Deadly Is the Diamond, Bermuda Grapevine, Murder Goes to Market, Strangers in Flight, Express to Danger.* London, 1949
37. *House of Storm.* New York and London, 1949
38. *Hunt with the Hounds.* New York, 1950
39. *Never Look Back.* New York and London, 1951
40. *Dead Men's Plans.* New York, 1952
41. *The Unknown Quantity.* New York and London, 1953
42. *Man Missing.* New York and London, 1954
43. *Postmark Murder.* New York and London, 1956
44. *Another Man's Murder.* New York, 1957
45. *Deadly Is the Diamond and Three Other Novelettes of Murder: Bermuda Grapevine, The Crimson Paw, Murder in Waltz Time.* New York, 1958
46. *Melora.* New York, 1959
47. *The Crimson Paw.* London, 1959
48. *Jury of One.* New York, 1960
49. *The Promise of Murder.* New York, 1961
50. *The Cup, The Blade, or the Gun.* New York, 1961
51. *The Crime at Honotassa.* London, 1962
52. *Enemy in the House.* New York, 1962
53. *Run Scared.* New York, 1963
54. *Call after Midnight.* New York, 1964
55. *R.S.V.P. Murder.* New York, 1965
56. *Witness at Large.* New York, 1966
57. *Woman on the Roof.* New York and London, 1968
58. *Message from Hong Kong.* New York and London, 1969
59. *El Rancho Rio.* New York, 1970
60. *Two Little Rich Girls.* New York, 1972
61. *The House by the Sea.* New York, 1972
62. *Murder in Waiting.* New York, 1973
63. *Danger Money.* New York and London, 1975
64. *Family Fortune.* New York, 1976
65. *Nine O'Clock Tide.* New York and London, 1978
66. *The Bayou Road.* New York and London, 1979
67. *Casa Madrone.* New York, 1980
68. *Family Affair.* New York and London, 1981
69. *Next of Kin.* New York, 1982

Eden, Dorothy
British, born April 3, 1912, died March 4, 1982
Pseudonym: Mary Paradise
1. *Singing Shadows.* London, 1940
2. *The Laughing Ghost.* London, 1943
3. *We Are for the Dark.* London, 1944
4. *Summer Sunday.* London, 1946
5. *Walk into My Parlor.* London, 1947
6. *The Schoolmaster's Daughters.* London, 1948
7. *Crow Hollow.* London, 1950
8. *The Voice of the Dolls.* London, 1950
9. *Cat's Prey.* London, 1952
10. *Lamb to the Slaughter.* London, 1953
11. *Bride by Candlelight.* London, 1954
12. *Darling Clementine.* London, 1955
13. *Death Is a Red Rose.* London, 1956
14. *The Pretty Ones.* London, 1957
15. *Listen to Danger.* London, 1958
16. *The Deadly Travellers.* London, 1959
17. *The Sleeping Bride.* London, 1959
18. *Samantha.* London, 1960
19. *Sleep in the Woods.* London, 1960
20. *Face of an Angel.* London, 1961
21. *Shadow of a Witch.* London, 1962
22. *Whistle for the Crows.* London, 1962
23. *Afternoon for Lizards.* London, 1962
24. *Lady of Mallow.* New York, 1962
25. *The Bird in the Chimney.* London, 1963
26. *Darkwater.* New York, 1964
27. *Bella.* London, 1964
28. *The Marriage Chest.* London, 1965
29. *Ravenscroft.* New York, 1965
30. *The Bridge of Fear.* New York, 1966
31. *Never Call it Loving.* London and New York, 1966
32. *The Brooding Lake.* New York, 1966
33. *The Night of the Letter.* New York, 1967
34. *Siege in the Sun.* London and New York, 1967
35. *Winterwood.* London and New York, 1967
36. *Yellow Is for Fear and Other Stories.* New York, 1968
37. *The Shadow Wife.* London and New York, 1968
38. *The Daughters of Ardmore Hall.* New York, 1968
39. *The Vines of Yarrabee.* London and New York, 1969
40. *Melbury Square.* London, 1970
41. *Waiting for Willa.* London and New York, 1970
42. *Afternoon Walk.* London and New York, 1971
43. *A Linnet Singing.* New York, 1972
44. *Speak to Me of Love.* London and New York, 1972
45. *The Millionaire's Daughter.* London and New York, 1074
46. *The Time of the Dragon.* London and New York, 1975
47. *The House on Hay Hill and Other Stories.* London and New York, 1976
48. *The Salamanca Drum.* London and New York, 1977
49. *The Storrington Papers.* New York, 1978
50. *Depart in Peace.* London, 1979
51. *The American Heiress.* London and New York, 1980
52. *An Important Family.* New York, 1982

Edson, J.T. (John Thomas)
British, born February 17, 1928
Pseudonyms: Rod Denver, Chuck Nolan
1. *Trail Boss.* London, 1961
2. *The Hard Riders.* London, 1962
3. *The Texan.* London, 1962
4. *Rio Guns.* London, 1962
5. *The Ysabel Kid.* London, 1962
6. *Quiet Town,* as Chuck Nolan. London, 1962
7. *Waco's Debt.* London, 1962
8. *Sagebrush Sleuth.* London, 1962
9. *Arizona Ranger,* as Rod Denver. London, 1962
10. *The Drifter.* London, 1963
11. *The Rio Hondo Kid.* London, 1963
12. *The Fastest Gun in Texas.* London, 1963
13. *Apache Rampage.* London, 1963
14. *The Half Breed.* London, 1963
15. *Gun Wizard.* London, 1963
16. *Gunsmoke Thunder.* London, 1963
17. *Wagons to Backsight.* London, 1964

18. *The Rushers*. London, 1964
19. *The Rio Hondo War*. London, 1964
20. *Waco Rides In*. London, 1964
21. *Trigger Fast*. London, 1964
22. *The Wildcats*. London, 1965
23. *The Peacemakers*. London, 1965
24. *Troubled Range*. London, 1965
25. *The Fortune Hunters*. London, 1965
26. *Slaughter's Way*. London, 1965
27. *The Man from Texas*. London, 1965
28. *The Trouble Busters*. London, 1965
29. *Trouble Trail*. London, 1965
30. *The Cow Thieves*. London, 1965
31. *The Bullwhip Breed*. London, 1965
32. *Guns in the Night*. London, 1966
33. *A Town Called Yellowdog*. London, 1966
34. *The Law of the Gun*. London, 1966
35. *Return to Backsight*. London, 1966
36. *The Devil Gun*. London, 1966
37. *The Colt and the Sabre*. London, 1967
38. *Comanche*. London, 1967
39. *The Fast Gun*. London, 1967
40. *Terror Valley*. London, 1967
41. *Sidewinder*. London, 1967
42. *The Floating Outfit*. London, 1967
43. *Hound Dog Man*. London, 1967
44. *The Big Hunt*. London, 1967
45. *Calamity Spells Trouble*. London, 1968
46. *The Bad Bunch*. London, 1968
47. *The Hooded Riders*. London, 1968
48. *Rangeland Hercules*. London, 1968
49. *McGraw's Inheritance*. London, 1968
50. *The Making of a Lawman*. London, 1968
51. *The Rebel Spy*. London, 1968
52. *The Professional Killers*. London, 1968
53. *The 1/4-Second Draw*. London, 1969
54. *The Deputies*. London, 1969
55. *The Bloody Border*. London, 1969
56. *The Town Tamers*. London, 1969
57. *The Small Texan*. London, 1969
58. *Cuchilo*. London, 1969
59. *Goodnight's Dream*. London, 1969
60. *From Hide to Horn*. London, 1969
61. *.44 Calibre Man*. London, 1969
62. *Cold Deck, Hot Lead*. London, 1969
63. *White Stallion, Red Mare*. London, 1970
64. *Under the Stars and Bars*. London, 1970
65. *Kill Dusty Fog!* London, 1970
66. *Back to the Bloody Border*. London, 1970
67. *Point of Contact*. London, 1970
68. *The Owlhoot*. London, 1970
69. *Run for the Border*. London, 1971
70. *Slip Gun*. London, 1971
71. *Bad Hombre*. London, 1971
72. *A Horse Called Mogollon*. London, 1971
73. *Hell in the Palo Duro*. London, 1971
74. *Two Miles to the Border*. London, 1972
75. *Go Back to Hell*. London, 1972
76. *The South Will Rise Again*. London, 1972
77. *To Arms, To Arms, in Dixie*. London, 1972
78. *Set Texas Back on Her Feet*. London, 1973
79. *Blonde Genius*, with Peter Clawson. London, 1973
80. *You're in Command Now, Mr. Fog*. London, 1973
81. *The Big Gun*. London, 1973
82. *The Hide and Tallow Man*. London, 1974
83. *The Floating Outfit*. New York, 1974
84. *The Quest for Bowie's Blade*. London, 1974
85. *Sixteen-Dollar Shooter*. London, 1974
86. *Young Ole Devil*. London, 1975
87. *Get Urrea*. London, 1975
88. *Ole Devil and the Caplocks*. London, 1975
89. *Bunduki*. London, 1975
90. *Bunduki and Dawn*. London, 1976
91. *Sacrifice for the Quagga God*. London, 1976
92. *Ole Devil and the Mule Train*. London, 1976
93. *Ole Devil at San Jacinto*. London, 1977
94. *Cap Fog, Meet Mr. J.G. Reeder*. London, 1977
95. *Doc Leroy, M.D.* London, 1977
96. *Set A-Foot*. London, 1978
97. *Beguinage*. London, 1978
98. *Beguinage Is Dead*. London, 1978
99. *Renegade*. New York, 1978
100. *Viridian's Trail*. New York, 1978
101. *The Remittance Kid*. London, 1978
102. *The Whip and the War Lance*. London, 1979
103. *The Gentle Giant*. London, 1979
104. *You're a Texas Ranger, Alvin Fog*. London, 1979
105. *J.T.'s Hundredth*. London, 1979
106. *J.T.'s Ladies*. London, 1980
107. *Fearless Master of the Jungle*. London, 1980
108. *Rapido Clint*. London, 1980
109. *The Justice of Company "Z"*. London, 1981
110. *Master of Triggeronometry*. London, 1981
111. *A Matter of Honour*. London, 1981
112. *Waco's Badge*. London, 1981
113. *White Indian*. London, 1981
114. *Old Mocassins on the Trail*. London, 1981

Ehrlich, Jack [John Gunther Ehrlich]
American, born April 6, 1930
1. *Revenge*. New York, 1958
2. *Court-Martial*. New York, 1959
3. *Parole*. New York, 1960
4. *Slow Burn*. New York, 1961
5. *Cry, Baby*. New York, 1962
6. *The Girl Cage*. New York, 1967
7. *Close Combat*. New York, 1969
8. *The Drowning*. New York, 1969
9. *The Fastest Gun in the Pulpit*. New York, 1972
10. *Bloody Vengence*. New York, 1973
11. *Laramie River Crossing*. New York, 1973
12. *The Chatham Killing*. New York, 1976
13. *Rebellion at Cripple Creek*. New York, 1979

Eliot, Anne [Lois Dwight Taylor]
American, born in 1903, died July 20, 1979
Other pseudonyms: Caroline Arnett; Lynn Avery; Nancy Dudley; Allen Dwight, with Turney Allen Taylor; Anne Lattin
1. *Spaniards' Mark*, as Allen Dwight. New York, 1933
2. *Linn Dickson, Confederate*, as Allen Dwight. New York, 1934
3. *The First Virginians*, as Allen Dwight. New York, 1936
4. *Drums in the Forest*, as Allen Dwight. New York, 1936
5. *Kentucky Cargo*, as Allen Dwight. New York, 1939
6. *Peter Liked to Draw*, as Anne Lattin. Chicago, 1953
7. *Linda Goes to the Hospital [Travels Alone, Goes to a TV Studio, Goes on a Cruise.]*, as Nancy Dudley. New York, 4 vols., 1953-58
8. *Linda's First Flight*, as Nancy Dudley. New York, 1956
9. *Peter's Policeman*, as Anne Lattin. Chicago, 1958
10. *The Silver Dagger*, as Allen Dwight. New York, 1959
11. *Cappy and the River*, as Lynn Avery. New York, 1960
12. *Jorie of Dogtown Common*, as Anne Eliot. New York, 1962
13. *Guns at Quebec*, as Allen Dwight. New York, 1962
14. *The Mystery of the Vanishing Horses*, as Lynn Avery. New York, 1963

15. *Soldier and Patriot: The Life of General Israel Putnam,* as Allan Dwight. New York, 1965
16. *To the Walls of Cartegena,* as Allen Dwight. Williamsburg (VA), 1967
17. *Return to Aylforth.* New York, 1967
18. *Sparky's Fireman,* as Anne Lattin. Chicago, 1968
19. *Shadows Waiting.* New York, 1969
20. *Stranger in Penbroke.* New York, 1971
21. *Incident at Villa Rahmana.* New York, 1972
22. *The Dark Beneath the Pines.* New York, 1974
23. *Melinda,* as Caroline Arnett. New York, 1975
24. *Clarissa,* as Caroline Arnett. New York, 1976
25. *Theodora,* as Caroline Arnett. New York, 1977
26. *Claudia,* as Caroline Arnett. New York, 1978
27. *Stephanie,* as Caroline Arnett. New York, 1979
28. *Christina,* as Caroline Arnett. New York, 1980

Elizabeth [Countess Mary Annette von Arnim, later Countess Russel]
British, born August 31, 1866, died February 9, 1941
Other pseudonym: Alice Cholmondeley
1. *Elizabeth and Her German Garden.* London and New York, 1898
2. *The Solitary Summer.* London and New York, 1899
3. *The April Baby's Book of Tunes, with the Story of How They Came to Be Written.* London and New York, 1900
4. *The Pious Pilgrimage.* Boston, 1901
5. *The Benefactress.* London and New York, 1901
6. *The Ordeal of Elizabeth.* New York, 1901
7. *The Adventures of Elizabeth in Rugen.* London and New York, 1904
8. *The Princess Priscilla's Fortnight.* London and New York, 1905
9. *Fraulein Schmidt and Mr. Anstruther, Being the Letters of an Independent Woman.* London and New York, 1907
10. *The Caravaners.* London and New York, 1909
11. *The Pastor's Wife.* London and New York, 1914
12. *Christine,* as Alice Cholmondeley. London and New York, 1917
13. *Christopher and Columbus.* London and New York, 1919
14. *In the Mountains,* published anonymously. London and New York, 1920
15. *Vera.* London and New York, 1921
16. *The Enchanted April.* London, 1922
17. *Love.* London and New York, 1925
18. *Introduction to Salley.* London and New York, 1926
19. *Expiration.* London and New York, 1929
20. *Father.* London and New York, 1931
21. *Jasmine Farm.* London and New York, 1934
22. *All the Dogs of My Life.* London and New York, 1936
23. *Mr. Skeffington.* London and New York, 1940
24. *One Thing in Common.* New York, 1941

Ellerbeck, Rosemary [Rosemary Anne L'Estrange Ellerbeck]
British
Pseudonyms: Anna L'Estrange, Nicola Thorne, Katherine Yorke
1. *Inclination to Murder.* London, 1965
2. *The Girls,* as Nicola Thorne. London and New York, 1967
3. *Bridie Climbing,* as Nicola Thorne. London, 1969
4. *In Love,* as Nicola Thorne. London, 1974
5. *Hammersleigh.* New York and London, 1976
6. *Return to Wuthering Heights,* as Anna L'Estrange. New York, 1977
7. *The Enchantress,* as Katherine Yorke. London and New York, 1979
8. *A Woman Like Us,* as Nicola Thorne. London and New York, 1979

9. *The Perfect Wife and Mother,* as Nicola Thorne. London, 1980
10. *Falcon Gold,* as Katherine Yorke. London, 1980
11. *Rose, Rose, Where Are You.* London and New York, 1981
12. *Lady of the Lakes,* as Katherine Yorke. London, 1981
13. *The Daughters of the House,* as Nicola Thorne. London and New York, 1981
14. *Where the Rivers Meet,* as Nicola Thorne. London, 1982

Elmore, Ernest (Carpenter)
Born in 1901, died in 1957
Pseudonym: John Bude
1. *The Steel Grubs.* London, 1928
2. *This Siren Song.* London, 1930
3. *The Baboon and the Fiddle.* London, 1932
4. *The Cornish Coast Murder,* as John Bude. London, 1935
5. *The Lake District Murder,* as John Bude. London, 1935
6. *The Sussex Downs Murder,* as John Bude. London, 1936
7. *The Cheltonham Square Murder,* as John Bude. London, 1937
8. *Loss of a Head,* as John Bude. London, 1938
9. *Hand on the Alibi,* as John Bude. London, 1939
10. *Green in Judgement.* London, 1939
11. *Death of a Cad,* as John Bude. London, 1940
12. *Death on Paper,* as John Bude. London, 1940
13. *Slow Vengeance,* as John Bude. London, 1941
14. *Death Knows No Calendar,* as John Bude. London, 1942
15. *Death Deals a Double,* as John Bude. London, 1943
16. *Death in White Pyjamas,* as John Bude. London, 1944
17. *Death in Ambush,* as John Bude. London, 1945
18. *Trouble A-Brewing,* as John Bude. London, 1946
19. *Snuffly Snorty Dog.* London, 1946
20. *Death Makes a Prophet,* as John Bude. London, 1947
21. *Dangerous Sunlight,* as John Bude. London, 1948
22. *Murder in Montparnasse,* as John Bude. London, 1949
23. *A Glut of Red Herrings,* as John Bude. London, 1949
24. *Christmas in Gilleybrook.* London, 1949
25. *Death Steals the Show,* as John Bude. London, 1950
26. *The Constable and the Lady,* as John Bude. London, 1951
27. *When the Case Was Opened,* as John Bude. London, 1952
28. *Death on the Riviera,* as John Bude. London, 1952
29. *Twice Dead,* as John Bude. London, 1953
30. *So Much in the Dark,* as John Bude. London, 1954
31. *The Lumpton Gobbelings.* London, 1954
32. *Two Ends to the Town,* as John Bude. London, 1955
33. *A Shift of Guilt,* as John Bude. London, 1956
34. *A Telegram from Le Touquet,* as John Bude. London, 1956
35. *Another Man's Shadow,* as John Bude. London, 1957
36. *A Twist of the Rope,* as John Bude. London, 1958
37. *The Night the Fog Came Down,* as John Bude. London and New York, 1958

Elston, Allen Vaughan
American, born July 28, 1887, died October 21, 1976
1. *Come Out and Fight.* New York, 1941
2. *Pacific Passage.* London, 1942
3. *Guns on the Cimarron.* Philadelphia, 1943
4. *Eagle's Eye.* Surrey (Eng), 1943
5. *Hit the Saddle.* Philadelphia, 1947
6. *Lost Harbours.* Surrey, 1947
7. *The Sheriff of San Miguel.* Philadelphia, 1949
8. *Ranch of the Roses.* Philadelphia, 1949
9. *Deadline at Durango.* Philadelphia, 1960
10. *Grass and Gold.* Philadelphia, 1951
11. *Roundup on the Picket Wire.* Philadelphia, 1952
12. *Saddle Up for Sunlight.* Philadelphia, 1952
13. *Stage Road to Denver.* Philadelphia, 1953
14. *Colorado Showdown.* New York, 1953

15. *Gold Brick Range.* New York, 1953
16. *Wagon Wheel Gap.* Philadelphia, 1954
17. *Long Lope to Lander.* Philadelphia, 1954
18. *Forbidden Valley.* Philadelphia, 1955
19. *The Wyoming Bubble.* Philadelphia, 1955
20. *The Marked Men.* Philadelphia, 1956
21. *Last Stage to Aspen.* Philadelphia, 1956
22. *Showdown.* New York, 1956
23. *Grand Mesa.* Philadelphia, 1957
24. *Rio Grande Deadline.* Philadelphia, 1957
25. *Wyoming Manhunt.* Philadelphia, 1958
26. *Gun Law at Laramie.* Philadelphia, 1959
27. *Beyond the Bitterroots.* Philadelphia and London, 1960
28. *Sagebrush Serenade.* Philadelphia, 1960
29. *Timberline Bonanza.* Philadelphia, 1961
30. *Treasure Coach from Deadwood.* Philadelphia, 1962
31. *Roundup on the Yellowstone.* Philadelphia, 1962
32. *The Seven Silver.* New York, 1964
33. *The Landseekers.* Philadelphia and London, 1964
34. *The Lawless Border.* New York, 1966
35. *Montana Passage.* New York, 1967
36. *Montana Manhunt.* New York, 1967
37. *Arizona Skyline.* New York, 1969
38. *Paradise Prairie.* New York, 1971
39. *The Big Pasture.* London, 1972
40. *Saddle Up for Steamboat.* New York, 1973

Erdman, Loula Grace
American, born in Missouri, died June 20, 1976
1. *Separate Star.* New York, 1944
2. *Fair Is the Morning.* New York, 1945
3. *The Years of the Locust.* New York, 1947
4. *Lonely Passage.* New York, 1948
5. *The Edge of Time.* New York, 1950
6. *The Wind Blows Free.* New York, 1952
7. *My Sky Is Blue.* New York, 1953
8. *Three at the Wedding.* New York, 1953
9. *The Far Journey.* New York, 1955
10. *The Wide Horizon.* New York, 1956
11. *The Short Summer.* New York, 1958
12. *The Good Land.* New York, 1959
13. *Many a Voyage.* New York, 1960
14. *The Man Who Told the Truth.* New York, 1962
15. *Life Was Simpler Then.* New York, 1963
16. *A Wonderful Thing and Other Stories.* New York, 1964
17. *Another Spring.* New York, 1966
18. *A Time to Write.* New York, 1969
19. *A Bluebird.* New York, 1973
20. *Save Weeping for Night.* New York, 1975

Ertz, Susan
British
1. *Madame Clair.* London and New York, 1923
2. *Nina.* London and New York, 1924
3. *After Noon.* London and New York, 1926
4. *Now East, Now West.* London and New York, 1927
5. *And Then Face to Face and Other Stories.* London, 1927
6. *The Wind of Complication.* New York, 1927
7. *The Galaxy.* London and New York, 1929
8. *Julian Probert.* London, 1931
9. *The Story of Julian.* New York, 1931
10. *Now We Set Out.* London, 1931
11. *The Proselyte.* London and New York, 1933
12. *Woman Alive.* London, 1935
13. *No Hearts to Break.* London and New York, 1937
14. *Big Frogs and Little Frogs.* London, 1938
15. *Black, White and Caroline.* London and New York, 1938
16. *One Fight More.* New York, 1939
17. *Anger in the Sky.* London and New York, 1943
18. *Two Names Under the Shore.* London, 1947
19. *Mary Hallam.* New York, 1947
20. *The Prodigal Heart.* London and New York, 1950
21. *The Undefended Gate.* London and New York, 1953
22. *Invitation to Folly.* New York, 1953
23. *Charmed Circle.* London and New York, 1956
24. *In the Cool of the Day.* New York, 1960
25. *Devices and Desires.* London, 1972
26. *Summer's Lease.* New York, 1972
27. *The Philosopher's Daughter.* London and New York, 1976

Estleman, Loren D.
American, born September 15, 1952
1. *The Oklahoma Punk.* Canoga Park (CA), 1976
2. *Sherlock Holmes Versus Dracula; or, The Adventure of the Sanguinary Count.* New York and London, 1978
3. *The Hider.* New York, 1978
4. *The High Rocks.* New York, 1979
5. *Dr. Jekyll and Mr. Holmes.* New York, 1979
6. *Motor City Blue.* Boston, 1980
7. *Stamping Ground.* New York, 1980
8. *Aces and Eights.* New York, 1981
9. *The Wolfer.* New York, 1981
10. *Angel Eyes.* Boston, 1981
11. *The Midnight Man.* Boston, 1982
12. *Murdock's Law.* New York, 1982

Estridge, Robin
British
Pseudonym: Philip Loraine
1. *The Future Is Tomorrow.* London, 1947
2. *The Publican's Wife.* London, 1948
3. *Meeting on the Shore.* London, 1949
4. *White Lie the Dead,* as Philip Loraine. London, 1950
5. *And to My Beloved Husband—,* as Philip Loraine. New York, 1950
6. *Exit with Intent: The Story of a Missing Comedian,* as Philip Loraine. London, 1950
7. *Return of a Hero.* London, 1950
8. *Sword Without Scabbard.* New York, 1950
9. *The Break in the Circle,* as Philip Loraine. London and New York, 1951
10. *The Dublin Nightmare,* as Philip Loraine. London, 1952
11. *Nightmare in Dublin,* as Philip Loraine. New York, 1952
12. *Outside the Law,* as Philip Loraine. New York, 1953
13. *The Olive Tree.* London and New York, 1953
14. *The Angel of Death,* as Philip Loraine. London and New York, 1961
15. *Day of the Arrow,* as Philip Loraine. London and New York, 1964
16. *The Eye of the Devil,* as Philip Loraine. London, 1966
17. *13,* as Philip Loraine. London, 1966
18. *W.I.L. One to Curtis,* as Philip Loraine. London and New York, 1967
19. *The Dead Men of Sestos,* as Philip Loraine. London and New York, 1968
20. *A Mafia Kiss,* as Philip Loraine. London and New York, 1969
21. *A Cuckoo's Child.* London, 1969
22. *Photographs Have Been Sent to Your Wife,* as Philip Loraine. London and New York, 1971
23. *Voices in an Empty Room,* as Philip Loraine. London, 1973
24. *Ask the Rattlesnake,* as Philip Loraine. London, 1975
25. *Wrong Man in the Mirror,* as Philip Loraine. New York, 1975

Evans, Max
American, August 29, 1925

1. *Southwest Wind.* San Antonio (TX), 1958
2. *Long John Dunn of Taos.* Los Angeles, 1959
3. *The Rounders.* New York, 1960
4. *The Hi Lo Country.* New York, 1961
5. *Three Short Novels: The Great Wedding, The One-Eyed Sky, My Pardner.* Boston, 1963
6. *The Mountain of Gold.* Dunwoody (GA), 1965
7. *Shadow of Thunder.* Chicago, 1969
8. *Sam Peckinpah, Master of Violence.* Vermillion, 1972
9. *Bobby Jack Smith, You Dirty Coward!* Los Angeles, 1974
10. *The White Shadow.* San Diego (CA), 1977

Evarts, Sr., Hal G. (George)
American, born August 24, 1887, died October 18, 1934
1. *The Cross Pull.* New York and London, 1920
2. *The Passing of the Old West.* Boston, 1921
3. *The Bald Face and Other Stories.* New York, 1921
4. *The Yellow Horde.* Boston and London, 1921
5. *The Settling of the Sage.* Boston and London, 1922
6. *Fur Sign.* Boston, 1922
7. *Tumbleweeds.* Boston, 1923
8. *Tomahawk Rights.* Boston, 1925
9. *Spanish Acres.* Boston, 1925
10. *The Painted Stallion.* Boston and London, 1926
11. *The Moccasin Telegraph.* Boston, 1927
12. *Fur Brigade.* Boston, 1928
13. *Jerbo, The Jumper.* Racine (WI), 1930
14. *Kobi of the Sea.* Racine, 1930
15. *Phantom, The White Mink.* Racine, 1930
16. *Swift, The Kit Fox.* Racine, 1930
17. *The Shaggy Legion.* Boston, 1930
18. *Shortgrass.* Boston and London, 1932
19. *Wolfdog.* New York and London, 1935

Evarts, Jr., Hal G. (George)
American, Born February 8, 1915
1. *Rolling Ahead.* Paris, 1945
2. *Renegade of Rainbow Basin.* New York, 1953
3. *Highgrader.* New York, 1954
4. *Apache Agent.* New York, 1955
5. *Fugitive's Canyon.* New York, 1955
6. *Ambush Rider.* New York, 1956
7. *The Night Raiders.* New York, 1956
8. *Man Without a Gun.* New York, 1957
9. *The Man from Yuma.* New York, 1958
10. *The Long Rope.* New York, 1959
11. *Jedediah Smith, Trail Blazer of the West.* New York, 1959
12. *Jim Clyman.* New York, 1959
13. *The Secret of the Himalayas.* New York, 1962
14. *The Blazing Land.* New York, 1960
15. *Turncoat.* New York, 1960
16. *The Silver Concubine.* New York, 1962
17. *Massacre Creek.* New York, 1962
18. *Colorado Crossing.* New York, 1963
19. *Treasure River.* New York, 1964
20. *The Branded Man.* New York, 1965
21. *The Talking Mountain.* New York, 1966
22. *Smugglers Road.* New York, 1968
23. *The Sundown Kid.* New York, 1969
24. *Mission to Tibet.* New York, 1970
25. *The Pegleg Mystery.* New York, 1972
26. *Big Foot.* New York, 1973
27. *The Purple Eagle Mystery.* New York, 1976
28. *Jay-Jay and the Peking Monster.* New York, 1978

Farnol, Jeffery [John Jeffery Farnol]
British, born February 10, 1878, died August 9, 1952
1. *My Lady Caprice.* London and New York, 1907
2. *The Broad Highway.* London, 1910
3. *The Money Moon.* London and Boston, 1911
4. *The Oubliette.* London, 1912
5. *The Amateur Gentleman.* London and Boston, 1913
6. *The Honourable Mr. Tawnish.* London and Boston, 1913
7. *Beltane the Smith.* London and Boston, 1915
8. *The Chronicles of the Imp.* London, 1915
9. *The Definite Object.* London and Boston, 1917
10. *Our Admiral Betty.* London and Boston, 1918
11. *Some War Impressions.* London, 1918
12. *Great Britain at War.* Boston, 1918
13. *The Geste of Duke Jocelyn.* London, 1919
14. *Black Bartlemy's Treasure.* London and Boston, 1920
15. *Martin Conisby's Vengeance.* London and Boston, 1921
16. *Peregrine's Progress.* London and Boston, 1922
17. *Sir John Dering.* London and Boston, 1923
18. *The Loring Mystery.* London and Boston, 1925
19. *The High Adventure.* London and Boston, 1926
20. *The Quest of Youth.* London and Boston, 1927
21. *Gyfford of Weare.* London, 1928
22. *Guyfford of Weare.* Boston, 1928
23. *Epics of the Fancy.* London, 1928
24. *Famous Prize Fights; or, Epics of "The Fancy."* Boston, 1928
25. *The Shadow and Other Stories.* London and Boston, 1929
26. *Over the Hills.* London and Boston, 1930
27. *The Jade of Destiny.* London, 1931
28. *A Jade of Destiny.* Boston, 1931
29. *Voices from the Dust, Being Romances of Old London.* London and Boston, 1932
30. *Charmian, Lady Vibart.* London and Boston, 1932
31. *The Way Beyond.* London and Boston, 1933
32. *Winds of Fortune.* London, 1934
33. *Winds of Chance.* Boston, 1934
34. *A Portrait of a Gentleman in Colours: The Romance of Mr. Lewis Berger.* London, 1935
35. *John o'the Green.* London and Boston, 1935
36. *A Pageant of Victory.* London and Boston, 1936
37. *The Crooked Furrow.* London, 1937
38. *Hove.* Privately printed, 1937
39. *A Book [New Book] for Jane.* London, 2 vols., 1937-39
40. *The Lonely Road.* London and New York, 1938
41. *The Happy Harvest.* London, 1939
42. *A Master of Business and Other Stories.* London and Boston, 1940
43. *Adam Penfeather, Buccaneer.* London, 1940
44. *Murder by Nail.* London, 1942
45. *Valley of Night.* New York, 1942
46. *The King Liveth.* London, 1943
47. *The "Piping Times."* London, 1945
48. *Heritage Perilous.* London, 1946
49. *My Lord of Wrybourne.* London, 1948
50. *Most Sacred of All.* New York, 1948
51. *The Fool Beloved.* London, 1949
52. *The Nineth Earl.* London, 1950
53. *The Glad Summer.* London, 1951
54. *Waif of the River.* London, 1952
55. *Justice by Midnight.* London, 1956

Faust, Frederick (Schiller)
American, born May 29, 1892, died May 12, 1944
Pseudonyms: Frank Austin, George Owen Baxter, Max Brand, Walter C. Butler, George Challis, Peter Dawson, Martin Dexter, Evan Evans, John Frederick, Frederick Frost, David Manning, Peter Henry Morland, Hugh Owen, Nicholas Silver
1. *The Untamed,* as Max Brand. New York, 1919
2. *Trailin',* as Max Brand. New York, 1920

3. *The Night Horseman*, as Max Brand. New York, 1920
4. *The Ten Foot Chain; or, Can Love Survive the Shackles?*, as Max Brand, with others. New York, 1920
5. *Riders of the Silences*, as John Frederick. New York, 1920
6. *The Seventh Man*, as Max Brand. New York, 1921
7. *Free Range Lanning*, as George Owen Baxter. New York, 1921
8. *The Gauntlet*, as George Owen Baxter. London, 1922
9. *The Village Street and Other Poems*. New York, 1922
10. *Alcatraz*, as Max Brand. New York, 1923
11. *Children of the Night*, as Max Brand. London, 1923
12. *Donnegan*, as George Owen Baxter. New York, 1923
13. *The Long, Long Trail*, as George Owen Baxter. New York, 1923
14. *Dan Barry's Daughter*, as Max Brand. New York, 1924
15. *Clung*, as Max Brand. London, 1924
16. *The Guide to Happiness*, as Max Brand. London, 1924
17. *Gun Gentleman*, as Max Brand. London, 1924
18. *The Range-Land Avenger*, as George Owen Baxter. New York, 1924
19. *Bill Hunter's Romance*, as David Manning. New York, 1924
20. *Jerry Peyton's Notched Inheritance*, as David Manning. New York, 1924
21. *His Third Majesty*, as Max Brand. London, 1925
22. *Beyond the Outpost*, as Peter Henry Morland. New York, 1925
23. *King Charlie*, as George Owen Baxter. London, 1925
24. *The Shadow of Silver Tip*, as George Owen Baxter. New York, 1925
25. *Wooden Guns*, as George Owen Baxter. New York, 1925
26. *The Brute*, as David Manning. New York, 1925
27. *Jim Curry's Test*, as David Manning. New York, 1925
28. *King Charlie's Riders*, as David Manning. New York, 1925
29. *The Bronze Collar*, as John Frederick. New York, 1925
30. *Fire-Brain*, as Max Brand. New York, 1926
31. *The White Wolf*, as Max Brand. New York, 1926
32. *Fate's Honeymoon*, as Max Brand. London, 1926
33. *Luck*, as Max Brand. London, 1926
34. *Black Jack*, as Max Brand. London, 1926
35. *Harrigan*, as Max Brand. London, 1926
36. *The Stranger at the Gate*, as Max Brand. London, 1926
37. *Train's Trust*, as George Owen Baxter. New York, 1926
38. *The Whispering Outlaw*, as George Owen Baxter. New York, 1926
39. *The Border Bandit*, as Evan Evans. New York, 1926
40. *Blackie and Red*, as David Manning. New York, 1926
41. *The Black Signal*, as David Manning. New York, 1926
42. *Ronicky Doone's Treasure*, as David Manning. New York, 1926
43. *The Splendid Rascal*, as George Challis. Indianapolis, 1926
44. *Monsieur*, as George Challis. Indianapolis, 1926
45. *The Blue Jay*, as Max Brand. New York and London, 1927
46. *The Garden of Eden*, as Max Brand. London, 1927
47. *Pride of Tyson*, as Max Brand. London, 1927
48. *The Trail to San Triste*, as George Owen Baxter. New York, 1927
49. *Bandit's Honor*, as David Manning. New York, 1927
50. *On the Trail of Four*, as David Manning. New York, 1927
51. *The Outlaw Tamer*, as David Manning. New York, 1927
52. *The Trap at Comanche Bend*, as David Manning. New York, 1927
53. *The Mountain Fugitive*, as David Manning. New York, 1927
54. *Western Tommy*, as David Manning. New York, 1927
55. *The Sword Lover*, as John Frederick. New York, 1927
56. *Border Guns*, as Max Brand. New York, 1928
57. *Pillar Mountain*, as Max Brand. New York, 1928
58. *Pleasant Jim*, as Max Brand. New York and London, 1928
59. *Lost Wolf*, as Peter Henry Morland. New York, 1928
60. *The Mustang Herder*, as David Manning. New York, 1928
61. *Senor Jingle Bells*, as David Manning. New York, 1928
62. *The Galloping Bronchos*, as David Manning. New York, 1929
63. *The Gun Tamer*, as Max Brand. New York, 1929
64. *Mistral*, as Max Brand. New York, 1929
65. *Tiger Man*, as George Owen Baxter. New York and London, 1929
66. *Destry Rides Again*, as Max Brand. New York, 1930
67. *The Outlaw of Buffalo Flat*, as Max Brand. New York, 1930
68. *Mystery Ranch*, as Max Brand. New York, 1930
69. *Mystery Valley*, as Max Brand. London, 1930
70. *The Rescue of Broken Arrow*, as Evan Evans. New York, 1930
71. *The Happy Valley*, as Max Brand. New York, 1931
72. *Smiling Charlie*, as Max Brand. New York and London, 1931
73. *The Killers*, as George Owen Baxter. New York and London, 1931
74. *Dionysus in Hades*. Oxford (Eng), 1931
75. *The Jackson Trail*, as Max Brand. New York, 1932
76. *Twenty Notches*, as Max Brand. New York and London, 1932
77. *Valley Vultures*, as Max Brand. New York and London, 1932
78. *The False Rider*, as Max Brand. New York, 1933
79. *The Longhorn Feud*, as Max Brand. New York and London, 1933
80. *The Outlaw*, as Max Brand. New York, 1933
81. *Slow Joe*, as Max Brand. New York and London, 1933
82. *Valley Thieves*, as Max Brand. New York, 1933
83. *Montana Rides!*, as Evan Evans. New York, 1933
84. *The Return of the Rancher*, as Frank Austin. New York, 1933
85. *The Thunderer*. New York, 1933
86. *Brothers on the Trail*, as Max Brand. New York, 1934
87. *War Party*, as Max Brand. New York, 1934
88. *Timbal Gulch Trail*, as Max Brand. New York and London, 1934
89. *Crooked Horn*, as Max Brand. London, 1934
90. *The Rancher's Revenge*, as Max Brand. New York, 1934
91. *Call of the Blood*, as George Owen Baxter. New York and London, 1934
92. *Red Devil of the Range*, as George Owen Baxter. New York, 1934
93. *Montana Rides Again*, as Evan Evans. New York, 1934
94. *The Sheriff Rides*, as Frank Austin. New York, 1934
95. *Hunted Riders*, as Max Brand. New York, 1935
96. *Dead Man's Treasure*, as Max Brand. New York, 1935
97. *Rustlers of Beacon Creek*, as Max Brand. New York, 1935
98. *Frontier Feud*, as Max Brand. New York, 1935
99. *The Seven of Diamonds*, as Max Brand. New York and London, 1935
100. *Brother of the Cheyennes*, as George Owen Baxter. New York, 1935
101. *King of the Range*, as Frank Austin. New York, 1935
102. *Cross Over Nine*, as Walter C. Butler. New York, 1935
103. *Happy Jack*, as Max Brand. New York and London, 1936
104. *The King Bird Rides*, as Max Brand. New York and London, 1936
105. *South of Rio Grande*, as Max Brand. New York, 1936
106. *The Song of the Whip*, as Evan Evans. New York and London, 1936
107. *The Night Flower*, as Walter C. Butler. New York, 1936
108. *Secret Agent Number One*, as Frederick Frost. Philadelphia, 1936
109. *The Streak*, as Max Brand. New York and London, 1937
110. *Trouble Trail*, as Max Brand. New York and London, 1937

111. *Rusty,* as George Owen Baxter. London, 1937
112. *Six Golden Angels,* as Max Brand. New York, 1937
113. *The Golden Knight,* as George Challis. New York, 1937
114. *Spy Meets Spy.* Philadelphia, 1937
115. *The Bamboo Whistle.* Philadelphia, 1937
116. *Dead or Alive,* as Max Brand. New York, 1938
117. *The Iron Trail,* as Max Brand. New York, 1938
118. *Riding the Iron Trail,* as Max Brand. London, 1938
119. *Singing Guns,* as Max Brand. New York and London, 1938
120. *The Naked Blade,* as George Challis. New York, 1938
121. *Fightin' Fool,* as Max Brand. New York, 1939
122. *Gunman's Gold,* as Max Brand. New York and London, 1939
123. *Marbleface,* as Max Brand. New York, 1939
124. *Poker Face,* as Max Brand. London, 1939
125. *Lanky for Luck,* as Max Brand. London, 1939
126. *Danger Trail,* as Max Brand. New York and London, 1940
127. *A Fairly Slick Guy,* as Max Brand. London, 1940
128. *The Dude,* as Max Brand. New York, 1940
129. *Riders of the Plains,* as Max Brand. New York, 1940
130. *Cleaned Out,* as Max Brand. London, 1940
131. *Wine on the Desert and Other Stories,* as Max Brand. New York, 1940
132. *Calling Dr. Kildare.* New York, 1940
133. *The Secret of Dr. Kildare.* New York, 1940
134. *The Border Kid,* as Max Brand. New York and London, 1941
135. *The Long Chance,* as Max Brand. New York, 1941
136. *Vengeance Trail,* as Max Brand. New York, 1941
137. *Dr. Kildare Takes Charge,* as Max Brand. New York, 1941
138. *Young Dr. Kildare,* as Max Brand. New York and London, 1941
139. *Silvertip,* as Max Brand. New York and London, 1942
140. *The Man from Mustang,* as Max Brand. New York, 1942
141. *Silvertip's Strike,* as Max Brand. New York, 1942
142. *The Safety Killer,* as Max Brand. London, 1942
143. *Striking Eagle,* as Max Brand. London, 1942
144. *Dr. Kildare's Crisis,* as Max Brand. New York, 1942
145. *Dr. Kildare's Trial,* as Max Brand. New York, 1942
146. *Silvertip's Roundup,* as Max Brand. New York, 1943
147. *Silvertip's Trap,* as Max Brand. New York, 1943
148. *Dr. Kildare's Search, and Dr. Kildare's Hardest Case,* as Max Brand. New York, 1943
149. *The Fighting Four,* as Max Brand. New York, 1944
150. *Silvertip's Chase,* as Max Brand. Philadelphia, 1944
151. *The Gate,* as Max Brand, with Mirza Ahmad Sohrab and Julie Chanler. New York, 1944
152. *Silvertip's Search,* as Max Brand. New York, 1945
153. *The Stolen Stallion,* as Max Brand. New York, 1945
154. *Mountain Riders,* as Max Brand. New York, 1946
155. *Valley of Vanishing Men,* as Max Brand. New York, 1947
156. *The Border Bandit,* as Evan Evans. New York, 1947
157. *The False Rider,* as Max Brand. New York, 1947
158. *Flaming Irons,* as Max Brand. New York, 1948
159. *Hired Hands,* as Max Brand. New York, 1948
160. *The Rescue of Broken Arrow,* as Evan Evans. New York, 1948
161. *The Bandit of the Black Hills,* as Max Brand. New York and London, 1949
162. *Seven Trails,* as Max Brand. New York, 1949
163. *Gunman's Legacy,* as Evan Evans. New York, 1949
164. *Smuggler's Trail,* as Evan Evans. New York, 1949
165. *Single Jack,* as Max Brand. New York, 1950
166. *Sixgun Legacy,* as Evan Evans. New York, 1950
167. *The Firebrand,* as George Challis. New York, 1950
168. *Sawdust and Sixguns,* as Evan Evans. New York, 1950
169. *The Hair-Trigger Kid,* as Max Brand. New York, 1951
170. *Tragedy Trail,* as Max Brand. New York, 1951
171. *Smoking Gun Trail,* as Evan Evans. London, 1951
172. *Lone Hand,* as Evan Evans. New York, 1951
173. *The Bait and The Trap,* as George Challis. New York, 1951
174. *Strange Courage,* as Evan Evans. New York, 1952
175. *The Gambler,* as Max Brand. New York, 1952
176. *Smiling Desperado,* as Max Brand. New York, 1953
177. *The Tenderfoot,* as Max Brand. New York, 1953
178. *Outlaw Valley,* as Evan Evans. New York, 1953
179. *Outlaw's Code,* as Evan Evans. New York, 1953
180. *The Gambler,* as Max Brand. New York, 1954
181. *The Invisible Outlaw,* as Max Brand. New York, 1954
182. *Outlaw Breed,* as Max Brand. New York, 1955
183. *Speedy,* as Max Brand. New York, 1955
184. *The Big Trail,* as Max Brand. New York, 1956
185. *Trail Partners,* as Max Brand. New York, 1956
186. *Blood on the Trail,* as Max Brand. New York, 1957
187. *Lucky Larribee,* as Max Brand. New York, 1957
188. *The Notebooks and Poems of Max Brand,* as Max Brand. New York, 1957
189. *The Long Chase,* as Max Brand. New York, 1960
190. *The White Cheyenne,* as Max Brand. New York, 1960
191. *Mighty Lobo,* as Max Brand. New York, 1962
192. *Tamer of the Wild,* as Max Brand. New York, 1962
193. *The Stranger,* as Max Brand. New York, 1963
194. *Golden Lightning,* as Max Brand. New York, 1964
195. *The Gentle Gunman,* as Max Brand. New York, 1964
196. *The Guns of Dorking Hollow,* as Max Brand. New York, 1965
197. *Torture Trail,* as Max Brand. New York, 1965
198. *Larramee's Ranch,* as Max Brand. New York, 1966
199. *Ride the Wild Trail,* as Max Brand. New York, 1966
200. *Steve Train's Ordeal,* as Max Brand. New York, 1967
201. *Max Brand's Best Stories,* as Max Brand. New York, 1967
202. *Rippon Rides Double,* as Max Brand. New York, 1968
203. *The Stingaree,* as Max Brand. New York, 1968
204. *Thunder Moon,* as Max Brand. New York, 1969
205. *Gunman's Reckoning,* as Max Brand. New York, 1970
206. *Trouble Kid,* as Max Brand. New York, 1970
207. *Ambush at Torture Canyon,* as Max Brand. **New** York, 1971
208. *Cheyenne Gold,* as Max Brand. New York, 1972
209. *Drifter's Vengeance,* as Max Brand. New York, 1972
210. *The Luck of the Spindrift,* as Max Brand. New York, 1972
211. *Big Game,* as Max Brand. New York, 1973
212. *The Granduca,* as Max Brand. New York, 1973
213. *The Phantom Spy,* as Max Brand. New York, 1973
214. *Dead Man's Treasure,* as Max Brand. London, 1975
215. *Storm on the Range,* as Max Brand. London, 1979

Felton, Ronald (Oliver)
British, born December 14, 1909
Pseudonym: Ronald Welch
1. *The Black Car Mystery,* as Ronald Welch. London, 1950
2. *The Clock Stood Still,* as Ronald Welch. London, 1951
3. *The Gauntlet,* as Ronald Welch. London and New York, 1951
4. *Knight Crusader,* as Ronald Welch. London, 1954
5. *Sker House.* London, 1954
6. *Ferdinand Magellan,* as Ronald Welch. London, 1955
7. *Captain of Dragoons,* as Ronald Welch. London and New York, 1956
8. *The Long Bow,* as Ronald Welch. Oxford (Eng), 1957
9. *Mohawk Valley,* as Ronald Welch. London and New York, 1958
10. *Captain of Foot,* as Ronald Welch. London, 1959
11. *Escape from France,* as Ronald Welch. London, 1960
12. *For the King,* as Ronald Welch. London, 1961
13. *Nicholas Carey,* as Ronald Welch. London and New York, 1963

14. *Bowman of Crecy,* as Ronald Welch. London, 1966
15. *The Hawk,* as Ronald Welch. London, 1967
16. *Sun of York,* as Ronald Welch. London, 1970
17. *The Galleon,* as Ronald Welch. London, 1971
18. *Tank Commander,* as Ronald Welch. London, 1972
19. *Zulu Warrior,* as Ronald Welch. Newton Abbot (Eng), 1974
20. *Ensign Carey,* as Ronald Welch. London, 1976

Field, Rachel (Lyman)
American, born September 19, 1894, died March 15, 1942
1. *Rise Up, Jennie Smith.* New York, 1918
2. *The Fifteenth Candle.* New York, 1921
3. *The Pointed People: Verses and Silhouettes.* New Haven (CT) and London, 1924
4. *An Alphabet for Boys and Girls.* New York and London, 1926
5. *Taxis and Toadstools: Verses and Decorations.* New York and London, 1926
6. *Eliza and the Elves.* New York, 1926
7. *The Magic Pawnshop: A New Year's Eve Fantasy.* New York, 1927
8. *A Little Book of Days.* New York and London, 1927
9. *Little Dog Toby.* New York, 1928
10. *Polly Patchwork.* New York, 1928
11. *Six Plays.* New York, 1924
12. *The Cross-Stitch Heart.* New York, 1927
13. *Hitty, Her First Hundred Years.* New York, 1929
14. *Pocket-Handkerchief Park.* New York, 1929
15. *Points East: Narratives of New England.* New York, 1930
16. *A Circus Ground.* Washington, D.C., 1930
17. *Patchwork Plays.* New York, 1930
18. *Calico Bush.* New York, 1931
19. *The Yellow Shop.* New York, 1931
20. *Hitty: The Life and Adventures of a Wooden Doll.* London, 1932
21. *The Bird Began to Sing.* New York, 1932
22. *Hepatica Hawkes.* New York, 1932
23. *Just Across the Street.* New York, 1933
24. *Fortune's Caravan.* New York, 1933
25. *God's Pocket: The Story of Captain Samuel Hadlock, Junior, of the Cranberry Isles, Maine.* New York, 1934
26. *Susanna B. and William C.* New York, 1934
27. *Branches Green.* New York, 1934
28. *Time Out of Mind.* New York, 1935
29. *Fear Is the Thorn.* New York, 1936
30. *First Class Matter.* New York, 1936
31. *To See Ourselves,* with Arthur Pederson. New York, 1937
32. *All This and Heaven Too.* New York, 1938
33. *The Bad Penny.* New York, 1938
34. *Christmas Time.* New York, 1941
35. *And Now Tomorrow.* New York, 1942
36. *Christmas in London.* Privately printed, 1946
37. *Ave Maria: An Interpretation from Walt Disney's "Fantasia" Inspired by the Music of Franz Schubert.* New York, 1940
38. *All Through the Night.* New York, 1940
39. *Prayer for a Child.* New York, 1944
40. *Poems.* New York, 1957
41. *The Rachel Field Story Book.* New York, 1958

Finley, Glenna
American, born June 12, 1925
1. *Death Strikes Out.* New York, 1957
2. *Career Wife.* New York, 1964
3. *Nurse Pro Tem.* New York, 1967
4. *A Tycoon for Ann.* New York, 1968
5. *Journey to Love.* New York, 1970
6. *Love's Hidden Fire.* New York, 1971
7. *Treasure of the Heart.* New York, 1971
8. *Love Lies North.* New York, 1972
9. *Bridal Affair.* New York, 1972
10. *Kiss a Stranger.* New York, 1972
11. *Love in Danger.* New York, 1973
12. *When Love Speaks.* New York, 1973
13. *The Romantic Spirit.* New York, 1973
14. *Surrender, My Love.* New York, 1974
15. *A Promising Affair.* New York, 1974
16. *Love's Magic Spell.* New York, 1974
17. *The Reluctant Maiden.* New York, 1975
18. *The Captured Heart.* New York, 1975
19. *Holiday for Love.* New York, 1976
20. *Love for a Rogue.* New York, 1976
21. *Storm of Desire.* New York, 1977
22. *Dare to Love.* New York, 1977
23. *To Catch a Bride.* New York, 1977
24. *Master of Love.* New York, 1978
25. *Beware My Heart.* New York, 1978
26. *The Marriage Merger.* New York, 1978
27. *Wildfire for Love.* New York, 1979
28. *Timed for Love.* New York, 1979
29. *Love's Temptation.* New York, 1979
30. *Stateroom for Two.* New York, 1980
31. *Affairs of Love.* New York, 1980
32. *Midnight Encounter.* New York, 1981
33. *Return Engagement.* New York, 1981
34. *One Way to Love.* New York, 1982

Franken, Rose (Dorothy)
American, born December 28, 1895
Pseudonyms: Margaret Grant, with W.B. Maloney; Franken Meloney, with W.B. Maloney
1. *Pattern.* New York, 1925
2. *Another Language.* New York, 1932
3. *Mr. Dooley, Jr.,* with Jane Lewin. New York, 1932
4. *Twice Born.* New York, 1935
5. *Call Back Love,* as Margaret Grant. New York, 1937
6. *Of Great Riches.* New York, 1937
7. *Gold Pennies.* New York, 1938
8. *Claudia: The Story of Marriage.* New York, 1939
9. *Strange Victory,* as Franken Meloney. New York, 1939
10. *When Doctors Disagree,* as Franken Meloney. New York, 1940
11. *Claudia and David.* New York, 1940
12. *Claudia.* New York, 1941
13. *American Breed,* as Franken Meloney. New York, 1941
14. *Another Claudia.* New York, 1943
15. *Outrageous Fortune.* New York, 1944
16. *Soldier's Wife.* New York, 1945
17. *Young Claudia.* New York, 1946
18. *The Hallams.* New York, 1948
19. *The Marriage of Claudia.* New York and London, 1948
20. *From Claudia to David.* London, 1949
21. *The Fragile Years.* New York, 1952
22. *Those Fragile Years.* London, 1952
23. *Rendezvous.* New York, 1954
24. *Intimate Story.* New York and London, 1955
25. *The Return of Claudia.* London, 1957
26. *The Antic Years.* New York, 1958
27. *When All Is Said and Done.* London, 1962
28. *You're Well Out of Hospital.* London and New York, 1966

Freeman, Cynthia (Bea Feinberg)
American, born in New York City
1. *A World Full of Strangers.* New York, 1975
2. *Fairytales.* New York, 1977
3. *The Days of Winter.* New York, 1978
4. *Portraits.* New York, 1979

5. *Come Pour the Wine.* New York, 1981
6. *No Time for Tears.* New York, 1981

Gallagher, Patricia
American
1. *The Sons and the Daughters.* New York and London, 1961
2. *Answer to Heaven.* London, 1962
3. *The Fires of Brimstone.* New York, 1966
4. *Shannon.* New York, 1967
5. *Shadows of Passion.* New York, 1971
6. *Summer of Sighs.* New York, 1971
7. *The Thicket.* New York, 1973
8. *Castles in the Air.* New York, 1976
9. *Mystic Rose.* New York, 1977
10. *No Greater Love.* New York, 1979
11. *All for Love.* New York, 1981

Garvice, Charles
British, born in 1833, died March 1, 1920
Pseudonyms: Charles Gibson, Caroline Hart
1. *Eve and Other Verses.* Privately printed, 1873
2. *Maurice Durant.* London, 1875
3. *One Love's Altar.* New York, 1892
4. *Paid For!* New York, 1892
5. *Married at Sight.* New York, 1894
6. *The Price of Honour,* as Charles Gibson. Cleveland (OH), no date
7. *His Love So True.* New York, 1896
8. *The Marquis.* New York, 1896
9. *Just a Girl.* London, 1898
10. *She Loved Him.* New York, 1899
11. *Claire.* New York, 1899
12. *Lorrie.* New York, 1899
13. *Modern Juliet.* New York, 1900
14. *Nell of Shorne Mills.* New York, 1900
15. *Nance.* London, 1900
16. *Her Heart's Desire.* London, 1900
17. *An Outcast of the Family.* London, 1900
18. *A Coronet of Shame.* London, 1900
19. *Leola Dale's Fortune.* New York, 1901
20. *Maida.* New York, 1901
21. *Only a Girl's Love.* New York, 1901
22. *For Her Only.* New York, 1902
23. *The Lady of Darracourt.* New York, 1902
24. *Jeanne.* New York, 1902
25. *Heir of Vering.* New York, 1902
26. *Woman's Soul.* New York, 1902
27. *So Nearly Lost.* New York, 1902
28. *So Fair, So False.* New York, 1902
29. *Love's Dilemma.* New York, 1902
30. *Martyred Love.* New York, 1902
31. *My Lady Pride.* New York, 1902
32. *Olivia.* New York, 1902
33. *In Cupid's Chains.* London, 1902
34. *Woven on Fate's Loom, and The Snowdrift.* New York, 1903
35. *Staunch of the Heart.* New York, 1903
36. *Her Ransom.* New York, 1903
37. *Led by Love.* New York, 1903
38. *Staunch as a Woman.* New York, 1903
39. *A Jest of Fate.* New York, 1904
40. *Her Humble Lover.* Cleveland (OH), 1904
41. *Love Decides.* London, 1904
42. *Linked by Fate.* London, 1904
43. *Love, The Tyrant.* London, 1905
44. *Edna's Secret Marriage.* New York, 1905
45. *The Other Woman.* New York, 1905
46. *When Love Meets Love.* New York, 1906
47. *A Girl of Spirit.* London, 1906
48. *Diana and Destiny.* London, 1906
49. *Where Love Leads.* London, 1907
50. *The Gold in the Gutter.* London, 1907
51. *Sacrifice to Art.* Chicago, 1908
52. *Sample of Prejudice.* Chicago, 1908
53. *Slave of the Lake.* Chicago, 1908
54. *Taming of Princess Olga.* Chicago, 1908
55. *Woman Decides.* Chicago, 1908
56. *My Lady of Snow.* Chicago, 1908
57. *Linnie.* Chicago, 1908
58. *Olivia and Others.* London, 1908
59. *A Love Comedy.* Chicago, 1908
60. *Marcia Drayton.* London, 1908
61. *Female Editor.* Chicago, 1908
62. *Leave Love to Itself.* Chicago, 1908
63. *First and Last.* Chicago, 1908
64. *In the Matter of a Letter.* Chicago, 1908
65. *Farmer Holt's Daughter.* Chicago, 1908
66. *Story of a Passion.* London, 1908
67. *Kyra's Fate.* London, 1908
68. *The Rugged Path.* London, 1908
69. *In Wolf's Clothing.* London, 1908
70. *Queen Kate.* London, 1909
71. *The Scribblers' Club.* London, 1909
72. *The Fatal Ruby.* London and New York, 1909
73. *By Dangerous Ways.* London, 1909
74. *A Fair Imposter.* London, 1909
75. *A Heritage of Hate.* London, 1909
76. *The Mistress of Court Regina.* London, 1909
77. *At Love's Cost.* London, 1909
78. *Ashes of Love.* New York, 1910
79. *A Hidden Terror,* as Caroline Hart. Cleveland, 1910
80. *Angela's Lover,* as Caroline Hart. Cleveland, no date
81. *For Love or Honor,* as Caroline Hart. Cleveland, no date
82. *From Want to Wealth,* as Caroline Hart. Cleveland, no date
83. *From Worse Than Death,* as Caroline Hart. Cleveland, no date
84. *Game of Love,* as Caroline Hart. Cleveland, no date
85. *Haunted Life,* as Caroline Hart. Cleveland, no date
86. *Hearts of Fire,* as Caroline Hart. Cleveland, no date
87. *Her Right to Love,* as Caroline Hart. Cleveland, no date
88. *Lil, The Dancing Girl,* as Caroline Hart. Cleveland, no date
89. *Lillian's Vow,* as Caroline Hart. Cleveland, no date
90. *Little Princess,* as Caroline Hart. Cleveland, no date
91. *Love's Rugged Path,* as Caroline Hart. Cleveland, no date
92. *Madness Of Love,* as Caroline Hart. Cleveland, no date
93. *Nameless Bess,* as Caroline Hart. Cleveland, no date
94. *Nobody's Wife,* as Caroline Hart. Cleveland, no date
95. *Redeemed by Love,* as Caroline Hart. Cleveland, no date
96. *Rival Heiresses,* as Caroline Hart. Cleveland, no date
97. *She Loved Not Wisely,* as Caroline Hart. Cleveland, no date
98. *Strange Marriage,* as Caroline Hart. Cleveland, no date
99. *That Awful Scar,* as Caroline Hart. Cleveland, no date
100. *Vengeance of Love,* as Caroline Hart. Cleveland, no date
101. *Women Who Came Between,* as Caroline Hart. Cleveland, no date
102. *Woman Wronged,* as Caroline Hart. Cleveland, no date
103. *Working Girl's Honor,* as Caroline Hart. Cleveland, no date
104. *Barriers Between.* London, 1910
105. *The Beauty of the Season.* London, 1910
106. *Better Than Life.* London, 1910
107. *Dulcie.* London, 1910
108. *The Earl's Daughter.* London, 1910
109. *A Girl from the South.* London, 1910
110. *The Heart of a Maid.* London, 1910
111. *Once in a Life.* London, 1910

112. *Only One Love.* London, 1910
113. *A Passion Flower.* London, 1910
114. *With All Her Heart.* London, 1910
115. *Floris.* London, 1910
116. *Signa's Sweetheart.* London, 1910
117. *Sweet as a Rose.* London, 1910
118. *A Farm in Creamland: A Book of the Devon Countryside.* London, 1911
119. *Leslie's Loyalty.* London, 1911
120. *Miss Estcourt.* London, 1911
121. *My Love Kitty.* London, 1911
122. *That Strange Girl.* London, 1911
123. *Voilet.* London, 1911
124. *Doris.* London, 1911
125. *Elaine.* London, 1911
126. *He Loves Me, He Loves Me Not.* London, 1911
127. *His Guardian Angel.* London, 1911
128. *Lord of Himself.* London, 1911
129. *The Other Girl.* London, 1911
130. *Sweet Cymbeline.* London, 1911
131. *A Wilful Maid.* London, 1911
132. *The Woman in It.* London, 1911
133. *Wounded Heart.* New York, 1911
134. *Breta's Double.* New York, no date
135. *His Perfect Trust.* Philadelphia, no date
136. *Imogene.* New York, no date
136. *Love of a Life Time.* Philadelphia, no date
137. *Lucille.* Chicago, no date
138. *Out of the Past.* New York, no date
139. *Price of Honor.* Philadelphia, no date
140. *Pride of Her Life.* New York, no date
141. *Royal Signet.* Philadelphia, no date
142. *The Spider and the Fly.* New York, no date
143. *Sydney.* New York, no date
144. *'Twixt Smile and Tear.* New York, no date
145. *Wasted Love.* New York, no date
146. *Love in a Snare.* London, 1912
147. *The Girl Without a Heart and Other Stories.* London, 1912
148. *A Relenting Fate and Other Stories.* London, 1912
149. *Fate.* London, 1912
150. *Fickle Fortune.* London, 1912
151. *In Fine Feathers.* London, 1912
152. *Stella's Fortune.* London, 1912
153. *Two Maids and a Man.* London, 1912
154. *The Verdict of the Heart.* London, 1912
155. *Country Love.* London, 1912
156. *Reuben.* London, 1912
157. *Nellie.* London, 1913
158. *All Is Not Fair in Love and Other Stories.* London, 1913
159. *The Tessacott Tragedy and Other Stories.* London, 1913
160. *The Loom of Fate.* London, 1913
161. *The Woman's Way.* London, 1914
162. *Iris.* London, 1914
163. *The Call of the Heart.* London, 1914
164. *In Exchange for Love.* London, 1914
165. *The One Girl in the World.* London, 1915
166. *Love, The Adventurous.* London, 1917
167. *Creatures of Destiny.* New York, no date
168. *Heart for Heart.* New York, no date
169. *Love and a Lie.* New York, no date
170. *Shadow of Her Life.* New York, no date
171. *'Twas Love's Fault.* New York, no date
172. *When Love Is Young.* New York, no date
173. *The Waster.* London, 1918
174. *The Girl in Love.* London, 1919
175. *The Girl in the 'bacca Shop.* London, 1920
176. *Miss Smith's Fortune and Other Stories.* London, 1920
177. *Wicked Sir Dare.* London, 1938

Gaskin, Catherine
Irish, born in 1929
1. *This Other Eden.* London, 1947
2. *With Every Year.* London, 1949
3. *Dust in the Sunlight.* London, 1950
4. *All Else Is Folly.* London and New York, 1950
5. *Daughter of the House.* London, 1952
6. *Sara Dane.* London, 1954
7. *Blake's Reach.* London and Philadelphia, 1958
8. *Corporation Wife.* London and New York, 1960
9. *I Know My Love.* London and New York, 1962
10. *The Tilsit Inheritance.* London and New York, 1963
11. *The File on Devlin.* London and New York, 1965
12. *Edge of Glass.* London and New York, 1967
13. *Fiona.* London and New York, 1970
14. *A Falcon for a Queen.* London and New York, 1970
15. *The Property of a Gentleman.* London and New York, 1972
16. *The Lynmara Legacy.* London, 1975
17. *The Summer of the Spanish Woman.* London and New York, 1977
18. *Family Affairs.* London and New York, 1980
19. *Promises.* London, 1982

Gavin, Catherine
British, born in 1907
1. *Louis Philippe, King of the French.* London, 1933
2. *Clyde Valley.* London, 1938
3. *The Hostile Shore.* London, 1940
4. *The Black Milestone.* London, 1941
5. *Britain and France: A Study of Twentieth Century Relations. The Entente Cordiale.* London, 1941
6. *Edward the Seventh: A Biography.* London, 1941
7. *The Mountain of Light.* London, 1944
8. *Liberated France.* London and New York, 1955
9. *Madeleine.* New York, 1957
10. *The Cactus and the Crown.* London and New York, 1962
11. *The Fortress.* London and New York, 1964
12. *The Moon into Blood.* London, 1966
13. *The Devil in Harbour.* London and New York, 1968
14. *The House of War.* London and New York, 1970
15. *Give Me the Daggers.* London and New York, 1972
16. *The Snow Mountain.* London, 1973
17. *Traitors' Gate.* London and New York, 1976
18. *None Dare Call It Treason.* London and New York, 1978
19. *How Sleep the Brave.* London and New York, 1980

Gellis, Roberta (Leah)
American, born in 1927
Pseudonyms: Max Daniels, Priscilla Hamilton, Leah Jacobs
1. *Knight's Honor.* New York, 1964
2. *Bond of Blood.* New York, 1965
3. *The Psychiatrist's Wife*, as Leah Jacobs. New York, 1966
4. *Sing Witch, Sing Death.* New York, 1975
5. *The Sword and the Swan.* Chicago, 1977
6. *Roselynde.* Chicago, 1978
7. *Alinor.* Chicago, 1978
8. *Joanna.* Chicago, 1978
9. *Space Guardian*, as Max Daniels. New York, 1978
10. *Gilliane.* Chicago and Feltham (Eng), 1979
11. *Offworld!* as Max Daniels. New York, 1979
12. *Love Token*, as Priscilla Hamilton. Chicago, 1979
13. *The English Heiress.* New York, 1980
14. *The Cornish Heiress.* New York, 1981
15. *Siren Song.* Chicago, 1981
16. *Rhiannon.* Chicago, 1982

Gibbs, Henry [Henry St. John Clair Rumbold-Gibbs]
British, born in 1910

Pseudonym: Simon Harvester
1. *Let Them Prey*, as Simon Harvester. London, 1942
2. *Epitaphs for Lemmings*, as Simon Harvester. London, 1943
3. *At a Farthing's Rate*. London, 1943
4. *Not to the Swift*. London, 1944
5. *From All Blindness*. London, 1944
6. *Maybe a Trumpet*, as Simon Harvester. London, 1945
7. *A Lantern for Diogenes*, as Simon Harvester. London, 1946
8. *Blue Days and Fair*. London, 1946
9. *Whatsoever Things Are True*, as Simon Harvester. London, 1947
10. *Know Then Thyself*. London, 1947
11. *Affectionately Yours, Fanny: Fanny Kemble and the Theatre*. London, 1947
12. *The Sequins Lost Their Lustre*, as Simon Harvester. London, 1948
13. *Children's Overture: A Study of Juvenile Delinquency in London Slums*. London, 1948
14. *Pawns in Ice*. London, 1948
15. *Man About Town*, as Simon Harvester. London, 1948
16. *A Breastplate for Aaron*, as Simon Harvester. London, 1949
17. *Good Men and True*, as Simon Harvester. London, 1949
18. *Ten-Thirty Sharp*. London, 1949
19. *Theatre Tapestry*. London, 1949
20. *Sheep May Safely Graze*, as Simon Harvester. London, 1950
21. *Withered Garland*. London, 1950
22. *Twilight in South Africa*. London and New York, 1950
23. *Obols for Charon*, as Simon Harvester. London, 1951
24. *The Vessel May Carry Explosives*, as Simon Harvester. London, 1951
25. *Witch Hunt*, as Simon Harvester. London, 1951
26. *Taps, Colonel Roberts*. London, 1951
27. *Cat's Cradle*, as Simon Harvester. London, 1952
28. *Traitor's Gate*, as Simon Harvester. London, 1952
29. *Cream and Cider*. London, 1952
30. *The Six-Mile Face*. London, 1952
31. *Disputed Barricade*. London, 1952
32. *Crescent in Shadow*. London, 1952
33. *Lucifer at Sunset*, as Simon Harvester. London, 1953
34. *Spider's Web*, as Simon Harvester. London, 1953
35. *Arrival in Suspicion*, as Simon Harvester. London, 1953
36. *Italy on Borrowed Time*. London, 1953
37. *Delay in Danger*, as Simon Harvester. London, 1954
38. *Cape of Shadows*. London, 1954
39. *Background to Bitterness: The Story of South Africa 1652-1954*. London and New York, 1954
40. *Africa on a Tightrope*. London, 1954
41. *The Bamboo Screen*, as Simon Harvester. London, 1955
42. *Tiger in the North*, as Simon Harvester. London, 1955
43. *The Splendour and the Dust*. London, 1955
44. *The Masks of Spain*. London, 1955
45. *Dragon Road*, as Simon Harvester. London, 1956
46. *The Paradise Men*, as Simon Harvester. London, 1956
47. *The Winds of Time*. London, 1956
48. *The Copper Butterfly*, as Simon Harvester. London, 1957
49. *The Golden Fear*, as Simon Harvester. London, 1957
50. *Thunder at Dawn*. London, 1957
51. *The Yesterday Walkers*, as Simon Harvester. London, 1958
52. *The Tumult and the Shouting*. London, 1958
53. *An Hour Before Zero*, as Simon Harvester. London, 1959
54. *Unsung Road*, as Simon Harvester. London, 1960
55. *The Chinese Hammer*, as Simon Harvester. London, 1960
56. *The Moonstone Jungle*, as Simon Harvester. London, 1961
57. *The Bamboo Prison*. London, 1961
58. *The Hills of India*. London, 1961
59. *Silk Road*, as Simon Harvester. London, 1962
60. *Troika*, as Simon Harvester. London, 1962
61. *Red Road*, as Simon Harvester. London, 1963
62. *The Mortal Fire*. London, 1963
63. *The Crimson Gate*. New York, 1963
64. *The Flying Horse*, as Simon Harvester. New York, 1964
65. *Flight in Darkness*, as Simon Harvester. London, 1964
66. *Assassins Road*, as Simon Harvester. London and New York, 1965
67. *Shadows in a Hidden Land*, as Simon Harvester. London and New York, 1966
68. *Treacherous Road*, as Simon Harvester. London, 1966
69. *Battle Road*, as Simon Harvester. London and New York, 1967
70. *Zion Road*, as Simon Harvester. London and New York, 1968
71. *Nameless Road*, as Simon Harvester. London, 1969
72. *Moscow Road*, as Simon Harvester. London, 1970
73. *Sahara Road*, as Simon Harvester. London and New York, 1972
74. *A Corner of the Playground*, as Simon Harvester. London, 1973
75. *Forgotten Road*, as Simon Harvester. London and New York, 1974
76. *Siberian Road*, as Simon Harvester. London and New York, 1976

Gibbs, Mary Ann [Marjory Elizabeth Sarah Bidwell]
British
Other pseudonym: Elizabeth Ford
1. *Fog*, as Elizabeth Ford. London, 1933
2. *The House with the Myrtle Trees*, as Elizabeth Ford. London, 1942
3. *The Blue Cockade: A Romantic Novel of 1780*, as Elizabeth Ford. London, 1943
4. *Queen's Harbour*, as Elizabeth Ford. London, 1944
5. *The Young Ladies Room*, as Elizabeth Ford. London, 1945
6. *The Irresponsibles*, as Elizabeth Ford. London, 1946
7. *Mountford Show*, as Elizabeth Ford. London, 1948
8. *Spring Comes to the Crescent*, as Elizabeth Ford. London, 1949
9. *So Deep Suspicion*, as Elizabeth Ford. London, 1950
10. *A Young Man with Ideas*. London, 1950
11. *Four Days in June*, as Elizabeth Ford. London, 1951
12. *Just Around the Corner*, as Elizabeth Ford. London, 1952
13. *Enchantment: A Pastoral*. London, 1952
14. *A Bit of a Bounder: An Edwardian Trifle*. London, 1952
15. *One Fine Day*, as Elizabeth Ford. London, 1954
16. *English Rose*, as Elizabeth Ford. London, 1953
17. *Meeting in the Spring*, as Elizabeth Ford. London, 1954
18. *Outrageous Fortune*, as Elizabeth Ford. London, 1955
19. *That Summer at Bacclesea*, as Elizabeth Ford. London, 1956
20. *The Empty Heart*, as Elizabeth Ford. London, 1957
21. *The Cottage at Drimble*, as Elizabeth Ford. London, 1957
22. *Butter Market House*, as Elizabeth Ford. London, 1958
23. *The Guardian*. London, 1958
24. *Young Lady with Red Hair*. London, 1959
25. *The Years of the Nannies*. London, 1960
26. *Heron's Nest*, as Elizabeth Ford. London, 1960
27. *Horatia*. London, 1961
28. *The Apothecary's Daughter*. London, 1962
29. *A Week by the Sea*, as Elizabeth Ford. London, 1962
30. *A Holiday Engagement: A Maplechester Novel*, as Elizabeth Ford. London, 1963
31. *Polly Kettle*. London, 1963
32. *No Room for Joanna: A Maplechester Novel*, as Elizabeth Ford. London, 1964
33. *The Amateur Governess*. London, 1964
34. *The House of Ravensbourne*. London, 1965
35. *The Sugar Mouse*. London, 1965
36. *A Country Holiday*, as Elizabeth Ford. London, 1966

37. *Dangerous Holiday*, as Elizabeth Ford. New York, 1967
38. *The Turbulent Messiters*, as Elizabeth Ford. London, 1967
39. *The Romantic Frenchman*. London, 1967
40. *The Sea Urchins*. London, 1968
41. *A Parcel of Land*. London, 1969
42. *A Lady in Berkshire*. London, 1970
43. *Limelight for Jane*, as Elizabeth Ford. London, 1970
44. *The Day of the Storm*, as Elizabeth Ford. London, 1971
45. *The Year of the Pageant*. London, 1971
46. *The Moon in a Bucket*. London, 1972
47. *The Green Beetle*, as Elizabeth Ford. London, 1972
48. *The Belvedere*, as Elizabeth Ford. London, 1973
49. *The Glass Palace*. London, 1973
50. *Young Ann*, as Elizabeth Ford. London, 1973
51. *A Wife for the Admiral*. London, 1974
52. *The Admiral's Lady*. New York, 1975
53. *The Nursery Maid*. London, 1975
54. *The Penniless Heiress*. London, 1975
55. *The Charming Couple*, as Elizabeth Ford. London, 1975
56. *The Amber Cat*, as Elizabeth Ford. London, 1976
57. *A Most Romantic City*. London and New York, 1976
58. *The Tempestuous Petticoat*. London, 1977
59. *Open Day at the Manor*, as Elizabeth Ford. London, 1977
60. *A Young Lady of Fashion*. London, 1978
61. *The Tulip Tree*. London and New York, 1979
62. *Dinah*. London and New York, 1981
63. *The Milliner's Shop*. London, 1981
64. *Renegade Girl*. New York, 1981
65. *The Marquess*. London, 1982

Gilbert, Anna [Marguerite Lazarus]
British, born in 1916
1. *Images of Rose*. London and New York, 1974
2. *The Look of Innocence*. London and New York, 1975
3. *A Family Likeness*. London, 1977
4. *Remembering Louise*. London and New York, 1978
5. *The Leavetaking*. London, 1979
6. *Flowers for Lilian*. London, 1980
7. *Miss Bede Is Staying*. London, 1982

Giles, Janice Holt
American, died in 1979
1. *The Enduring Hills*. Philadelphia, 1950
2. *Miss Willie*. Philadelphia, 1951
3. *Tara's Healing*. Philadelphia, 1951
4. *Harbin's Ridge*, with Henry Giles. Boston, 1951
5. *40 Acres and No Mule*. Philadelphia, 1952
6. *The Kentuckians*. Boston, 1953
7. *The Plum Thicket*. Boston, 1954
8. *Hannah Fowler*. Boston, 1956
9. *The Believers*. Boston, 1957
10. *The Land Beyond the Mountains*. Boston, 1958
11. *Johnny Osage*. Boston, 1960
12. *Savanna*. Boston, 1961
13. *Voyage to Santa Fe*. Boston, 1962
14. *A Little Better than Plumb: The Biography of a House*, with Henry Giles. Boston, 1963
15. *Find Me a River*. Boston, 1964
16. *Time of Glory*. Boston, 1966
17. *Special Breed*. Boston, 1966
18. *The Great Adventure*. Boston, 1966
19. *Shady Grove*. Boston, 1968
20. *Six-Horse Hitch*. Boston, 1969
21. *The Damned Engineers*. Boston, 1970
22. *Around Our House*, with Henry Giles. Boston, 1971
23. *The Kinta Years*. Boston, 1973
24. *Wellspring*. Boston, 1975

Glasscock, Anne
American, born February 19, 1924
Pseudonym: Michael Bonner
1. *Kennedy's Gold*, as Michael Bonner. New York, 1960
2. *The Iron Noose*, as Michael Bonner. New York and London, 1961
3. *Shadow of a Hawk*, as Michael Bonner. New York, 1963
4. *The Disturbing Death of Jenkin Delaney*, as Michael Bonner. New York, 1966

Gluyas, Constance
British, born in 1920
1. *The King's Brat*. Englewood Cliffs (NJ), 1972
2. *Born to Be King*. Englewood Cliffs, 1974
3. *My Lady Benbrook*. Englewood Cliffs, 1975
4. *Brief Is the Glory*. New York, 1975
5. *The House on Twyford Street*. New York, 1976
6. *My Lord Foxe*. New York, 1976
7. *Savage Eden*. New York, 1976
8. *Rogue's Mistress*. New York, 1977
9. *Woman of Fury*. New York, 1978
10. *Flame of the South*. New York, 1979
11. *Madame Tudor*. New York, 1979
12. *Lord Sin*. New York, 1980
13. *The Passionate Savage*. New York, 1980
14. *The Bridge to Yesterday*. New York, 1981

Glyn, Elinor
British, born in 1864, died September 23, 1943
1. *The Visits of Elizabeth*. London, 1900
2. *The Reflections of Ambrosine*. London and New York, 1902
3. *The Damsel and the Sage*. London and New York, 1903
4. *The Vicissitudes of Evangeline*. London and New York, 1905
5. *Beyond the Rocks*. London and New York, 1906
6. *Three Weeks*. London and New York, 1907
7. *The Sayings of Grandmama and Others*. London and New York, 1908
8. *Elizabeth Visits America*. London and New York, 1909
9. *His Hour*. London and New York, 1910
10. *The Reason Why*. London and New York, 1911
11. *Halcyone*. London and New York, 1912
12. *The Contract and Other Stories*. London, 1913
13. *The Sequence 1905-1912*. London, 1913
14. *Letters to Caroline*. London, 1914
15. *The Man and the Moment*. New York, 1914
16. *Three Things*. London and New York, 1915
17. *The Career of Katherine Bush*. New York, 1916
18. *Destruction*. London, 1918
19. *The Price of Things*. London, 1919
20. *Points of View*. London, 1920
21. *The Philosophy of Love*. London, 1920
22. *Man and Maid-Renaissance*. London, 1922
23. *The Elinor Glyn System of Writing*. New York, 1922
24. *The Great Moment*. London and Philadelphia, 1923
25. *The Philosophy of Love*. New York, 1923
26. *Letters from Spain*. London, 1924
27. *Six Days*. London and Philadelphia, 1924
28. *This Passion Called Love*. London and New York, 1925
29. *Love's Blindness*. London and New York, 1926
30. *It and Other Stories*. London and New York, 1927
31. *The Wrinkle Book; or, How to Keep Looking Young*. London, 1927
32. *The Flirt and the Flapper*. London, 1930
33. *Love's Hour*. London and New York, 1932
34. *Glorious Flames*. London, 1932
35. *Saint or Satyr? and Other Stories*. London, 1933
36. *Sooner or Later*. London, 1933
37. *Did She?* London, 1934

38. *Romantic Adventure*. London, 1936
39. *The Third Eye*. London, 1940
40. *Keep Young and Beautiful*, with Barbara Cartland. London, 1982

Godden, Rumer [Margaret Rumer Godden]
British, born in 1907
1. *Chinese Puzzle*. London, 1936
2. *The Lady and the Unicorn*. London, 1937
3. *Black Narcissus*. London and Boston, 1939
4. *Gypsy, Gypsy*. London and Boston, 1940
5. *Breakfast with the Nikolides*. London and Boston, 1942
6. *Rungli-Rungliot (Thus Far and No Further)*. London, 1943
7. *Bengal Journey: A Story of the Part Played by Women in the Province 1939-1945*. London, 1945
8. *Takes Three Tenses: A Fugue in Time*. Boston, 1945
9. *A Fugue in Time*. London, 1945
10. *The River*. London and Boston, 1946
11. *Rungliot Means in Paharia, Thus Far and No Further*. Boston, 1946
12. *The Doll's House*. London, 1947
13. *A Candle for St. Jude*. London and New York, 1948
14. *In Noah's Ark*. London and New York, 1949
15. *The Mousewife*. London and New York, 1951
16. *Kingfishers Catch Fire*. London and New York, 1953
17. *Impunity Jane: The Story of a Pocket Doll*. New York, 1954
18. *An Episode of Sparrows*. New York, 1955
19. *Hans Christian Andersen: A Great Life in Brief*. London and New York, 1955
20. *The Fairy Doll*. London and New York, 1956
21. *Mooltiki and Other Stories and Poems of India*. London and New York, 1957
22. *Mouse House*. New York, 1957
23. *The Greengage Summer*. London and New York, 1958
24. *The Story of Holly and Ivy*. London and New York, 1958
25. *Candy Floss*. London and New York, 1960
26. *China Court: The Hours of a Country House*. London and New York, 1961
27. *Miss Happiness and Miss Flower*. London and New York, 1961
28. *Thus Far and No Further*. London, 1961
29. *St. Jerome and the Lion*. London and New York, 1961
30. *The Battle of the Villa Fiorita*. London and New York, 1963
31. *Little Plum*. London and New York, 1963
32. *Home Is the Sailor*. London and New York, 1964
33. *Two under the Indian Sun*, with Jon Godden. London and New York, 1966
34. *Gone: A Thread of Stories*. New York, 1968
35. *Swans and Turtles: Stories*. London, 1968
36. *In This House of Brede*. London and New York, 1969
37. *The Kitchen Madonna*. London and New York, 1969
38. *Operation Sippacik*. London and New York, 1969
39. *The Tale of the Tales: The Beatrix Potter Ballet*. London, 1971
40. *Shiva's Pigeons: An Experience of India*, with Jon Godden. London and New York, 1972
41. *The Old Woman Who Lived in a Vinegar Bottle*. London and New York, 1972
42. *The Diddakoi*. London and New York, 1972
43. *Mr. McFadden's Hallowe'en*. London and New York, 1975
44. *The Peacock Spring*. London, 1975
45. *The Rocking Horse Secret*. London, 1977
46. *The Butterfly Lions: The Story of the Pekingese in History, Legend and Art*. London, 1977
47. *A Kindle of Kittens*. London, 1978
48. *Five for Sorrow, Ten for Joy*. London and New York, 1979
49. *Gulbadan: Portrait of a Rose Princess at the Mughal Court*. London, 1980
50. *The Dark Horse*. London, 1981
51. *The Dragon of Og*. London and New York, 1981

Gordon, Ethel Edison
American, born in 1915
1. *Where Does the Summer Go?* New York, 1967
2. *So Far from Home*. New York, 1968
3. *Freer's Cove*. New York, 1972
4. *The Chaperone*. New York, 1973
5. *The Birdwatcher*. New York, 1974
6. *The Freebody Heiress*. New York and London, 1974
7. *The French Husband*. New York, 1977
8. *The Venetian Lover*. New York, 1982

Goudge, Elizabeth
British, born in 1900
1. *The Fairies' Baby and Other Stories*. London, 1919
2. *Island Magic*. London and New York, 1934
3. *The Middle Window*. London, 1935
4. *A City of Bells*. London and New York, 1936
5. *A Pedlar's Pack and Other Stories*. London and New York, 1937
6. *Towers in the Mist*. London and New York, 1938
7. *Sister of the Angels: A Christmas Story*. London and New York, 1939
8. *The Bird in the Tree*. London and New York, 1940
9. *Smoky-House*. London and New York, 1940
10. *The Castle on the Hill*. London and New York, 1941
11. *The Golden Skylark and Other Stories*. London and New York, 1941
12. *The Well of the Star*. New York, 1941
13. *Henrietta's House*. London, 1942
14. *The Blue Hills*. New York, 1942
15. *The Ikon on the Wall and Other Stories*. London, 1943
16. *Green Dolphin Country*. London, 1944
17. *Green Dolphin*. New York, 1944
18. *The Elizabeth Goudge Reader*. New York, 1946
19. *The Little White Horse*. London, 1946
20. *Songs and Verses*. London, 1947
21. *At the Sign of the Dolphin: An Elizabeth Goudge Anthology*. London, 1947
22. *The Herb of Grace*. London, 1948
23. *Pilgrim's Inn*. New York, 1948
24. *Gentian Hill*. London and New York, 1949
25. *Make-Believe*. London, 1949
26. *The Reward of Faith and Other Stories*. London, 1950
27. *God So Loved the World: A Life of Christ*. London and New York, 1951
28. *The Valley of Song*. London, 1951
29. *White Wings: Collected Short Stories*. London, 1952
30. *The Heart of the Family*. London and New York, 1953
31. *The Rosemary Tree*. London and New York, 1956
32. *The White Witch*. London and New York, 1958
33. *My God and My All: The Life of St. Francis Assisi*. New York, 1959
34. *Saint Francis of Assisi*. London, 1959
35. *The Dean's Watch*. London and New York, 1960
36. *The Scent of Water*. London and New York, 1963
37. *Linnets and Valerians*. Leicester (Eng) and New York, 1964
38. *The Chapel of the Blessed Virgin Mary, Buckler's Hard, Beaulieu*. Privately printed, 1966
39. *A Christmas Book*. London and New York, 1967
40. *I Saw Three Ships*. Leicester and New York, 1969
41. *The Ten Gifts*, edited by Mary Baldwin. London and New York, 1969
42. *The Child from the Sea*. London and New York, 1970

Goudge, Elizabeth

43. *The Lost Angel.* London and New York, 1971
44. *The Joy of the Snow: An Autobiography.* London and New York, 1974
45. *Pattern of People: An Elizabeth Goudge Anthology.* London, 1979

Greig, Maysie [Jennifer Greig-Smith]

Australian, born in 1902

Other pseudonyms: Jennifer Ames, Ann Barclay, Mary Douglas Warre, Mary Douglas Warren

1. *Peggy of Beacon Hill.* Boston, 1924
2. *The Luxury Husband.* London and New York, 1928
3. *Ragamuffin.* London, 1929
4. *Satin Straps.* London and New York, 1929
5. *Jasmine—Take Care! or, A Girl Must Marry.* London, 1930
6. *Lovely Clay.* London, 1930
7. *A Nice Girl Comes to Town.* London and New York, 1930
8. *The Man She Bought.* New York, 1930
9. *This Way to Happiness.* London, 1931
10. *One-Man Girl.* London and New York, 1931
11. *The Women Money Buys.* New York, 1931
12. *A Girl Must Marry.* New York, 1931
13. *Faint Heart, Fair Lady.* London, 1932
14. *Laughing Cavalier.* London, 1932
15. *Little Sisters Don't Count.* London, 1932
16. *Cake Without Icing.* London and New York, 1932
17. *Pandora Lifts the Veil,* as Jennifer Ames. New York, 1932
18. *Professional Lover.* London and New York, 1933
19. *Parents Are a Problem.* London, 1933
20. *Love, Honour, and Obey.* New York, 1933
21. *A Bad Girl Leaves Town.* New York, 1933
22. *Anything But Love,* as Jennifer Ames. London, 1933
23. *Men Act That Way.* New York, 1933
24. *Cruise,* as Jennifer Ames. London, 1934
25. *Good Sport,* as Jennifer Ames. London, 1934
26. *Romance for Sale,* as Jennifer Ames. London, 1934
27. *Heart Appeal.* London, 1934
28. *She Walked into His Parlour.* London, 1934
29. *Good Sport,* as Maysie Greig. New York, 1934
30. *Romance for Sale,* as Maysie Greig. New York, 1934
31. *Ten Cent Love.* New York, 1934
32. *I Lost My Heart.* London, 1935
33. *I'll Get over It,* as Jennifer Ames. London, 1935
34. *Sweet Peril,* as Jennifer Ames. London, 1935
35. *Love and Let Me Go.* New York, 1935
36. *Marry in Haste.* London and New York, 1935
37. *Rich Man, Poor Girl.* London and New York, 1935
38. *Romance on a Cruise,* as Maysie Greig. New York, 1935
39. *Sweet Danger,* as Maysie Greig. New York, 1935
40. *I'll Get Over It,* as Maysie Greig. New York, 1936
41. *Other Men's Arms,* as Ann Barclay. London, 1936
42. *Swing High, Swing Low,* as Ann Barclay. London, 1936
43. *Challenge to Happiness.* London, 1936
44. *I Seek My Love,* as Jennifer Ames. London, 1936
45. *Tinted Dream,* as Jennifer Ames. London, 1936
46. *The Girl from Nowhere.* Hanley (Eng), 1936
47. *Odds on Love.* London and New York, 1936
48. *Workaday Lady.* London and New York, 1936
49. *Touching the Clouds.* New York, 1936
50. *Men as Her Stepping Stones,* as Ann Barclay. London, 1937
51. *Her World of Men,* as Jennifer Ames. London, 1937
52. *New Moon Through a Window.* London and New York, 1937
53. *Retreat from Love.* London, 1937
54. *The Pretty One.* London, 1937
55. *Dreams Get You Nowhere,* as Maysie Greig. New York, 1937
56. *Retreat from Love,* as Jennifer Ames. New York, 1937
57. *Doctor's Wife,* as Maysie Greig. New York, 1937
58. *Honeymoons Arranged,* as Maysie Greig. New York, 1938
59. *Her World of Men,* as Maysie Greig. New York, 1938
60. *Elder Sister,* as Jennifer Ames. London, 1938
61. *The Girl Men Talked About.* London, 1938
62. *Young Man Without Money.* London, 1938
63. *Stepping under Ladders.* London, 1938
64. *Other Women's Beauty.* London, 1938
65. *Strange Beauty.* New York, 1938
66. *Stranger Sweetheart,* as Jennifer Ames. London, 1938
67. *Stopover in Paradise.* New York, 1938
68. *Debutante in Uniform.* New York, 1938
69. *Men as Her Stepping Stones,* as Maysie Greig. New York, 1938
70. *Not One of Us,* as Maysie Greig. New York, 1939
71. *Bury the Past,* as Maysie Greig. New York, 1939
72. *A Man to Protect You.* New York, 1939
73. *Bury the Past,* as Jennifer Ames. London, 1939
74. *Dangerous Holiday,* as Jennifer Ames. London, 1939
75. *Not One of Us,* as Jennifer Ames. London, 1939
76. *Ask the Parlourmaid.* London, 1939
77. *Girl on His Hands.* London and New York, 1939
78. *Make the Man Notice You,* as Jennifer Ames. London, 1940
79. *Unmarried Couple.* New York, 1940
80. *Dangerous Cruise,* as Maysie Greig. New York, 1940
81. *Make the Man Notice You,* as Maysie Greig. New York, 1940
82. *A Fortune in Romance.* New York, 1940
83. *Honeymoon Alone,* as Jennifer Ames. London, 1940
84. *Ring Without Romance,* as Jennifer Ames. London, 1940
85. *Grand Relations.* London, 1940
86. *The Man Is Always Right.* London and New York, 1940
87. *Rich Twin, Poor Twin.* London and New York, 1940
88. *Reunion in Reno,* as Mary Douglas Warren. New York, 1941
89. *Too Many Women,* as Maysie Greig. New York, 1941
90. *Ring Without Romance,* as Maysie Greig. New York, 1941
91. *Honeymoon Alone,* as Maysie Greig. New York, 1941
92. *Too Many Women,* as Jennifer Ames. London, 1941
93. *Girl Without Credit.* New York, 1941
94. *This Desirable Bachelor.* London and New York, 1941
95. *Heaven Isn't Here.* New York, 1941
96. *The Rich Are Not Proud,* as Mary Douglas Warren. New York, 1942
97. *Heartbreak for Two.* New York, 1942
98. *Diplomatic Honeymoon,* as Maysie Greig. New York, 1942
99. *Diplomatic Honeymoon,* as Jennifer Ames. London, 1942
100. *No Retreat from Love.* New York, 1942
101. *Salute Me, Darling.* London, 1942
102. *The Wishing Star.* New York, 1942
103. *Pathway to Paradise.* New York, 1942
104. *Dark Sunlight,* as Jennifer Ames. London, 1943
105. *The Impossible Marriage.* London, 1943
106. *Professional Hero.* London and New York, 1943
107. *I've Always Loved You.* New York, 1943
108. *The Wishing Star,* as Mary Douglas Warre. London, 1943
109. *Restless Beauty,* as Jennifer Ames. London, 1944
110. *At the Same Time Tomorrow,* as Jennifer Ames. London, 1944
111. *Reluctant Millionaire.* London, 1944
112. *One Room for His Highness.* London, 1944
113. *At the Same Time Tomorrow,* as Maysie Greig. New York, 1944
114. *I Married Mr. Richardson,* as Jennifer Ames. London, 1945
115. *Journey in the Dark,* as Jennifer Ames. London, 1945
116. *Girl with a Million.* London, 1945
117. *I Loved Her Yesterday.* London, 1945

118. *Lovers in the Dark*, as Jennifer Ames. London, 1946
119. *Take Your Choice, Lady*, as Jennifer Ames. London, 1946
120. *Darling Clementine*. London, 1946
121. *Table for Two*. London and New York, 1946
122. *Fear Kissed My Lips*, as Jennifer Ames. London, 1947
123. *Candidate for Love*. New York, 1947
124. *Janice*. New York, 1947
125. *Heart in Darkness*, as Jennifer Ames. New York, 1947
126. *Castle in the Air*. London, 1947
127. *The Thirteenth Girl*. Hanley, 1947
128. *Take This Man*. London, 1947
129. *Shadow Across My Heart*, as Jennifer Ames. London, 1948
130. *She'll Take the High Road*, as Jennifer Ames. London, 1948
131. *I Met Him Again*. London, 1948
132. *Yours Forever*. London and New York, 1948
133. *Danger Wakes My Heart*, as Jennifer Ames. London, 1949
134. *Lips for a Stranger*, as Jennifer Ames. London, 1949
135. *Whispers in the Sun*. London and New York, 1949
136. *Too Much Alone*, as Jennifer Ames. London, 1950
137. *Danger in Eden*, as Jennifer Ames. New York, 1950
138. *Dark Carnival*. New York, 1950
139. *Flight to Happiness*, as Jennifer Ames. New York, 1950
140. *Southern Star*, as Mary Douglas Warren. New York, 1950
141. *The Manor Farm*, as Mary Douglas Warrren. New York, 1951
142. *After Tomorrow*, as Jennifer Ames. New York, 1951
143. *My Heart's Down Under*. London, 1951
144. *Dark Carnival*, as Jennifer Ames. London, 1951
145. *My Heart's Down Under*, as Jennifer Ames. New York, 1951
146. *It Happened One Flight*. London, 1951
147. *London, Here I Come*. London, 1951
148. *The Sunny Island*, as Mary Douglas Warren. New York, 1952
149. *The Frightened Heart*, as Jennifer Ames. London, 1952
150. *Wagon to a Star*. London, 1952
151. *Date with Danger*, as Maysie Greig. New York, 1952
152. *The Reluctant Cinderella*, as Jennifer Ames. New York, 1952
153. *Shadow Across My Heart*, as Mary Douglas Warren. New York, 1952
154. *This Fearful Paradise*, as Maysie Greig. New York, 1953
155. *Assignment to Love*, as Jennifer Ames. New York, 1953
156. *Wagon to a Star*, as Jennifer Ames. New York, 1953
157. *Salt Harbor*, as Mary Douglas Warren. New York, 1953
158. *The Fearful Paradise*, as Jennifer Ames. London, 1953
159. *Love Is a Gamble*, as Jennifer Ames. New York, 1954
160. *The High Road*, as Mary Douglas Warren. New York, 1954
161. *Flight into Fear*, as Jennifer Ames. London and New York, 1954
162. *Lovers under the Sun*. London, 1954
163. *That Girl in Nice*. London, 1954
164. *Shadows Across the Sun*, as Jennifer Ames. London, 1955
165. *Passport to Happiness*. New York, 1955
166. *Cloak and Dagger Lover*. London, 1955
167. *Shadow Over the Island*, as Mary Douglas Warren. New York, 1955
168. *Winds of Fear*, as Maysie Greig. New York, 1956
169. *Moon Over the Water*, as Mary Douglas Warren. New York, 1956
170. *Rough Seas to Sunrise*, as Jennifer Ames. London, 1956
171. *Night of Carnival*, as Jennifer Ames. London, 1956
172. *Kiss in Sunlight*. London, 1956
173. *Love on Dark Wings*, as Jennifer Ames. London, 1957
174. *Follow Your Dream*, as Jennifer Ames. New York, 1957
175. *Girl Without Money*. London, 1957
176. *No Dowry for Jennifer*. New York, 1957
177. *Beloved Knight*, as Jennifer Ames. London, 1958
178. *Love Is a Gambler*. London, 1958
179. *Doctor's Nurse*, as Jennifer Ames. London, 1959
180. *Love Is a Thief*. London, 1959
181. *Send for Miss Marshall*. London, 1959
182. *Follow Your Love*. New York, 1959
183. *Doctor in Exile*. London, 1960
184. *Catch Up to Love*. New York, 1960
185. *Kiss of Promise*. New York, 1960
186. *Love in a Far Country*, as Jennifer Ames. London, 1960
187. *Love in the East*, as Jennifer Ames. London, 1960
188. *Perilous Quest*, as Jennifer Ames. New York, 1960
189. *Overseas Nurse*, as Jennifer Ames. New York, 1961
190. *Her Heart's Desire*, as Jennifer Ames. New York, 1961
191. *Diana Goes to Tokyo*, as Jennifer Ames. London, 1961
192. *It Started in Hongkong*, as Jennifer Ames. London, 1961
193. *Cherry Blossom Love*. London, 1961
194. *Every Woman's Man*. London, 1961
195. *The Doctor Is a Lady*. London, 1962
196. *The Timid Cleopatra*, as Jennifer Ames. London, 1962
197. *Honeymoon in Manila*, as Jennifer Ames. London, 1962
198. *The Doctor Decides*, as Mary Douglas Warren. London, 1963
199. *Geisha in the House*, as Jennifer Ames. London, 1963
200. *Sinners in Paradise*, as Jennifer Ames. London, 1963
201. *Nurse at St. Catherine's*. London, 1963
202. *French Girl in Love*. London, 1963
203. *Every Woman's Doctor*. London, 1964
204. *Married Quarters*. London, 1964
205. *Nurse in Danger*. London, 1964
206. *The Two of Us*, as Jennifer Ames. London, 1964
207. *Happy Island*, as Jennifer Ames. London, 1964
208. *Nurse's Holiday*, as Jennifer Ames. London, 1965
209. *Nurse's Story*, as Jennifer Ames. London, 1965
210. *The Doctor and the Dancer*. London, 1965
211. *Ship's Doctor*. New York, 1966
212. *Doctor Brad's Nurse*, as Jennifer Ames. New York, 1966
213. *Doctor on Wings*. London, 1966
214. *Doctor Ted's Clinic*, as Jennifer Ames. London, 1967
215. *Girl in Jeopardy*. London, 1967
216. *The Sinister Island*, as Jennifer Ames. London, 1968
217. *The Golden Garden*. London, 1968
218. *Jilted*, as Jennifer Ames. London, 1968
219. *Screen Lover*. London, 1969
220. *The Girl Who Wasn't Welcome*. London, 1969
221. *Love Will Win*. London, 1969
222. *The Doctor Takes a Holiday*, as Jennifer Ames. London, 1969
223. *Never the Same*. London, 1970
224. *A Girl and Her Money*. London, 1971
225. *Love Me*. London, 1971
226. *Honeymoon for One*, as Jennifer Ames. New York, 1971
227. *Marriage Without a Ring*. London, 1972
228. *Write from the Heart*, as Jennifer Ames. London, 1972

Grimstead, Hettie
British
Pseudonym: Marsha Manning
1. *Painted Virgin*. London, 1931
2. *The Journey Home*. London, 1950
3. *Navy Blue Lady*. London, 1951
4. *The Twisted Road*. London, 1951
5. *The Captured Heart*. London, 1952
6. *Strangers May Kiss*. London, 1952
7. *The Passionate Summer*. London, 1953
8. *Song of Surrender*. London, 1953
9. *Candles for Love*. London, 1954
10. *Winds of Desire*. London, 1954
11. *Enchanted August*. London, 1955
12. *The Tender Pilgrim*. London, 1955

13. *The Burning Flame*. London, 1956
14. *Escape to Paradise*. London, 1956
15. *The Reluctant Bride*. London, 1957
16. *Scales of Love*. London, 1957
17. *The Unknown Heart*. London, 1958
18. *Tinsel Kisses*. London, 1958
19. *Kisses for Three*, as Marsha Manning. London, 1958
20. *Passport to Love*, as Marsha Manning. London, 1958
21. *The Heart Alone*, as Marsha Manning. London, 1959
22. *Skyscraper Hotel*, as Marsha Manning. London, 1959
23. *Dream Street*. London, 1959
24. *A Kiss in the Sun*. London, 1959
25. *Because You're Mine*, as Marsha Manning. London, 1960
26. *The Path to Love*. London, 1960
27. *Sweet Prisoner*. London, 1961
28. *Magic of the Moon*, as Marsha Manning. London, 1961
29. *Star of Desire*, as Marsha Manning. London, 1961
30. *Circle of Dreams*, as Marsha Manning. London, 1962
31. *Roses for the Bride*, as Marsha Manning. London, 1962
32. *The Golden Moment*. London, 1962
33. *Love Has Two Faces*. London, 1962
34. *Wedding for Three*. London, 1963
35. *Whisper to the Stars*. London, 1963
36. *Flower of the Heart*, as Marsha Manning. London, 1963
37. *Lucy in London*, as Marsha Manning. London, 1964
38. *Our Miss Penny*, as Marsha Manning. London, 1964
39. *When April Sings*. London, 1964
40. *The Door of the Heart*. London, 1965
41. *Once upon a Kiss*. London, 1965
42. *Sister Marion's Summer*, as Marsha Manning. London, 1965
43. *Lover, Come Lonely*, as Marsha Manning. London, 1965
44. *Full Summer's Kiss*, as Marsha Manning. London, 1966
45. *The Proud Lover*, as Marsha Manning. London, 1966
46. *Shake Down the Moon*. London, 1966
47. *The Sweetheart Tree*. London, 1966
48. *Four of Hearts*, as Marsha Manning. London and New York, 1967
49. *Dreams in the Sun*, as Marsha Manning. London, 1967
50. *Orchids for the Bride*. London, 1967
51. *The Tender Chord*. London, 1967
52. *Friend of the Bride*, as Marsha Manning. London, 1968
53. *Some Day, My Love*, as Marsha Manning. London, 1968
54. *Chase a Rainbow*. London, 1968
55. *Portrait of Paula*. London, 1968
56. *Yesterday's Lover*, as Marsha Manning. London, 1969
57. *Holiday Affair*, as Marsha Manning. London, 1969
58. *September's Girl*. London, 1969
59. *The Lovely Day*. London, 1970
60. *Roses for Breakfast*. London, 1970
61. *To Catch a Dream*, as Marsha Manning. London, 1970
62. *Summer Song*, as Marsha Manning. London, 1971
63. *Island Affair*. London, 1971
64. *Sweet Friday*, as Marsha Manning. London, 1972
65. *The Smiling Moon*, as Marsha Manning. London, 1972
66. *The Winter Rose*. London, 1972
67. *The Magic City*, as Marsha Manning. London, 1973
68. *Fires of Spring*. London, 1973
69. *Tuesday's Child*. London, 1973
70. *The Tender Vine*. London, 1974
71. *Dance of Summer*, as Marsha Manning. London, 1974
72. *Wedding of the Year*, as Marsha Manning. London, 1974
73. *Chance Encounter*, as Marsha Manning. London, 1975
74. *Sister Rose's Holiday*. London, 1975
75. *Day of Roses*, as Marsha Manning. London, 1976
76. *The Passionate Rivals*, as Marsha Manning. London, 1978

Grundy, Mabel Barnes [Mabel Sarah Barnes Grundy]
British

1. *A Thames Camp*. Bristol (Eng), 1902
2. *The Vacillations of Hazel*. Bristol, 1905
3. *Marguerite's Wonderful Year*. Bristol, 1906
4. *Hazel of Heatherland*. New York, 1906
5. *Dimbie and I—and Amelia*. New York, 1907
6. *Hilary on Her Own*. New York and London, 1908
7. *Gwenda*. New York, 1910
8. *The Third Miss Wenderby*. New York and London, 1911
9. *Patricia Plays a Part*. London, 1913
10. *Candytuft—I Mean Veronica*. London, 1914
11. *An Undressed Heroine*. London, 1916
12. *Her Mad Month*. London, 1917
13. *A Girl for Sale*. London, 1920
14. *The Great Husband Hunt*. London, 1922
15. *The Mating of Marcus*. London, 1923
16. *Sleeping Dogs*. London, 1924
17. *Three People*. London, 1926
18. *The Strategy of Suzanne*. London, 1929
19. *Pippa*. London, 1932
20. *Sally in a Service Flat*. London, 1934
21. *Private Hotel—Anywhere*. London, 1937
22. *Paying Pests*. London, 1941
23. *Mary Ann and Jane*. London, 1944
24. *The Two Miss Speckles*. London, 1946

Haas, Ben [Benjamin Leopold Haas]
American, born July 21, 1926, died October 27, 1977
Pseudonyms: John Benteen, Thorne Douglas, Richard Meade

1. *The Foragers*. New York, 1962
2. *KKK: A Study of the Klu Klux Klan*. Evanston (IL), 1963
3. *Look Away, Look Away*. New York, 1964
4. *The Last Valley*. London and Toronto, 1966
5. *The Troubled Summer*. Indianapolis, 1966
6. *Summer Always Ends*, as Richard Meade. New York, 1966
7. *Beyond the Danube*, as Richard Meade. London, 1967
8. *Cimarron Strip*, as Richard Meade. New York, 1967
9. *Rough Night in Jericho*, as Richard Meade. New York, 1967
10. *Big Bend*, as Richard Meade. New York, 1968
11. *The Danube Runs Red*, as Richard Meade. New York, 1968
12. *The Gun Runner*, as Richard Meade. London, 1969
13. *A Score of Arms*, as Richard Meade. London, 1969
14. *The Last Fraulein*, as Richard Meade. New York, 1970
15. *Exile's Quest*, as Richard Meade. New York, 1970
16. *The Belle from Catscratch*, as Richard Meade, with Jay Rutledge. New York, 1972
17. *The Chandler Heritage*. London and Toronto, 1972
18. *Daisy Canfield*. London and Toronto, 1973
19. *Calhoon*, as Thorne Douglas. New York, 1973
20. *The Big Drive*, as Thorne Douglas. New York, 1973
21. *Cartridge Creek*, as Richard Meade. New York, 1973
22. *Gaylord's Badge*, as Richard Meade. New York, 1975
23. *Killraine*, as Thorne Douglas. New York, 1975
24. *Night Riders*, as Thorne Douglas. New York, 1975
25. *The Mustang Men*, as Thorne Douglas. New York, 1977
26. *The House of Christina*. London and Toronto, 1977

Haggard, H. Rider [Henry Rider Haggard]
British, born in 1856, died May 14, 1925

1. *Cetywayo and His White Neighbors; or, Remarks on Recent Events in Zululand, Natal, and the Transvaal*. London, 1882
2. *Dawn*. London, 1884
3. *The Witch's Head*. London, 1884
4. *King Solomon's Mines*. London and New York, 1885
5. *She: A History of Adventure*. New York, 1885
6. *Allan Quatermain*. London and New York, 1887
7. *Jess*. London and New York, 1887

8. *A Tale of Three Lions, and On Going Back.* New York, 1887
9. *Mr. Meeson's Will.* New York, 1888
10. *Maiwa's Revenge.* New York and London, 1888
11. *My Fellow Laborer.* New York, 1888
12. *Colonel Quaritch, V.C.* New York, 1888
13. *Allan's Wife and Other Tales.* London and New York, 1889
14. *Cleopatra.* London and New York, 1889
15. *Black Heart and White Heart, and other Stories.* London, 1900
16. *Beatrice.* London and New York, 1890
17. *The World's Desire,* with Andrew Lang. London and New York, 1890
18. *Eric Brighteyes.* London and New York, 1891
19. *Nada the Lily.* New York and London, 1892
20. *Montezuma's Daughter.* New York and London, 1892
21. *The People of the Mist.* London and New York, 1894
22. *Church and the State: An Appeal to the Laity.* Privately printed, 1895
23. *Heart of the World.* New York, 1895
24. *Joan Haste.* London and New York, 1895
25. *The Wizard.* Bristol and New York, 1895
26. *Doctor Therne.* London and New York, 1898
27. *A Farmer's Year, Being His Commonplace Book for 1898.* London and New York, 1899
28. *Swallow.* New York and London, 1899
29. *The Spring of a Lion.* New York, 1899
30. *The New South Africa.* London, 1900
31. *A Winter Pilgrimage: . . . Travels Through Palestine, Italy, and the Island of Cyprus.* London and New York, 1901
32. *Lysbeth.* New York and London, 1901
33. *Rural England.* London and New York, 1902
34. *Pearl-Maiden.* London and New York, 1903
35. *The Brethren.* London and New York, 1904
36. *Stella Fregelius: A Tale of Three Destinies.* London and New York, 1904
37. *A Gardener's Year.* London and New York, 1905
38. *Report on the Salvation Army Colonies.* London, 1905
39. *Ayesha: The Return of She.* London and New York, 1905
40. *Benita: An African Romance.* London, 1906
41. *The Way of the Spirit.* London, 1906
42. *Fair Margaret.* London, 1907
43. *The Lady of the Heavens.* New York, 1908
44. *The Yellow God.* New York, 1908
45. *The Lady of Blossholme.* London, 1909
46. *Regeneration, Being an Account of the Social Work of the Salvation Army in Great Britain.* London, 1910
47. *Morning Star.* London and New York, 1910
48. *Queen Sheba's Ring.* London and New York, 1910
49. *Rural Denmark and Its Lessons.* London and New York, 1911
50. *The Mahatma and the Hare: A Dream Story.* London and New York, 1911
51. *Red Eve.* London and New York, 1911
52. *Marie.* London and New York, 1912
53. *Child of Storm.* London and New York, 1913
54. *A Call to Arms to the Men of East Anglia.* Privately printed, 1914
55. *The Wanderer's Necklace.* London and New York, 1914
56. *The Holy Flower.* London, 1915
57. *The After-War Settlement and the Employment of Ex-Service Men in the Oversea Dominions.* London, 1916
58. *The Ivory Child.* London and New York, 1916
59. *Finished.* London and New York, 1917
60. *Moon of Israel.* London and New York, 1918
61. *Love Eternal.* London and New York, 1918
62. *When the World Shook.* London and New York, 1919
63. *Smith and the Pharaohs and Other Tales.* Bristol (Eng), 1920
64. *The Ancient Allan.* London and New York, 1920
65. *The Virgin of the Sun.* London and New York, 1922
66. *Wisdom's Daughter.* London and New York, 1923
67. *Heu-Heu; or, The Monster.* London and New York, 1924
68. *Queen of the Dawn.* New York and London, 1925
69. *The Days of My Life: An Autobiography.* London and New York, 1926
70. *The Treasure of the Lake.* New York and London, 1926
71. *Allan and the Ice-Gods.* London and New York, 1927
72. *Mary of Marion Isle.* London and New York, 1929
73. *Belshazzar.* London and New York, 1930
74. *The Private Diaries of Sir H. Rider Haggard 1914-1915.* London and New York, 1980
75. *The Best Short Stories of Rider Haggard.* London, 1981

Haggard, William [Richard Henry Michael Clayton]
British, born August 11, 1907
1. *Slow Burner.* London and Boston, 1958
2. *The Telemann Touch.* London and Boston, 1958
3. *Venetian Blind.* London and New York, 1959
4. *Closed Circuit.* London and New York, 1960
5. *The Arena.* London and New York, 1961
6. *The Unquiet Sleep.* London and New York, 1962
7. *The High Wire.* London and New York, 1963
8. *The Antagonists.* London and New York, 1964
9. *The Powder Barrel.* London and New York, 1965
10. *The Hard Sell.* London, 1965
11. *The Power House.* London, 1966
12. *The Conspirators.* London, 1967
13. *A Cool Day for Killing.* London and New York, 1968
14. *The Doubtful Disciple.* London, 1969
15. *The Hardliners.* London and New York, 1970
16. *The Bitter Harvest.* London, 1971
17. *Too Many Enemies.* New York, 1972
18. *The Protectors.* London and New York, 1972
19. *The Old Masters.* London, 1973
20. *The Notch on the Knife.* New York, 1973
21. *The Kinsmen.* London and New York, 1974
22. *The Scorpion's Tail.* London and New York, 1975
23. *Yesterday's Enemy.* London and New York, 1976
24. *The Poison People.* London, 1978
25. *Visa to Limbo.* London, 1978
26. *The Median Line.* London, 1979

Haines, Pamela
British, born in 1929
1. *Tea At Gunter's.* London, 1974
2. *A Kind of War.* London, 1976
3. *Men on White Horses.* London, 1978
4. *The Kissing Gate.* London and New York, 1981

Hall, Oakley (Maxwell)
American, born July 1, 1920
Pseudonym: Jason Manor
1. *Murder City.* New York, 1949
2. *So Many Doors.* New York and London, 1950
3. *Corpus of Joe Bailey.* New York and London, 1953
4. *Too Dead to Run,* as Jason Manor. New York, 1953
5. *The Red Jaguar,* as Jason Manor. New York, 1954
6. *The Girl in the Red Jaguar,* as Jason Manor. New York, 1955
7. *The Pawns of Fear,* as Jason Manor. New York and London, 1955
8. *Mardios Beach.* New York and London, 1955
9. *No Halo for Me,* as Jason Manor. New York, 1956
10. *The Tramplers,* as Jason Manor. New York and London, 1956

Hall, Oakley

11. *Warlock.* New York, 1958
12. *The Downhill Racers.* New York and London, 1963
13. *The Pleasure Garden.* New York, 1966
14. *A Game for Eagles.* New York, 1970
15. *Report from Beau Harbor.* New York, 1971
16. *The Adelita.* New York, 1975
17. *Angle of Repose.* Water Gap (DE), 1976
18. *The Bad Lands.* New York, 1978
19. *Lullaby.* New York, 1982

Halleran, E.E. (Eugene Edward)
American, born February 28, 1905
Pseudonym: Evan Hall
1. *No Range Is Free.* Philadelphia, 1944
2. *Prairie Guns.* Philadelphia, 1944
3. *Thirteen Toy Pistols.* Philadelphia, 1945
4. *Outposts of Vengence.* Philadelphia, 1945
5. *Shadow of the Badlands.* Philadelphia, 1946
6. *Double Cross Trail.* Philadelphia, 1946
7. *Outlaw Guns.* Philadelphia, 1947
8. *Rustlers Canyon.* Philadelphia, 1948
9. *Outlaw Trail.* Philadelphia, 1949
10. *High Prairie.* Philadelphia, 1950
11. *Smoky Range.* Philadelphia, 1951
12. *Gunsmoke Valley.* London, 1952
13. *Straw Boss.* Philadelphia, 1952
14. *The Outlaw.* London, 1952
15. *Colorado Creek.* New York, 1953
16. *Winter Ambush.* Philadelphia, 1954
17. *Blazing Border.* Philadelphia, 1955
18. *Devil's Canyon.* Philadelphia, 1956
19. *Logan,* as Evan Hall. New York, 1956
20. *Wagon Captain.* New York, 1956
21. *The Hostile Hills.* New York, 1957
22. *Spanish Ridge.* New York, 1957
23. *Shadow of the Big Horn.* New York, 1960
24. *The Dark Raiders.* New York, 1960
25. *Convention Queen.* New York, 1960
26. *Warbonnet Creek.* New York, 1960
27. *Blood Brand.* New York, 1961
28. *Gringo Gun.* New York, 1961
29. *Boot Hill Silver.* New York, 1962
30. *Crimson Desert.* New York, 1962
31. *The Far Land.* New York, 1963
32. *Indian Fighter.* New York and London, 1964
33. *Summer of the Sioux.* London, 1965
34. *High Iron.* New York, 1965
35. *Red River Country.* New York, 1966
36. *The Pistoleros.* New York, 1967
37. *Outlaws of Empty Poke.* New York, 1969
38. *Cimarron Thunder.* New York, 1970

Hamilton, Donald (Bengtsson)
American, born March 24, 1916
1. *Date with Darkness.* New York, 1947
2. *The Steel Mirror.* New York, 1948
3. *Murder Twice Told.* New York, 1950
4. *Night Walker.* New York, 1954
5. *Rough Company.* London, 1954
6. *Smoky Valley.* New York, 1954
7. *Line of Fire.* New York, 1955
8. *Assignment: Murder.* New York, 1956
9. *Mad River.* New York, 1956
10. *The Big Country.* New York, 1957
11. *Death of a Citizen.* London and New York, 1960
12. *The Wrecking Crew.* New York, 1960
13. *The Man from Santa Clara.* New York, 1960
14. *Texas Fever.* New York, 1960
15. *The Removers.* New York, 1961
16. *Murderer's Row.* New York, 1962
17. *The Silencers.* New York, 1962
18. *The Ambushers.* New York, 1963
19. *The Ravagers.* New York, 1964
20. *The Shadowers.* New York and London, 1964
21. *The Devastators.* New York, 1965
22. *The Betrayers.* New York, 1966
23. *The Menacers.* New York and London, 1968
24. *The Interlopers.* New York and London, 1969
25. *On Guns and Hunting.* New York, 1970
26. *The Poisoners.* New York and London, 1971
27. *The Two-Shoot Gun.* New York, 1971
28. *The Intriguers.* New York and London, 1973
29. *The Intimidators.* New York and London, 1974
30. *The Terminators.* New York, 1975
31. *The Retaliators.* New York, 1976
32. *The Terrorizers.* New York, 1977

Hammett, Dashiell [Samuel Dashiell Hammett]
American, born May 27, 1894, died January 10, 1961
1. *Red Harvest.* New York and London, 1929
2. *The Dain Curse.* New York and London, 1929
3. *The Maltese Falcon.* New York and London, 1930
4. *The Glass Key.* New York and London, 1931
5. *The Thin Man.* New York and London, 1934
6. *Secret Agent X-9.* Philadelphia, 2 vols., 1934
7. *"Tempo in the Novel."* New York, 1940
8. *$106,000 Blood Money.* New York, 1943
9. *Blood Money.* Cleveland, 1943
10. *The Adventures of Sam Spade and Other Stories.* New York, 1944
11. *The Battle of the Aleutians.* Privately printed, 1944
12. *The Continental Op.* New York, 1945
13. *The Return of the Continental Op.* New York, 1945
14. *Watch on the Rhine.* New York, 1945
15. *Hammett Homicides.* New York, 1946
16. *Dead Yellow Women.* New York, 1947
17. *The Big Knock-Over.* New York, 1948
18. *Nightmare Town.* New York, 1948
19. *They Can Only Hang You Once.* New York, 1949
20. *The Creeping Siamese.* New York, 1950
21. *Woman in the Dark.* New York, 1951
22. *A Man Named Thin and Other Stories.* New York, 1962
23. *The Big Knockover: Selected Stories and Short Novels.* New York, 1966
24. *The Hammett Story Omnibus.* London, 1966
25. *The Big Knockover and The Continental Op.* New York, 2 vols., 1967

Hampson, Anne
British
1. *Eternal Summer.* London, 1969
2. *Precious Waif.* London, 1969
3. *Unwary Heart.* London, 1969
4. *The Autocrat of Melhurst.* London, 1969
5. *Gates of Steel.* London, 1970
6. *By Fountains Wild.* London, 1970
7. *Heaven Is High.* London, 1970
8. *Love Hath an Island.* London, 1970
9. *The Hawk and the Dove.* London, 1970
10. *Beyond the Sweet Waters.* London, 1970
11. *When the Bough Breaks.* London, 1970
12. *An Eagle Swooped.* London, 1970
13. *Isle of the Rainbows.* London, 1970
14. *Dark Hills Rising.* London, 1971
15. *The Rebel Bride.* London, 1971
16. *Stars of Springs.* London and Toronto, 1971

17. *Wings of the Night.* London, 1971
18. *Follow a Shadow.* London, 1971
19. *Gold Is the Sunrise.* London, 1971
20. *Petals Drifting.* London, 1971
21. *South of Mandraki.* London, 1971
22. *Waves of Fire.* London, 1971
23. *The Fair Island.* London, 1972
24. *Enchanted Dawn.* London, 1972
25. *Beloved Rake.* London, 1972
26. *The Plantation Boss.* London, 1972
27. *There Came a Tyrant.* London and Toronto, 1972
28. *Dark Avenger.* London, 1972
29. *Wife for a Penny.* London, 1972
30. *Hunter of the East.* London, 1973
31. *Boss of Bali Creek.* London, 1973
32. *Blue Hills of Sintra.* London, 1973
33. *Dear Stranger.* London and Toronto, 1973
34. *Stormy the Way.* London, 1973
35. *When Clouds Part.* London, 1973
36. *Master of Moonrock.* Toronto, 1973
37. *Windward Crest.* London, 1973
38. *A Kiss from Satan.* Toronto, 1973
39. *The Black Eagle.* London, 1973
40. *Dear Plutocrat.* London, 1973
41. *After Sundown.* Toronto, 1974
42. *Stars over Sarawak.* London and Toronto, 1974
43. *Fetters of Hate.* London, 1974
44. *Pride and Power.* London, 1974
45. *The Way of a Tyrant.* London and Toronto, 1974
46. *Moon Without Stars.* London, 1974
47. *Not Far from Heaven.* London, 1974
48. *Two of a Kind.* London, 1974
49. *Autumn Twilight.* London, 1975
50. *Flame of Fate.* London, 1975
51. *Jonty in Love.* London, 1975
52. *Reap the Whirlwind.* London, 1975
53. *South of Capricorn.* London, 1975
54. *Sunset Cloud.* London, 1976
55. *Song of the Waves.* London, 1976
56. *Dangerous Friendship.* Toronto, 1976
57. *Satan and the Nymph.* London, 1976
58. *A Man to Be Feared.* London and Toronto, 1976
59. *Isle at the Rainbow's End.* London, 1976
60. *Hills of Kalamata.* London, 1976
61. *Fire Meets Fire.* London, 1976
62. *Dear Benefactor.* London , 1976
63. *Call of the Outback.* London, 1976
64. *Call of the Veld.* London, 1977
65. *Harbour of Love.* London, 1977
66. *The Shadow Between.* London, 1977
67. *Sweet Is the Web.* London, 1977
68. *Moon Dragon.* London, 1978
69. *To Tame a Vixen.* London, 1978
70. *Master of Forrestmead.* London, 1978
71. *Under Moonglow.* London and Toronto, 1978
72. *For Love of a Pagan.* London, 1978
73. *Leaf in the Storm.* London and Toronto, 1978
74. *Above Rubies.* Toronto, 1978
75. *Fly Beyond the Sunset.* Toronto, 1978
76. *Isle of Desire.* Toronto, 1978
77. *South of the Moon.* Toronto, 1979
78. *Bride for a Night.* London, 1979
79. *Chateau in the Palms.* London, 1979
80. *Coolibah Creek.* London, 1979
81. *A Rose from Lucifer.* London, 1979
82. *Temple of Dawn.* London, 1979
83. *Call of the Heathen.* London, 1980
84. *The Laird of Locharrun.* London, 1980
85. *Pagan Lover.* London, 1980
86. *The Dawn Steals Softly.* New York and London, 1980
87. *Stormy Masquerade.* New York and London, 1980
88. *Second Tomorrow.* London, 1980
89. *Man of the Outback.* New York, 1980
90. *Where Eagles Nest.* New York, 1980
91. *Payment in Full.* New York and London, 1980
92. *Beloved Vagabond.* Toronto, 1981
93. *Man Without a Heart.* New York, 1981
94. *Shadow of Apollo.* New York, 1981

Hanshew, Thomas W.
American, born in 1857, died March 3, 1914
Pseudonym: Charlotte Mary Kingsley
1. *Young Mrs. Charnleigh.* New York, 1883
2. *Leonie; or, The Sweet Street Singer of New York.* New York, 1884
3. *A Wedded Widow; or, The Love That Lived.* New York, 1887
4. *Beautiful But Dangerous; or, The Heir of Shadowdene.* New York, 1891
5. *The World's Finger.* London and New York, 1901
6. *The Mallison Mystery.* London, 1903
7. *Arrol's Engagement,* as Charlotte Mary Kingsley. London, 1903
8. *The Horton Mystery.* New York, 1905
9. *The Great Ruby.* London, 1905
10. *The Shadow of a Dead Man.* London, 1906
11. *Fate and the Man.* London, 1910
12. *The Man of the Forty Faces.* London, 1910
13. *Cleek, The Man of the Forty Faces.* London, 1913
14. *Cleek of Scotland Yard.* London and New York, 1914
15. *Cleek's Greatest Riddles.* London, 1916
16. *Cleek's Government Cases.* New York, 1917
17. *The Master Detective.* New York, 1918
18. *The Forty-Niners; or, The Pioneer's Daughter.* Clyde (OH), no date
19. *Oath Bound; or, Faithful unto Death.* Clyde, no date
20. *Will-o'-the-Wisp; or, The Shot in the Dark.* Clyde, no date

Harbage, Alfred B. (Bennett)
American, born July 18, 1901, died May 2, 1976
Pseudonym: Thomas Kyd
1. *Thomas Killigrew: Cavalier Dramatist.* Philadelphia and London, 1930
2. *Sir William Davenant, Poet-Venturer.* Philadelphia and London, 1935
3. *Cavalier Drama.* New York and London, 1936
4. *Annals of English Drama, 975-1700.* Philadelphia, 1940
5. *Shakespeare's Audience.* New York, 1941
6. *Blood Is a Beggar,* as Thomas Kyd. Philadelphia, 1946
7. *Blood of Vintage,* as Thomas Kyd. Philadelphia, 1947
8. *As They Liked It: An Essay on Shakespeare and Morality.* New York, 1947
9. *Blood on the Bosom Devine,* as Thomas Kyd. Philadelphia, 1948
10. *Cover His Face,* as Thomas Kyd. Philadelphia, 1949
11. *Shakespeare and the Rival Traditions.* New York, 1952
12. *Theater for Shakespeare.* Toronto, 1955
13. *William Shakespeare: A Reader's Guide.* New York, 1963
14. *Conceptions of Shakespeare.* Cambridge, (MA), 1966
15. *Shakespeare Without Words and Other Essays.* Cambridge, 1972

Hardwick, Mollie
British
Pseudonyms: Mary Atkinson, John Drinkrow
1. *The Jolly Toper,* with Michael Hardwick. London, 1961

2. *The Sherlock Holmes Companion*, with Michael Hardwick. London, 1962
3. *Sherlock Holmes Investigates*, with Michael Hardwick. New York, 1963
4. *Four [and Four More] Sherlock Holmes Plays*, with Michael Hardwick. London, 2 vols., 1964-73
5. *The Man Who Was Sherlock Holmes*, with Michael Hardwick. London and New York, 1964
6. *The Charles Dickens Companion*, with Michael Hardwick. London, 1965
7. *The Plague and the Fire of London*, with Michael Hardwick. London, 1966
8. *Writers' Houses: A Literary Journey in England*, with Michael Hardwick. London, 1968
9. *Alfred Deller: A Singularity of Voice*, with Michael Hardwick. London, 1968
10. *Emma, Lady Hamilton*. London, 1969
11. *The Game's Afoot: Sherlock Holmes Plays*, with Michael Hardwick. London, 1969
12. *Dickens' England*, with Michael Hardwick. London and South Brunswick (NJ), 1970
13. *Charles Dickens ... As They Saw Him*, with Michael Hardwick. London, 1970
14. *Plays from Dickens*, with Michael Hardwick. London and New York, 1970
15. *The Private Life of Sherlock Homes*, with Michael Hardwick. London, 1970
16. *Mrs. Dizzy: The Life of Mary Ann Disraeli*. London and New York, 1972
17. *The Vintage Operetta Book*, as John Drinkrow. London, 1972
18. *The Thames-Side Book*, as Mary Atkinson. London, 1973
19. *The Bernard Shaw Companion*, with Michael Hardwick. London, 1973
20. *The Charles Dickens Encyclopedia*, with Michael Hardwick. London and New York, 1973
21. *Sarah's Story*. London, 1973
22. *The Vintage Musical Comedy Book*, as John Drinkrow. London, 1974
23. *Alice in Wonderland*, adaptation of the story by Lewis Carroll. London, 1974
24. *A Christmas Carol*. London, 1974
25. *The Years of Change*. London and New York, 1974
26. *Mrs. Bridge's Story*. London, 1975
27. *The War to End Wars*. London and New York, 1975
28. *The Gaslight Boys*, with Michael Hardwick. London, 1976
29. *The World of Upstairs, Downstairs*. Newton Abbot (Eng) and New York, 1976
30. *Thomas and Sarah*. London, 1978
31. *The Duchess of Duke Street*. London, 1976
32. *Beauty's Daughter: The Story of Lady Hamilton's "Lost" Daughter*. London, 1976
33. *Charlie Is My Darling*. London and New York, 1977
34. *The Atkinson Heritage*. London, 1978
35. *Sisters in Love*. London, 1979
36. *Dove's Nest*. London, 1980
37. *Lovers Meeting*. London and New York, 1979
38. *Juliet Bravo*. London, 1980
39. *Willowood*. London and New York, 1980
40. *Monday's Child*. London, 1981
41. *Calling Juliet Bravo*. London, 1981
42. *Juliet Bravo 2*. London, 1981

Hardy, W.G. (William George)
Canadian, born in 1895
1. *Abraham, Prince of Ur*. New York, 1935
2. *Turn Back the River*. New York and London, 1938
3. *All the Trumpets Sounded*. New York, 1942
4. *Education in Alberta*. Calgary (Canada), 1946
5. *The Unfulfilled*. Toronto, 1951
6. *The City of Libertines*. Toronto and New York, 1957
7. *From Sea unto Sea: Canada 1850-1920: The Road to Nationhood*. New York, 1960
8. *The Greek and Roman World: Ten Radio Talks*. Toronto, 1960
9. *Our Heritage from the Past*. Toronto, 1964
10. *Journey into the Past*. Toronto, 1965
11. *Origins and Ordeals of the Western World*. Cambridge (MA), 1968
12. *The Scarlet Mantle: A Novel of Julius Caesar*. Toronto, 1978
13. *The Bloodied Toga: A Novel of Julius Caesar*. Toronto, 1979

Harling, Robert
British, born in 1910
Pseudonym: Nicholas Drew
1. *The London Miscellany: A Nineteenth-Century Scrapbook*. London, 1937
2. *Home: A Victorian Vignette*. London, 1938
3. *Amateur Sailor*, as Nicholas Drew. London, 1944
4. *Notes on the Wood-Engravings of Eric Ravilious*. London, 1946
5. *The Steep Atlantick Stream*. London, 1946
6. *Edward Bawden*. London, 1950
7. *The Paper Palace*. London and New York, 1951
8. *The Dark Saviour*. London, 1952
9. *The Enormous Shadow*. London, 1955
10. *The Endless Colonnade*. London, 1958
11. *The Hollow Sunday*. London, 1967
12. *The Athenian Widow*. London, 1974
13. *The Letter Forms and Type Designs of Eric Gill*. Westerham (Eng), 1976
14. *The Summer Portrait*. London, 1979

Harrington, Joseph (James)
American, born in 1903
1. *Hawaiian Lover*. New York, 1932
2. *Scandal Rag*. New York, 1942
3. *The Last Known Address*. Philadelphia, 1965
4. *Blind Spot*. Philadelphia, 1966
5. *The Last Doorbell*. Philadelphia, 1969

Harris, Herbert
British, born August 25, 1911
1. *Who Kill to Live*. London, 1962
2. *Painted in Blood*. New York, 1972
3. *Serpents in Paradise*. London, 1975
4. *The Angry Battalion*. London, 1976

Harris, Marilyn
American, born June 4, 1931
1. *King's Ex*. New York and London, 1967
2. *In the Midst of Earth*. New York, 1969
3. *The Peppersalt Land*. New York, 1970
4. *The Runaway's Diary*. New York, 1971
5. *Hatter Fox*. New York, 1973
6. *The Conjurers*. New York, 1974
7. *Bledding Sorrow*. New York, 1976
8. *This Other Eden*. New York, 1977
9. *The Prince of Eden*. New York, 1978
10. *The Eden Passion*. New York, 1979
11. *The Women of Eden*. New York, 1980
12. *Eden Rising*. New York, 1982

Harris, Rosemary (Jeanne)
British, born February 20, 1923
1. *The Summer-House*. London, 1956

2. *Voyage to Cythera.* London, 1958
3. *Venus with Sparrows.* London, 1961
4. *All My Enemies.* London, 1967
5. *The Nice Girl's Story.* London, 1968
6. *A Wicked Pack of Cards.* London, 1969
7. *The Moon in the Cloud.* London, 1968
8. *The Shadow on the Sun.* London and New York, 1970
9. *The Seal-Singing.* London and New York, 1971
10. *The Child in the Bamboo Grove.* London, 1971
11. *The Bright and Morning Star.* London and New York, 1972
12. *The King's White Elephant.* London, 1973
13. *The Double Snare.* London, 1974
14. *The Lotus and the Grail: Legends from East to West.* London, 1974
15. *The Flying Ship.* London, 1975
16. *The Little Dog of Fo.* London, 1976
17. *Three Candles for the Dark.* London, 1976
18. *Want to Be a Fish.* London, 1977
19. *A Quest for Orion.* London, 1978
20. *Beauty and the Beast.* London, 1979
21. *Green Finger House.* London, 1980
22. *Tower of the Stars.* London, 1980
23. *The Enchanted Horse.* London, 1981

Harrison, Elizabeth [Edith Elizabeth Tatchell Harrison]
1. *Coffee at Dobree's.* London, 1965
2. *The Physicians.* London, 1966
3. *The Ravelston Affair.* London, 1967
4. *Emergency Call.* London, 1970
5. *Accident Call.* London, 1971
6. *Ambulance Call.* London, 1972
7. *Surgeon's Call.* London, 1973
8. *On Call.* London, 1974
9. *Hospital Call.* London, 1975
10. *Dangerous Call.* London, 1976
11. *To Mend a Heart.* London, 1977
12. *Young Doctor Goddard.* London, 1978
13. *A Doctor Called Caroline.* London, 1979

Harrison, Michael
Irish, born April 25, 1907
Pseudonym: Quentin Downes
1. *Weep for Lycidas.* London, 1934
2. *Spring in Tartarus: An Arabesque.* London, 1935
3. *All the Trees Were Green.* London, 1936
4. *Transit of Venus.* London, 1936
5. *Dawn Express: There and Back.* London, 1938
6. *What Are We Waiting For?* London, 1939
7. *Vernal Equinox.* London, 1939
8. *Gambler's Glory: The Story of John Law of Lauriston.* London, 1940
9. *Battered Caravanserai.* London, 1942
10. *Count Cagliostro, Nature's Unfortunate Child.* London, 1942
11. *Reported Safe Arrival: The Journal of a Voyage to Port X.* London, 1943
12. *So Linked Together.* London, 1944
13. *Higher Things.* London, 1945
14. *The House in Fishergate.* London, 1946
15. *Treadmill.* London, 1947
16. *They Would Be King.* London, 1947
17. *Post Office, Mauritius 1847: The Tale of Two Stamps.* London, 1947
18. *Sinecure.* London, 1948
19. *There's Glory for You!* London, 1949
20. *Things Less Noble: A Modern Love Story.* London, 1950
21. *Long Vacation.* London, 1951
22. *The Story of Christmas: Its Growth and Development from Earliest Times.* London, 1951
23. *The Darkened Room.* London, 1952
24. *No Smoke, No Fire,* as Quentin Downes. London, 1952
25. *Heads I Win.* London, 1953
26. *The Brain.* London, 1953
27. *Airborne at Kitty Hawk: The Story of the First Heavier-than-Air Flight Made by the Wright Brothers.* London, 1953
28. *Charles Dickens: A Sentimental Journey in Search of an Unvarnished Portrait.* London, 1953
29. *A New Approach to Stamp Collecting.* London, 1953
30. *They Hadn't a Clue.* London, 1954
31. *The Dividing Stone.* London, 1954
32. *A Hansom to St. James's.* London, 1954
33. *Beer Cookery: 101 Traditional Recipes.* London, 1954
34. *Peter Cheyney, Prince of Hokum: A Biography.* London, 1954
35. *In the Footsteps of Sherlock Holmes.* London, 1958
36. *The History of the Hat.* London, 1960
37. *London Beneath the Pavement.* London, 1961
38. *Rosa.* London, 1962
39. *Painful Details: Twelve Victorian Scandals.* London, 1962
40. *London by Gaslight 1861-1911.* London, 1963
41. *London Growing: The Development of a Metropolis.* London, 1965
42. *Mulberry: The Return in Triumph.* London, 1965
43. *Lord of London: A Biography of the Second Duke of Westminster.* London, 1966
44. *The Exploits of Chevalier Dupin.* Sauk City (WI), 1968
45. *Technical and Industrial Publicity.* London, 1968
46. *The London That Was Rome: The Imperial City Recreated by the New Archaeology.* London, 1971
47. *Fanfare of Strumpets.* London, 1971
48. *Murder in the Rue Royale.* London, 1972
49. *Clarence: The Life of H.R.H. the Duke of Clarence and Avondale 1864-1892.* London, 1972
50. *The London of Sherlock Holmes.* Newton Abbot (Eng) and New York, 1972
51. *The Roots of Witchcraft.* London, 1973
52. *The World of Sherlock Holmes.* London, 1973
53. *Clarence: Was He Jack the Ripper?* New York, 1974
54. *Theatrical Mr. Holmes: The World's Greatest Consulting Detective, Considered Against the Background of the Contemporary Theatre.* London, 1974
55. *Fire from Heaven; or, How Safe Are You from Burning?* London, 1976
56. *I, Sherlock Holmes.* New York, 1977

Harvey, John B.
British, born December 21, 1938
Pseudonyms: Jon Barton, William S. Brady, L.J. Coburn, J.B.Dancer, Jon Hart, William M. James, James Mann, John J. McLaglen, Thom Ryder, J.D.Sandon, Jonathan White
1. *Avenging Angel,* as Thom Ryder. London, 1975
2. *Angel Alone,* as Thom Ryder. London, 1975
3. *Amphetamines and Pearls.* London, 1976
4. *The Geranium Kiss.* London, 1976
5. *One of Our Dinosaurs Is Missing.* London, 1976
6. *Kill Hitler,* as Jon Barton. London, 1976
7. *Double Trouble,* as Jonathan White. London, 1976
8. *Double Dutch,* as Jonathan White. London, 1976
9. *Double Exposure,* as Jonathan White. London, 1976
10. *River of Blood,* as John J.McLaglen. London, 1976
11. *Shadow of the Vulture,* as John J.McLaglen. London, 1977
12. *Death in Gold,* as John J.McLaglen. London, 1977
13. *Forest of Death,* as Jon Barton. London, 1977
14. *Lightning Strikes,* as Jon Barton. London, 1977
15. *Double Up,* as Jonathan White. London, 1977
16. *Double Act,* as Jonathan White. London, 1977

Harvey, John B.

17. *Double Bed,* as Jonathan White. London, 1977
18. *Junkyard Angel.* London, 1977
19. *Neon Madman.* London, 1977
20. *Herbie Rides Again.* London, 1977
21. *Black Blood,* as Jon Hart. London, 1977
22. *High Slaughter,* as Jon Hart. London, 1977
23. *Triangle of Death,* as Jon Hart. London, 1977
24. *Guerilla Attack!* as Jon Hart. London, 1977
25. *Evil Breed,* as J.B. Dancer. London, 1977
26. *The Raiders,* as L.J. Coburn. London, 1977
27. *Bloody Shiloh,* as L.J. Coburn. London, 1978
28. *Judgement Day,* as J.B. Dancer. London, 1978
29. *Death Raid,* as Jon Hart. London, 1978
30. *Herbie Goes to Monte Carlo.* London, 1978
31. *Provence.* Berkhamsted (Eng), 1978
32. *Crossdraw,* as John J. McLaglen. London, 1978
33. *Vigilante,* as John J. McLaglen. London, 1979
34. *The Hanged Man,* as J.B. Dancer. London, 1979
35. *What About It, Sharon.* London, 1979
36. *Frame.* London, 1979
37. *Cannons in the Rain,* as J.D. Sandon. London, 1979
38. *Border Affair,* as J.D. Sandon. London, 1979
39. *Bloody Money,* as William S. Brady. London, 1979
40. *Blood Rising,* as William M. James. London, 1879
41. *Blood Brother,* as William M. James. London, 1980
42. *Killing Time,* as William S. Brady. London, 1980
43. *Blood Kin,* as William S. Brady. London, 1980
44. *Mazatlan,* as J.D. Sandon. London, 1980
45. *Cherokee Outlet.* London, 1980
46. *Blood Trail.* London, 1980
47. *Sundance,* as John J. McLaglen. London, 1980
48. *Billy the Kid,* as John J. McLaglen. London, 1980
49. *Till Death . . . ,* as John J. McLaglen. London, 1980
50. *Tago.* London, 1980
51. *The Silver Lie.* London, 1980
52. *Blood on the Border.* London, 1981
53. *Death Dragon,* as William M. James. London, 1981
54. *Desperadoes,* as William S. Brady. London, 1981
55. *Dead Man's Gold,* as William S. Brady. London, 1981
56. *Sierra Gold,* as William S. Brady. London, 1981
57. *Whiplash,* as William S. Brady. London, 1981
58. *Ride the Wide Country.* London, 1981
59. *Wheels of Thunder,* as J.D. Sandon. London, 1981
60. *Blind.* London, 1981
61. *Endgame,* as James Mann, with Laurence James. London, 1982

Hastings, Phyllis (Dora)
British
Pseudonyms: John Bedford, Julia Mayfield
1. *As Long as You Live.* London, 1951
2. *Far from Jupiter.* London, 1952
3. *Crowning Glory.* London, 1952
4. *Rapture in My Rags.* London and New York, 1954
5. *Dust Is My Pillow.* London and New York, 1955
6. *The Field of Roses.* London, 1955
7. *The Black Virgin of the Gold Mountain.* London, 1956
8. *The Innocent and the Wicked.* New York, 1956
9. *The Signpost Has Four Arms.* London, 1957
10. *The Forest of Stone,* as Julia Mayfield. London, 1957
11. *A Time for Pleasure.* New York, 1957
12. *The Happy Man.* London, 1958
13. *Golden Apollo.* London, 1958
14. *The Fountain of Youth.* London, 1959
15. *Sandals for My Feet.* London, 1960
16. *Long Barnaby.* London, 1961
17. *Looking [and More Looking] in Junk Shops,* as John Bedford. London, 2 vols., 1961-62
18. *The Night the Roof Blew Off.* London, 1962
19. *Talking about Teapots,* as John Bedford. London, 1964
20. *Collectors Pieces 1-12.* London, 12 vols., 1964-67
21. *London's Burning,* as John Bedford. London, 1966
22. *Delftware,* as John Bedford. London, 1966
23. *Their Flowers Were Always Black.* London, 1967
24. *The Swan River Story.* London, 1968
25. *All Earth to Love.* London, 1968
26. *Still Looking for Junk,* as John Bedford. London, 1969
27. *Day of the Dancing Sun.* London, 1971
28. *An Act of Darkness.* London, 1969
29. *The Stars Are My Children.* London, 1970
30. *The Temporary Boy.* London, 1971
31. *When the Gallows Is High.* London, 1971
32. *The Conservatory.* London, 1973
33. *The Gates of Morning.* London, 1973
34. *Bartholomew Fair.* London, 1974
35. *House of the Twelve Caesars.* London, 1975
36. *The Image-Maker.* London, 1976
37. *The Candles of the Night.* London, 1977
38. *The Death-Scented Flower.* London, 1977
39. *Field of the Forty Footsteps.* London, 1978
40. *The Stratford Affair.* London, 1978
41. *The Feast of the Peacock.* London, 1978
42. *Running Thursday.* London, 1980
43. *Buttercup Joe.* London, 1980
44. *Tiger's Heaven.* London, 1981
45. *The Overlooker.* London, 1982

Haycox, Ernest
American, born October 1, 1899, died October 13, 1950
1. *Free Grass.* New York, 1929
2. *Chaffee of Roaring Horse.* New York and London, 1930
3. *Whipering Range.* New York, 1930
4. *All Trails Cross.* London, 1931
5. *Starlight Rider.* New York, 1933
6. *Riders West.* New York, 1934
7. *Rough Air.* New York, 1934
8. *Smoky Pass.* London, 1934
9. *The Silver Desert.* New York, 1935
10. *Trail Smoke.* New York and London, 1936
11. *Deep West.* Boston and London, 1937
12. *Trouble Shooter.* Boston and London, 1937
13. *Man in the Saddle.* Boston, 1938
14. *Sundown Jim.* Boston and London, 1938
15. *The Border Trumpet.* Boston, 1939
16. *Rim of the Desert.* Boston, 1940
17. *Saddle and Ride.* Boston and London, 1940
18. *Trail Town.* Boston and London, 1941
19. *Alder Gulch.* Boston, 1942
20. *No Law and Order.* London, 1942
21. *American Character.* Eugene (OR), 1943
22. *Action by Night.* Boston and London, 1943
23. *The Wild Bunch.* Boston, 1943
24. *Bugles in the Afternoon.* Boston and London, 1944
25. *Canyon Passage.* Boston and London, 1945
26. *Long Storm.* Boston, 1946
27. *Rough Justice.* Boston, 1950
28. *By Rope and Lead.* Boston, 1951
29. *Murder on the Frontier.* Boston, 1952
30. *The Earthbreakers.* Boston, 1952
31. *Pioneer Loves.* Boston, 1952
32. *Rawhide Range.* New York, 1952
33. *Return of a Fighter.* New York, 1952
34. *Head of the Mountain.* New York, 1952
35. *Outlaw.* Boston, 1953
36. *The Grim Canyon.* New York, 1953
37. *Guns Up and the Hour of Fury.* New York, 1954

38. *Prairie Guns.* Boston, 1954
39. *Winds of Rebellion.* New York, 1954
40. *The Adventurers.* Boston, 1954
41. *Secret River, and The Trail of the Barefoot Pony.* New York, 1955
42. *Vengence Trail, and Invitation by Bullet.* New York, 1955
43. *A Rider of the High Mesa.* New York, 1956
44. *Gun Talk and Other Stories.* New York, 1956
45. *The Last Rodeo.* Boston, 1956
46. *Dead Man Range.* New York, 1957
47. *On the Prod.* New York, 1957
48. *Roaring Horse.* London, 1959
49. *Brand Fires on the Ridge.* Derby (CT), 1959
50. *Lone Rider.* New York, 1959
51. *Guns of the Tom Dee, and Valley of the Rogue.* New York, 1959
52. *The Best Western Stories of Ernest Haycox.* New York, 1960
53. *The Fuedists.* New York, 1960
54. *Frank Peace, Troubleshooter.* New York, 1963
55. *Outlaw Guns.* New York, 1963
56. *The Man from Montana.* New York, 1964
57. *Sixgun Duo.* New York, 1965
58. *Powder Smoke and Other Stories.* New York, 1966
59. *Trigger Trio.* New York, 1966
60. *Starlight and Gunflame.* New York, 1973
61. *Clint.* New York, 1973
62. *Frontier Blood.* New York, 1974
63. *Wipe Out the Brierlys.* New York, 1975

Hayes, Joseph (Arnold)
American, born August 2, 1918
Pseudonym: Joseph H. Arnold
1. *And Came the Spring.* New York, 1942
2. *Christmas at Home.* New York, 1943
3. *The Thompsons.* New York, 1943
4. *The Bridegroom Waits.* New York, 1943
5. *Kidnapped.* New York, 1944
6. *Sneak Date,* as Joseph H, Arnold. New York, 1944
7. *Come Rain or Shine.* New York, 1944
8. *Life of the Party.* New York, 1945
9. *Ask for Me Tomorrow.* New York, 1946
10. *Where's Laurie?* as Joseph H. Arnold. New York, 1946
11. *Come Over to Our House.* New York, 1946
12. *Home for Christmas.* New York, 1946
13. *A Woman's Privilege.* New York, 1947
14. *Quiet Summer.* New York, 1947
15. *Change of Heart.* New York, 1948
16. *Too Many Dates.* New York, 1950
17. *Curtain Going Up.* New York, 1950
18. *Turn Back the Clock.* New York, 1950
19. *June Wedding.* New York, 1951
20. *Once in Every Family.* New York, 1951
21. *Penny.* New York, 1951
22. *Too Young, Too Old.* Boston, 1952
23. *Mister Peepers.* New York, 1952
24. *Head in the Clouds.* New York, 1952
25. *The Desperate Hours.* New York and London, 1954
26. *The Desperate Hours.* New York, 1955
27. *Bon Voyage.* New York and London, 1957
28. *The Hours after Midnight.* New York, 1958
29. *Don't Go Away Mad.* New York, 1962
30. *Calculated Risk.* New York, 1963
31. *The Third Day.* New York, 1964
32. *The Deep End.* New York and London, 1967
33. *Like Any Other Fugitive.* New York, 1971
34. *The Long Dark Night.* New York and London, 1974
35. *Missing and Presumed Dead.* New York, 1975

36. *Impolite Comedy.* New York, 1977
37. *Island on Fire.* New York and London, 1979

Heald, Tim [Timothy Villiers Heald]
British, born January 28, 1944
1. *It's a Dog's Life.* London, 1971
2. *Unbecoming Habits.* London and New York, 1973
3. *Blue Blood Will Out.* London and New York, 1974
4. *Deadline.* London and New York, 1975
5. *Let Sleeping Dogs Die.* London and New York, 1976
6. *The Making of Space 1999.* New York, 1976
7. *Just Desserts.* London, 1977
8. *John Steed: An Authorized Biography.* London, 1977
9. *H.R.H.: The Man Who Will Be King.* New York, 1979

Heaven, Constance
British, born in 1911
Pseudonyms: Constance Fecher, Christina Merlin
1. *Queen's Delight,* as Constance Fecher. London, 1966
2. *Traitor's Son,* as Constance Fecher. London, 1967
3. *King's Legacy,* as Constance Fecher. London, 1967
4. *Player Queen,* as Constance Fecher. London, 1968
5. *Venture for a Crown.* New York., 1968
6. *Heir to Pendarrow.* New York, 1969
7. *Bright Star: A Portrait of Ellen Terry.* New York, 1970
8. *The Link Boys.* New York, 1971
9. *The Last Elizabethan: A Portrait of Sir Walter Ralegh.* New York, 1972
10. *Lion of Trevarrock,* as Constance Fecher. London, 1972
11. *The House of Kuragin.* London and New York, 1972
12. *The Leopard Dagger.* New York, 1973
13. *The Astrov Inheritance.* London, 1973
14. *Castle of Eagles.* London and New York, 1974
15. *The Place of Stones.* London and New York, 1975
16. *The Fires of Glenlochy.* London and New York, 1976
17. *The Queen and the Gypsy.* London and New York, 1977
18. *Lord of Ravensley.* London and New York, 1978
19. *Heir to Kuragin.* London, 1978
20. *The Spy Concerto,* as Christina Merlin. New York and London, 1980
21. *Sword of Mithras,* as Christina Merlin. London, 1982
22. *The Wildcliffe Bird.* London and New York, 1981
23. *The Ravensley Touch.* London and New York, 1982

Heckelmann, Charles N. (Newman)
American, born October 24, 1913
1. *Jungle Menace.* New York, 1937
2. *Clarksville's Battery; or, Baseball Versus Gangsters.* New York, 1937
3. *Ros Hackney, Halfback; or, How Clarksville's Captain Made Good.* New York, 1937
4. *The Winning Forward Pass; or, Onward to the Orange Bowl Game.* New York, 1940
5. *Home Run Hennessey; or, Winning the All-Star Game.* New York, 1941
6. *Touchdown to Victory; or, The Touchdown Express Makes Good.* New York, 1942
7. *Vengence Trail.* New York, 1944
8. *Lawless Range.* New York, 1945
9. *Six-Gun Outcast.* New York, 1946
10. *Deputy Marshall.* New York, 1947
11. *Guns of Arizona.* New York, 1949
12. *Outlaw Valley.* New York, 1950
13. *Danger Rides the Range.* New York, 1950
14. *Two-Bit Rancher.* New York, 1950
15. *Let the Guns Roar.* New York, 1950
16. *Fighting Ramrod.* New York, 1951
17. *Hell in His Holsters.* New York, 1952

18. *The Rawhider.* New York, 1952
19. *Hard Man with a Gun.* Boston, 1954
20. *Bullet Law.* Boston, 1955
21. *Trumpets in the Dawn.* New York, 1958
22. *The Big Valley.* Racine (WI), 1966
23. *The Glory Riders.* New York, 1967
24. *Writing Fiction for Profit.* New York, 1968
25. *Stranger from Durango.* New York, 1971
26. *Return to Arapahoe.* New York, 1980
27. *Wagons to Wind River.* New York, 1982

Hendryx, James B. (Beardsley)
American, born December 9, 1880, died March 1, 1963
1. *The Promise: A Tale of the Great Northwest.* New York, 1915
2. *Connie Morgan in Alaska.* New York, 1916
3. *The Gun-Brand: A Feud of the Frozen North.* New York, 1917
4. *The Texan: A Story of the Cattle Country.* New York, 1918
5. *Connie Morgan in the Lumber Camps.* New York, 1919
6. *The Golden Girl.* New York, 1920
7. *Prairie Flowers.* New York, 1920
8. *Connie Morgan in the Fur Country.* New York, 1921
9. *Snowdrift: A Story of the Land of the Strong Cold.* New York, 1922
10. *North.* New York, 1923
11. *Connie Morgan in the Cattle Country.* New York, 1923
12. *Connie Morgan with the Mounted.* London, 1924
13. *Marquard the Silent.* New York, 1924
14. *At the Foot of the Rainbow.* New York, 1924
15. *Beyond the Outposts.* London, 1924
16. *Without Gloves.* New York and London, 1924
17. *Connie Morgan with the Forest Rangers.* New York, 1925
18. *The Challenge of the North.* New York, 1925
19. *Oak and Iron: Of These Be the Breed of the North.* New York and London, 1925
20. *Downey of the Mounted.* New York and London, 1926
21. *Frozen Inlet Post.* New York and London, 1927
22. *Gold—and the Mounted.* New York and London, 1928
23. *Man of the North.* New York, 1929
24. *Connie Morgan Hits the Trail.* New York, 1929
25. *Connie Morgan, Prospector.* London, 1930
26. *Blood on the Yukon Trail.* New York, 1930
27. *In the Days of Gold.* London, 1930
28. *Corporal Downey Takes the Trail.* New York, 1931
29. *Raw Gold.* New York and London, 1933
30. *The Yukon Kid.* New York and London, 1934
31. *Connie Morgan in the Barren Lands.* London, 1934
32. *Outlaws on Halfaday Creek.* New York and London, 1935
33. *Connie Morgan in the Arctic.* New York and London, 1936
34. *Grubstake Gold.* New York, 1936
35. *Death Heads North.* No place, no date
36. *Blood of the North.* New York and London, 1938
37. *Black John of Halfaday Creek.* New York and London, 1939
38. *Edge of Beyond.* New York, 1939
39. *Hard Rock Man.* New York, 1940
40. *Devil's Gold.* London, 1940
41. *The Czar of Halfaday Creek.* New York, 1940
42. *Law and Order on Halfaday Creek.* New York, 1941
43. *Gambler's Chance.* New York, 1941
44. *New Rivers Calling.* New York, 1943
45. *Gold and Guns on Halfaday Creek.* New York, 1943
46. *Strange Doings on Halfaday Creek.* New York, 1943
47. *It Happened on Halfaday Creek.* New York, 1944
48. *The Way of the North.* New York, 1945
49. *Courage of the North.* New York, 1946
50. *Skullduggery on Halfaday Creek.* New York, 1946
51. *The Saga of Halfaday Creek.* New York, 1947
52. *On the Rim of the Artic.* New York, 1948
53. *Murder in the Outlands.* New York, 1949
54. *Justice on Halfaday Creek.* New York, 1949
55. *Badmen on Halfaday Creek.* New York, 1950
56. *Murder on Halfaday Creek.* New York, 1951
57. *The Stampeders.* New York, 1951
58. *Sourdough Gold.* New York, 1952
59. *The Long Chase.* New York, 1952
60. *Intrigue on Halfaday Creek.* New York, 1953
61. *Gold Is Where You Find It.* New York, 1953
62. *Good Men and Bad.* New York, 1954
63. *Terror on Halfaday Creek.* London, 1963

Henry, O. (William Sydney, or Sidney, Porter)
American, born September 11, 1862, died June 5, 1910
1. *Cabbages and Kings.* New York, 1904
2. *The Four Million.* New York, 1906
3. *Heart of the West.* New York, 1907
4. *The Trimmed Lamp.* New York, 1907
5. *The Voice of the City.* New York, 1908
6. *The Gentle Grafter.* New York, 1908
7. *Roads of Destiny.* New York, 1909
8. *Options.* New York, 1909
9. *Strictly Business: More Stories of the Four Million.* New York, 1910
10. *Whirligigs.* New York, 1910
11. *Let Me Feel Your Pulse.* New York, 1910
12. *The Two Women.* Boston, 1910
13. *Sixes and Sevens.* New York, 1911
14. *Rolling Stones.* New York, 1912
15. *The Complete Writings of O. Henry.* New York, 14 vols., 1917
16. *Waifs and Strays.* New York, 1917
17. *O. Henryana; Seven Odds and Ends: Poetry and Short Stories.* New York, 1920
18. *Letters to Lithopolis from O. Henry to Mabel Wagnalls.* New York and London, 1922
19. *Selected Stories.* New York, 1922
20. *Postscripts.* New York, 1923
21. *The Best of O. Henry.* London, 1929
22. *More O. Henry.* London, 1933
23. *O. Henry Encore: Stories and Illustrations.* Dallas, 1936
24. *The Best Short Stories of O. Henry.* New York, 1945
25. *The Pocket Book of O. Henry.* New York, 1948
26. *Cops and Robbers.* New York, 1948
27. *O. Henry Westerns.* London, 1961
28. *The Stories of O. Henry.* New York, 1965

Herron, Shaun
Canadian, born in 1912
1. *Miro.* New York, 1969
2. *The Hound and the Fox and the Harper.* New York, 1970
3. *The Miro Papers.* London, 1972
4. *Through the Dark and Hairy Wood.* New York, 1972
5. *The Whore-Mother.* New York, 1973
6. *The Bird in Last Year's Nest.* New York and London, 1974
7. *The Ruling Passion.* New York, 1978
8. *The MacDonnell.* London, 1978
9. *Aladale.* New York, 1979

Heuman, William
American, born February 11, 1912
Pseudonym: George Kramer
1. *Guns at Broken Bow.* New York, 1950
2. *Fighting Five.* New York, 1950
3. *Wonder Boy.* New York, 1951

4. *Red Runs the River.* New York, 1951
5. *Hunt the Man Down.* New York, 1951
6. *Roll the Wagons.* New York, 1951
7. *Maverick with a Star.* New York, 1952
8. *Secret of Death Valley.* New York, 1952
9. *South to Santa Fe.* New York, 1952
10. *Junior Quarterback.* New York, 1952
11. *Little League Champs.* Philadelphia, 1953
12. *Keelboats North.* New York, 1953
13. *On to Santa Fe.* New York, 1953
14. *Captain McRae: A Novel of the Northwest Frontier.* New York, 1954
15. *The Range Buster.* New York, 1954
16. *Ride for Texas.* New York, 1954
17. *Gunhand from Texas.* New York, 1954
18. *Bonanza on the Big Muddy.* New York, 1955
19. *The Girl from Frisco.* New York, 1955
20. *Night Stage.* New York, 1955
21. *Rimrock Town.* New York, 1955
22. *Wagon Train West.* New York, 1955
23. *Man in Blue.* New York, 1956
24. *Strictly from Brooklyn.* New York, 1956
25. *Rocky Malone.* Austin (TX), 1957
26. *Stagecoach West.* New York, 1957
27. *Violence Valley.* New York, 1957
28. *Heller from Texas.* New York, 1957
29. *Left End Luisetti.* Austin, 1958
30. *Guns of Hell Valley.* New York, 1958
31. *Rustler's Range.* New York, 1958
32. *Sabers in the Sun.* New York, 1958
33. *Wagon Wheel Drifter.* New York, 1958
34. *Then Came Mulvane.* New York, 1959
35. *Rimrock City.* New York, 1959
36. *Second String Hero.* Austin, 1959
37. *Missouri River Boy.* New York, 1959
38. *Back Court Man.* New York, 1960
39. *Bullets for Mulvane.* New York, 1960
40. *Pistoleers on Patrol.* New York, 1960
41. *Mulvane's War.* New York, 1960
42. *King of the West Side.* Grand Rapids (MI), 1961
43. *The Wonder Five.* New York, 1962
44. *Rookie Backstop.* New York, 1962
45. *Last Chance Valley.* New York, 1962
46. *Mulvane on the Prod.* New York, 1962
47. *Guns Along the Big Muddy.* New York, 1962
48. *Tall in the Saddle.* New York, 1963
49. *Powerhouse Five.* New York, 1963
50. *Famous American Athletes.* New York, 1963
51. *City High Five.* New York, 1964
52. *The Horse That Played the Outfield.* New York, 1964
53. *The Left Hander,* as George Kramer. New York, 1964
54. *Hardcase Holleran.* New York, 1964
55. *Crossfire Creek.* New York, 1964
56. *The Indians Carlisle.* New York, 1965
57. *Hillbilly Hurler.* New York, 1966
58. *Tall Team.* New York, 1966
59. *Scrambling Quarterback.* New York, 1967
60. *Backup Quarterback.* Austin, 1968
61. *Famous Coaches.* New York, 1968
62. *Custer, Man and Legend.* New York, 1968
63. *The "Go Ye" Men: The Life Story of Elmer Kile.* New York, 1968
64. *The Mountain Mission: The Story of Sam R. Hurley.* Joplin (MO), 1968
65. *Kid Battery,* as George Kramer. New York, 1968
66. *The Goofer Pitch.* New York, 1969
67. *Buffalo Soldier.* New York, 1969
68. *City High Champions.* New York, 1969
69. *Gridiron Stranger.* Philadelphia, 1970
70. *Home Run Henry.* New York, 1970
71. *Fastbreak Rebel.* New York, 1971
72. *Little League Hotshots.* New York, 1972
73. *Famous American Indians.* New York, 1972

Heyer, Georgette
British, born in 1902, died July 5, 1974
Pseudonym: Stella Martin
1. *The Black Moth.* London and Boston, 1921
2. *The Great Roxhythe.* London, 1922
3. *The Transformation of Philip Jettan,* as Stella Martin. London, 1923
4. *Instead of the Thorn.* London, 1923
5. *Simon the Coldheart.* London and Boston, 1925
6. *These Old Shades.* London and Boston, 1926
7. *Helen.* London and New York, 1928
8. *The Masqueraders.* London, 1928
9. *Beauvallet.* London, 1929
10. *Pastel.* London and New York, 1929
11. *Barren Corn.* London and New York, 1930
12. *The Conqueror.* London, 1931
13. *Footsteps in the Dark.* London, 1932
14. *Why Shoot the Butler?* London, 1933
15. *The Unfinished Clue.* London, 1934
16. *The Convenient Marriage.* London, 1934
17. *Devil's Cub.* London, 1934
18. *Regency Buck.* London, 1935
19. *Death in the Stocks.* London, 1935
20. *Behold, Here's Poison!* London and New York, 1936
21. *The Talisman Ring.* London, 1936
22. *An Infamous Army.* London, 1937
23. *They Found Him Dead.* London and New York, **1937**
24. *A Blunt Instrument.* London and New York, 1938
25. *Royal Escape.* London, 1938
26. *No Wind of Blame.* London and New York, 1939
27. *The Spanish Bride.* London and New York, 1940
28. *The Corinthian.* London, 1940
29. *Faro's Daughter.* London, 1941
30. *Beau Wyndham.* New York, 1941
31. *Envious Casca.* London and New York, 1941
32. *Penhallow.* London, 1942
33. *Friday's Child.* London, 1944
34. *The Reluctant Widow.* London and New York, 1946
35. *The Foundling.* London and New York, 1948
36. *Arabella.* London and New York, 1949
37. *The Grand Sophy.* London and New York, 1950
38. *The Quiet Gentleman.* London, 1951
39. *Duplicate Death.* London, 1951
40. *Detection Unlimited.* London, 1953
41. *Cotillion.* London and New York, 1953
42. *The Toll-Gate.* London and New York, 1954
43. *Bath Tangle.* London and New York, 1955
44. *Sprig Muslin.* London and New York, 1956
45. *April Lady.* London and New York, 1957
46. *Sylvester; or, The Wicked Uncle.* London and New York, 1957
47. *Venetia.* London, 1958
48. *The Unknown Ajax.* London, 1959
49. *Pistols for Two and Other Stories.* London, 1960
50. *A Civil Contract.* London, 1961
51. *The Nonesuch.* London, 1962
52. *False Colours.* London, 1963
53. *Frederica.* London and New York, 1965
54. *Black Sheep.* London, 1966
55. *Cousin Kate.* London, 1968
56. *Charity Girl.* London and New York, 1970
57. *Lady of Quality.* London and New York, 1972
58. *My Lord John.* London and New York, 1975

Hichens, Robert (Smythe)
    British, born in 1864, died July 20, 1950
1. *The Coastguard's Secret.* London, 1886
2. *The Green Carnation* (published anonymously). London and New York, 1894
3. *After Tomorrow, and The New Love.* New York, 1895
4. *An Imaginative Man.* London and New York, 1895
5. *The Folly of Eustace and Other Stories.* London and New York, 1896
6. *Byeways.* London and New York, 1897
7. *Flames: A London Phantasy.* London and Chicago, 1897
8. *The Medicine Man,* with H.D. Trail. New York, 1898
9. *The Londoner: An Absurdity.* London and Chicago, 1898
10. *The Daughter of Babylon,* with Wilson Barrett. London and Philadelphia, 1899
11. *The Slave.* London and Chicago, 1899
12. *Tongues of Conscience.* London and New York, 1900
13. *Homes of the Passing Show,* with others. London, 1900
14. *The Prophet of Berkeley Square: A Tragic Extravanganza.* London and New York, 1901
15. *Felix: Three Years of a Life.* London, 1902
16. *The Garden of Allah.* London and New York, 1904
17. *The Woman with the Fan.* London and New York, 1904
18. *The Black Spaniel and Other Stories.* London and New York, 1905
19. *The Call of the Blood.* London and New York, 1906
20. *Barbary Sheep.* New York, 1907
21. *A Spirit in Prison.* London and New York, 1908
22. *Egypt and Its Monuments.* London and New York, 1908
23. *Bella Donna.* London and Philadelphia, 1909
24. *The Knock on the Door.* London and Philadelphia, 1909
25. *The Holy Land.* London and New York, 1910
26. *The Dweller on the Threshold.* London and New York, 1911
27. *The Fruitful Vine.* London and New York, 1911
28. *The Near East.* London and New York, 1913
29. *The Way of Ambition.* London and New York, 1913
30. *The Hindu.* New York, 1917
31. *Snake-Bite and Other Stories.* London and New York, 1919
32. *Mrs. Marden.* London and New York, 1919
33. *The Spirit of the Time.* London and New York, 1921
34. *December Love.* London and New York, 1922
35. *The Last Time and Other Stories.* London, 1923
36. *After the Verdict.* London and New York, 1924
37. *The God Within Him.* London, 1926
38. *The Bacchante and the Nun.* London, 1927
39. *The Streets and Other Stories.* London, 1928
40. *Dr. Artz.* London and New York, 1929
41. *On the Screen.* London, 1929
42. *The Gates of Paradise and Other Stories.* London, 1930
43. *The Bracelet.* London and New York, 1930
44. *My Desert Friend and Other Stories.* London, 1931
45. *The First Lady Brendon.* London and New York, 1931
46. *Mortimer Brice: A Bit of His Life.* London and New York, 1932
47. *The Paradine Case.* London and New York, 1933
48. *The Gardenia and Other Stories.* London, 1934
49. *The Power to Kill.* London and New York, 1934
50. *The Afterglow and Other Stories.* London, 1935
51. *"Susie's" Career.* London, 1935
52. *The Sixth of October.* London and New York, 1936
53. *Daniel Airlie.* London and New York, 1937
54. *The Journey Up.* London and New York, 1938
55. *Secret Information.* London and New York, 1938
56. *That Which Is Hidden.* London, 1939
57. *The Million: An Entertainment.* London, 1940
58. *Married or Unmarried.* London, 1941
59. *A New Way of Life.* London and New York, 1942
60. *Veils.* London, 1943
61. *Harps in the Wind.* London, 1945
62. *Yesterday: The Autobiography of Robert Hichens.* London, 1947
63. *Incognito.* London, 1947
64. *Too Much Love of Living.* Philadelphia, 1947
65. *The Man in the Mirror and Other Stories.* London, 1950
66. *Beneath the Magic.* London, 1950
67. *The Mask.* London, 1951
68. *Nightbound.* London, 1951

Higgins, George V. (Vincent)
    American, born November 13, 1939
1. *The Friends of Eddie Coyle.* New York and London, 1972
2. *The Digger's Game.* New York and London, 1973
3. *Cogan's Trade.* New York and London, 1974
4. *A City on a Hill.* New York and London, 1975
5. *The Friends of Richard Nixon.* Boston, 1975
6. *The Judgment of Deke Hunter.* Boston and London, 1976
7. *Dreamland.* Boston, 1977
8. *A Year or So with Edgar.* New York, 1979
9. *Kennedy for the Defense.* New York, 1980

Hildick, Wallace (Edmund Wallace Hildick)
    British, born December 29, 1925
    Pseudonym: E.W. Hildick
1. *Jim Starling,* as E.W. Hildick. London, 1958
2. *Jim Starling and the Agency,* as E.W. Hildick. London, 1958
3. *Jim Starling and the Colonel,* as E.W. Hildick. London, 1960
4. *Jim Starling's Holiday,* as E.W. Hildick. London, 1960
5. *The Boy at the Window,* as E.W. Hildick. London, 1960
6. *Bed and Work.* London, 1962
7. *Jim Starling Takes Over,* as E.W. Hildick. London, 1963
8. *Jim Starling and the Spotted Dog,* as E.W. Hildick. London, 1963
9. *Jim Starling Goes to Town,* as E.W. Hildick. London, 1963
10. *Meet Lemon Kelly,* as E.W. Hildick. London, 1963
11. *Birdy Jones,* as E.W. Hildick. London, 1963
12. *Mapper Mundy's Treasure Hunt,* as E.W. Hildick. London, 1963
13. *A Town on the Never.* London, 1963
14. *Lemon Kelly Digs Deep,* as E.W. Hildick. London, 1964
15. *Louie's Lot,* as E.W. Hildick. London, 1965
16. *Lunch with Ashurbanipal.* London, 1965
17. *Word for Word: A Study of Authors' Alterations, with Exercises.* London, 1965
18. *The Questers,* as E.W. Hildick. Leicester (Eng), 1966
19. *Word for Word: The Rewriting of Fiction.* New York, 1966
20. *Close Look at Newspapers [Magazines and Comics, Television, Advertising],* as E.W. Hildick. London, 4 vols., 1966-69
21. *Calling Questers Four,* as E.W. Hildick. Leicester, 1967
22. *The Questers and the Whispering Spy,* as E.W. Hildick. Leicester, 1967
23. *Lucky Les: The Adventures of a Cat of Five Tales,* as E.W. Hildick. London, 1967
24. *Writing with Care: 200 Problems in the Use of English.* London and New York, 1967
25. *Lemon Kelly and the Home-Made Boy,* as E.W. Hildick. London, 1968
26. *Louie's S.O.S.,* as E.W. Hildick. London, 1968
27. *Birdy and the Group,* as E.W. Hildick. London, 1968
28. *Here Comes Parren,* as E.W. Hildick. London, 1968
29. *Back with Parren,* as E.W. Hildick. London, 1968
30. *Lemon Kelly,* as E.W. Hildick. New York, 1968
31. *Thirteen Types of Narrative.* London, 1968

32. *Birdy Swings North,* as E.W. Hildick. London, 1969
33. *Manhattan Is Missing,* as E.W. Hildick. New York, 1969
34. *Top Boy at Twisters Creek,* as E.W. Hildick. New York, 1969
35. *Monte Carlo or Bust!* London, 1969
36. *Those Daring Young Men in Their Jaunty Jalopies.* New York, 1969
37. *Birdy in Amsterdam,* as E.W. Hildick. London, 1970
38. *Ten Thousand Golden Cockerels,* as E.W. Hildick. London, 1970
39. *The Dragon That Lived under Manhattan,* as E.W. Hildick. New York, 1970
40. *The Secret Winners,* as E.W. Hildick. New York, 1970
41. *Children and Fiction: A Critical Study in Depth of the Artistic and Psychological Factors Involved in Writing Fiction for and About Children.* London. 1970
42. *The Secret Spenders,* as E.W. Hildick. New York, 1971
43. *The Prisoners of Gridling Gap: A Report, With Expert Comments from Doctor Ranulf Quitch,* as E.W. Hildick. New York, 1971
44. *My Kid Sister,* as E.W. Hildick. Cleveland, 1971
45. *Cokerheaton,* as E.W. Hildick. London, 1971
46. *Rushbrook,* as E. W. Hildick. London, 1971
47. *Storypacks: A New Concept in English Teaching,* as E.W. Hildick. London, 1971
48. *The Doughnut Dropout,* as E.W. Hildick. New York, 1972
49. *Kids Commune,* as E.W. Hildick. New York, 1972
50. *The Active-Enzyme Lemon-Freshened Junior High School Witch,* as E.W. Hildick. New York, 1973
51. *The Nose Knows,* as E.W. Hildick. New York, 1973
52. *Only the Best: Six Qualities of Excellence.* New York, 1973
53. *Birdy Jones and the New York Heads,* as E.W. Hildick. New York, 1974
54. *Dolls in Danger,* as E.W. Hildick. London, 1974
55. *Louie's Snowstorm,* as E.W. Hildick. New York, 1974
56. *Deadline for McGurk,* as E.W. Hildick. New York, 1975
57. *The Menaced Midget,* as E.W. Hildick. London, 1975
58. *The Case of the Condemned Cat,* as E.W. Hildick. London and New York, 1975
59. *Bracknell's Law.* New York, 1975
60. *Time Explorers Inc,* as E.W. Hildick. New York, 1976
61. *A Cat Called Amnesia,* as E.W. Hildick. New York, 1976
62. *The Case of the Nervous Newsboy,* as E.W. Hildick. London and New York, 1976
63. *The Great Rabbit Robbery,* as E.W. Hildick. London, 1976
64. *The Weirdown Experiment.* New York and London, 1976
65. *The Top-Flight Fully-Automated Junior High School Girl Detective,* as E.W. Hildick. New York, 1977
66. *The Case of the Invisible Dog,* as E.W. Hildick. London and New York, 1977
67. *Vandals.* London, 1977
68. *The Loop.* London, 1977
69. *Louie's Ransom,* as E.W. Hildick. New York, 1978
70. *The Case of the Secret Scribbler,* as E.W. Hildick. London and New York, 1978
71. *The Case of the Phantom Frog,* as E.W. Hildick. London and New York, 1979
72. *The Top-Flight Fully-Automated Girl Detective,* as E.W. Hildick. London, 1979

Hill, Grace Livingston
American, born in 1865, died February 23, 1947
Pseudonyms: Some books may display the name of Grace Livingston Hill-Lutz, Grace Livingston, or Marcia Macdonald

1. *Christian Endeavor Hour,* with R.G.F Hill. New York, 2 vols., 1895-96
2. *A Chautauqua Idyl.* Boston, 1887
3. *The Parkerstown Delegate.* Boston, 1892
4. *Katherine's Yesterday and Other Christian Endeavor Stories.* Boston, 1895
5. *In the Way.* Philadelphia, 1897
6. *Lone Point: A Summer Outing.* Philadelphia and London, 1898
7. *A Daily Rate.* Philadelphia, 1900
8. *An Unwilling Guest.* Philadelphia, 1902
9. *The Angel of His Presence.* Philadelphia, 1902
10. *The Story of a Whim.* Boston, 1903
11. *Because of Stephen.* Boston, 1904
12. *The Girl from Montana.* Boston, 1908
13. *Marcisa Schuyler.* Philadelphia, 1908
14. *Phoebe Dean.* Philadelphia, 1909
15. *Aunt Crete's Emancipation.* Boston, 1911
16. *Dawn of the Morning.* Philadelphia, 1911
17. *The Mystery of Mary.* Philadelphia, 1912
18. *Lo, Michael!* Philadelphia, 1913
19. *The Man of the Desert.* New York, 1914
20. *The Best Man.* Philadelphia, 1914
21. *Miranda.* Philadelphia, 1914
22. *The Obsession of Victoria Gracen.* Philadelphia, 1915
23. *The Finding of Jasper Holt.* Philadelphia, 1916
24. *A Voice in the Wilderness.* New York, 1916
25. *The Witness.* New York, 1917
26. *The Enchanted Barn.* Philadelphia, 1918
27. *The War Romance of the Salvation Army,* with Evangeline Booth. Philadelphia, 1919
28. *The Search.* Philadelphia, 1919
29. *The Red Signal.* Philadelphia, 1919
30. *Cloudy Jewel.* Philadelphia, 1920
31. *Exit Betty.* Philadelphia, 1920
32. *The Tryst.* Philadelphia, 1921
33. *The City of Fire.* Philadelphia, 1922
34. *Tomorrow about This Time.* Philadelphia, 1923
35. *The Big Blue Soldier.* Philadelphia., 1923
36. *Re-creations.* Philadelphia, 1924
37. *Ariel Custer.* Philadelphia, 1925
38. *Not under the Law.* Philadelphia, 1925
39. *A New Name.* Philadelphia, 1926
40. *Coming Through the Rye.* Philadelphia, 1926
41. *Job's Niece.* Philadelphia, 1927
42. *The White Flower.* Philadelphia, 1927
43. *The Honor Girl,* as Marcia Macdonald. Philadelphia, 1927
44. *Found Treasure,* as Marcia Macdonald. Philadelphia, 1928
45. *Crimson Roses.* Philadelphia, 1928
46. *Blue Ruin.* Philadelphia, 1928
47. *Out of the Storm,* as Marcia Macdonald. Philadelphia, 1929
48. *Duskin.* Philadelphia, 1929
49. *The Prodigal Girl.* Philadelphia, 1929
50. *The White Lady,* as Marcia Macdonald. Philadelphia, 1930
51. *Ladybird.* Philadelphia, 1930
52. *The Gold Shoe.* Philadelphia, 1930
53. *Silver Wings.* Philadelphia, 1931
54. *The Chance of a Lifetime.* Philadelphia, 1931
55. *Kerry.* Philadelphia, 1931
56. *Beggarman.* Philadelphia, 1932
57. *Her Wedding Garment.* Philadelphia, 1932
58. *The House Across the Hedge.* Philadelphia, 1932
59. *The Challengers.* Philadelphia, 1932
60. *Happiness Hill.* Philadelphia, 1932
61. *The Story of the Lost Star.* Philadelphia, 1932
62. *The Patch of Blue.* Philadelphia, 1932
63. *The Ransom.* Philadelphia, 1933
64. *Matched Pearls.* Philadelphia, 1933
65. *The Beloved Stranger.* Philadelphia, 1933
66. *Rainbow Cottage.* Philadelphia, 1934
67. *Amorelle.* Philadelphia, 1934

Hill, Grace Livingston

68. *The Christmas Bride.* Philadelphia, 1934
69. *Beauty for Ashes.* Philadelphia, 1935
70. *White Orchids.* Philadelphia, 1935
71. *The Strange Proposal.* Philadelphia, 1935
72. *April Gold.* Philadelphia, 1936
73. *Mystery Flowers.* Philadelphia, 1936
74. *The Substitute Guest.* Philadelphia, 1936
75. *Sunrise.* Philadelphia, 1937
76. *Daphne Deane.* Philadelphia, 1937
77. *Brentwood.* Philadelphia, 1937
78. *The Best Birthday: A Christmas Entertainment for Children.* Philadelphia, 1938
79. *Marigold.* Philadelphia, 1938
80. *The Minister's Son.* Philadelphia, 1938
81. *The Divided Battle.* Philadelphia, 1938
82. *Dwelling.* Philadelphia, 1938
83. *The Lost Message.* Philadelphia, 1938
84. *Maris.* Philadelphia, 1938
85. *Homing.* Philadelphia, 1938
86. *The Seventh Hour.* Philadelphia, 1939
87. *Patricia.* Philadelphia, 1939
88. *Stranger Within the Gates.* Philadelphia, 1939
89. *Head of the House.* Philadelphia, 1940
90. *Rose Falbraith.* Philadelphia, 1940
91. *Partners.* Philadelphia, 1940
92. *By Way of the Silverthorns.* Philadelphia, 1941
93. *In Tune with Wedding Bells.* Philadelphia, 1941
94. *Astra.* Philadelphia, 1941
95. *The Girl of the Woods.* Philadelphia, 1942
96. *Crimson Mountain.* Philadelphia, 1942
97. *The Street of the City.* Philadelphia, 1942
98. *Spice Box.* Philadelphia, 1943
99. *The Sound of the Trumpet.* Philadelphia, 1943
100. *Through These Fires.* Philadelphia, 1943
101. *More Than Conqueror.* Philadelphia, 1944
102. *Time of the Singing of Birds.* Philadelphia, 1944
103. *All Through the Night.* Philadelphia, 1945
104. *A Girl to Come Home To.* Philadelphia, 1945
105. *Bright Arrows.* Philadelphia, 1946
106. *Where Two Ways Met.* Philadelphia, 1947
107. *Mary Arden.* Philadelphia, 1948
108. *Miss Lavina's Call and Other Stories.* Philadelphia, 1949
109. *The Short Stories of Grace Livingston Hill.* New York, 1976

Hill, Pamela

British, born in 1920
Pseudonym: Sharon Fiske

1. *Flaming Janet: A Lady of Galloway.* London, 1954
2. *Shadow of Palaces: The Story of Francoise d'Aubigne, Marquise de Maintenon.* London, 1955
3. *Marjorie of Scotland.* London and New York, 1956
4. *Here Lies Margot.* London, 1957
5. *Madalena.* London, 1963
6. *Forget Not Ariadne.* London, 1965
7. *Julia.* London, 1967
8. *The Devil of Aske.* London, 1972
9. *The Malvie Inheritance.* London, 1973
10. *The Incumbent.* London, 1974
11. *Whitton's Folly.* London and New York, 1975
12. *Norah Stroyan.* London, 1976
13. *The Green Salamander.* London and New York, 1977
14. *Tsar's Woman.* London, 1977
15. *Strangers' Forest.* London and New York, 1978
16. *Daneclere.* London, 1978
17. *Homage to a Rose.* London, 1979
18. *Daughter of Midnight.* London, 1979
19. *Fire Opal.* London and New York, 1980
20. *A Place of Ravens.* London, 1980
21. *Summer Cypress,* as Sharon Fiske. London, 1981
22. *The House of Cray.* London and New York, 1982

Hillerman, Tony

American, born May 27, 1925

1. *The Blessing Way.* New York and London, 1970
2. *The Great Taos Bank Robbery and Other Affairs of Indian Country.* Albuquerque (NM), 1970
3. *The Fly on the Wall.* New York, 1971
4. *The Boy Who Made Dragonfly.* New York, 1972
5. *Dance Hall of the Dead.* New York, 1973
6. *New Mexico.* Portland (OR), 1975
7. *Rio Grande.* Portland (OR), 1976
8. *The Listening Woman.* New York, 1978

Hilton, James

British, born September 9, 1900
Pseudonym: Glen Trevor

1. *Catherine Herself.* London, 1920
2. *Storm Passage.* London, 1922
3. *The Passionate Year.* London, 1923
4. *The Dawn of Reckoning.* London, 1925
5. *The Meadows of the Moon.* London, 1926
6. *Terry.* London, 1927
7. *The Silver Flame.* London, 1928
8. *Murder at School: A Detective Fantasia.* London, 1931
9. *And Now Goodbye.* London, 1931
10. *Contango.* London, 1932
11. *Rage in Heaven.* New York, 1932
12. *Knight Without Armour.* London, 1933
13. *Lost Horizon.* London and New York, 1933
14. *Without Armour.* New York, 1934
15. *Good-bye, Mr. Chips.* London and Boston, 1934
16. *We Are Not Alone.* London and Boston, 1937
17. *To You, Mr. Chips.* London, 1938
18. *Mr. Chips Looks at the World.* Los Angeles, 1939
19. *Random Harvest.* London and Boston, 1941
20. *The Story of Dr. Wassell.* Boston, 1943
21. *Addresses on the Present War and Our Hopes for the Future.* New York, 1943
22. *So Well Remembered.* Boston, 1945
23. *Nothing So Strange.* Boston, 1947
24. *Twilight of the Wise.* London, 1949
25. *Morning Journey.* London and Boston, 1951
26. *Time and Time Again.* London and Boston, 1953
27. *The Duke of Edinburgh.* London, 1956
28. *The Story of Philip, Duke of Edinburgh.* Boston, 1956

Himes, Chester (Bomar)

American, born July 29, 1909

1. *If He Hollers Let Him Go.* New York, 1945
2. *Lonely Crusade.* New York, 1947
3. *Cast the First Stone.* New York, 1953
4. *The Third Generation.* Cleveland, 1954
5. *The Primitive.* New York, 1955
6. *For Love of Imabelle.* New York, 1959
7. *The Crazy Kill.* New York, 1959
8. *The Real Cool Killers.* New York, 1959
9. *All Shot Up.* New York, 1960
10. *The Big Gold Dream.* New York, 1960
11. *Pinktoes.* Paris (France), 1961
12. *Cotton Comes to Harlem.* New York and London, 1965
13. *A Rage in Harlem.* New York, 1965
14. *The Heat's On.* New York and London, 1966
15. *Run Man Run.* New York, 1966
16. *Blind Man with a Pistol.* New York and London, 1969
17. *Hot Day, Hot Night.* New York, 1970
18. *Come Back, Charleston Blue.* New York, 1970

19. *The Quality of Hurt.* New York, 1972
20. *Black on Black, Baby Sister, and Selected Writings.* New York and London, 1975
21. *My Life of Absurdity.* New York, 1976

Hintze, Naomi A. (Agans)
American, born in 1909
1. *Buried Treasure Waits for You.* Indianapolis (IN), 1962
2. *You'll Like My Mother.* New York, 1969
3. *The Stone Carnation.* New York, 1971
4. *Aloha Means Goodbye.* New York, 1972
5. *Listen, Please Listen.* New York, 1974
6. *The Psychic Realm: What Can You Believe?* with J. Gaither Pratt. New York, 1975
7. *Cry Witch.* New York, 1975
8. *Time Bomb,* with Peter van der Linde. New York, 1978

Hobart, Donald Bayne
1. *The Whistling Waddy: A Western Story.* New York, 1928
2. *Double Shuffle.* New York, 1928
3. *Hunchback House.* Racine (WI), 1929
4. *The Adventure Trail.* London, 1929
5. *The Clue of the Leather Noose.* Racine, 1930
6. *The Cell Murder Mystery.* New York, 1931
7. *The Horseshoe Trail.* New York, 1952
8. *Trail of the Twisted Horseshoes.* London, 1954
9. *Ruthless Range.* London, 1957
10. *Homicide Honeymoon.* New York, 1959
11. *Dark Trail.* New York, 1959
12. *Hardcase Guns.* New York, 1959
13. *Arizona Outlaw.* New York, 1961
14. *Six-Gun Empire.* New York, 1965
15. *Iron Horse Gunsmoke.* New York, 1965
16. *Vulture Valley.* New York, 1966
17. *Guns of the Big Hills.* New York, 1966
18. *Gallows Gold.* New York, 1966
19. *The Longhorn Trail.* New York, 1967
20. *Red River Guns.* New York, 1967
21. *Black Stallion Mesa.* New York, 1967
22. *Gunsmoke Country.* New York, 1967
23. *Guns Along the River.* New York, 1968
24. *Warrior Range.* New York, 1968
25. *Sinister Ranch.* New York, 1968

Hoch, Edward D. (Dentinger)
American, born February 22, 1930
1. *The Shattered Raven.* New York, 1969
2. *The Transvection Machine.* New York, 1971
3. *The Judges of Hades and Other Simon Ark Stories.* North Hollywood (CA), 1971
4. *City of Brass and Other Simon Ark Stories.* North Hollywood, 1971
5. *The Spy and the Thief.* New York, 1971
6. *The Fellowship of the Hand.* New York, 1973
7. *The Frankenstein Factory.* New York, 1975
8. *The Thefts of Nick Velvet.* Yonkers (NY), 1978
9. *The Monkey's Clue, and The Stolen Sapphire.* New York, 1978

Hocking, Anne [Mona Naomi Anne Messer Hocking]
British, born in 1890
Pseudonym: Mona Messer
1. *A Castle for Sale,* as Mona Messer. London and New York, 1930
2. *Mouse Trap,* as Mona Messer. London, 1931
3. *Eternal Compromise,* as Mona Messer. London and New York, 1932
4. *Cat's Paw.* London, 1933
5. *Death Duel.* London, 1933
6. *A Dinner of Herbs,* as Mona Messer. London, 1933
7. *Walk into My Parlour.* London, 1934
8. *The Hunt Is Up.* London, 1934
9. *Playing Providence,* as Mona Messer. London, 1934
10. *Wife of Richard,* as Mona Messer. London, 1934
11. *Without the Option.* London, 1935
12. *Cuckoo's Brood,* as Mona Messer. London, 1935
13. *Stranglehold.* London, 1936
14. *The House of En-Dor.* London, 1936
15. *Life Owes Me Something,* as Mona Messer. London, 1936
16. *As I Was Going to St. Ives.* London, 1937
17. *What a Tangled Web.* London, 1937
18. *Tomorrow Also,* as Mona Messer. London, 1937
19. *Ill Deeds Done.* London, 1938
20. *The Little Victims Play.* London, 1938
21. *Marriage Is Like That,* as Mona Messer. London, 1938
22. *So Many Doors.* London, 1939
23. *Old Mrs. Fitzgerald.* London, 1939
24. *Stranger's Vineyard,* as Mona Messer. London, 1939
25. *Deadly Is the Evil Tongue.* New York, 1940
26. *The Wicked Flee.* London, 1940
27. *The Gift of a Daughter,* as Mona Messer. London, 1940
28. *Miss Milverton.* London, 1941
29. *Night's Candles.* London, 1941
30. *Poison Is a Bitter Brew.* New York, 1942
31. *One Shall Be Taken.* London, 1942
32. *Death Loves a Shining Mark.* New York, 1943
33. *Nile Green.* London, 1943
34. *Six Green Bottles.* London, 1943
35. *The Vultures Gather.* London, 1945
36. *Death at the Wedding.* London, 1946
37. *Prussian Blue.* London, 1947
38. *The Finishing Touch.* New York, 1948
39. *At The Cedars.* London, 1949
40. *Death Disturbs Mr. Jefferson.* New York, 1950
41. *The Best Laid Plans.* New York, 1950
42. *Mediterranean Murder.* London, 1951
43. *Killing Kin.* New York, 1951
44. *There's Death in the Cup.* London, 1952
45. *Death among the Tulips.* London, 1953
46. *The Evil That Men Do.* London, 1953
47. *And No One Wept.* London, 1954
48. *Poison in Paradise.* London and New York, 1955
49. *A Reason for Murder.* London, 1955
50. *Murder at Mid-Day.* London, 1956
51. *Relative Murder.* London, 1957
52. *The Simple Way of Poison.* London and New York, 1957
53. *Epitaph for a Nurse.* London, 1958
54. *A Victim Must Be Found.* New York, 1959
55. *Poisoned Chalice.* London, 1959
56. *To Cease upon the Midnight.* London, 1959
57. *The Thin-Spun Life.* London, 1960
58. *Candidates for Murder.* London, 1961
59. *He Had to Die.* London, 1962
60. *Murder Cries Out.* London, 1968

Hodge, Jane Aiken
British, born in 1907
1. *Maulever Hall.* London and New York, 1964
2. *The Adventurers.* New York, 1965
3. *Watch the Wall, My Darling.* New York, 1966
4. *Here Comes a Candle.* London and New York, 1967
5. *The Winding Stair.* London, 1968
6. *Marry in Haste.* London, 1969
7. *Greek Wedding.* London and New York, 1970
8. *Savannah Purchase.* London and New York, 1971
9. *The Double Life of Jane Austen.* London, 1972

10. *Strangers in Company.* London and New York, 1973
11. *Shadow of a Lady.* New York, 1973
12. *One Way to Venice.* London, 1974
13. *Rebel Heiress.* London and New York, 1975
14. *Runaway Bride.* London and New York, 1976
15. *Judas Flowering.* London and New York, 1976
16. *Red Sky at Night: Lovers' Delight?* New York, 1977
17. *Last Act.* London and New York, 1979
18. *Wide Is the Water.* London and New York, 1981
19. *The Lost Garden.* London and New York, 1982

Hodgson, William Hope
British, born November 15, 1877, died April 17, 1918
1. *The Boats of the "Glen Carrig."* London, 1907
2. *The House on the Borderland.* London, 1908
3. *The Ghost Pirates.* London, 1909
4. *The Ghost Pirates, A Chaunty, and Another Story.* New York, 1909
5. *Carnacki, The Ghost Finder, and a Poem.* New York, 1910
6. *The Night Land.* London, 1912
7. *Poems and the Dream of X.* London and New York, 1912
8. *Carnacki, the Ghost Finder.* London, 1913
9. *Men of the Deep Waters.* London, 1914
10. *Cargunka and Poems and Anecdotes.* London and New York, 1914
11. *The Luck of the Strong.* London, 1916
12. *Captain Gault, Being the Exceedingly Private Log of a Sea-Captain.* London, 1917
13. *The Calling of the Sea.* London, 1920
14. *The Voice of the Ocean.* London, 1921
15. *Deep Waters.* Sauk City (WI), 1967
16. *Out of the Storm: Uncollected Fantasies.* West Kingston (RI), 1975
17. *Poems of the Sea.* London, 1977

Hoffman, Lee
American, born August 14, 1932
Pseudonym: Georgia York
1. *Gunfight at Laramie.* New York, 1966
2. *The Legend of Blackjack Sam.* New York, 1966
3. *Bred to Kill.* New York, 1967
4. *Telepower.* New York, 1967
5. *The Valdez Horses.* New York, 1967
6. *Dead Man's Gold.* New York, 1968
7. *The Yarborough Brand.* New York, 1968
8. *The Caves of Karst.* New York, 1969
9. *Wild Riders.* New York, 1969
10. *Loco.* New York, 1969
11. *Return to Broken Crossing.* New York, 1969
12. *West of Cheyenne.* New York, 1969
13. *Always the Blackknight.* New York, 1970
14. *Change Song.* New York, 1972
15. *Wiley's Move.* New York, 1973
16. *The Truth About the Cannonball Kid.* New York, 1975
17. *Fox.* New York, 1976
18. *Nothing But a Drifter.* New York, 1976
19. *Trouble Valley.* New York, 1976
20. *The Sheriff of Jack Hollow.* New York, 1977
21. *The Land Killer.* New York, 1978
22. *Savage Key*, as Georgia York. New York, 1979

Hogan, Ray [Robert Ray Hogan]
American, born December 14, 1908
Pseudonym: Clay Ringold
1. *Ex-Marshal.* New York, 1956
2. *The Friendless One.* New York, 1957
3. *Walk a Lonely Trail.* New York, 1957
4. *Land of Strangers.* New York, 1957
5. *Longhorn Law.* New York, 1957
6. *Marked Man.* New York, 1958
7. *Hangman's Valley.* New York, 1959
8. *Wanted: Alive.* New York, 1959
9. *Marshall Without a Badge.* New York, 1959
10. *Outlaw Marshall.* New York, 1959
11. *Guns Against the Sun.* New York, 1960
12. *Lead Reckoning.* New York, 1960
13. *The Ghost Raider.* New York, 1960
14. *The Shotgunner.* New York, 1960
15. *The Hasty Hangman.* New York, 1960
16. *Raider's Revenge.* New York, 1960
17. *Rebel Raid.* New York, 1961
18. *The Life and Death of Clay Allison.* New York, 1961
19. *The Ridge Runner.* New York, 1961
20. *Ride to the Gun.* New York, 1961
21. *Ambush at Riflestock.* New York, 1961
22. *Track the Man Down.* New York, 1961
23. *Marshal for Lawless.* New York, 1961
24. *The Jim Hendren Story.* New York, 1962
25. *Rebel in Yankee Blue.* New York, 1962
26. *Hell to Hallelujah.* New York, 1962
27. *New Gun for Kingdom City, and The Shotgunner.* New York, 1962
28. *Stranger in Apache Basin.* New York, 1963
29. *The Outside Gun.* New York, 1963
30. *The Life and Death of Johnny Ringo.* New York, 1963
31. *Trail of the Fresno Kid.* New York, 1963
32. *Last Gun at Cabresto.* New York, 1963
33. *Hoodoo Guns.* New York, 1964
34. *Johnny Ringo, Gentleman Outlaw.* London, 1964
35. *Man from Barranca Negra.* New York, 1964
36. *The Trackers.* New York, 1964
37. *Rebel Ghost.* New York, 1964
38. *Night Raider.* New York, 1964
39. *Tombstone Outlaw.* London, 1966
40. *Mosby's Last Raid.* New York, 1966
41. *Panhandle Pistolero.* New York, 1966
42. *Killer's Gun.* New York, 1966
43. *Dead Man on a Black Horse.* New York, 1966
44. *The Hellsfire Lawman.* New York, 1966
45. *Outlaw Mountain.* New York, 1967
46. *Legacy of the Slash M.* New York, 1967
47. *Border Bandit.* New York, 1967
48. *The Wolfer.* New York, 1967
49. *Devil's Butte.* New York, 1967
50. *Texas Lawman.* New York, 1967
51. *The Moon-Lighters.* New York, 1968
52. *Trouble at Tenkiller.* New York, 1968
53. *The Gunmaster.* New York, 1968
54. *The Hell Road.* New York, 1968
55. *Killer on Warbucket.* New York, 1968
56. *Return to Rio Fuego*, as Clay Ringold. New York, 1968
57. *Reckoning in Fire Valley*, as Clay Ringold. New York, 1969
58. *The Hooded Gun*, as Clay Ringold. New York, 1969
59. *The Man Who Killed the Marshal.* New York, 1969
60. *The Trail to Tucson.* New York, 1969
61. *Bloodrock Valley War.* New York, 1969
62. *Texas Guns.* New York, 1969
63. *The Rimrocker.* New York, 1970
64. *The Searching Guns.* New York, 1970
65. *Guns Along the Jicarilla.* New York, 1970
66. *Jackman's Wolf.* New York, 1970
67. *The Outlawed.* New York, 1970
68. *Three Cross.* New York, 1970
69. *Deputy of Violence.* New York, 1971
70. *Duel in Lagrima Valley.* New York, 1971
71. *A Bullet for Mr. Texas.* New York, 1971

72. *Marshal of Babylon.* New York, 1971
73. *Brandon's Posse.* New York, 1971
74. *A Man Called Ryker.* New York, 1971
75. *The Devil's Gunhand.* New York, 1972
76. *Passage to Dodge City.* New York, 1972
77. *The Night Hell's Corner Died.* New York, 1972
78. *The Hangman of San Sabal.* New York, 1972
79. *The Hell Merchant.* New York, 1972
80. *Lawman for Slaughter Valley.* New York, 1972
81. *Showdown at Texas Flat.* New York, 1972
82. *Conger's Woman.* New York, 1973
83. *The Guns of Stingaree.* New York, 1973
84. *Highroller's Man.* New York, 1973
85. *Skull Gold.* New York, 1973
86. *The Vengence Gun.* New York, 1973
87. *Day of Reckoning.* New York, 1973
88. *Man Without a Gun.* New York, 1974
89. *The Texas Brigade.* New York, 1974
90. *Wolf Lawman.* New York, 1974
91. *The Jenner Guns.* New York, 1974
92. *The Scorpion Killers.* New York, 1974
93. *The Tombstone Trail.* New York, 1974
94. *The Doomsday Marshal.* New York, 1975
95. *Honeymaker's Son.* New York, 1975
96. *The Proving Gun.* New York, 1975
97. *Betrayal in Tombstone.* New York, 1975
98. *Day of the Hangman.* New York, 1975
99. *The Last Comanchero.* New York, 1975
100. *Roxie Raker.* New York, 1975
101. *The Vigilante.* New York, 1975
102. *The Yesterday Rider.* New York, 1976
103. *High Green Gun.* New York, 1976
104. *The Regulator: Bill Thompson.* New York, 1976
105. *The Shotgun Rider.* New York, 1976
106. *The Iron Jehu.* New York, 1976
107. *The Doomsday Posse.* New York, 1977
108. *Omaha Crossing.* New York, 1977
109. *Tall Man Riding.* New York, 1977
110. *Bounty Hunter's Moon.* New York, 1977
111. *A Gun for Silver Rose.* New York, 1977
112. *The Peace Keeper.* New York, 1978
113. *The Glory Trail.* New York, 1978
114. *Adam Gann, Outlaw.* New York, 1978
115. *Gun Trap at Arabella.* New York, 1978
116. *The Raptons.* New York, 1979
117. *The Doomsday Trail.* New York, 1979
118. *The Hellborn.* New York, 1979
119. *Overkill at Saddlerock.* New York, 1979
120. *Brandon's Posse and the Hell Merchant.* New York, 1979
121. *Lawman's Choice.* New York, 1980
122. *Pilgrim.* New York, 1980
123. *Ragan's Law.* New York, 1980
124. *The Dead Gun.* New York, 1980
125. *Lawman for the Slaughter.* New York, 1980
126. *The Hell Raiser.* New York, 1980
127. *Outlaw's Pledge.* New York, 1981
128. *The Doomsday Bullet.* New York, 1981
129. *Decision at Doubtful Canyon.* New York, 1981
130. *Renegade Gun.* New York, 1982
131. *The Renegades.* New York, 1982
132. *Fortuna West, Lawman.* New York, 1983
133. *The Law and the Lynchburg.* New York, 1983

Holding, Elisabeth Sanxay
American, born June 8, 1889, died February 7, 1955
1. *Invincible Minnie.* New York and London, 1920
2. *Rosaleen among the Artists.* New York, 1921
3. *Angelica.* New York, 1921
4. *The Unlit Lamp.* New York, 1922
5. *The Shoals of Honor.* New York, 1926
6. *The Silk Purse.* New York, 1928
7. *Miasma.* New York, 1929
8. *Dark Power.* New York, 1930
9. *The Death Wish.* New York, 1934
10. *The Unfinished Crime.* New York, 1935
11. *The Strange Crime in Bermuda.* New York, 1937
12. *The Obstinate Murderer.* New York, 1938
13. *No Harm Intended.* London, 1939
14. *The Girl Who Had to Die.* New York, 1940
15. *Who's Afraid?* New York, 1940
16. *Trial by Murder.* New York, no date
17. *Speak of the Devil.* New York, 1941
18. *Kill Joy.* New York, 1942
19. *Lady Killer.* New York, 1942
20. *The Old Battle Ax.* New York, 1943
21. *Net of Cobwebs.* New York, 1945
22. *The Innocent Mrs. Duff.* New York, 1946
23. *Murder Is a Kill-Joy.* New York, 1946
24. *The Blank Wall.* New York, 1947
25. *Miss Kelly.* New York, 1947
26. *Too Many Bottles.* New York, 1951
27. *The Virgin Huntress.* New York, 1951
28. *The Party Was the Pay-Off.* New York, 1952
29. *Widow's Mite.* New York, 1953

Holding, James
American, born April 27, 1907
Pseudonym: Ellery Queen, Jr.
1. *The Lazy Little Zulu.* New York, 1962
2. *Cato the Kiwi Bird.* New York, 1963
3. *Mr. Moonlight and Omar.* New York, 1963
4. *The King's Contest and Other North African Tales.* London, 1964
5. *The Mystery of the False Fingertips.* London, 1964
6. *Sherlock on the Trail.* New York, 1964
7. *The Purple Bird Mystery,* as Ellery Queen, Jr. New York, 1965
8. *The Three Wishes of Hu.* New York, 1965
9. *The Sky-Eater and Other South Sea Tales.* London, 1966
10. *Poko and The Golden Demon.* London, 1968
11. *The Robber of Featherbed Lane.* New York, 1968
12. *The Mystery of the Dolphin Inlet.* New York, 1968
13. *A Bottle of Pop.* New York, 1972
14. *The Watchcat.* Middletown (CT), 1975

Holland, Isabelle
American, born in 1920
Pseudonym: Francesca Hunt
1. *Cecily.* Philadelphia, 1967
2. *Amanda's Choice.* Philadelphia, 1970
3. *The Man Without a Face.* Philadelphia, 1972
4. *The Mystery of Castle Renaldi,* as Francesca Hunt. Middletown (CT), 1972
5. *Heads You Win, Tails I Lose.* Philadelphia, 1973
6. *Of Love and Death and Other Journeys.* Philadelphia, 1975
7. *Journey for Three.* Boston, 1975
8. *Kilgaren.* New York, 1974
9. *Trelawny.* New York, 1974
10. *Moncrieff.* New York, 1975
11. *Darcourt.* New York, 1976
12. *Genelle.* New York, 1976
13. *The deMaury Papers.* New York, 1977
14. *Alan and the Animal Kingdom.* Philadelphia, 1977
15. *Hitchhike.* Philadelphia, 1977
16. *Tower Abbey.* New York, 1978
17. *Dinah and the Green Fat Kingdom.* Philadelphia, 1978

Holland, Isabelle

18. *Ask No Questions.* London, 1978
19. *The Marchinton Inheritance.* New York, 1979
20. *Counterpoint.* New York, 1980
21. *Now Is Not Too Late.* New York, 1980
22. *Summer of My First Love.* New York, 1981
23. *The Lost Madonna.* New York, 1981

Holland, Sheila
British, born December 22, 1937
Pseudonyms: Sheila Coates, Laura Hardy, Charlotte Lamb, Sheila Lancaster.

1. *Love in a Mist.* London, 1971
2. *Prisoner of the Heart.* London, 1972
3. *A Crown Usurped,* as Sheila Coates. London, 1972
4. *The Queen's Letter,* as Sheila Coates. London, 1973
5. *The Flight of the Swan,* as Sheila Coates. London, 1973
6. *A Lantern in the Night.* London, 1973
7. *Follow a Stranger,* as Charlotte Lamb. London and Toronto, 1973
8. *Carnival Coast,* as Charlotte Lamb. London and Toronto, 1973
9. *A Family Affair,* as Charlotte Lamb. London and Toronto, 1974
10. *Falcon on the Hill.* London, 1974
11. *Shadows at Dawn.* London, 1975
12. *The Growing Season.* London, 1975
13. *The Bells of the City,* as Sheila Coates. London, 1975
14. *The Gold of Apollo.* London, 1976
15. *The Caring Kind.* London, 1976
16. *Star-Crossed,* as Charlotte Lamb. London, 1976
17. *Sweet Sanctuary,* as Charlotte Lamb. London and Toronto, 1976
18. *Festival Summer,* as Charlotte Lamb. London and Toronto, 1977
19. *Florentine Spring,* as Charlotte Lamb. London and Toronto, 1977
20. *Hawk in a Blue Sky,* as Charlotte Lamb. London, 1977
21. *Kingfisher Morning,* as Charlotte Lamb. London, 1977
22. *Master of Comus,* as Charlotte Lamb. London, 1977
23. *The Devil and Miss Hay.* London, 1977
24. *Eleanor of Aquitaine.* London, 1978
25. *Maiden Castle.* Chicago, 1978
26. *Love's Bright Flame.* Chicago, 1978
27. *Dancing Hill.* Chicago, 1978
28. *Folly by Candlelight.* London, 1978
29. *Call Back Yesterday,* as Charlotte Lamb. London and Toronto, 1978
30. *Desert Barbarian,* as Charlotte Lamb. London and Toronto, 1978
31. *Disturbing Stranger,* as Charlotte Lamb. London, 1978
32. *Autumn Conquest,* as Charlotte Lamb. London, 1978
33. *The Long Surrender,* as Charlotte Lamb. London, 1978
34. *The Cruel Flame,* as Charlotte Lamb. London, 1978
35. *Duel of Desire,* as Charlotte Lamb. London, 1978
36. *The Devil's Arms,* as Charlotte Lamb. London, 1978
37. *Pagan Encounter,* as Charlotte Lamb. London, 1978
38. *Sophia.* Chicago, 1979
39. *Forbidden Fire,* as Charlotte Lamb. London, 1979
40. *The Silken Trap,* as Charlotte Lamb. London, 1979
41. *Dark Dominion,* as Charlotte Lamb. London, 1979
42. *Fever,* as Charlotte Lamb. London, 1979
43. *Dark Master,* as Charlotte Lamb. London, 1979
44. *Temptation,* as Charlotte Lamb. London and Toronto, 1979
45. *Twist of Fate,* as Charlotte Lamb. London, 1979
46. *Possession,* as Charlotte Lamb. London, 1979
47. *Love Is a Frenzy,* as Charlotte Lamb. London, 1979
48. *Frustration,* as Charlotte Lamb. London, 1979
49. *Sensation,* as Charlotte Lamb. London, 1979
50. *The Masque.* New York, 1979
51. *Dark Sweet Wanton,* as Sheila Lancaster. London, 1979
52. *The Tilthammer,* as Sheila Lancaster. London, 1980
53. *The Merchant's Daughter.* Chicago, 1980
54. *Miss Charlotte's Fancy.* Chicago, 1980
55. *Secrets to Keep.* Chicago, 1980
56. *Compulsion,* as Charlotte Lamb. London, 1980
57. *Crescendo,* as Charlotte Lamb. London, 1980
58. *Stranger in the Night,* as Charlotte Lamb. London, 1980
59. *Storm Centre,* as Charlotte Lamb. London and Toronto, 1980
60. *Seduction,* as Charlotte Lamb. London, 1980
61. *Savage Surrender,* as Charlotte Lamb. London and Toronto, 1980
62. *A Frozen Fire,* as Charlotte Lamb. London and Toronto, 1980
63. *Man's World,* as Charlotte Lamb. London, 1980
64. *Night Music,* as Charlotte Lamb. London, 1980
65. *Obsession,* as Charlotte Lamb. London, 1980
66. *Retribution,* as Charlotte Lamb. London and Toronto, 1981
67. *Illusion,* as Charlotte Lamb. Toronto, 1981
68. *Heartbreaker,* as Charlotte Lamb. Toronto, 1981
69. *Desire,* as Charlotte Lamb. London and Toronto, 1981
70. *Dangerous,* as Charlotte Lamb. London and Toronto, 1981
71. *Abduction,* as Charlotte Lamb. London and Toronto, 1981
72. *Burning Memories,* as Laura Hardy. London, 1981
73. *Playing with Fire,* as Laura Hardy. London, 1981
74. *Dream Master,* as Laura Hardy. London, 1982
75. *Tears and Red Roses,* as Laura Hardy. London, 1982
76. *Mistress of Fortune,* as Sheila Lancaster. London, 1982

Holman, C. Hugh [Clarence Hugh Holland]
American, born February 24, 1914
Pseudonym: Clarence Hunt

1. *Death Like Thunder.* New York, 1942
2. *Trout in the Milk.* New York, 1945
3. *Slay the Murderer.* New York, 1946
4. *Up This Crooked Way.* New York, 1946
5. *Another Man's Poison.* New York, 1947
6. *Small Town Corpse,* as Clarence Hunt. New York, 1951
7. *A Handbook to Literature.* New York, 1960
8. *Thomas Wolfe.* Minneapolis, 1960
9. *John P. Marquand.* Minneapolis, 1965
10. *Three Modes of Modern Southern Fiction.* Athens (GA), 1966
11. *The Roots of Southern Writing.* Athens, 1972
12. *"Detective Fiction as American Realism."* Bowling Green (OH), 1972
13. *The Loneliness at the Core: Studies in Thomas Wolfe.* Baton Rouge (LA), 1975
14. *The Immoderate Past.* Athens, 1977
15. *Windows on the World.* Knoxville (TN), 1979

Holt, Victoria [Eleanor Alice Hibbert]
British, born in 1906
Other pseudonyms: Eleanor Burford, Philippa Carr, Elbur Ford, Kathleen Kellow, Jean Plaidy, Ellalice Tate

1. *Daughter of Anna,* as Eleanor Burford. London, 1941
2. *Passionate Witness,* as Eleanor Burford. London, 1941
3. *The Married Lover,* as Eleanor Burford. London, 1942
4. *When All the World Is Young,* as Eleanor Burford. London, 1943
5. *So the Dreams Depart,* as Eleanor Burford. London, 1944
6. *Not in Our Stars,* as Eleanor Burford. London, 1945
7. *Together They Ride,* as Jean Plaidy. London, 1945
8. *Beyond the Blue Montains,* as Jean Plaidy. New York, 1947
9. *Dear Chance,* as Eleanor Burford. London, 1947
10. *Alexa,* as Eleanor Burford. London, 1948

11. *The House at Cupid's Cross,* as Eleanor Burford. London, 1949
12. *Murder Most Royal,* as Jean Plaidy. London, 1949
13. *The Goldsmith's Wife,* as Jean Plaidy. London and New York, 1950
14. *Believe the Heart,* as Eleanor Burford. London, 1950
15. *The Love Child,* as Eleanor Burford. London, 1950
16. *Poison in Pimlico,* as Elbur Ford. London, 1950
17. *Flesh and the Devil,* as Elbur Ford. London, 1950
18. *Saint or Sinner?* as Eleanor Burford. London, 1951
19. *Madame Serpent,* as Jean Plaidy. London and New York, 1951
20. *The Bed Disturbed,* as Elbur Ford. London, 1952
21. *The Italian Woman,* as Jean Plaidy. London, 1952
22. *Dear Delusion,* as Eleanor Burford. London, 1952
23. *Daughter of Satan,* as Jean Plaidy. London, 1952
24. *Bright Tomorrow,* as Eleanor Burford. London, 1952
25. *Danse Macabre,* as Kathleen Kellow. London, 1952
26. *Rooms at Mrs. Oliver's,* as Kathleen Kellow. London, 1953
27. *Such Bitter Business,* as Elbur Ford. London, 1953
28. *The Sixth Wife,* as Jean Plaidy. London, 1953
29. *Queen Jezebel,* as Jean Plaidy. London and New York, 1953
30. *Leave Me My Love,* as Eleanor Burford. London, 1953
31. *When We Are Married,* as Eleanor Burford. London, 1953
32. *Lilith,* as Kathleen Kellow. London, 1954
33. *The Spanish Bridegroom,* as Jean Plaidy. London, 1954
34. *St. Thomas's Eve,* as Jean Plaidy. London, 1954
35. *Castles in Spain,* as Eleanor Burford. London, 1954
36. *Heart's Afire,* as Eleanor Burford. London, 1954
37. *It Began in Vauxhall Gardens,* as Kathleen Kellow. London, 1955
38. *Gay Lord Robert,* as Jean Plaidy. London, 1955
39. *Royal Road to Fotheringay,* as Jean Plaidy, London, 1955
40. *When Other Hearts,* as Eleanor Burford. London, 1955
41. *Two Loves in Her Life,* as Eleanor Burford. London, 1955
42. *Begin to Live,* as Eleanor Burford. London, 1955
43. *Married in Haste,* as Eleanor Burford. London, 1956
44. *Call of the Blood,* as Kathleen Kellow. London, 1956
45. *The Wandering Prince,* as Jean Plaidy. London, 1956
46. *A Health unto His Majesty,* as Jean Plaidy. London, 1956
47. *Defenders of the Faith,* as Ellalice Tate. London, 1956
48. *The Scarlet Cloak,* as Ellalice Tate. London, 1957
49. *Rochester, The Mad Earl,* as Kathleen Kellow. London, 1957
50. *Here Lies Our Sovereign Lord,* as Jean Plaidy. London, 1957
51. *Flaunting Extravagant Queen (Marie Antoinette),* as Jean Plaidy. London, 1957
52. *To Meet a Stranger,* as Eleanor Burford. London, 1957
53. *The Queen of Diamonds,* as Ellalice Tate. London, 1958
54. *Pride of the Morning,* as Eleanor Burford. London, 1958
55. *Blaze of Noon,* as Eleanor Burford. London, 1958
56. *Madonna of the Seven Hills,* as Jean Plaidy. London, 1958
57. *Light on Lucrezia,* as Jean Plaidy. London, 1958
58. *A Triptych of Poisoners,* as Jean Plaidy. London, 1958
59. *Milady Chârlotte,* as Kathleen Kellow. London, 1959
60. *Madame du Barry,* as Ellalice Tate. London, 1959
61. *Louis, the Well-Beloved,* as Jean Plaidy. London, 1959
62. *The Road to Compiegne,* as Jean Plaidy. London, 1959
63. *The Dawn Chorus,* as Eleanor Burford. London, 1959
64. *Red Sky at Night,* as Eleanor Burford. London, 1959
65. *The Rise [Growth, End] of the Spanish Inquisition,* as Jean Plaidy. London, 3 vols., 1959-61
66. *The World's a Stage,* as Kathleen Kellow. London, 1960
67. *Night of Stars,* as Eleanor Burford. London, 1960
68. *Castile for Isabella,* as Jean Plaidy. London, 1960
69. *Mistress of Mellyn,* as Victoria Holt. New York and London, 1960
70. *Spain for the Sovereigns,* as Jean Plaidy. London, 1960
71. *The Young Elizabeth,* as Jean Plaidy. London and New York, 1961
72. *Meg Roper, Daughter of Sir Thomas More.* London, 1961
73. *This Was a Man,* as Ellalice Tate. London, 1961
74. *Daughters of Spain,* as Jean Plaidy. London, 1961
75. *Now That April's Gone,* as Eleanor Burford. London, 1961
76. *Katharine, The Virgin Widow,* as Jean Plaidy. London, 1961
77. *The King's Secret Matter,* as Jean Plaidy. London, 1962
78. *The Shadow of the Pomegranate,* as Jean Plaidy. London, 1962
79. *Who's Calling,* as Eleanor Burford. London, 1962
80. *Kirkland Revels,* as Victoria Holt. New York and London, 1962
81. *The Young Mary Queen of Scots.* London, 1962
82. *The Captive Queen of Scots,* as Jean Plaidy. London, 1963
83. *The Thistle and the Rose,* as Jean Plaidy. London, 1963
84. *Bride of Pendorric,* as Victoria Holt. New York and London, 1963
85. *Mary, Queen of France,* as Jean Plaidy. London, 1964
86. *The Murder in the Tower,* as Jean Plaidy. London, 1964
87. *Evergreen Gallant,* as Jean Plaidy. London, 1965
88. *The Legend of the Seventh Virgin,* as Victoria Holt. New York and London, 1965
89. *The Three Crowns,* as Jean Plaidy. London, 1965
90. *The Haunted Sister,* as Jean Plaidy. London, 1966
91. *The Queen's Favorites,* as Jean Plaidy. London, 1966
92. *Menfreya in the Morning,* as Victoria Holt. New York, 1966
93. *Queen in Waiting,* as Jean Plaidy. London, 1967
94. *The Princess of Celle,* as Jean Plaidy. London, 1967
95. *The King of the Castle,* as Victoria Holt. New York and London, 1967
96. *The Prince and the Quakeress,* as Jean Plaidy. London, 1968
97. *Caroline, The Queen,* as Jean Plaidy. London, 1968
98. *The Queen's Confession,* as Victoria Holt. New York and London, 1968
99. *Katharine of Aragon,* as Jean Plaidy. London, 1968
100. *Catherine de'Medici,* as Jean Plaidy. London, 1969
101. *The Shivering Sands,* as Victoria Holt. New York and London, 1969
102. *The Third George,* as Jean Plaidy. London, 1969
103. *Perdita's Prince,* as Jean Plaidy. London, 1969
104. *Sweet Lass of Richmond Hill,* as Jean Plaidy. London, 1970
105. *Indiscretions of the Queen,* as Jean Plaidy. London, 1970
106. *The Secret Woman,* as Victoria Holt. New York, 1970
107. *Isabella and Ferdinand,* as Jean Plaidy. London, 1970
108. *The Shadow of the Lynx,* as Victoria Holt. New York and London, 1971
109. *The Regent's Daughter,* as Jean Plaidy. London, 1971
110. *Goddess of the Green Room,* as Jean Plaidy. London, 1971
111. *The Miracle at St. Bruno's,* as Philippa Carr. London and New York, 1972
112. *The Captive of Kensington Palace,* as Jean Plaidy. London, 1972
113. *Victoria in the Wings,* as Jean Plaidy. London, 1972
114. *Charles II,* as Jean Plaidy. London, 1972
115. *On the Night of the Seventh Moon,* as Victoria Holt. New York, 1972
116. *The Curse of the Kings,* as Victoria Holt. New York and London, 1973
117. *The Queen and Lord M,* as Jean Plaidy. London, 1973
118. *The Queen's Husband,* as Jean Plaidy. London, 1973
119. *The Widow of Windsor,* as Jean Plaidy. London, 1974
120. *The Bastard King,* as Jean Plaidy. London, 1974
121. *The House of a Thousand Lanterns,* as Victoria Holt. New York and London, 1974
122. *The Lion Triumphant,* as Philippa Carr. London and New York, 1974

123. *The Witch from the Sea,* as Philippa Carr. London and New York, 1975
124. *Mary, Queen of Scots, The Fair Devil of Scotland,* as Jean Plaidy. London and New York, 1975
125. *The Lion of Justice,* as Jean Plaidy. London, 1975
126. *Lord of the Far Island,* as Victoria Holt. New York and London, 1975
127. *The Passionate Enemies,* as Jean Plaidy. London, 1976
128. *The Plantagenet Prelude,* as Jean Plaidy. London, 1976
129. *Lucrezia Borgia,* as Jean Plaidy. London, 1976
130. *The Pride of the Peacock,* as Victoria Holt. New York and London, 1976
131. *Saraband for Two Sisters,* as Philippa Carr. London and New York, 1976
132. *Lament for a Lost Lover,* as Philippa Carr. London and New York, 1977
133. *The Last of the Stuarts,* as Jean Plaidy. London, 1977
134. *The Devil on Horseback,* as Victoria Holt. New York and London, 1977
135. *The Revolt of the Eaglets,* as Jean Plaidy. London, 1977
136. *The Heart of the Lion,* as Jean Plaidy. London, 1977
137. *The Prince of Darkness,* as Jean Plaidy. London, 1978
138. *The Love-Child,* as Philippa Carr. London and New York, 1978
139. *The Battle of the Queens,* as Jean Plaidy. London, 1978
140. *My Enemy the Queen,* as Victoria Holt. New York and London, 1978
141. *The Spring of the Tiger,* as Victoria Holt. New York and London, 1979
142. *The Queen from Provence,* as Jean Plaidy. London, 1979
143. *Edward Longshanks,* as Jean Plaidy. London, 1979
144. *The Follies of the King,* as Jean Plaidy. London, 1980
145. *The Vow on the Heron,* as Jean Plaidy. London, 1980
146. *The Mask of the Enchantress,* as Victoria Holt. New York and London, 1980
147. *The Song of the Siren,* as Philippa Carr. London and New York, 1980
148. *The Drop of the Dice,* as Philippa Carr. London and New York, 1981
149. *Will You Love Me in September?* as Philippa Carr. New York, 1981
150. *The Judas Kiss,* as Victoria Holt. New York and London, 1981
151. *Passage to Pontefract,* as Jean Plaidy. London, 1981
152. *The Star of Lancaster,* as Jean Plaidy. London, 1981
153. *Epitaph for Three Women,* as Jean Plaidy. London, 1981
154. *Hammer of the Scots,* as Jean Plaidy. New York, 1981
155. *The Adultress,* as Philippa Carr. London, 1982
156. *Red Rose of Anjou,* as Jean Plaidy. London, 1982
157. *The Sun in Splendour,* as Jean Plaidy. London, 1982

Hope, Anthony [Sir Anthony Hope Hawkins]
British, born in 1863, died July 8, 1933
1. *A Man of Mark.* London, 1890
2. *Father Stafford.* London and New York, 1891
3. *Mr. Witt's Widow.* London and New York, 1892
4. *A Change of Air.* London, 1893
5. *Half a Hero.* London, 2 vols., 1893
6. *Sport Royal and Other Stories.* London, 1893
7. *Lover's Fate, and A Friend's Counsel.* Chicago, 1894
8. *The Dolly Dialogues.* London and New York, 1894
9. *The God in the Car.* London, 2 vols., 1894
10. *The Indiscretion of the Duchess.* Bristol (Eng) and New York, 1894
11. *The Prisoner of Zenda.* Bristol and New York, 1894
12. *The Lady of the Pool.* New York, 1894
13. *Comedies of Courtship.* London, 1896
14. *The Heart of Princess Osra and Other Stories.* London and New York, 1896
15. *The Chronicles of Count Antonio.* London and New York, 1895
16. *Phroso.* London and New York, 1897
17. *The Adventure of Lady Ursula.* New York, 1898
18. *Rupert of Hentzau.* Bristol and New York, 1898
19. *Simon Dale.* London and New York, 1898
20. *A Cut and a Kiss.* Boston, 1899
21. *The King's Mirror.* London and New York, 1899
22. *Quisanté.* London and New York, 1900
23. *Captain Dieppe.* New York, 1900
24. *Tristam of Blent.* London and New York, 1901
25. *The Intrusions of Peggy.* London and New York, 1902
26. *Double Harness.* London and New York, 1904
27. *A Servant of the Public.* London and New York, 1905
28. *Sophy of Kravonia.* Bristol and New York, 1906
29. *Tales of Two People.* London, 1907
30. *Helena's Path.* New York, 1907
31. *The Great Miss Driver.* London and New York, 1908
32. *Love's Logic and Other Stories.* New York, 1908
33. *Pilkerton's Peerage.* London, 1909
34. *Dialogue.* Privately printed, 1909
35. *Second String.* London and New York, 1910
36. *Mrs. Maxon Protests.* London and New York, 1911
37. *The New-German-Testament: Some Texts and a Commentary.* London, 1914
38. *Militarism, German and British.* London, 1915
39. *A Young Man's Year.* London and New York, 1915
40. *Why Italy Is with the Allies.* London, 1917
41. *Beaumaroy, Home from the Wars.* London, 1919
42. *Lucinda.* London and New York, 1920
43. *Selected Works.* London, 10 vols., 1925
44. *Little Tiger.* London and New York, 1925
45. *Memories and Notes.* London, 1927
46. *The Philosopher in the Apple Orchard: A Pastoral.* New York, 1936
47. *A Man and His Model.* New York, no date

Hopson, William L.
Pseudonym: John Sims
1. *Gun-Thrower.* New York and London, 1940
2. *Cowpoke Justice.* New York, 1941
3. *The Laughing Vaquero.* New York, 1943
4. *Sunset Ranch.* New York, 1943
5. *Silver Gulch.* New York, 1944
6. *Hell's Horseman.* New York, 1946
7. *Rambling Top Hand.* New York, 1946
8. *The Man from Sonora.* New York, 1946
9. *Notched Guns.* Chicago, 1947
10. *The Gringo Bandit.* New York, 1947
11. *Straight from Boothill.* New York, 1947
12. *Arizona Roundup.* New York, 1948
13. *N P Puncher.* New York, 1948
14. *The Tombstone Stage.* New York, 1948
15. *The Border Raider.* New York, 1948
16. *Big Matt McKee.* Stoke on Trent (Eng), 1949
17. *Horse Thief Masquerade.* New York, 1949
18. *The New Cowhand,* as John Sims. New York, 1949
19. *Outlaw of Hidden Valley,* as John Sims. New York, 1949
20. *Yucca City Outlaw.* New York, 1949
21. *Cattle-War Buckaroo.* New York, 1950
22. *A Thousand Head North.* Stoke on Trent, 1950
23. *Desperado on the Range.* New York, 1951
24. *Desert Campfire,* as John Sims. New York, 1951
25. *The Ranch Cat.* New York, 1951
26. *Killers Five.* New York, 1951
27. *The Last Apaches.* New York, 1951
28. *Gunfighter's Pay.* New York, 1952
29. *Hangtree Range,* as John Sims. New York, 1952

30. *High Saddle.* New York, 1952
31. *Cow Thief Empire.* New York, 1953
32. *Cry Viva.* New York, 1953
33. *Apache Greed.* New York, 1954
34. *Hangtree Ridge,* as John Sims. London, 1954
35. *A Gunman Rode North.* New York, 1954
36. *Apache Kill.* New York, 1954
37. *Bullet-Brand Empire.* New York, 1954
38. *Trouble Rides Tall.* New York, 1955
39. *Montana Gunslinger.* New York, 1956
40. *Vegas, Gunman Marshal.* New York, 1956
41. *Gunfire at Salt Fork.* New York, 1956
42. *Ramrod Vengence.* New York, 1957
43. *Backlash at Cajon Pass.* New York, 1958
44. *Long Ride to Abilene.* New York, 1958
45. *The Last Shoot-Out.* New York, 1958
46. *Twin Masquerade.* New York, 1959
47. *Six Shooter from Socorro.* London, 1959
48. *Mexico After Dark.* New York, 1964
49. *Trouble Takes All.* New York, 1964
50. *Desert Rampage.* New York, 1966
51. *Guns of the Clan.* New York, 1967
52. *Born Savage.* New York, 1970
53. *The Guns of MacCameron.* New York, 1971

Horgan, Paul
American, born August 1, 1903
1. *Lamb of God.* Privately printed, 1927
2. *Men of Arms.* Philadelphia, 1931
3. *The Fault of Angels.* New York, 1933
4. *No Quarter Given.* New York and London, 1935
5. *From the Royal City of the Holy Faith of Saint Francis of Assisi, Being Five Counts of Life in That Place.* Santa Fe (NM), 1936
6. *The Return of the Weed.* New York, 1936
7. *Lingering Walls.* London, 1936
8. *Main Line West.* New York and London, 1936
9. *A Lamp on the Plains.* New York and London, 1937
10. *Figures in a Landscape.* New York, 1940
11. *Far from Cibola.* New York and London, 1938
12. *The Habit of Empire.* Santa Fe and New York, 1938
13. *The Common Heart.* New York, 1942
14. *A Tree on the Plains: A Music Play for Americans.* Dallas (TX), 1943
15. *Look at America: The Southwest.* Boston, 1947
16. *The Devil in the Desert: A Legend of Life and Death in the Rio Grande.* New York, 1952
17. *One Red Rose for Christmas.* New York, 1952
18. *Great River: The Rio Grande in North American History.* New York, 2 vols., 1954
19. *Humble Powers: 3 Novelettes.* London, 1954
20. *The Saintmaker's Christmas Eve.* New York, 1955
21. *The Centuries of Santa Fe.* New York, 1956
22. *Rome Eternal.* New York, 1957
23. *Give Me Possession.* New York, 1957
24. *A Distant Trumpet.* New York and London, 1960
25. *One of the Quietest Things.* Los Angeles (CA), 1960
26. *Citizen of New Salem.* New York, 1961
27. *Abraham Lincoln: Citizen of New Salem.* London, 1961
28. *Mountain Standard Time.* New York and London, 1962
29. *Toby and the Nighttime.* New York and London, 1963
30. *Conquistadors in North American History.* New York, 1963
31. *Conquistadors in North America.* London, 1963
32. *Things as They Are.* New York, 1964
33. *Songs after Lincoln.* New York, 1965
34. *Peter Hurd: A Portrait Sketch from Life.* Austin, 1965
35. *Memories of the Future.* New York and London, 1966
36. *The Peachstone: Stories from Four Decades.* New York, 1967
37. *Everything to Live For.* New York, 1968
38. *Whitewater.* New York, 1970
39. *The Heroic Triad: Essays in the Social Energies of Three Southwestern Cultures.* New York, 1970
40. *Encounters with Stravinsky: A Personal Record.* New York and London, 1972
41. *Approaches to Writing.* New York, 1973
42. *Lamy of Santa Fe: His Life and Times.* New York, 1975
43. *The Thin Mountain Air.* New York, 1977
44. *Josiah Gregg and His Vision of the Early West.* New York, 1979
45. *Mexico Bay.* New York, 1982

Horler, Sydney
British, born July 18, 1888, died October 27, 1954
Pseudonyms: Peter Cavendish, Martin Heritage
1. *Standish of the Rangeland: A Story of Cowboy Pluck and Daring.* London, 1916
2. *Goal! A Romance of the English Cup Ties.* London, 1920
3. *The Breed of the Beverleys.* London, 1921
4. *A Legend of the League.* London, 1922
5. *McPhee.* London, 1922
6. *Love, The Sportsman.* London, 1923
7. *The Mystery of No. 1.* London, 1925
8. *The Ball of Fortune.* London, 1925
9. *School! School!* London, 1925
10. *The Order of the Octopus.* New York, 1926
11. *False-Face.* London and New York, 1926
12. *The House of Secrets.* London, 1926
13. *On the Ball!* London, 1926
14. *The Man Who Saved the Club.* London, 1926
15. *The Black Heart.* London, 1927
16. *In the Dark.* London, 1927
17. *Vivanti.* London and New York, 1927
18. *The Fellow Hagan!* London, 1927
19. *A Life for Sale.* New York, 1928
20. *Chipstead of the Lone Hand.* London, 1928
21. *The 13th Hour.* London, 1928
22. *The Curse of Doone.* London, 1928
23. *Miss Mystery.* London, 1928
24. *The House of Wingate,* as Martin Heritage. London, 1928
25. *Romeo and Julia,* as Peter Cavendish. London, 1928
26. *The Secret Service Man.* London, 1929
27. *Heart Cut Diamond.* London, 1929
28. *Lady of the Night.* London, 1929
29. *The Worst Man in the World.* London, 1929
30. *A House Divided.* New York, 1929
31. *Peril!* New York, 1930
32. *Checkmate.* London, 1930
33. *Danger's Bright Eyes.* London, 1930
34. *The Evil Chateau.* London, 1930
35. *The Murder Mask.* London, 1930
36. *The Screaming Skull and Other Stories.* London, 1930
37. *A Pro's Romance.* London, 1930
38. *The Exploits of Peter.* London, 1930
39. *Cavalier of Chance.* London, 1931
40. *Adventure Calling!* London, 1931
41. *The Man Who Walked with Death.* New York, 1931
42. *Princess after Dark.* London, 1931
43. *The Spy.* London, 1931
44. *The Temptation of Mary Cordon.* London, 1931
45. *Wolves of the Night.* London, 1931
46. *Vivanti Returns.* London, 1931
47. *The Mystery Mission and Other Stories.* London, 1931
48. *Midnight Love.* London, 1931
49. *Black Soul.* London, 1931
50. *The False Purple.* New York, 1932
51. *Gentleman-in-Waiting.* London, 1932

52. *High Stakes.* London, 1932
53. *Horror's Head.* London, 1932
54. *My Lady Dangerous.* London, 1932
55. *Tiger Standish.* London, 1932
56. *Writing for Money.* London, 1932
57. *The Formula.* London, 1933
58. *Harlequin of Death.* London and Boston, 1933
59. *Huntress of Death.* London, 1933
60. *The Menace.* London and Boston, 1933
61. *The Man Who Shook the Earth.* London, 1933
62. *Beauty and The Policeman.* London, 1933
63. *Excitement: An Impudent Autobiography.* London, 1933
64. *The Man from Scotland Yard.* London, 1934
65. *The Charlatan.* Boston, 1934
66. *The Secret Agent.* London and Boston, 1934
67. *S.O.S.* London, 1934
68. *The Prince of Plunder.* London and Boston, 1934
69. *Tiger Standish Comes Back.* London, 1934
70. *Song of the Scrum.* London, 1934
71. *Strictly Personal: An Indiscreet Diary.* London, 1934
72. *London's Underworld: The Record of a Month's Sojourn in the Crime Centres of the Metropolis.* London, 1934
73. *The Lessing Murder Case.* London, 1935
74. *Lord of Terror.* London, 1935
75. *The Mystery of the Seven Cafes: The Novel of the Famous Wireless Play.* London, 1935
76. *The Vampire.* London, 1935
77. *Dying to Live and Other Stories.* London, 1935
78. *The House in Greek Street.* London, 1935
79. *The Stroke Sinister and Other Stories.* London, 1935
80. *The Great Game.* London, 1935
81. *More Strictly Personal: Six Months of My Life.* London, 1935
82. *Death at Court Lady.* London, 1936
83. *The Grim Game.* London and Boston, 1936
84. *The Traitor.* London and Boston, 1936
85. *The Hidden Hand.* London, 1937
86. *Instruments of Darkness.* London, 1937
87. *They Called Him Nighthawk.* London, 1937
88. *The Destroyer, and The Red-Haired Death.* London, 1938
89. *The Evil Messenger.* London, 1938
90. *Dark Journey.* London, 1938
91. *A Gentleman for the Gallows.* London and New York, 1938
92. *Knaves and Co.* London, 1938
93. *The Phantom Forward.* London, 1939
94. *Terror on Tip-Toe.* London, 1939
95. *Tiger Standish Takes the Field.* London, 1939
96. *Here Is an S.O.S.* London, 1939
97. *The Man Who Died Twice.* London, 1939
98. *The Enemy Within the Gates.* London, 1940
99. *The Return of Nighthawk.* London, 1940
100. *Tiger Standish Steps on It.* London, 1940
101. *Malefactor's Row: A Book of Crime Studies.* London, 1940
102. *Enter the Ace.* London, 1941
103. *Nighthawk Strikes to Kill.* London, 1941
104. *Tiger Standish Does His Stuff.* London, 1941
105. *The Man Who Stayed to Supper: A Comedy.* London, 1941
106. *The Man Who Died Twice.* London, 1941
107. *Danger Preferred.* London, 1942
108. *Fear Walked Behind.* London, 1942
109. *The Man in White.* London, 1942
110. *The Night of Reckoning.* London, 1942
111. *Now Let Us Hate.* London, 1942
112. *The Hostage.* London, 1943
113. *High Hazard.* London, 1943
114. *The Man Who Preferred Cocktails.* London, 1943
115. *Murder Is So Simple.* London, 1943
116. *Tiger Standish Has a Party.* London, 1943
117. *Springtime Comes to William.* London, 1943
118. *The Man Who Mislaid the War.* London, 1943
119. *The Lady with the Limp.* London, 1944
120. *The Man with Dry Hands.* London, 1944
121. *Nighthawk Mops Up.* London, 1944
122. *A Bullet for the Countess.* London, 1945
123. *Virus X.* London, 1945
124. *Dark Danger.* New York, 1945
125. *Terror Comes to Twelvetrees.* London, 1945
126. *Murder for Sale.* London, 1945
127. *Marry the Girl.* London, 1945
128. *Great Adventure, and Out of a Dark Sky.* London, 1946
129. *High Pressure.* London, 1946
130. *Oh, Professor!* London, 1946
131. *Corridors of Fear.* London, 1947
132. *Ring Up Nighthawk.* London, 1947
133. *The Man with Three Wives.* London, 1947
134. *The Closed Door.* London, 1948
135. *Exit the Disguiser.* London, 1948
136. *The House with the Light.* London, 1948
137. *The Man Who Did Not Hang.* London, 1948
138. *Man Alive.* London, 1948
139. *The Man Who Loved Spiders.* London, 1949
140. *They Thought He Was Dead.* London, 1949
141. *Whilst the Crowd Roared.* Stoke on Trent (Eng), 1949
142. *A Man of Affairs.* London, 1949
143. *Master of Venom.* London, 1949
144. *Haloes for Hire.* London, 1949
145. *The Beacon Light.* London, 1949
146. *I Accuse the Doctors, Being a Candid Commentary on the Hostility Shown by the Leaders of the Medical Profession Towards the Healing Art of Osteopathy, and How the Public Suffers in Consequence.* London, 1949
147. *The Blanco Case.* London, 1950
148. *The High Game.* London, 1950
149. *The House of the Uneasy Dead.* London, 1950
150. *Nap on Nighthawk.* London, 1950
151. *Scarlett-Special Branch.* London, 1950
152. *Wedding Bells.* London, 1950
153. *The Devil Comes to Bolobyn.* London, 1951
154. *The Man in the Cloak.* London, 1951
155. *The House of Jackals.* London, 1951
156. *The Man of Evil.* London, 1951
157. *Murderer at Large.* London, 1951
158. *The Mystery of Mr. X.* London, 1951
159. *Scarlett Gets the Kidnapper.* London, 1951
160. *These Men and Women.* London, 1951
161. *Dr. Cupid.* London, 1951
162. *Girl Trouble.* London, 1951
163. *The Blade Is Bright.* London, 1952
164. *The Face of Stone.* London, 1952
165. *Hell's Brew.* London, 1952
166. *The Man Who Used Perfume.* London, 1952
167. *The Mocking Face of Murder.* London, 1952
168. *The Web.* London, 1952
169. *The Cage.* London, 1953
170. *The Dark Night.* London, 1953
171. *Death of a Spy.* London, 1953
172. *The Secret Hand.* London, 1954
173. *Nighthawk Swears Vengeance.* London, 1954
174. *The Man in the Hood.* London, 1955
175. *The Man in the Shadows.* London, 1955
176. *The Dark Hostess.* London, 1955

Horner, Lance
American, born in 1903, died in 1970
1. *The Street of the Sun.* New York, 1956
2. *Mandingo,* with Kyle Onstott. Richmond (VA), 1957

3. *The Tattooed Road.* Middleburg (VA), 1960
4. *Drum.* New York, 1962
5. *Master of Falconhurst.* New York, 1964
6. *Rogue Roman.* New York, 1965
7. *Child of the Sun.* New York, 1966
8. *The Black Sun.* New York, 1967
9. *The Mustee.* New York, 1967
10. *Heir to Falconhurst.* New York, 1968
11. *The Manhound.* New York, 1969
12. *Flight to Falconhurst.* New York, 1971
13. *Mistress of Falconhurst.* New York and London, 1973
14. *Golden Stud.* New York, 1975

Hornung, E.W. (Ernest William)
British, born June 7, 1866, died March 22, 1921
1. *A Bride from the Bush.* London and New York, 1890
2. *Under Two Skies.* London, 1892
3. *Tiny Luttrell.* London and New York, 2 vols., 1893
4. *The Boss of Taroomba.* London, 1894
5. *The Unbidden Guest.* ondon and New York, 1894
6. *The Rogue's March.* London and New York, 1896
7. *Irralie's Bushranger.* London and New York, 1896
8. *My Lord Duke.* London and New York, 1897
9. *Young Blood.* London and New York, 1898
10. *Some Persons Unknown.* London and New York, 1898
11. *Dead Men Tell No Tales.* London and New York, 1899
12. *The Amateur Cracksman.* London and New York, 1899
13. *The Belle of Toorak.* London, 1900
14. *Peccavi.* London and New York, 1900
15. *The Shadow of a Man.* New York, 1901
16. *The Black Mask.* London, 1901
17. *Raffles: Further Adventures of the Amateur Cracksman.* New York, 1901
18. *At Large.* New York, 1902
19. *The Shadow of the Rope.* London and New York, 1902
20. *Denis Dent.* London, 1903
21. *No Hero.* London and New York, 1903
22. *Stingaree.* London and New York, 1905
23. *A Thief in the Night.* London and New York, 1905
24. *Raffles, The Amateur Cracksman.* London, 1906
25. *Mr. Justice Raffles.* London and New York, 1909
26. *The Camera Fiend.* London and New York, 1911
27. *Fathers of Men.* London and New York, 1912
28. *The Thousandth Woman.* London and Indianapolis, 1913
29. *Witching Hill.* London and New York, 1913
30. *The Crime Doctor.* London and Indianapolis, 1914
31. *The Ballad of Ensign Joy.* New York, 1917
32. *Wooden Crosses.* London, 1918
33. *The Young Guard.* London, 1919
34. *Notes of a Camp-Follower on the Western Front.* London and New York, 1919
35. *Old Offenders and a Few Old Scores.* London, 1923
36. *E.W. Hornung and His Young Guard, 1914.* Crowthorne (Eng), 1941

Hosken, Clifford (James Wheeler)
British, born August 29, 1882, died June 9, 1950
Pseudonym: Richard Keverne
1. *Carteret's Cure,* as Richard Keverne. London and Boston, 1926
2. *Tales of Old Inns: The History, Legend, and Romance of Some of Our Older Hostelries,* as Richard Keverne. London, 1927
3. *William Cook, Antique Dealer,* as Richard Keverne. London, 1928
4. *The Strange Case of "William" Cook,* as Richard Keverne. New York, 1928
5. *The Havering Plot,* as Richard Keverne. London, 1928
6. *The Sanfield Scandal,* as Richard Keverne. London and New York, 1929
7. *The Man in the Red Hat,* as Richard Keverne. London and New York, 1930
8. *The Pretender.* London, 1930
9. *The Shadow Syndicate.* London and New York, 1930
10. *The Fleet Hall Inheritance,* as Richard Keverne. London and New York, 1931
11. *At the Blue Gates,* as Richard Keverne. London and New York, 1932
12. *Missing from His Home.* London, 1932
13. *Menace,* as Richard Keverne. London, 1933
14. *Artifex Intervenes: Three Detective Adventures,* as Richard Keverne. London, 1934
15. *He Laughed at Murder,* as Richard Keverne. London, 1934
16. *Crook Stuff,* as Richard Keverne. London, 1935
17. *White Gas,* as Richard Keverne. London, 1937
18. *More Crook Stuff,* as Richard Keverne. London, 1938
19. *Open Verdict,* as Richard Keverne. London, 1940
20. *The Black Cripple,* as Richard Keverne. London, 1941
21. *Crooks and Vagabonds,* as Richard Keverne. London, 1941
22. *The Lady in No. 4,* as Richard Keverne. London, 1944
23. *Coroner's Verdict: Accident,* as Richard Keverne. Philadelphia, 1945

Hough, Emerson
American, born June 28, 1857, died April 30, 1923
1. *Madre d'Oro: A Four-Act Spectacular Drama.* Chicago, 1889
2. *The Singing Mouse Stories.* New York, 1895
3. *The Story of the Cowboy.* New York and London, 1897
4. *The Girl at the Halfway House: A Story of the Plains.* New York, 1900
5. *The Mississippi Bubble.* Indianapolis, 1902
6. *The Way to the West and the Lives of Three Early Americans: Boone, Crockett, Carson.* Indianapolis, 1903
7. *The Law of the Land.* Indianapolis, 1904
8. *Heart's Desire.* New York and London, 1905
9. *The King of Gee-Whiz.* Indianapolis, 1906
10. *The Story of the Outlaw: A Study of the Western Desperado.* New York, 1907
11. *The Way of a Man.* New York, 1907
12. *The Cowboy.* New York, 2 vols., 1908
13. *The Sowing: A "Yankee's" View of England's Duty to Herself and to Canada.* Chicago, 1909
14. *54-40 or Fight.* Indianapolis, 1909
15. *The Purchase Price; or, The Cause of Compromise.* Indianapolis, 1910
16. *John Rawn, Prominent Citizen.* Indianapolis, 1912
17. *Getting a Wrong Start: A Truthful Autobiography.* New York, 1915
18. *Out of Doors.* New York, 1915
19. *Let Us Go Afield.* New York, 1916
20. *The Firefly's Light.* New York, 1916
21. *The Magnificent Adventure.* New York, 1916
22. *The Lady and the Pirate.* Indianapolis, 1917
23. *The Man Next Door.* New York and London, 1917
24. *The Broken Gate.* New York and London, 1917
25. *The Way Out: A Story of the Cumberlands Today.* New York and London, 1918
26. *The Indefinite American Attitude Toward the War and When Shall It Change?* New York, 1918
27. *The Passing of the Frontier: A Chronicle of the Old West.* New Haven (CT), 1918
28. *The Web.* Chicago, 1919
29. *The Sagebrusher.* New York and London, 1919
30. *Maw's Vacation: The Story of a Human Being in the Yellowstone.* St. Paul (MN), 1921

31. *The Covered Wagon.* New York and London, 1922
32. *North of 36.* New York and London, 1923
33. *Mother of Gold.* New York and London, 1924
34. *The Ship of Souls.* New York and London, 1925
35. *The American Rifle.* Albuquerque (NM), 1970

Hough, S.B. (Stanley Bennett)
British, born February 25, 1917
Pseudonyms: Rex Gordon, Bennett Stanley
1. *Frontier Incident.* London, 1951
2. *Moment of Decision.* London, 1952
3. *Mission in Guemo.* London, 1953
4. *Sea Struck,* as Bennett Stanley. New York, 1953
5. *The Seas South.* London, 1953
6. *The Alscott Experiment,* as Bennett Stanley. London, 1954
7. *Sea to Eden.* London, 1954
8. *The Primitives.* London, 1954
9. *Utopia 239,* as Rex Gordon. London, 1955
10. *Government Contract,* as Bennett Stanley. London, 1956
11. *Extinction Bomber.* London, 1956
12. *No Man Friday,* as Rex Gordon. London, 1956
13. *First on Mars,* as Rex Gordon. New York, 1957
14. *A Pound a Day Inclusive: The Modern Way to Holiday Travel.* London, 1957
15. *The Bronze Perseus.* London, 1959
16. *First to the Stars,* as Rex Gordon. New York, 1959
17. *Expedition Everyman: Your Way on Your Income to All the Desirable Places of Europe.* London, 1959
18. *Beyond the Eleventh Hour.* London, 1961
19. *The Worlds of Eclos,* as Rex Gordon. London, 1961
20. *First Through Time,* as Rex Gordon. New York, 1962
21. *The Tender Killer.* New York, 1963
22. *The Time Factor,* as Rex Gordon. London, 1964
23. *Expedition Everyman 1964.* London, 1964
24. *Where? An Independent Report on Holiday Resorts in Britain and the Continent.* London, 1964
25. *Dear Daughter Dead.* London, 1965
26. *Utopia Minus X,* as Rex Gordon. New York, 1967
27. *The Paw of God,* as Rex Gordon. London, 1967
28. *Sweet Sister Seduced.* London, 1968
29. *The Yellow Fraction,* as Rex Gordon. New York, 1969
30. *Fear Fortune, Father.* London, 1974

Household, Geoffrey (Edward West)
British, born November 30, 1900
1. *The Terror of Villadonga.* London, 1936
2. *The Spanish Cave.* Boston, 1936
3. *The Third Hour.* London, 1937
4. *The Salvation of Pisco Gabar and Other Stories.* London, 1938
5. *Rogue Male.* London and Boston, 1939
6. *Man Hunt.* New York, 1942
7. *Arabesque.* London and Boston, 1948
8. *The High Place.* London and Boston, 1950
9. *A Rough Shoot.* London and Boston, 1951
10. *A Time to Kill.* Boston, 1951
11. *Tales of Adventurers.* London and Boston, 1952
12. *Fellow Passenger.* London and Boston, 1955
13. *The Exploits of Xenophon.* New York, 1955
14. *Hang the Man High.* New York, 1957
15. *The Brides of Solomon and Other Stories.* London and Boston, 1958
16. *Against the Wind.* London, 1958
17. *Watcher in the Shadows.* London and Boston, 1960
18. *Xenophon's Adventure.* London, 1961
19. *Thing to Love.* London and Boston, 1963
20. *Olura.* London and Boston, 1965
21. *Sabres on the Sand and Other Stories.* London and Boston, 1966
22. *The Courtesy of Death.* London and Boston, 1967
23. *Prisoner of the Indies.* London and Boston, 1967
24. *Dance of the Dwarfs.* London and Boston, 1968
25. *Doom's Caravan.* London and Boston, 1971
26. *The Three Sentinels.* London and Boston, 1972
27. *The Lives and Times of Bernardo Brown.* London, 1973
28. *Red Anger.* London and Boston, 1975
29. *The Cats to Come.* London, 1975
30. *Escape into Daylight.* London and Boston, 1976
31. *Hostage-London: The Diary of Julian Despard.* London and Boston, 1977
32. *The Last Two Weeks of Georges Rivac.* London and Boston, 1978
33. *The Europe That Was.* Newton Abbot (Eng) and New York, 1979

Houston, Tex
1. *The Sheriff of Hammer County.* London, 1956
2. *Gunman Deputy.* London, 1957
3. *Gunslinger.* London, 1959

Howard, Mary [Mary Mussi]
British, born in 1907
Other pseudonym: Josephine Edgar
1. *Windier Skies.* London, 1930
2. *Dark Morality.* London, 1932
3. *Partners for Playtime.* London, 1938
4. *Strangers in Love.* London, 1939
5. *It Was Romance.* London, 1939
6. *The Untamed Heart,* as Mary Howard, London, 1940
7. *Far Blue Horizons.* London, 1940
8. *Uncharted Romance.* New York, 1941
9. *Devil in My Heart.* London and New York, 1941
10. *To-morrow's Hero.* London, 1941
11. *Reef of Dreams.* London, 1942
12. *Guy Is Life.* London and New York, 1943
13. *Have Courage, My Heart.* London, 1943
14. *Anna Heritage.* London, 1944
15. *The Wise Forget.* London, 1944
16. *Family Orchestra.* London and New York, 1945
17. *The Man from Singapore.* London, 1946
18. *Return to Love.* New York, 1946
19. *Weave Me Some Wings.* London, 1947
20. *The Clouded Moon.* New York, 1948
21. *Strange Paths.* London, 1948
22. *Star-Crossed.* London, 1949
23. *There Will I Follow.* London and New York, 1949
24. *Two Loves Have I.* London, 1950
25. *Bow to the Storm.* London, 1950
26. *Sixpence in Her Shoe.* London, 1950
27. *Promise of Delight.* London and New York, 1952
28. *The Gate Leads Nowhere.* London, 1953
29. *Fool's Haven.* London, 1954
30. *Sew a Fine Seam.* London, 1954
31. *Before I Kissed.* London, 1955
32. *The Grafton Girls.* London, 1956
33. *A Lady Fell in Love.* London, 1956
34. *Shadows in the Sun.* London, 1957
35. *Man of Stone.* London, 1958
36. *The Intruder.* London, 1959
37. *The House of Lies.* London, 1960
38. *More Than Friendship.* London, 1960
39. *Surgeon's Dilemma.* London, 1961
40. *The Pretenders.* London, 1962
41. *My Sister Sophie,* as Josephine Edgar. London, 1964
42. *The Big Man.* London, 1965
43. *The Dark Tower,* as Josephine Edgar. London, 1966
44. *The Interloper.* London, 1967

45. *The Dancer's Daughter,* as Josephine Edgar. London, 1968
46. *Time of Dreaming,* as Josephine Edgar. London, 1968
47. *The Repeating Pattern.* London, 1968
48. *The Bachelor Girls.* London, 1968
49. *The Pleasure Seekers.* London, 1970
50. *Home to My Country.* London, 1971
51. *The Devil's Innocents,* as Josephine Edgar. London, 1972
52. *A Right Grand Girl.* London, 1972
53. *The Cottager's Daughter.* New York, 1972
54. *The Stranger at the Gate,* as Josephine Edgar. London, 1973
55. *Soldiers and Lovers.* London, 1973
56. *Who Knows Sammy Halliday?* London, 1974
57. *The Lady of Wildersley,* as Josephine Edgar. London, 1975
58. *The Young Ones.* London, 1975
59. *Duchess,* as Josephine Edgar. London and New York, 1976
60. *The Spanish Summer.* London, 1977
61. *Countess,* as Josephine Edgar. London and New York, 1978
62. *Mr. Rodriguez.* London, 1979

Howard, Robert E. (Ervin)
American, born January 22, 1906, died June 12, 1936
1. *A Gent from Bear Creek.* London, 1937
2. *Skull-Face and Others.* Sauk City (WI), 1946
3. *Conan the Conqueror.* New York, 1950
4. *The Sword of Conan.* New York, 1952
5. *King Conan.* New York, 1953
6. *The Coming of Conan.* New York, 1953
7. *The Sword of Rhiannon.* London, 1954
8. *Conan the Barbarian.* New York, 1954
9. *Tales of Conan,* with L. Sprague de Camp. New York, 1955
10. *Always Comes Evening: The Collected Poems of Robert E. Howard.* Sauk City, 1958
11. *The Dark Man and Others.* Sauk City, 1963
12. *Almuric.* New York, 1964
13. *The Pride of Bear Creek.* West Kingston (RI), 1966
14. *Conan the Adventurer,* with L. Sprague de Camp. New York, 1966
15. *Etchings in Ivory.* Pasadena (CA), 1968
16. *Conan,* with L. Sprague de Camp and Lin Carter. New York, 1968
17. *Conan the Warrior,* with L. Sprague de Camp. New York, 1967
18. *Conan the Usurper,* with L. Sprague de Camp. New York, 1967
19. *King Kull,* with Lin Carter. New York, 1967
20. *Wolfshead.* New York, 1968
21. *Conan the Freebooter,* with L. Sprague de Camp. New York, 1968
22. *Conan the Wanderer,* with L. Sprague de Camp and Lin Carter. New York, 1968
23. *Red Shadows.* West Kingston, 1968
24. *Conan of Cimmeria,* with L. Sprague de Camp and Lin Carter. New York, 1969
25. *Singers in the Shadows.* West Kingston, 1970
26. *Red Blades of Black Cathay,* with Telvis Clyde Smith. West Kingston, 1971
27. *Marchers of Valhalla.* West Kingston, 1972
28. *Echoes from an Iron Harp.* West Kingston, 1972
29. *The Sowers of the Thunder.* West Kingston, 1973
30. *The Vultures: Showdown at Hell's Canyon.* Lakemont (GA), 1973
31. *A Song of the Naked Lands.* No place, 1973
32. *The Gold and the Gray.* No place, 1974
33. *The Incredible Adventures of Dennis Dorgan.* West Linn (OR), 1974
34. *The Lost Valley of Iskander.* West Linn, 1974
35. *The People of the Black Circle.* West Kingston, 1974
36. *Tigers of the Sea.* West Kingston, 1974
37. *Worms of the Earth.* West Kingston, 1974
38. *A Witch Shall Be Born.* West Kingston, 1975
39. *Red Nails.* West Kingston, 1975
40. *Vultures of Wapeton.* New York, 1976
41. *Swords of Shahrazar.* West Linn and London, 1976
42. *Black Vulmea's Vengence and Other Tales of Pirates.* West Kingston, 1976
43. *Skull-Face Omnibus.* London, 3 vols., 1976
44. *The Devil in Iron.* New York, 1976
45. *Son of the White Wolf.* West Linn, 1977
46. *The Hour of the Dragon.* New York, 1977
47. *The People of the Black Circle.* New York, 1977
48. *The Last Ride.* New York, 1978
49. *The Road of Azrael.* RI, 1979

Howatch, Susan (Elizabeth)
British, born July 14, 1940
1. *The Dark Shore.* New York, 1965
2. *The Waiting Sands.* New York, 1966
3. *Call in the Night.* New York, 1967
4. *The Shrouded Walls.* New York, 1968
5. *April's Grave.* New York, 1969
6. *The Devil on Lammas Night.* New York, 1970
7. *Penmarric.* New York and London, 1971
8. *Cahelmara.* New York and London, 1974
9. *The Rich Are Different.* New York and London, 1977
10. *Sins of the Fathers.* New York and London, 1980

Hoy, Elizabeth [Alice Nina Conarain]
Irish
1. *Love in Apron Strings.* London, 1933
2. *Roses in the Snow.* London, 1936
3. *Crown for a Lady.* London, 1937
4. *Sally in the Sunshine.* London, 1937
5. *Shadow of the Hills.* London, 1938
6. *Stars over Egypt.* London, 1938
7. *You Belong to Me.* London, 1939
8. *Mirage for Love.* London, 1939
9. *Runaway Bride.* London, 1939
10. *You Took My Heart.* London, 1939
11. *Enchanted Wilderness.* London, 1940
12. *Heart, Take Care!* London, 1940
13. *It Had to Be You.* London, 1940
14. *You Can't Lose Yesterday.* London, 1940
15. *I'll Find You Again.* London, 1941
16. *Take Love Easy.* London, 1941
17. *Come Back, My Dream.* London, 1942
18. *Hearts at Random.* London, 1942
19. *Proud Citadel.* London, 1942
20. *Ask Only Love.* London, 1943
21. *One Step from Heaven.* London, 1943
22. *Give Me New Wings.* London, 1944
23. *Sylvia Sorelle.* London, 1944
24. *Heart's Haven.* London, 1945
25. *It's Wise to Forget.* London, 1945
26. *Dear Stranger.* London, 1946
27. *Sword in the Sun.* London, 1946
28. *To Win a Paradise.* London, 1947
29. *The Dark Loch.* London, 1948
30. *Though I Bid Farewell.* London, 1948
31. *Background to Hyacinthe.* London, 149
32. *Immortal Morning.* London, 1949
33. *June for Enchantment.* London, 1949
34. *The Vanquished Heart.* London, 1949
35. *For Love's Sake Only.* New York, 1951
36. *Silver Maiden.* London, 1951
37. *When You Have Found Me.* London and New York, 1951
38. *White Hunter.* London, 1951

39. *The Enchanted.* London, 1952
40. *The Web of Love.* London, 1952
41. *Fanfare for Lovers.* London, 1953
42. *If Love Were Wise.* London, 1954
43. *So Loved and So Far.* London, 1954
44. *Snare the Wild Heart.* London, 1955
45. *Who Loves Believes.* London, 1955
46. *Young Doctor Kirkdene.* London, 1955
47. *Because of Doctor Danville.* London, 1955
48. *My Heart Has Wings.* London, 1957
49. *Do Something Dangerous.* London, 1958
50. *City of Dreams.* London, 1959
51. *Dark Horse, Dark Rider.* London, 1960
52. *Dear Fugitive.* London and Toronto, 1960
53. *The Door into the Rose Garden.* London, 1961
54. *Heart, Have You No Wisdom?* London, 1962
55. *Her Wild Voice Singing.* London, 1963
56. *Homeward the Heart.* London, 1964
57. *Flowering Desert.* London, 1965
58. *The Faithless One.* London, 1966
59. *My Secret Love.* London, 1967
60. *Honeymoon Holiday.* London, 1967
61. *Be More Than Dreams.* London, 1968
62. *Music I Hear with You.* London, 1969
63. *It Happened in Paris.* London, 1970
64. *African Dream.* London, 1971
65. *Into a Golden Land.* London and Toronto, 1971
66. *Immortal Flower.* London and Toronto, 1972
67. *That Island Summer.* London and Toronto, 1973
68. *The Girl in the Green Valley.* London, 1973
69. *Shadows on the Sand.* London and Toronto, 1974
70. *The Blue Hacaranda.* London and Toronto, 1975
71. *When the Dream Fades.* London, 1980

Huffaker, Clair
American, born in 1928
1. *Badge for a Gunfighter.* New York and London, 1957
2. *Rider from Thunder Mountain.* New York, 1957
3. *Cowboy.* New York and London, 1958
4. *Guns of Rio Conchos.* New York, 1958
5. *Posse from Hell.* New York, 1958
6. *Badman.* New York and London, 1958
7. *Flaming Lance.* New York, 1958
8. *Seven Ways from Sundown.* New York, 1960
9. *Good Lord, You're Upside Down!* New York, 1963
10. *Nobody Loves a Drunken Indian.* New York, 1967
11. *The Cowboy and the Cossack.* New York, 1973
12. *The War Wagon.* London, 1974
13. *One Time I Saw Morning Come Home: A Rememberance.* New York, 1974
14. *Guns from Thunder Mountain.* New York, 1975
15. *Rio Conchos.* London, 1975
16. *Clair Huffaker's Profiles of the American West.* New York, 1976

Hufford, Susan
American, born December 15, 1940
1. *Midnight Sailing.* New York, 1975
2. *The Devil's Sonata.* New York, 1976
3. *A Delicate Deceit.* New York, 1976
4. *Cove's End.* New York, 1977
5. *Satan's Sunset.* New York, 1977
6. *Skin Deep.* New York, 1978
7. *Trial of Innocence.* New York, 1978
8. *Melody of Malice.* New York, 1979
9. *Going All the Way.* New York, 1980

Hughes, Dorothy B. (Belle)
American, born August 10, 1904
1. *Dark Certainty.* New Haven (CT), 1931
2. *Pueblo on the Mesa: The First Fifty Years of the University of New Mexico.* Albuquerque (NM), 1939
3. *The So Blue Marble.* New York, 1940
4. *The Cross-Eyed Bear.* New York, 1940
5. *The Bamboo Blonde.* New York, 1941
6. *The Fallen Sparrow.* New York, 1942
7. *The Blackbirder.* New York, 1943
8. *The Delicate Ape.* New York, 1944
9. *Johnnie.* New York, 1944
10. *Dread Journey.* New York, 1945
11. *Ride the Pink Horse.* New York, 1946
12. *The Scarlet Imperial.* New York, 1946
13. *In a Lonely Place.* New York, 1947
14. *The Big Barbecue.* New York, 1949
15. *The Candy Kid.* New York, 1950
16. *The Davidian Report.* New York, 1952
17. *Kiss for a Killer.* New York, 1954
18. *The Body on the Bench.* New York, 1955
19. *The Expendable Man.* New York, 1963
20. *Erle Stanley Gardner: The Case of the Real Perry Mason.* New York, 1978

Hull, E.M. (Edith Maude)
British
1. *The Sheik.* London, 1919
2. *The Shadow of the East.* London and Boston, 1921
3. *The Desert Healer.* London and Boston, 1923
4. *The Sons of the Sheik.* Boston, 1925
5. *Camping in the Sahara.* London, 1926
6. *The Lion-Tamer.* London and New York, 1928
7. *The Captive of Sahara.* London and New York, 1931
8. *The Forest of Terrible Things.* London, 1939

Hull, Richard [Richard Henry Sampson]
British, born September 6, 1896, died in 1973
1. *The Murder of My Aunt.* London and New York, 1934
2. *Keep It Quiet.* London and New York, 1935
3. *Murder Isn't Easy.* London and New York, 1936
4. *The Ghost It Was.* London, 1936
5. *The Murderers of Monty.* London and New York, 1937
6. *Excellent Intentions.* London, 1938
7. *And Death Came Too.* London, 1939
8. *My Own Murderer.* London and New York, 1940
9. *The Unfortunate Murderer.* London, 1941
10. *Left-Handed Death.* London, 1946
11. *Last First.* London, 1947
12. *Until She Was Dead.* London, 1949
13. *A Matter of Nerves.* London, 1950
14. *Invitation to an Inquest.* London, 1950
15. *The Martineau Murders.* London, 1953

Hume, Fergus [Ferguson Wright Hume]
British, born July 8, 1859, died July 13, 1932
1. *The Mystery of a Hansom Cab.* Melbourne (Aus), 1886
2. *Professor Brankel's Secret.* Melbourne, 1886
3. *Madame Midas.* London and New York, 1888
4. *The Girl from Malta.* London and New York, 1889
5. *The Piccadilly Puzzle.* London and New York, 1889
6. *The Gentleman Who Vanished: A Psychological Phantasy.* London, 1890
7. *The Man with a Secret.* London, 3 vols., 1890
8. *Miss Mephistopheles.* London and New York, 1890
9. *Who God Hath Joined.* London, 3 vols., 1891
10. *The Year of Miracle: A Tale of the Year One Thousand Nine Hundred.* London and New York, 1891

11. *A Creature of the Night: An Italian Enigma.* London and New York, 1891
12. *The Fever of Life.* New York, 1891
13. *Monsieur Judas.* London and New York, 1891
14. *The Black Carnation.* London and New York, 1892
15. *Aladdin in London.* London and Boston, 1892
16. *Dowker-Detective.* New York, 1892
17. *The Island of Fantasy.* London, 3 vols., 1892
18. *When I Lived in Bohemia: Papers Selected from the Portfolio of Peter . . . , Esq.* Bristol and New York, 1892
19. *The Chronicles of Faeryland.* London, 1892
20. *A Speck of the Motley.* London, 1893
21. *The Harlequin Opal.* London, 3 vols., 1893
22. *The Chinese Jar.* London, 1893
23. *The Best of Her Sex.* London, 2 vols., 1894
24. *The Gates of Dawn.* London and New York, 1894
25. *The Lone Inn.* London, 1894
26. *A Midnight Mystery.* London, 1894
27. *The Mystery at Landy Court.* London, 1894
28. *The Cruise of the 'Liza Jane.* London, 1895
29. *The Masquerade Mystery.* London, 1895
30. *The Third Volume.* New York, 1895
31. *The Unwilling Bride.* New York, 1895
32. *The White Prior.* London, 1895
33. *The Expedition of Captain Flick.* London, 1895
34. *The Carbuncle Clue.* London, 1896
35. *A Marriage Mystery, Told from Three Points of View.* London, 1896
36. *Tracked by a Tattoo.* London, 1896
37. *The Dwarf's Chamber and Other Stories.* London, 1896
38. *Claude Duval of the Ninety-Five: A Romance of the Road.* London and New York, 1897
39. *The Tombstone Treasure.* London, 1897
40. *The Clock Struck One.* London, 1898
41. *The Devil-Stick.* London, 1898
42. *For the Defense.* Chicago, 1898
43. *Lady Jezebel.* London and New York, 1898
44. *The Rainbow Feather.* London and New York, 1898
45. *Hagar of the Pawn-Shop.* London, 1898
46. *The Indian Bangle.* London, 1899
47. *The Red-Headed Man.* London, 1899
48. *The Silent House in Pimlico.* London, 1900
49. *The Bishop's Secret.* London, 1900
50. *Bishop Pendle.* Chicago, 1900
51. *The Crimson Cryptogram.* London, 1900
52. *Shylock of the River.* London, 1900
53. *A Traitor in London.* London and New York, 1900
54. *The Lady from Nowhere.* London and New York, 1900
55. *The Vanishing of Tera.* London, 1900
56. *The Crime of the Crystal.* London, 1901
57. *The Golden Wang-Ho.* London, 1901
58. *The Millionare Mystery.* London and New York, 1901
59. *The Mother of Emeralds.* London, 1901
60. *The Pagan's Cup.* London and New York, 1902
61. *The Turnpike House.* London, 1902
62. *Woman: The Sphinx.* London, 1902
63. *The Jade Eye.* London, 1903
64. *The Miser's Will.* London, 1903
65. *The Silver Bullet.* London, 1903
66. *The Guilty House.* London, 1903
67. *The Yellow Holly.* London and New York, 1903
68. *The Coin of Edward VII.* London and New York, 1903
69. *The Mandarin's Fan.* London, 1904
70. *The Lonely Church.* London, 1904
71. *The Red Window.* London and New York, 1904
72. *The Wheeling Light.* London, 1904
73. *The Wooden Hand.* London, 1904
74. *The Fatal Song.* London, 1905
75. *Lady Jim of Curzon Street.* London, 1905
76. *The Opal Serpent.* London and New York, 1905
77. *The Scarlet Bat.* London, 1905
78. *The Secret Passage.* London and New York, 1905
79. *The White Room.* London, 1905
80. *The Black Patch.* London, 1906
81. *Jonah's Luck.* London, 1906
82. *The Mystery of the Shadow.* London and New York, 1906
83. *The Dancer in Red and Other Stories.* London, 1906
84. *Flies in the Web.* London, 1907
85. *The Purple Fern.* London, 1907
86. *The Sealed Message.* New York, 1907
87. *The Yellow Hunchback.* London, 1907
88. *The Amethyst Cross.* London, 1908
89. *The Crowned Skull.* London, 1908
90. *The Red Skull.* New York, 1908
91. *The Green Mummy.* London and New York, 1908
92. *The Mystery of a Motor Cab.* London, 1908
93. *The Sacred Herb.* London and New York, 1908
94. *The Devil's Ace.* London, 1909
95. *The Disappearing Eye.* London and New York, 1909
96. *The Top Dog.* London, 1909
97. *The Solitary Farm.* London and New York, 1909
98. *The Lonely Subaltern.* London, 1910
99. *The Mikado Jewel.* London, 1910
100. *The Peacock of Jewels.* London and New York, 1910
101. *The Spider.* London, 1910
102. *High Water Mark.* London, 1910
103. *The Jew's House.* London, 1911
104. *The Pink Shop.* London, 1911
105. *The Rectory Governess.* London, 1911
106. *Red Money.* New York, 1911
107. *The Steel Crown.* London and New York, 1911
108. *Across the Footlights.* London, 1912
109. *The Blue Talisman.* London, 1912
110. *Mother Mandarin.* London, 1912
111. *The Mystery Queen.* London and New York, 1912
112. *A Son of Perdition.* London, 1912
113. *The Curse.* London, 1913
114. *The Queer Street.* London, 1913
115. *The Thirteenth Guest.* London, 1913
116. *Seen in the Shadow.* London, 1913
117. *The 4 P.M. Express.* London, 1914
118. *Not Wanted.* London, 1914
119. *The Lost Parchment.* London and New York, 1914
120. *Answered: A Spy Story.* London, 1915
121. *The Caretaker.* London, 1915
122. *The Red Bicycle.* London, 1916
123. *The Silent Signal.* London, 1917
124. *The Grey Doctor.* London, 1917
125. *The Black Image.* London, 1918
126. *Heart of Ice.* London, 1918
127. *Next Door.* London, 1918
128. *Crazy-Quilt.* London, 1919
129. *The Master-Mind.* London, 1919
130. *The Dark Avenue.* London, 1920
131. *The Other Person.* London, 1920
132. *The Singing Head.* London, 1920
133. *The Woman Who Held On.* London, 1920
134. *Three.* London, 1921
135. *The Unexpected.* London, 1921
136. *A Trick of Time.* London, 1922
137. *The Moth-Woman.* London, 1923
138. *The Whispering Lane.* London, 1924
139. *The Caravan Mystery.* London, 1926
140. *The Last Straw.* London, 1932
141. *The Hurton Treasure Mystery.* London, 1937

Humphrey, William
American, born June 18, 1924
1. *The Last Husband and Other Stories.* New York and London, 1953
2. *Home from the Hill.* New York and London, 1958
3. *The Ordways.* New York and London, 1965
4. *A Time and a Place: Stories.* New York, 1968
5. *A Time and a Place: Stories of the Red River Country.* London, 1969
6. *The Spawning Run: A Fable.* New York and London, 1970
7. *Proud Flesh.* New York and London, 1973
8. *Ah, Wilderness! The Frontier in American Literature.* El Paso (TX), 1977
9. *Farther Off from Heaven.* New York and London, 1977
10. *My Moby Dick.* New York, 1978

Hunter, Elizabeth (Mary Teresa)
American, born in 1934
Pseudonym: Isobel Chace
1. *The African Mountain,* as Isobel Chace. London, 1960
2. *The Japenese Lantern,* as Isobel Chace. London, 1960
3. *Flamingoes on the Lake,* as Isobel Chace. London, 1961
4. *Cherry-Blossom Clinic.* London, 1961
5. *Spiced with Cloves.* London, 1962
6. *The Song and the Sea,* as Isobel Chace. London, 1962
7. *The Hospital of Fatima,* as Isobel Chace. London, 1963
8. *The Wild Land,* as Isobel Chace. London, 1963
9. *Watch the Wall, My Darling.* London, 1963
10. *A House for Sharing,* as Isobel Chace. London, 1964
11. *No Sooner Met.* London, 1965
12. *The Rhythm of Flamenco,* as Isobel Chace. London and Toronto. 1966
13. *The Spider's Web,* as Isobel Chace. London, 1966
14. *The Secret Marriage,* as Isobel Chace. London, 1966
15. *The Land of the Lotus-Eaters,* as Isobel Chace. London, 1966
16. *A Garland of Marigolds,* as Isobel Chace. London and Toronto. 1967
17. *There Were Nine Castles.* London, 1967
18. *Brittany Blue,* as Isobel Chace. London, 1967
19. *Oranges and Lemons,* as Isobel Chace. London, 1967
20. *The Saffron Sky,* as Isobel Chace. London and Toronto. 1968
21. *The Damask Rose,* as Isobel Chace. London, 1968
22. *A Handful of Silver,* as Isobel Chace. London, 1968
23. *The Legend of Katmandu,* as Isobel Chace. London, 1969
24. *Flower of Ethiopia,* as Isobel Chace. London, 1969
25. *Sugar in the Morning,* as Isobel Chace. London, 1969
26. *The Day That the Rain Came Down,* as Isobel Chace. London and Toronto, 1970
27. *The Flowering Cactus,* as Isobel Chace. London, 1970
28. *To Marry a Tiger,* as Isobel Chace. London, 1971
29. *The Wealth of the Islands,* as Isobel Chace. London, 1971
30. *Home Is Goodbye,* as Isobel Chace. London, 1971
31. *The Flamboyant Tree,* as Isobel Chace. London, 1972
32. *The English Daughter,* as Isobel Chace. London, 1972
33. *Cadence of Portugal,* as Isobel Chace. London, 1972
34. *A Pride of Lions,* as Isobel Chace. London, 1972
35. *The Tartan Touch,* as Isobel Chace. London, 1972
36. *The House of Scissors,* as Isobel Chace. London, 1972
37. *The Dragon's Cave,* as Isobel Chace. London, 1972
38. *The Edge of Beyond,* as Isobel Chace. London, 1973
39. *A Man of Kent,* as Isobel Chace. London, 1973
40. *The Crescent Moon.* London, 1973
41. *The Tree of Idleness.* London, 1973
42. *The Tower of the Winds.* London, 1973
43. *The Beads of Nemesis.* London, 1974
44. *The Bride Price.* London, 1974
45. *The Bonds of Matrimony.* London and Toronto, 1975
46. *The Spanish Inheritance.* London and Toronto, 1975
47. *The Voice in the Thunder.* London and Toronto, 1975
48. *The Sycamore Song.* London, 1975
49. *The Cornish Hearth,* as Isobel Chace. New York and London, 1975
50. *A Canopy of Rose Leaves,* as Isobel Chace. London, 1976
51. *The Clouded Veil,* as Isobel Chace. New York and London, 1976
52. *The Desert Castle,* as Isobel Chace. London, 1976
53. *Singing in the Wilderness,* as Isobel Chace. London and Toronto, 1976
54. *The Realms of Gold.* London, 1976
55. *Pride of Madeira.* Toronto, 1977
56. *The Whistling Thorn.* Toronto, 1977
57. *The Mouth of Truth.* Toronto, 1977
58. *Second Best Wife.* Toronto, 1978
59. *Bride in the Sun.* New York and London, 1980
60. *The Lion's Shadow.* London, 1980
61. *A Touch of Magic.* London, 1981

Hunter, Evan
American, born October 15, 1926
Pseudonyms:, Curt Cannon, Hunt Collins, Ezra Hannon, Richard Marsten, Ed McBain
1. *Find the Feathered Serpent,* as Ed McBain. Philadelphia, 1952
2. *The Big Fix,* as Richard Marsten. No place, 1952
3. *Don't Crowd Me,* as Richard Marsten. New York, 1953
4. *Rocket to Luna,* as Richard Marsten. Philadelphia, 1953
5. *Danger: Dinosaurs,* as Richard Marsten. Philadelphia, 1953
6. *Cut Me In,* as Hunt Collins. New York, 1954
7. *The Blackboard Jungle.* New York, 1954
8. *Runaway Black,* as Richard Marsten. New York, 1954
9. *The Proposition,* as Ed McBain. New York, 1955
10. *Murder in the Navy,* as Richard Marsten. New York, 1955
11. *Tomorrow and Tomorrow,* as Hunt Collins. New York, 1955
12. *Cop Hater,* as Ed McBain. New York, 1956
13. *The Mugger,* as Ed McBain. New York, 1956
14. *The Pusher,* as Ed McBain. New York, 1956
15. *So Nude, So Dead,* as Richard Marsten. New York, 1956
16. *The Spiked Heel,* as Richard Marsten. New York, 1956
17. *The Jungle Kids.* New York, 1956
18. *Tomorrow's World.* New York, 1956
19. *Second Ending.* New York and London, 1956
20. *The Con Man,* as Ed McBain. New York, 1957
21. *Vanishing Ladies,* as Richard Marsten. New York, 1957
22. *Killer's Choice,* as Ed McBain. New York, 1958
23. *Killer's Payoff,* as Ed McBain. New York, 1958
24. *April Robin Murders,* as Ed McBain. New York, 1958
25. *Lady Killer,* as Ed McBain. New York, 1958
26. *I'm Cannon—For Hire,* as Curt Cannon. New York, 1958
27. *Even the Wicked,* as Richard Marsten. New York, 1958
28. *I Like 'em Tough,* as Curt Cannon. New York, 1958
29. *Strangers When We Meet.* New York and London, 1958
30. *Killer's Wedge,* as Ed McBain. New York, 1959
31. *'Til Death,* as Ed McBain. New York, 1959
32. *King's Ransom,* as Ed McBain. New York, 1959
33. *A Matter of Conviction.* New York and London, 1959
34. *Big Man,* as Richard Marsten. New York, 1959
35. *Give the Boys a Great Big Hand,* as Ed McBain. New York, 1960
36. *The Heckler,* as Ed McBain. New York, 1960
37. *See Them Die,* as Ed McBain. New York, 1960
38. *The Last Spin and Other Stories.* London, 1960
39. *Lady, Lady, I Did It!* as Ed McBain. New York, 1961
40. *Mothers and Daughters.* New York and London, 1961

41. *The Remarkable Harry,* as Ed McBain. London, 1961
42. *The Wonderful Button,* as Ed McBain. New York, 1961
43. *Like Love,* as Ed McBain. New York, 1962
44. *The Empty Hours,* as Ed McBain. New York, 1962
45. *Ten Plus One,* as Ed McBain. New York, 1963
46. *Happy New Year, Herbie, and Other Stories.* New York, 1963
47. *Ax,* as Ed McBain. New York and London, 1964
48. *Buddwing.* New York and London, 1964
49. *The Sentries,* as Ed McBain. New York and London, 1965
50. *He Who Hesitates,* as Ed McBain. New York and London, 1965
51. *Doll,* as Ed McBain. New York, 1965
52. *Eighty Million Eyes,* as Ed McBain. New York and London, 1966
53. *The Young Savages.* New York, 1966
54. *The Paper Dragon.* New York, 1966
55. *A Horse's Head.* New York, 1967
56. *Fuzz.* New York and London, 1968
57. *The Paradise Party.* London, 1968
58. *Death of a Nurse,* as Ed McBain. New York, 1968
59. *Last Summer.* New York, 1968
60. *Shotgun,* as Ed McBain. New York and London, 1969
61. *Sons.* New York, 1969
62. *Jigsaw,* as Ed McBain. New York and London, 1970
63. *Hail, Hail, The Gang's All Here!* as Ed McBain. New York and London, 1971
64. *Nobody Knew You Were There.* New York and London, 1971
65. *The Beheading and Other Stories,* as Ed McBain. London, 1971
66. *Sadie When She Died,* as Ed McBain. New York and London, 1972
67. *Every Little Crook and Nanny.* New York and London, 1972
68. *The Easter Man: A Play and Six Stories,* as Ed McBain. New York, 1972
69. *Seven,* as Ed McBain. London, 1972
70. *Let's Hear It for the Deaf Man,* as Ed McBain. New York and London, 1973
71. *Hail to the Chief,* as Ed McBain. New York and London, 1973
72. *Come Winter.* New York, 1973
73. *Bread,* as Ed McBain. New York and London, 1974
74. *Streets of Gold.* New York, 1974
75. *Where There's Smoke,* as Ed McBain. New York and London, 1975
76. *Blood Relatives,* as Ed McBain. New York, 1975
77. *Doors,* as Ezra Hannon. New York, 1975
78. *Guns,* as Ed McBain. New York and London, 1976
79. *So Long as You Both Shall Live,* as Ed McBain. New York and London, 1976
80. *The Chisholms: A Novel of the Journey West.* New York and London, 1976
81. *Me and Mr. Stenner,* as Ed McBain. Philadelphia, 1976
82. *Long Time No See,* as Ed McBain. New York and London, 1977
83. *Goldilocks,* as Ed McBain. New York and London, 1978
84. *Calypso,* as Ed McBain. New York and London, 1979
85. *Walk Proud.* New York, 1979
86. *Ghosts,* as Ed McBain. London, 1980

Hurst, Fannie
American, born October 18, 1889, died February 23, 1968
1. *Just Around the Corner: Romance en Casserole.* New York, 1914
2. *Every Soul Hath Its Song.* New York, 1916
3. *Gaslight Sonatas.* New York and London, 1918
4. *Humoresque: A Laugh on Life with a Tear Behind It.* New York, 1919
5. *Star-Dust: The Story of an American Girl.* New York, 1921
6. *The Vertical City.* New York, 1922
7. *Lummox.* New York, 1923
8. *Appassionata.* New York and London, 1926
9. *Mannequin.* New York, 1926
10. *Song of Life.* New York and London, 1927
11. *A President Is Born.* New York and London, 1928
12. *Procession.* New York and London, 1929
13. *Five and Ten.* New York and London, 1929
14. *Back Street.* New York and London, 1931
15. *Imitation of Life.* New York, 1933
16. *Anitra's Dance.* New York and London, 1934
17. *No Food with My Meals.* New York, 1935
18. *Great Laughter.* New York, 1936
19. *We Are Ten.* New York, 1937
20. *Today Is Ladies' Day.* New York, 1939
21. *Lonely Parade.* New York and London, 1942
22. *White Christmas.* New York, 1942
23. *Hallelujah.* New York, 1944
24. *The Hands of Veronica.* New York and London, 1947
25. *Anywoman.* New York and London, 1950
26. *The Name Is Mary.* New York, 1951
27. *The Man with One Hand.* London, 1953
28. *Anatomy of Me: A Wonderer in Search of Herself.* New York, 1958
29. *Family!* New York, 1960
30. *God Must Be Sad.* New York, 1961
31. *Fool, Be Still.* New York, 1964

Hutten, Baroness von [Betsy Riddle]
American, born February 14, 1874, died January 26, 1957
1. *Miss Carmichael's Conscience: A Study in Fluctuations.* Philadelphia, 1900
2. *Marr'd in Making.* Philadelphia and London, 1901
3. *Our Lady of the Beeches.* Boston, 1902
4. *Violett: A Chronicle.* Boston, 1904
5. *Pam.* London, 1904
6. *Araby.* New York, 1904
7. *He and Hecuba.* New York, 1905
8. *What Became of Pam.* London, 1906
9. *The One Way Out.* New York, 1906
10. *The Halo.* New York and London, 1907
11. *Beechy; or, The Lordship of Love.* New York, 1909
12. *Kingsmead.* London and New York, 1909
13. *The Green Patch.* London and New York, 1910
14. *Sharrow.* London and New York, 1910
15. *Mrs. Drummond's Vocation.* London, 1913
16. *Maria.* London and New York, 1914
17. *Helping Hersey.* New York, 1914
18. *Bird's Fountain.* London and New York, 1915
19. *Mag Pye.* London and New York, 1917
20. *The Bag of Saffron.* London, 1917
21. *Happy House.* London, 1919
22. *Mothers-in-Law.* London and New York, 1922
23. *Pam at Fifty.* London and New York, 1924
24. *Julia.* London and New York, 1924
25. *Candy and Other Stories.* London, 1925
26. *Flies.* London, 1927
27. *Eddy and Edouard.* London, 1928
28. *The Loves of an Actress.* London, 1929
29. *Pam's Own Story.* London, 1930
30. *Swan House.* London, 1930
31. *The Curate's Egg: A Volume of Stories.* London, 1930
32. *In the Portico and Others.* London, 1931
33. *Monkey-Puzzle.* London, 1932
34. *Mice for Amusement.* London, 1933

35. *The Notorious Mrs. Gatacre and Other Stories.* London, 1933
36. *The Courtesan: The Life of Cora Pearl.* London, 1933
37. *The Mem.* London, 1934
38. *Die She Must.* London, 1934
39. *Cowardly Custard.* London, 1936
40. *The Elgin Marble.* London, 1937
41. *What Happened Is This.* London, 1938

Huxley, Elspeth (Josceline)
British, born July 23, 1907
1. *White Man's Country: Lord Delamere and the Making of Kenya.* London, 2 vols., 1935
2. *Atlantic Ordeal: The Story of Mary Cornish.* London, 1941
3. *East Africa.* London, 1941
4. *The Story of Five English Farmers.* London, 1941
5. *English Woman.* London, 1942
6. *Brave Deeds of the War.* London, 1943
7. *Race and Politics in Kenya: A Correspondence Between Elspeth Huxley and Margery Perham.* London, 1944
8. *Colonies: A Reader's Guide.* Cambridge (Eng), 1947
9. *Settlers of Kenya.* Nairobi and London, 1948
10. *The Sorcerer's Apprentice: A Journey Through East Africa.* London, 1948
11. *African Dilemmas.* London, 1948
12. *Four Guineas: A Journey Through West Africa.* London, 1954
13. *Kenya Today.* London, 1954
14. *What Are Trustee Nations?* London, 1955
15. *No Easy Way: A History of the Kenya Farmers' Association and Unga Limited.* Nairobi, 1957(?)
16. *The Flame Trees of Thika: Memories of an African Childhood.* London and New York, 1959
17. *A New Earth: An Experiment in Colonialism.* London and New York, 1960
18. *The Mottled Lizard.* London, 1962
19. *On the Edge of the Rift: Memories of Kenya.* New York, 1962
20. *Forks and Hope: An African Notebook.* London, 1964
21. *With Forks and Hope.* New York, 1964
22. *Back Street, New Worlds: A Look at Immigrants in Britain.* London, 1964
23. *Suki: A Little Tiger.* London and New York, 1964
24. *Brave New Victuals: An Inquiry into Modern Food Production.* London, 1965
25. *Their Shining Eldorado: A Journey Through Australia.* London and New York, 1967
26. *Love among the Daughters: Memories of the Twenties in England and America.* London and New York, 1968
27. *The Challenge of Africa.* London, 1971
28. *Livingstone and His African Journeys.* London and New York, 1974
29. *Florence Nightingale.* London, 1975
30. *Gallipot Eyes: A Wiltshire Diary.* London, 1976
31. *Scott of the Antarctic.* London, 1977
32. *Nellie: Letters from Africa.* London, 1980

Inglis, Susan [Doris Mackie]
1. *Married Man's Girl.* London, 1934
2. *The Marriage of Mary Chard.* London, 1935
3. *She Acted on Impulse.* London, 1936
4. *Uncertain Flame.* London, 1937
5. *Ice Girl.* London, 1938
6. *Tender Only to One.* London, 1938
7. *To Wear Your Ring.* London, 1938
8. *Put Love Aside.* London, 1939
9. *Too Many Men.* London, 1939
10. *Because I Love You.* London, 1940
11. *This Foolish Heart.* London, 1940
12. *Sara Steps In.* London, 1947
13. *Dick Heriot's Wife.* London, 1947
14. *Jill Takes a Chance.* London, 1949
15. *Deb and Destiny.* London, 1950
16. *Happiness Can't Wait.* London, 1950
17. *Three Men in Her Life.* London, 1951
18. *Highland Holiday.* London, 1952
19. *Sister Christine.* London, 1953
20. *The Loving Heart.* London, 1954
21. *Steven's Wife.* London, 1958
22. *The Secret Heart.* London, 1959
23. *The Old Hunting Lodge.* London, 1961

Irwin, Margaret (Emma Faith)
British, born in 1889, died December 11, 1967
1. *How Many Miles to Babylon?* London, 1913
2. *Come Out to Play.* London, 1914
3. *Out of the House.* London and New York, 1916
4. *The Happy Man: A Sketch for Acting.* London, 1921
5. *Still She Wished for Company.* London, 1924
6. *Who Will Remember?* New York, 1924
7. *These Mortals.* London, 1925
8. *South Molton Street.* London, 1927
9. *Knock Four Times.* London and New York, 1927
10. *Fire Down Below.* London and New York, 1928
11. *None So Pretty.* London and New York, 1930
12. *Royal Flush: The Story of Minette.* London and New York, 1932
13. *Check to the King of France.* London, 1933
14. *Minette.* London and New York, 1933
15. *Save the Children.* London, 1933
16. *The Proud Servant: The Story of Montrose.* London and New York, 1934
17. *Madame Fears the Dark: Seven Stories and a Play.* London, 1935
18. *Madame Fears the Dark.* London, 1936
19. *The Stranger Prince: The Story of Rupert of the Rhine.* London and New York, 1937
20. *The Bride: The Story of Louise and Montrose.* London and New York, 1939
21. *Mrs. Oliver Cromwell and Other Stories.* London, 1940
22. *The Gay Galliard: The Love Story of Mary Queen of Scots.* London, 1941
23. *Young Bess.* London, 1944
24. *Elizabeth, Captive Princess.* London and New York, 1948
25. *Elizabeth and the Prince of Spain.* London and New York, 1953
26. *Bloodstock and Other Stories.* London, 1953
27. *The Great Lucifer: A Portrait of Sir Walter Raleigh.* London and New York, 1960

Jackson, Shirley (Hardie)
American, born December 19, 1919, died August 8, 1965
1. *The Road Through the Wall.* New York, 1948
2. *The Lottery; or, The Adventures of James Harris.* New York, 1949
3. *Hangsaman.* New York and London, 1951
4. *The Lottery.* New York, 1952
5. *Life among the Savages.* New York, 1953
6. *The Bird's Nest.* New York, 1954
7. *The Witchcraft of Salem Village.* New York, 1956
8. *Raising Demons.* New York and London, 1957
9. *The Sundial.* New York and London, 1958
10. *The Haunting of Hill House.* New York, 1959
11. *The Bad Children: A Play in One Act for Bad Children.* Chicago, 1959
12. *Special Delivery: A Useful Book for Brand-New Mothers.* Boston, 1960

13. *9 Magic Wishes.* New York, 1963
14. *We Have Always Lived in the Castle.* New York, 1962
15. *Famous Sally.* New York, 1966
16. *The Magic of Shirley Jackson.* New York, 1966
17. *Come Along with Me.: Part of a Novel, Sixteen Stories, and Three Lectures.* New York, 1968

Jacob, Naomi (Ellington)
British, born July 1, 1884, died August 26, 1964
Pseudonym: Ellington Gray
1. *Jacob Ussher.* London, 1925
2. *Rock and Sand.* London, 1926
3. *Power.* London, 1927
4. *The Plough.* London, 1928
5. *Saffroned Bridesails,* as Ellington Gray. London, 1928
6. *The Man Who Found Himself.* London, 1929
7. *The Beloved Physician.* London, 1930
8. *That Wild Lie—.* London, 1930
9. *Roots.* London, 1931
10. *Seen Unknown. . . .* London, 1931
11. *Props.* London, 1932
12. *Young Emmanuel.* London, 1932
13. *Groping.* London, 1933
14. *Poor Straws!* London, 1933
15. *Me: A Chronicle about Other People.* London, 1933
16. *The Loaded Stick.* London, 1934
17. *Four Generations.* London and New York, 1934
18. *The Founder of the House.* London, 1935
19. *Me—in the Kitchen.* London, 1935
20. *Honour Comes Back—.* London and New York, 1935
21. *Our Marie: Marie Lloyd: A Biography.* London, 1936
22. *Time Piece.* London, 1936
23. *Barren Metal.* London and New York, 1936
24. *Fade Out.* London and New York, 1937
25. *The Lenient God.* London, 1937
26. *Me—Again.* London, 1937
27. *No Easy Way.* London, 1938
28. *More about Me.* London, 1939
29. *Straws in Amber.* London, 1939
30. *Full Meridian.* London, 1939
31. *This Porcelain Clay.* London and New York, 1939
32. *Shadow Drama,* by Nina Abbott, completed by Jacob. London, 1940
33. *Sally Scarth.* London, 1940
34. *Me—In War-Time.* London, 1940
35. *They Left the Land.* London and New York, 1940
36. *Under New Management.* London, 1941
37. *The Cap of Youth.* London and New York, 1941
38. *Balance Suspended,* by Nina Abbott, completed by Jacob. London, 1942
39. *Leopards and Spots.* London, 1942
40. *Private Follantz.* London, 1943
41. *White Wool.* London, 1944
42. *Me and the Mediterranean.* London, 1945
43. *Susan Crowther.* London, 1945
44. *Me—Over There.* London, 1947
45. *Honour's a Mistress.* London, 1947
46. *A Passage Perilous.* London, 1948
47. *Opera in Italy,* with James C. Robertson. London, 1948
48. *Gollantz: London, Paris, Milan.* London, 1948
49. *Me and Mine, You and Yours.* London, 1949
50. *Mary of Delight.* London, 1949
51. *Every Other Gift.* London, 1950
52. *Me—Looking Back.* London, 1950
53. *The Heart of the House.* London, 1951
54. *A Late Lark Singing.* London, 1952
55. *Impressions from Italy.* London, 1952
56. *Robert, Nana, and—Me.* London, 1952
57. *Just about Us.* London, 1953
58. *The Morning Will Come.* London, 1953
59. *Me—Likes and Dislikes.* London, 1954
60. *Antonia.* London, 1954
61. *Second Harvest.* London, 1954
62. *Tales of the Broad Acres.* London, 1955
63. *Prince China.* London, 1955
64. *The Irish Boy: A Romantic Biography.* London, 1955
65. *Wind on the Heath.* London, 1956
66. *Me—Yesterday and To-day.* London, 1957
67. *Gollantz and Partners.* London, 1958
68. *What's to Come.* London, 1958
69. *Search for a Background.* London, 1960
70. *Three Men and Jennie.* London, 1960
71. *Strange Beginning.* London, 1961
72. *Me—and the Stags.* London, 1962
73. *Great Black Oxen.* London, 1962
74. *Yolanda.* London, 1963
75. *Me—and the Swans.* London, 1963
76. *Me—Thinking Things Over.* London, 1964
77. *Long Shadows.* London, 1964
78. *Flavia.* London, 1965

Jakes, John (William)
American, born March 31, 1932
Pseudonyms: Alan Payne, Jay Scotland
1. *The Texans Ride North.* Philadelphia, 1952
2. *Wear a Fast Gun.* New York, 1956
3. *A Night for Treason.* New York, 1956
4. *The Devil Has Four Faces.* New York, 1958
5. *This'll Slay You,* as Alan Payne. New York, 1958
6. *The Seventh Man,* as Jay Scotland. New York, 1958
7. *The Imposter.* New York, 1959
8. *I, Barbarian,* as Jay Scotland. New York, 1959
9. *Johnny Havoc.* New York, 1960
10. *Strike the Black Flag,* as Jay Scotland. New York, 1961
11. *Johnny Havoc Meets Zelda.* New York, 1962
12. *Sir Scoundrel.* New York, 1962
13. *The Veils of Salome,* as Jay Scotland. New York, 1962
14. *Johnny Havoc and the Doll Who Had "It.".* New York, 1963
15. *G.I. Girls.* Derby (CT), 1963
16. *Arena,* as Jay Scotland. New York, 1963
17. *Traitor's Legion,* as Jay Scotland. New York, 1963
18. *Tiros: Weather Eye in Space.* New York, 1966
19. *When the Star Kings Die.* New York, 1967
20. *Famous Firsts in Sports.* New York, 1967
21. *Brak the Barbarian.* New York, 1968
22. *Making It Big.* New York, 1968
23. *Great War Correspondents.* New York, 1968
24. *The Asylum World.* New York, 1969
25. *Brak Versus the Mark of the Demons.* New York, 1969
26. *Brak the Barbarian Versus the Sorceress.* New York, 1969
27. *Great Women Reporters.* New York, 1969
28. *Secrets of Stardeep.* Philadelphia, 1969
29. *Brak the Barbarian—The Mark of the Demons.* London, 1970
30. *Brak the Barbarian—The Sorceress.* London, 1970
31. *The Hybrid.* New York, 1969
32. *The Last Magicians.* New York, 1969
33. *The Planet Wizard.* New York, 1969
34. *Tonight We Steal the Stars.* New York, 1969
35. *Black in Time.* New York, 1970
36. *Mask of Chaos.* New York, 1970
37. *Master of the Dark Gate.* New York, 1970
38. *Monte Cristo 99.* New York, 1970
39. *Six-Gun Planet.* New York, 1970
40. *Dracula, Baby.* Chicago, 1970

41. *Mention My Name in Atlantis.* New York, 1972
42. *Witch of the Dark Gate.* New York, 1972
43. *Conquest of the Planet of the Apes.* New York, 1972
44. *The Best of John Jakes.* New York, 1972
45. *Wind in the Willows.* Elgin (IL), 1972
46. *A Spell of Evil.* Chicago, 1972
47. *Violence.* Elgin, 1972
48. *Stranger with Roses.* Chicago, 1972
49. *Time Gate.* Philadelphia, 1972
50. *On Wheels.* New York, 1973
51. *Gaslight Girl.* Chicago, 1973
52. *Pardon Me, Is This Planet Taken?* Chicago, 1973
53. *Doctor, Doctor!* New York, 1973
54. *The Bastard.* New York, 1974
55. *Shepherd Song.* New York, 1974
56. *The Rebels.* New York, 1975
57. *The Seekers.* New York, 1975
58. *The Furies.* New York, 1976
59. *The Titans.* New York, 1976
60. *The Warriors.* New York, 1977
61. *King's Crusader,* as Jay Scotland. New York, 1977
62. *The Man from Cannae,* as Jay Scotland. New York, 1977
63. *Brak: When the Idols Walked.* New York, 1978
64. *The Lawless.* New York, 1978
65. *Excalibur!* New York, 1980
66. *The Americans.* New York, 1980
67. *Fortunes of Brak.* New York, 1980
68. *The Bastard Photostory.* New York, 1980
69. *North and South.* New York, 1982

James, P.D. (Phyllis Dorothy)
British, born August 3, 1920
1. *Cover Her Face.* London, 1962
2. *A Mind to Murder.* London, 1963
3. *Unnatural Causes.* London and New York, 1967
4. *Shroud for a Nightingale.* London and New York, 1971
5. *The Maul and the Pear Tree: The Ratcliffe Highway Murders, 1811.* London, 1971
6. *An Unsuitable Job for a Woman.* London, 1972
7. *The Black Tower.* London and New York, 1975
8. *Death of an Expert Witness.* London and New York, 1977

James, Will [Joseph Ernest Nephtali Dufault]
Canadian, born June 6, 1892, died September 3, 1942
1. *Cowboys North and South.* New York, 1924
2. *Drifting Cowboy.* New York and London, 1925
3. *Smoky the Cowhorse.* New York and London, 1926
4. *Cow Country.* New York and London, 1927
5. *Sand.* New York and London, 1929
6. *Lone Cowboy: My Life Story.* New York and London, 1930
7. *Sun Up: Tales of the Cow Camps.* New York and London, 1931
8. *Big Enough.* New York and London, 1931
9. *Uncle Bill: A Tale of Two Kinds of Cowboy.* New York and London, 1932
10. *All in a Day's Riding.* New York and London, 1933
11. *The Three Mustangeers.* New York, 1933
12. *In the Saddle with Uncle Bill.* New York and London, 1935
13. *Young Cowboy.* New York, 1935
14. *Home Ranch.* New York, 1935
15. *Scorpion, A Good Bad Horse.* New York and London, 1936
16. *Cowboy in the Making.* New York and London, 1937
17. *Look-See with Uncle Bill.* New York and London, 1938
18. *The Will James Cowboy Book.* New York, 1938
19. *Flint Spears, Cowboy Rodeo Contestant.* New York, 1938
20. *The Dark Horse.* New York and London, 1939
21. *My First Horse.* New York, 1940
22. *Horses I've Known.* New York, 1940
23. *The American Cowboy.* New York, 1942
24. *Book of Cowboy Stories.* New York, 1951

Jarrett, Cora
American, born February 21, 1877, died 19??
Pseudonym: Faraday Keene
1. *Peccadilloes,* as Faraday Keene. New York, 1929
2. *Night over Fitch's Pond.* Boston and London, 1933
3. *Pattern in Black and Red,* as Faraday Keene. Boston and London, 1934
4. *The Ginkgo Tree.* New York and London, 1935
5. *Strange Houses.* New York, 1936
6. *The Silver String.* New York, 1937
7. *I Asked No Other Thing.* New York, 1937
8. *Return in December.* New York, 1951

Jay, G.M. (Geraldine Mary)
Australian, born December 17, 1919
Pseudonyms: Geraldine Halls, Charlotte Jay
1. *The Knife Is Feminine.* London, 1951
2. *Beat Not the Bones.* London, 1952
3. *The Fugitive Eye.* London, 1953
4. *The Yellow Turban.* London and New York, 1955
5. *The Feast of the Dead.* London, 1956
6. *The Silk Project,* as Geraldine Halls. London, 1956
7. *The Brink of Silence,* as Charlotte Jay. New York, 1957
8. *The Man Who Walked Away.* London, 1958
9. *The Stepfather.* New York, 1958
10. *Arms for Adonis.* London, 1960
11. *A Hank of Hair.* London and New York, 1964
12. *The Cats of Benares,* as Geraldine Halls. London and New York, 1967
13. *The Cobra Kite,* as Geraldine Halls. London, 1971
14. *The Voice of the Crab,* as Geraldine Halls. London and New York, 1974
15. *The Last Summer of the Men Shortage,* as Geraldine Halls. London, 1976
16. *The Felling of Thawle,* as Geraldine Halls. London, 1979

Jeffries, Roderic
British, born October 21, 1906
Pseudonyms: Peter Alding, Jeffrey Ashford, Hastings Draper, Roderic Graeme, Graham Hastings
1. *Brandy Ahoy!* as Roderic Graeme. London, 1951
2. *Concerning Blackshirt,* as Roderic Graeme. London, 1952
3. *Blackshirt Wins the Trick,* as Roderic Graeme. London, 1953
4. *Blackshirt Passes By,* as Roderic Graeme. London, 1953
5. *Where's Brandy?* as Roderic Graeme. London, 1953
6. *Salute to Blackshirt,* as Roderic Graeme. London, 1954
7. *Brandy Goes a Cruising,* as Roderic Graeme. London, 1954
8. *The Amazing Mr. Blackshirt,* as Roderic Graeme. London, 1955
9. *Blackshirt Meets the Lady,* as Roderic Graeme. London, 1956
10. *Wiggery Pokery,* as Hastings Draper. London, 1956
11. *Paging Blackshirt,* as Roderic Graeme. London, 1957
12. *Blackshirt Helps Himself,* as Roderic Graeme. London, 1958
13. *Double for Blackshirt,* as Roderic Graeme. London, 1958
14. *Wigged and Gowned,* as Hastings Draper. London, 1958
15. *Twice Checked,* as Graham Hastings. London, 1959
16. *Blackshirt Sets the Pace,* as Roderic Graeme. London, 1959
17. *Blackshirt Sees It Through,* as Roderic Graeme. London, 1960
18. *Counsel for the Defence,* as Jeffrey Ashford. London, 1960
19. *Deadly Game,* as Graham Hastings. London, 1961
20. *Evidence of the Accused.* London, 1961
21. *Blackshirt Finds Trouble,* as Roderic Graeme. London, 1961

22. *Investigations Are Proceeding*, as Jeffrey Ashford. London, 1961
23. *Brief Help*, as Hastings Draper. London, 1961
24. *Exhibit No. Thirteen*. London, 1962
25. *Blackshirt Takes the Trail*, as Roderic Graeme. London, 1962
26. *The D.I.*, as Jeffrey Ashford. New York, 1962
27. *The Burden of Proof*, as Jeffrey Ashford. London and New York, 1962
28. *Police and Detection*. Leicester (Eng), 1962
29. *The Benefits of Death*. London, 1963
30. *Blackshirt on the Spot*, as Roderic Graeme. London, 1963
31. *Call for Blackshirt*, as Roderic Graeme. London, 1963
32. *Will Anyone Who Saw the Accident. . . .*, as Jeffrey Ashford. London, 1963
33. *An Embarrassing Death*. London, 1964
34. *Blackshirt Saves the Day*, as Roderic Graeme. London, 1964
35. *Enquiries Are Continuing*, as Jeffrey Ashford. London, 1964
36. *Against Time!* New York, 1964
37. *Dead Against the Lawyers*. London, 1965
38. *Danger for Blackshirt*, as Roderic Graeme. London, 1965
39. *The Superintendent's Room*, as Jeffrey Ashford. New York, 1965
40. *The Hands of Innocence*, as Jeffrey Ashford. London, 1965
41. *Police Dog*. Leicester and New York, 1965
42. *Death in the Coverts*. London, 1966
43. *Blackshirt at Large*, as Roderic Graeme. London, 1966
44. *Hit and Run*, as Jeffrey Ashford. London, 1966
45. *Consider the Evidence*, as Jeffrey Ashford. London and New York, 1966
46. *A Deadly Marriage*. London, 1967
47. *Blackshirt in Peril*, as Roderic Graeme. London, 1967
48. *Forget What You Saw*, as Jeffrey Ashford. London and New York, 1967
49. *The C.I.D. Room*, as Peter Alding. London, 1967
50. *All Leads Negative*, as Peter Alding. New York, 1967
51. *Police Car*. Leicester, 1967
52. *Patrol Car*. New York, 1967
53. *A Traitor's Crime*. London, 1968
54. *Circle of Danger*, as Peter Alding. London, 1968
55. *Grand Prix Monaco*, as Jeffrey Ashford. New York, 1968
56. *Blackshirt Stirs Things Up*, as Roderic Graeme. London, 1969
57. *Prisoner at the Bar*, as Jeffrey Ashford. London and New York, 1969
58. *Murder among Thieves*, as Peter Alding. London, 1969
59. *River Patrol*. New York, 1969
60. *Dead Man's Bluff*. London, 1970
61. *To Protect the Guilty*, as Jeffrey Ashford. London and New York, 1970
62. *Guilt Without Proof*, as Peter Alding. London, 1970
63. *Grand Prix Germany*, as Jeffrey Ashford. New York, 1970
64. *Bent Copper*, as Jeffrey Ashford. London and New York, 1971
65. *Despite the Evidence*, as Peter Alding. London, 1971
66. *Grand Prix United States*, as Jeffrey Ashford. New York, 1971
67. *Police Patrol Boat*. Leicester, 1971
68. *A Man Will Be Kidnapped Tomorrow*. London and New York, 1972
69. *Call Back to Crime*, as Peter Alding. London, 1972
70. *Trapped*. New York, 1972
71. *The Double Run*, as Jeffrey Ashford. London and New York, 1973
72. *Field of Fire*, as Peter Alding. London, 1973
73. *Grand Prix Britain*, as Jeffrey Ashford. New York, 1973
74. *Mistakenly in Mallorca*. London, 1974
75. *The Colour of Violence*, as Jeffrey Ashford. London and New York, 1974
76. *The Murder Line*, as Peter Alding. London, 1974
77. *Dick Knox at Le Mans*, as Jeffrey Ashford. New York, 1974
78. *Three Layers of Guilt*, as Jeffrey Ashford. London, 1975
79. *Six Days to Death*, as Peter Alding. London, 1975
80. *Two-Faced Death*. London, 1976
81. *Slow Down the World*, as Jeffrey Ashford. London and New York, 1976
82. *The Riddle of the Parchment*. London, 1976
83. *Troubled Deaths*. London, 1977
84. *Hostage to Death*, as Jeffrey Ashford. London and New York, 1977
85. *Murder Is Suspected*. London and New York, 1977
86. *The Boy Who Knew Too Much*. London, 1977
87. *The Anger of Fear*, as Jeffrey Ashford. London and New York, 1978
88. *Murder Begets Murder*. London and New York, 1979
89. *Ransom Town*, as Peter Alding. London and New York, 1979
90. *Eighteen Desperate Hours*. London, 1979
91. *The Missing Man*. London, 1980

Jenkins, W.F. (William Fitzgerald)
American, born June 16, 1896, died June 8, 1975
Pseudonym: Murray Leinster

1. *Scalps*, as Murray Leinster. New York, 1930
2. *Murder Mystery*, as Murray Leinster. New York, 1930
3. *Murder Madness*, as Murray Leinster. New York, 1931
4. *Murder Will Out*. London, 1932
5. *The Gamblin' Kid*. New York, 1933
6. *Mexican Trail*. New York, 1933
7. *Sword of Kings*. London, 1933
8. *Fighting Horse Valley*. New York, 1934
9. *Outlaw Sheriff*. New York, 1934
10. *Rustlin' Sheriff*. London, 1934
11. *The Kid Deputy*. New York and London, 1935
12. *Murder in the Family*. London, 1935
13. *No Clues*. London, 1935
14. *Wings of Chance*, as Murray Leinster. London, 1935
15. *Black Sheep*. New York and London, 1936
16. *Guns for Achin*. London, 1936
17. *The Man Who Feared*. New York, 1942
18. *The Murder of the U.S.A.* New York, 1946
19. *Outlaw Guns*, as Murray Leinster. New York, No date
20. *Texas Gun Slinger*, as Murray Leinster. New York, No date
21. *The Last Space Ship*, as Murray Leinster. New York, 1949
22. *Fight for Life*, as Murray Leinster. New York, No date
23. *Dallas*. New York, 1950
24. *Destroy the U.S.A.* New York, 1950
25. *Sidewise in Time*. Chicago, 1950
26. *Wanted—Dead or Alive!* London, 1951
27. *Son of the Flying "Y"*. New York, 1951
28. *Cattle Rustlers*. London, 1952
29. *Space Platform*. Chicago, 1953
30. *Space Tug*. Chicago, 1953
31. *Gateway to Elsewhere*, as Murray Leinster. New York, 1954
32. *The Forgotten Planet*, as Murray Leinster. New York, 1954
33. *The Brain-Stealers*, as Murray Leinster. New York, 1954
34. *Operation: Outer Space*, as Murray Leinster. Reading (PA), 1954
35. *The Black Galaxy*, as Murray Leinster. New York, 1954
36. *The Other Side of Here*, as Murray Leinster. New York, 1955
37. *Colonial Survey*, as Murray Leinster. New York, 1957
38. *The Planet Explorer*, as Murray Leinster. New York, 1957
39. *City on the Moon*. New York, 1957
40. *War with the Gizmos*, as Murray Leinster. New York, 1958
41. *Out of This World*. New York, 1958

Jenkins, W.F.

42. *The Monster from Earth's End*, as Murray Leinster. New York, 1959
43. *The Mutant Weapon*, as Murray Leinster. New York, 1959
44. *The Pirates of Zan*, as Murray Leinster. New York, 1959
45. *Four from Planet 5*, as Murray Leinster. New York, 1959
46. *Monsters and Such*. New York, 1959
47. *The Wailing Asteroid*, as Murray Leinster. New York, 1960
48. *Twists in Time*. New York, 1960
49. *Men into Space*. New York, 1960
50. *The Aliens*. New York, 1960
51. *Creatures of the Abyss*, as Murray Leinster. New York, 1961
52. *This World is Taboo*, as Murray Leinster. New York, 1961
53. *Talents, Incorporated*, as Murray Leinster. New York, 1962
54. *Operation Terror*, as Murray Leinster. New York, 1962
55. *The Duplicators*, as Murray Leinster. New York, 1964
56. *The Other Side of Nowhere*, as Murray Leinster. New York, 1964
57. *Time Tunnel*, as Murray Leinster. New York, 1964
58. *The Greeks Bring Gifts*, as Murray Leinster. New York, 1964
59. *Invaders of Space*, as Murray Leinster. New York, 1964
60. *Doctor to the Stars*. New York, 1964
61. *Space Captain*, as Murray Leinster. New York, 1966
62. *Checkpoint Lambda*, as Murray Leinster. New York, 1966
63. *Get Off My World!* New York, 1966
64. *Tunnel Through Time*. Philadelphia, 1966
65. *The Time Tunnel*, as Murray Leinster. New York, 1967
66. *Miners in the Sky*, as Murray Leinster. New York, 1967
67. *Space Gypsies*, as Murray Leinster. New York, 1967
68. *Timeslip!* as Murray Leinster. New York, 1967
69. *S.O.S. from Three Worlds*. New York, 1967
70. *Land of the Giants*, as Murray Leinster. New York, 1968
71. *The Hot Spot*, as Murray Leinster. New York, 1969
72. *Unknown Danger*, as Murray Leinster. New York, 1969
73. *The Best of Murray Leinster*. London, 1976

Jenks, George C. (Charles)
Born in 1850

1. *Double Curve Dan, The Pitcher Detective*. New York, 1883
2. *The Demon Doctor; or, Deadhold the "Kid" Detective*. New York, 1887
3. *The Giant Horseman; or, Tracking the Red Cross Gang*. New York, 1887
4. *The Climax*. New York, 1909
5. *The Deserters*. New York, 1912
6. *Stop Thief!* New York, 1913

Jepson, Selwyn
British, born in 1899

1. *The Qualified Adventurer*. London and New York, 1922
2. *Puppets of Fate*. London, 1922
3. *That Fellow MacArthur*. London, 1923
4. *The King's Red-Haired Girl*. London, 1923
5. *Golden-Eyes*. London, 1924
6. *The Sutton Papers*. New York, 1924
7. *Rogues and Diamonds*. London and New York, 1925
8. *Snaggletooth*. London, 1926
9. *The Death Gong*. London and New York, 1927
10. *Love—and Helen*. London and New York, 1928
11. *Tiger Dawn*. London, 1929
12. *I Met Murder*. London and New York, 1930
13. *The Floating Admiral*. London, 1931
14. *Rabbit's Paw*. London, 1932
15. *The Mystery of the Rabbit's Paw*. New York, 1932
16. *Heads and Tails*. London, 1933
17. *Love in Peril*. London, 1934
18. *The Wise Fool*. London, 1934
19. *Manchu Jade*. London, 1935
20. *Keep Murder Quiet*. London, 1940
21. *Man Running*. London, 1948
22. *Outrun the Constable*. New York, 1948
23. *Riviera Love Story*. London, 1948
24. *Tempering Steel*. London, 1949
25. *The Golden Dart*. London and New York, 1949
26. *The Hungry Spider*. New York, 1950
27. *Killer by Proxy*. New York, 1950
28. *Man Dead*. London and New York, 1951
29. *The Black Italian*. London and New York, 1954
30. *The Assassin*. London and Philadelphia, 1956
31. *A Noise in the Night*. London and Philadelphia, 1957
32. *The Laughing Fish*. London, 1960
33. *Verdict in Question*. New York, 1960
34. *Fear in the Wind*. London, 1964
35. *The Third Possibility*. London, 1965
36. *The Angry Millionaire*. New York, 1968
37. *Letter to a Dead Girl*. London, 1971

Jessup, Richard
American, born in 1925

1. *The Cunning and the Haunted*. New York, 1954
2. *A Rage to Die*. New York, 1955
3. *Cry Passion*. New York, 1956
4. *Night Boat to Paris*. New York, 1956
5. *Cheyenne Saturday*. New York, 1957
6. *Comanche Vengeance*. New York, 1957
7. *Long Ride West*. New York, 1957
8. *The Young Don't Cry*. New York, 1957
9. *The Man in Charge*. London, 1957
10. *Texas Outlaw*. New York, 1958
11. *Lowdown*. New York and London, 1958
12. *The Deadly Duo*. New York, 1959
13. *Sabadilla*. New York, 1960
14. *Chuka*. New York, 1961
15. *Port Angelique*. New York, 1961
16. *Wolf Cop*. New York, 1961
17. *The Cincinnati Kid*. Boston, 1963
18. *The Recreation Hall*. Boston, 1967
19. *Sailor*. Boston, 1969
20. *A Quiet Voyage Home*. Boston and London, 1970
21. *Foxway*. Boston, 1971
22. *The Hot Blue Sea*. New York, 1974
23. *Threat*. New York, 1981

Johnson, Barbara Ferry
American, born July 7, 1923

1. *Lionors*. New York, 1975
2. *Delta Blood*. New York, 1977
3. *Tara's Song*. New York, 1978
4. *Homeward Winds the River*. New York, 1979
5. *The Heirs of Love*. New York, 1980

Johnson, Dorothy M. (Marie)
American, born December 19, 1905

1. *Beulah Bunny Tells All*. New York, 1942
2. *Miss Bunny Intervens*. London, 1948
3. *Indian Country*. New York, 1953
4. *The Hanging Tree*. New York, 1957
5. *Famous Lawmen of the Old West*. New York, 1963
6. *Greece, Wonderland of the Past and Present*. New York, 1964
7. *Farewell to Troy*. Boston, 1964
8. *Some Went West*. New York, 1965
9. *Witch Princess*. Boston, 1967
10. *Flame on the Frontier: Short Stories of Pioneer Women*. New York, 1967
11. *Warrior for a Lost Nation: A Biography of Sitting Bull*. Philadelphia, 1969

12. *A Man Called Horse.* New York, 1970
13. *Western Badmen.* New York, 1970
14. *The Bloody Bozeman: The Perilous Trail to Montana's Gold.* New York, 1971
15. *Montana.* New York, 1971
16. *The Bedside Book of Bastards.* New York, 1973
17. *The Man Who Knew the Buckskin Kid.* London, 1976
18. *Buffalo Woman.* New York, 1977
19. *All the Buffalo Returning.* New York, 1979
20. *When You and I Were Young.* Whitefish (MT), 1982

Johnson, E. Richard [Emil Richard Johnson]
American, born in 1937
1. *Silver Street.* New York, 1968
2. *The Silver Street Killer.* London, 1969
3. *The Inside Man.* New York, 1969
4. *Mongo's Back in Town.* New York, 1969
5. *Cage Five Is Going to Break.* New York, 1970
6. *The God Keepers.* New York, 1970
7. *Case Load—Maximum.* New York, 1971
8. *The Judas.* New York, 1971
9. *The Cardinalli Contract.* New York, 1975

Johnston, Mary
American, born November 21, 1870, died May 9, 1936
1. *The Prisoners of Hope: A Tale of Colonial Virginia.* Boston, 1898
2. *To Have and to Hold.* Boston, 1900
3. *Audrey.* Boston and London, 1902
4. *Sir Mortimer.* New York and London, 1904
5. *The Goddess of Reason.* Boston and London, 1907
6. *An Address Read at Vicksburg.* . . . Privately printed, 1907
7. *Lewis Rand.* Boston and London, 1908
8. *The Status of Women.* Richmond (VA), 1909
9. *The Reason Why.* Privately printed, 1910(?)
10. *The Long Roll.* Boston, 1911
11. *To the House of Governors.* New York, 1912
12. *Cease Firing.* Boston and London, 1912
13. *Hagar.* Boston and London, 1913
14. *The Witch.* Boston and London, 1914
15. *The Fortunes of Garin.* Boston and London, 1915
16. *The Wanderers.* Boston and London, 1917
17. *Pioneers of the Old South: A Chronicle of English Colonial Beginnings.* New Haven (CT), 1918
18. *Foes.* New York, 1918
19. *Michael Forth.* New York, 1919
20. *Sweet Rocket.* New York and London, 1920
21. *Silver Cross.* Boston and London, 1922
22. *Croatan.* Boston, 1923
23. *The Slave Ship.* Boston, 1924
24. *The Great Valley.* Boston and London, 1926
25. *The Exile.* Boston and London, 1927
26. *Hunting Shirt.* Boston, 1931
27. *Miss Delicia Allen.* Boston and London, 1933
28. *Drury Randall.* Boston, 1934

Johnston, Norma
American
Pseudonym: Nicole St. John
1. *The Wishing Star.* New York, 1963
2. *The Wider Heart.* New York, 1964
3. *Ready or Not.* New York, 1965
4. *The Bridge Between.* New York, 1966
5. *The Keeping Days.* New York, 1973
6. *Glory in the Flower.* New York, 1974
7. *The Medici Ring,* as Nicole St. John. New York, 1975
8. *Of Time and of Seasons.* New York, 1975
9. *Strangers Dark and Gold.* New York, 1975
10. *Wychwood,* as Nicole St. John. New York, 1976
11. *A Striving after Wind.* New York, 1976
12. *The Sanctuary Tree.* New York, 1977
13. *Guinever's Gift,* as Nicole St. John. New York, 1977
14. *A Mustard Seed of Magic.* New York, 1977
15. *If You Love Me, Let Me Go.* New York, 1978
16. *The Swallow's Song.* New York, 1978
17. *Both Sides Now.* New York, 1978
18. *The Crucible Year.* New York, 1979
19. *Pride of Lions.* New York, 1979
20. *A Nice Girl Like You.* New York, 1980
21. *Myself and I.* New York, 1981

Johnston, Velda
Pseudonym: Veronica Jason
1. *Along a Dark Path.* New York, 1967
2. *House above Hollywood.* New York, 1968
3. *A Howling in the Woods.* New York, 1968
4. *I Came to the Castle.* New York, 1969
5. *The Light in the Swamp.* New York, 1970
6. *The Phantom Cottage.* New York, 1970
7. *The Face in the Shadows.* New York, 1971
8. *The People on the Hill.* New York, 1971
9. *The Mourning Trees.* New York, 1972
10. *The Late Mrs. Fonsell.* New York, 1972
11. *The White Pavilion.* New York, 1973
12. *Masquerade in Venice.* New York, 1973
13. *I Came to the Highlands.* New York, 1974
14. *The House on the Left Bank.* New York, 1975
15. *A Room with Dark Mirrors.* New York, 1975
16. *Deveron Hall.* New York, 1976
17. *The Frenchman.* New York and London, 1976
18. *The Etruscan Smile.* New York, 1977
19. *The Silver Dolphin.* New York, 1979
20. *The People from the Sea.* New York, 1979
21. *A Presence in an Empty Room.* New York, 1980
22. *The Stone Maiden.* New York, 1980
23. *The Fateful Summer.* New York, 1981
24. *So Wild a Heart,* as Veronica Jason. New York, 1981

Jones, Douglas C.
American, born December 6, 1924
1. *The Treaty of Medicine Lodge: The Story of the Great Treaty Council as Told by Eyewitnesses.* Norman (OK), 1966
2. *The Court-Martial of George Armstrong Custer.* New York, 1976
3. *Arrest Sitting Bull.* New York, 1977
4. *A Creek Called Wounded Knee.* New York, 1978
5. *Winding Stair.* New York, 1979
6. *The Winding Stair Massacre.* London, 1980
7. *Elkhorn Tavern.* New York, 1980
8. *Weedy Rough.* New York, 1981
9. *The Barefoot Brigade.* New York, 1982

Jones, Nard [Maynard Benedict Jones]
American, born April 12, 1904, died September 3, 1972
1. *Oregon Detour.* New York, 1930
2. *The Petlands.* New York, 1931
3. *Wheat Woman.* New York, 1933
4. *All Six Were Lovers.* New York, 1934
5. *Pulp, Paper, and People.* Privately printed, no date
6. *West, Young Man!* Portland (OR), 1937
7. *The Case of the Hanging Lady.* New York, 1938
8. *Swift Flows the River.* No place, 1940
9. *Scarlet Petticoat.* New York, 1941
10. *Still to the West.* New York, 1946
11. *Evergreen Land: A Portrait of the State of Washington.* New York, 1947

12. *The Island.* New York, 1948
13. *I'll Take What's Mine.* New York, 1954
14. *Ride the Dark Storm.* New York, 1955
15. *The Great Command: The Story of Marcus and Narcissa Whitman and the Oregon Country Pioneers.* Boston, 1959
16. *Rediscovering Washington State.* Olympia (WA), 1960
17. *Seattle.* New York, 1972

Joscelyn, Archie (Lynn)
American, born July 25, 1899
Pseudonyms: A.A. Archer, Al Cody, Tex Holt, Evelyn McKenna, Lynn Westland

1. *The Golden Bowl.* Cleveland, 1931
2. *Eric Hearle, Detective.* Cleveland, 1934
3. *Black Horse Rider.* New York and London, 1935
4. *Six-Gun Sovereignty.* New York, 1935
5. *Gun Sovereignty.* London, 1935
6. *The Law Man of Lonesome River.* New York, 1935
7. *Prisoner's Valley.* Cleveland, 1935
8. *The King of Thunder Valley.* New York and London, 1936
9. *Son of the Saddle,* as Lynn Westland. New York, 1936
10. *Three Men Murdered,* as A.A. Archer. New York, 1936
11. *Fire in My Heart,* as Evelyn McKenna. New York, 1936
12. *One Romantic Summer,* as Evelyn McKenna. New York, 1936
13. *Ranch of the Two Thumbs.* New York and London, 1937
14. *The Riding Devils.* New York and London, 1937
15. *Powdersmoke Pass,* as Lynn Westland. New York and London, 1937
16. *Dakota Marshal,* as Lynn Westland. New York, 1937
17. *The Enchanted Park,* as Evelyn McKenna. New York, 1937
18. *Cottonwood Canyon.* New York, 1938
19. *Hoot Owl Canyon.* New York, 1938
20. *Maverick Molloy,* as Lynn Westland. New York, 1938
21. *Quick on the Draw,* as Lynn Westland. London, 1938
22. *The Week-End Murders,* as A.A. Archer. New York, 1938
23. *The Heart E Horsemen.* New York, 1939
24. *Tenderfoot Bill.* New York, 1939
25. *King Cayuse,* as Lynn Westland. New York, 1939
26. *The Range of No Return,* as Lynn Westland. New York, 1939
27. *Guns of Lost Valley.* New York, 1940
28. *Double Diamond Brand.* New York, 1940
29. *Born to the Saddle.* New York and London, 1940
30. *The Nightmare Riders,* as Lynn Westland. New York, 1940
31. *Dead Man's Range.* New York, 1941
32. *The Sawbones of Desolate Range.* New York, 1941
33. *Yates of Red Dog.* New York, 1941
34. *King of the Rodeo,* as Lynn Westland. New York, 1941
35. *Shooting Valley.* New York, 1941
36. *Double Cross Tangles.* Kingswood (Eng), 1942
37. *Satan's Range.* New York, 1942
38. *Saddle River Spread,* as Lynn Westland. New York, 1942
39. *Shootin' Iron.* New York and London, 1942
40. *Trail to Bang-Up.* New York, 1943
41. *Valley Ranch.* New York, 1943
42. *Prentiss of the Box 8.* New York, 1943
43. *Gunsight Ranch,* as Lynn Westland. New York, 1943
44. *Trail to Montana,* as Lynn Westland. New York, 1943
45. *Troublesome Cowhand.* New York, 1944
46. *Blue River Riders.* New York, 1944
47. *Boss of the Northern Star.* New York, 1944
48. *Prairie Pinto,* as Lynn Westland. New York, 1944
49. *Wagon Train Westward,* as Lynn Westland. New York, 1944
50. *Rusty Mallory.* New York, 1945
51. *Sign of the Gun.* New York, 1945
52. *Over the Frontier Trail,* as Lynn Westland. New York, 1945
53. *Prairie Pioneers,* as Lynn Westland. New York, 1945
54. *Return to the Range,* as Lynn Westland. New York, 1945
55. *Death in the Saddle.* New York, 1946
56. *Judge Colt.* New York, 1946
57. *Long Loop Raiders,* as Lynn Westland. New York, 1946
58. *Empty Saddles,* as Al Cody. New York, 1946
59. *Thunder of Hoofs,* as Tex Holt. New York, 1946
60. *The Lone Pine Ranch,* as Lynn Westland. New York, 1947
61. *The Silver Cayuse,* as Lynn Westland. New York, 1947
62. *West of the Law,* as Al Cody. New York, 1947
63. *Bitter Creek,* as Al Cody. New York and London, 1947
64. *Thunder of Hooves.* London, 1948
65. *Smoky in the West.* New York, 1948
66. *Black River Ranch,* as Lynn Westland. New York, 1948
67. *Home Range,* as Lynn Westland. New York, 1948
68. *North from Montana,* as Lynn Westland. New York and London, 1948
69. *Disaster Trail,* as Al Cody. New York, 1948
70. *Outpost Trail,* as Al Cody. New York, 1948
71. *Dark Canyon,* as Tex Holt. New York, 1948
72. *Silvertip Ranch,* as Lynn Westland. New York, 1949
73. *The Marshal of Deer Creek,* as Al Cody. New York, 1949
74. *The Big Corral,* as Al Cody. New York, 1949
75. *Point West,* as Tex Holt. New York, 1949
76. *Border Wolves.* New York, 1950
77. *Death's Bright Angel.* Kingswood, 1950
78. *Shannahan's Feud.* Kingston (NY), 1950
79. *Texas Outlaw.* New York, 1950
80. *Stardance Post.* Kingswood, 1950
81. *Star Toter.* London, 1950
82. *Doomrock.* New York, 1950
83. *Texas Red,* as Lynn Westland. New York, 1950
84. *Sundown,* as Al Cody. New York, 1950
85. *Reservation Range,* as Al Cody. London, 1950
86. *Cactus on the Range,* as Tex Holt. New York, 1950
87. *Maverick Range.* Kingswood, 1951
88. *Vengeance Trail.* New York, 1951
89. *Outlaw's Holiday.* New York, 1951
90. *Gun Thunder Valley.* New York, 1951
91. *Hell for Leather.* New York, 1951
92. *Wagons West.* New York, 1951
93. *Trail Rider,* as Lynn Westland. Kingston (NY), 1951
94. *Hangman's Coulee,* as Al Cody. New York, 1951
95. *Forlorn Valley,* as Al Cody. London, 1951
96. *Red Man's Range,* as Al Cody. London, 1951
97. *Thunder River Trail,* as Al Cody. London, 1951
98. *The Golden Stagecoach.* London, 1952
99. *Hostage.* New York, 1952
100. *The Texan's Revenge.* New York, 1952
101. *Valley of the Sun.* Kingswood, 1952
102. *Forbidden River,* as Al Cody. New York, 1952
103. *The Thundering Hills,* as Al Cody. New York, 1952
104. *Outlaw Justice at Hangman's Coulee,* as Al Cody. New York, 1952
105. *Guns Blaze at Sundown,* as Al Cody. New York, 1952
106. *Outlaw Valley,* as Al Cody. Toronto, 1952
107. *Bad Man's Town,* as Al Cody. London, 1952
108. *Two Gun Vengeance.* New York, 1953
109. *Texas Showdown.* Toronto, 1953
110. *Gunman.* New York, 1953
111. *Canyon Man Hunt.* London, 1953
112. *The Claim Jumpers.* London, 1953
113. *Tough Sheriff Jameson,* as Lynn Westland. London, 1953
114. *Outlaw,* as Lynn Westland. London, 1953
115. *Ride to Blizzard,* as Lynn Westland. New York, 1953
116. *Legion of the Lawless,* as Lynn Westland. Toronto, 1953
117. *Riders of Stormhold,* as Al Cody. London, 1953
118. *Powder Burns,* as Al Cody. New York, 1953
119. *Outlaw Holiday.* London, 1954

120. *Trapper's Rendezvous.* New York, 1954
121. *Renegade Scout.* New York, 1954
122. *The Kempsey Outfit.* London, 1954
123. *The Dead Ride Hard,* as Lynn Westland. London, 1954
124. *Brand of Iron,* as Al Cody. New York and London, 1954
125. *Lost Valley,* as Al Cody. Toronto, 1954
126. *Cheyenne Justice.* New York and London, 1955
127. *The Silver Saddle.* London, 1955
128. *Guns on the Bitterroot,* as Al Cody. New York, 1955
129. *The Sundowners.* New York, 1956
130. *Hired Gun.* New York, 1956
131. *Wyoming Rendezvous.* London, 1956
132. *Whiplash War,* as Al Cody. New York, 1956
133. *Gunhand's Pay.* New York, 1957
134. *Six-Gun Sawbones.* New York, 1957
135. *Texas Revenge.* New York, 1957
136. *The Man From Salt Creek.* New York, 1957
137. *Cheyenne Kid.* New York, 1958
138. *Fighting Kid from Texas.* New York, 1958
139. *High Prairie.* New York, 1958
140. *River of the Sunset.* New York, 1958
141. *Montana Helltown,* as Al Cody. New York, 1958
142. *Bloody Wyoming,* as Al Cody. New York, 1958
143. *The Thief.* Rock Island (IL), 1958
144. *Dead Man's Trail.* New York, 1959
145. *Gunsmoke at Gila Gulch.* New York, 1959
146. *Wyoming Ambush,* as Al Cody. New York, 1959
147. *Winter Range,* as Al Cody. New York, 1959
148. *Gunsmoke on the Gila.* London, 1960
149. *Marshal of Broken Wheel.* New York and London, 1960
150. *The Crown.* Rock Island (IL), 1960
151. *Long Night at Lodge Pole,* as Al Cody. New York, 1961
152. *Gunsmoke Hill,* as Al Cody. New York, 1961
153. *Massacre Creek.* New York, 1962
154. *Gun Ranch,* as Lynn Westland. New York, 1962
155. *Homestead Range,* as Al Cody. New York, 1962
156. *Wyoming Outlaw,* as Al Cody. New York, 1962
157. *Sheriff of Red Wolf.* New York, 1963
158. *The Man Behind the Star.* New York, 1963
159. *A Sky Pilot for Powderhouse.* New York, 1963
160. *Rim of the Range.* New York, 1963
161. *Ambush of Satan's Hill.* New York, 1963
162. *The Heart of Texas,* as Lynn Westland. New York, 1963
163. *Powdersmoke Payoff,* as Lynn Westland. New York, 1963
164. *The Golden Saddle,* as Al Cody. New York, 1963
165. *This Land Is Mine,* as Tex Holt. New York, 1963
166. *The Silent Guns,* as Tex Holt. New York, 1963
167. *The Beast of Babylon.* Minneapolis (MN), 1963
168. *Gun in Hand.* London, 1964
169. *King of Silverhill.* New York, 1964
170. *Duel at Killman Creek.* New York, 1964
171. *Logan.* New York, 1964
172. *West from Deadwood.* New York, 1964
173. *Storm along the Rattlesnake.* New York, 1964
174. *Deadman's Gold,* as Lynn Westland. New York, 1964
175. *Thunder to the West,* as Lynn Westland. New York, 1964
176. *Squatter Sovereignty,* as Al Cody. New York, 1964
177. *Trail of the Innocents,* as Al Cody. New York, 1964
178. *Rimrock Vengeance.* New York, 1965
179. *The Sheriff of Singing River.* New York, 1965
180. *Smoke Against the Sky,* as Lynn Westland. New York, 1965
181. *The Red Gun,* as Lynn Westland. New York, 1965
182. *The Golden River.* New York, 1966
183. *The Gunhand.* New York, 1966
184. *The Renegade,* as Al Cody. New York, 1966
185. *Castle Midnight,* as Evelyn McKenna. New York, 1966
186. *Fort Fear.* New York, 1967
187. *Trail North.* New York, 1967
188. *Trouble at Sudden Creek.* New York, 1967
189. *Heritage in Powdersmoke,* as Lynn Westland. New York, 1967
190. *The Guns of Yesterday.* New York, 1968
191. *The Forbidden Frontier.* New York, 1968
192. *Bushwhack Range.* New York, 1968
193. *Lone Tree Renegade,* as Archie Joscelyn. New York, 1968
194. *Rogue's Range,* as Łynn Westland. New York, 1968
195. *Freeze-Out Creek.* New York, 1969
196. *Dragoon Pass,* as Lynn Westland. London, 1970
197. *Montana's Territory,* as Al Cody. New York, 1970
198. *The Ranch at Powder River,* as Al Cody. New York, 1972
199. *Empty Holsters.* New York, 1974
200. *Restless Spurs.* New York, 1974
201. *Gunsong at Twilight,* as Al Cody. New York, 1974
202. *Gunsmoke Holiday.* New York, 1975
203. *The Trail to Dismal River.* New York, 1975
204. *Return to Fort Yavapa,* as Al Cody. New York, 1975
205. *Lost River Canyon.* New York, 1976
206. *Kiowa Pass.* New York, 1976
207. *Broken Wheels.* New York, 1976
208. *Iron Horse Country,* as Al Cody. New York, 1976
209. *The Trail to Lost Horse Ranch.* New York, 1977
210. *Triple Cross Trail,* as Al Cody. New York, 1977
211. *Flame in the Forest,* as Al Cody. New York, 1977
212. *The Fort at the Dry,* as Al Cody. New York, 1977
213. *The Three McMahons,* as Al Cody. New York, 1977
214. *The Lost Herd.* New York, 1978
215. *The Hooded Falcon.* New York, 1978
216. *High Lonesome,* as Al Cody. New York, 1978
217. *The Mine at Lost Mountain,* as Al Cody. New York, 1978
218. *Return to Texas,* as Al Cody. New York, 1978
219. *West from Abilene,* as Al Cody. New York, 1978
220. *West of Sundown,* as Al Cody. New York, 1978

Kane, Frank
American, born July 19, 1912, died November 29, 1968
Pseudonym: Frank Boyd
1. *About Face.* New York, 1947
2. *Death About Face.* Kingston (NY), 1948
3. *Green Light for Death.* New York, 1949
4. *Slay Ride.* New York, 1950
5. *Bullet Proof.* New York, 1951
6. *Dead Weight.* New York, 1951
7. *Bare Trap.* New York, 1952
8. *Poisons Unknown.* New York, 1953
9. *Grave Danger.* New York, 1954
10. *Red Hot Ice.* New York, 1955
11. *Key Witness.* New York, 1956
12. *A Real Gone Guy.* New York, 1956
13. *Johnny Liddell's Morgue.* New York, 1956
14. *The Living End.* New York, 1957
15. *Liz.* Beacon, New York, 1958
16. *Syndicate Girl.* New York, 1958
17. *Trigger Mortis.* New York, 1958
18. *The Fatal Foursome.* New York, 1958
19. *Juke Box King.* New York, 1959
20. *The Line-Up.* New York, 1959
21. *The Flesh Peddlers,* as Frank Boyd. Derby (CT), 1959
22. *Johnny Staccato.* New York, 1960
23. *A Short Bier.* New York, 1960
24. *Time to Prey.* New York, 1960
25. *Due or Die.* New York, 1961
26. *The Mourning After.* New York, 1961
27. *Stacked Deck.* New York, 1961
28. *The Conspirators.* New York, 1962
29. *Crime of Their Life.* New York, 1962
30. *Dead Rite.* New York, 1962

31. *Ring-a-Ding-Ding.* New York, 1963
32. *Johnny Come Lately.* New York, 1963
33. *Hearse Class Male.* New York, 1968
34. *Barely Seen.* New York and London, 1964
35. *Final Curtain.* New York and London, 1964
36. *Fatal Undertaking.* New York, 1964
37. *The Guilt-Edged Frame.* New York, 1964
38. *Esprit de Corpse.* New York, 1965
39. *Two to Tangle.* New York, 1965
40. *Anatomy of the Whiskey Business.* Manhasset (NY), 1965
41. *Maid in Paris.* New York, 1966
42. *Travel Is for the Birds.* Manhasset, 1966
43. *Margin for Terror.* New York, 1967

Kane, Henry
American, born in 1918
Pseudonym: Anthony McCall
1. *A Halo for Nobody.* New York, 1947
2. *Armchair in Hell.* New York, 1948
3. *Report for a Corpse.* New York, 1948
4. *Hang by Your Neck.* New York, 1949
5. *Edge of Panic.* New York, 1950
6. *A Corpse for Christmas.* Philadelphia, 1951
7. *Until You Are Dead.* New York, 1951
8. *Laughter Came Screaming.* London, 1953
9. *My Business Is Murder.* New York, 1954
10. *Trilogy in Jeopardy.* London, 1955
11. *Trinity in Violence.* New York, 1955
12. *Too French and Too Deadly.* New York, 1955
13. *The Case of the Murdered Madame.* New York, 1955
14. *The Narrowing Lust.* London, 1956
15. *Who Killed Sweet Sue?* New York, 1956
16. *Martinis and Murder.* New York, 1956
17. *Sweet Charlie.* London, 1957
18. *The Deadly Finger.* New York, 1957
19. *The Finger.* London, 1957
20. *Death on the Double.* New York, 1957
21. *Death for Sale.* New York, 1957
22. *Murder of the Park Avenue Playgirl.* New York, 1957
23. *The Name Is Chambers.* New York, 1957
24. *Mask for Murder.* New York, 1957
25. *Sleep Without Dreams.* London, 1958
26. *Fistful of Death.* New York, 1958
27. *Triple Terror.* London, 1958
28. *The Dangling Man.* London, 1959
29. *Death Is the Last Lover.* New York, 1959
30. *Nirvana Can Also Mean Death.* London, 1959
31. *The Deadly Doll.* Rockville Centre (NY), 1959
32. *The Private Eyeful.* New York, 1959
33. *Peter Gunn.* New York, 1960
34. *Run for Doom.* London, 1960
35. *The Crumpled Cup.* London, 1961
36. *Death of a Flack.* New York and London, 1961
37. *My Darlin' Evangeline.* New York, 1961
38. *Perfect Crime.* London, 1961
39. *Dead in Bed.* New York, 1961
40. *Death of a Hooker.* London, 1961
41. *Kisses of Death.* New York, 1962
42. *Killer's Kiss.* London, 1962
43. *Death of a Dastard.* London, 1962
44. *How to Write a Song.* New York, 1962
45. *Never Give a Millionaire an Even Break.* New York, 1963
46. *Nobody Loves a Loser.* New York, 1963
47. *Snatch an Eye.* London, 1963
48. *Two Must Die.* New York, 1963
49. *Dirty Gertie.* London, 1963
50. *Frenzy of Evil.* London, 1963
51. *To Die or Not To Die.* New York, 1964
52. *Murder for the Millions.* London, 1964
53. *The Midnight Man.* New York, 1965
54. *Other Sins Only Speak.* London, 1965
55. *Prey by Dawn.* London, 1965
56. *Conceal and Disguise.* New York and London, 1966
57. *The Devil to Pay.* London, 1966
58. *Operation Delta,* as Anthony McCall. New York, 1966
59. *Homicide at Yuletide.* New York, 1966
60. *Unholy Trio.* New York, 1967
61. *Holocaust,* as Anthony McCall. New York, 1967
62. *Laughter in the Alehouse.* New York, 1968
63. *Don't Call Me Madame.* New York, 1969
64. *The Schack Job.* New York, 1969
65. *Who Dies There?* New York, 1969
66. *The Bomb Job.* New York, 1970
67. *Better Wed Than Dead.* New York, 1970
68. *Don't Go Away Dead.* New York, 1970
69. *Kiss! Kiss! Kill! Kill!* New York, 1970
70. *The Glow Job.* New York, 1971
71. *The Moonlighter.* New York, 1971
72. *The Tail Job.* New York, 1971
73. *The Virility Factor.* New York, 1971
74. *Come Kill with Me.* New York, 1972
75. *The Escort Job.* New York, 1972
76. *Kill for the Millions.* New York, 1972
77. *Decision.* New York, 1973
78. *A Kind of Rape.* New York, 1974
79. *The Violator.* New York, 1974
80. *The Avenger.* New York, 1975
81. *Lust of Power.* New York, 1975
82. *The Tripoli Documents.* New York, 1976

Kantor, MacKinlay
American, born February 4, 1904, died October 11, 1977
1. *Diversey.* New York, 1928
2. *El Goes South.* New York, 1930
3. *The Jaybird.* New York, 1932
4. *Long Remember.* New York and London, 1934
5. *The Voice of Bugle Ann.* New York and London, 1935
6. *Turkey in the Straw: A Book of American Ballads and Primitive Verse.* New York, 1935
7. *Arouse and Beware.* New York, 1936
8. *The Romance of Rosy Ridge.* New York, 1937
9. *The Boy in the Dark.* Webster Groves (MO), 1937
10. *The Noise of Their Wings.* New York, 1938
11. *Valedictory.* New York, 1939
12. *Cuba Libre.* New York, 1940
13. *Gentle Annie: A Western Novel.* New York, 1942
14. *Angleworms on Toast.* New York, 1942
15. *Happy Land.* New York, 1943
16. *Author's Choice: 40 Stories.* New York, 1944
17. *Glory for Me.* New York, 1945
18. *But Look, the Morn: The Story of a Childhood.* New York, 1947
19. *Midnight Lace.* New York, 1948
20. *Wicked Water: An American Primitive.* New York, 1949
21. *The Good Family.* New York, 1949
22. *One Wild Oat.* New York, 1950
23. *Signal Thirty-Two.* New York, 1950
24. *Lee and Grant at Appomattox.* New York, 1950
25. *Don't Touch Me.* New York, 1951
26. *Warwhoop: Two Short Novels of the Frontier.* New York, 1952
27. *Gettysburg.* New York, 1952
28. *The Daughter of Bugle Ann.* New York, 1953
29. *God and My Country.* Cleveland (OH), 1954
30. *Andersonville.* Cleveland, 1955

31. *Lobo*. Cleveland, 1957
32. *The Goss Boys*. London, 1958
33. *The Work of St. Francis*. Cleveland, 1958
34. *Silent Grow the Guns and Other Tales of the American Civil War*. New York, 1958
35. *Again the Bugle*. New York, 1958
36. *Frontier: Tales of the American Adventure*. New York, 1959
37. *The Unseen Witness*. London, 1959
38. *It's about Crime*. New York, 1960
39. *Spirit Lake*. Cleveland, 1961
40. *If the South Had Won the Civil War*. New York, 1961
41. *The Gun-Toter and Other Stories of the Missouri Hills*. New York, 1963
42. *Mission with LeMay: My Story*. New York, 1965
43. *Story Teller*. New York, 1967
44. *The Historical Novelist's Obligation to History*. Macon (GA), 1967
45. *Beauty Beast*. New York, 1968
46. *The Day I Met a Lion*. New York, 1968
47. *Missouri Bittersweet*. New York, 1969
48. *Hamilton County*. New York, 1970
49. *I Love You, Irene*. New York, 1972
50. *The Children Sing*. New York, 1973
51. *Valley Forge*. New York, 1975

Keating, H.R.F. (Henry Reymond Fitzwalter)
British, born October 31, 1926
1. *Death and the Visiting Firemen*. London, 1959
2. *Zen There Was Murder*. London, 1960
3. *A Rush on the Ultimate*. London, 1961
4. *The Dog It Was That Died*. London, 1962
5. *Death of a Fat God*. London, 1963
6. *The Perfect Murder*. London, 1964
7. *Is Skin-Deep, Is Fatal*. London and New York, 1965
8. *Inspecter Ghote's Good Crusade*. London and New York, 1966
9. *Inspector Ghote Hunts the Peacock*. London and New York, 1968
10. *Inspector Ghote Plays a Joker*. London and New York, 1969
11. *Understanding Pierre Teilhard de Chardin: A Guide to "The Phenomenon of Man."* London, 1969
12. *Inspector Ghote Breaks an Egg*. London, 1970
13. *The Strong Man*. London, 1971
14. *Inspector Ghote Goes by Train*. London, 1971
15. *Inspector Ghote Trusts the Heart*. London, 1972
16. *Bats Fly Up for Inspector Ghote*. London and New York, 1974
17. *The Underside*. London, 1974
18. *A Remarkable Case of Burglary*. London, 1975
19. *Murder Must Appetize*. London, 1975
20. *Filmi, Filmi, Inspector Ghote*. London, 1976
21. *"I.N.I.T.I.A.L.S."* New York, 1977
22. *A Long Walk to Wimbledon*. London, 1978
23. *"New Patents Pending."* London, 1978
24. *Inspector Ghote Draws a Line*. London and New York, 1979
25. *Sherlock Holmes: The Man and His World*. London and New York, 1979

Keene, Day
American, died ca. 1969
1. *This Is Murder, Mr. Herbert, and Other Stories*. New York, 1948
2. *Framed in Guilt*. New York, 1949
3. *Evidence Most Blind*. London, 1950
4. *Farewell to Passion*. New York, 1951
5. *My Flesh Is Sweet*. New York, 1951
6. *Love Me and Die*. New York, 1951
7. *To Kiss or Kill*. New York, 1951
8. *Hunt the Killer*. New York, 1952
9. *About Doctor Ferrel*. New York, 1952
10. *Home Is the Sailor*. New York, 1952
11. *If the Coffin Fits*. Hasbrouck Heights (NJ), 1952
12. *Naked Fury*. New York, 1952
13. *Wake Up to Murder*. New York, 1952
14. *Mrs. Homicide*. New York, 1953
15. *Strange Witness*. Hasbrouck Heights, 1953
16. *The Big Kiss-Off*. Hasbrouck Heights, 1954
17. *Death House Doll*. New York, 1954
18. *Homicidal Lady*. Hasbrouck Heights, 1954
19. *Joy House*. New York, 1954
20. *Notorious*. New York, 1954
21. *Sleep with the Devil*. New York, 1954
22. *There Was a Crooked Man*. New York, 1954
23. *His Father's Wife*. New York, 1954
24. *Who Has Wilma Lathrop?* New York, 1955
25. *The Dangling Carrot*. New York, 1955
26. *Murder on the Side*. New York, 1956
27. *Bring Him Back Dead*. New York, 1956
28. *Flight by Night*. New York, 1956
29. *It's a Sin to Kill*. New York, 1958
30. *Passage to Samoa*. New York, 1958
31. *Dead Dolls Don't Talk*. New York, 1959
32. *Dead in Bed*. New York, 1959
33. *Moran's Woman*. Rockville Centre (NY), 1959
34. *So Dead My Lovely*. New York, 1959
35. *Take a Step to Murder*. New York, 1959
36. *Too Black for Heaven*. Rockville Centre, 1959
37. *Too Hot to Hold*. New York, 1959
38. *The Brimstone Bed*. New York, 1960
39. *Payola*. New York, 1960
40. *Seed of Doubt*. New York, 1961
41. *Bye, Baby Bunting*. New York and London, 1963
42. *Carnival of Death*. New York, 1965
43. *Miami 59*. New York, 1959
44. *Chautauqua*. New York, 1960
45. *World Without Women*. New York, 1960
46. *Chicago 11*. New York, 1966
47. *Southern Daughter*. New York, 1967
48. *Live Again, Love Again*. New York, 1970
49. *Wild Girl*. New York, 1970

Kelland, Clarence Budington
American, born July 11, 1881, died February 18, 1964
1. *Quizzer No. 20, Being Questions and Answers on Insurance*. Detroit (MI), 1911
2. *Thirty Pieces of Silver*. New York, 1913
3. *Mark Tidd: His Adventures and Strategies [in the Backwoods, in Business, Tidd's Citadel, Editor, Manufacturer, in Italy, in Egypt, in Sicily]*. New York, 9 vols., 1913-28
4. *Into His Own: The Story of an Airedale*. Philadelphia, 1915
5. *The Hidden Spring*. New York, 1916
6. *Sudden Jim*. New York, 1917
7. *The Source*. New York, 1918
8. *The Little Moment of Happiness*. New York, 1919
9. *The Highflyers*. New York, 1919
10. *Efficiency Edgar*. New York, 1920
11. *Youth Challenges*. New York, 1920
12. *Catty Atkins [Riverman, Sailorman, Financier, Bandmaster]*. New York, 5 vols., 1920-24
13. *Scattergood Baines*. New York, 1921
14. *Conflict*. New York, 1922
15. *Contraband*. New York, 1923
16. *The Steadfast Heart*. New York, 1924
17. *Miracle*. New York and London, 1925

Kelland, Clarence Budington

18. *Rhoda Fair.* New York, 1926
19. *Dance Magic.* New York, 1927
20. *Jahala.* London, 1927
21. *Knuckles.* New York and London, 1928
22. *Dynasty.* New York, 1929
23. *Mr. Bundy.* London, 1929
24. *Hard Money.* New York, 1930
25. *Gold.* New York, 1931
26. *Speak Easily.* New York, 1932
27. *The Great Crooner.* New York, 1933
28. *Tombstone.* New York, 1933
29. *The Jealous House.* New York, 1934
30. *The Cat's Paw.* New York, 1934
31. *Dreamland.* New York, 1935
32. *Roxana.* New York, 1936
33. *Spotlight.* New York, 1937
34. *Mr. Deeds Goes to Town.* London, 1937
35. *Star Rising.* New York, 1938
36. *Arizona.* New York, 1939
37. *Skin Deep.* New York, 1939
38. *Valley of the Sun.* New York, 1940
39. *Scattergood.* New York, 1940
40. *Scattergood Baines Pulls the Strings.* New York, 1941
41. *House of Cards.* London, 1941
42. *Silver Spoon.* New York, 1941
43. *Sugarfoot.* New York, 1942
44. *Archibald the Great.* New York, 1943
45. *Heart on Her Sleeve.* New York, 1943
46. *Alias Jane Smith.* New York, 1944
47. *Double Treasure.* New York, 1946
48. *Land of the Torreones.* New York, 1946
49. *Murder for a Million.* Kingswood (Eng), 1947
50. *Merchant of Valor.* New York, 1947
51. *This Is My Son.* New York, 1948
52. *Desert Law.* New York, 1949
53. *The Comic Jest.* San Francisco, 1949
54. *Stolen Goods.* New York, 1950
55. *The Great Mail Robbery.* New York, 1951
56. *No Escape.* London, 1951
57. *The Key Man.* New York, 1952
58. *Dangerous Angel.* New York, 1953
59. *West of the Law.* New York, 1958
60. *Murder Makes an Entrance.* New York, 1955
61. *The Sinister Strangers.* Roslyn (NY), 1955
62. *The Case of the Nameless Corpse.* New York, 1956
63. *Death Keeps a Secret.* New York, 1956
64. *The Lady and the Giant.* New York, 1959
65. *Where There's Smoke.* New York, 1959
66. *Counterfeit Gentleman.* New York, 1960
67. *The Monitor Affair.* New York, 1960
68. *Mark of Treachery.* New York, 1961
69. *The Artless Heiress.* New York, 1962
70. *Party Man.* New York, 1962

Kelton, Elmer

American, born April 29, 1926
Pseudonyms: Alex Hawk, Lee McElroy

1. *Hot Iron.* New York, 1956
2. *Buffalo Wagons.* New York, 1957
3. *Barbed Wire.* New York, 1958
4. *Shadow of a Star.* New York, 1959
5. *The Texas Rifles.* New York and London, 1960
6. *Donovan.* New York, 1961
7. *Bitter Trail.* New York, 1962
8. *Horsehead Crossing.* New York, 1963
9. *Massacre at Goliad.* New York, 1965
10. *Llano River.* New York, 1966
11. *After the Bugles.* New York, 1967
12. *Captain's Rangers.* New York, 1969
13. *Shotgun Settlement,* as Alex Hawk. New York, 1969
14. *Hanging Judge.* New York, 1969
15. *The Day the Cowboys Quit.* New York, 1971
16. *Bowie's Mine.* New York, 1971
17. *Wagontongue.* New York, 1972
18. *Looking Back West: Selections from the Pioneer News-Observer.* San Angelo (TX), 1972
19. *The Time It Never Rained.* New York, 1973
20. *Manhunters.* New York, 1974
21. *Joe Pepper,* as Lee McElroy. New York, 1975
22. *Long Way to Texas,* as Lee McElroy. New York, 1976
23. *The Good Old Boys.* New York, 1978
24. *The Wolf and the Buffalo.* New York, 1980
25. *The Eyes of the Hawk,* as Lee McElroy. New York, 1981
26. *Frank C. McCarthy: The Old West.* Greenwich (CT), 1981

Kennedy, Margaret

British, born in 1896, died July 31, 1967

1. *A Century of Revolution 1789-1920.* London, 1922
2. *The Ladies of Lyndon.* London, 1923
3. *The Constant Nymph.* London, 1924
4. *Red Sky at Morning.* London and New York, 1927
5. *A Long Week-End.* London and New York, 1927
6. *Dewdrops.* London, 1928
7. *The Game and the Candle.* London, 1928
8. *The Fool of the Family.* London and New York, 1930
9. *Return I Dare Not.* London and New York, 1931
10. *A Long Time Ago.* London and New York, 1932
11. *Together and Apart.* London, 1936
12. *The Midas Touch.* London, 1938
13. *Where Stands a Winged Sentry.* New Haven (CT), 1941
14. *The Mechanized Muse.* London, 1942
15. *The Feast.* London and New York, 1950
16. *Lucy Carmichael.* New York and London, 1951
17. *Troy Chimneys.* New York, 1952
18. *The Oracles.* London, 1955
19. *The Heroes of Clone.* London, 1957
20. *Jane Austen.* London, 1950
21. *The Outlaws on Parnassus.* London, 1958
22. *A Night in Cold Harbour.* London and New York, 1960
23. *The Forgotten Smile.* London, 1961
24. *Not in the Calendar.* London and New York, 1964
25. *Women at Work.* London, 1966

Kennedy, Milward [Milward Rodon Kennedy Burge]

British, born June 21, 1894, died January 20, 1968
Other pseudonyms: Evelyn Elder, Robert Milward Kennedy

1. *The Bleston Mystery,* as Robert Milward Kennedy. London, 1928
2. *The Corpse on the Mat.* London, 1929
3. *The Man Who Rang the Bell.* New York, 1929
4. *Corpse Guards Parade.* London, 1929
5. *Half-Mast Murder.* London and New York, 1930
6. *Murder in Black and White,* as Evelyn Elder. London, 1931
7. *Death to the Rescue.* London, 1931
8. *Angel in the Case,* as Evelyn Elder. London, 1932
9. *The Murderer of Sleep.* London, 1932
10. *The Floating Admiral.* London, 1931
11. *Bull's Eye.* London and New York, 1933
12. *Ask a Policeman.* London and New York, 1933
13. *Corpse in Cold Storage.* London and New York, 1934
14. *Poison in the Parish.* London, 1935
15. *Sic Transit Gloria.* London, 1936
16. *The Scornful Corpse.* New York, 1936
17. *I'll Be Judge, I'll Be Jury.* London, 1937
18. *"Are Murders Meant?" and "Murderers in Fiction."* London, 1939

19. *Who Was Old Willy?* London, 1940
20. *It Began in New York.* London, 1943
21. *Escape to Quebec.* London, 1946
22. *The Top Boot.* London, 1950
23. *Two's Company.* London, 1952

Kenrick, Tony
British, born August 23, 1935
1. *The Only Good Body's A Dead One.* London, 1970
2. *A Tough One to Lose.* London and Indianapolis (IN), 1972
3. *Two for the Price of One.* London and Indianapolis, 1974
4. *Stealing Lillian.* London and New York, 1975
5. *The Kidnap Kid.* London, 1976
6. *The Seven Day Soldiers.* London and Chicago, 1976
7. *The Chicago Girl.* New York, 1976
8. *Two Lucky People.* London, 1978
9. *The Nighttime Guy.* London and New York, 1979
10. *The 81st Site.* New York and London, 1980

Kenyon, Michael
British, born June 26, 1931
Pseudonym: Daniel Forbes
1. *May You Die in Ireland.* London and New York, 1965
2. *The Whole Hog.* London, 1967
3. *The Trouble with Series Three.* New York, 1967
4. *Out of Season.* London, 1968
5. *Green Grass.* London, 1969
6. *The 100,000 Welcomes.* London and New York, 1970
7. *The Shooting of Dan McGrew.* London, 1972
8. *A Sorry State.* London and New York, 1974
9. *Mr. Big.* London, 1975
10. *Mr. Big,* as Daniel Forbes. New York, 1975
11. *Brainbox and Bull.* London, 1976
12. *The Rapist,* as Daniel Forbes. New York, 1977
13. *The Rapist.* London, 1977
14. *Deep Pocket.* London, 1978
15. *The Molehill File.* New York, 1978

Kersh, Gerald
American, born August 6, 1911, died November 5, 1968
1. *Jews Without Jehovah.* London, 1934
2. *Men Are So Ardent.* London, 1935
3. *Night and the City.* London, 1938
4. *I Got References.* London, 1939
5. *They Die with Their Boots Clean.* London, 1941
6. *The Nine Lives of Bill Nelson.* London, 1942
7. *The Dead Look On.* London and New York, 1943
8. *Brain and Ten Fingers.* London, 1943
9. *Selected Stories.* London, 1943
10. *Faces in a Dusty Picture.* London, 1944
11. *The Battle of the Singing Men.* London, 1944
12. *The Horrible Dummy and Other Stories.* London, 1944
13. *Sergeant Nelson of the Guards.* No place, 1945
14. *An Ape, A Dog, and a Serpent.* London, 1945
15. *Sergeant Nelson of the Guards.* Philadelphia, 1945
16. *The Weak and the Strong.* London, 1945
17. *Neither Man nor Dog.* London, 1946
18. *Clean, Bright, and Slightly Oiled.* London, 1946
19. *Prelude to a Certain Midnight.* New York and London, 1947
20. *Sad Road to the Sea.* London, 1947
21. *The Song of the Flea.* New York and London, 1948
22. *Clock Without Hands.* London, 1949
23. *The Thousand Deaths of Mr.Small.* New York, 1950
24. *The Brazen Bull.* London, 1952
25. *The Brighton Monster and Others.* London, 1953
26. *The Great Wash.* London, 1953
27. *The Secret Masters.* New York, 1953
28. *Guttersnipe: Little Novels.* London, 1954
29. *Men Without Bones and Other Stories.* London, 1955
30. *Fowlers End.* New York, 1957
31. *On an Odd Note.* New York, 1958
32. *The Ugly Face of Love and Other Stories.* London, 1960
33. *The Implacable Hunter.* London, 1961
34. *The Best of Gerald Kersh.* London, 1961
35. *The Terribly Wild Flowers: Nine Stories.* London, 1962
36. *More Than Once upon a Time.* London, 1964
37. *A Long Cool Day in Hell.* London, 1965
38. *The Hospitality of Miss Tolliver and Other Stories.* London, 1965
39. *The Angel and the Cuckoo.* New York, 1966
40. *Nightshade and Damnations.* New York, 1968
41. *Brock.* London, 1969

Kesey, Ken (Elton)
American, born September 17, 1935
1. *One Flew over the Cuckoo's Nest.* New York, 1962
2. *Sometimes a Great Notion.* New York, 1964
3. *Kesey's Garage Sale.* New York, 1973
4. *Ken Kesey.* Eugene (OR), 1977

Ketchum, Philip L.
American, born October 19, 1902, died December 13, 1969
Pseudonyms: Miriam Leslie, Mack Saunders
1. *Death in the Library.* New York, 1937
2. *Death at Dusk.* New York, 1938
3. *Death in the Night.* New York, 1939
4. *Kill at Dusk.* New York, 1946
5. *Good Night for Murder.* New York, 1946(?)
6. *Texan on the Prod.* New York, 1952
7. *Decision at Piute Wells.* New York, 1953
8. *Guns of the Barricade Bunch.* New York, 1953
9. *The Saddle Bum.* New York, 1954
10. *The Texas Gun.* New York, 1954
11. *Gun Law.* New York, 1954
12. *Desperation Valley.* New York, 1955
13. *Rider from Texas.* New York, 1955
14. *The Gunslinger.* New York, 1955
15. *The Great Axe Bretwalda.* Boston, 1955
16. *Longhorn Stampede.* New York, 1956
17. *The Night of the Coyotes.* New York, 1956
18. *The Big Gun.* New York, 1956
19. *The Elkhorn Feud.* New York, 1956
20. *Gun Trail,* as Mack Saunders. New York, 1956
21. *Dead Man's Trail.* New York, 1957
22. *Six-Gun Maverick.* New York, 1957
23. *Feud at Forked River.* New York, 1958
24. *The Dead-Shot Kid.* New York, 1959
25. *Gun Code.* New York, 1959
26. *Gunfire Man.* New York, 1959
27. *The Hard Man.* New York, 1959
28. *Apache Dawn.* New York, 1960
29. *Gunsmoke Territory.* New York, 1960
30. *The Buzzard Guns.* New York, 1960
31. *The Stalkers.* New York, 1961
32. *Harsh Reckoning.* New York, 1962
33. *Renegade Range.* Derby (CT), 1962
34. *Traitor Guns.* New York, 1962
35. *Quartet in White.* No place, 1963
36. *The Night Riders.* New York, 1966
37. *Wyoming.* New York, 1967
38. *The Man from Granite.* New York, 1967
39. *The Man Who Tamed Dodge.* New York, 1967
40. *The Man Who Turned Outlaw.* New York, 1967
41. *The Man Who Sold Leadville.* New York, 1968
42. *The Men of Moncada.* New York, 1968

43. *Cavanaugh Keep*, as Miriam Leslie. New York, 1968
44. *Cabot*. New York, 1969
45. *Mad Morgan's Hoard*. New York, 1969
46. *Support Your Local Sheriff*. New York, 1969
47. *Halfbreed*. New York, 1969
48. *Gila Crossing*. New York, 1969
49. *The Cougar Basin War*. New York, 1970
50. *Rattlesnake*. New York, 1970
51. *Buzzard Ridge*. New York, 1970
52. *Judgment Trail*. New York, 1971

Kevern, Barbara [Donald Lee Shepard]
American, born May 26, 1932
1. *Dark Eden*. New York, 1973
2. *Darkness Falling*. New York, 1974
3. *The Key*. New York, 1974
4. *The Devil's Vineyard*. New York, 1975

Keyes, Frances Parkinson
American, born June 21, 1885, died July 3, 1970
1. *The Old Gray Homestead*. Boston and London, 1919
2. *The Career of David Noble*. New York, 1921
3. *Letters from a Senator's Wife*. New York, 1924
4. *Queen Anne's Lace*. New York, 1930
5. *Silver Seas and Golden Cities: A Joyous Journey Through Latin Lands*. New York, 1931
6. *Lady Blanche Farm: A Romance of the Commonplace*. New York, 1931
7. *Senator Marlowe's Daughter*. New York, 1933
8. *The Safe Bridge*. New York, 1934
9. *The Happy Wanderer*. New York, 1935
10. *Honor Bright*. New York and London, 1936
11. *Capital Kaleidoscope: The Story of a Washington Hostess*. New York, 1937
12. *Written in Heaven: The Life on Earth of the Little Flower of Lisieux*. New York and London, 1937
13. *Pioneering People in Northern New England: A Series of Early Sketches*. Washington (DC), 1937
14. *Parts Unknown*. New York, 1938
15. *The Great Tradition*. New York and London, 1939
16. *Fielding's Folly*. New York and London, 1940
17. *Along a Little Way*. New York and London, 1940
18. *Bernadette, Maid of Lourdes*. New York, 1940
19. *The Grace of Guadalupe*. New York, 1941
20. *All That Glitters*. New York and London, 1941
21. *Crescent Carnival*. New York, 1942
22. *Also the Hills*. New York, 1943
23. *The River Road*. New York, 1945
24. *Came a Cavalier*. New York, 1947
25. *Once and Esplanade: A Cycle of Two Creole Weddings*. New York, 1947
26. *Dinner at Antoine's*. New York, 1948
27. *Joy Street*. New York, 1950
28. *The Cost of a Best Seller*. New York, 1950
29. *All This Is Louisiana*. New York, 1950
30. *Steamboat Gothic*. New York, 1952
31. *The Royal Box*. New York and London, 1954
32. *The Frances Parkinson Keyes Cookbook*. New York, 1955
33. *St. Anne: Grandmother of Our Savior*. New York, 1955
34. *Guadelupe to Lourdes*. St. Paul (MN), 1957
35. *The Land of Stones and Saints*. New York, 1957
36. *Blue Camellia*. New York and London, 1957
37. *Victorine*. New York, 1958
38. *Christmas Gift*. New York, 1959
39. *Mother Cabrini, Missionary to the World*. New York and London, 1959
40. *Station Wagon in Spain*. New York, 1959
41. *Roses in December*. New York and London, 1960
42. *The Chess Players*. New York, 1960
43. *The Rose and the Lily: The Lives and Times of Two South American Saints*. New York, 1961
44. *Madame Castel's Lodger*. New York, 1962
45. *The Restless Lady and Other Stories*. New York, 1963
46. *Three Ways of Love*. New York, 1963
47. *The Explorer*. New York, 1964
48. *Tongues of Fire*. New York, 1966
49. *I, the King*. New York and London, 1966
50. *The Heritage*. New York and London, 1968
51. *All Flags Flying: Reminiscences*. New York, 1972

Kidd, Flora
British
1. *Visit to Rowanbank*. London, 1966
2. *Whistle and I'll Come*. London, 1966
3. *Nurse at Rowanbank*. Toronto, 1966
4. *Love Alters Not*. London, 1967
5. *Wind So Gay*. London, 1968
6. *Strange as a Dream*. London, 1968
7. *When Birds Do Sing*. London, 1970
8. *Love Is Fire*. London, 1971
9. *My Heart Remembers*. London and Toronto, 1971
10. *The Dazzle on the Sea*. London and Toronto, 1971
11. *If Love Be Love*. London and Toronto, 1972
12. *Remedy for Love*. London and Toronto, 1972
13. *The Taming of Lisa*. London, 1972
14. *The Cave of the White Rose*. London, 1972
15. *Beyond the Sunset*. London and Toronto, 1973
16. *Night on the Mountain*. London, 1973
17. *The Legend of the Swans*. Toronto, 1974
18. *Gallant's Fancy*. London and Toronto, 1974
19. *The Paper Marriage*. Toronto, 1974
20. *Stranger in the Glen*. London and Toronto, 1975
21. *Enchantment in Blue*. London and Toronto, 1975
22. *The Bargain Bride*. London, 1976
23. *The Black Knight*. London, 1976
24. *The Dance of Courtship*. London and Toronto, 1976
25. *The Summer Wife*. London and Toronto, 1976
26. *Dangerous Pretence*. Toronto, 1977
27. *To Play with Fire*. London, 1977
28. *Jungle of Desire*. Toronto, 1977
29. *Marriage in Mexico*. London, 1978
30. *Castle of Temptation*. London, 1978
31. *Sweet Torment*. London and Toronto, 1978
32. *Canadian Affair*. London, 1978
33. *Passionate Encounter*. London and Toronto, 1979
34. *Stay Through the Night*. London, 1979
35. *Tangled Shadows*. London, 1979
36. *Together Again*. London and Toronto, 1979
37. *The Arranged Marriage*. London and Toronto, 1980
38. *The Silken Bond*. London and Toronto, 1980
39. *Wife by Contract*. London and Toronto, 1980
40. *Beyond Control*. London and Toronto, 1981
41. *Passionate Stranger*. London, 1981
42. *Personal Affair*. London, 1981

Kimbrough, Katheryn [John M. Kimbro]
American, born July 12, 1929
Other pseudonyms: Kym Allyson, Ann Ashton, Charlotte Bramwell, Jean Kimbro
1. *The House on Windswept Ridge*. New York, 1971
2. *The Twisted Cameo*. New York, 1971
3. *The Children of Houndstooth*. New York, 1972
4. *Thanesworth House*. New York, 1972
5. *The Broken Sphinx*. New York, 1972
6. *Cousin to Terror*, as Charlotte Bramwell. New York, 1972
7. *Stepmother's House*, as Charlotte Bramwell. New York, 1972

8. *Brother Sinister*, as Charlotte Bramwell. New York, 1973
9. *Heiress to Wolfskill.* New York, 1973
10. *The Phantom Flame of Wind House.* New York, 1973
11. *The Specter of Dolphin Cove.* New York, 1973
12. *Unseen Torment.* New York, 1974
13. *The Shadow over Pheasant Heath.* New York, 1974
14. *Augusta, The First.* New York, 1975
15. *Jane, the Courageous.* New York, 1975
16. *Margaret, The Faithful.* New York, 1975
17. *Patricia, the Beautiful.* New York, 1975
18. *Rachel, The Possessed.* New York, 1975
19. *Susannah, The Righteous.* New York, 1975
20. *Rebecca, The Mysterious.* New York, 1975
21. *A Shriek in the Midnight Tower.* New York, 1975
22. *The Haunted Portrait*, as Ann Ashton. New York, 1976
23. *The Moon Shadow*, as Kym Allyson. New York, 1976
24. *Twilight Return: An Astrological Gothic Novel: Cancer*, as Jean Kimbro. New York, 1976
25. *Night of Tears*, as John M. Kimbro. New York, 1976
26. *Joanne, The Unpredictable.* New York, 1976
27. *Olivia, The Tormented.* New York, 1976
28. *Harriet, The Haunted.* New York, 1976
29. *Nancy, The Daring.* New York, 1976
30. *Marcia, The Innocent.* New York, 1976
31. *Kate, The Curious.* New York, 1976
32. *Ilene, The Superstitious.* New York, 1977
33. *Millijoy, The Determined.* New York, 1977
34. *Barbara, The Valiant.* New York, 1977
35. *Ruth, The Unsuspecting.* New York, 1977
36. *Ophelia, The Anxious.* New York, 1977
37. *Dorothy, The Terrified.* New York, 1977
38. *Ann, The Gentle.* New York, 1978
39. *The Phantom Reflection*, as Ann Ashton. New York, 1978
40. *Nellie, The Obvious.* New York, 1978
41. *Isabelle, The Frantic.* New York, 1978
42. *Evelyn, The Ambitious.* New York, 1978
43. *Louise, The Restless.* New York, 1978
44. *Polly, The Worried.* New York, 1978
45. *Yvonne, The Confident.* New York, 179
46. *Joyce, The Beloved.* New York, 1979
47. *Augusta, The Second.* New York, 1979
48. *Carol, The Pursued.* New York, 1979
49. *Three Cries of Terror*, as Ann Ashton. New York, 1980
50. *Katherine, The Returned.* New York, 1980
51. *Peggy, The Concerned.* New York, 1981
52. *Concession*, as Ann Ashton. New York, 1981

King, C. Daly [Charles Daly King]
American, born in 1895
1. *Obelists at Sea.* London, 1932
2. *Obelists en Route.* London, 1934
3. *Obelists Fly High.* London and New York, 1935
4. *The Curious Mr. Tarrant.* London, 1935
5. *Careless Corpse: A Thanatophony.* London, 1937
6. *Arrogant Alibi.* London, 1938
7. *Bermuda Burial.* London, 1940
8. *The Oragean Vision.* New York, 1951

King, General Charles
American, born October 12, 1844, died March 18, 1933
1. *Campaigning with Crook.* Milwaukee (WI), 1880
2. *The Colonel's Daughter; or, Winning His Spurs.* Philadelphia, 1883
3. *Kitty's Conquest.* Philadelphia, 1884
4. *Famous and Decisive Battles of the World.* Philadelphia, 1884
5. *Marion's Faith.* Philadelphia, 1886
6. *The Deserter, and From the Ranks: Two Novels.* Philadelphia, 1888
7. *A War-Time Wooing.* New York, 1888
8. *Dunraven Ranch.* London, 1889
9. *Laramie; or, The Queen of Bedlam.* Philadelphia, 1889
10. *The Queen of Bedlam.* London, 1889
11. *Between the Lines.* New York, 1889
12. *Sunset Pass; or, Running the Gauntlet Through Apache Land.* New York, 1890
13. *Starlight Ranch and Other Stories of Army Life on the Frontier.* Philadelphia, 1890
14. *Campaigning with Crook and Stories of Army Life.* New York, 1890
15. *Major General George Crook, United States Army.* Privately printed, 1890
16. *Two Soldiers, and Dunraven Ranch: Two Novels.* Philadelphia, 1891
17. *Captain Blake.* Philadelphia, 1891
18. *Trials of a Staff Officer.* Philadelphia, 1891
19. *A Soldier's Secret, . . . An Army Portia: Two Novels.* Philadelphia, 1893
20. *Foes in Ambush.* Philadelphia, 1893
21. *Waring's Peril.* Philadelphia, 1894
22. *Cadet Days.* New York, 1894
23. *Captain Close, and Sergeant Croesus: Two Novels.* Philadelphia, 1895
24. *The Story of Fort Frayne.* New York and London, 1895
25. *Under Fire.* Philadelphia and London, 1895
26. *An Army Wife.* Chicago, 1896
27. *Trooper Ross and Signal Butte.* Philadelphia, 1896
28. *Trumpeter Fred.* Chicago, 1896
29. *A Garrison Tangle.* New York, 1896
30. *A Tame Surrender.* Philadelphia, 1896
31. *Warrior Gap.* New York, 1897
32. *A Wounded Name.* New York, 1898
33. *The General's Double.* Philadelphia, 1898
34. *Ray's Recruit.* Philadelphia, 1898
35. *A Trooper Galahad.* Philadelphia, 1899
36. *From School to Battlefield.* Philadelphia, 1899
37. *Fort Frayne.* New York, 1901
38. *Found in the Philippines.* New York, 1901
39. *In Spite of Foes; or, Ten Years' Trial.* Philadelphia, 1901
40. *Norman Holt.* New York, 1901
41. *Ray's Daughter: A Story of Manila Life.* Philadelphia, 1901
42. *The Way of the West.* Chicago, 1902
43. *The Iron Brigade.* New York, 1902
44. *The Conquering Corps Badge and Other Stories of the Philippines.* Milwaukee (WI), 1902
45. *Apache Princess.* New York, 1903
46. *A Daughter of the Sioux.* New York, 1903
47. *Comrades in Arms.* New York, 1904
48. *A Knight of Columbia.* New York, 1904
49. *A Soldier's Trial: An Episode of the Canteen Crusade.* New York, 1905
50. *A Broken Sword.* New York, 1905
51. *Tonio, Son of the Sierras.* New York and London, 1906
52. *Lieutenant Sandy Ray.* New York, 1906
53. *The Further Story of Lieutenant Sandy Ray.* New York, 1906
54. *The Rock of Chickamauga.* New York and London, 1907
55. *To the Front.* New York, 1908
56. *Lanier of the Cavalry; or, A Week's Arrest.* Philadelphia, 1909
57. *The True Ulysses S. Grant.* Philadelphia, 1914

King, Rufus (Frederick)
American, born January 3, 1893, died in 1966
1. *North Star: A Dog Story of the Canadian Northwest.* New York, 1925
2. *Whelp of the Winds: A Dog Story.* New York and London, 1926

3. *Mystery De Luxe.* New York, 1927
4. *Murder De Luxe.* London, 1927
5. *The Fatal Kiss Mystery.* New York, 1928
6. *Murder by the Clock.* New York and London, 1929
7. *A Woman Is Dead.* London, 1929
8. *Somewhere in This House.* New York, 1930
9. *Murder by Latitude.* New York, 1930
10. *Murder in the Willett Family.* New York, 1931
11. *Murder on the Yacht.* New York and London, 1932
12. *Valcour Meets Murder.* New York, 1932
13. *The Lesser Antilles Case.* New York, 1934
14. *Invitation to a Murder.* New York, 1934
15. *Profile of a Murder.* New York, 1935
16. *The Case of the Constant God.* New York, 1936
17. *Crime of Violence.* New York, 1937
18. *I Want a Policeman.* New York, 1937
19. *Murder Masks Miami.* New York and London, 1939
20. *Holiday Homicide.* New York, 1940
21. *Diagnosis: Murder.* New York, 1941
22. *Design in Evil.* New York, 1942
23. *A Variety of Weapons.* New York, 1943
24. *The Case of the Dowager's Etchings.* New York, 1944
25. *Murder Challenges Valcour.* New York, 1944
26. *A Murder in This House.* New York, 1945
27. *The Deadly Dove.* New York, 1945
28. *Museum Piece No. 13.* New York, 1946
29. *Secret Beyond the Door.* New York, 1947
30. *Lethal Lady.* New York, 1947
31. *The Case of the Redoubled-Cross.* New York, 1949
32. *Duenna to a Murder.* New York and London, 1951
33. *Never Walk Alone.* New York, 1951
34. *Malice in Wonderland.* New York, 1958
35. *The Steps to Murder.* New York, 1960
36. *The Faces of Danger.* New York, 1964

Kirk, Russell (Amos)
American, born October 19, 1918
1. *Randolph of Roanoke: A Study of Conservative Thought.* Chicago, 1951
2. *The Intelligent Woman's Guide to Conservatism.* New York, 1957
3. *The American Cause.* Chicago, 1957
4. *Old House of Fear.* New York, 1961
5. *The Surly Sullen Bell: Ten Stories and Sketches, Uncanny or Uncomfortable, with a Note on the Ghostly Tale.* New York, 1962
6. *Confessions of a Bohemian Tory: Episodes and Relections of a Vagrant Career.* New York, 1963
7. *Lord of the Hollow Dark.* New York, 1979
8. *The Princess of All Lands.* Sauk City (WI), 1979

Knibbs, H.H. (Henry Herbert)
American, born October 24, 1874, died May 17, 1945
Pseudonym: Henry K. Herbert
1. *First Poems,* as Henry K. Herbert. Rochester (NY), 1908
2. *Lost Farm Camp.* Boston and London, 1912
3. *Stephen March's Way.* Boston, 1913
4. *Overland Red.* Boston, 1914
5. *Songs of the Outlands: Ballads of the Hoboes and Other Verse.* Boston, 1914
6. *Sundown Slim.* Boston, 1915
7. *Riders of the Stars: A Book of Western Verse.* Boston, 1916
8. *Tang of Life.* Boston, 1918
9. *Jim Waring of Sonora Town.* New York, No date
10. *The Ridin' Kid from Powder River.* Boston, 1919
11. *Songs of the Trail.* Boston, 1920
12. *Partners of Chance.* Boston, 1921
13. *Saddle Songs and Other Verse.* Boston, 1922
14. *Wild Horses.* Boston and London, 1924
15. *Temescal.* Boston and London, 1925
16. *The Sungazers.* Boston and London, 1926
17. *Sunny Mateel.* Boston and London, 1927
18. *Songs of the Lost Frontier.* London, 1930
19. *Gentlemen, Hush!* Boston, 1933
20. *The Tonto Kid.* Boston, 1936

Knight, Alanna
British
Pseudonym: Margaret Hope
1. *Legend of the Loch.* London, 1969
2. *The October Witch.* London and New York, 1971
3. *This Outward Angel.* New York, 1972
4. *Castle Clodha.* London and New York, 1972
5. *Lament for Lost Lovers.* London, 9172
6. *The White Rose.* London, 1973
7. *A Stranger Came By.* London, 1974
8. *The Passionate Kindness.* Aylesbury (Eng), 1974
9. *A Drink for the Bridge.* London, 1976
10. *The Wicked Wynsleys.* New York, 1977
11. *The Queen's Captain,* as Margaret Hope. New York, 1978
12. *Girl on an Empty Swing.* Macclesfield (Eng), 1978
13. *Hostage Most Royal,* as Margaret Hope. New York, 1979
14. *The Shadow Queen,* as Margaret Hope. New York, 1979
15. *The "Black Duchess."* London and New York, 1980
16. *Castle of Foxes.* New York, 1981
17. *Colla's Children.* London, 1982

Knox, Bill [William Knox]
British, born February 20, 1928
Pseudonyms: Michael Kirk, Robert MacLeod, Noah Webster
1. *Deadline for a Dream.* London, 1957
2. *The Cockatoo Crime.* London, 1958
3. *Death Department.* London, 1959
4. *Leave It to the Hangman.* London and New York, 1960
5. *Death Calls the Shots.* London, 1961
6. *Die for Big Betsy.* London, 1961
7. *In at the Kill.* New York, 1961
8. *Life Begins at Midnight.* London, 1961
9. *Little Drops of Blood.* London and New York, 1962
10. *Sanctuary Isle.* London, 1962
11. *Ecurie Ecosse: The Story of Scotland's International Racing Team.* London, 1962
12. *The Grey Sentinels.* New York, 1963
13. *The Man in the Bottle.* London, 1963
14. *The Killing Game.* New York, 1963
15. *The Drum of Ungara.* New York, 1963
16. *The Scavengers.* London and New York, 1964
17. *Cave of Bats,* as Robert MacLeod. London, 1964
18. *Drum of Power.* London, 1964
19. *Final Diagnosis.* London, 1964
20. *The Taste of Proof.* London and New York, 1965
21. *Devilweed.* London and New York, 1966
22. *The Deep Fall.* London, 1966
23. *The Ghost Car.* New York, 1966
24. *Lake of Fury,* as Robert MacLeod. London, 1966
25. *Blacklight.* London and New York, 1967
26. *Justice on the Rocks.* London and New York, 1967
27. *Isle of Dragons,* as Robert MacLeod. London, 1967
28. *The Klondyker.* London, 1968
29. *Figurehead.* New York, 1968
30. *The Iron Sanctuary,* as Robert MacLeod. New York, 1968
31. *Court of Murder.* London, 1968
32. *The Tallyman.* London and New York, 1969
33. *Blueback.* London and New York, 1969
34. *Place of Mists,* as Robert MacLeod. London, 1970

35. *Children of the Mist.* London. 1970
36. *Who Shot the Bull?* New York, 1970
37. *Seafire.* London, 1970
38. *A Property in Cyprus,* as Noah Webster. London, 1970
39. *To Kill a Witch.* London, 1971
40. *Flickering Death,* as Noah Webster. New York, 1971
41. *Path of Ghosts,* as Robert MacLeod. London and New York, 1971
42. *Stormtide.* London, 1972
43. *A Killing in Malta,* as Noah Webster. London and New York, 1972
44. *Draw Batons!* London and New York, 1973
45. *Nest of Vultures,* as Robert MacLeod. London, 1973
46. *A Burial in Portugal,* as Noah Webster. London and New York, 1973
47. *Whitewater.* London and New York, 1974
48. *All Other Perils,* as Michael Kirk. London, 1974
49. *The View from Daniel Pike.* London and New York, 1974
50. *Rally to Kill.* London and New York, 1975
51. *A Witchdance in Bavaria,* as Noah Webster. London, 1975
52. *Hellspout.* London and New York, 1976
53. *Dragonship,* as Michael Kirk. London, 1976
54. *Pilot Error.* London and New York, 1977
55. *Witchrock.* London. 1977
56. *A Pay-Off in Switzerland,* as Robert MacLeod. London and New York, 1977
57. *Salvage Job,* as Michael Kirk. London, 1978
58. *Live Bait.* New York, 1979
59. *Incident in Iceland,* as Noah Webster. New York, 1979

Knox, Ronald A. (Arbuthnott)
British, born February 17, 1888, died August 24, 1957
1. *Signa Severa.* Privately printed, 1906
2. *Remigium Alarum.* Oxford (Eng), 1910
3. *Juxta Salices.* Privately printed, 1910
4. *A Still More Sporting Adventure!* Oxford, 1911
5. *Naboth's Vineyard in Pawn.* London, 1913
6. *The Church in Bondage.* London, 1914
7. *An Hour at the Front.* London, 1914
8. *Reunion All Round: or, Jael's Hammer Laid Aside.* London, 1914
9. *Ten Minutes at the Front.* London, 1916
10. *An Apologia.* Privately Printed, 1917
11. *Sanctions: A Frivolity.* London, 1924
12. *A Book of Acrostics.* London, 1924
13. *The Viaduct Murder.* London, 1925
14. *Other Eyes Than Ours.* London, 1926
15. *An Open-Air Pulpit.* London, 1926
16. *The Three Taps: A Detective Story Without a Moral.* London and New York, 1927
17. *The Footsteps at the Lock.* London, 1928
18. *Anglican Cobwebs.* London, 1928
19. *Essays in Satire.* London, 1928
20. *Miracles.* New York, 1928
21. *The Rich Young Man: A Fantasy.* London, 1928
22. *On Getting There.* London, 1929
23. *Caliban in Grub Street.* London and New York, 1930
24. *The Floating Admiral.* London, 1931
25. *Broadcast Minds.* London, 1932
26. *The Body in the Silo.* London, 1934
27. *Settled Out of Court.* New York, 1934
28. *Still Dead.* London and New York, 1934
29. *Six Against the Yard,* with others. London, 1936
30. *Six Against Scotland Yard.* New York, 1936
31. *Double Cross Purposes.* London, 1937
32. *Nazi and Nazarene.* London, 1940
33. *God and the Atom.* London and New York, 1945
34. *The Trials of a Translator.* New York and London, 1949
35. *Stimuli.* London and New York, 1951
36. *Off the Record.* London, 1953
37. *Bridegroom and Bride.* London and New York, 1957
38. *On English Translation.* Oxford, 1957
39. *Literary Distractions.* London and New York, 1958

Krause, Herbert (Arthur)
American, born May 25, 1905, died September 22, 1976
1. *Wind Without Rain.* Indianapolis (IN), 1939
2. *Neighbor Boy.* Iowa City (IA), 1939
3. *The Thresher.* Indianapolis, 1946
4. *The Oxcart Trail.* Indianapolis, 1954
5. *Myth and Reality on the High Plains.* Northfield (MN), 1962

Kyne, Peter B. (Bernard)
American, born October 12, 1880, died November 25, 1957
1. *The Three Godfathers.* New York, 1913
2. *The Long Chance.* New York, 1914
3. *Cappy Ricks; or, The Subjugation of Matt Peasley.* New York, 1916
4. *Webster—Man's Man.* New York, 1917
5. *Ireland uber Alles: A Tale of the Sea.* London, 1917
6. *The French Wounded Emergency Book.* San Francisco, 1917
7. *The Valley of the Giants.* New York, 1918
8. *The Stolen Ship.* London, 1919
9. *The Green-Pea Pirates.* New York, 1919
10. *Captain Scaggs.* New York, no date
11. *Peter B. Kyne.* New York, 1919
12. *Kindred of the Dust.* New York and London, 1920
13. *The Go-Getter.* New York and London, 1921
14. *The Pride of Palomar.* New York and London, 1921
15. *Cappy Ricks Retires.* New York and London, 1922
16. *Never the Twain Shall Meet.* New York and London, 1923
17. *The Enchanted Hill.* New York and London, 1924
18. *The Understanding Heart.* New York and London, 1926
19. *Made of Money.* London, 1927
20. *They Also Serve.* New York, 1927
21. *Money to Burn.* New York, 1928
22. *Tide of Empire.* New York and London, 1928
23. *The Silent Comrade.* New York and London, 1929
24. *Jim the Conqueror.* New York and London, 1929
25. *The Parson of Panamint and Other Stories.* New York and London, 1929
26. *The Thunder of God.* New York, 1930
27. *Outlaws of Eden.* New York, 1930
28. *Golden Dawn.* New York and London, 1930
29. *The Gringo Privateer, and Island of Desire.* New York, 1931
30. *Lord of Lonely Valley.* New York and London, 1932
31. *Two Make a World.* New York, 1932
32. *Comrades of the Storm.* New York and London, 1933
33. *Cappy Ricks Comes Back.* New York and London, 1934
34. *The Golden West: Three Novels.* New York, 1935
35. *The Cappy Ricks Special.* New York, 1935
36. *Soldiers, Sailors, and Dogs.* New York, 1936
37. *Dude Woman.* New York and London, 1940
38. *The Book I Never Wrote.* Privately printed, 1942

La Farge, Oliver (Hazard Perry)
American, December 19, 1901, died August 2, 1963
1. *Tribes and Temples: A Record of the Expedition to Middle America Conducted by the Tulane University of Louisiana in 1925.* New Orleans, 2 vols., 1926-27
2. *Laughing Boy.* Boston, 1929
3. *Sparks Fly Upward.* Boston, 1931
4. *The Year Bearer's People.* New Orleans, 1931
5. *Long Pennant.* Boston, 1933
6. *All the Young Men.* Boston, 1935

La Farge, Oliver

7. *An Alphabet for Writing the Navajo Language.* Washington (DC), 1936
8. *The Enemy Gods.* Boston, 1937
9. *As Long as the Grass Shall Grow.* New York, 1940
10. *The Copper Pot.* Boston, 1942
11. *War below Zero: The Battle for Greenland.* Boston, 1944
12. *Raw Material.* Boston, 1945
13. *Santa Eulalia: The Religion of a Cuchumatan Indian Town.* Chicago, 1947
14. *The Eagle in the Egg.* Boston, 1949
15. *Cochise of Arizona: The Pipe of Peace Is Broken.* New York, 1953
16. *The Mother Ditch.* Boston, 1954
17. *A Pictorial History of the American Indian.* New York, 1956
18. *Behind the Mountains.* Boston, 1956
19. *A Pause in the Desert: A Collection of Short Stories.* Boston, 1957
20. *Santa Fe: The Autobiography of a Southwestern Town.* Norman (OK), 1959
21. *The American Indian.* New York, 1960
22. *The Door in the Wall: Stories.* Boston, 1965
23. *The Man with the Calabash Pipe: Some Observations.* Boston, 1966

L'Amour, Louis [Louis Dearborn LaMoore]
American, born in 1908
Other pseudonyms: Tex Burns, Jim Mayo

1. *Smoke from This Altar.* Oklahoma City (OK), 1939
2. *Westward the Tide.* Kingswood, Surrey (Eng), 1950
3. *Hopalong Cassidy and the Riders of High Rock,* as Tex Burns. New York, 1951
4. *Hopalong Cassidy and the Rustlers of West Fork,* as Tex Burns. New York and London, 1951
5. *Hopalong Cassidy and the Trail to Seven Pines,* as Tex Burns. New York, 1951
6. *Hopalong Cassidy, Trouble Shooter,* as Tex Burns. New York, 1952
7. *Hondo.* New York, 1953
8. *Showdown at Yellow Butte,* as Jim Mayo. New York, 1953
9. *Crossfire Trail.* New York, 1954
10. *Utah Blaine,* as Jim Mayo. New York, 1954
11. *Kilkenny.* New York, 1954
12. *Heller with a Gun.* New York, 1955
13. *To Tame a Land.* New York, 1955
14. *Guns of the Timberlands.* New York, 1955
15. *The Burning Hills.* New York, 1956
16. *Silver Canyon.* New York, 1956
17. *Last Stand at Papago Wells.* New York, 1957
18. *The Tall Stranger.* New York, 1957
19. *Sitka.* New York, 1957
20. *Radigan.* New York, 1958
21. *The First Fast Draw.* New York and London, 1959
22. *Taggart.* New York and London, 1959
23. *The Daybreakers.* London, 1960
24. *Flint.* New York, 1960
25. *Sackett.* New York, 1961
26. *Shalako.* New York and London, 1962
27. *Killoe.* New York and London, 1962
28. *High Lonesome.* New York, 1962
29. *Lando.* New York, 1962
30. *How the West Was Won.* New York and London, 1963
31. *Fallon.* New York and London, 1963
32. *Catlow.* New York and London, 1963
33. *Dark Canyon.* New York, 1963
34. *Mojave Crossing.* New York and London, 1964
35. *Hanging Woman Creek.* New York and London, 1964
36. *Kiowa Trail.* New York and London, 1964
37. *The High Graders.* New York and London, 1965
38. *The Sackett Brand.* New York and London, 1965
39. *The Key-Lock Man.* New York, 1965
40. *Kid Rodelo.* New York, 1966
41. *Mustang Man.* New York and London, 1966
42. *Kilrone.* New York and London, 1966
43. *The Broken Gun.* New York and London, 1966
44. *The Skyliners.* New York and London, 1967
45. *Matagorda.* New York, 1967
46. *Brionne.* New York and London, 1968
47. *Chancy.* New York and London, 1968
48. *Down the Long Hills.* New York and London, 1968
49. *The Empty Land.* New York and London, 1969
50. *The Lonely Men.* New York, 1969
51. *Conagher.* New York and London, 1969
52. *The Man Called Noon.* New York and London, 1970
53. *Reilly's Luck.* New York, 1970
54. *Galloway.* New York and London, 1970
55. *North to the Rails.* New York and London, 1971
56. *Under the Sweetwater Rim.* New York and London, 1971
57. *Tucker.* New York, 1971
58. *Callaghen.* New York and London, 1972
59. *Ride the Dark Trail.* New York and London, 1972
60. *Treasure Mountain.* New York, 1972
61. *The Ferguson Rifle.* New York and London, 1973
62. *The Man from Skibbereen.* New York and London, 1973
63. *The Quick and the Dead.* New York, 1973
64. *The Californios.* New York and London, 1974
65. *Sackett's Land.* New York, 1974
66. *War Party.* New York and London, 1975
67. *The Man from the Broken Hills.* New York, 1975
68. *Over on the Dry Side.* New York, 1975
69. *Rivers West.* New York and London, 1975
70. *To the Far Blue Mountains.* New York, 1976
71. *Where the Long Grass Blows.* New York, 1976
72. *The Rider of Lost Creek.* New York and London, 1976
73. *Sackett's Gold.* New York, 1977
74. *Fair Blows the Wind.* New York, 1978
75. *Borden Chantry.* London, 1978
76. *The Mountain Valley War.* London, 1978
77. *Bendigo Shafter.* New York and London, 1979
78. *The Iron Marshal.* New York and London, 1979
79. *The Proving Trail.* New York and London, 1979
80. *The Warrior's Path.* New York, 1980
81. *Yondering.* New York and London, 1980
82. *The Strong Shall Live: A Collection of Short Stories.* London, 1980
83. *Comstock Lode.* New York, 1981
84. *The Cherokee Trail.* New York, 1982

Lane, Roumelia

1. *Rose of the Desert.* London, 1967
2. *Hideway Heart.* London, 1967
3. *House of the Winds.* London and Toronto, 1968
4. *A Summer of Love.* London, 1968
5. *Terminus Tehran.* London, 1969
6. *Sea of Zanj.* London and Toronto, 1969
7. *The Scented Hills.* London, 1970
8. *Café Mimosa.* London and Toronto, 1971
9. *In the Shade of the Palms.* London, 1972
10. *Nurse at Noongwalla.* London, 1973
11. *Across the Lagoon.* London and Toronto, 1974
12. *Stormy Encounter.* London, 1974
13. *Where the Moonflower Weaves.* London, 1974
14. *Harbour of Deceit.* London and Toronto, 1975
15. *The Tenant of San Mateo.* London and Toronto, 1976
16. *Himalayan Moonlight.* London, 1977
17. *Bamboo Wedding.* Toronto, 1977

18. *The Brightest Star.* London, 1978
19. *Hidden Rapture.* London, 1978
20. *Second Spring.* London, 1980

Langley, John
1. *Rustler's Brand.* London, 1954
2. *Riders of Red Range.* London, 1955
3. *Six-Gun Trial.* London, 1958
4. *Six-Gun Feud.* London, 1959
5. *Kit of Slash K.* London, 1960
6. *Heir to Bar 60.* London, 1960
7. *Six-Gun Law.* London, 1960
8. *Six-Gun War.* London, 1960
9. *Six-Gun Gamble.* London, 1963
10. *Six-Gun Strife.* London, 1963
11. *Six-Gun Champion.* London, 1964
12. *Six-Gun Citadel.* London, 1964
13. *Six-Gun Smoke.* London, 1965
14. *Six-Gun Cavalier.* London, 1965
15. *Six-Gun Vengeance.* London, 1966
16. *Six-Gun Salute.* London, 1967
17. *The Badlands Gang.* London, 1970

Lathen, Emma [Mary J. Latis and Martha Hennissart]
Other pseudonym: R.B. Dominic
1. *Banking on Death.* New York, 1961
2. *A Place for Murder.* New York and London, 1963
3. *Accounting for Murder.* New York, 1964
4. *Death Shall Overcome.* New York, 1966
5. *Murder Makes the Wheels Go Round.* New York and London, 1966
6. *Murder Against the Grain.* New York and London, 1967
7. *A Stitch in Time.* New York and London, 1968
8. *Come to Dust.* New York, 1968
9. *Murder Sunny Side Up,* as R.B. Dominic. New York and London, 1968
10. *When in Greece.* New York and London, 1969
11. *Murder to Go.* New York, 1969
12. *Murder in High Place,* as R.B. Dominic. London, 1969
13. *Pick Up Sticks.* New York, 1970
14. *Ashes to Ashes.* New York and London, 1971
15. *The Longer the Thread.* New York, 1971
16. *There Is No Justice,* as R.B. Dominic. New York, 1971
17. *Murder Out of Court,* as R.B. Dominic. London, 1971
18. *Murder Without Icing.* New York, 1972
19. *Sweet and Low.* New York and London, 1974
20. *Epitaph for a Lobbyist,* as R.B. Dominic. New York and London, 1974
21. *By Hook or by Crook.* New York and London, 1975
22. *Murder Out of Commission,* as R.B. Dominic. New York and London, 1976
23. *Double, Double, Oil and Trouble.* New York, 1978

Latimer, Jonathan (Wyatt)
American, born October 23, 1906
Pseudonym: Peter Coffin
1. *Murder in the Madhouse.* New York and London, 1935
2. *Headed for a Hearse.* New York, 1935
3. *The Lady in the Morgue.* New York, 1936
4. *The Search for My Great Uncle's Head,* as Peter Coffin. New York, 1937
5. *The Dead Don't Care.* New York and London, 1938
6. *Red Gardenias.* New York and London, 1939
7. *Dark Memory.* New York and London, 1940
8. *Solomon's Vineyard.* London, 1941
9. *The Fifth Grave.* New York, 1950
10. *Some Dames Are Deadly.* New York, 1955
11. *Sinners and Shrouds.* New York, 1955
12. *Black Is the Fashion for Dying.* New York, 1959
13. *The Mink-Lined Coffin.* London, 1960

La Tourrette, Jacqueline
American, born May 5, 1926
1. *The Josesph Stone.* New York, 1971
2. *A Matter of Sixpence.* New York, 1972
3. *The Madonna Creek Witch.* New York, 1973
4. *The Previous Lady.* New York, 1974
5. *The Pompeii Scroll.* New York, 1975
6. *Shadows in Umbria.* New York, 1979
7. *The Wild Harp.* New York, 1981

Lawrence, Hilda [Hildegarde Lawrence]
American, born ca. 1906
1. *Blood Upon the Snow.* New York, 1944
2. *A Time to Die.* New York, 1945
3. *The Pavilion.* New York, 1946
4. *Death of a Doll.* New York, 1947
5. *Duet of Death.* New York and London, 1949
6. *Death Has Four Hands and The Bleeding House.* New York, 2 vols., 1950

Lea, Tom
American, born July 11, 1907
1. *John W. Norton, American Painter 1876-1934.* Chicago, 1935
2. *George Catlin Westward Bound a Hundred Years Ago.* El Paso (TX), 1939
3. *Randado.* El Paso, 1941
4. *A Grizzly from the Coral Sea.* El Paso, 1944
5. *Peleliu Landing.* El Paso, 1945
6. *A Calendar of Twelve Travelers Through the Pass of the North.* El Paso, 1946
7. *The Brave Bulls.* Boston, 1949
8. *Bullfight Manual for Spectators.* El Paso, 1949
9. *The Wonderful Country.* Boston, 1950
10. *Western Beef Cattle: A Series of Eleven Paintings.* Dallas (TX), 1950
11. *Tom Lea: A Portfolio of Six Paintings.* Austin (TX), 1953
12. *The Stained Glass Designs in the McKee Chapel, Church of Saint Clement, El Paso, Texas.* El Paso, 1953
13. *The King Ranch.* Boston, 1957
14. *The Primal Yoke.* Boston, 1960
15. *Maud Durlin Sullivan 1872-1944: Pioneer Southwestern Librarian: A Tribute.* Los Angeles (CA), 1962
16. *The Hands of Cantu.* Boston and London, 1964
17. *A Picture Gallery.* Boston, 1968
18. *In the Crucible of the Sun.* Kingsville (TX), 1974

Leasor, James [Thomas James Leasor]
British, born December 20, 1923
1. *Not Such a Bad Day.* Leicester (Eng), 1946
2. *The Monday Story.* London, 1951
3. *Author by Profession.* London, 1952
4. *Wheels of Fortune: A Brief Account of the Life and Times of William Morris, Viscount Nuffield.* London, 1954
5. *NTR: Nothing to Report.* London, 1955
6. *The Sergeant Major: A Biography of R.S.M. Ronald Brittain, M.B.E., Coldstream Guards.* London, 1955
7. *The Red Fort: An Account of the Siege of Delhi in 1857.* London, 1956
8. *The One That Got Away.* London, 1956
9. *The Millionth Chance: The Story of the R. 101.* London and New York, 1957
10. *Mutiny at the Red Fort.* London, 1959
11. *War at the Top.* London, 1959
12. *The Clock with Four Hands.* New York, 1959

13. *The Strong Delusion.* London, 1960
14. *Conspiracy of Silence,* with Peter Eton. London, 1960
15. *Wall of Silence.* Indianapolis (IN), 1960
16. *The Plague and the Fire.* New York, 1961
17. *Rudolf Hess, The Uninvited Envoy.* London, 1962
18. *The Uninvited Envoy.* New York, 1962
19. *Passport to Oblivion.* London, 1964
20. *Where the Spies Are.* London, 1965
21. *Passport to Peril.* London, 1966
22. *Spylight.* Philadelphia, 1966
23. *Passport in Suspense.* London, 1967
24. *The Yang Meridian.* New York, 1968
25. *Passport for a Pilgrim.* London, 1968
26. *Singapore: The Battle That Changed the World.* London and New York, 1968
27. *The Don't Make Them Like That Any More.* London, 1969
28. *A Week of Love, Being Seven Adventures of Jason Love.* London, 1969
29. *Never Had a Spanner on Her.* London, 1970
30. *Love-All.* London, 1971
31. *Follow the Drum.* London and New York, 1972
32. *Host of Extras.* London, 1973
33. *Mandarin-Gold.* London, 1973
34. *The Chinese Widow.* London, 1975
35. *Green Beach.* London and New York, 1975
36. *Jade Gate.* London, 1976
37. *Boarding Party.* London and Boston, 1978

le Carre, John [David John Moore Cornwell]
British, born October 19, 1931
1. *Call for the Dead.* London, 1961
2. *A Murder of Quality.* London, 1962
3. *The Spy Who Came In from the Cold.* London, 1963
4. *The Looking-Glass War.* London and New York, 1965
5. *The Deadly Affair.* London, 1966
6. *A Small Town in Germany.* London and New York, 1968
7. *The Naive and Sentimental Lover.* London, 1971
8. *Tinker, Tailor, Soldier, Spy.* London and New York, 1974
9. *The Honourable Schoolboy.* London and New York, 1977
10. *Smiley's People.* London, 1980

Lee, Elsie
American, born January 24, 1912
Pseudonyms: Elsie Cromwell, Norman Daniels, Jane Gordon, Lee Sheridan
1. *How to Get the Most Out of Your Tape Recording,* as Lee Sheridan with Michael Sheridan. Flushing (NY), 1958
2. *More Fun with Your Tape Recorders and Stereo,* as Lee Sheridan with Michael Sheridan. Los Angeles (CA), 1958
3. *The Exciting World of Rocks and Gems.* Los Angeles, 1959
4. *Easy Gourmet Cooking.* New York, 1962
5. *The Bachelor's Cookbook,* as Lee Sheridan with Michael Sheridan. New York, 1962
6. *The Blood Red Oscar.* New York, 1962
7. *Sam Benedict: Cast the First Stone,* as Norman Daniels. New York, 1963
8. *A Comedy of Terrors.* New York, 1964
9. *The Masque of the Red Death.* New York, 1964
10. *Muscle Beach.* New York, 1964
11. *Season of Evil.* New York, 1965
12. *Dark Moon, Lost Lady.* New York, 1965
13. *Clouds over Vellanti.* New York, 1965
14. *The Curse of Carranca.* New York, 1966
15. *Mansion of the Golden Window.* New York, 1966
16. *At Home with Plants: A Guide to Successful Indoor Gardening.* New York and London, 1966
17. *The Drifting Sands.* New York, 1966
18. *Sinister Abbey.* New York, 1967
19. *The Spy at the Villa Miranda.* New York, 1967
20. *Doctor's Office.* New York, 1968
21. *Second Easy Gourmet Cookbook.* New York, 1968
22. *The Governess,* as Elsie Cromwell. New York, 1969
23. *Satan's Coast.* New York, 1969
24. *Fulfillment.* New York, 1969
25. *Barrow Sinister.* New York, 1969
26. *Ivorstone Manor,* as Elsie Cromwell. New York, 1970
27. *Silence Is Golden.* New York, 1971
28. *Wingarden.* New York, 1971
29. *The Diplomatic Lover.* New York, 1971
30. *Star of Danger.* New York, 1971
31. *Book of Simple Gourmet Cookery.* New York, 1971
32. *The Passions of Medora Graeme.* New York, 1972
33. *A Prior Betrothal.* New York, 1973
34. *The Wicked Guardian.* New York, 1973
35. *Second Season.* New York, 1973
36. *Two Hearts Apart,* as Jane Gordon. London, 1973
37. *Party Cookbook.* New York, 1974
38. *An Eligible Connection.* Bath (Eng), 1974
39. *Roomates.* New York, 1976
40. *The Nabob's Widow.* New York, 1976
41. *Mistress of Mount Fair.* New York, 1977

Lee, Wayne (Cyril)
American, born July 2, 1917
Pseudonym: Lee Sheldon
1. *Bachelor Bait.* Franklin (OH), 1951
2. *Prairie Vengeance.* New York, 1954
3. *Poor Willie.* Minneapolis (MN), 1954
4. *Deadwood.* Minneapolis, 1955
5. *Hold the Phone.* Minneapolis, 1955
6. *Broken Wheel Ranch.* New York, 1956
7. *Big News.* Minneapolis, 1957
8. *Slugging Backstop.* New York, 1957
9. *His Brother's Guns.* New York, 1958
10. *Killer's Range.* New York, 1958
11. *Bat Masterson.* Racine (WI), 1960
12. *Gun Brand.* New York, 1961
13. *Blood on the Prairie.* New York, 1962
14. *A Stranger in Stirrup.* New York, 1962
15. *Thunder in the Backfield.* New York, 1962
16. *The Gun Tamer.* New York, 1963
17. *Devil Wire.* New York, 1963
18. *The Hostile Land.* New York, 1964
19. *Gun in His Hand.* New York, 1964
20. *Warpath West.* New York, 1965
21. *The Fast Gun.* New York, 1965
22. *The Brand of a Man.* New York, 1966
23. *Trail of the Skulls.* New York, 1966
24. *Mystery at Scorpion Creek.* New York, 1966
25. *Showdown at Julesburg Station.* New York, 1967
26. *Return to Gunpoint.* New York, 1967
27. *Only the Brave.* New York, 1967
28. *Doomed Planet,* as Lee Sheldon. New York, 1967
29. *Sudden Guns.* New York, 1968
30. *Trouble at the Flying H.* New York, 1969
31. *Stage to Lonesome Butte.* New York, 1969
32. *Showdown at Sunrise.* New York, 1971
33. *The Buffalo Hunters.* New York, 1972
34. *Suicide Trail.* New York, 1972
35. *Wind over Rimfire.* New York, 1973
36. *Son of a Gunman.* New York, 1973
37. *Law of the Prairie.* New York, 1974
38. *Die-Hard.* New York, 1975
39. *Scotty Philip: The Man Who Saved the Buffalo.* Caldwell (ID), 1975
40. *Law of the Lawless.* New York, 1977

41. *Skirmish at Fort Kearny.* New York, 1977
42. *Gun Country.* New York, 1978
43. *Petticoat Wagon Train.* New York, 1978
44. *The Violent Man.* New York, 1978
45. *Ghost of a Gunfighter.* New York, 1979
46. *McQuaid's Gun.* New York, 1980
47. *Trails of the Smoky Hill.* Caldwell, 1980
48. *Shadow of a Gun.* New York, 1981
49. *Guns at Genesis.* New York, 1981
50. *Putnam's Ranch War.* New York, 1982

Lehman, Paul Evan
   Pseudonym: Paul Evan
1. *Idaho.* New York, 1933
2. *Cowboy Idaho.* London, 1933
3. *Blood of the West.* New York and London, 1934
4. *Son of a Cowthief.* New York and London, 1935
5. *The Cougar of Canyon Caballo.* New York, 1936
6. *Texas Men.* New York, 1936
7. *Valley of the Hunted Men.* New York, 1937
8. *Wolves of the Chaparral.* New York and London, 1938
9. *Calamity Range.* New York and London, 1939
10. *Vultures of Paradise Valley.* London, 1940
11. *Brand of the Outlaw.* New York, 1942
12. *Trail of the Outlaw.* New York, 1942
13. *Cow Kingdom.* London, 1943
14. *West of the Wolverine.* London, 1945
15. *Only the Brave.* New York and London, 1947
16. *The Cold Trail.* Kingston (NY), 1949
17. *The Devil's Doorstep.* New York and London, 1949
18. *Montana Man.* New York, 1949
19. *Passion in the Dust.* New York, 1949
20. *Brother of the Kid.* New York, 1950
21. *The Siren of Silver Valley.* Kingston, 1950
22. *Vengeance Valley.* Kingston, 1950
23. *The Man from the Badlands.* New York, 1951
24. *Range Justice.* Toronto, 1951
25. *Law of the .45.* Toronto, 1951
26. *Redrock Gold.* London, 1951
27. *Gun Law.* Toronto, 1952
28. *The Doves of War.* New York, 1952
29. *Faces in the Dust.* New York and London, 1952
30. *The Twisted Trail,* as Paul Evan. New York, 1952
31. *Fightin' Sons of Texas.* New York, 1953
32. *Pistols of the Pecos.* New York, 1953
33. *By Means of a Gun.* London, 1953
34. *Stagecoach to Hellfire Pass.* New York, 1953
35. *Vultures on Horseback.* New York, 1953
36. *This Range Is Mine,* as Paul Evan. New York, 1953
37. *This Is My Range.* London, 1953
38. *Gunsmoke Kingdom,* as Paul Evan. New York, 1953
39. *Bullets Don't Bluff.* New York, 1954
40. *Texas Vengeance.* London, 1954
41. *Fighting Buckaroo.* Toronto, 1954
42. *Outlaws of Lost River,* as Paul Evan. New York, 1954
43. *Trojans from Texas.* Kingswood (Eng), 1955
44. *The Fighting Texan.* New York, 1955
45. *Call of the West,* as Paul Evan. New York, 1955
46. *Gunsmoke over Sabado,* as Paul Evan. New York, 1955
47. *Bandit in Black.* London, 1956
48. *The Gunhand.* New York, 1956
49. *Pistol Law.* New York, 1956
50. *The Vengeance Trail.* New York, 1956
51. *Lynch Law,* as Paul Evan. New York, 1956
52. *Outlaw Loot.* New York, 1956
53. *Rustlers of the Rio Grande.* New York, 1957
54. *Law in the Saddle.* Toronto, 1957
55. *Thunder Creek Range,* as Paul Evan. New York, 1957
56. *West of the Pecos,* as Paul Evan. New York, 1957
57. *Gun-Whipped.* New York, 1958
58. *The Tough Texan.* New York, 1958
59. *The Young Texan.* New York, 1958
60. *Renegade Marshal.* New York, 1958
61. *Thunderbolt Range.* New York, 1958
62. *Law of the Gun,* as Paul Evan. New York, 1958
63. *Troubled Range.* New York, 1959
64. *Gunsmoke at Buffalo Basin.* New York, 1959
65. *The Manhunter.* New York, 1959
66. *Action at the Bitterroot.* New York, 1959
67. *Poverty Range.* New York, 1960
68. *Colt '60.* New York, 1961
69. *Law of the Six-Gun.* New York, 1962
70. *Outlaw's Revenge.* New York, 1965
71. *Range War at Keno.* New York, 1965
72. *Cowhand Justice.* New York, 1968
73. *Hot Triggers.* New York, 1968

Lemarchand, Elizabeth (Wharton)
   British, born October 22, 1906
1. *Death of an Old Girl.* London, 1967
2. *The Affacombe Affair.* London, 1968
3. *Alibi for a Corpse.* London, 1969
4. *Death on Doomsday.* London, 1971
5. *Cyanide with Compliments.* London, 1972
6. *Let or Hindrance.* London, 1973
7. *No Vacation from Murder.* New York, 1974
8. *Buried in the Past.* London, 1974
9. *Step in the Dark.* London, 1976
10. *Unhappy Returns.* London, 1977
11. *Suddenly While Gardening.* London, 1978

LeMay, Alan
   American, born June 3, 1899, died April 27, 1964
1. *Painted Ponies.* New York, 1927
2. *Old Father of Waters.* New York, 1928
3. *Pelican Coast.* New York, 1929
4. *One of Us Is a Murderer.* New York and London, 1930
5. *Bug Eye.* New York, 1931
6. *Gunsight Trail.* New York and London, 1931
7. *Winter Range.* New York and London, 1932
8. *Cattle Kingdom.* New York and London, 1933
9. *Thunder in the Dust.* New York and London, 1934
10. *The Smoky Years.* New York and London, 1935
11. *Deep Water Island.* New York and London, 1936
12. *Empire for a Lady.* New York, 1937
13. *Useless Cowboy.* New York, 1943
14. *Hell for Breakfast.* New York, 1947
15. *Wild Justice.* New York, 1948
16. *The Searchers.* New York, 1954
17. *The Unforgiven.* New York, 1957
18. *The Siege at Dancing Bird.* London, 1959
19. *By Dim and Flaring Lamps.* New York, 1962

Leonard, Elmore
   American, born October 11, 1925
1. *The Bounty Hunters.* Boston, 1953
2. *The Law at Randado.* Boston, 1955
3. *Escape from Five Shadows.* Boston, 1956
4. *Last Stand at Saber River.* New York, 1959
5. *Lawless River.* London, 1959
6. *Stand on the Saber.* London, 1960
7. *Hombre.* New York, 1961
8. *Valdez Is Coming.* London, 1969
9. *The Big Bounce.* New York and London, 1969
10. *The Moonshine War.* New York, 1969
11. *Forty Lashes Less One.* New York, 1972

12. *Mr. Majestyk.* New York, 1974
13. *Fifty-Two Pickup.* New York and London, 1974
14. *Swag.* New York, 1976
15. *Ryan's Rules.* New York, 1976
16. *The Hunted.* New York, 1977
17. *Unknown Man No. 89.* New York and London, 1977
18. *The Switch.* New York, 1978
19. *Gunsights.* New York, 1979
20. *City Primeval.* New York, 1980
21. *Gold Coast.* New York, 1980
22. *Split Images.* New York, 1982
23. *Cat Chaser.* New York, 1982

Le Queux, William (Tufnell)
British, born July 2, 1864, died October 13, 1927
1. *Guilty Bonds.* London, 1891
2. *Strange Tales of a Nihilist.* London and New York, 1892
3. *The Great War in England in 1897.* London, 1894
4. *The Temptress.* London and New York, 1895
5. *Zoraida: A Romance of the Harem and the Great Sahara.* London and New York, 1895
6. *Stolen Souls.* London and New York, 1895
7. *Devil's Dice.* London, 1896
8. *A Secret Service.* London, 1896
9. *Whoso Findeth a Wife.* London, 1897
10. *A Madonna of the Music Halls.* London, 1897
11. *The Eye of Ishtar.* London and New York, 1897
12. *If Sunners Entice Thee.* London, 1898
13. *The Great White Queen.* London, 1898
14. *Scribes and Pharisees.* London and New York, 1898
15. *The Veiled Man.* London, 1899
16. *The Bond of Black.* London and New York, 1899
17. *Wiles of the Wicked.* London, 1899
18. *The Day of Temptation.* London and New York, 1899
19. *England's Peril.* London, 1899
20. *Secrets of Monte Carlo.* London, 1899
21. *An Eye for an Eye.* London, 1900
22. *In White Raiment.* London, 1900
23. *Of Royal Blood.* London, 1900
24. *The Gamblers.* London, 1901
25. *The Sign of the Seven Sins.* Philadelphia, 1901
26. *Her Majesty's Minister.* London and New York, 1901
27. *The Court of Honour.* London, 1901
28. *The Under-Secretary.* London, 1902
29. *The Unnamed.* London, 1902
30. *The Tickencote Treasure.* London, 1903
31. *The Three Glass Eyes.* London, 1903
32. *The Seven Secrets.* London, 1903
33. *The Idol of the Town.* London, 1903
34. *Secrets of the Foreign Office.* London, 1903
35. *As We Forgave Them.* London, 1904
36. *The Closed Book.* London and New York, 1904
37. *The Hunchback of Westminster.* London, 1904
38. *The Man from Downing Street.* London, 1904
39. *The Red Hat.* London, 1904
40. *The Sign of the Stranger.* London, 1904
41. *The Valley of the Shadow.* London, 1905
42. *Who Giveth This Woman?* London, 1905
43. *The Spider's Eye.* London, 1905
44. *Sins of the City.* London, 1905
45. *The Mask.* London, 1905
46. *Behind the Throne.* London, 1905
47. *The Czar's Spy.* London and New York, 1905
48. *Confessions of a Ladies' Man, Being the Adventures of Cuthbert Croom, of His Majesty's Diplomatic Service.* London, 1905
49. *The Great Court Scandal.* London, 1906
50. *The House of the Wicked.* London, 1906
51. *The Mysterious Mr. Miller.* London, 1906
52. *The Mystery of a Motor-Car.* London, 1906
53. *Whatsoever a Man Soweth.* London, 1906
54. *The Woman at Kensington.* London, 1906
55. *The Invasion of 1910, with a Full Account of the Siege of London.* London, 1906
56. *The Secret of the Square.* London, 1907
57. *The Great Plot.* London, 1907
58. *Whosoever Loveth.* London, 1907
59. *The Count's Chauffeur.* London, 1907
60. *An Observer in the Near East.* London, 1907
61. *The Near East.* New York, 1907
62. *The Lady in the Car, in Which the Amours of a Mysterious Motorist Are Related.* London and Phiadelphia, 1908
63. *The Crooked Way.* London, 1908
64. *The Looker-On.* London, 1908
65. *The Pauper of Park Lane.* London and New York, 1908
66. *Stolen Sweets.* London, 1908
67. *The Woman in the Way.* London, 1908
68. *The Red Room.* London, 1909
69. *The House of Whispers.* London, 1909
70. *Fatal Thirteen.* London, 1909
71. *Spies of the Kaiser: Plotting the Downfall of England.* London, 1909
72. *The Great God Gold.* Boston, 1910
73. *Lying Lips.* London, 1910
74. *The Unknown Tomorrow.* London, 1910
75. *Treasure of Israel.* London, 1910
76. *Hushed Up!* London, 1911
77. *The Money-Spider.* London and Boston, 1911
78. *Revelations of the Secret Service.* London, 1911
79. *The Indiscretions of a Lady's Maid.* London, 1911
80. *The Death-Doctor.* London, 1912
81. *Fatal Fingers.* London, 1912
82. *The Mystery of Nine.* London, 1912
83. *Without Trace.* London, 1912
84. *The Balkan Trouble; or, An Observer in the Near East.* London, 1912
85. *The Price of Power, Being Chapters from the Secret History of the Imperial Court of Russia.* London, 1913
86. *The Room of Secrets.* London, 1913
87. *The Lost Million.* London, 1913
88. *Mysteries.* London, 1913
89. *The White Lie.* London, 1914
90. *Sons of Satan.* London, 1914
91. *The Hand of Allah.* London, 1914
92. *Her Royal Highness.* London, 1914
93. *The Maker of Secrets.* London, 1914
94. *The Four Faces.* London and New York, 1914
95. *The German Spy.* London, 1914
96. *The War of the Nations.* Vol. 1. London, 1914
97. *German Atrocities: A Record of Shameless Deeds.* London, 1914
98. *The Double Shadow.* London, 1915
99. *At the Sign of the Sword.* London and New York, 1915
100. *The Mysterious Three.* London, 1915
101. *The Mystery of the Green Ray.* London, 1915
102. *The Sign of Silence.* London, 1915
103. *The White Glove.* London, 1915
104. *German Spies in England: An Exposure.* London, 1915
105. *Britain's Deadly Peril: Are We Told the Truth?* London, 1915
106. *The Devil's Spawn: How Italy Will Defeat Them.* London, 1915
107. *"Cinders" of Harley Street.* London, 1916
108. *The Zeppelin Destroyer.* London, 1916
109. *Number 70, Berlin.* London, 1916
110. *The Place of Dragons.* London, 1916

111. *The Spy Hunter.* London, 1916
112. *The Man about Town.* London, 1916
113. *Annette of the Argonne.* London, 1916
114. *The Broken Thread.* London, 1916
115. *The Way to Win.* London, 1916
116. *Behind the German Lines.* London, 1917
117. *The Breath of Suspicion.* London, 1917
118. *The Devil's Carnival.* London, 1917
119. *No Greater Love.* London, 1917
120. *Two in a Tangle.* London, 1917
121. *Rasputin, The Rascal Monk.* London, 1917
122. *The Bomb-Makers.* London, 1917
123. *Beryl of the Biplane.* London, 1917
124. *Hushed Up at German Headquarters.* London, 1917
125. *The Rainbow Mystery: Chronicles of a Colour-Criminologist.* London, 1917
126. *The Scandal-Monger.* London, 1917
127. *The Secrets of Potsdam.* London, 1917
128. *More Secrets of Potsdam.* London, 1917
129. *Further Secrets of Potsdam.* London, 1917
130. *Donovan of Whitehall.* London, 1917
131. *The Yellow Ribbon.* London, 1918
132. *The Secret Life of the Ex-Tsaritza.* London, 1918
133. *The Sister Disciple.* London, 1918
134. *The Stolen Statesman.* London, 1918
135. *The Little Blue Goddess.* London, 1918
136. *The Minister of Evil: The Secret History of Rasputin's Betrayal of Russia.* London, 1918
137. *Bolo, The Super-Spy.* London, 1918
138. *The Catspaw.* London, 1918
139. *Sant of the Secret Service.* London, 1918
140. *Love Intrigues of the Kaiser's Sons.* London and New York, 1918
141. *Cipher Six.* London, 1919
142. *The Doctor of Pimlico.* London, 1919
143. *The Forbidden Word.* London, 1919
144. *The King's Incognito.* London, 1919
145. *The Lure of Love.* London, 1919
146. *Rasputinism in London.* London, 1919
147. *The Secret Shame of the Kaiser.* London, 1919
148. *Secrets of the White Tsar.* London, 1919
149. *The Hotel X.* London, 1919
150. *Mysteries of the Great City.* London, 1919
151. *The Heart of a Princess.* London, 1920
152. *The Intriguers.* London, 1920
153. *No. 7, Saville Square.* London, 1920
154. *The Red Widow; or, The Death-Dealers of London.* London, 1920
155. *The Terror of the Air.* London, 1920
156. *Whither Thou Goest.* London, 1920
157. *In Secret.* London, 1920
158. *The Secret Telephone.* New York, 1920
159. *Society Intrigues I Have Known.* London, 1920
160. *This House to Let.* London, 1921
161. *The Lady-in-Waiting.* London, 1921
162. *The Open Verdict.* London, 1921
163. *The Power of the Borgias: The Story of the Great Film.* London, 1921
164. *Mademoiselle of Monte Carlo.* London and New York, 1921
165. *The Fifth Finger.* London and New York, 1921
166. *The Luck of the Secret Service.* London, 1921
167. *The Elusive Four: The Exciting Exploits of Four Thieves.* London, 1921
168. *The Golden Face.* London and New York, 1922
169. *The Stretton Street Affair.* New York, 1922
170. *Three Knots.* London, 1922
171. *The Voice from the Void.* London, 1922
172. *The Young Archduchess.* London and New York, 1922
173. *Tracked by Wireless.* London and New York, 1922
174. *The Gay Triangle: The Romance of the First Air Adventurers.* London, 1922
175. *Landru: His Secret Love Affairs.* London, 1922
176. *Where the Desert Ends.* London, 1923
177. *The Bronze Face.* London, 1923
178. *Behind the Bronze Door.* New York, 1923
179. *Bleke, The Butler, Being the Exciting Adventures of Robert Bleke During Certain Years of His Service in Various Families.* London, 1923
180. *Things I Know about Kings, Celebrities, and Crooks.* London, 1923
181. *The Crystal Claw.* London and New York, 1924
182. *Fine Feathers.* London, 1924
183. *A Woman's Debt.* London, 1924
184. *The Valrose Mystery.* London, 1925
185. *The Marked Man.* London, 1925
186. *The Blue Bungalow.* London, 1925
187. *The Broadcast Mystery.* London, 1925
188. *The Fatal Face.* London, 1926
189. *Hidden Hands.* London, 1926
190. *The Dangerous Game.* New York, 1926
191. *The Letter E.* London, 1926
192. *The Mystery of Mademoiselle.* London, 1926
193. *The Scarlet Sign.* London, 1926
194. *The Black Owl.* London, 1926
195. *The Office Secret.* London, 1927
196. *The House of Evil.* London, 1927
197. *The Lawless Hand.* London, 1927
198. *Blackmailed.* London, 1927
199. *The Chameleon.* London, 1927
200. *The Tattoo Mystery.* New York, 1927
201. *Poison Shadows.* New York, 1927
202. *The Crimes Club: A Record of Secret Investigations into Some Amazing Crimes, Mostly Withheld from the Public.* London, 1927
203. *Engelberg: The Crown Jewel of the Alps.* London, 1927
204. *Interlaken: The Alpine Wonderland: A Novelist's Jottings.* Interlaken (Switzerland), no date
205. *Concerning This Woman.* London, 1928
206. *The Rat Trap.* London, 1928
207. *The Secret Formula.* London, 1928
208. *The Sting.* London and New York, 1928
209. *Twice Tried.* London, 1928
210. *The Peril of Helen Marklove and Other Stories.* London, 1928
211. *The Amazing Count.* London, 1929
212. *The Crinkled Crown.* London and New York, 1929
213. *The Golden Three.* London, 1930
214. *The Factotum and Other Stories.* London, 1931

Leslie, Doris
British, born ca. 1902, died May 31, 1982
1. *The Starling.* London and New York, 1927
2. *Fools in Mortar.* London and New York, 1928
3. *The Echoing Green.* London, 1929
4. *Terminus.* London, 1931
5. *Puppets Parade.* London, 1932
6. *Full Flavour.* London and New York, 1934
7. *Fair Company.* London and New York, 1936
8. *Concord in Jeopardy.* London and New York, 1938
9. *Another Cynthia: The Adventures of Cynthia, Lady Ffulkes 1780-1850.* London and New York, 1939
10. *Royal William: The Story of a Democrat.* London, 1940
11. *House in the Dust.* London and New York, 1942
12. *Polonaise.* London, 1943
13. *Folly's End.* London, 1944
14. *The Peverills.* London, 1946

15. *Wreath for Arabella.* London, 1948
16. *That Enchantress.* London, 1950
17. *The Great Corinthian: A Portrait of the Prince Regent.* London, 1952
18. *A Toast to Lady Mary.* London, 1954
19. *Peridot Flight.* London, 1956
20. *Tales of Grace and Favour.* London, 1956
21. *As the Tree Falls.* London, 1958
22. *The Perfect Wife.* London, 1960
23. *I Return.* London, 1962
24. *This for Caroline.* London, 1964
25. *Paragon Street.* London, 1965
26. *The Sceptre and the Rose.* London, 1967
27. *The Marriage of Martha Todd.* London, 1968
28. *The Rebel Princess.* London, 1970
29. *A Young Wives' Tale.* London, 1971
30. *The Desert Queen.* London, 1972
31. *The Dragon's Head.* London, 1973
32. *The Incredible Duchess.* London, 1974
33. *Call Back Yesterday.* London, 1975
34. *Notorious Lady.* London, 1976
35. *The Warrior King.* London, 1977
36. *Crown of Thorns.* London, 1979

Lesser, Milton
American, born August 7, 1928
Pseudonyms: Andrew Frazer, Stephen Marlowe, Jason Ridgway, and C.H. Thames
1. *Earthbound.* Philadelphia, 1952
2. *The Star Seekers.* Philadelphia, 1953
3. *Catch the Brass Ring.* New York, 1954
4. *Turn Left for Murder.* New York, 1955
5. *Model for Murder.* Hasbrouck Heights (NJ), 1955
6. *The Second Longest Night.* New York, 1955
7. *Dead on Arrival.* New York, 1956
8. *Mecca for Murder.* New York, 1956
9. *Violence Is Golden,* as C.H. Thames. New York, 1956
10. *Killers Are My Meat.* New York, 1957
11. *Murder Is My Dish.* New York, 1957
12. *Trouble Is My Name.* New York, 1957
13. *Violence Is My Business.* New York, 1958
14. *Terror Is My Trade.* New York, 1958
15. *West Side Jungle,* as Jason Ridgway. New York, 1958
16. *Blonde Bait.* New York, 1959
17. *Double in Trouble.* New York, 1959
18. *Find Eileen Hardin—Alive!* as Andrew Frazer. New York, 1959
19. *Passport to Peril.* New York, 1959
20. *Homicide Is My Game.* New York, 1959
21. *Danger Is My Line.* New York, 1960
22. *Death Is My Comrade.* New York, 1960
23. *The Fall of Marty Moon,* as Andrew Frazer. New York, 1960
24. *Peril Is My Pay.* New York, 1960
25. *Adam's Fall,* as Jason Ridgway. New York, 1960
26. *Stadium Beyond the Stars.* Philadelphia, 1960
27. *Manhunt Is My Mission.* New York, 1961
28. *People in Glass Houses,* as Jason Ridgway. New York, 1961
29. *Spacemen Go Home.* New York, 1961
30. *Jeopardy Is My Job.* New York, 1962
31. *Hardly a Man Is Now Alive,* as Jason Ridgway. New York, 1962
32. *Lost Worlds and the Men Who Found Them.* Racine (WI), 1962
33. *Blood of My Brother,* as C.H. Thames. New York, 1963
34. *Francesca.* New York and London, 1963
35. *The Shining,* as Stephen Marlowe. New York, 1963
36. *Walt Disney's Strange Animals of Australia.* Racine (WI), 1963
37. *Drum Beat—Berlin.* New York, 1964
38. *Drum Beat—Dominique.* New York, 1965
39. *Secret of the Black Planet.* New York, 1965
40. *Drum Beat—Madrid.* New York, 1966
41. *The Search for Bruno Heidler.* New York, 1966
42. *The Treasure of the Cosa Nostra,* as Jason Ridgway. New York, 1966
43. *Drum Beat—Erica.* New York, 1967
44. *Come Over, Red Rover.* New York, 1968
45. *Drum Beat—Marianne.* New York, 1968
46. *The Summit.* New York, 1970
47. *The Man with No Shadow.* Englewood Cliffs (NJ) and London, 1974
48. *The Cawthorn Journals.* Englewood Cliffs, 1975
49. *Translation.* Englewood Cliffs, 1976

Levin, Ira
American, born August 27, 1929
1. *A Kiss Before Dying.* New York, 1953
2. *No Time for Sergeants.* New York, 1956
3. *Interlock.* New York, 1958
4. *Critic's Choice.* New York, 1961
5. *General Seeger.* New York, 1962
6. *Rosemary's Baby.* New York and London, 1967
7. *Dr. Cook's Garden.* New York, 1968
8. *This Perfect Day.* New York and London, 1970
9. *The Stepford Wives.* New York and London, 1972
10. *Veronica's Room.* New York, 1974
11. *The Boys from Brazil.* New York and London, 1976

Lewin, Michael Z.
American, born July 21, 1942
1. *How to Beat College Tests: A Practical Guide to Ease the Burden of Useless Courses.* New York, 1970
2. *Ask the Right Question.* New York, 1971
3. *The Way We Die Now.* New York and London, 1973
4. *The Enemies Within.* New York and London, 1974
5. *The Next Man.* New York, 1976
6. *Night Cover.* New York and London, 1976
7. *"Soft-Boiled But Still an Egg."* New York, 1977
8. *The Silent Salesman.* New York and London, 1978

Lewis, Alfred Henry
American, born January 20, 1857, died December 23, 1914
Pseudonym: Quin
1. *Wolfville.* New York and London, 1897
2. *The Old Plantation Home: A Story of Southern Life Just After the War,* as Quin. Nashville (TN), 1899
3. *Sandburrs.* New York, 1900
4. *Richard Croker.* New York, 1901
5. *Wolfville Days.* New York, 1902
6. *Wolfville Nights.* New York, 1902
7. *The Black Lion Inn.* New York, 1903
8. *Peggy O'Neal.* Philadelphia, 1903
9. *The Boss, and How He Came to Rule New York.* New York, 1903
10. *The President.* New York, 1904
11. *The Sunset Trail.* New York, 1905
12. *The Throwback: A Romance of the Southwest.* New York, 1906
13. *The Story of Paul Jones: An Historical Romance.* New York and London, 1906
14. *Confessions of a Detective.* New York, 1906
15. *When Men Grew Tall; or, The Story of Andrew Jackson.* New York, 1907
16. *Wolfville Folks.* New York, 1908
17. *An American Patrician; or, The Story of Aaron Burr.* New York, 1908

18. *The Apaches of New York.* New York, 1912
19. *Faro Nell and Her Friends: Wolfville Stories.* New York, 1913
20. *Nation-Famous New York Murders.* New York, 1914
21. *Old Wolfville: Chapters from the Fiction of Alfred Henry Lewis.* Yellow Springs (OH), 1968
22. *Wolfville Yarns.* Kent (OH), 1968

Lewis, C. Day [Cecil Day Lewis]
British, born in 1904, died May 22, 1972
Pseudonym: Nicholas Blake

1. *Beechen Vigil and Other Poems.* London, 1925
2. *Country Comets.* London, 1928
3. *Transitional Poem.* London, 1929
4. *From Feathers to Iron.* London, 1931
5. *The Magnetic Mountain.* London, 1933
6. *Dick Willoughby.* Oxford (Eng), 1933
7. *A Hope for Poetry.* Oxford, 1934
8. *A Hope for Poetry and Collected Poems.* New York, 1935
9. *Collected Poems, 1929-1933.* London, 1935
10. *Collected Poems, 1929-1935, with A Hope for Poetry.* New York, 1935
11. *A Time to Dance and Other Poems.* London, 1935
12. *A Question of Proof,* as Nicholas Blake. London and New York, 1935
13. *Revolution in Writing.* London, 1935
14. *Thou Shell of Death,* as Nicholas Blake. London, 1936
15. *Shell of Death,* as Nicholas Blake. New York, 1936
16. *The Friendly Tree.* London, 1936
17. *Noah and the Waters.* London, 1936
18. *A Time to Dance, Noah and the Waters and Other Poems, with an Essay, Revolution in Writing.* New York, 1936
19. *Imagination and Thinking,* with L. Susan Stebbing. London, 1936
20. *We're Not Going to Do Nothing: A Reply to Mr. Aldous Huxley's Pamphlet "What Are You Going to Do about It?"* London, 1936
21. *Starting Point.* London, 1937
22. *There's Trouble Brewing,* as Nicholas Blake. London and New York, 1937
23. *The Beast Must Die,* as Nicholas Blake. London and New York, 1938
24. *Overtures to Death and Other Poems.* London, 1938
25. *Child of Misfortune.* London, 1939
26. *The Smiler with the Knife,* as Nicholas Blake. London and New York, 1939
27. *Malice in Wonderland,* as Nicholas Blake. London, 1940
28. *The Summer Camp Mystery,* as Nicholas Blake. New York, 1940
29. *Poems in Wartime.* London, 1940
30. *Selected Poems.* London, 1940
31. *The Case of the Abominable Snowman,* as Nicholas Blake. London, 1941
32. *The Corpse in the Snowman,* as Nicholas Blake. New York, 1941
33. *Word over All.* London, 1943
34. *(Poems).* London, 1943
35. *Poetry for You: A Book for Boys and Girls on the Enjoyment of Poetry.* Oxford, 1944
36. *Short Is the Time Poems, 1936-1943.* New York, 1945
37. *Minute for Murder,* as Nicholas Blake. London, 1947
38. *The Poetic Image.* London and New York, 1947
39. *Enjoying Poetry: A Reader's Guide.* London, 1947
40. *The Colloquial Element in English Poetry.* Newcastle upon Tyne (Eng), 1947
41. *Poems, 1943-1947.* London and New York, 1948
42. *Collected Poems, 1929-1936.* London, 1948
43. *Head of a Traveller,* as Nicholas Blake. London and New York, 1949
44. *The Otterbury Incident.* London, 1948
45. *Selected Poems.* London, 1951
46. *The Poet's Task.* Oxford, 1951
47. *The Grand Manner.* Nottingham (Eng), 1952
48. *The Dreadful Hollow,* as Nicholas Blake. London and New York, 1953
49. *An Italian Visit:* London and New York, 1953
50. *The Lyrical Poetry of Thomas Hardy.* London, 1953
51. *The Whisper in the Gloom,* as Nicholas Blake. London and New York, 1954
52. *Collected Poems.* London, 1954
53. *Christmas Eve.* London, 1954
54. *Notable Images of Virtue: Emily Bronte, George Meredith, W.B. Yeats.* Toronto, 1954
55. *Catch and Kill,* as Nicholas Blake. New York, 1955
56. *A Tangled Web,* as Nicholas Blake. London and New York, 1956
57. *End of Chapter,* as Nicholas Blake. London and New York, 1957
58. *The Newborn: D.M.B., 29th April, 1957.* London, 1957
59. *Pegasus and Other Poems.* London, 1957
60. *The Poet's Way to Knowledge.* Cambridge (Eng), 1957
61. *A Penknife in My Heart,* as Nicholas Blake. London, 1958
62. *The Window's Cruise,* as Nicholas Blake. London and New York, 1959
63. *Death and Daisy Bland,* as Nicholas Blake. New York, 1960
64. *The Buried Day.* London and New York, 1960
65. *The Worm of Death,* as Nicholas Blake. London and New York, 1961
66. *The Gate and Other Poems.* London, 1962
67. *The Deadly Joker,* as Nicholas Blake. London, 1963
68. *The Sad Variety,* as Nicholas Blake. London and New York, 1964
69. *Malice with Murder,* as Nicholas Blake. New York, 1964
70. *Requiem for the Living.* New York, 1964
71. *On Not Saying Anything.* Cambridge, 1964
72. *A Marriage Song for Albert and Barbara.* Cambridge, 1965
73. *The Room and Other Poems.* London, 1965
74. *The Lyric Impulse.* Cambridge and London, 1965
75. *Thomas Hardy,* with R.A. Scott-James. London, 1965
76. *The Morning after Death,* as Nicholas Blake. London and New York, 1966
77. *C. Day Lewis: Selections from His Poetry.* London, 1967
78. *Selected Poems.* New York, 1967
79. *The Abbey That Refused to Die: A Poem.* County Mayo (Ireland), 1967
80. *The Private Wound,* as Nicholas Blake. London and New York, 1968
81. *A Need for Poetry?* Hull (Eng), 1968
82. *On Translating Poetry: A Lecture.* Abingdon-on-Thames (Eng), 1970
83. *The Whispering Roots.* London, 1970
84. *The Whispering Roots and Other Poems.* New York, 1970
85. *Going My Way.* London, 1970
86. *The Poems of C. Day Lewis.* London, 1977

Lewis, Maynah
British, born April 14, 1919

1. *No Place for Love.* London, 1963
2. *Give Me This Day.* London, 1964
3. *See the Bright Morning.* London, 1965
4. *Make Way for Tomorrow.* London, 1966
5. *The Long, Hot Days.* London, 1966
6. *The Future Is Forever.* London, 1967
7. *Till Then, My Love.* London, 1968
8. *Of No Fixed Abode.* London, 1968
9. *Symphony for Two Players.* London, 1969
10. *A Corner of Eden.* London, 1970

11. *A Pride of Innocence.* London, 1971
12. *Too Late for Tears.* London, 1972
13. *The Town That Nearly Died.* London, 1973
14. *The Miracle of Lac Blanche.* London, 1973
15. *The Unforgiven.* London, 1974
16. *The Other Side of Paradise.* London, 1975
17. *Yesterday Came Suddenly.* London, 1975
18. *A Woman of Property.* London, 1976
19. *These My Children.* London, 1977
20. *Love Has Two Faces.* London, 1981
21. *Barren Harvest.* London, 1981
22. *Hour of the Siesta.* London, 1982

Lewis, Roy [John Royston Lewis]
British, born January 17, 1933
Pseudonyms: David Springfield, J.R. Lewis
1. *A Lover Too Many.* London, 1969
2. *Law of the Retailer: An Outline for Students and Business Men,* as J.R. Lewis. London, 1964
3. *Cases for Discussion,* as J.R. Lewis. Oxford (Eng), 1965
4. *An Introduction to Business Law,* as J.R. Lewis. London, 1965
5. *Law in Action,* as J.R. Lewis. London, 1965
6. *Questions and Answers on Civil Procedure,* as J.R. Lewis. London, 1966
7. *Building Law,* as J.R. Lewis. London, 1966
8. *Democracy: The Theory and the Practice,* as J.R. Lewis. London, 1966
9. *Managing Within the Law,* as J.R. Lewis. London, 1967
10. *Principles of Registered Land Conveyancing,* as J.R. Lewis. London, 1967
11. *Company Law,* as J.R. Lewis. London, 1967
12. *Revision Notes for Ordinary Level British Constitution,* as J.R. Lewis. London, 1967
13. *Civil and Criminal Procedure,* as J.R. Lewis. London, 1968
14. *Landlord and Tenant,* as J.R. Lewis. London, 1968
15. *Outlines of Equity,* as J.R. Lewis. London, 1968
16. *Mercantile and Commercial Law,* as J.R. Lewis. London, 1969
17. *A Wolf by the Ears.* London, 1970
18. *The Company Executive and the Law,* as David Springfield. London, 1970
19. *Error of Judgment.* London, 1971
20. *The Fenokee Project.* London, 1971
21. *A Fool for a Client.* London, 1972
22. *The Secret Singing.* London, 1972
23. *Blood Money.* London, 1973
24. *Of Singular Purpose.* London, 1973
25. *Law for the Retailer,* as J.R. Lewis. No place, 1974
26. *A Question of Degree.* London, 1974
27. *Double Take.* London, 1975
28. *A Part of Virtue.* London, 1975
29. *Witness My Death.* London, 1976
30. *A Distant Banner.* London, 1976
31. *Law for the Construction Industry,* as J.R. Lewis. London, 1976
32. *Administrative Law for the Construction Industry,* as J.R. Lewis. London, 1976
33. *Nothing but Foxes.* London, 1977
34. *An Uncertain Sound.* London, 1978
35. *An Inevitable Fatality.* London, 1978
36. *The Teaching of Public Administration in Further and Higher Education,* as J.R. Lewis. London, 1979

Lewty, Marjorie
British, born April 8, 1906
1. *Never Call It Loving.* London, 1958
2. *The Million Stars.* London, 1959
3. *The Imperfect Secretary.* London, 1959
4. *The Lucky One.* London, 1961
5. *This Must Be for Ever.* London, 1962
6. *Alex Rayner, Dental Nurse.* London and Toronto, 1965
7. *Dental Nurse at Denley's.* London, 1968
8. *Town Nurse—Country Nurse.* London, 1970
9. *The Extraordinary Engagement.* London, 1972
10. *The Rest Is Magic.* London, 1973
11. *All Made of Wishes.* London and Toronto, 1974
12. *Flowers in Stony Places.* London and Toronto, 1975
13. *The Fire in the Diamond.* London and Toronto, 1976
14. *To Catch a Butterfly.* London and Toronto, 1977
15. *The Time and the Loving.* London, 1977
16. *The Short Engagement.* London and Toronto, 1978
17. *A Very Special Man.* London, 1979
18. *A Certain Smile.* London, 1979
19. *Prisoner in Paradise.* London, 1980
20. *Love Is a Dangerous Game.* London, 1980
21. *Beyond the Lagoon.* London, 1981

Ley, Alice Chetwynd
British, born October 12, 1913
1. *The Jewelled Snuff Box.* London, 1959
2. *The Georgian Rake.* London, 1960
3. *The Guinea Stamp.* London, 1961
4. *Master of Liversedge.* London, 1966
5. *The Clandestine Betrothal.* London, 1967
6. *The Toast of the Town.* London, 1969
7. *Letters for a Spy.* London, 1970
8. *A Season at Brighton.* London, 1971
9. *Tenant of Chesdene Manor.* London, 1974
10. *The Beau and the Bluestocking.* London, 1975
11. *At Dark of the Moon.* London, 1977
12. *An Advantageous Marriage.* London, 1977
13. *A Regency Scandal.* New York and London, 1979
14. *A Conformable Wife.* New York, 1981

Linebarger, P.M.A. (Paul Myron Anthony)
American, born July 11, 1913, died August 6, 1966
Pseudonyms: Felix C. Forrest, Carmichael Smith, Cordwainer Smith
1. *The Political Doctrines of Sun Yat-Sen,* as P.M.A. Linebarger. Baltimore (MD), 1937
2. *Government in Republican China,* as P.M.A. Linebarger. New York, 1938
3. *The China of Chiang Kai-shek,* as P.M.A. Linebarger. Boston, 1941
4. *Ria,* as Felix C. Forrest. New York, 1947
5. *Carola,* as Felix C. Forrest. New York, 1948
6. *Atomsk,* as Carmichael Smith. New York, 1949
7. *Far Eastern Governments and Politics,* with Djang Chu and Ardath W. Burks, as P.M.A. Linebarger. New York, 1952
8. *Psychological Warfare,* as P.M.A. Linebarger. Washington (DC), 1954
9. *You Will Never Be the Same,* as Cordwainer Smith. Evanston (IL), 1963
10. *The Planet Buyer,* as Cordwainer Smith. New York, 1964
11. *Space Lords,* as Cordwainer Smith. New York, 1965
12. *Quest of the Three Worlds,* as Cordwainer Smith. New York, 1966
13. *The Underpeople,* as Cordwainer Smith. New York, 1968
14. *Under Old Earth and Other Explorations,* as Cordwainer Smith. New York, 1970
15. *Stardreamer,* as Cordwainer Smith. New York, 1971
16. *The Best of Cordwainer Smith,* as Cordwainer Smith. New York, 1975
17. *Norstrilia,* as Cordwainer Smith. New York, 1975
18. *The Instrumentality of Mankind,* as Cordwainer Smith. New York, 1979

Lindsay, Rachel
Pseudonyms: Roberta Leigh, Janey Scott
1. *In Name Only,* as Roberta Leigh. London, 1951
2. *Dark Inheritance,* as Roberta Leigh. London, 1952
3. *The Vengeful Heart,* as Roberta Leigh. London, 1952
4. *The Widening Stream.* London, 1952
5. *Beloved Ballerina,* as Roberta Leigh. London, 1953
6. *And Then Came Love,* as Roberta Leigh. London, 1954
7. *Alien Corn.* London, 1954
8. *Healing Hands.* London, 1955
9. *Mask of Gold.* London, 1956
10. *Pretence,* as Roberta Leigh. London, 1956
11. *Stacy,* as Roberta Leigh. London, 1958
12. *Castle in the Trees.* London, 1958
13. *House of Lorraine.* London, 1959
14. *The Taming of Laura.* London, 1959
15. *Memory of Love,* as Janey Scott. London, 1959
16. *Melody of Love,* as Janey Scott. London, 1960
17. *A Time to Love,* as Janey Scott. London, 1960
18. *Business Affair.* London, 1960
19. *Heart of a Rose.* London, 1961
20. *Sara Gay—Model Girl [in Mayfair, in New York, in Monte Carlo],* as Janey Scott. London, 4 vols., 1961
21. *Song in My Heart.* London, 1961
22. *Lesley Forrest. M.D.* New York, 1962
23. *Moonlight and Magic.* London, 1962
24. *Design for Murder.* London, 1964
25. *No Business to Love.* London, 1966
26. *Love and Lucy Granger.* London, 1967
27. *Price of Love.* London, 1967
28. *My Heart's a Dancer,* as Roberta Leigh. London, 1970
29. *Love and Dr. Forrest.* London, 1971
30. *The Latitude of Love.* London, 1971
31. *A Question of Marriage.* London, 1972
32. *Cage of Gold.* London, 1973
33. *Chateau in Provence.* London, 1973
34. *Cinderella in Mink,* as Roberta Leigh. London, 1973
35. *If Dreams Came True,* as Roberta Leigh. London, 1974
36. *Shade of the Palms,* as Roberta Leigh. London and Toronto, 1974
37. *Food for Love.* Toronto, 1974
38. *Heart of the Lion,* as Roberta Leigh. Toronto, 1975
39. *Man in a Million,* as Roberta Leigh. London, 1975
40. *Temporary Wife,* as Roberta Leigh. London and Toronto, 1975
41. *Affair in Venice.* London and Toronto, 1975
42. *Love in Disguise.* London and Toronto, 1975
43. *Innocent Deception.* London and Toronto, 1975
44. *Prince for Sale.* London and Toronto, 1975
45. *The Marquis Takes a Wife.* London, 1976
46. *Roman Affair.* London, 1976
47. *Tinsel Star.* London, 1976
48. *A Man to Tame.* London, 1976
49. *Cupboard Love,* as Roberta Leigh. London and Toronto, 1976
50. *To Buy a Bride,* as Roberta Leigh. London and Toronto, 1976
51. *The Unwilling Bridegroom,* as Roberta Leigh. London, 1976
52. *Man Without a Heart,* as Roberta Leigh. London, 1976
53. *Girl for a Millionare,* as Roberta Leigh. Toronto, 1977
54. *Too Young to Love,* as Roberta Leigh. Toronto, 1977
55. *Forbidden Love.* Toronto, 1977
56. *Prescription for Love.* London and Toronto, 1977
57. *Facts of Love,* as Roberta Leigh. London, 1978
58. *Night of Love,* as Roberta Leigh. London, 1978
59. *The Savage Aristocrat,* as Roberta Leigh. London, 1978
60. *Not a Marrying Man,* as Roberta Leigh. Toronto, 1978
61. *Love in Store,* as Roberta Leigh. New York, 1978
62. *Rough Diamond Lover.* Toronto, 1978
63. *An Affair to Forget.* Toronto, 1978
64. *Forgotten Marriage.* Toronto, 1978
65. *Brazilian Affair.* Toronto, 1978
66. *Flower of the Desert,* as Roberta Leigh. New York, 1979
67. *My Sister's Keeper.* London, 1979
68. *Man of Ice.* London and Toronto, 1980
69. *Love and No Marriage,* as Roberta Leigh. New York, 1980
70. *Rent a Wife,* as Roberta Leigh. London, 1980
71. *Wife for a Year,* as Roberta Leigh. London, 1980
72. *Love Match,* as Roberta Leigh. New York, 1980
73. *Confirmed Bachelor,* as Roberta Leigh. Toronto, 1981
74. *Untouched Wife.* Toronto, 1981

Linington, Elizabeth [Barbara Elizabeth Linington]
American, born March 11, 1921
Pseudonyms: Anne Blaisdell, Lesley Egan, Egan O'Neill, Dell Shannon
1. *The Proud Man.* New York, 1955
2. *The Long Watch.* New York, 1956
3. *Monsieur Janvier.* New York, 1957
4. *The Anglophile,* as Egan O'Neill. New York, 1957
5. *The Pretender.* London, 1957
6. *The Kingbreaker.* New York, 1958
7. *Case Pending,* as Dell Shannon. New York and London, 1960
8. *Nightmare,* as Anne Blaisdell. New York, 1961
9. *The Ace of Spades,* as Dell Shannon. New York, 1961
10. *A Case for Appeal,* as Lesley Egan. New York and London, 1961
11. *Forging an Empire: Elizabeth I.* Chicago, 1961
12. *Extra Kill,* as Dell Shannon. New York and London, 1962
13. *Knave of Hearts,* as Dell Shannon. New York, 1962
14. *Against the Evidence,* as Lesley Egan. New York, 1962
15. *The Borrowed Alibi,* as Lesley Egan. New York and London, 1962
16. *Death of a Busybody,* as Dell Shannon. New York and London, 1963
17. *Double Bluff,* as Dell Shannon. New York, 1963
18. *Run to Evil,* as Lesley Egan. New York and London, 1963
19. *Greenmask!* New York, 1964
20. *No Evil Angel.* New York, 1964
21. *Mark of Murder,* as Dell Shannon. New York, 1964
22. *Root of All Evil,* as Dell Shannon. New York, 1964
23. *The Death-Bringers,* as Dell Shannon. New York, 1965
24. *Death by Inches,* as Dell Shannon. New York, 1965
25. *My Name Is Death,* as Lesley Egan. New York and London, 1965
26. *Detective's Due,* as Lesley Egan. New York, 1965
27. *Come to Think of It.* Boston, 1965
28. *Date with Death.* New York and London, 1966
29. *Coffin Corner,* as Dell Shannon. New York, 1966
30. *With a Vengeance,* as Dell Shannon. New York, 1966
31. *Some Avenger, Rise!* New York, 1966
32. *Something Wrong.* New York, 1967
33. *Chance to Kill,* as Dell Shannon. New York, 1967
34. *Rain with Violence,* as Dell Shannon. New York, 1967
35. *The Nameless Ones,* as Lesley Egan. New York, 1967
36. *Policeman's Lot.* New York, 1968
37. *Kill with Kindness,* as Dell Shannon. New York, 1968
38. *A Serious Investigation,* as Lesley Egan. New York, 1968
39. *Schooled to Kill,* as Dell Shannon. New York, 1969
40. *Crime on Their Hands,* as Dell Shannon. New York, 1969
41. *The Wine of Violence,* as Lesley Egan. New York, 1969
42. *Unexpected Death,* as Dell Shannon. New York, 1970
43. *In the Death of a Man,* as Lesley Egan. New York and London, 1970
44. *Practice to Deceive.* New York and London, 1971
45. *Whim to Kill,* as Dell Shannon. New York and London, 1971

Linington, Elizabeth

46. *The Ringer*, as Dell Shannon. New York, 1971
47. *Malicious Mischief*, as Lesley Egan. New York, 1971
48. *Murder with Love*, as Dell Shannon. New York and London, 1972
49. *With Intent to Kill*, as Dell Shannon. New York, 1972
50. *Paper Chase*, as Lesley Egan. New York, 1972
51. *Crime by Chance*. Philadelphia, 1973
52. *No Holiday for Crime*, as Dell Shannon. New York, 1973
53. *Spring of Violence*, as Dell Shannon. New York, 1973
54. *Crime File*, as Dell Shannon. New York, 1974
55. *Deuces Wild*, as Dell Shannon. New York and London, 1975
56. *Streets of Death*, as Dell Shannon. New York, 1976
57. *Scenes of Crime*, as Lesley Egan. New York, 1976
58. *Perchance of Death*. New York, 1977
59. *Appearances of Death*, as Dell Shannon. New York, 1977
60. *The Blind Search*, as Lesley Egan. New York, 1977
61. *Cold Trail*, as Dell Shannon. New York, 1978
62. *A Dream Apart*, as Lesley Egan. New York, 1978
63. *Look Back on Death*, as Lesley Egan. New York, 1978
64. *No Villain Need Be*. New York, 1979
65. *Felony at Random*, as Dell Shannon. New York and London, 1979
66. *The Hunters and the Hunted*, as Lesley Egan. New York, 1979

Little, Constance and Gwyneth

1. *The Grey Mist Murders*. New York, 1938
2. *The Black-Headed Pins*. New York, 1938
3. *The Black Gloves*. New York, 1939
4. *Black Corridors*. New York, 1940
5. *The Black Paw*. New York and London, 1941
6. *The Black Shrouds*. New York, 1941
7. *The Black Thumb*. New York, 1942
8. *The Black Rustle*. New York, 1943
9. *The Black Lady*. London, 1944
10. *The Black Honeymoon*. New York and London, 1944
11. *Great Black Kanba*. New York, 1944
12. *The Black Express*. London, 1945
13. *The Black Eye*. New York, 1945
14. *The Black Stocking*. New York, 1946
15. *The Black Goatee*. New York and London, 1947
16. *The Black Coat*. New York, 1948
17. *The Black Piano*. New York and London, 1948
18. *The Black House*. New York and London, 1950
19. *The Black Smith*. New York, 1950
20. *The Blackout*. New York, 1951
21. *The Black Dream*. New York, 1952
22. *The Black Curl*. New York, 1953
23. *The Black Iris*. New York and London, 1953

Lofts, Norah

British, born August 27, 1904
Pseudonyms: Juliet Astley, Peter Curtis

1. *I Met a Gypsy*. London and New York, 1935
2. *Here Was a Man: A Romantic History of Sir Walter Raleigh*. London and New York, 1936
3. *White Hell of Pity*. London and New York, 1937
4. *Requiem for Idols*. London and New York, 1938
5. *Out of This Nettle*. London, 1938
6. *Blossom Like the Rose*. London and New York, 1939
7. *Hester Roon*. London and New York, 1940
8. *Dead March in Three Keys*, as Peter Curtis. London, 1940
9. *The Road to Revelation*. London, 1941
10. *The Brittle Glass*. London, 1942
11. *You're Best Alone*, as Peter Curtis. London, 1943
12. *Michael and All the Angels*. London, 1943
13. *Jassy*. London and New York, 1944
14. *Lady Living Alone*, as Peter Curtis. London, 1945
15. *To See a Fine Lady*. London and New York, 1946
16. *Silver Nutmeg*. London and New York, 1947
17. *A Calf for Venus*. London and New York, 1949
18. *Women in the Old Testament: Twenty Psychological Portraits*. London and New York, 1949
19. *Esther*. New York, 1950
20. *The Lute Player*. London and New York, 1951
21. *Bless This House*. London and New York, 1954
22. *Winter Harvest*. New York, 1955
23. *Queen in Waiting*. London, 1955
24. *Afternoon of an Autocrat*. London and New York, 1956
25. *Scent of Cloves*. New York, 1957
26. *Heaven in Your Hand and Other Stories*. New York, 1958
27. *The Town House*. London and New York, 1959
28. *No Question of Murder*. New York, 1959
29. *The Devil's Own*, as Peter Curtis. London and New York, 1960
30. *The House at Old Vine*. London and New York, 1961
31. *The House at Sunset*. New York, 1962
32. *The Concubine: A Novel Based upon the Life of Anne Boleyn*. New York, 1963
33. *How Far to Bethehem?* London and New York, 1965
34. *The Witches*. London, 1966
35. *Eternal France: A History of France 1789-1944*, with Margery Weiner. New York, 1968
36. *The Lost Ones*. London, 1969
37. *Madselin*. London, 1969
38. *The King's Pleasure*. New York, 1969
39. *The Bride of Moat House*. New York, 1969
40. *Lovers All Untrue*. London and New York, 1970
41. *The Little Wax Doll*. London and New York, 1970
42. *The Story of Maude Reed*. London, 1971
43. *A Rose for Virtue*. London and New York, 1971
44. *Rupert Hatton's Story*. London, 1972
45. *Charlotte*. London, 1972
46. *Nethergate*. London and New York, 1973
47. *Is Anybody There?* London, 1974
48. *Crown of Aloes*. London and New York, 1974
49. *Walk into My Parlour*. London, 1975
50. *Knight's Acre*. London and New York, 1975
51. *The Homecoming*. London, 1975
52. *Checkmate*. London, 1975
53. *The Fall of Midas*, as Juliet Astley. New York, 1975
54. *The Lonely Furrow*. London, 1976
55. *Domestic Life in England*. London and New York, 1976
56. *Gad's Hall*. London, 1977
57. *Queens of Britian*. London, 1977
58. *Emma Hamilton*. London and New York, 1978
59. *Copsi Castle*, as Juliet Astley. London and New York, 1978
60. *Haunted House*. London, 1978
61. *Anne Boleyn*. New York and London, 1979
62. *Day of the Butterfly*. London, 1979
63. *A Wayside Tavern*. London and New York, 1980
64. *The Old Priory*. London, 1981
65. *The Claw*. London, 1981

London, Jack [John Griffith London]

American, born January 12, 1876, died November 22, 1916

1. *The Son of the Wolf: Tales of the Far North*. Boston, 1900
2. *The God of His Fathers and Other Stories*. New York, 1901
3. *The Cruise of the Dazzler*. New York, 1902
4. *A Daughter of the Snows*. Philadelphia, 1902
5. *Children of the Frost*. New York, 1902
6. *The Call of the Wild*. New York and London, 1903
7. *The Kempton-Wace Letters*. New York and London, 1903
8. *The People of the Abyss*. New York and London, 1903
9. *The Faith of Men and Other Stories*. New York and London, 1904

10. *The Sea-Wolf.* New York and London, 1904
11. *The Tramp.* New York, 1904
12. *The Scab.* Chicago, 1904
13. *The Game.* New York and London, 1905
14. *Tales of the Fish Patrol.* New York, 1905
15. *Jack London: A Sketch of His Life and Work.* London, 1905
16. *War of the Classes.* New York and London, 1905
17. *White Fang.* New York, 1906
18. *The Apostate.* Chicago, 1906
19. *Moon-Face and Other Stories.* New York and London, 1906
20. *Scorn of Women.* New York, 1906
21. *What Life Means to Me.* Princeton (NJ), 1906
22. *Love of Life and Other Stories.* New York, 1907
23. *Before Adam.* New York, 1907
24. *The Road.* New York, 1907
25. *The Iron Heel.* New York and London, 1908
26. *Jack London: Who He Is and What He Has Done.* New York, 1908(?)
27. *Martin Eden.* New York, 1909
28. *Revolution.* Chicago, 1909
29. *Burning Daylight.* New York, 1910
30. *Lost Face.* New York, 1910
31. *Theft.* New York and London, 1910
32. *Revolution and Other Essays.* New York, 1910
33. *Adventure.* London and New York, 1911
34. *When God Laughs and Other Stories.* New York, 1911
35. *South Sea Tales.* New York, 1911
36. *The Strength of the Strong.* Chicago, 1911
37. *The Cruise of the Snark.* New York and London, 1911
38. *Smoke Bellew.* New York, 1912
39. *The Dream of Debs.* Chicago, 1912
40. *The House of Pride and Other Tales of Hawaii.* New York, 1912
41. *A Son of the Sun.* New York, 1912
42. *The Abysmal Brute.* New York, 1913
43. *John Barleycorn.* New York, 1913
44. *The Valley of the Moon.* New York and London, 1913
45. *The Night Born. . . .* New York, 1913
46. *Jack London by Himself.* New York and London, 1913
47. *The Mutiny of the Elsinore.* New York, 1914
48. *The Strength of the Strong.* New York, 1914
49. *An Odyssey of the North.* London, 1915
50. *The Scarlet Plague.* New York and London, 1915
51. *The Jacket.* London, 1915
52. *The Star Rover.* New York, 1915
53. *The Little Lady of the Big House.* New York and London, 1916
54. *The Turtles of Tasman.* New York, 1916
55. *The Acorn-Planters: A California Forest Play. . . .* New York and London, 1916
56. *Jerry of the Islands.* New York and London, 1917
57. *Michael, Brother of Jerry.* New York, 1917
58. *The Human Drift.* New York, 1917
59. *Hearts of Three.* London, 1918
60. *The Red One.* New York, 1918
61. *On the Makaloa Mat.* New York, 1919
62. *Smoke and Shorty.* London, 1920
63. *Island Tales.* London, 1920
64. *Dutch Courage and Other Stories.* New York, 1922
65. *London's Essays of Revolt.* New York, 1926
66. *Jack London, American Rebel: A Collection of His Social Writings.* New York, 1947
67. *The Adventures of Captain Grief.* Cleveland (OH), 1954
68. *Jack London's Tales of Adventure.* New York, 1956
69. *Short Stories.* New York, 1960
70. *Stories of Hawaii.* New York, 1965
71. *Great Short Works of Jack London.* New York, 1965
72. *Letters from Jack London, Containing an Unpublished Correspondence Between London and Sinclair Lewis.* New York, 1965
73. *Jack London Reports: War Correspondence, Sports Articles, and Miscellaneous Writings.* New York, 1970
74. *Daughters of the Rich.* Oakland (CA), 1971
75. *Jack London's Articles and Short Stories in the (Oakland) High School Aegis.* Cedar Springs (MI), 1971
76. *Gold.* Oakland, 1972
77. *Goliah: A Utopian Essay.* Berkeley (CA), 1973
78. *Curious Fragments: Jack London's Tales of Fantasy Fiction.* Port Washington (NY), 1975
79. *The Science Fiction of Jack London.* Boston, 1975
80. *No Mentor But Myself: A Collection of Articles, Essays, Reviews, and Letters on Writing and Writers.* Port Washington, 1979
81. *Revolution: Stories and Essays.* London, 1979
82. *Jack London on the Road: The Tramp Diary and Other Hobo Writings.* Logan (UT), 1979
83. *Jack London's Yukon Women.* New York, 1982

London, Laura [Thomas Dale Curtis and Sharon Curtis]
Americans, Thomas born November 11, 1952, Sharon born March 6, 1951
1. *A Heart Too Proud.* New York, 1978
2. *The Bad Baron's Daughter.* New York, 1978
3. *Moonlight Mist.* New York, 1979
4. *Love's a Stage.* New York, 1980
5. *The Gypsy Heiress.* New York, 1981

Loring, Emilie
American, died March 14, 1951
1. *For the Comfort of the Family: A Vacation Experiment.* New York, 1914
2. *The Mother in the House.* Boston, 1917
3. *The Trail of Conflict.* Philadelphia, 1922
4. *Here Comes the Sun!* Philadelphia, 1924
5. *The Dragon-Slayer.* London, 1924
6. *A Certain Crossroad.* Philadelphia, 1925
7. *The Solitary Horseman.* Philadelphia, 1927
8. *Gay Courage.* Philadelphia, 1928
9. *Where's Peter?* Philadelphia, 1928
10. *Swift Water.* Philadelphia, 1929
11. *Lighted Windows.* Philadelphia, 1930
12. *Fair Tomorrow.* Philadelphia, 1931
13. *Uncharted Seas.* Philadelphia, 1932
14. *Hilltops Clear.* Philadelphia, 1933
15. *Come One, Fortune!* London, 1933
16. *We Ride the Gale!* Philadelphia, 1934
17. *With Banners.* Philadelphia, 1934
18. *It's a Great World!* Philadelphia, 1935
19. *Give Me One Summer.* Philadelphia, 1936
20. *As Long as I Live.* Philadelphia, 1937
21. *Today Is Yours.* Boston, 1938
22. *High of Heart.* Boston, 1938
23. *Across the Years.* Boston, 1939
24. *There Is Always Love.* Boston, 1940
25. *Star in Your Eyes.* Boston, 1941
26. *Where Beauty Dwells.* Boston, 1941
27. *When Hearts Are Light Again.* Boston, 1943
28. *Keeper of the Faith.* Boston, 1944
29. *Beyond the Sound of Guns.* Boston, 1945
30. *Bright Skies.* Boston, 1946
31. *Beckoning Trails.* Boston, 1947
32. *I Hear Adventure Calling.* Boston, 1948
33. *Love Came Laughing.* Bosotn, 1949
34. *To Love and to Honor.* Boston, 1950
35. *For All Your Life.* Boston, 1952

36. *I Take This Man.* Boston, 1954
37. *My Dearest Love.* Boston, 1954
38. *The Shadow of Suspicion.* Boston, 1955
39. *What Then Is Love.* Boston, 1954
40. *Look to the Stars.* Boston, 1957
41. *Behind the Cloud.* Boston, 1958
42. *With This Ring.* Boston, 1959
43. *How Can the Heart Forget?* Boston, 1960
44. *Throw Wide the Door.* Boston, 1962
45. *Follow Your Heart.* Boston, 1963
46. *A Candle in Her Heart.* Boston, 1964
47. *Forever and a Day.* Boston, 1965
48. *Spring Always Comes.* Boston, 1966
49. *A Key to Many Doors.* Boston, 1967
50. *In Times Like These.* Boston, 1968
51. *Love with Honor.* Boston, 1969
52. *No Time for Love.* Bosotn, 1970
53. *Forsaking All Others.* Boston, 1971
54. *The Shining Years.* Boston. 1972

Lorrimer, Clair [Patricia Denise Clark]
British, born February 21, 1921
Other pseudonym: Patricia Robins
1. *The Adventures of the Three Baby Bunnies,* as Patricia Robins. London, 1934
2. *Seven Days Leave,* as Patricia Robins. London, 1943
3. *To the Stars,* as Patricia Robins. London, 1944
4. *See No Evil,* as Patricia Robins. London, 1945
5. *Tree Fairies,* as Patricia Robins. London, 1945
6. *Sea Magic,* as Patricia Robins. London, 1946
7. *The Heart of a Rose,* as Patricia Robins. London, 1947
8. *Statues of Snow,* as Patricia Robins. London, 1947
9. *Three Loves,* as Patricia Robins. London, 1949
10. *Awake My Heart,* as Patricia Robins. London, 1950
11. *Beneath the Moon,* as Patricia Robins. London, 1951
12. *The Fair Deal,* as Patricia Robins. London, 1952
13. *Heart's Desire,* as Patricia Robins. London, 1953
14. *So This Is Love,* as Patricia Robins. London, 1953
15. *Heaven in Our Hearts,* as Patricia Robins. London, 1954
16. *One Who Cares,* as Patricia Robins. London, 1954
17. *Love Cannot Die,* as Patricia Robins. London, 1955
18. *The Foolish Heart,* as Patricia Robins. London, 1956
19. *Give All To Love,* as Patricia Robins. London, 1956
20. *Where Duty Lies,* as Patricia Robins. London, 1957
21. *He Is Mine,* as Patricia Robins. London, 1957
22. *Lonely Quest,* as Patricia Robins. London, 1959
23. *Lady Chatterley's Daughter,* as Patricia Robins. London, 1961
24. *The Last Chance,* as Patricia Robins. London, 1961
25. *The Long Wait,* as Patricia Robins. London, 1962
26. *The Runaways,* as Patricia Robins. London, 1962
27. *Seven Loves,* as Patricia Robins. London,. 1962
28. *With All My Love,* as Patricia Robins. London, 1962
29. *The Constant Heart,* as Patricia Robins. London, 1964
30. *Second Love,* as Patricia Robins. London, 1964
31. *The Night Is Mine,* as Patricia Robins. London, 1964
32. *There Is But One,* as Patricia Robins. London, 1965
33. *No More Loving,* as Patricia Robins. London, 1965
34. *Topaze Island,* as Patricia Robins. London, 1966
35. *The 100 Reward,* as Patricia Robins. Exeter (Eng), 1966
36. *The Uncertain Joy,* as Patricia Robins. London, 1966
37. *Forbidden,* as Patricia Robins. London, 1967
38. *A Voice in the Dark.* London, 1967
39. *Sapphire in the Sand,* as Patricia Robins. London, 1968
40. *Laugh on Friday,* as Patricia Robins. London, 1969
41. *No Stone Unturned,* as Patricia Robins. London, 1969
42. *Cinnabar House,* as Patricia Robins. London, 1970
43. *Under the Sky,* as Patricia Robins. London, 1970
44. *The Crimson Tapestry,* as Patricia Robins. London, 1972
45. *Play Fair with Love,* as Patricia Robins. London, 1972
46. *None But He,* as Patricia Robins. London, 1973
47. *The Shadow Falls.* New York, 1974
48. *Relentless Storm.* New York, 1975
49. *The Secret of Quarry House.* New York, 1976
50. *Mavreen.* London, 1976
51. *Tamarisk.* London, 1978
52. *Chantal.* London, 1980
53. *The Garden.* London, 1980
54. *The Chatelaine.* London, 1981
55. *The Wilderling.* London, 1982

Lovesey, Peter
British, born September 10, 1936
Pseudonyn: Peter Lear
1. *The Kings of Distance: A Study of Five Great Runners.* London, 1968
2. *The Guide to British Track and Field Literature 1275-1968.* London, 1969
3. *Wobble to Death.* London and New York, 1970
4. *The Detective Wore Silk Drawers.* London and New York, 1971
5. *Abracadaver.* London and New York, 1972
6. *Mad Hatter's Holiday: A Novel of Murder in Victorian Brighton.* London and New York, 1973
7. *Invitation to a Dynamite Party.* London, 1974
8. *The Tick of Death.* New York, 1974
9. *A Case of Spirits.* London and New York, 1975
10. *Swing, Swing Together.* London and New York, 1976
11. *Goldengirl,* as Peter Lear. London, 1977
12. *"The Historian: Once upon a Crime."* New York, 1977
13. *Waxwork.* London and New York, 1978
14. *The Official Centenary History of the Amateur Athletic Association.* London, 1979

Low, Dorothy Mackie [Lois Dorothea Low]
British, born July 15, 1916
Other pseudonyms: Zoe Cass, Lois Paxton
1. *Isle for a Stranger.* London, 1962
2. *Dear Liar.* London, 1963
3. *A Ripple on the Water.* London, 1964
4. *The Intruder.* London, 1965
5. *The Man Who Died Twice,* as Lois Paxton. London, 1968
6. *A House in the Country.* London, 1970
7. *The Quiet Sound of Fear,* as Lois Paxton. London and New York, 1971
8. *Who Goes There?* London, 1972
9. *Island of the Seven Hills,* as Zoe Cass. New York, 1974
10. *The Silver Leopard,* as Zoe Cass. New York, 1976
11. *A Twist in the Silk,* as Zoe Cass. London, 1980

Lowndes, Marie [Marie Adelaide Belloc Lowndes]
British, born in 1868, died November 14, 1947
Pseudonym: Philip Curtin
1. *H.R.H. the Prince of Wales: An Account of His Career* (published anonymously). London and New York, 1898
2. *The Philosophy of the Marquise.* London, 1899
3. *T.R.H. the Prince and Princess of Wales* (published anonymously). London, 1902
4. *The Heart of Penelope.* London, 1904
5. *Barbara Rebell.* London, 1905
6. *The Pulse of Life.* London, 1908
7. *The Uttermost Farthing.* London, 1908
8. *Studies in Wives.* London, 1909
9. *When No Man Pursueth.* London, 1910
10. *Jane Oglander.* London and New York, 1911
11. *The Chink in the Armour.* London and New York, 1912

12. *Mary Pechell.* London and New York, 1912
13. *The Lodger.* London and New York, 1913
14. *The End of Her Honeymoon.* New York, 1913
15. *Studies in Love and Terror.* London and New York, 1913
16. *Noted Murder Mysteries,* as Philip Curtin. London, 1914
17. *Told in Gallant Deeds: A Child's History of the War.* London, 1914
18. *Good Old Anna.* London, 1915
19. *The Red Cross Barge.* London, 1916
20. *Lilla: A Part of Her Life.* London, 1916
21. *Love and Hatred.* London and New York, 1917
22. *Out of the War?* London, 1918
23. *From the Vasty Deep.* London, 1920
24. *The Lonely House.* London and New York, 1920
25. *What Timmy Did.* London, 1921
26. *Why They Married.* London, 1923
27. *The Terriford Mystery.* London and New York, 1924
28. *Bread of Deceit.* London, 1925
29. *Some Men and Women.* London, 1925
30. *What Really Happened?* London and New York, 1926
31. *The Story of Ivy.* London, 1927
32. *Thou Shalt Not Kill.* London, 1927
33. *Cressida: No Mystery.* London, 1928
34. *Duchess Laura: Certain Days of Her Life.* London, 1929
35. *Love's Revenge.* London, 1929
36. *One of Those Ways.* London and New York, 1929
37. *The Key: A Love Drama.* London, 1930
38. *With All John's Love.* London, 1930
39. *Why Be Lonely?* with F.S.A. Lowndes. London, 1931
40. *Letty Lynton.* London and New York, 1931
41. *Vanderlyn's Adventure.* New York, 1931
42. *Jenny Newstead.* London and New York, 1932
43. *What Really Happened.* London, 1932
44. *Love Is a Flame.* London, 1932
45. *The Reason Why.* London, 1932
46. *Duchess Laura: Further Days from Her Life.* New York, 1933
47. *Another Man's Wife.* London and New York, 1934
48. *The Chianti Flask.* New York, 1934
49. *Who Rides on a Tiger?* New York, 1935
50. *And Call It Accident.* New York, 1936
51. *The Second Key.* New York, 1936
52. *The Marriage-Broker.* London, 1937
53. *The Empress Eugenie.* New York, 1938
54. *Motive.* London, 1938
55. *Lizzie Borden: A Study in Conjecture.* New York, 1939
56. *Reckless Angel.* New York, 1939
57. *The Christine Diamond.* London and New York, 1940
58. *"I, Too, Have Lived in Arcadia:" A Record of Love and of Childhood.* London, 1941
59. *Before the Storm.* New York, 1941
60. *What of the Night?* New York, 1943
61. *Where Love and Friendship Dwelt.* London and New York, 1943
62. *A Labour of Hercules.* London, 1943
63. *The Merry Wives of Westminster.* London, 1946
64. *A Passing World.* London, 1948
65. *She Dwelt with Beauty.* London, 1949
66. *The Young Hilaire Belloc.* London, 1956

Ludlum, Robert
American, born May 25, 1927
Pseudonyms: Jonathan Ryder, Michael Shepherd
1. *The Scarlatti Inheritance.* Cleveland and London, 1971
2. *The Osterman Weekend.* Cleveland and London, 1972
3. *The Matlock Paper.* New York and London, 1973
4. *Trevayne,* as Jonathan Ryder. New York, 1973
5. *The Cry of the Halidon,* as Jonathan Ryder. New York and London, 1974
6. *The Rhinemann Exchange.* New York, 1974
7. *The Road to Gandolfo,* as Michael Shepherd. New York, 1975
8. *The Gemini Contenders.* New York and London, 1976
9. *The Chancellor Manuscript.* New York, 1977
10. *The Matarese Circle.* New York and London, 1979

Lyall, Gavin (Tudor)
British, born May 9, 1932
1. *The Wrong Side of the Sky.* London and New York, 1961
2. *The Most Dangerous Game.* New York, 1963
3. *Midnight Plus One.* London and New York, 1965
4. *Shooting Script.* London and New York, 1966
5. *Venus with Pistol.* London and New York, 1969
6. *Blame the Dead.* London, 1972
7. *Judas Country.* London and New York, 1975
8. *Operation Warboard.* London and New York, 1976

Lynn, Margaret [Gladys Starkey Battye]
Born in 1915
1. *To See a Stranger.* London, 1961
2. *Stranger by Night.* London, 1963
3. *Whisper of Darkness.* London, 1965
4. *A Light in the Window.* London, 1967
5. *Sunday Evening.* London, 1969
6. *Sweet Epitaph.* London, 1971

Macardle, Dorothy (Margaret Callan)
Irish, born in 1899, died December 23, 1958
1. *Tragedies of Kerry 1922-1923.* Dublin (Ireland), 1924
2. *Earth-Bound: Nine Stories of Ireland.* Worcester (MA), 1924
3. *Witch's Brew.* London, 1931
4. *Ann Kavanagh.* New York, 1937
5. *The Children's Guest.* London, 1940
6. *Uneasy Freehold.* London, 1941
7. *The Loving-Cup.* London, 1943
8. *The Seed Was Kind.* London, 1944
9. *Fantastic Summer.* London, 1946
10. *Dark Enchantment.* London and New York, 1953
11. *Shakepeare, Man and Boy.* London, 1961

MacDonald, John D. (Dann)
American, born July 24, 1916
1. *The Brass Cupcake.* New York, 1950
2. *Judge Me Not.* New York, 1951
3. *Murder for the Bride.* New York, 1951
4. *Weep for Me.* New York, 1951
5. *Wine of the Dreamers.* New York, 1951
6. *The Damned.* New York, 1952
7. *Ballroom of the Skies.* New York, 1952
8. *Dead Low Tide.* New York, 1953
9. *The Neon Jungle.* New York, 1953
10. *Planet of the Dreamers.* New York, 1953
11. *Cancel All Our Vows.* New York, 1953
12. *All These Condemned.* New York, 1954
13. *Area of Suspicion.* New York, 1954
14. *Contrary Pleasure.* New York, 1954
15. *A Bullet for Cinderella.* New York, 1955
16. *Cry Hard, Cry Fast.* New York, 1955
17. *April Evil.* New York, 1956
18. *Border Town Girl.* New York, 1956
19. *Murder in the Wind.* New York, 1956
20. *You Live Once.* New York, 1956
21. *Hurricane.* London, 1957
22. *Death Trap.* New York, 1957
23. *The Empty Trap.* New York, 1957
24. *The Price of Murder.* New York, 1957
25. *A Man of Affairs.* New York, 1957

26. *Clemmie.* New York, 1958
27. *The Executioners.* New York, 1958
28. *Soft Touch.* New York, 1958
29. *The Deceivers.* New York, 1958
30. *The Beach Girls.* New York, 1959
31. *The Crossroads.* New York, 1959
32. *Deadly Welcome.* New York, 1959
33. *Please Write for Details.* New York, 1959
34. *The End of the Night.* New York, 1960
35. *The Only Girl in the Game.* New York, 1960
36. *Slam the Big Door.* New York, 1960
37. *On the Make.* New York, 1960
38. *One Monday We Killed Them All.* New York, 1961
39. *Where Is Janice Gantry?* New York, 1961
40. *You Kill Me.* New York, 1961
41. *Man-Trap.* London, 1961
42. *A Flash of Green.* New York, 1962
43. *The Girl, The Gold Watch, and Everything.* New York, 1962
44. *A Key to the Suite.* New York, 1962
45. *Cape Fear.* New York, 1962
46. *The Drowner.* New York, 1963
47. *On the Run.* New York, 1963
48. *I Could Go On Singing.* New York, 1963
49. *The Deep Blue Goodby.* New York, 1964
50. *Nightmare in Pink.* New York, 1964
51. *A Purple Place for Dying.* New York, 1964
52. *The Quick Red Fox.* New York, 1964
53. *A Deadly Shade of Gold.* New York, 1965
54. *Bright Orange for the Shroud.* New York, 1965
55. *The House Guests.* New York, 1965
56. *Darker Than Amber.* New York, 1966
57. *One Fearful Yellow Eye.* New York, 1966
58. *End of the Tiger and Other Stories.* New York, 1966
59. *The Last One Left.* New York, 1967
60. *Three for McGee.* New York, 1967
61. *Pale Gray for Guilt.* New York, 1968
62. *The Girl in the Plain Brown Wrapper.* New York, 1968
63. *No Deadly Drug.* New York, 1968
64. *Dress Her in Indigo.* New York, 1969
65. *The Long Lavender Look.* New York and London, 1970
66. *Five Star Fugitive.* London, 1970
67. *Seven.* New York, 1971
68. *A Tan and Sandy Silence.* New York, 1972
69. *The Scarlet Ruse.* New York, 1973
70. *The Turquoise Lament.* Philadelphia, 1973
71. *McGee.* London, 1975
72. *The Dreadful Lemon Sky.* Philadelphia, 1975
73. *Condominium.* Philadelphia, 1977
74. *The Empty Copper Sea.* Philadelphia, 1978
75. *The Green Ripper.* Philadelphia, 1979

MacDonald, Philip
British, born in 1899
Pseudonyms: Oliver Fleming, Anthony Lawless, Martin Porlock
1. *Ambrotox and Limping Dick,* as Oliver Fleming. London, 1920
2. *The Spandau Quid,* as Oliver Fleming. London, 1923
3. *The Rasp.* London, 1924
4. *Queen's Mate.* London, 1926
5. *Patrol.* London and New York, 1927
6. *The White Crow.* New York, 1928
7. *Likeness of Exe.* London, 1929
8. *The Link.* London and New York, 1930
9. *The Noose.* London and New York, 1930
10. *Rynox.* London, 1930
11. *The Rynox Murder Mystery.* New York, 1931
12. *The Choice.* London, 1931
13. *The Polferry Riddle.* New York, 1931
14. *Harbour,* as Anthony Lawless. London and New York, 1931
15. *Persons Unknown.* New York, 1931
16. *Murder Gone Mad.* London and New York, 1931
17. *The Wraith.* London and New York, 1931
18. *The Crime Conductor.* New York, 1931
19. *Mystery at Friar's Pardon,* as Martin Porlock. London, 1931
20. *Moonfisher.* London, 1931
21. *Rope to Spare.* London and New York, 1932
22. *The Polferry Mystery.* London, 1932
23. *The Mase.* London, 1932
24. *Mystery in Kensington Gore,* as Martin Porlock. London, 1932
25. *Escape,* as Martin Porlock. New York, 1932
26. *The Rynox Mystery.* London, 1933
27. *Death on My Left.* London and New York, 1933
28. *R.I.P.* London, 1933
29. *Menace.* New York, 1933
30. *X v. Rex,* as Martin Porlock. London, 1933
31. *Mystery of the Dead Police,* as Martin Porlock. New York, 1933
32. *The Mystery of Mr. X,* as Martin Porlock. London, 1934
33. *The Last Patrol.* London, 1934
34. *The Nursemaid Who Disappeared.* London, 1938
35. *Warrant for X.* New York, 1938
36. *The Dark Wheel.* London and New York, 1948
37. *Something to Hide.* New York, 1952
38. *Fingers of Fear and Other Stories.* London, 1953
39. *Guest in the House.* New York, 1955
40. *The Man Out of the Rain and Other Stories.* New York, 1955
41. *No Time for Terror.* New York, 1956
42. *The List of Adrian Messenger.* New York, 1959
43. *Sweet and Deadly.* Rockville Centre (NY), 1959
44. *Death and Chicanery.* New York, 1962

MacGill, Mrs. Patrick [Margaret MacGill]
Pseudonym: Margaret Gibbons
1. *The "Good-Night" Stories,* as Margaret Gibbons. London, 1912
2. *The Rose of Glenconnel.* London, 1916
3. *An Anzac's Bride.* London, 1917
4. *Whom Love Hath Chosen.* London, 1919
5. *The Bartered Bride.* London, 1920
6. *Each Hour a Peril.* London, 1921
7. *The Flame of Life.* London, 1921
8. *Hidden Fires.* London, 1921
9. *The Highest Bidder.* London, 1921
10. *His Dupe.* London, 1922
11. *Molly of the Lone Pine.* London, 1922
12. *Shifting Sands.* London, 1922
13. *A Lover on Loan.* London, 1923
14. *Her Undying Past.* London, 1924
15. *Love—and Carol.* London, 1925
16. *Her Dancing Partner.* London, 1926
17. *Love's Defiance.* London, 1926
18. *The Ukelele Girl.* London, 1927
19. *Dancers in the Dark.* London, 1929
20. *Painted Butterflies.* London, 1931
21. *Hollywood Madness.* London, 1936

MacInnes, Helen (Clark)
American, born October 7, 1907
1. *Above Suspicion.* Boston and London, 1941
2. *Assignment in Brittany.* Boston and London, 1941
3. *While Still We Live.* Boston, 1944
4. *The Unconquerable.* London, 1944

5. *Horizon.* London, 1945
6. *Friends and Lovers.* Boston, 1947
7. *Rest and Be Thankful.* Boston and London, 1949
8. *Neither Five Nor Three.* New York and London, 1951
9. *I and My True Love.* New York and London, 1953
10. *Pray for a Brave Heart.* New York and London, 1955
11. *North from Rome.* New York and London, 1958
12. *Decision at Delphi.* New York and London, 1961
13. *The Venetian Affair.* New York, 1963
14. *Home Is the Hunter.* New York, 1964
15. *The Double Image.* New York and London, 1966
16. *The Salzburg Connection.* New York, 1968
17. *Message from Malaga.* New York and London, 1971
18. *Snare of the Hunter.* New York and London, 1974
19. *Agent in Place.* New York and London, 1976
20. *Prelude to Terror.* New York and London, 1978

Mackinlay, Leila (Antoinette Sterling)
British, born September 5, 1910
Pseudonym: Brenda Grey
1. *Little Mountebank.* London, 1930
2. *Fame's Fetters.* London, 1931
3. *Madame Juno.* London, 1931
4. *An Exotic Young Lady.* London, 1932
5. *Willed to Wed.* London, 1933
6. *Modern Micawbers,* as Brenda Grey. London, 1933
7. *The Pro's Daughter.* London, 1934
8. *Shadow Lawn.* London, 1934
9. *Love Goes South.* London, 1935
10. *Into the Net.* London, 1935
11. *Night Bell.* London, 1936
12. *Young Man's Slave.* London, 1936
13. *Doubting Heart.* London, 1937
14. *Apron-Strings.* London, 1937
15. *Caretaker Within.* London, 1938
16. *Theme Song.* London, 1938
17. *Only Her Husband.* London, 1939
18. *The Reluctant Bride.* London, 1939
19. *Man Always Pays.* London, 1940
20. *Woman at the Wheel.* London, 1940
21. *Ridin' High.* London, 1941
22. *None Better Loved.* London, 1941
23. *Time on Her Hands.* London, 1942
24. *The Brave Live On.* London, 1942
25. *Green Limelight.* London, 1943
26. *Lady of the Torch.* London, 1944
27. *Two Walk Together.* London, 1945
28. *Piper's Pool.* London, 1946
29. *Piccadilly Inn.* London, 1946
30. *Blue Shutters.* London, 1947
31. *Echo of Applause.* London, 1948
32. *Peacock Hill.* London, 1948
33. *Restless Dream.* London, 1949
34. *Pilot's Point.* London, 1949
35. *Six Wax Candles.* London, 1950
36. *Spider Dance.* London, 1950
37. *Guilt's Pavilions.* London, 1951
38. *Five Houses.* London, 1952
39. *Unwise Wanderer.* London, 1952
40. *Cuckoo Cottage.* London, 1953
41. *She Married Another.* London, 1953
42. *Midnight Is Mine.* London, 1954
43. *Fiddler's Green.* London, 1954
44. *Vagabond Daughter.* London, 1955
45. *Musical Productions.* London, 1955
46. *Riddle of a Lady.* London, 1955
47. *Man of the Moment.* London, 1956
48. *She Moved to Music.* London, 1956
49. *Divided Duty.* London, 1957
50. *Mantle of Innocence.* London, 1957
51. *Love on a Shoestring.* London, 1958
52. *The Secret in Her Life.* London, 1958
53. *Seven Red Roses.* London, 1959
54. *Uneasy Conquest.* London, 1959
55. *Food of Love.* London, 1960
56. *Spotlight on Susan.* London, 1960
57. *Beauty's Tears.* London, 1961
58. *Spring Rainbow.* London, 1961
59. *Vain Delights.* London, 1962
60. *Broken Armour.* London, 1963
61. *False Relations.* London, 1963
62. *Fool of Virtue.* London, 1964
63. *Practice for Sale.* London, 1964
64. *Stardust in Her Eyes,* as Brenda Grey. London, 1964
65. *Girl of His Choice,* as Brenda Grey. London, 1965
66. *Ring of Hope.* London, 1965
67. *No Room for Loneliness.* London, 1965
68. *An Outside Chance.* London, 1966
69. *How High the Moon,* as Brenda Grey. London, 1966
70. *Throw Your Bouquet,* as Brenda Grey. London, 1967
71. *A Very Special Person,* as Brenda Grey. London, 1967
72. *The Third Boat.* London, 1967
73. *Mists of the Moor.* London, 1967
74. *Shadow of a Smile,* as Brenda Grey. London, 1968
75. *Frost at Dawn.* London, 1968
76. *Homesick for a Dream.* London, 1968
77. *Wanted—Girl Friday.* London, 1968
78. *Farewell to Sadness.* London, 1970
79. *The Silken Purse.* London, 1970
80. *Tread Softly on Dreams,* as Brenda Grey. London, 1970
81. *Son of Summer,* as Brenda Grey. London, 1970
82. *Mixed Singles,* as Brenda Grey. London, 1971
83. *Bridal Wreath.* London, 1971
84. *Husband in Name,* as Brenda Grey. London, 1972
85. *Strange Involvement.* London, 1972
86. *Birds of Silence.* London, 1974
87. *Fortune's Slave.* London, 1975
88. *Twilight Moment.* London, 1976
89. *The Uphill Path.* London, 1979

MacLean, Alistair (Stuart)
Swiss, born in 1922
Pseudonym: Ian Stuart
1. *H.M.S. Ulysses.* London, 1955
2. *The Guns of Navarone.* London and New York, 1957
3. *South by Java Head.* London and New York, 1958
4. *The Last Frontier.* London, 1959
5. *The Secret Ways.* New York, 1959
6. *Night Without End.* London and New York, 1960
7. *Fear Is the Key.* London and New York, 1961
8. *The Snow on the Ben,* as Ian Stuart. London, 1961
9. *The Dark Crusader,* as Ian Stuart. London, 1961
10. *The Black Shrike,* as Ian Stuart. New York, 1961
11. *The Golden Rendezvous.* London and New York, 1962
12. *The Satan Bug,* as Ian Stuart. London and New York, 1962
13. *All about Lawrence of Arabia.* London, 1962
14. *Lawrence of Arabia.* New York, 1962
15. *Ice Station Zebra.* London and New York, 1963
16. *When Eight Bells Toll.* London and New York, 1966
17. *When Eagles Dare.* London and New York, 1967
18. *Force 10 from Navarone.* London and New York, 1968
19. *Puppet on a Chain.* London and New York, 1969
20. *Caravan to Vaccares.* London and New York, 1970
21. *Bear Island.* London and New York, 1971
22. *Captain Cook.* London and New York, 1972
23. *The Way to Dusty Death.* London and New York, 1973

MacLean, Alistair

24. *Breakheart Pass.* London and New York, 1974
25. *Circus.* London and New York, 1975
26. *The Golden Gate.* London and New York, 1976
27. *Death from Disclosure,* as Ian Stuart. London, 1976
28. *Seawitch.* London and New York, 1977
29. *Goodbye California.* London, 1977
30. *Flood Tide,* as Ian Stuart. London, 1977
31. *Sand Trap,* as Ian Stuart. London, 1977
32. *Fatal Switch,* as Ian Stuart. London, 1978
33. *A Weekend to Kill,* as Ian Stuart. London, 1978

MacLeod, Charlotte (Matilda)
American, born November 12, 1922
Pseudonyms: Alisa Craig, Matilda Hughes

1. *Mystery of the White Knight.* New York, 1965
2. *The Food of Love,* as Matilda Hughes. New York, 1965
3. *Next Door to Danger.* New York, 1965
4. *Headlines for Caroline,* as Matilda Hughes. New York, 1967
5. *The Fat Lady's Ghost.* New York, 1968
6. *Mouse's Vineyard.* New York, 1968
7. *Ask Me No Questions.* Philadelphia, 1971
8. *Brass Pounder.* Boston, 1971
9. *Astrology for Sceptics.* New York, 1972
10. *King Devil.* New York, 1978
11. *Rest You Merry.* New York, 1978
12. *The Family Vault.* New York, 1979
13. *The Luck Runs Out.* New York, 1979
14. *We Dare Not Go a-Hunting.* New York, 1980
15. *The Withdrawing Room.* New York, 1980
16. *A Pint of Murder,* as Alisa Craig. New York, 1980
17. *The Grub-and-Stakers Move a Mountain,* as Alisa Craig. New York, 1981
18. *Murder Goes Mumming,* as Alisa Craig. New York, 1981
19. *The Palace Guard.* New York, 1981
20. *Wrack and Rune.* New York, 1982

MacLeod, Jean S.
British, born January 20, 1908
Pseudonym: Catherine Airlie

1. *Life for Two.* London, 1936
2. *Human Symphony.* London, 1937
3. *Summer Rain.* London, 1938
4. *Sequel to Youth.* London, 1938
5. *Mist Across the Hills.* London, 1938
6. *Dangerous Obsession.* London, 1938
7. *Run Away from Love.* London, 1939
8. *Return to Spring.* London, 1939
9. *The Rainbow Isle.* London, 1939
10. *The Whim of Fate.* London, 1940
11. *Silent Bondage.* London, 1940
12. *The Lonely Farrow.* London, 1940
13. *Heatherbloom.* London, 1940
14. *The Reckless Pilgrim.* London, 1941
15. *The Shadow of a Vow.* London, 1941
16. *One Way Out.* London, 1941
17. *Forbidden Rapture.* London, 1941
18. *Penalty for Living.* London, 1942
19. *Blind Journey.* London, 1942
20. *Bleak Heritage.* London, 1942
21. *Reluctant Folly.* London, 1942
22. *Unseen To-morrow.* London, 1943
23. *The Rowan Tree.* London, 1943
24. *Flower o' the Broom.* London, 1943
25. *The Circle of Doubt.* London, 1943
26. *Lamont of Ardgoyne.* London, 1944
27. *Two Paths.* London, 1944
28. *Brief Fulfillment.* London, 1945
29. *The Bridge of Years.* London, 1945
30. *This Much to Give.* London, 1945
31. *One Love.* London, 1945
32. *The Tranquil Haven.* London, 1946
33. *Sown in the Wind.* London, 1946
34. *The House of Oliver.* London, 1947
35. *And We in Dreams.* London, 1947
36. *The Chalet in the Sun.* London, 1948
37. *Ravenscrag.* London, 1948
38. *The Wild Macraes,* as Catherine Airlie. London, 1948
39. *From Such a Seed,* as Catherine Airlie. London, 1949
40. *Above the Lattice.* London, 1949
41. *To-morrow's Bargain.* London, 1949
42. *Katherine.* London, 1950
43. *The Valley of Palms.* London, 1950
44. *The Restless Years,* as Catherine Airlie. London, 1950
45. *Fabric of Dreams,* as Catherine Airlie. London, 1951
46. *Roadway to the Past.* London, 1951
47. *Once to Every Heart.* London, 1951
48. *Cameron of Gare.* London, 1952
49. *Music at Midnight.* London, 1952
50. *Strange Recompense,* as Catherine Airlie. London, 1952
51. *The Green Rushes,* as Catherine Airlie. London, 1953
52. *Hidden in the Wind,* as Catherine Airlie. London, 1953
53. *The Silent Valley.* London, 1953
54. *The Stranger in Their Midst.* London, 1953
55. *Dear Doctor Everett.* London, 1954
56. *The Man in Authority.* London, 1954
57. *A Wind Sighing,* as Catherine Airlie. London, 1954
58. *Nobody's Child,* as Catherine Airlie. London, 1954
59. *The Valley of Desire,* as Catherine Airlie. London, 1955
60. *The Ways of Love,* as Catherine Airlie. London, 1955
61. *After Long Journeying.* London, 1955
62. *Master of Glenkeith.* London, 1955
63. *The Way in the Dark.* London, 1956
64. *My Heart's in the Highlands.* London, 1956
65. *The Mountain of Stars,* as Catherine Airlie. London, 1956
66. *The Unguarded Hour,* as Catherine Airlie. London, 1956
67. *Land of Heart's Desire,* as Catherine Airlie. London, 1957
68. *Journey in the Sun.* London, 1957
69. *The Prisoner of Love.* London, 1958
70. *Red Lotus,* as Catherine Airlie. London, 1958
71. *The Last of the Kintyres,* as Catherine Airlie. London, 1959
72. *The Gated Road.* London, 1959
73. *Air Ambulance.* London and Toronto, 1959
74. *The Little Doctor.* London and Toronto, 1960
75. *Nurse Lang.* Toronto, 1960
76. *The White Cockade.* London, 1960
77. *Shadow on the Sun,* as Catherine Airlie. London, 1960
78. *One Summer's Day,* as Catherine Airlie. London, 1961
79. *The Country of the Heart,* as Catherine Airlie. London, 1961
80. *The Silver Dragon.* London, 1961
81. *Slave of the Wind.* London, 1962
82. *The Dark Fortune.* London, 1962
83. *Mountain Clinic.* Toronto, 1962
84. *The Unlived Year,* as Catherine Airlie. London, 1962
85. *Passing Stranger,* as Catherine Airlie. London, 1963
86. *The Wheels of Chance,* as Catherine Airlie. London, 1964
87. *Sugar Island.* London and Toronto, 1964
88. *The Black Cameron.* London and Toronto, 1964
89. *Crane Castle.* London and Toronto, 1965
90. *The Wolf of Heimra.* London, 1965
91. *Doctor's Daughter.* Toronto, 1965
92. *The Tender Glory.* London, 1965
93. *The Sea Change,* as Catherine Airlie. London, 1965
94. *Doctor Overboard,* as Catherine Airlie. Toronto, 1966
95. *The Drummer of Corrae.* London and Toronto, 1966
96. *Lament for a Lover.* London and Toronto, 1967

97. *Nurse Jane in Teneriffe,* as Catherine Airlie. Toronto, 1967
98. *The Master of Keills.* London, 1967
99. *The Bride of Mingalay.* London and Toronto, 1967
100. *The Moonflower.* London, 1967
101. *Summer Island.* London, 1968
102. *The Joshua Tree.* London, 1970
103. *The Fortress.* London, 1970
104. *The Way Through the Valley.* London and Toronto, 1971
105. *The Scent of Juniper.* London, 1971
106. *Moment of Decision.* Toronto, 1972
107. *Adam's Daughter.* London, 1972
108. *The Rainbow Days.* London and Toronto, 1973
109. *Over the Castle Wall.* London, 1974
110. *Time Suspended.* London, 1974
111. *The Phantom Pipes.* London, 1975
112. *Journey into Spring.* Toronto, 1976
113. *Island Stranger.* London, 1977
114. *Viking Song.* London, 1977
115. *The Ruaig Inheritance.* London, 1978
116. *Search for Yesterday.* London and Toronto, 1978
117. *Meeting in Madrid.* London, 1979
118. *Brief Enchantment.* London, 1979
119. *Black Sand, White Sand.* London, 1981

Maddocks, Margaret (Kathleen Avern)
British, born August 10, 1906
1. *Come Lasses and Lads.* London, 1944
2. *The Quiet House.* London, 1947
3. *Remembered Spring.* London, 1949
4. *Fair Shine the Day.* London, 1952
5. *Piper's Tune.* London, 1954
6. *A Summer Gone.* London, 1957
7. *The Frozen Fountain.* London, 1959
8. *Larksbrook.* London, 1962
9. *The Green Grass.* London, 1963
10. *November Tree.* London, 1964
11. *The Silver Answer.* London, 1965
12. *Dance Barefoot.* London, 1966
13. *Fool's Enchantment.* London, 1968
14. *Thea.* London, 1969
15. *The Weathercock.* London, 1971
16. *A View of the Sea.* London, 1973
17. *The Moon Is Square.* London, 1975
18. *An Unlessoned Girl.* London, 1977

Mainwaring, Daniel
American, born in 1902, died in 1978
Pseudonyn: Geoffrey Homes
1. *One Against the Earth.* New York, 1933
2. *The Doctor Died at Dusk,* as Geoffrey Homes. New York, 1936
3. *The Man Who Murdered Himself,* as Geoffrey Homes. New York and London, 1936
4. *The Man Who Didn't Exist,* as Geoffrey Homes. New York, 1937
5. *The Man Who Murdered Goliath,* as Geoffrey Homes. New York, 1938
6. *Then There Were Three,* as Geoffrey Homes. New York, 1938
7. *No Hands on the Clock,* as Geoffrey Homes. New York, 1939
8. *Finders Keepers,* as Geoffrey Homes. New York, 1940
9. *Forty Whacks,* as Geoffrey Homes. New York, 1941
10. *The Street of the Crying Woman,* as Geoffrey Homes. New York, 1942
11. *Seven Died,* as Geoffrey Homes. London, 1943
12. *The Hill of the Terrified Monk,* as Geoffrey Homes. New York, 1943
13. *Six Silver Handles,* as Geoffrey Homes. New York, 1944
14. *Build My Gallows High,* as Geoffrey Homes. New York, 1946
15. *Stiffs Don't Vote,* as Geoffrey Homes. New York, 1947
16. *The Case of the Mexican Knife,* as Geoffrey Homes. New York, 1948
17. *Dead as a Dummy,* as Geoffrey Homes. New York, 1949
18. *The Case of the Unhappy Angels,* as Geoffrey Homes. New York, 1950

Maling, Arthur (Gordon)
American, born June 11, 1923
1. *Decoy.* New York, 1969
2. *Go-Between.* New York, 1970
3. *Loophole.* New York, 1971
4. *The Snowman.* New York, 1973
5. *Dingdong.* New York, 1974
6. *Bent Man.* New York, 1975
7. *Ripoff.* New York, 1976
8. *Schroeder's Game.* New York and London, 1977
9. *Lucky Devil.* New York, 1978
10. *The Rheingold Route.* New York and London, 1979
11. *The Koberg Link.* New York, 1979

Manley-Tucker, Audrie
Pseudonym: Linden Howard
1. *Leonie.* London, 1958
2. *Lost Melody.* London, 1959
3. *A Love Song in Springtime.* London, 1960
4. *Piper's Gate.* London, 1960
5. *Dark Bondage.* London, 1961
6. *A Memory of Summer.* London, 1961
7. *The Promise of Morning.* London, 1962
8. *Candlemas Street.* London, 1963
9. *The Loved and the Cherished.* London, 1964
10. *A Rainbow in My Hand.* London, 1965
11. *Shadow of Yesterday.* London, 1965
12. *Champagne Girl.* London, 1967
13. *Love, Spread Your Wings.* London, 1967
14. *Door Without a Key.* London, 1967
15. *Julie Barden, District Nurse.* London, 1968
16. *Return to Sender.* London, 1968
17. *Julie Barden, Doctor's Wife.* London, 1969
18. *A Room Without a Door.* London, 1970
19. *Assistance Unlimited.* London, 1971
20. *Every Goose a Swan.* London, 1972
21. *Shetland Summer.* London, 1973
22. *The Piper in the Hills.* London, 1974
23. *Life Begins Tomorrow.* London, 1975
24. *Foxglove Country,* as Linden Howard. New York, 1977
25. *Two for Joy.* London, 1979
26. *The Devil's Lady,* as Linden Howard. London and New York, 1980
27. *Tamberlyn.* London, 1981

Marlowe, Dan J. (James)
American, born July 10, 1914
1. *Doorway to Death.* New York, 1959
2. *Killer with a Key.* New York, 1959
3. *Doom Service.* New York, 1960
4. *The Fatal Frails.* New York, 1960
5. *Shake a Crooked Town.* New York, 1961
6. *Backfire.* New York, 1961
7. *The Name of the Game Is Death.* New York, 1962
8. *Strongarm.* New York, 1963
9. *Never Live Twice.* New York, 1964
10. *Death Deep Down.* New York, 1965
11. *Four for the Money.* New York, 1966

12. *The Vengeance Man.* New York, 1966
13. *The Raven Is a Blood Red Bird.* New York, 1967
14. *Route of the Red Gold.* New York, 1967
15. *One Endless Hour.* New York, 1969
16. *Operation Fireball.* New York, 1969
17. *Flashpoint.* New York, 1970
18. *Operation Breakthrough.* New York, 1971
19. *Operation Drumfire.* New York and London, 1972
20. *Operation Checkmate.* New York, 1972
21. *Operation Flashpoint.* New York and London, 1972
22. *Operation Stranglehold.* New York, 1973
23. *Operation Whiplash.* New York, 1973
24. *Operation Overkill.* London, 1973
25. *Operation Hammerlock.* New York, 1974
26. *Operation Deathmaker.* New York, 1975
27. *Operation Endless Hour.* New York, 1975

Marlowe, Derek
British, born May 21, 1938
1. *A Dandy in Aspic.* London and New York, 1966
2. *The Memoirs of Venus Lackey.* London and New York, 1968
3. *A Single Summer with L.B.: The Summer of 1816.* London, 1969
4. *Echoes of Celandine.* London and New York, 1970
5. *A Single Summer with Lord B.* New York, 1970
6. *Do You Remember England?* London and New York, 1972
7. *Somebody's Sister.* London and New York, 1974
8. *Nightshade.* London, 1975
9. *The Disappearance.* London, 1977
10. *The Rich Boy from Chicago.* London, 1980

Marlowe, Hugh [Henry Patterson]
British, born July 27, 1929
Other pseudonyms: Martin Fallon, James Graham, Jack Higgins, Harry Paterson
1. *Sad Wind from the Sea,* as Harry Paterson. London, 1959
2. *Cry of the Hunter,* as Harry Paterson. London, 1960
3. *The Thousand Faces of Night,* as Harry Paterson. London, 1961
4. *Comes the Dark Stranger,* as Harry Paterson. London, 1962
5. *Hell Is Too Crowded,* as Harry Paterson. London, 1962
6. *Hell Is Too Crowded,* as Jack Higgins. New York, 1962
7. *The Testament of Caspar Schultz,* as Martin Fallon. London and New York, 1962
8. *The Testament of Caspar Schultz,* as Jack Higgins. New York, 1962
9. *Pay the Devil,* as Harry Paterson. London, 1963
10. *The Dark Side of the Island,* as Harry Paterson. London, 1963
11. *The Dark Side of the Island,* as Jack Higgins. New York, 1963
12. *Seven Pillars to Hell.* London and New York, 1963
13. *Year of the Tiger,* as Martin Fallon. London and New York, 1963
14. *Year of the Tiger,* as Jack Higgins. New York, 1963
15. *A Phoenix in the Blood,* as Harry Paterson. London, 1964
16. *Thunder at Noon,* as Harry Paterson. London, 1964
17. *Wrath of the Lion,* as Harry Paterson. London, 1964
18. *Wrath of the Lion,* as Jack Higgins. New York, 1964
19. *Passage by Night.* London and New York, 1964
20. *The Graveyard Shift,* as Harry Paterson. London, 1965
21. *The Keys of Hell,* as Martin Fallon. London and New York, 1965
22. *The Keys of Hell,* as Jack Higgins. New York, 1965
23. *The Iron Tiger,* as Harry Paterson. London, 1966
24. *The Iron Tiger,* as Jack Higgins. New York, 1966
25. *A Candle for the Dead.* London and New York, 1966
26. *Midnight Never Comes,* as Martin Fallon. London, 1966
27. *Midnight Never Comes,* as Jack Higgins. New York, 1966
28. *Brought in Dead,* as Harry Paterson. London, 1967
29. *Dark Side of the Street,* as Martin Fallon. London, 1967
30. *Dark Side of the Street,* as Jack Higgins. New York, 1967
31. *Hell Is Always Today,* as Harry Paterson. London, 1968
32. *Hell Is Always Today,* as Jack Higgins. New York, 1968
33. *East of Desolation,* as Jack Higgins. London, 1968
34. *The Violent Enemy.* London, 1969
35. *A Fine Night for Dying,* as Martin Fallon. London, 1969
36. *A Fine Night for Dying,* as Jack Higgins. New York, 1969
37. *In the Hour Before Midnight,* as Jack Higgins. London, 1969
38. *The Sicilian Heritage,* as Jack Higgins. New York, 1970
39. *Night Judgment at Sinos,* as Jack Higgins. London, 1970
40. *A Game for Heroes,* as James Graham. London and New York, 1970
41. *Toll for the Brave,* as Harry Paterson. London, 1971
42. *Toll for the Brave,* as Jack Higgins. New York, 1971
43. *The Last Place God Made,* as Jack Higgins. London, 1971
44. *The Wrath of God,* as James Graham. London and New York, 1971
45. *The Savage Day,* as Jack Higgins. London and New York, 1972
46. *The Khufra Run,* as James Graham. London, 1972
47. *A Prayer for the Dying,* as Jack Higgins. London, 1973
48. *Bloody Passage,* as James Graham. London, 1974
49. *The Run to Morning,* as James Graham. New York, 1974
50. *The Eagle Has Landed,* as Jack Higgins. London and New York, 1975
51. *The Valhalla Exchange,* as Harry Paterson. New York, 1976
52. *The Valhalla Exchange,* as Jack Higgins. New York, 1976
53. *Storm Warning,* as Jack Higgins. London and New York, 1976
54. *Day of Judgement,* as Jack Higgins. London, 1978
55. *To Catch a King,* as Jack Higgins. New York, 1979
56. *To Catch a King,* as Harry Paterson. London, 1979
57. *The Cretan Lover,* as Jack Higgins. London and New York, 1980

Marquand, John (Phillips)
American, born November 10, 1893, died July 16, 1960
1. *Prince and Boatswain: Sea Tales from the Recollections of Rear-Admiral Charles E. Clark.* Greenfield (MA), 1915
2. *The Unspeakable Gentleman.* New York and London, 1922
3. *Four of a Kind.* New York, 1923
4. *The Black Cargo.* New York and London, 1925
5. *Lord Timothy Dexter of Newburyport, Mass.* New York and London, 1926
6. *Do Tell Me, Doctor Johnson.* Privately printed, 1928
7. *Warning Hill.* Boston, 1930
8. *Haven's End.* Boston, 1933
9. *Ming Yellow.* Boston and London, 1935
10. *No Hero.* Boston, 1935
11. *Thank You, Mr. Moto.* Boston, 1936
12. *Think Fast, Mr. Moto.* Boston, 1937
13. *The Late George Apley: A Novel in the Form of a Memoir.* Boston and London, 1937
14. *Mr. Moto Is So Sorry.* Boston, 1938
15. *Wickford Point.* Boston and London, 1939
16. *Mr. Moto Takes a Hand.* London, 1940
17. *Don't Ask Questions.* London, 1941
18. *Last Laugh, Mr. Moto.* Boston, 1942
19. *H.M. Pulham, Esquire.* Boston and London, 1942
20. *So Little Time.* Boston, 1943
21. *Repent in Haste.* Boston, 1945
22. *B.F.'s Daughter.* Boston, 1946
23. *The Late George Apley.* New York, 1946

24. *Polly Fulton.* London, 1947
25. *It's Loaded, Mr. Bauer.* London, 1949
26. *Point of No Return.* Boston and London, 1949
27. *Sun, Sea, and Sand.* New York, 1950
28. *Melville Goodwin, USA.* Boston, 1951
29. *Federalist Newburyport; or, Can Historical Fiction Remove a Fly from Amber?* New York, 1952
30. *Sincerely, Willis Wayde.* Boston and London, 1955
31. *Thirty Years.* Boston, 1954
32. *Stopover: Tokyo.* Boston and London, 1957
33. *Life at Happy Knoll.* Boston, 1957
34. *Women and Thomas Harrow.* Boston, 1958
35. *Timothy Dexter Revisited.* Boston, 1960
36. *The Last of Mr. Moto.* New York, 1963
37. *Right You Are, Mr. Moto.* New York, 1977

Marsh, Jean [Evelyn Marshall]
British, born December 2, 1897
Other pseudonym: Lesley Bourne
1. *The Shore House Mystery.* London, 1931
2. *Murder Next Door.* London, 1933
3. *Death Stalks the Bride.* London, 1943
4. *On the Trail of the Albatross.* London, 1950
5. *Secret of the Pygmy Herd.* London, 1951
6. *Identity Unwanted.* London, 1951
7. *Death Visits the Circus.* London, 1953
8. *The Pattern Is Murder.* London, 1954
9. *Death Among the Stars.* London, 1955
10. *Death at Peak Hour.* London, 1957
11. *Trouble for Tembo,* as Lesley Bourne. London, 1958
12. *Adventure with a Boffin.* London, 1962
13. *The Valley of Silent Sound.* London, 1962
14. *Sand Against the Wind.* London, 1973
15. *Loving Partnership.* London, 1978
16. *The Family at Castle Trevissa.* London, 1979
17. *Bewdley, XV Century Sanctuary Town.* Kinver, 1979
18. *All Saints' Centenary.* Kinver, 1980
19. *Sawdust and Dreams.* London, 1980
20. *Mistress of Tanglewood.* London, 1981
21. *Unbidden Dreams.* London, 1980
22. *The Rekindled Flame.* London, 1982
23. *This Foolish Love.* London, 1982

Marsh, Ngaio [Edith Ngaio Marsh]
Born in New Zealand, April 23, 1899
1. *A Man Lay Dead.* London, 1934
2. *Enter a Murderer.* London, 1935
3. *The Nursing-Home Murder.* London, 1935
4. *Death in Ecstasy.* London, 1936
5. *Vintage Murder.* London, 1937
6. *Artists in Crime.* London and New York, 1938
7. *Death in a White Tie.* London and New York, 1938
8. *Overture to Death.* London and New York, 1939
9. *Death at the Bar.* London and Boston, 1940
10. *Death of a Peer.* Boston, 1940
11. *Surfeit of Lampreys.* London, 1941
12. *Death and the Dancing Footman.* Boston, 1941
13. *New Zealand.* London, 1942
14. *Colour Scheme.* London and Boston, 1943
15. *Died in the Wool.* London and Boston, 1945
16. *A Play Toward: A Note on Play Production.* Christchurch (New Zealand), 1946
17. *Final Curtain.* London and Boston, 1947
18. *Swing, Brother, Swing.* London, 1949
19. *A Wreath for Rivera.* Boston, 1949
20. *Opening Night.* London, 1951
21. *Night at the Vulcan.* Boston, 1951
22. *Spinsters in Jeopardy.* Boston, 1953
23. *The Bride of Death.* New York, 1955
24. *Scales of Justice.* London and Boston, 1955
25. *Death of a Fool.* Boston, 1956
26. *Off with His Head.* London, 1957
27. *Singing in the Shrouds.* Boston, 1958
28. *False Scent.* Boston and London, 1960
29. *Perspectives: The New Zealander and the Visual Arts.* Auckland (New Zealand), 1960
30. *Hand in Glove.* Boston and London, 1962
31. *Dead Water.* Boston, 1963
32. *New Zealand.* New York, 1964
33. *Black and Honeydew: An Autobiography.* Boston, 1965
34. *Killer Dolphin.* Boston, 1966
35. *Death at the Dolphin.* London, 1967
36. *Clutch of Constables.* London, 1968
37. *When in Rome.* London, 1970
38. *Tied Up in Tinsel.* London and Boston, 1972
39. *Black as He's Painted.* London and Boston, 1975
40. *Last Ditch.* Boston and London, 1977
41. *Grave Mistake.* Boston and London, 1978

Marshall, Edison (Tesla)
American, born August 28, 1894, died October 29, 1967
Pseudonym: Hall Hunter
1. *The Voice of the Pack.* Boston and London, 1920
2. *The Strength of the Pines.* Boston and London, 1921
3. *The Snowshoe Trail.* Boston and London, 1921
4. *Sheperds of the Wild.* Boston and London, 1922
5. *The Sky Line of Spruce.* Boston, 1922
6. *The Heart of Little Shikara and Other Stories.* Boston, 1922
7. *The Land of Forgotten Men.* Boston, 1923
8. *The Isle of Retribution.* Boston and London, 1923
9. *The Death Bell.* New York, 1924
10. *Seward's Folly.* Boston and London, 1924
11. *The Sleeper of the Moonlit Ranges.* New York and London, 1925
12. *Ocean Gold.* New York, 1925
13. *Campfire Courage: The Woodsmoke Boys in the Canadian Rockies.* New York, 1926
14. *Child of the Wild: A Story of Alaska.* New York and London, 1926
15. *The Deadfall.* New York and London, 1927
16. *The Far Call.* New York and London, 1928
17. *The Fish Hawk.* New York and London, 1929
18. *Singing Arrows.* New York and London, 1930
19. *The Missionary.* New York and London, 1930
20. *The Doctor of Lonesome River.* New York and London, 1931
21. *The Deputy at Snow Mountain.* New York and London, 1932
22. *Forlorn Island.* New York and London, 1932
23. *The Light in the Jungle.* New York, 1933
24. *The Splendid Quest.* New York, 1934
25. *Ogden's Strange Story.* New York, 1934
26. *Dian of the Lost Land.* New York, 1935
27. *Sam Campbell, Gentlemen.* New York, 1935
28. *The Stolen God.* New York, 1936
29. *The White Brigand.* New York, 1937
30. *Darzee, Girl of India.* New York, 1937
31. *The Jewel of Malabar.* New York and London, 1938
32. *Benjamin Blake.* New York, 1941
33. *Great Smith.* New York, 1943
34. *The Upstart.* New York, 1945
35. *Shikar and Safari: Reminiscences of Jungle Hunting.* New York, 1947
36. *Yankee Pasha: The Adventures of Jason Starbuck.* New York, 1948
37. *Castle in the Swamp: A Tale of Old Carolina.* New York, 1948

38. *Gypsy Sixpence.* New York, 1949
39. *Love Stories of India.* New York, 1950
40. *The Infinite Woman.* New York, 1950
41. *The Viking.* New York, 1951
42. *The Bengal Tiger: A Tale of India,* as Hall Hunter. New York, 1952
43. *American Captain.* New York, 1954
44. *Caravan to Xanadu: A Novel of Marco Polo.* New York, 1954
45. *The Gentleman.* New York and London, 1956
46. *The Heart of the Hunter.* New York, 1956
47. *The Inevitable Hour: A Novel of Martinique.* New York, 1957
48. *Princess Sophia.* New York, 1958
49. *The Pagan King.* New York, 1959
50. *Earth Giant.* New York, 1960
51. *West with the Vikings.* New York, 1961
52. *The Conqueror.* New York, 1962
53. *Cortez and Marina.* New York, 1963
54. *The Lost Colony.* New York, 1964

Marshall, Rosamond (Van der Zee)
American, born October 17, 1902, died November 13, 1957
1. *None But the Brave: A Story of Holland.* Boston, 1942
2. *Kitty.* New York, 1943
3. *The Treasure of Shafto.* New York, 1946
4. *Duchess Hotspur.* New York, 1946
5. *Celeste.* New York, 1949
6. *Laird's Choice.* New York, 1951
7. *Bond of the Flesh.* New York, 1952
8. *Jane Hadden.* New York, 1952
9. *The Temptress.* New York, 1952
10. *The General's Wench.* New York, 1953
11. *The Dollmaster.* New York, 1954
12. *The Loving Meddler.* New York, 1954
13. *Rogue Cavalier.* New York, 1955
14. *The Rib of the Hawk.* New York, 1956
15. *Captain Ironhand.* New York and London, 1957
16. *The Bixby Girls.* New York, 1957

Martin, Rhona
British, born June 3, 1922
1. *Gallows Wedding.* London, 1978
2. *Margo Walk.* London, 1981

Mason, A.E.W. (Alfred Edward Woodley)
British, born May 7, 1865, died November 22, 1948
1. *A Romance of Wastdale.* London and New York, 1895
2. *The Courtship of Morrice Buckler.* London, 1896
3. *Lawrence Clavering.* London and New York, 1897
4. *The Philanderers.* London and New York, 1897
5. *The Watchers.* Bristol and New York, 1899
6. *Miranda of the Balcony.* London and New York, 1899
7. *Parson Kelly.* London and New York, 1900
8. *Ensign Knightley and Other Stories.* London and New York, 1901
9. *Clementina.* London and New York, 1901
10. *The Four Feathers.* London and New York, 1902
11. *The Truants.* London and New York, 1904
12. *Running Water.* London and New York, 1907
13. *The Broken Road.* London and New York, 1907
14. *At the Villa Rose.* London and New York, 1910
15. *The Clock.* New York, 1910
16. *Making Good.* New York, 1910
17. *The Turnstile.* London and New York, 1912
18. *The Witness for the Defence.* London, 1913
19. *The Four Corners of the World.* London and New York, 1917
20. *The Episode of the Thermometer.* New York, 1918
21. *The Summons.* London and New York, 1920
22. *The Royal Exchange.* London, 1920
23. *The Winding Stair.* London and New York, 1923
24. *The House of the Arrow.* London and New York, 1924
25. *No Other Tiger.* London and New York, 1927
26. *The Prisoner in the Opal.* London and New York, 1928
27. *The Dean's Elbow.* London, 1930
28. *The Three Gentlemen.* London and New York, 1932
29. *The Sapphire.* London and New York, 1933
30. *Dilemmas.* London, 1934
31. *They Wouldn't Be Chessmen.* London and New York, 1935
32. *Sir George Alexander and the St. James' Theatre.* London, 1935
33. *Fire over England.* London and New York, 1936
34. *The Drum.* London and New York, 1937
35. *Konigsmark.* London, 1938
36. *The Secret Fear.* New York, 1940
37. *The Life of Francis Drake.* London, 1941
38. *Musk and Amber.* London and New York, 1942
39. *The House in Lordship Lane.* London and New York, 1946

Masur, Harold Q.
American, born January 29, 1909
1. *Bury Me Deep.* New York, 1947
2. *Suddenly a Corpse.* New York, 1949
3. *You Can't Live Forever.* New York, 1950
4. *So Rich, So Lovely, and So Dead.* New York, 1952
5. *The Big Money.* New York, 1954
6. *Tall, Dark, and Deadly.* New York, 1956
7. *The Last Gamble.* New York, 1958
8. *The Last Breath.* London, 1958
9. *Murder on Broadway.* New York, 1959
10. *Send Another Hearse.* New York and London, 1960
11. *The Name Is Jordan.* New York, 1962
12. *Make a Killing.* New York and London, 1964
13. *The Legacy Lenders.* New York and London, 1967
14. *The Attorney.* New York, 1973

Mather, Anne
Pseudonym: Caroline Fleming
1. *Caroline.* London, 1965
2. *Beloved Stranger.* London, 1966
3. *Design for Loving.* London, 1966
4. *Masquerade.* London, 1966
5. *The Arrogance of Love.* London, 1968
6. *Dark Venetian,* as Caroline Fleming. London, 1969
7. *The Enchanted Island.* London, 1969
8. *Dangerous Rhapsody.* London, 1969
9. *Legend of Lexandros.* London, 1969
10. *Dangerous Enchantment.* London, 1969
11. *Tangled Tapestry.* London, 1969
12. *The Arrogant Duke.* London and Toronto, 1970
13. *Charlotte's Hurricane.* London, 1970
14. *Lord of Zaracus.* London, 1970
15. *Sweet Revenge.* London, 1970
16. *Who Rides the Tiger.* London, 1970
17. *Moon Witch.* London, 1970
18. *Master of Falcon's Head.* London, 1970
19. *The Reluctant Governess.* London, 1971
20. *The Pleasure and the Pain.* London, 1971
21. *The Sanchez Tradition.* London, 1971
22. *Storm in a Rain Barrel.* London, 1971
23. *Dark Enemy.* London, 1971
24. *All the Fire.* London, 1971
25. *The High Valley.* London, 1971
26. *The Autumn of the Witch.* London, 1972
27. *Living with Adam.* London, 1972

28. *A Distant Sound of Thunder.* London, 1972
29. *Monkshood.* London, 1972
30. *Prelude to Enchantment.* London, 1972
31. *The Night of the Bulls.* London, 1972
32. *Jake Howard's Wife.* London, 1973
33. *A Savage Beauty.* London, 1973
34. *Chase a Green Shadow.* London, 1973
35. *White Rose of Winter.* London, 1973
36. *Mask of Scars.* London, 1973
37. *The Waterfalls of the Moon.* London, 1973
38. *The Shrouded Web.* London, 1973
39. *Seen by Candlelight.* Toronto, 1974
40. *Legacy of the Past.* Toronto, 1974
41. *Leopard in the Snow.* London and Toronto, 1974
42. *The Japanese Screen.* London, 1974
43. *Rachel Trevellyan.* London, 1974
44. *Silver Fruit upon Silver Trees.* London, 1974
45. *Dark Moonless Night.* London, 1974
46. *Witchstone.* London, 1974
47. *No Gentle Possession.* Toronto, 1975
48. *Pale Dawn, Dark Sunset.* London and Toronto, 1975
49. *Take What You Want.* London, 1975
50. *Come the Vintage.* London, 1975
51. *Dark Castle.* London, 1975
52. *Country of the Falcon.* London, 1975
53. *For the Love of Sara.* London, 1975
54. *Valley Deep, Mountain High.* London, 1976
55. *The Smouldering Flame.* London, 1976
56. *Wild Enchantress.* London, 1975
57. *Beware the Beast.* London, 1976
58. *Devil's Mount.* London, 1976
59. *Forbidden.* London, 1976
60. *Come Running.* London, 1976
61. *Alien Wife.* Toronto, 1977
62. *The Medici Lover.* London and Toronto, 1977
63. *Born Out of Love.* Toronto, 1977
64. *A Trial Marriage.* Toronto, 1977
65. *Devil in Velvet.* London, 1977
66. *Loren's Baby.* London and Toronto, 1978
67. *Rooted in Dishonour.* London and Toronto, 1978
68. *Proud Harvest.* London and Toronto, 1978
69. *Scorpions' Dance.* London and Toronto, 1978
70. *Captive Destiny.* London, 1978
71. *Fallen Angel.* London, 1978
72. *Apollo's Seed.* London, 1979
73. *Hell or High Water.* London, 1979
74. *The Judas Trap.* London, 1979
75. *Lure of Eagles.* London and Toronto, 1979
76. *Melting Fire.* London, 1979
77. *Images of Love.* London and Toronto, 1980
78. *Sandstorm.* London and Toronto, 1980
79. *Spirit of Atlantis.* London and Toronto, 1980
80. *Whisper of Darkness.* London and Toronto, 1980
81. *Castles of Sand.* London, 1981
82. *Forbidden Flame.* London and Toronto, 1981
83. *A Haunting Compulsion.* London and Toronto, 1981
84. *Innocent Obsession.* London and Toronto, 1981
85. *Edge of Temptation.* London and Toronto, 1982

Mather, Berkely [John Evan Weston Davies]
British
1. *The Achilles Affair.* London and New York, 1959
2. *The Pass Beyond Kashmir.* London and New York, 1960
3. *Geth Straker and Other Stories.* London, 1962
4. *The Road and the Star.* London and New York, 1965
5. *Genghis Khan.* London and New York, 1965
6. *The Gold of Malabar.* London and New York, 1967
7. *The Springers.* London, 1968
8. *A Spy for a Spy.* New York, 1968
9. *The Break in the Line.* London, 1970
10. *The Break.* New York, 1970
11. *The Terminators.* London and New York, 1970
12. *Snowline.* London and New York, 1973
13. *The White Dacoit.* London, 1974
14. *With Extreme Prejudice.* London, 1975
15. *The Memsahib.* London and New York, 1977
16. *The Pagoda Tree.* London, 1979

Maugham, Robin [Robert Cecil Romer Maugham]
British, born May 17, 1916
Other pseudonym: David Griffin
1. *The 1946 MS.* London, 1943
2. *Come to Dust.* London, 1945
3. *Approach to Palestine.* London, 1947
4. *Nomad.* London, 1947
5. *The Servant.* London, 1948
6. *North African Notebook.* London, 1948
7. *Line on Ginger.* London, 1949
8. *Journey to Siwa.* London, 1950
9. *The Rough and the Smooth.* London and New York, 1951
10. *Behind the Mirror.* London and New York, 1955
11. *The Man with Two Shadows.* London, 1958
12. *Odd Man In.* London, 1958
13. *The Servant.* London, No date
14. *A Lonesome Road.* London, 1959
15. *The Slaves of Timbuktu.* London and New York, 1961
16. *November Reef: A Novel of the South Seas.* London, 1962
17. *The Joyita Mystery.* London, 1962
18. *Mister Lear.* London, 1963
19. *The Green Shade.* London and New York, 1966
20. *Somerset and All the Maughams.* London and New York, 1966
21. *The Wrong People,* as David Griffin. New York, 1967
22. *The Intruder.* London, 1968
23. *The Second Window.* London and New York, 1968
24. *The Link: A Victorian Mystery.* London and New York, 1969
25. *Enemy!* London, 1971
26. *Testament: Cairo 1898.* London, 1972
27. *The Last Encounter.* London, 1972
28. *Escape from the Shadows: Robin Maugham, His Autobiography.* London, 1972
29. *The Barrier.* London, 1973
30. *The Black Tent and Other Stories.* London, 1973
31. *The Sign.* London and New York, 1974
32. *Search for Nirvana.* London, 1975
33. *Knock on Teak.* London, 1976
34. *Lovers in Exile.* London, 1977
35. *Conversations with Willie: Recollections of W. Somerset Maugham.* London and New York, 1978
36. *The Dividing Line.* London, 1979

Maugham, W. Somerset [William Somerset Maugham]
British, born January 25, 1874, died December 16, 1965
1. *Liza of Lambeth.* London, 1897
2. *The Making of a Saint.* Boston and London, 1898
3. *Orientations.* London, 1899
4. *The Hero.* London, 1901
5. *Mrs. Craddock.* London, 1902
6. *A Man of Honour.* London, 1903
7. *The Merry-Go-Round.* London, 1904
8. *The Land of the Blessed Virgin: Sketches and Impressions of Andalusia.* London, 1905
9. *The Bishop's Apron: A Study in the Origins of a Great Family.* London, 1906
10. *The Explorer.* London, 1907

Maugham, W. Somerset

11. *The Magician.* London, 1908
12. *Lady Frederick.* London, 1911
13. *Jack Straw.* London, 1911
14. *Mrs. Dot.* London and Chicago, 1912
15. *The Explorer: A Melodrama.* London and Chicago, 1912
16. *Penelope.* London and Chicago, 1912
17. *Smith.* London and Chicago, 1913
18. *The Tenth Man: A Tragic Comedy.* London and Chicago, 1913
19. *Landed Gentry.* London and Chicago, 1913
20. *The Land of Promise.* London, 1913
21. *Of Human Bondage.* New York and London, 1915
22. *The Moon and Sixpence.* London and New York, 1919
23. *The Unknown.* London and New York, 1920
24. *The Trembling of the Leaf: Little Stories of the South Sea Islands.* New York and London, 1921
25. *The Circle.* London and New York, 1921
26. *Caesar's Wife.* London, 1922
27. *East of Suez.* London and New York, 1922
28. *On a Chinese Screen.* New York and London, 1922
29. *The Unattainable.* London, 1923
30. *Our Betters.* London, 1923
31. *Home and Beauty.* London, 1923
32. *Loaves and Fishes.* London, 1924
33. *The Painted Veil.* New York and London, 1925
34. *The Casuarina Tree.* London and New York, 1926
35. *The Constant Wife.* London and New York, 1927
36. *The Letter.* London and New York, 1927
37. *Ashenden; or, The British Agent.* London and New York, 1928
38. *Sadie Thompson and Other Stories of the South Seas.* London, 1928
39. *The Sacred Flame.* New York and London, 1928
40. *Cakes and Ale; or, The Skeleton in the Cupboard.* London and New York, 1930
41. *The Letter: Stories of Crime.* London, 1930
42. *The Bread-Winner.* London, 1930
43. *The Gentleman in the Parlour: A Record of a Journey from Rangoon to Haiphong.* London and New York, 1930
44. *Six Stories Written in the First Person Singular.* New York and London, 1931
45. *The Book-Bag.* No place, 1932
46. *The Narrow Corner.* London and New York, 1932
47. *For Services Rendered.* London, 1932
48. *Ah King: Six Stories.* London and New York, 1933
49. *Rain and Other Stories.* London, 1933
50. *Sheppey.* London, 1933
51. *The Judgement Seat.* London, 1934
52. *East and West: Collected Short Stories.* New York, 1934
53. *Altogether.* London, 1934
54. *Don Fernando; or, Variations on Some Spanish Themes.* London and New York, 1935
55. *Cosmopolitans.* New York, 1936
56. *Cosmopolitans: Very Short Stories.* London, 1936
57. *My South Sea Island.* Chicago, 1936
58. *Theatre.* New York and London, 1937
59. *The Favorite Short Stories of W. Somerset Maugham.* New York, 1937
60. *Six Comedies.* New York, 1937
61. *The Summing Up.* London and New York, 1938
62. *Christmas Holiday.* London and New York, 1939
63. *The Mixture as Before.* London and New York, 1940
64. *Books and You.* London and New York, 1940
65. *France at War.* London and New York, 1940
66. *Up at the Villa.* New York and London, 1941
67. *Strictly Personal.* New York, 1941
68. *The Hour Before the Dawn.* New York, 1942
69. *The Somerset Maugham Sampler.* New York, 1943
70. *The Razor's Edge.* New York and London, 1944
71. *The Unconquered.* New York, 1944
72. *The Somerset Maugham Pocket Book.* New York, 1944
73. *Then and Now.* London and New York, 1946
74. *Of Human Bondage, with a Digression on the Art of Fiction.* Washington (DC), 1946
75. *Creatures of Circumstance.* London and New York, 1947
76. *Catalina: A Romance.* London, 1948
77. *East of Suez: Great Stories of the Tropics.* New York, 1948
78. *Here and There: Short Stories.* London, 1948
79. *Great Novelists and Their Novels: Essays on the Ten Greatest Novels of the World and the Men and Women Who Wrote Them.* Philadelphia, 1948
80. *A Writer's Notebook.* London and New York, 1949
81. *Trio: Stories and Screen Adaptations.* London and New York, 1950
82. *A Maugham Reader.* New York, 1950
83. *The Writer's Point of View.* London, 1951
84. *The World Over: Stories of Manifold Places and People.* New York, 1952
85. *The Vagrant Mood: Six Essays.* London, 1952
86. *The Noble Spaniard.* London, 1953
87. *Ten Novels and Their Authors.* London, 1954
88. *Mr. Maugham Himself.* New York, 1954
89. *The Partial View.* London, 1954
90. *The Art of Fiction.* New York, 1955
91. *A Fragment of Autobiography.* London, 1956
92. *The Best Short Stories.* New York, 1957
93. *Points of View.* London, 1958
94. *Points of View: Five Essays.* New York, 1959
95. *Purely for My Pleasure.* London and New York, 1962
96. *Selected Prefaces and Introductions.* New York, 1963
97. *A Maugham Twelve: Stories.* London, 1966
98. *Wit and Wisdom.* London, 1966
99. *Cakes and Ale.* New York, 1967
100. *Essays on Literature.* New York and London, 1967
101. *Malaysian Stories.* Singapore, 1969
102. *Seventeen Lost Stories.* New York, 1969

May, Wynne [Winifred Jean May]
1. *A Cluster of Palms.* London, 1967
2. *The Highest Peak.* London, 1967
3. *The Valley of Aloes.* London and Toronto, 1967
4. *Tawny Are the Leaves.* London, 1968
5. *Tamboti Moon.* London and New York, 1969
6. *Where Breezes Falter.* London, 1970
7. *Sun, Sea and Sand.* London, 1970
8. *The Tide at Full.* London, 1971
9. *A Grain of Gold.* London, 1971
10. *A Slither of Silk.* London, 9172
11. *A Bowl of Stars.* London and Toronto, 1973
12. *A Plume of Dust.* London and Toronto, 1975
13. *A Plantation of Vines.* Toronto, 1977
14. *Island of Cyclones.* London, 1979
15. *A Scarf of Flame.* London, 1979

Maybury, Anne [Anne Buxton]
British
Other pseudonym: Katherine Troy
1. *The Best Love of All.* London, 1932
2. *The Enchanted Kingdom.* London, 1932
3. *The Love That Is Stronger Than Life.* London, 1932
4. *Love Triumphant.* London, 1932
5. *The Way of Compassion.* London, 1933
6. *The Second Winning.* London, 1933
7. *Farewell to Dreams.* London, 1934
8. *Harness the Winds.* London, 1934
9. *Catch at a Rainbow.* London, 1935

10. *Come Autumn—Come Winter.* London, 1935
11. *The Garden of Wishes.* London, 1935
12. *The Starry Wood.* London, 1935
13. *The Wondrous To-Morrow.* London, 1936
14. *Give Me Back My Dreams.* London, 1936
15. *Lovely Destiny.* London, 1936
16. *The Stars Grow Pale.* London, 1936
17. *This Errant Heart.* London, 1937
18. *This Lovely Hour.* London, 1937
19. *I Dare Not Dream.* London, 1937
20. *Oh, Darling Joy!* London, 1937
21. *Lady, It Is Spring!* London, 1938
22. *The Shadow of My Loving.* London, 1938
23. *They Dreamed Too Much.* London, 1938
24. *Chained Eagle.* London, 1939
25. *Gather Up the Years.* London, 1939
26. *Return to Love.* London, 1939
27. *The Barrier Between Us.* London, 1940
28. *Dare to Marry.* London, 1940
29. *I'll Walk with My Love.* London, 1940
30. *Dangerous Living.* London, 1941
31. *The Secret of the Rose.* London, 1941
32. *All Enchantments Die.* London, 1941
33. *To-Day We Live.* London, 1942
34. *Arise, Oh Sun!* London, 1942
35. *A Lady Fell in Love.* London, 1943
36. *Journey into Morning.* London, 1944
37. *Can I Forget You?* London, 1944
38. *The Valley of Roses.* London, 1945
39. *The Young Invader.* London, 1947
40. *The Winds of Spring.* London, 1948
41. *Storm Heaven.* London, 1949
42. *The Sharon Women.* London, 1950
43. *First, The Dream.* London, 1951
44. *Goodbye, My Love.* London, 1952
45. *The Music of Our House.* London, 1952
46. *Her Name Was Eve.* London, 1953
47. *The Heart Is Never Fair.* London, 1954
48. *Prelude to Louise.* London, 1954
49. *Follow Your Hearts.* London, 1955
50. *The Other Juliet.* London, 1955
51. *Forbidden.* London, 1956
52. *Dear Lost Love.* London, 1957
53. *Beloved Enemy.* London, 1957
54. *The Stars Cannot Tell.* London, 1958
55. *My Love Has a Secret.* London, 1958
56. *The Gay of Heart.* London, 1959
57. *The Rebel Heart.* London, 1959
58. *Shadow of a Stranger.* London, 1960
59. *Bridge to the Moon.* London, 1960
60. *Stay Until Tomorrow.* London, 1961
61. *The Night My Enemy.* London, 1962
62. *I Am Gabriella!* London, 1962
63. *Green Fire.* London, 1963
64. *My Dearest Elizabeth.* London, 1964
65. *The Bridges of Bellenmore.* New York, 1964
66. *Pavilion at Monkshood.* New York, 1965
67. *Jessica.* London, 1965
68. *The Moonlit Door.* London and New York, 1967
69. *The Minerva Stone.* London and New York, 1968
70. *Ride a White Dolphin.* London and New York, 1971
71. *The Terracotta Palace.* London and New York, 1971
72. *Walk in the Paradise Garden.* New York, 1972
73. *The Midnight Dancers.* New York, 1973
74. *Jessamy Court.* New York, 1974
75. *The Jewelled Daughter.* London and New York. 1976
76. *Dark Star.* New York, 1977
77. *Radiance.* New York, 1979

McBain, Laurie (Lee)
American, born October 15, 1949
1. *Devil's Desire.* New York, 1975
2. *Moonstruck Madness.* New York, 1977
3. *Tears of Gold.* New York and London, 1979
4. *Chance the Winds of Fortune.* New York, 1980
5. *Dark Before the Rising Sun.* New York, 1982

McCloy, Helen (Worrell Clarkson)
American, born June 6, 1904
Pseudonym: Helen Clarkson
1. *Dance of Death.* New York, 1938
2. *Design for Dying.* London, 1938
3. *The Man in the Moonlight.* New York and London, 1940
4. *The Deadly Truth.* New York, 1941
5. *Who's Calling.* New York, 1942
6. *Cue for Murder.* New York, 1942
7. *Do Not Disturb.* New York, 1943
8. *The Goblin Market.* New York, 1943
9. *Panic.* New York, 1944
10. *The One That Got Away.* New York, 1945
11. *She Walks Alone.* New York, 1948
12. *Through a Glass Darkly.* New York, 1950
13. *Better Off Dead.* New York, 1951
14. *Alias Basil Willing.* New York, 1951
15. *Unfinished Crime.* New York, 1954
16. *He Never Came Back.* London, 1954
17. *The Long Body.* New York, 1955
18. *Two-Thirds of a Ghost.* New York, 1956
19. *The Slayer and the Slain.* New York, 1957
20. *Wish You Were Dead.* New York, 1958
21. *The Last Day,* as Helen Clarkson. New York, 1959
22. *Before I Die.* New York and London, 1963
23. *The Singing Diamonds and Other Stories.* New York, 1965
24. *Surprise, Surprise.* New York, 1965
25. *The Further Side of Fear.* New York and London, 1967
26. *Mr. Splitfoot.* New York, 1968
27. *A Question of Time.* New York and London, 1971
28. *A Change of Heart.* New York and London, 1973
29. *The Sleepwalker.* New York and London, 1974
30. *Minotaur Country.* New York and London, 1975
31. *The Changeling Conspiracy.* New York, 1976
32. *Cruel as the Grave.* London, 1977
33. *The Imposter.* New York, 1977
34. *The Smoking Mirror.* New York and London, 1979

McClure, James (Howe)
British, born October 9, 1939
1. *The Steam Pig.* London, 1971
2. *The Caterpillar Cop.* London, 1972
3. *Four and Twenty Virgins.* London, 1973
4. *The Gooseberry Fool.* London and New York, 1974
5. *Snake.* London, 1975
6. *Rogue Eagle.* London and New York, 1976
7. *Killers.* London, 1976
8. *The Sunday Hangman.* London and New York, 1977
9. *"Book One: To Be Continued" and "Corella of the 87th."* New York, 1977

McCoy, Horace
American, born April 14, 1897, died in 1959
1. *They Shoot Horses, Don't They?* New York and London, 1935
2. *No Pockets in a Shroud.* London, 1937
3. *I Should Have Stayed Home.* New York and London, 1938
4. *Kiss Tomorrow Goodbye.* New York, 1948
5. *Scalpel.* New York, 1952
6. *Corruption City.* New York, 1959
7. *I Should Have Stayed Home.* New York, 1978

McCutchan, Philip [Donald Philip McCutchan]
British, born October 13, 1920
Pseudonyms: Robert Conington Galway, Duncan MacNeil, T.I.G. Wigg
1. *Whistle and I'll Come.* London, 1957
2. *The Kid.* London, 1958
3. *A Job with the Boys,* as T.I.G. Wigg. London, 1958
4. *Storm South.* London, 1959
5. *On Course for Danger.* London and New York, 1959
6. *Gibraltar Road.* London, 1960
7. *For the Sons of Gentlemen,* as T.I.G. Wigg. London, 1960
8. *Redcap.* London, 1961
9. *Hopkinson and the Devil of Hate.* London, 1961
10. *A Rum for the Captain,* as T.I.G. Wigg. London, 1961
11. *Bluebolt One.* London, 1962
12. *Leave the Dead Behind Us.* London, 1962
13. *Marley's Empire.* London, 1963
14. *The Man from Moscow.* London, 1963
15. *Warmaster.* London, 1963
16. *Assignment New York,* as Robert Conington Galway. London, 1963
17. *Assignment London,* as Robert Conington Galway. London, 1963
18. *Moscow Coach.* London, 1964
19. *Bowering's Breakwater.* London, 1964
20. *Sladd's Evil.* London, 1965
21. *Assignment Andalusia,* as Robert Conington Galway. London, 1965
22. *A Time for Survival.* London, 1966
23. *The Dead Line.* London and New York, 1966
24. *Skyprobe.* London, 1966
25. *Assignment Malta,* as Robert Conington Galway. London, 1966
26. *Poulter's Passage.* London, 1967
27. *The Day of the Coastwatch.* London, 1968
28. *The Screaming Dead Balloons.* London and New York, 1968
29. *Assignment Gaolbreak,* as Robert Conington Galway. London, 1968
30. *The Bright Red Businessmen.* London and New York, 1969
31. *The All-Purpose Bodies.* London, 1969
32. *Assignment Argentina,* as Robert Conington Galway. London, 1969
33. *Assignment Fenland,* as Robert Conington Galway. London, 1969
34. *Assignment Seabed,* as Robert Conington Galway. London, 1969
35. *Drums along the Khyber,* as Duncan MacNeil. London, 1969
36. *Hartinger's Mouse.* London, 1970
37. *Man, Let's Go On.* London, 1970
38. *Half a Bag of Stringer.* London, 1970
39. *Assignment Sydney,* as Robert Conington Galway. London, 1970
40. *Assignment Death Squad,* as Robert Conington Galway. London, 1970
41. *Lieutenant of the Line,* as Duncan MacNeil. London, 1970
42. *This Drakotny.* London, 1971
43. *The Negative Man,* as Robert Conington Galway. London, 1971
44. *Sadhu on the Mountain Peak,* as Duncan MacNeil. London, 1971
45. *The German Helmet.* London, 1972
46. *The Oil Bastards.* London, 1972
47. *The Gates of Kunarja,* as Duncan MacNeil. London, 1972
48. *Pull My String.* London, 1973
49. *The Red Daniel,* as Duncan MacNeil. London, 1973
50. *Coach North.* London, 1974
51. *Beware, Beware the Bight of Benin.* London, 1974
52. *Call for Simon Shard.* London, 1974
53. *Subaltern's Choice,* as Duncan MacNeil. London and New York, 1974
54. *Beware the Bight of Benin.* New York, 1975
55. *A Very Big Bang.* London, 1975
56. *Halfhyde's Island.* London, 1975
57. *By Command of the Viceroy,* as Duncan MacNeil. London and New York, 1975
58. *Blood Run East.* London, 1976
59. *The Guns of Arrest.* London and New York, 1976
60. *The Mullah from Kashmir,* as Duncan MacNeil. London, 1976
61. *Tall Ships: The Golden Age of Sail.* London and New York, 1976
62. *The Eros Affair.* London, 1977
63. *Halfhyde to the Narrows.* London and New York, 1977
64. *Wolf in the Fold,* as Duncan MacNeil. London and New York, 1977
65. *Blackmail North.* London, 1978
66. *Halfhyde for the Queen.* London and New York, 1978
67. *Charge of Cowardice,* as Duncan MacNeil. London and New York, 1978
68. *Sunstrike.* London, 1979
69. *Halfhyde Ordered South.* London, 1979
70. *The Restless Frontier,* as Duncan MacNeil. London, 1979
71. *Great Yachts.* London and New York, 1979

McCutcheon, George Barr
American, born July 26, 1866, died October 23, 1928
Pseudonym: Richard Greaves
1. *Graustark: The Story of a Love Behind a Throne.* Chicago, 1901
2. *Castle Craneycrow.* Chicago, 1902
3. *Brewster's Millions,* as Richard Greaves. Chicago, 1903
4. *The Sherrods.* New York, 1903
5. *Beverly of Graustark.* New York and London, 1904
6. *The Day of the Dog.* New York, 1904
7. *Nedra.* New York and London, 1905
8. *The Purple Parasol.* New York, 1905
9. *Cowardice Court.* New York, 1906
10. *Jane Cable.* New York and London, 1906
11. *The Flyers.* New York and London, 1907
12. *The Daughter of Anderson Crow.* New York and London, 1907
13. *The Husbands of Edith.* New York, 1908
14. *The Man from Brodney's.* New York and London, 1908
15. *The Alternative.* New York, 1909
16. *Truxton King: A Story of Graustark.* New York and London, 1909
17. *The Butterfly Man.* New York, 1910
18. *The Rose in the Ring.* New York and London, 1910
19. *Mary Midthorne.* New York and London, 1911
20. *What's-His-Name.* New York and London, 1911
21. *Her Weight in Gold.* No place, 1911
22. *The Hollow of Her Hand.* New York and London, 1912
23. *A Fool and His Money.* New York and London, 1913
24. *Black Is White.* New York, 1914
25. *The Prince of Graustark.* New York and London, 1914
26. *Mr. Bingle.* New York and London, 1915
27. *From the Housetops.* New York and London, 1916
28. *The Light That Lies.* New York, 1916
29. *Green Fancy.* New York, 1917
30. *The City of Masks.* New York, 1918
31. *Shot with Crimson.* New York, 1918
32. *The Court of New York.* London, 1919
33. *Sherry.* New York, 1919
34. *West Wind Drift.* New York, 1920
35. *Anderson Crow, Detective.* New York, 1920

36. *Quill's Window.* New York, 1921
37. *Yollop.* New York, 1922
38. *Viola Gwyn.* New York and London, 1922
39. *Oliver October.* New York, 1923
40. *East of the Setting Sun: A Story of Graustark.* New York, 1924
41. *Anderson, The Joker, in Three Yarns.* Chicago, 1924
42. *Romeo in Moon Village.* New York, 1925
43. *The Inn of the Hawk and Raven: A Tale of Old Graustark.* New York, 1926
44. *Kindling and Ashes; or, The Heart of Barbara Wayne.* New York, 1926
45. *Blades.* New York and London, 1928
46. *The Merivales.* New York, 1929
47. *Books Once Were Men: An Essay for Booklovers.* New York, 1931

McDonald, Gregory
American, born February 15, 1937
1. *Running Scared.* New York, 1964
2. *Fletch.* Indianapolis (IN), 1974
3. *Confess, Fletch.* New York, 1976
4. *Flynn.* New York, 1977
5. *Fletch's Fortune.* London and New York, 1978
6. *Fletch Forever.* New York, 1978
7. *Love among the Mashed Potatoes.* New York, 1978

McEvoy, Marjorie
British
Pseudonym: Marjorie Harte
1. *No Castle of Dreams.* London, 1960
2. *A Red, Red Rose.* London, 1960
3. *The Meaning of a Kiss.* London, 1961
4. *A Call for the Doctor,* as Marjorie Harte. London, 1961
5. *Forever Faithful.* London, 1962
6. *Goodbye, Doctor Garland,* as Marjorie Harte. London, 1962
7. *Nurse in the Orient,* as Marjorie Harte. London, 1962
8. *Softly Treads Danger.* London, 1963
9. *Calling Nurse Stewart.* London, 1963
10. *Doctors in Conflict,* as Marjorie Harte. London, 1963
11. *Masquerade for a Nurse,* as Marjorie Harte. London, 1964
12. *No Orchids for a Nurse,* as Marjorie Harte. London, 1964
13. *Strange Journey,* as Marjorie Harte. New York, no date
14. *Doctor Mysterious,* as Marjorie Harte. London, 1965
15. *Moon over the Danube.* London, 1966
16. *Who Walks by Moonlight?* London, 1966
17. *Brazilian Stardust.* New York, 1967
18. *Dusky Cactus.* London, 1968
19. *The Grenfell Legacy.* London, 1968
20. *Cover Girl,* as Marjorie Harte. London, 1968
21. *The White Castello.* London, 1969
22. *Castle Doom.* New York, 1970
23. *The Hermitage Bell.* New York, 1971
24. *My Love Johnny.* London, 1971
25. *Eaglescliffe.* New York, 1971
26. *No Eden for a Nurse,* as Marjorie Harte. London, 1971
27. *Peril at Polvellyn.* New York, 1973
28. *The Chinese Box.* New York, 1973
29. *The Closing Web,* as Marjorie Harte. New York, 1973
30. *Ravensmount.* New York, 1974
31. *The Wych Stone.* New York, 1974
32. *The Queen of Spades.* New York, 1975
33. *Echoes from the Past.* New York, 1979
34. *Calabrian Summer.* New York, 1980

McGivern, William P. (Peter)
American, born December 6, 1927
Pseudonym: Bill Peters

1. *But Death Runs Faster.* New York, 1948
2. *Heaven Ran Last.* New York, 1949
3. *The Whispering Corpse.* New York, 1950
4. *Very Cold for May.* New York, 1950
5. *Shield for Murder.* New York, 1951
6. *Blondes Die Young,* as Bill Peters. New York, 1952
7. *The Crooked Frame.* New York, 1952
8. *The Big Heat.* New York and London, 1953
9. *Margin of Terror.* New York, 1953
10. *Rogue Cop.* New York, 1954
11. *The Darkest Hour.* New York, 1955
12. *Waterfront Cop.* New York, 1956
13. *The Seven File.* New York, 1956
14. *Night Extra.* New York, 1957
15. *Odds Against Tomorrow.* New York, 1957
16. *Mention My Name in Mombasa: The Unscheduled Adventures of an American Family Abroad.* New York, 1958
17. *Savage Streets.* New York, 1959
18. *Seven Lies South.* New York, 1960
19. *The Road to the Snail.* New York, 1961
20. *Killer on the Turnpike.* New York, 1961
21. *A Pride of Place.* New York, 1962
22. *Police Special.* New York, 1962
23. *A Choice of Assassins.* New York, 1963
24. *The Caper of the Golden Bulls.* New York, 1966
25. *Lie Down, I Want to Talk to You.* New York, 1967
26. *Chicago-7.* London, 1970
27. *Caprifoil.* New York, 1972
28. *Reprisal.* New York, 1973
29. *Night of the Juggler.* New York and London, 1975
30. *Soldiers of '44.* New York and London, 1979

McNeile, H.C. (Herman Cyril)
British, born September 28, 1888, died August 14, 1937
Pseudonym: Sapper
1. *The Lieutenant and Others,* as Sapper. London, 1915
2. *Sergeant Michael Cassidy, R.E,* as Sapper. London, 1915
3. *Michael Cassidy, Sergeant,* as Sapper. New York, 1916
4. *Men, Women, and Guns,* as Sapper. London and New York, 1916
5. *No Man's Land,* as Sapper. London and New York, 1917
6. *The Human Torch,* as Sapper. London and New York, 1918
7. *Mufti.* London and New York, 1919
8. *Bull-Dog Drummond: The Adventures of a Demobilized Officer Who Found Peace Dull.* London and New York, 1920
9. *The Man in Ratcatcher and Other Stories.* London and New York, 1921
10. *The Black Gang.* London and New York, 1922
11. *Jim Maitland.* London, 1923
12. *The Dinner Club,* as Sapper. London and New York, 1923
13. *The Third Round.* London, 1924
14. *Bulldog Drummond's Third Round,* as Sapper. New York, 1924
15. *Out of the Blue,* as Sapper. London and New York, 1925
16. *The Final Count,* as Sapper. London and New York, 1926
17. *Jim Brent,* as Sapper. London, 1926
18. *Word of Honour,* as Sapper. London and New York, 1926
19. *The Saving Clause,* as Sapper. London, 1927
20. *The Female of the Species,* as Sapper. London and New York, 1928
21. *Temple Tower,* as Sapper. London and New York, 1929
22. *Tiny Carteret,* as Sapper. London and New York, 1930
23. *The Finger of Fate,* as Sapper. London, 1930
24. *Sapper's War Stories,* as Sapper. London, 1930
25. *The Island of Terror,* as Sapper. London, 1931
26. *Guardians of the Treasure,* as Sapper. New York, 1931
27. *The Return of Bull-Dog Drummond,* as Sapper. London, 1932

McNeile, H.C.

28. *Bulldog Drummond Returns,* as Sapper. New York, 1932
29. *Knock-Out,* as Sapper. London, 1933
30. *Bulldog Drummond Strikes Back,* as Sapper. New York, 1933
31. *Ronald Standish,* as Sapper. London, 1933
32. *When Carruthers Laughed,* as Sapper. London, 1934
33. *51 Stories,* as Sapper. London, 1934
34. *Bulldog Drummond at Bay,* as Sapper. London and New York, 1935
35. *Ask for Ronald Standish,* as Sapper. London, 1936
36. *Challenge,* as Sapper. London and New York, 1937

McShane, Mark
British, born November 28, 1929
Pseudonym: Marc Lovell

1. *The Straight and the Crooked.* London, 1960
2. *Seance on a Wet Afternoon.* London, 1961
3. *The Passing of Evil.* London, 1961
4. *Seance.* New York, 1962
5. *Untimely Ripped.* London, 1962
6. *The Girl Nobody Knows.* New York, 1965
7. *Night's Evil.* New York and London, 1966
8. *The Crimson Madness of Little Doom.* New York, 1966
9. *The Way to Nowhere.* London, 1967
10. *Ill Met by a Fish Shop on George Street.* New York, 1968
11. *The Ghost of Megan,* as Marc Lovell. New York, 1968
12. *The Singular Case of the Multiple Dead.* New York, 1969
13. *Memory of Megan,* as Marc Lovell. New York, 1970
14. *The Man Who Left Well Enough.* New York, 1971
15. *The Imitation Thieves,* as Marc Lovell. New York, 1971
16. *Seance for Two.* New York, 1972
17. *A Presence in the House,* as Marc Lovell. New York, 1972
18. *The Othello Complex.* Paris, 1974
19. *The Headless Snowman.* Paris, 1974
20. *An Enquiry into the Existence of Vampires,* as Marc Lovell. New York, 1974
21. *Dreamers in a Haunted House,* as Marc Lovell. New York, 1975
22. *Lashed But Not Leashed.* New York, 1976
23. *Vampires in the Shadows,* as Marc Lovell. London, 1976
24. *The Blind Hypnotist,* as Marc Lovell. New York, 1976
25. *Lifetime.* New York, 1977
26. *The Second Vanetti Affair,* as Marc Lovell. New York, 1977
27. *The Guardian Spectre,* as Marc Lovell. New York, 1977
28. *Fog Sinister,* as Marc Lovell. New York, 1977
29. *A Voice from the Living,* as Marc Lovell. New York, 1978
30. *The Hostage Game.* New York, 1979
31. *And They Say You Can't Buy Happiness,* as Marc Lovell. London, 1979
32. *Hand over Mind,* as Marc Lovell. New York, 1979

Meade, L.T. [Elizabeth Thomasina Meade]
Irish, born in 1854, died October 26, 1914

1. *Lotty's Last Home.* London, 1875
2. *David's Little Lad.* London, 1877
3. *A Knight of Today.* London, 1877
4. *Scamp and I: A Story of City By-Ways.* London, 1877
5. *Bel Marjory.* London, 1878
6. *The Children's Kingdom.* London, 1878
7. *Your Brother and Mine: A Cry from the Great City.* London, 1878
8. *Water Lilies and Other Tales.* London, 1878
9. *Dot and Her Treasures.* London, 1879
10. *Water Gipsies: A Story of Canal Life in England.* New York, 1879
11. *Andrew Harvey's Wife.* London, 1880
12. *A Dweller in Tents.* London, 1880
13. *Mou-Setse: A Negro Hero.* London, 1880
14. *The Floating Light of Ringfinnan, and Guardian Angels.* Edinburgh (Scotland), 1880
15. *Mother Herring's Chicken.* London and New York, 1881
16. *A London Baby: The Story of King Roy.* London, 1882
17. *The Children's Pilgrimage.* London, 1883
18. *How It All Came Round.* London and New York, 1883
19. *Hermie's Rose-Buds and Other Stories.* London, 1883
20. *The Autocrat of the Nursery.* London, 1884
21. *A Band of Three.* London, 1884
22. *Scarlet Anemones.* London, 1884
23. *The Two Sisters.* London. 1884
24. *The Angel of Love.* London, 1885
25. *A Little Silver Trumpet.* London, 1885
26. *A World of Girls: The Story of a School.* London, 1886
27. *Daddy's Boy.* London, 1887
28. *The O'Donnell's of Inchfawn.* London and New York, 1887
29. *The Palace Beautiful.* London, 1887
30. *Sweet Nancy.* London, 1887
31. *Deb and the Duchess.* London, 1888
32. *Nobody's Neighbours.* London, 1888
33. *A Farthingful.* London, 1889
34. *The Golden Lady.* London, 1889
35. *The Lady of the Forest.* London and New York, 1889
36. *The Little Princess of Tower Hill.* London, 1889
37. *Polly, A New-Fashioned Girl.* London, 1889
38. *Poor Miss Carolina.* London, 1889
39. *The Beresford Prize.* London, 1890
40. *Dickory Dock.* London, 1890
41. *Engaged to Be Married.* London, 1890
42. *Frances Kane's Fortune.* London and New York, 1890
43. *Heart of Gold.* London and New York, 1890
44. *Just a Love Story.* London, 1890
45. *Marigold.* London, 1890
46. *The Honourable Miss.* New York, 1890
47. *A Girl of the People.* London and New York, 1890
48. *Hepsy Gipsy.* London, 1891
49. *A Life for a Love.* New York, 1891
50. *The Children of Wilton Chase.* London and New York, 1891
51. *A Sweet Girl-Graduate.* London, 1891
52. *Little Mary and Other Stories.* London, 1891
53. *Bashful Fifteen.* London and New York, 1892
54. *Four on an Island.* London and New York, 1892
55. *Jill, A Flower Girl.* New York, 1892
56. *The Medicine Lady.* London and New York, 3 vols., 1892
57. *Out of the Fashion.* London and New York, 1892
58. *A Ring of Rubies.* London and New York, 1892
59. *Beyond the Blue Mountains.* London, 1893
60. *A Young Mutineer.* London and New York, 1893
61. *This Troublesome World.* New York, 1893
62. *Betty, A School Girl.* London, 1894
63. *In an Iron Grip.* London, 2 vols., 1894
64. *Red Rose and Tiger Lily.* London and New York, 1894
65. *A Soldier of Fortune.* London, 3 vols., 1894
66. *Girls, New and Old.* London and New York, 1895
67. *A Princess of the Gutter.* London, 1895
68. *The Least of These and Other Stories.* Cincinnati (OH), 1895
69. *Catalina, Art Student.* London, 1896
70. *A Girl in Ten Thousand.* Edinburgh, 1896
71. *Good Luck.* London, 1896
72. *A Little Mother to the Others.* London, 1896
73. *Merry Girls of England.* London, 1896
74. *Playmates.* London, 1896
75. *The White Tzar.* London, 1896
76. *The House of Surprises.* London, 1896
77. *Bad Little Hannah.* London, 1897
78. *A Handful of Silver.* Edinburgh, 1897

79. *The Way of a Woman.* London, 1897
80. *Wild Kitty.* London, 1897
81. *Cave Perilous.* London, 1898
82. *A Bunch of Cherries.* London and New York, 1898
83. *The Cleverest Woman in England.* London, 1898
84. *The Girls of St. Wode's.* London, 1898
85. *Mary Gifford, M.B.* London, 1898
86. *The Rebellion of Lil Carrington.* London, 1898
87. *The Siren.* London, 1898
88. *Adventuress.* London, 1899
89. *All Sorts.* London, 1899
90. *The Temptation of Olive Latimer.* New York, 1899
91. *The Desire of Man: An Impossibility.* London, 1899
92. *Light o' the Morning: The Story of an Irish Girl.* London, 1899
93. *The Odds and the Evens.* London, 1899
94. *A Public School Boy.* London, 1899
95. *Wages.* London, 1900
96. *A Plucky Girl.* Philadelphia, 1900
97. *The Beauforts.* London, 1900
98. *A Brave Poor Thing.* London, 1900
99. *Daddy's Girl.* London, 1900
100. *Miss Nonentity.* London, 1900
101. *Seven Maids.* London, 1900
102. *A Sister of the Red Cross: A Tale of the South African War.* London, 1900
103. *The Time of Roses.* London, 1900
104. *Wheels of Iron.* London, 1901
105. *The Blue Diamond.* London, 1901
106. *Cosey Corner; or, How They Kept a Farm.* London, 1901
107. *Girls of the True Blue.* London and New York, 1901
108. *The New Mrs. Lascelles.* London, 1901
109. *A Stumble by the Way.* London, 1901
110. *A Very Naughty Girl.* London, 1901
111. *Drift.* London, 1902
112. *Girls of the Forest.* London, 1902
113. *Margaret.* London, 1902
114. *The Pursuit of Penelope.* London, 1902
115. *Queen Rose.* London, 1902
116. *The Rebel of the School.* London, 1902
117. *The Squire's Little Girl.* London, 1902
118. *Through Peril for a Wife.* London, 1902
119. *The Princess Who Gave Away All, and The Naughty One of the Family.* London, 1902
120. *The Witch Maid.* London, 1903
121. *The Burden of Her Youth.* London, 1903
122. *By Mutual Consent.* London, 1903
123. *A Gay Charmer.* London, 1903
124. *The Manor School.* London and New York, 1903
125. *Peter the Pilgrim.* London, 1903
126. *Resurgam.* London, 1903
127. *Rosebury.* London, 1903
128. *That Brilliant Peggy.* London, 1903
129. *Stories from the Old, Old Bible.* London, 1903
130. *A Maid of Mystery.* London, 1904
131. *The Adventures of Miranda.* London, 1904
132. *At the Back of the World.* London, 1904
133. *Castle Poverty.* London, 1904
134. *The Girls of Mrs. Pritchard's School.* London, 1904
135. *Love Triunphant.* London, 1904
136. *A Madcap.* London and New York, 1904
137. *A Modern Tomboy.* London, 1904
138. *Nurse Charlotte.* London, 1904
139. *Petronella, and the Coming of Polly.* London, 1904
140. *The Lady Cake-Maker.* London, 1904
141. *Wilfull Cousin Kate.* London, 1905
142. *Bess of Delaney's.* London, 1905
143. *A Bevy of Girls.* London and New York, 1905
144. *Dumps: A Plain Girl.* London and New York, 1905
145. *His Mascot.* London, 1905
146. *Little Wife Hester.* London, 1905
147. *Loveday: The Story of an Heiress.* London, 1905
148. *Old Readymoney's Daughter.* London, 1905
149. *The Other Woman.* London, 1905
150. *Virginia.* London, 1905
151. *The Colonel and the Boy.* London, 1906
152. *The Face of Juliet.* London, 1906
153. *The Girl and Her Fortune.* London, 1906
154. *The Heart of Helen.* London, 1906
155. *The Hill-Top Girl.* London, 1906
156. *The Home of Sweet Content.* London, 1906
157. *In the Flower of Her Youth.* London, 1906
158. *The Maid with the Goggles.* London, 1906
159. *Sue.* London, 1906
160. *Turquoise and Ruby.* London and New York, 1906
161. *Victory.* London, 1906
162. *The Colonel's Conquest.* Philadelphia, 1907
163. *The Curse of the Feverals.* London, 1907
164. *A Girl from America.* London, 1907
165. *The Home of Silence.* London, 1907
166. *Kindred Spirits.* London, 1907
167. *The Lady of Delight.* London, 1907
168. *Little Josephine.* London, 1907
169. *The Little School-Mothers.* London and Philadelphia, 1907
170. *The Love of Susan Cardigan.* London, 1907
171. *The Red Cap of Liberty.* London, 1907
172. *The Red Ruth.* London, 1907
173. *The Scamp Family.* London, 1907
174. *Three Girls from School.* London, 1907
175. *The Aim of Her Life.* London, 1908
176. *Betty of the Rectory.* London, 1908
177. *The Court-Harman Girls.* London, 1908
178. *The Courtship of Sybil.* London, 1908
179. *Hetty Beresford.* London, 1908
180. *Sarah's Mother.* London, 1908
181. *The School Favourite.* London, 1908
182. *The School Queens.* London, 1908
183. *A Lovely Fiend and Other Stories.* London, 1908
184. *Wild Heather.* London, 1909
185. *Oceana's Girlhood.* New York, 1909
186. *Aylwyn's Friends.* London, 1909
187. *Betty Vivian: A Story of Haddo Court School.* London, 1909
188. *Blue of the Sea.* London, 1909
189. *Brother or Husband.* London, 1909
190. *The Fountain of Beauty.* London, 1909
191. *I Will Sing a New Song.* London, 1909
192. *The Princess of the Revels.* London, 1909
193. *The Stormy Petrel.* London, 1909
194. *The A.B.C. Girl.* London, 1910
195. *Belinda Treherne.* London, 1910
196. *A Girl of Today.* London, 1910
197. *Lady Anne.* London, 1910
198. *Miss Gwendoline.* London, 1910
199. *Nance Kennedy.* London, 1910
200. *Pretty-Girl and the Others.* London, 1910
201. *Rose Regina.* London, 1910
202. *A Wild Irish Girl.* London and New York, 1910
203. *A Bunch of Cousins, and The Barn "Boys."* London, 1911
204. *Desborough's Wife.* London, 1911
205. *The Doctor's Children.* London and Philadelphia, 1911
206. *For Dear Dad.* London, 1911
207. *The Girl from Spain.* London, 1911
208. *The Girls of Merton College.* New York, 1911
209. *Mother and Son.* London, 1911
210. *Ruffles.* London, 1911

211. *The Soul of Margaret Rand.* London, 1911
212. *Daddy's Girl and Consuelo's Quest of Happiness.* New York, 1911
213. *Corporal Violet.* London, 1912
214. *A Girl of the People.* London, 1912
215. *Kitty O'Donovan.* London and New York, 1912
216. *Lord and Lady Kitty.* London, 1912
217. *Love's Cross Roads.* London, 1912
218. *Peggy from Kerry.* London and New York, 1912
219. *The Chesterton Girl Graduates.* New York, 1913
220. *The Girls of Abinger Close.* London, 1913
221. *The Girls of King's Royal.* New York, 1913
222. *The Passion of Kathleen Duveen.* London, 1913
223. *A Band of Mirth.* London, 1914
224. *Col. Tracy's Wife.* London, 1914
225. *Elizabeth's Prisoner.* London, 1914
226. *A Girl of High Adventure.* London, 1914
227. *Her Happy Face.* London, 1914
228. *The Queen of Joy.* London and New York, 1914
229. *The Wooing of Monica.* London, 1914
230. *The Darling of the School.* London, 1915
231. *The Daughter of a Soldier: A Colleen of South Ireland.* New York, 1915
232. *Greater Than Gold.* London, 1915
233. *Jill the Irresistible.* New York, 1915
234. *Hollyhock.* London, 1916
235. *Madge Mostyn's Nieces.* London, 1916
236. *The Maid Indomitable.* London, 1916
237. *Mother Mary.* London, 1916
238. *Daughters of Today.* London, 1916
239. *Better Than Riches.* London, 1917
240. *The Fairy Godmother.* London, 1917
241. *Miss Patricia.* London, 1925
242. *Roses and Thorns.* London, 1928
243. *In Time of Roses.* New York, no date

Meggs, Brown (Moore)
American, born October 20, 1930
1. *Saturday Games.* New York, 1974
2. *The Matter of Paradise.* New York, 1975
3. *Aria.* New York, 1978

Meyer, Nicholas
American, born December 24, 1945
1. *Target Practice.* New York, 1974
2. *The Seven-Per-Cent Solution, Being a Reprint from the Reminiscences of John H. Watson, M.D.* New York, 1974
3. *The West End Horror: A Posthumous Memoir of John H. Watson, M.D.* New York and London, 1976
4. *Black Orchid.* New York, 1977

Meynell, Laurence (Walter)
British, born August 9, 1899
Pseudonyms: Valerie Baxter, Robert Eton, Geoffrey Ludlow, A. Stephen Tring
1. *Mockbeggar.* London, 1924
2. *Lois.* London and New York, 1927
3. *The Ballad of Pen Fields, with a Plan of the Battlefield.* Privately printed, 1927
4. *Bluefeather.* London and New York, 1928
5. *Death's Eye.* London, 1929
6. *The Shadow and the Stone.* New York, 1929
7. *Camouflage.* London, 1930
8. *Mystery at Newton Ferry.* Philadelphia, 1930
9. *Asking for Trouble.* London, 1931
10. *Consummate Rose.* London, 1931
11. *Storm Against the Wall.* London and Philadelphia, 1931
12. *The House on the Cliff.* London and Philadelphia, 1932
13. *Paid in Full.* London, 1933
14. *So Many Doors.* Philadelphia, 1933
15. *Watch the Wall.* London, 1933
16. *Gentlemen Go By.* Philadelphia, 1934
17. *Odds on Bluefeather.* London, 1934
18. *Inside Out! or, Mad as a Hatter,* as Geoffrey Ludlow. London, 1934
19. *The Pattern,* as Robert Eton. London, 1934
20. *Third Time Unlucky!* London, 1935
21. *The Dividing Air,* as Robert Eton. London, 1935
22. *On the Night of the 18th....* London and New York, 1936
23. *Woman Had to Do It!* as Geoffrey Ludlow. London, 1936
24. *The Bus Leaves for the Village,* as Robert Eton. London, 1936
25. *The Door in the Wall.* London and New York, 1937
26. *The House in the Hills.* London, 1937
27. *Not in Our Stars,* as Robert Eton. London, 1937
28. *The Dandy.* London, 1938
29. *The Hut.* London, 1938
30. *The Journey,* as Robert Eton. London, 1938
31. *Palace Pier,* as Robert Eton. London, 1938
32. *His Aunt Came Late.* London, 1939
33. *And Be a Villain.* London, 1939
34. *The Legacy,* as Robert Eton. London, 1939
35. *The Faithful Years,* as Robert Eton. London, 1939
36. *The Corner of Paradise Place,* as Robert Eton. London, 1940
37. *The Creaking Chair.* London, 1941
38. *The Dark Square.* London, 1941
39. *Strange Landing.* London, 1946
40. *The Evil Hour.* London, 1947
41. *St. Lynn's Advertiser,* as Robert Eton. London, 1947
42. *The Old Gang,* as A. Stephen Tring. London, 1947
43. *The Bright Face of Danger.* London, 1948
44. *The Echo in the Cave.* London, 1949
45. *The Dragon at the Gate,* as Robert Eton. London, 1949
46. *Penny Dreadful,* as A. Stephen Tring. London, 1949
47. *The Lady on Platform One.* London, 1950
48. *Party of Eight.* London, 1950
49. *Bedfordshire.* London, 1950
50. *The Cave by the Sea,* as A. Stephen Tring. London, 1950
51. *The Man No One Knew.* London, 1951
52. *Famous Cricket Grounds.* London, 1951
53. *"Plum" Warner.* London, 1951
54. *Barry's Exciting Year [Gets His Wish, Great Day],* as A. Stephen Tring. London, 3 vols., 1951-54
55. *The Frightened Man.* London, 1952
56. *Danger round the Corner.* London, 1952
57. *Smoky Joe.* London, 1952
58. *Builder and Dreamer: A Life of Isambard Kingdom Brunel.* London, 1952
59. *Young Master Carver: A Boy in the Reign of Edward III,* as A. Stephen Tring. London, 1952
60. *Too Clever by Half.* London, 1953
61. *Exmoor.* London, 1953
62. *Smoky Joe in Trouble.* London, 1953
63. *Policeman in the Family.* London, 1953
64. *Rolls, Man of Speed: A Life of Charles Stewart Rolls.* London, 1953
65. *Penny Triumphant [Penitent, Puzzled, Dramatic, in Italy, and the Pageant, Says Goodbye],* as A. Stephen Tring. London, 7 vols., 1953-61
66. *Give Me the Knife.* London, 1954
67. *Under the Hollies.* London, 1954
68. *Bridge under the Water.* London, 1954
69. *Jane: Young Author,* as Valerie Baxter. London, 1954
70. *Where Is She Now?* London, 1955
71. *Isambard Kingdom Brunel.* London, 1955

72. *The Hon. C.S. Rolls.* London, 1955
73. *Great Men of Staffordshire.* London, 1955
74. *The First Men to Fly: A Short History of Wilbur and Orville Wright.* London, 1955
75. *The Kite Man,* as A. Stephen Tring. Oxford (Eng), 1955
76. *Elizabeth: Young Policewoman,* as Valerie Baxter. London, 1955
77. *Saturday Out.* London, 1956
78. *The Sun Will Shine.* London, 1956
79. *Animal Doctor.* London, 1956
80. *Smoky Joe Goes to School.* London, 1956
81. *James Brindley: The Pioneer of Canals.* London, 1956
82. *Shirley: Young Bookseller,* as Valerie Baxter. London, 1956
83. *The Breaking Point.* London, 1957
84. *Our Patron Saints.* London, 1957
85. *Thomas Telford: The Life Story of a Great Engineer.* London, 1957
86. *Sonia Back Stage.* London, 1957
87. *Frankie and the Green Umbrella,* as A. Stephen Tring. London, 1957
88. *Hester: Ship's Officer,* as Valerie Baxter. London, 1957
89. *One Step from Murder.* London, 1958
90. *Farm Animals.* London, 1958
91. *The Young Architect.* London, 1958
92. *District Nurse Carter.* London, 1958
93. *Nurse Ross Takes Over.* London, 1958
94. *Pictures for Sale,* as A. Stephen Tring. London, 1958
95. *The Hunted King.* London, 1959
96. *Nurse Ross Shows the Way.* London, 1959
97. *Monica Anson, Travel Agent.* London, 1959
98. *Peter's Busy Day,* as A. Stephen Tring. London, 1959
99. *The Abandoned Doll.* London, 1960
100. *The House in Marsh Road.* London, 1960
101. *Nurse Ross Saves the Day.* London, 1960
102. *Bandaberry.* London, 1960
103. *The Pit in the Garden.* London, 1961
104. *Ted's Lucky Ball,* as A. Stephen Tring. London, 1961
105. *Moon over Ebury Square.* London, 1962
106. *Nurse Ross and the Doctor.* London, 1962
107. *Virgin Luck.* London, 1963
108. *Sleep of the Unjust.* London, 1963
109. *The Dancers in the Reeds.* London, 1963
110. *Good Luck, Nurse Ross.* London, 1963
111. *Airmen on the Run: True Stories of Evasion and Escape by British Airmen of World War II.* London, 1963
112. *The Man with the Sack,* as A. Stephen Tring. London, 1963
113. *More Deadly Than the Male.* London, 1964
114. *Scoop.* London, 1964
115. *Double Fault.* London, 1965
116. *The Empty Saddle.* London, 1965
117. *Break for Summer.* London, 1965
118. *Die by the Book.* London, 1966
119. *The Imperfect Aunt.* London, 1966
120. *Shadow in the Sun.* London, 1966
121. *The Suspect Scientist.* London, 1966
122. *Chad,* as A. Stephen Tring. London, 1966
123. *The Mauve Front Door.* London, 1967
124. *Week-end in the Scampi Belt.* London, 1967
125. *The Man in the Hut.* London, 1967
126. *Death of a Philanderer.* London, 1968
127. *Of Malicious Intent.* London, 1969
128. *Peter and the Picture Thief.* London, 1969
129. *The Shelter.* London, 1970
130. *The Curious Crime of Miss Julia Blossom.* London, 1970
131. *The Beginning of Words: How English Grew.* London, 1970
132. *Jimmy and the Election.* London, 1970
133. *Tony Trotter and the Kitten.* London, 1971
134. *The End of the Long Hot Summer.* London, 1972
135. *Death by Arrangement.* London and New York, 1972
136. *A Little Matter of Arson.* London, 1972
137. *A View from the Terrace.* London, 1972
138. *The Fatal Flaw.* London, 1973
139. *The Thirteen Trumpeters.* London, 1973
140. *The Fortunate Miss East.* London, 1973
141. *The Woman in Number Five.* London, 1974
142. *The Fairly Innocent Little Man.* London, 1974
143. *The Great Cup Tie.* London, 1974
144. *Burlington Square.* New York, 1975
145. *The Footpath.* London, 1975
146. *Don't Stop for Hooky Hefferman.* London, 1975
147. *Hooky and the Crock of Gold.* London, 1975
148. *The Lost Half Hour.* London, 1976
149. *The Vision Splendid.* London, 1976
150. *The Folly of Henrietta Dale.* London, 1976
151. *The Little Kingdom.* London, 1977
152. *Folly to Be Wise.* London, 1977
153. *Hooky Gets the Wooden Spoon.* London and New York, 1977
154. *Papersnake.* London, 1978
155. *The Dangerous Year.* London, 1978
156. *The Sisters.* London, 1979
157. *Hooky and the Villainous Chauffeur.* London, 1979

Miles, Lady [Favell Mary Miles]
British, died January 3, 1969
1. *The Red Flame.* London, 1921
2. *Red, White, and Grey.* London, 1921
3. *Ralph Carey.* London, 1922
4. *Stony Ground.* London, 1923
5. *The Fanatic.* London, 1924
6. *Tread Softly.* London, 1926
7. *Love's Cousin.* London, 1927
8. *Dark Dream.* London, 1929
9. *Lorna Neale.* London, 1932
10. *This Flower.* London, 1933
11. *The Second Lesson.* London, 1936

Millar, Margaret (Ellis)
American, born February 5, 1915
1. *The Invisible Worm.* New York, 1941
2. *The Weak-Eyed Bat.* New York, 1942
3. *The Devil Loves Me.* New York, 1942
4. *Wall of Eyes.* New York, 1943
5. *Fire Will Freeze.* New York, 1944
6. *The Iron Gates.* New York, 1945
7. *Experiment in Springtime.* New York, 1947
8. *It's All in the Family.* New York, 1948
9. *The Cannibal Heart.* New York, 1949
10. *Taste of Fears.* London, 1950
11. *Do Evil in Return.* New York, 1950
12. *Rose's Last Summer.* New York, 1952
13. *The Lively Corpse.* New York, No date
14. *Vanish in an Instant.* New York, 1952
15. *Wives and Lovers.* New York, 1954
16. *Beast in View.* New York and London, 1955
17. *An Air That Kills.* New York, 1957
18. *The Soft Talkers.* London, 1957
19. *The Listening Walls.* New York and London, 1959
20. *A Stranger in My Grave.* New York and London, 1960
21. *How Like an Angel.* New York and London, 1962
22. *The Fiend.* New York and London, 1964
23. *The Birds and Beasts Were There.* New York, 1968
24. *Beyond This Point Are Monsters.* New York, 1970
25. *Ask for Me Tomorrow.* New York, 1976
26. *The Murder of Miranda.* New York, 1979

Millhiser, Marlys (Joy)
American, born May 27, 1938
1. *Michael's Wife.* New York, 1972
2. *Nella Waits.* New York, 1974
3. *Willing Hostage.* New York, 1976
4. *The Mirror.* New York, 1978
5. *Nightmare Country.* New York, 1981

Milne, A.A. (Alan Alexander)
British, born January 18, 1882, died January 31, 1956
1. *Lovers in London.* London, 1905
2. *The Day's Play.* London, 1910
3. *The Holiday Round.* London, 1912
4. *Once a Week.* London, 1914
5. *Happy Days.* New York, 1915
6. *Once on a Time.* London, 1917
7. *First Plays.* London and New York, 1919
8. *Not That It Matters.* London, 1919
9. *If I May.* London, 1920
10. *Mr. Pim.* London, 1921
11. *Wurzel-Flummery.* London and New York, 1921
12. *Second Plays.* London, 1921
13. *The Sunny Side.* London, 1921
14. *The Red House Mystery.* London and New York, 1922
15. *Three Plays.* New York, 1922
16. *Success.* London, 1923
17. *The Artist: A Duologue.* London and New York, 1923
18. *The Man in the Bowler Hat: A Terribly Exciting Affair.* London and New York, 1923
19. *When We Were Very Young.* London and New York, 1924
20. *To Have the Honour.* London and New York, 1925
21. *Ariadne; or, Business First.* London and New York, 1925
22. *For the Luncheon Interval: Cricket and Other Verses.* London and New York, 1925
23. *A Gallery of Children.* London and Philadelphia, 1925
24. *Portrait of a Gentleman in Slippers: A Fairy Tale.* London and New York, 1926
25. *Four Plays.* London, 1926
26. *Winnie-the-Pooh.* London and New York, 1926
27. *The Princess and the Woodcutter.* London, 1927
28. *Now We Are Six.* London and New York, 1927
29. *The Ivory Door: A Legend.* New York, 1928
30. *The Ascent of Man.* London, 1928
31. *The House at Pooh Corner.* London and New York, 1928
32. *Mr. Pim Passes By.* London, 1929
33. *The Secret and Other Stories.* London and New York, 1929
34. *The Fourth Wall: A Detective Story.* New York, 1929
35. *Toad of Toad Hall.* London and New York, 1929
36. *By Way of Introduction.* London and New York, 1929
37. *Those Were the Days: The Day's Play, The Holiday Round, Once a Week, The Sunny Side.* London and New York, 1929
38. *Michael and Mary.* London, 1930
39. *When I Was Very Young.* London and New York, 1930
40. *The Very Young Calendar 1930.* New York, 1930
41. *Four Plays.* New York, 1932
42. *Four Days' Wonder.* London and New York, 1933
43. *Two People.* London and New York, 1933
44. *A.A. Milne.* London, 1933
45. *Peace with Honour: An Enquiry into the War Convention.* London and New York, 1934
46. *Other People's Lives.* London and New York, 1935
47. *More Plays.* London, 1935
48. *Miss Marlow at Play.* London and New York, 1936
49. *Miss Elizabeth Bennet.* London, 1936
50. *Sarah Simple.* London, 1939
51. *It's Too Late Now: The Autobiography of a Writer.* London, 1939
52. *Autobiography.* New York, 1939
53. *Behind the Lines.* London and New York, 1940
54. *War with Honour.* London, 1940
55. *The Ugly Duckling.* London, 1941
56. *War Aims Unlimited.* London, 1941
57. *One Year's Time.* London, 1942
58. *Chloe Marr.* London and New York, 1946
59. *Sneezles and Other Selections.* New York, 1947
60. *Going Abroad?* London, 1947
61. *Birthday Party and Other Stories.* New York, 1948
62. *The Norman Church.* London, 1948
63. *Books for Children: A Reader's Guide.* London, 1948
64. *A Table near the Band and Other Stories.* London and New York, 1950
65. *Before the Flood.* London and New York, 1951
66. *Year In, Year Out.* London and New York, 1952
67. *On Lewis Carroll.* Lexington, 1964
68. *Prince Rabbit, and The Princess Who Could Not Laugh.* London and New York, 1966

Mitchell, Gladys (Maude Winifred)
British, born April 19, 1901
Pseudonyms: Stephen Hockaby, Malcolm Torrie
1. *Speedy Death.* London and New York, 1929
2. *The Mystery of a Butcher's Shop.* London, 1929
3. *The Longer Bodies.* London, 1930
4. *The Saltmarsh Murders.* London, 1932
5. *Ask a Policeman.* London and New York, 1933
6. *Marsh Hay*, as Stephen Hockaby. London, 1933
7. *Death at the Opera.* London, 1934
8. *Death in the Wet.* Philadelphia, 1934
9. *Seven Stars and Orion*, as Stephen Hockaby. London, 1934
10. *The Devil at Saxon Wall.* London, 1935
11. *Gabriel's Hold*, as Stephen Hockaby. London, 1935
12. *Dead Men's Morris.* London, 1936
13. *Shallow Brown*, as Stephen Hockaby. London, 1936
14. *Outlaws of the Border.* London, 1936
15. *Come Away, Death.* London, 1937
16. *St. Peter's Finger.* London, 1938
17. *Printer's Error.* London, 1939
18. *Grand Master*, as Stephen Hockaby. London, 1939
19. *Brazen Tongue.* London, 1940
20. *The Three Fingerprints.* London, 1940
21. *Hangman's Curfew.* London, 1941
22. *When Last I Died.* London, 1941
23. *Laurels Are Poison.* London, 1942
24. *The Worsted Viper.* London, 1943
25. *Sunset over Soho.* London, 1943
26. *My Father Sleeps.* London, 1944
27. *The Rising of the Moon.* London, 1945
28. *Here Comes a Chopper.* London, 1946
29. *Death and the Maiden.* London, 1947
30. *The Dancing Druids.* London, 1948
31. *Holiday River.* London, 1948
32. *Tom Brown's Body.* London, 1949
33. *The Seven Stones Mystery.* London, 1949
34. *Groaning Spinney.* London, 1950
35. *The Malory Secret.* London, 1950
36. *The Devil's Elbow.* London, 1951
37. *Pam at Storne Castle.* London, 1951
38. *The Echoing Strangers.* London, 1952
39. *Merlin's Furlong.* London, 1953
40. *Faintley Speaking.* London, 1954
41. *Caravan Creek.* London, 1954
42. *On Your Marks.* London, 1954
43. *Watson's Choice.* London, 1955
44. *Twelve Horses and the Hangman's Noose.* London, 1956
45. *The Twenty-Third Man.* London, 1957

46. *Spotted Hemlock.* London, 1958
47. *The Man Who Grew Tomatoes.* London and New York, 1959
48. *The Light-Blue Hills.* London, 1959
49. *Say It with Flowers.* London, 1960
50. *The Nodding Canaries.* London, 1961
51. *My Bones Will Keep.* London and New York, 1962
52. *Adders on the Heath.* London and New York, 1963
53. *Death of a Delft Blue.* London, 1964
54. *Pageant of Murder.* London and New York, 1965
55. *The Croaking Raven.* London, 1966
56. *Heavy as Lead,* as Malcolm Torrie. London, 1966
57. *Skeleton Island.* London, 1967
58. *Late and Cold,* as Malcolm Torrie. London, 1967
59. *Three Quick and Five Dead.* London, 1968
60. *Your Secret Friend,* as Malcolm Torrie. London, 1968
61. *Dance to Your Daddy.* London, 1969
62. *Churchyard Salad,* as Malcolm Torrie. London, 1969
63. *Gory Dew.* London, 1970
64. *Shades of Darkness,* as Malcolm Torrie. London, 1970
65. *Lament for Leto.* London, 1971
66. *Bismarck Herrings,* as Malcolm Torrie. London, 1971
67. *A Hearse on May-Day.* London, 1972
68. *The Murder of Busy Lizzie.* London, 1973
69. *A Javelin for Jonah.* London, 1974
70. *Winking at the Brim.* London, 1974
71. *Convent on Styx.* London, 1975
72. *Late, Late in the Evening.* London, 1976
73. *Noonday and Night.* London, 1977
74. *Fault in the Structure.* London, 1977
75. *"Why Do People Read Detective Stories?"* New York, 1977
76. *Wraiths and Changelings.* London, 1978
77. *Mingled with Venom.* London, 1978
78. *Nest of Vipers.* London, 1979
79. *The Mudflats of the Dead.* London, 1979

Mitchell, Margaret (Munnerlyn)
American, born in 1900, died August 16, 1949
1. *Gone with the Wind.* New York and London, 1936
2. *Margaret Mitchell's "Gone with the Wind" Letters 1936-1949.* New York and London, 1976

Moore, Doris Langley [Doris Elizabeth Langley Moore]
British
Pseudonym: A Gentlewoman
1. *The Technique of the Love Affair,* as A Gentlewoman. London and New York, 1928
2. *Pandora's Letter Box, Being a Discourse on Fashionable Life.* London, 1929
3. *A Winter's Passion.* London, 1932
4. *The Bride's Book; or, Young Housewife's Compendium.* London, 1932
5. *The Pleasure of Your Company: A Text-Book of Hospitality.* London, 1933
6. *E. Nesbit: A Biography.* London, 1933
7. *The Unknown Eros.* London, 1935
8. *Our Loving Duty.* London, 1936
9. *They Knew Her When: A Game of Snakes and Ladders.* London, 1938
10. *The Vulgar Heart: An Enquiry into the Sentimental Tendencies of Public Opinion.* London, 1945
11. *Not at Home.* London, 1948
12. *The Woman in Fashion.* London, 1949
13. *All Done by Kindness.* London, 1951
14. *Pleasure: A Discursive Guide Book.* London, 1953
15. *The Child in Fashion.* London, 1953
16. *A Game of Snakes and Ladders.* London, 1955
17. *My Caravaggio Style.* London and Philadelphia, 1959
18. *The Great Byron Adventure.* Philadelphia, 1959
19. *Marie and the Duke of H—: The Daydream Love Affair of Marie Bashkirtseff.* London and Philadelphia, 1966
20. *Ada, Countess of Lovelace: Byron's Legitimate Daughter.* London, 1977

Morland, Nigel
British, born June 24, 1905
Pseudonyms: Mary Dane, John Donavan, Norman Forrest, Roger Garnett, Vincent McCall, Neal Shepherd
1. *The Goofus Man: A Fantasy for Children.* London, 1930
2. *Cachexia: A Collection of Prose Poems.* Paris (France), 1930
3. *Dawn Was Theirs.* Paris, 1931
4. *People We Have Never Met: A Book of Superficial Cameos.* Paris, 1931
5. *Abrakadabra! Verse for Modern Children.* Paris, 1932
6. *"Mary!" A Story of the Magdalene.* Paris, 1932
7. *The Phantom Gunman.* London, 1935
8. *The Moon Murders.* London, 1935
9. *The Street of the Leopard.* London, 1936
10. *The Clue of the Bricklayer's Aunt.* London, 1936
11. *Death Took a Publisher,* as Norman Forrest. London, 1936
12. *Finger Prints: An Introduction to Scientific Criminology.* London, 1936
13. *How to Write Detective Novels.* London, 1936
14. *Death Took a Greek God,* as Norman Forrest. London, 1937
15. *The Clue in the Mirror.* London, 1937
16. *The Case of the Rusted Room,* as John Donavan. London and New York, 1937
17. *Death in Piccadilly,* as Roger Garnett. London, 1937
18. *Starr Bedford Dies,* as Roger Garnett. London, 1937
19. *The Conquest of Crime.* London, 1937
20. *The Case Without a Clue.* London and New York, 1938
21. *Death Traps the Killer,* as Mary Dane. London, 1938
22. *A Rope for the Hanging.* London, 1938
23. *The Case of the Beckoning Dead,* as John Donavan. London and New York, 1938
24. *The Case of the Talking Dust,* as John Donavan. London, 1938
25. *The Killing of Paris Norton,* as Roger Garnett. London, 1938
26. *The Croaker,* as Roger Garnett. London, 1938
27. *Death Flies Low,* as Neal Shepherd. London, 1938
28. *Death Walks Softly,* as Neal Shepherd. London, 1938
29. *A Knife for the Killer.* London, 1939
30. *Murder at Radio City.* New York, 1939
31. *The Case of the Coloured Wind,* as John Donavan. London, 1939
32. *Danger—Death at Work,* as Roger Garnett. London, 1939
33. *Death Rides Swiftly,* as Neal Shepherd. London, 1939
34. *Crime Against Children: An Aspect of Sexual Criminology.* London, 1939
35. *A Gun for a God.* London, 1940
36. *Murder in Wardour Street.* New York, 1940
37. *The Clue of the Careless Hangman.* London, 1940
38. *The Case of the Violet Smoke,* as John Donavan. New York, 1940
39. *The Case of the Plastic Man,* as John Donavan. London, 1940
40. *Exit to Music: A Problem in Detection,* as Neal Shepherd. London, 1940
41. *The Careless Hangman.* New York, 1941
42. *Dumb Alibi.* New York, 1941
43. *The Corpse on the Flying Trapeze.* London and New York, 1941
44. *The Case of the Plastic Mask,* as John Donavan. New York, 1941
45. *A Coffin for the Body.* London, 1943

46. *A Man Died Talking,* as Roger Garnett. London, 1943
47. *Death Takes a Star.* London, 1943
48. *The Sooper's Cases.* London, 1943
49. *The Laboratory Murder and Other Stories.* London, 1944
50. *Corpse in the Circus.* London, 1945
51. *Eleven Thrilling Mysteries,* as Vincent McCall. London, 1945
52. *Death Spoke Sweetly.* London, 1946
53. *Murder Runs Wild.* London, 1946
54. *Strangely She Died.* London, 1946
55. *Smash and Grab,* as Vincent McCall. London, 1946
56. *The Corpse in the Circus and Other Stories.* London, 1946
57. *The Big Killing.* Hounslow (Eng), 1946
58. *Mrs. Pym of Scotland Yard.* London, 1946
59. *How Many Coupons for a Shroud?* London, 1946
60. *Dressed to Kill.* London, 1947
61. *The Hatchet Murders.* London, 1947
62. *26 Three Minute Thrillers: A Collection of Ingenious Puzzle Yarns.* London, 1947
63. *Eve Finds the Killer,* as Roger Garnett. London, 1947
64. *The Case of the Innocent Wife.* London, 1947
65. *Exit to Music and Other Stories.* London, 1947
66. *Death's Sweet Music.* London, 1947
67. *Dusky Death.* London, 1948
68. *She Didn't Like Dying.* London, 1948
69. *Fish Are So Trusting.* London, 1948
70. *No Coupons for a Shroud.* London, 1949
71. *Two Dead Charwomen.* London, 1949
72. *Death Takes an Editor.* London, 1949
73. *The Corpse Was No Lady.* London, 1950
74. *An Outline of Scientific Criminology.* London and New York, 1950
75. *Blood on the Stars.* London, 1951
76. *Death When She Wakes.* London, 1951
77. *He Hanged His Mother on Monday.* London, 1951
78. *The Lady Had a Gun.* London, 1951
79. *Call Him Early for the Murder.* London, 1952
80. *A Girl Died Singing.* London, 1952
81. *The Dead Have No Friends,* as John Donavan. London, 1952
82. *The Moon Was Made for Murder.* London, 1953
83. *Sing a Song of Cyanide.* London, 1953
84. *Hangman's Clutch.* London, 1954
85. *Background to Murder.* London, 1955
86. *Death for Sale.* London, 1957
87. *Look in Any Doorway.* London, 1957
88. *This Friendless Lady.* London, 1957
89. *A Bullet for Midas.* London, 1958
90. *Death and the Golden Boy.* London, 1958
91. *That Nice Miss Smith.* London, 1958
92. *Science in Crime Detection.* London, 1958
93. *Death to the Ladies.* London, 1959
94. *The Concrete Maze.* London, 1960
95. *So Quiet a Death.* London, 1960
96. *The Dear, Dead Girls.* London, 1961
97. *An Outline of Sexual Criminology.* Oxford (Eng), 1966
98. *Pattern of Murder.* London, 1966
99. *Mrs. Pym and Other Stories.* Henley-on-Thames (Eng), 1976
100. *An International Pattern of Murder.* Hornchurch (Eng), 1977
101. *Who's Who in Crime Fiction.* London, 1980

Morrissey, J.L. (Joseph Lawrence)
American
Pseudonyms: Henry Richards, Richard Saxon
1. *City of the Hidden Eyes.* London, 1964
2. *Cosmic Crusade,* as Richard Saxon. London, 1964
3. *Future for Sale,* as Richard Saxon. London, 1964
4. *The Hour of the Phoenix,* as Henry Richards. London, 1964
5. *The Stars Came Down,* as Richard Saxon. London, 1964

Murray, Frances [Rosemary Booth]
British, born February 10, 1928
1. *Ponies on the Heather.* London, 1966
2. *The Dear Colleague.* London and New York, 1972
3. *The Burning Lamp.* London and New York, 1973
4. *The Heroine's Sister.* London and New York, 1975
5. *Ponies and Parachutes.* London, 1975
6. *Red Rowan Berry.* London, 1976
7. *White Hope.* London, 1978
8. *Castaway.* London, 1978

Neihardt, John G. (Gneisenau)
American, born January 8, 1881, died November 3, 1973
1. *The Divine Enchantment: A Mystical Poem.* New York, 1900
2. *The Lonesome Trail.* New York and London, 1907
3. *A Bundle of Myrrh.* New York, 1907
4. *Man Song.* New York, 1909
5. *The River and I.* New York, 1910
6. *The Dawn Builder.* New York, 1911
7. *Life's Lure.* New York, 1914
8. *The Song of Hugh Glass.* New York, 1915
9. *The Quest.* New York, 1916
10. *The Song of Three Friends.* New York, 1919
11. *The Splendid Warfaring: The Story of the Exploits and Adventures of Jedidiah Smith and His Comrades.* New York, 1920
12. *Two Mothers.* New York, 1921
13. *Indian Tales and Others.* New York, 1925
14. *The Song of the Indian Wars.* New York, 1925
15. *Collected Poems.* New York, 1926
16. *The Song of the Messiah.* New York, 1935
17. *Black Elk Speaks, Being the Life Story of a Holy Man of the Oglala Sioux.* New York, 1932
18. *The Song of Jed Smith.* New York, 1941
19. *A Cycle of the West.* New York, 1949
20. *When the Tree Flowered: An Authentic Tale of the Old Sioux World.* New York, 1951
21. *Eagle Voice.* London, 1953
22. *Lyric and Dramatic Poems.* Lincoln (NB), 1965
23. *The Mountain Men.* Lincoln, 1971
24. *The Twilight of the Sioux.* Lincoln, 1971
25. *All Is But a Beginning: Youth Remembered 1881-1901.* New York, 1972
26. *Patterns and Coincidences: A Sequel to All Is But a Beginning.* Columbia, 1978

Newton, D.B. (Dwight Bennett)
American, born January 14, 1916
Psuedonyms: Dwight Bennett, Clement Hardin, Ford Logan, Hank Mitchum, Dan Temple
1. *Guns of the Rimrock.* New York, 1946
2. *The Gunmaster of Saddleback.* New York and London, 1948
3. *Range Boss.* New York, 1949
4. *The Trail Beyond Boothill.* London, 1949
5. *Shotgun Guard.* Philadelphia, 1950
6. *Stormy Range,* as Dwight Bennett. New York, 1951
7. *Stagecoach Guard.* London, 1951
8. *Six Gun Gamble.* Philadelphia, 1951
9. *Border Graze,* as Dwight Bennett. New York, 1952
10. *Lost Wolf River,* as Dwight Bennett. New York, 1952
11. *Range Feud.* London, 1953
12. *Guns Along the Wickiup.* New York, 1953
13. *Hellbent for a Hangrope,* as Clement Hardin. New York, 1954
14. *Rainbow Rider.* London, 1954
15. *Fire in the Desert,* as Ford Logan. New York, 1954
16. *Top Hand,* as Dwight Bennett. New York, 1955

17. *Outlaw River*, as Dan Temple. New York, 1955
18. *The Outlaw Breed*. New York, 1955
19. *The Man from Idaho*, as Dan Temple. New York, 1956
20. *The Avenger*, as Dwight Bennett. New York, 1956
21. *Bullet Lease*, as Dan Temple. New York, 1957
22. *Cross Me in Gunsmoke*, as Clement Hardin. New York, 1957
23. *The Lurking Gun*, as Clement Hardin. New York, 1961
24. *Cherokee Outlet*, as Dwight Bennett. New York, 1961
25. *The Love Goddess*. New York, 1962
26. *The Badge Shooters*, as Clement Hardin. New York, 1962
27. *Maverick Brand*. Derby (CT), 1962
28. *On the Dodge*. New York, 1962
29. *The Oregon Rifles*, as Dwight Bennett. New York, 1962
30. *Guns of Warbonnet*. New York, 1963
31. *Rebel Trail*, as Dwight Bennett. New York, 1963
32. *Gun and Star*, as Dan Temple. New York, 1964
33. *The Savage Hills*. New York, 1964
34. *Bullets in the Wind*. New York, 1964
35. *Fury at Three Forks*. New York, 1964
36. *Outcast of Ute Bend*, as Clement Hardin. New York, 1965
37. *Crooked River Canyon*, as Dwight Bennett. New York, 1966
38. *The Ruthless Breed*, as Clement Hardin. New York, 1966
39. *The Manhunters*. New York, 1966
40. *Hideout Valley*. New York, 1967
41. *The Paxman Feud*, as Clement Hardin. New York, 1967
42. *The Oxbow Deed*, as Clement Hardin. New York, 1967
43. *The Tabbart Brand*. New York, 1967
44. *Ambush Reckoning*, as Clement Hardin. New York, 1968
45. *The Wolf Pack*. New York, 1968
46. *Shotgun Freighter*. New York, 1968
47. *The Judas Horse*. New York, 1969
48. *Sheriff of Sentinel*, as Clement Hardin. New York, 1969
49. *Legend in the Dust*, as Dwight Bennett. New York, 1970
50. *Colt Wages*, as Clement Hardin. New York, 1970
51. *Stage Line to Rincon*, as Clement Hardin. New York, 1971
52. *The Big Land*, as Dwight Bennett. New York, 1972
53. *Syndicate Gun*. New York, 1972
54. *The Guns of Ellsworth*, as Dwight Bennett. New York, 1973
55. *Massacre Valley*. New York, 1973
56. *Range Tramp*. New York, 1973
57. *Hangman's Knot*, as Dwight Bennett. New York, 1975
58. *Trail of the Bear*. New York, 1975
59. *The Land Grabbers*. New York, 1975
60. *The Cheyenne Encounter*, as Dwight Bennett. New York, 1976
61. *Bounty on Bannister*. New York, 1977
62. *West of the Railhead*, as Dwight Bennett. New York, 1977
63. *Triple Trouble*. New York, 1978
64. *The Texans*, as Dwight Bennett. New York, 1979
65. *Disaster Creek*, as Dwight Bennett. New York, 1981
66. *Station 1: Dodge City*, as Hank Mitchum. New York, 1982
67. *Station 2: Laredo*, as Hank Mitchum. New York, 1982

Nickson, Arthur (Thomas)
Pseudonyms: Arthur Hodson, Roy Peters, John Saunders, Matt Winstan
1. *Tin Star Sheriff*. London, 1956
2. *Silver Town*. London, 1957
3. *Gold Trail*. London, 1957
4. *The Big Herd*, as Matt Winstan. London, 1957
5. *Gunslick Gambler*, as Matt Winstan. London, 1958
6. *No Star for the Deputy*. London, 1958
7. *Rusty Hines Hits the Trail*. London, 1958
8. *Rusty Hines—Trouble Shooter*. London, 1959
9. *One-Gun Justice*, as Matt Winstan. London, 1959
10. *Vengeance Rode West*, as Matt Winstan. London, 1959
11. *Two Gun Marshal*, as John Saunders. London, 1959
12. *New Trails Blaze West*, as Matt Winstan. London, 1960
13. *Dust Was His Shroud*. London, 1960
14. *Guns Blaze at Noon*. London, 1960
15. *A Colt for the Kid*, as John Saunders. London, 1960
16. *Guns in High Summer*, as John Saunders. London, 1961
17. *The Next Stage Out*, as John Saunders. London, 1961
18. *Lone Killer*. London, 1961
19. *Bounty Hunter's Trail*. London, 1961
20. *Pay Off in Lead*, as Matt Winstan. London, 1961
21. *Gunsmoke on the Iron Trail*. London, 1961
22. *Arizona Gun Feud*. London, 1962
23. *Bandit Trail*, as Matt Winstan. London, 1962
24. *Trail to Boot Hill*, as Matt Winstan. London, 1962
25. *Arizona Feud*, as John Saunders. London, 1962
26. *Gunfight at Nolan's Canyon*. London, 1963
27. *Two Deputies Came Riding*. London, 1963
28. *Drive to Dodge City*, as Matt Winstan. London, 1963
29. *No Branding Fire*, as Matt Winstan. London, 1963
30. *Gunman's Bluff*, as Roy Peters. London, 1963
31. *Shootup in Cleaver Valley*, as Roy Peters. London, 1964
32. *The Shotgun Marshal*, as Roy Peters. London, 1964
33. *Stranger in Oak City*, as Roy Peters. London, 1964
34. *Guns at Salt Flats*, as Matt Winstan. London, 1964
35. *Silvercrop*, as Arthur Hodson. London, 1964
36. *Arizona Hideout*. London, 1964
37. *Gun Trail*. London, 1964
38. *Gold-Lust City*, as Matt Winstan. London, 1965
39. *Range Tramp*. London, 1965
40. *Lynch Law Justice*, as John Saunders. London, 1965
41. *Cattle Doctor*, as Roy Peters. London, 1965
42. *Rail War*, as Roy Peters. London, 1965
43. *Buffalo!*, as Roy Peters. London, 1966
44. *Vigilante Justice*, as Roy Peters. London, 1966
45. *Gunslick Marshal*, as Matt Winstan. London, 1966
46. *Greenhorn Sheriff*, as Matt Winstan. London, 1966
47. *Ride a Crooked Trail*. London, 1966
48. *Colt Justice*, as Matt Winstan. London, 1967
49. *Sandy Creek Rustlers*. London, 1967
50. *West to Arizona*, as Roy Peters. London, 1967
51. *Women Ain't Angels*, as Roy Peters. London, 1967
52. *Silver Stampede*, as Roy Peters. London, 1968
53. *Alias Sam Smith*, as Roy Peters. London, 1968
54. *Land Grab*, as Matt Winstan. London, 1968

Nichols, John
American, born July 23, 1940
1. *The Sterile Cuckoo*. New York, 1965
2. *The Wizard of Loneliness*. New York, 1966
3. *The Milagro Beanfield War*. New York, 1974
4. *The Magic Journey*. New York, 1978
5. *The Ghost in the Music*. New York, 1979
6. *If Mountains Die*. New York, 1979
7. *The Nirvana Blues*. New York, 1981
8. *The Last Beautiful Days of Autumn*. New York, 1982

Nicole, Christopher (Robin)
British, born December 7, 1930
Pseudonyms: Robin Cade, Peter Grange, Mark Logan, Christina Nicholson, Andrew York
1. *West Indian Cricket*. London, 1957
2. *Off White*. London, 1959
3. *Ratoon*. London and New York, 1962
4. *Dark Noon*. London, 1963
5. *Amyot's Cry*. London, 1964
6. *Blood Amyot*. London, 1964
7. *The Amyot Crime*. London, 1965
8. *The West Indies: Their People and History*. London, 1965
9. *White Boy*. London, 1966

10. *King Creole*, as Peter Grange. London, 1966
11. *The Eliminator*, as Andrew York. London, 1966
12. *The Co-Ordinator*, as Andrew York. London and Philadelphia, 1967
13. *The Predator*, as Andrew York. London and Philadelphia, 1968
14. *The Self-Lovers*. London, 1968
15. *The Devil's Emissary*, as Peter Grange. London, 1968
16. *The Deviator*, as Andrew York. London and Philadelphia, 1969
17. *The Dominator*, as Andrew York. London, 1969
18. *The Thunder and the Shouting*. London and New York, 1969
19. *The Doom Fishermen*, as Andrew York. London, 1969
20. *Operation Destruct*, as Andrew York. New York, 1969
21. *The Tumult at the Gate*, as Peter Grange. London, 1970
22. *The Longest Pleasure*. London, 1970
23. *Manhunt for a General*, as Andrew York. London, 1970
24. *Operation Manhunt*, as Andrew York. New York, 1970
25. *The Face of Evil*. London, 1971
26. *The Infiltrator*, as Andrew York. London and New York, 1971
27. *Where the Cavern Ends*, as Andrew York. London and New York, 1971
28. *The Expurgator*, as Andrew York. London, 1972
29. *The Captivator*, as Andrew York. London, 1972
30. *Appointment in Kiltone*, as Andrew York. London, 1972
31. *Operation Neptune*, as Andrew York. New York, 1972
32. *The Golden Goddess*, as Peter Grange. London, 1973
33. *Lord of the Golden Fan*. London, 1973
34. *Introduction to Chess*. London, 1973
35. *The Fear Dealers*, as Robin Cade. London and New York, 1974
36. *Caribee*. London and New York, 1974
37. *The Fascinator*, as Andrew York. London and New York, 1975
38. *Dark Passage*, as Andrew York. New York, 1975
39. *The Devil's Own*. London and New York, 1975
40. *Mistress of Darkness*. London and New York, 1976
41. *Tricolour*, as Mark Logan. London and New York, 1976
42. *Guillotine*, as Mark Logan. London and New York, 1976
43. *Tallant for Trouble*, as Andrew York. London and New York, 1977
44. *Black Dawn*. London and New York, 1977
45. *The Power and the Passion*, as Christina Nicholson. London and New York, 1977
46. *Tallant for Disaster*, as Andrew York. London and New York, 1978
47. *Sunset*. London and New York, 1978
48. *Brumaire*, as Mark Logan. London and New York, 1978
49. *The Savage Sands*, as Christina Nicholson. London and New York, 1978
50. *The Secret Memoirs of Lord Byron*. Philadelphia, 1978

Niven, Frederick (John)
British, born March 31, 1878, died January 30, 1944
1. *The Lost Cabin Mine*. London, 1908
2. *The Island Providence*. London, 1910
3. *A Wilderness of Monkeys*. London and New York, 1911
4. *Above Your Heads*. London, 1912
5. *Dead Men's Bells*. London, 1912
6. *Hands Up*. London and New York, 1913
7. *Ellen Adair*. London, 1913
8. *The Porcelain Lady*. London, 1913
9. *Justice of the Peace*. London, 1914
10. *The S.S. Glory*. London, 1915
11. *Two Generations*. London, 1916
12. *Cinderella of Skookum Creek*. London, 1916
13. *Maple-Leaf Songs*. London, 1917
14. *Sage-Brush Stories*. London, 1917
15. *Penny Scot's Treasure*. London, 1918
16. *The Lady of the Crossing: A Novel of the New West*. London and New York, 1919
17. *A Tale That Is Told*. London, 1920
18. *The Wolfer*. New York, 1923
19. *Treasure Trail*. New York, 1923
20. *A Lover of the Land and Other Poems*. New York, 1925
21. *Queer Fellows*. London, 1927
22. *Wild Honey*. New York, 1927
23. *Go North, Where the World Is Young*. Privately printed, no date
24. *The Story of Alexander Selkirk*. London, 1929
25. *Canada West*. London, 1930
26. *The Three Marys*. London, 1930
27. *The Paisley Shawl*. London and New York, 1931
28. *The Rich Wife*. London, 1932
29. *Mrs. Barry*. London and New York, 1933
30. *Triumph*. London and New York, 1934
31. *The Flying Years*. London, 1935
32. *Old Soldier*. London, 1936
33. *Colour in the Canadian Rockies*, with Walter J. Phillips. Toronto, 1937
34. *The Staff at Simon's*. London, 1937
35. *Coloured Spectacles*. London, 1938
36. *The Story of Their Days*. London, 1939
37. *Mine Inheritance*. London, 1940
38. *Brothers in Arms, Being the Account Written by James Niven . . . of Glasgow, in the 18th Century*. London, 1942
39. *Under Which King*. London, 1943
40. *The Transplanted*. London, 1944

Nolan, Frederick
British
Pseudonym: Fredrick H. Christian
1. *The Life and Death of John Henry Tunstall*, as Frederick H. Christian. Albuquerque (NM), 1965
2. *Lone Star Western Annual*, as Frederick H. Christian. London, 1966
3. *Sudden Strikes Back*, as Frederick H. Christian. London, 1966
4. *Sudden—Troubleshooter*, as Frederick H. Christian. London, 1967
5. *Sudden at Bay*, as Frederick H. Christian. London, 1968
6. *Sudden—Apache Fighter*, as Frederick H. Christian. London, 1969
7. *Sudden—Dead or Alive*, as Frederick H. Christian. London, 1970
8. *Send Angel*, as Frederick H. Christian. London, 1972
9. *Kill Angel*, as Frederick H. Christian. London, 1972
10. *Find Angel*, as Frederick H. Christian. London, 1973
11. *Trap Angel*, as Frederick H. Christian. London, 1973
12. *Frame Angel*, as Frederick H. Christian. London, 1974
13. *The Ritter Double-Cross*. London, 1974
14. *The Oshawa Project*. London, 1974
15. *No Place to Be a Cop*. London, 1974
16. *The Algonquin Project*. New York, 1975
17. *The Pilgrim Fathers*, as Frederick H. Christian. London, 1975
18. *Kill Petrosino*. London, 1975
19. *Hang Angel*, as Frederick H. Christian. New York and London, 1975
20. *Hunt Angel*, as Frederick H. Christian. New York and London, 1975
21. *Take Angel*, as Frederick H. Christian. London, 1975
22. *Warn Angel*, as Frederick H. Christian. London, 1975
23. *Stop Angel*, as Frederick H. Christian. New York and London, 1976

24. *The Mittenwald Incident*. New York and London, 1976
25. *Jay J. Ames, Investigator*, as told to Fredrick Nolan. New York, 1976
26. *The Sound of Their Music: The Story of Rodgers and Hammerstein*, as Frederick H. Christian. New York and London, 1978
27. *Battle of the Alamo*, as Frederick H. Christian. London, 1978
28. *Carver's Kingdom*. London, 1978
29. *Ride Clear of Durango*, as Frederick H. Christian. Los Angeles (CA), 1979
30. *Bad Day at Agua Caliente*, as Frederick H. Christian. Los Angeles, 1979
31. *Brass Target*. New York, 1979
32. *Ride Out to Vengeance*, as Frederick H. Christian. Los Angeles, 1979
33. *Ambush in Purgatory*, as Frederick H. Christian. Los Angeles, 1979
34. *Showdown at Trinidad*, as Frederick H. Christian. Los Angeles, 1979
35. *White Nights, Red Dawn*. New York, 1980
36. *Shoot-Out at Silver King*, as Frederick H. Christian. Los Angeles, 1980
37. *Massacre in Madison*, as Frederick H. Christian. Los Angeles, 1980

Norris, Frank [Benjamin Franklin Norris]
American, born March 5, 1870, died October 25, 1902
1. *Yvernelle: A Legend of Feudal France*. Philadelphia, 1891
2. *Moran of the Lady Letty: A Story of Adventure off the California Coast*. New York, 1898
3. *Shanghaied*. London, 1899
4. *Blix*. New York, 1899
5. *McTeague: A Story of San Francisco*. New York and London, 1899
6. *A Man's Woman*. New York and London, 1900
7. *The Octopus: A Story of California*. New York and London, 1901
8. *A Deal in Wheat and Other Stories of the New and Old West*. New York and London, 1903
9. *The Pit: A Story of Chicago*. New York and London, 1903
10. *The Responsibilities of the Novelist and Other Literary Essays*. New York and London, 1903
11. *The Joyous Miracle*. New York and London, 1906
12. *The Third Circle*. New York and London, 1909
13. *Vandover and the Brute*. New York and London, 1914
14. *The Surrender of Santiago: An Account of the Historic Surrender of Santiago to General Shafter, July 17, 1898*. San Francisco, 1917
15. *Collected Writings*. New York, 1928
16. *Two Poems and "Kim" Reviewed*. San Francisco (CA), 1930
17. *Frank Norris of "The Wave": Stories and Sketches from the San Francisco Weekly, 1893-1897*. San Francisco, 1931
18. *The Letters of Frank Norris*. San Francisco, 1956
19. *The Literary Criticism of Frank Norris*. Austin (TX), 1964
20. *A Novelist in the Making: A Collection of Student Themes and the Novels Blix and Vandover and the Brute*. Cambridge (MA), 1971

Nye, Nelson (Coral)
American, born September 28, 1907
Pseudonyms: Clem Colt, Drake C. Denver
1. *Two-Fisted Cowpoke*. New York, 1936
2. *The Killer of Cibecue*. New York, 1936
3. *The Sheriff of Navajo County*. London, 1937
4. *The Leather Slapper*. New York and London, 1937
5. *Quick-Fire Hombre*. New York and London, 1937
6. *The Star Packers*, as Drake C. Denver. New York, 1937
7. *The Waddy from Roarin' Fork*. London, 1938
8. *G Stands for Gun*. New York and London, 1938
9. *Gun-Smoke*, as Clem Colt. New York, 1938
10. *Gun-Smoke*. London, 1938
11. *The Shootin' Sheriff*, as Clem Colt. New York, 1938
12. *Prairie Dust*. London, 1938
13. *The Bar Nothing Brand*, as Clem Colt. New York, 1939
14. *No Wire Range*, as Drake C. Denver. London, 1939
15. *Center-Fire Smith*, as Clem Colt. New York, 1939
16. *The Bandit of Bloody Run*. New York, 1939
17. *Smoke-Wagon Kid*. London, 1939
18. *Hair-Trigger Realm*, as Clem Colt. New York, 1940
19. *Turbulent Guns*, as Drake C. Denver. London, 1940
20. *Trigger-Finger Law*, as Clem Colt. New York, 1940
21. *The Feud at Sleepy Cat*, as Drake C. Denver. New York, 1940
22. *Tinbadge*, as Drake C. Denver. New York, 1941
23. *Wildcats of Tonto Basin*, as Drake C. Denver. New York, 1941
24. *The Five Diamond Brand*, as Clem Colt. New York, 1941
25. *Triggers for Six*, as Clem Colt. New York, 1941
26. *Pistols for Hire*. New York, 1941
27. *Gunfighter Breed*. New York, 1942
28. *Salt River Ranny*. New York, 1942
29. *Gun Quick*, as Drake C. Denver. New York, 1942
30. *The Desert Desperadoes*, as Drake C. Denver. New York, 1942
31. *Lost Water*, as Drake C. Denver. London, 1942
32. *The Sure-Fire Kid*, as Clem Colt. New York, 1942
33. *Trigger Talk*, as Clem Colt. New York, 1942
34. *Rustlers' Roost*, as Clem Colt. New York, 1943
35. *Guns of Horse Prairie*, as Clem Colt. New York, 1943
36. *Come A-Smokin'*. London, 1943
37. *Beneath the Belt*. London, 1943
38. *Gunslick Mountain*. London, 1944
39. *Wild Horse Shorty*. New York and London, 1944
40. *Cartridge-Case Law*. New York, 1944
41. *The Renegade Cowboy*, as Clem Colt. New York, 1944
42. *Fiddle-Back Ranch*, as Clem Colt. New York, 1944
43. *Maverick Canyon*, as Clem Colt. New York, 1944
44. *Breed of the Chaparral*, as Drake C. Denver. New York, 1946
45. *Once in the Saddle*, as Clem Colt. New York, 1946
46. *Blood of Kings*. New York, 1946
47. *The Barber of Tubac*. New York, 1947
48. *Coyote Song*, as Clem Colt. New York, 1947
49. *Outstanding Modern Quarter Horse Sires*. New York, 1948
50. *Saddle Bow Slim*, as Clem Colt. New York, 1948
51. *The Gun Wolf of Tubac*. New York, 1949
52. *Breed of the Chaparral*, as Clem Colt. London, 1949
53. *Gunman, Gunman*. Golden (CO), 1949
54. *Long Rope*, as Drake C. Denver. London, 1949
55. *Champions of the Quarter Tracks*. New York, 1950
56. *Riders by Night*. New York, 1950
57. *Rustlers of K.C. Ranch*. London, 1950
58. *Caliban's Colt*. New York, 1950
59. *Horses Is Fine People*. London, 1950
60. *A Bullet for Billy the Kid*. New York, 1950
61. *Thief River*. New York, 1951
62. *Born to Trouble*. New York, 1951
63. *Wide Loop*. New York, 1952
64. *Plunder Valley*. New York, 1952
65. *Desert of the Damned*. New York, 1952
66. *Tough Company*, as Clem Colt. New York, 1952
67. *Strawberry Roan*, as Clem Colt. New York and London, 1953
68. *No Tomorrow*, as Clem Colt. London, 1953
69. *The Crazy K*. London, 1953

70. *Smoke Talk*, as Clem Colt. New York, 1954
71. *Smoke Talk*. London, 1954
72. *Six-Gun Buckaroo*, as Clem Colt. New York, 1954
73. *The One-Shot Kid*. New York, 1954
74. *Hired Hand*. New York and London, 1954
75. *The Red Sombrero*. New York, 1954
76. *Quick Trigger Country*, as Clem Colt. New York, 1955
77. *Quick Trigger Country*. London, 1955
78. *The Texas Tornado*. New York, 1955
79. *The Lonely Grass*. New York, 1955
80. *The Parson of Gunbarrel Basin*. New York and London, 1955
81. *Gunshot Trail*. New York, 1955
82. *Tornado on Horseback*. New York, 1955
83. *The No-Gun Fighter*. New York, 1956
84. *Ranger's Revenge*. New York, 1956
85. *Blood Sky*. London, 1956
86. *Arizona Dead-Shot*. New York, 1957
87. *South Fork*. London, 1957
88. *Bandido*. New York, 1957
89. *Maverick Marshall*. New York, 1958
90. *Guns of Arizona*. New York, 1958
91. *Gunfighter Brand*. New York, 1958
92. *Horses, Women, and Guns*. New York, 1959
93. *The Overlanders*. New York, 1959
94. *Long Run*. New York, 1959
95. *Ride the Wild Plains*. London, 1959
96. *The Last Bullet*. New York, 1960
97. *River of Horns*. London, 1960
98. *The Wolf that Rode*. New York, 1960
99. *Johnny Get Your Gun*. London, 1960
100. *Gunfight at the OK Corral*. New York, 1960
101. *Not Grass Alone*. New York, 1961
102. *The Irreverent Scout*. London, 1961
103. *Trouble on the Tonto Rim*. New York, 1961
104. *Gun-Hunt for the Sundance Kid*. New York, 1962
105. *Rafel*. New York, 1962
106. *Man on the Skewbald Mare*. No place, no date
107. *Death Comes Riding*. London, 1962
108. *Your Western Horse: His Ways and His Rider*. New York, 1963
109. *The Seven Six-Gunners*. New York, 1963
110. *Death Valley Slim, The Kid From Lincoln County*. New York and London, 1963
111. *Bancroft's Banco*. New York, 1963
112. *Wild River*. London, 1963
113. *The Complete Book of the Quarter Horse*. New York, 1964
114. *Treasure Trail from Tucson*. New York, 1964
115. *Weeping Widow Mine*. London, 1964
116. *Sudden Country*. New York, 1964
117. *Gun Feud at Tiedown, Rogue's Rondezvous*. New York, 1964
118. *Ambush at Yuma's Chimney*. New York, 1965
119. *The Bravo Brand*. London, 1965
120. *The Marshal of Pioche*. New York, 1966
121. *Iron Hand*. New York, 1966
122. *Single Action*. New York, 1967
123. *The Trail of Lost Skulls*. New York, 1967
124. *Shotgun Law*, as Drake C. Denver. New York, 1967
125. *Rider on the Roan*. New York, 1967
126. *A Lost Mine Named Salvation*. New York, 1968
127. *The Trouble at Pena Blanca*. New York, 1969
128. *Wolftrap*. New York, 1969
129. *Gringo*. New York, 1969
130. *Loco*. New York, 1969
131. *Ramrod*. New York, 1969
132. *Boss Gun*. New York, 1969
133. *Arizona Renegade*. New York, 1969
134. *The Texas Gun*. New York, 1970
135. *Trouble at Quinn's Crossing*. New York, 1971
136. *Hellbound for Ballarat*. New York, 1971
137. *Kelly*. New York, 1971
138. *The Clifton Contract*. New York, 1972
139. *Speed and the Quarter Horse: A Payload of Sprinters*. Caldwell (ID), 1973
140. *The Gun Wolf*. New York, 1980
141. *The Palominas Pistolero*. London, 1980
142. *Great Moments in Quarter Racing History*. New York, 1981
143. *Frontier Scout*. New York, 1982

Obets, Bob
1. *Blood Moon Range*. New York, 1957
2. *Rails to the Rio*. New York, 1965

O'Conner, Jack [John Woolf O'Conner]
American, born January 22, 1902, died January 20, 1978
1. *Conquest: A Novel of the Old Southwest*. New York, 1930
2. *Boom Town: A Novel of the Southwestern Silver Boom*. New York, 1938
3. *Game in the Desert*. New York, 1939
4. *Hunting in the Southwest*. New York, 1945
5. *Hunting in the Rockies*. New York, 1947
6. *Sporting Guns*. New York, 1947
7. *The Rifle Book*. New York, 1949
8. *The Big Game Rifle*. New York, 1952
9. *Sportsman's Arms and Ammunition Manual*. New York, 1952
10. *Outdoor Life Shooting Book*. New York, 1957
11. *The Complete Book of Rifles and Shotguns*. New York, 1961
12. *The Big Game of North America*. New York, 1962
13. *Big Game Hunts*. New York, 1963
14. *The Shotgun Book*. New York, 1965
15. *The Art of Hunting Big Game in North America*. New York, 1967
16. *Horse and Buggy West: A Boyhood on the Last Frontier*. New York, 1969
17. *The Hunting Rifle*. New York, 1970
18. *Sheep and Sheep Hunting*. New York, 1974
19. *The Big Game Animals of North America*. New York, 1977

O'Connor, Richard
American, born March 10, 1915, died February 15, 1975
Pseudonyms: Frank Archer, John Burke, Patrick Wayland
1. *Thomas: Rock of Chickamauga*. New York, 1948
2. *Hood: Cavalier General*. New York, 1949
3. *Sheridan: The Inevitable*. Indianapolis (IN), 1953
4. *High Jinks on the Klondike*. Indianapolis, 1954
5. *Guns of Chickamauga*. New York, 1955
6. *Gold, Dice, and Women*. London, 1955
7. *Down to Eternity: How the Poor Edwardian and His World Died with the Titanic*. New York, 1956
8. *Bat Masterson*. New York, 1957
9. *Johnstown the Day the Dam Broke*. Philadelphia, 1957
10. *Company Q*. New York, 1957
11. *Officers and Ladies*. New York, 1958
12. *Hell's Kitchen: The Roaring Days of New York's Wild West Side*. Philadelphia, 1958
13. *Wild Bill Hickok*. New York, 1959
14. *The Vandal*. New York, 1960
15. *Pat Garrett: A Biography of the Famous Marshall and the Killer of Billy the Kid*. New York, 1960
16. *Black Jack Pershing*. New York, 1961
17. *Gould's Millions*. New York, 1962
18. *The Scandalous Mr. Bennett*. New York, 1962
19. *Courtroom Warrior: The Combative Career of William Travers Jerome*. Boston, 1963

20. *Jack London: A Biography.* Boston, 1964
21. *Counterstroke,* as Patrick Wayland. New York, 1964
22. *Double Defector,* as Patrick Wayland. New York, 1964
23. *The Malabang Pearl,* as Frank Archer. New York, 1964
24. *Out of the Blue,* as Frank Archer. New York, 1964
25. *The Waiting Game,* as Patrick Wayland. New York, 1965
26. *The Widow Watchers,* as Frank Archer. New York, 1965
27. *Bret Harte: A Biography.* Boston, 1966
28. *The Turquoise Spike,* as Frank Archer. New York, 1967
29. *Ambrose Bierce: A Biography.* Boston, 1967
30. *The Lost Revolutionary: A Biography of John Reed,* with Dale L. Walker. New York, 1967
31. *Young Bat Masterson.* New York, 1967
32. *Sitting Bull: War Chief of the Sioux.* New York, 1968
33. *The German Americans: An Informal History.* Boston, 1968
34. *John Lloyd Stephen: Explorer of Lost Worlds.* New York, 1968
35. *Gentleman Johnny Burgoyne.* New York, 1969
36. *The Common Sense of Tom Paine.* New York, 1969
37. *Pacific Destiny: An Informal History of the U.S. in the Far East, 1776-1968.* Boston, 1969
38. *Winged Legend: The Story of Amelia Earhart,* as John Burke. New York, 1970
39. *The First Hurrah: A Biography of Alfred E. Smith.* New York, 1970
40. *John Steinbeck.* New York, 1970
41. *O. Henry: The Legendary Life of William S. Porter.* New York, 1970
42. *The Irish: Portrait of a People.* New York, 1971
43. *The Oil Barons: Men of Greed and Grandeur.* Boston, 1971
44. *The Cactus Throne: The Tragedy of Maximillian and Carlotta.* New York, 1971
45. *Ernest Hemingway.* New York, 1971
46. *Sinclair Lewis.* New York, 1971
47. *Buffalo Bill: The Noblest Whiteskin,* as John Burke. New York, 1972
48. *Duet in Drinks: The Flamboyant Saga of Lillian Russell and Diamond Jim Brady in America's Gilded Age,* as John Burke. New York, 1972
49. *The Naked Crusader,* as Frank Archer. New York, 1972
50. *Iron Wheels and Broken Men: The Railroad Barons and the Plunder of the West.* New York, 1973
51. *The Spirit Soldiers: A Historical Narrative of the Boxer Rebellion.* New York, 1973
52. *The Golden Summer: An Antic History of Newport.* New York, 1974
53. *Heywood Broun: A Biography.* New York, 1975

Olsen, T.V. (Theodore Victor)
American, born April 25, 1932
Pseudonyms: Joshua Stark, Christopher Storm, Cass Willoughby
1. *Haven of the Hunted.* New York, 1956
2. *The Man from Nowhere.* New York, 1959
3. *McGiven.* New York, 1960
4. *High Lawless.* New York, 1960
5. *Gunswift.* New York, 1960
6. *Ramrod Rider.* New York, 1961
7. *Brand of the Star.* New York, 1961
8. *Brothers of the Sword.* New York, 1962
9. *Savage Sierra.* New York, 1962
10. *The Young Duke,* as Christopher Storm. New York, 1963
11. *Break the Young Land,* as Joshua Stark. New York, 1964
12. *A Man Called Brazos.* New York, 1964
13. *The Sex Rebels,* as Christopher Storm. New York, 1964
14. *Campus Motel,* as Christopher Storm. New York, 1965
15. *Canyon of the Gun.* New York, 1965
16. *The Stalking Moon.* New York, 1965
17. *The Hard Men.* New York, 1966
18. *The Lockhart Breed,* as Joshua Stark. New York, 1967
19. *Bitter Grass.* New York, 1967
20. *Autumn Passion,* as Cass Willoughby. New York, 1966
21. *Blizzard Pass.* New York, 1968
22. *Arrow in the Sun.* New York, 1969
23. *Young Duke,* as Christopher Storm. London, 1970
24. *Keno,* as Joshua Stark. New York, 1970
25. *Soldier Blue.* New York, 1970
26. *A Man Named Yuma.* New York, 1971
27. *Eye of the Wolf.* New York, 1971
28. *Summer of the Drums.* New York, 1972
29. *There Was a Season.* New York, 1972
30. *Starbucks Brand.* New York, 1973
31. *Mission to the West.* New York, 1973
32. *Run to the Mountain.* New York, 1974
33. *Track the Man Down.* New York, 1975
34. *Westward They Rode.* New York, 1976
35. *Day of the Buzzard.* New York, 1976
36. *Bonner's Stallion.* New York, 1977
37. *Allegories for One Man's Moods.* Rhinelander (WI), 1979
38. *Roots of the North.* Rhinelander, 1979
39. *Rattlesnake.* New York, 1979
40. *Our First Hundred Years.* Rhinelander, 1981
41. *Blood of the Breed.* New York, 1982

Onstott, Kyle
American, born January 12, 1887, died in 1966
1. *Your Dog as a Hobby,* with Irving C. Ackerman. New York, 1940
2. *Beekeeping as a Hobby.* New York, 1941
3. *The Art of Breeding Better Dogs.* Washington (DC), 1946
4. *Mandingo,* with Lance Horner. Richmond (VA), 1957

O'Rourke, Frank
American, born October 16, 1916
Pseudonyms: Kevin O'Conner, Frank O'Malley, Patrick O'Malley
1. *"E" Company.* New York, 1945
2. *Flashing Spikes.* New York, 1948
3. *Action at Three Peaks.* New York, 1948
4. *Thunder on the Buckhorn.* New York, 1949
5. *The Team.* New York, 1949
6. *The Best Go First,* as Frank O'Malley. New York, 1950
7. *Bonus Rookie.* New York, 1950
8. *The Greatest Victory and Other Baseball Stories.* New York, 1950
9. *Blackwater.* New York, 1950
10. *The Gun.* New York, 1951
11. *The Football Gravy Train.* New York, 1951
12. *Never Come Back.* New York, 1952
13. *The Heavenly World Series and Other Baseball Stories.* New York, 1952
14. *Nine Good Men.* New York, 1952
15. *Concannon.* New York, 1952
16. *Warbonnet Law.* New York, 1952
17. *Gold under Skull Peak.* New York, 1952
18. *Gunsmoke over Big Muddy.* New York, 1952
19. *Violence at Sundown.* New York, 1953
20. *Latigo.* New York, 1953
21. *Ride West.* New York, 1953
22. *Gun Hand.* New York, 1953
23. *The Catcher, and the Manager: Two Baseball Fables.* New York, 1953
24. *High Dive.* New York, 1954
25. *Thunder in the Sun.* New York, 1954
26. *High Vengeance.* New York, 1954
27. *The Big Fifty.* New York, 1955

28. *Dakota Rifle.* New York, 1955
29. *Car Deal.* New York, 1955
30. *The Last Round.* New York, 1956
31. *The Diamond Hitch.* New York, 1956
32. *Concannon,* as Frank O'Malley. New York, 1956
33. *Hard Men.* New York, 1956
34. *Battle Royal.* New York, 1956
35. *The Last Chance.* New York, 1956
36. *Segundo.* New York, 1956
37. *Legend in the Dust.* New York, 1957
38. *The Bravados.* New York, 1957
39. *The Man Who Found His Way.* New York, 1957
40. *The Last Ride.* New York, 1958
41. *A Texan Came Riding.* New York, 1958
42. *Ambuscade.* New York, 1959
43. *Desperate Rider.* New York, 1959
44. *Violent Country.* New York, 1959
45. *The Far Mountains.* New York, 1959
46. *The Bride Stealer.* New York, 1960
47. *Window in the Dark.* New York, 1960
48. *The Springtime Fancy.* New York, 1961
49. *The Great Bank Robbery.* New York, 1961
50. *Gunlaw Hill.* New York, 1961
51. *Bandoleer Crossing.* New York, 1961
52. *The Affair of the Red Mosaic,* as Patrick O'Malley. New York, 1961
53. *The Affair of Swan Lake,* as Patrick O'Malley. New York, 1962
54. *New Departure,* as Kevin O'Conner. New York, 1962
55. *The Bright Morning.* New York, 1963
56. *A Private Anger, and Flight and Pursuit.* New York, 1963
57. *The Affair of Jolie Madame,* as Patrick O'Malley. New York, 1963
58. *The Affair of Chief Strongheart,* as Patrick O'Malley. New York, 1964
59. *The Affair of John Donne,* as Patrick O'Malley. New York, 1964
60. *Instant Gold.* New York, 1964
61. *A Mule for Marquesa.* New York, 1964
62. *The Affair of the Blue Pig,* as Patrick O'Malley. New York, 1965
63. *The Affair of the Bumbling Briton,* as Patrick O'Malley. New York, 1965
64. *The Duchess Says No.* New York, 1965
65. *P's Progress.* New York, 1966
66. *The Swift Runner.* Philadelphia, 1969
67. *The Abduction of Virginia Lee.* Philadelphia, 1970
68. *The Shotgun Man.* New York, 1976
69. *Badger.* New York, 1977

Ostenso, Martha
American, born September 17, 1900, died November 24, 1963
1. *A Far Land.* New York, 1924
2. *Wild Geese.* New York, 1925
3. *The Passionate Flight.* London, 1925
4. *The Dark Dawn.* New York, 1926
5. *The Mad Carews.* New York, 1927
6. *The Young May Moon.* New York, 1929
7. *The Waters Under the Earth.* New York, 1930
8. *Prologue to Love.* New York, 1932
9. *There's Always Another Year.* New York, 1933
10. *The White Reef.* New York, 1934
11. *The Stone Field.* New York, 1937
12. *The Mandrake Root.* New York, 1938
13. *Love Passed This Way.* New York, 1942
14. *And They Shall Walk: The Life Story of Sister Kenny.* New York, 1943
15. *O River, Remember!* New York, 1943
16. *Milk Route.* New York, 1948
17. *The Sunset Tree.* New York, 1949
18. *A Man Had Tall Sons.* New York, 1958

Overholser, Wayne D.
American, born September 4, 1906
Pseudonyms: John S. Daniels, Lee Leighton, Mark Morgan, Wayne Roberts, Dan J. Stevens, Joseph Wayne
1. *Buckaroo's Code.* New York, 1947
2. *West of the Rimrock.* New York, 1949
3. *Gun Crazy.* New York, 1950
4. *Draw or Drag.* New York, 1950
5. *The Sweet Bitter Land,* as Joseph Wayne. New York, 1950
6. *Oregon Trunk,* as Dan J. Stevens. New York, 1950
7. *The Snake Stomper,* as Joseph Wayne. New York, 1951
8. *Gunplay Valley,* as Joseph Wayne. New York, 1951
9. *Wild Horse Range,* as Dan J. Stevens. New York, 1951
10. *Steel to the South.* New York, 1951
11. *By Gun and Spur,* as Joseph Wayne. New York, 1952
12. *Gun and Spur,* as Joseph Wayne. London, 1952
13. *Fabulous Gunmen.* New York, 1952
14. *Gunflame,* as John S. Daniels. Philadelphia, 1952
15. *The Nester,* as John S. Daniels. Philadelphia, 1953
16. *Law Man,* as Lee Leighton. New York, 1953
17. *Fighting Man,* as Mark Morgan. New York, 1953
18. *Valley of Guns.* New York, 1953
19. *The Long Wind,* as Joseph Wayne. New York, 1953
20. *Bunch Grass,* as Joseph Wayne. New York, 1954
21. *The Colt Slinger,* as Joseph Wayne. New York, 1954
22. *The Violent Land.* New York, 1954
23. *Tough Hand.* New York, 1954
24. *The Land Grabbers,* as John S. Daniels. Philadelphia, 1955
25. *Guns at Lariat,* as Joseph Wayne. London, 1955
26. *The Return of the Kid,* as Joseph Wayne. New York, 1955
27. *Cast a Long Shadow.* New York, 1955
28. *Blood Money,* as Dan J. Stevens. New York, 1956
29. *Beyond the Pass,* as Lee Leighton. New York, 1956
30. *Gunlock.* New York, 1956
31. *Silent River,* as Wayne Roberts, with Robert Greenleaf Athearn. New York, 1956
32. *The Lone Deputy.* New York, 1957
33. *Desperate Man.* New York, 1957
34. *Showdown at Stony Creek,* as Joseph Wayne, with Lewis B. Patten. New York, 1957
35. *The Man from Yesterday,* as John S. Daniels. New York, 1957
36. *Tomahawk,* as Lee Leighton, with Lewis B. Patten. New York, 1958
37. *Colorado Gold,* as Lee Leighton, with Chad Merriman. New York, 1958
38. *Smoke of the Gun,* as John S. Daniels. New York, 1958
39. *Hearn's Valley.* New York, 1958
40. *Hangman's Mesa,* as Dan J. Stevens. Derby (CT), 1959
41. *Ute Country,* as John S. Daniels. New York, 1959
42. *Pistol Johnny,* as Joseph Wayne. New York, 1960
43. *Fight for the Valley,* as Lee Leighton. New York, 1960
44. *War in Sandoval County.* New York, 1960
45. *The Judas Gun.* New York, 1960
46. *The Gun and the Man,* as Joseph Wayne, with Lewis B. Patten. New York, 1960
47. *Standoff at the River.* New York, 1961
48. *The Killer Marshall.* New York, 1961
49. *The Bitter Night.* New York, 1961
50. *The Gunfighters,* as John S. Daniels. London, 1961
51. *The Gun and the Law,* as Joseph Wayne, with Lewis B. Patten. New York and London, 1961
52. *Gut Shot,* as Lee Leighton. New York, 1962

53. *Land of Promises*, as Joseph Wayne. New York, 1962
54. *The Bad Man*, as Joseph Wayne. New York, 1962
55. *The Trial of Billy Peale*. New York, 1962
56. *A Gun for Johnny Deere*. New York, 1963
57. *To the Far Mountains*. New York, 1963
58. *Gun Trap at Bright Water*, as Dan J. Stevens. New York, 1963
59. *Proud Journey*, as Joseph Wayne. New York, 1963
60. *The Crossing*, as John S. Daniels. New York, 1963
61. *Trail's End*, as John S. Daniels. New York, 1964
62. *Deadman Junction*, as Joseph Wayne. New York, 1964
63. *Land Beyond the Law*, as Dan J. Stevens. New York, 1964
64. *Day of Judgement*. New York, 1965
65. *The Hunted*, as John S. Daniels. New York, 1965
66. *War Party*, as John S. Daniels. New York, 1966
67. *Colorado Incident*. London, 1966
68. *Brand 99*. New York, 1966
69. *Stage to Durango*, as Dan J. Stevens. New York, 1966
70. *Deadline*, as Dan J. Stevens. New York, 1966
71. *Big Ugly*, as Lee Leighton. New York, 1966
72. *Hanging at Pulpit Rock*, as Lee Leighton. New York, 1967
73. *Killer from Owl Creek*, as Dan J. Stevens. New York, 1967
74. *Ride into Danger*. New York and London, 1967
75. *Summer of the Sioux*. New York, 1967
76. *Red Is the Valley*, as Joseph Wayne. New York, 1967
77. *North to Deadwood*. New York, 1968
78. *Stranger in Rampart*, as Dan J. Stevens. New York, 1968
79. *The Day the Killers Came*, as John S. Daniels. New York, 1968
80. *The Three Sons of Adam Jones*, as John S. Daniels. New York, 1969
81. *The Dry Fork Incident*, as Dan J. Stevens. New York, 1969
82. *Bitter Journey*, as Lee Leighton. New York, 1969
83. *Killer Guns*, as Lee Leighton. New York, 1969
84. *The Meeker Massacre*, with Lewis B. Patten. New York, 1969
85. *Buckskin Man*. New York, 1969
86. *You'll Never Hang Me*, as Lee Leighton. New York, 1971
87. *The Long Trail North*. New York, 1972
88. *The Noose*. New York, 1972
89. *Hunter's Moon*, as Dan J. Stevens. New York, 1973
90. *Sun on the Wall*. New York, 1973
91. *Cassidy*, as Lee Leighton. New York, 1973
92. *Greenhorn Marshall*, as Lee Leighton. New York, 1974
93. *Red Snow*. New York, 1976
94. *The Mason County War*. New York, 1976
95. *The Dry Gulcher*. New York, 1977
96. *The Trouble Kid*. New York, 1978
97. *The Diablo Ghost*. New York, 1978
98. *The Cattle Queen Fued*. New York, 1979
99. *Nightmare in Broken Bow*. New York, 1980
100. *Revenge in Crow City*. New York, 1980
101. *Danger Patrol*. New York, 1982

Ovstedal, Barbara
Pseudonym: Rosalind Laker, Barbara Paul
1. *Sovereign's Key*, as Rosalind Laker. London, 1969
2. *Far Seeks the Heart*, as Rosalind Laker. London, 1970
3. *Sail a Jeweled Ship*, as Rosalind Laker. London, 1971
4. *The Shripney Lady*, as Rosalind Laker. London, 1972
5. *Red Cherry Summer*. London, 1973
6. *Valley of the Reindeer*. London, 1973
7. *Norway*. London and New York, 1973
8. *Souvenir from Sweden*. London, 1974
9. *Fair Wind of Love*, as Rosalind Laker. London, 1974
10. *The Seventeenth Stair*, as Barbara Paul. London and New York, 1975
11. *The Smuggler's Bride*, as Rosalind Laker. New York, 1975
12. *The Curse of Halewood*, as Barbara Paul. London, 1976
13. *Ride the Blue Riband*, as Rosalind Laker. New York, 1977
14. *The Frenchwoman*, as Barbara Paul. London and New York, 1977
15. *A Wild Cry of Love*, as Barbara Paul. London, 1978
16. *Warwyck's Woman*, as Rosalind Laker. New York, 1978
17. *To Love a Stranger*, as Barbara Paul. New York, 1979
18. *Claudine's Daughter*, as Rosalind Laker. New York and London, 1979
19. *Warwyck's Choice*, as Rosalind Laker. New York, 1980
20. *Fly Banners of Silk*, as Rosalind Laker. New York, 1981
21. *Gilded Splendour*, as Rosalind Laker. New York, 1982

Palmer, John Leslie
British, born in 1885, died August 5, 1944
Pseudonyms: Francis Beeding, with Hilary Adam St. George Saunders; Christopher Haddon; David Pilgrim, with Hilary Adam St. George Saunders
1. *The Censor and the Theatres*. London, 1912
2. *The Comedy of Manners*. London, 1913
3. *The Future of the Theatre*. London, 1913
4. *Comedy*. London, 1914
5. *Over the Hills*. London, 1914
6. *Peter Paragon: A Tale of Youth*. London and New York, 1915
7. *Bernard Shaw: An Epitath*. London, 1915
8. *George Bernard Shaw, Harlequin or Patriot?* New York, 1915
9. *Rudyard Kipling*. London, 1915
10. *The King's Men*. London and New York, 1916
11. *The Happy Fool*. London and New York, 1922
12. *Looking after Joan*. London and New York, 1923
13. *The Seven Sleepers*, as Francis Beeding. London and Boston, 1925
14. *The Little White Hag*, as Francis Beeding. London and Boston, 1926
15. *Jennifer*. London and New York, 1926
16. *The Hidden Kingdom*, as Francis Beeding. London and Boston, 1927
17. *The House of Dr. Edwardes*, as Francis Beeding. London, 1927
18. *Studies in the Contemporary Theatre*. London and Boston, 1927
19. *The Six Proud Walkers*, as Francis Beeding. London and Boston, 1928
20. *The Five Flamboys*, as Francis Beeding. London and Boston, 1929
21. *Pretty Sinister*, as Francis Beeding. London and Boston, 1929
22. *The Four Armourers*, as Francis Beeding. London and Boston, 1930
23. *The League of Discontent*, as Francis Beeding. London and Boston, 1930
24. *Moliere: His Life and Works*. London and New York, 1930
25. *Death Walks in Eastrepps*, as Francis Beeding. London and New York, 1931
26. *The Three Fishers*, as Francis Beeding. London and Boston, 1931
27. *Timothy*. London, 1931
28. *Murder Intended*, as Francis Beeding. London and Boston, 1932
29. *Take It Crooked*, as Francis Beeding. London and Boston, 1932
30. *The Emerald Clasp*, as Francis Beeding. London and Boston, 1933
31. *The Two Undertakers*, as Francis Beeding. London and Boston, 1933
32. *The One Sane Man*, as Francis Beeding. London and Boston, 1934

Palmer, John Leslie

33. *Mr. Bobadil*, as Francis Beeding. London, 1934
34. *The Street of the Serpents*, as Francis Beeding. New York, 1934
35. *Ben Jonson*. London and New York, 1934
36. *Death in Four Letters*, as Francis Beeding. London and New York, 1935
37. *The Norwich Victims*, as Francis Beeding. London and New York, 1935
38. *The Eight Crooked Trenches*, as Francis Beeding. London and New York, 1936
39. *The Nine Waxed Faces*, as Francis Beeding. London and New York, 1936
40. *The Hesperides: A Looking-Glass Fugue*. London, 1936
41. *The Erring Under-Secretary*, as Francis Beeding. London, 1937
42. *Hell Let Loose*, as Francis Beeding. London and New York, 1937
43. *No Fury*, as Francis Beeding. London, 1937
44. *Murdered: One by One*, as Francis Beeding. New York, 1937
45. *So Great a Man*, as David Pilgrim. London and New York, 1937
46. *The Big Fish*, as Francis Beeding. London, 1938
47. *Heads Off at Midnight*, as Francis Beeding. New York, 1938
48. *The Black Arrows*, as Francis Beeding. London and New York, 1938
49. *The Ten Holy Terrors*, as Francis Beeding. London and New York, 1939
50. *Under the Long Barrow*, as Christopher Haddon. London, 1939
51. *The Man in the Purple Gown*. New York, 1939
52. *Mandragora*. London, 1940
53. *The Man with Two Names*. New York, 1940
54. *Not a Bad Show*, as Francis Beeding. London, 1940
55. *The Secret Weapon*, as Francis Beeding. New York, 1940
56. *Eleven Were Brave*, as Francis Beeding. London, 1940
57. *No Common Glory*, as David Pilgrim. London and New York, 1941
58. *The Twelve Disguises*, as Francis Beeding. London and New York, 1942
59. *Coffin for One*, as Francis Beeding. New York, 1943
60. *The Grand Design*, as David Pilgrim. London and New York, 1944
61. *Spellbound*, as Francis Beeding. Cleveland (OH), 1945
62. *There Are Thirteen*, as Francis Beeding. London and New York, 1946
63. *The Emperor's Servant*, as David Pilgrim. London, 1946

Patten, Lewis B. (Byford)
American, born January 13, 1915
Pseudonyms: Lewis Ford, Lee Leighton, Joseph Wayne

1. *Massacre at White River*. New York, 1952
2. *Gunmen's Grass*, as Lewis Ford. New York, 1954
3. *Gene Autry and the Ghost Riders*. Racine (WI), 1955
4. *Gunfighter from Montana*, as Lewis Ford. New York, 1955
5. *Gunsmoke Empire*. New York, 1955
6. *Back Trail*. London, 1956
7. *White Warrior*. New York, 1956
8. *Rope Law*. New York, 1956
9. *Maverick Empire*, as Lewis Ford. New York, 1957
10. *Guns of the Vengeful*. London, 1957
11. *The Massacre at San Pablo*. New York, 1957
12. *Pursuit*. New York, 1957
13. *Showdown at Stony Creek*, as Joseph Wayne, with Wayne D. Overholser. New York, 1957
14. *Valley of Violent Men*. New York, 1957
15. *Gun Proud*. New York, 1957
16. *Home Is the Outlaw*. New York, 1958
17. *Five Rode West*. New York, 1958
18. *Sunblade*. New York, 1958
19. *Showdown at War Cloud*. New York, 1958
20. *Tomahawk*, as Lee Leighton, with Wayne D. Overholser. New York, 1958
21. *Fighting Rawhide*. New York, 1959
22. *The Man Who Rode Alone*. New York, 1959
23. *The Ruthless Men*. New York, 1959
24. *Savage Star*. New York, 1959
25. *Top Man with a Gun*. New York, 1959
26. *Hangman's Country*. New York and London, 1960
27. *The Gun and the Man*, as Joseph Wayne, with Wayne D. Overholser. New York, 1960
28. *Savage Town*. New York, 1960
29. *Range 45*. London, 1960
30. *Renegade Gun*. New York, 1961
31. *The Savage Country*. London, 1961
32. *Law of the Gun*. New York, 1961
33. *The Angry Horseman*. New York, 1961
34. *The Angry Horseman*, as Lewis Ford. London, 1961
35. *The Gun and the Law*, as Joseph Wayne, with Wayne D. Overholser. New York and London, 1961
36. *The Gold Magnet*. London, 1962
37. *Flame in the West*. New York, 1962
38. *Savage Vengence*. London, 1962
39. *The Ruthless Range*. New York, 1963
40. *The Tarnished Star*. New York, 1963
41. *The Scaffold at Hangman's Creek*. New York and London, 1963
42. *Vengence Rider*. New York, 1963
43. *Gun's at Grey Butte*. New York and London, 1963
44. *Wagon's East*. New York, 1964
45. *Ride for Vengence*. New York, 1964
46. *Proudly They Die*. New York and London, 1964
47. *Outlaw Canyon*. London, 1964
48. *Giant on Horseback*. New York, 1964
49. *The Killer from Yuma*. New York, 1964
50. *The Arrogant Guns*. New York, 1965
51. *No God in Saguaro*. New York and London, 1966
52. *Death Waited at Rialto Creek*. New York, 1966
53. *The Odds Against Circle L*. New York, 1966
54. *Prodigal Gunfighter*. New York, 1966
55. *Deputy from Furnace Creek*. New York, 1967
56. *The Star and the Gun*. New York, 1967
57. *Bones of the Buffalo*. New York, 1967
58. *Ambush Creek*. New York, 1967
59. *Cheyenne Drums*. New York, 1968
60. *Death of a Gunfighter*. New York, 1968
61. *The Red Sabbath*. New York, 1968
62. *The Meeker Massacre*, with Wayne D. Overholser. New York, 1969
63. *The Youngerman Guns*. New York, 1969
64. *Posse from Poison Creek*. New York, 1969
65. *Apache Hostage*. New York, 1970
66. *A Death in Indian Wells*. New York, 1970
67. *Red Runs the River*. New York, 1970
68. *Six Ways of Dying*. New York, 1970
69. *Showdown at Mesilla*. New York, 1971
70. *Ride the Hot Wind*. New York, 1971
71. *The Trial of Judas Wiley*. New York, 1972
72. *The Cheyenne Pool*. New York, 1972
73. *The Hide Hunters*. New York, 1973
74. *The Gun of Jesse Hand*. New York, 1973
75. *The Ordeal of Jason Ord*. New York, 1973
76. *The Tired Gun*. New York, 1973
77. *Hands of Geronimo*. New York, 1974
78. *Two for Vengeance*. New York, 1974
79. *Bounty Man*. New York, 1974

80. *Death Stalks Yellowhorse.* New York, 1974
81. *The Angry Town of Pawnee Bluffs.* New York, 1974
82. *Lynching at Broken Butte.* New York, 1974
83. *The Orphans of Coyote Creek.* New York, 1975
84. *Vow of Vengeance.* New York, 1975
85. *The Gallows at Graneros.* New York, 1975
86. *The Trap.* New York, 1976
87. *Ride a Crooked Trail.* New York, 1976
88. *The Lawless Breed.* New York, 1976
89. *Ambush at Soda Creek.* New York, 1976
90. *Man Outgunned.* New York, 1976
91. *Hunt the Man Down.* New York, 1977
92. *Guilt of a Killer Town, and Massacre Ridge.* New York, 1977
93. *Villa's Rifles.* New York, 1977
94. *The Trial at Apache Junction.* New York, 1977
95. *The Killings at Coyote Springs.* New York, 1977
96. *Cheyenne Captives.* New York, 1978
97. *Death Rides a Black Horse.* New York, 1978
98. *The Law in Cottonwood.* New York, 1978
99. *The Trial of the Apache Kid.* New York, 1979
100. *Rifles of Revenge.* New York, 1979
101. *Track of the Hunter.* New York, 1980

Pattullo, George
Canadian, born October 29, 1879, died July 30, 1967
1. *The Untamed: Range Life in the Southwest.* New York, 1911
2. *The Sheriff of Badger.* New York, 1912
3. *One Man's War: The Diary of a Leatherneck,* with J.E. Rendinell. New York, 1928
4. *Tight Lines!* Privately printed, 1938
5. *Horrors of Moonlight.* Privately printed, 1939
6. *A Good Rooster Crows Everywhere.* Privately printed, 1939
7. *All Our Yesterdays.* San Antonio (TX), 1948
8. *Era of Infamy.* San Antonio, 1952
9. *Morning After Cometh.* San Antonio, 1954
10. *How Silly Can We Get?* San Antonio, 1956
11. *Always New Frontiers.* Nevada, 1951
12. *Giant Afraid.* San Antonio (TX), 1957
13. *Some Men in Their Time.* San Antonio, 1959

Pendower, Jacques
British, born December 30, 1899, died in 1976
Pseudonyms: Cathleen Carstairs, Tom Curtis, Penn Dower, T.C.H. Jacobs, Marilyn Pender, Anne Penn.
1. *The Terror of Torlands,* as T.C.H. Jacobs. London, 1930
2. *The Bronkhorst Case,* as T.C.H. Jacobs. London, 1931
3. *Scorpion's Trail,* as T.C.H. Jacobs. London, 1932
4. *The Kestrel House Mystery,* as T.C.H. Jacobs. London, 1932
5. *Documents of Murder,* as T.C.H. Jacobs. New York, 1933
6. *Sinister Quest,* as T.C.H. Jacobs. London and New York, 1934
7. *The 13th Chime,* as T.C.H. Jacobs. London and New York, 1935
8. *Silent Terror,* as T.C.H. Jacobs. London, 1936
9. *Appointment with the Hangman,* as T.C.H. Jacobs. London and New York, 1936
10. *The Laughing Men,* as T.C.H. Jacobs. London, 1937
11. *Identity Unknown,* as T.C.H. Jacobs. London, 1938
12. *Traitor Spy,* as T.C.H. Jacobs. London, 1939
13. *Brother Spy,* as T.C.H. Jacobs. London, 1940
14. *The Broken Knife,* as T.C.H. Jacobs. London, 1941
15. *The Grensen Murder Case,* as T.C.H. Jacobs. London, 1943
16. *Reward for Treason,* as T.C.H. Jacobs. London, 1944
17. *The Black Box,* as T.C.H. Jacobs. London, 1946
18. *The Curse of Khatra,* as T.C.H. Jacobs. London, 1947
19. *With What Motive?* as T.C.H. Jacobs. London, 1948
20. *Dangerous Fortune,* as T.C.H. Jacobs. London, 1949
21. *The Red Eyes of Kali,* as T.C.H. Jacobs. London, 1950
22. *Lock the Door, Mademoiselle,* as T.C.H. Jacobs. London, 1951
23. *Blood and Sun-Tan,* as T.C.H. Jacobs. London, 1952
24. *Lady, What's Your Game?* as T.C.H. Jacobs. London, 1952
25. *Lone Star Ranger,* as Penn Dower. London, 1952
26. *No Sleep for Elsa,* as T.C.H. Jacobs. London, 1953
27. *Bret Malone, Texas Marshal,* as Penn Dower. London, 1953
28. *Gunsmoke over Alba,* as Penn Dower. London, 1953
29. *Bandit Gold,* as Tom Curtis. London, 1953
30. *The Woman Who Waited,* as T.C.H. Jacobs. London, 1954
31. *Good Knight, Sailor,* as T.C.H. Jacobs. London, 1954
32. *Texas Stranger,* as Penn Dower. London, 1954
33. *Indian Moon,* as Penn Dower. London, 1954
34. *Gunman's Glory,* as Tom Curtis. London, 1954
35. *Trail End,* as Tom Curtis. London, 1954
36. *Results of an Accident,* as T.C.H. Jacobs. London, 1955
37. *Death in the Mews,* as T.C.H. Jacobs. London, 1955
38. *The Dark Avenue.* London, 1955
39. *Hunted Woman.* London, 1955
40. *Malone Rides In,* as Penn Dower. London, 1955
41. *Frontier Mission,* as Tom Curtis. London, 1955
42. *Border Justice,* as T.C.H. Jacobs. London, 1955
43. *Cavalcade of Murder,* as T.C.H. Jacobs. London, 1955
44. *Cause for Suspicion,* as T.C.H. Jacobs. London, 1956
45. *Two-Gun Marshal,* as Penn Dower. London, 1956
46. *Desperate Venture,* as T.C.H. Jacobs. London, 1956
47. *Pageant of Murder,* as T.C.H. Jacobs. London, 1956
48. *Aspects of Murder,* as T.C.H. Jacobs. London, 1956
49. *Broken Alibi,* as T.C.H. Jacobs. London and New York, 1957
50. *Guns in Vengeance,* as Penn Dower. London, 1957
51. *Ride and Seek,* as Tom Curtis. London, 1957
52. *Phantom Marshal,* as Tom Curtis. London, 1957
53. *Deadly Race,* as T.C.H. Jacobs. London, 1958
54. *Mission in Tunis.* London, 1958
55. *Frontier Marshal,* as Penn Dower. London, 1958
56. *Gun Business,* as Tom Curtis. London, 1958
57. *Black Trinity,* as T.C.H. Jacobs. London, 1959
58. *Double Diamond.* London, 1959
59. *The Long Shadow.* London, 1959
60. *Lone Star Law,* as Tom Curtis. London, 1959
61. *Women Are Like That,* as T.C.H. Jacobs. London, 1960
62. *Anxious Lady.* London, 1960
63. *It Began in Spain,* as Kathleen Carstairs. London, 1960
64. *The Devouring Flame,* as Marilyn Pender. London, 1960
65. *Dangerous Delusion,* as Anne Penn. London, 1960
66. *Let Him Stay Dead,* as T.C.H. Jacobs. London, 1961
67. *The Tattooed Man,* as T.C.H. Jacobs. London, 1961
68. *Target for Terror,* as T.C.H. Jacobs. London, 1961
69. *The Widow from Spain.* London, 1961
70. *A Question of Loyalty,* as Marilyn Pender. London, 1961
71. *Prove Your Love,* as Anne Penn. London, 1961
72. *Third Time Lucky,* as Kathleen Carstairs. London, 1962
73. *The Red Net,* as T.C.H. Jacobs. London, 1962
74. *Murder Market,* as T.C.H. Jacobs. London, 1962
75. *Death on the Moor.* London, 1962
76. *The Perfect Wife.* London, 1962
77. *The Golden Vision,* as Marilyn Pender. London, 1962
78. *Rebel Nurse,* as Marilyn Pender. London, 1962
79. *The Secret Power,* as T.C.H. Jacobs. London, 1963
80. *Danger Money,* as T.C.H. Jacobs. London, 1963
81. *Operation Carlo.* London, 1963
82. *The Elusive Monsieur Drago,* as T.C.H. Jacobs. London, 1964
83. *Sinister Talent.* London, 1964

Pendower, Jacques

84. *Master Spy.* London, 1964
85. *Bandit Brothers,* as Penn Dower. London, 1964
86. *Final Payment,* as T.C.H. Jacobs. London, 1965
87. *Spy Business.* London, 1965
88. *Ashes in the Cellar,* as T.C.H. Jacobs. London, 1966
89. *Sweet Poison,* as T.C.H. Jacobs. London, 1966
90. *Out of This World.* London, 1966
91. *Shadows of Love,* as Kathleen Carstairs. London, 1966
92. *Dangerous Love,* as Marilyn Pender. London, 1966
93. *Mystery Patient,* as Anne Penn. London, 1966
94. *Death of a Scoundrel,* as T.C.H. Jacobs. London, 1967
95. *Wild Week-End,* as T.C.H. Jacobs. London, 1967
96. *Betrayed.* New York, 1967
97. *Traitor's Island.* London, 1967
98. *Try Anything Once.* London, 1967
99. *A Trap for Fools.* London, 1968
100. *House of Horror,* as T.C.H. Jacobs. London, 1969
101. *The Black Devil,* as T.C.H. Jacobs. London, 1969
102. *The Golden Statuette.* London, 1969
103. *Diamonds for Danger.* London, 1970
104. *She Came by Night.* London, 1971
105. *Cause for Alarm.* London, 1971
106. *Security Risk,* as T.C.H. Jacobs. London, 1972
107. *Date with Fear.* London, 1974

Perry, George Sessions
American, born May 5, 1910, died December 13, 1956
1. *Walls Rise Up.* New York, 1939
2. *Hold Autumn in Your Hand.* New York, 1941
3. *30 Days Hath September,* with Dorothy Cameron Disney. New York, 1942
4. *Texas: A World in Itself.* New York, 1942
5. *Where Away: A Modern Odyssey,* with Isabel Leighton. New York, 1944
6. *Hackberry Cavalier.* New York, 1944
7. *Cities of America.* New York, 1947
8. *Families of America: Where They Come From and How They Live.* New York, 1949
9. *My Granny Van: The Running Battle of Rockdale, Texas.* New York, 1949
10. *The Story of Texas A and M.* New York, 1951
11. *Tale of a Foolish Farmer.* New York, 1951
12. *The Story of Texas.* New York, 1956

Pocock, Roger [Henry Roger Ashwell Pocock]
British, born November 9, 1865, died in 1941
1. *Tales of Western Life, Lake Superior, and the Canadian Prairie,* as H.R.A Pocock. Ottawa (Canada), 1888
2. *Rottenness: A Study of America and England.* London, 1896
3. *The Blackguard.* London, 1896
4. *The Dragon-Slayer.* London, 1896
5. *The Artic Night.* London, 1896
6. *A Frontiersman.* London, 1903
7. *Following the Frontier.* New York, 1903
8. *Curly: A Tale of the Arizona Desert.* London, 1904
9. *Sword and Dragon.* London, 1909
10. *The Chariot of the Sun: A Fantasy.* London, 1910
11. *Jesse of the Cariboo.* London, 1911
12. *A Man in the Open.* Indianapolis (IN), 1912
13. *Captains of Adventure.* Indianapolis, 1913
14. *Canada's Fighting Troops.* London, 1914
15. *The Splendid Blackguard.* London, 1915
16. *The Cheerful Blackguard.* Indianapolis, 1915
17. *Horses.* London, 1917
18. *The Wolf Trail.* New York, 1923
19. *Chorus to Adventures: Being the Later Life of Roger Pocock ("A Frontiersman").* London, 1931

Portis, Charles (McColl)
American, born December 28, 1933
1. *Norwood.* New York, 1967
2. *True Grit.* New York, 1968
3. *The Dog of the South.* New York, 1970

Potter, Margaret (Edith)
British. Born June 21, 1926
Pseudonyms: Anne Betteridge, Anne Melville, Margaret Newman
1. *Murder to Music,* as Margaret Newman. London, 1959
2. *The Foreign Girl,* as Anne Betteridge. London, 1960
3. *The Young Widow,* as Anne Betteridge. London, 1961
4. *Spring in Morocco,* as Anne Betteridge. London, 1962
5. *The Long Dance of Love,* as Anne Betteridge. London, 1963
6. *The Younger Sister,* as Anne Betteridge. London, 1964
7. *Return to Delphi,* as Anne Betteridge. London, 1964
8. *Single to New York,* as Anne Betteridge. London, 1965
9. *The Chains of Love,* as Anne Betteridge. London, 1965
10. *The Truth Game,* as Anne Betteridge. London, 1966
11. *A Portuguese Affair,* as Anne Betteridge. London, 1966
12. *A Little Bit of Luck,* as Anne Betteridge. London, 1967
13. *Shooting Star,* as Anne Betteridge. London, 1968
14. *The Touch-and-Go Year.* London, 1968
15. *Love in a Rainy Country,* as Anne Betteridge. London, 1969
16. *The Blow-and-Grow Year.* London, 1969
17. *Sirocco,* as Anne Betteridge. London, 1970
18. *The Girl Outside,* as Anne Betteridge. London, 1971
19. *Sandy's Safari.* London, 1971
20. *Journey from a Foreign Land,* as Anne Betteridge. London, 1972
21. *The Sacrifice,* as Anne Betteridge. London, 1973
22. *The Stranger on the Beach,* as Anne Betteridge. London, 1974
23. *A Time of Their Lives,* as Anne Betteridge. London, 1974
24. *The Story of the Stolen Necklace.* London, 1974
25. *Trouble on Sunday.* London, 1974
26. *Smoke over Shap.* London, 1975
27. *The Temp,* as Anne Betteridge. London, 1976
28. *The Motorway Mob.* London, 1976
29. *The Lorimer Line,* as Anne Melville. London and New York, 1977
30. *A Place for Everyone,* as Anne Betteridge. London, 1977
31. *Tony's Special Place.* London, 1977
32. *The Tiger and the Goat,* as Anne Betteridge. London, 1978
33. *The Lorimer Legacy,* as Anne Melville. London, 1979
34. *Alexa,* as Anne Melville. New York, 1979
35. *Lorimers at War,* as Anne Melville. London, 1980
36. *Lorimers in Love,* as Anne Melville. London, 1981
37. *Blaize,* as Anne Melville. New York, 1981

Powell, James
American, born April 25, 1942
1. *A Man Made for Trouble.* Canoga Park (CA), 1976
2. *Deathwind.* New York, 1979
3. *Stage to Seven Springs.* New York and London, 1979
4. *Vendetta.* New York, 1980
5. *The Malpais Rider.* New York, 1981
6. *The Hunt.* New York, 1982

Prebble, John (Edward Curtis)
British, born June 23, 1915
1. *Where the Sea Breaks.* London, 1944
2. *The Edge of Darkness.* London, 1947
3. *The Edge of Night.* New York, 1948
4. *Age Without Pity.* London and New York, 1950
5. *The Mather Story.* London, 1954

6. *The Brute Streets.* London, 1954
7. *Mongaso, Man Who Is Always Moving: The Story of an African Hunter.* London, 1956
8. *Elephants and Ivory.* New York, 1956
9. *The High Girders.* London, 1956
10. *Disaster at Dundee.* New York, 1957
11. *Spanish Stirrup.* New York, 1958
12. *My Great-Aunt Appearing Day and Other Stories.* London, 1958
13. *The Buffalo Soldiers.* London and New York, 1959
14. *Culloden.* London, 1961
15. *The Highland Clearances.* London, 1963
16. *Glencoe: The Story of the Massacre.* London and New York, 1966
17. *The Darian Disaster.* London, 1968
18. *The Lion in the North: A Personal View of Scotland's History.* London and New York, 1971
19. *The Massacre of Glencoe.* London, 1972
20. *Spanish Stirrup and Other Stories.* London and New York, 1973
21. *Mutiny: Highland Regiments in Revolt 1743-1804.* London, 1975

Prescott, John (Brewster)
American, born July 29, 1919
1. *The Beautiful Ship: A Story of the Great Lakes.* New York, 1952
2. *Meeting in the Mountains.* New York, 1953
3. *The Renegade.* New York, 1954
4. *Journey by the River.* New York, 1954
5. *Guns of Hell Valley.* New York, 1957
6. *Wagon Train.* New York, 1957
7. *Ordeal.* New York, 1958
8. *Valley of Wrath.* New York, 1961
9. *Lion in the Hills.* New York, 1961
10. *Mountain-Lion: A Puma Called Rust.* London, 1962
11. *Treasure of the Black Hills.* New York, 1962

Pritchard, John Wallace
American, born December 4, 1912
Pseudonym: Ian Wallace
1. *Every Crazy Wind.* New York, 1952
2. *Off to Work,* with Paul H. Voelker. Pittsburgh, 1962
3. *Croyd,* as Ian Wallace. New York, 1967
4. *Dr. Orpheus,* as Ian Wallace. New York, 1968
5. *Deathstar Voyage,* as Ian Wallace. New York, 1969
6. *The Purloined Prince,* as Ian Wallace. New York, 1971
7. *Pan Sagittarius,* as Ian Wallace. New York, 1973
8. *A Voyage to Dari,* as Ian Wallace. New York, 1974
9. *The World Asunder,* as Ian Wallace. New York, 1976
10. *The Sign of the Mute Medusa,* as Ian Wallace. New York, 1977
11. *Z-Sting,* as Ian Wallace. New York, 1978
12. *Heller's Leap,* as Ian Wallace. New York, 1979
13. *The Lucifer Rocket,* as Ian Wallace. New York, 1980

Purdum, Herbert R.
1. *My Brother John.* New York, 1966
2. *A Hero for Henry.* New York, 1968

Queen, Ellery [Frederic Dannay and Manfred B. Lee]
Americans: Frederic Dannay, born Daniel Nathan, October 20, 1905; Manfred Bennington Lee, born Manfred Lepofsky, January 11, 1905, died April 3, 1971
Other pseudonym: Barnaby Ross
1. *The Roman Hat Mystery.* New York and London, 1929
2. *The French Powder Mystery.* New York and London, 1930
3. *The Dutch Shoe Mystery.* New York and London, 1931
4. *The Greek Coffin Mystery.* New York and London, 1932
5. *The Tragedy of X,* as Barnaby Ross. New York and London, 1932
6. *The Tragedy of Y,* as Barnaby Ross. New York and London, 1932
7. *The Tragedy of Z,* as Barnaby Ross. New York and London, 1933
8. *Drury Lane's Last Case.* New York and London, 1933
9. *The Egyptian Cross Mystery.* New York, 1933
10. *The American Gun Mystery.* New York and London, 1933
11. *The Siamese Twin Mystery.* New York, 1933
12. *The Chinese Orange Mystery.* New York and London, 1934
13. *The Adventures of Ellery Queen.* New York, 1934
14. *The Spanish Cape Mystery.* New York and London, 1935
15. *Halfway House.* New York and London, 1936
16. *The Door Between.* New York and London, 1937
17. *The Devil to Pay.* New York and London, 1938
18. *Ellery Queen's Big Book.* New York, 1938
19. *The Four of Hearts.* New York, 1938
20. *The Dragon's Teeth.* New York and London, 1939
21. *Calamity Town.* Boston and London. 1942
22. *The New Adventures of Ellery Queen.* New York and London, 1940
23. *More Adventures of Ellery Queen.* New York, 1940
24. *There Was an Old Woman.* Boston, 1943
25. *Ellery Queen's Mystery Parade.* Cleveland (OH), 1944
26. *The Murderer Is a Fox.* Boston and London, 1945
27. *The Case Book of Ellery Queen.* New York, 1945
28. *Ten Days' Wonder.* Boston and London, 1948
29. *Cat of Many Tails.* Boston and London, 1949
30. *Double, Double.* Boston and London, 1950
31. *Death at the Rodeo.* New York, 1951
32. *The Origin of Evil.* Boston and London, 1951
33. *The King Is Dead.* Boston and London, 1952
34. *Calender of Crime.* Boston and London, 1952
35. *The Scarlet Letters.* Boston and London, 1953
36. *QBI: Queen's Bureau of Investigation.* Boston, 1954
37. *The Virgin Heiress.* New York, 1954
38. *The Glass Village.* Boston and London, 1954
39. *The Quick and the Dead.* New York, 1956
40. *Inspector Queen's Own Case.* New York and London, 1956
41. *The Wrightsville Murders.* Boston, 1956
42. *The Hollywood Murders.* Philadelphia, 1957
43. *The Finishing Stroke.* New York and London, 1958
44. *The Case of the Seven Murders.* New York, 1958
45. *The New York Murders.* Boston, 1958
46. *The XYZ Murders,* as Barnaby Ross. Philadelphia, 1961
47. *The Bizarre Murders.* Philadelphia, 1962
48. *The Player on the Other Side.* New York and London, 1963
49. *And on the Eighth Day.* New York and London, 1964
50. *Queens Full.* New York, 1965
51. *The Fourth Side of the Triangle.* New York and London, 1965
52. *A Study in Terror.* New York, 1966
53. *Sherlock Holmes Versus Jack the Ripper.* London, 1967
54. *Face to Face.* New York and London, 1967
55. *The House of Brass.* New York and London, 1968
56. *QED: Queen's Experiments in Detection.* New York, 1968
57. *Cop Out.* Cleveland and London, 1969
58. *The Last Woman in His Life.* Cleveland and London, 1970
59. *A Fine and Private Place.* Cleveland and London, 1971

Raine, William MacLeod
American, born June 22, 1871, died July 25, 1954
1. *A Daughter of Raasay: A Tale of the '45.* New York, 1902
2. *For Love and Honour.* London, 1904
3. *Wyoming.* New York, 1908

Raine, William MacLeod

4. *Ridgway of Montana.* New York, 1909
5. *Bucky O'Conner: A Tale of the Unfenced Border.* New York, 1910
6. *A Texas Ranger.* New York, 1911
7. *Mavericks.* New York, 1912
8. *Brand Blotters.* New York, 1912
9. *Crooked Trails and Straight.* New York, 1913
10. *The Vision Splendid.* New York, 1913
11. *The Pirate of Panama.* New York, 1914
12. *A Daughter of the Dons: A Story of New Mexico Today.* New York, 1914
13. *The Highgrader.* New York, 1915
14. *Steve Yeager.* Boston, 1915
15. *The Yukon Trail.* Boston, 1917
16. *The Sheriff's Son.* Boston, 1918
17. *A Man Four-Square.* Boston, 1919
18. *The Big-Town Round-Up.* Boston, 1920
19. *Oh, You Tex!* Boston, 1920
20. *Tangled Trails.* Boston and London, 1921
21. *Gunsight Pass.* Boston and London, 1921
22. *Man-Size.* Boston and London, 1922
23. *The Fighting Edge.* Boston, 1922
24. *Ironheart.* Boston and London, 1923
25. *The Desert's Price.* New York and London, 1924
26. *Troubled Waters.* London, 1924
27. *Roads of Doubt.* New York and London, 1925
28. *Bonanza: A Story of the Gold Trail.* New York and London, 1926
29. *The Last Shot.* New York and London, 1926
30. *The Return of the Range Rider.* London, 1926
31. *Judge Colt.* New York and London, 1927
32. *Grip of the Yukon.* New York, 1928
33. *Colorado.* New York and London, 1928
34. *Texas Man.* New York, 1928
35. *Roaring River.* London, 1928
36. *Famous Sheriffs and Western Outlaws.* New York, 1929
37. *The Fighting Tenderfoot.* New York and London, 1929
38. *Rutledge Trails the Ace of Spades.* New York, 1930
39. *Cattle,* with Will C. Barnes. New York, 1930
40. *Cattle, Cowboys, and Rangers.* New York, 1930
41. *The Knife Through the Ace.* London, 1930
42. *The Valiant.* Boston and London, 1930
43. *Beyond the Rio Grande.* Boston, 1931
44. *Badman.* London, 1931
45. *The Black Tolts.* Boston and London, 1932
46. *Under Northern Stars.* Boston, 1932
47. *The Broad Arrow.* Boston and London, 1933
48. *For Honour and Life.* Boston, 1933
49. *Banded Stars.* London, 1933
50. *The Trail of Danger.* Boston and London, 1934
51. *Border Breed.* Boston and London, 1935
52. *Square-Shooter.* Boston and London, 1935
53. *To Ride the River With.* Boston, 1936
54. *Sorreltop.* London, 1936
55. *Run of the Brush.* Boston and London, 1936
56. *Bucky Follows a Cold Trail.* Boston, 1937
57. *Cool Customer.* London, 1937
58. *King of the Bush.* Boston, 1937
59. *Sons of the Saddle.* Boston and London, 1938
60. *On the Dodge.* Boston and London, 1938
61. *The River Bend Feud.* Boston and London, 1939
62. *Riders of Buck River.* Boston, 1940
63. *Riders of the Rim Rocks.* London, 1940
64. *Trail's End.* Boston and London, 1940
65. *Guns of the Frontier: The Story of How Law Came to the West.* Boston, 1940
66. *45-Caliber Law: The Way of Life of the Frontier Peace Officer.* Evanston (IL), 1941
67. *They Called Him Blue Blazes.* Boston, 1941
68. *Cry Murder in the Marketplace.* London, 1941
69. *Justice Deferred.* London, 1941
70. *Gone to Texas.* London, 1942
71. *The Damyank.* Boston, 1942
72. *Hell and High Water.* Boston and London, 1943
73. *Courage Scout.* Boston and London, 1944
74. *Who Wants to Live Forever?* Boston and London, 1945
75. *Plantation Guns.* London, 1945
76. *Clattering Hoofs.* Boston and London, 1946
77. *Cry Murder.* New York, 1947
78. *This Nettle Danger.* Boston, 1947
79. *Top Rider.* London, 1948
80. *The Outlaw Trail.* London, 1947
81. *Gunsmoke Trail.* New York, 1948
82. *He Threw a Long Shadow.* London, 1948
83. *Rustlers Gap.* New York, 1949
84. *The Bandit Trail.* Boston, 1949
85. *Saddletramp.* London, 1949
86. *Powdersmoke Feud.* New York, 1950
87. *Rangers Luck.* Boston and London, 1950
88. *Texas Breed.* New York, 1950
89. *Saddlebum.* Boston, 1951
90. *Jingling Spurs.* Boston, 1951
91. *His Spurs a-Jingling.* London, 1951
92. *Glory Hole.* London, 1951
93. *Challenge to Danger.* Boston, 1952
94. *Arizona Guns.* New York, 1952
95. *The Six-Gun Kid.* New York, 1952
96. *Range Beyond the Law.* New York, 1952
97. *Justice Comes to Tomahawk.* Boston, 1952
98. *Rawhide Justice.* London, 1952
99. *Gun Showdown.* New York, 1952
100. *The Texas Kid.* New York, 1952
101. *Dry Bones in the Valley.* Boston and London, 1953
102. *West of the Law.* New York, 1953
103. *Reluctant Gunman.* Boston, 1954
104. *Boldly They Rode.* London, 1954
105. *High Grass Valley.* Boston and London, 1955
106. *Whipsaw.* New York, 1955
107. *Bullet Ambush.* New York, 1958
108. *The Tough Tenderfoot.* New York, 1958
109. *Pistol Pardners.* New York, 1959
110. *Drygulch Trail.* New York, 1960
111. *Six-Gun Feud.* New York, 1964
112. *Ride the River.* New York, 1973
113. *A Gun for Tom Fallon.* New York, 1974

Rathborne, St. George (Henry)
American, born December 26, 1854, died December 16, 1938
Pseudonyms: Hugh Allen; Duke Duncan; Aleck Forbes; Lieutenant Keene; Marline Manly; Warne Miller, M.D.; Harry St. George; Col. J.M. Travers

1. *Old Shadow,* as Marline Manley. Chicago, 1871
2. *Crack Skull Bob,* as Marline Manley. New York, 1872
3. *Bouncing Dick,* as Marline Manley. New York, 1873(?)
4. *Dave Barton,* as Marline Manley. New York, 1873(?)
5. *Gray Wolf,* as Marline Manley. Chicago, 1877
6. *Howdega,* as Marline Manley. Chicago, 1877
7. *The Mohawk Rangers,* as Marline Manley. Chicago, 1877
8. *Old Solitary,* as Marline Manley. Chicago, 1877
9. *The Young Gold Hunters,* as Marline Manley. Chicago, 1877
10. *Kit Carson's Last Bullet,* as Marline Manley. Chicago, 1878
11. *The Marked Moccasin,* as Marline Manley. New York, 1878
12. *The Winding Trail,* as Marline Manley. Chicago, 1878
13. *The Young Lion Hunters,* as Marline Manley. Chicago, 1878

14. *Winged Moccasin*, as Marline Manley. Chicago, 1878
15. *Old Iron Arm*, as Harry St.George. Chicago, 1878
16. *Traps and Trails*, as Harry St.George. Chicago, 1878
17. *Old Hickory*, as Harry St.George. New York, 1878
18. *Wabash Trailers*, as Harry St.George. Chicago, 1878
19. *The White Slave*, as Harry St.George. Chicago, 1878
20. *Skipper Sandy*, as Harry St.George. Chicago, 1878
21. *Forest Phantom*, as Harry St.George. Chicago, 1878
22. *The Texan Rifles*, as Harry St.George. Chicago, 1878
23. *Rattling Rube*, as Harry St.George. New York, 1878(?)
24. *The Head Hunter*, as Duke Duncan. Chicago, 1878
25. *Little Silver Knife*, as Lieutenant Keene. Chicago, 1878
26. *The Water Witch*, as Lieutenant Keene. Chicago, 1878
27. *Silver Bullet*, as Lieutenant Keene. Chicago, 1879
28. *The Snake Charmer*, as Lieutenant Keene. Chicago, 1879
29. *Daring Davy*, as Harry St. George. New York, 1879
30. *Prince of Detectives*, as Harry St. George. Chicago, 1879
31. *Leadville Luke*, as Marline Manley. Chicago, 1879
32. *The Money Maker*, as Marline Manley. Chicago, 1879
33. *Payne's Trail*, as Marline Manley. Chicago, 1879
34. *Prairie Coyote*, as Marline Manley. Chicago, 1879
35. *Mexican Mose*, as Marline Manley. New York, No date
36. *The Hunted Detective*, as Duke Duncan. Chicago, 1880
37. *Kit Carson's Ghost*, as Marline Manley. Chicago, 1880
38. *Gold Dust*, as Lieutenant Keene. Chicago, 1880
39. *Leadville Luke's Last Shot*, as Marline Manley. Chicago, 1880
40. *Leadville Luck's Luck*, as Marline Manley. Chicago, 1880
41. *Moccasin Mat*, as Marline Manley. Chicago, 1880
42. *The Red Sagamore*, as Marline Manley. Chicago, 1880
43. *Hickory Harry*, as Harry St.George. New York, 1880
44. *Thunderbolt Tom*, as Harry St.George. New York, 1880
45. *The White Wampum*, as Harry St.George. New York, 1880
46. *The Fire Witch*, as Harry St.George. Chicago, 1881
47. *Pandy Ellis, The Prairie Ranger*, as Marline Manley. New York, No date
48. *Little Hurricane*, as Marline Manley. Chicago, 1881
49. *The Phantom Smuggler*, as Marline Manley. Chicago, 1881
50. *Prairie Whirlwind*, as Marline Manley. Chicago, 1881
51. *Rope and Rifle*, as Marline Manley. Chicago, 1881
52. *Tavern League*, as Marline Manley. Chicago, 1881
53. *Charley Charlton*, as Col. J.M. Travers. New York, 1881
54. *The Creole Brothers*, as Col. J.M. Travers. New York, 1881
55. *The Black Hercules*, as Col. J.M. Travers. New York, 1882
56. *Fred Baxter*, as Col. J.M. Travers. New York, 1882
57. *The Lost Island*, as Col. J.M. Travers. New York, 1882
58. *The Girl Spy*, as Marline Manley. Chicago, 1882
59. *Night Riders*, as Marline Manley. Chicago, 1882
60. *Battle Smoke; or, The War Correspondent Among Guerrillas*, as Hugh Allen. New York, 1883
61. *The Pittsburg Landing*, as Duke Duncan. New York, 1883
62. *Fredericksburg*, as Aleck Forbes. New York, 1883
63. *Roaring Ralph Rockwood*, as Harry St.George. New York, 1884
64. *The Snow-Shoe Trail*. New York, 1884
65. *Custer's Last Shot*, as Col. J.M. Travers. New York, 1884
66. *Detective Jack Anderson*, as Col. J.M. Travers. New York, 1884
67. *Gotham Detectives in New Orleans*, as Col. J.M. Travers. New York, 1884
68. *Jack Sharp, Keenest Detective in Gotham*, as Col. J.M. Travers. New York, 1884
69. *A House of Mystery*, as Col. J.M. Travers. New York, 1884
70. *Old Gold Eyes, The Miner Detective*, as Col. J.M. Travers. New York, 1884
71. *The Diamond Detective*, as Col. J.M. Travers. New York, 1885
72. *Tom Barker, The Detective from the Bowery*, as Col. J.M. Travers. New York, 1885
73. *Jockey Joe*, as Warne Miller, M.D. New York, 1885
74. *Old Broadbrim's Latest Trail*, as Warne Miller, M.D. New York, 1885
75. *Gypsy Jock*, as Warne Miller, M.D. New York, 1886
76. *Old Revenue, The Niagara Falls Detective*, as Warne Miller, M.D. New York, 1886
77. *Tracked by the Dead*, as Warne Miller, M.D. New York, 1886
78. *Silas Quirk, The Diamond Detective*, as Warne Miller, M.D. New York, No date
79. *Detective Jack Anderson* (not the same as #66.), as Col. J.M. Travers. New York, 1886
80. *Old Broadbrim's Double Game*, as Col. J.M. Travers. New York, 1886
81. *Old Saddlebags, The Circuit Rider Detective*, as Col. J.M. Travers. New York, 1886
82. *Sombrero Sam, The Cowboy Detective*, as Col. J.M. Travers. New York, 1886
83. *Tom Throttle, The Engineer Detective*, as Col. J.M. Travers. New York, 1886
84. *Tracked at Midnight*, as Col. J.M. Travers. New York, 1886
85. *Jack Sharp in Florida*, as Col. J.M. Travers. New York, 1887
86. *Blue Blazes*, as Marline Manley. New York, 1887(?)
87. *Killpatrick's Best Bower*, as Marline Manley. New York, 1887
88. *The Young Tiger Hunters*, as Marline Manley. New York, 1888
89. *Paddling in Florida*. New York, 1889
90. *The Great Travers Case*, as Col. J.M. Travers. New York, 1890
91. *Doctor Jack*. New York, 1890
92. *The Poker King*, as Marline Manley. New York, 1890
93. *Rube Burrow's League*, as Marline Manley. New York, 1891
94. *The Cartaret Affair*. Chicago, 1891
95. *The Colonel by Brevet*. St. Paul (MN), 1892
96. *The Detective and the Poisoner*. Chicago, 1892
97. *The Man from Wall Street*. Chicago, 1892
98. *The Color Bearer*, as Aleck Forbes. New York, 1893
99. *The Cresent Star*, as Warne Miller, M.D. New York, 1893
100. *The Boy Cruisers*. New York, 1893
101. *Baron Sam*. New York, 1893
102. *Captain Tom*. New York, 1893
103. *Doctor Jack's Wife*. New York, 1893
104. *Major Matterson of Kentucky*. St. Paul (MN), 1893
105. *Miss Caprice*. New York, 1893
106. *Mynheer Joe*. New York and London, 1893
107. *The Bachelor of the Midway*. New York, 1894
108. *Monsieur Bob*. St. Paul and London, 1894
109. *Entangled in Crime*, as Warne Miller, M.D. New York, 1895
110. *The Fair Maid of Fez*. New York, 1895
111. *The Stranglers of Ohio*, as Marline Manley. New York, 1895
112. *Old Specie*, as Marline Manley. New York, No date
113. *Vestibule Limited Company*, as Marline Manley. New York, No date
114. *Witch or Wife*. Chicago, 1895
115. *Mrs. Bob*. New York, 1896
116. *Her Rescue from the Turks*. New York and London, 1896
117. *The Great Mogul*. New York and London, 1896
118. *A Bar-Sinister*. New York, 1897
119. *A Goddess of Africa*. Boston and London, 1897
120. *Masked in Mystery*. New York and London, 1897
121. *A Son of Mars*. New York and London, 1897
122. *Squire John*. New York, 1897
123. *The Girl from Hong Kong*. New York and London, 1898
124. *Saved by the Sword*. New York and London, 1898

125. *The Spider's Web.* New York, 1898
126. *A Fair Revolutionist.* New York and London, 1898
127. *A Chase for a Bride.* New York, 1899
128. *Miss Fairfax of Virginia.* New York, 1899
129. *A Sailor's Sweetheart.* New York, 1900
130. *Under Egyptian Skies.* New York, 1900
131. *Paddling Under Palmettos.* New York and London, 1901
132. *Sunset Ranch.* New York, 1901
133. *Chums of the Prairie.* New York and London, 1902
134. *The Gulf Cruisers.* New York, 1902
135. *Rival Canoe Boys.* New York, 1902
136. *The Young Range Riders.* New York and London, 1902
137. *Shifting Winds.* New York, 1902
138. *A Brazilian Free-Lance.* London, 1903
139. *The Witch from India.* New York and London, 1903
140. *A Filibuster in Tatters.* London, 1903
141. *For Love and Glory.* New York and London, 1903
142. *A Yankee Consul.* London, 1903
143. *Kinkaid, from Peking.* New York and London, 1903
144. *Well Worth Winning.* New York and London, 1903
145. *Dr. Jack's Paradise Mine.* New York and London, 1904
146. *My Florida Sweetheart.* New York and London, 1904
147. *The Red Slippers.* New York, 1904
148. *For Love of a Duchess.* London, 1904
149. *The Young Castaways.* Akron (OH), 1905
150. *The Young Voyagers of the Nile.* Akron, 1905
151. *Down in Dixie.* New York, 1905
152. *Favorite of Fortune.* New York, 1905
153. *Rival Toreadors.* New York, 1905
154. *Wizard of the Moors.* New York, 1905
155. *Adrift on a Junk; or, Boy Sailors of the China Sea.* Akron, 1905
156. *Down the Amazon.* Akron, 1905
157. *Dr. Jack and Company.* New York, 1906
158. *Dr. Jack's Talisman.* New York, 1906
159. *An American Monte Cristo.* London, 1909
160. *Campmates in Michigan.* Chicago, No date
161. *American Nabob.* New York, No date
162. *At Sword's Points.* New York, No date
163. *Back to Old Kentucky.* New York, No date
164. *Canoe and Campfire.* New York, No date
165. *Captain of the Kaiser.* New York, No date
166. *Champions in Arms.* New York, No date
167. *Daughter of Russia.* New York, No date
168. *Dr. Jack's Widow.* New York, No date
169. *Filipe's Pretty Sister.* New York, No date
170. **Little Miss Millions.** New York, No date
171. *Montezuma's Mines.* New York, No date
172. *My Hildegarde.* New York, No date
173. *Nabob of Singapore.* New York, No date
174. *Teddy's Enchantress.* New York, No date
175. *Voyagers of Fortune.* New York, No date
176. *Warrior Bold.* New York, No date
177. *Winning of Isolde.* New York, No date
178. *Canoe Mates in Canada.* Chicago, 1912
179. *The House Boat Boys.* Chicago, 1912
180. *Chums in Dixie.* Chicago, 1912
181. *The Young Fur Traders.* Chicago, 1912
182. *Tom Turner's Adventures with the Radio.* Racine (WI), 1924
183. *Carried by Storm.* Cleveland, no date
184. *Jeff Clayton's Strong Arm.* Cleveland, no date
185. *Rocky Mountain Boys.* Chicago, no date
186. *Texan Thoroughbred.* Cleveland, no date
187. *Under Troubled Skies.* Cleveland, no date
188. *The Pioneer Boys of the Ohio; Mississippi; on the Great Lakes; Missouri; Yellowstone; Columbia; Colorado; Kansas,* as Harrison Adams. Boston, 8 vols., 1912-28

Reese, John
American, born December 18, 1910, died August 15, 1951
Pseudonyms: John Jo Carpenter, Cody Kennedy, Jr.
1. *Sheehan's Mill.* New York, 1943
2. *Signal Guns at Sunup,* as John Jo Carpenter. New York, 1950
3. *Big Mutt.* Philadelphia, 1952
4. *The Shouting Duke.* Philadelphia, 1952
5. *The High Passes.* Boston, 1954
6. *Three Wild Ones.* Philadelphia, 1963
7. *Dinky.* Philadelphia, 1964
8. *Rich Man's Range.* New York, 1966
9. *Sure Shot Shapiro.* New York, 1968
10. *Sunblind Range.* New York, 1968
11. *The Looters.* New York, 1968
12. *Pity Us All.* New York, 1969
13. *Singalee.* New York, 1969
14. *Horses, Honor, and Women.* New York, 1970
15. *Sierra Showdown.* New York, 1971
16. *Jesus on Horseback: The Mooney County Saga.* New York, 1971
17. *The Wild One.* New York, 1972
18. *Big Hitch.* New York, 1972
19. *Springfield .45-70.* New York, 1972
20. *They Don't Shoot Cowards.* New York, 1973
21. *Weapon Heavy.* New York, 1973
22. *Angel Range; The Blowholers; The Land Baron.* New York, 3 vols., 1973-74
23. *The Sharpshooter.* New York, 1974
24. *Lonesome Cowboy.* New York, 1975
25. *Texas Fold.* New York, 1975
26. *Wes Hardin's Gun.* New York, 1975
27. *Hangman's Springs.* New York, 1976
28. *Blacksnake Man.* New York, 1976
29. *A Sheriff for All the People.* New York, 1976
30. *Omar, Fats, and Trixie.* New York, 1976
31. *Halter Broke.* New York, 1977
32. *The Cherokee Diamondback.* New York, 1977
33. *Sequoia Shootout.* New York, 1977
34. *A Pair of Deuces.* New York, 1978
35. *Deadeye.* New York, 1978
36. *Legacy of a Land Hog.* New York, 1979
37. *This Wild Land,* as Cody Kennedy Jr. New York, 1979
38. *The Warrior Flame,* as Cody Kennedy Jr. New York, 1980
39. *The Conquering Clan,* as Cody Kennedy Jr. New York, 1980
40. *Two Thieves and a Puma.* New York, 1980
41. *Maximum Range.* New York, 1981

Repp, Ed [Earl Edward Earl Repp]
American, born May 22, 1900, died February 19, 1979
Pseudonym: John Cody
1. *Cyclone Jim.* New York, 1935
2. *Hell on the Pecos.* New York, 1935
3. *Gun Hawk.* New York, 1936
4. *Hell in the Saddle.* New York and London, 1936
5. *Suicide Ranch.* New York, 1936
6. *Empty Holsters,* as John Cody. New York, 1936
7. *The Radium Pool.* Los Angeles (CA), 1949
8. *Stellar Missiles.* Los Angeles, 1949
9. *Canyon of the Forgotten.* London, 1950
10. *Don Hurricane.* London, 1950
11. *Hell's Hacienda.* London, 1951
12. *Six-Gun Law.* London, 1951
13. *Colt Carrier of the Rio.* London, 1952
14. *Desperado.* London, 1954

Rhodes, Eugene Manlove
American, born January 19, 1869, died June 27, 1934

1. *Good Men and True*. New York, 1910
2. *Bransford in Arcadia; or The Little Eohippus*. New York, 1914
3. *The Desire of the Moth*. New York, 1916
4. *West Is West*. New York, 1917
5. *Bransford of Rainbow Range*. New York, 1920
6. *The Come On*. New York, 1920
7. *Say Now Shibboleth*. Chicago, 1921
8. *Stepsons of Light*. Boston, 1921
9. *Copper Streak Trail*. Boston, 1922
10. *Once in the Saddle*. Boston, 1927
11. *The Trusty Knaves*. Boston, 1933
12. *Beyond the Desert*. Boston, 1934
13. *Penalosa*. Santa Fe (NM), 1934
14. *The Proud Sheriff*. Boston and London, 1935
15. *The Little World Waddies*. El Paso (TX), 1946
16. *The Best Novels and Stories of Eugene Manlove Rhodes*. Boston, 1949
17. *Sunset Land*. New York, 1955
18. *The Rhodes Reader: Stories of Virgins, Villains, and Varmints*. Norman (OK), 1957
19. *The Line of Least Resistence*. Chicago, 1958
20. *The Brave Adventure*. Clarendon (TX), 1971

Richmond, Roe [Roaldus Frederick Richmond]
American, born January 10, 1910
1. *Conestoga Cowboy*. New York, 1949
2. *Maverick Heritage*. New York, 1951
3. *Riders of Red Butte*. New York, 1951
4. *Island Fortress: The Story of Francis Marion*. Philadelphia, 1952
5. *Mojave Guns*. New York, 1952
6. *The Utah Kid*. New York, 1953
7. *Death Rides the Dondrino*. Boston, 1954
8. *Montana Bad Man*. New York, 1957
9. *The Hard Men*. New York, 1958
10. *Wyoming Way*. New York, 1958
11. *Lash of Idaho*. New York, 1958
12. *Forced Gigolos*. Chicago, 1960
13. *The Kansan*. New York, 1960
14. *The Deputy*. New York, 1960
15. *The Wild Breed*. New York, 1961
16. *The Blazing Star*. Chicago, 1963
17. *War in the Panhandle*. New York, 1979
18. *Legacy of a Gunfighter*. New York, 1980
19. *Showdown at Fire Hill*. New York, 1980
20. *Rio Grande Riptide*. New York, 1980
21. *Crusade on the Chisolm*. New York, 1980
22. *Hell on a Holiday*. New York, 1980
23. *Guns at Goliad*. New York, 1980
24. *Nevada Qween High*. New York, 1980
25. *An End to Summer*. New York, 1980
26. *The Blaze of Autumn*. New York, 1980
27. *Kelleway's Luck*. New York, 1981
28. *Life-Line of Texas*. New York, 1981
29. *Staked Plains Rendevous*. New York, 1981

Richter, Conrad (Michael)
American, born October 13, 1890, died October 30, 1968
1. *Human Vibration: The Mechanics of Life and Mind*. New York, 1925
2. *Brothers of No Kin and Other Stories*. New York, 1924
3. *Early Americana and Other Stories*. New York, 1936
4. *The Sea of Grass*. New York and London, 1937
5. *The Trees*. New York and London, 1940
6. *Tacey Cromwell*. New York, 1942
7. *The Free Man*. New York, 1943
8. *The Fields*. New York, 1946
9. *Smoke Over the Prairie and Other Stories*. London, 1947
10. *Always Young and Fair*. New York, 1947
11. *The Town*. New York, 1950
12. *The Light in the Forest*. New York, 1953
13. *The Mountain on the Desert*. New York, 1955
14. *The Lady*. New York and London, 1957
15. *The Waters of Kronos*. New York and London, 1960
16. *A Simple Honorable Man*. New York and London, 1962
17. *The Grandfathers*. New York and London, 1964
18. *A Country of Strangers*. New York and London, 1966
19. *The Awakening Land*. New York, 1966
20. *Over the Blue Mountain*. New York, 1967
21. *The Aristocrat*. New York, 1968
22. *The Rawhide Knot and Other Stories*. New York, 1978

Rigsby, Howard [Vechel Howard Rigsby]
American, born November 11, 1909, died November 7, 1975
Pseudonyms: Mark Howard, Vechel Howard
1. *Voyage to Leandro*. New York, 1939
2. *Kill and Tell*. New York, 1951
3. *Murder for the Holidays*. New York, 1951
4. *Rage in Texas*. New York, 1953
5. *As a Man Falls*. New York, 1954
6. *Lucinda*. New York, 1954
7. *The Lone Gun*. New York, 1956
8. *The Avenger*. New York, 1957
9. *The Reluctant Gun*. New York, 1957
10. *Sundown at Crazy Horse*. New York, 1957
11. *Tall in the West*. New York, 1958
12. *Naked to My Pride*. New York, 1958
13. *Clash of Shadows*. Philadelphia, 1959
14. *Murder on Her Mind*, as Vechel Howard. New York, 1959
15. *Murder with Love*, as Vechel Howard. New York, 1959
16. *Stage to Painted Creek*. New York, 1959
17. *A Time for Passion*, as Mark Howard. New York, 1960
18. *The Last Sunset*. New York, 1961
19. *The Tulip Tree*. New York, 1963
20. *Calliope Reef*. New York, 1967

Roan, Tom
American
Pseudonym: Adam Rebel
1. *Whispering Range*. New York, 1934
2. *Montana Outlaw*. New York, 1934
3. *The Rio Kid*. New York and London, 1935
4. *Smoky River*. New York and London, 1935
5. *The Dragon Strikes Back*. New York and London, 1936
6. *Roaring Frontier*. London, 1937
7. *Riverboat Gambler*. New York and London, 1938
8. *Gun Lord of Silver River*. London, 1943
9. *The Gun Ghost*. London, 1952
10. *Gamblers in Gunsmoke*. New York, 1952
11. *Lawless Old Wyoming*. London, 1952
12. *Slave Girl*. New York, 1952
13. *The Blue Dragon of Fan Wong*. London, 1953
14. *Greedy Fingers*. London, 1953
15. *Perils of the Barbary Coast*. London, 1953
16. *Outlaw in the Saddle*. New York and London, 1953
17. *Stable Boy*, as Adam Rebel. London, 1955
18. *Wyoming Gun*. New York, 1955
19. *Thunder in the Valley*. London, 1955
20. *Rawhiders*. New York, 1958

Robertson, Frank C. (Chester)
American, born January 12, 1890, died July 29, 1969
Pseudonyms: Robert Crane, Frank Chester Field
1. *The Foreman of the Forty-Bar*. New York, 1925
2. *The Cleanup on Deadman*. New York, 1926

3. *The Outlaws of Flower-Pot Canyon.* New York, 1926
4. *The Boss of the Tumbling H.* New York, 1927
5. *On the Trail to Chief Joseph.* New York, 1927
6. *The Fall of Buffalo Horn.* New York, 1928
7. *The Man Branders.* New York, 1928
8. *The Boss of the Flying M.* London, 1928
9. *The Boss of the Ten Mile Basin.* London, 1928
10. *The Boss of the Double E.* London, 1928
11. *Brand of the Open Hand.* New York, 1928
12. *The Far Horizon.* London, 1929
13. *The Hidden Cabin.* London, 1929
14. *The Silver Cow.* New York, 1929
15. *Clawhammer.* New York, 1930
16. *Riders of the Sunset Trail.* London, 1930
17. *Wildhorse Henderson.* London, 1930
18. *The Bandit of Bayhorse Basin.* London, 1931
19. *Deadman's Grove.* London, 1931
20. *The Mormon Trail.* London, 1931
21. *The Range Defender.* London, 1931
22. *We Want That Range.* New York, 1931
23. *The Fight for River Range.* New York and London, 1932
24. *Outlaw's Trail.* London, 1932
25. *Prairie Princess.* London, 1932
26. *Red Rustlers.* New York and London, 1932
27. *Shoot-up!* London, 1932
28. *The Powder Burner.* London, 1932
29. *The Trouble Grabber.* New York, 1932
30. *Back to the West.* London, 1933
31. *Cowboy Courage.* London, 1933
32. *Freewater Range.* New York and London, 1933
33. *Larruping Leather.* New York, 1933
34. *Song of the Leather.* London, 1933
35. *Outlaw Ranch.* New York, 1934
36. *Renegade Riders.* London, 1934
37. *Ex-Rustler.* London, 1934
38. *Range Justice.* London, 1934
39. *Thunder in the West,* as Robert Crane. New York and London, 1934
40. *Wild Riding Hunt.* New York, 1934
41. *Brothers of the Range.* London, 1935
42. *Forbidden Trails.* New York, 1935
43. *The Rocky Road to Jericho,* as Frank Chester Field. New York, 1935
44. *Trail Boss.* London, 1935
45. *Wild Blood,* as Robert Crane. New York and London, 1935
46. *Stormy Range,* as Robert Crane. London, 1936
47. *Deadman's Canyon,* as Robert Crane. London, 1936
48. *Freedom of the Range,* as Robert Crane. London, 1936
49. *Squaw Pass War,* as Robert Crane. London, 1936
50. *Trigger Artist,* as Robert Crane. London, 1936
51. *Bandits of the Barrens.* London, 1936
52. *Branded Men.* New York, 1936
53. *Randy of Roaring River.* London, 1936
54. *Silver Zone.* New York and London, 1936
55. *The Clean-up on Deadman,* as Robert Crane. London, 1937
56. *The Outlaw of Antler.* New York and London, 1937
57. *Moose River Range.* London, 1937
58. *Too Many Brands,* as Robert Crane. London, 1937
59. *Blocked Trails,* as Robert Crane. London, 1937
60. *Cache at Flower-Pot Canyon,* as Robert Crane. London, 1937
61. *The Fighting O'Farrels,* as Robert Crane. London, 1937
62. *He Built Himself a Loop,* as Robert Crane. London, 1937
63. *Diana of the Ophir Hills,* as Robert Crane. London, 1937
64. *The Man from Skull Valley,* as Robert Crane. London, 1937
65. *Desert Waters,* as Robert Crane. London, 1938
66. *Thunder on the Range.* New York, 1938
67. *The Pride of Pine Creek.* New York, 1938
68. *Range Rebellion.* London, 1938
69. *Lookou for Outlaws.* London, 1938
70. *Roundup and Trail.* London, 1938
71. *Fighting Jack Warbonnet.* New York, 1939
72. *Romance of Surprise Ranch,* as Robert Crane. London, 1939
73. *Six-Gun Challenge: and Bob Gates, Outlaw,* as Robert Crane. London, 1939
74. *Rip Roarin' Rincon.* New York, 1939
75. *Bullets for Silver.* London, 1939
76. *The Cabin in the Canyon.* London, 1939
77. *The Firebrand from Burnt Creek.* New York and London, 1940
78. *Cowboy Comes A-Fightin.* New York, 1940
79. *Rifle Law.* London, 1940
80. *Poison Valley.* New York, 1941
81. *Pilgrims of Poison Valley.* London, 1941
82. *Snake River to Hell.* New York, 1941
83. *Outlaw Country.* London, 1941
84. *Cowman's Jackpot.* New York, 1942
85. *Greener Grows the Grass.* London, 1942
86. *Vigilante War in Buena Vista.* New York, 1942
87. *The Roaring Sixties.* London, 1942
88. *Grizzly Meadows.* New York, 1943
89. *Rustlers on the Loose.* London, 1943
90. *Kingdom for a Horse.* London, 1943
91. *Getly's Gold.* New York and London, 1944
92. *The Noose Hangs High.* London, 1944
93. *Round-Up In the River.* New York and London, 1945
94. *The Lost Range.* New York, 1946
95. *Hoof-Beats in the Night.* London, 1946
96. *Boomerang Jail.* New York and London, 1947
97. *Man Bait.* London, 1948
98. *Rope Crazy.* New York and London, 1948
99. *The Longhorns of Hate.* New York, 1949
100. *The Sheriff of Crow Country.* London, 1949
101. *The Way of an Outlaw.* London, 1949
102. *The Road to Paint Rock.* London, 1950
103. *A Ram in the Thicket: An Autobiography.* New York, 1950
104. *Wrangler on the Prod.* New York, 1950
105. *Quicker on the Draw.* London, 1950
106. *Hangman of the Humbug.* New York, 1951
107. *Idaho Range.* London, 1951
108. *Riders Against the Sky.* London, 1951
109. *Where Desert Blizzards Blow.* New York, 1952
110. *Reach for the Skies.* London, 1952
111. *Saddle on a Cloud.* New York and London, 1952
112. *Crooked Water.* London, 1953
113. *Sagebrush Sorrel.* New York, 1953
114. *Ride Out and Die.* London, 1953
115. *The Cruel Winds of Winter.* London, 1954
116. *Hero's Walk,* as Robert Crane. New York, 1954
117. *The Double Brand.* London, 1954
118. *Horn Silver.* London, 1955
119. *Rock River Feud.* London, 1955
120. *Squatters Rights.* London, 1956
121. *Boot Hill Bound.* London, 1957
122. *Disaster Valley.* New York and London, 1957
123. *Lawman's Pay.* New York, 1957
124. *The Young Nighthawk.* London, 1957
125. *Deadhorse Mesa.* London, 1958
126. *The Bandits of Crown Cliffs.* London, 1959
127. *Wagon Trail to Danger.* London, 1959
128. *The Poker Game.* London, 1960
129. *Soapy Smith, King of the Frontier Con Men,* with Mary Beth Harris. New York, 1961
130. *Rawhide.* New York, 1961

131. *Boom Towns of the Great Basin,* with Mary Beth Harris. Denver (CO), 1962
132. *Hornet Creek.* London, 1962
133. *Cariboo.* London, 1962
134. *A Man Called Paladin.* London, 1963
135. *Fort Hall, Gateway to the Oregon Country.* New York, 1963
136. *Fugitives of Green Valley.* London, 1963
137. *Feud at Blue Canyon.* New York, 1963
138. *Showdown.* London, 1963
139. *Hoodlums at Hogup.* London, 1964
140. *Waylands Law.* London, 1964
141. *Sheriff's Deputy.* London, 1965
142. *Windy Jake's Legacy.* London, 1965
143. *Bullets on the Blackfoot.* London, 1966
144. *Bloody Ambush,* as Robert Crane. New York, 1966
145. *The Bud Valley Bible.* London, 1966
146. *Outlaw Sanctuary.* London, 1967
147. *The Valley of Frightened Men.* London, 1967

Roderus, Frank
American, born September 21, 1942
1. *Journey to Utah.* New York, 1977
2. *The 33 Brand.* New York, 1977
3. *The Keystone Kid.* New York, 1978
4. *Easy Money.* New York, 1978
5. *Home to Texas.* New York, 1978
6. *Duster.* Independence (MO), 1977
7. *The Name Is Hart.* New York, 1979
8. *Hell Creek Cabin.* New York, 1979
9. *Sheepherding Man.* New York and London, 1980
10. *Jason Evers, His Own Story.* New York, 1980
11. *Old Kyle's Boy.* New York and London, 1981
12. *Cowboy.* New York, 1981

Ross, Sinclair
Canadian, born January 22, 1908
1. *As for Me and My House.* New York, 1941
2. *The Well.* Toronto, 1958
3. *The Lamp at Noon and Other Stories.* Toronto, 1968
4. *Whir of Gold.* Toronto, 1970
5. *Sawbones Memorial.* Toronto, 1974
6. *The Race.* Ottawa (Canada), 1982

Ross, Zola (Helen)
American, born May 9, 1912
Pseudonyms: Helen Arre, Z.H. Ross
1. *Three Down Vulnerable,* as Z.H. Ross. Indianapolis, 1946
2. *Overdue for Death,* as Z.H. Ross. Indianapolis, 1947
3. *One Corpse Missing,* as Z.H. Ross. Indianapolis, 1948
4. *Bonanza Queen: A Novel of the Comstock Lode.* Indianapolis, 1949
5. *The Mystery of Catesby Island,* with Lucile McDonald. New York, 1950
6. *Tonapah Lady.* Indianapolis, 1950
7. *Reno Crescent.* Indianapolis, 1951
8. *Stormy Year,* with Lucile McDonald. New York, 1952
9. *The Green Land.* Indianapolis, 1952
10. *The Corpse by the River,* as Helen Arre. New York, 1953
11. *Friday's Child,* with Lucile McDonald. New York, 1954
12. *No Tears at the Funeral,* as Helen Arre. New York, 1954
13. *Cassy Scandal.* Indianapolis, 1954
14. *The Golden Witch.* Indianapolis, 1955
15. *Murder in Mink,* as Z.H. Ross. Indianapolis, 1956
16. *Write it Murder,* as Helen Arre. New York, 1956
17. *A Land to Tame.* Indianapolis, 1956
18. *Mystery of the Long House,* with Lucile McDonald. New York, 1956
19. *Pigtail Pioneer,* with Lucile McDonald. Philadelphia, 1956
20. *Wing Harbor,* with Lucile McDonald. New York, 1957
21. *Spokane Saga.* Indianapolis, 1957
22. *The Golden Shroud,* as Helen Arre. New York, 1958
23. *The Courting of Ann Maria,* with Lucile McDonald. New York, 1958
24. *Assignment in Ankara,* with Lucile McDonald. New York, 1959
25. *Stolen Letters,* with Lucile McDonald. New York, 1959
26. *Murder by the Book,* as Helen Arre. New York, 1960
27. *Winters Answer,* with Lucile McDonald. New York, 1961
28. *The Sunken Forest,* with Lucile McDonald. New York, 1968
29. *For Glory and the King,* with Lucile McDonald. New York, 1969

Rowland, Donald S. (Sydney)
British, born September 23, 1928
Pseudonyms: Annette Adams, Jack Basset, Hazel Baxter, Karla Benton, Helen Berry, Lewis Brant, Alison Bray, William Brayce, Fenton Brockley, Oliver Bronson, Chuck Buchanan, Rod Caley, Roger Carlton, Janita Cleve, Sharon Court, Vera Craig, Wesley Craille, John Delaney, John Dryden, Freda Fenton, Charles Field, Graham Garner, Burt Kroll, Helen Langley, Henry Lansing, Harvey Lant, Irene Lynn, Hank Madison, Stuart McHugh, Chuck Mason, G.J. Morgan, Glebe Morgan, Edna Murray, Lorna Page, Olive Patterson, Alvin Porter, Alex Random, W.J. Rimmer, Donna Rix, Matt Rockwell, Charles Roscoe, Minerva Rosetti, Norford Scott, Valerie Scott, Bart Segundo, Bart Shane, Frank Shaul, Clinton Spurr, Roland Starr, J.D. Stevens, Mark Suffling, Kay Talbot, Will Travers, Sarah Vine, Elaine Vinson, Rick Walters, Neil Webb
1. *The Battle Done.* London, 1958
2. *Vengence for Water Valley.* London, 1961
3. *Drygulch Valley.* London, 1961
4. *Gunsmoke Payoff.* London, 1961
5. *Murder Range.* London, 1961
6. *12 Platoon.* London, 1962
7. *Both Feet in Hell.* London, 1962
8. *Not for Glory.* London, 1962
9. *Showdown at Singing Springs.* London, 1962
10. *Rough Justice.* London, 1963
11. *The Long Trail.* London, 1963
12. *Lonely Star.* London and New York, 1964
13. *Empty Saddles.* London, 1964
14. *Boss of Border Country,* as Bart Segundo. London, 1964
15. *Black Sundown,* as Frank Shaul. London, 1964
16. *Kingdom of Grass,* as Charles Field. London, 1964
17. *Gunsmoke Law,* as Charles Roscoe. London, 1964
18. *Bitter Valley,* as J.D.Stevens. London, 1964
19. *Rogue Rancher,* as Will Travers. London, 1964
20. *Danger Trail,* as Neil Webb. London, 1964
21. *Blood in the Dust,* as Lewis Brant. London, 1964
22. *Dark Prairie,* as Lewis Brant. London, 1964
23. *Vengeance Gun,* as Clinton Spurr. London, 1964
24. *The Hell Raisers,* as Clinton Spurr. London, 1965
25. *Trail Fever,* as Clinton Spurr. London, 1965
26. *Hard to Kill,* as Lewis Brant. London, 1965
27. *Gun Crazy,* as Will Travers. London, 1965
28. *Twisted Trail,* as J.D.Stevens. London, 1965
29. *Shoot First,* as J.D.Stevens. London, 1965
30. *Heartbreak Range,* as J.D.Stevens. London, 1965
31. *Cattleman's Country,* as Charles Roscoe. London, 1965
32. *Gunswift Justice,* as Charles Roscoe. London, 1965
33. *Saddle Tramp,* as Charles Field. London, 1965
34. *Star Brand Killer,* as Charles Field. London, 1965
35. *Bullets at Dry Creek.* New York, 1965
36. *Cattlemen's Creed,* as Oliver Bronson. London, 1965

37. *Raw Deal,* as Oliver Bronson. London, 1965
38. *Rope Branded,* as Neil Webb. London, 1965
39. *Thunder Canyon,* as Neil Webb. London, 1965
40. *Quick on the Draw,* as John Dryden. London, 1965
41. *Wild Loop Range,* as John Dryden. London, 1965
42. *Roughshod,* as Norford Scott. London, 1965
43. *Tight Rein,* as Norford Scott. London, 1966
44. *Whip-Hand,* as Norford Scott. London, 1966
45. *Hard Ridden,* as John Dryden. London, 1966
46. *Trigger Law,* as Neil Webb. London, 1966
47. *High Stakes,* as Neil Webb. London, 1966
48. *Big Saddle,* as Neil Webb. London, 1966
49. *Bullet Proof,* as Neil Webb. London, 1966
50. *Draw or Die,* as Charles Roscoe. London, 1966
51. *Showdown,* as Will Travers. London, 1966
52. *Gold Fever,* as Will Travers. London, 1966
53. *Trail End,* as Charles Field. London, 1966
54. *Crossfire.* London, 1966
55. *Range Hog,* as William Brayce. London, 1966
56. *Saddle Pard,* as Frank Shaul. London, 1966
57. *Brave Star,* as Chuck Buchanan. London, 1966
58. *Lonesome Valley,* as Rod Caley. London, 1966
59. *Hell-Bent,* as Wesley Craille. London, 1966
60. *Bleak Range,* as Henry Lansing. London, 1966
61. *The Sidewinders,* as W.J.Rimmer. London, 1966
62. *Trigger Help,* as Matt Rockwell. London, 1966
63. *Gunsmoke Pass,* as Rick Walters. London, 1966
64. *Gunshot Pay-Off,* as Lewis Brant. London, 1966
65. *Bitter Round-Up,* as Lewis Brant. London, 1966
66. *Gun Hand,* as Lewis Brant. London, 1966
67. *Short Rope,* as Clinton Spurr. London, 1966
68. *Shooting Trouble,* as Jack Bassett. London, 1966
69. *Forked Trail,* as Jack Bassett. London, 1966
70. *Water Rights,* as Burt Kroll. London, 1966
71. *Greenhorn Gun,* as Burt Kroll. London, 1966
72. *Range Fury,* as Harvey Lant. London, 1966
73. *High, Wide, and Handsome,* as Harvey Lant. London, 1966
74. *Slaughter Trail,* as Harvey Lant. London, 1966
75. *Riding High,* as Hank Madison. London, 1966
76. *Wanted—Dead or Alive,* as Hank Madison. London, 1966
77. *Gun Shy,* as Stuart McHugh. London, 1966
78. *Prairie Wolf,* as Stuart McHugh. London, 1966
79. *Back Trail,* as Chuck Mason. London, 1966
80. *The Law Dealer,* as Chuck Mason. London, 1966
81. *Gunman Notorious,* as Chuck Mason. London, 1966
82. *The Corpse Maker,* as Alvin Porter. London, 1966
83. *Bitter Feud,* as Alvin Porter. London, 1967
84. *Riding Through,* as Alvin Porter. London, 1967
85. *Crooked Spurs,* as Alvin Porter. London, 1967
86. *Ride Hard—Shoot Fast,* as Chuck Mason. London, 1967
87. *Hell Branded,* as Chuck Mason. London, 1967
88. *Gun Lightning,* as Chuck Mason. London, 1967
89. *Riding for a Fall,* as Stuart McHugh. London, 1967
90. *Running Wild,* as Stuart McHugh. London, 1967
91. *Fighting Mad,* as Hank Madison. London, 1967
92. *Killer in the County,* as Hank Madison. London, 1967
93. *Gunsmoke Legacy,* as Hank Madison. London, 1967
94. *Bad Medicine,* as Harvey Lant. London, 1967
95. *Gun Range,* as Harvey Lant. London, 1967
96. *Hungry Guns,* as Burt Kroll. London, 1967
97. *No Quarter,* as Jack Bassett. London, 1967
98. *Gunsmoke Creek,* as Jack Bassett. London, 1967
99. *Saddle Scum,* as Jack Bassett. London, 1967
100. *Shoot and Run,* as Clinton Spurr. London, 1967
101. *Killer Brand,* as Clinton Spurr. London, 1967
102. *Gun Fever,* as Clinton Spurr. London, 1967
103. *The Back Shooter,* as Lewis Brant. London, 1967
104. *Gun Trail,* as Lewis Brant. London, 1967
105. *Law of the Holster.* New York, 1967
106. *Kicking Horse Country,* as Norford Scott. London, 1967
107. *Vengeance of the Diamond M,* as Norford Scott. London, 1967
108. *Saddled for Hell,* as Norford Scott. London, 1967
109. *Gun Rogues.* London, 1967
110. *Big Tracks,* as Jack Bassett. London, 1968
111. *Undercover Law,* as Chuck Mason. London, 1968
112. *Coyote Trail,* as Burt Kroll. London, 1968
113. *Snake Breed,* as Burt Kroll. London, 1968
114. *Lawman Courageous,* as Frank Shaul. London, 1968
115. *Island of Decision,* as Annette Adams. London, 1968
116. *Doctor of the Heart,* as Annette Adams. London, 1968
117. *Helicopter Nurse,* as Hazel Baxter. London, 1968
118. *The Heart Healer,* as Annette Adams. London, 1968
119. *Locum in Love,* as Hazel Baxter. London, 1968
120. *Surgeon's Help,* as Hazel Baxter. London, 1968
121. *Where the Heart Lies,* as Helen Langley. London, 1968
122. *Highland Love,* as Helen Berry. London, 1968
123. *Doctor Needs a Wife,* as Helen Berry. London, 1968
124. *Occupation: Nurse,* as Helen Berry. London, 1968
125. *Wayward Nurse,* as Helen Berry. London, 1968
126. *Prescription for Love,* as Alison Bray. London, 1968
127. *Doctor's Destiny,* as Alison Bray. London, 1968
128. *Surgeon's Honour,* as Alison Bray. London, 1968
129. *The Nurse Inherits,* as Freda Fenton. London, 1968
130. *Nurse Hopeful,* as Freda Fenton. London, 1968
131. *Romantic Doctor,* as Irene Lynn. London, 1968
132. *Patient Lover,* as Edna Murray. London, 1968
133. *Love Thy Doctor,* as Edna Murray. London, 1968
134. *Married to Medicine,* as Edna Murray. London, 1968
135. *Emergency Nurse,* as Edna Murray. London, 1968
136. *Ward Sister,* as Edna Murray. London, 1968
137. *Love Is a Doctor,* as Lorna Page. London, 1968
138. *Doctor of Decision,* as Lorna Page. London, 1968
139. *Mystery Clinic,* as Olive Patterson. London, 1968
140. *Runaway Doctor,* as Olive Patterson. London, 1968
141. *Her Favorite Doctor,* as Kay Talbot. London, 1968
142. *Doctor's Slave,* as Kay Talbot. London, 1968
143. *Hospital Romance,* as Kay Talbot. London, 1969
144. *Dental Nurse,* as Kay Talbot. London, 1969
145. *Country Doctor,* as Kay Talbot. London, 1969
146. *Nurse Errant,* as Olive Patterson. London, 1969
147. *Temporary Nurse,* as Lorna Page. London, 1969
148. *The Nurse Investigates,* as Lorna Page. London, 1969
149. *Loving Nurse,* as Edna Murray. London, 1969
150. *Tropical Nurse,* as Irene Lynn. London, 1969
151. *Doctor Abroad,* as Freda Fenton. London, 1969
152. *Doctor's Inheritance,* as Freda Fenton. London, 1969
153. *District Nurse,* as Freda Fenton. London, 1969
154. *Impulsive Nurse,* as Freda Fenton. London, 1969
155. *Highland Nurse,* as Helen Berry. London, 1969
156. *Presciption for Nurse,* as Allison Bray. London, 1969
157. *Hospital Sister,* as Allison Bray. London, 1969
158. *Doctor in Doubt,* as Hazel Baxter. London, 1969
159. *Night Sister,* as Hazel Baxter. London, 1969
160. *Overseas Nurse,* as Sarah Vine. London, 1969
161. *Terror Law,* as Norford Scott. London, 1969
162. *Death Wore Spurs,* as Clinton Spurr. London, 1969
163. *Part-Time Nurse,* as Vera Craig. London, 1969
164. *Enchanted Nurse,* as Vera Craig. London, 1969
165. *Nurse in Jeopardy,* as Vera Craig. London, 1969
166. *Unselfish Nurse,* as Vera Craig. London, 1970
167. *Case Nurse,* as Vera Craig. London, 1970
168. *Winged Nurse,* as Helen Berry. London, 1970
169. *Operation Omina,* as Roland Starr. New York, 1970
170. *Passionate Nurse,* as Kay Talbot. London, 1970
171. *Heartbreak Nurse,* as Kay Talbot. London, 1970

172. *Fortunate Nurse,* as Lorna Page. London, 1970
173. *Doctor's Prescription,* as Lorna Page. London, 1970
174. *Doctor Duty,* as Irene Lynn. London, 1970
175. *Doctor in Bondage,* as Irene Lynn. London, 1970
176. *Nurse at Crag House,* as Allison Bray. London, 1970
177. *Poor Little Rich Nurse,* as Allison Bray. London, 1970
178. *Doctor's Endeavor,* as Hazel Baxter. London, 1970
179. *Island Nurse,* as Edna Murray. London, 1970
180. *Faithful Nurse,* as Edna Murray. London, 1970
181. *Cruise Nurse,* as Edna Murray. London, 1970
182. *Nurse in Danger,* as Edna Murray. London, 1970
183. *Temptation Doctor,* as Olive Patterson. London, 1970
184. *Nurse in Torment,* as Olive Patterson. London, 1971
185. *Romantic Island,* as Karla Benton. London, 1971
186. *Nurse on Loan,* as Karla Benton. London, 1971
187. *African Love Song,* as Janita Cleve. London, 1971
188. *For Love or Money,* as Janita Cleve. London, 1971
189. *Love Thy Neighbour,* as Janita Cleve. London, 1971
190. *Daughter of Destiny,* as Sharon Court. London, 1971
191. *Pathway to Love,* as Sharon Court. London, 1971
192. *Doctor of the Isles,* as Donna Rix. London, 1971
193. *Conflict of Love,* as Donna Rix. London, 1971
194. *Ski Lift to Love,* as Valerie Scott. London, 1971
195. *Race to Love,* as Valerie Scott. London, 1971
196. *Lover's Quest,* as Elaine Vinson. London, 1971
197. *Enchanted Isle,* as Elaine Vinson. London, 1971
198. *Island of Desire,* as Elaine Vinson. London, 1972
199. *Nurse on Skis,* as Elaine Vinson. London, 1972
200. *Doctor in Her Life,* as Valerie Scott. London, 1972
201. *Career Nurse,* as Donna Rix. London, 1972
202. *Surgical Nurse,* as Sharon Court. London, 1972
203. *Nurse in Need,* as Sharon Court. London, 1972
204. *Dutiful Nurse,* as Sharon Court. London, 1972
205. *Nurse at Pinewood,* as Janita Cleve. London, 1972
206. *Nurse Abroad,* as Karla Benton. London, 1972
207. *Glen Hall,* as Vera Craig. London, 1972
208. *Trigger Fever,* as Clinton Spurr. London, 1972
209. *Hell Star,* as Chuck Mason. London, 1972
210. *Gunsmoke Showdown,* as Burt Kroll. London, 1972
211. *Angry Guns,* as Harvey Lant. London, 1972
212. *Arizona Pay-Off,* as Hank Madison. London, 1972
213. *Man from Texas,* as Hank Madison. London, 1973
214. *Resident Nurse,* as Janita Cleve. London, 1973
215. *The Straightshooter,* as Hank Madison. London, 1973
216. *Nurse in Clover,* as Donna Rix. London, 1973
217. *Heart of a Nurse,* as Donna Rix. London, 1973
218. *Nurse Courageous,* as Donna Rix. London, 1973
219. *Pistol Range,* as Harvey Lant. London, 1973
220. *Fighting Marshall,* as Harvey Lant. London, 1973
221. *Gun Hell,* as Harvey Lant. London, 1973
222. *Shoot on Sight,* as Burt Kroll. London, 1973
223. *Mocking Bird Creek,* as Burt Kroll. London, 1973
224. *Wyoming Wild,* as Clinton Spurr. London, 1973
225. *The Loner,* as Clinton Spurr. London, 1973
226. *The Ambusher,* as Clinton Spurr. London, 1973
227. *Bleak Valley,* as Neil Webb. London, 1973
228. *Guns of Hate,* as Neil Webb. London, 1973
229. *Doubtful Nurse,* as Elaine Vinson. London, 1973
230. *Killer Streak,* as John Dryden. London, 1973
231. *Range Rights,* as John Dryden. London, 1973
232. *Gun for Hire,* as Chuck Mason. London, 1973
233. *Carefree Doctor,* as Karla Benton. London, 1973
234. *Nurse in Love,* as Karla Benton. London, 1973
235. *Hangrope Fever,* as Chuck Mason. London, 1973
236. *Quick Triggers,* as Chuck Mason. London, 1973
237. *Depot in Space.* London, 1973
238. *Heiress to Crag Castle,* as Minerva Rosetti. New York, 1973
239. *Now and Forever,* as Vera Craig. New York, 1973
240. *Mysterious Nurse,* as Valerie Scott. London, 1973
241. *Secretive Nurse,* as Valerie Scott. London, 1973
242. *Dedicated Nurse,* as Valerie Scott. London, 1974
243. *Land of Enchantment,* as Vera Craig. New York, 1974
244. *Path of Peril,* as Vera Craig. New York, 1974
245. *The Love Barrier,* as Vera Craig. New York, 1974
246. *Omina Uncharted,* as Roland Starr. London, 1974
247. *Master of Space.* London, 1974
248. *Mansion to Menace.* New York, 1974
249. *Star Quest,* as Fenton Brockley. London, 1974
250. *Gun Trap,* as Chuck Mason. London, 1974
251. *Fast Draw Law,* as Chuck Mason. London, 1974
252. *Backlash,* as Chuck Mason. London, 1974
253. *The Wildloopers,* as John Dryden. London, 1974
254. *Desperate Gun,* as Hank Madison. London, 1974
255. *Range Grab,* as Harvey Lant. London, 1974
256. *Broken-Down Cowboy,* as Burt Kroll. London, 1974
257. *Lone-Wolf Lawman,* as Burt Kroll. London, 1974
258. *Crooked Brand,* as John Dryden. London, 1974
259. *Close Call,* as Clinton Spurr. London, 1974
260. *Running Iron,* as Clinton Spurr. London, 1974
261. *Gun Wolves,* as Neil Webb. London, 1974
262. *Space Probe,* as Graham Garner. London, 1974
263. *Star Cluster Seven,* as Alex Random. London, 1974
264. *Starfall Muta,* as Graham Garner. London, 1975
265. *Dark Constellation,* as Alex Random. London, 1975
266. *Cradle of Stars,* as Alex Random. London, 1975
267. *Time Facter,* as Roland Starr. London, 1975
268. *Killer Law,* as Neil Webb. London, 1975
269. *Gringo Basin,* as Lewis Brant. London, 1975
270. *Gunslick,* as Lewis Brant. London, 1975
271. *Hell on Wheels,* as G.J. Morgan. London, 1975
272. *Border Fury,* as G.J. Morgan. London, 1975
273. *Trail of Death,* as G.J. Morgan. London, 1975
274. *Beyond Tomorrow,* as Roger Carlton. London, 1975
275. *Star Arrow,* as Roger Carlton. London, 1975
276. *Project Oceanus,* as Mark Suffling. London, 1975
277. *Space Crusader,* as Mark Suffling. London, 1975
278. *Space Venturer.* London, 1976
279. *Nightmare Planet.* London, 1976
280. *Shale Creek Showdown,* as Lewis Brant. London, 1976
281. *The Sarbo Gang,* as Harvey Lant. London, 1976
282. *Blood on the Saddle,* as Hank Madison. London, 1976
283. *Rifts of Time,* as Graham Garner. London, 1976
284. *Frontier Law,* as Hank Madison. London, 1976
285. *Hostile Range,* as Neil Webb. London, 1976
286. *Gun Wild.* London, 1976
287. *Return from Omina,* as Roland Starr. London, 1976
288. *Hell Tracks,* as Clinton Spurr. London, 1976
289. *Death in Oak Ridge,* as Chuck Mason. London, 1976
290. *The Deadly Stranger,* as John Delaney. London, 1976
291. *The Hard Bounty,* as John Delaney. London, 1976
292. *Oregon Outrage,* as John Delaney. London, 1977
293. *Blood Brand,* as John Delaney. London, 1977
294. *Die-Hard Lawman,* as Alvin Porter. London, 1977
295. *Heller from Texas,* as Chuck Mason. London, 1977
296. *Trail to Boot Hill,* as Burt Kroll. London, 1977
297. *Trail of No Return,* as Charles Roscoe. London, 1977
298. *Smoke of the .45,* as Norford Scott. London, 1977
299. *Bullets at Sunset,* as Lewis Brant. London, 1977
300. *Gun Handy,* as Neil Webb. London, 1977
301. *Lawless Land,* as John Delaney. London, 1978
302. *Hell Town,* as Clinton Spurr. London, 1978
303. *Impetuous Nurse,* as Allison Bray. London, 1978
304. *Nurse in Conflict,* as Lorna Page. London, 1978
305. *Doctor's Orders,* as Vera Craig. London, 1978
306. *Doctor from the Past,* as Donna Rix. London, 1978
307. *Doctor in Her Heart,* as Valerie Scott. London, 1978

308. *Doctor's Dilemma*, as Valerie Scott. London, 1979
309. *Nurse in the Clouds*, as Valerie Scott. London, 1979
310. *Nurse in the Glenn*, as Donna Rix. London, 1979
311. *Love in Ward Two*, as Vera Craig. London, 1979
312. *Nurse in Charge*, as Lorna Page. London, 1979
313. *Reluctant Doctor*, as Alison Bray. London, 1979
314. *Hair-Triggered*, as Lewis Brant. London, 1979
315. *Hell on the Border*, as Harvey Lant. London, 1979
316. *Hell Rider*, as Hank Madison. London, 1979
317. *Iron Rails*, as Bart Shane. Ipswich (Eng), 1979
318. *Rails West*, as Bart Shane. Ipswich, 1980
319. *Duty Nurse*, as Irene Lynn. London, 1980
320. *Railhead*, as Bart Shane. Ipswich, 1980
321. *Gunsmoke Marshall*, as Harvey Lant. London, 1980
322. *Lawless Range*, as Hank Madison. London, 1980
323. *Gun Wages*, as Burt Kroll. London, 1980
324. *Bloodthirsty Range*, as Lewis Brant. London, 1980
325. *The Rail Rogues*, as Glebe Morgan. New York, 1980
326. *Gun Boss*, as Charles Roscoe. London, 1980
327. *Border Bandit*, as Norford Scott. London, 1980
328. *Railroad Marshall*, as Clinton Spurr. London, 1980
329. *Hell on the Range*, as Chuck Mason. London, 1980
330. *Devil's Brood*, as Alvin Porter. London, 1980
331. *Gunsmoke and Rawhide*, as Alvin Porter. London, 1981
332. *Gunman's Law*, as Chuck Mason. London, 1981
333. *Flaming Range*, as Burt Kroll. London, 1981
334. *Gun Thunder*, as Harvey Lant. London, 1981
335. *Ambush Range*, as Burt Kroll. London, 1981
336. *Sixgun Bart*, as Frank Shaul. London, 1981
337. *Hardcase Law*, as Neil Webb. London, 1981
338. *Gun Hatred*, as Neil Webb. London, 1981
339. *Killer Trail*, as Charles Roscoe. London, 1981
340. *Hard Range*, as Norford Scott. London, 1981
341. *Bullet Justice*, as Hank Madison. London, 1982
342. *Range Justice*, as Alvin Porter. London, 1982
343. *Hard Law*, as Hank Madison. London, 1982
344. *Gun Wranglers*, as Norford Scott. London, 1982
345. *Six-Gun Showdown*, as Charles Roscoe. London, 1982
346. *Hostile Hills*, as Clinton Spurr. London, 1982
347. *Texas Ranger*, as Jack Bassett. London, 1982
348. *Cowboy Law*, as Lewis Brant. London, 1982
349. *Tough Country*, as Rod Caley. London, 1982

Rushing, Jane Gilmore
American, born November 15, 1925
1. *Walnut Grove*. New York, 1964
2. *Against the Moon*. New York, 1968
3. *Tamzen*. New York, 1972
4. *Mary Dove*. New York and London, 1974
5. *The Raincrow*. New York, 1977
6. *Covenant of Grace*. New York, 1982

Russell, Charles M. (Marion)
American, born March 19, 1864, died October 24, 1926
1. *Rawhide Rawlins Stories*. Great Falls (MT), 1921
2. *More Rawhides*. Great Falls, 1925
3. *Trails Plowed Under*. New York and London, 1927
4. *Good Medicine: The Illustrated Letters of Charles M. Russel*. New York, 1929
5. *Good Medicine: Memories of the Real West*. New York, 1936
6. *Forty Pen and Ink Drawings*. Pasadena (CA), 1947
7. *Rawhide Rawlins Rides Again; or Behind the Swinging Doors: A Collection of Charlie Russel's Favorite Stories*. Pasadena, 1948
8. *Paper Talk: Illustrated Letters*. Fort Worth (TX), 1962

Ryan, Marah Ellis
American, born February 27, 1866, died July 11, 1934

1. *Merze: The Story of an Actress*. Chicago, 1889
2. *In Love's Domain*. Chicago, 1890
3. *A Pagan of the Alleghenies*. Chicago, 1891
4. *Told in the Hills*. Chicago, 1891
5. *Squaw Elouise*. Chicago, 1892
6. *A Flower of France: A Story of Old Louisiana*. Chicago, 1894
7. *A Chance Child, Comrades, Hendrex and Margotte, and Persephone*. Chicago, 1896
8. *The Bondwoman*. Chicago, 1899
9. *That Girl Montana*. Chicago, 1901
10. *Miss Moccasins*. Chicago, 1904
11. *My Quaker Maid*. Chicago, 1906
12. *For the Soul of Rafael*. Chicago and London, 1906
13. *Indian Love Letters*. Chicago, 1907
14. *The Flute of the Gods*. Chicago, 1909
15. *The Woman of the Twilight*. Chicago and London, 1913
16. *The House of the Dawn*. Chicago, 1914
17. *The Druid Path*. Chicago and London, 1917
18. *The Treasure Trail: A Romance of the Land of Gold and Sunshine*. Chicago, 1918
19. *The Dancer of Tuluum*. Chicago, 1924

Sabatini, Rafael
British, born April 29, 1875, died February 13, 1950
1. *The Lovers of Yvonne*. London, 1902
2. *The Suitors of Yvonne*. New York, 1902
3. *The Tavern Knight*. London, 1904
4. *Bardelys the Magnificent*. London, 1906
5. *The Trampling of the Lilies*. London, 1906
6. *Love-at-Arms*. London, 1907
7. *The Shame of Molly*. London, 1908
8. *St. Martin's Summer*. London, 1909
9. *Anthony Wilding*. London, 1910
10. *Arms and the Maid; or, Anthony Wilding*. New York, 1910
11. *The Lion's Skin*. London and Boston, 1911
12. *The Life of Cesare Borgia of Grance*. London, 1911
13. *The Justice of the Duke*. London, 1912
14. *The Strolling Saint*. London, 1913
15. *Torquemada and the Spanish Inquisition*. London and New York, 1913
16. *The Gates of Doom*. London, 1914
17. *The Sea-Hawk*. London and Philadelphia, 1915
18. *The Banner of the Bull: Three Episodes in the Career of Cesare Borgia* London and Philadelphia, 1915
19. *The Snare*. London and Philadelphia, 1915
20. *The Historical Nights' Entertainment*, 1st-3rd Series. Boston, 3 vols., 1917-38
21. *Scaramouche: a Romance of the French Revolution*. London and Boston, 1921
22. *Captain Blood, His Odyssey*. London and Boston, 1922
23. *Fortune's Fool*. London and Boston, 1923
24. *Mistress Wilding*. Boston, 1924
25. *The Urbinian*. Boston, 1924
26. *The Carolinian*. London and Boston, 1925
27. *The Tyrant: An Episode in the Life of Cesare Borgia*. London, 1925
28. *Bellarion the Fortunate*. London and Boston, 1926
29. *The Nuptials of Corbal*. London and Boston, 1927
30. *The Hounds of God*. London and Boston, 1928
31. *The Romantic Prince*. London and Boston, 1929
32. *The Reaping*. London, 1929
33. *The Minion*. London, 1930
34. *The King's Minion*. Boston, 1930
35. *Captain Blood Returns*. Boston, 1931
36. *Stories of Love, Intrigue, and Battle, Being Selected Works of Rafael Sabatini*. Boston, 1931
37. *The Chronicles of Captain Blood*. London, 1932

38. *The Black Swan.* London and Boston, 1932
39. *The Stalking Horse.* London and Boston, 1933
40. *Venetian Masque.* London and Boston, 1934
41. *Heroic Lives.* London and Boston, 1934
42. *Chivalry.* London and Boston, 1935
43. *The Fortunes of Captain Blood.* London and Boston, 1936
44. *The Lost King.* London and Boston, 1937
45. *The Sword of Islam.* London and Boston, 1939
46. *The Marquis of Carabas.* London, 1940
47. *Master-at-Arms.* Boston, 1940
48. *Columbus.* London and Boston, 1942
49. *King in Prussia.* London, 1944
50. *The Birth of Mischief.* Boston, 1945
51. *Turbulent Tales.* London, 1946
52. *The Gamester.* London and Boston, 1949
53. *Saga of the Sea.* London, 1953
54. *Sinner, Saint, and Jester.* London, 1954
55. *In the Shadow of the Guillotine.* London, 1955

Saberhagen, Fred [Frederick Thomas Saberhagen]
American, born May 18, 1930
1. *The Golden People.* New York, 1964
2. *The Water of Thought.* New York, 1965
3. *Berserker.* New York, 1967
4. *The Broken Lands.* New York, 1968
5. *Brother Assassin.* New York, 1969
6. *Brother Berserker.* London, 1969
7. *The Black Mountains.* New York, 1971
8. *Changeling Earth.* New York, 1973
9. *Berserker's Planet.* New York, 1975
10. *The Dracula Tape.* New York, 1975
11. *The Book of Saberhagen.* New York, 1975
12. *Specimens.* New York, 1976
13. *The Holmes-Dracula File.* New York, 1978
14. *The Veils of Azlaroc.* New York, 1978
15. *The Empire of the East.* New York, 1979
16. *Love Conquers All.* New York, 1979
17. *Mask of the Sun.* New York, 1979
18. *Berserker Man.* New York, 1979
19. *An Old Friend of the Family.* New York, 1979
20. *The Ultimate Enemy.* New York, 1979
21. *A Matter of Taste.* New York, 1980
22. *Thorn.* New York, 1980

Sachs, Marilyn
American, born December 18, 1927
1. *Amy Moves In.* New York, 1964
2. *Laura's Luck.* New York, 1965
3. *Amy and Laura.* New York, 1966
4. *Veronica Ganz.* New York, 1968
5. *Peter and Veronica.* New York, 1969
6. *Marv.* New York, 1970
7. *The Bear's House.* New York, 1971
8. *The Truth about Mary Rose.* New York and London, 1973
9. *A Pocket Full of Seeds.* New York, 1973
10. *Matt's Mitt.* New York, 1975
11. *Dorrie's Book.* New York, 1975
12. *A December Tale.* New York, 1976

Sale, Richard (Bernard)
American, born December 17, 1911
1. *Not Too Narrow, Not Too Deep.* New York and London, 1936
2. *Is a Ship Burning?* London, 1937
3. *Cardinal Rock.* London, 1940
4. *Destination Unknown.* Kingswood (Eng), 1943
5. *Lazarus No. 7.* New York, 1942
6. *Sailor, Take Warning.* London, 1942
7. *Passing Strange.* New York, 1942
8. *Death Looks In.* London, 1943
9. *Lazarus Murder Seven.* Kingston, 1943
10. *Benefit Performance.* New York, 1946
11. *Home Is the Hangman.* New York, 1949
12. *Murder at Midnight.* New York, 1950
13. *The Oscar.* New York, 1963
14. *For the President's Eyes Only.* New York, 1971
15. *The Man Who Raised Hell.* London, 1971

Salkey, Andrew [Felix Andrew Salkey]
American, born January 30, 1928
1. *A Quality of Violence.* London, 1959
2. *Escape to an Autumn Pavement.* London, 1960
3. *Hurricane.* London, 1964
4. *Earthquake.* London, 1965
5. *Drought.* London, 1966
6. *The Shark Hunters.* London, 1966
7. *Riot.* London, 1967
8. *The Late Emancipation of Jerry Stover.* London, 1968
9. *The Adventures of Catullus Kelly.* London, 1969
10. *Jonah Simpson.* London, 1969
11. *Havana Journal.* London, 1971
12. *Anancy's Score.* London, 1973
13. *Jamaica.* London, 1973
14. *Joey Tyson.* London, 1974
15. *Come Home.* London, 1975
16. *Land.* London, 1976
17. *The River that Disappeared.* London, 1977

Sallis, James
American, born December 21, 1944
1. *A Few Last Words.* London, 1969
2. *Down Home: Country-Western.* New York, 1971

Sanders, Dorothy Lucy
Australian, born May 4, 1907
Pseudonyms: Shelley Dean, Lucy Walker
1. *Fairies on the Doorstep.* Sydney (Australia), 1948
2. *The Randy.* Sydney, 1948
3. *Six for Heaven,* as Lucy Walker. London, 1952
4. *Shining River,* as Lucy Walker. London, 1954
5. *The One Who Kisses,* as Lucy Walker. London, 1954
6. *Sweet and Faraway,* as Lucy Walker. London, 1955
7. *Come Home, Dear!* as Lucy Walker. London, 1956
8. *Waterfall,* as Lucy Walker. London, 1956
9. *Heaven Is Here,* as Lucy Walker. London and New York, 1957
10. *Ribbons in Her Hair.* London, 1957
11. *Master of Ransome,* as Lucy Walker. London and New York, 1958
12. *Orchard Hill,* as Lucy Walker. New York, 1958
13. *The Stranger from the North,* as Lucy Walker. London, 1959
14. *Kingdom of the Heart,* as Lucy Walker. London, 1959
15. *Pepper Tree Bay.* London, 1959
16. *Love in a Cloud,* as Lucy Walker. London, 1960
17. *The Loving Heart,* as Lucy Walker. London, 1960
18. *The Moonshiner,* as Lucy Walker. London, 1961
19. *Wife to Order,* as Lucy Walker. London, 1961
20. *Monday in Summer.* London, 1961
21. *The Distant Hills,* as Lucy Walker. London, 1962
22. *Down in the Forest,* as Lucy Walker. London, 1962
23. *Cupboard Love,* as Lucy Walker. New York, 1963
24. *The Call of the Pines,* as Lucy Walker. London, 1963
25. *Follow Your Star,* as Lucy Walker. London, 1963
26. *The Man from Outback,* as Lucy Walker. London, 1964
27. *A Man Called Masters,* as Lucy Walker. London, 1965

28. *The Other Girl,* as Lucy Walker. London, 1965
29. *Reaching for the Stars,* as Lucy Walker. London, 1966
30. *The Ranger in the Hills,* as Lucy Walker. London, 1966
31. *South Sea Island,* as Shelley Dean. London, 1966
32. *Island in the South,* as Shelley Dean. London, 1967
33. *The River Is Down,* as Lucy Walker. London, 1967
34. *Home at Sundown,* as Lucy Walker. London, 1968
35. *The Gone-Away Man,* as Lucy Walker. London, 1969
36. *Joyday for Jodi,* as Lucy Walker. London, 1971
37. *The Mountain That Went to the Sea,* as Lucy Walker. London, 1971
38. *The Bell Branch,* as Lucy Walker. London, 1971
39. *Girl Alone,* as Lucy Walker. London, 1973
40. *Pool of Dreams,* as Lucy Walker. New York, 1973
41. *The Runaway Girl,* as Lucy Walker. London and New York, 1975
42. *Gamma's Girl,* as Lucy Walker. London, 1977
43. *So Much Love,* as Lucy Walker. New York, 1977

Sanders, Lawrence
American, born in 1920
1. *Handbook of Creative Crafts,* with Richard Carol. New York, 1968
2. *The Anderson Tapes.* New York, 1970
3. *The Pleasures of Helen.* New York, 1971
4. *Love Songs.* New York, 1972
5. *The First Deadly Sin.* New York, 1973
6. *The Tomorrow File.* New York, 1975
7. *The Tangent Objective.* New York, 1976
8. *The Second Deadly Sin.* New York, 1977
9. *The Marlow Chronicles.* New York, 1977
10. *The Tangent Factor.* New York, 1978
11. *The Sixth Commandment.* New York and London, 1979

Sandoz, Mari (Susette)
American, born in 1901, died March 10, 1966
1. *Old Jules.* Boston, 1935
2. *Slogum House.* Boston, 1937
3. *Capital City.* Boston, 1939
4. *Crazy Horse: The Strange Man of the Oglalas: A Biography.* New York, 1942
5. *The Tom-Walker.* New York, 1947
6. *Cheyenne Autumn.* New York, 1953
7. *Winter Thunder.* Philadelphia, 1954
8. *The Buffalo Hunters: The Story of the Hide Men.* New York, 1954
9. *Miss Morissa, Doctor of the Gold Trail.* New York, 1955
10. *The Horsecatcher.* Philadelphia, 1957
11. *The Cattlemen from the Rio Grande Across the Far Marias.* New York, 1958
12. *Hostiles and Friendlies: Selected Short Writings.* Lincoln, 1959
13. *Son of the Gamblin' Man: The Youth of an Artist.* New York, 1960
14. *These Were the Sioux.* New York, 1961
15. *Love Song to the Plains.* New York, 1961
16. *The Far Looker.* New York, 1962
17. *The Story Catcher.* Philadelphia, 1963
18. *The Beaver Men: Spearheads of Empire.* New York, 1964
19. *Old Jules Country: A Selection from Old Jules and Thirty Years of Writing since the Book Was Published.* New York, 1965
20. *The Battle of the Little Bighorn.* Philadelphia, 1966
21. *The Christmas of the Phonograph Records: A Recollection.* Lincoln (NB), 1966
22. *Sandhill Sundays and Other Recollections.* Lincoln, 1970
23. *The Great Council.* Rushville (NB), 1970

Santee, Ross
American, born August 16, 1888, died June 28, 1965
1. *Spike: The Story of a Cowpuncher's Dog.* New York, No date
2. *Men and Horses.* New York, 1926
3. *Cowboy.* New York, 1928
4. *The Pooch.* New York, 1931
5. *The Bar X Golf Course.* New York, 1933
6. *Sleepy Black: The Story of a Horse.* New York, 1933
7. *The Bubbling Spring.* New York, 1949
8. *Rusty: A Cowboy of the Old West.* New York, 1949
9. *Apache Land.* New York, 1949
10. *Hardrock and Silver Sage.* New York, 1951
11. *Lost Pony Tracks.* New York, 1953
12. *Dog Days.* New York, 1955
13. *The Rummy Kid Goes Home and Other Stories of the Southwest.* New York, 1965

Sarban, John W. (Wall)
British
1. *Ringstones and Other Curious Tales.* London and New York, 1951
2. *The Sound of His Horn.* London, 1952
3. *The Doll Maker and Other Tales of the Uncanny.* London, 1953
4. *The Doll Maker.* New York, 1960

Sargent, Pamela
American, born March 20, 1948
1. *Cloned Lives.* New York, 1976
2. *Starshadows and Blue Roses.* New York, 1977
3. *The Sudden Star.* New York, 1979
4. *The White Death.* London, 1980
5. *Watchstar.* New York, 1980

Saville, Malcolm [Leonard Malcolm Saville]
British, born February 21, 1901
1. *Mystery at Witchend.* London, 1943
2. *Seven White Gates.* London, 1944
3. *Country Scrap Book.* London, 1944
4. *Spy in the Hills.* New York, 1945
5. *The Gay Dolphin Adventure.* London, 1945
6. *Trouble at Townsend.* London, 1945
7. *Open-Air Scrap Book.* London, 1945
8. *Seaside Scrap Book.* London, 1946
9. *Jane's Country Year.* London, 1946
10. *The Secret of Grey Walls.* London, 1947
11. *The Riddle of the Painted Box.* London, 1947
12. *Redshank's Warning.* London, 1948
13. *Two Fair Plaits.* London, 1948
14. *Lone Pine Five.* London, 1949
15. *Strangers at Snowfell.* London, 1949
16. *The Master of Maryknoll.* London, 1950
17. *The Sign of the Alpine Rose.* London, 1950
18. *The Flying Fish Adventure.* London, 1950
19. *Adventure of the Life-Boat Service.* London, 1950
20. *All Summer Through.* London, 1951
21. *The Elusive Grasshopper.* London, 1951
22. *The Buckinghams at Ravenswyke.* London, 1952
23. *The Luck of Sallowby.* London, 1952
24. *Coronation Gift Book.* London, 1952
25. *The Ambermere Treasure.* London, 1953
26. *Christmas at Nettleford.* London, 1953
27. *The Secret of the Hidden Pool.* London, 1953
28. *The Neglected Mountain.* London, 1953
29. *Spring Comes to Nettleford.* London, 1954
30. *The Long Passage.* London, 1954
31. *Susan, Bill and the Ivy-Clad Oak [Wolf-dog, Golden Clock, Vanishing Boy, Dark Stranger, "Saucy Kate," Bright Star Circus, Pirates Bold].* London, 8 vols., 1954-61
32. *Saucers over the Moor.* London, 1955

33. *Where the Bus Stopped.* Oxford (Eng), 1955
34. *The Secret of Buzzard Scar.* London, 1955
35. *Young Johnnie Bimbo.* London, 1956
36. *Wings over Witchend.* London, 1956
37. *Lone Pine London.* London, 1957
38. *Treasure at the Mill.* London, 1957
39. *The Fourth Key.* London, 1957
40. *The Secret of the Gorge.* London, 1958
41. *King of Kings.* London, 1958
42. *Mystery Mine.* London, 1959
43. *Four-and-Twenty Blackbirds.* London, 1959
44. *Small Creatures.* London, 1959
45. *Sea Witch Comes Home.* London, 1960
46. *Country Book.* London, 1961
47. *Seaside Book.* London, 1962
48. *Not Scarlet But Gold.* London, 1962
49. *A Palace for the Buckinghams.* London, 1963
50. *Three Towers in Tuscany.* London, 1963
51. *The Purple Valley.* London, 1964
52. *Treasure at Amorys.* London, 1964
53. *Dark Danger.* London, 1965
54. *White Fire.* London, 1966
55. *The Thin Grey Man.* London and New York, 1966
56. *Man with Three Fingers.* London, 1966
57. *Strange Story.* London, 1967
58. *The Secret of the Ambermere Treasure.* New York, 1967
59. *The Secret of Galleybird Pit.* London, 1968
60. *Power of Three.* London, 1968
61. *Rye Royal.* London, 1969
62. *Strangers at Witchend.* London, 1970
63. *The Dagger and the Flame.* London, 1970
64. *The Secret of Villa Rosa.* London, 1971
65. *Where's My Girl?* London, 1972
66. *Diamond in the Sky.* London, 1974

Sawyer, Ruth
American, born August 5, 1880, died June 3, 1970
1. *The Primrose Ring.* New York and London, 1915
2. *Seven Miles to Arden.* New York and London, 1916
3. *This Way to Christmas.* New York and London, 1916
4. *Herself, Himself, and Myself: A Romance.* New York and London, 1917
5. *A Child's Year Book.* New York and London, 1917
6. *Doctor Danny.* New York and London, 1918
7. *Leerie.* New York and London, 1920
8. *The Silver Sixpence.* New York and London, 1921
9. *Tale of the Enchanted Bunnies.* New York and London, 1923
10. *Four Ducks on a Pond.* New York and London, 1928
11. *Gladiola Murphy.* New York and London, 1930
12. *Folkhouse.* New York and London, 1932
13. *The Luck of the Road.* New York and London, 1934
14. *Tono Antonio.* New York, 1934
15. *Gallant: The Story of Storm Veblen.* New York and London, 1936
16. *Roller Skates.* New York, 1936
17. *Picture Tales from Spain.* New York, 1936
18. *The Year of Jubilo.* New York, 1940
19. *The Least One.* New York, 1941
20. *The Long Christmas.* New York, 1941
21. *The Way of the Storyteller.* New York, 1942
22. *The Christmas Anna Angel.* New York, 1944
23. *This Is the Christmas: A Serbian Folk Tale.* Boston, 1945
24. *Old Con and Patrick.* New York, 1946
25. *The Little Red Horse.* New York, 1950
26. *Maggie Rose, Her Birthday Christmas.* New York, 1952
27. *Journey Cake, Ho!* New York, 1953
28. *A Cottage for Betsy.* New York, 1954
29. *The Enchanted Schoolhouse.* New York, 1956
30. *The Year of the Christmas Dragon.* New York, 1960
31. *Dietrich of Berne and the Dwarf-King Laurin: Hero Tales of the Austrian Tirol,* with Emmy Molles. New York, 1963
32. *Daddles: The Story of a Plain Hound-Dog.* Boston, 1964
33. *Lucinda's Year of Jubilo.* London, 1965
34. *Joy to the World: Christmas Legends.* Boston, 1966
35. *My Spain: A Story-Teller's Year of Collecting.* New York, 1967

Saunders, Hilary Adam St. George
British, born January 14, 1898, died December 16, 1951
Pseudonyms: Francis Beeding, with John Leslie Palmer; David Pilgrim, with John Leslie Palmer
1. *The Seven Sleepers,* as Francis Beeding. London and Boston, 1925
2. *The Little White Hag,* as Francis Beeding. London and Boston, 1926
3. *The Hidden Kingdom,* as Francis Beeding. London and Boston, 1927
4. *The House of Dr. Edwardes,* as Francis Beeding. London, 1927
5. *The Six Proud Walkers,* as Francis Beeding, with John Leslie Palmer. London and Boston, 1928
6. *The Five Flamboys,* as Francis Beeding. London and Boston, 1929
7. *Pretty Sinister,* as Francis Beeding. London and Boston, 1929
8. *The Four Armourers,* as Francis Beeding. London and Boston, 1930
9. *The League of Discontent,* as Francis Beeding. London and Boston, 1930
10. *Death Walks in Eastrepps,* as Francis Beeding. London and New York, 1931
11. *The Three Fishers,* as Francis Beeding. London and Boston, 1931
12. *The Devil and X.Y.Z.,* with Barum Browne (Geoffrey Dennis). London and New York, 1931
13. *Murder Intended,* as Francis Beeding. London and Boston, 1932
14. *Take It Crooked,* as Francis Beeding. London and Boston, 1932
15. *The Emerald Clasp,* as Francis Beeding. London and Boston, 1933
16. *The Two Undertakers,* as Francis Beeding. London and Boston, 1933
17. *The One Sane Man,* as Francis Beeding. London and Boston, 1934
18. *Mr. Bobadil,* as Francis Beeding. London, 1934
19. *The Street of the Serpents,* as Francis Beeding. New York, 1934
20. *Death in Four Letters,* as Francis Beeding. London and New York, 1935
21. *The Norwich Victims,* as Francis Beeding. London and New York, 1935
22. *The Death-Riders,* with Cornelius Cofyn (John de Vere Loder). London and New York, 1935
23. *The Eight Crooked Trenches,* as Francis Beeding. London and New York, 1936
24. *The Nine Waxed Faces,* as Francis Beeding. London and New York, 1936
25. *The Erring Under-Secretary,* as Francis Beeding. London, 1937
26. *Hell Let Loose,* as Francis Beeding. London and New York, 1937
27. *No Fury,* as Francis Beeding. London, 1937
28. *Murdered: One by One,* as Francis Beeding. New York, 1937

29. *So Great a Man*, as David Pilgrim. London and New York, 1937
30. *The Big Fish*, as Francis Beeding. London, 1938
31. *Heads Off at Midnight*, as Francis Beeding. New York, 1938
32. *The Black Arrows*, as Francis Beeding. London and New York, 1938
33. *The Ten Holy Terrors*, as Francis Beeding. London and New York, 1939
34. *Not a Bad Show*, as Francis Beeding. London, 1940
35. *The Secret Weapon*, as Francis Beeding. New York, 1940
36. *Eleven Were Brave*, as Francis Beeding. London, 1940
37. *No Common Glory*, as David Pilgrim. London and New York, 1941
38. *The Twelve Disguises*, as Francis Beeding. London and New York, 1942
39. *Coffin for One*, as Francis Beeding. New York, 1943
40. *The Grand Design*, as David Pilgrim. London and New York, 1944
41. *Pioneers! O Pioneers!* London and New York, 1944
42. *Spellbound*, as Francis Beeding. Cleveland, 1945
43. *There Are Thirteen*, as Francis Beeding. London and New York, 1946
44. *The Emperor's Servant*, as David Pilgrim. London, 1946
45. *The Sleeping Bacchus*. London, 1951

Saxton, Josephine
British, born June 11, 1935
1. *The Hieros Gamos of Sam and An Smith*. New York, 1969
2. *Vector for Seven; or, the Weltanshauung of Mrs. Amelia Mortimer and Friends*. New York, 1971
3. *Group Feast*. New York, 1971
4. *The Space-Time Journal*. London, 1972
5. *The Travails of Jane Saint*. London, 1981

Sayers, Dorothy L. (Leigh)
British, born July 13, 1893, died December 17, 1957
1. *Op. 1*. Oxford (Eng), 1916
2. *Catholic Tales and Christian Songs*. Oxford, 1918
3. *Whose Body?* New York and London, 1923
4. *Clouds of Witness*. London, 1926
5. *Unnatural Death*. London, 1927
6. *The Dawson Pedigree*. New York, 1928
7. *The Unpleasantness at the Bellona Club*. London and New York, 1928
8. *Lord Peter Views the Body*. London, 1928
9. *The Documents in the Case*, with Robert Eustace. London and New York, 1930
10. *Strong Poison*. London and New York, 1930
11. *The Five Red Herrings*. London, 1931
12. *Suspicious Characters*. New York, 1931
13. *The Floating Admiral*, with others. London, 1931
14. *Have His Carcase*. London and New York, 1932
15. *Murder Must Advertise*. London and New York, 1933
16. *Ask a Policeman*, with others. London and New York, 1933
17. *Hangman's Holiday*. London and New York, 1933
18. *The Nine Tailors*. London and New York, 1934
19. *Gaudy Night*. London, 1935
20. *Six Against the Yard*, with others. London, 1936
21. *Six Against Scotland Yard*. New York, 1936
22. *Papers Relating to the Family of Wimsey*. Privately printed, 1936
23. *Busman's Honeymoon*. London and New York, 1937
24. *An Account of Lord Mortimer Wimsey, The Hermit of the Wash*. Privately printed, 1937
25. *In the Teeth of the Evidence and Other Stories*. London, 1939
26. *Double Death: A Murder Story*, with others. London, 1939
27. *Strong Meat*. London, 1939
28. *The Mysterious English*. London, 1941
29. *The Mind of the Maker*. London and New York, 1941
30. *The Other Six Deadly Sins*. London, 1943
31. *Lord, I Thank Thee—*. Stamford (CT), 1943
32. *Even the Parrot: Exemplary Conversations for Enlightened Children*. London, 1944
33. *Unpopular Opinions*. London, 1946
34. *A Treasury of Sayers Stories*. London, 1958
35. *A Matter of Eternity: Selections from the Writings of Dorothy L. Sayers*. Grand Rapids (MI), 1969
36. *Lord Peter: A Collection of All the Lord Peter Wimsey Stories*. New York, 1972
37. *Striding Folly*. London, 1972

Sayers, James Denson
Pseudonyms: Denver Bardwell, Dan James
1. *Can the White Race Survive?* Washington (DC), 1929
2. *Gun-Smoke in Sunset Valley*, as Denver Bardwell. New York and London, 1935
3. *Killers on the Diamond A*, as Denver Bardwell. New York, 1935
4. *Gun Thunder on the Rio*, as Dan James. New York, 1935
5. *Beyond Midnight Chasm*, as Denver Bardwell. New York, 1936
6. *Rancho Bonita*, as Denver Bardwell. New York, 1936
7. *Rustlers on the Smoky Trail*, as Dan James. New York, 1936
8. *Stranger at Storm Ranch*, as Dan James. New York, 1936
9. *Storm Ranch*, as Denver Bardwell. London, 1937
10. *West of the Sunset*, as Dan James. London, 1937
11. *The Exile Returns West*, as Denver Bardwell. London, 1937
12. *Range War in Squaw Valley*, as Dan James. London, 1938
13. *Rivers Westward*, as Denver Bardwell. New York and London, 1939
14. *Coyote Hunter*, as Denver Bardwell. New York and London, 1940
15. *Prairie Fire*, as Denver Bardwell. New York, 1940
16. *Eagle Trail*, as Denver Bardwell. New York, 1951
17. *Calamity at Devil's Crossing*, as Denver Bardwell. Kingswood (Eng), 1951
18. *Owl-Hoot Pay-Off*, as Denver Bardwell. Kingswood, 1952
19. *Where the Sun Sets*, as Denver Bardwell. Kingswood, 1952
20. *Trouble at Choctaw Bend*, as Dan James. New York and London, 1952
21. *Shadow Guns*, as Dan James. New York, 1953
22. *Gunsmoke Mesa*, as Denver Bardwell. Kingswood, 1954
23. *Bullet Valley*, as Denver Bardwell. London, 1971

Scarborough, Dorothy
American, born in 1877, died November 7, 1935
1. *Fugitive Verses*. Waco (TX), 1912
2. *From a Southern Porch*. New York, 1919
3. *In the Land of Cotton*. New York, 1923
4. *The Wind*, anonymous. New York, 1925
5. *On the Trail of Negro Folk-Songs*. Cambridge (MA), 1925
6. *Impatient Griselda*. New York, 1927
7. *Can't Get a Red Bird*. New York, 1929
8. *The Stretch-Berry Smile*. Indianapolis (IN), 1932
9. *The Story of Cotton*. New York, 1933

Scarry, Richard (McClure)
American, born June 5, 1919
1. *The Great Big Car and Truck Book*. New York, 1951
2. *Rabbit and His Friends*. New York, 1953
3. *Nursery Tales*. New York, 1958
4. *Naughty Bunny*. New York and London, 1959
5. *Tinker and Tanker*. New York, 1960
6. *Hickory Dickory Clock Book*. New York, 1961
7. *Tinker and Tanker Out West*. New York, 1961

8. *Tinker and Tanker and Their Space Ship.* New York, 1961
9. *Tinker and Tanker and the Pirates.* New York, 1961
10. *Manners.* New York, 1962
11. *Tinker and Tanker, Knights of the Round Table.* New York, 1963
12. *Tinker and Tanker in Africa.* New York, 1963
13. *Best Wordbook Ever.* New York, 1963
14. *What Animals Do.* New York, 1963
15. *A Tinker and Tanker Coloring Book.* New York, 1963
16. *The Rooster Struts.* New York, 1963
17. *Polite Elephant.* New York, 1964
18. *The Golden Happy Book of Animals.* New York, 1964
19. *Animals.* London, 1964
20. *Animal Mother Goose.* New York, 1964
21. *Best Nursery Rhymes Ever.* New York, 1964
22. *Teeny Tiny Tales.* New York, 1965
23. *The Santa Claus Book.* New York, 1965
24. *The Bunny Book.* New York, 1965
25. *Busy Busy World.* New York, 1965
26. *Is This the House of Mistress Mouse?* New York, 1966
27. *Storybook Dictionary.* New York, 1966
28. *The Egg in the Hole Book.* New York, 1967
29. *Planes.* New York, 1967
30. *Trains.* New York, 1967
31. *Boats.* New York, 1967
32. *Cars.* New York, 1967
33. *Best Storybook Ever.* New York, 1968
34. *The Early Bird.* New York, 1968
35. *The Great Pie Robbery.* New York and London, 1969
36. *The Supermarket Mystery.* New York and London, 1969
37. *Great Big Schoolhouse.* New York and London, 1969
38. *Cars.* London, 1969
39. *Planes.* London, 1969
40. *What Do People Do All Day?* New York and London, 1969
41. *ABC Word Book.* New York, 1971
42. *Great Big Air Book.* New York and London, 1971
43. *Look and Learn Library (Best Stories Ever, Fun with Words, Going Places, Things to Know).* New York, 4 vols., 1971
44. *Funniest Storybook Ever.* New York and London, 1972
45. *Nicky Goes to the Doctor.* New York and London, 1972
46. *Hop Aboard, Here We Go!* New York and London, 1972
47. *Silly Stories.* New York, 1973
48. *Babykins and His Family.* New York, 1973
49. *Find Your ABC's.* New York,. 1973
50. *Please and Thank You Book.* New York, 1973
51. *Best Rainy Day Book Ever.* New York, 1974
52. *European Word Book.* London, 1974
53. *Cars and Trucks and Things That Go.* New York and London, 1974
54. *Great Steamboat Mystery.* New York, 1975
55. *Animal Nursery Tales.* New York and London, 1975
56. *Best Counting Book Ever.* New York, 1975
57. *Early Words.* New York, 1976
58. *Color Book.* New York, 1976
59. *Laugh and Learn Library.* London, 1976
60. *Look-Look Books.* New York, 1976
61. *Busiest People Ever.* New York, 1976
62. *Favorite Storybook.* New York and London, 1976
63. *Busy Town, Busy People.* New York and London, 1976
64. *Picture Dictionary.* London, 1976
65. *Teeny Tiny ABC.* New York and London, 1976
66. *Little ABC.* New York and London, 1976
67. *Things to Know.* New York and London, 1976
68. *Best Make-It Book Ever.* New York, 1977

Schachner, Nat [Nathan Schachner]
American, born January 16, 1895, died October 2, 1955

1. *Aaron Burr.* New York, 1937
2. *By the Dim Lamps.* New York, 1941
3. *The King's Messenger.* Philadelphia, 1942
4. *The Sun Shines West.* New York, 1943
5. *The Wanderer: A Novel of Dante and Beatrice.* New York, 1944
6. *Space Lawyer.* New York, 1953

Schaefer, Jack (Warner)
American, born November 19, 1907
1. *Shane.* Boston, 1949
2. *First Blood.* Boston, 1953
3. *The Canyon.* Boston, 1953
4. *The Big Range.* Boston, 1953
5. *The Pioneers.* Boston, 1954
6. *The Canyon and Other Stories.* London, 1955
7. *Company of Cowards.* Boston, 1957
8. *The Kean Land and Other Stories.* Boston, 1959
9. *Old Ramon.* Boston, 1960
10. *The Plainsmen.* Boston, 1963
11. *Monte Walsh.* Boston, 1963
12. *The Great Endurance Horse Race.* Santa Fe, 1963
13. *Stubby Pringle's Christmas.* Boston, 1964
14. *Heroes Without Glory: Some Goodmen of the Old West.* Boston, 1965
15. *Adolphe Francis Alphonse Bandelier.* Santa Fe, 1966
16. *Collected Stories.* Boston, 1966
17. *Mavericks.* Boston, 1967
18. *New Mexico.* New York, 1967
19. *An American Bestiary.* Boston, 1975

Scherf, Margaret (Louise)
American, born April 1, 1908
1. *The Corpse Grows a Beard.* New York, 1940
2. *The Case of the Kippered Corpse.* New York, 1941
3. *They Came to Kill.* New York, 1942
4. *The Owl in the Cellar.* New York, 1945
5. *Always Murder a Friend.* New York, 1948
6. *Murder Makes Me Nervous.* New York, 1948
7. *Gilbert's Last Toothache.* New York, 1949
8. *For the Love of Murder.* New York, No date
9. *The Gun in Daniel Webster's Bust.* New York, 1949
10. *The Curious Custard Pie.* New York, 1950
11. *The Green Plaid Pants.* New York, 1951
12. *The Corpse with One Shoe.* Roslyn (NY), 1951
13. *The Elk and the Evidence.* New York, 1952
14. *Dead: Senate Office Building.* New York, 1953
15. *The Case of the Hated Senator.* New York, 1954
16. *Glass on the Stairs.* New York, 1954
17. *The Cautious Overshoes.* New York, 1956
18. *Judicial Body.* New York, 1957
19. *Never Turn Your Back.* New York, 1959
20. *Wedding Train.* New York, 1960
21. *The Diplomat and the Gold Piano.* New York, 1963
22. *The Mystery of the Velvet Box.* New York, 1963
23. *The Mystery of the Empty Trunk.* New York, 1964
24. *Death and the Diplomat.* London, 1964
25. *The Corpse in the Flannel Nightgown.* New York, 1965
26. *The Mystery of the Shaky Staircase.* New York, 1965
27. *The Banker's Bones.* New York, 1968
28. *The Beautiful Birthday Cake.* New York, 1971
29. *To Cache a Millionaire.* New York, 1972
30. *If You Want a Murder Well Done.* New York, 1974
31. *Don't Wake Me Up While I'm Driving.* New York, 1977
32. *The Beaded Banana.* New York, 1978

Schlee, Ann
British, born May 26, 1934

Schlee, Ann

1. *The Strangers.* London, 1971
2. *The Consul's Daughter.* London and New York, 1972
3. *The Guns of Darkness.* London, 1973
4. *Ask Me No Questions.* London, 1976
5. *Lost.* London, 1977

Schlein, Miriam
American
Pseudonym: Lavinia Stanhope

1. *A Day at the Playground.* New York, 1951
2. *Tony's Pony.* New York, 1952
3. *Shapes.* New York, 1952
4. *Go with the Sun.* New York, 1952
5. *The Four Little Foxes.* New York, 1953
6. *When Will the World Be Mine?* New York, 1953
7. *Fast Is Not a Ladybug: A Book about Fast and Slow Things.* New York, 1953
8. *The Sun Looks Down.* Nashville (TN), 1954
9. *How Do You Travel?* Nashville, 1954
10. *Elephant Herd.* New York, 1954
11. *Heavy Is a Hippopotamus.* New York, 1954
12. *Oomi, The New Hunter.* New York, 1955
13. *Little Red Nose.* New York, 1955
14. *Puppy's House.* Chicago, 1955
15. *Big Talk.* New York, 1955
16. *Lazy Day.* New York, 1955
17. *It's about Time.* New York, 1955
18. *City Boy, Country Boy.* Chicago, 1955
19. *Henry's Ride.* Nashville, 1956
20. *Deer in the Snow.* New York and London, 1956
21. *Something for Now, Something for Later.* New York, 1956
22. *Little Rabbit, The High Jumper.* New York, 1957
23. *Amazing Mr. Pelgrew.* New York and London, 1957
24. *A Bunny, A Bird, A Funny Cat.* London and New York, 1957
25. *Here Comes Night.* Chicago, 1957
26. *The Big Cheese.* New York, 1958
27. *The Bumblebee's Secret.* New York and London, 1958
28. *Home, The Tale of a Mouse.* New York, 1958
29. *Herman McGregor's World.* Chicago, 1958
30. *The Raggle Taggle Fellow.* New York and London, 1959
31. *Little Dog Little.* New York, 1959
32. *The Fisherman's Day.* Chicago, 1959
33. *Kittens, Cubs, and Babies.* New York, 1959
34. *The Sun, The Wind, The Sea, and the Rain.* New York and London, 1960
35. *My Family.* New York, 1960
36. *Laurie's New Brother.* New York and London, 1961
37. *Amuny, Boy of Old Egypt.* New York and London, 1961
38. *Fast Is Not a Ladybird.* Kingswood (Eng), 1961
39. *The Pile of Junk.* New York and London, 1962
40. *Snow Time.* Chicago, 1962
41. *The Snake in the Carpool.* New York and London, 1963
42. *The Way Mothers Are.* Chicago, 1963
43. *Who?* New York, 1963
44. *The Big Green Thing.* New York, 1963
45. *Big Lion, Little Lion.* Chicago, 1964
46. *Billy, The Littlest One.* Chicago, 1966
47. *The Best Place.* Chicago, 1968
48. *My House.* Chicago, 1971
49. *Moon-Months and Sun-Days.* New York, 1972
50. *Juju-Sheep and the Python's Moonstone, and Other Moon Stories from Different Times and Different Places.* Chicago, 1973
51. *The Rabbit's World.* New York, 1973
52. *What's Wrong with Being a Skunk?* New York, 1974
53. *The Girl Who Would Rather Climb Trees.* New York, 1975
54. *Bobo the Troublemaker.* New York, 1976
55. *Careers in a Department Store,* as Lavinia Stanhope. Milwaukee (WI), 1976
56. *Giraffe, The Silent Giant.* New York, 1976

Schmidt, Stanley (Albert)
American, born March 7, 1944

1. *Newton and the Quasi-Apple.* New York, 1975
2. *The Sins of the Fathers.* New York, 1976
3. *Lifeboat Earth.* New York, 1978

Schmitz, James H. (Henry)
American, born October 15, 1911

1. *Agent of Vega.* New York, 1960
2. *A Tale of Two Clocks.* New York, 1962
3. *The Universe Against Her.* New York, 1964
4. *A Nice Day for Screaming and Other Tales of the Hub.* Philadelphia, 1965
5. *The Witches of Karres.* Philadelphia, 1966
6. *The Demon Breed.* New York, 1968
7. *A Pride of Monsters.* New York, 1970
8. *The Eternal Frontiers.* New York, 1973
9. *The Lion Game.* New York, 1973
10. *The Telzey Toy.* New York, 1973
11. *Legacy.* New York, 1979

Scortia, Thomas N. (Nicholas)
American, born August 29, 1926

1. *What Mad Oracle?* Evanston (IL), 1961
2. *Artery of Fire.* New York, 1972
3. *Earthwreck!* New York, 1974
4. *The Glass Inferno,* with Frank M. Robinson. New York, 1974
5. *Caution! Inflammable.* New York, 1975
6. *The Prometheus Crisis,* with Frank M. Robinson. New York, 1975
7. *The Nightmare Factor,* with Frank M. Robinson. New York and London, 1978
8. *The Gold Crew,* with Frank M. Robinson. New York, 1980

Scott, R.T.M. (Reginald Thomas Maitland)
Canadian, born August 14, 1882

1. *Secret Service Smith.* New York, 1923
2. *The Black Magician.* New York, 1925
3. *Ann's Crime.* New York, 1926
4. *Aurelius Smith - Detective.* New York, 1927
5. *Smith of the Secret Service.* London, 1929
6. *The Mad Monk.* New York, 1931
7. *Murder Stalks the Mayor.* London, 1935
8. *The Agony Column Murders.* New York, 1946
9. *The Nameless Ones.* New York, 1947

Seale, Sara [A.D.L. MacPherson]

1. *Beggars May Sing.* London, 1932
2. *Chase the Moon.* London, 1933
3. *Summer Spell.* London, 1937
4. *Grace Before Meat.* London, 1938
5. *This Merry Bond.* London, 1938
6. *Spread Your Wings.* London, 1939
7. *Green Grass Growing.* London, 1940
8. *Stormy Petrel.* London, 1941
9. *Barn Dance.* London, 1941
10. *The Silver Sty.* London, 1941
11. *House of Glass.* London, 1944
12. *Folly to Be Wise.* London, 1946
13. *The Reluctant Orphan.* London, 1947
14. *The English Tutor.* London, 1948
15. *The Gentle Prisoner.* London, 1949
16. *These Delights.* London, 1949

17. *Then She Fled Me.* London, 1950
18. *The Young Amanda.* London, 1950
19. *The Dark Stranger.* London, 1951
20. *Wintersbride.* London, 1951
21. *The Lordly One.* London, 1952
22. *The Forbidden Island.* London, 1953
23. *Turn to the West.* London, 1953
24. *The Truant Spirit.* London, 1954
25. *Time of Grace.* London, 1955
26. *Child Friday.* London, 1956
27. *Sister to Cinderella.* London, 1956
28. *I Know My Love.* London, 1957
29. *Trevallion.* London, 1957
30. *Lucy Lamb.* London, 1958
31. *Charity Child.* London, 1959
32. *Dear Dragon.* London, 1959
33. *Cloud Castle.* London, 1960
34. *The Only Charity.* London, 1961
35. *Valentine's Day.* London, 1962
36. *The Reluctant Landlord.* London, 1962
37. *Doctor's Ward.* London and Toronto, 1962
38. *Orphan Bride.* Toronto, 1962
39. *By Candlelight.* London, 1963
40. *The Youngest Bridesmaid.* London, 1963
41. *The Third Uncle.* London, 1964
42. *To Catch a Unicorn.* London, 1964
43. *Green Girl.* London, 1965
44. *The Truant Bride.* London, 1966
45. *Penny Plain.* London, 1967
46. *That Young Person.* London, 1969
47. *The Queen of Hearts.* Toronto, 1969
48. *Dear Professor.* London, 1970
49. *Mr. Brown.* London, 1971
50. *The Unknown Mr. Brown.* Toronto, 1972
51. *My Heart's Desire.* Toronto, 1976

Searls, Hank [Henry Hunt Searls, Jr.]
American, born August 10, 1922
1. *The Big X.* New York and London, 1959
2. *The Crowded Sky.* New York and London, 1960
3. *The Astronaut.* London, 1960
4. *The Pilgrim Project.* New York, 1964
5. *The Hero Ship.* Cleveland (OH) and London, 1969
6. *The Lost Prince: Young Joe, The Forgotten Kennedy.* Cleveland, 1969
7. *Pentagon.* New York, 1971
8. *Never Kill a Cop.* New York, 1977
9. *Overboard.* New York and London, 1977
10. *Jaws 2.* Universal City (CA) and London, 1978
11. *Firewind.* New York, 1981

Seed, Jenny [Cecile Eugenie Seed]
Born in South Africa, May 18, 1930
1. *The Dancing Mule.* London, 1964
2. *The Always-late Train.* Parow, 1965
3. *Small House, Big Garden.* London, 1965
4. *Peter the Gardner.* London, 1966
5. *Tombi's Song.* London, 1966
6. *To the Rescue.* London, 1966
7. *Stop Those Children!* London, 1966
8. *Timothy and Tinker.* London, 1967
9. *The River Man.* London, 1968
10. *The Voice of the Great Elephant.* London, 1968
11. *Canvas City.* London, 1968
12. *The Prince of the Bay.* London, 1970
13. *Vengeance of the Zulu King.* New York, 1970
14. *Kulumi the Brave: A Zulu Tale.* London and New York, 1970
15. *The Great Thirst.* London, 1971
16. *The Red Dust Soldiers.* London, 1972
17. *The Broken Spear.* London, 1972
18. *The Sly Green Lizard.* London, 1973
19. *The Bushman's Dream: African Tales of the Creation.* London, 1974
20. *Warriors on the Hills.* London, 1975
21. *The Unknown Land.* London, 1976
22. *Strangers in the Land.* London, 1977

Seeley, Mabel
American, born March 25, 1903
1. *The Listening House.* New York, 1938
2. *The Crying Sisters.* New York, 1939
3. *The Whispering Cup.* New York, 1940
4. *The Chuckling Fingers.* New York, 1941
5. *Eleven Came Back.* New York and London, 1943
6. *Woman of Property.* New York, 1947
7. *The Beckoning Door.* New York and London, 1950
8. *The Stranger Beside Me.* New York, 1951
9. *The Whistling Shadow.* New York, 1954
10. *The Blonde with the Deadly Past.* New York, 1955

Seelye, John (Douglas)
American, born January 1, 1931
1. *The True Adventures of Huckleberry Finn, as told by John Seelye.* Evanston (IL), 1970
2. *The Kid.* New York and London, 1972
3. *Dirty Tricks; or, Nick Noxin's Natural Nobility.* New York, 1974
4. *Mark Twain in the Movies: A Meditation with Pictures.* New York, 1977

Seifert, Elizabeth
American, born June 19, 1897
Pseudonym: Ellen Ashley
1. *Young Doctor Galahad.* New York, 1938
2. *Young Doctor.* London, 1939
3. *A Great Day.* New York, 1939
4. *Thus Doctor Mallory.* New York, 1940
5. *Doctor Mallory.* London, 1941
6. *Hillbilly Doctor.* New York, 1940
7. *Doctor Bill.* London, 1941
8. *Bright Scalpel.* New York, 1941
9. *Healing Hands.* London, 1942
10. *Army Doctor.* New York, 1942
11. *Surgeon in Charge.* New York, 1942
12. *A Certain Doctor French.* New York, 1943
13. *Bright Banners.* New York, 1943
14. *Girl in Overalls: A Novel of Women in Defense Today,* as Ellen Ashley. New York, 1943
15. *Girl Intern.* New York, 1944
16. *Dr. Ellison's Decision.* New York, 1944
17. *Dr. Woodward's Ambition.* New York, 1945
18. *Orchard Hill.* New York, 1945
19. *Old Doc.* New York, 1946
20. *Dusty Spring.* New York, 1946
21. *Doctor Chris.* London, 1946
22. *Take Three Doctors.* New York, 1947
23. *So Young, So Fair.* New York, 1947
24. *The Glass and the Trumpet.* New York, 1948
25. *Hospital Zone.* New York, 1948
26. *The Bright Coin.* New York, 1949
27. *The Doctor Dares.* London, 1950
28. *Homecoming.* New York, 1950
29. *Pride of the South.* London, 1950
30. *The Story of Andrea Fields.* New York, 1950
31. *Miss Doctor.* New York, 1951

32. *Woman Doctor.* London, 1951
33. *Doctor of Mercy.* New York, 1951
34. *The Strange Loyalty of Dr. Carlisle.* New York, 1952
35. *The Doctor Takes a Wife.* New York, 1952
36. *Doctor Mollie.* London, 1952
37. *The Case of Dr. Carlisle.* London, 1953
38. *The Doctor Disagrees.* New York, 1953
39. *Lucinda Marries the Doctor.* New York, 1953
40. *Doctor at the Crossroads.* New York, 1954
41. *Marriage for Three.* New York, 1954
42. *A Doctor in the Family.* New York, 1955
43. *Challenge for Doctor Mays.* New York, 1955
44. *A Doctor for Blue Jay Cove.* New York, 1956
45. *A Call for Doctor Barton.* New York, 1956
46. *Doctor Mays.* London, 1957
47. *Substitute Doctor.* New York, 1957
48. *The Doctor's Husband.* New York, 1957
49. *Doctor's Orders.* London, 1958
50. *The New Doctor.* New York, 1958
51. *Love Calls the Doctor.* New York, 1958
52. *Doctor Jamie.* London, 1959
53. *Home-Town Doctor.* New York, 1959
54. *Doctor on Trial.* London, 1959
55. *When Doctors Marry.* New York, 1960
56. *Doctors on Parade.* New York, 1960
57. *The Doctor's Bride.* New York, 1960
58. *The Doctor Makes a Choice.* New York, 1961
59. *Dr. Jeremy's Wife.* New York, 1961
60. *The Honor of Dr. Shelton.* New York, 1962
61. *The Doctor's Strange Secret.* New York, 1962
62. *Dr. Scott, Surgeon on Call.* New York, 1963
63. *Legacy for a Doctor.* New York, 1963
64. *Katie's Young Doctor.* New York, 1964
65. *A Doctor Comes to Bayard.* New York, 1964
66. *Doctor Samaritan.* New York, 1965
67. *Ordeal of Three Doctors.* New York, 1965
68. *Surgeon on Call.* London, 1965
69. *Hegerty, M.D.* New York, 1966
70. *Pay the Doctor.* New York, 1966
71. *Doctor with a Mission.* New York, 1967
72. *The Rival Doctors.* New York, 1967
73. *The Doctor's Confession.* New York, 1968
74. *To Wed a Doctor.* New York, 1968
75. *Bachelor Doctor.* New York, 1969
76. *For Love of a Doctor.* New York, 1969
77. *Doctor's Kingdom.* New York, 1970
78. *The Doctor's Two Lives.* New York, 1970
79. *Doctor in Judgment.* New York, 1971
80. *The Doctor's Second Love.* New York, 1971
81. *Doctor's Destiny.* New York, 1972
82. *The Doctor's Reputation.* New York, 1972
83. *The Doctor's Private Life.* New York, 1973
84. *The Two Faces of Dr. Collier.* New York, 1973
85. *The Doctor and Mathilda.* New York, 1974
86. *Doctor in Love.* New York, 1974
87. *The Doctor's Daughter.* New York, 1974
88. *Four Doctors, Four Wives.* New York, 1975
89. *The Doctor's Affair.* New York, 1975
90. *Two Doctors and a Girl.* New York, 1976
91. *The Doctor's Desperate Hour.* New York, 1976
92. *Doctor Tuck.* New York, 1977
93. *The Doctors of Eden Place.* New York, 1977
94. *The Doctors Were Brothers.* New York, 1978
95. *Rebel Doctor.* New York, 1978
96. *The Doctor's Promise.* New York, 1979
97. *The Problems of Doctor A.* New York, 1979

Selden, George [George Selden Thompson]
American, born May 14, 1929
1. *The Dog That Could Swim Under Water.* New York, 1956
2. *The Garden under the Sea.* New York, 1957
3. *The Cricket in Times Square.* New York, 1960
4. *I See What I See!* New York, 1962
5. *The Mice, The Monks, and the Christmas Tree.* New York and London, 1963
6. *Sparrow Socks.* New York, 1965
7. *Oscar Lobster's Fair Exchange.* New York and London, 1966
8. *The Dunkard.* New York, 1968
9. *Tucker's Countryside.* New York, 1969
10. *The Genie of Sutton Place.* New York, 1973
11. *Harry Cat's Pet Puppy.* New York, 1974

Sellings, Arthur [Robert Arthur Ley]
British, born in 1921, died September 24, 1968
Other pseudonym: Martin Luther
1. *Time Transfer and Other Stories.* London, 1956
2. *Telepath.* New York, 1962
3. *The Silent Speakers.* London, 1963
4. *The Uncensored Man.* London, 1964
5. *The Quy Effect.* London, 1966
6. *Intermind,* as Martin Luther. New York, 1967
7. *The Power of X.* London, 1968
8. *The Long Eureka.* London, 1968
9. *Junk Day.* London, 1970

Seltzer, Charles Alden
American, born August 15, 1875, died February 9, 1942
Pseudonym: Hiram Hopkins
1. *The Council of Three.* New York, 1900
2. *Sparks of Fun: A Series of Humorous Letters,* as Hiram Hopkins. Cleveland (OH), 1901
3. *The Two-Gun Man.* New York, 1911
4. *The Range Riders.* New York, 1911
5. *The Coming of the Law.* New York, 1912
6. *The Triangle Cupid.* New York, 1912
7. *The Trail to Yesterday.* New York, 1913
8. *The Boss of the Lazy Y.* Chicago, 1915
9. *The Range Boss.* Chicago, 1916
10. *The Vengeance of Jefferson Gawne.* Chicago, 1917
11. *"Firebrand" Trevison.* Chicago, 1918
12. *The Ranchman.* Chicago, 1919
13. *The Trail Horde.* Chicago, 1920
14. *"Beau" Rand.* Chicago, 1921
15. *"Drag" Harlem.* Chicago, 1921
16. *Square Deal Sanderson.* Chicago and London, 1922
17. *West!* New York, 1922
18. *Brass Commandments.* New York and London, 1923
19. *Channing Comes Through.* New York, 1924
20. *The Way of the Buffalo.* New York and London, 1924
21. *Lonesome Ranch.* London, 1924
22. *Last Hope Ranch.* New York and London, 1925
23. *Trailing Back.* London, 1925
24. *The Valley of the Stars.* New York and London, 1926
25. *The Gentleman from Virginia.* New York and London, 1926
26. *Slow Burgess.* London, 1926
27. *Land of the Free.* New York and London, 1927
28. *The Mesa.* New York, 1928
29. *Mystery Range.* New York and London, 1928
30. *The Raider.* New York and London, 1929
31. *The Red Brand.* New York, 1929
32. *Pedro the Magnificent.* London, 1929
33. *Gone North.* New York and London, 1930
34. *A Son of Arizona.* New York and London, 1931
35. *Double Cross Ranch.* New York and London, 1932

36. *War on Wishbone Range.* New York, 1932
37. *Breath of the Desert.* London, 1932
38. *Clear the Trail.* New York and London, 1933
39. *West of Apache Pass.* New York and London, 1934
40. *Silverspurs.* New York and London, 1935
41. *Kingdom in the Cactus.* New York, 1936
42. *Parade of the Empty Boots.* New York, 1937
43. *Arizona Jim.* New York and London, 1939
44. *Treasure Ranch.* New York, 1940
45. *So Long, Sucker.* New York, 1941
46. *Gun-Law for Lavercombe.* New York, 1962
47. *Ferguson's Trail.* New York, 1964
48. *Sure Shot.* New York, 1964
49. *Law of the Gun.* New York, 1966
50. *Revenge Ambush.* New York, 1967
51. *Hellfire.* New York, 1967
52. *Gold Rock Ambush.* New York, 1968
53. *Night of Vengeance.* New York, 1968
54. *The Loner.* New York, 1968
55. *Desert Rider.* New York, 1968

Selwyn, Francis
British, born August 20, 1935
1. *Cracksman on Velvet.* London and New York, 1974
2. *Sergeant Verity and the Cracksman.* London, 1975
3. *Sergeant Verity and the Imperial Diamond.* London, 1975
4. *Sergeant Verity Presents His Compliments.* London and New York, 1977
5. *Sergeant Verity and the Blood Royal.* London and New York, 1979

Senarens, Luis P. (Philip)
American, April 24, 1865, died in 1935
Pseudonym: Captain Howard
1. *A.D.T.; or, The Messenger Boy Detective,* as Captain Howard. New York, 1882
2. *The Girl Detective,* as Captain Howard. New York, 1882
3. *The Mystery of One Night,* as Captain Howard. New York, 1882
4. *Young Vidocq,* as Captain Howard. New York, 1882
5. *Frank Reade, Jr. and His Steam Wonder.* New York, 1884
6. *Frank Reade, Jr. and His Electric Boat.* New York, 1884
7. *Frank Reade, Jr. and His Adventures with His Latest Invention.* New York, 1884
8. *Frank Reade, Jr. and His Airship.* New York, 1884
9. *Frank Reade, Jr.'s Marvel; or, Above and Below Water.* New York, 1884
10. *Frank Reade, Jr. in the Clouds.* New York, 1885
11. *Frank Reade, Jr. with His New Steam Horse among the Cowboys; or, The League of the Plains.* New York, 1892
12. *Frank Reade, Jr. with His New Steam Horse in the Great American Desert; or, The Sandy Trail of Death.* New York, 1892
13. *Frank Reade, Jr. with His New Steam Horse and the Mystery of the Underground Ranch.* New York, 1892
14. *Frank Reade, Jr. with His New Steam Horse in Search of an Ancient Mine.* New York, 1892
15. *Frank Reade, Jr. with His New Steam Horse in the North-West; or, Wild Adventures among the Blackfeet.* New York, 1892
16. *Frank Reade, Jr.'s Electric Air Canoe; or, The Search for the Valley of Diamonds.* New York, 1892
17. *Jack Wright, the Boy Inventor, and His Under-Water Ironclad; or, The Treasure of the Sandy Sea.* New York, 1892
18. *Jack Wright and His Electric Deer; or, Fighting the Bandits of the Black Hills.* New York, 1892
19. *Jack Wright and His Prairie Engine; or, Among the Bushmen of Australia.* New York, 1892
20. *Jack Wright and His Electric Air Schooner; or, The Mystery of a Magic Mine.* New York, 1892
21. *Jack Wright and His Electric Sea-Motor; or, The Search for a Drifting Wreck.* New York, 1892
22. *Jack Wright and His Ocean Sleuth-Hound; or, Tracking an Underwater Treasure.* New York, 1892
23. *Jack Wright and His Dandy of the Deep; or, Driven Afloat in the Sea of Fire.* New York, 1892
24. *Jack Wright and His Electric Torpedo Ram; or, The Sunken City of the Atlantic.* New York, 1892
25. *Jack Wright and His Deep Sea Monitor; or, Searching for a Ton of Gold.* New York, 1892
26. *Jack Wright, The Boy Inventor, Exploring Central Asia in His Magnetic Hurricane.* New York, 1892
27. *Jack Wright and His Ocean Plunger; or, The Harpoon Hunters of the Arctic.* New York, 1892
28. *Jack Wright and His Electric "Sea-Ghost;" or, A Strange Under-Water Journey.* New York, 1892
29. *Jack Wright, The Boy Inventor, and His Deep Sea Diving Bell; or, The Buccaneers of the Gold Coast.* New York, 1892
30. *Jack Wright, The Boy Inventor, and His Electric Tricycle-Boat; or, The Treasure of the Sun-Worshippers.* New York, 1892
31. *Jack Wright and His Undersea Wrecking Raft; or, The Mystery of a Scuttled Ship.* New York, 1892
32. *Jack Wright and His Terror of the Seas; or, Fighting for a Sunken Fortune.* New York, 1892
33. *Jack Wright and His Electric Diving Boat; or, Lost under the Ocean.* New York, 1892
34. *Jack Wright and His Submarine Yacht; or, The Fortune Hunters of the Red Sea.* New York, 1892
35. *Jack Wright and His Electric Gunboat; or, The Search for a Stolen Girl.* New York, 1893
36. *Frank Reade, Jr.'s New Electric Submarine Boat "The Explorer;" or, To the North Pole under the Ice.* New York, 1893
37. *Frank Reade, Jr.'s New Electric Van; or, Hunting Wild Animals in the Jungles of India.* New York, 1893
38. *Frank Reade, Jr.'s "White Cruiser" of the Clouds; or, The Search for the Dog-Faced Men.* New York, 1893
39. *Frank Reade, Jr.'s Deep Sea Diver the "Tortoise;" or, the Search for a Sunken Island.* New York, 1893
40. *Frank Reade, Jr.'s New Electric Terror the "Thunderer;" or, The Search for the Tartar's Captive.* New York, 1893
41. *Frank Reade, Jr. and His Air-Ship.* New York, 1893
42. *Frank Reade, Jr.'s Latest Air Wonder the "Kite;" or, A Six Weeks' Flight over the Andes.* New York, 1893
43. *Frank Reade, Jr.'s New Electric Invention the "Warrior;" or, Fighting the Apaches in Arizona.* New York, 1893
44. *Frank Reade, Jr.'s "Sea Serpent;" or, The Search for Sunken Gold.* New York, 1893
45. *Fighting the Slave Hunters; or, Frank Reade, Jr. in Central Africa.* New York, 1893
46. *Around the World Under Water; or, The Wonderful Cruise of a Submarine Boat.* New York, 1893
47. *Lost in the Land of Fire; or, Across the Pampas in the Electric Turret.* New York, 1893
48. *Six Weeks in the Great Whirlpool; or, Strange Adventures in a Submarine Boat.* New York, 1893
49. *Chased Across the Sahara; or, The Bedouins' Captive.* New York, 1893
50. *The Mystic Brand; or, Frank Reade, Jr. and His Overland Stage upon the Staked Plains.* New York, 1893
51. *Frank Reade, Jr. and His New Torpedo Boat; or, At War with the Brazilian Rebels.* New York, 1893
52. *Frank Reade, Jr. and His Magnetic Gun-Carriage; or, Working for the U.S. Mail.* New York, 1893

53. *Frank Reade, Jr. and His Engine of the Clouds; or, Chased Around the World in the Sky.* New York, 1893
54. *The Sunken Pirate; or, Frank Reade, Jr. in Search of Treasure at the Bottom of the Sea.* New York, 1893
55. *Frank Reade, Jr. and His Electric Air-Boat; or, Hunting Wild Beasts for a Circus.* New York, 1893
56. *Jack Wright and His Electric Sea Launch; or, A Desperate Cruise for Life.* New York, 1893
57. *Jack Wright and His Electric Bicycle-Boat; or, Searching for Captain Kidd's Gold.* New York, 1893
58. *Jack Wright and His Electric Side-Wheel Boat; or, Fighting the Brigands of the Coral Isles.* New York, 1893
59. *Jack Wright's Wonder of the Waves; or, The Flying Dutchman of the Pacific.* New York, 1893
60. *Jack Wright and His Electric Exploring Ship; or, A Cruise around Greenland.* New York, 1893
61. *Jack Wright and His Electric Man-of-War; or, Fighting the Sea Robbers of the Frozen Coast.* New York, 1893
62. *Jack Wright and His Submarine Torpedo-Tug; or, Winning a Government Reward.* New York, 1893
63. *Jack Wright and His Electric Sea Demon; or, Daring Adventures under the Ocean.* New York, 1893
64. *Jack Wright and His Electric "Whale"; or, The Treasure Trove of the Polar Sea.* New York, 1893
65. *Jack Wright and His Electric Marine "Rover;" or, 50,000 Miles in Ocean Perils.* New York, 1893
66. *Jack Wright and His Electric Deep Sea Cutter; or, Searching for a Pirate's Treasure.* New York, 1893
67. *Jack Wright and His Electric Monarch of the Ocean; or, Cruising for a Million in Gold.* New York, 1893
68. *Jack Wright and His Electric Devil-Fish; or, Fighting the Smugglers of Alaska.* New York, 1893
69. *Jack Wright and His Electric Demon of the Plains; or, Wild Adventures among the Cowboys.* New York, 1893
70. *Jack Wright and His Electric Balloon Ship; or, 30,000 Leagues above the Earth.* New York, 1893
71. *Jack Wright and His Electric Locomotive; or, The Lost Mine of Death Valley.* New York, 1893
72. *Jack Wright and His Iron-Clad Air-Motor; or, Searching for a Lost Explorer.* New York, 1893
73. *Jack Wright and His Electric Tricycle; or, Fighting the Stranglers of the Crimson Desert.* New York, 1893
74. *Jack Wright and His Electric Dynamo Boat; or, The Mystery of a Buried Sea.* New York, 1893
75. *Jack Wright and His Flying Torpedo; or, The Black Demons of Dismal Swamp.* New York, 1893
76. *Jack Wright and His Prairie Privateer; or, Fighting the Western Road-Agents.* New York, 1893
77. *Jack Wright and His Naval Cruiser; or, Fighting the Pirates of the Pacific.* New York, 1893
78. *Jack Wright, The Boy Inventor, and His Whaleback Privateer; or, Cruising in the Behring Sea.* New York, 1893
79. *Frank Reade, Jr. and His Electric Car; or, Outwitting a Desperate Gang.* New York, 1894
80. *Lost in the Mountains of the Moon; or, Frank Reade, Jr.'s Great Trip with His New Air-Ship, the "Scud."* New York, 1894
81. *100 Miles below the Surface of the Sea; or, The Marvelous Trip of Frank Reade, Jr.'s "Hardshell" Submarine Boat.* New York, 1894
82. *Abandoned in Alaska; or, Frank Reade, Jr.'s Thrilling Search for a Lost Gold Claim with His New Electric Wagon.* New York, 1894
83. *Around the Arctic Circle; or, Frank Reade, Jr.'s Most Famous Trip with His Air-Ship, The "Orbit."* New York, 1894
84. *Under the Four Oceans; or, Frank Reade, Jr.'s Submarine Chase of a "Sea Devil."* New York, 1894
85. *From the Nile to the Niger; or, Frank Reade, Jr. Lost in the Soudan with His "Overland Omnibus."* New York, 1894
86. *The Chase of a Comet; or, Frank Reade, Jr.'s Most Wonderful Aerial Trip with His New Air-Ship, The "Flash."* New York, 1894
87. *Lost in the Great Undertow; or, Frank Reade, Jr.'s Submarine Cruise in the Gulf Stream.* New York, 1894
88. *From Tropic to Tropic; or, Frank Reade, Jr.'s Latest Tour with His Bicycle Car.* New York, 1894
89. *To the End of the Earth in an Air-Ship; or, Frank Reade, Jr.'s Great Mid-Air Flight.* New York, 1894
90. *The Underground Sea; or, Frank Reade, Jr.'s Subterranean Cruise in His Submarine Boat.* New York, 1894
91. *The Mysterious Mirage; or, Frank Reade, Jr.'s Desert Search for a Secret City with His New Overland Chaise.* New York, 1894
92. *The Electric Island; or, Frank Reade, Jr.'s Search for the Greatest Wonder on Earth with His Air-Ship, The "Flight."* New York, 1894
93. *For Six Weeks Buried in a Deep Sea Cave; or, Frank Reade, Jr.'s Great Submarine Search.* New York, 1894
94. *The Galleon's Gold; or, Frank Reade, Jr.'s Deep Sea Search.* New York, 1894
95. *Across Australia with Frank Reade, Jr. in His New Electric Car; or, Wonderful Adventures in the Antipodes.* New York, 1894
96. *Frank Reade, Jr.'s Greatest Flying Machine; or, Fighting the Terror of the Coast.* New York, 1894
97. *Jack Wright and His Winged Gunboat; or, A Voyage to an Unknown Land.* New York, 1894
98. *Jack Wright and His Electric Flyer; or, Racing in the Clouds for a Boy's Life.* New York, 1894
99. *Jack Wright, The Boy Inventor's Electric Sledge Boat; or, Wild Adventures in Alaska.* New York, 1894
100. *Jack Wright and His Electric Express Wagon; or, Wiping Out the Outlaws of Deadwood.* New York, 1894
101. *Jack Wright and His Submarine Explorer; or, A Cruise at the Bottom of the Ocean.* New York, 1894
102. *Jack Wright and His Demon of the Air; or, A Perilous Trip in the Clouds.* New York, 1894
103. *Jack Wright and His Electric Ripper; or, Searching for a Treasure in the Jungle.* New York, 1894
104. *Jack Wright and His King of the Sea; or, Diving for Old Spanish Gold.* New York, 1894
105. *Jack Wright and His Electric Balloons; or, Cruising in the Clouds for a Mountain Treasure.* New York, 1894
106. *Jack Wright and His Imp of the Ocean; or, The Wreckers of Whirlpool Reef.* New York, 1894
107. *Jack Wright and His Electric Cab; or, Around the Globe on Wheels.* New York, 1894
108. *Jack Wright and His Flying Phantom; or, Searching for a Lost Balloonist.* New York, 1894
109. *Jack Wright and His Submarine Warship; or, Chasing the Demons of the Sea of Gold.* New York, 1894
110. *Jack Wright and His Prairie Yacht; or, Fighting the Indians of the Sea of Grass.* New York, 1894
111. *Jack Wright and His Electric Air Rocket; or, The Boy Exile of Siberia.* New York, 1894
112. *Jack Wright and His Submarine Destroyer; or, Warring Against the Japanese Pirates.* New York, 1894
113. *Jack Wright and His Electric Battery Diver; or, A Two Months' Cruise Under Water.* New York, 1894
114. *Jack Wright and His Electric Stage; or, Leagued Against the James Boys.* New York, 1894
115. *Jack Wright and His Wheel of the Wind; or, The Jewels of the Volcano Dwellers.* New York, 1894
116. *Jack Wright and the Head-Hunters of the African Coast; or, The Electric Pirate Chaser.* New York, 1894

117. *3,000 Pounds of Gold; or, Jack Wright and His Electric Bat, Fighting the Cliff-Dwellers of the Sierras.* New York, 1894
118. *Jack Wright and the Wild Boy of the Woods; or, Exposing a Strange Mystery with the Electric Cart.* New York, 1894
119. *Jack Wright among the Demons of the Ocean with His Electric Sea-Fighter.* New York, 1894
120. *Jack Wright, The Wizard of Wrightstown and His Electric Dragon; or, A Wild Race to Save a Fortune.* New York, 1894
121. *Jack Wright's Electric Land-Clipper; or, Exploring the Mysterious Gobi Desert.* New York, 1894
122. *On the Great Meridian with Frank Reade, Jr. in His New Air-Ship; or, A Twenty-Five Thousand Mile Trip in Mid-Air.* New York, 1895
123. *Under the Indian Ocean with Frank Reade, Jr.; or, A Cruise in a Submarine Boat.* New York, 1895
124. *Astray in the Selvas; or, The Wild Experiences of Frank Reade, Jr., Barney and Pomp, in South America with the Electric Car.* New York, 1895
125. *Lost in a Comet's Tail; or, Frank Reade, Jr.'s Strange Adventure with His New Air-Ship.* New York, 1895
126. *Six Sunken Pirates; or, Frank Reade, Jr.'s Marvelous Adventures in the Deep Sea.* New York, 1895
127. *Beyond the Gold Coast; or, Frank Reade, Jr.'s Overland Trip with His Electric Phaeton.* New York, 1895
128. *Latitude 90; or, Frank Reade, Jr.'s Most Wonderful Mid-Air Flight.* New York, 1895
129. *Afloat in a Sunken Forest; or, With Frank Reade, Jr. on a Submarine Cruise.* New York, 1895
130. *Across the Desert of Fire; or, Frank Reade, Jr.'s Marvelous Trip to a Strange Country.* New York, 1895
131. *Over Two Continents; or, Frank Reade, Jr.'s Long Distance Flight with His New Air-Ship.* New York, 1895
132. *The Coral Labyrinth; or, Lost with Frank Reade, Jr. in a Deep Sea Cave.* New York, 1895
133. *Along the Orinoco; or, with Frank Reade, Jr. in Venezuela.* New York, 1895
134. *Across the Earth; or, Frank Reade, Jr.'s Latest Trip with His New Air-Ship.* New York, 1895
135. *1,000 Fathoms Deep; or, With Frank Reade, Jr. in the Sea of Gold.* New York, 1895
136. *The Island in the Air; or, Frank Reade, Jr.'s Trip to the Tropics.* New York, 1895
137. *In the Wild Man's Land; or, With Frank Reade, Jr. in the Heart of Australia.* New York, 1895
138. *The Sunken Isthmus; or, With Frank Reade, Jr. in the Yucatan Channel, with His New Submarine Yacht, The "Sea Diver."* New York, 1895
139. *The Lost Caravan; or, Frank Reade, Jr. on the Staked Plains with His "Electric Racer."* New York, 1895
140. *The Transient Lake; or, Frank Reade, Jr.'s Adventures in a Mysterious Country with His Air-Ship, The "Spectre."* New York, 1895
141. *The Weird Island; or, Frank Reade, Jr.'s Strange Submarine Search for a Deep Sea Wonder.* New York, 1895
142. *The Abandoned Country; or, Frank Reade, Jr. Exploring a New Continent.* New York, 1895
143. *Over the Steppes; or, Adrift in Asia with Frank Reade, Jr.* New York, 1895
144. *The Unknown Sea; or, Frank Reade, Jr.'s Under-Water Cruise.* New York, 1895
145. *In the Black Zone; or, Frank Reade, Jr.'s Quest for the Mountain of Ivory.* New York, 1895
146. *The Lost Navigators; or, Frank Reade, Jr.'s Mid-Air Search with His New Air-Ship, The "Sky Flyer."* New York, 1895
147. *The Magic Island; or, Frank Reade, Jr.'s Deep Sea Trip of Mystery.* New York, 1895
148. *Through the Tropics; or, Frank Reade, Jr.'s Adventures in the Gran Chaco.* New York, 1895
149. *In White Latitudes; or, Frank Reade, Jr.'s Ten Thousand Mile Flight over the Frozen North.* New York, 1895
150. *Below the Sahara; or, Frank Reade, Jr. Exploring an Underground River, with His Submarine Boat.* New York, 1895
151. *The Black Mogul; or, Through India with Frank Reade, Jr. Aboard His "Electric Boomer."* New York, 1895
152. *The Missing Planet; or, Frank Reade, Jr.'s Quest for a Fallen Star with His New Air-Ship, "The Zenith."* New York, 1895
153. *The Black Squadron; or, Frank Reade, Jr. in the Indian Ocean with His Submarine Boat, The "Rocket."* New York, 1895
154. *The Prairie Pirates; or, Frank Reade, Jr.'s Trip to Texas with His Electric Vehicle, The "Detective."* New York, 1895
155. *Over the Orient; or, Frank Reade, Jr.'s Travels in Turkey with His New Air-Ship.* New York, 1895
156. *The Black Whirlpool; or, Frank Reade, Jr.'s Deep Sea Search for a Lost Ship.* New York, 1895
157. *The Silent City; or, Frank Reade, Jr.'s Visit to a Strange People with His New Electric "Flyer."* New York, 1895
158. *The White Desert; or, Frank Reade, Jr.'s Trip to the Land of Tombs.* New York, 1895
159. *Under the Gulf of Guinea; or, Frank Reade, Jr. Exploring the Sunken Reef of Gold with His New Submarine Boat.* New York, 1895
160. *The Yellow Khan; or, Frank Reade, Jr. among the Thugs in Central India.* New York, 1895
161. *Frank Reade, Jr. in Japan, with His War Cruiser of the Clouds.* New York, 1895
162. *Frank Reade, Jr. in Cuba; or, Helping the Patriots with His Latest Air-Ship.* New York, 1895
163. *Chasing a Pirate; or, Frank Reade, Jr. on a Desperate Cruise.* New York, 1895
164. *In the Land of Fire; or, Frank Reade, Jr. among the Head Hunters.* New York, 1895
165. *7,000 Miles Underground; or, Frank Reade, Jr. Exploring a Volcano.* New York, 1895
166. *The Demon of the Clouds; or, Frank Reade, Jr. and the Ghosts of Phantom Island.* New York, 1895
167. *The Cloud City; or, Frank Reade, Jr.'s Most Wonderful Discovery.* New York, 1895
168. *The White Atoll; or, Frank Reade, Jr. in the South Pacific.* New York, 1895
169. *The Monarch of the Moon; or, Frank Reade, Jr.'s Exploits in Africa with His Electric "Thunderer."* New York, 1895
170. *37 Bags of Gold; or, Frank Reade, Jr. Hunting for a Lost Steamer.* New York, 1895
171. *The Lost Lake; or, Frank Reade, Jr.'s Trip to Alaska.* New York, 1895
172. *The Caribs' Cave; or, Frank Reade, Jr.'s Submarine Search for the Reef of Pearls.* New York, 1895
173. *The Desert of Death; or, Frank Reade, Jr. Exploring an Unknown Land.* New York, 1895
174. *A Trip to the Sea of the Sun; or, With Frank Reade, Jr. on a Perilous Cruise.* New York, 1895
175. *Skull and Cross-Bones; or, Jack Wright's Diving-Bell and the Pirates.* New York, 1895
176. *Jack Wright, The Boy Inventor, and His Phantom Frigate; or, Fighting the Coast Wreckers of the Gulf.* New York, 1895
177. *Jack Wright and His Air-Ship on Wheels; or, A Perilous Journey to Cape Farewell.* New York, 1895
178. *Jack Wright and His Electric Roadster in the Desert of Death; or, Chasing the Australian Brigand.* New York, 1895
179. *Jack Wright's Ocean Marvel; or, The Mystery of a Frozen Island.* New York, 1895

Senarens, Luis P.

180. *Jack Wright and His Electric Soaring Machine; or, A Daring Flight Through Miles of Peril.* New York, 1895
181. *Jack Wright and His Electric Battery Car; or, Beating the Express Train Robbers.* New York, 1895
182. *Jack Wright and His Electric Sea Horse; or, Seven Weeks in Ocean Perils.* New York, 1895
183. *Jack Wright and His Electric Balloon Boat; or, A Dangerous Voyage Above The Clouds.* New York, 1895
184. *In the Jungles of India; or, Jack Wright as a Wild Animal Hunter.* New York, 1895
185. *50,000 Leagues under the Sea; or, Jack Wright's Most Dangerous Voyage.* New York, 1895
186. *Jack Wright, The Boy Inventor, Working for the Union Pacific Railroad; or, Over the Continent in the "Electric."* New York, 1895
187. *Over the South Pole; or, Jack Wright's Search for a Lost Explorer with His Flying Boat.* New York, 1895
188. *Jack Wright and His Electric Air Monitor; or, The Scourge of the Pacific.* New York, 1895
189. *The Boy Lion Fighter; or, Jack Wright in the Swamps of Africa.* New York, 1895
190. *Jack Wright and His Electric Submarine Ranger; or, Afloat among the Cannibals of the Deep.* New York, 1895
191. *The Demon of the Sky; or, Jack Wright's $10,000 Wager.* New York, 1895
192. *Adrift in the Land of Snow; or, Jack Wright and His Sledge-boat on Wheels.* New York, 1896
193. *The Floating Terror; or, Jack Wright Fighting the Buccaneers of the Venezuelan Coast.* New York, 1896
194. *Lost in the Polar Circle; or, Jack Wright and His Aerial Explorer.* New York, 1896
195. *Jack Wright, The Boy Inventor, and the Smugglers of the Border Lakes; or, The Second Cruise of the Whaleback "Comet."* New York, 1896
196. *The Fatal Blue Diamond; or, Jack Wright among the Demon Worshippers with His Electric Motor.* New York, 1896
197. *Running the Blockade; or, Jack Wright Helping the Cuban Filibusters.* New York, 1896
198. *Flying Avenger; or, Jack Wright Fighting for Cuba.* New York, 1896
199. *Jack Wright and His New Electric Horse; or, A Perilous Trip over Two Continents.* New York, 1896
200. *Over the Sahara Desert; or, Jack Wright Fighting the Slave Hunters.* New York, 1896
201. *Diving for a Million; or, Jack Wright and His Electric Ocean Liner.* New York, 1896
202. *The Black Lagoon; or, Frank Reade, Jr.'s Submarine Search for a Sunken City in Russia.* New York, 1896
203. *The Mysterious Brand; or, Frank Reade, Jr. Solving a Mexican Mystery.* New York, 1896
204. *Across the Milky Way; or, Frank Reade, Jr.'s Great Astronomical Trip with His Air-Ship, "The Shooting Star."* New York, 1896
205. *Under the Great Lakes; or, Frank Reade, Jr. Latest Submarine Cruise.* New York, 1896
206. *The Magic Mine; or, Frank Reade, Jr.'s Trip up the Yukon with His Electric Combination Traveller.* New York, 1896
207. *Across Arabia; or, Frank Reade, Jr.'s Search for the Forty Thieves.* New York, 1896
208. *The Silver Sea; or, Frank Reade, Jr.'s Submarine Cruise in Unknown Waters.* New York, 1896
209. *In the Tundras; or, Frank Reade, Jr.'s Latest Trip Through Northern Asia.* New York, 1896
210. *The Circuit of Cancer; or, Frank Reade, Jr.'s Novel Trip Around the World in His New Air-Ship, The "Flight."* New York, 1896
211. *The Sacred Sea; or, Frank Reade, Jr.'s Submarine Exploits among the Dervishes of India.* New York, 1896
212. *The Land of Dunes; or, With Frank Reade, Jr. in the Desert of Gobi.* New York, 1896
213. *Six Days under Havana Harbor; or, Frank Reade, Jr.'s Secret Service Work for Uncle Sam.* New York, 1896
214. *The Sinking Star; or, Frank Reade, Jr.'s Trip into Space with His New Air-Ship "Saturn."* New York, 1896
215. *In the Gran Chaco; or, Frank Reade, Jr. in Search of a Missing Man.* New York, 1896
216. *The Lost Oasis; or, With Frank Reade, Jr. in the Australian Desert.* New York, 1896
217. *The Isle of Hearts; or, Frank Reade, Jr. in a Strange Sea with His Submarine Boat.* New York, 1896
218. *Jack Wright and Frank Reade, Jr., The Two Young Inventors; or, Brains Against Brains.* New York, 1896

Sendak, Maurice (Bernard)
American, born June 10, 1928
1. *Kenny's Window.* New York, 1956
2. *Very Far Away.* New York, 1957
3. *The Sign on Rosie's Door.* New York, 1960
4. *The Nutshell Library.* New York, 4 vols., 1962
5. *Where the Wild Things Are.* New York, 1963
6. *Higglety Pigglety Pop! or, There Must Be More to Life.* New York, 1967
7. *In the Night Kitchen.* New York, 1970
8. *Ten Little Rabbits.* Philadelphia, 1970
9. *Fantasy Sketches.* Philadelphia, 1970
10. *Pictures.* New York, 1971
11. *Some Swell Pup:, Are You Sure You Want a Dog?* New York, 1976
12. *Seven Little Monsters.* New York and London, 1977

Seredy, Kate
American, born November 10, 1899, died March 7, 1975
1. *The Good Master.* New York, 1935
2. *Listening.* New York, 1936
3. *The White Stag.* New York, 1937
4. *The Singing Tree.* New York, 1939
5. *A Tree for Peter.* New York, 1941
6. *The Open Gate.* New York, 1943
7. *The Chestry Oak.* New York, 1948
8. *Gypsy.* New York, 1951
9. *Philomena.* New York, 1955
10. *The Tenement Tree.* New York, 1959
11. *A Brand-New Uncle.* New York, 1961
12. *Lazy Tinka.* New York, 1962

Serling, Rod [Edward Rodman Serling]
American, born December 25, 1924, died June 28, 1975
1. *Patterns: Four Television Plays.* New York, 1957
2. *Stories from the Twilight Zone.* New York, 1960
3. *More Stories from the Twilight Zone.* New York, 1961
4. *Requiem for a Heavyweight.* New York and London, 1962
5. *New Stories from the Twilight Zone.* New York, 1962
6. *From the Twilight Zone.* New York, 1962
7. *The Season to Be Wary.* Boston, 1967
8. *The Lonely, in Writing for Television.* New York, 1970
9. *Night Gallery.* New York, 1971
10. *A Storm in Summer.* Toronto, 1972
11. *Night Gallery 2.* New York, 1972

Serviss, Garrett P. (Putnam)
American, born March 24, 1851, died May 25, 1929
1. *Astronomy with an Opera-Glass.* New York, 1888
2. *Wonders of the Lunar Worlds; or, A Trip to the Moon.* New York, 1892
3. *The Moon Metal.* New York, 1900
4. *A Columbus of Space.* New York and London, 1911

5. *The Second Deluge.* New York and London, 1912
6. *Riding Through Space: The Earth's Scenic Voyage.* Springfield (OH), 1923
7. *Edison's Conquest of Mars.* Los Angeles (CA), 1947
8. *Invasion of Mars.* Reseda (CA), 1969

Seton, Anya
British
1. *My Theodosia.* Boston, 1941
2. *Dragonwyck.* Boston, 1944
3. *The Turquoise.* Boston and London, 1946
4. *The Hearth and the Eagle.* Boston and London, 1948
5. *Foxfire.* Boston and London, 1951
6. *Katherine.* Boston and London, 1954
7. *The Mistletoe and Sword: A Story of Roman Britain.* New York, 1955
8. *The Winthrop Woman.* Boston and London, 1958
9. *Washington Irving.* Boston, 1960
10. *Devil Water.* Boston and London, 1962
11. *Avalon.* Boston, 1965
12. *Green Darkness.* Boston and London, 1972
13. *Smouldering Fires.* New York, 1975

Seton, Ernest Thompson [Ernest Evan Thompson Seton]
American, born August 14, 1860, died October 23, 1946
1. *A List of Animals in Manitoba.* Toronto, 1886
2. *The Birds of Manitoba.* Washington, 1891
3. *Wild Animals I Have Known, Being the Personal Histories of Lobo, Silverspot, Raggylug, Bingo, The Springfield Fox, The Pacing Mustang, Wully, and Redruff.* New York, 1899
4. *The Trail of the Sandhill Stag.* New York and London, 1899
5. *Raggylug the Cottontail Rabbit and Other Animal Stories.* London, 1900
6. *The Biography of a Grizzly.* New York and London, 1900
7. *Lives of the Hunted.* New York, 1901
8. *Pictures of Wild Animals.* New York, 1901
9. *Bird Portraits.* Boston, 1901
10. *Two Little Savages.* Montreal and New York, 1903
11. *How to Play Indian.* Philadelphia, 1903
12. *Monarch, The Big Bear of Tallac.* New York, 1904
13. *The Red Book; or, How to Play Indian.* New York, 1904
14. *Animal Heroes, Being the Histories of a Cat, a Dog, a Pigeon, a Lynx, Two Wolves, and a Reindeer.* New York, 1905
15. *Woodmyth and Fable.* Toronto and New York, 1905
16. *The Birch-Bark Roll of the Woodcraft Indians.* New York, 1906
17. *The Natural History of the Ten Commandments.* New York, 1907
18. *The Biography of a Silver-Fox; or, Domino Reynard of Golden Town.* New York and London, 1909
19. *The War Dance and the Fire-Fly Dance.* New York, 1910
20. *Rolf in the Woods.* New York and London, 1911
21. *Wild Animals at Home.* Toronto, New York and London, 1913
22. *The White Reindeer, Arnaux, and The Boy and the Lynx.* London, 1915
23. *The Slum Cat, Snap, and The Winnipeg Wolf.* London, 1915
24. *Wild Animal Ways.* New York and London, 1916
25. *The Preacher of Cedar Mountain: a Tale of the Open Country.* New York and London, 1917
26. *Woodland Tales.* New York and London, 1921
27. *Bannertail: The Story of a Grey Squirrel.* New York, 1922
28. *Katug the Snow Child.* Oxford (Eng), 1929
29. *Krag, The Kootenay Ram and Other Animal Stories.* London, 1929
30. *Animals Worth Knowing.* New York, 1934
31. *Johnny Bear, Lobo, and Other Stories.* New York, 1935
32. *Great Historic Animals: Mainly about Wolves.* New York, 1937
33. *The Biography of an Arctic Fox.* New York, 1937
34. *Mainly about Wolves.* London, 1937
35. *Trail and Camp-Fire Stories.* New York and London, 1940
36. *The Trail of an Artist-Naturalist: The Autobiography of Ernest Thompson Seton.* New York, 1940
37. *Santana, The Hero Dog of France.* Los Angeles, 1945
38. *Animal Tracks and Hunter Signs.* New York, 1958
39. *Ernest Thompson Seton, Naturalist.* New York, 1959
40. *By a Thousand Fires: Nature Notes and Extracts from the Life and Unpublished Journals.* New York, 1967
41. *The Worlds of Ernest Thompson Seton.* New York, 1976

Seuss, Dr. [Theodore Seuss Geisel]
American, born March 2, 1904
Pseudonym: Theo LeSeig
1. *And to Think That I Saw It on Mulberry Street.* New York, 1937
2. *The 500 Hats of Bartholomew Cubbins.* New York, 1938
3. *The King's Stilts.* New York, 1939
4. *The Seven Lady Godivas.* New York, 1939
5. *Horton Hatches the Egg.* New York, 1940
6. *McElligot's Pool.* New York, 1947
7. *Thidwick, The Big-Hearted Moose.* New York, 1948
8. *Bartholomew and the Oobleck.* New York, 1949
9. *If I Ran the Zoo.* New York, 1950
10. *Scrambled Eggs Super!* New York, 1953
11. *Horton Hears a Who!* New York, 1954
12. *On Beyond Zebra.* New York, 1955
13. *If I Ran the Circus.* New York, 1956
14. *Signs of Civilization!* La Jolla (CA), 1956
15. *The Cat in the Hat.* New York, 1957
16. *How the Grinch Stole Christmas.* New York, 1957
17. *The Cat in the Hat Comes Back!* New York, 1958
18. *Yertle the Turtle and Other Stories.* New York, 1958
19. *Happy Birthday to You!* New York, 1959
20. *One Fish, Two Fish, Red Fish, Blue Fish.* New York, 1960
21. *Green Eggs and Ham.* New York, 1960
22. *Ten Apples Up on Top!* as Theo LeSeig. New York, 1961
23. *The Sneetches and Other Stories.* New York, 1961
24. *Sleep Book.* New York, 1962
25. *Hop on Pop.* New York, 1963
26. *ABC.* New York, 1963
27. *The Cat in the Hat Dictionary, by the Cat Himself,* with Philip D. Eastman. New York, 1964
28. *I Wish I Had Duck Feet,* as Theo LeSeig. New York, 1965
29. *The Fox in Socks.* New York, 1965
30. *I Had Trouble in Getting to Solla Sollew.* New York, 1965
31. *Come Over to My House,* as Theo LeSeig. New York, 1966
32. *The Cat in the Hat Songbook.* New York, 1967
33. *Lost World Revisited: A Forward Looking Backward Glance.* New York, 1967
34. *The Foot Book.* New York, 1968
35. *The Eye Book,* as Theo LeSeig. New York, 1968
36. *I Can Lick 30 Tigers Today and Other Stories.* New York, 1969
37. *My Book about Me—By Me, Myself. I Wrote It! I Drew It!* New York, 1969
38. *Mr. Brown Can Moo! Can You?* New York, 1970
39. *I Can Draw It Myself.* New York, 1970
40. *The Lorax.* New York, 1971
41. *I Can Write—By Me, Myself,* as Theo LeSeig. New York, 1971
42. *In a People House,* as Theo LeSeig. New York, 1972
43. *Marvin K. Mooney, Will You Please Go Now?* New York, 1972

Seuss, Dr.

44. *The Many Mice of Mr. Brice*, as Theo LeSeig. New York, 1973
45. *Did I Ever Tell You How Lucky You Are?* New York, 1973
46. *The Shape of Me and Other Stuff.* New York, 1973
47. *Wacky Wednesday*, as Theo LeSeig. New York, 1974
48. *There's a Wocket in My Pocket!* New York, 1974
49. *Great Day for Up!* New York, 1974
50. *Would You Rather Be a Bullfrog?* as Theo LeSeig. New York, 1975
51. *Oh, The Thinks You Can Think.* New York, 1975
52. *Hooper Humperdink . . . ? Not Him!* New York, 1976
53. *The Cat's Quizzer.* New York, 1976
54. *Please Try to Remember the First of Octember,* as Theo LeSeig. New York, 1977

Severn, David [David Storr Unwin]
British, born December 3, 1918

1. *Rick Afire!* London, 1942
2. *A Cabin for Crusoe.* London, 1943
3. *Wagon for Five.* London, 1944
4. *A Hermit in the Hills.* London, 1945
5. *Forest Holiday.* London, 1946
6. *Ponies and Poachers.* London, 1947
7. *Bill Badger and the Pine Martins [Bathing Pool, Burried Treasure].* London, 3 vols., 1947-50
8. *Wily Fox and the Baby Show [Christmas Party, Missing Fireworks].* London, 3 vols., 1947-50
9. *The Cruise of the "Maiden Castle."* London, 1948
10. *Treasure for Three.* London, 1949
11. *Dream Gold.* London, 1949
12. *Crazy Castle.* London, 1951
13. *Burglers and Bandicoots.* London, 1952
14. *Drumbeats!* London, 1953
15. *The Governor's Wife,* as David Unwin. London, 1954
16. *Blaze of Broadfurrow Farm.* London, 1955
17. *Walnut Tree Meadow.* London, 1955
18. *A View of the Heath,* as David Unwin. London, 1956
19. *The Future Took Us.* London, 1958
20. *The Green-Eyed Gryphon.* London, 1958
21. *Foxy-Boy.* London, 1959
22. *Three at the Sea.* London, 1959
23. *Jeff Dickson, Cowhand.* London, 1963
24. *Clouds over the Alberhorn.* London, 1963
25. *The Wild Valley.* New York, 1963
26. *A Dog for a Day.* London, 1965
27. *The Girl in the Grove.* London, 1974
28. *The Wishing Bone.* London, 1977

Sewell, Helen (Moore)
American, born June 27, 1896, died February 24, 1957

1. *A Head for Happy.* New York, 1931
2. *Blue Barns.* New York, 1933
3. *Ming and Mehitable.* New York, 1936
4. *Peggy and the Pony.* New York and London, 1937
5. *Jimmy and Jemima.* New York, 1940
6. *Peggy and the Pup.* New York and London, 1941
7. *Birthdays for Robin.* New York, 1943
8. *Belinda the Mouse.* New York and London, 1944
9. *Three Tall Tales.* New York, 1947

Shannon, Monica
American, died August 13, 1965

1. *California Fairy Tales.* New York and London, 1926
2. *Eyes for the Dark.* New York, 1928
3. *Goose Grass Rhymes.* New York, 1930
4. *Tawnymore.* New York, 1931
5. *Dobry.* New York, 1935
6. *More Tales from California.* New York, 1935

Sharkey, Jack [John Michael Sharkey]
American, born May 6, 1931

1. *The Secret Martians.* New York, 1960
2. *Murder, Maestro, Please.* New York and London, 1960
3. *Death for Auld Lang Syne.* New York, 1962
4. *The Addams Family.* New York, 1965
5. *Ultimatum in 2050 A.D.* New York, 1965

Sharmat, Marjorie Weinman
American, born November 12, 1928

1. *Rex.* New York, 1967
2. *Goodnight Andrew, Goodnight Craig.* New York, 1969
3. *Gladys Told Me to Meet Her Here.* New York, 1970
4. *A Hot Thirsty Day.* New York and London, 1971
5. *51 Sycamore Lane.* New York and London, 1971
6. *Getting Something on Maggie Marmelstein.* New York, 1971
7. *A Visit with Rosalind.* New York, 1972
8. *Nate the Great.* New York, 1972
9. *Sophie and Gussie.* New York, 1973
10. *Morris Brookside, A Dog.* New York, 1973
11. *Morris Brookside Is Missing.* New York, 1974
12. *Nate the Great Goes Undercover.* New York, 1974
13. *I Want Mama.* New York, 1974
14. *Walter the Wolf.* New York, 1975
15. *I'm Not Oscar's Friend Anymore.* New York, 1975
16. *Nate the Great and the Lost List.* New York, 1975
17. *Burton and Dudley.* New York, 1975
18. *Maggie Marmelstein for President.* New York, 1975
19. *The Lancelot Closes at Five.* New York, 1976
20. *The Trip and Other Sophie and Gussie Stories.* New York, 1976
21. *Edgemont.* New York, 1976
22. *Mooch the Messy.* New York, 1976
23. *I Don't Care.* New York, 1977
24. *I'm Terrific.* New York, 1977
25. *Nate the Great and the Phony Clue.* New York, 1977

Sharp, Margery
British, born in 1905

1. *Rhododendron Pie.* London and Boston, 1930
2. *Fanfare for Tin Trumpets.* London, 1932
3. *The Nymph and the Nobleman.* London, 1932
4. *The Flowering Thorn.* London, 1933
5. *Sophy Cassmajor.* London and Boston, 1934
6. *Four Gardens.* London and Boston, 1935
7. *The Nutmeg Tree.* London and Boston, 1937
8. *Harlequin House.* London and Boston, 1939
9. *The Stone of Chastity.* London and Boston, 1940
10. *Three Companion Pieces: Sophy Cassmajor, The Tigress on the Hearth, and The Nymph and the Nobleman.* Boston, 1941
11. *Cluny Brown.* London and Boston, 1944
12. *Britannia Mews.* London and Boston, 1946
13. *The Foolish Gentlewoman.* London and Boston, 1948
14. *Lise Lillywhite.* London and Boston, 1951
15. *The Gypsy in the Parlour.* London and Boston, 1954
16. *The Eye of Love.* London and Boston, 1957
17. *The Rescuers.* London and Boston, 1959
18. *Melisande.* London and Boston, 1960
19. *Something Light.* London, 1960
20. *Martha in Paris.* London, 1962
21. *Miss Bianca.* London and Boston, 1962
22. *The Turret.* Boston, 1963
23. *Martha, Eric and George.* London and Boston, 1964
24. *The Sun in Scorpio.* London and Boston, 1965
25. *Lost at the Fair.* Boston, 1965
26. *Miss Bianca in the Salt Mines.* London and Boston, 1966
27. *In Pious Memory.* Boston, 1967

28. *Rosa.* London, 1969
29. *Miss Bianca in the Orient.* London and Boston, 1970
30. *Miss Bianca in the Antarctic.* London, 1970
31. *The Innocents.* London, 1971
32. *Miss Bianca and the Bridesmaid.* London and Boston, 1972
33. *The Lost Chapel Picnic and Other Stories.* London and Boston, 1973
34. *The Magical Cockatoo.* London, 1974
35. *The Children Next Door.* London, 1974
36. *The Faithful Servants.* London and Boston, 1975
37. *Bernard the Brave.* London, 1976
38. *Summer Visits.* London, 1977

Shaver, Richard S. (Sharpe)
American, born in 1907, died November 5, 1975
1. *I Remember Lemuria, and The Return of Sathanas.* Evanston (IL), 1948

Shaw, Bob [Robert Shaw]
British, born December 31, 1931
1. *Night Walk.* New York, 1967
2. *The Two-Timers.* New York, 1968
3. *Shadow of Heaven.* New York, 1969
4. *The Palace of Eternity.* New York, 1969
5. *One Million Tomorrows.* New York, 1970
6. *The Ground Zero Man.* New York, 1971
7. *Other Days, Other Eyes.* New York and London, 1972
8. *Tomorrow Lies in Ambush.* New York and London, 1973
9. *Orbitsville.* New York and London, 1975
10. *A Wreath of Stars.* London, 1976
11. *Cosmic Kaleidoscope.* London, 1976
12. *Medusa's Children.* London, 1977
13. *Who Goes Here?* London, 1977
14. *Ship of Strangers.* London, 1978
15. *Vertigo.* London, 1978
16. *Dagger of the Mind.* London, 1979

Shaw, Felicity
British, born in 1918
Pseudonym: Anne Morice
1. *The Happy Exiles.* London and New York, 1956
2. *Sun Trap.* London, 1958
3. *Death in the Grand Manor,* as Anne Morice. London, 1970
4. *Murder in Married Life,* as Anne Morice. London, 1971
5. *Death of a Gay Dog,* as Anne Morice. London, 1971
6. *Murder on French Leave,* as Anne Morice. London, 1972
7. *Death and the Dutiful Daughter,* as Anne Morice. London, 1973
8. *Death of a Heavenly Twin,* as Anne Morice. London and New York, 1974
9. *Killing with Kindness,* as Anne Morice. London, 1974
10. *Nursery Tea and Poison,* as Anne Morice. London and New York, 1975
11. *Death of a Wedding Guest,* as Anne Morice. London and New York, 1976
12. *Murder in Mimicry,* as Anne Morice. London and New York, 1977
13. *Scared to Death,* as Anne Morice. London, 1977
14. *Murder by Proxy,* as Anne Morice. London and New York, 1978
15. *Murder in Outline,* as Anne Morice. London, 1979

Sheckley, Robert
American, born July 16, 1928
1. *Untouched by Human Hands.* New York, 1954
2. *Citizen in Space.* New York, 1955
3. *Pilgrimage to Earth.* New York, 1957
4. *Immortality Delivered.* New York, 1958
5. *Immortality Inc.* New York, 1959
6. *The Status Civilization.* New York, 1960
7. *Store of Infinity.* New York, 1960
8. *Notions: Unlimited.* New York, 1960
9. *Calibre .50.* New York, 1961
10. *Dead Run.* New York, 1961
11. *Live Gold.* New York, 1962
12. *The Man in the Water.* Evanston (IL), 1962
13. *Journey Beyond Tomorrow.* New York, 1962
14. *Shards of Space.* New York and London, 1962
15. *White Death.* New York, 1963
16. *The Tenth Victim.* New York, 1965
17. *The Game of X.* New York, 1965
18. *Mindswap.* New York and London, 1966
19. *Time Limit.* New York and London, 1967
20. *Dimension of Miracles.* New York, 1968
21. *The People Trap.* New York, 1968
22. *Can You Feel Anything When I Do This?* New York, 1971
23. *The Robert Sheckley Omnibus.* London, 1973
24. *Options.* New York, 1975
25. *Crompton Divided.* New York, 1978
26. *Journey of Joenes.* London, 1978
27. *The Alchemical Marriage of Alistair Crompton.* London, 1978
28. *Futuropolis.* New York, 1978
29. *The Robot Who Looked Like Me.* London, 1978
30. *The Wonderful Worlds of Robert Sheckley.* New York, 1979

Shellabarger, Samuel
American, born May 18, 1888, died March 20, 1954
Pseudomyms: John Esteven, Peter Loring
1. *The Door of Death,* as John Esteven. New York, 1928
2. *The Chevalier Bayard: A Study in Fading Chivalry.* New York, 1928
3. *The Black Gale.* New York, 1929
4. *Voodoo,* as John Esteven. New York, 1930
5. *By Night at Dinsmore,* as John Esteven. New York and London, 1935
6. *Lord Chesterfield.* New York and London, 1935
7. *While Murder Waits,* as John Esteven. London, 1936
8. *Grief Before Night,* as Peter Loring. Philadelphia, 1938
9. *Graveyard Watch,* as John Esteven. New York, 1938
10. *Blind Man's Night,* as John Esteven. London, 1938
11. *Lord Chesterfield and Manners.* Claremont (CA), 1938
12. *Miss Rolling Stone,* as Peter Loring. Philadelphia, 1939
13. *He Travels Alone.* London, 1939
14. *Assurance Double Sure,* as John Esteven. London, 1939
15. *Captain from Castile.* Boston, 1945
16. *Prince of Foxes.* Boston, 1947
17. *The King's Cavalier.* Boston, 1950
18. *Blaise of France.* London, 1950
19. *Lord Chesterfield and His World.* Boston, 1951
20. *Lord Vanity.* Boston, 1953
21. *The Token.* Boston, 1955
22. *Tolbecken.* Boston, 1956

Shelley, John L. (Lascola)
American, born in 1907
1. *Gunpoint!* New York, 1956
2. *The Average Gun.* New York, 1959
3. *Cavalry Sergeant.* New York, 1960
4. *The Rimlanders.* New York, 1961
5. *The Dying Breed.* New York, 1962
6. *Hired Gun.* New York, 1963
7. *A Gun for Billy Hardin.* New York, 1965
8. *The Relentless Rider,* with David Shelly. New York, 1965
9. *Saddle Tramp.* New York, 1965
10. *The Siege at Gunhammer.* New York, 1967
11. *Ironhand.* New York, 1970

Sherriff, R.C. (Robert Charles)
  British, born June 6, 1896, died November 13, 1975
  1. *Journey's End*, with Vernon Bartlett. London and New York, 1930
  2. *Badger's Green*. London, 1930

Shiras, Wilmar H. (House)
  American, born September 23, 1908
  Pseudonym: Jane Howes
  1. *Slow Dawning*, as Jane Howes. St. Louis (MO), 1946
  2. *Children of the Atom*. New York, 1953

Short, Luke [Frederick Dilley Glidden]
  American, born in 1908, died August 18, 1975
  1. *The Feud at Single Shot*. New York and London, 1936
  2. *Guns of the Double Diamond*. London, 1937
  3. *Bull-Foot Ambush*. London, 1938
  4. *Misery Lode*. London, 1938
  5. *Weary Range*. London, 1939
  6. *The Gold Rustlers*. London, 1939
  7. *Six Guns of San Jon*. New York and London, 1939
  8. *Flood-Water*. London, 1939
  9. *Hard Money*. New York, 1940
  10. *Bounty Guns*. London, 1940
  11. *Brand of Empire*. London, 1940
  12. *War on the Cimarron*. New York, 1940
  13. *Dead Freight for Piute*. New York, 1940
  14. *Western Freight*. London, 1941
  15. *Gunman's Chance*. New York, 1941
  16. *Hardcase*. New York, 1942
  17. *Ride the Man Down*. New York, 1942
  18. *Sunset Graze*. New York, 1942
  19. *Ramrod*. New York, 1943
  20. *Blood on the Moon*. London, 1943
  21. *Bought with a Gun*. London, 1943
  22. *Gauntlet of Fire*. London, 1944
  23. *And the Wind Blows Free*. New York, 1945
  24. *Hard Case*. London, 1945
  25. *Coroner Creek*. New York, 1946
  26. *Station West*. Boston and London, 1947
  27. *High Vermilion*. Boston and London, 1948
  28. *Fiddlefoot*. Boston and London, 1949
  29. *Hands Off!* New York, 1949
  30. *The Rustlers*. New York, 1949
  31. *Ambush*. Boston, 1950
  32. *Vengeance Valley*. Boston, 1950
  33. *Bull-Whip*. New York, 1950
  34. *Trumpets West!* New York, 1951
  35. *Play a Lone Hand*. Boston, 1951
  36. *Barren Land Murders*. New York, 1951
  37. *Saddle by Starlight*. Boston, 1952
  38. *Savage Range*. New York, 1952
  39. *Raw Land*. New York, 1952
  40. *King Colt*. New York, 1953
  41. *Bold Rider*. New York, 1953
  42. *Silver Rock*. Boston, 1953
  43. *The Man on the Blue*. New York, 1954
  44. *Marauder's Moon*. New York, 1955
  45. *Cattle, Guns, and Men*. New York, 1955
  46. *Rimrock*. New York, 1955
  47. *The Branded Men*. New York, 1956
  48. *Barren Land Showdown*. New York, 1957
  49. *The Whip*. New York, 1957
  50. *Summer of the Smoke*. New York, 1958
  51. *First Claim*. New York and London, 1960
  52. *Desert Crossing*. New York, 1961
  53. *Last Hunt*. New York, 1962
  54. *The Some-Day Country*. New York, 1964
  55. *Trigger Country*. London, 1965
  56. *First Campaign*. New York and London, 1965
  57. *Paper Sheriff*. New York and London, 1966
  58. *Debt of Honor*. New York, 1967
  59. *The Primrose Try*. New York, 1967
  60. *The Guns of Hanging Lake*. New York, 1968
  61. *Donovan's Gun*. New York, 1968
  62. *The Deserters*. New York, 1969
  63. *Three for the Money*. New York, 1970
  64. *The Outrider*. New York, 1971
  65. *Man from the Desert*. New York, 1971
  66. *The Stalkers*. New York, 1973
  67. *The Man from Two Rivers*. New York, 1974
  68. *Trouble Country*. New York, 1976

Shrake, Edwin
  American, born September 6, 1931
  1. *Blood Reckoning*. New York, 1962
  2. *But Not for Love*. New York and London, 1964
  3. *Blessed McGill*. New York, 1968
  4. *Strange Peaches*. New York, 1972
  5. *Peter Arbiter*. Austin, 1973
  6. *Limo*, with Dan Jenkins. New York, 1976

Shute, Nevil [Nevil Shute Norway]
  British, born January 17, 1899, died January 12, 1960
  1. *Marazan*. London, 1926
  2. *So Disdained*. London, 1928
  3. *Mysterious Aviator*. Boston, 1928
  4. *Lonely Road*. London and New York, 1932
  5. *Ruined City*. London, 1938
  6. *Kindling*. New York, 1938
  7. *What Happened to the Corbetts*. London, 1939
  8. *Ordeal*. New York, 1939
  9. *Landfall: A Channel Story*. London and New York, 1940
  10. *An Old Captivity*. London and New York, 1940
  11. *Pied Piper*. New York, 1941
  12. *Pastoral*. London and New York, 1944
  13. *Most Secret*. London and New York, 1945
  14. *The Chequer Board*. London and New York, 1947
  15. *No Highway*. London and New York, 1948
  16. *A Town Like Alice*. London, 1950
  17. *The Legacy*. New York, 1950
  18. *Round The Bend*. London and New York, 1951
  19. *The Far Country*. London and New York, 1952
  20. *In the Wet*. London and New York, 1953
  21. *Slide Rule: The Autobiography of an Engineer*. London and New York, 1954
  22. *Requiem for a Wren*. London, 1955
  23. *The Breaking Wave*. New York, 1955
  24. *Beyond the Black Stump*. London and New York, 1956
  25. *On the Beach*. London and New York, 1957
  26. *The Rainbow and the Rose*. London and New York, 1958
  27. *Trustee from the Toolroom*. London and New York, 1960
  28. *Stephen Morris*. London and New York, 1961

Siller, Van [Hilda Van Siller]
  British
  1. *Echo of a Bomb*. New York, 1943
  2. *Good Night, Ladies*. New York, 1943
  3. *Under a Cloud*. New York, 1944
  4. *Somber Memory*. New York, 1945
  5. *One Alone*. New York, 1946
  6. *The Curtain Between*. New York, 1947
  7. *Fatal Bride*. New York, 1948
  8. *Paul's Apartment*. New York, 1948
  9. *The Last Resort*. Philadelphia, 1951
  10. *Fatal Lover*. New York, 1953

11. *Bermuda Murder*. London, 1956
12. *Murder Is My Business*. London, 1958
13. *The Widower*. New York, 1958
14. *The Road*. London, 1960
15. *A Complete Stranger*. New York, 1965
16. *The Lonely Breeze*. New York, 1965
17. *The Murders at Hibiscus Key*. London, 1965
18. *The Mood for Murder*. New York, 1966
19. *The Red Geranium*. London, 1966
20. *The Builtmore Call*. London, 1967
21. *Sudden Storm*. London, 1968
22. *The Watchers*. New York and London, 1969
23. *Whisper of Death*. New York, 1969
24. *It Had to Be You*. New York, 1970
25. *The Old Friend*. New York, 1973
26. *Deception of Death*. London, 1974
27. *The Hell with Elaine*. New York, 1974

Silverberg, Robert
American, born January 15, 1935
Pseudonyms: Walter Chapman, Ivar Jorgensen, Calvin M. Knox, David Osborne, Lee Sebastian

1. *Revolt on Alpha C*. New York, 1955
2. *The Thirteenth Immortal*. New York, 1957
3. *Master of Life and Death*. New York, 1957
4. *The Shrouded Planet*. New York, 1957
5. *Invaders from Earth*. New York, 1958
6. *Starman's Quest*. New York, 1958
7. *Invincible Barriers*, as David Osborne. New York, 1958
8. *Stepsons of Terra*. New York, 1958
9. *Aliens from Space*, as David Osborne. New York, 1958
10. *Starhaven*, as Ivar Jorgensen. New York, 1958
11. *Lest We Forget Thee, Earth*, as Calvin M. Knox. New York, 1958
12. *The Dawning Light*. New York, 1959
13. *The Planet Killers*. New York, 1959
14. *The Plot Against Earth*, as Calvin M. Knox. New York, 1959
15. *Lost Race of Mars*. Philadelphia, 1960
16. *Treasures Beneath the Sea*. Racine (WI), 1960
17. *Collision Course*. New York, 1961
18. *First American into Space*. Derby (CT), 1961
19. *The Seed of Earth*. New York, 1962
20. *Recalled to Life*. New York, 1962
21. *Next Stop the Stars*. New York, 1962
22. *Lost Cities and Vanished Civilizations*. Philadelphia, 1962
23. *The Silent Invaders*. New York, 1963
24. *The Fabulous Rockefellers*. Derby, 1963
25. *Sunken History: The Story of Underwater Archaeology*. Philadelphia, 1963
26. *15 Battles That Changed the World*. New York, 1963
27. *Home of the Red Man: Indian North America Before Columbus*. Greenwich (CT), 1963
28. *Empires in the Dust*. Philadelphia, 1963
29. *Regan's Planet*. New York, 1964
30. *One of Our Asteroids Is Missing*, as Calvin M. Knox. New York, 1964
31. *Godling, Go Home!* New York, 1964
32. *The Great Doctors*. New York, 1964
33. *Akhnaten, The Rebel Pharaoh*. Philadelphia, 1964
34. *The Man Who Found Ninevah: The Story of Austen Henry Layard*. New York, 1964
35. *Man Before Adam*. Philadelphia, 1964
36. *Time of the Green Freeze*. New York, 1965
37. *Conquerors from the Darkness*. New York, 1965
38. *To Worlds Beyond*. Philadelphia, 1965
39. *The Loneliest Continent*, as Walter Chapman. New York, 1965
40. *Scientists and Scoundrels: A Book of Hoaxes*. New York, 1965
41. *The World of Coral*. New York, 1965
42. *The Mask of Akhnaten*. New York, 1965
43. *Socrates*. New York, 1965
44. *The Old Ones: Indians of the American Southwest*. Greenwich, 1965
45. *Men Who Mastered the Atom*. New York, 1965
46. *The Great Wall of China*. Philadelphia, 1965
47. *Niels Bohr, The Man Who Mapped the Atom*. Philadelphia, 1965
48. *Forgotten by Time: A Book of Living Fossils*. New York, 1966
49. *Frontiers of Archaeology*. Philadelphia, 1966
50. *Kublai Khan, Lord of Xanadu*, as Walter Chapman. Inianapolis (IN), 1966
51. *The Long Rampart: The Story of the Great Wall of China*. Philadelphia, 1966
52. *Rivers*, as Lee Sebastian. New York, 1966
53. *Bridges*. Philadelphia, 1966
54. *To the Rock of Darius: The Story of Henry Rawlinson*. New York, 1966
55. *Needle in a Timestack*. New York, 1966
56. *The Gate of Worlds*. New York, 1967
57. *To Open the Sky*. New York, 1967
58. *Thorns*. New York, 1967
59. *Those Who Watch*. New York, 1967
60. *The Time-Hoppers*. New York, 1967
61. *Planet of Death*. New York, 1967
62. *The Dawn of Medicine*. New York, 1967
63. *The Adventures of Nat Palmer, Antarctic Explorer*. New York, 1967
64. *The Auk, The Dodo, and the Oryx*. New York, 1967
65. *The Golden Dream: Seekers of El Dorado*. Indianapolis, 1967
66. *Men Against Time: Salvage Archaeology in the United States*. New York, 1967
67. *The Morning of Mankind*. Greenwich, 1967
68. *The World of the Rain Forest*. New York, 1967
69. *Light for the World: Edison and the Power Industry*. Princeton (NJ), 1967
70. *Four Men Who Changed the Universe*. New York, 1968
71. *Hawksbill Station*. New York, 1968
72. *The Masks of Time*. New York, 1968
73. *Whom the Gods Would Slay*, as Ivar Jorgensen. New York, 1968
74. *Ghost Towns of the American West*. New York, 1968
75. *Mound Builders of Ancient America*. Greenwich, 1968
76. *The South Pole*, as Lee Sebastian. New York, 1968
77. *Stormy Voyager: The Story of Charles Wilkes*. Philadelphia, 1968
78. *The World of the Ocean Depths*. New York, 1968
79. *The Challenge of Climate: Man and His Environment*. New York, 1969
80. *Vanishing Giants: The Story of the Sequoias*. New York, 1969
81. *Wonders of Ancient Chinese Science*. New York, 1969
82. *The World of Space*. New York, 1969
83. *Bruce of the Blue Nile*. New York, 1969
84. *The Anvil of Time*. London, 1969
85. *Up the Line*. New York, 1969
86. *Nightwings*. New York, 1969
87. *Across a Billion Years*. New York, 1969
88. *The Man in the Maze*. New York and London, 1969
89. *Three Survived*. New York, 1969
90. *To Live Again*. New York, 1969
91. *The Calibrated Alligator*. New York, 1969
92. *Dimension Thirteen*. New York, 1969

93. *If I Forget Thee, O Jerusalem: American Jews and the State of Israel.* New York, 1970
94. *World's Fair 1992.* Chicago, 1970
95. *Downward to the Earth.* New York, 1970
96. *Tower of Glass.* New York, 1970
97. *Vornan-19.* London, 1970
98. *Parsecs and Parables.* New York, 1970
99. *The Cube Root of Uncertainty.* London, 1970
100. *Mammoths, Mastodons, and Man.* New York, 1970
101. *The Pueblo Revolt.* New York, 1970
102. *The Seven Wonders of the Ancient World.* New York, 1970
103. *Moonferns and Starsongs.* New York, 1971
104. *The World Inside.* New York, 1971
105. *A Time of Changes.* New York, 1971
106. *Son of Man.* New York, 1971
107. *The Deadly Sky,* as Ivar Jorgensen. New York, 1971
108. *Before the Sphinx.* New York, 1971
109. *Clocks for the Ages: How Scientists Date the Past.* New York, 1971
110. *To the Western Shore: Growth of the United States 1776-1853.* New York, 1971
111. *Into Space,* with Arthur C. Clark. New York, 1971
112. *The Book of Skulls.* New York, 1972
113. *Dying Inside.* New York, 1972
114. *The Second Trip.* New York, 1972
115. *The Reality Trip and Other Implausibilities.* New York, 1972
116. *John Muir: Prophet among the Glaciers.* New York, 1972
117. *The Longest Voyage: Circumnavigation in the Age of Discovery.* Indianapolis, 1972
118. *The Realm of Prester John.* New York, 1972
119. *The World Within the Ocean Wave.* New York, 1972
120. *The World Within the Tide Pool.* New York, 1972
121. *Valley Beyond Time.* New York, 1973
122. *Unfamiliar Territory.* New York, 1973
123. *Earth's Other Shadow.* New York, 1973
124. *Born with the Dead.* New York, 1974
125. *Sundance.* Nashville (TN), 1974
126. *Drug Themes in Science Fiction.* Rockville (MD), 1974
127. *The Stochastic Man.* New York, 1975
128. *Sunrise on Mercury.* Nashville, 1975
129. *The Feast of St. Dionysus.* New York, 1975
130. *Shadrach in the Furnace.* Indianapolis, 1976
131. *The Shores of Tomorrow.* Nashville, 1976
132. *The Best of Robert Silverberg.* New York, 1976
133. *Capricorn Games.* New York, 1976
134. *The Songs of Summer.* London, 1979
135. *Lord Valentine's Castle.* New York and London, 1980

Simak, Clifford D. (Donald)
American, born August 3, 1904
1. *The Creator.* Los Angeles, 1946
2. *Cosmic Engineers.* New York, 1950
3. *Time and Again.* New York, 1951
4. *Empire.* New York, 1951
5. *City.* New York, 1952
6. *First He Died.* New York, 1953
7. *Ring Around the Sun.* New York, 1953
8. *Strangers in the Universe.* New York, 1956
9. *The Worlds of Clifford Simak.* New York, 1960
10. *Time is the Simplest Thing.* New York, 1961
11. *The Trouble with Tycho.* New York, 1961
12. *Aliens for Neighbours.* London, 1961
13. *They Walked Like Men.* New York, 1962
14. *Other Worlds of Clifford Simak.* New York, 1962
15. *All the Traps of Earth.* New York, 1962
16. *Way Station.* New York, 1963
17. *The Solar System: Our New Front Yard.* New York, 1963
18. *All the Traps of Earth and The Night of the Puudly.* London, 2 vols., 1964
19. *Worlds Without End.* New York, 1964
20. *All Flesh Is Grass.* New York, 1965
21. *Best Science Fiction Stories of Clifford Simak.* New York, 1965
22. *Why Call Them Back from Heaven?* New York and London, 1967
23. *The Werewolf Principle.* New York, 1967
24. *The Goblin Reservation.* New York, 1968
25. *So Bright the Vision.* New York, 1968
26. *Out of Their Minds.* New York, 1970
27. *Destiny Doll.* New York, 1971
28. *A Choice of Gods.* New York, 1972
29. *Cemetery World.* New York, 1973
30. *Our Children's Children.* New York, 1974
31. *Enchanted Pilgrimage.* New York, 1975
32. *The Best of Clifford D. Simak.* London, 1975
33. *Shakespeare's Planet.* New York, 1976
34. *A Heritage of Stars.* New York, 1977
35. *Skirmish: The Great Short Fiction of Clifford D. Simak.* New York, 1977
36. *Mastodonia.* New York, 1978
37. *Catface.* London, 1978
38. *The Fellowship of the Talisman.* New York, 1978
39. *The Visitors.* New York, 1980
40. *Project Pope.* New York, 1981

Simon, Roger L. (Lichtenberg)
American, born in 1943
1. *Heir.* New York, 1968
2. *The Mama Tass Manifesto.* New York, 1970
3. *The Big Fix.* New York, 1973
4. *Wild Turkey.* New York, 1975
5. *Peking Duck.* New York and London, 1979

Simpson, Helen [Helen de Guerry Simpson]
Born in Australia, December 1, 1897, died October 14, 1940
1. *Acquittal.* London and New York, 1925
2. *The Baseless Fabric.* London and New York, 1925
3. *Cups, Wands, and Swords.* London, 1927
4. *Enter Sir John,* with Clemence Dane. London and New York, 1928
5. *Mumbudget.* London, 1928
6. *The Desolate House.* London, 1929
7. *Desires and Devices.* New York, 1930
8. *Printer's Devil,* with Clemence Dane. London, 1930
9. *Author Unknown.* New York, 1930
10. *'Vantage Striker.* London, 1931
11. *The Prime Minister Is Dead.* New York, 1931
12. *Re-Enter Sir John,* with Clemence Dane. London and New York, 1932
13. *Boomerang.* London and New York, 1932
14. *Ask a Policeman,* with others. London and New York, 1933
15. *The Woman and the Beast, Viewed from Three Angles.* London, 1933
16. *The Spanish Marriage.* London and New York, 1933
17. *Saraband for Dead Lovers.* London and New York, 1935
18. *Imaginary Biographies,* with others. London, 1936
19. *Under Capricorn.* London, 1937
20. *A Woman among Wild Men: Mary Kingsley.* London, 1938
21. *A Woman Looks Out.* London, 1940
22. *Maid No More.* London and New York, 1940

Sims, George (Frederick Robert)
British, born August 3, 1923
1. *The Swallow Lovers.* London, 1942
2. *Poems.* London, 1944

3. *The Immanent Goddess.* London, 1944
4. *Some Cadences: Poems Written in 1945.* Reading (Eng), 1960
5. *The Terrible Door.* London and New York, 1964
6. *Sleep No More.* London and New York, 1966
7. *The Last Best Friend.* London, 1967
8. *The Sand Dollar.* London, 1969
9. *Deadhand.* London, 1971
10. *Hunters Point.* London, 1973
11. *The End of the Web.* London and New York, 1976
12. *Rex Mundi.* London, 1978

Sinclair, Olga (Ellen)
British, born January 23, 1923
Pseudonym: Ellen Clare

1. *The Man at the Manor.* London, 1967
2. *Gypsies.* Oxford (Eng), 1967
3. *Man of the River.* London, 1968
4. *Hearts by the Tower.* London, 1968
5. *Night of the Black Tower.* New York, 1968
6. *Bitter Sweet Summer.* London, 1970
7. *Dancing in Britain.* Oxford, 1970
8. *Children's Games.* Oxford, 1972
9. *Wild Dream.* London, 1973
10. *Tenant of Binningham Hall.* London, 1975
11. *Toys and Toymaking.* Oxford, 1975
12. *Where the Cigale Sings.* London, 1976
13. *My Dear Fugitive.* London, 1976
14. *Never Fall in Love.* London, 1977
15. *Master of Melthorpe.* London, 1979
16. *Gypsy Julie.* London, 1979
17. *Ripening Vine,* as Ellen Clare. London, 1981
18. *Gypsy Girl.* London, 1981

Sinclair, Upton
American, born September 20, 1878, died November 25, 1968
Pseudonym: Frederick Garrison

1. *Springtime and Harvest: A Romance.* New York, 1901
2. *King Midas.* New York and London, 1901
3. *Prince Hagen.* Boston and London, 1903
4. *The Journal of Arthur Stirling.* New York and London, 1903
5. *Manassas.* New York and London, 1904
6. *The Toy and the Man.* Westwood (MA), 1904
7. *Our Bourgeois Literature.* Chicago, 1905
8. *The Jungle.* New York and London, 1906
9. *A Captain of Industry.* Girard (KS) and London, 1906
10. *Colony Customs.* Englewood (NJ), 1906
11. *The Helicon Home Colony.* Englewood, 1906
12. *A Home Colony: A Prospectus.* New York, 1906
13. *What Life Means to Me.* Girard, 1906
14. *The Overman.* New York, 1907
15. *The Industrial Republic.* New York and London, 1907
16. *The Metropolis.* New York and London, 1908
17. *The Money Changers.* New York and London, 1908
18. *Prince Hagen.* Privately printed, 1909
19. *Good Health and How We Won It,* with Michael Williams. New York, 1909
20. *The Art of Health.* London, 1909
21. *War: A Manifesto Against It.* Girard and London, 1909
22. *Strength and Health.* New York, 1910
23. *Samuel the Seeker.* New York and London, 1910
24. *Love's Pilgrimage.* New York, 1911
25. *Four Letters about "Love's Pilgrimage."* Privately printed, 1911
26. *The Fasting Cure.* New York and London, 1911
27. *Plays of Protest.* New York, 1912
28. *Sylvia.* Philadelphia, 1913
29. *Damaged Goods.* Philadelphia and London, 1913
30. *Sylvia's Marriage.* Philadelphia, 1914
31. *The Sinclair-Astor Letters: Famous Correspondence Between Socialist and Millionaire.* Girard, 1914
32. *The Social Problem as Seen from the Viewpoint of Trade Unionism, Capital, and Socialism,* with others. New York, 1914
33. *Upton Sinclair: Biographical and Critical Opinions.* Privately printed, 1917
34. *King Coal.* New York and London, 1917
35. *Jimmie Higgins.* London, 1918
36. *The Profits of Religion.* Privately printed, 1918
37. *The Spy.* London, 1919
38. *Russia: A Challenge.* Girard, 1919
39. *The High Cost of Living.* Girard, 1919
40. *The Brass Check.* London, 1919
41. *100%: The Story of a Patriot.* London, 1920
42. *The Associated Press and Labor.* Privately printed, 1920
43. *Press-titution.* Girard, 1920
44. *The Crimes of the "Times": A Test of Newspaper Decency.* Privately printed, 1921
45. *Mind and Body.* New York, 1921
46. *The McNeal-Sinclair Debate on Socialism.* Girard, 1921
47. *They Call Me Carpenter.* New York and London, 1922
48. *The Book of Life.* Pasadena (CA), 1922
49. *Love and Society.* Pasadena, 1922
50. *The Goose-Step: A Study of American Education.* Privately printed, 1922
51. *Biographical Letter and Critical Opinions.* Privately printed, 1922
52. *Hell: A Verse Drama and Photo-Play.* Privately printed, 1923
53. *The Millennium: A Comedy of the Year 2000.* Girard, 1924
54. *The Pot Boiler.* Girard, 1924
55. *Singing Jailbirds.* Privately printed, 1924
56. *The Goslings.* Privately printed, 1924
57. *The Schools of Los Angeles.* Privately printed, 1924
58. *Mammonart.* Privately printed, 1925
59. *Letters to Judd.* Privately printed, 1926
60. *The Spokesman's Secretary.* Privately printed, 1926
61. *Oil!* New York and London, 1927
62. *Money Writes!* New York, 1927
63. *Boston.* New York, 1928
64. *Mountain City.* New York, 1929
65. *The Pulitzer Prize and "Special Pleading."* Privately printed, 1929
66. *Peter Gudge Becomes a Secret Agent.* Moscow (USSR), 1930
67. *Mental Radio.* New York and London, 1930
68. *The Wet Parade.* New York and London, 1931
69. *Roman Holiday.* New York and London, 1931
70. *Socialism and Culture.* Girard, 1931
71. *Upton Sinclair on "Comrade" Kautsky.* Moscow, 1931
72. *American Outpost.* New York, 1932
73. *Candid Reminiscences: My First Thirty Years.* London, 1932
74. *I, Governor of California, and How I Ended Poverty.* New York and London, 1933
75. *Upton Sinclair Presents William Fox.* Privately printed, 1933
76. *The Way Out—What Lies Ahead for America?* New York and London, 1933
77. *EPIC Plan for California.* New York, 1934
78. *EPIC Answers: How to End Poverty in California.* Los Angeles, 1934
79. *Immediate EPIC.* Los Angeles, 1934
80. *The Lie Factory Starts.* Los Angeles, 1934

81. *An Upton Sinclair Anthology.* New York and London, 1934
82. *Upton Sinclair's Last Will and Testament.* Los Angeles, 1934
83. *We, People of America, and How We Ended Poverty: A True Story of the Future.* Pasadena, 1934
84. *Depression Island.* Pasadena, 1935
85. *I, Candidate for Governor, and How I Got Licked.* New York, 1935
86. *How I Got Licked and Why.* London, 1935
87. *What God Means to Me: An Attempt at a Working Religion.* New York and London, 1936
88. *Co-op: A Novel of Living Together.* New York and London, 1936
89. *The Gnomobile.* New York and London, 1936
90. *The Flivver King.* Girard, 1937
91. *No Paseran!* New York, 1937
92. *Terror in Russia: Two Views,* with Eugene Lyons. New York, 1938
93. *Little Steel.* New York and London, 1938
94. *Our Lady.* Emmaus (PA) and London, 1938
95. *Upton Sinclair on the Soviet Union.* New York, 1938
96. *Expect No Peace!* Girard, 1939
97. *Marie Antoinette.* New York and London, 1939
98. *Telling the World.* London, 1939
99. *What Can Be Done about America's Economic Troubles?* Girard, 1939
100. *Your Million Dollars.* Privately printed, 1939
101. *Letters to a Millionaire.* London, 1939
102. *Is the American Form of Capitalism Essential to the American Form of Democracy?* Girard, 1940
103. *Peace or War in America?* Girard, 1940
104. *World's End.* New York and London, 1940
105. *Between Two Worlds.* New York and London, 1941
106. *Songs of Our Nation,* as Frederick Garrison. New York, 1941
107. *Dragon's Teeth.* New York and London, 1942
108. *Wide Is the Gate.* New York and London, 1943
109. *Index to the Lanny Budd Story,* with others. New York, 1943
110. *To Solve the German Problem—A Free State?* Privately printed, 1943
111. *Presidential Agent.* New York, 1944
112. *Dragon Harvest.* New York and London, 1945
113. *A World to Win.* New York, 1946
114. *Presidential Mission.* New York, 1947
115. *One Clear Call.* New York, 1948
116. *Marie and Her Lover.* Girard. 1948
117. *A Giant's Strength.* Girard and London, 1948
118. *Limbo on the Loose: A Midsummer Night's Dream.* Girard, 1948
119. *O Shepherd, Speak!* New York, 1949
120. *This World of 1949 and What to Do about It.* Girard, 1949
121. *Another Pamela; or, Virtue Still Rewarded.* New York and London, 1950
122. *The Enemy Had It Too.* New York, 1950
123. *A Personal Jesus: Portrait and Interpretation.* New York, 1952
124. *The Return of Lanny Budd.* New York and London, 1953
125. *What Didymus Did.* London, 1954
126. *Radio Liberation Speech to the Peoples of the Soviet Union.* New York, 1955
127. *The Cup of Fury.* Great Neck (NY), 1956
128. *It Happened to Didymus.* New York, 1958
129. *Theirs Be the Guilt.* New York, 1959
130. *My Lifetime in Letters.* Columbia (MO), 1960
131. *Affectionately Eve.* New York, 1961
132. *Secret Life of Jesus.* Philadelphia, 1962
133. *The Autobiography of Upton Sinclair.* New York, 1962
134. *Three Plays.* Moscow, 1965
135. *August 22nd.* New York, 1965
136. *The Coal War: A Sequel to King Coal.* Boulder (CO), 1976

Singer, Isaac Bashevis
American, born July 14, 1904
1. *The Family Moskat.* New York, 1950
2. *Satan in Goray.* New York, 1955
3. *Gimpel the Fool and Other Stories.* New York, 1957
4. *The Magician of Lublin.* New York, 1960
5. *The Spinoza of Market Street and Other Stories.* New York, 1961
6. *The Slave.* New York, 1962
7. *Short Friday and Other Stories.* New York, 1964
8. *Zlateh the Goat and Other Stories.* New York, 1966
9. *Selected Short Stories.* New York, 1966
10. *In My Father's Court.* New York, 1966
11. *Mazel and Shlimazel; or, The Milk of a Lioness.* New York, 1967
12. *The Fearsome Inn.* New York, 1967
13. *The Manor.* New York, 1967
14. *When Schlemiel Went to Warsaw and Other Stories.* New York, 1968
15. *The Seance and Other Stories.* New York, 1968
16. *A Day of Pleasure: Stories of a Boy Growing Up in Warsaw.* New York, 1969
17. *A Friend of Kafka and Other Stories.* New York, 1970
18. *Joseph and Koza; or, The Sacrifice to the Vistula.* New York, 1970
19. *Elijah the Slave: A Hebrew Legend Retold.* New York, 1970
20. *The Estate.* New York and London, 1970
21. *Alone in the Wild Forest.* New York, 1971
22. *The Topsy-Turvy Emperor of China.* New York, 1971
23. *The Wicked City.* New York, 1972
24. *Enemies: A Love Story.* New York, 1972
25. *The Fools of Chelm and Their History.* New York, 1973
26. *A Crown of Feathers and Other Stories.* New York, 1973
27. *The Hasidim: Paintings, Drawings, and Etchings,* with Ira Moskowitz. New York, 1973
28. *Why Noah Chose the Dove.* New York, 1974
29. *Passions and Other Stories.* New York, 1975
30. *A Tale of Three Wishes.* New York, 1976
31. *A Little Boy in Search of God: Mysticism in a Personal Light.* New York, 1976
32. *Naftali the Storyteller and His Horse, Sus, and Other Stories.* New York, 1976

Sladek, John (Thomas)
American, born December 15, 1937
Pseudonyms: Thom Demijohn, Cassandra Knye
1. *The House That Fear Built,* as Cassandra Knye, with Thomas M. Disch. New York, 1966
2. *The Castle and the Key,* as Cassandra Knye. New York, 1967
3. *The Reproductive System.* London, 1968
4. *Black Alice,* as Thom Demijohn, with Thomas M. Disch. New York, 1968
5. *Mechasm.* New York, 1969
6. *The Muller-Fokker Effect.* London, 1970
7. *The Steam-Driven Boy and Other Strangers.* London, 1973
8. *The New Apocrypha: Guide to Strange Science and Occult Beliefs.* London, 1973
9. *Black Aura.* London, 1974
10. *Keep the Giraffe Burning.* London, 1977
11. *Invisible Green.* London, 1977

12. *Roderick; or, The Education of a Young Machine.* London, 1980
13. *The Best of John Sladek.* New York, 1981

Slaughter, Frank G. (Gill)
American, born February 25, 1908
Pseudonyms: G. Arnold Haygood, C.V. Terry
1. *That None Should Die.* New York, 1941
2. *Spencer Brade, M.D.* New York, 1942
3. *Air Surgeon.* New York, 1943
4. *Battle Surgeon.* New York, 1944
5. *A Touch of Glory.* New York, 1945
6. *In a Dark Garden.* New York, 1946
7. *The New Science of Surgery.* New York, 1946
8. *The Golden Isle.* New York, 1947
9. *Medicine for Moderns: The New Science of Psychosomatic Medicine.* New York, 1947
10. *Sangaree.* New York, 1948
11. *Divine Mistress.* New York, 1949
12. *The New Way to Mental and Physical Health.* New York, 1949
13. *The Stubborn Heart.* New York, 1950
14. *Immortal Magyar: Semmelweis, Conqueror of Childbed Fever.* New York, 1950
15. *Fort Everglades.* New York and London, 1951
16. *The Road to Bithynia: A Novel of Luke, The Beloved Physician.* New York, 1951
17. *East Side General.* New York, 1952
18. *Storm Haven.* New York, 1953
19. *The Galileans: A Novel of Mary Magdalene.* New York, 1953
20. *Your Body and Your Mind.* New York, 1953
21. *The Song of Ruth.* New York, 1954
22. *Buccaneer Surgeon,* as C.V. Terry. New York, 1954
23. *Apalachee Gold: The Fabulous Adventures of Cabeza de Vaca.* New York, 1954
24. *The Healer.* New York and London, 1955
25. *Flight from Natchez.* New York, 1955
26. *Buccaneer Doctor,* as C.V. Terry. London, 1955
27. *Darien Venture,* as C.V. Terry. New York and London, 1955
28. *The Golden Ones,* as C.V. Terry. New York, 1955
29. *The Scarlet Cord: A Novel of the Woman of Jericho.* New York and London, 1956
30. *The Warrior.* New York, 1956
31. *Science and Surgery.* New York, 1956
32. *The Flaming Frontier.* London, 1957
33. *The Mapmaker: A Novel of the Days of Prince Henry, The Navigator.* New York, 1957
34. *Sword and Scalpel.* New York and London, 1957
35. *Daybreak.* New York and London, 1958
36. *Deep Is the Shadow,* as G. Arnold Haygood. New York, 1959
37. *The Crown and the Cross: The Life of Christ.* Cleveland (OH) and London, 1959
38. *The Thorn of Arimathea.* New York and London, 1959
39. *Lorena.* New York, 1959
40. *The Deadly Lady of Madagascar,* as C.V. Terry. New York and London, 1959
41. *Pilgrims in Paradise.* New York, 1960
42. *Puritans in Paradise.* London, 1960
43. *The Land and the Promise: The Greatest Stories from the Bible.* Cleveland, 1960
44. *Epidemic!* New York and London, 1961
45. *The Curse of Jezebel: A Novel of the Biblical Queen of Evil.* New York, 1961
46. *Semmelweis, Conqueror of Childbed Fever.* New York, 1961
47. *Queen of Evil.* London, 1962
48. *Tomorrow's Miracle.* New York and London, 1962
49. *David, Warrior and King: A Biblical Biography.* Cleveland, 1962
50. *Devil's Harvest.* New York and London, 1963
51. *Upon This Rock: A Novel of Simon Peter, Prince of the Apostles.* New York, 1963
52. *A Savage Place.* New York and London, 1964
53. *Constantine: The Miracle of the Flaming Cross.* New York, 1965
54. *The Purple Quest: A Novel of Seafaring Adventure in the Ancient World.* New York and London, 1965
55. *Surgeon U.S.A.* New York, 1966
56. *War Surgeon.* London, 1967
57. *Doctor's Wives.* New York, 1967
58. *God's Warrior.* New York and London, 1967
59. *The Sins of Herod: A Novel of Rome and the Early Church.* New York, 1968
60. *Surgeon's Choice: A Novel of Medicine Tomorrow.* New York and London, 1969
61. *Countdown.* New York and London, 1970
62. *Code Five.* New York, 1971
63. *Convention, M.D.: A Novel of Medical In-Fighting.* New York, 1972
64. *Women in White.* New York, 1974
65. *Lifeblood.* London, 1974
66. *Stonewall Brigade.* New York, 1975
67. *Shadow of Evil.* New York, 1975
68. *Plague Ship.* New York, 1976
69. *Devil's Gamble.* New York, 1977
70. *The Passionate Rebel.* New York and London, 1979
71. *Gospel Fever: A Novel about America's Most Beloved TV Evangelist.* New York, 1980
72. *Doctor's Daughters.* New York, 1981

Slesar, Henry
American, born June 12, 1927
1. *Gray Flannel Shroud.* New York, 1959
2. *Enter Murderers.* New York, 1960
3. *A Bouquet of Clean Crimes and Neat Murders.* New York, 1960
4. *A Crime for Mothers and Others.* New York, 1962
5. *The Bridge of Lions.* New York, 1963
6. *The Seventh Mask.* New York, 1969
7. *The Thing at the Door.* New York, 1974

Sloane, William M. [William Milligan Sloane III]
American, born August 15, 1906, died September 25, 1974
1. *Back Home: A Ghost Play.* New York, 1931
2. *Runner in the Snow: A Play of the Supernatural.* Boston, 1931
3. *Digging Up the Dirt.* New York, 1931
4. *Crystal Clear.* New York, 1932
5. *Ballots for Bill: A Light-Hearted Comedy of Politics.* New York, 1933
6. *The Silence of God: A Play for Christmas.* Boston, 1933
7. *Art for Art's Sake.* Boston, 1934
8. *The Invisible Clue.* New York, 1934
9. *Gold Stars for Glory.* Boston, 1935
10. *To Walk the Night.* New York, 1937
11. *The Edge of Running Water.* New York, 1939
12. *The Unquiet Corpse.* New York, 1946
13. *The Rim of Morning.* New York, 1964

Slobodkin, Louis
American, born February 19, 1903, died May 8, 1975
1. *The Friendly Animals.* New York, 1944
2. *Magic Michael.* New York, 1944

3. *Clear the Track for Michael's Magic Train.* New York, 1945
4. *Fo'castle Waltz.* New York, 1945
5. *The Adventures of Arab.* New York, 1946
6. *The Seaweed Hat.* New York, 1947
7. *Hustle and Bustle.* New York, 1948
8. *Bixxy and the Secret Message.* New York, 1949
9. *Sculpture: Principles and Practice.* Cleveland (OH), 1949
10. *Mr. Mushroom.* New York, 1950
11. *Dinny and Danny.* New York, 1951
12. *Our Friendly Friends.* New York, 1951
13. *The Spaceship under the Apple Tree.* New York, 1952
14. *Circus, April 1st.* New York, 1953
15. *The Horse with High-Heeled Shoes.* New York, 1954
16. *Mr. Petersand's Cats and Kittens.* New York, 1954
17. *The Amiable Giant.* New York, 1955
18. *Millions and Millions and Millions!* New York, 1955
19. *The Little Mermaid Who Could Not Sing.* New York, 1956
20. *One Is Good But Two Are Better.* New York, 1956
21. *Melvin the Moose Child.* New York, 1957
22. *Thank You—You're Welcome.* New York, 1957
23. *The Space Ship Returns to the Apple Tree.* New York and London, 1958
24. *The Wide-Awake Owl.* New York, 1958
25. *The First Book of Drawing.* New York, 1958
26. *Trick or Treat.* New York and London, 1959
27. *Excse Me! Certainly!* New York, 1959
28. *Gogo, The French Sea Gull.* New York, 1960
29. *Nomi and the Lovely Animals.* New York, 1960
30. *Up High and Down Low.* New York, 1960
31. *A Good Place to Hide.* New York, 1961
32. *Picco, The Sad Italian Pony.* New York, 1961
33. *The Three-Seated Space Ship.* New York, 1962
34. *The Late Cuckoo.* New York, 1962
35. *Luigi and the Long-Nosed Soldier.* New York and London, 1963
36. *Moon Blossom and the Golden Penny.* New York, 1963
37. *The Polka-Dot Goat.* New York and London, 1964
38. *Colette and the Princess.* New York, 1965
39. *Yasu and the Strangers.* New York and London, 1965
40. *Round Trip Space Ship.* New York and London, 1968
41. *The Space Ship in the Park.* New York and London, 1972
42. *Wilbur the Warrior.* New York, 1972

Slobodkina, Esphyr
American, born September 22, 1908
1. *Caps for Sale.* New York, 1940
2. *The Wonderful Feast.* New York, 1955
3. *Little Dog Lost, Little Dog Found.* New York, 1956
4. *The Clock.* New York and London, 1956
5. *The Little Dinghy.* New York and London, 1958
6. *Behind the Dark Window Shade.* New York, 1958
7. *Billie.* New York, 1959
8. *Pinky and the Petunias.* New York, 1959
9. *Moving Day for the Middlemans.* New York and London, 1960
10. *Jack and Jim.* New York and London, 1961
11. *The Long Island Ducklings.* New York, 1961
12. *Boris and His Balalaika.* New York and London, 1964
13. *The Flame, The Breeze, and the Shadow.* Chicago, 1969
14. *Notes for a Biographer.* Great Neck (NY), 1977

Smith, Clark Ashton
American, born January 13, 1893, died August 14, 1961
1. *The Star-Treader and Other Poems.* San Francisco, 1912
2. *Odes and Sonnets.* San Francisco, 1918
3. *Ebony and Crystal: Poems in Verse and Prose.* Privately printed, 1922
4. *Sandalwood.* Privately printed, 1925
5. *The Immortals of Mercury.* New York, 1932
6. *The Double Shadow and Other Fantasies.* Privately printed, 1933
7. *The White Sybil.* Everett (PA), 1935(?)
8. *Nero and Other Poems.* Lakeport (CA), 1937
9. *Out of Space and Time.* Sauk City (WI), 1942
10. *Lost Worlds.* Sauk City, 1944
11. *Genius Loci.* Sauk City, 1948
12. *The Dark Chateau and Other Poems.* Sauk City, 1951
13. *Spells and Philtres.* Sauk City, 1958
14. *The Abominations of Yondo.* Sauk City, 1960
15. *Tales of Science and Sorcery.* Sauk City, 1964
16. *Poems in Prose.* Sauk City, 1965
17. *Other Dimensions.* Sauk City, 1970
18. *The Mortuary.* Glendale (CA), 1971
19. *Grotesques and Fantastiques.* Saddle River (NJ), 1973
20. *Planets and Dimensions: Collected Essays.* Baltimore (MD), 1973
21. *Klarkash-ton and Monstro Kigriv.* Saddle River, 1974
22. *Prince Alcouz and the Magician.* Glendale, 1977

Smith, E.E. (Edward Elmer)
American, born May 1, 1890, died August 31, 1965
1. *What Does This Convention Mean? A Speech Delivered at the Chicago 1940 World's Science Fiction Convention.* Privately printed, 1941
2. *The Skylark of Space,* with Mrs. Lee Hawkins Garby. Providence (RI), 1946
3. *Spacehounds of IPC.* Reading (PA), 1947
4. *Skylark Three.* Reading, 1948
5. *Triplanetary.* Reading, 1948
6. *Skylark of Valeron.* Reading, 1949
7. *First Lensman.* Reading, 1950
8. *Galactic Patrol.* Reading, 1950
9. *Gray Lensman.* Reading, 1951
10. *Second Stage Lensman.* Reading, 1953
11. *Children of the Lens.* Reading, 1954
12. *The Vortex Blaster.* New York, 1960
13. *The Galaxy Primes.* New York, 1965
14. *Subspace Explorers.* New York, 1965
15. *Skylark DuQuesne.* New York, 1966
16. *Masters of the Vortex.* New York, 1968
17. *The Best of E.E. "Doc" Smith.* London, 1975
18. *Masters of Space.* London, 1976
19. *Imperial Stars.* New York, 1976

Smith, George H. (Henry)
American, born October 27, 1922
Pseudonyms: M.J. Deer, Jerry Jason, Diana Summers
1. *1976: Year of Terror.* New York, 1961
2. *Scourge of the Blood Cult.* New York, 1961
3. *The Coming of the Rats.* New York, 1961
4. *Doomsday Wing.* Derby (CT), 1963
5. *A Place Called Hell,* as M.J. Deer, with Mary J. Deer Smith. New York, 1963
6. *Flames of Desire,* as M.J. Deer, with Mary J. Deer Smith. New York, 1963
7. *The Unending Night.* Derby, 1964
8. *The Forgotten Planet.* New York, 1965
9. *The Psycho Makers,* as Jerry Jason. New York, 1965
10. *The Four Day Weekend.* New York, 1966
11. *The Sex and Savagery of Hell's Angels.* San Diego (CA), 1966
12. *Druid's World.* New York, 1967
13. *Bayou Belle.* New York, 1967
14. *Those Sexy Saucer People.* San Diego, 1967
15. *Who Is Ronald Reagan?* New York, 1968

16. *Kar Kaballa.* New York, 1969
17. *Witch Queen of Lochlann.* New York, 1969
18. *Martin Luther King, Jr.* New York, 1971
19. *The New Barbarians.* London, 1973
20. *Bikers at War.* London, 1976
21. *The Second War of the Worlds.* New York, 1978
22. *The Island Snatchers.* New York, 1978
23. *Wild Is the Heart,* as Diana Summers. Chicago, 1978
24. *Love's Wicked Ways,* as Diana Summers. Chicago, 1979

Smith, George O. (Oliver)
American, born April 9, 1911
1. *Venus Equilateral.* Philadelphia, 1947
2. *Pattern for Conquest: An Interplanetary Adventure.* New York, 1949
3. *Nomad.* Philadelphia, 1950
4. *Operation Interstellar.* Chicago, 1950
5. *Hellflower.* New York, 1953
6. *Highways in Hiding.* New York, 1956
7. *The Space Plague.* New York, 1957
8. *Troubled Star.* New York, 1957
9. *Fire in the Heavens.* New York, 1958
10. *The Path of Unreason.* New York, 1958
11. *Lost in Space.* New York, 1959
12. *The Fourth "R."* New York, 1959
13. *Mathematics, The Language of Science.* New York, 1961
14. *The Brain Machine.* New York, 1968
15. *Scientists' Nightmares.* New York, 1972
16. *The Complete Venus Equilateral.* New York, 1976

Smith, Joan
American, born in 1938
1. *An Affair of the Heart.* New York, 1977
2. *Escapade.* New York, 1977
3. *La Comtesse.* New York, 1978
4. *Imprudent Lady.* New York, 1978
5. *Dame Durden's Daughter.* New York, 1978
6. *Aunt Sophie's Diamonds.* New York, 1979
7. *Flowers of Eden.* New York, 1979
8. *Sweet and Twenty.* New York, 1979
9. *Talk of the Town.* New York, 1979
10. *Aurora.* New York, 1980
11. *Babe.* New York, 1980
12. *Endure My Heart.* New York, 1980
13. *Lace for Milady.* New York, 1980
14. *Delsie.* New York, 1981
15. *Lover's Vows.* New York, 1981
16. *Love's Way.* New York, 1982

Smith, Shelley [Nancy Hermione Bodington]
British, born July 12, 1912
1. *Background for Murder.* London, 1942
2. *Death Stalks a Lady.* London, 1945
3. *This Is the House.* London, 1945
4. *Come and Be Killed!* London, 1946
5. *He Died of Murder!* London 1947
6. *The Woman in the Sea.* London and New York, 1948
7. *Man with a Calico Face.* New York, 1950
8. *How Many Miles to Babylon?* London and New York, 1950
9. *Man Alone.* London, 1952
10. *The Crooked Man.* New York, 1952
11. *An Afternoon to Kill.* London, 1953
12. *The Party at No. 5.* London, 1954
13. *The Cellar at No.5.* New York, 1954
14. *The Lord Have Mercy.* London, 1956
15. *Rachel Weeping: A Triptych.* London and New York, 1957

16. *The Shrew Is Dead.* New York, 1959
17. *The Ballad of the Running Man.* London, 1961
18. *A Grave Affair.* London, 1971
19. *A Game of Consequences.* London, 1978

Snedeker, Caroline Dale
American, born March 23, 1871, died January 22, 1956
Pseudonym: Caroline Dale Owen
1. *The Coward of Thermopylar.* New York, 1911
2. *The Spartan.* New York, 1912
3. *Seth Way,* as Caroline Dale Owen. Boston, 1917
4. *The Perilous Seat.* New York and London, 1923
5. *Theras and His Town.* New York, 1924
6. *Downright Dencey.* New York, 1927
7. *The Beckoning Road.* New York, 1929
8. *The Black Arrowhead: Legends of Long Island.* New York, 1929
9. *The Town of the Fearless.* New York, 1931
10. *The Forgotten Daughter.* New York, 1933
11. *Uncharted Ways.* New York, 1935
12. *The White Isle.* New York, 1940
13. *Luke's Quest.* New York, 1947
14. *A Triumph for Flavius.* New York, 1955
15. *Lysis Goes to the Play.* New York, 1962

Snow, Charles H. (Horace)
Born in 1877
Pseudonyms: H.C. Averill, Charles Ballew, Robert Cole, James Dillard, Allen Forrest, Russ Hardy, John Harlow, Ranger Lee, Gary Marshall, Wade Smith, Dan Wardle, Chester Wills
1. *Dust of Gold.* London, 1928
2. *Rustlers and Ruby Silver.* London, 1930
3. *The Rider of San Felipe.* Boston, 1930
4. *Days of '50.* London, 1930
5. *The Fighting Sheriff.* London, 1931
6. *The Sheriff of Chispa Loma.* Philadelphia, 1931
7. *Roaring Guns.* London, 1931
8. *The Cowboys from Alamos.* London, 1932
9. *Don Jim.* London and Philadelphia, 1932
10. *The Invisible Band.* London, 1932
12. *The Silent Shot.* London, 1932
13. *Red Gold,* as Charles Ballew. London, 1932
14. *Stocky of Lone Tree Ranch.* Philadelphia, 1932
15. *The Lakeside Murder.* London, 1933
16. *Beyond Arizona.* London, 1933
17. *The Gold-Pan Nugget.* London, 1933
18. *The Nevadans.* London, 1933
19. *Pay Dirt Creek.* London, 1933
20. *The Scorpion's Sting.* London, 1933
21. *Tamer of Bad Men.* London, 1933
22. *The Gambler of Red Gulch,* as Charles Ballew. London, 1933
23. *One Crazy Cowboy,* as Charles Ballew. London and New York, 1933
24. *The Black Riders of the Range.* London, 1934
25. *The Bonanza Murder Case.* London, 1934
26. *The Gold of Alamito.* London, 1934
27. *The Highgraders.* London, 1934
28. *Hollow Stump Mystery.* London, 1934
29. *The Outlaws of Inspiration.* London, 1934
30. *Rubies and Red Blood.* London, 1934
31. *Smugglers' Ranch.* London and Philadelphia, 1934
32. *From Ragtown to Rugby,* as Charles Ballew. London, 1934
33. *Sheriff Blood,* as Charles Ballew. London, 1934
34. *The Bandit of Paloduro,* as Charles Ballew. New York, 1934
35. *Flaming Six-Gun,* as Gary Marshall. London, 1934
36. *Runaway Horses,* as Gary Marshall. London, 1934

37. *The Scarlet Ace*, as Gary Marshall. London, 1934
38. *The Watchers of Gold Gulch*, as Gary Marshall. London, 1934
39. *Dogs of Discord*, as Charles Ballew. London, 1935
40. *Rim-Fire Rides*, as Charles Ballew. London, 1935
41. *Texas Spurs*, as Charles Ballew. New York, 1935
42. *The Treasure of Aspen Canyon*, as Charles Ballew. London and New York, 1935
43. *Cactus Thorns*. London, 1935
44. *Six-Guns of Sandoval*. Philadelphia, 1935
45. *Cardigan-Cowboy*. London and Philadelphia, 1935
46. *The Gold Raiders*. London, 1935
47. *The Iron-Nerved Maverick*. London, 1935
48. *Murder on the Castle Ranch*. London, 1935
49. *The Sign of the Death Circle*. London, 1935
50. *Signal Smokes*. London, 1935
51. *Blood of the Sotone*, as Gary Marshall. London, 1935
52. *The Gallant Outlaw*, as Gary Marshall. London, 1935
53. *One Fightin' Cowboy*, as Gary Marshall. London, 1935
54. *Raiders of the Tonto Rim*, as Gary Marshall. New York, 1935
55. *The Red Spider of Quartz Gulch*, as Gary Marshall. London, 1935
56. *The Saga of Sunny Jim*, as Gary Marshall. London, 1935
57. *The Sheriff's Daughter*, as Gary Marshall. London, 1935
58. *Border Blood*, as Gary Marshall. London, 1936
59. *Argonaut Gold*. London and Philadelphia, 1936
60. *The Desert Castle Mystery*. London, 1936
61. *Hidden Pay*. London, 1936
62. *Law on the Mines*. London, 1936
63. *Red Husky*. London, 1936
64. *The Riders of Sunset Mesa*. London, 1936
65. *The Seven Peaks*. London, 1936
66. *Rim-Fire, Detective*, as Charles Ballew. London, 1936
67. *Rim-Fire on the Range*, as Charles Ballew. London, 1936
68. *Rim-Fire, Sheriff*, as Charles Ballew. London, 1936
69. *Rim-Fire, Six Guns*, as Charles Ballew. London, 1936
70. *The Fighting Tenderfoot*, as Gary Marshall. London, 1936
71. *Powder Smoke*, as Gary Marshall. London, 1936
72. *Raging River*, as Gary Marshall. London, 1936
73. *Rangeland Gold*, as Gary Marshall. London, 1936
74. *The Capture of the King*, as Gary Marshall. London, 1937
75. *The Feud of Lone Lake Valley*, as Gary Marshall. London, 1937
76. *Nesters of Chunk Valley*, as Gary Marshall. London, 1937
77. *Nevada Gold*, as Gary Marshall. London, 1937
78. *The Outlaw Chief*, as Gary Marshall. London, 1937
79. *Rough Ranges*, as Gary Marshall. London, 1937
80. *The Vigilantes of Gold Gulch*. Philadelphia, 1937
81. *Rim-Fire Fights*, as Charles Ballew. London, 1937
82. *Rim-Fire Horns In*, as Charles Ballew. London, 1937
83. *Rim-Fire, Ranchero*, as Charles Ballew. London, 1937
84. *Rim-Fire Roams*, as Charles Ballew. London, 1937
85. *Bandits of Bedrock*. London, 1937
86. *The Brush Creek Murders*. London, 1937
87. *The Fire Cloud, and Thoroughbreds*. London, 1937
88. *Romance Rides a Red Horse, and Azalia Blossoms*. London, 1937
89. *Sheriff of Olancha*. London, 1937
90. *Steel of the North, and Mesquite's Loop*. London, 1937
91. *Terry Orcutt's Guns*. London, 1937
92. *The Trail to Abilene*. London and Philadelphia, 1937
93. *Trails of '56*. London, 1937
94. *Haunted Canyon*, as Ranger Lee. London, 1937
95. *Wild Riders*, as Ranger Lee. London, 1937
96. *Thundering Hoofs*, as Ranger Lee. New York, 1937
97. *Rebel on the Range*, as Ranger Lee. New York, 1938
98. *Big Strike*. London, 1938
99. *Guns in the Chaparral*. London, 1938
100. *Six Bars of Gold*. London, 1938
101. *White Mountains*. London, 1938
102. *Rim-Fire on the Desert*, as Charles Ballew. London, 1938
103. *Rim-Fire Slips*, as Charles Ballew. London, 1938
104. *Rim-Fire and Slats*, as Charles Ballew. London, 1938
105. *Border Feud*. Philadelphia, 1938
106. *Empty Cartridges*, as Gary Marshall. London, 1938
107. *The Girl from Garrison's*, as Gary Marshall. London, 1938
108. *The Rider from Rincon*, as Gary Marshall. London, 1938
109. *Rimrock Range*, as Gary Marshall. London, 1938
110. *Two Horizons*, as H.C. Averill. London, 1938
111. *Marauders of the Mesas*, as Ranger Lee. London, 1939
112. *The Red Gash Outlaws*, as Ranger Lee. London and New York, 1939
113. *Copper Range*, as Gary Marshall. London, 1939
114. *Devils of Desolation*, as Gary Marshall. London, 1939
115. *Gun-Slinger*, as Gary Marshall. London, 1939
116. *Painted Hills*, as Gary Marshall. London, 1939
117. *Riders of the Range*. Philadelphia, 1939
118. *The Bandit of Matagorda*. London, 1939
119. *Irregular Ranger*. London, 1939
120. *Roaring Range*. London, 1939
121. *Three Rivers Range*. London, 1939
122. *Frontier Regiment*, as Charles Ballew. London, 1939
123. *Guns along the Border*, as Charles Ballew. London, 1939
124. *Rim-Fire in Mexico*, as Charles Ballew. London, 1939
125. *Rim-Fire Presides*, as Charles Ballew. London, 1939
126. *Rouse River Range*, as Charles Ballew. London, 1939
127. *Outlaws of Red Canyon*. Philadelphia, 1940
128. *Grizzly*. London, 1940
129. *She Was Sheriff*. London, 1940
130. *Top Hand*. London, 1940
131. *War on the Penasco*. London, 1940
132. *Blood Stain Trails*, as Charles Ballew. London, 1940
133. *Wolf of the Mesas*, as Charles Ballew. London, 1940
134. *Black Butte*, as Gary Marshall. London, 1940
135. *The New Range Boss*, as Gary Marshall. London, 1940
136. *Boots On*, as Gary Marshall. London, 1940
137. *Outlaws of the Bad Lands*, as Ranger Lee. London, 1940
138. *Renegade Ranger*, as Ranger Lee. London, 1940
139. *The Sixth Bandit*, as Ranger Lee. London, 1940
140. *The Man of the Bay*, as Ranger Lee. London, 1941
141. *Badland Bill*, as Ranger Lee. New York, 1941
142. *The Girl of the Lazy L*, as Gary Marshall. London, 1941
143. *Six-Gun Smoke*, as Gary Marshall. London, 1941
144. *Rim-Fire Runs*, as Charles Ballew. London, 1941
145. *Sheriff of Yavisa*. Philadelphia, 1941
146. *Dillard of Circle 22*. London, 1941
147. *Fightin' Bob*. London, 1941
148. *Free Range*, as Ranger Lee. London, 1942
149. *Rustler's Luck*, as Ranger Lee. London, 1942
150. *The Wide Loop*, as Ranger Lee. London, 1942
151. *The Mystery of Devil's Canyon*. London, 1942
152. *The Brand Stealer*. Philadelphia, 1942
153. *Crowfoot Range*. London, 1942
154. *Outlaws of Sugar Loaf*. Philadelphia, 1942
155. *The New Sheriff*, as Charles Ballew. London, 1942
156. *Rim-Fire Gets 'em*, as Charles Ballew. London, 1942
157. *Barbed Wire*, as Gary Marshall. London, 1942
158. *Desperadoes of Diablo*, as Gary Marshall. London, 1942
159. *B Diamond Ranch*, as Wade Smith. London, 1942
160. *The Red Steer*, as Wade Smith. London, 1942
161. *Three Bar Cross*, as Wade Smith. London, 1943
162. *The Prospector of Signal Mountain*, as Gary Marshall. London, 1943
163. *Red Mesas*, as Gary Marshall. London, 1943
164. *Wild Range*, as Charles Ballew. London, 1943

165. *Wolves of Grey Bluff,* as Charles Ballew. London, 1943
166. *The Girl of the Bar D Bar.* London, 1943
167. *Horsethief Pass.* London, 1943
168. *Rebel of Ronde Valley.* Philadelphia, 1943
169. *The Bar D Boss,* as Ranger Lee. New York, 1943
170. *Red Shirt,* as Ranger Lee. London, 1943
171. *The Silver Train,* as Ranger Lee. London, 1943
172. *Wild Country,* as Wade Smith. London, 1944
173. *Just Dusty,* as Ranger Lee. London, 1944
174. *Buckshot,* as Gary Marshall. London, 1944
175. *Double-Cross Brand.* London, 1944
176. *Horse Thieves of Rock River,* as Charles Ballew. London, 1944
177. *Outlaw Town,* as Charles Ballew. London, 1944
178. *Rim-Fire on the Prod,* as Charles Ballew. London, 1944
179. *Rim-Fire Returns,* as Charles Ballew. London, 1944
180. *Boss of the Diamond Ranch,* as Wade Smith. London, 1949
181. *Five Finger Valley,* as Wade Smith. London, 1949
182. *Red Mountain,* as H.C. Averill. London, 1949
183. *Buffalo Valley,* as Gary Marshall. London, 1949
184. *The Horsethief.* London, 1949
185. *The Highgrade Murder.* London, 1949
186. *Mystery of Limestone Mountain,* as Charles Ballew. London, 1949
187. *Robbers' Ranch,* as Charles Ballew. London, 1949
188. *Valley of Tumbling Waters,* as Charles Ballew. London, 1949
189. *Crimson Dust,* as Ranger Lee. London, 1949
190. *Rustler King,* as Russ Hardy. London, 1949
191. *Sycamore Canyon,* as Russ Hardy. London, 1949
192. *Silver on the Sage,* as Chester Wills. London, 1949
193. *Treasure of the Pine Country,* as Chester Wills. London, 1949
194. *Shoot-up at Two Rivers,* as Chester Wills. London, 1950
195. *Hidden River,* as Wade Smith. London, 1950
196. *Montana Gunsmoke,* as Wade Smith. London, 1950
197. *Feud of the San Grigorio,* as H.C. Averill. London, 1950
198. *Yuba Diggings,* as H.C. Averill. London, 1950
199. *The Claim Jumpers,* as Ranger Lee. London, 1950
200. *The Ranch in the Canyon,* as Ranger Lee. London, 1950
201. *Rim-Fire and The Bear,* as Charles Ballew. London, 1950
202. *Gold Dust and Bear Meat.* London, 1950
203. *The Mysterious Missile.* London, 1950
204. *The Old Breed,* as Gary Marshall. London, 1950
205. *Old Panther-Foot,* as Gary Marshall. London, 1950
206. *Montana Skies,* as Wade Smith. London, 1951
207. *Below the Border,* as Wade Smith. London, 1951
208. *Down Mexico Way,* as Gary Marshall. London, 1951
209. *Hair Trigger,* as Gary Marshall. London, 1951
210. *Frontier Meetin' House.* London, 1951
211. *The Mountain Murder Case.* London, 1951
212. *Roaming Rider.* London, 1951
213. *Under the Big Red Rim.* London, 1951
214. *Bandit of Mormon Mesa,* as Charles Ballew. London, 1951
215. *Rustlers and Powder Smoke,* as Charles Ballew. London, 1951
216. *Brothers of the Sage,* as Ranger Lee. London, 1951
217. *Wild Range Country,* as Ranger Lee. London, 1951
218. *The Big Drive North,* as Chester Wills. London, 1951
219. *The Devil's Trail,* as Chester Wills. London, 1952
220. *Picture Rock,* as Chester Wills. London, 1952
221. *Outlaws of Clover Valley,* as Wade Smith. London, 1952
222. *The Trail of the Cimarron Kid,* as Wade Smith. London, 1952
223. *Brand of the Red Bird,* as H.C. Averill. London, 1952
224. *The New Marshal,* as Ranger Lee. London, 1952
225. *Wild Horse War,* as Ranger Lee. London, 1952
226. *The Mesa Trail.* London, 1952
227. *Snake Brand.* London, 1952
228. *Mountain Gold,* as Gary Marshall. London, 1952
229. *Blizzard,* as Russ Hardy. London, 1952
230. *Sagebrush Desert,* as Gary Marshall. London, 1953
231. *Cloudburst,* as Gary Marshall. London, 1953
232. *Black Sage Range,* as Charles Ballew. London, 1953
233. *Rim-Fire Abstains,* as Charles Ballew. London, 1953
234. *The Slash K Ranch,* as Charles Ballew. London, 1953
235. *Feud at Carson's Ranch.* London, 1953
236. *The Buckhorn Murder Case.* London, 1953
237. *Saga of the Sierras.* London, 1953
238. *Big Horse,* as Ranger Lee. London, 1953
239. *End of a Lawless Trail,* as Ranger Lee. London, 1953
240. *The Outlaw Brothers,* as Wade Smith. London, 1953
241. *Tough Tenderfoot,* as Wade Smith. London, 1953
242. *Empty Guns,* as Chester Wills. London, 1953
243. *The Long Rifle,* as Chester Wills. London, 1953
244. *The Bandit of High Lonesome,* as Chester Wills. London, 1954
245. *Call of the Mountains,* as Chester Wills. London, 1954
246. *The Bandit of Big Bend,* as Wade Smith. London, 1954
247. *Feudin' in the Hills,* as H.C. Averill. London, 1954
248. *Big War for Little Ranch,* as Ranger Lee. London, 1954
249. *Sagebrush Empire,* as Gary Marshall. London, 1954
250. *Line Fence,* as Gary Marshall. London, 1954
251. *The Forty-Niner.* London, 1954
252. *The Castle in the Sagebrush,* as Charles Ballew. London, 1954
253. *Sails in the Desert,* as Charles Ballew. London, 1954
254. *Twice Murdered.* London, 1954
255. *The Notched Stick,* as Russ Hardy. London, 1954
256. *The Twenty and One,* as Dan Wardle. London, 1954
257. *Five Bars of Gold,* as Dan Wardle. London, 1955
258. *The Hard Trail,* as Russ Hardy. London, 1955
259. *Tiger of the West,* as Russ Hardy. London, 1955
260. *Dead Man's Saddle,* as Wade Smith. London, 1955
261. *Tawny Men from Texas,* as Wade Smith. London, 1955
262. *Bedrock Courage,* as H.C. Averill. London, 1955
263. *The Empty Scabbard,* as Ranger Lee. London, 1955
264. *Panther Canyon,* as Ranger Lee. London, 1955
265. *Battle of High Mesa.* London, 1955
266. *Red Fire Stampede.* London, 1955
267. *Shotgun.* London, 1955
268. *Mountain Valley,* as Charles Ballew. London, 1955
269. *Bandits of the Brush Country,* as Gary Marshall. London, 1955
270. *Lost Loot,* as Gary Marshall. London, 1955
271. *Coarse Gold,* as Chester Wills. London, 1955
272. *Mountain Vengeance,* as Chester Wills. London, 1955
273. *Spear for a Tiger,* as Dan Wardle. London, 1956
274. *Bones of Amazing Valley,* as Chester Wills. London, 1956
275. *The Man from Arizona,* as Chester Wills. London, 1956
276. *The Long Trail to Battle,* as Wade Smith. London, 1956
277. *War for Water,* as Wade Smith. London, 1956
278. *Trouble Country,* as H.C. Averill. London, 1956
279. *Texan Sheriff,* as Gary Marshall. London, 1956
280. *Trouble in the Mountains,* as Gary Marshall. London, 1956
281. *Cattle on the Plains,* as Charles Ballew. London, 1956
282. *The Bushwhacker,* as Charles Ballew. London, 1956
283. *Red Ring Dynamite.* London, 1956
284. *Rustler Bait.* London, 1956
285. *Vengeance Trail,* as Robert Cole. London, 1956
286. *The Dagger of Wild Valley,* as Ranger Lee. London, 1956
287. *The Four Diamond Brand,* as Ranger Lee. London, 1956
288. *The Red Trail,* as Russ Hardy. London, 1956
289. *The Wheels Roll West,* as Allen Forrest. London, 1956
290. *Apache Trail,* as Allen Forrest. London, 1957
291. *Return of the Rancho,* as Russ Hardy. London, 1957
292. *Pack Train,* as Russ Hardy. London, 1957

293. *Hidden Gold*, as Russ Hardy. London, 1957
294. *The Prisoner at Quartz Mountain*, as H.C. Averill. London, 1957
295. *Redistribution Bullet*, as H.C. Averill. London, 1957
296. *Boom Camp*, as Ranger Lee. London, 1957
297. *The Longhorns*, as Ranger Lee. London, 1957
298. *The Hangman's Tree*, as Robert Cole. London, 1957
299. *Hell's Half Acre*. London, 1957
300. *Last of an Outlaw Brand*. London, 1957
301. *Rustlers of Moon River*. London, 1957
302. *Kelly of the Badlands*, as Charles Ballew. London, 1957
303. *The Valley of Ten Thousand Horses*, as Charles Ballew. London, 1957
304. *Big Cactus*, as Wade Smith. London, 1957
305. *Wildcat Silver*, as Wade Smith. London, 1957
306. *The Fighting Doctor of Dobetown*, as Chester Wills. London, 1957
307. *The Fighting Prospector*, as Chester Wills. London, 1957
308. *From War to Longhorns*, as James Dillard. London, 1957
309. *Gold in the Canyon*, as James Dillard. London, 1957
310. *Nevada Cowboy*, as John Harlow. London, 1957
311. *Dead Man's Mine*, as John Harlow. London, 1958
312. *Trail into Mexico*, as John Harlow. London, 1958
313. *Indian Fighter*, as Allen Forrest. London, 1958
314. *Arizona Gold*, as Chester Wills. London, 1958
315. *Raiders of Big Mesa*, as Chester Wills. London, 1958
316. *The Man Hunter*, as Wade Smith. London, 1958
317. *Wrong Man for Murder*, as H.C. Averill. London, 1958
318. *The Fight for Monitor Mountain*, as Charles Ballew. London, 1958
319. *Fight for Pay Ground*, as Charles Ballew. London, 1958
320. *Range Beyond the Mountains*, as Charles Ballew. London, 1958
321. *The Caves of Pinnacle Peak*. London, 1958
322. *Gangster in the Desert*. London, 1958
323. *Into the Gunsmoke*. London, 1958
324. *Scars on the West*. London, 1958
325. *The Lost River Trail*, as Ranger Lee. London, 1958
326. *Trouble Ranch*, as Russ Hardy. London, 1958
327. *Outlaws at Bravo*, as Ranger Lee. London, 1959
328. *Bear Trap*, as Ranger Lee. London, 1959
329. *Winter in the Ghost Camp*. London, 1959
330. *Tenon's Task*. London, 1959
331. *Blood on the Saddle*, as Charles Ballew. London, 1959
332. *The Highwayman of Cedar Creek*, as Charles Ballew. London, 1959
333. *Bunch Grass Range*, as H.C. Averill. London, 1959
334. *Guns at Sulpher Creek*, as H.C. Averill. London, 1959
335. *The Fence Buster*, as Wade Smith. London, 1959
336. *Marauder from Mexico*, as Wade Smith. London, 1959
337. *Prospector from the Pine Mountain*, as Chester Wills. London, 1959
338. *Stagecoach for Oro Grande*, as Chester Wills. London, 1959
339. *The Back Trail*, as Chester Wills. London, 1960
340. *Lone Mountain Gold*, as Wade Smith. London, 1960
341. *Made of Sheriff's Stuff*, as Wade Smith. London, 1960
342. *Long Trails*, as H.C. Averill. London, 1960
343. *Pay Ground and Powder Smoke*, as H.C. Averill. London, 1960
344. *Horsethief of Varson Valley*. London, 1960
345. *Last of the Outlaws Trail*. London, 1960
346. *Robbery in the Mountains*. London, 1960
347. *Frontier Wall of Fire*, as Charles Ballew. London, 1960
348. *Lawman of the Mountains*, as Charles Ballew. London, 1960
349. *Rifles at Cow Tail*, as Charles Ballew. London, 1960
350. *Justice Comes to Cactus City*, as Ranger Lee. London, 1960
351. *The Sheriff's Hunch*, as Wade Smith. London, 1961
352. *The Taming of Wild River*, as Wade Smith. London, 1961
353. *Mustang Valley*, as H.C. Averill. London, 1961
354. *Trail's End*, as H.C. Averill. London, 1961
355. *War to the Last Man*, as H.C. Averill. London, 1961
356. *Skeletons in the Desert*, as Ranger Lee. London, 1961
357. *Quick Rifle*, as Ranger Lee. London, 1961
358. *Cabin Fever*, as Charles Ballew. London, 1961
359. *The Gold of Poverty Flat*, as Charles Ballew. London, 1961
360. *The Trail-Blazer*, as Charles Ballew. London, 1961
361. *Battle at Yellow Creek*. London, 1961
362. *Guns and Black Gold*. London, 1961
363. *Guns in the Sage*. London, 1961
364. *Pay from the Grass Roots*. London, 1961
365. *Hair Trigger Country*, as Chester Wills. London, 1961
366. *Sagebrush Funeral*, as Chester Wills. London, 1961
367. *Smoking Them Out*, as Chester Wills. London, 1962
368. *Powder Burns in Wyoming*, as Chester Wills. London, 1962
369. *Baron of Big Cedar Basin*, as Wade Smith. London, 1962
370. *Law Arrives in Elkhorn*, as H.C. Averill. London, 1962
371. *Penning the Outlaw*, as H.C. Averill. London, 1962
372. *Death of a Rancher*. London, 1962
373. *Gun Holds High Hand*. London, 1962
374. *Jailbreak in Gold Horn*. London, 1962
375. *Danger Trail*, as Charles Ballew. London, 1962
376. *Gunslinger's Last Battle*, as Charles Ballew. London, 1962
377. *Ride That Buckskin*, as Charles Ballew. London, 1962
378. *Fighters of Ghost Camp*, as Ranger Lee. London, 1962
379. *Prospector Trail*, as James Dillard. London, 1962
380. *The Gold of Oro Fino*, as James Dillard. London, 1962
381. *The Treasure of Eagle Peak*, as James Dillard. London, 1963
382. *Guns in Arizona*, as H.C. Averill. London, 1963
383. *Rustlers on the Bar-S*, as H.C. Averill. London, 1963
384. *Dead Men Ride*, as Charles Ballew. London, 1963
385. *Bushwhacker Bullet*, as Charles Ballew. London, 1963
386. *Monitor Mountain*, as Charles Ballew. London, 1963
387. *Mountain Trouble*, as Charles Ballew. London, 1963
388. *Sourdough Pay-Off*, as Charles Ballew. London, 1963
389. *Showdown at Cedar Creek*, as Charles Ballew. London, 1963
390. *Gun on the Mantel*. London, 1963
391. *Riding the Back Trail*. London, 1963
392. *The Wrong Man*, as H.C. Averill. London, 1963
393. *The Ghost of Tom Peck Canyon*, as Chester Wills. London, 1963
394. *Ride to Red Rock*, as Chester Wills. London, 1963
395. *Sagebrush Gunsmoke*, as H.C. Averill. London, 1964
396. *Through Panther Pass*, as H.C. Averill. London, 1964
397. *California Trail*, as H.C. Averill. London, 1964
398. *Bad Medicine in Wyoming*, as Charles Ballew. London, 1964
399. *Death in the Canyon*. London, 1964
400. *Gold Beyond the Mountains*. London, 1964
401. *Law on a Rampage*. London, 1964
402. *Gunsight Moon*, as Charles Ballew. London, 1964
403. *War on the Flying O*, as Charles Ballew. London, 1964
404. *Barred from the Range*, as H.C. Averill. London, 1965
405. *Arizona Hunter*, as Charles Ballew. London, 1965
406. *Feud and Flood*, as Charles Ballew. London, 1965
407. *The Trail Together*, as Charles Ballew. London, 1965
408. *The Dry Diggings Nugget*. London, 1965
409. *Smoke Signals from Timberline*. London, 1965
410. *Tangled Ropes*. London, 1965
411. *The Shot in the Back*, as H.C. Averill. London, 1966
412. *The Brand Was IXL*, as H.C. Averill. London, 1966
413. *Big Range Country*. London, 1966
414. *Flame in the Storm*. London, 1966
415. *Law Comes to Silver Blade*. London, 1966
416. *The Tenderfoot Called Rawhide*, as Charles Ballew. London, 1966
417. *Beyond the Rimrock*, as Charles Ballew. London, 1967

418. *Faro at Cottonwood Springs,* as Charles Ballew. London, 1967
419. *Happy Ranch.* London, 1967

Snyder, Zilpha Keatley
American, born May 11, 1928
1. *Season of Ponies.* New York, 1964
2. *The Velvet Room.* New York, 1965
3. *Black and Blue Magic.* New York, 1966
4. *The Egypt Game.* New York, 1967
5. *Eyes in the Fishbowl.* New York, 1968
6. *Today Is Saturday.* New York, 1969
7. *The Changeling.* New York, 1970
8. *The Headless Cupid.* New York, 1971
9. *The Witches of Worm.* New York, 1972
10. *The Princess and the Giants.* New York, 1973
11. *The Truth about Stone Hollow.* New York, 1974
12. *Below the Root.* New York, 1975
13. *And All Between.* New York, 1976
14. *Until the Celebration.* New York, 1977

Sobol, Donald J.
American, born October 4, 1924
1. *The Double Quest.* New York, 1957
2. *The Lost Dispatch.* New York, 1958
3. *The First Book of Medieval Man.* New York, 1959
4. *The First Book of Medieval Britain.* London, 1960
5. *Two Flags Flying.* New York, 1960
6. *The Wright Brothers at Kitty Hawk.* New York, 1961
7. *The First Book of the Barbarian Invaders.* A.D. *375-511.* New York, 1962
8. *The First Book of Stocks and Bonds,* with Rose Sobol. New York, 1963
9. *Lock, Stock, and Barrel.* Philadelphia, 1965
10. *Secret Agents Four.* New York, 1967
11. *Greta the Strong.* Chicago, 1970
12. *Milton, The Model A.* New York, 1971
13. *The Amazons of Greek Mythology.* South Brunswick (NJ) and London, 1972
14. *True Sea Adventures.* Nashville (TN), 1975

Sohl, Jerry [Gerald Allan Sohl]
American, born December 2, 1913
Pseudonyms: Nathan Butler, Sean Mei Sullivan
1. *The Haploids.* New York, 1952
2. *Costigan's Needle.* New York, 1953
3. *The Transcendent Man.* New York, 1953
4. *The Altered Ego.* New York, 1954
5. *Point Ultimate.* New York, 1955
6. *The Mars Monopoly.* New York, 1956
7. *The Time Dissolver.* New York, 1957
8. *Prelude to Peril.* New York, 1957
9. *The Odious Ones.* New York, 1959
10. *One Against Herculum.* New York, 1959
11. *Night Slaves.* New York, 1965
12. *The Lemon Eaters.* New York and London, 1967
13. *The Anomaly.* New York, 1971
14. *The Spun Sugar Hole.* New York, 1971
15. *The Resurrection of Frank Borchard.* New York, 1973
16. *Dr. Josh,* as Nathan Butler. New York, 1973
17. *Underhanded Chess.* New York, 1973
18. *Supermanchu, Master of Kung Fu,* as Sean Mei Sullivan. New York, 1974
19. *Mamelle,* as Nathan Butler. New York, 1974
20. *Underhanded Bridge.* New York, 1975
21. *I, Aleppo.* Toronto, 1976
22. *Blow-Dry,* as Nathan Butler. New York, 1976
23. *Mamelle, The Goddess,* as Nathan Butler. New York, 1977

Sorensen, Virginia
American, born February 17, 1912
1. *A Little Lower Than the Angels.* New York, 1942
2. *On This Star.* New York, 1946
3. *The Neighbors.* New York, 1947
4. *The Evening and the Morning.* New York, 1949
5. *The Proper Gods.* New York, 1951
6. *Curious Missie.* New York, 1953
7. *The House Next Door: Utah, 1896.* New York, 1954
8. *Many Heavens.* New York, 1954
9. *Plain Girl.* New York, 1955
10. *Miracles on Maple Hill.* New York, 1956
11. *Kingdom Come.* New York, 1960
12. *Where Nothing is Long Ago: Memories of a Mormon Childhood.* New York, 1963
13. *Lotte's Locket.* New York, 1964
14. *Around the Corner.* New York, 1971
15. *The Man with the Key.* New York, 1974
16. *Companions of the Road.* New York, 1978

Speare, Elizabeth George
American, born November 21, 1908
1. *The Witch of Blackbird Pond.* Boston, 1958
2. *Calico Captive.* Boston, 1959
3. *Child Life in New England, 1790-1840.* Sturbridge (MA), 1961
4. *The Bronze Bow.* Boston, 1961
5. *Life in Colonial America.* New York, 1963
6. *The Prospering.* Boston, 1967

Spearman, Frank H. (Hamilton)
American, born September 26, 1859, died December 29, 1937
1. *Divorce.* New York, no date
2. *The Nerve of Foley and Other Railroad Stories.* New York, 1900
3. *Held for Others, Being Stories of Railroad Life.* New York, 1901
4. *Doctor Bryson.* New York, 1902
5. *The Daughter of a Magnate.* New York, 1903
6. *The Close of the Day.* New York, 1904
7. *The Strategy of Great Railroads.* New York, 1904
8. *Whispering Smith.* New York, 1906
9. *Robert Kimberly.* New York, 1911
10. *The Mountain Divide.* New York, 1912
11. *Merrilie Dawes.* New York, 1913
12. *Nan of Music Mountain.* New York and London, 1916
13. *Laramie Holds the Range.* New York and London, 1921
14. *The Marriage Verdict.* New York and London, 1923
15. *Selwood of Sleepy Cat.* New York and London, 1925
16. *Flambeau Jim.* New York, 1927
17. *Spanish Lover.* New York, 1930
18. *Hell's Desert.* New York, 1933
19. *Gunlock Ranch.* New York and London, 1935
20. *Carmen of the Rancho.* New York and London, 1938

Spence, Bill [William John Duncan Spence]
British, born April 20, 1923
Pseudonyms: Jim Bowden, Floyd Rogers, Duncan Spence
1. *Dark Hell,* as Duncan Spence. London, 1959
2. *The Return of the Sheriff,* as Jim Bowden. London, 1960
3. *Wayman's Ford,* as Jim Bowden. London, 1960
4. *Two Gun Justice,* as Jim Bowden. London, 1961
5. *Roaring Valley,* as Jim Bowden. London, 1962
6. *Revenge in Red Springs,* as Jim Bowden. London, 1962
7. *Black Water Canyon,* as Jim Bowden. London, 1963
8. *Arizona Gold,* as Jim Bowden. London, 1963

9. *Trail of Revenge*, as Jim Bowden. London, 1964
10. *The Man from Cheyenne Wells*, as Floyd Rogers. London, 1964
11. *Revenge Rider*, as Floyd Rogers. London, 1964
12. *Brazo Feud*, as Jim Bowden. London, 1965
13. *Guns Along the Brazo*, as Jim Bowden. London, 1967
14. *The Stage Riders*, as Floyd Rogers. London, 1967
15. *Gun Loose*, as Jim Bowden. London, 1969
16. *Valley of Revenge*, as Jim Bowden. London, 1971
17. *Trail to Texas*, as Jim Bowden. London, 1973
18. *Thunder in Montana*, as Jim Bowden. London, 1973
19. *Montana Justice*, as Floyd Rogers. London, 1973
20. *Hangman's Gulch*, as Floyd Rogers. London, 1974
21. *Showdown in Salt Fork*, as Jim Bowden. London, 1975
22. *Hired Gun*, as Jim Bowden. London, 1976
23. *Incident at Bison Creek*, as Jim Bowden. London, 1977
24. *Romantic Ryedale*, with Joan Spence. York (Eng), 1977
25. *Cap*, as Jim Bowden. London, 1978
26. *Dollars of Death*, as Jim Bowden. London, 1979
27. *Incident at Elk River*, as Floyd Rogers. London, 1979
28. *Renegade Riders*, as Jim Bowden. London, 1980
29. *Gunfight at Elm Creek*, as Jim Bowden. London, 1980
30. *Harpooned: The Story of Whaling*. London, 1980
31. *Bomber's Moon*. London, 1981
32. *The Shadow of Eagle Rock*, as Jim Bowden. London, 1982

Sperry, Armstrong
American, born November 7, 1897, died in April 1976
1. *One Day with Manu*. Philadelphia, 1933
2. *One Day with Jambi in Sumatra*. Philadelphia, 1934
3. *One Day with Tuktu, An Eskimo Boy*. Philadelphia, 1935
4. *All Sail Set*. Philadelphia, 1936
5. *Wagons Westward: The Old Trail to Santa Fe*. Philadelphia, 1936
6. *Call It Courage*. Philadelphia, 1936
7. *Little Eagle, A Navajo Boy*. Philadelphia, 1938
8. *Lost Lagoon*. New York, 1939
9. *Coconut, The Wonder Tree*. New York, 1942
10. *The Boy Who Was Afraid*. London, 1942
11. *Bamboo, The Grass Tree*. New York, 1942
12. *No Brighter Glory*. New York, 1942
13. *Storm Canvas*. Philadelphia, 1944
14. *Hull-Down for Action*. New York, 1945
15. *The Rain Forest*. New York, 1947
16. *Danger to Windward*. Philadelphia, 1947
17. *Black Falcon*. Philadelphia, 1949
18. *The Voyages of Christopher Columbus*. New York, 1950
19. *River of the West*. Philadelphia, 1952
20. *Thunder Country*. New York, 1952
21. *Frozen Fire*. New York, 1956

Spicer, Bart
American, born in 1918
Pseudonyn: Jay Barbette
1. *The Dark Light*. New York, 1949
2. *Blues for the Prince*. New York, 1950
3. *The Golden Door*. London and New York, 1951
4. *Black Sheep, Run*. New York, 1951
5. *The Long Green*. New York, 1952
6. *Final Copy*, as Jay Barbette. New York, 1950
7. *Dear Dead Days*, as Jay Barbette. New York, 1953
8. *Shadow of Fear*. London, 1953
9. *The Taming of Carney Wilde*. New York, 1954
10. *The Wild Ohio*. New York and London, 1954
11. *The Day of the Dead*. New York, 1955
12. *Death's Long Shadow*, as Jay Barbette. New York, 1955
13. *The Tall Captains*. New York, 1957
14. *Brother to the Enemy*. New York, 1958
15. *The Deadly Doll*, as Jay Barbette. New York, 1958
16. *Exit, Running*. New York, 1959
17. *Look Behind You*, as Jay Barbette. New York, 1960
18. *The Day Before Thunder*. New York, 1960
19. *Act of Anger*. New York, 1962
20. *The Burned Man*. New York, 1966
21. *Kellogg Junction*. New York, 1969
22. *Festival*. New York, 1970
23. *The Adversary*. New York and London, 1974

Spillane, Mickey [Frank Morrison Spillane]
American, born March 9, 1918
1. *I, The Jury*. New York, 1947
2. *My Gun Is Quick*. New York, 1950
3. *Vengeance Is Mine!* New York, 1950
4. *The Big Kill*. New York, 1951
5. *The Long Wait*. New York, 1951
6. *One Lonely Night*. New York, 1951
7. *Kiss Me, Deadly*. New York, 1952
8. *The Deep*. New York and London, 1961
9. *The Girl Hunters*. New York and London, 1962
10. *Me, Hood!* London, 1963
11. *Day of the Guns*. New York, 1964
12. *The Flier*. London, 1964
13. *Return of the Hood*. London, 1964
14. *The Snake*. New York and London, 1964
15. *Bloody Sunrise*. New York and London, 1965
16. *The Death Dealers*. New York, 1965
17. *Killer Mine*. London, 1965
18. *The By-Pass Control*. New York, 1966
19. *The Twisted Thing*. New York and London, 1966
20. *The Body Lovers*. New York and London, 1967
21. *The Delta Factor*. New York, 1967
22. *The Tough Guys*. New York, 1969
23. *Survival . . . Zero!* New York and London, 1970
24. *The Erection Set*. New York and London, 1972
25. *The Last Cop Out*. New York and London, 1973

Spinrad, Norman
American, born September 15, 1940
1. *The Solarians*. New York, 1966
2. *Agent of Chaos*. New York, 1967
3. *The Men in the Jungle*. New York, 1967
4. *Bug Jack Barron*. New York, 1969
5. *The Last Hurrah of the Golden Horde*. New York, 1970
6. *Fragments of America*. North Hollywood (CA), 1970
7. *The Iron Dream*. New York, 1972
8. *No Direction Home*. New York, 1975
9. *Passing Through the Flame*. New York, 1975
10. *Experiment Perilous: Three Essays on Science Fiction*. New York, 1976
11. *Riding the Torch*. New York, 1978
12. *A World Between*. New York, 1979
13. *The Star-Spangled Future*. New York, 1979
14. *Songs from the Stars*. New York, 1980

Sprigg, Christopher St. John
British, born October 20, 1907, died February 12, 1937
Pseudonym: Christopher Caudwell
1. *The Airship: Its Design, History, Operation, and Future*, as Christopher Caudwell. London, 1931
2. *Crime in Kensington*. London, 1933
3. *Pass the Body*. New York, 1933
4. *Fatality in Fleet Street*. London, 1933
5. *The Perfect Alibi*. London and New York, 1934
6. *Death of an Airman*. London, 1934
7. *British Airways*, as Christopher Caudwell. London and New York, 1934

8. *Great Flights,* as Christopher Caudwell. London, 1935
9. *Death of a Queen.* London, 1935
10. *The Corpse with the Sunburnt Face.* London and New York, 1935
11. *This My Hand,* as Christopher Caudwell. London, 1936
12. *The Six Queer Things.* London and New York, 1937
13. *Poems,* as Christopher Caudwell. London, 1939

Spykman, E.C. (Elizabeth Choate)
American, born July 17, 1896, died August 7, 1965
1. *A Lemon and a Star.* New York, 1955
2. *The Wild Angel.* New York, 1957
3. *Westover.* Middlebury, (CT), 1959
4. *Terrible, Horrible Edie.* New York, 1960
5. *Edie on the Warpath.* New York, 1966

Stableford, Brian M. (Michael)
American, born July 25, 1948
1. *Cradle of the Sun.* New York and London, 1969
2. *The Blind Worm.* New York and London, 1970
3. *The Days of Glory.* New York, 1971
4. *In the Kingdom of the Beasts.* New York, 1971
5. *Day of Wrath.* New York, 1971
6. *To Challenge Chaos.* New York, 1972
7. *Halcyon Drift.* New York, 1972
8. *Rhapsody in Black.* New York, 1973
9. *Promised Land.* New York, 1974
10. *The Paradise Game.* New York, 1974
11. *The Fenris Device.* New York, 1974
12. *Swan Song.* New York, 1975
13. *Man in a Cage.* New York, 1975
14. *The Face of Heaven.* London, 1976
15. *The Mind-Riders.* New York, 1976
16. *The Florians.* New York, 1976
17. *Critical Threshold.* New York, 1977
18. *The Realms of Tartarus.* New York, 1977
19. *Wildeblood's Empire.* New York, 1977
20. *The City of the Sun.* New York, 1978
21. *The Last Days of the Edge of the World.* London, 1978
22. *Balance of Power.* New York, 1979
23. *The Walking Shadow.* London, 1979
24. *The Paradox of Sets.* New York, 1979
25. *A Clash of Symbols: The Triumph of James Blish.* San Bernardino (CA), 1979
26. *Optiman.* New York, 1980

Stafford, Jean
American, born July 1, 1915, died March 26, 1979
1. *Boston Adventure.* New York, 1944
2. *The Mountain Lion.* New York, 1947
3. *The Catherine Wheel.* New York and London, 1952
4. *Children Are Bored on Sunday.* New York, 1953
5. *New Short Novels,* with others. New York, 1954
6. *Stories,* with others. New York, 1956
7. *A Book of Stories.* London, 1957
8. *Elephi: The Cat with the High I.Q.* New York, 1962
9. *The Lion and the Carpenter and Other Tales from the Arabian Nights Retold.* New York and London, 1962
10. *Bad Characters.* New York, 1964
11. *Selected Stories.* London, 1966
12. *A Mother in History.* New York and London, 1966
13. *The Collected Stories of Jean Stafford.* New York, 1969

Starrett, Vincent [Charles Vincent Emerson Starrett]
American, born October 26, 1886, died January 4, 1974
1. *Arthur Machen: A Novelist of Ecstasy and Sin.* Chicago, 1918
2. *The Escape of Alice: A Christmas Fantasy.* Privately printed, 1919
3. *Ambrose Bierce.* Chicago, 1920
4. *The Unique Hamlet: A Hitherto Unchronicled Adventure of Mr. Sherlock Holmes.* Privately printed, 1920
5. *A Student of Catalogues.* Privately printed, 1921
6. *Stephen Crane: A Bibliography.* Philadelphia, 1923
7. *Buried Caesars: Essays in Literary Appreciation.* Chicago, 1923
8. *Coffins for Two.* Chicago, 1924
9. *Seaports in the Moon: A Fantasia on Romantic Themes.* New York, 1928
10. *Murder on "B" Deck.* New York, 1929
11. *Ambrose Bierce: A Bibliography.* Philadelphia, 1929
12. *Penny Wise and Book Foolish.* New York, 1929
13. *All About Mother Goose.* Privately printed, 1930
14. *The Blue Door.* New York, 1930
15. *Dead Man Inside.* New York, 1931
16. *The End of Mr. Garment.* New York, 1932
17. *The Private Life of Sherlock Holmes.* New York, 1933
18. *The Great Hotel Murder.* New York and London, 1935
19. *Snow for Christmas.* Privately printed, 1935
20. *Midnight and Percy Jones.* New York, 1936
21. *The Laughing Buddha.* Mount Morris (IL), 1937
22. *Persons from Porlock.* Chicago, 1938
23. *Oriental Encounter: Two Essays in Bad Taste.* Chicago, 1938
24. *Books Alive.* New York, 1940
25. *Bookman's Holiday: The Private Satisfactions of an Incurable Collector.* New York, 1942
26. *Autolycus in Limbo.* New York, 1943
27. *The Case Book of Jimmie Lavender.* New York, 1944
28. *Murder In Peking.* New York, 1946
29. *Books and Bipeds.* New York, 1947
30. *Stephen Crane: A Bibliography,* with Ames W. Williams. Glendale (CA), 1948
31. *Sonnets and Other Verse.* Chicago, 1949
32. *Best Loved Books of the Twentieth Century.* New York, 1955
33. *The Great All-Star Animal League Ball Game.* New York, 1957
34. *Book Column.* New York, 1958
35. *Born in a Bookshop: Chapters from the Chicago Renascence.* Norman (OK), 1965
36. *The Quick and the Dead.* Sauk City (WI), 1965
37. *Late, Later and Possibly Last: Essays.* St. Louis (MO), 1973
38. *Sincerely Tony/Faithfully Vincent: The Correspondence of Anthony Boucher and Vincent Starrett.* Chicago, 1975

Stasheff, Christopher
American, born in January, 1944
1. *The Warlock in Spite of Himself.* New York, 1969
2. *King Kobold.* New York, 1971
3. *A Wizard in Bedlam.* New York, 1979

Steel, Danielle
American
1. *Going Home.* New York, 1973
2. *Passion's Promise.* New York, 1977
3. *Now and Forever.* New York, 1978
4. *The Promise.* New York and London, 1978
5. *Season of Passion.* New York and London, 1979
6. *The Ring.* New York, 1980
7. *Golden Moments.* London, 1980
8. *Loving.* New York, 1980
9. *To Love Again.* New York, 1980
10. *Remembrance.* New York, 1981
11. *Palomino.* New York, 1981
12. *Summer's End.* New York, 1981
13. *Love: Poems.* New York, 1981
14. *A Perfect Stranger.* New York, 1982
15. *Once in a Lifetime.* New York, 1982

Steele, Mary Q. (Quintard)
American, born May 8, 1922
Pseudonym: Wilson Gage
1. *The Secret of the Indian Mound [Crossbone Hill, Fiery Gorge]*, as Wilson Gage. Cleveland (OH), 3 vols, 1958-60
2. *A Wild Goose Tale*, as Wilson Gage. Cleveland, 1961
3. *Dan and the Miranda*, as Wilson Gage. Cleveland, 1962
4. *Miss Osbone-the-Mop*, as Wilson Gage. Cleveland, 1963
5. *Big Blue Island*, as Wilson Gage. Cleveland, 1964
6. *The Ghost of Five Owl Farm*, as Wilson Gage. Cleveland, 1966
7. *Journey Outside.* New York, 1969
8. *Mike's Toads*, as Wilson Gage. New York, 1970
9. *The Living Year: An Almanac for My Survivors.* New York, 1972
10. *The First of the Penguins.* New York, 1973
11. *Because of the Sand Witches There.* New York, 1975
12. *The Eye in the Forest.* New York, 1975
13. *The True Men.* New York, 1976
14. *Squash Pie*, as Wilson Gage. New York, 1976
15. *Down in the Boondocks*, as Wilson Gage. New York, 1977

Steele, William O. (Owen)
American, born December 22, 1917
1. *The Golden Root.* New York, 1951
2. *The Buffalo Knife.* New York, 1952
3. *Over-Mountain Boy.* New York, 1952
4. *Wilderness Journey.* New York, 1953
5. *The Story of Daniel Boone.* New York, 1953
6. *John Sevier, Pioneer Boy.* Indianapolis (IN), 1953
7. *Francis Marion: Young Swamp Fox.* Indianapolis, 1954
8. *Winter Danger.* New York, 1954
9. *The Story of Leif Ericson.* New York, 1954
10. *Tomahawks and Trouble.* New York, 1955
11. *We Were There on the Oregon Trail.* New York, 1955
12. *David Crockett's Earthquake.* New York, 1956
13. *De Soto: Child of the Sun.* New York, 1956
14. *We Were There with the Pony Express.* New York, 1956
15. *The Lone Hunt.* New York, 1956
16. *Flaming Arrows.* New York, 1957
17. *Daniel Boone's Echo.* New York, 1957
18. *The Perilous Road.* New York, 1958
19. *Andy Jackson's Water Well.* New York, 1959
20. *The Far Frontier.* New York, 1959
21. *The Spooky Thing.* New York, 1960
22. *Westward Adventure: The True Stories of Six Pioneers.* New York, 1962
23. *The Year of the Bloody Sevens.* New York, 1963
24. *Wayah of the Real People.* Williamsburg (VA), 1964
25. *The No-Name Man of the Mountain.* New York, 1964
26. *Trail Through Danger.* New York, 1965
27. *Tomahawk Border.* Williamsburg, 1966
28. *The Old Wilderness Road: An American Journey.* New York, 1968
29. *Hound Dog Zip to the Rescue.* Champaign (IL), 1970
30. *The Wilderness Tattoo: A Narrative of Juan Ortiz.* New York, 1972
31. *Henry Woodward of Carolina: Surgeon, Trader, Indian Chief.* Columbia (SC), 1972
32. *Triple Trouble for Hound Dog Zip.* Champaign, 1972
33. *John's Secret Treasure.* New York, 1975
34. *The Eye in the Forest*, with Mary Q. Steele. New York, 1975
35. *The Man with the Silver Eyes.* New York, 1976

Steelman, Robert J. (James)
American, born March 7, 1914
1. *Stages South.* New York, 1956
2. *Apache Wells.* New York, 1959
3. *Winter of the Sioux.* New York, 1959
4. *Call of the Arctic.* New York, 1960
5. *Ambush at Three Rivers.* New York, 1964
6. *Cheyenne Vengeance.* New York, 1974
7. *Dakota Territory.* New York, 1974
8. *The Fox Dancer.* New York, 1975
9. *Sun Boy.* New York, 1975
10. *Portrait of a Sioux.* New York, 1976
11. *Lord Apache.* New York, 1977
12. *The Galvanized Reb.* New York, 1977
13. *White Medicine Man.* New York, 1979
14. *Surgeon to the Sioux.* New York, 1979
15. *The Great Yellowstone Steamboat Race.* New York, 1980
16. *The Man They Hanged.* New York, 1980
17. *The Prairie Baroness.* New York, 1981
18. *The Santee Massacre.* New York, 1982

Steen, Marguerite
British, born May 12, 1894, died August 4, 1975
Pseudonyms: Lennox Dryden, Jane Nicholson
1. *The Gilt Cage.* London, 1926
2. *Duel in the Dark.* London, 1928
3. *Dark Duel.* New York, 1929
4. *The Reluctant Madonna.* London, 1929
5. *They That Go Down.* London, 1930
6. *Ancestors*, as Lennox Dryden. London, 1930
7. *They That Go Down in Ships.* New York, 1931
8. *When the Wind Blows.* London, 1931
9. *Unicorn.* London, 1931
10. *The Wise and the Foolish Virgins.* London and Boston, 1932
11. *Oakfields Plays, Including the Inglemere Christmas Play.* London, 1932
12. *Spider.* London and Boston, 1933
13. *Stallion.* London and Boston, 1933
14. *Peepshow.* London, 1933
15. *Hugh Walpole: A Study.* London and New York, 1933
16. *The Lost One: A Biography of Mary—Perdita—Robinson.* London, 1933
17. *Matador.* London and Boston, 1934
18. *The One-Eyed Moon.* London and Boston, 1935
19. *The Tavern.* London, 1935
20. *Return of a Heroine.* London and Indianapolis (IN), 1936
21. *Who Would Have Daughters?* London, 1937
22. *The Marriage Will Not Take Place.* London, 1938
23. *Family Ties.* London, 1939
24. *A Kind of Insolence and Other Stories.* London, 1940
25. *French for Love.* London, 1940
26. *The Sun Is My Undoing.* London and New York, 1941
27. *Shelter*, as Jane Nicholson. London and New York, 1941
28. *William Nicholson.* London, 1943
29. *Rose Timson.* London, 1946
30. *Bell Timson.* New York, 1946
31. *Granada Window.* London, 1949
32. *Twilight on the Floods.* London and New York, 1949
33. *The Swan.* London, 1951
34. *Phoenix Rising.* London, 1952
35. *Jehovah Blues.* New York, 1952
36. *Anna Fitzalan.* London and New York, 1953
37. *Bulls of Parral.* London and New York, 1954
38. *The Unquiet Spirit.* London, 1955
39. *Little White King.* London and Cleveland (OH), 1956
40. *The Tower.* London, 1959
41. *The Woman in the Back Seat.* London and New York, 1959
42. *A Pride of Terrys: A Family Saga.* London, 1962
43. *A Candle in the Sun.* London and New York, 1964

44. *Looking Glass: An Autobiography.* London, 1966
45. *Pier Glass: More Autobiography.* London, 1968

Stegner, Wallace (Earle)
American, born February 18, 1909
1. *Remembering Laughter.* Boston and New York, 1937
2. *The Potter's House.* Muscatine, 1938
3. *On a Darkling Plain.* New York, 1940
4. *Fire and Ice.* New York, 1941
5. *Mormon Country.* New York, 1942
6. *The Big Rock Candy Mountain.* New York, 1943
7. *Second Growth.* Boston, 1947
8. *The Preacher and the Slave.* Boston, 1950
9. *The Women on the Wall.* Boston, 1950
10. *The City of the Living.* Boston, 1956
11. *New Short Novels 2,* with others. New York, 1956
12. *A Shooting Star.* New York and London, 1961
13. *Wolf Willow: A History, A Story, and A Memory of the Last Plains Frontier.* New York, 1962
14. *The Gathering of Zion: The Story of the Mormon Trail.* New York, 1964
15. *All the Little Live Things.* New York, 1967
16. *Angel of Repose.* New York and London, 1971
17. *The Uneasy Chair: A Biography of Bernard DeVoto.* New York, 1974
18. *Ansel Adams: Images 1923-1974.* Greenwich (CT), 1974
19. *The Spectator Bird.* New York, 1976
20. *Recapitulation.* New York, 1979
21. *American Places,* with Page Stegner. New York and London, 1981
22. *One Way to Spell Man.* New York, 1982

Stein, Aaron Marc
American, born November 15, 1906
Pseudonymns: George Bagby, Hampton Stone
1. *Murder at the Piano,* as George Bagby. New York, 1935
2. *Ring Around a Murder,* as George Bagby. New York, 1936
3. *Murder Half Baked,* as George Bagby. New York, 1937
4. *Murder on the Nose,* as George Bagby. New York, 1938
5. *Bird Walking Weather,* as George Bagby. New York, 1939
6. *The Corpse with the Purple Thighs,* as George Bagby. New York, 1939
7. *The Corpse Wore a Wig,* as George Bagby. New York, 1940
8. *The Sun Is a Witness.* New York, 1940
9. *Up to No Good.* New York, 1941
10. *Here Comes the Corpse,* as George Bagby. New York, 1941
11. *Red Is for Killing,* as George Bagby. New York, 1941
12. *The Bloody Wig Murders,* as George Bagby. No place, 1942
13. *Murder Calling "50,"* as George Bagby. New York, 1942
14. *Only the Guilty.* New York, 1942
15. *The Case of the Absent-Minded Professor.* New York, 1943
16. *. . . and High Water.* New York, 1946
17. *Dead on Arrival,* as George Bagby. New York, 1946
18. *The Original Carcase,* as George Bagby. New York, 1946
19. *The Twin Killing,* as George Bagby. New York, 1947
20. *We Saw Him Die.* New York, 1947
21. *Death Takes a Paying Guest.* New York, 1947
22. *The Cradle and the Grave.* New York, 1948
23. *The Starting Gun,* as George Bagby. New York, 1948
24. *In Cold Blood,* as George Bagby. New York, 1948
25. *The Corpse in the Corner Saloon,* as Hampton Stone. New York, 1948
26. *The Girl with the Hole in Her Head,* as Hampton Stone. New York, 1949
27. *The Needle That Wouldn't Hold Still,* as Hampton Stone. New York, 1950
28. *Drop Dead,* as George Bagby. New York, 1949
29. *Coffin Corner,* as George Bagby. New York, 1949
30. *The Second Burial.* New York, 1949
31. *Days of Misfortune.* New York, 1949
32. *Blood Will Tell,* as George Bagby. New York, 1950
33. *Three—Blood.* New York, 1950
34. *Frightened Amazon.* New York, 1950
35. *Shoot Me Dacent.* New York, 1951
36. *Pistols for Two.* New York, 1951
37. *Death Ain't Commercial,* as George Bagby. New York, 1951
38. *Scared to Death,* as George Bagby. New York, 1952
39. *The Corpse with Sticky Fingers,* as George Bagby. New York, 1952
40. *Mask for Murder.* New York, 1952
41. *The Dead Thing in the Pool.* New York, 1952
42. *The Corpse That Refused to Stay Dead,* as Hampton Stone. New York, 1952
43. *The Corpse Who Had Too Many Friends,* as Hampton Stone. New York, 1953
44. *Death Meets 400 Rabbits.* New York, 1953
45. *Give the Little Corpse a Great Big Hand,* as George Bagby. New York, 1953
46. *A Big Hand for the Corpse,* as George Bagby. Roslyn, 1953
47. *A Body for the Bride,* as George Bagby. New York, 1954
48. *Dead Drunk,* as George Bagby. New York, 1953
49. *The Body in the Basket,* as George Bagby. New York, 1954
50. *A Dirty Way to Die,* as George Bagby. New York, 1955
51. *Moonmilk and Murder.* New York, 1955
52. *Shadow on the Window,* as George Bagby. Roslyn, 1955
53. *The Man Who Had Too Much to Lose,* as Hampton Stone. New York and London, 1955
54. *The Strangler Who Couldn't Let Go,* as Hampton Stone. New York, 1956
55. *Dead Storage,* as George Bagby. New York, 1956
56. *Cop Killer,* as George Bagby. New York, 1956
57. *Dead Wrong,* as George Bagby. New York, 1957
58. *The Strangler,* as Hampton Stone. London, 1957
59. *The Girl Who Kept Knocking Them Dead,* as Hampton Stone. New York and London, 1957
60. *Sitting Up Dead.* New York, 1958
61. *The Three-Time Losers,* as George Bagby. New York and London, 1958
62. *Never Need an Enemy.* New York, 1959
63. *The Real Gone Goose,* as George Bagby. New York, 1959
64. *The Man Who Was Three Jumps Ahead,* as Hampton Stone. New York, 1959
65. *Evil Genius,* as George Bagby. New York, 1961
66. *The Man Who Looked Death in the Eye,* as Hampton Stone. New York, 1961
67. *Home and Murder.* New York, 1962
68. *The Babe with the Twistable Arm,* as Hampton Stone. New York, 1962
70. *Murder's Little Helper,* as George Bagby. New York, 1963
71. *Blood on the Stars.* New York and London, 1964
72. *The Real Serendipitous Kill,* as Hampton Stone. New York, 1964
73. *Mysteriouser and Mysteriouser,* as George Bagby. New York, 1965
74. *Murder in Wonderland,* as George Bagby. London, 1965
75. *Dirty Pool,* as George Bagby. New York, 1966
76. *I Fear the Greeks.* New York, 1966
77. *The Kid Was Last Seen Hanging Ten,* as Hampton Stone. New York, 1966
78. *The Funniest Killer in Town,* as Hampton Stone. New York, 1967
79. *Executioner's Rest.* London, 1967
80. *Deadly Delight.* New York, 1967
81. *Bait for Killer,* as George Bagby. London, 1967
82. *Corpse Candle,* as George Bagby. New York, 1967

83. *Another Day—Another Death,* as George Bagby. New York and London, 1968
84. *Snare Andalucian.* New York, 1968
85. *Faces of Death.* London, 1968
86. *Kill Is a Four-Letter Word.* New York, 1968
87. *The Corpse Was No Bargain at All,* as Hampton Stone. New York, 1968
88. *Honest Reliable Corpse,* as George Bagby. New York and London, 1969
89. *Killer Boy Was Here,* as George Bagby. New York, 1970
90. *Alp Murder.* New York, 1970
91. *The Swinger Who Swung by the Neck,* as Hampton Stone. New York, 1970
92. *The Kid Who Came Home with a Corpse,* as Hampton Stone. New York, 1972
93. *The Finger.* New York, 1973
94. *Lock and Key.* New York, 1973
95. *Coffin Country.* New York and London, 1976
96. *Two in the Bush,* as George Bagby. New York and London, 1976
97. *Innocent Bystander,* as George Bagby. New York, 1976
98. *My Dead Body,* as George Bagby. New York, 1976
99. *Lend Me Your Ears.* New York, 1977
100. *The Tough Get Going,* as George Bagby. New York, 1977
101. *Better Dead,* as George Bagby. New York, 1978
102. *Body Search.* New York and London, 1978
103. *Nowhere?* New York and London, 1978
104. *Chill Factor.* New York, 1978
105. *Guaranteed to Fade,* as George Bagby. New York, 1978
106. *I Could Have Died,* as George Bagby. New York, 1979
107. *Mugger's Day,* as George Bagby. New York, 1979
108. *The Rolling Heads.* New York and London, 1979
109. *One Dip Dead.* New York, 1979
110. *The Cheating Butcher.* New York, 1980

Steinbeck, John (Ernst)
American, born February 27, 1902, died September 20, 1968
1. *Cup of Gold: A Life of Henry Morgan, Buccaneer, with Occasional Reference to History.* New York, 1929
2. *The Pastures of Heaven.* New York, 1932
3. *To a God Unknown.* New York, 1933
4. *Tortilla Flat.* New York and London, 1935
5. *In Dubious Battle.* New York and London, 1936
6. *Saint Katy the Virgin.* New York, 1936
7. *Of Mice and Men.* New York and London, 1937
8. *The Red Pony.* New York, 1937
9. *The Long Valley.* New York, 1938
10. *Their Blood Is Strong.* San Francisco, 1938
11. *The Grapes of Wrath.* New York and London, 1939
12. *John Steinbeck Replies.* New York, 1940
13. *Sea of Cortez: A Leisurely Journal of Travel and Research,* with Edward F. Ricketts. New York, 1941
14. *Bombs Away: The Story of a Bomber Team.* New York, 1942
15. *The Moon Is Down.* New York and London, 1942
16. *The Viking Portable Library Steinbeck.* New York, 1943
17. *The Steinbeck Pocket Book.* New York, 1943
18. *Cannery Row.* New York and London, 1945
19. *The Portable Steinbeck.* New York, 1946
20. *The Wayward Bus.* New York and London, 1947
21. *The Pearl.* New York, 1947
22. *The First Watch.* Los Angeles, 1947
23. *Vanderbilt Clinic.* New York, 1947
24. *A Russian Journal.* New York, 1948
25. *The Indispensable Steinbeck.* New York, 1950
26. *Burning Bright: A Play in Story Form.* New York, 1950
27. *The Steinbeck Omnibus.* London, 1951
28. *The Log from the Sea of Cortez.* New York, 1951
29. *East of Eden.* New York and London, 1952
30. *The Short Novels.* New York, 1953
31. *Sweet Thursday.* New York and London, 1954
32. *The Short Reign of Pippin IV: A Fabrication.* New York and London, 1957
33. *Once There Was a War.* New York, 1958
34. *The Winter of Our Discontent.* New York and London, 1961
35. *Travels with Charley in Search of America.* New York and London, 1962
36. *Journal of a Novel: The East of Eden Letters.* New York, 1969
37. *Steinbeck: A Life in Letters.* New York and London, 1975

Steptoe, John (Lewis)
American, born September 14, 1950
1. *Stevie.* New York, 1969
2. *Uptown.* New York, 1970
3. *Train Ride.* New York, 1971
4. *Birthday.* New York, 1972
5. *My Special Best Words.* New York, 1974
6. *Marcia.* New York, 1976

Stevens, James (Floyd)
American, born November 15, 1892, died December 31, 1971
1. *Paul Bunyan.* New York, 1925
2. *Mattock.* New York, 1927
3. *Brawny-Man.* New York, 1928
4. *Homer in the Sagebrush.* New York, 1928
5. *The Saginaw Paul Bunyan.* New York, 1932
6. *Timber! The Way of Life in the Lumber Camps.* Evanston (IL), 1942
7. *Paul Bunyan's Bears.* Seattle (WA), 1947
8. *Big Jim Turner.* New York, 1948

Stevenson, Anne
1. *Ralph Dacre.* New York and London, 1967
2. *Flash of Splendour.* London, 1968
3. *A Relative Stranger.* New York and London, 1970
4. *A Game of Statues.* New York and London, 1972
5. *The French Inheritance.* New York and London, 1974
6. *Coil of Serpents.* New York and London, 1977
7. *Mask of Treason.* New York, 1979
8. *Turkish Rondo.* New York and London, 1981

Stevenson, Florence
American
Pseudonyms: Zandra Colt, Lucia Curzon, Zabrina Faire
1. *The Story of Aida, Based on the Opera by Giuseppe Verdi.* New York, 1965
2. *Ophelia.* New York, 1968
3. *Feast of Eggshells.* New York, 1970
4. *The Curse of the Concullens.* New York, 1970
5. *The Witching Hour.* New York, 1971
6. *Where Satan Dwells.* New York, 1971
7. *Bianca,* with Patricia Hagan Murray. New York, 1973
8. *Kilmeny in the Dark Wood.* New York, 1973
9. *Altar of Evil.* New York, 1973
10. *The Mistress of Devil's Manor.* New York, 1973
11. *The Sorcerer of the Castle.* New York, 1974
12. *Dark Odyssey.* New York, 1974
13. *The Ides of November.* New York, 1975
14. *A Shadow on the House.* New York, 1975
15. *Witch's Crossing.* New York, 1975
16. *The Silent Watcher.* New York, 1975
17. *A Darkness on the Stairs.* New York, 1976
18. *The House at Luxor.* New York, 1976
19. *Dark Encounter.* New York, 1977

20. *The Horror from the Tombs.* New York, 1977
21. *Call Me Counselor.* Philadelphia, 1977
22. *Julie.* New York, 1978
23. *The Golden Galatea.* New York, 1979
24. *Lady Blue,* as Zabrina Faire. New York, 1979
25. *The Midnight Match,* as Zabrina Faire. New York, 1979
26. *The Romany Rebel,* as Zabrina Faire. New York, 1979
27. *Enchanting Jenny,* as Zabrina Faire. New York, 1979
28. *Wicked Cousin,* as Zabrina Faire. New York, 1980
29. *Athena's Airs,* as Zabrina Faire. New York, 1980
30. *Bold Pursuit,* as Zabrina Faire. New York, 1980
31. *The Moonlight Variations.* New York, 1981
32. *Pretender to Love.* New York, 1981
33. *Pretty Kitty.* New York, 1981
34. *Tiffany's True Love.* New York, 1981
35. *The Chadbourne Luck,* as Lucia Curzon. New York, 1981
36. *Adverse Alliance,* as Lucia Curzon. New York, 1981
37. *The Mourning Bride,* as Lucia Curzon. New York, 1982
38. *The Cactus Rose,* as Zandra Colt. New York, 1982

Stewart, J.I.M. (John Innes Mackintosh)
British, born September 30, 1906
Pseudonym: Michael Innes

1. *Death at the President's Lodging,* as Michael Innes. London, 1936
2. *Seven Suspects,* as Michael Innes. New York, 1937
3. *Hamlet, Revenge!* as Michael Innes. London and New York, 1937
4. *Lament for a Maker,* as Michael Innes. London and New York, 1938
5. *Stop Press,* as Michael Innes. London, 1939
6. *The Spider Strikes,* as Michael Innes. New York, 1939
7. *The Secret Vanguard,* as Michael Innes. London, 1940
8. *There Came Both Mist and Snow,* as Michael Innes. London, 1940
9. *A Comedy of Terrors,* as Michael Innes. New York, 1940
10. *Appleby on Ararat,* as Michael Innes. London and New York, 1941
11. *The Daffodil Affair,* as Michael Innes. London and New York, 1942
12. *The Weight of the Evidence,* as Michael Innes. New York, 1943
13. *Educating the Emotions.* Adelaide (Australia), 1944
14. *Appleby's End,* as Michael Innes. London and New York, 1945
15. *From London Far,* as Michael Innes. London, 1946
16. *The Unsuspected Chasm,* as Michael Innes. New York, 1946
17. *What Happened at Hazelwood?* as Michael Innes. London and New York, 1946
18. *A Night of Errors,* as Michael Innes. New York, 1947
19. *The Journeying Boy,* as Michael Innes. London, 1949
20. *The Case of the Journeying Boy,* as Michael Innes. New York, 1949
21. *Character and Motive in Shakespeare: Some Recent Appraisals Examined.* London, 1949
22. *Three Tales of Hamlet,* as Michael Innes. London, 1950
23. *Operation Pax,* as Michael Innes. London, 1951
24. *The Paper Thunderbolt,* as Michael Innes. New York, 1951
25. *A Private View,* as Michael Innes. London, 1952
26. *One-Man Show,* as Michael Innes. New York, 1952
27. *Christmas at Candleshoe,* as Michael Innes. London and New York, 1953
28. *Appleby Talking: Twenty-Three Detective Stories,* as Michael Innes. London, 1954
29. *Dead Man's Shoes,* as Michael Innes. New York, 1954
30. *Mark Lambert's Supper.* London, 1954
31. *The Man from the Sea,* as Michael Innes. London and New York, 1955
32. *The Guardians.* London, 1955
33. *Old Hall, New Hall,* as Michael Innes. London, 1956
34. *A Question of Queens,* as Michael Innes. New York, 1956
35. *Appleby Talks Again: Eighteen Detective Stories,* as Michael Innes. London, 1956
36. *Death by Moonlight,* as Michael Innes. New York, 1957
37. *Appleby Plays Chicken,* as Michael Innes. London, 1957
38. *Death on a Quiet Day,* as Michael Innes. New York, 1957
39. *A Use of Riches.* London and New York, 1957
40. *James Joyce.* London, 1957
41. *The Long Farewell,* as Michael Innes. London and New York, 1958
42. *Hare Sitting Up,* as Michael Innes. London and New York, 1959
43. *The Man Who Wrote Detective Stories and Other Stories.* London and New York, 1959
44. *The New Sonia Wayward,* as Michael Innes. London, 1960
45. *The Case of Sonia Wayward,* as Michael Innes. New York, 1960
46. *Silence Observed,* as Michael Innes. London and New York, 1961
47. *The Man Who Won the Pools.* London and New York, 1961
48. *The Last of Sonia Wayward,* as Michael Innes. New York, 1962
49. *A Connoisseur's Case,* as Michael Innes. London, 1962
50. *The Crabtree Affair,* as Michael Innes. New York, 1962
51. *The Last Tresilians.* London and New York, 1963
52. *Thomas Love Peacock.* London, 1963
53. *Eight Modern Writers.* London and New York, 1963
54. *Money from Holme,* as Michael Innes. London, 1964
55. *An Acre of Grass.* London, 1965
56. *The Bloody Wood,* as Michael Innes. London and New York, 1966
57. *A Change of Heir,* as Michael Innes. London and New York, 1966
58. *The Aylwins.* London, 1966
59. *Rudyard Kipling.* London and New York, 1966
60. *Vanderlyn's Kingdom.* London, 1967
61. *Appleby at Allington,* as Michael Innes. London, 1968
62. *Death by Water,* as Michael Innes. New York, 1968
63. *Joseph Conrad.* London and New York, 1968
64. *A Family Affair,* as Michael Innes. London, 1969
65. *Picture of Guilt,* as Michael Innes. New York, 1969
66. *Cucumber Sandwiches and Other Stories.* London and New York, 1969
67. *Death at the Chase,* as Michael Innes. London and New York, 1970
68. *An Awkward Lie,* as Michael Innes. London and New York, 1971
69. *Avery's Mission.* London and New York, 1971
70. *Thomas Hardy: A Critical Biography.* London and New York, 1971
71. *Shakespeare's Lofty Scene.* London, 1971
72. *The Open House,* as Michael Innes. London and New York, 1972
73. *A Palace of Art.* London, 1972
74. *Appleby's Answer,* as Michael Innes. London and New York, 1973
75. *Mungo's Dream,* as Michael Innes. London and New York, 1973
76. *Appleby's Other Story,* as Michael Innes. London and New York, 1974
77. *The Mysterious Commission,* as Michael Innes. London, 1974
78. *The Gaudy.* London, 1974
79. *The Appleby File,* as Michael Innes. London, 1975
80. *Young Pattullo.* London, 1975

81. *The Gay Phoenix,* as Michael Innes. London, 1976
82. *A Memorial Service.* London and New York, 1976
83. *Honeybath's Haven,* as Michael Innes. London, 1977
84. *The Madonna of the Astrolabe.* London and New York, 1977
85. *The Amperstand Papers,* as Michael Innes. London, 1978
86. *Full Term.* London, 1978
87. *Going It Alone,* as Michael Innes. London, 1979
88. *Our England Is a Garden and Other Stories.* London, 1979

Stewart, Mary (Florence Elinor)
British, born September 17, 1916
1. *Madam, Will You Talk?* London, 1955
2. *Wildfire at Midnight.* London and New York, 1956
3. *Thunder on the Right.* London, 1957
4. *Nine Coaches Waiting.* London, 1958
5. *My Brother Michael.* London and New York, 1960
6. *The Ivy Tree.* London, 1961
7. *The Moon-Spinners.* London, 1962
8. *This Rough Magic.* London and New York, 1964
9. *Airs above the Ground.* London and New York, 1965
10. *The Gabriel Hounds.* London and New York, 1967
11. *The Wind Off the Small Isles.* London, 1968
12. *The Crystal Cave.* London and New York, 1970
13. *The Little Broomstick.* Leicester (Eng), 1971
14. *The Hollow Hills.* London and New York, 1973
15. *Ludo and the Star Horse.* Leicester, 1974
16. *Touch Not the Cat.* London and New York, 1976
17. *The Last Enchantment.* London and New York, 1979

Stine, Hank [Henry Eugene Stine]
American, born April 13, 1945
1. *Season of the Witch.* New York, 1968
2. *Thrill City.* New York, 1969
3. *A Day in the Life.* New York, 1970

Stockton, Frank R. [Francis Richard Stockton]
American, born April 5, 1834, died April 20, 1902
1. *Ting-a-Ling.* Boston, 1870
2. *Roundabout Rambles in Lands of Fact and Fancy.* New York, 1872
3. *What Might Have Been Expected.* New York, 1874
4. *Tales Out of School.* New York, 1875
5. *Rudder Grange.* New York, 1879
6. *A Jolly Friendship.* New York and London, 1880
7. *The Floating Prince and Other Fairy Tales.* New York and London, 1881
8. *Ting-a-Ling Tales.* New York, 1882
9. *The Lady or the Tiger? and Other Stories.* New York, 1884
10. *The Transferred Ghost.* New York, 1884
11. *The Story of Viteau.* New York and London, 1884
12. *The Bee-Man of Orn and Other Fanciful Tales.* New York, 1887
13. *The Queen's Museum.* New York, 1887
14. *The Dusantes.* New York and London, 1888
15. *Amos Kilbright, His Adscititious Experiences, with Other Stories.* New York and London, 1888
16. *The Great War Syndicate.* New York and London, 1889
17. *Personally Conducted.* New York and London, 1889
18. *The Stories of the Three Burglars.* New York and London, 1890
19. *The Merry Chanter.* New York and London, 1890
20. *Ardis Claverden.* New York and London, 1890
21. *The House of Martha.* Boston and London, 1891
22. *The Squirrel Inn.* New York and London, 1891
23. *The Rudder Grangers Abroad.* New York and London, 1891
24. *The Clocks of Rondaine and Other Stories.* New York and London, 1892
25. *The Watchmaker's Wife and Other Stories.* New York, 1893
26. *The Shadrach and Other Stories.* London, 1893
27. *Pomona's Travels.* New York and London, 1894
28. *Fanciful Tales.* New York, 1894
29. *The Adventures of Captain Horn.* New York and London, 1895
30. *A Chosen Few.* New York, 1895
31. *Mrs. Cliff's Yacht.* New York and London, 1896
32. *Captain Chap; or, The Rolling Stones.* Philadelphia and London, 1896
33. *New Jersey, from the Discovery of the Scheyichbi to Recent Times.* New York, 1896
34. *Stories of New Jersey.* New York, 1896
35. *A Story-Teller's Pack.* New York and London, 1897
36. *The Great Stone of Sardis.* New York and London, 1898
37. *The Girl at Cobhurst.* New York and London, 1898
38. *The Associate Hermits.* New York and London, 1898
39. *The Buccaneers and Pirates of Our Coasts.* New York, 1898
40. *The Young Master of Hyson Hall.* Philadelphia, 1899
41. *The Vizier of the Two-Horned Alexander.* New York and London, 1899
42. *A Bicycle in Cathay.* New York, 1900
43. *Afield and Afloat.* New York and London, 1901
44. *Kate Bonnet.* New York and London, 1902
45. *John Gayther's Garden.* New York and London, 1903
46. *The Captain's Toll Gate.* New York and London, 1903
47. *The Magic Egg and Other Stories.* New York, 1907
48. *Stories of the Spanish Main.* New York, 1913
49. *The Poor Count's Christmas.* New York, 1927

Stoker, Bram
Irish, born November 8, 1847, died April 20, 1945
1. *The Duties of Clerks of Petty Sessions in Ireland.* Privately printed, 1879
2. *Under the Sunset.* London, 1881
3. *A Glimpse of America.* London, 1886
4. *The Snake's Pass.* London and New York, 1890
5. *The Watter's Mou'.* London and New York, 1894
6. *Crooken Sands.* New York, 1894
7. *The Man from Shorrox's.* New York, 1894
8. *The Shoulder of Shasta.* London, 1895
9. *Dracula.* London, 1897
10. *Miss Betty.* London, 1898
11. *The Mystery of the Sea.* London and New York, 1902
12. *The Jewel of Seven Stars.* London, 1903
13. *The Man.* London, 1905
14. *Lady Athlyne.* London and New York, 1908
15. *Snowbound: The Record of a Theatrical Touring Party.* London, 1908
16. *The Gates of Life.* New York. 1908
17. *The Lady of the Shroud.* London, 1909
18. *Famous Imposters.* London and New York, 1910
19. *The Lair of the White Worm.* London, 1911
20. *Dracula's Guest and Other Weird Stories.* London, 1914
21. *The Garden of Evil.* New York, 1966
22. *Dracula's Curse.* New York, 1968
23. *The Bram Stoker Bedside Companion: Stories of Fantasy and Horror.* London, 1973

Stolz, Mary (Slattery)
American, born March 24, 1920
1. *To Tell Your Love.* New York, 1950
2. *The Organdy Cupcakes.* New York, 1951
3. *The Sea Gulls Woke Me.* New York, 1951
4. *The Leftover Elf.* New York, 1952
5. *In a Mirror.* New York, 1953
6. *Truth and Consequence.* New York, 1953
7. *Ready or Not.* New York, 1953

8. *Pray Love, Remember.* New York, 1954
9. *Two by Two.* Boston, 1954
10. *A Love or a Season.* New York, 1964
11. *Rosemary.* New York, 1955
12. *Hospital Zone.* New York, 1956
13. *The Day and the Way We Met.* New York, 1956
14. *Good-by, My Shadow.* New York, 1957
15. *Because of Madeline.* New York, 1957
16. *And Love Replied.* New York, 1958
17. *Second Nature.* New York, 1958
18. *Emmitt's Pig.* New York, 1959
19. *Some Merry-Go-Round Music.* New York, 1959
20. *The Beautiful Friend and Other Stories.* New York, 1960
21. *A Dog on Barkham Street.* New York, 1960
22. *Belling the Tiger.* New York, 1961
23. *Wait for Me, Michael.* New York, 1961
24. *The Great Rebellion.* New York, 1961
25. *Fredou.* New York, 1962
26. *Pigeon Flight.* New York, 1962
27. *Siri, The Conquistador.* New York, 1963
28. *The Bully of Barkham Street.* New York, 1963
29. *Who Wants Music on Monday?* New York, 1963
30. *The Mystery of the Woods.* New York, 1964
31. *The Noonday Friends.* New York, 1965
32. *Maximilian's World.* New York, 1966
33. *A Wonderful, Terrible Time.* New York, 1967
34. *Say Something.* New York, 1968
35. *The Dragons of the Queen.* New York, 1969
36. *The Story of a Singular Hen and Her Peculiar Children.* New York, 1969
37. *Juan.* New York, 1970
38. *By the Highway Home.* New York, 1971
39. *Leap Before You Look.* New York, 1972
40. *Lands End.* New York, 1973
41. *The Edge of Next Year.* New York, 1974
42. *Cat in the Mirror.* New York, 1975
43. *Ferris Wheel.* New York, 1977

Stong, Phil [Philip Duffield Stong]
American, born January 27, 1899, died April 26, 1957
1. *State Fair.* New York and London, 1932
2. *The Stranger's Return.* New York and London, 1933
3. *Village Tale.* New York and London, 1934
4. *Farm Boy.* New York, 1934
5. *The Farmer in the Dell.* New York, 1935
6. *Week-end.* New York, 1935
7. *Honk: The Story of a Moose.* New York, 1935
8. *Career.* New York and London, 1936
9. *Buckskin Breeches.* New York and London, 1937
10. *The Rebellion of Lennie Barlow.* New York, 1937
11. *No-Sitch, The Hound.* New York, 1936
12. *High Water.* New York, 1937
13. *County Fair.* New York, 1938
14. *Edgar, The 7:58.* New York, 1938
15. *Young Settler.* New York, 1938
16. *Horses and Americans.* New York, 1939
17. *Ivanhoe Keeler.* New York, 1939
18. *The Long Lane.* New York, 1939
19. *Cowhand Goes to Town.* New York, 1939
20. *The Hired Man's Elephant.* New York, 1939
21. *If School Keeps.* New York, 1940
22. *Hawkeyes: A Biography of the State of Iowa.* New York, 1940
23. *The Princess.* New York, 1941
24. *Captain Kidd's Cow.* New York, 1941
25. *One Destiny.* New York, 1942
26. *The Iron Mountain.* New York, 1942
27. *Way Down Cellar.* New York, 1942
28. *Missouri Canary.* New York, 1943
29. *Marta of Muscovy: The Fabulous life of Russia's First Empress.* New York, 1945
30. *Censored, The Goat.* New York, 1945
31. *Gold in Them Hills, Being an Irreverent History of the Great 1849 Gold Rush.* New York, 1947
32. *Positive Pete!* New York, 1947
33. *Jessamy John.* New York, 1947
34. *The Prince and the Porker.* New York, 1950
35. *Forty Pounds of Gold.* New York, 1951
36. *Hirum the Hillbilly.* New York, 1951
37. *Return in August.* New York, 1953
38. *Mississippi Pilot.* New York, 1954
39. *Blizzard.* New York, 1955
40. *A Beast Called an Elephant.* New York, 1955
41. *The Adventures of "Horse" Barsby.* New York, 1956
42. *Mike: The Story of a Young Circus Acrobat.* New York, 1957

Stout, Rex (Todhunter)
American, born December 1, 1886, died October 27, 1975
1. *How Like a God.* New York, 1929
2. *Seed on the Wind.* New York, 1930
3. *Golden Remedy.* New York, 1931
4. *Forest Fire.* New York, 1933
5. *Fer-de-Lance.* New York, 1934
6. *The President Vanishes.* New York, 1934
7. *The League of Frightened Men.* New York and London, 1935
8. *O Careless Love!* New York, 1935
9. *The Rubber Band.* New York and London, 1936
10. *The Red Box.* New York and London, 1937
11. *The Hand in the Glove.* New York, 1937
12. *Too Many Cooks.* New York and London, 1938
13. *Mr. Cinderella.* New York, 1938
14. *Crime on Her Hands.* London, 1939
15. *Some Buried Caesar.* New York and London, 1939
16. *Mountain Cat.* New York, 1939
17. *Double for Death.* New York, 1939
18. *Over My Dead Body.* New York and London, 1940
19. *Where There's a Will.* New York, 1940
20. *The Broken Vase.* New York, 1941
21. *Alphabet Hicks.* New York, 1941
22. *Black Orchids.* New York, 1942
23. *Not Quite Dead Enough.* New York, 1944
24. *The Red Bull.* New York, 1945
25. *The Silent Speaker.* New York, 1946
26. *Too Many Women.* New York, 1947
27. *And Be a Villain.* New York, 1948
28. *More Deaths Than One.* London, 1949
29. *The Second Confession.* New York, 1949
30. *Trouble in Triplicate.* New York and London, 1949
31. *Three Doors to Death.* New York and London, 1950
32. *In the Best Families.* New York, 1950
33. *Curtains for Three.* New York, 1950
34. *Even in the Best Families.* London, 1951
35. *Murder by the Book.* New York, 1951
36. *Triple Jeopardy.* New York, 1951
37. *Prisoner's Base.* New York, 1952
38. *Out Goes She.* London, 1953
39. *The Golden Spiders.* New York, 1953
40. *Three Men Out.* New York, 1954
41. *The Black Mountain.* New York, 1954
42. *Before Midnight.* New York, 1955
43. *Might As Well Be Dead.* New York, 1956
44. *Three Witnesses.* New York and London, 1956
45. *Three for the Chair.* New York, 1957
46. *If Death Ever Slept.* New York, 1957

47. *Champagne for One.* New York, 1958
48. *And Four to Go.* New York, 1958
49. *Crime and Again.* London, 1959
50. *Plot It Yourself.* New York, 1959
51. *Murder in Style.* London, 1960
52. *Three at Wolfe's Door.* New York, 1960
53. *Too Many Clients.* New York, 1960
54. *To Kill Again.* New York, 1960
55. *The Final Deduction.* New York, 1961
56. *Gambit.* New York, 1962
57. *Homicide Trinity.* New York, 1962
58. *The Mother Hunt.* New York, 1963
59. *Trio for Blunt Instruments.* New York, 1964
60. *A Right to Die.* New York, 1964
61. *The Doorbell Rang.* New York, 1965
62. *The Sound of Murder.* New York, 1965
63. *Death of a Doxy.* New York, 1966
64. *The Father Hunt.* New York, 1968
65. *Death of a Dude.* New York, 1969
66. *Please Pass the Guilt.* New York, 1973
67. *The Nero Wolfe Cook Book,* with others. New York, 1973
68. *A Family Affair.* New York, 1975
69. *Justice Ends at Home and Other Stories.* New York, 1977

Strange, John Stephen [Dorothy Stockbridge Tillett]
American, born in 1896
1. *Paths of June.* New York, 1920
2. *The Man Who Killed Fortescue.* New York, 1928
3. *The Clue of the Second Murder.* New York, 1929
4. *The Strangler Fig.* New York, 1930
5. *Murder on the Ten-Yard Line.* New York, 1931
6. *Murder Game.* London, 1931
7. *Black Hawthorn.* New York, 1933
8. *The Chinese Jar Mystery.* London, 1934
9. *For the Hangman.* New York, 1934
10. *The Bell in the Fog.* New York, 1936
11. *Silent Witnesses.* New York, 1938
12. *The Corpse and the Lady.* London, 1938
13. *Rope Enough.* New York, 1938
14. *A Picture of the Victim.* New York, 1940
15. *Murder Gives a Lovely Light.* New York, 1941
16. *Look Your Last.* New York, 1943
17. *Murder at World's End.* New York, 1943
18. *The Ballot Box Murders.* New York, 1943
19. *Angry Dust.* New York, 1946
20. *Make My Bed Soon.* New York and London, 1948
21. *All Men Are Liars.* New York, 1948
22. *Come to Judgement.* London, 1949
23. *Unquiet Grave.* New York, 1949
24. *Uneasy Is the Grave.* London, 1950
25. *Reasonable Doubt.* New York and London, 1951
26. *Deadly Beloved.* New York and London, 1952
27. *Let The Dead Past—.* New York, 1953
28. *Dead End.* London, 1953
29. *The Fair and the Dead.* New York, 1953
30. *Catch the Gold Ring.* New York, 1955
31. *A Handful of Silver.* London, 1955
32. *Night of Reckoning.* New York, 1958
33. *Eye Witness.* New York, 1961
34. *The House on 9th Street.* New York, 1976

Strete, Craig
American
1. *If All Else Fails, We Can Whip the Horse's Eyes and Make Him Cry and Sleep.* Amsterdam (NY), 1976
2. *The Bleeding Man and Other Science Fiction Stories.* New York, 1977
3. *When Grandfather Journeys into Winter.* New York, 1979

Stribling, T.S. (Theodore Sigismond)
American, born March 4, 1881, died July 10, 1965
1. *The Cruise of the Dry Dock.* Chicago, 1917
2. *Birthright.* New York, 1922
3. *Fombombo.* New York and London, 1923
4. *Red Sand.* New York and London, 1924
5. *Teeftallow.* New York and London, 1926
6. *Bright Metal.* New York and London, 1928
7. *East Is East.* New York, 1928
8. *Strange Moon.* New York and London, 1929
9. *Clues of the Caribbees, Being Certain Criminal Investigations of Henry Poggioli, Ph.D.* New York, 1929
10. *Backwater.* New York and London, 1930
11. *The Forge.* New York and London, 1931
12. *The Store.* New York and London, 1932
13. *Unfinished Cathedral.* New York and London, 1934
14. *The Sound Wagon.* New York, 1935
15. *These Bars of Flesh.* New York, 1938
16. *Best Dr. Poggioli Detective Stories.* New York, 1975

Sturgeon, Theodore [Edward Hamilton Waldo]
American, born February 26, 1918
Other pseudonyms: Frederick R. Ewing, Ellery Queen
1. *Without Sorcery.* Philadelphia, 1948
2. *The Dreaming Jewels.* New York, 1950
3. *More Than Human.* New York, 1953
4. *E Pluribus Unicorn.* New York, 1953
5. *Caviar.* New York, 1955
6. *A Way Home.* New York and London, 1955
7. *I, Libertine,* as Frederick R. Ewing. New York, 1956
8. *The King and Four Queens.* New York, 1956
9. *Thunder and Roses.* London, 1957
10. *The Synthetic Man.* New York, 1957
11. *The Cosmic Rape.* New York, 1958
12. *A Touch of Strange.* New York, 1958
13. *Aliens 4.* New York, 1959
14. *Venus Plus X.* New York, 1960
15. *Beyond.* New York, 1960
16. *Voyage to the Bottom of the Sea.* New York, 1961
17. *Not Without Sorcery.* New York, 1961
18. *Some of Your Blood.* New York, 1961
19. *. . . and My Fear Is Great; Baby Is Three.* New York, 1963
20. *The Player on the Other Side,* as Ellery Queen. New York, 1963
21. *Sturgeon in Orbit.* New York, 1964
22. *The Joyous Invasions.* London, 1965
23. *Starshine.* New York, 1966
24. *The Rare Breed.* New York, 1966
25. *Sturgeon Is Alive and Well.* New York, 1971
26. *The Worlds of Theodore Sturgeon.* New York, 1972
27. *Sturgeon's West.* New York, 1973
28. *To Here and the Easel.* London, 1973
29. *Visions and Venturers.* New York, 1978
30. *Maturity.* Minneapolis (MN), 1979
31. *The Golden Helix.* New York, 1979
32. *The Stars Are the Styx.* New York, 1979

Sublette, C.M. (Clifford MacClellan)
American, born August 16, 1887, died in 1939
1. *The Scarlet Cockerel.* Boston, 1925
2. *The Bright Face of Danger.* Boston, 1926
3. *The Golden Chimney.* Boston, 1931
4. *Greenhorn's Hunt.* Indianapolis (IN), 1934
5. *Perilous Journey: A Tale of the Mississippi River and the Natchez Trace.* Indianapolis, 1943

Suddaby, Donald
British, born in 1900, died March 17, 1964

Pseudonym: Alan Griff
1. *Scarlet-Dragon: A Little Chinese Phantasy.* Blackburn (Eng), 1923
2. *Lost Men in the Grass,* as Alan Griff. London, 1940
3. *Masterless Swords: Variations on a Theme.* London, 1947
4. *New Tales of Robin Hood.* London, 1950
5. *The Star Raiders.* London, 1950
6. *The Death of Metal.* London, 1952
7. *Merry Jack Jugg, Highwayman.* London, 1954
8. *Village Fanfare: or, The Man from the Future.* London, 1954
9. *The Moon of Snowshoes.* London, 1956
10. *Prisoners of Saturn.* London, 1957
11. *Fresh News from Sherwood.* London, 1959
12. *Crowned with White Olive.* London, 1961
13. *Tower of Babel.* London, 1962
14. *A Bell in the Forest.* London, 1964
15. *Robin Hood's Master Stroke.* London, 1965

Swarthout, Glendon (Fred)
American, born April 8, 1918
1. *Willow Run.* New York, 1943
2. *They Came to Cordura.* New York and London, 1958
3. *Where the Boys Are.* New York and London, 1960
4. *Welcome to Thebes.* New York, 1962
5. *The Ghost and the Magic Saber,* with Kathryn Swarthout. New York, 1963
6. *The Cadillac Cowboys.* New York, 1964
7. *The Eagle and the Iron Cross.* New York, 1966
8. *Whichaway,* with Kathryn Swarthout. New York, 1966
9. *Loveland.* New York, 1968
10. *The Button Boat,* with Kathryn Swarthout. New York, 1969
11. *Bless the Beasts and Children.* New York and London, 1970
12. *The Tin Lizzie Troop.* New York and London, 1972
13. *TV Thompson,* with Kathryn Swarthout. New York, 1972
14. *Luck and Pluck.* New York and London, 1973
15. *The Shootist.* New York and London, 1975
16. *The Melodeon.* New York and London, 1977
17. *Skeletons.* New York and London, 1979
18. *Cadbury's Coffin,* with Kathryn Swarthout. New York, 1982

Symons, Julian (Gustave)
British, born May 30, 1912
1. *Confusions about X.* London, 1939
2. *The Second Man.* London, 1943
3. *The Immaterial Murder Case.* London, 1945
4. *A Man Called Jones.* London, 1947
5. *Bland Beginning.* London and New York, 1949
6. *The Thirty-First of February.* London and New York, 1950
7. *A.J.A. Symons: His Life and Speculations.* London, 1950
8. *Charles Dickens.* London and New York, 1951
9. *Thomas Carlyle: The Life and Ideas of a Prophet.* London and New York, 1952
10. *The Broken Penny.* London and New York, 1953
11. *The Narrowing Circle.* London and New York, 1954
12. *Horatio Bottomley.* London, 1955
13. *The Paper Chase.* London, 1956
14. *Bogue's Fortune.* New York, 1957
15. *The Colour of Murder.* London and New York, 1957
16. *The General Strike: A Historical Portrait.* London, 1957
17. *The Gigantic Shadow.* London, 1958
18. *The Pipe Dream.* New York, 1959
19. *The 100 Best Crime Stories.* London, 1959
20. *The Progress of a Crime.* London and New York, 1960
21. *The Thirties: A Dream Revolved.* London, 1960
22. *A Reasonable Doubt: Some Criminal Cases Re-examined.* London, 1960
23. *Murder! Murder!* London, 1961
24. *The Killing of Francie Lake.* London, 1962
25. *The Plain Man.* New York, 1962
26. *The Detective Story in Britain.* London, 1962
27. *Buller's Campaign.* London, 1963
28. *The End of Solomon Grundy.* London and New York, 1964
29. *The Belting Inheritance.* London and New York, 1965
30. *Francis Quarles Investigates.* London, 1965
31. *England's Pride: The Story of the Gordon Relief Expedition.* London, 1965
32. *Crime and Detection: An Illustrated History from 1840.* London, 1966
33. *A Pictorial History of Crime.* New York, 1966
34. *Critical Occasions.* London, 1966
35. *The Man Who Killed Himself.* London and New York, 1967
36. *The Man Whose Dreams Came True.* London, 1968
37. *The Man Who Lost His Wife.* London, 1970
38. *The Players and the Game.* London and New York, 1972
39. *Bloody Murder.* London, 1972
40. *Mortal Consequences.* New York, 1972
41. *Notes from Another Country.* London, 1972
42. *The Plot Against Roger Rider.* London and New York, 1973
43. *The Object of an Affair and Other Poems.* Edinburgh (Scotland), 1974
44. *A Three-Pipe Problem.* London and New York, 1975
45. *Ellery Queen Presents Julian Symons' How To Trap a Crook and Twelve Other Mysteries.* New York, 1977
46. *The Blackheath Poisonings.* London, 1978
47. *The Tell-Tale Heart: The Life and Works of Edgar Allan Poe.* London and New York, 1978

Tall, Stephen [Compton Newby Crook]
American, born June 14, 1908
1. *The Stardust Voyages.* New York, 1975
2. *The Ramsgate Paradox.* New York, 1976
3. *The People Beyond the Wall.* New York, 1980

Tate, Joan
British, born September 23, 1922
1. *Jenny.* London, 1964
2. *The Crane.* London, 1964
3. *The Rabbit Boy.* London, 1964
4. *Coal Hoppy.* London, 1964
5. *The Next-Doors.* London, 1964
6. *The Silver Grill.* London, 1964
7. *Picture Charlie.* London, 1964
8. *Lucy.* London, 1964
9. *The Tree.* London, 1966
10. *The Holiday.* London, 1966
11. *Tad.* London, 1966
12. *Bill.* London, 1966
13. *Mrs. Jenny.* London, 1966
14. *Bits and Pieces.* London, 1967
15. *The New House.* Stockholm (Sweden), 1967
16. *The Soap Box Car.* Stockholm, 1967
17. *The Old Car.* Stockholm, 1967
18. *The Great Birds.* Stockholm, 1967
19. *The Train.* Stockholm, 1967
20. *Polly.* Stockholm, 1967
21. *The Circus and Other Stories.* London, 1967
22. *Letters to Chris.* London, 1967
23. *Wild Martin and the Crow.* London, 1967
24. *Luke's Garden.* London, 1967
25. *Sam and Me.* London, 1968
26. *Out of the Sun.* London, 1969
27. *Whizz Kid.* London, 1969

28. *The Letter.* Stockholm, 1969
29. *Puddle's Tiger.* Stockholm, 1969
30. *The Caravan.* Stockholm, 1969
31. *Edward and the Uncles.* Stockholm, 1969
32. *The Secret.* Stockholm, 1969
33. *Clipper.* London, 1969
34. *Ring on My Finger.* London, 1971
35. *The Long Road Home.* London, 1971
36. *Gramp.* London, 1971
37. *Wild Boy.* London, 1972
38. *Wump Day.* London, 1972
39. *Your Town.* Newton Abbot (Eng), 1972
40. *How Do You Do?* Paderborn (Eng), 1973
41. *Ben and Annie.* Leicester (Eng), 1973
42. *Tina and David.* Nashville (TN), 1973
43. *Not the Usual Kind of Girl.* New York, 1973
44. *Dad's Camel.* London, 1973
45. *Jock and the Rock Cakes.* Leicester, 1973
46. *Grandpa and My Little Sister Bee.* Leicester, 1973
47. *Taxi!* Paderborn, 1973
48. *Night Out.* Stockholm, 1973
49. *The Match.* Stockholm, 1973
50. *Dina.* Stockholm, 1973
51. *Journal for One.* Stockholm, 1973
52. *The Man Who Rang the Bell.* Stockholm, 1973
53. *Ginger Mock.* London, 1974
54. *The Runners.* Newton Abbot, 1974
55. *Dirty Dan.* Stockholm, 1974
56. *Sandy's Trumpet.* Stockholm, 1974
57. *Zena.* Stockholm, 1974
58. *The Thinking Box.* Stockholm, 1974
59. *Going Up.* Stockholm, 3 vols, 1969-74
60. *The Living River.* London, 1974
61. *Your Dog.* London, 1975
62. *The New House.* London, 1976
63. *The House That Jack Built.* London, 1976
64. *Crow and the Brown Boy.* London, 1976
65. *Polly and the Barrow Boy.* London, 1976
66. *Billogs.* London, 1976
67. *You Can't Explain Everything.* London, 1976
68. *See You and Other Stories.* London, 1977
69. *On Your Own 1.* Exeter (Eng), 1977

Tate, Peter
British
1. *The Thinking Seat.* New York, 1969
2. *Country Love and Poison Rain.* New York, 1973
3. *Moon on an Iron Meadow.* New York, 1974
4. *Seagulls under Glass.* New York, 1975
5. *Faces in the Flames.* New York, 1976
6. *Greencomber.* New York, 1979

Tattersall, Jill [Honor Jill Tattersall]
British, born December 18, 1931
1. *A Summer's Cloud.* London, 1965
2. *Enchanter's Castle.* London, 1966
3. *The Midnight Oak.* London, 1967
4. *Lyonesse Abbey.* London and New York, 1968
5. *A Time at Tarragon.* London, 1969
6. *Lady Ingram's Retreat.* London, 1970
7. *Midsummer Masque.* London and New York, 1972
8. *The Wild Hunt.* London and New York, 1974
9. *The Witches of All Saints.* London and New York, 1975
10. *The Shadows of Castle Fosse.* New York and London, 1976
11. *Chanters Chase.* New York and London, 1978
12. *Dark at Noon.* New York and London, 1979
13. *Damnation Reef.* New York, 1979
14. *Lady Ingram's Room.* New York, 1981

Taylor, Phoebe Atwood
American, born May 18, 1909, died January 9, 1976
Pseudonym: Alice Tilton
1. *The Cape Cod Mystery.* Indianapolis (IN), 1931
2. *Death Lights a Candle.* Indianapolis, 1932
3. *The Mystery of the Cape Cod Players.* New York, 1933
4. *The Mystery of the Cape Cod Tavern.* New York, 1934
5. *Sandbar Sinister.* New York, 1934
6. *The Tinkling Symbol.* New York and London, 1935
7. *Deathblow Hill.* New York, 1935
8. *The Crimson Patch.* New York and London, 1936
9. *Out of Order.* New York, 1936
10. *Figure Away.* New York, 1937
11. *Octagon House.* New York, 1937
12. *Beginning with a Bash,* as Alice Tilton. London, 1937
13. *The Annulet of Guilt.* New York, 1938
14. *Banbury Bog.* New York, 1938
15. *The Cut Direct,* as Alice Tilton. New York and London, 1938
16. *Spring Harrowing.* New York and London, 1939
17. *Cold Steal,* as Alice Tilton. New York, 1939
18. *The Criminal C.O.D.* New York and London, 1940
19. *The Deadly Sunshade.* New York, 1940
20. *The Left Leg,* as Alice Tilton. New York, 1940
21. *The Perennial Boarder.* New York, 1941
22. *The Hollow Chest,* as Alice Tilton. New York, 1941
23. *The Six Iron Spiders.* New York, 1942
24. *Three Plots for Asey Mayo.* New York, 1942
25. *Going, Going, Gone.* New York, 1943
26. *File for Record,* as Alice Tilton. New York, 1943
27. *Dead Ernest,* as Alice Tilton. New York, 1944
28. *Proof of the Pudding.* New York and London, 1945
29. *The Asey Mayo Trio.* New York and London, 1946
30. *Punch with Care.* New York, 1946
31. *The Iron Clew,* as Alice Tilton. New York, 1947
32. *The Iron Hand,* as Alice Tilton. London, 1947
33. *Diplomatic Corpse.* Boston and London, 1951

Taylor, Robert Lewis
American, born September 24, 1912
1. *Adrift in a Boneyard.* New York, 1947
2. *Doctor, Lawyer, Merchant, Chief.* New York, 1948
3. *W.C. Fields: His Follies and Fortunes.* New York, 1949
4. *The Running Pianist.* New York, 1950
5. *Professor Fodorski: A Politico-Sporting Romance.* New York, 1950
6. *The Bright Sands.* New York and London, 1954
7. *Center Ring: The People of the Circus.* New York, 1956
8. *The Travels of Jamie McPheeters.* New York, 1958
9. *A Journey to Matecumbe.* New York and London, 1961
10. *Two Roads to Guadalupe.* New York, 1964
11. *A Roaring in the Wind, Being a History of Alder Gulch, Montana, in Its Great and Shameful Days.* New York, 1978

Taylor, Sydney (Brenner)
American, born October 31, 1904
1. *All-of-a-Kind Family.* Chicago, 1951
2. *More All-of-a-Kind Family.* Chicago, 1954
3. *All-of-a-Kind Family Uptown.* Chicago, 1958
4. *Mr. Barney's Beard.* Chicago, 1961
5. *Now That You Are Eight.* New York, 1963
6. *A Papa Like Every One Else.* Chicago, 1966
7. *The Dog Who Came to Dinner.* Chicago, 1966
8. *All-of-a-Kind Family Downtown.* Chicago, 1972

Taylor, Theodore
American, born June 23, 1921
1. *The Magnificent Miyscher.* New York, 1954

2. *The Body Trade.* New York, 1958
3. *People Who Make Movies.* New York, 1967
4. *The Cay.* New York, 1969
5. *The Children's War.* New York, 1971
6. *The Maldonado Miracle.* New York, 1973
7. *Teetoncey.* New York, 1974
8. *Teetoncey and Ben o'Neal.* New York, 1975
9. *The Odyssey of Ben O'Neal.* New York, 1977

Telfair, Richard
1. *Wyoming Jones.* New York, 1958
2. *Day of the Gun.* New York, 1958
3. *The Secret of Apache Canyon.* New York, 1959
4. *Wyoming Jones for Hire.* New York, 1959
5. *The Bloody Medallion.* New York, 1959
6. *The Corpse That Talked.* New York, 1959
7. *Scream Bloody Murder.* New York, 1960
8. *Sundance.* New York, 1960
9. *Good Luck, Sucker.* New York, 1961
10. *The Slavers.* New York, 1961
11. *Target for Tonight.* New York, 1962

Tenn, William [Philip Klass]
American, born in 1920
1. *Of All Possible Worlds.* New York, 1955
2. *The Human Angle.* New York, 1956
3. *Time in Advance.* New York, 1958
4. *A Lamp for Medusa.* New York, 1968
5. *Of Men and Monsters.* New York, 1968
6. *The Seven Sexes.* New York, 1968
7. *The Square Root of Man.* New York, 1968
8. *The Wooden Star.* New York, 1968

Tennant, Emma (Christina)
British, born October 20, 1937
Pseudonym: Catherine Aydy
1. *The Colour of Rain,* as Catherine Aydy. London, 1964
2. *The Time of the Crack.* London, 1973
3. *The Last of the Country House Murders.* London, 1974
4. *Hotel de Dream.* London, 1976
5. *The Crack.* London, 1978
6. *The Bad Sister.* London and New York, 1978
7. *Wild Nights.* London, 1979
8. *Alice Fell.* London, 1980
9. *The Boggart.* London, 1980

Tevis, Walter (Stone)
American, born February 28, 1928
1. *The Hustler.* New York, 1959
2. *The Man Who Fell to Earth.* New York and London, 1963
3. *Mockingbird.* New York and London, 1980
4. *Far from Home.* New York, 1981

Tey, Josephine [Elizabeth Mackintosh]
British, born in 1887, died February 13, 1952
Other pseudonym: Gordon Daviot
1. *The Man in the Queue,* as Gordon Daviot. London and New York, 1929
2. *Kif: An Unvarnished History.* London and New York, 1929
3. *The Expensive Halo.* London and New York, 1931
4. *A Shilling for Candles: The Story of a Crime.* London, 1936
5. *Claverhouse.* London, 1937
6. *Miss Pym Disposes.* London, 1946
7. *The Franchise Affair.* London, 1948
8. *Brat Farrar.* London, 1949
9. *To Love and Be Wise.* London, 1950
10. *Come and Kill Me.* New York, 1951
11. *The Daughter of Time.* London, 1951
12. *The Singing Sands.* London, 1952
13. *The Privateer.* London and New York, 1952

Thane, Elswyth
American, born May 16, 1900
1. *Riders of the Wind.* New York, 1926
2. *Echo Answers.* New York and London, 1927
3. *His Elizabeth.* New York and London, 1928
4. *Cloth of Gold.* New York and London, 1929
5. *Bound to Happen.* New York and London, 1930
6. *The Tudor Wench.* London, 1933
7. *Queen's Folly.* New York and London, 1937
8. *Tryst.* New York and London, 1939
9. *England Was an Island Once.* New York, 1940
10. *Remember Today: Leaves from a Guardian Angel's Notebook.* New York, 1941
11. *From This Day Forward.* New York, 1941
12. *Dawn's Early Light.* New York, 1943
13. *Yankee Stranger.* New York, 1944
14. *Ever After.* New York, 1945
15. *The Light Heart.* New York, 1947
16. *The Bird Who Made Good.* New York, 1947
17. *Kissing Kin.* New York, 1948
18. *Reluctant Farmer.* New York, 1950
19. *This Was Tomorrow.* New York, 1951
20. *Homing.* New York, 1957
21. *Melody.* New York, 1950
22. *The Lost General.* New York, 1953
23. *Letter to a Stranger.* New York, 1954
24. *Duell.* No place, 1959
25. *Washington's Lady.* New York, 1960
26. *Potomac Squire.* New York, 1963
27. *Mount Vernon Family.* New York, 1968
28. *The Virginia Colony.* New York, 1969
29. *The Strength of the Hills.* New York, 1976

Thayer, Lee [Emma Redington Thayer]
American, born April 5, 1874, died November 18, 1973
1. *Alice and the Wonderland People.* New York, 1914
2. *When Mother Lets Us Draw.* New York, 1916
3. *The Mystery of the Thirteenth Floor.* New York, 1919
4. *The Unlatched Door.* New York, 1920
5. *That Affair at "The Cedars."* New York, 1921
6. *Q.E.D.* New York, 1922
7. *The Puzzle.* London, 1923
8. *The Sinister Mark.* New York and London, 1923
9. *The Key.* New York and London, 1924
10. *Doctor S.O.S.* New York and London, 1925
11. *Poison.* New York and London, 1926
12. *Alias Dr. Ely.* New York and London, 1927
13. *The Darkest Spot.* New York and London, 1928
14. *Dead Men's Shoes.* New York and London, 1929
15. *They Tell No Tales.* New York and London, 1930
16. *The Last Shot.* New York and London, 1931
17. *Set a Thief.* New York, 1931
18. *To Catch a Thief.* London, 1932
19. *The Glass Knife.* New York and London, 1932
20. *The Scrimshaw Millions.* New York, 1932
21. *Counterfeit.* New York, 1933
22. *The Counterfeit Bill.* London, 1934
23. *Hell-Gate Tides.* New York and London, 1933
24. *The Second Bullet.* New York, 1934
25. *The Second Shot.* London, 1935
26. *Dead Storage.* New York, 1935
27. *The Death Weed.* London, 1935
28. *Sudden Death.* New York, 1935
29. *Red-Handed.* London, 1936

30. *Dark of the Moon.* New York, 1936
31. *Dead End Street, No Outlet.* New York, 1936
32. *Murder in the Mirror.* London, 1936
33. *Last Trump.* New York and London, 1937
34. *Death in the Gorge.* London, 1937
35. *A Man's Enemies.* New York, 1937
36. *This Man's Doom.* London, 1938
37. *Ransom Racket.* New York and London, 1938
38. *That Strange Sylvester Affair.* New York, 1938
39. *Lightning Strikes Twice.* New York and London, 1939
40. *Stark Murder.* New York, 1939
41. *Guilty.* New York, 1940
42. *X Marks the Spot.* New York, 1940
43. *Hallowe'en Homicide.* New York, 1941
44. *Persons Unknown.* New York, 1941
45. *Murder Is Out.* New York, 1942
46. *Murder on Location.* New York, 1942
47. *Accessory after the Fact.* New York, 1943
48. *Hanging's Too Good.* New York, 1943
49. *A Plain Case of Murder.* New York, 1944
50. *Five Bullets.* New York, 1944
51. *Accident, Manslaughter, or Murder?* New York, 1945
52. *A Hair's Breadth.* New York, 1946
53. *The Jaws of Death.* New York, 1946
54. *Murder Stalks the Circle.* New York, 1947
55. *Out, Brief Candle!* New York, 1948
56. *Pig in a Poke.* New York, 1948
57. *Evil Root.* New York, 1949
58. *Within the Vault.* New York, 1950
59. *Too Long Endured.* New York, 1950
60. *Death Within the Vault.* London, 1951
61. *Do Not Disturb.* New York, 1951
62. *Guilt Edged.* New York, 1951
63. *Clancy's Secret Mission.* London, 1952
64. *Blood on the Knight.* New York, 1952
65. *Guilt-Edged Murder.* London, 1953
66. *The Prisoner Pleads "Not Guilty."* New York, 1953
67. *Dead Reckoning.* New York, 1954
68. *No Holiday for Death.* New York, 1954
69. *Murder on the Pacific.* London, 1955
70. *Who Benefits?* New York, 1955
71. *Fatal Alibi.* London, 1956
72. *Guilt Is Where You Find It.* New York, 1957
73. *Still No Answer.* New York, 1958
74. *Web of Hate.* London, 1959
75. *Two Ways to Die.* New York, 1959
76. *Dead on Arrival.* New York, 1960
77. *And One Cried Murder.* New York, 1961
78. *Dusty Death.* New York, 1966
79. *Death Walks in Shadow.* London, 1966

Thomas, Ross
American, born February 19, 1926
Pseudonym: Oliver Bleeck
1. *The Cold War Swap.* New York, 1966
2. *Spy in the Vodka.* London, 1967
3. *Cast a Yellow Shadow.* New York, 1967
4. *The Seersucker Whipsaw.* New York, 1967
5. *The Singapore Wink.* New York and London, 1969
6. *The Brass Go-Between,* as Oliver Bleeck. New York, 1969
7. *The Fools in Town Are on Our Side.* London, 1970
8. *The Backup Men.* New York and London, 1971
9. *Protocol for a Kidnapping,* as Oliver Bleeck. New York and London, 1971
10. *The Procane Chronicle,* as Oliver Bleeck. New York, 1972
11. *The Thief Who Painted Sunlight,* as Oliver Bleeck. London, 1972
12. *The Porkchoppers.* New York, 1972
13. *If You Can't Be Good.* New York, 1973
14. *The Highbinders,* as Oliver Bleeck. New York and London, 1974
15. *The Money Harvest.* New York and London, 1975
16. *Yellow-Dog Contract.* New York, 1976
17. *St. Ives,* as Oliver Bleeck. New York, 1976
18. *No Questions Asked,* as Oliver Bleeck. New York and London, 1976
19. *Chinaman's Chance.* New York and London, 1978
20. *The Eighth Dwarf.* New York and London, 1979

Thomason, Jr., John W. (William)
American, born February 28, 1893, died March 12, 1944
1. *Fix Bayonets!* New York, 1926
2. *Red Pants and Other Stories.* New York, 1927
3. *Marines and Others.* New York, 1929
4. *Jeb Stuart.* New York, 1930
5. *Salt Winds and Gobi Dust.* New York, 1934
6. *Gone to Texas.* New York, 1937
7. *Lone Star Preacher, Being a Chronicle of the Acts of Praxiteles Swan.* New York, 1941
8. *—and a Few Marines.* New York, 1943
9. *Texas Rebel.* New York, 1961
10. *A Thomason Sketchbook: Drawings.* Austin (TX), 1969

Thompson, Thomas
American, born February 24, 1913
1. *Range Drifter.* New York, 1949
2. *Broken Valley.* New York, 1949
3. *Sundown Riders.* New York, 1950
4. *Gunman Brand.* New York, 1951
5. *Shadow of the Butte.* New York, 1952
6. *The Steel Web.* New York, 1953
7. *King of Abilene.* New York, 1953
8. *Trouble Rider.* New York, 1954
9. *They Brought Their Guns.* New York, 1954
10. *Forbidden Valley.* New York, 1955
11. *Born to Gunsmoke.* New York, 1956
12. *Rawhide Rider.* New York, 1957
13. *Brand of a Man.* New York, 1958
14. *Bitter Water.* New York and London, 1960
15. *Bonanza: One Man with Courage.* New York, 1966
16. *Gun of the Stranger.* London, 1960
17. *Moment of Glory.* New York, 1961

Thomson, Basil (Home)
British, born April 21, 1861, died March 26, 1939
1. *The Diversions of a Prime Minister.* Edinburgh (Scotland), 1894
2. *South Sea Yarns.* Edinburgh, 1894
3. *A Court Intrigue.* London, 1896
4. *The Indiscretions of Lady Asneath.* London, 1898
5. *Savage Island: An Account of a Sojourn in Niue and Tonga.* London, 1902
6. *The Fijians: A Study of the Decay of Custom.* London, 1908
7. *Queer People.* London, 1922
8. *Mr. Pepper, Investigator.* London, 1925
9. *The Criminal.* London, 1925
10. *Carfax Abbey.* London, 1928
11. *The Metal Flask.* London, 1929
12. *The Prince from Overseas.* London, 1930
13. *P.C. Richardson's First Case.* London and New York, 1933
14. *The Kidnapper.* London, 1933
15. *Richardson Scores Again.* London, 1934
16. *Richardson's Second Case.* New York, 1934
17. *Inspector Richardson, C.I.D.* London, 1934
18. *The Case of Naomi Clynes.* New York, 1934

19. *Richardson Goes Abroad.* London, 1935
20. *The Case of the Dead Diplomat.* New York, 1935
21. *Richardson Solves a Dartmoor Mystery.* London, 1935
22. *The Story of Scotland Yard.* London, 1935
23. *The Gold Repeater: A Detective Story for Boys.* London, 1936
24. *The Dartmoor Enigma.* New York, 1936
25. *Death in the Bathroom.* London, 1936
26. *Who Killed Stella Pomeroy?* New York, 1936
27. *The Scene Changes.* New York, 1937
28. *Milliner's Hat Mystery.* London, 1937
29. *The Mystery of the French Milliner.* New York, 1937
30. *A Murder Arranged.* London, 1937
31. *When Thieves Fall Out.* New York, 1937

Thomson, June
British, born June 24, 1930
1. *Not One of Us.* New York, 1971
2. *Death Cap.* London, 1973
3. *The Long Revenge.* London, 1974
4. *Case Closed.* London and New York, 1977
5. *A Question of Identity.* New York, 1977
6. *Deadly Relations.* London, 1979
7. *The Habit of Loving.* New York, 1979

Thorpe, Kay
1. *Devon Interlude.* London, 1968
2. *The Last of the Mallorys.* London and Toronto, 1968
3. *Opportune Marriage.* London, 1968
4. *Rising Star.* London and Toronto, 1969
5. *Curtain Call.* London and Toronto, 1971
6. *Not Wanted on Voyage.* London and Toronto, 1972
7. *Olive Island.* London, 1972
8. *Sawdust Season.* London and Toronto, 1972
9. *Man in a Box.* London, 1972
10. *An Apple in Eden.* London, 1973
11. *The Man at Kambala.* London, 1973
12. *Remember This Stranger.* London, 1974
13. *The Iron Man.* London, 1974
14. *The Shifting Sands.* London and Toronto, 1975
15. *Sugar Cane Harvest.* London, 1975
16. *The Royal Affair.* Toronto, 1976
17. *Safari South.* London, 1976
18. *The River Lord.* Toronto, 1977
19. *Storm Passage.* Toronto, 1977.
20. *Lord of La Pampa.* London, 1977
21. *Bitter Alliance.* London, 1978
22. *Full Circle.* London, 1978
23. *Timber Boss.* London and Toronto, 1978
24. *The Wilderness Trail.* London, 1978
25. *Caribbean Encounter.* Toronto, 1978
26. *The Dividing Line.* London, 1979
27. *The Man from Tripoli.* London and Toronto, 1979
28. *This Side of Paradise.* London, 1979
29. *Chance Meeting.* London and Toronto, 1980
30. *No Passing Fancy.* London, 1980
31. *Copper Lake.* London and Toronto, 1981
32. *Floodtide.* Toronto, 1981

Thorpe, Sylvia [June Sylvia Thimblethorpe]
British, born in 1926
1. *The Scandalous Lady Robin.* London, 1950
2. *The Sword and the Shadow.* London, 1951
3. *Beggar on Horseback.* London, 1953
4. *Smuggler's Moon.* London, 1955
5. *The Golden Panther.* London, 1956
6. *Sword of Vengeance.* London, 1957
7. *Rogues' Covenant.* London, 1957
8. *Captain Gallant.* London, 1958
9. *Beloved Rebel.* London, 1959
10. *Romantic Lady.* London, 1960
11. *The Devil's Bondsman.* London, 1961
12. *The Highwayman.* London, 1962
13. *The House at Bell Orchard.* London, 1962
14. *The Reluctant Adventuress.* London, 1963
15. *Fair Shine the Day.* London, 1964
16. *Spring Will Come Again.* London, 1965
17. *Strangers on the Moor.* New York, 1966
18. *The Changing Tide.* London, 1967
19. *Dark Heritage.* London, 1968
20. *No More A-Roving.* London, 1970
21. *The Scarlet Domino.* London, 1970
22. *The Scapegrace.* London, 1971
23. *Dark Enchantress.* London, 1973
24. *The Silver Nightingale.* London and New York, 1974
25. *The Witches of Conyngton.* London, 1976
26. *Tarrington Chase.* London, 1977
27. *A Flash of Scarlet.* New York, 1978
28. *The Varleigh Medallion.* London and New York, 1979
29. *The Avenhurst Inheritance.* London, 1981

Thurber, James (Grover)
American, born December 8, 1884, died November 2, 1961
1. *Is Sex Necessary? or, Why You Feel the Way You Do,* with E.B. White. New York, 1929
2. *The Owl in the Attic and Other Perplexities.* New York and London, 1931
3. *The Seal in the Bedroom and Other Predicaments.* New York and London, 1932
4. *My Life and Hard Times.* New York and London, 1933
5. *The Middle-aged Man on the Flying Trapeze: A Collection of Short Piece.* New York and London, 1935
6. *Let Your Mind Alone! and Other More or Less Inspirational Pieces.* New York and London, 1937
7. *Cream of Thurber. . . .* London, 1939
8. *The Last Flower: A Parable in Pictures.* New York and London, 1939
9. *Fables for Our Time and Famous Poems Illustrated.* New York and London, 1940
10. *My World and Welcome to It.* New York and London, 1942
11. *Men, Women, and Dogs: A Book of Drawings.* New York, 1943
12. *Many Moons.* New York, 1943
13. *The Great Quillow.* New York, 1944
14. *The Thurber Carnival.* New York and London, 1945
15. *The White Deer.* New York, 1945
16. *The Beast in Me, and Other Animals: A New Collection of Pieces and Drawings about Human Beings and Less Alarming Creatures.* New York, 1948
17. *The 13 Clocks.* New York, 1950
18. *The Thurber Album: A New Collection of Pieces about People.* New York and London, 1952
19. *Thurber Country: A New Collection of Pieces about Males and Females, Mainly of Our Own Species.* New York and London, 1953
20. *Thurber on Humor.* Columbus (OH), 1953(?)
21. *Thurber's Dogs: A Collection of the Master's Dogs, Written and Drawn, Real and Imaginary, Living and Long Ago.* New York and London, 1955
22. *A Thurber Garland.* London, 1955
23. *The Wonderful O.* New York and London, 1955
24. *Further Fables for Our Time.* New York and London, 1956
25. *Alarms and Diversions.* New York and London, 1957
26. *The Years with Ross.* Boston and London, 1959
27. *Lanterns and Lances.* New York and London, 1961
28. *Credos and Curios.* New York and London, 1962

Tidyman, Ernest
American, born January 1, 1928
1. *Flower Power.* New York, 1968
2. *The Anzio Death Trap.* New York, 1968
3. *Shaft.* New York, 1970
4. *Absolute Zero.* New York, 1971
5. *Shaft among the Jews.* New York, 1972
6. *Shaft's Big Score.* New York and London, 1972
7. *Shaft Has a Ball.* New York and London, 1973
8. *Goodbye, Mr. Shaft.* New York, 1973
9. *High Plains Drifter.* New York and London, 1973
10. *Shaft's Carnival of Killers.* New York, 1974
11. *Line of Duty.* Boston and London, 1974
12. *Dummy.* Boston and London, 1974
13. *The Last Shaft.* London, 1975
14. *Starstruck.* London, 1975
15. *Table Stakes.* Boston, 1979

Tippette, Giles
American, born August 25, 1934
Pseudonym: Wilson Young
1. *The Bank Robber.* New York, 1970
2. *The Spikes Gang.* New York, 1971
3. *The Trojan Cow.* New York, 1971
4. *The Brave Men.* New York, 1972
5. *Saturday's Children.* New York, 1973
6. *Austin Davis,* as Wilson Young. New York, 1974
7. *The Sunshine Killers,* as Wilson Young. New York, 1974
8. *The Survivalist.* New York, 1975
9. *The Mercenaries.* New York, 1976
10. *Wilson's Gold.* New York, 1980
11. *Wilson's Luck.* New York, 1980
12. *Wilson's Choice.* New York, 1981
13. *Wilson's Revenge.* New York, 1981
14. *Wilson's Woman.* New York, 1982
15. *The Texas Bank Robbing Company.* New York, 1982

Titus, Eve
American, born July 16, 1922
Pseudonym: Nancy Lord
1. *Anatole.* New York, 1956
2. *Anatole and the Cat.* New York, 1957
3. *Basil of Baker Street.* New York, 1958
4. *My Dog and I,* as Nancy Lord. New York, 1958
5. *Anatole and the Robot.* New York, 1960
6. *Anatole over Paris.* New York, 1961
7. *The Mouse and the Lion.* New York, 1962
8. *Basil and the Lost Colony.* New York, 1964
9. *Anatole and the Poodle.* New York, 1964
10. *Anatole and the Piano.* New York, 1966
11. *The Two Stonecutters.* New York, 1967
12. *Anatole and the Thirty Thieves.* New York and London, 1969
13. *Mr. Shaw's Shipshape Shoeshop.* New York, 1970
14. *Anatole and the Toyshop.* New York, 1970
15. *Basil and the Pygmy Cats.* New York, 1971
16. *Why the Wind God Wept.* New York, 1972
17. *Anatole in Italy.* New York, 1973
18. *Basil in Mexico.* New York, 1976

Todd, Barbara Euphan
British, died February 2, 1976
Pseudonyms: Barbara Bower, Euphan
1. *The 'normous Saturday Fairy Book,* with Marjory Royce and Moira Meighn. London, 1924
2. *The 'normous Sunday Story Book,* with Marjory Royce and Moira Meighn. London, 1925
3. *The Very Good Walkers,* with Marjory Royce. London, 1925
4. *Hither and Thither.* London, 1927
5. *Mr. Blossom's Shop.* London, 1929
6. *Happy Cottage,* with Marjory Royce. London, 1930
7. *South Country Secrets,* as Euphan, with Klaxon. London, 1935
8. *The Touchstone,* with Klaxon. London, 1935
9. *The Seventh Daughter,* as Euphan. London, 1935
10. *Worzel Gummidge; or, The Scarecrow of Scatterbrook.* London, 1936
11. *Worzel Gummidge Again.* London, 1937
12. *The Mystery Train.* London, 1937
13. *The Splendid Picnic.* London, 1937
14. *Stories of the Coronations,* as Euphan. London, 1937
15. *More about Worzel Gummidge.* London, 1938
16. *Mr. Dock's Garden.* Leeds (Eng), 1939
17. *Gertrude the Greedy Goose.* London, 1939
18. *The House That Ran Behind,* with Esther Boumphrey. London, 1943
19. *Miss Ranskill Comes Home,* as Barbara Bower. London, 1946
20. *Worzel Gummidge, The Scarecrow of Scatterbrook Farm.* New York, 1947
21. *Worzel Gummidge and Saucy Nancy.* London, 1947
22. *Worzel Gummidge Takes a Holiday.* London, 1949
23. *Aloysius Let Loose.* London, 1950
24. *Earthy Mangold and Worzel Gummidge.* London, 1954
25. *Worzel Gummidge and the Railway Scarecrows.* London, 1955
26. *Worzel Gummidge at the Circus.* London, 1956
27. *The Boy with the Green Thumb.* London, 1956
28. *The Wizard and the Unicorn.* London, 1957
29. *Worzel Gummidge and the Treasure Ship.* London, 1958
30. *The Shop Around the Corner.* London, 1959
31. *Detective Worzel Gummidge.* London, 1963
32. *The Shop by the Sea.* London, 1966
33. *The Clock Shop.* Kingswood (Eng), 1967
34. *The Shop on Wheels.* Kingswood, 1968
35. *The Box in the Attic.* Kingswood, 1970
36. *The Wand from France.* Kingswood, 1972

Tolbert, Frank X. [Frank Xavier Tolbert, Sr.]
American, born July 27, 1912
1. *Neiman-Marcus: The Story of the Proud Dallas Store.* New York, 1953
2. *Bigamy Jones.* New York, 1954
3. *The Staked Plain.* New York, 1958
4. *The Day of San Jacinto.* New York, 1959
5. *Dick Dowling at Sabine Press.* New York, 1962
6. *The Story of Lyne Taliaferro (Tol) Barret, Who Drilled Texas' First Oil Well.* Dallas, 1966
7. *A Bowl of Red.* New York, 1966

Tolkien, J.R.R. (John Ronald Reuel)
British, born January 3, 1892, died September 2, 1973
1. *A Middle English Vocabulary.* London and New York, 1922
2. *Songs for the Philologists,* with others. London, 1936
3. *The Hobbit; or, There and Back Again.* London, 1937
4. *Beowulf: The Monsters and the Critics.* London, 1937
5. *Farmer Giles of Ham.* London, 1949
6. *The Lord of the Rings: The Fellowship of the Ring.* London and Boston, 1954
7. *The Lord of the Rings: The Two Towers.* London and Boston, 1955
8. *The Lord of the Rings: The Return of the King.* London and Boston, 1956
9. *The Adventures of Tom Bombadil and Other Verses from the Red Book.* London, 1962
10. *Tree and Leaf.* London, 1964

11. *The Tolkien Reader.* New York, 1966
12. *Smith of Wootton Major.* London and Boston, 1967
13. *The Road Goes Ever On.* Boston, 1967
14. *Bilbo's Last Song.* London and Boston, 1974
15. *Tree and Leaf, Smith of Wootton Major, The Homecoming of Beorhtnoth Beorhthelm's Son.* London, 1975
16. *The Father Christmas Letters.* London and Boston, 1976
17. *The Silmarillion.* London and Boston, 1977

Tomalin, Ruth
British
Pseudonym: Ruth Leaver
1. *Threnody for Dormice.* London, 1947
2. *The Day of the Rose: Essays and Portraits.* London, 1947
3. *Green Ink,* as Ruth Leaver. London, 1951
4. *Deer's Cry.* London, 1952
5. *All Souls.* London, 1952
6. *W.H. Hudson.* London and New York, 1954
7. *The Sound of Pens,* as Ruth Leaver. London, 1955
8. *The Daffodil Bird.* London, 1959
9. *The Sea Mice.* London, 1962
10. *The Garden House.* London, 1964
11. *The Spring House.* London, 1968
12. *Away to the West.* London, 1972
13. *A Green Wishbone.* London, 1975
14. *A Stranger Thing.* London, 1975
15. *The Snake Crook.* London, 1976

Tompkins, Walker A. (Allison)
American, born July 10, 1909
1. *Ozar, The Aztec.* London, 1935
2. *Red-Hot Holsters.* Akron (OH), 1938
3. *The Border Eagle.* New York, 1939
4. *Deadhorse Express.* New York, 1940
5. *Wyoming Trail.* New York, 1940
6. *Senor Desperado: A Novel of Early California.* London, 1940
7. *The Phantom Sheriff.* New York, 1941
8. *Thundergust Trail.* New York, 1942
9. *The Wyoming Raiders.* New York, 1942
10. *Border Bonanza.* New York, 1943
11. *Ghost Mine Gold.* New York, 1943
12. *Texas Tumbleweed.* New York, 1943
13. *Six-Gun Legacy.* London, 1943
14. *Trouble on Funeral Range.* New York, 1944
15. *The Scout of Terror Trail.* New York, 1944
16. *Texas Guns.* London, 1945
17. *Lion of the Lavabeds.* New York, 1947
18. *Flaming Canyon.* Philadelphia, 1948
19. *West of Texas Law.* Philadelphia, 1948
20. *West of the Law.* London, 1948
21. *Santa Fe Trail.* New York, 1948
22. *Manhunt West.* Philadelphia, 1949
23. *The Paintin' Pistoleer: Humorous Tales of the Old West.* New York, 1949
24. *Rider.* Philadelphia, 1950
25. *Roy Rogers and the Ghost of Mystery Rancho.* Racine (WI), 1950
26. *Border Ambush.* Philadelphia, 1951
27. *Prairie Marshal.* Philadelphia, 1952
28. *Haunted Corral.* London, 1952
29. *Pistol Empire.* London, 1952
30. *Gold on the Hoof.* Philadelphia and London, 1953
31. *Guns of Massacre Gap.* London, 1953
32. *One Against a Bullet Horde.* New York, 1954
33. *Texas Renegade.* Philadelphia, 1954
34. *Deadwood.* New York, 1954
35. *SOS at Midnight.* Philadelphia, 1957
36. *CQ Ghost Ship.* Philadelphia, 1960
37. *Santa Barbara's Royal Rancho.* Berkeley (CA), 1960
38. *DX Brings Danger.* Philadelphia, 1962
39. *California's Wonderful Corner.* Charlotte (NC), 1962
40. *Santa Barbara Yesterdays.* Santa Barbara (CA), 1962
41. *Fourteen at the Table.* Privately printed, 1964
42. *Goleta: The Good Land.* Goleta (CA), 1966
43. *Stearns Wharf Centennial.* Santa Barbara, 1972
44. *Mattei's Tavern: Where Road Met Rail.* Santa Barbara, 1974
45. *It Happened in Old Santa Barbara.* Santa Barbara, 1976
46. *Continuing Quest.* Santa Barbara, 1977
47. *When Disaster Strikes.* Santa Barbara, 1981
48. *Stagecoach Days in Santa Barbara County.* Santa Barbara, 1982

Torday, Ursula
British
Pseudonyms: Paula Allardyce, Charity Blackstock, Lee Blackstock, Charlotte Keppel
1. *The Ballad-Maker of Paris.* London, 1935
2. *No Peace for the Wicked.* London, 1937
3. *The Mirror of the Sun.* London, 1938
4. *After the Lady,* as Paula Allardyce. London, 1954
5. *The Doctor's Daughter,* as Paula Allardyce. London, 1955
6. *A Game of Hazard,* as Paula Allardyce. London, 1955
7. *Adam and Evelina,* as Paula Allardyce. London, 1956
8. *The Man of Wrath,* as Paula Allardyce. London, 1956
9. *Dewey Death,* as Charity Blackstock. London, 1956
10. *Miss Fenny,* as Charity Blackstock. London, 1957
11. *The Lady and the Pirate,* as Paula Allardyce. London, 1957
12. *Southarn Folly,* as Paula Allardyce. London, 1957
13. *Beloved Enemy,* as Paula Allardyce. London, 1958
14. *My Dear Miss Emma,* as Paula Allardyce. London, 1958
15. *The Woman in the Woods,* as Lee Blackstock. New York, 1958
16. *All Men Are Murderers,* as Charity Blackstock. New York, 1958
17. *The Foggy, Foggy Dew,* as Charity Blackstock. London, 1958
18. *Death My Lover,* as Paula Allardyce. London, 1959
19. *A Marriage Has Been Arranged,* as Paula Allardyce. London, 1959
20. *The Foggy, Foggy Dew, and Dewey Death,* as Charity Blackstock. New York, 1959
21. *The Shadow of Murder,* as Charity Blackstock. London, 1959
22. *The Bitter Conquest,* as Charity Blackstock. London, 1959
23. *The Briar Patch,* as Charity Blackstock. London, 1960
24. *Young Lucifer,* as Charity Blackstock. Philadelphia, 1960
25. *Johnny Danger,* as Paula Allardyce. London, 1960
26. *The Exorcism,* as Charity Blackstock. London, 1961
27. *Witches' Sabbath,* as Paula Allardyce. London, 1961
28. *The Gentle Highwayman,* as Paula Allardyce. London, 1961
29. *A House Possessed,* as Charity Blackstock. Philadelphia, 1962
30. *The Gallant,* as Charity Blackstock. London, 1962
31. *Mr. Christopoulos,* as Charity Blackstock. London, 1963
32. *Adam's Rib,* as Paula Allardyce. London, 1963
33. *The Factor's Wife,* as Charity Blackstock. London, 1964
34. *The English Wife,* as Charity Blackstock. New York, 1964
35. *The Respectable Miss Parkington-Smith,* as Paula Allardyce. London, 1964
36. *When the Sun Goes Down,* as Charity Blackstock. London, 1965
37. *Monkey on a Chain,* as Charity Blackstock. New York, 1965
38. *Octavia; or, The Trials of a Romantic Novelist,* as Paula Allardyce. London, 1965

39. *The Knock at Midnight*, as Charity Blackstock. London, 1966
40. *The Moonlighters*, as Paula Allardyce. London, 1966
41. *The Children*. Boston, 1966
42. *Wednesday's Children*. London, 1967
43. *Party in Dolly Creek*, as Charity Blackstock. London, 1967
44. *The Widow*, as Charity Blackstock. New York, 1967
45. *Six Passengers for the "Sweet Bird,"* as Paula Allardyce. London, 1967
46. *Waiting at the Church*, as Paula Allardyce. London, 1968
47. *The Melon in the Cornfield*, as Charity Blackstock. London, 1969
48. *The Lemmings*, as Charity Blackstock. New York, 1969
49. *The Daughter*, as Charity Blackstock. New York, 1970
50. *The Ghost of Archie Gilroy*, as Paula Allardyce. London, 1970
51. *The Encounter*, as Charity Blackstock. New York, 1971
52. *The Jungle*, as Charity Blackstock. London and New York, 1972
53. *The Lonely Strangers*, as Charity Blackstock. New York, 1972
54. *Miss Jonas's Boy*, as Paula Allardyce. London, 1972
55. *The Gentle Sex*, as Paula Allardyce. London, 1974
56. *Madam, You Must Die*, as Charlotte Keppel. London, 1974
57. *Loving Sands, Deadly Sands*, as Charlotte Keppel. New York, 1975
58. *People in Glass Houses*, as Charity Blackstock. London and New York, 1975
59. *Legacy of Pride*, as Paula Allardyce. New York, 1975
60. *Gentleman Rogue*, as Paula Allardyce. New York, 1975
61. *Eliza*, as Paula Allardyce. New York, 1975
62. *My Name Is Clary Brown*, as Charlotte Keppel. New York, 1976
63. *When I Say Goodbye, I'm Clary Brown*, as Charlotte Keppel. London, 1977
64. *Ghost Town*, as Charity Blackstock. London and New York, 1976
65. *Paradise Row*, as Paula Allardyce. New York, 1976
66. *Emily*, as Paula Allardyce. New York, 1976
67. *The Carradine Affair*, as Paula Allardyce. New York, 1976
68. *I Met Murder on the Way*, as Charity Blackstock. London, 1977
69. *The Shirt Front*, as Charity Blackstock. New York, 1977
70. *Miss Philadelphia Smith*, as Paula Allardyce. London, 1977
71. *Shadowed Love*, as Paula Allardyce. New York, 1977
72. *Haunting Me*, as Paula Allardyce. London, 1978
73. *Miss Charley*, as Charity Blackstock. London, 1979
74. *The Rebel Lover*, as Paula Allardyce. Chicago, 1979
75. *The Rogue's Lady*, as Paula Allardyce. Chicago, 1979
76. *With Fondest Thoughts*, as Charity Blackstock. London, 1980
77. *The Vixen's Revenge*, as Paula Allardyce. Chicago, 1980
78. *I Could Be Good to You*, as Charlotte Keppel. London and New York, 1980
79. *The Villains*, as Charlotte Keppel. Loughton (Eng), 1980
80. *The Ghosts of Fontenoy*, as Charlotte Keppel. Loughton, 1981
81. *Dream Towers*, as Charity Blackstock. London, 1981

Townsend, John Rowe
British, born May 10, 1922
1. *Gumble's Yard*. London, 1961
2. *Hell's Edge*. London, 1963
3. *Widdershins Crescent*. London, 1965
4. *Written for Children: An Outline of English Children's Literature*. London, 1965
5. *The Hallersage Sound*. London, 1966
6. *Good-bye to the Jungle*. Philadelphia, 1967
7. *Pirate's Island*. London and Philadelphia, 1968
8. *The Intruder*. London, 1969
9. *Trouble in the Jungle*. Philadelphia, 1969
10. *Goodnight, Prof. Love*. London, 1970
11. *Goodnight, Prof. Dear*. Philadelphia, 1971
12. *A Sense of Story: Essays on Contemporary Writers for Children*. London and Philadelphia, 1971
13. *The Summer People*. London and Philadelphia, 1972
14. *A Wish for Wings*. London, 1972
15. *Forest of the Night*. London, 1974
16. *Noah's Castle*. London, 1975
17. *Top of the World*. London, 1976
18. *The Xanadu Manuscript*. London, 1977
19. *The Visitors*. Philadelphia, 1977

Train, Arthur (Cheney)
American, born September 6, 1875, died December 22, 1945
1. *McAllister and His Double*. New York and London, 1905
2. *The Prisoner at the Bar*. New York, 1906
3. *Mortmain*. New York, 1907
4. *True Stories of Crime from the District Attorney's Office*. New York and London, 1908
5. *The Butler's Story*. New York and London, 1909
6. *The Confessions of Artemas Quibble*. New York, 1911
7. *"C.Q.;" or, In the Wireless House*. New York, 1912
8. *Courts, Criminals, and the Camorra*. New York and London, 1912
9. *The Man Who Rocked the Earth*, with Robert William Wood. New York, 1915
10. *The World and Thomas Kelly*. New York, 1917
11. *The Earthquake*. New York, 1918
12. *Tutt and Mr. Tutt*. New York, 1920
13. *As It Was in the Beginning*. New York, 1921
14. *The Hermit of Turkey Hollow*. New York, 1921
15. *By Advice of Counsel*. New York, 1921
16. *Courts and Criminals*. New York, 1921
17. *Tut, Tut! Mr. Tutt*. New York, 1923
18. *His Children's Children*. New York and London, 1923
19. *The Needle's Eye*. New York, 1924
20. *The Lost Gospel*. New York, 1925
21. *On the Trail of the Bad Men*. New York, 1925
22. *Page Mr. Tutt*. New York, 1926
23. *The Blind Goddess*. New York, 1926
24. *When Tutt Meets Tutt*. New York, 1927
25. *High Winds*. New York and London, 1927
26. *Ambition*. New York and London, 1928
27. *The Horns of Ramadan*. New York, 1928
28. *Illusion*. New York and London, 1929
29. *Paper Profits*. New York and London, 1930
30. *The Adventures of Ephraim Tutt*. New York, 1930
31. *Puritan's Progress*. New York, 1931
32. *Princess Pro Tem*. New York, 1932
33. *The Strange Attacks on Herbert Hoover*. New York, 1932
34. *No Matter Where*. New York, 1933
35. *Tutt for Tutt*. New York, 1934
36. *Jacob's Ladder*. New York, 1935
37. *Manhattan Murder*. New York, 1936
38. *Mr. Tutt Takes the Stand*. New York, 1936
39. *Mr. Tutt's Case Book*. New York, 1936
40. *Murderers' Medicine*. London, 1937
41. *Old Man Tutt*. New York, 1938
42. *From the District Attorney's Office*. London, 1939
43. *My Day in Court*. New York, 1939
44. *Tassels on Her Boots*. New York and London, 1940
45. *Mr. Tutt Comes Home*. New York, 1941
46. *Yankee Lawyer—Autobiography of Ephraim Tutt*. New York, 1943
47. *Mr. Tutt Finds a Way*. New York, 1945

48. *The Moon Maker,* with Robert William Wood. Hamburg (NY), 1958
49. *Mr. Tutt at His Best.* New York, 1961

Tranter, Nigel (Godwin)
British, born November 23, 1909
Pseudonym: Nye Tredgold

1. *The Fortalices and Early Mansions of Southern Scotland 1400-1650.* Edinburgh (Scotland), 1935
2. *Trespass.* Edinburgh, 1937
3. *Mammon's Daughter.* London, 1939
4. *Harsh Heritage.* London, 1939
5. *Eagles Feathers.* London, 1941
6. *Watershed.* London, 1941
7. *The Gilded Fleece.* London, 1942
8. *Delayed Action.* London, 1944
9. *Tinker's Pride.* London, 1945
10. *Man's Estate.* London, 1946
11. *Flight of Dutchmen.* London, 1947
12. *Island Twilight.* London, 1947
13. *Root and Branch.* London, 1948
14. *Colours Flying.* London, 1948
15. *The Chosen Course.* London, 1949
16. *Thirsty Range,* as Nye Tredgold. London, 1949
17. *Fair Game.* London, 1950
18. *High Spirits.* London, 1950
19. *The Freebooters.* London, 1950
20. *Heartbreak Valley,* as Nye Tredgold. London, 1950
21. *Tidewrack.* London, 1951
22. *Fast and Loose.* London, 1951
23. *Bridal Path.* London, 1952
24. *Cheviot Chase.* London, 1952
25. *The Big Corral,* as Nye Tredgold. London, 1952
26. *Trail Herd,* as Nye Tredgold. London, 1952
27. *Ducks and Drakes.* London, 1953
28. *The Queen's Grace.* London, 1953
29. *Desert Doublecross,* as Nye Tredgold. London, 1953
30. *Rum Week.* London, 1954
31. *The Night Riders.* London, 1954
32. *Cloven Hooves,* as Nye Tredgold. London, 1954
33. *There Are Worse Jungles.* London, 1955
34. *Rio d'Oro.* London, 1955
35. *Dynamite Trail,* as Nye Tredgold. London, 1955
36. *The Long Coffin.* London, 1956
37. *Rancher Renegade,* as Nye Tredgold. London, 1956
38. *MacGregor's Gathering.* London, 1957
39. *The Enduring Flame.* London, 1957
40. *Trailing Trouble,* as Nye Tredgold. London, 1957
41. *Dead Reckoning,* as Nye Tredgold. London, 1957
42. *Balefire.* London, 1958
43. *The Stone.* London, 1958
44. *Bloodstone Trail,* as Nye Tredgold. London, 1958
45. *Spaniards' Isle.* Leicester (Eng), 1958
46. *The Man Behind the Curtain.* London, 1959
47. *The Clansman.* London, 1959
48. *Border Rising.* Leicester, 1959
49. *Spanish Galleon.* London, 1960
50. *The Flockmasters.* London, 1960
51. *Nestor the Monster.* Leicester, 1960
52. *Kettle of Fish.* London, 1961
53. *The Master of Gray.* London, 1961
54. *Birds of a Feather.* Leicester, 1961
55. *The Deer Poachers.* London, 1961
56. *Drug on the Market.* London, 1962
57. *Gold for Prince Charlie.* London, 1962
58. *Something Very Fishy.* London, 1962
59. *The Fortified House in Scotland.* Edinburgh, 4 vols., 1962-66
60. *The Courtesan.* London, 1963
61. *Give a Dog a Bad Name.* London, 1963
62. *Chain of Destiny.* London, 1964
63. *Silver Island.* London, 1964
64. *Smoke Across the Highlands.* New York, 1964
65. *The Pegasus Book of Scotland.* London, 1964
66. *Past Master.* London, 1965
67. *Pursuit.* London, 1965
68. *Outlaw of The Highlands: Rob Roy.* London, 1965
69. *A Stake in the Kingdom.* London, 1966
70. *Lion Let Loose.* London, 1967
71. *Fire and High Water.* London, 1967
72. *Tinker Tess.* London, 1967
73. *Cable from Kabul.* London, 1968
74. *Black Douglas.* London, 1968
75. *To the Rescue.* London, 1968
76. *Land of the Scots.* London and New York, 1968
77. *The Steps to the Empty Throne.* London, 1969
78. *The Path of the Hero King.* London, 1970
79. *The Price of the King's Peace.* London, 1971
80. *The Queen's Scotland.* London 4 vols., 1971-77
81. *The Young Montrose.* London, 1972
82. *Portrait of the Border Country.* London, 1972
83. *Montrose, The Captain-General.* London, 1973
84. *The Wisest Fool.* London, 1974
85. *The Wallace.* London, 1975
86. *Lords of Misrule.* London, 1976
87. *A Folly of Princes.* London, 1977
88. *The Captive King.* London, 1977
89. *Macbeth the King.* London, 1978
90. *Margaret the Queen.* London, 1979
91. *Portrait of the Lothians.* London, 1979
92. *David the Prince.* London, 1980
93. *True Thomas.* London, 1981
94. *Nigel Tranter's Scotland: A Very Personal View.* Glasgow (Scotland), 1981
95. *The Patriot.* London, 1982

Travers, P.L. (Pamela Lyndon)
British, born in 1906

1. *Mary Poppins.* London and New York, 1934
2. *Mary Poppins Comes Back.* London and New York, 1935
3. *Moscow Excursion.* London and New York, 1935
4. *Happy Ever After.* New York, 1940
5. *I Go by Sea, I Go by Land.* London and New York, 1941
6. *Aunt Sass.* New York, 1941
7. *Mary Poppins Opens the Door.* New York, 1943
8. *Ah Wong.* New York, 1943
9. *Mary Poppins in the Park.* London and New York, 1952
10. *The Fox at the Manger.* New York, 1962
11. *Mary Poppins from A to Z.* New York, 1962
12. *Friend Monkey.* New York, 1971
13. *About Sleeping Beauty.* New York, 1975
14. *Mary Poppins in the Kitchen: A Cookery Book with a Story.* New York, 1975

Treadgold, Mary
British, born April 16, 1910

1. *We Couldn't Leave Dinah.* London, 1941
2. *Left Til Called For.* New York, 1941
3. *No Ponies.* London, 1946
4. *The "Polly Harris."* London, 1949
5. *The Running Child.* London, 1951
6. *The Mystery of the "Polly Harris."* New York, 1951
7. *The Heron Ride.* London, 1962
8. *The Winter Princess.* Leicester (Eng), 1962
9. *Return to the Heron.* London, 1963
10. *The Weather Boy.* Leicester, 1964

Treadgold, Mary

11. *Maid's Ribbons.* London, 1965
12. *Elegant Patty.* London, 1967
13. *Poor Patty.* London, 1968
14. *This Summer, Last Summer.* London, 1968
15. *The Humbugs.* London, 1968
16. *The Rum Day of the Vanishing Pony.* Leicester, 1970

Trease, Geoffrey [Robert Geoffrey Trease]
British, born August 11, 1909
1. *The Supreme Prize and Other Poems.* London, 1926
2. *Bows Against the Barons.* London, 1934
3. *Comrades for the Charter.* London, 1934
4. *The Unsleeping Sword.* London, 1934
5. *Walking in England.* Wisbech (Eng), 1935
6. *Call to Arms.* London, 1935
7. *Red Comet.* Moscow (USSR), 1936
8. *Missing from Home.* London, 1937
9. *The Christmas Holiday Mystery.* London, 1937
10. *Mystery on the Moors.* London, 1937
11. *Detectives of the Dales.* London, 1938
12. *In the Land of the Mogul.* Oxford (Eng), 1938
13. *North Sea Spy.* London, 1939
14. *Such Divinity.* London, 1939
15. *Only Natural.* London, 1940
16. *Cue for Treason.* Oxford, 1940
17. *Clem Voroshilov, The Red Marshal.* London, 1940
18. *Running Deer.* London, 1941
19. *The Grey Adventure.* Oxford, 1942
20. *Black Night, Red Morning.* Oxford, 1944
21. *Army Without Banners.* London, 1945
22. *Trumpets in the West.* Oxford and New York, 1947
23. *Silver Guard.* Oxford, 1948
24. *The Hills of Varna.* London, 1948
25. *Shadows of the Hawk.* New York, 1949
26. *The Mystery of Moorside Farm.* Oxford, 1949
27. *No Boats on Bannermere.* London, 1949
28. *The Secret Fiord.* London, 1949
29. *Fortune, My Foe: The Story of Sir Walter Raleigh.* London, 1949
30. *Under Black Banner.* London, 1950
31. *The Crown of Violet.* London, 1952
32. *Web of Traitors.* New York, 1952
33. *The Baron's Hostage.* London, 1952
34. *Black Banner Players.* London, 1952
35. *The New House at Hardale.* London, 1953
36. *The Silken Secret.* Oxford, 1953
37. *Black Banner Abroad.* London, 1954
38. *The Fair Flower of Danger.* Oxford, 1955
39. *Word to Caesar.* London, 1956
40. *Message to Hadrian.* New York, 1956
41. *The Gates of Bannerdale.* London, 1956
42. *Snared Nightingale.* London, 1957
43. *Mist over Athelney.* London, 1958
44. *Escape to King Alfred.* New York, 1958
45. *So Wild the Heart.* London and New York, 1959
46. *The Maythorn Story.* London, 1960
47. *Thunder of Valmy.* London, 1960
48. *Victory at Valmy.* New York, 1961
49. *Change at Maythorn.* London, 1962
50. *Follow My Black Plume.* London and New York, 1963
51. *A Thousand for Sicily.* London and New York, 1964
52. *Seven Stages.* London, 1964
53. *The Dutch Are Coming.* London, 1965
54. *Bent Is the Bow.* London, 1965
55. *This Is Your Century.* London and New York, 1965
56. *The Red Towers of Granada.* London, 1966
57. *The White Nights of St. Petersburg.* London and New York, 1967
58. *The Grand Tour.* London and New York, 1967
59. *The Runaway Serf.* London, 1968
60. *Byron: A Poet Dangerous to Know.* London and New York, 1969
61. *A Masque for the Queen.* London, 1970
62. *The Condottieri: Soldiers of Fortune.* London, 1970
63. *A Whiff of Burnt Boats: An Early Autobiography.* London and New York, 1971
64. *Horsemen on the Hills.* London, 1971
65. *A Ship to Rome.* London, 1972
66. *A Voice in the Night.* London, 1973
67. *Popinjay Stairs.* London, 1973
68. *Laughter at the Door: A Continued Autobiography.* London and New York, 1974
69. *The Chocolate Boy.* London, 1975
70. *The Iron Tsar.* London, 1975
71. *When the Drums Beat.* London, 1976
72. *Violet for Bonaparte.* London, 1976
73. *The Seas of Morning.* London, 1976
74. *The Spy Catchers.* London, 1976
75. *The Field of the Forty Footsteps.* London, 1977
76. *The Claws of the Eagle.* London, 1977

Treat, Lawrence
American, born December 21, 1903
1. *Bringing Sherlock Home.* New York, 1930
2. *Run Far, Run Fast.* New York, 1937
3. *B as in Banshee.* New York, 1940
4. *D as in Dead.* New York, 1941
5. *H as in Hangman.* New York, 1942
6. *O as in Omen.* New York, 1943
7. *Wail for the Corpses.* New York, 1943
8. *The Leather Man.* New York, 1944
9. *V as in Victim.* New York, 1945
10. *H as in Hunted.* New York, 1946
11. *Q as in Quicksand.* New York, 1947
12. *T as in Trapped.* New York, 1947
13. *F as in Flight.* New York, 1948
14. *Over the Edge.* New York, 1948
15. *Trial and Terror.* New York, 1949
16. *Big Shot.* New York, 1951
17. *Weep for a Wanton.* New York, 1956
18. *Lady, Drop Dead.* New York and London, 1960
19. *Venus Unarmed.* New York, 1961
20. *P as in Police.* New York, 1970

Treece, Henry
British, born December 22, 1911, died June 10, 1966
1. *38 Poems.* London, 1940
2. *Towards a Personal Armageddon.* Prairie City (IL), 1941
3. *Invitation and Warning.* London, 1942
4. *The Black Seasons.* London, 1945
5. *Collected Poems.* New York, 1946
6. *I Cannot Go Hunting Tomorrow: Short Stories.* London, 1946
7. *How I See Apocalypse.* London, 1946
8. *The Haunted Garden.* London, 1947
9. *Dylan Thomas: "Dog among the Fairies."* London, 1949
10. *The Exiles.* London, 1952
11. *The Dark Island.* London and New York, 1952
12. *The Rebels.* London, 1953
13. *Legions of the Eagle.* London, 1954
14. *The Eagles Have Flown.* London, 1954
15. *Desperate Journey.* London, 1954
16. *Ask for King Billy.* London, 1955
17. *Viking's Dawn.* London, 1955
18. *Hounds of the King.* London, 1955
19. *The Golden Strangers.* London, 1956

20. *The Great Captains.* London and New York, 1956
21. *Men of the Hills.* London, 1957
22. *The Road to Miklagard.* London and New York, 1957
23. *Hunter Hunted.* London, 1957
24. *Don't Expect Any Mercy!* London, 1958
25. *The Children's Crusade.* London, 1958
26. *The Return of Robinson Crusoe.* London, 1958
27. *The Further Adventures of Robinson Crusoe.* New York, 1958
28. *Red Queen, White Queen.* London and New York, 1958
29. *Perilous Pilgrimage.* New York, 1959
30. *The Bombard.* London, 1959
31. *Ride to Danger.* New York, 1959
32. *Wickham and the Armada.* London, 1959
33. *Castles and Kings.* London, 1959
34. *The Savage Warriors.* New York, 1959
35. *The Pagan Queen.* New York, 1959
36. *The Master of Badger's Hall.* New York, 1959
37. *A Fighting Man.* London, 1960
38. *Viking's Sunset.* London and New York, 1960
39. *Red Settlement.* London, 1960
40. *The Invaders.* New York, 1960
41. *Jason.* London and New York, 1961
42. *The Jet Beads.* Leicester (Eng), 1961
43. *The Golden One.* London, 1961
44. *Man with a Sword.* London, 1962
45. *War Dog.* Leicester, 1962
46. *The Amber Princess.* New York, 1962
47. *The Crusades.* London and New York, 1962
48. *Electra.* London, 1963
49. *Horned Helmet.* Leicester and New York, 1963
50. *Know About the Crusades.* London, 1963
51. *Oedipus.* London, 1964
52. *The Last of the Vikings.* Leicester, 1964
53. *The Burning of Njal.* London and New York, 1964
54. *The Eagle King.* New York, 1965
55. *The Bronze Sword.* London, 1965
56. *Splintered Sword.* Leicester, 1965
57. *Killer in Dark Glasses.* London, 1965
58. *Bang, You're Dead!* London, 1966
59. *The Queen's Brooch.* London, 1966
60. *The Last Viking.* New York, 1966
61. *The Green Man.* London and New York, 1966
62. *Swords from the North.* London and New York, 1967
63. *The Windswept City.* London, 1967
64. *Vinland the Good.* London, 1967
65. *Westward to Vinland.* New York, 1967
66. *The Dream-Time.* Leicester, 1967
67. *The Centurion.* New York, 1967
68. *The Invaders: Three Stories.* Leicester and New York, 1972

Trench, John (Chenevix)
British, born October 17, 1920
1. *Docken Dead.* London, 1953
2. *Dishonoured Bones.* London, 1954
3. *What Rough Beast.* London and New York, 1957
4. *History for Postmen.* London, 1961
5. *The Bones of Britain.* London, 1962
6. *Beyond the Atlas.* London and New York, 1963

Tresselt, Alvin
American, born September 30, 1916
1. *Rain Drop Splash.* New York, 1946
2. *White Snow, Bright Snow.* New York, 1947
3. *Johnny Maple-Leaf.* New York, 1948
4. *The Wind and Peter.* New York, 1948
5. *Bonnie Bess, The Weathervane Horse.* New York, 1949
6. *Sun Up.* New York, 1949
7. *Little Lost Squirrel.* New York, 1950
8. *Follow the Wind.* New York, 1950
9. *Hi, Mr. Robin!* New York, 1950
10. *Autumn Harvest.* New York, 1951
11. *A Day with Daddy.* New York, 1953
12. *Follow the Road.* New York, 1953
13. *I Saw the Sea Come In.* New York, 1954
14. *Wake Up Farm!* New York, 1955
15. *Wake Up City!* New York, 1957
16. *The Rabbit Story.* New York, 1957
17. *The Frog in the Well.* New York, 1958
18. *The Smallest Elephant in the World.* New York, 1959
19. *Timothy Robbins Climbs the Mountain.* New York, 1960
20. *An Elephant Is Not a Cat.* New York, 1962
21. *Under the Trees and Through the Grass.* New York, 1962
22. *How Far Is Far?* New York, 1964
23. *The Mitten: An Old Ukrainian Folktale.* New York, 1964
24. *Hide and Seek Fog.* New York, 1965
25. *The Old Man and the Tiger.* New York, 1965
26. *A Thousand Lights and Fireflies.* New York, 1965
27. *The Tears of the Dragon.* New York, 1967
28. *The World in the Candy Egg.* New York, 1967
29. *Legend of the Willow Plate,* with Nancy Cleaver. New York, 1968
30. *The Crane Maiden.* New York, 1968
31. *Helpful Mr. Bear.* New York, 1968
32. *Ma Lien and the Magic Brush.* New York, 1968
33. *How Rabbit Tricked His Friends.* New York, 1969
34. *The Rolling Rice Ball.* New York, 1969
35. *The Fisherman Under the Sea.* New York, 1969
36. *The Fox Who Traveled.* New York, 1968
37. *It's Time Now!* New York, 1969
38. *The Land of Lost Buttons.* New York, 1970
39. *Eleven Hungry Cats.* New York, 1970
40. *Gengoroh and the Thunder God.* New York, 1970
41. *The Beaver Pond.* New York, 1971
42. *A Sparrow's Magic.* New York, 1970
43. *The Hare and the Bear and Other Stories.* New York, 1971
44. *Stories from the Bible.* New York, 1971
45. *Ogre and His Bride.* New York, 1971
46. *Lum Fu and the Golden Mountain.* New York, 1971
47. *The Little Mouse Who Tarried.* New York, 1971
48. *Wonder Fish from the Sea.* New York, 1971
49. *The Dead Tree.* New York, 1972
50. *The Little Green Man.* New York, 1972
51. *The Nutcracker.* New York, 1974

Trevor, Elleston
British, born February 17, 1920
Pseudonyms: Trevor Burgess, Mansell Black, T. Dudley-Smith, Roger Fitzalan, Adam Hall, Howard North, Simon Rattray, Warwick Scott, Caesar Smith
1. *Into the Happy Glade,* as T. Dudley-Smith. London, 1943
2. *Animal Life Stories (Rippleswim the Otter, Scamper-foot the Pine Marten, Shadow the Fox).* London. 3 vols., 1943-45
3. *Over the Wall,* as T. Dudley-Smith. London, 1943
4. *Double Who Double Crossed,* as T. Dudley-Smith. London, 1944
5. *By a Silver Stream,* as T. Dudley-Smith. London, 1944
6. *Elleston Trevor Miscellany.* London, 1944
7. *Wumpus.* London, 1945
8. *Deep Wood.* London, 1945
9. *Heather Hill.* London, 1946
10. *The Immortal Error.* London, 1946
11. *More about Wumpus.* London, 1947
12. *Escape to Fear,* as T. Dudley-Smith. London, 1948
13. *Now Try the Morgue,* as T. Dudley-Smith. London, 1948

14. *The Island of the Pines.* London, 1948
15. *The Secret Travelers.* London, 1948
16. *Where's Wumpus?* London, 1948
17. *Badger's Beech.* London, 1948
18. *The Wizard of the Wood.* London, 1948
19. *Badger's Moon.* London, 1949
20. *Ant's Castle.* London, 1949
21. *The Mystery of the Missing Book,* as Trevor Burgess. London, 1950
22. *Chorus of Echoes.* London and New York, 1950
23. *Mole's Castle.* London, 1951
24. *Sweethallow Valley.* London, 1951
25. *Challenge of the Firebrand.* London, 1951
26. *Secret Arena.* London, 1951
27. *Image in the Dust,* as Warwick Scott. London, 1951
28. *Knight Sinister,* as Simon Rattray. London and New York, 1951
29. *Dead on Course,* as Mansell Black. London, 1951
30. *Redfern's Miracle.* London and New York, 1951
31. *Tiger Street.* London and New York, 1951
32. *Sinister Cargo,* as Mansell Black. London, 1951
33. *The Domesday Story,* as Warwick Scott. London, 1952
34. *A Blaze of Roses.* London and New York, 1952
35. *Queen in Danger,* as Simon Rattray. London and New York, 1952
36. *The Passion and the Pity.* London, 1953
37. *Bishop in Check,* as Simon Rattray. London and New York, 1953
38. *The Racing Wraith,* as Trevor Burgess. London, 1953
39. *Dead Silence,* as Simon Rattray. London, 1954
40. *A Spy at Monk's Court,* as Trevor Burgess. London, 1954
41. *Naked Canvas,* as Warwick Scott. London, 1954
42. *The Big Pick-Up.* London and New York, 1955
43. *Squadron Airborne.* London, 1955
44. *Dead Circuit,* as Simon Rattray. London, 1955
45. *Forbidden Kingdom.* London, 1955
46. *The Killing-Ground.* London, 1956
47. *Gale Force.* London, 1956
48. *Heat Wave,* as Caesar Smith. London, 1957
49. *The Pillars of Midnight.* London, 1957
50. *Dream of Death.* London, 1958
51. *Badger's Wood.* London, 1958
52. *Silhouette.* London, 1959
53. *The V.I.P.* London, 1959
54. *The Crystal City.* London, 1959
55. *Green Glades.* London, 1959
56. *The Billboard Madonna.* London, 1960
57. *The Mind of Max Duvine.* London, 1960
58. *The Burning Shore.* London, 1961
59. *The Pasang Run.* New York, 1962
60. *The Volcanoes of San Domingo,* as Adam Hall. London, 1963
61. *Squirrel's Island.* London, 1963
62. *The Flight of the Phoenix.* London and New York, 1964
63. *The Berlin Memorandum,* as Adam Hall. London, 1965
64. *The Quiller Memorandum.* New York, 1965
65. *The Second Chance.* London, 1965
66. *Weave a Rope of Sand.* London, 1965
67. *The Shoot.* London and New York, 1966
68. *The 9th Directive,* as Adam Hall. London, 1966
69. *The Freebooters.* London and New York, 1967
70. *A Blaze of Arms,* as Roger Fitzalan. London, 1967
71. *A Place for the Wicked.* London, 1968
72. *The Striker Portfolio,* as Adam Hall. New York, 1968
73. *Bury Him among Kings.* London and New York, 1970
74. *The Fire-Raiser.* London, 1970
75. *The Warsaw Document,* as Adam Hall. London and New York, 1971
76. *Pawn in Jeopardy,* as Adam Hall. Chicago, 1972
77. *Cockpit,* as Adam Hall. Chicago, 1972
78. *Doomsday,* as Adam Hall. Chicago, 1972
79. *Rook's Gambit,* as Adam Hall. Chicago, 1972
80. *The Tango Briefing,* as Adam Hall. London and New York, 1973
81. *Expressway,* as Howard North. London and New York, 1973
82. *The Mandarin Cypher,* as Adam Hall. London and New York, 1975
83. *The Paragon.* London, 1975
84. *Night Stop.* New York, 1975
85. *The Kobra Manifesto.* London and New York, 1976
86. *The Theta Syndrome.* New York and London, 1977
87. *Blue Jay Summer.* London and New York, 1977
88. *Seven Witnesses.* London, 1977

Trevor, Meriol [Lucy Meriol Trevor]
British, born April 15, 1919
1. *The Forest and the Kingdom.* London, 1949
2. *Hunt the King, Hide the Fox.* London, 1950
3. *The Fires and the Stars.* London, 1951
4. *Sun Slower, Sun Faster.* London, 1955
5. *The Other Side of the Moon.* London, 1956
6. *The Last of Britain.* London and New York, 1956
7. *The New People.* London and New York, 1957
8. *Merlin's Ring.* London, 1957
9. *The Treasure Hunt.* London, 1957
10. *Midsummer, Midwinter.* Aldington (Eng), 1957
11. *A Narrow Place.* London, 1958
12. *The Caravan War.* London, 1958
13. *Four Odd Ones.* London, 1958
14. *The Sparrow Child.* London, 1958
15. *Shadows and Images.* London, 1960
16. *Newman: Pillar of the Cloud.* London and New York, 1962
17. *The Rose Round.* London, 1963
18. *William's Wild Day Out.* London, 1963
19. *The Midsummer Maze.* London and New York, 1964
20. *Lights in a Dark Town.* London, 1964
21. *The King of the Castle.* London, 1966
22. *The City and the World.* London, 1970
23. *The Holy Images.* London, 1971
24. *The Two Kingdoms.* London, 1973
25. *The Fugitives.* London, 1973
26. *The Marked Man.* London and New York, 1974
27. *The Enemy at Home.* London and New York, 1974
28. *The Forgotten Country.* London, 1975
29. *The Fortunate Marriage.* London and New York, 1976
30. *The Treacherous Paths.* London, 1976
31. *The Civil Prisoners.* London and New York, 1977

Trimble, Louis (Preston)
American, born March 2, 1917
Pseudonyms: Stuart Brock, Gerry Travis
1. *Sports of the World.* Los Angeles, 1939
2. *Fit to Kill.* New York, 1941
3. *Date for Murder.* New York, 1942
4. *Tragedy in Turquoise.* New York, 1942
5. *Tarnished Love,* as Gerry Travis. New York, 1942
6. *Design for Dying.* New York, 1945
7. *Murder Trouble.* New York, 1945
8. *Give Up the Body.* Seattle (WA), 1946
9. *You Can't Kill a Corpse.* New York, 1946
10. *The Valley of Violence.* Philadelphia, 1948
11. *Death Is My Lover,* as Stuart Brock. New York, 1948
12. *Just Around the Corner,* as Stuart Brock. New York, 1948
13. *Railtown Sheriff.* New York, 1949
14. *The Tide Can't Wait.* New York, 1949

15. *The Case of the Blank Cartridge.* New York, 1949
16. *Blondes Are Skin Deep.* New York, 1950
17. *Gunsmoke Justice.* Philadelphia, 1950
18. *Gaptown Law.* Philadelphia, 1950
19. *Fighting Cowman.* New York, 1953
20. *Crossfire.* New York, 1953
21. *Bring Back Her Body,* as Stuart Brock. New York, 1953
22. *Double-Cross Ranch.* New York, 1954
23. *Bullets on Bunchgrass.* New York, 1954
24. *Action at Boundary Peak.* New York, 1955
25. *Whispering Canyon.* New York, 1955
26. *Forbidden Range.* New York, 1956
27. *Stab in the Dark.* New York, 1956
28. *The Virgin Victim.* New York, 1956
29. *A Lovely Mask for Murder,* as Gerry Travis. New York, 1956
30. *Killer's Choice,* as Stuart Brock. New York, 1956
31. *Nothing to Lose But My Life.* New York, 1957
32. *The Big Bite,* as Gerry Travis. New York, 1957
33. *The Smell of Trouble.* New York, 1958
34. *Mountain Ambush.* New York, 1958
35. *Cargo for the Styx.* New York, 1959
36. *The Corpse Without a Country.* New York, 1959
37. *Orbit Deferred.* New York, 1959
38. *Till Death Do Us Part.* New York, 1959
39. *The Duchess of Skid Row.* New York, 1960
40. *Girl on a Slay Ride.* New York, 1960
41. *Love Me and Die.* New York, 1960
42. *Montana Gun.* New York, 1961
43. *Deadman Canyon.* New York, 1961
44. *The Surfside Caper.* New York, 1961
45. *Siege at High Meadow.* New York, 1962
46. *The Man from Colorado.* New York, 1963
47. *Wild Horse Range.* New York, 1963
48. *The Dead and the Deadly.* New York, 1963
49. *Trouble at Gunsight.* New York, 1964
50. *The Desperate Deputy of Cougar Hill.* New York, 1965
51. *The Holdout in the Diablos.* New York, 1965
52. *Showdown in the Cayuse.* New York, 1966
53. *Standoff at Massacre Buttes.* New York, 1967
54. *Marshal of Sangaree.* New York, 1968
55. *West to the Pecos.* New York, 1968
56. *Anthropol.* New York, 1968
57. *The Hostile Peaks.* New York, 1969
58. *Trouble Valley.* New York, 1970
59. *The Noblest Experiment in the Galaxy.* New York, 1970
60. *The Ragbag Army.* New York, 1971
61. *Guardians of the Gate,* with Jacqueline Trimble. New York, 1972
62. *The City Machine.* New York, 1972
63. *The Wandering Variables.* New York, 1972
64. *The Bodelan Way.* New York, 1974
65. *The Lonesome Mountains.* New York, 1974

Tripp, Miles (Barton)
British, born May 5, 1923
Pseudonyms: John Michael Brett, Michael Brett
1. *Faith Is a Windsock.* London, 1952
2. *The Image of Nan.* London, 1955
3. *A Glass of Red Wine.* London, 1960
4. *Kilo Forty.* London, 1963
5. *Diecast,* as Michael Brett. New York, 1963
6. *The Skin Dealer.* London, 1964
7. *A Plague of Demons,* as Michael Brett. London, 1965
8. *A Quartet of Three.* London, 1965
9. *The Chicken.* London, 1966
10. *A Cargo of Spent Evil,* as John Michael Brett. London, 1966

11. *The Fifth Point of the Compass.* London, 1967
12. *One Is One.* London, 1968
13. *Malice and the Maternal Instinct.* London, 1969
14. *The Eighth Passenger: A Flight of Recollection and Discovery.* London, 1969
15. *A Man Without Friends.* London, 1970
16. *Five Minutes with a Stranger.* London, 1971
17. *The Claws of God.* London, 1972
18. *Obsession.* London, 1973
19. *Woman at Risk.* London, 1974
20. *A Woman in Bed.* London, 1976
21. *The Once a Year Man.* London, 1977
22. *The Wife-Smuggler.* London, 1978
23. *Cruel Victim.* London, 1979

Trollope, Joanna (Joanna Potter)
British, born December 9, 1943
Other pseudonym: Caroline Harvey
1. *Eliza Stanhope.* London, 1978
2. *Parson Harding's Daughter.* London, 1979
3. *Leaves from the Valley.* London, 1980
4. *Charlotte, Alexandra,* as Caroline Harvey. London, 1980
5. *Mistaken Virtues.* New York, 1980
6. *The City of Gems.* London, 1981

Tubb, E.C. (Edwin Charles)
British, born October 15, 1919
Pseudonyms: Chuck Adams, Jud Cary, J.F. Clarkson, James S. Farrow, James R. Fenner, Charles S. Graham, Charles Grey, Volsted Gridban, Gill Hunt, E.F. Jackson, Gregory Kern, King Lang, Mike Lantry, P. Lawrence, Chet Lawson, Arthur Maclean, Carl Maddox, M.L. Powers, Paul Schofield, Brian Shaw, Roy Sheldon, John Stevens, Edward Thomson
1. *Saturn Patrol,* as King Lang. London, 1951
2. *Planetfall,* as Gill Hunt. London, 1951
3. *Argentis,* as Brian Shaw. London, 1952
4. *Alien Impact.* London, 1952
5. *Atom War on Mars.* London, 1952
6. *Alien Universe,* as Volsted Gridban. London, 1952
7. *Reverse Universe,* as Volsted Gridban. London, 1952
8. *The Mutants Rebel.* London, 1953
9. *Venusian Adventure.* London, 1953
10. *Planetoid Disposals Ltd.,* as Volsted Gridban. London, 1953
11. *DeBracy's Drug,* as Volsted Gridban. London, 1953
12. *Fugitive of Time,* as Volsted Gridban. London, 1953
13. *The Wall,* as Charles Grey. London, 1953
14. *Dynasty of Doom,* as Charles Grey. London, 1953
15. *The Tormented City,* as Charles Grey. London, 1953
16. *Space Hunger,* as Charles Grey. London, 1953
17. *I Fight for Mars,* as Charles Grey. London, 1953
18. *The Extra Man,* as Charles Grey. London, 1954
19. *The Hand of Havoc,* as Charles Grey. London, 1954
20. *Enterprise 2115,* as Charles Grey. London, 1954
21. *Alien Life.* London, 1954
22. *The Living World,* as Carl Maddox. London, 1954
23. *World at Bay.* London, 1954
24. *The Metal Eater,* as Roy Sheldon. London, 1954
25. *Journey to Mars.* London, 1954
26. *Menace from the Past,* as Carl Maddox. London, 1954
27. *City of No Return.* London, 1954
28. *The Stellar Legion.* London, 1954
29. *The Hell Planet.* London, 1954
30. *The Resurrected Man.* London, 1954
31. *Alien Dust.* London, 1955
32. *The Fighting Fury,* as Paul Schofield. London, 1955
33. *Assignment New York,* as Mike Lantry. London, 1955
34. *Comanche Capture,* as E.F. Jackson. London, 1955

35. *Sands of Destiny*, as Jud Cary. London, 1955
36. *Men of the Long Rifle*, as J. F. Clarkson. London, 1955
37. *The Space-Born.* New York, 1956
38. *Scourge of the South*, as M.L. Powers. London, 1956
39. *Vengeance Trail*, as James S. Farrow. London, 1956
40. *Quest for Quantrell*, as John Stevens. London, 1956
41. *Trail Blazers*, as Chuck Adams. London, 1956
42. *Drums of the Prairie*, as P. Lawrence. London, 1956
43. *Men of the West*, as Chet Lawson. London, 1956
44. *Wagon Trail*, as Charles S. Graham. London, 1957
45. *Colt Vengeance*, as James R. Fenner. London, 1957
46. *The Mechanical Monarch*, as Charles Grey. New York, 1958
47. *Touch of Evil*, as Arthur Maclean. London, 1959
48. *Target Death.* London, 1961
49. *Lucky Strike.* London, 1961
50. *Calculated Risk.* London, 1961
51. *Too Tough to Handle.* London, 1962
52. *The Dead Keep Faith.* London, 1962
53. *The Spark of Anger.* London, 1962
54. *Full Impact.* London, 1962
55. *I Vow Vengeance.* London, 1962
56. *Gunflash.* London, 1962
57. *Hit Back.* London, 1962
58. *One Must Die.* London, 1962
59. *Suicide Squad.* London, 1962
60. *Airbourne Commando.* London, 1963
61. *No Higher Stakes.* London, 1963
62. *Penalty of Fear.* London, 1963
63. *Moon Base.* London and New York, 1964
64. *Ten from Tomorrow.* London, 1966
65. *Death Is a Dream.* London and New York, 1967
66. *The Winds of Gath.* New York, 1967
67. *Gath.* London, 1968
68. *C.O.D. Mars.* New York, 1968
69. *Derai.* New York, 1968
70. *S.T.A.R. Flight.* New York, 1969
71. *Toyman.* New York, 1969
72. *Escape into Space.* London, 1969
73. *Kalin.* New York, 1969
74. *The Jester at Scar.* New York, 1970
75. *Lallia.* New York, 1971
76. *Technos.* New York, 1972
77. *Century of the Manikin.* New York, 1972
78. *A Scatter of Stardust.* New York, 1972
79. *Mayenne.* New York, 1973
80. *Veruchia.* New York, 1973
81. *Jondelle.* New York, 1973
82. *Galaxy of the Lost*, as Gregory Kern. New York, 1973
83. *Slave Ship from Sergan*, as Gregory Kern. New York, 1973
84. *Monster from Metelaze*, as Gregory Kern. New York, 1973
85. *Zenya.* New York, 1974
86. *Enemy Within the Skull*, as Gregory Kern. New York, 1974
87. *Jewel of Jarhan*, as Gregory Kern. New York, 1974
88. *Seetee Alert!* as Gregory Kern. New York, 1974
89. *The Gholan Gate*, as Gregory Kern. New York, 1974
90. *The Eater of Worlds*, as Gregory Kern. New York, 1974
91. *Earth Enslaved*, as Gregory Kern. New York, 1974
92. *Planet of Dread*, as Gregory Kern. New York, 1974
93. *Spawn of Laban*, as Gregory Kern. New York, 1974
94. *The Genetic Buccaneer*, as Gregory Kern. New York, 1974
95. *A World Aflame*, as Gregory Kern. New York, 1974
96. *Breakaway.* London and New York, 1975
97. *Eloise.* New York, 1975
98. *Eye of the Zodiac.* New York, 1975
99. *Collision Course.* London, 1975
100. *The Ghosts of Epidoris*, as Gregory Kern. New York, 1975
101. *Mimics of Dephene*, as Gregory Kern. New York, 1975
102. *Beyond the Galactic Lens*, as Gregory Kern. New York, 1975
103. *Atilus the Slave*, as Edward Thomson. London, 1975
104. *Atilus the Gladiator*, as Edward Thomson. London, 1975
105. *Das Kosmiche Duelle*, as Gregory Kern. Bergisch Gladbach (Germany), 1976
106. *Jack of Swords.* New York, 1976
107. *Alien Seed.* London, 1976
108. *Spectrum of a Forgotten Sun.* New York, 1976
109. *Rogue Planet.* London, 1976
110. *Earthfall.* London, 1977
111. *Haven of Darkness.* New York, 1977
112. *Prison of Light.* New York, 1977
113. *The Primitive.* London, 1977
114. *Incident on Ath.* New York, 1978
115. *The Quillian Sector.* New York, 1978
116. *Gladiator,* as Edward Thomson. London, 1978
117. *Stellar Assignment.* London, 1979
118. *Web of Sand.* New York, 1979
119. *Death Wears a White Face.* London, 1979
120. *Iduna's Universe.* New York, 1979
121. *The Luck Machine.* London, 1980
122. *The Terra Data.* New York, 1980
123. *The Life Buyer.* London, 1980

Tucker, Wilson [Arthur Wilson "Bob" Tucker]
American, born November 23, 1914
1. *The Chinese Doll.* New York, 1946
2. *To Keep or Kill.* New York, 1947
3. *The Dove.* New York, 1948
4. *The Stalking Man.* New York, 1949
5. *Red Herring.* New York, 1951
6. *The City in the Sea.* New York, 1951
7. *The Long Loud Silence.* New York, 1952
8. *The Time Masters.* New York, 1953
9. *Wild Talent.* New York, 1954
10. *The Science Fiction Subtreasury.* New York, 1954
11. *Man from Tomorrow.* New York, 1955
12. *Time Bomb.* New York, 1955
13. *Time: X.* New York, 1955
14. *The Man in My Grave.* New York, 1956
15. *Tomorrow Plus X.* New York, 1957
16. *The Hired Target.* New York, 1957
17. *The Lincoln Hunters.* New York, 1958
18. *To the Tombaugh Station.* New York, 1960
19. *Last Stop.* New York, 1963
20. *A Processional of the Damned.* New York, 1965
21. *The Warlock.* New York, 1967
22. *The Year of the Quiet Sun.* New York, 1970
23. *This Witch.* New York, 1971
24. *Ice and Iron.* New York, 1974

Tudor, Tasha
American
1. *Pumpkin Moonshine.* New York and London, 1938
2. *Alexander the Gander.* New York and London, 1939
3. *The Country Fair.* New York and London, 1940
4. *A Tale of Easter.* New York and London, 1941
5. *Snow Before Christmas.* New York and London, 1941
6. *Dorcas Porcus.* New York and London, 1942
7. *The White Goose.* New York and London, 1943
8. *Linsey Woolsey.* New York, 1946
9. *Thistly B.* New York, 1949
10. *The Dolls' Christmas.* New York and London, 1950
11. *Amanda and the Bear.* New York and London, 1951
12. *Edgar Allan Crow.* New York, 1953
13. *A Is for Annabelle.* New York, 1954
14. *1 Is One.* New York, 1956
15. *Around the Year.* New York, 1957
16. *Becky's Birthday.* New York, 1960

17. *Becky's Christmas.* New York, 1961
18. *First Delights.* New York, 1966
19. *Corgiville Fair.* New York, 1971

Tunis, John R. (Roberts)
American, born December 7, 1889, died February 4, 1975
1. *$port$, Heroics, and Hysterics.* New York, 1928
2. *American Girl.* New York, 1930
3. *Was College Worth While?* New York, 1936
4. *The Iron Duke.* New York, 1938
5. *The Duke Decides.* New York, 1939
6. *Champion's Choice.* New York, 1940
7. *The Kid from Tomkinsville.* New York, 1940
8. *Choosing a College.* New York, 1940
9. *Sport for the Fun of It.* New York, 1940
10. *Democracy and Sport.* New York, 1941
11. *This Writing Game: Selections from Twenty Years of Freelancing.* New York, 1941
12. *World Series.* New York, 1941
13. *All-American.* New York, 1942
14. *Million-Miler: The Story of an Air Pilot.* New York, 1942
15. *Keystone Kids.* New York, 1943
16. *Lawn Games.* New York, 1943
17. *Rookie of the Year.* New York, 1944
18. *Yea! Wildcats!* New York, 1944
19. *A City for Lincoln.* New York, 1945
20. *The Kid Comes Back.* New York, 1946
21. *Highpockets.* New York, 1948
22. *Son of the Valley.* New York, 1949
23. *Young Razzle.* New York, 1949
24. *The Other Side of the Fence.* New York, 1953
25. *Go, Team Go!* New York, 1954
26. *Buddy and the Old Pro.* New York, 1955
27. *Schoolboy Johnson.* New York, 1958
28. *The American Way of Sport.* New York, 1958
29. *Silence over Dunkerque.* New York, 1962
30. *A Measure of Independence.* New York, 1964
31. *His Enemy, His Friend.* New York, 1967
32. *Grand National.* New York, 1973

Turkle, Brinton
American, born August 15, 1915
1. *Obadiah the Bold.* New York, 1965
2. *The Magic of Millicent Musgrave.* New York, 1967
3. *The Fiddler of High Lonesome.* New York, 1968
4. *Thy Friend, Obadiah.* New York, 1969
5. *The Sky Dog.* New York, 1969
6. *Mooncoin Castle: or, Skulduggery Rewarded.* New York, 1970
7. *The Adventures of Obadiah.* New York, 1972
8. *It's Only Arnold.* New York, 1973
9. *Deep in the Forest.* New York, 1976

Turner, Philip (William)
British, born December 3, 1925
Pseudonym: Stephen Chance
1. *Colonel Sheperton's Clock.* London, 1964
2. *The Christmas Story: A Carol Service for Children.* London, 1964
3. *The Grange at High Force.* London, 1965
4. *Peter Was His Nickname.* London, 1965
5. *Sea Peril.* London, 1966
6. *The Bible Story.* London, 1968
7. *Steam on the Line.* London and Cleveland (OH), 1968
8. *Illustrated Bible Stories.* New York, 1969
9. *War on the Darnel.* London and New York, 1969
10. *Wig-wig and Homer.* London, 1969
11. *Devil's Nob.* London, 1970
12. *Septimus and the Danedyke Mystery,* as Stephen Chance. London, 1971
13. *Septimus and the Minster Ghost,* as Stephen Chance. London, 1972
14. *Powder Quay.* London, 1971
15. *Dunkirk Summer.* London, 1973
16. *Septimus and the Stone of Offering,* as Stephen Chance. London, 1976
17. *Skull Island.* London, 1977

Tuttle, W.C. (Wilbur Coleman)
American, born November 11, 1883
1. *Reddy Brant, His Adventures.* New York, 1920
2. *The Medicine Man.* London, 1925
3. *Straight Shooting.* New York, 1926
4. *Sad Sontag Plays His Hunch.* New York, 1926
5. *Ghost Trails.* London, 1926
6. *The Flood of Fate.* London, 1926
7. *Sun Dog Loot.* London, 1926
8. *The Devil's Payday.* New York, No date
9. *Law of the Range.* New York, No date
10. *Powder Law.* New York, No date
11. *Sontag of Sundown.* New York, No date
12. *Spawn of the Desert.* New York, No date
13. *Tramps of the Range.* New York, No date
14. *Thicker Than Water.* Boston, 1927
15. *Hashknife of the Double Bar 8.* London, 1927
16. *The Dead-Line.* London, 1927
17. *Rustler's Roost.* London, 1927
18. *Hashknife Lends a Hand.* London, 1927
19. *The Morgan Trail.* Boston, 1928
20. *Hashknife of the Canyon Trail.* London, 1928
21. *Lo Lo Valley.* London, 1929
22. *Hidden Blood.* London, 1929
23. *Tumbling River Range.* London, 1929
24. *The Mystery of the Red Triangle.* London, 1929
25. *The Keeper of Red Horse Pass.* London, 1930
26. *Spooky Riders.* London, 1930
27. *The Red Head From Sun Dog.* Boston and London, 1930
28. *Hashknife of Stormy River.* London, 1931
29. *The Valley of Twisted Trails.* Boston, 1931
30. *Singing River.* London, 1931
31. *Mystery at JHC Ranch.* Boston, 1932
32. *Bluffer's Luck.* London, 1932
33. *The Silver Bar Mystery.* London, 1932
34. *Loot of the Lazy F.* London, 1933
35. *The Santa Dolores Stage.* Boston, 1934
36. *Rifled Gold.* Boston and London, 1934
37. *Horse-Shoe Luck.* London, 1934
38. *The Turquoise Trail.* London, 1935
39. *Henry the Sheriff.* Boston, 1936
40. *Rocky Rhodes.* London, 1936
41. *Wild Horse Valley.* Boston, 1938
42. *Wandering Dogies.* Boston, 1938
43. *Shotgun Gold.* Boston, 1940
44. *The Tin God of Twisted River.* Boston, 1941
45. *The Valley of Vanishing Herds.* Boston, 1942
46. *The Wolf Pack of Lobo Butte.* Boston, 1945
47. *Wolf Creek Valley.* London, 1946
48. *The Trouble Trailer.* Boston and London, 1946
49. *Straws in the Wind.* Boston and London, 1948
50. *Gun Feud.* New York, 1951
51. *The Trail of Deceit.* Boston, 1951
52. *Salt for the Tiger.* New York, 1952
53. *Renegade Sheriff.* New York, 1953
54. *The Singing Kid.* Kingswood, 1953
55. *Thunderbird Range.* New York, 1954
56. *Mission River Justice.* New York, 1955

57. *The Shadow Shooter.* London, 1955
58. *Ghost Guns.* London, 1957
59. *The Shame of Arizona.* London, 1957
60. *Danger Trail.* London, 1958
61. *The King of Dancing Valley.* London, 1958
62. *Me and Rudolph.* New York, 1958
63. *The Rim Rider.* London, 1959
64. *Silver Buckshot.* London, 1959
65. *The Deputy.* New York, 1959
66. *Dynamite Days.* London, 1960
67. *The Trail to Kingdom Come.* London, 1960
68. *Outlaw Empire.* New York, 1960
69. *Galloping Gold.* London, 1961
70. *Gold at K-Bar-T.* London, 1961
71. *Diamond Hitch.* London, 1962
72. *Passengers for Painted Rock.* London, 1962
73. *The House of the Hawk.* London, 1963
74. *West of the Aztec Pass.* London, 1963
75. *Piperock Tales.* New York, 1963
76. *Double Trouble.* London, 1964
77. *Valley of Suspicion.* London, 1964
78. *Arizona Drifters.* London, 1964
79. *Double-Crossers of Ghost Tree.* London, 1965
80. *Road to the Moon.* London, 1965
81. *Stockade.* London, 1965
82. *Buckshot Range.* London, 1966
83. *The Payroll of Fate.* London, 1966
84. *Montana Man.* New York, 1966
85. *The Lone Wolf.* London, 1967
86. *Lucky Pardners.* London, 1967
87. *Medicine Maker.* London, 1967
88. *The King of Blue Grass Valley.* London, 1977
89. *Vanishing Brands.* London, 1977
90. *Red Trail of a 41.* London, 1978

Twain, Mark (Samuel Langhorne Clemens)
American, born November 30, 1835, died April 21, 1910
1. *The Celebrated Jumping Frog of Calaveras County and Other Sketches.* New York, 1867
2. *The Innocents Abroad; or, The New Pilgrims' Progress.* Hartford (CT), 1869
3. *Mark Twain's (Burlesque) Autobiography and First Romance.* New York, 1871
4. *Memoranda: From the Galaxy.* Toronto, 1871
5. *The Innocents at Home.* London, 1872
6. *Roughing It.* London and Hartford, 1872
7. *A Curious Dream and Other Sketches.* London, 1872
8. *Screamers: A Gathering of Scraps of Humour, Delicious Bits, and Short Stories.* London, 1872
9. *The Gilded Age: A Tale of Today,* with Charles Dudley Warner. Hartford, 1873
10. *Sketches.* New York, 1874
11. *Sketches, New and Old.* Hartford, 1875
12. *The Adventures of Tom Sawyer.* London and Hartford, 1876
13. *Old Times on the Mississippi.* Toronto, 1876
14. *A True Story and the Recent Carnival of Crime.* Boston, 1877
15. *Punch, Brothers, Punch! and Other Sketches.* New York, 1878
16. *An Idle Excursion.* Toronto, 1878
17. *A Tramp Abroad.* Hartford and London, 1880
18. *Date 1601: Conversations as It Was by the Social Fireside in the Time of the Tudors.* Privately printed, 1880
19. *The Prince and the Pauper.* London and Boston, 1881
20. *A Curious Experience.* Toronto, 1881
21. *The Stolen White Elephant Etc.* London and Boston, 1882
22. *Life on the Mississippi.* London and Boston, 1883
23. *The Adventures of Huckleberry Finn.* London, 1884
24. *A Connecticut Yankee in King Arthur's Court.* New York and London, 1889
25. *Facts for Mark Twain's Memory Builder.* New York, 1891
26. *The American Claimant.* New York and London, 1892
27. *Merry Tales.* New York, 1892
28. *The £1,000,000 Bank-Note and Other New Stories.* New York and London, 1893
29. *Pudd'nhead Wilson: A Tale.* London, 1894
30. *The Tragedy of Pudd'nhead Wilson.* Hartford, 1894
31. *Tom Sawyer Abroad.* New York and London, 1894
32. *Personal Recollections of Joan of Arc. . . .* New York and London, 1896
33. *Tom Sawyer Abroad, Tom Sawyer, Detective, and Other Stories.* New York, 1896
34. *Tom Sawyer, Detective, as Told by Huck Finn, and Other Tales.* London, 1897
35. *How to Tell a Story and Other Essays.* New York, 1897
36. *Following the Equator: A Journey Around the World.* Hartford, 1897
37. *More Tramps Abroad.* London, 1897
38. *The Pains of Lowly Life.* London, 1900
39. *English as She Is Taught.* Boston, 1900
40. *The Man That Corrupted Hadleyburg and Other Stories and Essays.* New York and London, 1900
41. *To the Person Sitting in Darkness.* New York, 1901
42. *Edmund Burke on Croker, and Tammany.* New York, 1901
43. *A Double Barreled Detective Story.* New York and London, 1902
44. *My Debut as a Literary Person, with Other Essays and Stories.* Hartford, 1903
45. *Extracts from Adam's Diary.* New York and London, 1904
46. *A Dog's Tale.* London and New York, 1904
47. *Mark Twain on Vivisection.* New York, 1905
48. *King Leopold's Soliloquy: A Defense of His Congo Rule.* Boston, 1905
49. *Editorial Wild Oats.* New York, 1905
50. *Eve's Diary.* New York and London, 1906
51. *The $30,000 Bequest and Other Stories.* New York, 1906
52. *What Is Man?* New York, 1906
53. *Mark Twain on Spelling.* New York, 1906
54. *A Horse's Tale.* New York and London, 1907
55. *Christian Science, with Notes Containing Corrections to Date.* New York and London, 1907
56. *Extract from Captain Stormfield's Visit to Heaven.* New York and London, 1909
57. *Is Shakespeare Dead? From My Autobiography.* New York and London, 1909
58. *Mark Twain's Speeches.* New York and London, 1910
59. *Queen Victoria's Jubilee.* Privately printed, 1910
60. *Letter to the California Pioneers.* Oakland (CA), 1911
61. *The Mysterious Stranger: A Romance.* New York, 1916
62. *What Is Man? and Other Essays.* New York, 1917
63. *Mark Twain's Letters, Arranged with Comment.* New York, 2 vols., 1917
64. *The Curious Republic of Gondour and Other Whimsical Sketches.* New York, 1919
65. *Letters.* London, 1920
66. *Moments with Mark Twain.* New York, 1920
67. *The Mysterious Stranger and Other Stories.* New York and London, 1922
68. *Europe and Elsewhere.* New York and London, 1923
69. *Mark Twain's Autobiography.* New York and London, 2 vols., 1924
70. *Sketches of the Sixties by Bret Harte and Mark Twain . . . from "The Californian," 1864-67.* San Francisco, 1926
71. *The Quaker City Holy Land Excursion: An Unfinished Play.* Privately printed, 1927

72. *The Adventures of Thomas Jefferson Snodgrass.* Chicago, 1928
73. *A Boy's Adventure.* Privately printed, 1928
74. *The Suppressed Chapter of "Following the Equator."* Privately printed, 1928
75. *A Letter from Mark Twain to His Publisher, Chatto and Windus.* San Francisco, 1929
76. *Mark Twain the Letter Writer.* Boston, 1932
77. *The Family Mark Twain.* New York, 1935
78. *The Mark Twain Omnibus.* New York, 1935
79. *Representative Selections.* New York, 1935
80. *Mark Twain's Notebook.* New York, 1935
81. *Letters from the Sandwich Islands, Written for the "Sacramento Union."* San Francisco, 1937
82. *The Washoe Giant in San Francisco, Being Heretofore Uncollected Sketches. . . ."* San Francisco, 1938
83. *Mark Twain's Western Years, Together with Hitherto Unreprinted Clemens Western Items.* Stanford (CA), 1938
84. *Letters from Honolulu Written for the "Sacramento Union."* Honolulu (HI), 1939
85. *Jim Smiley and His Jumping Frog.* Chicago, 1940
86. *Mark Twain in Eruption: Hitherto Unpublished Pages about Men and Events.* New York, 1940
87. *Travels with Mr. Brown, Being Heretofore Uncollected Sketches Written for the San Francisco "Alta California" in 1866 and 1867.* New York, 1940
88. *Republican Letters.* Webster Groves (CA), 1941
89. *Letters to Will Brown.* Austin (TX), 1941
90. *Letters in the "Muscatine Journal."* Chicago, 1942
91. *Washington in 1868.* Webster Groves and London, 1943
92. *A Murder, A Mystery, and a Marriage.* Privately printed, 1945
93. *Mark Twain, Business Man.* Boston, 1946
94. *The Letters of Quintus Curtius Snodgrass.* Dallas (TX), 1946
95. *The Portable Mark Twain.* New York, 1946
96. *Mark Twain in Three Moods: Three New Items of Twainiana.* San Marino (CA), 1948
97. *The Love Letters of Mark Twain.* New York, 1949
98. *Mark Twain to Mrs. Fairbanks.* San Marino, 1949
99. *Report from Paradise.* New York, 1952
100. *Mark Twain to Uncle Remus 1881-1885.* Atlanta, 1953
101. *Twins of Genius.* East Lansing, 1953
102. *The Complete Short Stories.* New York, 1957
103. *Mark Twain of the "Enterprise."* . . . Berkeley, 1957
104. *Traveling with Innocents Abroad: Mark Twain's Original Reports from Europe and the Holy Land.* Norman (OK), 1958
105. *The Autobiography of Mark Twain.* New York, 1959
106. *The Art, Humor, and Humanity of Mark Twain.* Norman, 1959
107. *Mark Twain and the Government.* Caldwell (ID), 1960
108. *Mark Twain-Howells Letters: The Correspondence of Samuel L. Clemens and William Dean Howells 1872-1910.* Cambridge (MA), 2 vols., 1960
109. *Your Personal Mark Twain.* New York, 1960
110. *Life as I Find It: Essays, Sketches, Tales, and Other Material.* New York, 1961
111. *The Complete Humorous Sketches and Tales.* New York, 1961
112. *Ah Sin.* San Francisco, 1961
113. *The Travels of Mark Twain.* New York, 1961
114. *Contributions to "The Galaxy," 1868-1871.* Gainesville (FL), 1961
115. *Mark Twain on the Art of Writing.* Buffalo (NY), 1961
116. *Letters to Mary.* New York, 1961
117. *The Pattern for Mark Twain's "Roughing It": Letters from Nevada by Samuel and Orion Clemens, 1861-1862.* Berkeley, 1961
118. *Letters from the Earth.* New York, 1962
119. *Mark Twain on the Damned Human Race.* New York, 1962
120. *Selected Shorter Writings.* Boston, 1962
121. *Simon Wheeler, Detective.* New York, 1963
122. *The Complete Essays.* New York, 1963
123. *Mark Twain's San Francisco.* New York, 1963
124. *The Forgotten Writings of Mark Twain.* New York, 1963
125. *The Complete Novels.* New York, 2 vols., 1964
126. *The Adventures of Colonel Sellers, Being Twain's Share of "The Gilded Age."* New York, 1965
127. *On the Poetry of Mark Twain, with Selections from His Verse.* Urbana (IL), 1966
128. *General Grant by Matthew Arnold, with a Rejoinder by Mark Twain.* Carbondale (IL), 1966
129. *Letters from Hawaii.* New York, 1966
130. *Which Was the Dream? and Other Symbolic Writings of the Later Years.* Berkeley (CA), 1967
131. *The Complete Travel Books.* New York, 1967
132. *Letters to His Publishers, 1867-1894.* Berkeley, 1967
133. *Mark Twain's Satires and Burlesques.* Berkeley, 1967
134. *Mark Twain's Mysterious Stranger Manuscripts.* Berkeley, 1969
135. *Mark Twain's Hannibal, Huck, and Tom.* Berkeley, 1969
136. *Clemens of the "Call:" Mark Twain in California.* Berkeley, 1969
137. *Correspondence with Henery Huttleston Rogers, 1893-1009.* Berkeley, 1969
138. *Man Is the Only Animal That Blushes—or Needs to: The Wisdom of Mark Twain.* Los Angeles, 1970
139. *Mark Twain's Quarrel with Heaven: Captain Stormfield's Visit to Heaven and Other Sketches.* New Haven (CT), 1970
140. *Everybody's Mark Twain.* South Brunswick (NJ) and London, 1972
141. *Fables of Man.* Berkeley, 1972
142. *A Pen Warmed Up in Hell: Mark Twain in Protest.* New York, 1972
143. *The Choice Humorous Works of Mark Twain.* London, 1973
144. *Mark Twain's Notebooks and Journals.* Berkeley, 1975
145. *Letters from the Sandwich Islands.* Norfolk Island (Australia), 1975
146. *Mark Twain Speaking.* Iowa City (IA), 1976
147. *The Mammoth Cod, and Address to the Stomach Club.* Milwaukee (WI), 1976
148. *The Comic Mark Twain Reader.* New York, 1977
149. *Mark Twain Speaks for Himself.* West Lafayette (IN), 1978

Tyre, Nedra
American
1. *Red Wine First.* New York, 1947
2. *Mouse in Eternity.* New York, 1952
3. *Death Is a Lover.* New York, 1953
4. *Death of an Intruder.* New York, 1953
5. *Journey to Nowhere.* New York and London, 1954
6. *Hall of Death.* New York, 1960
7. *Reformatory Girls.* New York, 1962
8. *Everyone Suspect.* New York, 1964
9. *Twice So Fair.* New York, 1971

Uchida, Yoshiko
American, born November 24, 1921
1. *The Dancing Kettle and Other Japanese Folk Tales.* New York, 1949
2. *New Friends for Susan.* New York, 1951
3. *We Do Not Work Alone: Kanjiro Kawai.* Kyoto (Japan), 1953
4. *The Magic Listening Cap: More Folk Tales from Japan.* New York, 1955

5. *The Full Circle*. New York, 1957
6. *Takao and the Grandfather's Sword*. New York, 1958
7. *The Promised Year*. New York, 1959
8. *Mik and the Prowler*. New York, 1960
9. *Rokubei and the Thousand Rice Bowls*. New York, 1962
10. *The Forever Christmas Tree*. New York, 1963
11. *Sumi's Prize*. New York, 1964
12. *The Sea of Gold and Other Tales from Japan*. New York, 1965
13. *Sumi's Special Happening*. New York, 1966
14. *In-Between Miya*. New York, 1967
15. *Sumi and the Goat and the Tokyo Express*. New York, 1969
16. *Hisako's Mysteries*. New York, 1969
17. *Makoto, The Smallest Boy*. New York, 1970
18. *Journey to Topaz*. New York, 1971
19. *Samurai of Gold Hill*. New York, 1972
20. *The History of Sycamore Church*. El Cerrito (CA), 1974
21. *The Birthday Visitor*. New York, 1975
22. *The Rooster Who Understood Japanese*. New York, 1976

Ude, Wayne
American, born March 23, 1946
1. *Buffalo and Other Stories*. Amherst (NY), 1975
2. *Becoming Coyote*. Amherst, 1979

Udry, Janice (May)
American, born June 14, 1928
1. *Little Bear and the Beautiful Kite*. Racine (WI), 1955
2. *A Tree Is Nice*. New York, 1956
3. *Theodore's Parents*. New York, 1958
4. *The Moon Jumpers*. New York, 1959
5. *Danny's Pig*. New York, 1960
6. *Alfred*. Chicago, 1960
7. *Let's Be Enemies*. New York, 1961
8. *Is Susan Here?* New York and London, 1962
9. *The Mean Mouse and Other Mean Stories*. New York, 1962
10. *End of the Line*. Chicago, 1962
11. *Betsy-Back-in-Bed*. Chicago, 1963
12. *Next Door to Laura Linda*. Chicago, 1965
13. *What Mary Jo Shared*. Chicago, 1966
14. *If You're a Bear*. Chicago, 1967
15. *Mary Ann's Mud Day*. New York, 1967
16. *What Mary Jo Wanted*. Chicago, 1968
17. *Glenda*. New York, 1969
18. *Emily's Autumn*. Chicago, 1969
19. *The Sunflower Garden*. New York, 1969
20. *Mary Jo's Grandmother*. Chicago, 1970
21. *Angie*. New York, 1971
22. *How I Faded Away; or, The Invisible Boy*. Chicago, 1976
23. *Oh No, Cat!* New York, 1976

Uhnak, Dorothy
American, born in 1933
1. *Policewoman: A Young Woman's Initiation into the Realities of Justice*. New York, 1964
2. *The Bait*. New York and London, 1968
3. *The Witness*. New York, 1969
4. *The Ledger*. New York, 1970
5. *Law and Order*. New York and London, 1973
6. *The Investigation*. New York, 1977

Underwood, Michael [John Michael Evelyn]
British, born June 2, 1916
1. *Murder on Trial*. London, 1954
2. *Murder Made Absolute*. London, 1955
3. *Death on Remand*. London, 1956
4. *False Witness*. London, 1957
5. *Lawful Pursuit*. London and New York, 1958
6. *Arm of the Law*. London, 1959
7. *Cause of Death*. London, 1960
8. *Death by Misadventure*. London, 1960
9. *Adam's Case*. London and New York, 1961
10. *The Case Against Phillip Quest*. London, 1962
11. *Girl Found Dead*. London, 1963
12. *The Crime of Colin Wise*. London and New York, 1964
13. *The Unprofessional Spy*. London and New York, 1964
14. *The Anxious Conspirator*. London and New York, 1965
15. *A Crime Apart*. London, 1966
16. *The Man Who Died on Friday*. London, 1967
17. *The Man Who Killed Too Soon*. London, 1968
18. *The Shadow Game*. London, 1969
19. *The Silent Liars*. London and New York, 1970
20. *Shem's Demise*. London, 1970
21. *A Trout in the Milk*. London, 1971
22. *Reward for a Defector*. London, 1973
23. *A Pinch of Snuff*. London and New York, 1974
24. *The Juror*. London and New York, 1975
25. *Menaces, Menaces*. London and New York, 1976
26. *Murder with Malice*. London and New York, 1977
27. *The Fatal Trip*. London and New York, 1977
28. *Crooked Wood*. London and New York, 1978
29. *Anything but the Truth*. London, 1978
30. *Smooth Justice*. London and New York, 1979
31. *Victim of Circumstance*. London and New York, 1980

Ungerer, Tomi [Jean Thomas Ungerer]
American and French, born November 28, 1931
1. *The Mellops Go Flying*. New York, 1957
2. *The Mellops Go Diving for Treasure*. New York, 1957
3. *The Mellops Strike Oil*. New York, 1958
4. *Crictor*. New York, 1958
5. *Adelaide*. New York, 1959
6. *Emile*. New York, 1960
7. *Christmas Eve at the Mellops'*. New York and London, 1960
8. *Rufus*. New York, 1961
9. *Snail, Where Are You?* New York, 1962
10. *The Three Robbers*. New York, 1962
11. *The Mellops Go Spelunking*. New York and London, 1963
12. *One, Two, Where's My Shoe?* New York and London, 1964
13. *Orlando the Brave Vulture*. New York, 1966
14. *Moon Man*. London, 1966
15. *The Party*. New York, 1966
16. *Zeralda's Ogre*. New York, 1967
17. *Ask Me A Question*. New York, 1968
18. *Fornicon*. New York, 1969
19. *The Hat*. New York, 1970
20. *I Am Papa Snap and These Are My Favorite No-such Stories*. New York, 1971
21. *No Kiss for Mother*. New York, 1973

Unwin, Nora S. (Spicer)
British, born February 22, 1907
1. *Round the Year: Verses and Pictures*. London, 1939
2. *Lucy and the Little Red Horse, with Mrs. Mouse and Family and Lucy and the Fairy Feasts*. London, 1943
3. *Doughnuts for Lin*. New York, 1950
4. *Proud Pumpkin*. New York, 1953
5. *Poquito, The Little Mexican Duck*. New York, 1959
6. *Two too Many*. New York, 1962
7. *Joyful the Morning*. New York, 1963
8. *The Way of the Shepherd: The Story of the Twenty-Third Psalm*. New York, 1963
9. *The Midsummer Witch*. New York, 1966
10. *Sinbad the Cygnet*. New York, 1970

Upfield, Arthur W. (William)
Australian, born September 1, 1888, died February 13, 1964
1. *The House of Cain.* London, 1928
2. *The Barrakee Mystery.* London, 1929
3. *The Beach of Atonement.* London, 1930
4. *The Sands of Windee.* London, 1931
5. *A Royal Abduction.* London, 1932
6. *Gripped by Drought.* London, 1932
7. *Wings above the Diamantina.* Sydney (Australia), 1936
8. *Winged Mystery.* London, 1937
9. *Mr. Jelly's Business.* Sydney, 1937
10. *Wind of Evil.* Sydney, 1937
11. *The Bone Is Pointed.* Sydney, 1938
12. *The Mystery of the Swordfish Reef.* Sydney, 1939
13. *Bushranger of the Skies.* Sydney, 1940
14. *Wings above the Claypan.* New York, 1943
15. *Murder Down Under.* New York, 1943
16. *No Footprints in the Bush.* New York, 1944
17. *Death of a Swagman.* New York, 1945
18. *The Devil's Steps.* New York, 1946
19. *An Author Bites the Dust.* Sydney and New York, 1948
20. *The Mountains Have a Secret.* New York, 1948
21. *The Widows of Broome.* New York, 1950
22. *The Bachelors of Broken Hill.* New York, 1950
23. *The New Shoe.* New York, 1951
24. *Venom House.* New York, 1952
25. *Murder Must Wait.* London and New York, 1953
26. *Death of a Lake.* London and New York, 1954
27. *Sinister Stones.* New York, 1954
28. *Cake in the Hatbox.* London, 1955
29. *The Battling Prophet.* London, 1956
30. *The Man of Two Tribes.* London and New York, 1956
31. *Bony Buys a Woman.* London, 1957
32. *The Bushman Who Came Back.* New York, 1957
33. *Bony and the Black Virgin.* London, 1959
34. *Bony and the Mouse.* London, 1959
35. *Journey to the Hangman.* New York, 1959
36. *Bony and the Kelly Gang.* London, 1960
37. *Valley of Smugglers.* New York, 1960
38. *Bony and the White Savage.* London, 1961
39. *The White Savage.* New York, 1961
40. *The Will of the Tribe.* New York, 1962
41. *Madman's Bend.* London, 1963
42. *The Body at Madman's Bend.* New York, 1963
43. *The Lake Frome Monster.* London, 1966

Upton, Bertha (Hudson)
American, born in 1849, died in 1912
1. *The Adventures of Two Dutch Dolls—and a Golliwogg.* London and New York, 1895
2. *The Golliwogg's Bicycle Club.* London and New York, 1896
3. *The Vege-Men's Revenge.* London and New York, 1897
4. *Little Hearts.* London and New York, 1897
5. *The Golliwogg at the Sea-side.* London and New York, 1898
6. *The Golliwogg in War!* London and New York, 1899
7. *The Golliwogg's Polar Adventures.* London and New York, 1900
8. *The Golliwogg's Auto-Go-Cart.* London and New York, 1901
9. *The Golliwogg's Air Ship.* London and New York, 1902
10. *The Golliwogg's Circus.* London and New York, 1903
11. *The Golliwogg in Holland.* London and New York, 1904
12. *The Golliwogg's Fox Hunt.* London and New York, 1905
13. *The Golliwogg's Desert Island.* London and New York, 1906
14. *The Golliwogg's Christmas.* London and New York, 1907
15. *The Golliwogg in the African Jungle.* London and New York, 1909

Vaizey, Mrs. George de Horne [Jessie Bell Vaizey]
British, born in 1857

1. *A Rose-Coloured Thread.* London, 1898
2. *About Peggy Saville.* London, 1900
3. *Sisters Three.* London, 1900
4. *Tom and Some Other Girls: A Public School Story.* London and New York, 1901
5. *More about Peggy.* London, 1901
6. *A Houseful of Girls.* London, 1902
7. *Pixie O'Shaughnessy.* London, 1903
8. *More about Pixie.* London, 1903
9. *The Daughters of a Genius: Story of a Brave Endeavour.* London, and Philadelphia, 1903
10. *How Like the King.* London, 1905
11. *The Heart of Una Sackville.* London, 1907
12. *The Fortunes of the Farrells.* London, 1907
13. *Betty Trevor.* London, 1907
14. *Big Game: A Story for Girls.* London, 1908
15. *Flaming June.* London, 1908
16. *The Conquest of Chrystabel.* London, 1909
17. *Old Friends and New.* London, 1909
18. *A Question of Marriage.* London, 1910
19. *Etheldreda the Ready: A School Story.* London and New York, 1910
20. *Cynthia Charrington.* London and New York, 1911
21. *A Honeymoon in Hiding.* London and New York, 1911
22. *The Adventures of Billie Belshaw.* London, 1912
23. *A College Girl.* London, 1913
24. *An Unknown Lover.* London and New York, 1913
25. *Grizel Married.* London, 1914
26. *Lady Cassandra.* London, 1914
27. *The Love Affairs of Pixie.* London, 1914
28. *Salt of Life.* London, 1915
29. *The Independence of Claire.* London, 1915
30. *What a Man Wills.* London and New York, 1915
31. *The Lady of the Basement Flat.* London, 1917
32. *Harriet Mannering's Paying Guests.* London, 1917
33. *The Right Arm and Other Stories.* London, 1918

Van Slyke, Helen (Lenore)
American, born July 9, 1919, died in 1979
Pseudonym: Sharon Ashton
1. *The Rich and the Righteous.* New York, 1971
2. *All Visitors Must Be Announced.* New York, 1972
3. *The Heart Listens.* New York, 1973
4. *The Santa Ana Wind,* as Sharon Ashton. New York, 1974
5. *The Mixed Blessing.* New York, 1975
6. *The Best Place to Be.* New York and London, 1976
7. *The Best People.* New York, 1976
8. *Always Is Not Forever.* New York, 1977
9. *Sisters and Strangers.* New York, 1978
10. *A Necessary Woman.* New York and London, 1979
11. *No Love Lost.* Philadelphia and London, 1980
12. *Public Smiles, Private Tears.* New York, 1982

Van Stockum, Hilda
American, born February 9, 1908
1. *A Day on Skates.* New York and London 1934
2. *The Cottage at Bantry Bay.* New York, 1938
3. *Francie on the Run.* New York, 1939
4. *Kersti and Saint Nicholas.* New York, 1940
5. *Pegeen.* New York, 1941
6. *Andries.* New York, 1942
7. *Gerrit and the Organ.* New York, 1943
8. *The Mitchells.* New York, 1945
9. *Canadian Summer.* New York, 1948
10. *Angel's Alphabet.* New York, 1948
11. *Patsy and the Pup.* New York, 1950
12. *King Oberon's Forest.* New York, 1957
13. *Friendly Gables.* New York, 1960

14. *Little Old Bear*. New York, 1962
15. *The Winged Watchman*. New York, 1962
16. *Jeremy Bear*. London, 1963
17. *Bennie and the New Baby*. London, 1964
18. *New Baby Is Lost*. London, 1964
19. *Mogo's Flute*. New York, 1966
20. *Penengro*. New York, 1972
21. *Rufus Round and Round*. London, 1973
22. *The Borrowed House*. New York, 1975

Vance, Jack [John Holbrook Vance]
American
Pseudonyms: Peter Held, Ellery Queen, Alan Wade
1. *The Dying Earth*. New York, 1950
2. *The Space Pirate*. New York, 1953
3. *Vandals of the Void*. Philadelphia, 1953
4. *To Live Forever*. New York, 1956
5. *Isle of Peril*, as Alan Wade. New York, 1957
6. *Take My Face*, as Peter Held. New York, 1957
7. *Big Planet*. New York, 1957
8. *The Languages of Pao*. New York, 1958
9. *Slaves of the Klau*. New York, 1958
10. *The Man in the Cage*. New York, 1960
11. *The Five Gold Bands*. New York, 1963
12. *The Dragon Masters*. New York, 1963
13. *The Houses of Iszm and Son of the Tree*. New York, 1964
14. *The Four Johns*, as Ellery Queen. New York, 1964
15. *The Star King*. New York, 1964
16. *The Killing Machine*. New York, 1964
17. *Future Tense*. New York, 1964
18. *The World Between and Other Stories*. New York, 1965
19. *A Room to Die In*, as Ellery Queen. New York, 1965
20. *Monsters in Orbit*. New York, 1965
21. *Space Opera*. New York, 1965
22. *The Madman Theory*, as Ellery Queen. New York, 1966
23. *The Fox Valley Murders*. Indianapolis (IN), 1966
24. *The Blue World*. New York, 1966
25. *The Brains of Earth*. New York, 1966
26. *The Eyes of the Overworld*. New York, 1966
27. *The Many Worlds of Magnus Ridolph*. New York, 1966
28. *The Pleasant Grove Murders*. Indianapolis, 1967
29. *The Last Castle*. New York, 1967
30. *The Palace of Love*. New York, 1967
31. *City of the Chasch*. New York, 1968
32. *The Deadly Isles*. Indianapolis, 1969
33. *Emphyrio*. New York, 1969
34. *Servants of the Wankh*. New York, 1969
35. *The Dirdir*. New York, 1969
36. *The Pnume*. New York, 1970
37. *Eight Fantasms and Magics*. New York, 1970
38. *Bad Ronald*. New York, 1973
39. *The Anome*. New York, 1973
40. *The Brave Free Men*. New York, 1973
41. *Trullion: Alastor 2262*. New York, 1973
42. *The Asutra*. New York, 1974
43. *The Worlds of Jack Vance*. New York, 1973
44. *The Gray Prince*. Indianapolis, 1974
45. *Marune: Alastor 933*. New York, 1975
46. *Showboat World*. New York, 1975
47. *Four Men Called John*. London, 1976
48. *Maske: Thaery*. New York, 1976
49. *The Best of Jack Vance*. New York, 1976
50. *Wyst: Alastor 1716*. New York, 1978
51. *Green Magic*. San Francisco, 1979
52. *The Face*. New York, 1979
53. *The House On Lily Street*. San Francisco, 1979
54. *The View from Chickweed's Window*. San Francisco, 1979

Vance, Louis Joseph
American, born September 19, 1879, died December 16, 1933
1. *Terence O'Rourke, Gentleman Adventurer*. New York, 1905
2. *The Private War*. New York and London, 1906
3. *The Brass Bowl*. Indianapolis (IN) and London, 1907
4. *The Black Bag*. Indianapolis and London, 1908
5. *The Bronze Bell*. New York and London, 1909
6. *The Pool of Flame*. New York, 1909
7. *No Man's Land*. New York and London, 1910
8. *The Fortune Hunter*. New York and London, 1910
9. *Marrying Money*. London, 1911
10. *Cynthia-of-the-Minute*. New York and London, 1911
11. *The Bandbox*. Boston and London, 1912
12. *The Destroying Angel*. Boston, 1912
13. *The Day of Days*. Boston, 1913
14. *Joan Thursday*. Boston and London, 1913
15. *The Lone Wolf*. Boston, 1914
16. *The Trey o' Hearts*. New York, 1914
17. *Nobody*. New York, 1915
18. *Sheep's Clothing*. Boston, 1915
19. *The False Faces*. New York, 1918
20. *The Dark Mirror*. New York, 1920
21. *Bean Revel*. London, 1920
22. *Alias the Lone Wolf*. New York and London, 1921
23. *Red Masquerade*. New York and London, 1921
24. *Linda Lee Incorporated*. New York, 1922
25. *Baroque*. New York and London, 1923
26. *The Lone Wolf Returns*. New York, 1923
27. *Mrs. Paramour*. New York, 1924
28. *The Road to En-Dor*. New York, 1924
29. *The Dark Power*. London, 1925
30. *The Dead Ride Hard*. Philadelphia, 1926
31. *White Fire*. New York and London, 1926
32. *They Call It Love*. Philadelphia, 1927
33. *Lip Service*. London, 1928
34. *The Woman in the Shadow*. Philadelphia, 1930
35. *Speaking of Women*. Philadelphia, 1930
36. *The Lone Wolf's Son*. Philadelphia, 1931
37. *The Trembling Flame*. Philadelphia, 1931
38. *Detective*. Philadelphia, 1932
39. *Encore the Lone Wolf*. Philadelphia, 1933
40. *The Lone Wolf's Last Prowl*. Philadelphia, 1934
41. *The Street of Strange Faces*. Philadelphia and London, 1934

Vance, William E.
Pseudonym: George Cassidy
1. *The Branded Lawman*. New York, 1952
2. *Avenger from Nowhere*. New York, 1953
3. *Hard-Rock Rancher*. New York, 1953
4. *Apache War Cry*. New York, 1955
5. *Way Station West*. New York, 1955
6. *Homicide Lost*. New York, 1956
7. *Outlaws Welcome!* New York, 1958
8. *Day of Blood*. Derby (CT), 1961
9. *Outlaw Brand*. New York, 1964
10. *Outlaw Country*. New York, 1964
11. *The Wolf Slayer*. New York, 1964
12. *Tracker*. New York, 1964
13. *The Wild Riders of Savage Valley*. New York, 1965
14. *Son of a Desperado*. New York, 1966
15. *No Man's Brand*. New York, 1967
16. *The Raid at Crazyhorse*. New York, 1967
17. *Drifter's Gold*. New York, 1979
18. *Death Stalks the Cheyenne Trail*. New York, 1980
19. *King of the Mountain*, as George Cassidy. New York, 1980
20. *Law and Outlaw*. New York, 1982

Van Dine, S.S. [Willard Huntington Wright]
American, born in 1888, died April 11, 1939
1. *Europe after 8:15,* with H.L. Mencken and George Jean Nathan. New York, 1914
2. *Modern Painting: Its Tendency and Meaning.* New York, 1915
3. *What Nietzsche Taught.* New York, 1915
4. *The Man of Promise.* New York, 1916
5. *The Creative Will: Studies in the Philosophy and Syntax of Aesthetics.* New York, 1916
6. *The Forum Exhibition of Modern American Painters, March Thirteenth to March Twenty-fifth, 1916.* New York, 1916
7. *Informing a Nation.* New York, 1917
8. *Misinforming a Nation.* New York, 1917
9. *The Future of Painting.* New York, 1923
10. *The Benson Murder Case.* New York and London, 1926
11. *The Canary Murder Case.* New York and London, 1927
12. *The Green Murder Case.* New York and London, 1928
13. *The Bishop Murder Case.* New York and London, 1929
14. *The Scarab Murder Case.* New York and London, 1930
15. *The Kennel Murder Case.* New York and London, 1933
16. *The Dragon Murder Case.* New York, 1933
17. *The Casino Murder Case.* New York and London, 1934
18. *The Garden Murder Case.* New York and London, 1935
19. *The President's Mystery Story,* with others. New York, 1935
20. *The Kidnap Murder Case.* New York and London, 1936
21. *The Gracie Allen Murder Case.* New York and London, 1938
22. *The Winter Murder Case.* New York and London, 1939
23. *The Smell of Murder.* New York, 1950

van Vogt, A.E. (Alfred Elton)
American, born April 26, 1912
1. *Slan.* Sauk City (WI), 1946
2. *The Weapon Makers.* Providence (RI), 1947
3. *The Book of Ptath.* Reading (PA), 1947
4. *The World of A.* New York, 1948
5. *Out of the Unknown.* Los Angeles, 1948
6. *The Voyage of the Space Beagle.* New York, 1950
7. *Masters of Time.* Reading, 1950
8. *The House That Stood Still.* New York, 1950
9. *The Weapon Shops of Isher.* New York, 1951
10. *Mission: Interplanetary.* New York, 1952
11. *The Mixed Men.* New York, 1952
12. *Away and Beyond.* New York, 1952
13. *Destination: Universe!* New York, 1952
14. *The Universe Maker.* New York, 1953
15. *Planets for Sale.* New York, 1954
16. *One Against Eternity.* New York, 1955
17. *Mission to the Stars.* New York, 1955
18. *The Pawns of Null-A.* New York, 1956
19. *The Hypnotism Handbook.* Los Angeles, 1956
20. *Empire of the Atom.* Chicago, 1957
21. *The Mind Cage.* New York, 1957
22. *Triad.* New York, 1959
23. *The War Against the Rull.* New York, 1959
24. *Siege of the Unseen.* New York, 1959
25. *Earth's Last Fortress.* New York, 1960
26. *The Mating Cry.* New York, 1960
27. *The Wizard of Linn.* New York, 1962
28. *The Violent Man.* New York, 1962
29. *The Beast.* New York, 1963
30. *Two Hundred Million A.D.* New York, 1964
31. *The Twisted Men.* New York, 1964
32. *Rogue Ship.* New York, 1965
33. *Monsters.* New York, 1965
34. *The Players of Null-A.* New York, 1966
35. *The Winged Man.* New York, 1966
36. *The Universe Maker, and The Proxy Intelligence.* London, 1967
37. *A van Vogt Omnibus.* London, 1967
38. *The Far-Out Worlds of A.E. van Vogt.* New York, 1968
39. *The World of Null-A.* London, 1969
40. *Moonbeast.* London, 1969
41. *The Silkie.* New York, 1969
42. *Quest for the Future.* New York, 1970
43. *Children of Tomorrow.* New York, 1970
44. *The Sea Thing and Other Stories.* London, 1970
45. *The Battle of Forever.* New York, 1971
46. *More Than Superhuman.* New York, 1971
47. *The Proxy Intelligence and Other Mind Benders.* New York, 1971
48. *M-33 in Andromeda.* New York, 1971
49. *The Darkness on Diamondia.* New York, 1972
50. *The Book of van Vogt.* New York, 1972
51. *The Money Personality.* West Nyack (NY), 1972
52. *Future Glitter.* New York, 1973
53. *Two Science Fiction Novels.* London, 1973
54. *The Secret Galactics.* Englewood Cliffs (NJ), 1974
55. *The Man with a Thousand Names.* New York, 1974
56. *The Worlds of A.E. van Vogt.* New York, 1974
57. *The Best of A.E. van Vogt.* London, 1974
58. *Reflections of A.E. van Vogt.* Lakemont (GA), 1975
59. *The Undercover Aliens.* London, 1976
60. *Earth Factor X.* New York, 1976
61. *The Blal.* New York, 1976
62. *The Best of A.E. van Vogt.* New York, 1976
63. *The Gryb.* New York, 1976
64. *Tyranopolis.* London, 1977
65. *The Anarchistic Colossus.* New York, 1977
66. *Supermind.* New York, 1977
67. *Pendulum.* New York, 1978
68. *Renaissance.* New York, 1979
69. *Lost: Fifty Suns.* New York, 1979
70. *Cosmic Encounter.* New York, 1980

Varley, John
American, born in 1947
1. *The Ophiuchi Hotline.* New York, 1977
2. *Titan.* New York, 1978
3. *The Persistence of Vision.* New York, 1978
4. *In the Hall of the Martian Kings.* London, 1978
5. *The Barbie Murders and Other Stories.* New York, 1980
6. *Wizard.* New York, 1980

Verney, John
British, born September 30, 1913
1. *Verney Abroad.* London, 1954
2. *Going to the Wars: A Journey in Various Directions.* London and New York, 1955
3. *Look at Houses.* London, 1959
4. *Friday's Tunnel.* London, 1959
5. *February's Road.* London, 1961
6. *Every Advantage.* London, 1961
7. *The Mad King of Chichiboo.* London and New York, 1963
8. *ismo.* London, 1964
9. *A Dinner of Herbs.* London, 1966
10. *Fine Day for a Picnic.* London, 1968
11. *Seven Sunflower Seeds.* London, 1968
12. *Samson's Hoard.* London, 1973

Vernon, Roger Lee
American, born in 1924
1. *The Space Frontier.* New York, 1955
2. *Robot Hunt.* New York, 1959

Verrill, A. Hyatt [Alpheus Hyatt Verrill]
American, born July 23, 1871, died November 14, 1954
Pseudonym: Ray Ainsbury
1. *Gasolene Engines: Their Operation, Use, and Care.* New York, 1912
2. *Knots, Splices, and Rope Work.* New York, 1912
3. *Harper's Book for Young Naturalists [Gardeners].* New York, 2 vols., 1913-14
4. *Harper's Wireless [Aircraft, Gasoline Engine] Book.* New York, 3 vols., 1913-14
5. *The American Crusoe.* New York, 1914
6. *Cuba Past and Present.* New York, 1914
7. *South and Central American Trade Conditions of Today.* New York, 1914
8. *Porto Rico Past and Present.* New York, 1914
9. *Cruise of the Cormorant.* New York, 1915
10. *In Morgan's Wake.* New York, 1915
11. *Uncle Abner's Legacy.* New York, 1915
12. *Pets for Pleasure and Profit.* New York, 1915
13. *The Boys' Outdoor Vacation Book.* New York, 1915
14. *The Amateur Carpenter.* New York, 1915
15. *The Boy Collector's Handbook.* New York, 1915
16. *Isles of Spice and Palm.* New York, 1915
17. *The Golden City.* New York, 1916
18. *Marooned in the Forest.* New York, 1916
19. *Jungle Chums.* New York, 1916
20. *A-B-C of Automobile Driving.* New York, 1916
21. *The Real Story of the Whaler.* New York, 1916
22. *The Ocean and Its Mysteries.* New York, 1916
23. *The Book of the Motor Boat [Sailboat].* New York, 2 vols., 1916
24. *The Book of the West Indies.* New York, 1917
25. *The Book of Camping.* New York, 1917
26. *The Trail of the Cloven Foot.* New York, 1918
27. *How to Operate a Motor Car.* Philadelphia, 1918
28. *Getting Together with Latin America.* New York, 1918
29. *The Tail of the White Indians.* New York, 1920
30. *Islands and Their Mysteries.* New York, 1920
31. *Panama, Past and Present.* New York, 1921
32. *The Boys' Book of Whalers [Carpentry, Buccaneers].* New York, 3 vols., 1922-23
33. *Radio for Amateurs.* New York and London, 1922
34. *Rivers and Their Mysteries.* New York, 1922
35. *The Home Radio.* New York, 1922
36. *The Boy Adventurers in the Forbidden Land [in the Land of El Dorado, in the Unknown Land].* New York, 3 vols., 1922-24
37. *The Deep Sea Hunters [in the Frozen Sea, in the South Seas].* New York, 3 vols., 1922-24
38. *The Radio Detectives [in the Jungle, Southward Bound, under the Sea].* New York, 4 vols., 1922
39. *The Boy Adventurers in the Land of the Monkey Men.* New York, 1923
40. *In the Wake of the Buccaneers.* New York, 1923
41. *The Real Story of the Pirate.* New York, 1923
42. *Smugglers and Smuggling.* New York and London, 1924
43. *Love Stories of Some Famous Pirates.* London, 1924
44. *The Home Radio Up to Date.* New York, 1927
45. *Panama [Cuba, Jamaica, West Indies] of Today.* New York, 4 vols., 1927-31
46. *The American Indian.* New York, 1927
47. *Old Civilization of the New World.* Indianapolis (IN) and London, 1929
48. *Thirty Years in the Jungle.* London, 1929
49. *Great Conquerors of South and Central America.* New York, 1929
50. *Lost Treasure.* New York, 1930
51. *Gasoline-Engine Book for Boys.* New York, 1930
52. *Under Peruvian Skies.* London, 1930
53. *Secret Treasure.* New York, 1931
54. *The Inquisition.* New York, 1931
55. *Barton's Mills: A Saga of the Pioneers.* New York, 1932
56. *The Incas' Treasure House.* Boston, 1932
57. *Romantic and Historic Maine [Florida, Virginia].* New York, 3 vols., 1933-35
58. *Before the Conquerors.* New York, 1935
59. *Our Indians.* New York, 1935
60. *They Found Gold.* New York, 1936
61. *The Heart of Old New England.* New York, 1936
62. *Along New England Shores.* New York, 1936
63. *Strange Sea Shells [Insects, Reptiles, Birds, Fish, Animals] and Their Stories.* Boston and London, 6 vols., 1936-39
64. *The Treasure of the Bloody Gut.* New York, 1937
65. *My Jungle Trails.* Boston and London, 1937
66. *Foods America Gave the World.* Boston, 1937
67. *Minerals, Metals, and Gems.* Boston, 1939
68. *Carib Gold.* London, 1939
69. *Wonder Plants and Plant Wonders.* New York, 1939
70. *Perfumes and Spices.* Boston, 1940
71. *Wonder Creatures of the Sea.* New York, 1940
72. *Strange Prehistoric Animals and Their Stories.* Boston, 1948
73. *The Bridge of Light.* Reading, 1950
74. *The Strange Story of Our Earth.* Boston, 1952
75. *America's Ancient Civilization.* New York and London, 1954
76. *When the Moon Ran Wild,* as Ray Ainsbury. London, 1962

Veryan, Patricia [Patricia V. Bannister]
British/American, born November 21, 1923
1. *The Lord and the Gypsy.* New York, 1978
2. *Love's Duet.* New York, 1979
3. *Debt of Honour.* London, 1980
4. *Mistress of Willowvale.* New York, 1980
5. *A Perfect Match.* London, 1981
6. *Nanette.* New York, 1981
7. *Feather Castles.* New York, 1982

Vickers, Roy C.
British, born in 1888(?), died in 1965
Pseudonyms: David Durham, Sefton Kyle and John Spencer
1. *Lord Roberts: The Story of His Life.* London, 1914
2. *The Mystery of the Scented Death.* London, 1921
3. *The Vengeance of Henry Jarroman.* London, 1923
4. *The Woman Accused,* as David Durham. London, 1923
5. *Hounded Down,* as David Durham. London, 1923
6. *Ishmael's Wife.* London, 1924
7. *A Murder for a Million.* London, 1924
8. *The Exploits of Fidelity Dove,* as David Durham. London, 1924
9. *Four Past Four.* London, 1925
10. *The Pearl-Headed Pin,* as David Durham. London, 1925
11. *Dead Man's Dower,* as Sefton Kyle. London, 1925
12. *His Other Wife.* London, 1926
13. *The Unforbidden Sin.* London, 1926
14. *The White Raven.* London, 1927
15. *Guilty, But—,* as Sefton Kyle. London, 1927
16. *The Radingham Mystery.* London, 1928
17. *A Girl of These Days.* London, 1929
18. *The Rose in the Dark.* London, 1930
19. *The Gold Game.* London, 1930
20. *The Hawk,* as Sefton Kyle. London and New York, 1930
21. *The Deputy for Cain.* London, 1931
22. *The Marriage for the Defence.* London, 1932
23. *The Whispering Death,* as John Spencer. London, 1932
24. *The Vengeance of Mrs. Danvers,* as Sefton Kyle. London, 1932
25. *The Bloomsbury Treasure,* as Sefton Kyle. London, 1932

26. *Swell Garrick*, as John Spencer. London, 1933
27. *Bardelow's Heir.* London, 1933
28. *Red Hair*, as Sefton Kyle. London, 1933
29. *Money Buys Everything.* London, 1934
30. *The Life He Stole*, as Sefton Kyle. London, 1934
31. *Kidnap Island.* London, 1935
32. *Hide Those Diamonds!* London, 1935
33. *The Man in the Red Mask.* London, 1935
34. *The Forgotten Honeymoon*, as David Durham. London, 1935
35. *The Man Without a Name*, as Sefton Kyle. London, 1935
36. *Silence*, as Sefton Kyle. London, 1935
37. *The Durand Case*, as Sefton Kyle. London, 1936
38. *Number Seventy-Three*, as Sefton Kyle. London, 1936
39. *Terror of Tongues!* London, 1937
40. *The Girl in the News.* London, 1937
41. *I'll Never Tell.* London, 1937
42. *The Body in the Safe*, as Sefton Kyle. London, 1937
43. *The Notorious Miss Walters*, as Sefton Kyle. London, 1937
44. *The Enemy Within.* London, 1938
45. *The Life Between.* London, 1938
46. *The Girl Who Dared*, as David Durham. London, 1938
47. *During His Majesty's Pleasure*, as Sefton Kyle. London, 1938
48. *Missing!* as Sefton Kyle. London, 1938
49. *Against the Law*, as David Durham. London, 1939
50. *Miss X*, as Sefton Kyle. London, 1939
51. *The Judge's Dilemma*, as Sefton Kyle. London, 1939
52. *Playgirl Wanted.* London, 1940
53. *She Walked in Fear.* London, 1940
54. *The Shadow over Fairholme*, as Sefton Kyle. London, 1940
55. *The Girl Known as D 13*, as Sefton Kyle. London, 1940
56. *Brenda Gets Married.* London, 1941
57. *A Date with Danger.* London, 1942
58. *War Bride.* London, 1942
59. *The Price of Silence*, as Sefton Kyle. London, 1942
60. *Love Was Married*, as Sefton Kyle. London, 1943
61. *The Department of Dead Ends.* New York, 1947
62. *Six Came to Dinner.* London, 1948
63. *Gold and Wine.* London, 1949
64. *Murder of a Snob.* London, 1949
65. *Murdering Mr. Velfrage.* London, 1950
66. *Maid to Murder.* New York, 1950
67. *They Can't Hang Caroline.* London, 1950
68. *Murder Will Out.* London, 1950
69. *The Sole Survivor, and the Kynsard Affair.* Roslyn (NY), 1951
70. *Murder in Two Flats.* London and New York, 1952
71. *Eight Murders in the Suburbs.* London, 1954
72. *Double Image and Other Stories.* London and Roslyn, 1955
73. *Six Murders in the Suburbs.* Roslyn, 1958
74. *Seven Chose Murder.* London and Roslyn, 1959
75. *Find the Innocent.* London, 1959
76. *Best Detective Stories.* London, 1965

Vidal, Gore (Eugene Luther)
American, born October 3, 1925
Pseudonym: Edgar Box
1. *Williwaw.* New York, 1946
2. *In a Yellow Wood.* New York, 1947
3. *The City and the Pillar.* New York, 1948
4. *The Season of Comfort.* New York, 1949
5. *Dark Green, Bright Red.* New York and London, 1950
6. *A Search for the King: A Twelfth Century Legend.* New York, 1950
7. *The Judgement of Paris.* New York, 1952
8. *Death in the Fifth Position*, as Edgar Box. New York, 1952
9. *Death Before Bedtime*, as Edgar Box. New York, 1953
10. *Death Likes It Hot*, as Edgar Box. New York, 1954
11. *Messiah.* New York, 1954
12. *A Thirsty Evil: Seven Short Stories.* New York, 1956
13. *Visit to a Small Planet.* Boston, 1956
14. *The Best Man: A Play about Politics.* Boston, 1960
15. *Three: Williwaw, A Thirsty Evil, Julian the Apostate.* New York, 1962
16. *Three Plays.* London, 1962
17. *Romulus: A New Comedy.* New York, 1962
18. *Rocking the Boat.* Boston, 1962
19. *Julian.* Boston, 1964
20. *Washington, D.C.* Boston, 1967
21. *Myra Breckenridge.* Boston, 1968
22. *Weekend.* New York, 1968
23. *Sex, Death and Money.* New York, 1968
24. *Reflections upon a Sinking Ship.* Boston and London, 1969
25. *Two Sisters: A Memoir in the Form of a Novel.* Boston and London, 1970
26. *Burr.* New York, 1973
27. *Myron.* New York, 1974
28. *1876.* New York and London, 1976
29. *Matters of Fact and Fiction, Essays 1973-1976.* New York and London, 1977
30. *Great American Families*, with Others. New York and London, 1977
31. *Kalki.* New York and London, 1978

Vinge, Joan D. [Joan Carol Dennison Vinge]
1. *The Outcasts of Heaven Belt.* New York, 1978
2. *Fireship.* New York, 1978
3. *Eyes of Amber and Other Stories.* New York, 1979
4. *The Snow Queen.* New York and London, 1980

Vining, Elizabeth Gray
American, born October 6, 1902
Pseudonym: Elizabeth Janet Gray
1. *Merediths' Ann*, as Elizabeth Janet Gray. New York and London, 1927
2. *Tangle Garden*, as Elizabeth Janet Gray. New York, 1928
3. *Tilly-Tod*, as Elizabeth Janet Gray. New York, 1929
4. *Meggy MacIntosh*, as Elizabeth Janet Gray. New York, 1930
5. *Jane Hope*, as Elizabeth Janet Gray. New York, 1933
6. *Young Walter Scott.* New York, 1935
7. *Beppy Marlowe of Charles Town*, as Elizabeth Janet Gray. New York, 1936
8. *Penn.* New York, 1938
9. *The Contributions of the Quakers.* Philadelphia, 1939
10. *The Fair Adventure*, as Elizabeth Janet Gray. New York, 1940
11. *Adam of the Road*, as Elizabeth Janet Gray. New York, 1942
12. *Sandy*, as Elizabeth Janet Gray. New York, 1945
13. *Windows for the Crown Prince.* Philadelphia and London, 1952
14. *The World in Tune.* Wallingford (PA), 1952
15. *The Virginia Exiles.* Philadelphia, 1955
16. *Friend of Life: The Biography of Rufus M. Jones.* Philadelphia, 1958
17. *The Cheerful Heart*, as Elizabeth Janet Gray. New York, 1959
18. *Return to Japan.* Philadelphia, 1960
19. *Japanese Young People Today.* Philadelphia, 1961
20. *I Will Adventure*, as Elizabeth Janet Gray. New York, 1962
21. *Take Heed of Loving Me.* Philadelphia, 1964
22. *Flora: A Biography.* Philadelphia, 1966
23. *Flora MacDonald, Her Life in the Highlands of America.* London, 1967
24. *I, Roberta.* Philadelphia, 1967

25. *William Penn: Mystic.* Wallingford, 1969
26. *Quiet Pilgrimage.* Philadelphia, 1970
27. *The Taken Girl.* New York, 1972
28. *The May Masse Collection: Creative Publishing for Children.* Emporia (KS), 1972
29. *Mr. Whittier.* New York, 1974

Viorst, Judith (Stahl)
American
1. *Projects: Space.* New York, 1962
2. *150 Science Experiments Step-by-Step.* New York, 1963
3. *The Natural World: A Guide to North American Wildlife.* New York, 1965
4. *The Village Square.* New York, 1965
5. *The Changing Earth.* New York, 1967
6. *It's Hard to be Hip over Thirty and Other Tragedies of Married Life.* Cleveland (OH), 1968
7. *Sunday Morning.* New York, 1968
8. *I'll Fix Anthony.* New York, 1969
9. *The Washington D.C., Underground Gourmet.* New York, 1970
10. *Try It Again, Sam.* New York, 1970
11. *People and Other Aggravations.* New York, 1971
12. *The Tenth Good Thing about Barney.* New York, 1971
13. *Yes, Married: A Saga of Love and Complaint.* New York, 1972
14. *Alexander and the Terrible, Horrible, No Good, Very Bad Day.* New York, 1972
15. *My Mama Says There Aren't Any Zombies, Ghosts, Vampires, Creatures, Demons, Monsters, Fiends, Goblins, or Things.* New York, 1973
16. *Rosie and Michael.* New York, 1974
17. *How Did I Get to be Forty and Other Atrocities.* New York, 1976
18. *A Visit from St. Nicholas.* New York, 1977

Vonnegut, Jr., Kurt
American, born November 11, 1922
1. *Player Piano.* New York, 1952
2. *Utopia 14.* New York, 1954
3. *The Sirens of Titan.* New York, 1959
4. *Canary in a Cat House.* New York, 1961
5. *Mother Night.* New York, 1962
6. *Cat's Cradle.* New York and London, 1963
7. *God Bless You, Mr. Rosewater; or, Pearls Before Swine.* New York and London, 1965
8. *Welcome to the Monkey House: A Collection of Short Works.* New York, 1968
9. *Slaughterhouse-Five; or, The Children's Crusade.* New York, 1969
10. *Happy Birthday, Wanda June.* New York, 1971
11. *Between Time and Timbuktu; or, Prometheus-5: A Space Fantasy.* New York, 1972
12. *Breakfast of Champions; or, Goodbye, Blue Monday.* New York, 1973
13. *Slapstick; or, Lonesome No More.* New York, 1976
14. *Jailbird.* New York and London, 1979

Waber, Bernard
American, born September 27, 1924
1. *Lorenzo.* Boston, 1961
2. *The House on East 88th Street.* Boston, 1962
3. *Rich Cat, Poor Cat.* Boston, 1963
4. *How to Go About Laying an Egg.* Boston, 1963
5. *Just Like Abraham Lincoln.* Boston, 1964
6. *Lyle, Lyle, Crocodile.* Boston, 1965
7. *Lyle and the Birthday Party.* Boston, 1966
8. *"You Look Ridiculous," Said the Rhinoceros to the Hippopotamus.* Boston, 1966
9. *An Anteater Named Arthur.* Boston, 1967
10. *Cheese.* Boston, 1967
11. *A Rose for Mr. Bloom.* Boston, 1968
12. *Lovable Lyle.* Boston, 1969
13. *A Firefly Named Torchy.* Boston, 1970
14. *Nobody Is Perfick.* Boston, 1971
15. *Ira Sleeps Over.* Boston, 1972
16. *Lyle Finds His Mother.* Boston, 1974
17. *I Was All Thumbs.* Boston, 1975
18. *But Names Will Never Hurt Me.* Boston, 1976
19. *Goodbye, Funny Dumpy-Lumpy.* Boston, 1977
20. *Mice on My Mind.* Boston, 1977

Wade, Henry [Henry Lancelot Aubrey-Fletcher]
British, born September 10, 1887, died May 30, 1969
1. *The Verdict of You All.* London, 1926
2. *A History of the Foot Guards to 1856,* as H.L. Aubrey-Fletcher. London, 1927
3. *The Missing Partners.* London and New York, 1928
4. *The Duke of York's Steps.* London and New York, 1929
5. *The Dying Alderman.* New York and London, 1930
6. *The Floating Admiral,* with others. London, 1931
7. *No Friendly Drop.* London, 1931
8. *The Hanging Captain.* London, 1932
9. *Mist on the Saltings.* London, 1933
10. *Policeman's Lot.* London, 1933
11. *Constable, Guard Thyself!* London, 1934
12. *Heir Presumptive.* London, 1935
13. *Bury Him Darkly.* London, 1936
14. *The High Sheriff.* London, 1937
15. *Released for Death.* London, 1938
16. *Here Comes the Copper.* London, 1938
17. *Lonely Magdalen.* London, 1940
18. *New Graves at Great Norne.* London, 1947
19. *Diplomat's Folly.* London, 1951
20. *Be Kind to the Killer.* London, 1952
21. *Too Soon to Die.* London, 1953
22. *Gold Was Our Grave.* London and New York, 1954
23. *A Dying Fall.* London and New York, 1955
24. *The Litmore Snatch.* London and New York, 1957

Wade, Robert
American, born in 1920
Pseudonyms: Wade Miller, with Bill Miller; Will Daemer, with Bill Miller; Whit Masterson; Bob Wade; Dale Wilmer, with Bill Miller
1. *Deadly Weapon,* as Wade Miller. New York, 1946
2. *Guilty Bystander,* as Wade Miller. New York, 1947
3. *Pop Goes the Queen,* as Bob Wade, with Bill Miller. New York, 1947
4. *Fatal Step,* as Wade Miller. New York, 1948
5. *Uneasy Street,* as Wade Miller. New York, 1948
6. *Devil on Two Sticks,* as Wade Miller. New York, 1949
7. *Killer's Choice,* as Wade Miller. New York, 1950
8. *Calamity Fair,* as Wade Miller. New York, 1950
9. *Devil May Care,* as Wade Miller. New York, 1950
10. *Murder Charge,* as Wade Miller. New York, 1950
11. *Stolen Woman,* as Wade Miller. New York, 1950
12. *The Case of the Lonely Lovers,* as Will Daemer. New York, 1951
13. *The Killer,* as Wade Miller. New York, 1951
14. *Shoot to Kill,* as Wade Miller. New York, 1951
15. *The Tiger's Wife,* as Wade Miller. New York, 1951
16. *Memo for Murder,* as Dale Wilmer. Hasbrouck Heights (NJ), 1951
17. *Branded Woman,* as Wade Miller. New York, 1952
18. *The Big Guy,* as Wade Miller. New York, 1953
19. *South of the Sun.* New York and London, 1953

20. *Dead Fall*, as Dale Wilmer. New York, 1954
21. *Jungle Heat*, as Dale Wilmer. New York, 1954
22. *Mad Baxter*, as Wade Miller. New York, 1955
23. *All Through the Night*, as Whit Masterson, with Bill Miller. New York, 1955
24. *Dead, She Was Beautiful*, as Whit Masterson, with Bill Miller. New York, 1955
25. *Badge of Evil*, as Whit Masterson, with Bill Miller. New York and London, 1956
26. *Kiss Her Goodbye*, as Wade Miller. New York, 1956
27. *A Cry in the Night*, as Whit Masterson, with Bill Miller. New York, 1956
28. *A Shadow in the Wild*, as Whit Masterson, with Bill Miller. New York and London, 1957
29. *Touch of Evil*, as Whit Masterson, with Bill Miller. New York, 1958
30. *Kitten with a Whip*, as Wade Miller. New York, 1959
31. *The Dark Fantastic*, as Whit Masterson, with Bill Miller. New York, 1959
32. *Sunner Take All*, as Wade Miller. New York, 1960
33. *A Hammer in His Hand*, as Whit Masterson, with Bill Miller. New York and London, 1960
34. *Evil Come, Evil Go*, as Whit Masterson. New York and London, 1961
35. *Nightmare Cruise*, as Wade Miller. New York, 1961
36. *The Sargasso People*, as Wade Miller. London, 1961
37. *The Girl from Midnight*, as Wade Miller. New York, 1962
38. *Man on a Nylon String*, as Whit Masterson. New York and London, 1963
39. *The Stroke of Seven*. New York, 1965
40. *711—Officer Needs Help*, as Whit Masterson. New York, 1965
41. *Killer with a Badge*, as Whit Masterson. London, 1966
42. *Warning Shot*, as Whit Masterson. New York, 1967
43. *Play Like You're Dead*, as Whit Masterson. New York, 1967
44. *The Last One Kills*, as Whit Masterson. New York, 1969
45. *Knave of Eagles*. New York, 1969
46. *The Death of Me Yet*, as Whit Masterson. New York, 1970
47. *The Gravy Train*, as Whit Masterson. New York, 1971
48. *Why She Cries, I Do Not Know*, as Whit Masterson. New York, 1972
49. *The Undertaker Wind*, as Whit Masterson. New York, 1973
50. *The Man With Two Clocks*, as Whit Masterson. New York, 1974
51. *The Great Train Hijack*, as Whit Masterson. New York, 1976
52. *Hunter of the Blood*, as Whit Masterson. New York, 1977
53. *The Slow Gallows*, as Whit Masterson. New York, 1979

Wagoner, David (Russell)
American, June 5, 1926
1. *Dry Sun, Dry Wind*. Bloomington (IN), 1953
2. *The Man in the Middle*. New York, 1954
3. *Money, Money, Money*. New York, 1955
4. *Rock*. New York, 1958
5. *A Place to Stand*. Bloomington, 1958
6. *Poems*. Portland (OR), 1959
7. *The Nesting Ground*. Bloomington, 1963
8. *The Escape Artist*. New York and London, 1965
9. *Staying Alive*. Bloomington, 1966
10. *Baby, Come On Inside*. New York, 1968
11. *New and Selected Poems*. Bloomington, 1969
12. *Working Against Time*. London, 1970
13. *Where Is My Wandering Boy Tonight?* New York, 1970
14. *Riverbed*. Bloomington, 1972
15. *Sleeping in the Woods*. Bloomington, 1974
16. *The Road to Many a Wonder*. New York, 1974
17. *Tracker*. Boston, 1975
18. *A Guide to Dungeness Spit*. Port Townsend (WA), 1975
19. *Traveling Light*. Port Townsend, 1976
20. *Collected Poems 1956-1976*. Bloomington, 1976
21. *Whole Hog*. Boston, 1976
22. *Who Shall Be the Sun? Poems Based on the Lore, Legends, and Myths of Northwest Coast and Plateau Indians*. Bloomington, 1978
23. *In Broken Country*. Boston, 1979
24. *The Hanging Garden*. Boston, 1980
25. *Landfall*. Boston, 1981

Wahl, Jan
American, born April 1, 1933
1. *The Beast Book*. New York, 1964
2. *Pleasant Fieldmouse*. New York, 1964
3. *The Howards Go Sledding*. New York, 1964
4. *Hello, Elephant*. New York, 1964
5. *Cabbage Moon*. New York, 1965
6. *The Muffletumps: The Story of Four Dolls*. New York, 1966
7. *Christmas in the Forest*. New York, 1967
8. *Pocahontas in London*. New York, 1967
9. *The Furious Flycycle*. New York, 1968
10. *Push Kitty*. New York, 1968
11. *Cobweb Castle*. New York, 1968
12. *Rickety Rackety Rooster*. New York, 1968
13. *Runaway Jonah and Other Tales*. New York, 1968
14. *A Wolf of My Own*. New York, 1969
15. *How the Children Stopped the Wars*. New York, 1969
16. *The Fishermen*. New York, 1969
17. *May Horses*. New York, 1969
18. *The Norman Rockwell Storybook*. New York, 1969
19. *The Prince Who Was a Fish*. New York, 1970
20. *The Mulberry Tree*. New York, 1970
21. *The Wonderful Kite*. New York, 1970
22. *Doctor Rabbit*. New York, 1970
23. *The Animals' Peace Day*. New York, 1970
24. *Abe Lincoln's Beard*. New York, 1971
25. *Anna Help Ginger*. New York, 1971
26. *Crabapple Night*. New York, 1971
27. *Margaret's Birthday*. New York, 1971
28. *The Six Voyages of Pleasant Fieldmouse*. New York, 1971
29. *Lorenzo Bear and Company*. New York, 1971
30. *The Very Peculiar Tunnel*. New York, 1972
31. *Magic Heart*. New York, 1972
32. *Grandmother Told Me*. Boston, 1972
33. *Cristobal and the Witch*. New York, 1972
34. *Juan Diego and the Lady*. New York, 1972
35. *S.O.S. Bobomobile! or, The Further Adventures of Melvin Spitznagle and Professor Mickimecki*. New York, 1973
36. *Crazy Brobobalou*. New York, 1973
37. *The Five in the Forest*. Chicago, 1974
38. *Pleasant Fieldmouse's Halloween Party*. New York, 1974
39. *Mooga Mega Mekki*. Chicago, 1974
40. *Jeremiah Knucklebones*. New York, 1974
41. *The Woman with the Eggs*. New York, 1975
42. *The Muffletump Storybook*. Chicago, 1975
43. *The Clumpets Go Sailing*. New York, 1975
44. *The Bear, The Wolf, and the Mouse*. Chicago, 1975
45. *The Screeching Door; or, What Happened at the Elephant Hotel*. New York, 1975
46. *The Muffletump's Christmas Party*. Chicago, 1975
47. *Follow Me, Cried Bee*. New York, 1976
48. *Great-Grandmother Cat Tales*. New York, 1976
49. *Grandpa's Indian Summer*. Englewood Cliffs (NJ), 1976
50. *The Pleasant Fieldmouse Storybook*. Englewood Cliffs, 1977
51. *Doctor Rabbit's Foundling*. New York, 1977

52. *Carrot Nose.* New York, 1977
53. *Frankenstein's Dog.* Englewood Cliffs, 1977
54. *The Muffletumps' Halloween Scare.* Chicago, 1977
55. *Dracula's Cat.* Englewood Cliffs, 1977
56. *Pleasant Fieldmouse's Valentine Trick.* New York, 1977

Wainwright, John
British, born February 25, 1921
Pseudonym: Jack Ripley
1. *Death in a Sleeping City.* London, 1965
2. *Ten Steps to the Gallows.* London, 1965
3. *Evil Intent.* London, 1966
4. *The Crystallised Carbon Pig.* London, 1966
5. *Talent for Murder.* London and New York, 1967
6. *The Worms Must Wait.* London, 1967
7. *Web of Silence.* London, 1968
8. *Edge of Extinction.* London, 1968
9. *The Darkening Glass.* London, 1968
10. *The Take-Over Men.* London, 1969
11. *The Big Tickle.* London, 1969
12. *Freeze Thy Blood Less Coldly.* London, 1970
13. *Prynter's Devil.* London, 1970
14. *The Last Buccaneer.* London, 1971
15. *Dig the Grave and Let Him Lie.* London, 1971
16. *Davis Doesn't Live Here Any More,* as Jack Ripley. London, 1971
17. *The Pig Got Up and Slowly Walked Away,* as Jack Ripley. London, 1971
18. *Night Is a Time to Die.* London, 1972
19. *Requiem for a Loser.* London, 1972
20. *My Word, You Should Have Seen Us,* as Jack Ripley. London, 1972
21. *My God, How the Money Rolls In,* as Jack Ripley. London, 1972
22. *A Pride of Pigs.* London, 1973
23. *High-Class Kill.* London, 1973
24. *The Devil You Don't.* London, 1973
25. *A Touch of Malice.* London, 1973
26. *The Evidence I Shall Give.* London, 1974
27. *Cause for a Killing.* London, 1974
28. *Kill the Girls and Make Them Cry.* London, 1974
29. *The Hard Hit.* London, 1974
30. *Square Dance.* London and New York, 1975
31. *Death of a Big Man.* London and New York, 1975
32. *Landscape with Violence.* London, 1975
33. *Coppers Don't Cry.* London, 1975
34. *Acquittal.* London and New York, 1976
35. *Walther P.38.* London, 1976
36. *Who Goes Next?* London and New York, 1976
37. *The Bastard.* London and New York, 1976
38. *Pool of Tears.* London and New York, 1977
39. *A Nest of Rats.* London and New York, 1977
40. *Do Nothin' till You Hear from Me.* London and New York, 1977
41. *The Day of the Peppercorn Kill.* London, 1977
42. *The Jury People.* London and New York, 1978
43. *Thief of Time.* London and New York, 1978
44. *Death Certificate.* London, 1978
45. *A Ripple of Murders.* London, 1978
46. *Brainwash.* London and New York, 1979
47. *Duty Elsewhere.* London and New York, 1979
48. *Tension.* London, 1979
49. *The Reluctant Sleeper.* London, 1979
50. *Home Is the Hunter, and The Big Kayo.* London, 1979
51. *Take Murder. . . .* London, 1979

Waldo, Dave [David Waldo Clarke]
British, born August 13, 1907
1. *Modern English Writers.* London, 1947
2. *William Shakespeare.* London, 1950
3. *The Man from Thunder River.* London, 1951
4. *Warbonnet.* London, 1952
5. *Ride On, Stranger.* London, 1953
6. *The Long Riders.* London, 1957
7. *Lariat.* London, 1958
8. *Beat the Drum Slowly.* London, 1961
9. *Ride the High Hills.* London, 1961
10. *No Man Rides Alone.* London, 1965
11. *Once in the Saddle.* London, 1968

Walker, David (Harry)
Canadian, born February 9, 1911
1. *The Storm and the Silence.* Boston, 1949
2. *Geordie.* London and Boston, 1952
3. *Digby.* London and Boston, 1953
4. *Harry Black.* London and Boston, 1954
5. *Sandy Was a Soldier's Boy.* London and Boston, 1957
6. *Where the High Winds Blow.* London and Boston, 1960
7. *Dragon Hill.* Boston, 1962
8. *Storms of Our Journey and Other Stories.* Boston, 1962
9. *Winter of Madness.* London and Boston, 1964
10. *Mallabec.* London and Boston, 1965
11. *Come Back, Geordie.* London and Boston, 1966
12. *Devil's Plunge.* London, 1968
13. *CAB-Intersec.* Boston, 1968
14. *Pirate Rock.* London and Boston, 1969
15. *Big Ben.* Boston, 1969
16. *The Lord's Pink Ocean.* London and Boston, 1972
17. *Black Dougal.* London, 1973
18. *Ash.* London and Boston, 1976
19. *Pot of Gold.* London, 1977

Wallace, Edgar [Richard Horatio Edgar Wallace]
British, born April 1, 1875, died February 10, 1932
1. *The Mission That Failed! A Tale of the Raid and Other Poems.* Cape Town (South Africa), 1898
2. *Nicholson's Nek.* Cape Town, 1900
3. *War! and Other Poems.* Cape Town, 1900
4. *Writ in Barracks.* London, 1900
5. *Unofficial Despatches.* London, 1901
6. *Smithy.* London, 1905
7. *The Four Just Men.* London, 1906
8. *Angel Esquire.* Bristol and New York, 1908
9. *The Council of Justice.* London, 1908
10. *Captain Tatham of Tatham Island.* London, 1909
11. *The Duke in the Suburbs.* London, 1909
12. *Smithy Abroad: Barrack Room Sketches.* London, 1909
13. *The Nine Bears.* London, 1910
14. *The Other Man.* New York, 1911
15. *Sanders of the River.* London, 1911
16. *The People of the River.* London, 1912
17. *Private Selby.* London, 1912
18. *The Fourth Plague.* London, 1913
19. *Grey Timothy.* London, 1913
20. *The River of Stars.* London, 1913
21. *Pallard the Punter.* London, 1914
22. *The Admirable Carfew.* London, 1914
23. *Bosambo of the River.* London, 1914
24. *Smithy, Not to Mention Nobby Clark and Spud Murphy.* London, 1914
25. *Smithy's Friend Nobby.* London, 1914
26. *Bones, Being Further Adventures in Mr. Commissioner Sanders' Country.* London, 1915
27. *The Man Who Bought London.* London, 1915
28. *The Melody of Death.* Bristol (Eng), 1915
29. *Smithy and the Hun.* London, 1915

30. *The Island of Galloping Gold.* London, 1916
31. *The Clue of the Twisted Candle.* Boston, 1916
32. *A Debt Discharged.* London, 1916
33. *The Tomb of Ts'in.* London, 1916
34. *Nobby.* London, 1916
35. *The Just Men of Cordova.* London, 1917
36. *Kate Plus Ten.* London and Boston, 1917
37. *The Secret House.* London, 1917
38. *The Keepers of the King's Peace.* London, 1917
39. *Lieutenant Bones.* London, 1918
40. *Down under Donovan.* London, 1918
41. *The Man Who Knew.* Boston, 1918
42. *Those Folk of Bulboro.* London, 1918
43. *Tam o' the Scouts.* London, 1918
44. *The Green Rust.* London, 1919
45. *The Adventures of Heine.* London, 1919
46. *Tam of the Scouts.* Boston, 1919
47. *The Fighting Scouts.* London, 1919
48. *The Daffodil Mystery.* London, 1920
49. *Jack o' Judgment.* London, 1920
50. *The Daffodil Murder.* Boston, 1921
51. *The Book of All Power.* London, 1921
52. *Bones in London.* London, 1921
53. *The Law of the Four Just Men.* London, 1921
54. *Sandi, The King Maker.* London, 1922
55. *The Angel of Terror.* Boston and London, 1922
56. *Number Six.* London, 1922
57. *Captains of Souls.* Boston, 1922
58. *The Crimson Circle.* London, 1922
59. *The Flying Fifty-Five.* London, 1922
60. *Mr. Justice Maxell.* London, 1922
61. *The Valley of Ghosts.* London, 1922
62. *The Clue of the New Pin.* Boston and London, 1923
63. *The Green Archer.* London, 1923
64. *The Missing Million.* London, 1923
65. *Bones of the River.* London, 1923
66. *Chick.* London, 1923
67. *The Books of Bart.* London, 1923
68. *Educated Evans.* London, 1924
69. *The Dark Eyes of London.* London, 1924
70. *Double Dan.* London, 1924
71. *Diana of Kara-Kara.* Boston, 1924
72. *The Face in the Night.* London, 1924
73. *Room 13.* London, 1924
74. *Flat 2.* New York, 1924
75. *The Sinister Man.* London, 1924
76. *The Three Oaks Mystery.* London, 1924
77. *A King by Night.* London, 1925
78. *The Strange Countess.* London, 1925
79. *The Three Just Men.* London, 1925
80. *Blue Hand.* London, 1925
81. *The Daughters of the Night.* London, 1925
82. *The Fellowship of the Frog.* London, 1925
83. *The Gaunt Stranger.* London, 1925
84. *The Hairy Arm.* Boston, 1925
85. *The Mind of Mr. J.G. Reeder.* London, 1925
86. *The Missing Millions.* Boston, 1925
87. *The Black Avons.* London, 1925
88. *The Ringer.* New York, 1926
89. *Eve's Island.* London, 1926
90. *The Avenger.* London, 1926
91. *Barbara on Her Own.* London, 1926
92. *The Black Abbot.* London, 1926
93. *The Day of Uniting.* London, 1926
94. *The Door with Seven Locks.* London and New York, 1926
95. *The Joker.* London, 1926
96. *The Man from Morocco.* London, 1926
97. *The Million Dollar Story.* London, 1926
98. *The Northing Tramp.* London, 1926
99. *Penelope of the Polyantha.* London, 1926
100. *The Square Emerald.* London, 1926
101. *The Terrible People.* London and New York, 1926
102. *We Shall See!* London, 1926
103. *The Yellow Snake.* London, 1926
104. *More Educated Evans.* London, 1926
105. *Mrs. William Jones and Bill.* London, 1926
106. *Sanders.* London, 1926
107. *People: A Short Autobiography.* London, 1926
108. *This England.* London, 1927
109. *The Brigand.* London, 1927
110. *Big Foot.* London, 1927
111. *The Girl from Scotland Yard.* New York, 1927
112. *The Feathered Serpent.* London, 1927
113. *The Forger.* London, 1927
114. *The Hand of Power.* London, 1927
115. *The Man Who Was Nobody.* London, 1927
116. *The Ringer.* London, 1927
117. *The Squeaker.* London, 1927
118. *Terror Keep.* London and New York, 1927
119. *The Traitor's Gate.* London and New York, 1927
120. *Good Evans!* London, 1927
121. *The Mixer.* London, 1927
122. *The Double.* London, 1928
123. *The Clever One.* New York, 1928
124. *The Squealer.* New York, 1928
125. *The Thief in the Night.* London, 1928
126. *The Flying Squad.* London, 1928
127. *The Gunner.* London, 1928
128. *The Twister.* London, 1928
129. *Again Sanders.* London, 1928
130. *Again the Three Just Men.* London, 1928
131. *Elegant Edward.* London, 1928
132. *The Orator.* London, 1928
133. *Tam.* London, 1928
134. *Again the Ringer.* London, 1929
135. *The Educated Man—Good Evans!* London, 1929
136. *The Golden Hades.* London, 1929
137. *Gunman's Bluff.* New York, 1929
138. *The Green Ribbon.* London, 1929
139. *The India-Rubber Men.* London, 1929
140. *The Terror.* London, 1929
141. *The Murder Book of Mr. J. G. Reeder.* New York, 1929
142. *Four Square Jane.* London, 1929
143. *The Big Four.* London, 1929
144. *The Black.* London, 1929
145. *The Ghost of Down Hill.* London, 1929
146. *The Cat Burglar.* London, 1929
147. *Circumstantial Evidence.* London, 1929
148. *Fighting Snub Reilly.* London, 1929
149. *The Governor of Chi-Foo.* London, 1929
150. *The Little Green Man.* London, 1929
151. *Planetoid 127.* London, 1929
152. *The Prison-Breakers.* London, 1929
153. *Forty-Eight Short Stories.* London, 1929
154. *For Information Received.* London, 1929
155. *The Lady of Little Hell.* London, 1929
156. *The Lone House Mystery.* London, 1929
157. *Red Aces.* London, 1929
158. *The Reporter.* London, 1929
159. *The Flying Squad.* London, 1929
160. *The Man Who Changed His Name.* London, 1929
161. *The Squeaker.* London, 1929
162. *The Calendar.* London, 1930
163. *The Clue of the Silver Key.* London, 1930
164. *The Silver Key.* New York, 1930
165. *The Lady of Ascot.* London, 1930

166. *White Face.* London, 1930
167. *Mr. Commissioner Sanders.* New York, 1930
168. *The Iron Grip.* London, 1930
169. *Killer Kay.* London, 1930
170. *The Stretelli Case and Other Mystery Stories.* Cleveland (OH), 1930
171. *The Lady Called Nita.* London, 1930
172. *The Law of the Three Just Men.* New York, 1931
173. *On the Spot.* London and New York, 1931
174. *The Coat of Arms.* London, 1931
175. *The Devil Man.* London and New York, 1931
176. *The Ringer Returns.* New York, 1931
177. *The Man at the Carlton.* London, 1931
178. *The Arranways Mystery.* New York, 1932
179. *The Life and Death of Charles Peace.* London, 1932
180. *The Frightened Lady.* London, 1932
181. *When the Gangs Came to London.* London and New York, 1932
182. *The Guv'nor and Other Stories.* London, 1932
183. *Mr. Reeder Returns.* New York, 1932
184. *Sergeant Sir Peter.* London, 1932
185. *The Steward.* London, 1932
186. *The Calendar.* London, 1932
187. *The Case of the Frightened Lady.* London, 1932
188. *My Hollywood Diary.* London, 1932
189. *The Guv'nor and Mr. J. G. Reeder Returns.* New York, 2 vols., 1933-34
190. *Again the Three Just Men.* New York, 1933
191. *The Last Adventure.* London, 1934
192. *The Woman from the East and Other Stories.* London, 1934
193. *Nig-Nog.* Cleveland, 1934
194. *Criminal at Large.* New York, 1934
195. *The Forest of Happy Dreams.* London, 1935
196. *The Undisclosed Client.* London, 1962
197. *Sergeant Dunn C.I.D.* London, 1962
198. *Again the Three.* London, 1968
199. *An African Millionare.* London, 1972
200. *The Man Who Married His Cook and Other Stories.* London, 1976

Walling, R.A.J. (Robert Alfred John)
British, born January 11, 1869, died September 4, 1949
1. *Flaunting Moll and Other Stories.* London, 1898
2. *A Sea-Dog of Devon: A Life of Sir John Hawkins.* London and New York, 1907
3. *George Borrow: The Man and His Work.* London, 1908
4. *That Dinner-Party at Bardolph's.* London, 1927
5. *The Strong Room.* London, 1927
6. *That Dinner at Bardolph's.* New York, 1928
7. *Murder at the Keyhole.* New York and London, 1929
8. *The Man with the Squeaky Voice.* New York and London, 1930
9. *The Stroke of One.* London and New York, 1931
10. *The Fatal Five Minutes.* London and New York, 1932
11. *Behind the Yellow Blind.* London, 1932
12. *Murder at Midnight.* New York, 1932
13. *Adventures of a Rubberneck.* Plymouth (MA), 1932
14. *The Charm of Brittany.* London, 1933
15. *Prove It, Mr. Tolefree.* New York, 1933
16. *Follow the Blue Car.* London, 1933
17. *In Time for Murder.* New York, 1933
18. *The Tolliver Case.* London, 1934
19. *Legacy of Death.* New York, 1934
20. *VIII to IX.* London, 1934
21. *The Bachelor Flat Mystery.* New York, 1934
22. *The Five Suspects.* London, 1935
23. *The Cat and the Corpse.* London, 1935
24. *The Corpse in the Green Pajamas.* New York, 1935
25. *The Corpse in the Coppice.* New York, 1935
26. *The West Country.* London and New York, 1935
27. *Mr. Tolefree's Reluctant Witnesses.* London, 1936
28. *The Corpse with the Floating Foot.* New York, 1936
29. *The Corpse in the Crimson Slippers.* London and New York, 1936
30. *The Corpse with a Dirty Face.* London and New York, 1936
31. *The Mystery of Mr. Mock.* London, 1937
32. *Bury Him Deeper.* London, 1937
33. *Marooned with Murder.* New York, 1937
34. *Green Hills of England.* London, 1937
35. *The Crime in Cumberland Court.* London, 1938
36. *The Coroner Doubts.* London, 1938
37. *The Corpse with the Blue Cravat.* New York, 1938
38. *More Than One Serpent.* London, 1938
39. *The Corpse with the Grimy Glove.* New York, 1938
40. *Dust in the Vault.* London, 1939
41. *The Corpse with the Blistered Hand.* New York, 1939
42. *They Liked Entwhistle.* London, 1939
43. *The Corpse with the Red-Headed Friend.* New York, 1939
44. *Why Did Trethewy Die?* London, 1940
45. *The Spider and the Fly.* New York, 1940
46. *By Hook or by Crook.* London, 1941
47. *By Hook or Crook.* New York, 1941
48. *Castle-Dinas.* London, 1942
49. *The Corpse with the Eerie Eye.* New York, 1942
50. *The Doodled Asterisk.* London, 1943
51. *A Corpse by Any Other Name.* New York, 1943
52. *A Corpse Without a Clue.* London and New York, 1944
53. *The Late Unlamented.* London and New York, 1948
54. *The Corpse with the Missing Watch.* New York, 1949
55. *The Story of Plymouth.* London and New York, 1950

Walsh, J.M. (James Morgan)
British, born in 1897, died August 29, 1952
Pseudonyms: H. Haverstock Hill, Stephen Maddock, and George M. White
1. *The Brethren of the Compass,* with E.J. Blyth. London, 1925
2. *The White Mask.* London, 1925
3. *The Company of Shadows.* London, 1926
4. *The Mystery of the Crystal Skull,* as George M. White. London, 1926
5. *The Hairpin Mystery.* London, 1926
6. *Anne of Flying Gap,* as H. Haverstock Hill. London, 1926
7. *Spoil of the Desert,* as H. Haverstock Hill. London, 1927
8. *The Hand of Doom.* London, 1927
9. *The Images of Han.* London, 1927
10. *The Black Cross.* London, 1928
11. *The Crimes of Cleopatra's Needle.* London, 1928
12. *The Purple Stain.* London, 1928
13. *The Silver Greyhound.* London, 1928
14. *The Golden Isle,* as H. Haverstock Hill. London, 1928
15. *The Week-End Crime Book,* with Audrey Baldwin. London, 1929
16. *Golden Harvest,* as H. Haverstock Hill. London, 1929
17. *The Mystery Man.* London, 1929
18. *The Mystery of the Green Caterpillars.* London, 1929
19. *The Tempania Mystery.* London, 1929
20. *The Secret of the Crater,* as H. Haverstock Hill. London, 1930
21. *The Black Ghost.* London, 1930
22. *Exit Simeon Hex.* London, 1930
23. *The Man Behind the Curtain.* London, 1931
24. *Mystery House.* London, 1931
25. *The Whisperer.* London, 1931
26. *Vandals of the Void.* London, 1931

27. *Vanguard to Neptune.* London, 1932
28. *The Girl of the Islands.* London, 1932
29. *The League of Missing Men.* London, 1932
30. *Lady Incognito.* London, 1932
31. *A Woman of Destiny,* as Stephen Maddock. London, 1933
32. *King's Messenger.* London, 1933
33. *The Secret Service Girl.* London, 1933
34. *Spies Are Abroad.* London, 1933
35. *The Man from Whitehall.* London, 1934
36. *Spies in Pursuit.* London, 1934
37. *Danger after Dark,* as Stephen Maddock. London, 1934
38. *Gentlemen of the Night,* as Stephen Maddock. London, 1934
39. *The White Siren,* as Stephen Maddock. London, 1934
40. *Conspirators in Capri,* as Stephen Maddock. London, 1935
41. *The Eye of the Keyhole,* as Stephen Maddock. London, 1935
42. *The Silent Man.* London, 1935
43. *Spies Never Return.* London, 1935
44. *Tiger in the Night.* London, 1935
45. *The Half Ace.* London, 1936
46. *Spies' Vendetta.* London, 1936
47. *Conspirators Three,* as Stephen Maddock. London, 1936
48. *Forbidden Frontiers,* as Stephen Maddock. London, 1936
49. *Conspirators at Large,* as Stephen Maddock. London, 1937
50. *Chalk-Face.* London, 1937
51. *Spies in Spain.* London, 1937
52. *Island of Spies.* London, 1937
53. *Black Dragon.* London, 1938
54. *Dial 999.* London, 1938
55. *Doorway to Danger,* as Stephen Maddock. London, 1938
56. *Lamp-Post 592,* as Stephen Maddock. London, 1938
57. *Spies along the Severn,* as Stephen Maddock. London, 1939
58. *Bullets for Breakfast.* London, 1939
59. *King's Enemies.* London, 1939
60. *Secret Weapons.* London, 1940
61. *Spades at Midnight,* as Stephen Maddock. London, 1940
62. *Date with a Spy,* as Stephen Maddock. London, 1941
63. *Death at His Elbow.* London, 1941
64. *Spies from the Skies.* London, 1941
65. *Danger Zone.* London, 1942
66. *Step Aside to Death,* as Stephen Maddock. London, 1942
67. *Drums Beat at Dusk,* as Stephen Maddock. London, 1943
68. *Island Alert.* London, 1943
69. *Face Value.* London, 1944
70. *Something on the Stairs,* as Stephen Maddock. London, 1944
71. *Mutton Dressed as Lamb, and Live Bait.* London, 1944
72. *I'll Never Like Friday Again,* as Stephen Maddock. London, 1945
73. *Whispers in the Dark.* London, 1945
74. *The Man Who Grew Bulbs.* London, 1945
75. *Express Delivery.* London, 1946
76. *Overture to Trouble,* as Stephen Maddock. London, 1946
77. *Exit Only,* as Stephen Maddock. London, 1947
78. *Once in Tiger Bay.* London, 1947
79. *Six Characters for an Actress.* London, 1947
80. *Walking Shadow.* London, 1948
81. *East of Piccadilly,* as Stephen Maddock. London, 1948
82. *Keep Your Fingers Crossed,* as Stephen Maddock. London, 1949
83. *Time to Kill.* London, 1949
84. *Return to Tiger Bay.* London, 1950
85. *Private Line,* as Stephen Maddock. London, 1950
86. *Public Mischief,* as Stephen Maddock. London, 1951
87. *Next, Please.* London, 1951
88. *Close Shave,* as Stephen Maddock. London, 1952
89. *King of Tiger Bay.* London, 1952

Walsh, Sheila
British, born October 10, 1928
Pseudonym: Sophie Leyton
1. *The Golden Songbird.* London and New York, 1975
2. *Madalena.* London, 1976
3. *The Sergeant Major's Daughter.* London, 1977
4. *A Fine Silk Purse.* London, 1978
5. *The Incomparable Miss Brady.* London and New York, 1980
6. *Lady Cecily's Dilemma,* as Sophie Leyton. London, 1980
7. *The Rose Domino.* New York, 1981

Walsh, Thomas (Francis Morgan)
American, born in 1908
1. *Nightmare in Manhattan.* Boston, 1950
2. *The Night Watch.* Boston and London, 1952
3. *The Dark Window.* Boston and London, 1956
4. *Dangerous Passenger.* Boston, 1959
5. *The Eye of the Needle.* New York, 1961
6. *A Thief in the Night.* New York, 1962
7. *To Hide a Rogue.* New York, 1964
8. *The Tenth Point.* New York and London, 1965
9. *The Resurrection Man.* New York, 1966
10. *The Face of The Enemy.* New York, 1966
11. *The Action of the Tiger.* New York, 1968

Walters, Hugh [Walter Llewellyn Hughes]
British, born June 15, 1910
1. *Blast Off at Woomera.* London, 1957
2. *Blast-Off at 0300.* New York, 1958
3. *The Domes of Pico.* London, 1958
4. *Menace from the Moon.* New York, 1959
5. *Operation Columbus.* London, 1960
6. *First on the Moon.* New York, 1961
7. *Moon Base One.* London, 1961
8. *Outpost on the Moon.* New York, 1962
9. *Expedition Venus.* London and New York, 1962
10. *Destination Mars.* London and New York, 1963
11. *Terror by Satellite.* London and New York, 1964
12. *Mission to Mercury.* London and New York, 1965
13. *Journey to Jupiter.* London, 1965
14. *Spaceship to Saturn.* London and New York, 1967
15. *The Mohole Mystery.* London, 1968
16. *The Mohole Menace.* New York, 1969
17. *Nearly Neptune.* London, 1969
18. *Neptune One Is Missing.* New York, 1969
19. *First Contact?* London, 1971
20. *Passage to Pluto.* London and Nashville (TN), 1973
21. *Tony Hale, Space Detective.* London, 1973
22. *Murder on Mars.* London, 1975
23. *Boy Astronaut.* London, 1977
24. *The Caves of Drach.* London, 1977
25. *The Last Disaster.* London, 1978
26. *The Blue Aura.* London, 1979
27. *First Family on the Moon.* London, 1979

Wambaugh, Joseph [Joseph Aloysius Wambaugh, Jr.]
American, born January 22, 1937
1. *The New Centurions.* Boston, 1970
2. *The Blue Knight.* Boston, 1972
3. *The Onion Field.* New York, 1973
4. *The Choirboys.* New York, 1975
5. *The Black Marble.* New York and London, 1978

Wandrei, Donald
American, born in 1908
1. *Ecstasy and Other Poems.* Athol (MA), 1928
2. *Dark Odyssey.* St. Paul (MN), 1931
3. *The Eye and the Finger.* Sauk City (WI), 1944

4. *The Web of Easter Island.* Sauk City, 1948
5. *Poems for Midnight.* Sauk City, 1964
6. *Strange Harvest.* Sauk City, 1965

Warren, Charles Marquis
American, born December 16, 1912
1. *Only the Valiant.* New York, 1943
2. *Valley of the Shadow.* New York, 1948
3. *Deadhead.* New York, 1949

Warriner, Thurman
British
Pseudonym: Simon Troy
1. *Method in His Murder.* London and New York, 1950
2. *Ducats in Her Coffin.* London, 1951
3. *Death's Dateless Night.* London, 1952
4. *Road to Rhuine,* as Simon Troy. London and New York, 1952
5. *The Doors of Sleep.* London, 1955
6. *Half-Way to Murder,* as Simon Troy. London, 1955
7. *Death's Bright Angel.* London, 1956
8. *Tonight and Tomorrow,* as Simon Troy. London, 1957
9. *She Died, Of Course.* London, 1958
10. *The Golden Lantern.* London, 1958
11. *Drunkard's End,* as Simon Troy. London, 1960
12. *Heavenly Bodies.* London, 1960
13. *Second Cousin Removed,* as Simon Troy. London, 1961
14. *Waiting for Oliver,* as Simon Troy. London, 1962
15. *Don't Play with the Rough Boys,* as Simon Troy. London, 1963
16. *Cease upon the Midnight,* as Simon Troy. London, 1964
17. *No More A-roving,* as Simon Troy. London, 1965
18. *Sup with the Devil,* as Simon Troy. London, 1967
19. *Swift to Its Close,* as Simon Troy. London and New York, 1969
20. *Blind Man's Garden,* as Simon Troy. London, 1970

Waterloo, Stanley
American, born May 21, 1846, died October 11, 1913
1. *How It Looks.* New York, 1888
2. *A Man and a Woman.* Chicago, 1892
3. *An Odd Situation.* Chicago, 1893
4. *Honest Money.* Chicago, 1895
5. *The Story of Ab: A Tale in the Time of the Cave Men.* Chicago, 1897
6. *Armageddon.* Chicago, 1898
7. *The Wolf's Long Howl.* Chicago, 1899
8. *The Launching of a Man.* Chicago, 1899
9. *The Seekers.* Chicago, 1900
10. *These Are My Jewels.* Chicago, 1902
11. *The Cassoway.* Chicago, 1906
12. *A Son of the Ages.* New York and London, 1914

Waters, Frank (Joseph)
American, born July 25, 1902
1. *Fever Pitch.* New York, 1930
2. *The Wild Earth's Nobility: A Novel of the Old West.* New York, 1935
3. *Below Grass Roots.* New York, 1937
4. *Midas of the Rockies: The Story of Stratton and Cripple Creek.* New York, 1937
5. *Dust Within the Rock.* New York, 1940
6. *People of the Valley.* New York, 1941
7. *The Man Who Killed the Deer.* New York, 1942
8. *River Lady,* with Houston Branch. New York, 1942
9. *The Colorado.* New York, 1946
10. *The Yogi of Cockroach Court.* New York, 1947
11. *Diamond Head,* with Houston Branch. New York, 1948
12. *Masked Gods: Navajo and Pueblo Ceremonialism.* Albuquerque (NM), 1950
13. *The Earp Brothers of Tombstone: The Story of Mrs. Virgil Earp.* New York, 1960
14. *Book of the Hopi.* New York, 1963
15. *Leon Gaspard.* Flagstaff (AZ), 1964
16. *The Woman at Otowi Crossing.* Denver (CO), 1966
17. *Pumpkin Seed Point.* Chicago, 1969
18. *Frank Waters.* Austin (TX), 1969
19. *Conversations with Frank Waters.* Chicago, 1971
20. *Pike's Peak: A Family Saga.* Chicago, 1971

Watkins, William Jon
American, born July 19, 1942
1. *Five Poems.* Chula Vista (CA), 1968
2. *The Judas Wheel.* New York, 1969
3. *Ecodeath,* with Gene Snyder. New York, 1972
4. *Clickwhistle.* New York, 1973
5. *The God Machine.* New York, 1973
6. *A Fair Advantage.* Englewood Cliffs (NJ), 1975
7. *The Litany of Sh'reev,* with Gene Snyder. New York, 1976
8. *Tricentennial.* New York, 1977
9. *What Rough Beast.* Chicago, 1980
10. *Suburban Wilderness.* New York, 1981

Watkins-Pitchford, D.J. (Denys James)
British, born July 25, 1905
Pseudonyms: BB, Michael Traherne
1. *Wild Lone,* as BB. London and New York, 1938
2. *Sky Gipsy: The Story of a Wild Goose,* as BB. London, 1939
3. *Manka, The Sky Gipsy,* as BB. New York, 1939
4. *The Little Grey Men,* as BB. London, 1942
5. *The Idle Countryman,* as BB. London, 1943
6. *Brendon Chase,* as BB. London, 1944
7. *The Wayfaring Tree,* as BB. London, 1945
8. *A Stream in Your Garden,* as BB. London, 1948
9. *Down the Bright Stream,* as BB. London, 1948
10. *Meeting Hill: BB's Fairy Book,* as BB. London, 1948
11. *Be Quiet and Go A-Angling,* as Michael Traherne. London, 1949
12. *Confessions of a Carp Fisher,* as BB. London, 1950
13. *Tide's Ending,* as BB. London and New York, 1950
14. *Letters from Compton Deverell,* as BB. London, 1950
15. *Wind in the Wood,* as BB. London, 1952
16. *Dark Estuary,* as BB. London, 1953
17. *The Forest of Boland Light Railway,* as BB. London, 1955
18. *The Forest of the Railway,* as BB. New York, 1957
19. *Monty Woodpig's Caravan,* as BB. London, 1957
20. *Ben the Bullfinch,* as BB. London, 1957
21. *Wandering Wind,* as BB. London, 1957
22. *Alexander,* as BB. Oxford (Eng), 1957
23. *Monty Woodpig and His Bumblebuzz Car,* as BB. London, 1958
24. *Mr. Bumstead,* as BB. London, 1958
25. *A Carp Water: Wood Pool and How to Fish It,* as BB. London, 1958
26. *The Autumn Road to the Isles,* as BB. London, 1959
27. *The Wizard of Boland,* as BB. London, 1959
28. *Bill Badger's Winter Cruise,* as BB. London, 1959
29. *Bill Badger and the Pirates,* as BB. London, 1960
30. *Bill Badger's Finest Hour,* as BB. London, 1961
31. *The Badgers of Bearshanks,* as BB. London, 1961
32. *The White Road Westwards,* as BB. London, 1961
33. *Bill Badger's Whispering Reeds Adventure,* as BB. London, 1962
34. *Lepus, The Brown Hare,* as BB. London, 1962
35. *September Road to Caithness and the Western Sea,* as BB. London, 1962

36. *Bill Badger's Big Mistake*, as BB. London, 1963
37. *The Summer Road to Whales*, as BB. London, 1964
38. *The Pegasus Book of the Countryside*, as BB. London, 1964
39. *Bill Badger and the Big Store Robbery*, as BB. London, 1967
40. *The Whopper*, as BB. London, 1967
41. *A Summer on the Nene*, as BB. London, 1967
42. *At the Back o' Ben Dee*, as BB. London, 1968
43. *Bill Badger's Voyage to the World's End*, as BB. London, 1969
44. *The Tyger Tray*, as BB. London, 1971
45. *The Pool of the Black Witch*, as BB. London, 1974
46. *Lord of the Forest*, as BB. London, 1975

Watson, Clyde
American, born July 25, 1947
1. *Father Fox's Pennyrhymes*. New York, 1971
2. *Tom Fox and the Apple Tree*. New York, 1972
3. *Quips and Quirks*. New York, 1975
4. *Hickory Stick Rag*. New York, 1976
5. *Binary Numbers*. New York, 1977

Watson, Colin
British, born February 1, 1920
1. *Coffin, Scarcely Used*. London, 1958
2. *Bump in the Night*. London, 1960
3. *Hopjoy Was Here*. London, 1962
4. *The Puritan*. London, 1966
5. *Lonelyheart 4122*. London and New York, 1967
6. *Charity Ends at Home*. London and New York, 1968
7. *The Flaxborough Crab*. London, 1969
8. *Just What The Doctor Ordered*. New York, 1969
9. *Snobbery with Violence: Crime Stories and Their Audience*. London, 1971
10. *Broomsticks over Flaxborough*. London, 1972
11. *Kissing Covens*. New York, 1972
12. *The Naked Nuns*. London, 1975
13. *Six Nuns and a Shotgun*. New York, 1975
14. *One Man's Meat*. London, 1977
15. *It Shouldn't Happen to a Dog*. New York, 1977
16. *Blue Murder*. London, 1979

Watson, Ian
British, born April 20, 1943
1. *Japan: A Cat's Eye View*. Osaka (Japan), 1969
2. *The Embedding*. London, 1973
3. *The Jonah Kit*. London, 1975
4. *The Martian Inca*. London and New York, 1977
5. *Alien Embassy*. London, 1977
6. *Japan Tomorrow*. Osaka, 1977
7. *Miracle Visitors*. London and New York, 1978
8. *God's World*. London, 1979
9. *The Very Slow Time Machine*. London and New York, 1979
10. *The Gardens of Delight*. London, 1980
11. *Under Heaven's Bridge*, with Michael Bishop. London, 1980

Watts, Peter (Christopher)
British, born December 19, 1919
Pseudonyms: Matt Chisholm, Cy James, Luke Jones, Duncan Mackinlock, Tom Owen
1. *Out of Yesterday*. London, 1950
2. *Half Breed*, as Matt Chisholm. London, 1958
3. *High Peak*, as Matt Chisholm. London, 1958
4. *Hodge*, as Matt Chisholm. London, 1958
5. *Riders at the Ford*, as Matt Chisholm. London, 1958
6. *The Dread and the Glory*, as Tom Owen. London, 1959
7. *Hang a Man High*, as Matt Chisholm. London, 1959
8. *The Saga of Trench Godden*, as Matt Chisholm. London, 1959
9. *Blood on the Land*, as Matt Chisholm. London, 1959
10. *Joe Blade*, as Matt Chisholm. London, 1959
11. *Never Give Ground*, as Matt Chisholm. London, 1959
12. *Wild Mustanger*, as Matt Chisholm. London, 1959
13. *The Law of Ben Hodge*, as Matt Chisholm. London, 1959
14. *A Posse of Violent Men*, as Matt Chisholm. London, 1960
15. *Fury at Tombstone*, as Matt Chisholm. London, 1960
16. *Pursuit in the Sun*, as Matt Chisholm. London, 1960
17. *Prayer for a Gunman*, as Matt Chisholm. London, 1960
18. *Hangrope for a Gunman*, as Matt Chisholm. London, 1960
19. *Circus of Horror*, as Tom Owen. London, 1960
20. *Island of Hell*, as Duncan Mackinlock. London, 1961
21. *Advance to Death*, as Matt Chisholm. London, 1961
22. *A Rage of Guns*, as Matt Chisholm. London, 1961
23. *Three Canyons to Death*, as Luke Jones. London, 1961
24. *The Brasada Guns*, as Cy James. London, 1961
25. *The Gun Is My Brother*, as Cy James. London, 1961
26. *The Violent Hills*, as Cy James. London, 1961
27. *Brasada*, as Luke Jones. London, 1962
28. *The Long Night Through*. London, 1962
29. *Bitter Range*, as Matt Chisholm. London, 1962
30. *Three for Vengeance*, as Matt Chisholm. London, 1963
31. *The Proud Horseman*, as Matt Chisholm. London, 1963
32. *The Hard Men*, as Matt Chisholm. London, 1963
33. *Death at Noon*, as Matt Chisholm. London, 1963
34. *The Hangman Rides Tall*, as Matt Chisholm. London, 1963
35. *Death Rides Fast*, as Cy James. London, 1964
36. *Ride the Far Country*, as Cy James. London, 1964
37. *Hellion*, as Cy James. London, 1964
38. *The Battle of Red Rock*, as Matt Chisholm. London, 1964
39. *Hangrope Posse*, as Cy James. London, 1965
40. *Gun-Rage*, as Cy James. London, 1965
41. *Indians!*, as Matt Chisholm. London, 1965
42. *The Corgi Sports Almanac*, as Matt Chisholm. London, 1965
43. *Blood Creek*, as Cy James. London, 1965
44. *Gun Hand*, as Cy James. London, 1965
45. *Savage Horseman*, as Cy James. London, 1966
46. *Man in the Saddle*, as Cy James. London, 1966
47. *The Running Gun*, as Cy James. London, 1966
48. *My Gun Is Justice*, as Cy James. London, 1966
49. *The Last Gun*, as Matt Chisholm. London, 1966
50. *Scream and Shout*. London, 1966
51. *Cash McCord*, as Matt Chisholm. London, 1966
52. *Spur to Death*, as Matt Chisholm. London, 1966
53. *Hunted*, as Matt Chisholm. London, 1966
54. *Gun Marshal*, as Matt Chisholm. London, 1967
55. *Kiowa*, as Matt Chisholm. London, 1967
56. *Indian Scout*, as Matt Chisholm. London, 1967
57. *Apache Kill*, as Matt Chisholm. London, 1967
58. *Range War*, as Matt Chisholm. London, 1967
59. *Tough to Kill*, as Matt Chisholm. London, 1968
60. *Gun Lust*, as Matt Chisholm. London, 1968
61. *A Bullet for Brody*, as Matt Chisholm. London, 1968
62. *Spur*, as Matt Chisholm. London, 1968
63. *The Trail of Fear*, as Matt Chisholm. London, 1968
64. *Rage of McAllister*, as Matt Chisholm. London, 1969
65. *McAllister Strikes*, as Matt Chisholm. London, 1969
66. *Hell for McAllister*, as Matt Chisholm. London, 1969
67. *McAllister Justice*, as Matt Chisholm. London, 1969
68. *Kill McAllister*, as Matt Chisholm. London, 1969
69. *McAllister Rides*, as Matt Chisholm. London, 1969
70. *McAllister Makes War*, as Matt Chisholm. London, 1969
71. *McAllister's Fury*, as Matt Chisholm. London, 1969
72. *McAllister Fights*, as Matt Chisholm. London, 1969
73. *The Cimmaron Kid*, as Cy James. London, 1969
74. *Gunsmoke for McAllister*, as Matt Chisholm. London, 1969
75. *Blood on McAllister*, as Matt Chisholm. London, 1969

76. *McAllister Says No,* as Matt Chisholm. London, 1970
77. *Danger for McAllister,* as Matt Chisholm. London, 1970
78. *McAllister Gambles,* as Matt Chisholm. London, 1970
79. *Hang McAllister,* as Matt Chisholm. London and New York, 1970
80. *Shoot McAllister,* as Matt Chisholm. London, 1970
81. *Trail of McAllister,* as Matt Chisholm. London, 1970
82. *Stampede,* as Matt Chisholm. London, 1970
83. *Trail West,* as Cy James. London, 1970
84. *Longhorn,* as Cy James. London, 1970
85. *Gun,* as Cy James. London, 1971
86. *The Brave Ride Tall,* as Cy James. London, 1971
87. *Blood at Sunset,* as Cy James. London, 1971
88. *Hard Texas Trail,* as Matt Chisholm. London, 1971
89. *Riders West,* as Matt Chisholm. London, 1971
90. *One Notch to Death,* as Matt Chisholm. London, 1972
91. *One Man—One Gun,* as Matt Chisholm. London, 1972
92. *Thunder in the West,* as Matt Chisholm. London, 1972
93. *McAllister Runs Wild,* as Matt Chisholm. London, 1972
94. *Brand McAllister,* as Matt Chisholm. London, 1972
95. *Battle of McAllister,* as Matt Chisholm. London, 1972
96. *McAllister Trapped,* as Matt Chisholm. London, 1973
97. *Vengeance of McAllister,* as Matt Chisholm. London, 1973
98. *A Breed of Men,* as Matt Chisholm. London, 1973
99. *Battle Fury,* as Matt Chisholm. London, 1973
100. *Blood on the Hills,* as Matt Chisholm. London, 1973
101. *McAllister Must Die,* as Matt Chisholm. London, 1974
102. *The McAllister Legend,* as Matt Chisholm. London, 1974
103. *A Dictionary of the Old West 1850-1900.* London, 1977
104. *The Indian Incident,* as Matt Chisholm. London, 1978
105. *The True Book of the Wild West,* as Matt Chisholm. London, 1978
106. *The Tucson Conspiracy,* as Matt Chisholm. London, 1978
107. *The Pecos Manhunt,* as Matt Chisholm. London, 1979
108. *The Laredo Assignment,* as Matt Chisholm. London, 1979
109. *The Colorado Virgins,* as Matt Chisholm. London, 1979
110. *The Mexican Proposition,* as Matt Chisholm. London, 1979
111. *The Nevada Mustang,* as Matt Chisholm. London, 1979
112. *The Arizona Climax,* as Matt Chisholm. London, 1980
113. *The Cheyenne Trap,* as Matt Chisholm. London, 1980
114. *The Montana Deadlock,* as Matt Chisholm. London, 1980
115. *The Navaho Trail,* as Matt Chisholm. London, 1981
116. *The Last Act,* as Matt Chisholm. London, 1981
117. *McAllister Never Surrenders,* as Matt Chisholm. London, 1981
118. *McAllister and Cheyenne Death,* as Matt Chisholm. London, 1981
119. *McAllister and the Spanish Gold,* as Matt Chisholm. London, 1981
120. *McAllister and the Comanche Crossing,* as Matt Chisholm. London, 1981
121. *McAllister and Quarry,* as Matt Chisholm. London, 1981
122. *Die-Hard,* as Matt Chisholm. London, 1981
123. *Wolf-Bait,* as Matt Chisholm. London, 1981
124. *Fire-Brand,* as Matt Chisholm. London, 1981

Waugh, Hillary (Baldwin)
American, born June 22, 1920
Pseudonyms: Elissa Grandower, H. Baldwin Taylor, Harry Walker
1. *Madam Will Not Dine Tonight.* New York, 1947
2. *Hope to Die.* New York, 1948
3. *If I Live to Dine.* Hasbrouck Heights (NJ), 1949
4. *The Odds Run Out.* New York, 1949
5. *Last Seen Wearing....* New York, 1952
6. *A Rag and a Bone.* New York, 1954
7. *The Case of the Missing Gardener,* as Harry Walker. New York, 1954
8. *Rich Man, Dead Man.* New York, 1956
9. *Rich Man, Murder.* London, 1956
10. *The Case of the Brunette Bombshell.* New York, 1957
11. *The Eighth Mrs. Bluebeard.* New York, 1958
12. *The Girl Who Cried Wolf.* New York, 1958
13. *Sleep Long, My Love.* New York, 1959
14. *Road Block.* New York, 1960
15. *That Night It Rained.* New York, 1961
16. *Murder on the Terrace.* London, 1961
17. *The Late Mrs. D.* New York and London, 1962
18. *Born Victim.* New York, 1962
19. *Jigsaw.* London, 1962
20. *Death and Circumstances.* New York and London, 1963
21. *Prisoner's Plea.* New York, 1963
22. *The Missing Man.* New York and London, 1964
23. *The Duplicate,* as H. Baldwin Taylor. New York, 1964
24. *End of a Party.* New York and London, 1965
25. *Girl on the Run.* New York, 1965
26. *Pure Poison.* New York, 1966
27. *The Triumvirate,* as H. Baldwin Taylor. New York and London, 1966
28. *The Trouble with Tycoons,* as H. Baldwin Taylor. New York, 1967
29. *The Missing Tycoon,* as H. Baldwin Taylor. London, 1967
30. *The Con Game.* New York and London, 1968
31. *"30" Manhattan East.* New York, 1968
32. *Run When I Say Go.* New York and London, 1969
33. *The Young Prey.* New York, 1969
34. *Finish Me Off.* New York, 1970
35. *The Shadow Guest.* New York and London, 1971
36. *Parrish for the Defense.* New York, 1974
37. *A Bride for Hampton House.* New York, 1975
38. *Seaview Manor,* as Elissa Grandower. New York, 1976
39. *The Summer at Raven's Roost,* as Elissa Grandower. New York, 1976
40. *The Secret Room of Morgate House,* as Elissa Grandower. New York, 1977
41. *Doctor on Trial.* New York, 1977
42. *Madman at My Door.* New York, 1978
43. *Blackbourne Hall,* as Elissa Grandower. New York, 1979

Way, Margaret
1. *Blaze of Silk.* London, 1970
2. *King Country.* London, 1970
3. *The Time of the Jacaranda.* London and Toronto, 1970
4. *Return to Belle Amber.* London, 1971
5. *Summer Magic.* London, 1971
6. *Bauhinia Junction.* London, 1971
7. *The Man from Bahl Bahla.* London and Toronto, 1971
8. *Noonfire.* London, 1972
9. *Ring of Jade.* London and Toronto, 1972
10. *A Man Like Daintree.* London, 1972
11. *Copper Moon.* London, 1972
12. *The Rainbow Bird.* London, 1972
13. *Storm over Mandargi.* London, 1973
14. *Sweet Sundown.* London, 1974
15. *The Love Theme.* London and Toronto, 1974
16. *McCabe's Kingdom.* London, 1974
17. *Wind River.* Toronto, 1974
18. *Reeds of Honey.* London and Toronto, 1975
19. *Storm Flower.* London, 1975
20. *A Lesson in Loving.* London, 1975
21. *Flight into Yesterday.* London and Toronto, 1976
22. *The Man on Half-Moon.* London, 1976
23. *Red Cliffs of Malpara.* London and Toronto, 1976
24. *Swan's Reach.* Toronto, 1977
25. *One Way Ticket.* Toronto, 1977
26. *The Awakening Flame.* London and Toronto, 1978

27. *Wake the Sleeping Tiger.* London, 1978
28. *The Wild Swan.* London and Toronto, 1978
29. *Ring of Fire.* London, 1978
30. *Portrait of Jaime.* Toronto, 1978
31. *Mutiny in Paradise.* Toronto, 1978
32. *Black Ingo.* Toronto, 1978
33. *Blue Lotus.* London, 1979
34. *The Butterfly and the Baron.* London, 1979
35. *Valley of the Moon.* London, 1979
36. *White Magnolia.* London, 1979
37. *The Winds of Heaven.* London, 1979
38. *The Golden Puma.* London, 1980
39. *Flamingo Park.* London, 1980
40. *Lord of the High Valley.* London, 1980
41. *Temple of Fire.* London, 1980
42. *Shadow Dance.* Toronto, 1981
43. *A Season for Change.* Toronto, 1981

Wayne, Jenifer [Anne Jenifer Wayne]
British, born in 1917
1. *This Is the Law: Stories of Wrongdoers by Fault or Folly.* London, 1948
2. *The Shadows and Other Poems.* London, 1959
3. *Clemence and Ginger.* London, 1960
4. *The Day the Ceiling Fell Down.* London, 1961
5. *The Night the Rain Came In.* London, 1963
6. *Kitchen People.* London, 1963
7. *Merry by Name.* London, 1964
8. *The Ghost Next Door.* London, 1965
9. *Saturday and the Irish Aunt.* London, 1966
10. *Someone in the Attic.* London, 1967
11. *Ollie.* London, 1969
12. *Sprout.* London, 1970
13. *Something in the Barn.* London, 1971
14. *Sprout's Window-Cleaner.* London, 1971
15. *Sprout and the Dog-Sitter.* London, 1972
16. *Brown Bread and Butter in the Basement: A Twenties Childhood.* London, 1973
17. *The Smoke in Albert's Garden.* London, 1974
18. *Sprout and the Helicopter.* London, 1975
19. *Sprout and the Conjuror.* London, 1976
20. *Sprout and the Magician.* New York, 1977

Webb, Jack
American, born April 2, 1920
Pseudonyms: John Farr, Tex Grady
1. *The Big Sin.* New York, 1952
2. *The Naked Angel.* New York, 1953
3. *Such Women Are Dangerous.* London, 1954
4. *The Damned Lovely.* New York, 1954
5. *High Mesa,* as Tex Grady. New York, 1952
6. *The Broken Doll.* New York, 1955
7. *Don't Feed the Animals,* as John Farr. New York, 1955
8. *Naked Fear,* as John Farr. New York, 1955
9. *The Zoo Murders,* as John Farr. London, 1956
10. *The Bad Blond.* New York, 1956
11. *She Shark,* as John Farr. New York, 1956
12. *The Brass Halo.* New York, 1957
13. *The Lady and the Snake,* as John Farr. New York, 1957
14. *The Deadly Combo,* as John Farr. New York, 1958
15. *The Deadly Sex.* New York, 1959
16. *The Delicate Darling.* New York, 1959
17. *One for My Dame.* New York, 1961
18. *The Gilded Witch.* Evanston (IL) and London, 1963
19. *Make My Bed Soon.* New York, 1963

Webb, Jean Francis
American, born October 1, 1910
Pseudonyms: Ethel Hamill, Roberta Morrison, Lee Davis Willoughby
1. *Love They Must.* New York, 1933
2. *Forty Brothers.* Menasha (WI), 1934
3. *No Match for Murder.* New York, 1942
4. *Reveille for Romance,* as Ethel Hamill. New York, 1946
5. *Challenge to Love,* as Ethel Hamill. New York, 1946
6. *Little Women.* New York, 1949
7. *Anna Lucasta.* New York, 1949
8. *King Solomon's Mines.* New York, 1950
9. *Honeymoon in Honolulu,* as Ethel Hamill. New York, 1950
10. *Tower in the Forest,* as Ethel Hamill. New York, 1951
11. *Nurse on Horseback,* as Ethel Hamill. New York, 1952
12. *The Dancing Mermaid,* as Ethel Hamill. New York, 1952
13. *Bluegrass Doctor,* as Ethel Hamill. New York, 1953
14. *The Minister's Daughter,* as Ethel Hamill. New York, 1953
15. *Gloria and the Bullfighter,* as Ethel Hamill. New York, 1954
16. *A Nurse Comes Home,* as Ethel Hamill. New York, 1954
17. *Golden Feathers.* New York, 1954
18. *Nurse Elizabeth Comes Home.* London, 1955
19. *Runaway Nurse,* as Ethel Hamill. New York, 1955
20. *The Hawaiian Islands from Monarchy to Democracy.* New York, 1956
21. *A Nurse for Galleon Key,* as Ethel Hamill. New York, 1957
22. *The Golden Image,* as Ethel Hamill. New York, 1959
23. *Aloha Nurse,* as Ethel Hamill. New York, 1961
24. *Tower of Dreams,* as Ethel Hamill. London, 1961
25. *Sudden Love,* as Ethel Hamill. New York, 1962
26. *Kaiulani, Crown Princess of Hawaii.* New York, 1962
27. *The Nurse from Hawaii,* as Ethel Hamill. New York, 1964
28. *Will Shakespeare and His America.* New York, 1964
29. *All for Love,* as Ethel Hamill. New York, 1965
30. *Tree of Evil,* as Roberta Morrison. New York, 1966
31. *The Craigshaw Curse.* New York, 1968
32. *Carnavaron's Castle.* New York, 1969
33. *Roses from a Haunted Garden.* New York, 1971
34. *Somewhere Within This House.* New York, 1973
35. *The Bride of Cairngore.* New York, 1974
36. *Is This Coffin Taken?* New York, 1978
37. *The Cajuns,* as Lee Davis Willoughby. New York, 1981
38. *The Dark House.* New York, 1982

Webster, Jean [Alice Jane Chandler Webster]
American, born July 24, 1876, died June 11, 1916
1. *When Patty Went to College.* New York, 1903
2. *The Wheat Princess.* New York, 1905
3. *Jerry, Junior.* New York, 1907
4. *The Four-Pools Mystery.* New York, 1908
5. *Much Ado about Peter.* New York, 1909
6. *Just Patty.* New York, 1911
7. *Daddy-Long-Legs.* New York, 1912
8. *Dear Enemy.* New York and London, 1915
9. *Jerry.* London, 1916
10. *Vitriol and Lilacs.* Cleveland (OH), 1943

Weinbaum, Stanley G. (Grauman)
American, born in 1900, died December 14, 1935
1. *Dawn of Flame.* New York, 1936
2. *The New Adam.* Chicago, 1939
3. *The Black Flame.* Reading (PA), 1948
4. *A Martian Odyssey and Others.* Reading, 1949
5. *The Dark Other.* Los Angles (CA), 1950
6. *The Red Peri.* Reading, 1952
7. *The Best of Stanley G. Weinbaum.* New York, 1974

Weir, Rosemary
British, born July 22, 1905
Pseudonym: Catherine Bell

Weir, Rosemary

1. *The Secret Journey.* London, 1957
2. *The Secret of Cobbetts Farm.* London, 1957
3. *No. 10 Green Street.* London, 1958
4. *Island of Birds.* London, 1959
5. *The Honeysuckle Line.* London, 1959
6. *The Hunt for Harry.* London, 1959
7. *Robert's Rescued Railway.* New York, 1960
8. *Great Days in Green Street.* London, 1960
9. *Pineapple Farm.* London, 1960
10. *Little Lion's Real Island.* London, 1960
11. *A Dog of Your Own: or, Dogs Without Tears: Do's and Don't's for Young Dog Owners.* London, 1960
12. *The House in the Middle of the Road.* London, 1961
13. *Albert the Dragon.* London and New York, 1961
14. *What a Lark.* Leicester (Eng), 1961
15. *Tania Takes the Stage.* London, 1961
16. *Top Secret.* London, 1962
17. *The Star and the Flame.* London, 1962
18. *Soap Box Derby.* Leicester, 1962
19. *Black Sheep.* London, 1963
20. *The Smallest Dog on Earth.* London and New York, 1963
21. *The Young David Garrick.* London, 1963
22. *Mystery of the Black Sheep.* New York, 1964
23. *Further Adventures of Albert the Dragon.* London and New York, 1964
24. *Mike's Gang.* London and New York, 1965
25. *A Patch of Green.* London, 1965
26. *Devon Venture,* as Catherine Bell. London, 1965
27. *The Real Game.* Leicester, 1965
28. *The Heirs of Ashton Manor.* New York, 1966
29. *The Boy from Nowhere.* London and New York, 1966
30. *High Courage.* London and New York, 1967
31. *Pyewacket.* London and New York, 1967
32. *Boy on a Brown Horse.* London, 1967
33. *The Foxwood Flyer.* London, 1968
34. *Albert the Dragon and the Centaur.* London and New York, 1968
35. *No Sleep for Angus.* London and New York, 1969
36. *Summer of the Silent Hands.* Leicester, 1969
37. *The Lion and the Rose.* New York, 1970
38. *The Man Who Built a City: A Life of Sir Christopher Wren.* New York, 1971
39. *The Three Red Herrings.* Nashville (TN), 1972
40. *Blood Royal.* New York, 1973
41. *Uncle Barney and the Sleep-Destroyer.* London, 1974
42. *Uncle Barney and the Shrink-Drink.* London, 1977
43. *Albert and the Dragonettes.* London, 1977

Welch, James
American, born in 1940

1. *Riding the Earthboy 40.* Cleveland (OH), 1971
2. *Winter in the Blood.* New York, 1974
3. *The Death of Jim Loney.* New York, 1979

Welcome, John [John Needham Huggard Brennan]
Irish, born June 22, 1914

1. *Red Coats Galloping.* London, 1949
2. *Mr. Merston's Money.* London, 1951
3. *Mr. Merston's Hounds.* London, 1953
4. *The Cheltenham Gold Cup: The Story of a Great Steeplechase.* London, 1957
5. *Run for Cover.* London, 1958
6. *Stop at Nothing.* London, 1959
7. *Beware of Midnight.* London and New York, 1961
8. *Cheating at Cards: The Cases in Court.* London, 1963
9. *Great Scandals of Cheating at Cards: Famous Court Cases.* New York, 1964
10. *Hard to Handle.* London, 1964
11. *Wanted for Killing.* London, 1965
12. *Fred Archer: His Life and Times.* London, 1967
13. *Hell Is Where You Find It.* London, 1968
14. *On the Stretch.* London, 1969
15. *Neck or Nothing: The Extraordinary Life and Times of Bob Sievier.* London, 1970
16. *Go for Broke.* London and New York, 1972
17. *The Sporting Empress: The Story of Elizabeth of Austria and Bay Middleton.* London, 1975
18. *A Light-Hearted Guide to British Racing.* London, 1975
19. *Grand National.* London, 1976
20. *Bellary Bay.* London and New York, 1979

Wellman, Manly Wade
American, born May 21, 1903
Pseudonym: Gans T. Field

1. *The Invading Asteroid.* New York, 1932
2. *Romance in Black,* as Gans T. Field. London, 1946
3. *A Double Life.* Chicago, 1947
4. *Find My Killer.* New York, 1947
5. *The Sleuth Patrol.* New York, 1947
6. *The Mystery of Lost Valley.* New York, 1948
7. *Sojarr of Titan.* New York, 1949
8. *Giant in Gray: A Biography of Wade Hampton of South Carolina.* New York, 1949
9. *The Beasts from Beyond.* London, 1950
10. *The Raiders of Beaver Lake.* New York, 1950
11. *The Devil's Planet.* London, 1951
12. *The Haunting of Drowning Creek.* New York, 1951
13. *Wild Dogs of Drowning Creek.* New York, 1952
14. *The Last Mammoth.* New York, 1953
15. *Grey Riders: Jeb Stuart and His Men.* New York, 1954
16. *Rebel Mail Runner.* New York, 1954
17. *Dead and Gone: Classic Crimes of North Carolina.* Chapel Hill (NC), 1954
18. *Fort Sun Dance.* New York and London, 1955
19. *Flag on the Levee.* New York, 1955
20. *To Unknown Lands.* New York, 1956
21. *Young Squire Morgan.* New York, 1956
22. *Rebel Boast: First at Bethel—Last at Appomattox.* New York, 1956
23. *Twice in Time.* New York, 1957
24. *Lights over Skeleton Ridge.* New York, 1957
25. *Fastest on the River.* New York, 1957
26. *The Ghost Battalion: A Story of the Iron Scouts.* New York, 1958
27. *The Life and Times of Sir Archie,* with Elizabeth Amis Blanchard. Chapel Hill, 1958
28. *Giants from Eternity.* New York, 1959
29. *The Dark Destroyers.* New York, 1959
30. *Ride, Rebels!* New York, 1959
31. *The County of Warren, North Carolina, 1586-1917.* Chapel Hill, 1959
32. *They Took Their Stand: The Founders of the Confederacy.* New York, 1959
33. *The Rebel Songster,* with Frances Wellman. New York, 1959
34. *Candle of the Wicked.* New York, 1960
35. *Appomattox Road.* New York, 1960
36. *Third String Center.* New York, 1960
37. *Harpers Ferry, Prize of War.* Charlotte (NC), 1960
38. *Island in the Sky.* New York, 1961
39. *Rifles at Ramsour's Mill.* New York, 1961
40. *Many Are the Hearts.* Raleigh (NC), 1961
41. *The County of Gaston,* with Robert F. Cope. Gastonia (NC), 1961
42. *Not at These Hands.* New York, 1962
43. *Battle for King's Mountain.* New York, 1962
44. *Clash on the Catawba.* New York, 1962

45. *The County of Moore 1847-1947.* Southern Pines (NC), 1962
46. *Who Fears the Devil?* Sauk City (WI), 1963
47. *The River Pirates.* New York, 1963
48. *Settlement on Shocco.* Winston-Salem (NC), 1963
49. *The South Fork Rangers.* New York, 1963
50. *The Master of Scare Hollow.* New York, 1964
51. *A True Story of the Revolting and Bloody Crimes of Sergeant Stanlas, U.S.A.* Wichita (KS), 1964
52. *The Great Riverboat Race.* New York, 1965
53. *Mystery at Bear Paw Gap.* New York, 1965
54. *Battle at Bear Paw Gap.* New York, 1966
55. *The Specter of Bear Paw Gap.* New York, 1966
56. *Winston-Salem in History: The Founders.* Winston-Salem, 1966
57. *Jamestown Adventure.* New York, 1967
58. *The Solar Invasion.* New York, 1968
59. *Brave Horse: A Story of Janus.* New York, 1968
60. *Carolina Pirate.* New York, 1968
61. *Frontier Reporter.* New York, 1969
62. *Mountain Feud.* New York, 1969
63. *Napoleon of the West: A Story of the Aaron Burr Conspiracy.* New York, 1970
64. *Fast Break Five.* New York, 1971
65. *Worse Things Waiting.* Chapel Hill, 1973
66. *The Kingdom of Madison.* Chapel Hill, 1973
67. *The Story of Moore County.* Southern Pines, 1974
68. *Sherlock Holmes's War of the Worlds,* with Wade Wellman. New York, 1975
69. *The Beyonders.* New York, 1977
70. *The Old Gods Waken.* New York, 1979
71. *After Dark.* New York, 1980

Wellman, Paul I. (Iselin)
American, born October 14, 1898, died September 16, 1966
1. *Death on the Prairie.* New York, 1934
2. *Death on the Desert.* New York, 1935
3. *Bronco Apache.* New York, 1936
4. *Jubal Troop.* New York and London, 1939
5. *The Trampling Herd: The Story of the Cattle Range in America.* New York, 1939
6. *Angel with Spurs.* Philadelphia, 1942
7. *The Bowl of Brass.* Philadelphia, 1942
8. *The Callaghan, Yesterday and Today.* Encinal (TX), 1944(?)
9. *The Walls of Jericho.* Philadelphia, 1947
10. *Death on Horseback: Seventy Years of War for the American West.* Philadelphia, 1947
11. *The Chain.* New York, 1949
12. *The Iron Mistress.* New York, 1951
13. *Good Soldiers Do Die.* Dallas (TX), 1951
14. *The Comancheros.* New York, 1952
15. *The Female: A Novel of Another Time.* New York, 1953
16. *The Female City.* London, 1954
17. *The Indian Wars of the West.* New York, 1954
18. *Glory, God, and Gold.* New York, 1954
19. *Jericho's Daughters.* New York, 1956
20. *Portage Bay.* New York and London, 1957
21. *Ride the Red Earth.* New York, 1958
22. *Gold in California.* Boston, 1958
23. *The Fiery Flower.* New York, 1959
24. *Indian Wars and Warriors: East [and West].* Boston, 2 vols., 1959
25. *Stuart Symington: Portrait of a Man with a Mission.* New York, 1960
26. *Race to the Golden Spike.* Boston, 1961
27. *A Dynasty of Western Outlaws.* New York, 1961
28. *The Blazing Southwest.* London, 1961
29. *Magnificent Destiny.* New York, 1962
30. *The Greatest Cattle Drive.* Boston, 1964
31. *Spawn of Evil.* New York and London, 1964
32. *The Devil's Desciples.* London, 1965
33. *The House Divides: The Age of Jackson and Lincoln.* New York and London, 1966
34. *The Buckstones.* New York, 1967

Wells, Carolyn
American, born June 18, 1869, died March 26, 1942
Pseudonym: Rowland Wright
1. *The Story of Betty.* New York, 1899
2. *The Jingle Book.* New York, 1899
3. *Idle Idylls.* New York, 1900
4. *Folly in Fairyland.* Philadelphia and London, 1901
5. *The Merry-Go-Round.* New York, 1901
6. *Mother Goose's Menagerie.* Boston, 1901
7. *Patty Fairfield.* New York, 1901
8. *The Pete and Polly Stories.* Chicago, 1902
9. *A Phenomenal Fauna.* New York, 1902
10. *Eight Girls and a Dog.* New York, 1902
11. *Folly in the Forest.* Philadelphia, 1902
12. *Trotty's Trip.* Philadelphia, 1902
13. *Abeniki Caldwell.* New York, 1902
14. *Children of Our Town.* New York, 1902
15. *The Bumblepuppy Book.* London, 1903
16. *Patty at Home.* New York, 1904
17. *In the Reign of Queen Dick.* New York, 1904
18. *The Staying Guests.* New York, 1904
19. *Folly for the Wise.* Indianapolis (IN), 1904
20. *The Gordon Elopement,* with Harry Parsons Taber. New York, 1904
21. *The Dorrance Domain.* Boston, 1905
22. *The Matrimonial Bureau,* with Harry Parsons Taber. Boston and London, 1905
23. *Patty in the City.* New York, 1905
24. *At the Sign of the Sphinx.* New York, 1906
25. *Dorrance Doings.* Boston, 1906
26. *Rubaiyat of a Motor Car.* New York, 1906
27. *The Emily Emmins Papers.* New York, 1907
28. *Fluffy Ruffles.* New York, 1907
29. *Marjorie's Vacation.* New York, 1907
30. *Rainy Day Diversions.* New York, 1907
31. *Patty in Paris.* New York, 1907
32. *Patty's Friends.* New York, 1908
33. *Patty's Summer Days.* New York, 1908
34. *The Carolyn Wells Year Book of Old Favorites and New Fancies for 1909.* New York, 1908
35. *The Happy Chaps.* New York, 1908
36. *Dick and Dolly.* New York, 1909
37. *Marjorie's New Friend.* New York, 1909
38. *Marjorie's Busy Days.* New York, 1909
39. *Patty's Pleasure Trip.* New York, 1909
40. *Pleasant Day Diversions.* New York, 1909
41. *The Rubaiyat of a Bridge.* New York, 1909
42. *The Seven Ages of Childhood.* New York, 1909
43. *The Clue.* Philadelphia, 1909
44. *Betty's Happy Year.* New York, 1910
45. *Dick and Dolly's Adventures.* New York, 1910
46. *Marjorie in Command.* New York, 1910
47. *Patty's Success.* New York, 1910
48. *Marjorie's Maytime.* New York, 1911
49. *Patty's Motor Car.* New York, 1911
50. *The Gold Bag.* Philadelphia, 1911
51. *Patty's Butterfly Days.* New York, 1912
52. *The Lover's Baedeker and Guide to Arcady.* New York, 1912
53. *Marjorie at Seacote.* New York, 1912
54. *A Chain of Evidence.* Philadelphia, 1912
55. *The Maxwell Mystery.* Philadelphia, 1913

56. *Christmas Carollin'.* New York, 1913
57. *The Eternal Feminine.* New York, 1913
58. *Girls and Gayety.* New York, 1913
59. *The Technique of the Mystery Story.* Springfield (MA), 1913
60. *Patty's Social Session.* New York, 1913
61. *Pleasing Prose.* New York, 1913
62. *The Re-Echo Club.* New York, 1913
63. *Patty's Suitors.* New York, 1914
64. *Anybody But Anne.* Philadelphia, 1914
65. *Jolly Plays for Holidays.* Boston, 1914
66. *The White Alley.* Philadelphia, 1915
67. *Two Little Women.* New York, 1915
68. *Patty's Romance.* New York, 1915
69. *Patty's Fortune.* New York, 1916
70. *Two Little Women and Treasure House.* New York, 1916
71. *The Bride of a Moment.* New York, 1916
72. *The Curved Blades.* Philadelphia, 1916
73. *Faulkner's Folly.* Philadelphia, 1917
74. *The Mark of Cain.* New York, 1917
75. *Two Little Women on a Holiday.* New York, 1917
76. *Baubles.* New York, 1917
77. *Doris of Dobbs Ferry.* New York, 1917
78. *Patty Blossom.* New York, 1917
79. *Patty-Bride.* New York, 1918
80. *The Room with the Tassels.* New York, 1918
81. *Vicky Van.* Philadelphia, 1918
82. *The Diamond Pin.* Philadelphia, 1919
83. *Patty and Azalea.* New York, 1919
84. *The Man Who Fell Through the Earth.* New York, 1919
85. *In the Onyx Lobby.* New York and London, 1920
86. *The Disappearance of Kimball Webb,* as Rowland Wright. New York, 1920
87. *Raspberry Jam.* Philadelphia, 1920
88. *The Come Back.* New York and London, 1920
89. *Ptomaine Street: A Tale of Warble Petticoat.* Philadelphia, 1921
90. *The Luminous Face.* New York, 1921
91. *The Mystery of the Sycamore.* Philadelphia, 1921
92. *The Mystery Girl.* Philadelphia, 1922
93. *The Meaning of Thanksgiving.* Philadelphia, 1922
94. *Queen Christmas.* Philadelphia, 1922
95. *The Sweet Girl Graduate.* Philadelphia, 1922
96. *The Vanishing of Betty Varian.* New York, 1922
97. *A Concise Bibliography of the Works of Walt Whitman.* New York, 1922
98. *The Affair at Flower Acres.* New York, 1923
99. *Feathers Left Around.* Philadelphia, 1923
100. *More Lives Than One.* New York, 1923
101. *Spooky Hollow.* Philadelphia, 1923
102. *Wheels Within Wheels.* New York, 1923
103. *The Fourteenth Key.* New York, 1924
104. *The Furthest Fury.* Philadelphia, 1924
105. *The Moss Mystery.* New York, 1924
106. *Prillilgirl.* Philadelphia, 1924
107. *Cross Word Puzzle Book.* New York, 1924
108. *Anything But the Truth.* Philadelphia, 1925
109. *The Daughter of the House.* Philadelphia, 1925
110. *Face Cards.* New York, 1925
111. *Book of American Limericks.* New York, 1925
112. *The Bronze Hand.* Philadelphia, 1926
113. *The Red-Haired Girl.* Philadelphia, 1926
114. *The Vanity Case.* New York, 1926
115. *All at Sea.* Philadelphia, 1927
116. *The Sixth Commandment.* New York, 1927
117. *Where's Emily?* Philadelphia, 1927
118. *A Book of Charades.* New York, 1927
119. *The Crime in the Crypt.* Philadelphia, 1928
120. *Deep-Lake Mystery.* New York, 1928
121. *The Tannahill Tangle.* Philadelphia, 1928
122. *Sleeping Dogs.* New York, 1929
123. *The Tapestry Room Murder.* Philadelphia, 1929
124. *Triple Murder.* Philadelphia, 1929
125. *The Doomed Five.* Philadelphia, 1930
126. *The Doorstep Murders.* New York, 1930
127. *The Ghosts' High Noon.* Philadelphia, 1930
128. *Horror House.* Philadelphia, 1931
129. *The Skeleton at the Feast.* New York, 1931
130. *The Umbrella Murder.* Philadelphia, 1931
131. *Fuller's Earth.* Philadelphia, 1932
132. *The Roll-Top Desk Mystery.* Philadelphia, 1932
133. *The Broken O.* Philadelphia, 1933
134. *The Clue of the Eyelash.* Philadelphia, 1933
135. *The Master Murderer.* Philadelphia, 1933
136. *All for Fun: Brain Teasers.* New York, 1933
137. *Eyes in the Wall.* Philadelphia, 1934
138. *The Elusive Vicky Van.* London, 1934
139. *In the Tiger's Cage.* Philadelphia, 1934
140. *The Visiting Villain.* Philadelphia, 1934
141. *The Beautiful Derelict.* Philadelphia, 1935
142. *For Goodness' Sake.* Philadelphia, 1935
143. *The Wooden Indian.* Philadelphia, 1935
144. *The Huddle.* Philadelphia, 1936
145. *Money Musk.* Philadelphia, 1936
146. *Murder in the Bookshop.* Philadelphia, 1936
147. *The Mystery of the Tarn.* Philadelphia, 1937
148. *The Radio Studio Murder.* Philadelphia, 1937
149. *The Rest of My Life.* Philadelphia, 1937
150. *Gilt-Edged Guilt.* Philadelphia, 1938
151. *The Killer.* Philadelphia, 1938
152. *The Missing Link.* Philadelphia, 1938
153. *Calling All Suspects.* Philadelphia, 1939
154. *Crime Tears On.* Philadelphia, 1939
155. *The Importance of Being Murdered.* Philadelphia, 1939
156. *Crime Incarnate.* Philadelphia, 1940
157. *Devil's Work.* Philadelphia, 1940
158. *Murder on Parade.* Philadelphia, 1940
159. *Murder Plus.* Philadelphia, 1940
160. *The Black Night Murders.* Philadelphia, 1941
161. *Murder at the Casino.* Philadelphia, 1941
162. *Murder Will In.* Philadelphia, 1942
163. *Who Killed Caldwell?* Philadelphia, 1942

Wells, H.G. (Herbert George)
British. September 21, 1866, died August 13, 1946
1. *Text-Book of Biology.* London, 2 vols., 1893
2. *The Time Machine: An Invention.* London and New York, 1895
3. *The Stolen Bacillus and Other Incidents.* London, 1895
4. *The Wonderful Visit.* London and New York, 1895
5. *Select Conversations with an Uncle(Now Extinct) and Two Other Reminiscences.* New York and London, 1895
6. *The Island of Doctor Moreau.* London and New York, 1896
7. *The Wheels of Chance.* London and New York, 1896
8. *The Invisible Man: A Grotesque Romance.* London and New York, 1897
9. *The Plattner Story and Others.* London, 1897
10. *Thirty Strange Stories.* New York, 1897
11. *Certain Personal Matters: A Collection of Material, Mainly Autobiographical.* London, 1897
12. *The War of the Worlds.* London and New York, 1898
13. *When the Sleeper Wakes.* London and New York, 1899
14. *Tales of Space and Time.* London and New York, 1899
15. *A Cure for Love.* New York, 1899
16. *The Vacant Country.* New York, 1899
17. *Love and Mr. Lewisham.* London and New York, 1900
18. *The First Men in the Moon.* London and Indianapolis (IN), 1901

19. *Anticipations of the Reaction of Mechanical and Scientific Progress upon Human Life and Thought.* London, 1901
20. *The Sea Lady: A Tissue of Moonshine.* London and New York, 1902
21. *The Discovery of the Future.* London, 1902
22. *Twelve Stories and a Dream.* London, 1903
23. *Mankind in the Making.* London, 1903
24. *The Food of the Gods, and How It Came to Earth.* London and New York, 1904
25. *A Modern Utopia.* London and New York, 1905
26. *Kipps.* London and New York, 1905
27. *In the Days of the Comet.* London and New York, 1906
28. *The Future in America: A Search after Realities.* London and New York, 1906
29. *Faults of the Fabian.* Privately Printed, 1906
30. *Socialism and the Family.* London, 1906
31. *Reconstruction of the Fabian Society.* Privately printed, 1906
32. *This Misery of Boots.* London, 1907
33. *Will Socialism Destroy the Home?* London, 1907
34. *The War in the Air, and Particularly How Mr. Bert Smallways Fared While It Lasted.* London and New York, 1908
35. *Tono-Bungay.* London and New York, 1908
36. *New Worlds for Old.* London and New York, 1908
37. *First and Last Things: A Confession of Faith and Rule of Life.* London and New York, 1908
38. *Ann Veronica.* London and New York, 1909
39. *The Sleeper Wakes.* London, 1910
40. *The History of Mr. Polly.* London and New York, 1910
41. *The Country of the Blind and Other Stories.* London, 1911
42. *The Door in the Wall and Other Stories.* New York, 1911
43. *The New Machiavelli.* London and New York, 1911
44. *Floor Games.* London, 1911
45. *Marriage.* London and New York, 1912
46. *The Labour Unrest.* London, 1912
47. *The Passionate Friends.* London and New York, 1913
48. *War and Common Sense.* London, 1913
49. *Liberalism and Its Party.* London, 1913
50. *Little Wars.* London and Boston, 1913
51. *The World Set Free: A Story of Mankind.* London and New York, 1914
52. *The Wife of Sir Isaac Harman.* London and New York, 1914
53. *An Englishman Looks at the World, Being a Series of Unrestrained Remarks upon Contemporary Matters.* London, 1914
54. *Social Forces in England and America.* New York, 1914
55. *The War That Will End War.* London and New York, 1914
56. *The War and Socialism.* London, 1915
57. *The Peace of the World.* London, 1915
58. *Boon.* London and New York, 1915
59. *Bealby.* London and New York, 1915
60. *The Research Magnificent.* London and New York, 1915
61. *Mr. Britling Sees It Through.* London and New York, 1916
62. *What Is Coming? A Forecast of Things after the War.* London and New York, 1916
63. *The Elements of Reconstruction.* London, 1916
64. *The Soul of a Bishop.* London and New York, 1917
65. *War and the Future.* London, 1917
66. *Italy, France, and Britain at War.* New York, 1917
67. *God the Invisible King.* London and New York, 1917
68. *Joan and Peter.* London and New York, 1918
69. *In the Fourth Year: Anticipations of a World Peace.* London and New York, 1918
70. *Anticipations of a World Peace.* London, 1918
71. *British Nationalism and the League of Nations.* London, 1918
72. *The Undying Fire.* London and New York, 1919
73. *History Is One.* Boston, 1919
74. *The Outline of History, Being a Plain History of Life and Mankind.* London and New York, 2 vols., 1920
75. *Russia in the Shadows.* London, 1920
76. *The Salvaging of Civilisation.* London and New York, 1921
77. *The New Teaching of History, with a Reply to Some Recent Criticism of "The Outline of History."* London, 1921
78. *The Secret Places of the Heart.* London and New York, 1922
79. *Tales of the Unexpected [of Life and Adventure, of Wonder].* London, 3 vols., 1922-23
80. *Washington and the Hope of Peace.* London, 1922
81. *Washington and the Riddle of Peace.* New York, 1922
82. *The World, Its Debts, and the Rich Men.* London, 1922
83. *A Short History of the World.* London and New York, 1922
84. *Men Like Gods.* London and New York, 1923
85. *Socialism and the Scientific Motive.* Privately printed, 1923
86. *The Dream.* London and New York, 1924
87. *The Story of a Great Schoolmaster, Being a Plain Account of the Life and Ideas of Sanderson of Oundle.* London and New York, 1924
88. *A Year of Prophesying.* London, 1924
89. *Christina Alberta's Father.* London and New York, 1925
90. *A Forecast of the World's Affairs.* New York, 1925
91. *The World of William Clissold.* London, 3 vols., 1926
92. *Mr. Belloc Objects to "The Outline of History."* London, 1926
93. *Complete Short Stories.* London, 1927
94. *Meanwhile: The Picture of a Lady.* London and New York, 1927
95. *Democracy under Revision.* London and New York, 1927
96. *Wells' Social Anticipations.* New York, 1927
97. *Mr. Blettsworthy on Rampole Island.* London and New York, 1928
98. *The Book of Catherine Wells.* London, 1928
99. *The Way the World Is Going: Guesses and Forecasts of the Years Ahead.* London, 1928
100. *The Open Conspiracy: Blue Prints for a World Revolution.* London and New York, 1928
101. *The Short Stories of H.G. Wells.* New York, 1929
102. *The King Who Was a King: The Book of a Film.* London, 1929
103. *The Common Sense of World Peace.* London, 1929
104. *Imperialism and the Open Conspiracy.* London, 1929
105. *The Adventures of Tommy.* London and New York, 1929
106. *The Science of Life: A Summary of Contemporary Knowledge about Life and Its Possibilities,* with Julian Huxley and G.P. Wells. London, 3 vols., 1929-30
107. *The Autocracy of Mr. Parham.* London and New York, 1930
108. *The Way to World Peace.* London, 1930
109. *What Are We to Do with Our Lives?* London and New York, 1931
110. *The Work, Wealth, and Happiness of Mankind.* New York, 2 vols., 1931
111. *The Blupington of Blup.* London, 1932
112. *What Should Be Done Now?* New York, 1932
113. *The Shape of Things to Come: The Ultimate Resolution.* London and New York, 1933
114. *Experiment in Autobiography: Discoveries and Conclusions of a Very Ordinary Brain since 1866.* London, 2 vols. and New York 1 vol., 1934
115. *Things to Come.* London and New York, 1935
116. *The New America: The New World.* London and New York, 1935
117. *The Croquet Player.* London, 1936
118. *Man Who Could Work Miracles.* London and New York, 1936

Wells, H.G.

119. *The Outline of Man's Work and Wealth.* New York, 1936
120. *The Anatomy of Frustration: A Modern Synthesis.* London and New York, 1936
121. *The Idea of a World Encyclopedia.* London, 1936
122. *Star Begotten: A Biological Fantasia.* London and New York, 1937
123. *Brynhild.* London and New York, 1937
124. *The Camford Visitation.* London, 1937
125. *The Brothers.* London and New York, 1938
126. *Apropos of Dolores.* London and New York, 1938
127. *World Brain.* London and New York, 1938
128. *The Holy Terror.* London and New York, 1939
129. *The Country of the Blind.* London, 1939
130. *Travels of a Republican Radical in Search of Hot Water.* London, 1939
131. *Babes in the Darkling Wood.* London and New York, 1940
132. *All Aboard for Ararat.* London, 1940
133. *The Rights of Man; or, What are We Fighting For?* London, 1940
134. *The Common Sense of War and Peace: World Revolution or War Unending?* London, 1940
135. *You Can't Be Too Careful: A Sample of Life 1901-1951.* London, 1941
136. *The Pocket History of the World.* New York, 1941
137. *Guide to the New World: A Handbook of Constructive World Revolution.* London, 1941
138. *The Outlook for Homo Sapiens.* London, 1942
139. *Science and the World-Mind.* London, 1942
140. *The Conquest of Time.* London, 1942
141. *The New Rights of Man.* Girard (KS), 1942
142. *Crux Ansata: An Indictment of the Roman Catholic Church.* London, 1943
143. *The Mosley Outrage.* London, 1943
144. *Marxism vs. Liberalism.* New York, 1945
145. *The Happy Turning: A Dream of Life.* London, 1945
146. *Mind at the End of Its Tether.* London, 1945
147. *The Desert Daisy.* Urbana (IL), 1957
148. *28 Science Fiction Stories.* London, 1958
149. *Selected Short Stories.* London, 1958
150. *The Valley of Spiders.* London, 1964
151. *Hoopdriver's Holiday.* Lafayette (IN), 1964
152. *Journalism and Prophecy 1893-1946.* Boston, 1964
153. *The Cone.* London, 1965
154. *Best Science Fiction Stories of H.G. Wells.* New York, 1966
155. *The Wealth of Mr. Waddy.* Carbondale (IL), 1969

Wentworth, Patricia (Dora Amy Elles)
British, born in 1878, died January, 28, 1961
1. *A Marriage under the Terror.* London and New York, 1910
2. *A Child's Rhyme Book.* London, 1910
3. *A Little More Than Kin.* London, 1911
4. *More Than Kin.* New York, 1911
5. *The Devil's Wind.* London, 1912
6. *The Fire Within.* London, 1913
7. *Simon Heriot.* London, 1914
8. *Queen Anne Is Dead.* London, 1915
9. *Earl or Chieftain? The Romance of Hugh O'Neill.* Dublin (Ireland), 1919
10. *The Astonishing Adventure of Jane Smith.* London and Boston, 1923
11. *The Red Lacquer Case.* London, 1924
12. *The Annam Jewel.* London, 1924
13. *The Black Cabinet.* London, 1925
14. *The Dower House Mystery.* London, 1925
15. *The Amazing Chance.* London, 1926
16. *Anne Belinda.* London, 1927
17. *Hue and Cry.* London and Philadelphia, 1927
18. *Grey Mask.* London, 1928
19. *Will-o'-the-Wisp.* London and Philadelphia, 1928
20. *Fool Errant.* London and Philadelphia, 1929
21. *Beggar's Choice.* London, 1930
22. *The Coldstone.* London and Philadelphia, 1930
23. *Kingdom Lost.* Philadelphia, 1930
24. *Danger Calling.* London and Philadelphia, 1931
25. *Nothing Venture.* London and Philadelphia, 1932
26. *Red Danger.* London, 1932
27. *Red Shadow.* Philadelphia, 1932
28. *Seven Green Stones.* London, 1933
29. *Outrageous Fortune.* Philadelphia, 1933
30. *Walk with Care.* London and Philadelphia, 1933
31. *Fear by Night.* London and Philadelphia, 1934
32. *Devil-in-the-Dark.* London, 1934
33. *Touch and Go.* Philadelphia, 1934
34. *Blindfold.* London and Philadelphia, 1935
35. *Red Stefan.* London and Philadelphia, 1935
36. *Hole and Corner.* London and Philadelphia, 1936
37. *Dead or Alive.* London and Philadelphia, 1936
38. *The Case Is Closed.* London and Philadelphia, 1937
39. *Down Under.* London and Philadelphia, 1937
40. *Mr. Zero.* London and Philadelphia, 1938
41. *Run!* London and Philadelphia, 1938
42. *The Blind Side.* London and Philadelphia, 1939
43. *Lonesome Road.* London and Philadelphia, 1939
44. *Who Pays the Piper?* London, 1940
45. *Account Rendered.* Philadelphia, 1940
46. *Rolling Stone.* London and Philadelphia, 1940
47. *Unlawful Occasions.* London, 1941
48. *Weekend with Death.* Philadelphia, 1941
49. *In the Balance.* Philadelphia, 1941
50. *Danger Point.* London, 1942
51. *Pursuit of a Parcel.* London and Philadelphia, 1942
52. *The Chinese Shawl.* London and Philadelphia, 1943
53. *Miss Silver Deals with Death.* Philadelphia, 1943
54. *The Key.* Philadelphia, 1944
55. *The Clock Strikes Twelve.* Philadelphia, 1944
56. *She Came Back.* Philadelphia, 1945
57. *Silence in Court.* Philadelphia, 1945
58. *Beneath the Hunter's Moon: Poems.* London, 1945
59. *Pilgrim's Rest.* Philadelphia, 1946
60. *Latter End.* Philadelphia, 1947
61. *Wicked Uncle.* Philadelphia, 1947
62. *The Case of William Smith.* Philadelphia, 1948
63. *The Traveller Returns.* London, 1948
64. *Eternity Ring.* Philadelphia, 1948
65. *Miss Silver Comes to Stay.* Philadelphia, 1949
66. *The Catherine Wheel.* Philadelphia, 1949
67. *Spotlight.* London, 1949
68. *The Brading Collection.* Philadelphia, 1950
69. *Through the Wall.* Philadelphia, 1950
70. *Anna, Where Are You?* Philadelphia, 1951
71. *The Ivory Dagger.* Philadelphia, 1951
72. *The Watersplash.* Philadelphia, 1951
73. *Dark Threat.* New York, 1951
74. *Ladies' Bane.* Philadelphia, 1952
75. *Vanishing Point.* Philadelphia, 1953
76. *Out of the Past.* Philadelphia, 1953
77. *The Pool of Dreams: Poems.* London, 1953
78. *The Benevent Treasure.* Philadelphia, 1954
79. *The Silent Pool.* Philadelphia, 1954
80. *Poison in the Pen.* Philadelphia, 1955
81. *The Listening Eye.* Philadelphia, 1955
82. *The Gazebo.* Philadelphia, 1956
83. *The Fingerprint.* Philadelphia, 1956
84. *The Alington Inheritance.* Philadelphia, 1956
85. *The Girl in the Cellar.* London, 1961
86. *Death at Deep End.* New York, 1963
87. *The Summerhouse.* New York, 1967

Wersba, Barbara
American, born August 19, 1932
1. *The Boy Who Loved the Sea.* New York, 1961
2. *The Brave Balloon of Benjamin Buckley.* New York, 1963
3. *The Land of Forgotten Beasts.* New York, 1964
4. *A Song for Clowns.* New York, 1965
5. *Do Tigers Ever Bite Kings?* New York, 1966
6. *The Dream Watcher.* New York, 1968
7. *Run Softly, Go Fast.* New York, 1970
8. *Let Me Fall Before I Fly.* New York, 1971
9. *Amanda Dreaming.* New York, 1973
10. *The Country of the Heart.* New York, 1975
11. *Tunes for a Small Harmonica.* New York, 1976

West, Joyce (Tarlton)
British
Pseudonym: Manu Gilbert
1. *Sheep Kings.* Wellington (New Zealand), 1936
2. *Drovers Road.* London, 1953
3. *Fatal Lady,* with Mary Scott. Hamilton (New Zealand), 1960
4. *The Year of the Shining Cuckoo.* Hamilton, 1961
5. *Such Nice People,* with Mary Scott. Hamilton, 1962
6. *Cape Lost.* Auckland (New Zealand) and London, 1963
7. *The Mangrove Murder,* with Mary Scott. Auckland and London, 1963
8. *No Red Herrings,* with Mary Scott. London, 1964
9. *Who Put It There?* with Mary Scott. Hamilton and London, 1965
10. *The Golden Country.* Hamilton and London, 1965
11. *Lineman's Ticket,* as Manu Gilbert. Hamilton, 1967
12. *The Sea Islanders.* London and New York, 1970

West, Kingsley
1. *A Time for Vengeance.* New York, 1961
2. *South to Gunsight Pass.* London, 1961
3. *Ride West to Pueblo.* London, 1962
4. *Showdown at Gila Bend.* New York, 1963
5. *Killer's Kingdom.* London, 1963
6. *Latigo's Day.* London, 1963
7. *Comanche River.* New York and London, 1965
8. *Arroyo Hondo.* New York, 1966
9. *Arroyo West.* New York, 1976

West, Tom [Fred East]
American, born in 1895
Pseudonym: Roy Manning
1. *Meddling Maverick.* New York, 1944
2. *Bushwhack Basin.* New York, 1945
3. *Trigger Trail,* as Roy Manning. Philadelphia, 1945
4. *Trouble Trail.* New York, 1946
5. *Renegade Ranch.* New York, 1946
6. *Vengeance Valley,* as Roy Manning. Philadelphia, 1946
7. *Renegade Range.* London, 1947
8. *Six-Gun Showdown.* New York, 1947
9. *Tangled Trail,* as Roy Manning. Philadelphia, 1947
10. *Powdersmoke Pay-Off.* New York, 1948
11. *Spectre Spread.* New York, 1948
12. *Botched Brand.* New York, 1949
13. *Six Gun Sheriff,* as Roy Manning. Philadelphia, 1949
14. *Ghost Gold.* New York, 1950
15. *Red Range,* as Roy Manning. Philadelphia, 1950
16. *Vulture Valley.* New York, 1951
17. *Flaming Feud.* New York, 1951
18. *The Marshal of Vengeance Valley,* as Roy Manning. London, 1951
19. *Ghost Gun.* New York, 1952
20. *Gunsmoke Gold.* New York, 1952
21. *The Desperado Code,* as Roy Manning. New York, 1953
22. *Lobo Legacy.* New York, 1954
23. *Outlaw Brand.* New York, 1956
24. *Beware of This Tenderfoot,* as Roy Manning. New York, 1956
25. *Torture Trail.* New York, 1957
26. *Draw and Die!* as Roy Manning New York, 1958
27. *Lead in His Fists.* New York, 1958
28. *Slick on the Draw.* New York, 1958
29. *Twisted Trail.* New York, 1959
30. *The Cactus Kid.* New York, 1959
31. *Nothing But My Gun.* New York, 1960
32. *The Gun from Nowhere.* New York, 1961
33. *Killer's Canyon.* New York, 1961
34. *Battling Buckaroos.* New York, 1962
35. *Triggering Texan.* New York, 1963
36. *Lobo Man.* New York, 1963
37. *Sidewinder Showdown.* New York, 1964
38. *The Man at Rope's End.* New York, 1964
39. *Lost Loot of Kittycat Ranch.* New York, 1965
40. *Buchwhack Brand.* New York, 1965
41. *The Toughest Town in the Territory.* New York, 1965
42. *Bitter Brand.* New York, 1966
43. *Rattlesnake Range.* New York, 1966
44. *Hangrope Heritage.* New York, 1966
45. *Crossfire at Barbed M.* New York, 1967
46. *Showdown at Serano.* New York, 1967
47. *Heroes on Horseback: The Story of the Pony Express.* New York, 1969
48. *The Buzzard's Nest.* London, 1970
49. *Dead Man's Double Cross.* London, 1970
50. *Don't Cross My Line.* London, 1970
51. *Renegade Roundup.* London, 1970
52. *The Black Buzzards.* London, 1970
53. *Write His Name in Gunsmoke.* New York, 1972
54. *Lone Gun.* New York, 1974
55. *Payoff at Piute.* New York, 1977
56. *Battle at Rattlesnake Pass.* New York, 1979
57. *Sagebrush Showdown.* New York, 1979
58. *Trigger Tyrant.* New York, 1979

West, Wallace George
American, born May 22, 1900
1. *Betty Boop in Snow-White.* Racine (WI), 1934
2. *Alice in Wonderland.* Racine, 1934
3. *Paramount Newsreel Men with Admiral Byrd in Little America.* Racine, 1934
4. *Jimmy Allen in the Sky Parade.* New York, 1936
5. *Thirteen Hours by Air.* New York, 1936
6. *Our Good Neighbors in Latin America.* New York, 1942
7. *Our Good Neighbors in Soviet Russia.* New York, 1945
8. *Down to the Sea in Ships.* New York, 1947
9. *The Bird of Time.* New York, 1959
10. *Find a Career in Electronics.* New York, 1959
11. *Lords of Atlantis.* New York, 1960
12. *The Memory Bank.* New York, 1961
13. *Clearing the Air.* New York, 1961
14. *Outposts in Space.* New York, 1962
15. *River of Time.* New York, 1963
16. *The Time-Lockers.* New York, 1964
17. *Conserving Our Waters.* New York, 1964
18. *The Everlasting Exiles.* New York, 1967
19. *The Amazing Inventor from Laurel Creek.* New York, 1967

Westerman, Percy (Francis)
British, born in 1876, died February 22, 1959
1. *A Lad of Grit.* London, 1908
2. *The Winning of Goldenspurs.* London, 1911
3. *The Young Cavalier.* London, 1911

4. *The Flying Submarine.* London, 1912
5. *Captured at Tripoli.* London, 1912
6. *The Quest of the "Golden Hope."* London, 1912
7. *The Sea Monarch.* London, 1912
8. *The Scouts of Seal Island.* London, 1913
9. *The Rival Submarines.* London, 1913
10. *The Stolen Cruiser.* London, 1913
11. *When East Meets West.* London, 1913
12. *Under King Henry's Banners.* London, 1914
13. *The Sea-Girt Fortress.* London, 1914
14. *The Sea Scouts of the "Petrel."* London, 1914
15. *The Log of a Snob.* London, 1914
16. *'Gainst the Might of Spain.* London, 1914
17. *Building the Empire.* London, 1914
18. *The Dreadnought of the Air.* London, 1914
19. *The Dispatch-Riders.* London, 1915
20. *The Fight for Constantinople.* London, 1915
21. *The Nameless Island.* London, 1915
22. *A Sub. of the R.N.R.* London, 1915
23. *Rounding Up the Raider.* London, 1916
24. *The Secret Battleplane.* London, 1916
25. *The Treasures of the "San Philipo."* London, 1916
26. *A Watch-Dog of the North Sea.* London, 1917
27. *Deeds of Pluck and Daring in the Great War.* London, 1917
28. *The Fritz Strafers.* London, 1918
29. *Under the White Ensign.* London, 1918
30. *Billy Barcroft, R.N.A.S.* London, 1918
31. *A Lively Bit of the Front.* London, 1918
32. *The Secret Channel and Other Stories.* London, 1918
33. *The Submarine Hunters.* London, 1918
34. *To the Fore with the Tanks!* London, 1918
35. *Wilmshurst of the Frontier Force.* London, 1918
36. *With Beatty off Jutland.* London, 1918
37. *Winning His Wings.* London, 1919
38. *The Thick of the Fray at Zeebruge, April 1918.* London, 1919
39. *A Sub and a Submarine.* London, 1919
40. *'Midst Arctic Perils.* London, 1919
41. *The Airship "Golden Hind."* London, 1920
42. *The Mystery Ship.* London, 1920
43. *The Salving of the "Fusi Yama."* London, 1920
44. *Sea Scouts All.* London, 1920
45. *Sea Scouts Abroad.* London, 1921
46. *The Third Officer.* London, 1921
47. *Sea Scouts Up-Channel.* London, 1922
48. *The Wireless Officer.* London, 1922
49. *The War of the Wireless Waves.* London, 1923
50. *The Pirate Submarine.* London, 1923
51. *A Cadet of the Mercantile Marine.* London, 1923
52. *Clipped Wings.* London, 1923
53. *Captain Cain.* London, 1924
54. *The Good Ship "Golden Effort."* London, 1924
55. *The Mystery of Stockmere School.* London, 1924
56. *Sinclair's Luck.* London, 1924
57. *The Treasure of the Sacred Lake.* London, 1924
58. *Unconquered Wings.* London, 1924
59. *Clinton's Quest.* London, 1925
60. *East in the "Golden Gain."* London, 1925
61. *The Boys of the "Puffin."* London, 1925
62. *The Buccaneers of Boya.* London, 1925
63. *Annesley's Double.* London and New York, 1926
64. *King of Kilba.* London, 1926
65. *The Luck of the "Golden Dawn."* London, 1926
66. *The Riddle of the Air.* London, 1926
67. *The Sea Scouts of the "Kestrel."* London, 1926
68. *Tireless Wings.* London, 1926
69. *The Terror of the Seas.* London, 1927
70. *Mystery Island.* London, 1927
71. *Captain Blundell's Treasure.* London, 1927
72. *Chums of the "Golden Vanity."* London, 1927
73. *In the Clutches of the Dyaks.* London, 1927
74. *The Junior Cadet.* London, 1928
75. *On the Wings of the Wind.* London, 1928
76. *A Shanghai Adventure.* London, 1928
77. *Pat Stobart in the "Golden Dawn."* London, 1928
78. *Rivals of the Reef.* London, 1929
79. *Captain Starlight.* London, 1929
80. *Captain Sang.* London, 1930
81. *Leslie Dexter, Cadet.* London, 1930
82. *A Mystery of the Broads.* London, 1930
83. *The Secret of the Plateau.* London, 1931
84. *The Senior Cadet.* London, 1931
85. *In Defiance of the Ban.* London, 1931
86. *All Hands to the Boats!* London, 1932
87. *The Amir's Ruby.* London, 1932
88. *Fosdyke's Gold.* London, 1932
89. *King for a Month.* London, 1933
90. *Rocks Ahead!* London, 1933
91. *The White Arab.* London, 1933
92. *The Disappearing Dhow.* London, 1933
93. *Chasing the "Pleiad."* London, 1933
94. *The Westow Talisman.* London, 1934
95. *Tales of the Sea.* London, 1934
96. *Andy-All-Alone.* London, 1934
97. *The Black Hawk.* London, 1934
98. *Standish of the Air Police.* London, 1935
99. *The Red Pirate.* London, 1935
100. *Sleuths of the Air.* London, 1935
101. *On Board the "Golden Effort."* London, 1935
102. *The Call of the Sea.* London, 1935
103. *Captain Flick.* London, 1936
104. *His First Ship.* London, 1936
105. *Midshipman Raxworthy.* London, 1936
106. *Ringed by Fire.* London, 1936
107. *Winged Might.* London, 1937
108. *Under Fire in Spain.* London, 1937
109. *The Last of the Buccaneers.* London, 1937
110. *Midshipman Webb's Treasure.* London, 1937
111. *Haunted Harbor.* London, 1937
112. *His Unfinished Voyage.* London, 1937
113. *Cadet Alan Carr.* London, 1938
114. *Standish Gets His Man.* London, 1938
115. *Sea Scouts Alert!* London, 1938
116. *Standish Loses His Man.* London, 1939
117. *In Eastern Seas.* London, 1939
118. *The Bulldog Breed.* London, 1939
119. *At Grips with the Swastika.* London, 1940
120. *Eagles' Talons.* London, 1940
121. *In Dangerous Waters.* London, 1940
122. *When the Allies Swept the Seas.* London, 1940
123. *Standish Pulls It Off.* London, 1940
124. *The War—And Alan Carr.* London, 1940
125. *War Cargo.* London, 1941
126. *Sea Scouts at Dunkirk.* London, 1941
127. *Standish Holds On.* London, 1941
128. *Fighting for Freedom.* London, 1941
129. *Alan Carr in the Near East.* London, 1942
130. *Destroyer's Luck.* London, 1942
131. *On Guard for England.* London, 1942
132. *Secret Flight.* London, 1942
133. *With the Commandoes.* London, 1943
134. *Sub-Lieutenant John Cloche.* London, 1943
135. *Alan Carr in Command.* London, 1943
136. *Alan Carr in the Arctic.* London, 1943
137. *Combined Operations.* London, 1944

138. *Engage the Enemy Closely*. London, 1944
139. *Secret Convoy*. London, 1944
140. *One of the Many*. London, 1945
141. *Operations Successfully Executed*. London, 1945
142. *By Luck and Pluck*. London, 1946
143. *Return to Base*. London, 1946
144. *Squadron Leader*. London, 1946
145. *Unfettered Night*. London, 1947
146. *Trapped in the Jungle*. London, 1947
147. *The Phantom Submarine*. London, 1947
148. *The "Golden Gleaner."* London, 1948
149. *First Over*. London, 1948
150. *Mystery of the Key*. London, 1948
151. *Missing, Believed Lost*. London, 1949
152. *Contraband*. London, 1949
153. *Beyond the Burma Road*. London, 1949
154. *Sabarinda Island*. London, 1950
155. *Mystery of Nix Hall*. London, 1950
156. *By Sea and Air*. London, 1950
157. *Desolation Island*. London, 1950
158. *Held to Ransom*. London, 1951
159. *The Isle of Mystery*. London, 1951
160. *Working Their Passage*. London, 1951
161. *Sabotage!* London, 1952
162. *Round the World in the "Golden Gleaner."* London, 1952
163. *Dangerous Cargo*. London, 1952
164. *Bob Strickland's Log*. London, 1953
165. *The Missing Diplomat*. London, 1953
166. *Rolling Down to Rio*. London, 1953
167. *Wrested from the Deep*. London, 1954
168. *A Midshipman of the Fleet*. London, 1954
169. *The Ju-Ju Hand*. London, 1954
170. *The Dark Scout*. London, 1954
171. *Daventry's Quest*. London, 1955
172. *The Lure of the Lagoon*. London, 1955
173. *Held in the Frozen North*. London, 1956
174. *The Mystery of the "Sempione."* London, 1957
175. *Jack Craddock's Commission*. London, 1958
176. *Mistaken Identity*. London, 1959

Westlake, Donald E. (Edwin)
American, born July 12, 1933
Pseudonyms: Curt Clark, Tucker Coe, Timothy J. Culver, Richard Stark
1. *The Mercenaries*. New York, 1960
2. *Killing Time*. New York, 1961
3. *361*. New York and London, 1962
4. *The Smashers*. New York, 1962
5. *The Hunter*, as Richard Stark. New York, 1962
6. *Killy*. New York, 1963
7. *The Man with the Getaway Face*, as Richard Stark. New York, 1963
8. *The Outfit*, as Richard Stark. New York, 1963
9. *The Mourner*, as Richard Stark. New York, 1963
10. *The Operator*. New York, 1964
11. *Pity Him Afterwards*. New York, 1964
12. *The Score*, as Richard Stark. New York, 1964
13. *The Fugitive Pigeon*. New York, 1965
14. *The Jugger*, as Richard Stark. New York, 1965
15. *The Busy Body*. New York and London, 1966
16. *The Spy in the Ointment*. New York, 1966
17. *The Seventh*, as Richard Stark. New York, 1966
18. *The Handle*, as Richard Stark. New York, 1966
19. *Kinds of Love, Kinds of Death*, as Tucker Coe. New York, 1966
20. *God Save the Mark*. New York, 1967
21. *Point Blank*, as Richard Stark. London, 1967
22. *The Rare Coin Score*, as Richard Stark. New York, 1967
23. *The Damsel*, as Richard Stark. New York, 1967
24. *The Green Eagle Score*, as Richard Stark. New York, 1967
25. *Anarchaos*, as Curt Clark. New York, 1967
26. *Philip*. New York, 1967
27. *The Black Ice Score*, as Richard Stark. New York, 1968
28. *Murder among Children*, as Tucker Coe. New York and London, 1968
29. *The Curious Facts Preceding My Execution and Other Fictions*. New York, 1968
30. *The Dame*, as Richard Stark. New York and London, 1969
31. *Who Stole Sassi Manoon?* New York, 1969
32. *Somebody Owes Me Money*. New York, 1969
33. *Up Your Banners*. New York, 1969
34. *The Split*, as Richard Stark. London, 1969
35. *The Sour Lemon Score*, as Richard Stark. New York and London, 1969
36. *The Blackbird*, as Richard Stark. New York, 1969
37. *The Hot Rock*. New York, 1970
38. *Adios, Sheherazade*. New York, 1970
39. *Ex Officio*, as Timothy J. Culver. New York, 1970
40. *Wax Apple*, as Tucker Coe. New York, 1970
41. *I Gave at the Office*. New York, 1971
42. *The Steel Hit*, as Richard Stark. London, 1971
43. *Killtown*, as Richard Stark. London, 1971
44. *Deadly Edge*, as Richard Stark. New York, 1971
45. *Slayground*, as Richard Stark. New York, 1971
46. *Lemons Never Lie*, as Richard Stark. Cleveland, 1971
47. *A Jade in Aries*, as Tucker Coe. New York, 1971
48. *Bank Shot*. New York and London, 1972
49. *Cops and Robbers*. New York and London, 1972
50. *Run Lethal*, as Richard Stark. London, 1972
51. *Plunder Squad*, as Richard Stark. New York, 1972
52. *Don't Lie to Me*, as Tucker Coe. New York, 1972
53. *Under an English Heaven*. New York and London, 1972
54. *Gangway*, with Brian Garfield. New York, 1973
55. *Help I Am Being Held Prisoner*. New York, 1974
56. *Jimmy the Kid*. New York, 1974
57. *Butcher's Moon*, as Richard Stark. New York, 1974
58. *Two Much!* New York, 1975
59. *Brothers Keepers*. New York, 1975
60. *Dancing Aztecs*. New York, 1976
61. *Enough*. New York, 1977
62. *Nobody's Perfect*. New York, 1977
63. *A New York Dance*. London, 1979

Weston, Carolyn
American
1. *Tormented*. New York, 1956
2. *Face of My Assassin*, with Jan Huckins. New York, 1959
3. *Danju Gig*. New York, 1969
4. *Spy in Black*. London, 1972
5. *Poor, Poor Ophelia*. New York, 1972
6. *Susannah Screaming*. New York, 1975
7. *Rouse the Demon*. New York, 1976

Westwood, Gwen
British, born June 27, 1915
1. *Monkey Business*. London, 1965
2. *The Gentle Dolphin*. London, 1965
3. *The Red Elephant Blanket*. London, 1966
4. *The Pumpkin Eater*. London, 1966
5. *Narni of the Desert*. London, 1967
6. *A Home for Digby*. London, 1968
7. *Keeper of the Heart*. London and Toronto, 1969
8. *Bright Wilderness*. London, 1969
9. *The Emerald Cuckoo*. London, 1970
10. *Castle of the Unicorn*. London and Toronto, 1971
11. *Pirate of the Sun*. London and Toronto, 1972
12. *Citadel of Swallows*. London and Toronto, 1973

13. *Sweet Roots and Honey.* London, 1974
14. *Ross of Silver Ridge.* London, 1975
15. *Blossoming Gold.* London and Toronto, 1976
16. *Bride of Bonamour.* London and Toronto, 1977
17. *A Place for Lovers.* London, 1978
18. *Forgotten Bride.* London, 1980
19. *Zulu Moon.* London, 1980

Wheatley, Dennis (Yates)
British, born January 8, 1897. November 11, 1977
1. *The Forbidden Territory.* New York and London, 1933
2. *Such Power Is Dangerous.* London, 1933
3. *Old Rowley: A Private Life of Charles II.* London, 1933
4. *Black August.* New York and London, 1934
5. *The Fabulous Valley.* London, 1934
6. *The Devil Rides Out.* London, 1934
7. *The Eunuch of Stamboul.* London and Boston, 1935
8. *They Found Atlantis.* London and Philadelphia, 1936
9. *Murder Off Miami.* London, 1936
10. *File on Bolitho Blane.* New York, 1936
11. *Contraband.* London, 1936
12. *The Secret War.* London, 1937
13. *Who Killed Robert Prentice?* London, 1937
14. *File on Robert Prentice.* New York, 1937
15. *Red Eagle: A Life of Marshal Voroshilov.* London, 1937
16. *A Private Life of Charles II.* London, 1938
17. *Invasion.* London, 1938
18. *Uncharted Seas.* London, 1938
19. *The Malinsay Massacre.* London, 1938
20. *The Golden Spaniard.* London, 1938
21. *The Quest of Julian Day.* London, 1939
22. *Herewith the Clues!* London, 1939
23. *Sixty Days to Live.* London, 1939
24. *Blockade.* London, 1939
25. *The Scarlet Imposter.* London, 1940
26. *Three Inquisitive People.* London, 1940
27. *Faked Passports.* London, 1940
28. *The Black Baroness.* London, 1940
29. *Total War.* London, 1941
30. *Strange Conflict.* London, 1941
31. *The Sword of Fate.* London, 1941
32. *"V" for Vengeance.* London and New York, 1942
33. *Mediterranean Nights.* London, 1942
34. *Gunmen, Gallants, and Ghosts.* London, 1943
35. *The Man Who Missed the War.* London, 1945
36. *Codeword—Golden Fleece.* London, 1946
37. *Come into My Parlour.* London, 1946
38. *The Launching of Roger Brook.* London, 1947
39. *The Shadow of Tyburn Tree.* London, 1948
40. *The Haunting of Toby Jugg.* London, 1948
41. *The Seven Ages of Justerini's.* London, 1949
42. *The Rising Storm.* London, 1949
43. *The Second Seal.* London, 1950
44. *Alibi.* London, 1951
45. *The Man Who Killed the King.* London, 1951
46. *Star of Ill-Omen.* London, 1952
47. *To the Devil—A Daughter.* London, 1953
48. *Curtain of Fear.* London, 1953
49. *The Island Where Time Stands Still.* London, 1954
50. *The Dark Secret of Josephine.* London, 1955
51. *The Ka of Gifford Hillary.* London, 1956
52. *The Prisoner in the Mask.* London, 1957
53. *Traitors' Gate.* London, 1958
54. *The Rape of Venice.* London, 1959
55. *The Satanist.* London, 1960
56. *Stranger Than Fiction.* London, 1959
57. *Saturdays with Bricks and Other Days under Shell-Fire.* London, 1961
58. *Vendetta in Spain.* London, 1961
59. *Mayhem in Greece.* London, 1962
60. *The Sultan's Daughter.* London, 1963
61. *Bill for the Use of a Body.* London, 1964
62. *They Used Dark Forces.* London, 1964
63. *Dangerous Inheritance.* London, 1965
64. *The Wanton Princess.* London, 1966
65. *Unholy Crusade.* London, 1967
66. *The White Witch of the South Seas.* London, 1968
67. *Evil in a Mask.* London, 1969
68. *Gateway to Hell.* London, 1970
69. *The Ravishing of Lady Mary Ware.* London, 1971
70. *The Devil and All His Works.* London and New York, 1971
71. *The Strange Story of Linda Lee.* London, 1972
72. *The Irish Witch.* London, 1973
73. *Desperate Measures.* London, 1974
74. *The Young Man Said.* London, 1977
75. *Officer and Temporary Gentleman.* London, 1978
76. *Drink and Ink.* London, 1979

Whitaker, Rod (Rodney Whitaker)
American, born January 12, 1925
Pseudonyms: Nicholas Seare, Trevanian
1. *The Language of Film.* Englewood Cliffs (NJ), 1970
2. *The Eiger Sanction,* as Trevanian. New York, 1972
3. *The Loo Sanction,* as Trevanian. New York, 1973
4. *Thirteen Thirty Nine or So, Being an Apology for A Pedlar,* as Nicholas Seare. New York, 1975
5. *The Main,* as Trevanian. New York, 1976
6. *Shibumi,* as Trevanian. New York and London, 1979

White, Eliza Orne
American, born August 2, 1856, died Died January 23, 1947
1. *Miss Brooks.* Boston, 1890
2. *Winterborough.* Boston, 1892
3. *The Coming of Theodora.* Boston, 1895
4. *When Molly Was Six.* Boston, 1894
5. *A Little Girl of Long Ago.* Boston, 1896
6. *The Browning Courtship and Other Stories.* Boston, 1897
7. *A Lover of the Truth.* Boston, 1898
8. *Ednah and Her Brothers.* Boston, 1900
9. *John Forsyth's Aunts.* New York and London, 1901
10. *Lesley Chilton.* Boston, 1903
11. *An Only Child.* Boston, 1905
12. *A Borrowed Sister.* Boston, 1906
13. *The Wares of Edgefield.* Boston, 1909
14. *Brothers in Fur.* Boston, 1910
15. *The Enchanted Mountain.* Boston, 1911
16. *The First Step.* Boston, 1914
17. *The Blue Aunt.* Boston, 1918
18. *The Strange Year.* Boston, 1920
19. *Peggy in Her Blue Frock.* Boston, 1921
20. *Tony.* Boston, 1924
21. *Joan Morse.* Boston, 1926
22. *Diana's Rosebush.* Boston, 1927
23. *The Adventures of Andrew.* Boston, 1928
24. *Sally in Her Fur Coat.* Boston, 1929
25. *The Green Door.* Boston, 1930
26. *When Abigail Was Seven.* Boston, 1931
27. *The Four Young Kendalls.* Boston, 1932
28. *Where Is Adelaide?* Boston, 1933
29. *Lending Mary.* Boston, 1934
30. *Ann Frances.* Boston, 1935
31. *Nancy Alden.* Boston, 1936
32. *The Farm Beyond the Town.* Boston, 1937
33. *Helen's Gift House.* Boston, 1938
34. *Patty Makes a Visit.* Boston, 1939

35. *The House Across the Valley*. Boston, 1940
36. *I: The Autobiography of a Cat*. Boston, 1941
37. *Training Sylvia*. Boston, 1942
38. *When Esther Was a Little Girl*. Boston, 1944

White, E.B. (Elwyne Brooks)
American, born July 11, 1899
1. *Is Sex Necessary? or, Why You Feel the Way You Do*, with James Thurber. New York, 1929
2. *The Lady Is Cold: Poems*. New York and London, 1929
3. *Ho Hum*. New York, 1931
4. *Another Ho Hum*. New York, 1932
5. *Alice Through the Cellophane*. New York, 1933
6. *Every Day Is Saturday*. New York, 1934
7. *Farewell to Model T*. New York, 1936
8. *The Fox of Peapack and Other Poems*. New York and London, 1938
9. *Quo Vadimus? or, The Case for the Bicycle*. New York and London, 1939
10. *One Man's Meat*. New York, 1942
11. *Stuart Little*. New York, 1945
12. *Here Is New York*. New York, 1949
13. *Charlotte's Web*. New York and London, 1952
14. *The Second Tree from the Corner*. New York and London, 1954
15. *An E.B. White Reader*. New York, 1966
16. *The Trumpet of the Swan*. New York and London, 1970
17. *Letters of E.B. White*. New York, 1976

White, Ethel Lina
British, born in 1887, died in 1944
1. *The Wish-Bone*. London, 1927
2. *'Twill Soon Be Dark*. London, 1929
3. *The Eternal Journey*. London, 1930
4. *Put Out the Light*. London, 1931
5. *Fear Stalks the Village*. London, 1932
6. *Some Must Watch*. London, 1933
7. *The First Time He Died*. London, 1935
8. *Wax*. London and New York, 1935
9. *The Wheel Spins*. London and New York, 1936
10. *The Elephant Never Forgets*. London, 1937
11. *The Third Eye*. London and New York, 1937
12. *Step in the Dark*. London, 1938
13. *While She Sleeps*. London and New York, 1940
14. *She Faded Into Air*. London and New York, 1941
15. *Midnight House*. London, 1942
16. *Her Heart in Her Throat*. New York, 1942
17. *The Man Who Loved Lions*. London, 1943
18. *The Man Who Was Not There*. New York, 1943
19. *They See in Darkness*. London, 1944
20. *The Spiral Staircase*. Cleveland (OH), 1946
21. *The Lady Vanishes*. London, 1962
22. *The Unseen*. New York, 1966
23. *Sinister Light*. New York, 1966

White, James
British, born April 7, 1928
1. *The Secret Visitors*. New York, 1957
2. *Second Ending*. New York, 1962
3. *Hospital Station*. New York, 1962
4. *Star Surgeon*. New York, 1963
5. *Deadly Litter*. New York, 1964
6. *Open Prison*. London, 1965
7. *Escape Orbit*. New York, 1965
8. *The Watch Below*. London and New York, 1966
9. *All Judgment Fled*. London, 1968
10. *The Aliens Among Us*. New York, 1969
11. *Tomorrow Is Too Far*. London and New York, 1971
12. *Major Operation*. New York, 1971
13. *Dark Inferno*. London, 1972
14. *Lifeboat*. New York, 1972
15. *The Dream Millennium*. London and New York, 1974
16. *Monsters and Medics*. London and New York, 1977
17. *Underkill*. London, 1979
18. *Ambulance Ship*. New York, 1979

White, Jon Manchip [Jon Ewbank Manchip White]
British, born June 22, 1924
1. *Dragon and Other Poems*. London, 1943
2. *Salamander*. London, 1946
3. *The Rout of San Romano*. Aldington (Eng), 1952
4. *Ancient Egypt*. London, 1952
5. *Mask of Dust*. London, 1953
6. *Last Race*. New York, 1953
7. *Anthropology*. London, 1954
8. *Build Us a Dam*. London, 1955
9. *The Girl from Indiana*. London, 1956
10. *No Home but Heaven*. London, 1957
11. *The Mercenaries*. London, 1958
12. *Hour of the Rat*. London, 1962
13. *Everyday Life in Ancient Egypt*. London, 1963
14. *The Rose in the Brandy Glass*. London, 1965
15. *Nightclimber*. London and New York, 1968
16. *Diego Velazquez, Painter and Courtier*. **London and Chicago**, 1969
17. *The Land God Made in Anger: Reflections on a Journey Through South West Africa*. London and Chicago, 1969
18. *The Game of Troy*. London and New York, 1971
19. *The Mountain Lion*. London, 1971
20. *Cortes and the Downfall of the Aztec Empire*. London and New York, 1971
21. *The Garden Game*. London, 1973
22. *Send for Mr. Robinson*. London and New York, 1974
23. *A World Elsewhere: One Man's Fascination with the American Southwest*. New York, 1975
24. *Everyday Life of the North American Indian*. London, 1979
25. *The Moscow Papers*. Canoga Park (CA), 1979

White, Lionel
American, born July 9, 1905
1. *The Snatchers*. New York, 1953
2. *To Find a Killer*. New York, 1954
3. *Love Trap*. New York, 1955
4. *The Big Caper*. New York, 1955
5. *Clean Break*. New York and London, 1955
6. *Flight into Terror*. New York, 1955
7. *Operation—Murder*. New York, 1956
8. *The House Next Door*. New York, 1956
9. *Right for Murder*. London, 1957
10. *Death Takes the Bus*. New York, 1957
11. *Hostage for a Hood*. New York, 1957
12. *Too Young to Die*. New York, 1958
13. *Coffin for a Hood*. New York, 1958
14. *Invitation to Violence*. New York and London, 1958
15. *The Merriweather File*. New York, 1959
16. *Rafferty*. New York, 1959
17. *Run, Killer, Run*. New York, 1959
18. *Lament for a Virgin*. New York and London, 1960
19. *Steal Big*. New York, 1960
20. *The Time of Terror*. New York, 1960
21. *Marilyn K*. Derby (CT), 1960
22. *A Grave Undertaking*. New York, 1961
23. *A Death at Sea*. New York, 1961
24. *Obsession*. New York, 1962
25. *The Money Trap*. New York, 1963
26. *The Ransomed Madonna*. New York, 1964

27. *The House on K Street.* New York, 1965
28. *A Party to Murder.* New York, 1966
29. *The Night of the Rape.* New York, 1967
30. *The Crimshaw Memorandum.* New York, 1967
31. *Hijack.* New York, 1969
32. *Death of a City.* Indianapolis (IN), 1970
33. *The Mexico Run.* New York, 1974
34. *A Rich and Dangerous Game.* New York, 1974
35. *Jailbreak.* London, 1976

White, Stewart Edward
American, born March 12, 1873, died September 18, 1946
1. *The Claim Jumpers: A Romance.* New York, 1901
2. *The Westerners.* New York and London, 1901
3. *The Blazed Trail.* New York and London, 1902
4. *Conjuror's House: A Romance of the Free Forest.* New York and London, 1903
5. *The Forest.* New York, 1903
6. *The Magic Forest: A Modern Fairy Story.* New York, 1903
7. *Blazed Trail Stories, and Stories of the Wild Life.* New York, 1904
8. *The Silent Places.* New York and London, 1904
9. *The Mountains.* New York and London, 1904
10. *The Pass.* New York and London, 1906
11. *Camp and Trail.* New York, 1907
12. *Arizona Nights.* New York and London, 1907
13. *The Mystery,* with Samuel Hopkins Adams. New York and London, 1907
14. *The Riverman.* New York and London, 1908
15. *The Rules of the Game.* New York, 1910
16. *The Adventures of Bobby Orde.* New York, 1911
17. *The Cabin.* New York, 1911
18. *The Sign at Six.* Indianapolis (IN) and London, 1912
19. *The Land of Footprints.* New York, 1912
20. *African Camp Fires.* New York, 1913
21. *Gold.* New York, 1913
22. *The Gray Dawn.* New York and London, 1915
23. *The Rediscovered Country.* New York and London, 1915
24. *Bobby Orde.* London, 1916
25. *The Leopard Woman.* New York and London, 1916
26. *Simba.* New York, 1918
27. *White Magic.* London, 1918
28. *The Forty-Niners: A Chronicle of the California Trail and El Dorado.* New Haven (CT), 1918
29. *The Killer.* New York, 1919
30. *The Rose Dawn.* New York, 1920
31. *On Tiptoe: A Romance of the Redwoods.* New York and London, 1922
32. *Daniel Boone, Wilderness Scout.* New York, 1922
33. *The Glory Hole.* New York and London, 1924
34. *Skookum Chuck.* New York and London, 1925
35. *Credo.* New York and London, 1925
36. *Secret Harbor.* New York and London, 1926
37. *Lions in the Path: A Book of Adventure on the High Veldt.* New York, 1926
38. *Back of Beyond.* New York and London, 1927
39. *The Story of California.* New York, 1927
40. *Why Be a Mud Turtle?* New York, 1928
41. *The Shepper-Newfounder.* New York, 1931
42. *Wild Animals.* Burlingame (CA), 1932
43. *The Long Rifle.* New York and London, 1932
44. *Ranchero.* New York and London, 1933
45. *Folded Hills.* New York and London, 1934
46. *Pole Star,* with Harry DeVighne. New York, 1935
47. *The Hold-up.* San Francisco, 1937
48. *Old California in Picture and Story.* New York, 1937
49. *Across the Unknown,* with Harwood White. New York, 1939
50. *Wild Geese Calling.* New York and London, 1940
51. *Stampede.* New York, 1942
52. *The Saga of Andy Burnett.* New York, 1947
53. *The Unobstructed Universe.* New York, 1940
54. *The Road I Know.* New York, 1942
55. *Speaking for Myself.* New York, 1943
56. *The Stars Are Still There.* New York, 1946
57. *With Folded Wings.* New York, 1947
58. *The Job of Living.* New York, 1948

White, Ted [Theodore Edwin White]
American, born February 4, 1938
Pseudonyms: Ron Archer, Norman Edwards
1. *Invasion from 2500,* as Norman Edwards, with Terry Carr. Derby (CT), 1964
2. *Android Avenger.* New York, 1965
3. *Phoenix Prime.* New York, 1966
4. *The Sorceress of Qar.* New York, 1966
5. *The Jewels of Elsewhen.* New York, 1967
6. *Lost in Space,* as Ron Archer, with Dave Van Arnam. New York, 1967
7. *Sideslip,* with Dave Van Arnam. New York, 1968
8. *Captain America: The Great Gold Steal.* New York, 1968
9. *The Spawn of the Death Machine.* New York, 1968
10. *No Time Like Tomorrow.* New York, 1969
11. *By Furies Possessed.* New York, 1970
12. *Star Wolf!* New York, 1971
13. *Trouble on Project Ceres.* Philadelphia, 1971
14. *Forbidden World,* with David Bischoff. New York, 1978

White, T.H. (Terence Hanbury)
British, born May 29, 1906, died January 17, 1964
Pseudonym: James Aston
1. *Loved Helen and Other Poems.* London and New York, 1929
2. *The Green Bay Tree; or, The Wicked Man Touches Wood.* Cambridge (Eng), 1929
3. *Dead Mr. Nixon.* London, 1931
4. *Darkness at Pemberley.* London, 1932
5. *They Winter Abroad,* as James Aston. London and New York, 1932
6. *First Lesson,* as James Aston. London, 1932
7. *Farewell Victoria.* London, 1933
8. *Earth Stopped; or, Mr. Marx's Sporting Tour.* London, 1934
9. *Gone to Ground.* London and New York, 1935
10. *England Have My Bones.* London and New York, 1936
11. *Burke's Steerage; or, The Amateur Gentleman's Introduction to Noble Sports and Pastimes.* London, 1938
12. *The Sword in the Stone.* London, 1938
13. *The Witch in the Wood.* New York, 1939
14. *The Ill-Made Knight.* New York, 1940
15. *Mistress Masham's Repose.* New York, 1946
16. *The Elephant and the Kangaroo.* New York, 1947
17. *The Age of Scandal: An Excursion Through a Minor Period.* London and New York, 1950
18. *The Goshawk.* London, 1951
19. *The Scandalmonger.* London and New York, 1952
20. *The Master: An Adventure Story.* London and New York, 1957
21. *The Once and Future King.* London and New York, 1958
22. *The Godstone and the Blackymor.* London and New York, 1959
23. *America at Last: The American Journal of T.H. White.* New York, 1965
24. *The White/Garnett Letters.* London and New York, 1968
25. *The Book of Merlyn.* Austin (TX) and London, 1977

Whitechurch, Victor L. (Lorenzo)
  British, born March 12, 1868, died in May 1933
1. *The Course of Justice.* London, 1903
2. *The Canon in Residence.* London, 1904
3. *The Locum Tenens.* London, 1906
4. *Concerning Himself: The Story of an Ordinary Man.* London, 1909
5. *The Canon's Dilemma and Other Stories.* London, 1909
6. *Off the Main Road: a Village Comedy.* London, 1911
7. *Left in Charge.* London and New York, 1912
8. *Thrilling Stories of the Railway.* London, 1912
9. *A Downland Corner.* London, 1912
10. *Three Summers: A Romance.* London, 1915
11. *If Riches Increase.* London, 1923
12. *The Templeton Case.* London and New York, 1924
13. *A Bishop Out of Residence.* London, 1924
14. *Downland Echoes.* London, 1924
15. *The Adventures of Captain Ivan Koravitch.* Edinburgh (Scotland), 1925
16. *Concerning Right and Wrong: A Plain Man's Creed.* London, 1925
17. *The Dean and Jecinora.* London and New York, 1926
18. *The Crime at Diana's Pool.* London and New York, 1927
19. *Shot on the Downs.* London, 1927
20. *Mixed Relations.* London, 1928
21. *The Robbery at Rudwick House.* New York, 1929
22. *First and Last.* London, 1929
23. *Murder at the Pageant.* London, 1930
24. *The Floating Admiral,* with others. London, 1931
25. *Murder at the College.* London, 1932
26. *Murder at Exbridge.* New York, 1932

Whitfield, Raoul
  American, born in 1897, died in 1945
1. *Green Ice.* New York, 1930
2. *Wings of Gold.* New York, 1930
3. *Silver Wings.* New York, 1930
4. *Danger Zone.* New York, 1931
5. *Death in a Bowl.* New York, 1931
6. *The Virgin Kills.* New York, 1932
7. *Danger Circus.* New York, 1933
8. *The Green Ice Murders.* New York, 1947

Whitney, Phyllis A. (Ayame)
  American, born September 9, 1903
1. *A Place for Ann.* Boston, 1941
2. *A Star for Ginny.* Boston, 1942
3. *A Window for Julie.* Boston, 1943
4. *Red is for Murder.* New York, 1943
5. *The Silver Inkwell.* Boston, 1945
6. *Willow Hill.* New York, 1947
7. *Writing Juvenile Fiction.* Boston, 1947
8. *Ever After.* Boston, 1948
9. *Mystery of the Gulls.* Philadelphia, 1949
10. *Linda's Homecoming.* Philadelphia, 1950
11. *The Island of Dark Woods.* Philadelphia, 1951
12. *Love Me, Love Me Not.* Boston, 1952
13. *Mystery of the Black Diamonds.* Philadelphia, 1954
14. *Step to the Music.* New York, 1953
15. *A Long Time Coming.* Philadelphia, 1954
16. *Mystery on the Isle of Skye.* Philadelphia, 1955
17. *The Quicksilver Pool.* New York, 1955
18. *The Trembling Hills.* New York, 1956
19. *Skye Cameron.* New York, 1957
20. *The Fire and the Gold.* New York, 1956
21. *The Highest Dream.* Philadelphia, 1956
22. *Mystery of the Green Cat.* Philadelphia, 1957
23. *Black Diamonds.* Leicester (Eng), 1957
24. *Secret of the Samurai Sword.* Philadelphia, 1958
25. *The Moonflower.* New York, 1958
26. *Creole Holiday.* Philadelphia, 1959
27. *Mystery of the Haunted Pool.* Philadelphia, 1960
28. *The Mask and the Moonflower.* London, 1960
29. *Thunder Heights.* New York, 1960
30. *Secret of the Tiger's Eye.* Philadelphia, 1961
31. *Blue Fire.* New York, 1961
32. *Mystery of the Golden Horn.* Philadelphia, 1962
33. *Window on the Square.* New York, 1962
34. *Seven Tears for Apollo.* New York, 1963
35. *Mystery of the Hidden Hand.* Philadelphia, 1963
36. *Secret of the Emerald Star.* Philadelphia, 1964
37. *Black Amber.* New York, 1964
38. *Sea Jade.* New York, 1965
39. *The Red Carnelian.* New York, 1965
40. *Mystery of the Angry Idol.* Philadelphia, 1965
41. *Columbella.* New York, 1966
42. *Secret of the Spotted Shell.* Philadelphia, 1967
43. *Mystery of the Strange Traveler.* Philadelphia, 1967
44. *Silverhill.* New York, 1967
45. *Hunter's Green.* New York, 1968
46. *Secret of Goblin Glen.* Philadelphia, 1968
47. *The Mystery of the Crimson Ghost.* Philadelphia, 1969
48. *Secret of the Missing Footprint.* Philadelphia, 1969
49. *The Winter People.* New York, 1969
50. *Lost Island.* New York, 1970
51. *The Vanishing Scarecrow.* Philadelphia, 1971
52. *Nobody Likes Trina.* Philadelphia, 1972
53. *Listen for the Whisper.* New York and London, 1972
54. *Snowfire.* New York and London, 1973
55. *Mystery of the Scowling Boy.* Philadelphia, 1973
56. *The Turquoise Mask.* New York, 1974
57. *Secret of Haunted Mesa.* Philadelphia, 1975
58. *Spindrift.* New York and London, 1975
59. *The Golden Unicorn.* New York and London, 1976
60. *Writing Juvenile Stories and Novels.* Boston, 1976
61. *The Stone Bull.* New York and London, 1977
62. *Secret of the Stone Face.* Philadelphia, 1977

Whitson, John H. (Harvey)
  American, born December 28, 1854, died May 2, 1936
1. *Captain Cactus.* New York, 1888
2. *Huckleberry, The Foot Hills Detective.* New York, 1888
3. *The Silver Sport.* New York, 1888
4. *Happy Hans, The Dutch Vidocq.* New York, 1889
5. *Prince Primrose.* New York, 1889
6. *Signal Sam.* New York, 1890
7. *Kansas Karl, The Detective King.* New York, 1890
8. *Stuttering Sam.* New York, 1891
9. *The River Rustlers.* New York, 1891
10. *Kent Kirby.* New York, 1892
11. *Lodestone Lem.* New York, 1892
12. *The Rustler of Rolling Stone.* New York, 1892
13. *Singer Sam.* New York, 1892
14. *Teamster Tom.* New York, 1892
15. *The Doctor Detective in Texas.* New York, 1893
16. *The King-Pin of the Leadville Lions.* New York, 1894
17. *The Crescent City.* New York, 1894
18. *The Six-Shot Spotter.* New York, 1895
19. *The Texan Detective.* New York, 1895
20. *The Texan Firebrand.* New York, 1895
21. *The Tramp's Trump-Trick.* New York, 1895
22. *The Young Rider.* Elgin (IL), 1899
23. *With Fremont the Pathfinder.* Boston, 1903
24. *Barbara, A Woman of the West.* Boston, 1903
25. *The Rainbow Chasers.* Boston, 1904
26. *Campaigning with Tippecanoe.* New York, 1904

Whitson, John H.

27. *A Courier of Empire.* Boston, 1904
28. *Justin Wingate, Ranchman.* Boston, 1905
29. *The Castle of Doubt.* Boston, 1907

Whittington, Harry

American, born February 4, 1915
Pseudonyms: Ashley Carter, Tabor Evans, Whit Harrison, Kel Holland, Harriet Kathryn Myers, Blaine Stevens, Clay Stuart, Hondo Wells, Harry White, Hallam Whitney

1. *Vengeance Valley.* New York, 1945
2. *Slay Ride for a Lady.* Kingston (NY), 1950
3. *The Brass Monkey.* Kingston, 1951
4. *Call Me Killer.* Hasbrouck Heights (NJ), 1951
5. *Fires That Destroy.* New York, 1951
6. *The Lady Was a Tramp.* Kingston, 1951
7. *Married to Murder.* New York, 1951
8. *Murder Is My Mistress.* Hasbrouck Heights, 1951
9. *Satan's Widow.* New York, 1951
10. *Forever Evil.* New York, 1951
11. *Swamp Kill,* as Whit Harrison. New York, 1951
12. *Body and Passion,* as Whit Harrison. New York, 1951
13. *Nature Girl,* as Whit Harrison. New York, 1952
14. *Sailor's Weekend,* as Whit Harrison. New York, 1952
15. *Army Girl,* as Whit Harrison. New York, 1952
16. *Girl on Parole,* as Whit Harrison. New York, 1952
17. *Rapture Alley,* as Whit Harrison. New York, 1952
18. *Drawn to Evil.* New York, 1952
19. *Mourn the Hangman.* Hasbrouck Heights, 1952
20. *Violent Night,* as Whit Harrison. New York, 1952
21. *Backwoods Hussy,* as Hallam Whitney. New York, 1952
22. *So Dead My Love!* New York, 1953
23. *Vengeful Sinner.* New York, 1953
24. *Cracker Girl.* Beacon (NY), 1953
25. *Wild Oats.* Beacon, 1953
26. *Prime Sucker.* Beacon, 1953
27. *This Woman Is Mine.* New York, 1953
28. *Strip the Town Naked,* as Whit Harrison. Beacon, 1953
29. *Shanty Road,* as Whit Harrison. New York, 1953
30. *Shack Road,* as Hallam Whitney. New York, 1953
31. *Sinner's Club,* as Hallam Whitney. New York, 1953
32. *City Girl,* as Hallam Whitney. New York, 1953
33. *Backwoods Shack,* as Hallam Whitney. New York, 1954
34. *Naked Island.* New York, 1954
35. *You'll Die Next!* New York, 1954
36. *Saddle the Storm.* New York, 1954
37. *Shadow at Noon,* as Harry White. New York, 1955
38. *The Naked Jungle.* New York, 1955
39. *One Got Away.* New York, 1955
40. *The Wild Seed,* as Hallam Whitney. New York, 1956
41. *Brute in Brass.* New York, 1956
42. *Desire in the Dust.* New York, 1956
43. *The Humming Box.* New York, 1956
44. *Saturday Night Town.* New York, 1956
45. *A Woman on the Place.* New York, 1956
46. *Mink.* Paris (France), 1956
47. *Across That River.* New York, 1957
48. *Man in the Shadow.* New York, 1957
49. *One Deadly Dawn.* New York, 1957
50. *Play for Keeps.* New York and London, 1957
51. *Temptations of Valerie.* New York, 1957
52. *Teen-Age Jungle.* New York, 1958
53. *Web of Murder.* New York, 1958
54. *Star Lust.* No place, 1958
55. *Trouble Rides Tall.* New York and London, 1958
56. *Strictly for the Boys.* No place, 1959
57. *Native Girl.* New York, 1959
58. *Shack Road Girl.* New York, 1959
59. *Backwoods Tramp.* New York, 1959
60. *Halfway to Hell.* New York, 1959
61. *Strange Bargain.* New York, 1959
62. *Strangers on Friday.* New York and London, 1959
63. *A Ticket to Hell.* New York, 1959
64. *Connolly's Woman.* New York, 1960
65. *Die, Lover.* New York, 1960
66. *Vengeance Is the Spur.* New York and London, 1960
67. *The Devil Wears Wings.* New York and London, 1960
68. *Heat of Night.* New York, 1960
69. *Hell Can Wait.* New York, 1960
70. *A Night for Screaming.* New York, 1960
71. *Nita's Place.* New York, 1960
72. *Rebel Woman.* New York, 1960
73. *Guerrilla Girls.* New York, 1960
74. *Any Woman He Wanted,* as Whit Harrison. Beacon, 1960
75. *A Woman Possessed,* as Whit Harrison. Beacon, 1961
76. *God's Back Was Turned.* New York, 1961
77. *Journey into Violence.* New York, 1961
78. *The Young Nurses.* New York, 1961
79. *Desert Stake-out.* New York, 1961
80. *Searching Rider.* New York, 1961
81. *A Trap for Sam Dodge.* New York, 1962
82. *Wild Sky.* New York, 1962
83. *Cross the Red Creek.* New York, 1962
84. *Small Town Nurse,* as Harriet Kathryn Myers. New York, 1962
85. *A Haven for the Damned.* New York, 1962
86. *Hot as Fire, Cold as Ice.* New York, 1962
87. *69 Babylon Park.* New York, 1962
88. *Dry Gulch Town.* New York, 1963
89. *Prairie Raiders,* as Hondo Wells. New York, 1963
90. *Don't Speak to Strange Girls.* New York and London, 1963
91. *The Fall of the Roman Empire.* New York and London, 1964
92. *High Fury.* New York, 1964
93. *Hangrope Town.* New York, 1964
94. *His Brother's Wife,* as Clay Stuart. Beacon, 1964
95. *The Tempted,* as Kel Holland. Beacon, 1964
96. *The Doomsday Affair.* New York and London, 1965
97. *Wild Lonesome.* New York, 1965
98. *Valley of the Savage Men.* New York, 1965
99. *Lisa,* as Hallam Whitney. New York, 1965
100. *Doomsday Mission.* New York, 1967
101. *The Bitter Mission of Captain Burden.* New York, 1968
102. *Smell of Jasmine.* New York, 1968
103. *Treachery Trail.* Racine (WI), 1968
104. *Charro.* New York, 1969
105. *Golden Stud,* as Ashley Carter, with Lance Horner. New York, 1975
106. *Master of Black Oaks,* as Ashley Carter. New York, 1976
107. *The Sword of the Golden Stud,* as Ashley Carter. New York, 1977
108. *Secret of Blackoaks,* as Ashley Carter. New York, 1978
109. *Panama,* as Ashley Carter. New York, 1978
110. *Taproots of Falconhurst,* as Ashley Carter. New York, 1979
111. *The Outlanders,* as Blaine Stevens. New York, 1979
112. *Scandal of Falconhurst,* as Ashley Carter. New York, 1980
113. *Longarm on the Humboldt,* as Tabor Evans. New York, 1981
114. *Longarm and the Golden Lady,* as Tabor Evans. New York, 1981
115. *Longarm and the Blue Norther,* as Tabor Evans. New York, 1981
116. *Heritage of Blackoaks,* as Ashley Carter. New York and London, 1981
117. *Embrace the Wind,* as Blaine Stevens. New York, 1982
118. *Longarm in Silver City,* as Tabor Evans. New York, 1982
119. *Longarm in Boulder Canyon,* as Tabor Evans. New York, 1982

120. *Longarm in the Big Thicket*, as Tabor Evans. New York, 1982

Wibberley, Leonard [Patrick O'Connor]
Irish, born April 9, 1915
Pseudonyms: Leonard Holton, Patrick O'Conner, Christopher Webb
1. *The Lost Harpooner*, as Patrick O'Conner. New York, 1947
2. *The King's Beard*. New York, 1952
3. *The Secret of the Hawk*. New York, 1953
4. *The Coronation Book: The Dramatic Story in History and Legend*. New York, 1953
5. *Deadman's Cave*. New York, 1954
6. *The Flight of the Peacock*, as Patrick O'Conner. New York, 1954
7. *The Society of Foxes*, as Patrick O'Conner. New York, 1954
8. *The Epics of Everest*. New York, 1954
9. *Mrs. Searwood's Secret Weapon*. Boston, 1954
10. *The Wound of Peter Wayne*. New York, 1955
11. *The Watermelon Mystery*, as Patrick O'Conner. New York, 1955
12. *The Mouse That Roared*. Boston, 1955
13. *The Wrath of Grapes*. London, 1955
14. *McGillicuddy McGotham*. Boston, 1956
15. *Gunpowder for Washington*, as Patrick O'Conner. New York, 1956
16. *The Black Tiger*, as Patrick O'Conner. New York, 1956
17. *The Life of Winston Churchill*. New York, 1956
18. *Mexican Road Race*, as Patrick O'Conner. New York, 1957
19. *Kevin O'Conner and the Light Brigade*. New York, 1957
20. *John Barry, Father of the Navy*. New York, 1957
21. *Take Me to Your President*. New York, 1957
22. *Matt Tyler's Chronicle*, as Christopher Webb. New York, 1958
23. *Black Tiger at Le Mans*, as Patrick O'Conner. New York, 1958
24. *Wes Powell, Conqueror of the Grand Canyon*. New York, 1958
25. *Beware of the Mouse*. New York, 1958
26. *The Coming of the Green*. New York, 1958
27. *The Five-Dollar Watch Mystery*, as Patrick O'Conner. New York, 1959
28. *John Treegate's Musket*. New York, 1959
29. *The Quest of Excalibur*. New York, 1959
30. *The Saint Maker*, as Leonard Holton. New York, 1959
31. *No Garlic in the Soup*. New York, 1959
32. *The Land That Isn't There: An Irish Adventure*. New York, 1960
33. *A Pact with Satan*, as Leonard Holton. New York, 1960
34. *The Hands of Cormac Joyce*. New York, 1960
35. *Mark Toyman's Inheritance*, as Christopher **Webb**. New York, 1960
36. *Pete Treegate's War*. New York, 1960
37. *Black Tiger at Bonneville*, as Patrick O'Conner. New York, 1960
38. *Secret of the Doubting Saint*, as Leonard Holton. New York, 1961
39. *Treasure at Twenty Fathoms*, as Patrick O'Conner. New York, 1961
40. *Sea Captain from Salem*. New York, 1961
41. *The Time of the Lamb*. New York, 1961
42. *Zebulon Pike, Soldier and Explorer*. New York, 1961
43. *Stranger at Killknock*. New York, 1961
44. *Yesterday's Land: A Baja California Adventure*. New York, 1961
45. *Treegate's Raiders*. New York, 1962
46. *The River of Pee Dee Jack*, as Christopher Webb. New York, 1962
47. *Black Tiger at Indianapolis*, as Patrick O'Conner. New York, 1962
48. *The Ballad of the Pilgrim Cat*. New York, 1962
49. *The Mouse on the Moon*. New York, 1962
50. *Ventures into the Deep: The Thrill of Skuba Diving*. New York, 1962
51. *Quest of the Otter*, as Christopher Webb. New York, 1963
52. *The Shepherd's Reward*. New York, 1963
53. *Young Man from the Piedmont: The Youth of Thomas Jefferson*. New York, 1963
54. *Deliver Us from Wolves*, as Leonard Holton. New York, 1963
55. *Ah Julian! A Memoir of Julian Brodetsky*. New York, 1963
56. *Flowers by Request*, as Leonard Holton. New York, 1964
57. *A Feast of Freedom*. New York, 1964
58. *The Raising of the Dubhe*, as Patrick O'Conner. New York, 1964
59. *A Dawn in the Trees: Thomas Jefferson, The Years 1776 to 1789*. New York, 1964
60. *Fiji: Islands of the Dawn*. New York, 1964
61. *Seawind from Hawaii*, as Patrick O'Conner. New York, 1965
62. *The Island of the Angels*. New York, 1965
63. *The Gales of Spring: Thomas Jefferson, The Years 1789 to 1801*. New York, 1965
64. *The "Ann and Hope" Mutiny*, as Christopher Webb. New York, 1966
65. *Time of the Harvest: Thomas Jefferson, The Years 1801 to 1826*. New York, 1966
66. *The Centurion*. New York, 1966
67. *Out of the Depths*, as Leonard Holton. New York, 1966
68. *Toward a Distant Island: A Sailor's Odyssey*. New York, 1966
69. *The "Ann and Hope" Mutiny*, as Christopher Webb. New York, 1966
70. *Something to Read*. New York, 1967
71. *Encounter Near Venus*. New York, 1967
72. *The Road from Toomi*. New York, 1967
73. *South Swell*, as Patrick O'Conner. New York, 1967
74. *Adventures of an Elephant Boy*. New York, 1968
75. *A Touch of Jonah*, as Leonard Holton. New York, 1968
76. *Attar of the Ice Valley*. New York and London, 1969
77. *Hound of the Sea*. New York, 1969
78. *The Mouse on Wall Street*. New York, 1969
79. *Beyond Hawaii*, as Patrick O'Conner. New York, 1969
80. *A Car Called Carmellia*, as Patrick O'Conner. New York, 1970
81. *Eusebius, The Phoenician*, as Christopher Webb. New York, 1970
82. *A Problem in Angels*, as Leonard Holton. New York, 1970
83. *Journey to Untor*. New York, 1970
84. *Leopard's Prey*. New York, 1971
85. *Voyage by Bus*. New York, 1971
86. *Meeting with a Great Beast*. New York, 1971
87. *Black Jack Rides Again*. Chicago, 1971
88. *The Mirror of Hell*, as Leonard Holton. New York, 1972
89. *The Shannon Sailor's: A Voyage to the Heart of Ireland*. New York, 1972
90. *Flint's Island*. New York, 1972
91. *Red Pawns*. New York, 1973
92. *The Testament of Theophilus*. New York, 1973
93. *Merchant of Rome*. New York, 1974
94. *The Last Stand of Father Felix*. New York, 1974
95. *The Devil to Play*, as Leonard Holton. New York, 1974
96. *Guarneri, Violin Maker of Genius*. New York, 1974
97. *1776—And All That*. New York, 1975
98. *Once, In a Garden*. New York, 1975
99. *The Last Battle*. New York, 1976
100. *A Corner of Paradise*, as Leonard Holton. New York, 1977
101. *One in Four*. New York, 1977

Wiggin, Kate Douglas
American, born September 28, 1856, died August 24, 1923
1. *The Story of Patsy: A Reminiscence.* San Francisco 1883
2. *The Birds' Christmas Carol.* San Francisco, 1887
3. *A Summer in a Canon.* Boston, 1889
4. *Timothy's Quest.* Boston, 1890
5. *The Story Hour,* with Nora A. Smith. Boston, 1890
6. *The Relation of Kindergarten to the Public School.* San Francisco, 1891
7. *Children's Rights: A Book of Nursery Logic,* with Nora A. Smith. Boston and London, 1892
8. *Polly Oliver's Problem.* Boston and London, 1893
9. *A Cathedral Courtship, and Penelope's English Experiences.* Boston and London, 1893
10. *The Village Watch-Tower.* Boston and London, 1895
11. *Marm Lisa.* Boston and London, 1896
12. *Nine Love Songs and a Carol.* Boston and London, 1896
13. *Penelope's Progress.* Boston and London, 1898
14. *Penelope's Irish Experiences.* Boston and London, 1901
15. *The Diary of a Goosegirl.* Boston and London, 1902
16. *Rebecca of Sunnybrook Farm.* Boston and London, 1903
17. *Half-a-Dozen Housekeepers.* Philadelphia and London, 1903
18. *The Affair at the Inn,* with others. Boston and London, 1904
19. *Rose o' the River.* Boston and London, 1905
20. *New Chronicles of Rebecca.* Boston and London, 1907
21. *The Old Peabody Pew: A Christmas Romance of a Country Church.* Boston and London, 1907
22. *Susanna and Sue.* Boston and London, 1909
23. *Robinetta,* with others. Boston and London, 1911
24. *Mother Carey's Chickens.* Boston, 1911
25. *A Child's Journey with Dickens.* Boston and London, 1912
26. *The Story of Waitstill Baxter.* Boston and London, 1913
27. *The Romance of a Christmas Card.* Boston and London, 1916
28. *Ladies in Waiting.* Boston and London, 1919
29. *Quilt of Happiness.* Boston, 1923
30. *Love by Express.* Buxton (ME), 1923
31. *My Garden of Memory: An Autobiography.* Boston, 1923
32. *Creeping Jenny and Other New England Stories.* Boston, 1924
33. *Twilight Stories,* with Nora A. Smith. Boston, 1925
34. *More about Rebecca of Sunnybrook Farm.* London, 1930

Wilcox, Collin
American, born September 21, 1924
Pseudonym: Carter Wick
1. *The Black Door.* New York, 1967
2. *The Third Figure.* New York, 1968
3. *The Lonely Hunter.* New York, 1969
4. *The Disappearance.* New York, 1970
5. *Dead Aim.* New York, 1971
6. *Hiding Place.* New York, 1973
7. *McCloud.* New York, 1973
8. *Long Way Down.* New York, 1974
9. *The New Mexico Connection.* New York and London, 1974
10. *Aftershock.* New York, 1975
11. *The Faceless Man,* as Carter Wick. New York, 1975
12. *The Third Victim.* New York, 1976
13. *Doctor, Lawyer. . . .* New York, 1977
14. *The Watcher.* New York, 1978
15. *Twospot,* with Bill Pronzini. New York, 1978
16. *Night Games.* New York, 1979
17. *Power Plays.* New York, 1979

Wilder, Laura Ingalls
American, born February 7, 1867, died January 10, 1957
1. *Little House in the Big Woods.* New York, 1932
2. *Farmer Boy.* New York, 1933
3. *Little House on the Prairie.* New York, 1935
4. *On the Banks of Plum Creek.* New York, 1937
5. *By the Shores of Silver Lake.* New York, 1939
6. *The Long Winter.* New York, 1940
7. *Little Town on the Prairie.* New York, 1941
8. *These Happy Golden Years.* New York, 1943
9. *The First Four Years.* New York, 1971

Wilhelm, Kate
American, born June 8, 1928
1. *The Mile-Long Spaceship.* New York, 1963
2. *More Bitter Than Death.* New York, 1963
3. *The Clone,* with Ted Thomas. New York, 1965
4. *The Nevermore Affair.* New York, 1966
5. *Andover and the Android.* London, 1966
6. *The Killer Thing.* New York, 1967
7. *The Killing Thing.* London, 1967
8. *The Downstairs Room.* New York, 1968
9. *Let the Fire Fall.* New York, 1969
10. *Year of the Cloud,* with Ted Thomas. New York, 1970
11. *Abyss.* New York, 1971
12. *Margaret and I.* Boston, 1971
13. *City of Cain.* Boston, 1974
14. *The Infinity Box.* New York, 1975
15. *The Clewiston Test.* New York, 1976
16. *Where Late the Sweet Birds Sang.* New York, 1976
17. *Fault Lines.* New York, 1977
18. *Somerset Dreams and Other Fictions.* New York, 1978
19. *Juniper Time.* New York, 1979

Willard, Barbara
British, born March 12, 1909
1. *Love in Ambush,* with Elizabeth Helen Devas. London, 1930
2. *Ballerina.* London, 1931
3. *Candle Flame.* London, 1932
4. *Name of Gentleman.* London, 1933
5. *Joy Befall Thee.* London, 1934
6. *As Far as in Me Lies.* London, 1936
7. *The Dogs Do Bark.* London, 1938
8. *Set Piece.* London, 1938
9. *Girl Out Back.* New York, 1958
10. *Operator.* London, 1958
11. *Man on the Run.* New York, 1958
12. *Talk of the Town.* New York, 1958
13. *All the Way.* New York, 1958
14. *Man in Motion.* London, 1959
15. *Stain of Suspicion.* London, 1959
16. *Uncle Sagamore and His Girls.* New York, 1959
17. *The Concrete Flamingo.* London, 1960
18. *Aground.* New York, 1960
19. *The Sailcloth Shroud.* New York and London, 1960
20. *Nude on Thin Ice.* New York, 1961
21. *The Long Saturday Night.* New York, 1962
22. *Dead Calm.* New York, 1963
23. *The Wrong Venus.* New York, 1966
24. *Don't Just Stand There.* London, 1967
25. *And the Deep Blue Sea.* New York, 1971
26. *Man on a Leash.* New York, 1973

Williams, Claudette
1. *Spring Gambit.* New York, 1976
2. *Sassy.* New York, 1977
3. *Sunday's Child.* New York, 1977
4. *After the Storm.* New York, 1977
5. *Blades of Passion.* New York, 1978
6. *Cotillion for Mandy.* New York, 1978
7. *Myriah.* New York, 1978

8. *Cassandra.* New York and London, 1979
9. *Jewelene.* New York, 1979
10. *Lacey.* New York, 1979
11. *Mary, Sweet Mary.* New York, 1980
12. *Naughty Lady Ness.* New York, 1980
13. *Passion's Pride.* New York, 1980
14. *Desert Rose, English Moon.* New York, 1981

Williams, Gordon
British, born June 30, 1929
Pseudonym: P.B. Yuill, with Terry Venables

1. *The Last Day of Lincoln Charles.* London, 1965
2. *The Camp.* London and New York, 1966
3. *The Man Who Had Power Over Women.* London, 1966
4. *From Scenes Like These.* London, 1968
5. *The Siege of Trencher's Farm.* London and New York, 1969
6. *The Upper Pleasure Garden.* London and New York, 1970
7. *They Used to Play on Grass,* with Terry Venables. London, 1971
8. *Walk, Don't Walk.* London and New York, 1972
9. *The Boneless Keeper,* as P.B. Yuill. London, 1974
10. *Hazell Plays Solomon,* as P.B. Yuill. London, 1974
11. *Big Morning Blues.* London, 1974
12. *Hazell and The Three Card Trick,* as P.B. Yuill. London, 1975
13. *Hazell and the Menacing Jester,* as P.B. Yuill. London, 1976
14. *The Duellists.* London, 1977
15. *The Micronauts.* New York, 1978
16. *The Microcolony.* New York, 1979

Williams, Jay
American, born May 31, 1914
Pseudonym: Michael Delving

1. *The Stolen Oracle.* New York, 1943
2. *The Counterfeit African.* New York and London, 1944
3. *The Sword and the Scythe.* New York, 1946
4. *The Roman Moon Mystery.* New York, 1948
5. *The Good Yeoman.* New York, 1948
6. *The Magic Gate.* New York, 1949
7. *Eagle Jake and Indian Pete.* New York, 1947
8. *Augustus Caesar.* Evanston (IL), 1951
9. *Fall of the Sparrow.* New York, 1951
10. *The Rogue from Padua.* Boston, 1952
11. *The Siege.* Boston, 1955
12. *A Change of Climate.* New York and London, 1956
13. *The Witches.* New York, 1957
14. *Solomon and Sheba.* New York, 1959
15. *The Battle for the Atlantic.* New York, 1959
16. *The Tournament of the Lions.* New York, 1960
17. *Medusa's Head.* New York, 1960
18. *The Forger.* New York, 1961
19. *Knights of the Crusades.* New York, 1962
20. *Puppy Pie.* New York, 1962
21. *I Wish I Had Another Name.* New York, 1962
22. *Joan of Arc.* New York, 1963
23. *Tomorrow's Fire.* New York, 1964
24. *Leonardo da Vinci.* New York, 1965
25. *The Question Box.* New York, 1965
26. *Philbert the Fearful.* New York, 1966
27. *What Can You Do with a Word?* New York, 1966
28. *The Spanish Armada.* New York and London, 1966
29. *Smiling, The Boy Fell Dead,* as Michael Delving. New York, 1966
30. *The Cookie Tree.* New York, 1967
31. *Life in the Middle Ages.* New York, 1966
32. *To Catch a Bird.* New York, 1968
33. *The King with Six Friends.* New York, 1968
34. *The Sword of King Arthur.* New York, 1968
35. *The Horn of Roland.* New York, 1968
36. *Uniad.* New York, 1968
37. *The World of Titian.* New York and London, 1968
38. *The Devil Finds Work,* as Michael Delving. New York, 1969
39. *The Good-for-Nothing Prince.* New York, 1969
40. *The Practical Princess.* New York, 1969
41. *School for Sillies.* New York, 1969
42. *A Box Full of Infinity.* New York, 1970
43. *Stupid Marco.* New York, 1970
44. *Die Like A Man,* as Michael Delving. New York, 1970
45. *The Silver Whistle.* New York, 1971
46. *A Present from a Bird.* New York, 1971
47. *The Hawkstone.* New York, 1971
48. *The Youngest Captain.* New York, 1972
49. *Magical Storybook.* New York, 1972
50. *The Hero from Otherwhere.* New York, 1972
51. *Seven at One Blow.* New York, 1972
52. *A Shadow of Himself,* as Michael Delving. New York and London, 1972
53. *Petronella.* New York, 1973
54. *Forgetful Fred.* New York, 1974
55. *The People of the Ax.* New York, 1974
56. *A Bag Full of Nothing.* New York, 1974
57. *Stage Left.* New York, 1974
58. *Bored to Death,* as Michael Delving. New York, 1975
59. *Wave of Fatalities.* London, 1975
60. *The China Expert,* as Michael Delving. London, 1976
61. *Everyone Knows What a Dragon Looks Like.* New York, 1976
62. *The Burgler Next Door.* New York, 1976
63. *Moon Journey.* London, 1976
64. *Daylight Robbery.* London, 1977
65. *The Reward Worth Having.* New York, 1977
66. *The Time of the Kraken.* New York and London, 1977
67. *Pettifur.* New York, 1977

Williams, Jeanne [Dorothy Jeanne Williams]
American, born April 10, 1930
Pseudonyms: Megan Castell, Jeanne Crecy, Jeanne Foster, Kristin Michaels, Deirdre Rowan, J.R. Williams

1. *Tame the Wild Stallion,* as J.R. Williams. Englewood Cliffs (NJ), 1957
2. *To Buy a Dream.* New York, 1958
3. *Promise of Tomorrow.* New York, 1959
4. *Mission in Mexico,* as J.R. Williams. Englewood Cliffs, 1959
5. *The Horse Talker,* as J.R. Williams. Englewood Cliffs, 1961
6. *The Confederate Fiddle,* as J.R. Williams. Englewood Cliffs, 1962
7. *Oh, Susanna!* as J.R. Williams. New York, 1963
8. *River Guns.* London, 1963
9. *Coyote Winter.* New York, 1965
10. *Beasts with Music.* New York, 1967
11. *Oil Patch Partners.* New York, 1968
12. *New Medicine.* New York, 1971
13. *Hands of Terror,* as Jeanne Crecy. New York, 1972
14. *Trails of Tears: American Indians Driven from their Lands.* New York, 1972
15. *Lady Gift,* as Jeanne Crecy. London, 1973
16. *The Lightning Tree,* as Jeanne Crecy. New York, 1973
17. *Dragon's Mount,* as Deirdre Rowan. New York, 1973
18. *Freedom Trail.* New York, 1973
19. *Silver Wood,* as Deirdre Rowan. New York, 1974
20. *Shadow of the Volcano,* as Deirdre Rowan. New York, 1975
21. *The Winter Keeper,* as Jeanne Crecy. New York, 1975
22. *To Begin with Love,* as Kristin Michaels. New York, 1975

23. *The Night Hunters,* as Jeanne Crecy. New York, 1975
24. *My Face Beneath the Stone,* as Jeanne Crecy. New York, 1975
25. *The Evil among Us,* as Jeanne Crecy. New York, 1975
26. *Winter Wheat.* New York, 1975
27. *Enchanted Twilight,* as Kristin Michaels. New York, 1976
28. *A Special Kind of Love,* as Kristin Michaels. New York, 1976
29. *Ravensgate,* as Deirdre Rowan. New York, 1976
30. *A Lady Bought with Rifles.* New York, 1976
31. *Time of the Burning Mask,* as Deirdre Rowan. New York, 1976
32. *A Woman Clothed in Sun.* New York, 1977
33. *Song of the Heart,* as Kristin Michaels. New York, 1977
34. *Enchanted Journey,* as Kristin Michaels. New York, 1977
35. *Voyage to Love,* as Kristin Michaels. New York, 1978
36. *Bride of Thunder.* New York, 1978
37. *Make Believe Love,* as Kristin Michaels. New York, 1978
38. *Daughter of the Sword.* New York, 1979
39. *The Queen of a Lonely Country,* as Megan Castell. New York, 1980
40. *The Valiant Woman.* New York, 1980
41. *Deborah Leigh,* as Jeanne Foster. New York, 1981
42. *Magic Side of the Moon,* as Kristin Michaels. New York, 1981
43. *Harvest of Fury.* New York, 1981
44. *Eden Richards,* as Jeanne Foster. New York, 1982
45. *Mating of Hawks.* New York, 1982

Williams, John (Edward)
American, born August 29, 1922
1. *Nothing But the Night.* Denver (CO), 1948
2. *The Broken Landscape.* Denver, 1949
3. *Butcher's Crossing.* New York and London, 1960
4. *The Necessary Lie.* Denver, 1965
5. *Stoner.* New York, 1965
6. *Augustus.* New York, 1972

Williams, John A. (Alfred)
American, born December 5, 1925
1. *The Angry Ones.* New York, 1960
2. *Night Song.* New York, 1961
3. *Africa: Her History, Lands, and People.* New York, 1962
4. *Sissie.* New York, 1963
5. *This Is My Country, Too.* New York, 1965
6. *The Man Who Cried I Am.* Boston, 1967
7. *Journey Out of Anger.* London, 1968
8. *Sons of Darkness, Sons of Light.* Boston, 1969
9. *The Most Native of Sons: A Biography of Richard Wright.* New York, 1970
10. *Captain Blackman.* New York, 1972
11. *Flashbacks: A Twenty-Year Diary of Article Writing.* New York, 1973
12. *Romare Bearden.* New York, 1973
13. *Mothersill and the Foxes.* New York, 1975
14. *One for New York.* Chatham (NJ), 1975
15. *Minorities in the City.* New York, 1975
16. *The Junior Bachelor Society.* New York, 1976

Williams, Robert Moore
American, born June 19, 1907
1. *The Chaos Fighters.* New York, 1955
2. *Conquest of the Space Sea.* New York, 1955
3. *Doomsday Eve.* New York, 1957
4. *The Blue Atom.* New York, 1958
5. *The Void Beyond and Other Stories.* New York, 1958
6. *World of the Masterminds.* New York, 1960
7. *To the End of Time.* New York, 1960
8. *The Day They H-Bombed Los Angeles.* New York, 1961
9. *The Darkness Before Tomorrow.* New York, 1962
10. *King of the Fourth Planet.* New York, 1962
11. *Walk Up the Sky.* New York, 1962
12. *The Star Wasps.* New York, 1963
13. *Flight from Yesterday.* New York, 1963
14. *The Lunar Eye.* New York, 1964
15. *The Second Atlantis.* New York, 1965
16. *Vigilante—21st Century.* New York, 1967
17. *Zanthar of the Many Worlds.* New York, 1967
18. *Zanthar of the Edge of Never.* New York, 1968
19. *The Bell from Infinity.* New York, 1968
20. *Zanthar at Moon's Madness.* New York, 1968
21. *Zanthar at Trip's End.* New York, 1968
22. *Beachhead Planet.* New York and London, 1970
23. *Jongor of Lost Land.* New York, 1970
24. *The Return of Jongor.* New York, 1970
25. *Jongor Fights Back.* New York, 1970
26. *When Two Worlds Meet.* New York, 1970
27. *Love Is Forever, We Are for Tonight.* New York, 1970
28. *Now Comes Tomorrow.* New York and London, 1971

Williams, Ursula Moray
British, born April 19, 1911
1. *Jean-Pierre.* London, 1931
2. *For Brownies: Stories and Games for the Pack and Everybody Else.* London, 1932
3. *The Pettabomination.* London, 1933
4. *Kelpie, The Gipsies' Pony.* London, 1934
5. *More for Brownies.* London, 1934
6. *Anders and Marta.* London, 1935
7. *Adventures of Anne.* London, 1935
8. *The Twins and Their Ponies.* London, 1936
9. *Sandy-on-the-Shore.* London, 1936
10. *Tales for the Sixes and Sevens.* London, 1936
11. *Dumpling.* London, 1937
12. *Elaine of La Signe.* London, 1937
13. *Adventures of Boss and Dingbat.* London, 1937
14. *Adventures of the Little Wooden Horse.* London, 1938
15. *Adventures of Puffin.* London, 1939
16. *Peter and the Wanderlust.* London, 1939
17. *Elaine of the Mountains.* Philadelphia, 1939
18. *Pretenders' Island.* London, 1940
19. *A Castle for John-Peter.* London, 1941
20. *Gobbolino the Witch's Cat.* London, 1942
21. *The Three Toymakers.* London, 1945
22. *Malkin's Mountain.* London, 1948
23. *The Story of Laughing Dandino.* London, 1948
24. *Jockin the Jester.* London, 1951
25. *The Binklebys at Home.* London, 1951
26. *The Binklebys on the Farm.* London, 1953
27. *The Secrets of the Wood.* London, 1955
28. *Grumpa.* Leicester (Eng), 1955
29. *Goodbody's Puppet Show.* London, 1956
30. *Golden Horse with a Silver Tail.* London, 1957
31. *Hobbie.* Leicester, 1958
32. *The Moonball.* London, 1958
33. *The Noble Hawks.* London, 1959
34. *The Nine Lives of Island MacKenzie.* London, 1959
35. *Island MacKenzie.* New York, 1960
36. *The Earl's Falconer.* New York, 1961
37. *Peter on the Road.* London, 1963
38. *Beware of This Animal.* London, 1964
39. *Johnnie Tigerskin.* London, 1964
40. *O for a Mouseless House!* London, 1964
41. *High Adventure.* London, 1965
42. *Cruise of the "Happy-Go-Gay."* London, 1967
43. *A Crown for a Queen.* London and New York, 1968

44. *The Toymaker's Daughter*. London, 1968
45. *Mog*. London, 1969
46. *Boy in a Barn*. London and New York, 1970
47. *Johnnie Golightly and His Crocodile*. London, 1970
48. *Trafic Jam*. London, 1971
49. *Man on a Steeple*. London, 1971
50. *Mrs. Townsend's Robber*. London, 1971
51. *Out of the Shadows*. London, 1971
52. *Castle Merlin*. London and Nashville (TN), 1972
53. *A Picnic with the Aunts*. London, 1972
54. *The Kidnapping of My Grandmother*. London, 1972
55. *Children's Parties, and Games for a Rainy Day*. London, 1972
56. *Tiger-Nanny*. Leicester, 1973
57. *Grandpapa's Folly and the Woodworm-Bookworm*. London, 1974
58. *The Line*. London, 1974
59. *No Ponies for Miss Pobjoy*. London, 1975

Williams, Valentine [George Valentine Williams]
British, born October 20, 1883, died November 20, 1946
Pseudonyms: Douglas Valentine, Vedette
1. *With Our Army in Flanders*. London, 1915
2. *Adventures of an Ensign*, as Vedette. Edinburgh (Scotland), 1917
3. *The Man with the Clubfoot*, as Douglas Valentine. London, 1918
4. *The Secret Hand: Some Further Adventures By Desmond Okewood of the British Secret Service*, as Douglas Valentine. London, 1918
5. *Okewood of the Secret Service*. New York, 1919
6. *The Return of Clubfoot*. London, 1922
7. *The Yellow Streak*. London and Boston, 1922
8. *Island Gold*. Boston, 1923
9. *The Orange Divan*. London and Boston, 1923
10. *Clubfoot the Avenger*. London and Boston, 1924
11. *The Three of Clubs*. London and Boston, 1924
12. *The Red Mass*. London and Boston, 1925
13. *Mr. Ramosi*. London and Boston, 1926
14. *The Pigeon House*. London, 1926
15. *The Key Man*. Boston, 1926
16. *The Eye in Attendance*. London and Boston, 1927
17. *The Crouching Beast*. London and Boston, 1928
18. *Mannequin*. London, 1930
19. *The Mysterious Miss Morrisot*. Boston, 1930
20. *The Knife Behind the Curtain: Tales of Secret Service and Crime*. London and Boston, 1930
21. *Death Answers the Bell*. London, 1931
22. *The Gold Comfit Box*. London, 1932
23. *The Mystery of the Gold Box*. Boston, 1932
24. *The Clock Ticks On*. London and Boston, 1933
25. *Fog*, with Dorothy Rice Sims. London and Boston, 1933
26. *The Portcullis Room*. London and Boston, 1934
27. *Masks Off at Midnight*. London and Boston, 1934
28. *The Clue of the Rising Moon*. London and Boston, 1935
29. *Dead Man Manor*. London and Boston, 1936
30. *The Spider's Touch*. London and Boston, 1936
31. *Mr. Treadgold Cuts In*. London, 1937
32. *The Curiosity of Mr. Treadgold*. Boston, 1937
33. *The World of Action: The Autobiography of Valentine Williams*. London and Boston, 1938
34. *The Fox Prowls*. London and Boston, 1939
35. *Double Death*, with others. London, 1939
36. *Courier to Marrakesh*. London, 1944
37. *Skeleton Out of the Cupboard*. London, 1946

Williamson, Jack [John Stewart Williamson]
American, born April 29, 1908
Pseudonym: Will Stewart
1. *Lady in Danger*. London, no date
2. *The Girl from Mars*, with Miles J. Breuer. New York, 1929
3. *The Legion of Space*. Reading (PA), 1947
4. *Darker Than You Think*. Reading, 1948
5. *The Humanoids*. New York, 1949
6. *The Green Girl*. New York, 1950
7. *The Cometeers*. Reading, 1950
8. *Seetee Shock,* as Will Stewart. New York, 1950
9. *Seetee Ship,* as Will Stewart. New York, 1950
10. *Dragon's Island*. New York, 1951
11. *The Legion of Time*. Reading, 1952
12. *Undersea Quest,* with Frederik Pohl. New York, 1954
13. *Dome Around America*. New York, 1955
14. *Star Bridge,* with James E. Gunn. New York, 1955
15. *Undersea Fleet,* with Frederik Pohl. New York, 1956
16. *Undersea City,* with Frederik Pohl. New York, 1958
17. *The Legion of Time and After World's End*. London, 2 vols., 1961
18. *The Trial of Terra*. New York, 1962
19. *Golden Blood*. New York, 1964
20. *The Reign of Wizardry*. New York, 1964
21. *The Reefs of Space*. New York, 1964
22. *Starchild*. New York, 1965
23. *Bright New Universe*. New York, 1967
24. *One Against the Legion*. New York, 1967
25. *Trapped in Space*. New York, 1968
26. *The Not-Men*. New York, 1968
27. *Rogue Star*. New York, 1969
28. *The Pandora Effect*. New York, 1969
29. *People Machines*. New York, 1971
30. *The Moon Children*. New York, 1972
31. *H.G. Wells, Critic of Progress*. Baltimore (MD), 1973
32. *Farthest Star,* with Frederik Pohl. New York, 1975
33. *The Early Williamson*. New York, 1975
34. *The Power of Blackness*. New York, 1976
35. *The Best of Jack Williamson*. New York, 1978
36. *Brother to Demons, Brother to Gods*. Indianapolis (IN), 1979
37. *The Humanoid Touch*. New York, 1980

Willis, Ted [Edward Henry Willis; Baron Willis of Chislehurst]
British, born January 13, 1918
1. *Fighting Youth of Russia*. London, 1942
2. *The Blue Lamp*. London, 1950
3. *The Lady Purrs*. London and Boston, 1950
4. *George Comes Home*. London, 1955
5. *The Devil's Churchyard*. London, 1957
6. *Doctor in the House*. London and New York, 1957
7. *Seven Gates to Nowhere*. London, 1958
8. *Hot Summer Night*. London, 1959
9. *Brothers-in-Law*. London, 1959
10. *The Eyes of Youth*. London, 1960
11. *Dixon of Dock Green: My Life,* with Charles Hatton. London, 1960
12. *Dixon of Dock Green: A Novel,* with Paul Graham. London, 1961
13. *Doctor ar Sea*. London and New York, 1961
14. *The Little Goldmine*. London, 1962
15. *Woman in a Dressing Gown*. London, 1964
16. *Dead on Saturday*. London, 1970
17. *Whatever Happened to Tom Mix? The Story of One of My Lives*. London, 1970
18. *Black Beauty*. London, 1972
19. *Death May Surprise Us*. London, 1974
20. *Westminster One*. New York, 1975
21. *The Left-Handed Sleeper*. London, 1975
22. *Man-Eater*. London, 1976

23. *The Churchill Commando.* London and New York, 1977
24. *The Buckingham Palace Connection.* London and New York, 1978
25. *The Lions of Judah.* London, 1979

Wills, Cecil M. [Maitland Cecil Melville Wills]
British, born in 1891
1. *Author in Distress.* London, 1934
2. *Number 18.* London, 1934
3. *Death at the Pelican.* London, 1934
4. *Death Treads—.* London, 1935
5. *Then Came the Police.* London, 1935
6. *The Chamois Murder.* London, 1935
7. *Fatal Accident.* London, 1936
8. *Defeat of a Detective.* London, 1936
9. *On the Night in Question.* London, 1937
10. *A Body in the Dawn.* London, 1938
11. *The Case of the Calabar Bean.* London, 1939
12. *The Case of the R.E. Pipe.* London, 1940
13. *The Clue of the Lost Hour.* London, 1949
14. *The Clue of the Golden Ear-Ring.* London, 1950
15. *Who Killed Brother Treasurer?* London, 1951
16. *What Say the Jury?* London, 1951
17. *The Dead Voice.* London, 1952
18. *It Pays to Die.* London, 1953
19. *Death on the Line.* London, 1954
20. *Death in the Dark.* London, 1955
21. *Midsummer Murder.* London, 1956
22. *The Tiger Strikes Again.* London, 1957
23. *Mere Murder.* London, 1958
24. *The Case of the Empty Beehive.* London, 1959
25. *Death of a Best Seller.* London, 1959
26. *The Colonel's Foxhound.* London, 1960
27. *Justice in Jeopardy.* London, 1961

Wilson, Barbara Ker
British, born September 24, 1929
1. *Scottish Folk Tales and Legends.* London and New York, 1954
2. *Path-Through-the-Woods.* London and New York, 1958
3. *The Wonderful Cornet.* London, 1958
4. *The Lovely Summer.* London and New York, 1960
5. *Look at Books.* London, 1960
6. *Writing for Children.* London, 1960
7. *Noel Streatfield.* London, 1961
8. *Last Year's Broken Toys.* London, 1962
9. *Beloved of the Gods.* London, 1965
10. *Legends of the Round Table.* London, 1966
11. *Greek Fairy Tales.* London, 1966
12. *A Family Likeness.* London, 1967
13. *Animal Folk Tales.* London, 1968
14. *The Biscuit-Tin Family.* Cleveland (OH), 1968
15. *Australia, Wonderland Down Under.* New York, 1969
16. *Hiccups and Other Stories: Thirty Tales for Little Children.* London, 1971
17. *Tales Told to Kabbarli: Aboriginal Legends.* Sydney (Australia), London and New York, 1972
18. *The Magic Fishbones.* London, 1972
19. *The Magic Bird.* London, 1973

Wilson, Colin (Henry)
British, born June 26, 1931
1. *The Outsider.* London and Boston, 1956
2. *Religion and the Rebel.* London and Boston, 1957
3. *The Age of Defeat.* London, 1959
4. *The Stature of Man.* Boston, 1959
5. *Ritual in the Dark.* London and Boston, 1960
6. *Encyclopedia of Murder,* with Patricia Pitman. London, 1961
7. *Adrift in Soho.* London and Boston, 1961
8. *Origins of the Sexual Impulse.* London and Boston, 1963
9. *The World of Violence.* London, 1963
10. *The Violent World of Hugh Greene.* Boston, 1963
11. *Man Without a Shadow: The Diary of an Existentialist.* London, 1963
12. *The Sex Diary of Gerard Sorme.* New York, 1963
13. *Rasputin and the Fall of the Romanovs.* London and New York, 1964
14. *Brandy of the Damned: Discoveries of a Musical Eclectic.* London, 1964
15. *Necessary Doubt.* London and New York, 1964
16. *Beyond the Outsider: The Philosophy of the Future.* London and Boston, 1965
17. *Eagle and Earwig.* London, 1965
18. *Introduction to the New Existentialism.* London, 1966
19. *Sex and the Intelligent Teenager.* London, 1966
20. *Voyage to a Beginning.* London, 1966
21. *The Glass Cage: An Unconventional Detective Story.* London, 1966
22. *The Mind Parasites.* London and Sauk City (WI), 1967
23. *Bernard Shaw: A Reassessment.* London and New York, 1969
24. *A Casebook of Murder.* London, 1969
25. *Poetry and Mysticism.* San Francisco, 1969
26. *The Philosopher's Stone.* London, 1969
27. *Strindberg.* London, 1970
28. *The Killer.* London, 1970
29. *Lingard.* New York, 1970
30. *The God of the Labyrinth.* London, 1970
31. *The Occult.* New York and London, 1971
32. *The Hedonists.* New York, 1971
33. *The Black Room.* London, 1971
34. *Order of Assassins: The Psychology of Murder.* London, 1972
35. *L'Amour: The Ways of Love.* New York, 1972
36. *Strange Powers.* London, 1973
37. *Tree by Tolkien.* London, 1973
38. *Hermann Hesse.* London and Philadelphia, 1974
39. *Wilhelm Reich.* London and Philadelphia, 1974
40. *Jorge Luis Borges.* London and Philadelphia, 1974
41. *A Book of Booze.* London, 1974
42. *The Schoolgirl Murder Case.* London and New York, 1974
43. *The Return of Lloigor.* London, 1974
44. *The Unexplained.* Lake Oswego (OR), 1975
45. *Mysterious Powers.* London and Danbury (CT), 1975
46. *They Had Strange Powers.* New York, 1975
47. *The Craft of the Novel.* London, 1975
48. *Enigmas and Mysteries.* London and New York, 1976
49. *The Geller Phenomenon.* London, 1976
50. *The Space Vampires.* London and New York, 1976
51. *Science Fiction as Existentialism.* Hayes, 1978

Wilson, Harry Leon
American, born May 1, 1867, died June 19, 1939
1. *Zigzag Tales from the East to the West.* New York, 1894
2. *The Spenders: A Tale of the Third Generation.* Boston and London, 1902
3. *The Lions of the Lord: A Tale of the Old West.* Boston, 1903
4. *The Seeker.* New York, 1904
5. *The Boss of Little Arcady.* Boston and London, 1905
6. *Ewing's Lady.* New York, 1907
7. *Bunker Bean.* New York, 1913
8. *Ruggles of Red Gap.* New York, 1915
9. *Somewhere in Red Gap.* New York and London, 1916
10. *Ma Pettengill.* New York and London, 1919
11. *The Wrong Twin.* New York and London, 1921

12. *Merton of the Movies.* New York and London, 1922
13. *Oh, Doctor!* New York and London, 1923
14. *So This Is Golf!* New York and London, 1923
15. *Professor, How Could You!* New York, 1924
16. *Ma Pettengill Talks.* New York, 1925
17. *The Man from Home.* New York, 1925
18. *Cousin Jane.* New York, 1925
19. *Lone Tree.* New York, 1929
20. *Two Black Sheep.* New York, 1931
21. *When in the Course—.* New York, 1940

Wilson, Richard
American, born September 23, 1920
1. *The Girls from Planet 5.* New York, 1955
2. *Those Idiots from Earth.* New York, 1957
3. *And Then the Town Took Off.* New York, 1960
4. *30-Day Wonder.* New York, 1960
5. *Time Out for Tomorrow.* New York, 1962

Wilson, Robert Anton
American, born January 18, 1932
1. *Playboy's Book of Forbidden Worlds.* Chicago, 1972
2. *Sex and Drugs.* Chicago, 1973
3. *The Sex Magician.* Los Angeles, 1974
4. *The Book of the Breast.* Chicago, 1974
5. *Cosmic Trigger: The Final Secret of the Illuminati.* Berkeley (CA), 1977

Winsor, Kathleen
American, born October 16, 1919
1. *Forever Amber.* New York, 1944
2. *Star Money.* New York and London, 1950
3. *The Lovers.* New York and London, 1952
4. *America, With Love.* New York, 1957
5. *Wanderers Eastward, Wanderers West.* New York and London, 1965
6. *Calais.* New York, 1979

Winspear, Violet
British
1. *Lucifer's Angel.* London and Toronto, 1961
2. *Wife Without Kisses.* London, 1961
3. *The Strange Waif.* London, 1962
4. *House of Strangers.* London, 1963
5. *Beloved Tyrant.* London, 1964
6. *Cap Flamingo.* London, 1964
7. *Love's Prisoner.* London, 1964
8. *Nurse at Cap Flamingo.* Toronto, 1965
9. *Bride's Dilemma.* London, 1965
10. *Desert Doctor.* London and Toronto, 1965
11. *The Tower of the Captive.* London, 1966
12. *The Viking Stranger.* London, 1966
13. *Tender Is the Tyrant.* London, 1967
14. *The Honey Is Bitter.* London, 1967
15. *Beloved Castaway.* London, 1968
16. *Court of the Veils.* London, 1968
17. *The Dangerous Delight.* London, 1968
18. *Pilgrim's Castle.* London, 1969
19. *The Unwilling Bride.* London, 1969
20. *Blue Jasmine.* London, 1969
21. *Dragon Bay.* London, 1969
22. *Palace of the Peacocks.* London and Toronto, 1969
23. *The Chateau of St. Avrell.* London, 1970
24. *The Cazalet Bride.* London and Toronto, 1970
25. *Tawny Sands.* London, 1970
26. *Black Douglas.* London, 1971
27. *Dear Puritan.* London, 1971
28. *Bride to Lucifer.* London, 1971
29. *The Castle of the Seven Lilacs.* London and Toronto, 1971
30. *Raintree Valley.* London, 1971
31. *The Little Nobody.* London, 1972
32. *The Pagan Island.* London and Toronto, 1972
33. *Rapture of the Desert.* London, 1972
34. *The Silver Slave.* London and Toronto, 1972
35. *The Glass Castle.* London, 1973
36. *Devil in a Silver Room.* London and Toronto, 1973
37. *Forbidden Rapture.* London, 1973
38. *The Kisses and the Wine.* London and Toronto, 1973
39. *Palace of the Pomegranate.* London, 1974
40. *The Girl at Golden Hawk.* London, 1974
41. *The Noble Savage.* London, 1974
42. *Satan Took a Bride.* London, 1975
43. *Dearest Demon.* London, 1975
44. *The Devil's Darling.* London and Toronto, 1975
45. *Darling Infidel.* London and Toronto, 1976
46. *The Burning Sands.* London, 1976
47. *The Child of Judas.* London and Toronto, 1976
48. *The Sun Tower.* London, 1976
49. *The Sin of Cynara.* London and Toronto, 1976
50. *The Loved and the Feared.* London, 1977
51. *Love Battle.* London, 1977
52. *Love in a Stranger's Arms.* London and Toronto, 1977
53. *Passionate Sinner.* London, 1977
54. *Time of the Temptress.* London, 1977
55. *The Valdez Marriage.* London, 1978
56. *The Awakening of Alice.* London and Toronto, 1978
57. *Desire Has No Mercy.* London, 1979
58. *The Sheik's Captive.* London, 1979
59. *Love Is the Honey.* London and Toronto, 1980
60. *A Girl Possessed.* London, 1980
61. *Love's Agony.* London and Toronto, 1981

Winston, Daoma
American, born November 3, 1922
1. *Tormented Lovers.* Derby (CT), 1962
2. *Love Her, She's Yours.* Derby, 1963
3. *The Secrets of Cromwell Crossing.* New York, 1965
4. *Sinister Stone.* New York, 1966
5. *The Wakefield Witches.* New York, 1966
6. *The Mansion of Smiling Masks.* New York, 1967
7. *Shadow of an Unknown Woman.* New York, 1967
8. *The Castle of Closing Doors.* New York, 1967
9. *The Carnaby Curse.* New York, 1967
10. *Shadow on Mercer Mountain.* New York, 1967
11. *Pity My Love.* New York, 1967
12. *The Trificante Treasure.* New York, 1968
13. *Moderns.* New York, 1968
14. *The Long and Living Shadow.* New York, 1968
15. *Bracken's World.* New York, 1969
16. *Mrs. Berrigan's Dirty Book.* New York, 1970
17. *Beach Generation.* New York, 1970
18. *Wild Country.* New York, 1970
19. *Dennison Hill.* New York, 1970
20. *House of Mirror Images.* New York, 1970
21. *Sound Stage.* New York, 1970
22. *The Love of Lucifer.* New York, 1970
23. *The Vampire Curse.* New York, 1971
24. *Flight of a Fallen Angel.* New York, 1971
25. *The Devil's Daughter.* New York, 1971
26. *The Devil's Princess.* New York, 1971
27. *Seminar in Evil.* New York, 1972
28. *The Victim.* New York, 1972
29. *The Return.* New York, 1972
30. *The Inheritance.* New York, 1972
31. *Kingdom's Castle.* New York, 1972
32. *Skeleton Key.* New York, 1972

33. *The Mayeroni Myth.* New York, 1972
34. *Moorhaven.* New York, 1973
35. *The Trap.* New York, 1973
36. *The Unforgotten.* New York, 1973
37. *The Haversham Legacy.* New York, 1974
38. *Mills of the Gods.* New York, 1974
39. *Emerald Station.* New York, 1974
40. *The Golden Valley.* New York, 1975
41. *Death Watch.* New York, 1975
42. *A Visit after Dark.* New York, 1975
43. *Walk Around the Square.* New York, 1975
44. *Gallows Way.* New York, 1976
45. *The Dream Killers.* New York, 1976
46. *The Adventuress.* New York, 1978
47. *The Lotteries.* New York and London, 1980
48. *A Sweet Familiarity.* New York, 1981
49. *Mira.* New York, 1982

Winther, Sophus K. (Keith)
American, born June 24, 1893
1. *The Realistic War Novel.* Seattle, 1930
2. *Eugene O'Neill: A Critical Study.* New York, 1934
3. *Take All to Nebraska.* New York, 1935
4. *Mortgage Your Heart.* New York, 1937
5. *This Passion Never Dies.* New York, 1938
6. *Beyond the Garden Gate.* New York, 1946

Wister, Owen
American, born July 14, 1860, died July 21, 1938
1. *The New Swiss Family Robinson.* Cambridge (MA), 1882
2. *The Dragon of Wantley: His Rise, His Voracity, and His Downfall.* Philadelphia, 1892
3. *Lin McLean.* New York, 1897
4. *Red Men and White.* New York and London, 1896
5. *The Jimmyjohn Boss and Other Stories.* New York and London, 1900
6. *Ulysses S. Grant.* Boston, 1900
7. *The Virginian: A Horseman of the Plains.* New York and London, 1902
8. *Done in the Open.* New York, 1903
9. *Musk-Ox, Bison, Sheep, and Goat,* with Caspar W. Whitney and George Bird Grinnell. New York, 1904
10. *Lady Baltimore.* New York and London, 1906
11. *How Doth the Simple Spelling Bee.* New York and London, 1907
12. *Mother.* New York, 1907
13. *The Seven Ages of Washington: A Biography.* New York, 1907
14. *Members of the Family.* New York and London, 1911
15. *The Pentecost of Calamity.* New York and London, 1915
16. *A Straight Deal; or, The Ancient Grudge.* New York and London, 1920
17. *Indispensable Information for Infants; or, Easy Entrance to Eden.* New York, 1921
18. *Neighbors Henceforth.* New York and London, 1922
19. *When West Was West.* New York and London, 1928
20. *Theodore Roosevelt.* London, 1930
21. *Owen Wister Out West: His Journals and Letters.* Chicago, 1958
22. *The West of Owen Wister: Selected Short Stories.* Lincoln, 1972

Witting, Clifford
British, born in 1907
1. *Murder in Blue.* London and New York, 1937
2. *Midsummer Murder.* London, 1937
3. *The Case of the Michaelmas Goose.* London, 1938
4. *Catt Out of the Bag.* London, 1939

5. *Measure for Murder.* London, 1941
6. *Subject: Murder.* London, 1945
7. *Let X Be The Murderer.* London, 1947
8. *Dead on Time.* London, 1948
9. *The Knights of St. Perran.* London, 1948
10. *A Bullet for Rhino.* London, 1950
11. *The Case of the Busy Bees.* London, 1952
12. *Silence after Dinner.* London, 1953
13. *Mischief in the Offing.* London, 1958
14. *There Was a Crooked Man.* London, 1960
15. *Driven to Kill.* London, 1961
16. *Villainous Saltpetre.* London, 1962
17. *Crime in Whispers.* London, 1964
18. *The Facts of English,* with Ronald Ridout. London, 1964
19. *English Proverbs Explained,* with Ronald Ridout. London, 1967

Wolfe, Gene (Rodman)
American, born May 7, 1931
1. *Operation ARES.* New York, 1970
2. *The Fifth Head of Cerberus.* New York, 1972
3. *Peace.* New York, 1975
4. *The Devil in a Forest.* Chicago, 1976
5. *The Island of Doctor Death and Other Stories.* New York, 1980
6. *The Shadow of the Torturer.* New York, 1980
7. *The Claw of the Conciliator.* New York, 1981
8. *Gene Wolfe's Book of Days.* New York, 1981

Wollheim, Donald A. (Allen)
American, born October 1, 1914
Pseudonym: David Grinnell
1. *The Secret of Saturn's Rings [the Martian Moons, the Ninth Planet].* Philadelphia, 3 vols., 1954-59
2. *One Against the Moon.* Cleveland (OH), 1956
3. *Across Time,* as David Grinnell. New York, 1957
4. *The Edge of Time,* as David Grinnell. New York, 1958
5. *The Martian Missile,* as David Grinnell. New York, 1959
6. *Destiny's Orbit.* New York, 1961
7. *Destination: Saturn,* as David Grinnell, with Lin Carter. New York, 1967
8. *Two Dozen Dragon Eggs.* Reseda (CA), 1969
9. *To Venus! To Venus!* as David Grinnell. New York, 1970

Wood, Lorna
British, born June 16, 1913
1. *The Crumb-Snatchers.* London, 1933
2. *Gilded Sprays.* London, 1935
3. *The Hopeful Travelers.* London, 1936
4. *The Smiling Rabbit and Other Stories.* London, 1939
5. *The Traveling Tree and Other Stories.* London, 1943
6. *Ameliaranne Goes Digging.* London, 1948
7. *The Finicky Mouse and Other Stories.* London, 1949
8. *The Handkerchief Man.* London, 1951
9. *The People in the Garden.* London, 1954
10. *Rescue by Broomstick.* London, 1954
11. *The Hag Calls for Help.* London, 1957
12. *Holiday on Hot Bricks.* London, 1958
13. *Seven-League Ballet Shoes.* London, 1959
14. *Climb by Candlelight.* London, 1959
15. *Hags on Holiday.* London, 1960
16. *The Golden-Haired Family.* London, 1961
17. *Hag in the Castle.* London, 1962
18. *Hags by Starlight.* London, 1970
19. *The Dogs of Pangers.* London, 1970
20. *The Brave Adventures of a Shoemaker's Boy.* London, 1971
21. *Pangers Pup.* London, 1972

Woodiwiss, Kathleen E.
American
1. *The Flame and the Flower.* New York, 1972
2. *The Wolf and the Dove.* New York, 1974
3. *Shanna.* New York and London, 1977
4. *Ashes in the Wind.* New York, 1979

Woods, Sara [Sara Bowen-Judd]
British, born March 7, 1922
1. *Bloody Instructions.* London, 1962
2. *Malice Domestic.* London, 1962
3. *The Taste of Fears.* London, 1963
4. *The Third Encounter.* New York, 1963
5. *Error of the Moon.* London, 1963
6. *Trusted Like the Fox.* London, 1964
7. *This Little Measure.* London, 1964
8. *The Windy Side of the Law.* London and New York, 1965
9. *Though I Know She Lies.* London, 1965
10. *Enter Certain Murders.* London and New York, 1966
11. *Let's Choose Executors.* London, 1966
12. *The Case Is Altered.* London and New York, 1967
13. *And Shame the Devil.* London, 1967
14. *Knives Have Edges.* London, 1968
15. *Past Praying For.* London and New York, 1968
16. *Tarry and Be Hanged.* London, 1969
17. *An Improbable Fiction.* London, 1970
18. *Serpent's Tooth.* London, 1971
19. *The Knavish Crows.* London, 1971
20. *They Love Not Poison.* London and New York, 1972
21. *Yet She Must Die.* London, 1973
22. *Enter the Corpse.* London, 1973
23. *Done to Death.* London, 1974
24. *A Show of Violence.* London and New York, 1975
25. *My Life Is Done.* London, 1975
26. *The Law's Delay.* London and New York, 1977
27. *A Thief or Two.* London and New York, 1977
28. *Exit Murderer.* London and New York, 1978
29. *The Fatal Writ.* London and New York, 1979
30. *Proceed to Judgment.* London and New York, 1979

Woolf, Douglas
American, born March 23, 1922
1. *The Hypocritic Days.* Majorca, 1955
2. *Wall to Wall.* New York, 1962
3. *Signs of a Migrant Worrier.* Eugene (OR), 1965
4. *John-Juan.* Kyoto (Japan), 1967
5. *Ya! and John-Juan.* New York, 1971
6. *Spring of the Lamb, with Broken Field Runner: A Douglas Woolf Notebook.* Highlands (NC), 1972
7. *On Us.* Santa Barbara (CA), 1977
8. *HAD.* Eugene, 1977
9. *Future Preconditional.* Toronto, 1978

Woolrich, Cornell [George Hopley]
American, born in 1903, died in 1968
Other pseudonyms: George Hopley, William Irish
1. *Cover Charge.* New York, 1926
2. *Children of the Ritz.* New York, 1927
3. *Times Square.* New York, 1929
4. *A Young Man's Heart.* New York, 1930
5. *The Time of Her Life.* New York, 1931
6. *Manhattan Love Song.* New York, 1932
7. *The Bride Wore Black.* New York, 1940
8. *The Black Curtain.* New York, 1941
9. *Black Alibi.* New York, 1942
10. *Phantom Lady,* as William Irish. Philadelphia, 1942
11. *The Black Angel.* New York, 1943
12. *I Wouldn't Be in Your Shoes,* as William Irish. Philadelphia, 1943
13. *The Black Path of Fear.* New York, 1944
14. *Deadline at Dawn,* as William Irish. Philadelphia, 1944
15. *And So to Death,* as William Irish. New York, 1944
16. *After-Dinner Story,* as William Irish. Philadelphia, 1944
17. *Night Has a Thousand Eyes,* as George Hopley. New York, 1945
18. *If I Should Die Before I Wake,* as William Irish. New York, 1945
19. *The Dancing Detective,* as William Irish. Philadelphia, 1946
20. *Borrowed Crimes,* as William Irish. New York, 1946
21. *Waltz into Darkness,* as William Irish. Philadelphia, 1947
22. *Rendezvous in Black.* New York, 1948
23. *I Married a Dead Man,* as William Irish. Philadelphia, 1948
24. *Six Times Death,* as William Irish. New York, 1948
25. *Dead Man Blues,* as William Irish. Philadelphia, 1948
26. *The Blue Ribbon,* as William Irish. Philadelphia, 1949
27. *Dilemma of the Dead Lady,* as William Irish. Hasbrouck Heights (NJ), 1950
28. *Somebody on the Phone,* as William Irish. Philadelphia, 1950
29. *Fright,* as George Hopley. New York and London, 1950
30. *Savage Bride.* New York, 1950
31. *Nightmare,* as William Irish. New York, 1950
32. *Six Nights of Mystery,* as William Irish. New York, 1950
33. *You'll Never See Me Again,* as William Irish. New York, 1951
34. *Strangler's Serenade,* as William Irish. New York, 1951
35. *The Night I Died,* as William Irish. London, 1951
36. *Deadly Night Call,* as William Irish. Hasbrouck Heights, 1951
37. *Eyes That Watch You,* as William Irish. New York, 1952
38. *Bluebeard's Seventh Wife,* as William Irish. New York, 1952
39. *Beware the Lady.* New York, 1953
40. *Nightmare.* New York, 1956
41. *Violence.* New York, 1958
42. *Hotel Room.* New York, 1958
43. *Death Is My Dancing Partner.* New York, 1959
44. *Beyond the Night.* New York, 1959
45. *The Doom Stone.* New York, 1960
46. *The Best of William Irish,* as William Irish. Philadelphia, 1960
47. *The Ten Faces of Cornell Woolrich.* New York, 1965
48. *The Dark Side of Love.* New York, 1965
49. *Nightwebs.* New York, 1971
50. *Angels of Darkness.* New York, 1979

Worboys, Anne [Annette Isobel Worboys]
British
Pseudonyms: Annette Eyre, Vicky Maxwell, Anne Eyre Worboys
1. *Dream of Petals Whim,* as Anne Eyre Worboys. London, 1961
2. *Palm Rock and Paradise,* as Anne Eyre Worboys. London, 1961
3. *Call for a Stranger,* as Anne Eyre Worboys. London, 1962
4. *Three Strings to a Fortune,* as Annette Eyre. London, 1962
5. *Visit to Rata Creek,* as Annette Eyre. London, 1964
6. *The Valley of Yesterday,* as Annette Eyre. London, 1965
7. *A Net to Catch the Wind,* as Annette Eyre. London, 1966
8. *Return to Bellbird Country,* as Annette Eyre. London, 1966
9. *The House of Five Pines,* as Annette Eyre. London, 1967
10. *The River and Wilderness,* as Annette Eyre. London, 1967
11. *A Wind from the Hill,* as Annette Eyre. London, 1968
12. *Thorn-Apple,* as Annette Eyre. London, 1968
13. *Tread Softly in the Sun,* as Annette Eyre. London, 1969
14. *The Little Millstones,* as Annette Eyre. London, 1970
15. *Dolphin Bay,* as Annette Eyre. London, 1970
16. *Rainbow Child,* as Annette Eyre. London, 1971

17. *The Magnolia Room*, as Annette Eyre. London, 1972
18. *Venetian Inheritance*, as Annette Eyre. London, 1973
19. *Chosen Child*, as Vicky Maxwell. London, 1973
20. *Flight to the Villa Mistra*, as Vicky Maxwell. London, 1973
21. *The Lion of Delos*. New York, 1974
22. *The Way of the Tamarisk*, as Vicky Maxwell. London, 1974
23. *Give Me Your Love*, as Annette Eyre. New York, 1975
24. *Every Man a King*. London, 1975
25. *High Hostage*, as Vicky Maxwell. London, 1976
26. *Rendezvous with Fear*. New York, 1977
27. *The Barrancourt Destiny*. London, 1977
28. *The Other Side of Summer*, as Vicky Maxwell. London, 1977
29. *The Bhunda Jewels*. London, 1980
30. *Run, Sarah, Run*. New York, 1981

Wormser, Richard (Edward)
Born in 1908, died in 1977
Pseudonym: Ed Friend
1. *The Man with the Wax Face*. New York, 1934
2. *The Communist's Corpse*. New York and London, 1935
3. *All's Fair. . . .* New York, 1937
4. *Pass Through Manhattan*. New York, 1940
5. *Trem McRae and the Golden Cinders*. Philadelphia, 1940
6. *The Hanging Heiress*. New York, 1949
7. *The Lonesome Quarter*. New York, 1951
8. *The Longhorn Trail*, with Dan Gordon. New York, 1955
9. *Slattery's Range*. London, 1957
10. *The Widow Wore Red*. New York, 1958
11. *The Body Looks Familiar*. New York, 1958
12. *Battalion of Saints*. New York, 1961
13. *The Late Mrs. Five*. New York, 1960
14. *Drive East on 66*. New York, 1961
15. *Thief of Bahgdad*. New York, 1961
16. *The Last Days of Sodom and Gomorrah*. New York and London, 1962
17. *Three Cornered War*. New York, 1962
18. *Perfect Pigeon*. New York, 1962
19. *Pan Satyrus*. New York, 1963
20. *A Nice Girl Like You*. New York and London, 1963
21. *McLintock*. New York, 1963
22. *Bedtime Story*. London, 1964
23. *Ride a Northbound Horse*. New York and London, 1964
24. *Operation Crossbow*. New York, 1965
25. *Torn Curtain*. New York and London, 1966
26. *The Wild Wild West*. New York, 1966
27. *Alvarez Kelly*, as Ed Friend. New York, 1966
28. *The Infernal Light*, as Ed Friend. New York, 1966
29. *The Scalphunters*, as Ed Friend. New York, 1968
30. *The Kidnapped Circus*. New York, 1968
31. *Southwest Cookery; or, At Home on the Range*. New York, 1969
32. *The Most Deadly Game*, as Ed Friend. New York, 1970
33. *The Ranch by the Sea*. New York, 1970
34. *Gone to Texas*. New York, 1970
35. *The Black Mustanger*. New York, 1971
36. *The Takeover*. New York, 1971
37. *The Invader*. New York, 1972
38. *Double Decker*. New York, 1974
39. *Tubac*. Tubac (AZ), 1975
40. *On the Prod*. New York, 1978

Wren, P.C. (Percival Christopher)
British, born in 1885, died November 22, 1941
1. *The Indian Teacher's Guide to the Theory and Practice of Mental, Moral, and Physical Education*. Bombay (India), 1910
2. *Dew and Mildew: Semi-Detached Stories from Karabad, India*. London, 1912
3. *Father Gregory; or, Lures and Failures: A Tale of Hindostan*. London, 1913
4. *Snake and Sword*. London, 1914
5. *The Wages of Virtue*. London, 1916
6. *Driftwood Spars*. London, 1916
7. *Stepsons of France*. London and New York, 1917
8. *The Young Stagers, Being Further Faites and Gestes of the Junior Curlton Club of Karabad, India . . .* London, 1917
9. *Cupid in Africa; or, The Baking of Bertram in Love and War—A Character Study*. London, 1920
10. *With the Prince Through Canada, New Zealand, and Australia*. Bombay, 1922
11. *The Snake and the Sword*. New York, 1923
12. *Beau Geste*. London, 1924
13. *Beau Sabreur*. London and New York, 1926
14. *Dew and Mildew: A Loose-Knit Tale of Hindustan*. New York, 1927
15. *Beau Ideal*. London and New York, 1928
16. *Soldiers of Misfortune: The Story of Otho Belleme*. London and New York, 1929
17. *Good Gestes: Stories of Beau Geste, His Brothers, and Certain of their Comrades in the French Foreign Legion*. London and New York, 1929
18. *Mysterious Waye: The Story of "The Unsetting Sun."* London and New York, 1930
19. *The Mammon of Righteousness: The Story of Coxe and the Box*. London, 1930
20. *Mammon*. New York, 1930
21. *Valiant Dust*. London and New York, 1932
22. *Action and Passion*. London and New York, 1933
23. *Flawed Blades: Tales from the Foreign Legion*. London and New York, 1933
24. *Beggars' Horses*. London, 1934
25. *Port o' Missing Men: Strange Tale of the Stranger Regiment*. London, 1934
26. *Sinbad the Soldier*. London and Boston, 1935
27. *Explosion*. London, 1935
28. *Spanish Maine*. London, 1935
29. *The Desert Heritage*. Boston, 1935
30. *Fort in the Jungle: The Extraordinary Adventures of Sinbad Dysari in Tonkin*. London and Boston, 1936
31. *Bubble Reputation*. London, 1936
32. *The Courtenay Treasure*. Boston, 1936
33. *The Man of a Ghost*. London, 1937
34. *The Spur of Pride*. Boston, 1937
35. *Worth Wile*. London, 1937
36. *To the Hilt*. Boston, 1937
37. *Cardboard Castle*. London and Boston, 1938
38. *Rough Shooting: True Tales and Strange Stories*. London, 1938
39. *Paper Prison*. London, 1939
40. *The Man the Devil Didn't Want*. Philadelphia, 1940
41. *The Disappearance of General Jason*. London, 1940
42. *Two Feet from Heaven*. London, 1940
43. *Odd—But Even So: Stories Stranger Than Fiction*. London, 1941
44. *The Dark Woman*. Philadelphia, 1943
45. *The Hunting of Henri*. London, 1944
46. *Stories of the Foreign Legion*. London, 1947
47. *Dead Men's Boot and Other Tales from the Foreign Legion*. London, 1949

Wright, Austin Tappan
American, born August 20, 1883, died September 18, 1931
1. *Islandia*. New York, 1942

Wright, Harold Bell
American, born May 4, 1872, died May 24, 1944

1. *That Printer of Udell's: A Story of the Middle West.* Chicago, 1903
2. *The Shepherd of the Hills.* Chicago, 1907
3. *The Calling of Dan Matthews.* Chicago, 1909
4. *The Uncrowned King.* Chicago, 1910
5. *The Winning of Barbara Worth.* Chicago, 1911
6. *Their Yesterdays.* Chicago, 1912
7. *The Eyes of the World.* Chicago, 1914
8. *When a Man's a Man.* Chicago and London, 1916
9. *The Re-creation of Brian Kent.* Chicago, 1919
10. *Helen of the Old House.* London and New York, 1921
11. *The Mine with the Iron Door: A Romance.* London and New York, 1923
12. *A Son of His Father.* London and New York, 1925
13. *God and the Groceryman.* London and New York, 1927
14. *Long Ago Told (Huh-Kew ah-Kah): Legends of the Papago Indians.* London and New York, 1929
15. *Exit.* London and New York, 1930
16. *Ma Cinderella.* London and New York, 1932
17. *To My Sons.* London and New York, 1934
18. *The Man Who Went Away.* New York, 1942
19. *The Devil's Highway,* with John Lebar. New York, 1932

Wright, S. Fowler [Sydney Fowler Wright]
British, born January 6, 1874, died February 25, 1965
Pseudonyms: Sydney Fowler, Alan Seymour
1. *Scenes from the Morte d'Arthur,* as Alan Seymour. London, 1919
2. *Some Songs of Bilitis.* Birmingham (Eng), 1921
3. *The Amphibians: A Romance of 500,000 Years Hence.* London, 1925
4. *The Song of Songs and Other Poems.* London, 1925
5. *The Ballad of Elaine.* London, 1926
6. *Deluge.* London, 1927
7. *The Island of Captain Sparrow.* New York and London, 1928
8. *The World Below.* London, 1929
9. *Dawn.* New York, 1929
10. *The Riding of Lancelot: A Narrative Poem.* London, 1929
11. *Police and Public: A Political Pamphlet.* London, 1929
12. *Elfwin.* London and New York, 1930
13. *The King Against Anne Bickerton,* as Sydney Fowler. London, 1930
14. *The Case of Anne Bickerton,* as Sydney Fowler. New York, 1930
15. *Dream; or, The Simian Maid.* London, 1931
16. *Seven Thousand in Israel.* London, 1931
17. *Red Ike,* with J.M. Denwood. London, 1931
18. *Under the Brutchstone.* New York, 1931
19. *The Bell Street Murders,* as Sydney Fowler. London and New York, 1931
20. *By Saturday,* as Sydney Fowler. London, 1931
21. *The Hanging of Constance Hillier,* as Sydney Fowler. London, 1931
22. *Crime & Co.,* as Sydney Fowler. New York, 1931
23. *The Hand-Print Mystery,* as Sydney Fowler. London, 1932
24. *Beyond the Rim.* London, 1932
25. *The New Gods Lead,* as Sydney Fowler. London, 1932
26. *The Life of Walter Scott: A Biography.* London, 1932
27. *Lord's Right in Languedoc.* London, 1933
28. *Power.* London, 1933
29. *Arresting Delia,* as Sydney Fowler. London and New York, 1933
30. *The Secret of the Screen,* as Sydney Fowler. London, 1933
31. *David.* London, 1934
32. *Who Else But She?* as Sydney Fowler London, 1934
33. *Three Witnesses,* as Sydney Fowler. London, 1935
34. *The Attic Murder,* as Sydney Fowler. London, 1936
35. *Was Murder Done?,* as Sydney Fowler. London, 1936
36. *Post-Mortem Evidence,* as Sydney Fowler. London, 1936
37. *The Screaming Lake.* London, 1937
38. *Megiddo's Ridge.* London, 1937
39. *Four Callers in Razor Street,* as Sydney Fowler. London, 1937
40. *The Hidden Tribe.* London, 1938
41. *The Adventures of Wyndham Smith.* London, 1938
42. *The Jordans Murder,* as Sydney Fowler. London, 1938
43. *The Murder in Bethnal Square,* as Sydney Fowler. London, 1938
44. *Ordeal of Barata.* London, 1939
45. *The Wills of Jane Kanwhistle,* as Sydney Fowler. London, 1939
46. *Should We Surrender Colonies?* London, 1939
47. *The Rissole Mystery,* as Sydney Fowler. London, 1941
48. *A Bout with the Mildew Gang,* as Sydney Fowler. London, 1941
49. *The Siege of Malta: Founded on an Unfinished Romance by Sir Walter Scott.* London, 1942
50. *Second Bout with the Mildew Gang,* as Sydney Fowler. London, 1942
51. *Dinner in New York,* as Sydney Fowler. London, 1943
52. *The End of the Mildew Gang,* as Sydney Fowler. London, 1944
53. *The Adventure in the Blue Room,* as Sydney Fowler. London, 1945
54. *The Vengeance of Gwa.* London, 1945
55. *Justice, and The Rat.* London, 1945
56. *Too Much for Mr. Jellipot,* as Sydney Fowler. London, 1945
57. *The Witchfinder.* London, 1946
58. *Who Murdered Reynard?* as Sydney Fowler London, 1947
59. *The Throne of Saturn.* Sauk City (WI), 1949
60. *Spiders' War.* New York, 1954
61. *The Dwellers.* London, 1954
62. *With Cause Enough,* as Sydney Fowler. London, 1954

Wrightson, Patricia [Alice Patricia Wrightson]
Australian, born June 21, 1921
1. *The Crooked Snake.* Sydney (Australia) and London, 1955
2. *The Bunyip Hole.* Sydney and London, 1958
3. *The Rocks of Honey.* Sydney, 1960
4. *The Feather Star.* London, 1962
5. *Down to Earth.* New York and London, 1965
6. *I Own the Racecourse!* London, 1968
7. *A Racecourse for Andy.* New York, 1968
8. *An Older Kind of Magic.* London and New York, 1972
9. *The Nargun and the Stars.* London, 1973
10. *The Ice is Coming.* New York and London, 1977

Wylie, Philip (Gordon)
American, born May 12, 1902, died October 26, 1971
1. *Heavy Laden.* New York, 1928
2. *Babes and Sucklings.* New York, 1929
3. *Gladiator.* New York, 1930
4. *The Murderer Invisible.* New York, 1931
5. *Footprint of Cinderella.* New York, 1931
6. *The Savage Gentleman.* New York, 1932
7. *Five Fatal Words,* with Edwin Balmer. New York, 1932
8. *When Worlds Collide,* with Edwin Balmer. New York, 1933
9. *After Worlds Collide,* with Edwin Balmer. New York, 1934
10. *Finnley Wrenn: A Novel in a New Manner.* New York, 1934
11. *The Golden Hoard,* with Edwin Balmer. New York, 1934
12. *As They Reveled.* New York, 1936
13. *Too Much of Everything.* New York and London, 1936
14. *The Shield of Silence,* with Edwin Balmer. New York, 1936

15. *An April Afternoon.* New York, 1938
16. *Danger Mansion.* New York, 1940
17. *The Big Ones Get Away!* New York, 1940
18. *The Other Horseman.* New York, 1941
19. *Salt Water Daffy.* New York, 1941
20. *Generation of Vipers.* New York, 1942
21. *Corpses at Indian Stones.* New York, 1943
22. *Night unto Night.* New York, 1944
23. *Fish and Tin Fish: Crunch and Des Strike Again.* New York, 1944
24. *Fifth Mystery Book,* with others. New York, 1944
25. *Selected Short Stories.* New York, 1944
26. *Crunch and Des: Stories of Florida Fishing.* New York, 1948
27. *Opus 21.* New York, 1949
28. *The Disappearance.* New York and London, 1951
29. *Three to be Read.* New York, 1951
30. *Denizens of the Deep: True Tales of Deep-Sea Fishing.* New York, 1953
31. *Tomorrow!* New York, 1954
32. *The Best of Crunch and Des.* New York, 1954
33. *The Answer.* New York and London, 1956
34. *Treasure Cruise and Other Crunch and Des Stories.* New York, 1956
35. *The Innocent Ambassadors.* New York, 1957
36. *9 Rittenhouse Square.* New York, 1959
37. *Triumph.* New York, 1963
38. *They Both Were Naked.* New York, 1965
39. *The Party.* New York, 1966(?)
40. *Autumn Romance.* New York, 1967
41. *The Magic Animal.* New York, 1968
42. *The Spy Who Spoke Porpoise.* New York, 1969
43. *Los Angeles: A.D. 2017.* New York, 1971
44. *Sons and Daughters of Mom.* New York, 1971
45. *The End of the Dream.* New York, 1972

Wynd, Oswald (Morris)
   Scottish, born in 1913
   Pseudonym: Gavin Black
1. *Black Fountains,* as Gavin Black. New York, 1947
2. *Red Sun South,* as Gavin Black. New York, 1948
3. *The Stubborn Flower,* as Gavin Black. London, 1949
4. *Friend of the Family,* as Gavin Black. New York, 1949
5. *When Ape Is King.* London, 1949
6. *The Gentle Pirate,* as Gavin Black. New York, 1951
7. *Stars in the Heather.* Edinburgh (Scotland), 1956
8. *Moon of the Tiger,* as Gavin Black. London and New York, 1958
9. *Summer Can't Last,* as Gavin Black. London, 1960
10. *The Devil Came on Sunday,* as Gavin Black. London and New York, 1961
11. *Suddenly, At Singapore,* as Gavin Black. London, 1961
12. *Dead Man Calling,* as Gavin Black. London and New York, 1962
13. *A Wall in the Long Dark Night.* London, 1962
14. *A Dragon for Christmas,* as Gavin Black. London and New York, 1963
15. *The Eyes Around Me,* as Gavin Black. London and New York, 1964
16. *Death the Red Flower.* London and New York, 1965
17. *You Want to Die, Johnny?* as Gavin Black. London and New York, 1966
18. *A Wind of Death,* as Gavin Black. London and New York, 1967
19. *Walk Softly, Men Praying.* London and New York, 1967
20. *Sumatra Seven Zero.* London and New York, 1968
21. *The Cold Jungle,* as Gavin Black. London and New York, 1969
22. *The Hawser Pirates,* as Gavin Black. London and New York, 1970
23. *A Time for Pirates,* as Gavin Black. London and New York, 1971
24. *The Bitter Tea,* as Gavin Black. New York, 1972
25. *The Forty Days.* London, 1972
26. *The Golden Cockatrice,* as Gavin Black. London, 1974
27. *A Big Wind for Summer,* as Gavin Black. London and New York, 1975
28. *A Moon for Killers,* as Gavin Black. London, 1976
29. *Killer Moon,* as Gavin Black. London, 1977
30. *The Ginger Tree,* as Gavin Black. London and New York, 1977
31. *Gale Force,* as Gavin Black. London, 1978
32. *Night Run from Java,* as Gavin Black. London, 1979

Wyndham, John [John Wyndham Parkes Lucas Beynon Harris]
   British, born July 10, 1903, died March 11, 1969
   Pseudonyms: John Beynon, Johnson Harris, Lucas Parkes
1. *The Secret People,* as John Beynon. London, 1935
2. *Foul Play Suspected,* as John Beynon. London, 1935
3. *Planet Plane,* as John Beynon. London, 1936
4. *Love in Time,* as Johnson Harris. London, 1946
5. *The Day of the Triffids.* New York and London, 1951
6. *Revolt of the Triffids.* New York, 1952
7. *Stowaway to Mars.* London, 1953
8. *The Kraken Wakes.* London, 1953
9. *Out of the Deeps.* New York, 1953
10. *Jizzle.* London, 1954
11. *Re-Birth.* New York, 1955
12. *The Chrysalids.* London, 1955
13. *The Seeds of Time.* London, 1956
14. *Tales of Gooseflesh and Laughter.* New York, 1956
15. *The Midwich Cuckoos.* London, 1957
16. *The Outward Urge,* as John Wyndham and Lucas Parkes. New York and London, 1959
17. *Trouble with Lichen.* New York and London, 1960
18. *Village of the Damned.* New York, 1960
19. *Consider Her Ways and Others.* London, 1961
20. *The Infinite Moment.* New York, 1961
21. *Chocky.* New York, 1968
22. *The Best of John Wyndham.* London, 1973
23. *Sleepers of Mars.* London, 1973
24. *Wanderers of Time.* London, 1973
25. *The Man from Beyond and Other Stories.* London, 1975
26. *Exiles on Asperus.* London, 1979
27. *Web.* London, 1979

Wyndham, Lee [Jane Lee Hyndman]
   American, born December 16, 1912
1. *Sizzling Pan Ranch.* New York, 1951
2. *Slipper under Glass.* New York, 1952
3. *Golden Slippers.* New York, 1953
4. *Buttons and Beaux,* with Louise Barnes Gallagher. New York, 1953
5. *Silver Yankee.* Philadelphia, 1953
6. *A Dance for Susie.* New York, 1953
7. *Showboat Holiday.* Philadelphia, 1954
8. *Binkie's Billions.* New York, 1954
9. *Susie and the Dancing Cat.* New York, 1954
10. *Camel Bird Ranch.* New York, 1955
11. *Susie and the Ballet Family.* New York, 1955
12. *First Steps in Ballet,* with Thalia Mara. New York, 1955
13. *Ballet Teacher.* New York, 1956
14. *The Lost Birthday Present.* New York, 1957
15. *Lady Architect.* New York, 1957
16. *Games and Stunts for All Occasions.* Philadelphia, 1957
17. *Year 'round Party Book.* Philadelphia, 1957

18. *On Your Toes, Susie.* New York, 1958
19. *Dance to My Measure.* New York, 1958
20. *Candy Stripers.* New York, 1958
21. *Ballet for You.* New York, 1959
22. *The Timid Dragon.* New York, 1960
23. *The Little Wise Man,* with Robert Wyndham. Indianapolis (IN), 1960
24. *Chip Nelson and the Contrary Indians.* New York, 1960
25. *The How and Why Wonderbook of Ballet.* New York, 1961
26. *Susie and the Ballet Horse.* New York, 1961
27. *Bonnie.* New York, 1961
28. *Beth Hilton, Model.* New York, 1961
29. *Folk Tales of India.* Indianapolis, 1962
30. *The Family at Seven Chimneys House.* New York, 1963
31. *Thanksgiving.* Champaign (IL), 1963
32. *Folk Tales of China.* Indianapolis, 1963
33. *Tales from the Arabian Nights.* Racine (WI), 1965
34. *Writing for Children and Teenagers.* Cincinnati (OH), 1968
35. *Mourka, The Mighty Cat.* New York, 1969
36. *Russian Tales of Fabulous Beasts and Marvels.* New York, 1969
37. *Florence Nightingale, Nurse to the World.* New York, 1969
38. *The Winter Child: An Old Russian Folk Tale.* New York, 1970
39. *Tales the People Tell in Russia.* New York, 1970
40. *Tales the People Tell in China.* New York, 1971
41. *Holidays in Scandinavia.* Champaign, 1975

Wynne, May [Mabel Winifred Knowles]
British, born in January 1875, died 19??
Pseudonym: Lester Lurgan

1. *Love's Objects; or, Some Thoughts for Young Girls.* London, 1899
2. *In the Shadows; or, Thoughts for Mourners.* London, 1900
3. *Sympathy.* London, 1901
4. *Mollie's Adventures.* London, 1903
5. *For Faith and Navarre.* London, 1904
6. *Ronald Lindsay.* London, 1905
7. *A King's Tragedy.* London, 1905
8. *The Temptation of Philip Carr.* London, 1905
9. *Theodore.* London, 1906
10. *Maid of Brittany.* London, 1906
11. *The Goal.* London, 1907
12. *When Terror Ruled.* London, 1907
13. *Henry of Navarre: A Romance of August, 1572,* as Mabel W. Knowles. New York, 1908
14. *Let Erin Remember.* London, 1908
15. *The Tailor of Vitre.* London, 1908
16. *For Church and Chieftain.* London, 1909
17. *For Charles the Rover.* London, 1909
18. *The Gipsy Count.* New York, 1909
19. *A Blot on the Escutcheon.* New York, No date
20. *A King's Masquerade.* London, 1910
21. *Mistress Cynthia.* London, 1910
22. *Bohemian Blood,* as Lester Lurgan. London, 1910
23. *The Mill-Owner,* as Lester Lurgan. London, 1910
24. *Jimmie: The Tales of a Little Black Bear.* London, 1910
25. *The League of the Triangle,* as Lester Lurgan. London, 1911
26. *The Gallant Graham.* London, 1911
27. *Honour's Fetters.* London, 1911
28. *The Claim That Won.* London, 1912
29. *Hey for Cavaliers!* London, 1912
30. *The Red Fleur-de-Lys.* London, 1912
31. *A Message from Mars,* as Lester Lurgan. London, 1912
32. *The Ban,* as Lester Lurgan. London, 1912
33. *The Wrestler on the Shore,* as Lester Lurgan. London, 1912
34. *Phil's Cousin: A Holiday Tale.* London, 1912
35. *The Story of Heather.* London, 1912
36. *Crackers: The Tale of a Mischievous Monkey.* London, 1912
37. *The Brave Brigands.* London, 1913
38. *The Destiny of Claude.* London, 1913
39. *The Secret of the Zenana.* London, 1913
40. *The Life and Reign of Victoria the Good.* London, 1913
41. *Goring's Girl.* London, 1914
42. *The Hero of Urbino.* London, 1914
43. *Murray Finds a Chum.* London, 1914
44. *The Silent Captain.* London, 1914
45. *The Regent's Gift.* London, 1915
46. *Tony's Chums.* London, 1915
47. *When Auntie Lil Took Charge.* London, 1915
48. *Foes of Freedom.* London, 1916
49. *An English Girl in Serbia.* London, 1916
50. *The Gipsy King.* London, 1917
51. *The Lyons Mail.* London, 1917
52. *Marcel of the "Zephyrs."* London, 1917
53. *The Master Wit: A Story of Boccaccio.* London, 1917
54. *Penance.* London, 1917
55. *A Spy for Napoleon.* London, 1917
56. *The Taint of Tragedy.* London, 1917
57. *Three's Company.* London, 1917
58. *The "Veiled Lady."* London, 1918
59. *The King of a Day.* London, 1918
60. *Queen Jennie.* London, 1918
61. *Stranded in Belgium.* London, 1918
62. *A Cousin from Canada.* London, 1918
63. *The Honour of the School.* London, 1918
64. *The Red Whirlpool.* London, 1919
65. *The Curse of Gold.* London, 1919
66. *Dick.* London, 1919
67. *Phyllis in France.* London, 1919
68. *Robin the Prodigal.* London, 1919
69. *A Run for His Money.* London, 1919
70. *The Heroine of Chelton School.* London, 1919
71. *The Little Girl Beautiful.* London, 1919
72. *Nan and Ken.* London, 1919
73. *Nipper and Co.* London, 1919
74. *Scouts for Serbia.* London, 1919
75. *Comrades from Canada.* London, 1919
76. *The Seven Champions of Christendom.* London, 1919
77. *The Adventures of Dolly Dingle.* London, 1920
78. *A Prince of Intrigue: A Romance of Mazeppa.* London, 1920
79. *Adventures of Two.* London, 1920
80. *A Gallant of Spain.* London, 1920
81. *Janie's Great Mistake.* London, 1920
82. *The Girls of Beechcroft School.* London, 1920
83. *Roseleen at School.* London, 1920
84. *Three Bears and Gwen.* London, 1920
85. *Mervyn, Jock, or Joe.* London, 1921
86. *Mog Megone.* London, 1921
87. *My Lady's Honour.* London, 1921
88. *The Spendthrift Duke.* London, 1921
89. *Little Ladyship.* London, 1921
90. *Lost in the Jungle.* London, 1921
91. *The Red Rose of Lancaster.* London, 1922
92. *A Trap for Navarre.* London, 1922
93. *A King in the Lists.* London, 1922
94. *The Girls of the Veldt Farm.* London, 1922
95. *Peggy's First Term.* London, 1922
96. *Angela Goes to School.* London, 1922
97. *Christmas at Holford.* London, 1922
98. *The Ambitions of Jill.* London, 1923
99. *The Witch-Finder.* London, 1923
100. *Girls in the Wild.* London, 1923
101. *The Best of Chums.* London, 1923
102. *A Heather Holiday.* London, 1923

103. *Blundering Bettina.* London, 1924
104. *The Girl Who Played the Game.* London, 1924
105. *Bertie, Bobby, and Belle.* London, 1924
106. *The Girls of Clanways Farm.* London, 1924
107. *Kits at Clynton Court School.* London, 1924
108. *The Sunshine Children.* London, 1924
109. *Three and One Over.* London, 1924
110. *Two and a Chum.* London, 1924
111. *Jill the Hostage.* London, 1925
112. *Hootie Toots of Hollow Tree.* Philadelphia, 1925
113. *Rachel Lee.* London, 1925
114. *The Girls of Old Grange School.* London, 1925
115. *Over the Hills and Far Away.* London, 1925
116. *Dare-All Jack and the Cousins.* London, 1925
117. *Hazel Asks Why.* London, 1926
118. *Gwennola.* London, 1926
119. *Carol of Hollydene School.* London, 1926
120. *The Secret of Carrock School.* London, 1926
121. *Diccon the Impossible.* London, 1926
122. *The Girl over the Wall.* London, 1926
123. *Jean Plays Her Part.* London, 1926
124. *The Fires of Youth.* London, 1927
125. *Plotted in Darkness.* London, 1927
126. *King Mandarin's Challenge.* London, 1927
127. *A Royal Traitor.* London, 1927
128. *Love's Penalty.* London, 1927
129. *Dinah's Secret.* London, 1927
130. *Jean of the Lumber Camp.* London, 1927
131. *Robin Hood to the Rescue.* Exeter (Eng), 1927
132. *Terry the Black Sheep.* London, 1928
133. *The Girls of Mackland Court.* London, 1928
134. *The Terror of the Moor.* London, 1928
135. *Gipsy-Spelled.* London, 1929
136. *The House of Whispers.* London, 1929
137. *Red Fruit.* London, 1929
138. *Little Sally Mandy's Christmas Present.* Philadelphia, 1929
139. *The Guide's Honour.* London, 1929
140. *Hamlet: A Romance from Shakespeare's Play.* London, 1930
141. *A Term to Remember.* London, 1930
142. *Two Girls in the Hawk's Den.* London, 1930
143. *Bobbety the Brownie.* London, 1930
144. *Juliet of the Mill.* London, 1931
145. *The Masked Rider.* Chicago, 1931
146. *Patient Pat Joins the Circus.* Philadelphia, 1931
147. *Peter Rabbit and the Big Black Crows.* Philadelphia, 1931
148. *The Peter Rabbit Playtime Story Book.* Philadelphia, 1931
149. *Girls of the Pansy Patrol.* London, 1931
150. *Patsy from the Wilds.* London, 1931
151. *The Girl Upstairs.* London, 1932
152. *The Unseen Witness.* London, 1932
153. *Stella Maris.* London, 1932
154. *Who Was Wendy?* London, 1932
155. *The Heart of Glenayrt.* London, 1932
156. *The Old Brigade.* London, 1932
157. *The Secret of Marigold Marnell.* London, 1932
158. *Pixie's Mysterious Mission.* London, 1933
159. *Enter Jenny Wren.* London, 1933
160. *Wendy's Adventure in Scotland.* London, 1933
161. *An Adventurous Holiday.* London, 1933
162. *The School Mystery.* London, 1933
163. *Malys Rockell.* London, 1934
164. *The Smugglers of Penreen.* London, 1934
165. *Comrades to Robin Hood.* London, 1934
166. *Up to Val.* London, 1935
167. *Tangled Fates.* London, 1935
168. *Flower o' the Moor.* London, 1935
169. *The Choice of Mavis.* London, 1935
170. *The Mysterious Island.* London, 1935
171. *Their Girl Chum.* London, 1935
172. *Under Cap'n Drake.* London, 1935
173. *Bunny the Aunt.* London, 1936
174. *The Haunted Ranch.* London, 1936
175. *Thirteen for Luck.* London, 1936
176. *Vivette on Trial.* London, 1936
177. *"Peter." The New Girl.* London, 1936
178. *The Daring of Star.* London, 1936
179. *The Secret of Brick House.* London, 1937
180. *Temptation.* London, 1937
181. *Two Maids of Rosemarkie.* London, 1937
182. *The Luck of Penrayne.* London, 1937
183. *Audrey on Approval.* London, 1937
184. *The Girl Sandy.* London, 1938
185. *Whither?* London, 1938
186. *The Lend-a-Hand Holiday.* London, 1938
187. *Heather the Second.* London, 1938
188. *The Unexpected Adventure.* London, 1939
189. *The Term of Many Adventures.* London, 1939
190. *The Coming of Verity.* London, 1940
191. *Love Dismayed.* London, 1942
192. *Echoed from the Past.* London, 1944
193. *The Pursuing Shadow.* London, 1944
194. *Little Brown Tala.* London, 1944
195. *The Unsuspected Witness.* London, 1945
196. *The Secret of the Caves.* London, 1945
197. *Brown Tala Finds Little Tulsi.* London, 1945
198. *Ginger Ellen.* London, 1947
199. *Little Brown Tala Stories.* London, 1947
200. *Patch the Piebald.* Croydon (Eng), 1947
201. *Playing the Game.* Croydon, 1947
202. *Snow Fairies.* London, 1947
203. *The Great Adventure.* London, 1948
204. *Sally Comes to School.* London, 1949
205. *The Furry Fairies.* London, 1949
206. *Merion Plays the Game.* London, 1950
207. *Secrets of the Rockies.* London, 1954

Yarbro, Chelsea Quinn
American, born September 15, 1942
Pseudonym: Vanessa Pryor
1. *Time of the Fourth Horseman.* New York, 1976
2. *Ogilvie, Tallant, and Moon.* New York, 1976
3. *False Dawn.* New York, 1978
4. *Hotel Transylvania: A Novel of Forbidden Love.* New York, 1978
5. *Cautionary Tales.* New York, 1978
6. *Music When Sweet Voices Die.* New York, 1979
7. *The Palace.* New York, 1979
8. *Messages from Michael.* Chicago, 1979
9. *Blood Games.* New York, 1980
10. *Ariosto.* New York, 1980
11. *Dead and Buried.* New York, 1980
12. *Sins of Omission.* New York, 1980
13. *Path of the Eclipse.* New York, 1981
14. *Tempting Fate.* New York, 1982
15. *A Taste of Wine,* as Vanessa Pryor. New York, 1982

Yates, A.G. (Alan Geoffrey)
British, born in 1923
Pseudonyms: Carter Brown, Peter Carter Brown, Peter Carter-Brown (You are likely to find any one of these pseudonyms with these titles.)
1. *Venus Unarmed.* Sydney (Australia), 1953
2. *The Mermaid Murmurs Murder.* Sydney, 1953
3. *The Lady Is Chased.* Sydney, 1953
4. *The Frame Is Beautiful.* Sydney, 1953
5. *Fraulein Is Feline.* Sydney, 1953
6. *Wreath for Rebecca.* Sydney, ca.1953

7. *The Black Widow Weeps.* Sydney, ca.1953
8. *Penthouse Passout.* Sydney, ca.1953
9. *Shady Lady.* Sydney, ca.1953
10. *Strip Without Tease.* Sydney, ca.1953
11. *Trouble Is a Dame.* Sydney, ca.1953
12. *Lethal in Love.* Sydney, ca.1953
13. *Murder—Paris Fashion.* Sydney, 1954
14. *Nemesis Wore Nylons.* Sydney, 1954
15. *Maid for Murder.* Sydney, 1954
16. *Murder Is My Mistress.* Sydney, 1954
17. *Homicide House.* Sydney, 1954
18. *A Morgue Amour.* Sydney, 1954
19. *The Killer Is Kissable.* Sydney, 1954
20. *Curtains for a Chorine.* Sydney, 1955
21. *Shamus, Your Slip Is Showing.* Sydney, 1955
22. *Cutie Cashed His Chips.* Sydney, 1955
23. *Honey, Here's Your Hearse!* Sydney, 1955
24. *The Two-Timing Blonde.* Sydney, 1955
25. *Sob-Sister Cries Murder.* Sydney, 1955
26. *The Blonde.* Sydney, 1955
27. *Curves for the Coroner.* Sydney, 1955
28. *Miss Called Murder.* Sydney, 1955
29. *Swan Song for a Siren.* Sydney, 1955
30. *A Bullet for My Baby.* Sydney, 1955
31. *Kiss and Kill.* Sydney, 1955
32. *Kiss Me Deadly.* Sydney, 1955
33. *The Wench Is Wicked.* Sydney, 1955
34. *Hot Seat for a Honey.* Sydney, 1956
35. *The Minx Is Murder.* Sydney, 1957
36. *The Savage Salome.* Sydney and New York, 1961
37. *The Million Dollar Babe.* New York, 1961
38. *Charlie Sent Me!* Sydney and New York, 1963

Yates, Dornford (Cecil William Mercer)
British, born August 7, 1885, died March 5, 1960
1. *The Brother of Daphne.* London, 1914
2. *The Courts of Idleness.* London, 1920
3. *Anthony Lyveden.* London, 1921
4. *Berry and Co.* London, 1921
5. *Jonah and Co.* London, 1922
6. *Valerie French.* London, 1923
7. *And Five Were Foolish.* London, 1924
8. *As Other Men Are.* London, 1925
9. *The Stolen March.* London, 1926
10. *Blind Corner.* London and New York, 1927
11. *Perishable Goods.* London and New York, 1928
12. *Blood Royal.* London, 1929
13. *Summer Fruit.* New York, 1929
14. *Maiden Stakes.* London, 1929
15. *Fire Below.* London, 1930
16. *By Royal Command.* New York, 1931
17. *Adele & Co.* New York, 1931
18. *Safe Custody.* London and New York, 1932
19. *Storm Music.* London and New York, 1934
20. *She Fell among Thieves.* London and New York, 1935
21. *And Berry Came Too.* London and New York, 1936
22. *She Painted Her Face.* London and New York, 1937
23. *This Publican.* London, 1938
24. *The Devil in Satin.* New York, 1938
25. *Gale Warning.* London, 1939
26. *Shoal Water.* London, 1940
27. *Period Stuff.* London, 1942
28. *An Eye for a Tooth.* London, 1943
29. *The House That Berry Built.* London and New York, 1945
30. *Red in the Morning.* London, 1946
31. *Were Death Denied.* New York, 1946
32. *The Berry Scene.* London and New York, 1947
33. *Cost Price.* London, 1949
34. *The Laughing Bacchante.* New York, 1949
35. *Lower Than Vermin.* London, 1950
36. *As Berry and I Were Saying.* London, 1952
37. *Ne'er-Do-Well.* London, 1954
38. *Wife Apparent.* London, 1956
39. *B-Berry and I Look Back.* London, 1958

Yates, Elizabeth
American, born December 6, 1905
1. *High Holiday.* London, 1938
2. *Hans and Frieda in the Swiss Mountains.* New York and London, 1939
3. *Climbing Higher.* London, 1939
4. *Quest in the North-land.* New York, 1940
5. *Haven for the Brave.* New York, 1941
6. *Under the Little Fir and Other Stories.* New York, 1942
7. *Around the Year in Iceland.* Boston, 1942
8. *Patterns on the Wall.* New York, 1943
9. *Mountain Born.* New York, 1943
10. *Wind of Spring.* New York, 1945
11. *Nearby.* New York, 1947
12. *Once in the Year.* New York, 1947
13. *Joseph.* New York, 1947
14. *The Young Traveler in the U.S.A.* London, 1948
15. *Beloved Bondage.* New York, 1948
16. *Guardian Heart.* New York, 1950
17. *The Christmas Story.* New York, 1950
18. *Children of the Bible.* New York, 1950
19. *Amos Fortune, Free Man.* New York, 1950
20. *A Place for Peter.* New York, 1952
21. *David Livingstone.* Evanston (IL), 1952
22. *Brave Interval.* New York, 1952
23. *Hue and Cry.* New York, 1953
24. *Rainbow 'round the World: A Story of UNICEF.* Indianapolis (IN), 1954
25. *Prudence Crandall, Woman of Courage.* New York, 1955
26. *The Carey Girl.* New York, 1956
27. *Gifts of True Love: Based on the Old Carol "The Twelve Days of Christmas."* Wallingford (PA), 1958
28. *Pebble in a Pool: The Widening Circles of Dorothy Canfield Fisher's Life.* New York, 1958
29. *The Lighted Heart.* New York, 1960
30. *Someday You'll Write.* New York, 1962
31. *The Next Fine Day.* New York, 1962
32. *Sam's Secret Journal.* New York, 1964
33. *Carolina's Courage.* New York, 1964
34. *Howard Thurman: Portrait of a Practical Dreamer.* New York, 1964
35. *Carolina and the Indian Doll.* London, 1965
36. *Up the Golden Stair.* New York, 1966
37. *Is There a Doctor in the Barn? A Day in the Life of Forrest F. Tenney.* No place, no date.
38. *D.M.V.* New York, 1966
39. *An Easter Story.* New York, 1967
40. *With Pipe, Paddle, and Song.* New York, 1968
41. *New Hampshire.* New York, 1969
42. *On That Night.* New York, 1969
43. *Sarah Whitcher's Story.* New York, 1971
44. *The Lady from Vermont.* Battleboro (?) (CT), 1971
45. *Skeezer, Dog with a Mission.* New York, 1973
46. *The Road Through Sandwich Notch.* Battleboro (?), 1973
47. *A Book of Hours.* New York, 1976
48. *Call It Zest.* Battleboro (?), 1977

Yerby, Frank (Garvin)
American, born September 5, 1916
1. *The Foxes of Harrow.* New York, 1946
2. *The Vixens.* New York, 1947

3. *The Golden Hawk.* New York, 1948
4. *Pride's Castle.* New York, 1949
5. *Floodtide.* New York, 1950
6. *A Woman Called Fancy.* New York, 1951
7. *The Saracen Blade.* New York, 1952
8. *The Devil's Laughter.* New York, 1953
9. *Benton's Row.* New York, 1954
10. *Bride of Liberty.* New York, 1954
11. *The Treasure of Pleasant Valley.* New York, 1955
12. *Captain Rebel.* New York, 1956
13. *Fairoaks.* New York, 1957
14. *The Serpent and the Staff.* New York, 1958
15. *Jarrett's Jade.* New York, 1959
16. *Gillian.* New York, 1960
17. *The Garfield Honor.* New York, 1961
18. *Griffin's Way.* New York, 1962
19. *The Old Gods Laugh: A Modern Romance.* New York and London, 1964
20. *An Odor of Sanctity.* New York, 1965
21. *Goat Song: A Novel of Ancient Greece.* New York, 1967
22. *Judas, My Brother: The Story of the Thirteenth Disciple.* New York and London, 1969
23. *Speak Now.* New York, 1969
24. *The Dahomean.* New York, 1971
25. *The Man from Dahomey.* London, 1971
26. *The Girl from Storyville: A Victorian Novel.* New York and **London**, 1972
27. *The Voyage Unplanned.* New York and London, 1974
28. *Tobias and the Angel.* New York and London, 1975
29. *A Rose for Ana Maria.* New York and London, 1976
30. *Hail the Conquering Hero.* New York, 1977
31. *A Darkness at Ingraham's Crest.* New York, 1979
32. *Western: A Saga of the Great Plains.* New York, 1982

Yolen, Jane
American, born February 11, 1939
1. *Pirates in Petticoats.* New York, 1963
2. *See This Little Line?* New York, 1963
3. *The Witch Who Wasn't.* New York and London, 1964
4. *Gwinellen, The Princess Who Could Not Sleep.* New York, 1965
5. *Trust a City Kid.* New York, 1966
6. *Isabel's Noel.* New York, 1967
7. *The Emperor and the Kite.* Cleveland (OH), 1967
8. *The Minstrel and the Mountain.* Cleveland and Edinburgh (Scotland), 1968
9. *Greyling.* Cleveland, 1968
10. *The Longest Name on the Block.* New York, 1968
11. *World on a String: The Story of Kites.* Cleveland, 1968
12. *It All Depends.* New York, 1969
13. *The Wizard of Washington Square.* New York, 1969
14. *The Inway Investigators: or, The Mystery at McCracken's Place.* New York, 1969
15. *The Seventh Mandarin.* New York and London, 1970
16. *Hobo Toad and the Motorcycle Gang.* New York, 1970
17. *The Bird of Time.* New York, 1971
18. *The Girl Who Loved the Wind.* New York, 1972
19. *Friend: The Story of George Fox and the Quakers.* New York, 1972
20. *The Wizard Islands.* New York, 1973
21. *Writing Books for Children.* Boston, 1973
22. *The Girl Who Cried Flowers and Other Tales.* New York, 1974
23. *The Rainbow Rider.* New York, 1974
24. *The Adventures of Eeka Mouse.* Stamford (CT), 1974
25. *The Boy Who Had Wings.* New York, 1974
26. *The Magic Three of Solatia.* New York, 1974
27. *The Little Spotted Fish.* New York, 1975
28. *The Transfigured Hart.* New York, 1975
29. *Ring Out! A Book of Bells.* New York, 1975
30. *Moon Ribbon and Other Tales.* New York, 1976
31. *Milkweed Days.* New York, 1976
32. *Simple Gifts: The Story of the Shakers.* New York, 1976
33. *The Sultan's Perfect Tree.* New York, 1977
34. *The Seeing Stick.* New York, 1977
35. *The Hundredth Dove and Other Tales.* New York, 1977
36. *The Giant's Farm.* New York, 1977
37. *Hannah Dreaming.* Springfield (MA), 1977
38. *An Invitation to the Butterfly Ball.* New York and Kingswood (Eng), 1977

Yorke, Margaret [Margaret Beda Nicholson]
British, born January 30, 1924
1. *Summer Flight.* London, 1957
2. *Pray, Love, Remember.* London, 1958
3. *Christopher.* London, 1959
4. *Deceiving Mirror.* London, 1960
5. *The China Doll.* London, 1961
6. *Once a Stranger.* London, 1962
7. *The Birthday.* London, 1963
8. *Full Circle.* London, 1965
9. *No Fury.* London, 1967
10. *The Apricot Bed.* London, 1968
11. *The Limbo Ladies.* London, 1969
12. *Dead in the Morning.* London, 1970
13. *Silent Witness.* London, 1972
14. *Grave Matters.* London, 1973
15. *Mortal Remains.* London, 1974
16. *No Medals for the Major.* London, 1974
17. *The Small Hours of the Morning.* London and New York, 1975
18. *Cast for Death.* London and New York, 1976
19. *The Cost of Silence.* London and New York, 1977
20. *The Point of Murder.* London, 1978
21. *The Come-On.* New York, 1979
22. *Death on Account.* London, 1979

Young, Delbert Alton
1. *Mutiny on Hudson Bay.* Toronto, 1964
2. *The Mounties.* Toronto and London, 1968
3. *Last Voyage of the Unicorn.* Toronto, 1969
4. *The Ghost Ship.* Toronto, 1972
5. *According to Hakluyt.* Toronto, 1973

Young, Gordon (Ray)
Pseudonym: Hugh Richmond
1. *Savages.* New York, 1921
2. *Wild Blood.* Indianapolis (IN), 1921
3. *Tajola.* London, 1922
4. *Hurricane Williams.* Indianapolis, 1922
5. *Seibert of the Island.* London, 1924
6. *Crooked Shadows.* New York, 1924
7. *Days of '49.* New York, 1925
8. *Pearl-Hunger.* London, 1925
9. *The Vengeance of Hurricane Williams.* New York and London, 1925
10. *Standish of the Star Y.* London, 1926
11. *La Rue of the Eighty-Eight.* London, 1927
12. *Treasure.* London, 1927
13. *Fighting Blood.* New York, 1932
14. *The Fighting Fool.* London, 1933
15. *Red Clark o'Tulluco.* New York and **London**, 1933
16. *Red Clark Rides Alone.* New York, 1933
17. *Red Clark of the Arrowhead.* New York and **London**, 1935
18. *Huroc the Avenger.* London, 1936
19. *Red Clark on the Border.* New York and **London**, 1937
20. *Red Clark, Range Boss.* New York, 1938
21. *Red Clark, Boss!* London, 1938

22. *Red Clark, Two-Gun Man.* New York, 1939
23. *Red Clark for Luck.* New York, 1940
24. *Mr. Beamish,* as Hugh Richmond. New York, 1940
25. *Red Clark Takes a Hand.* New York, 1941
26. *Iron Rainbow.* New York, 1942
27. *Tall in the Saddle.* New York, 1943
28. *Red Clark at the Showdown.* New York, 1947
29. *Red Clark in Paradise.* New York, 1947
30. *Holster Law.* New York, no date
31. *Gunman from Tulluco.* New York, 1948
32. *Quarter Horse.* New York, 1948
33. *Red Clark to the Rescue.* New York, 1948
34. *Trouble Rides Double.* London, 1948
35. *Roaring Guns.* New York, 1949
36. *Wanted—Dead or Alive!* New York, 1949
37. *Guns of the Arrowhead.* New York, 1950
38. *Fast on the Draw.* New York, 1950
39. *Trouble on the Border.* New York, 1951
40. *Range Boss.* New York, 1951
41. *Two-Gun Man.* New York, 1952
42. *Hell on Hoofs.* New York, 1953

Zagat, Arthur Leo
American, born in 1895, died April 3, 1949
1. *Seven Out of Time.* Reading (PA), 1949

Zangwill, Israel
British, born January 21, 1864, died August 1, 1926
1. *Motza Kleis,* with Louis Cowen. London, 1882
2. *The Premier and the Painter: A Fantastic Romance,* with Louis Cowen. London, 1888
3. *The Bachelors' Club.* London and New York, 1891
4. *"A Doll's House" Repaired,* with Eleanor Marx Aveling. London, 1891
5. *Hebrew, Jew, Israelite.* London, 1892
6. *The Old Maids' Club.* London and New York, 1892
7. *Children of the Ghetto, Being Pictures of a Peculiar People.* London, 3 vols., 1892
8. *Merely Mary Ann.* London, 1893
9. *Ghetto Tragedies.* London, 1893
10. *The Great Demonstration,* with Louis Cowen. London, 1893
11. *The King of Schnorrers: Grotesques and Fantasies.* London and New York, 1894
12. *Joseph the Dreamer.* London, 1895
13. *The Master.* London and New York, 1895
14. *The Position of Judaism.* New York, 1895
15. *Without Prejudice.* London and New York, 1896
16. *The People's Saviour.* New York, 1898
17. *The Celibates' Club, Being the United Stories of "The Bachelors' Club" and "The Old Maids' Club."* London, 1898
18. *Dreamers of the Ghetto.* London and New York, 1898
19. *They That Walk in Darkness: Ghetto Tragedies.* London and New York, 1899
20. *Six Persons.* London, 1899
21. *The Mantle of Elijah.* London and New York, 1900
22. *The Grey Wig: Stories and Novelettes.* London and New York, 1903
23. *Merely Mary Ann.* New York and London, 1904
24. *The Serio-Comic Governess.* New York, 1904
25. *The East African Question: Zionism and England's Offer.* New York, 1904
26. *What Is the ITO?* London, 1905
27. *Ghetto Comedies.* London and New York, 1907
28. *A Land of Refuge.* London, 1907
29. *Talked Out!* London, 1907
30. *One and One Are Two.* London, 1907
31. *Old Fogeys and Old Bogeys.* London, 1909
32. *The Lock on the Ladies.* London, 1909
33. *Report on the Purpose of Jewish Settlement in Cyrenaica.* London, 1909
34. *Be Fruitful and Multiply.* London, 1909
35. *Italian Fantasies.* London and New York, 1910
36. *Sword and Spirit.* London, 1910
37. *The War God.* London, 1911
38. *The Next Religion.* London and New York, 1912
39. *The Hithertos.* London, 1912
40. *The Problem of the Jewish Race.* New York, 1912
41. *Report of the Commission for Jewish Settlement in Angora.* London, 1913
42. *Plaster Saints: A High Comedy.* London, 1914
43. *The War and the Women.* New York, 1915
44. *The War for the World.* London and New York, 1916
45. *The Principle of Nationalities.* London and New York, 1917
46. *The Service of the Synagogue,* with Nina Davis Salaman and Elsie Davis. New York, 3 vols., 1917
47. *Chosen Peoples: The Hebraic Ideal "Versus" the Teutonic.* London, 1918
48. *Hands Off Russia.* London, 1919
49. *Jinny the Carrier: A Folk Comedy of Rural England.* London and New York, 1919
50. *The Jewish Pogroms in the Ukraine,* with others. Washington (DC), 1919
51. *The Voice of Jerusalem.* London, 1920
52. *The Cockpit.* London and New York, 1921
53. *Watchman, What of the Night?* New York, 1923
54. *The Forcing House; or, The Cockpit Continued.* London and New York, 1923
55. *Is the Ku Klux Klan Constructive or Destructive? A Debate Between Imperial Wizard Evans,* with others. Gerard (KS), 1924
56. *Too Much Money.* London, 1924
57. *We Moderns.* London, 1925
58. *Now and Forever: A Conversation with Mr. Israel Zangwill on the Jew and the Future.* New York, 1925
59. *Our Own.* New York, 1926
60. *Speeches, Articles, and Letters.* London, 1937
61. *Zangwill in the Melting-Pot: Selections.* London, no date

Zebrowski, George
American, born December 28, 1945
1. *The Omega Point.* New York, 1972
2. *The Star Web.* Toronto, 1975
3. *Ashes and Stars.* New York, 1977
4. *The Monadic Universe and Other Stories.* New York, 1977
5. *Macrolife.* New York, 1979

Zelazny, Roger (Joseph)
American, born May 13, 1937
1. *This Immortal.* New York, 1966
2. *The Dream Master.* New York, 1966
3. *Lord of Light.* New York, 1967
4. *Four for Tomorrow.* New York, 1967
5. *Isle of the Dead.* New York, 1969
6. *Creatures of Light and Darkness.* New York, 1969
7. *Damnation Alley.* New York, 1969
8. *A Rose for Ecclesiastes.* London, 1969
9. *Nine Princes in Amber.* New York, 1970
10. *Jack of Shadows.* New York, 1971
11. *The Doors of His Face, The Lamps of His Mouth, and Other Stories.* New York, 1971
12. *The Guns of Avalon.* New York, 1972
13. *Today We Choose Faces.* New York, 1973
14. *To Die in Italbar.* New York, 1973
15. *Sign of the Unicorn.* New York, 1975
16. *Doorways in the Sand.* New York, 1976
17. *The Hand of Oberon.* New York, 1976

18. *Bridge of Ashes.* New York, 1976
19. *Deus Irae,* with Philip K. Dick. New York, 1976
20. *My Name Is Legion.* New York, 1976
21. *The Courts of Chaos.* New York, 1978
22. *The Illustrated Roger Zelazny,* with Gray Morrow. New York, 1978
23. *The Chronicles of Amber.* New York, 2 vols., 1979
24. *The Bells of Shoredam.* San Francisco, 1979
25. *Roadmarks.* New York, 1979
26. *Changeling.* New York, 1980
27. *The Last Defender of Camelot.* New York, 1980

Zinberg, Len [Leonard S. Zinberg]
American, born in 1911, died January 7, 1968
Pseudonyms: Steve April, Ed Lacy
1. *Walk Hard—Talk Loud.* Indianapolis (IN), 1940
2. *What D'ya Know for Sure.* New York, 1947
3. *Strange Desires.* New York, 1948
4. *Hold with the Hares.* New York, 1948
5. *The Woman Aroused,* as Ed Lacy. New York, 1951
6. *Sin in Their Blood,* as Ed Lacy. New York, 1952
7. *Strip for Violence,* as Ed Lacy. New York, 1953
8. *Enter Without Desire,* as Ed Lacy. New York, 1954
9. *Go for the Body,* as Ed Lacy. New York, 1954
10. *Route 13,* as Steve April. New York, 1954
11. *The Best That Ever Did It,* as Ed Lacy. New York, 1955
12. *Visa to Death,* as Ed Lacy. New York, 1956
13. *The Men from the Boys,* as Ed Lacy. New York, 1956
14. *Lead with Your Left,* as Ed Lacy. New York and London, 1957
15. *Room to Swing,* as Ed Lacy. New York, 1957
16. *Breathe No More, My Lady,* as Ed Lacy. New York, 1958
17. *Devil for the Witch,* as Ed Lacy. London, 1958
18. *Be Careful How You Live,* as Ed Lacy. New York and London, 1958
19. *Shakedown for Murder,* as Ed Lacy. New York, 1958
20. *Blonde Bait,* as Ed Lacy. Rockville Centre (NY), 1959
21. *Death in Passing,* as Ed Lacy. London, 1959
22. *The Big Fix,* as Ed Lacy. New York, 1960
23. *A Deadly Affair,* as Ed Lacy. New York, 1960
24. *Dead End,* as Ed Lacy. New York, 1960
25. *Bugged for Murder,* as Ed Lacy. New York, 1961
26. *The Freeloaders,* as Ed Lacy. New York, 1961
27. *South Pacific Affair,* as Ed Lacy. New York, 1961
28. *The Sex Castle,* as Ed Lacy. New York, 1963
29. *Too Hot to Handle,* as Ed Lacy. New York, 1963
30. *Moment of Untruth,* as Ed Lacy. New York, 1964
31. *Sleep in Thunder,* as Ed Lacy. New York, 1964
32. *Pity the Honest,* as Ed Lacy. London, 1964
33. *Harlem Underground,* as Ed Lacy. New York, 1965
34. *Double Trouble,* as Ed Lacy. London, 1965
35. *The Hotel Dwellers,* as Ed Lacy. New York, 1966
36. *In Black and Whitey,* as Ed Lacy. New York, 1967
37. *The Napalm Bugle,* as Ed Lacy. New York, 1968
38. *The Big Bust,* as Ed Lacy. New York, 1969
39. *Shoot It Again,* as Ed Lacy. New York, 1969

Zindel, Paul
American, born May 15, 1936
1. *The Pigman.* New York, 1968
2. *My Darling, My Hamburger.* New York, 1969
3. *I Never Loved Your Mind.* New York, 1970
4. *I Love My Mother.* New York, 1975
5. *Pardon Me, You're Stepping on My Eyeball!* New York and London, 1976
6. *Confessions of a Teenage Baboon.* New York, 1977

Zion, Gene [Eugene Zion]
American, born October 5, 1913
1. *All Falling Down.* New York, 1951
2. *Hide and Seek Day.* New York, 1954
3. *The Summer Snowman.* New York, 1955
4. *Harry, The Dirty Dog.* New York, 1956
5. *Really Spring.* New York, 1956
6. *Jeffie's Party.* New York, 1957
7. *Dear Garbage Man.* New York, 1957
8. *No Roses for Harry!* New York, 1958
9. *Dear Dustman.* London, 1962
10. *The Plant Sitter.* New York, 1959
11. *Harry and the Lady Next Door.* New York, 1960
12. *The Meanest Squirrel I Ever Met.* New York, 1962
13. *The Sugar Mouse Cake.* New York, 1964
14. *Harry by the Sea.* New York, 1965

Zolotow, Charlotte
American, born June 26, 1915
Pseudonyms: Sara Abbot, Charlotte Bookman
1. *The Park Book.* New York, 1944
2. *But Not Billy.* New York and London, 1944
3. *The Storm Book.* New York, 1952
4. *The Magic Word.* New York, 1952
5. *The City Boy and the Country Horse,* as Charlotte Bookman. New York, 1952
6. *Indian, Indian.* New York, 1952
7. *The Quiet Mother and the Noisy Little Boy.* New York, 1953
8. *One Step, Two. . . .* New York, 1955
9. *Not a Little Monkey.* New York, 1957
10. *Over and Over.* New York, 1957
11. *Do You Know What I'll Do?* New York, 1958
12. *Sleepy Book.* New York, 1958
13. *The Bunny Who Found Easter.* Berkeley (CA), 1959
14. *Aren't You Glad.* New York, 1960
15. *The Little Black Puppy.* New York, 1960
16. *Big Brother.* New York, 1960
17. *The Three Funny Friends.* New York, 1961
18. *The Night When Mother Went Away.* New York, 1961
19. *The Man with the Purple Eyes.* New York, 1961
20. *Mr. Rabbit and the Lovely Present.* New York, 1962
21. *The Sky Was Blue.* New York, 1963
22. *The Quarreling Book.* New York, 1963
23. *The White Marble.* New York and London, 1963
24. *A Tiger Called Thomas.* New York, 1963
25. *In My Garden.* New York, 1960
26. *When the Wind Stops.* New York, 1962
27. *I Have a Horse of My Own.* New York and London, 1964
28. *The Poodle Who Barked at the Wind.* New York, 1964
29. *A Rose, A Bridge, and a Wild Black Horse.* New York and London, 1964
30. *When I Have a Little Girl [a Son].* New York, 2 vols., 1965-67
31. *Someday.* New York, 1965
32. *If It Weren't for You.* New York, 1966
33. *Big Sister and Little Sister.* New York, 1966
34. *Flocks of Birds.* New York and London, 1966
35. *I Want to Be Little.* New York and London, 1967
36. *Summer Is. . . .* New York and London, 1967
37. *All That Sunlight.* New York, 1967
38. *The New Friend.* New York and London, 1968
39. *My Friend John.* New York, 1968
40. *The Hating Book.* New York, 1969
41. *The Old Dog,* as Sara Abbot. New York, 1969
42. *Some Things Go Together.* New York, 1969
43. *A Week in Yani's World: Greece.* New York and London, 1969

44. *A Week in Lateef's World: India.* New York, 1970
45. *Where I Begin,* as Sara Abbot. New York, 1970
46. *River Winding.* New York and London, 1970
47. *You and Me.* New York, 1971
48. *Wake Up and Goodnight.* New York, 1971
49. *A Father Like That.* New York, 1971
50. *William's Doll.* New York, 1972
51. *Hold My Hand.* New York, 1972
52. *The Beautiful Christmas Tree.* Berkeley, 1972
53. *Janey.* New York, 1973
54. *My Grandson Lew.* New York, 1974
55. *The Unfriendly Book.* New York, 1975
56. *It's Not Fair.* New York, 1976
57. *May I Visit?* New York, 1976

Appendix A:

A Reading Guide

Following is an extensive listing of books, annual publications, and periodicals, as a guide to the many different fiction genres with which The Collector's Bookshelf *deals. Notable are the genres of science fiction, westerns, the "dime novel," mysteries and detective fiction, the occult, folklore, so-called "women's fiction" (the historical romance, Gothic novels, etc.), juvenile fiction, and children's books.*

Also included are guides to book collecting, some of which will be valuable to those who collect books for a profit.

Adams, Ramon F. *More Burrs Under the Saddle: Books and Histories of the West.* 1979.

Aldiss, Brian. *Billion Year Spree: A History of Science Fiction.* 1973.

Aldiss, Brian, and Harry Harrison. *Hell's Cartographers: Some Personal Histories of Science Fiction Writers.* 1975.

American Book Collector, The. Morteus Press, 274 Madison Avenue, New York, N.Y.

American Book Prices Current. Annual.

Amis, Kingsley. *The James Bond Dossier.* 1965.

Anderson, Rachel. *The Purple Heart Throbs: The Sub-Literature of Love.* London, Hodder and Stoughton, 1974.

Antiquarian Book Monthly Review. ABMR Publications, Ltd., 52 St. Clement's, Oxford, England, OX4 1AG.

Antique Trader Weekly, The, PO Box 1050, Dubuque, Iowa.

Ash, Brian. *Who's Who in Science Fiction.* 1976.

Attebery, Brian. *The Fantasy Tradition in American Literature.* 1980.

Bain, Robert, ed. *Southern Writers: A Biographical Dictionary.* 1979.

Barron, Neil. *Anatomy of Wonders: A Critical Guide to Science Fiction.* 1981.

Baynton-Williams, Roger. *Investing in Maps.* 1969.

Bleiler, Everett F. *The Checklist of Science Fiction and Supernatural Fiction.* 1979.

Bleiler, Everett F. *The Guide to Supernatural Fiction.* 1982.

Blum, Eleanor. *Basic Books in the Mass Media: An Annotated Selected Booklist.* 1980.

Book Arts Review. 15 Bleeker Street, New York, N.Y. 10012.

Book Collector, The. 90-91 Great Russell Street, London, England, WC1b 3PY.

Bradley, Van Allen. *The Book Collector's Handbook of Values.* Latest edition.

Brandes, George Morris Cohen. *Main Currents in Nineteenth-Century Literature.* 6 vols., 1972.

Breen, John L. *What About Murder? A Guide to Books About Mystery and Detective Fiction.* 1981.

Britton, Anne, and Marion Collin. *Romantic Fiction.* London, Boardman, 1960.

Bruccoli, Mathew, et al. *Dictionary of Literary Biography.* 19 vols., 1978-82.

———. *First Printings of American Authors.* 4 vols., 1977-78.

Bruccoli, Matthew, and C. E. Frazer Clark, Jr. *Pages: Inside the World of Books, Writers, and Writing.* 1976.

Bruns, Hank F. *Angling Books of the Americas.* 1983.

Burke, W. J., and W. D. Howe. *American Authors and Books.* 1972. Latest edition.

Cecil, Mirabel. *Heroines in Love 1750-1974.* London, Joseph, 1974.

Clareson, Thomas D. *Science Fiction Criticism: An Annotated Checklist.* 1972.

Clarie, Thomas C. *Occult Bibliography: An Annotated List of Books Published in English, 1971-75.* 1978.

Clark, Joseph D. *Beastly Folklore.* 1968.

Cohen, Norman. *Long Steel Rail: The Railroad in American Folksong.* 1981.

Cohen, Sara Blacher, ed. *Comic Relief: Humor in Contemporary American Literature.* 1978.

Collectors News. PO Box 156, Grundy Center, Iowa 50638.

Commire, Anne. *Yesterday's Authors of Books for Children.* 1976.

Cook, Michael L. *Dime Novel Round-up: An Annotated Index 1931-1981.* 1982.

———. *Mystery Fanfare: A Composite Annotated Index to Mystery and Related Fanzines, 1963-1981.* 1982.

———. *Murder by Mail: Inside the Mystery Book Clubs.* 1979.

Coven, Brenda. *American Women Dramatists of the Twentieth Century: A Bibliography.* 1982.

Cowart, David, and Thomas L. Wymer. *Twentieth-Century American Science Fiction Writers.* 2 vols., 1981.

Cunningham, Eugene. *Triggernometry.* Latest printing.

Currey, L. W. *Science Fiction and Fantasy Authors: A Bibliography of First Printings.* 1979.

Dahl, Svend. *History of the Book.* 1968.
Davis, David B. *Homicide in American Fiction, 1798–1860: A Study in Social Values.* 1968.
Day, A. Grove. *Books About Hawaii: Fifty Basic Authors.* 1977.
———. *Pacific Islands Literature: One Hundred Basic Books.* 1971.
Debo, Angle. *A History of the Indians of the United States.* 1979.
Derleth, August. *A Praed Street Dossier.* 1968.
De Vinne, Theodore L. *The Practice of Typography: A Treatise on Title Pages.* 1968.
De Waal, Ronald B. *The World Bibliography of Sherlock Holmes and Dr. Watson.* 1975.
Dinan, John A. *The Pulp Western: A Popular History of the Western Fiction Magazine in America.* 1981.
Dobyns, Henry F., and Robert C. Euler. *Indians of the Southwest: A Critical Bibliography.* 1981.
Dow, George Francis. *Slave Ships and Slaving.* 1968.
Drazan, Joseph G. *The Pacific Northwest: An Index to People and Places in Books.* 1979.
Duff. E. Gordon. *Early Printed Books.* 1968.
Duffy, John. *The Healers: A History of American Medicine.* 1979.

Earle, Alice M. *Stage-Coach and Tavern Days.* 1968.
Eastman, Mary H. *Index to Fairy Tales, Myths and Legends.* 3 vols., 1926, 1937, 1952.
Eisenstein, Elizabeth. *The Printing Press as an Agent of Change.* 2 vols., 1979.
Ellery Queen's Book of First Appearances. 1982.

Fairbanks, Carol, and Eugene A. Engeldinger. *Black American Fiction: A Bibliography.* 1978.
Faunce, Patricia S. *Women and Ambition: A Bibliography.* 1980.
Faye, Christopher U. *Fifteenth-Century Printed Books at the University of Illinois.* 1949.
Feiffer, Jules. *The Great Comic Book Heroes.* 1965.
Fisher, Vardis, and Opal Laurel Holmes. *Gold Rushes and Mining Camps of the Early American West.*
Flanagan, Cathleen C., and John T. Flanagan. *American Folklore: A Bibliography, 1950–74.* 1977.
Foster, Thomas Henry. *Beadles, Bibles and Bibliophiles.* 1948.
Foundation: The Review of Science Fiction. North East London Polytechnic, Longbridge Road, Dagenham, Essex, England, RM8 2AS.
14th-Century English Mystics Newsletter. Department of English, University of Iowa, Iowa City, Iowa 52242.
Franklin, V. Benjamin. *Boston Printers, Publishers and Booksellers, 1640–1800.* 1980.
Franklin, Linda C. *Antiques and Collectibles: A Bibliography of Works in English, 16th Century to 1976.* 1978.

Gee, Ernest Richard. *Early American Sporting Books, 1734–1844.* 1975.
Georges, Robert A., and Stephen Stern. *American Immigrant and Ethnic Folklore: An Annotated Bibliography.* 1982.
Glover, Dorothy, and Graham Greene. *Victorian Detective Fiction: A Catalogue.* 1966.
Goodwater, Leanne. *Women in Antiquity: An Annotated Bibliography.* 1975.
Goulart, Ron. *Cheap Thrills: An Informal History of the Pulp Magazines.* 1972.
———. *The Hardboiled Dicks: An Anthology and Study of Pulp Detective Fiction.* 1965.
Greenfeld, Beth, and Juliann E. Fleenor, eds. *The Female Gothic.* St. Albans, Vt., Eden Press, 1982.
Greiner, Donald, ed. *American Poets Since World War II.* 2 vols., 1980.
Gribbin, Lenore S. *Who's Whodunit: A List of 3,218 Detective Story Writers and Their 1,000 Pseudonyms.* 1968.
Grimes, Janet, and Diva Daims. *Novels in English by Women, 1891–1920: A Preliminary Check-list.* 1979.
Grobani, Anton. *Guide to Baseball Literature.* 1975.
———. *Guide to Football Literature.* 1975.
Grumet, Robert Steven. *Native Americans of the Northwest Coast: A Critical Bibliography.* 1980.
Gunn, Dewey W. *Mexico in American and British Letters: A Bibliography of Fiction and Travel Books.* 1974.

Hackett, Alice Payne, and James Henry Burke. *Eighty Years of Best Sellers.* New York, Bowker, 1977.
Hancer, K. *The Paperback Price Guide.* Annual.
Harlequin 30th Anniversary 1949–1979: The First 30 Years of the World's Best Romance Fiction. Toronto, Harlequin, 1979.
Hart, James D. *The Popular Book: A History of America's Literary Taste.* New York, Oxford University Press, 1950.
Heard, J. Norman. *Bookman's Guide to Americana.* The most recent editions.
Hubin, Allen J. *The Bibliography of Crime Fiction, 1749–1975.* 1979.
Hudgeons, Thomas E. *Official Price Guide to Old Books & Autographs.* Latest edition.

International Collector's Alert, 100076 Boca Entrada Boulevard, Boca Raton, Fla. 33433.
Isaac Asimov's Science Fiction Magazine, 380 Lexington Avenue, New York, N.Y. 10017.

Journal of Modern Literature, 1241 Humanities Building, Temple University, Philadelphia, Pa. 19122.

Kirkpatrick, Daniel, ed. *Twentieth-Century Children's Writers.* 1978.

LeFontaine, Joseph Raymond. *A Handbook for Booklovers.* 1988.
———. *International Book Collector's Directory.* 1983.
———. *Turning Paper to Gold.* 1987.
Lowery, Lawrence F. *The Collector's Guide to Big Little Books and Similar Books.* Latest edition.

Mann, Peter H. *The Romantic Novel: A Survey of Reading Habits* and *A Survey: The Facts About Romantic Fiction.* London, Mills and Boon, 2 vols., 1969–1974.
Matthews, Jack. *Collecting Rare Books for Fun and Profit.* 1981. (In my opinion the best book on the subject ever written for the neophyte.)
Mcgrath, Daniel F., ed. *Bookman's Price Index.* Latest editions.
Moers, Ellen. *Literary Women.* New York, Doubleday, 1976; London, W. H. Allen, 1977.
Molnor, John E. *Author-Title Index to Joseph Sabin's Dictionary of Books Relating to America.* 3 vol., 1974.
Mossman, Jennifer, ed. *Pseudonyms and Nicknames Dictionary.* 2 vols., 1982.
Mussell, Kay. *Women's Gothic and Romantic Fiction: A Reference Guide.* Westport, Conn., Greenwood Press, 1981.

Nye, Russell B., ed. *New Dimensions in Popular Culture.* Bowling Green, Ohio, Popular Press, 1972.
———. *The Unembarrassed Muse: The Popular Arts in America.* New York, Dial Press, 1970.

Pelton, Robert W. *Collecting Autographs for Fun and Profit.* 1987.
Peters, Jean, ed. *Book Collecting: A Modern Guide.* 1977.

Radcliffe, Elsa J. *Gothic Novels of the Twentieth Century: An Annotated Bibliography.* Metuchen, N.J., Scarecrow Press, 1979.

Raymond, Joseph. *International Book Collector's Directory.* Latest edition.

Reilly, John M., ed. *Twentieth-Century Crime and Mystery Writers.* 1980.

Ritchie, Claire. *Writing the Romantic Novel.* London, Bond Street, 1962.

Romantic Times: The Complete Newspaper for Readers of Romantic Fiction, 163 Joralemon Street, Suite 1234, Brooklyn Heights, N.Y. 11201.

Sabin, Joseph. *A Dictionary of Books Relating to America.* 2 vols., latest edition.

Sampson, George, ed. *The Concise Cambridge History of English Literature.* Latest edition.

Science Fiction Books Published in Britain, Aardvark House, 2 Cowper Road, Cambridge, England, CB1 3SN.

Sharp, Harold S. *Handbook of Pseudonyms and Personal Nicknames.* 5 vols., 1972–82.

Smith, Curtis, ed. *Twentieth-Century Science Fiction Writers.* 1981.

Smith, Herbert F. *The Popular American Novel 1865–1920.* Boston, Twayne, 1980.

Tebbell, J. A. *History of Book Publishing in the United States, 1630–1980.* 4 vols., 1972–1981.

Vinson, James, et al. *Twentieth-Century Romance and Gothic Writers.* 1982.

Vinson, James. *Twentieth-Century Western Writers.* 1982.

Vinson, James, and D. L. Kirkpatrick, eds. *Contemporary Novelists.* Latest edition.

Wolff, R. L. *Nineteenth-Century Fiction: A Bibliographic Catalogue.* 2 vols., 1980.

Appendix B:
About the Collector's Bookshelf Value Guide

The companion book, *The Collector's Bookshelf Value Guide,* is an indexed and coded cross-reference to *The Collector's Bookshelf. The Value Guide* provides the current market value for every book title listed for every author in *The Collector's Bookshelf.* The values are current as of October 1990 and are in United States currency. The two volumes together provide value information for over 33,000 book titles that have a current market value of nearly one million dollars.

Why is This Information Important?

First, even if your only purpose in buying any used book is to read it and then discard it, you still ought to be aware of whether you have unintentionally acquired a valuable gem. Wouldn't it be nice to discover that the book you paid fifty cents for was actually worth $150, and you could sell it for somewhere between $75 and $150? This has happened to me many, many times over the years. It's possible to pay pennies for books that are worth thousands of dollars.

Next, if you are a serious collector, you need to know the proper value for any book you are buying. Is the price being asked fair, a great bargain, or too high? And if you're planning on selling something from your collection you need to know the fair market value.

If you're a dealer, you need this information also. You don't want to pay too much for anything you buy to resell, and you want to price it fairly. If you price it too high you may never sell it, and if too low you're giving away your fair profit.

Librarians also need to know fair book values. A good part of the acquisitions budget of many libraries is devoted to replacing books that are worn out or missing. They need to know fair values. And if you intend to sell a book to a library, you certainly need to know its fair value so you don't "give it away."

All these are reasons to obtain a copy of *The Collector's Bookshelf Value Guide.*

Following this Appendix you will find an order card, which will let you order your own copy directly from the publisher. There is also a form you can return so that you can be notified when the *Value Guide* is revised to reflect changes in the overall market. This is expected to occur every two years.

ORDER FORM

The Collector's Bookshelf Value Guide

The Collector's Bookshelf Value Guide can be obtained from your book-dealer or directly from Prometheus Books. Returning this form will ensure that you will be notified whenever the *Value Guide* is updated. If you already own the *Value Guide* and simply want to be notified of updates, please write "already own" next to "Amount enclosed."

Please enclose $16.95 plus $1.85 postage and handling. Prices are subject to change without notice.

Send to _____
(Please type or print clearly)

Address _____

City _____ State _____ Zip _____

Amount enclosed _____

Charge my ☐ VISA ☐ MasterCard

Account # ☐☐☐☐☐☐☐☐☐☐☐☐☐☐☐☐

Exp. Date _____ / _____ Tel. _____

Signature _____

Prometheus Books
59 John Glenn Dr., Amherst, New York 14228

Phone orders call toll free: (800) 421-0351

Please allow 3–6 weeks for delivery